ANDERSONVILLE

BOOKS BY MacKINLAY KANTOR

Fiction

DIVERSEY · EL GOES SOUTH · THE JAYBIRD

LONG REMEMBER · THE VOICE OF BUGLE ANN

AROUSE AND BEWARE · THE ROMANCE OF ROSY RIDGE

THE NOISE OF THEIR WINGS · HERE LIES HOLLY SPRINGS

VALEDICTORY · CUBA LIBRE · GENTLE ANNIE · HAPPY LAND

AUTHOR'S CHOICE · GLORY FOR ME · MIDNIGHT LACE

WICKED WATER · THE GOOD FAMILY · ONE WILD OAT

SIGNAL THIRTY-TWO · DON'T TOUCH ME · WARWHOOP

THE DAUGHTER OF BUGLE ANN · GOD AND MY COUNTRY

Juvenile

ANGLEWORMS ON TOAST

LEE AND GRANT AT APPOMATTOX

GETTYSBURG

Autobiographical

BUT LOOK, THE MORN

Verse

TURKEY IN THE STRAW

CIVIL WAR
BOOK CLUB

STOCKADE EDITION

AUTOGRAPHED BY THE AUTHOR

FOR MEMBERS OF THE

CIVIL WAR BOOK CLUB

MacKINLAY KANTOR

ANDERSONVILLE

THE WORLD PUBLISHING COMPANY

CLEVELAND AND NEW YORK

Library of Congress Catalog Card Number: 55-8257

FIRST EDITION

TO IRENE

"The future historian who shall undertake to write an unbiased story of the War between the States, will be compelled to weigh in the scales of justice all its parts and features; and if the revolting crimes . . . have indeed been committed, the perpetrators must be held accountable. Be they of the South or of the North, they can not escape history."

—R. RANDOLPH STEVENSON, formerly surgeon in the Army of the Confederate States of America.

I

Sometimes there was a compulsion which drew Ira Claffey from his plantation and sent him to walk the forest. It came upon him at eight o'clock on this morning of October twenty-third; he responded, he yielded, he climbed over the snake fence at the boundary of his sweet potato field and went away among the pines.

Ira Claffey had employed no overseer since the first year of the war, and had risen early this morning to direct his hands in the potato patch. Nowadays there were only seven and one-half hands on the place, house and field, out of a total Negro population of twelve souls; the other four were an infant at the breast and three capering children of shirt-tail size.

Jem and Coffee he ordered to the digging, and made certain that they were thorough in turning up the harvest and yet gentle in lifting the potatoes. Nothing annoyed Ira Claffey like storing a good thirty-five bushels in a single mound and then losing half of them through speedy decay.

In such a manner, he thought, have some of our best elements and institutions perished. One bruise, one carelessness, and rot begins. Decay is a secret but hastening act in darkness; then one opens up the pine bark and pine straw—or shall we say, the Senate?—and observes a visible wastage and smell, a wet and horrid mouldering of the potatoes. Or shall we say, of the men?

In pursuit of his own husbandry on this day, Ira carried a budding knife in his belt. While musing in bed the night before, he had been touched with ambition: he would bud a George the Fourth peach upon a Duane's Purple plum.

Veronica was not yet asleep, but reading her Bible by candlelight beside him. He told her about it.

But, Ira, does not the Duane's Purple ripen too soon? Aren't those the trees just on the other side of the magnolias?

No, no, my dear. Those are Prince's Yellow Gage. The Duane's Purple matures in keeping with the George Fourths. I'd warrant you about the second week of July. Say about the tenth. I should love to see that skin. Such a fine red cheek on the George Fourths, and maybe dotted with that lilac bloom and yellow specks—

But she was not hearing him, she was weeping. He turned to watch her; he sighed, he put out one big hand and touched the thick gray-yellow braid which weighted on her white-frilled shoulder. It was either Moses or Sutherland whom she considered now. Dully he wondered which one.

She said, on receiving the communication of his thought, though he had said nothing— She spoke Suthy's name.

Oh, said Ira. I said nothing to make you think—

The Prince's Yellow Gage. He fancied them so. When they were still green he'd hide them in the little waist he wore. Many's the time I gave him a belting—

She sobbed a while longer, and he stared into the gloom beyond the bed curtains, and did his best to forget Suthy. Suthy was the eldest. Sixteenth Georgia. It was away up at the North, at a place no one had ever heard of before, a place called Gettysburg.

In recent awareness of bereavement had lain the germ of retreat and restlessness, perhaps; but sometimes Ira spirited himself off into the woods when he was fleeing from no sadness or perplexity. He had gone like that since he could first remember. Oh, pines were taller forty-five years ago . . . when he was only three feet tall, the easy nodding grace of their foliage was reared out of all proportion, thirty times his stature. And forests were wilder, forty-five years ago, over in Liberty County, and he went armed with a wooden gun which old Jehu had carved and painted as a Christmas gift for him. It had a real lock, a real flint; it snapped and the sparks flew. Ira Claffey slew brigades of redcoats with this weapon; he went as commander of a force of small blacks; he was their general.

Hi, them's British, Mastah Iry.

Where?

Yonder in them 'simmons!

Take them on the flank.

Hi, what you say we do, Mastah?

He wasn't quite sure what he wanted them to do. Something about the flank. His Uncle Sutherland talked about a flank attack in some wild distant spot known as the Carolinas. . . . Of course this was later on, perhaps only forty years ago, when Ira Claffey was ten. . . .

Charge those redcoats! They advanced upon the persimmon brake in full cry and leaping; and once there came terror when a doe soared out of the thicket directly in their faces, and all the little darkies scattered like quail, and Ira came near to legging it after them.

In similar shades he had been Francis Marion, and surely his own boys had scuttled here in identical pursuits. It was a good place to be, treading alone on the clay-paved path curving its way to the closest branch of Sweetwater Creek. God walked ahead and behind and with him, near, powerful, silent . . . *words of my mouth, and the meditation of my heart, be acceptable in thy sight, O Lord, my strength, and my redeemer.*

He had budded the peach upon the plum as he wished to do, though he feared that it was a trifle too late in the season for success. He budded each of the two selected trees five times, and then went back to the potato field. Coffee and Jem were doing well enough, but they were plaguèd slow; Ira had been emphatic about the tenderness he required of them, and they handled the big sulphur-colored Brimstones as if they were eggs. Well, he thought, I shan't speed them on this. Better forty bushels well-dug and well-stored than eighty bushels bumped and scratched and ready to spoil as soon as they're covered.

Keep on with it until I return, and mind about no bruising. I shall look up some pine straw—where it's thickest and easy to scoop—and we'll fetch the cart after the nooning.

Yassah.

Frost had not yet killed the vines. Some planters always waited for a killing frost before they dug, but Ira was certain that the crop kept better if dug immediately before the frost struck.

He was newly come into his fifty-first year; the natal day had been observed on October sixth. Black Naomi chuckled mysteriously in the kitchen; there had been much talk about, Mistess, can I please speak with you a minute *alone?* He had to pretend that he was blind and deaf, and owned no suspicion that delicate and hard-to-come-by substances were being lavished in his honor. The fragrant Lady Baltimore cake appeared in time, borne by Ira Claffey's daughter because she would not trust the wenches with this treasure.

There they sat, the three surviving Claffeys left at home, sipping their roast-grain coffee and speaking words in praise of the cake, and now Ira had lived for half a century . . . fifty years stuffed with woe and work and dreams and peril. He sought to dwell in recollection only on the benefits accruing. With Veronica and Lucy he tried to keep his imaginings away from far-off roads where horses and men were in tragic operation.

The best I've tasted since the Mexican War.

Poppy, you always say that. About everything.

Come, come, Lucy. Do I indeed?

You do, agreed his wife, and gave him her wan smile above the home-dipped candles.

Yes, sir, chimed in Lucy. It's always the best and the worst and the biggest and all such things, but always dated from that old war.

After this night, said Ira, I presume that I should date everything from my fiftieth birthday?

Poppy, love, you don't look even on the outskirts of fifty. Scarcely a shred of gray in your hair.

Well, my dear, I don't have much hair left to me.

That's no certain indication of encroaching age. Is it, Mother? Take

Colonel Tollis. I declare, he can't be aged over thirty-one or two, and yet he's got less hair than—

Lucy. Do you consider it ladylike, to discuss baldness so—so intimately?

Well, I declare—

So it had gone; they uttered their little jests and remonstrances; they had their affection; the stringy candles sank and died in chipped gilt candelabra, and in the end Ira Claffey sat alone in his library and treated himself to port. He had tasted no port since the previous winter (there was so little of it left now) and he made a silent gesture and toasted each of his sons in turn as they stared from ambrotype frames beside him. His hand went down and rubbed along his right leg; it caressed his shabby fawn-colored pantaloons above the knotted hole which for years he had bandaged afresh each day. I'd be with you, fifty or no fifty, he tried to tell his sons, reaching to them across uncharted distances and dimensions. I'd be among the muskets if it hadn't been for Monterey. I wonder who that Mexican was! I wonder if he is living still—sorrowing as I am sorrowing, going through repeated and sometimes doleful mimicry. Still able to love, however? Not so frequently? But still able, and most eager at times.

The wine affected Ira Claffey because he drank so little of it in this time of strife and paucity. He thought of Veronica and the fever which came over him sometimes in darkness, the drawing up of her night-dress, the muffled hysteria of their encounter, the shame which she always admitted afterward because she had been taught that carnal enjoyment was lewd and Ira could never persuade her otherwise. He thought of the mistress he had had in Milledgeville when he was in the Legislature, he thought of pretty strumpets he'd known in the brief time when he was a soldier, he thought of the first brown girl he ever lay with at seventeen or thereabouts in age.

How do you countenance such goings-on? You, professedly a religious man—

I suppose each of us must be guilty of certain sins. We'd be less than human if we weren't blemished a bit. And I strive earnestly not to envy, not to grow little snips and slips and buds and seeds of jealousy. I deplore cruelty, and own no avarice—at least none I'm conscious of. But lust—

I'm steeped in that particular brand of iniquity. At least—when I was younger— And now, now, tonight, the night I'm fifty—

Silently he opened the library door and looked across the dark hall. Lucy and her mother were scraping lint at the big table in the crowded parlor; they had a servant helping them, but Lucy was yawning. He felt a fire as he saw that yawn. Soon, then— To bed, to bed! Incestuous sheets, sweet prince? Nay, my Veronica and I lie within the embrace of a mortal primness known as Holy Wedlock.

Thus we contrived eight children, and thus the four small graves within the red rusty fence—the longest no longer than my walking stick— Thus we had four children to grow to full stature—or close to it— Thus we came to another war.

I was a Stephens man from the first, but what possible difference can that make now, to Mr. Stephens or to me?

I was no Secessionist. Quite the contrary. But dress yourselves in gray, Suthy and Badger and Moses, and be off with your shooting-irons. Scrape the raw white fabric, Lucy. Put up the calves-foot jelly for the wounded, my Veronica. And cry and cry, and read your Bible, and pray again, and cry once more. . . .

Mist had condensed thickly after a chilly night, and Ira walked through it like a swimmer moving erect, walking rapidly though lamely, a man with broad round powerful shoulders, and carrying his head tipped forward as if to resist the weight of the flat-brimmed black hat pulled low on his forehead. His brow was channeled horizontally by four distinct wrinkles like deep narrow scars. His pale eyes shone from a covert of long dark lashes and coffee-colored eyebrows. His nose was insignificant, his wide full-lipped mouth the best feature in a round smooth face. Ira Claffey demonstrated the manner of a keen-eyed hunter who was forever on the watch for birds and expected that a covey would go crackling up and out, only a few steps ahead.

He would have been able to name the week—and possibly the day—of the year; he would have been able to name it by evidence before him if startled quickly awake from a century's repose. The long-leaved pines themselves, their banks of dark green plush in milky distance, with the outer tips of pine needles touched by autumnal tan, and yet this tan was invisible until you came close. Sunflowers, the little susie flowers still blooming spiritedly; sodden cornfields shrunken merciless, every ragged stalk of fodder soaked with mist; sandy, clayey bare spots in yard and gardens standing out silvery—ir.tense spots, never casual, but seeming to have been cleared and stamped recently, and for a special purpose . . . eight o'clock in the morning, as told by his silver watch, with the sun burning low and solid in a cloudless sky but with farthermost groves still fogged; jack-oaks half green and looking withered and scrofulous; the scrub swamp gums well turned at this date, and some of them burning in artificial pinks; tulip trees half green; some of the buttonwoods verdant as in summer.

The air hung clammy, but still good because it was wild, unprovoked by many men or their machines or structures. Ira heard the squeal of a train whistle (the service was untidy and uncertain on this Southwestern line from Macon to Americus and Albany. Claffey could not have told you with accuracy just how many trains jounced puffing up and down the line each day; at least he knew that the service was sadly confused because of military necessity) and far above the hill and western pines there frothed some woodsmoke as the cars halted at Anderson Station. Nothing much there except a wretched store, several houses, and a pyramid of old sawdust from Yeoman's mill, no longer operating.

. . . Air good because it was wild, and because deer had run through it, and turkeys also. It was long since the Creeks trotted those easy slopes, but you could still smell them when fall came on. Cold weather was their time, the time of Indian ghosts, and Ira loved to sense them; he loved the ghosts as well as any boy and better than some. More than the Indians, however: air was tanged with sweet-gum and persimmons and nut trees and dry goober vines and thistles. Ira Claffey worshipped vegetation; he understood the small or wide-spread miracles appurtenant to chlorophyll, photosynthesis . . . oh, list to the botanizing, the rub or splitting of cotyledons! . . . Any plant was his love, some were near to being his spiritual mistresses (he remembered making love and crushing infinitesimal purplish flowers while they did it; he and a slave girl, when he was young, when he was very young; but he could never get a white woman to lie with him in grass and blossoms, though he had tried. Ladies wanted beds). More than these affections, too: Ira had an enormous respect for vegetation beyond loving it; yet he was disciplined and sensible, and recognized that weeds must be ripped out, and some trees also.

Here, in the last field at his left hand, once the cotton had flourished . . . dry toughness of the stalks, the long long picking-sacks, the dark hands going like beaks to bite and swallow the cotton. No cotton now, markets were gone. A few good melon vines had volunteered and come running over the ground, squarely over the bottom rail of the fence; and more gourd vines and some pumpkins had volunteered from another quarter, and doubtless cucumbers as well, though Ira Claffey hadn't checked. They interbred as all gourds will. Now their awful progeny rotted amid visible ruins of a cotton planter's hopes. They were not melons, not pumpkins; they were monsters; not even the hungriest hand would eat them. Children came and kicked them loose and rolled them around. The green worms had come, too, and the green worms worked their especial penetrating assassination: once the air was admitted to these fruit, spoilage was hurried. The bastard product of vines lay exposed where leaves had fallen, like bulbous rotting bodies—skulls, perhaps—and they made an almost visible awfulness of odor. Ah, said Ira Claffey to himself, I didn't realize that this was such a horror. Well, there's no pride in having an old field turned into a sink, even though we have nothing to plant in it. Send Coffee down here post haste with a cart and let him get rid of these nuisances; he can dump them into the swamp

—bury them, if necessary. . . . No, Coffee's instructed with the Brimstones, I shan't take him from potato digging, I'll take Jonas from the woodpile and send him instead.

He left the orbs and jellies of noxious cross-breeds behind him thankfully, and turned north on a path which led from northern limits of his own plantation . . . pines cool in their brittle dignity, and a stile to be mounted over. This was a serious obstacle because his right leg could not be made to bend past forty-five degrees at the knee without pain. Something about a quadriceps tendon fastening itself to a femur; Ira did not know; he was no surgeon. He wrinkled his small nose, thinking of surgeons and probes which looked something like knitting needles—uncompanionable needles, to say the least.

Halfway down the northern slope of this ridge was where the stile bothered him; now he lurched on a downward path through land belonging to the McWhorters, the Yeomans, the Biles. Wilderness barely fit for pasture, these eminences were; no one was ever quite certain just where the joining lines ran, and no survey had been made since the earliest times. The McWhorter heirs lived in Americus and did nothing about their woodland except to pay microscopic taxes; the Yeoman place no longer operated as a plantation, with both the young-middle-aged men gone to the army and their wives dwelling with cousins in Tattnall County. The Biles were old, sedentary, retiring—their house stood two miles away, and they lived off their garden-patch with two slovenly house servants to bear them company. Ira Claffey himself had given them meat as a neighborly gift in winter and trusted that some other folks had done the same.

Irvine Yeoman, aged forty-one, had died in the same battle which claimed Sutherland Claffey—that Gettysburg place. For the moment Ira had forgotten.

In speculation on death (even secret half-realized contemplation of the misery) and on the scrawny barrenness which fell over remote holdings like this when war ruled, Ira desired keenly all faith and sustenance which the forest might give. . . . No deer here nowadays; one had not been shot in these woods for years. Raccoons and bobcats and other vermin, the spotted skunks and weasels darting at night on urgent autumnal errands . . . but lean stringy dancing legs of the deer went piercing other thickets. It was a miraculous thing how a deer could be frightened loose and go rising and plunging through tough jagged windfalls from some old hurricane; then you'd go and examine the route where he'd run, and you wouldn't think that a rat could have gotten through there; but the deer had, and the remarkable mechanism of his small hooves and elastic sinews was even now carrying him at a fool's pace through tighter fences of tumbled roots and pine boughs at the other end of the wilderness.

The Sweetwater branch to be crossed, a fine fair small stream to visit, generous in its treatment of roots of gums and willows which marked its way. Ira went across on the trunk of a tree he'd had his hands fell for that very purpose: to make a bridge where strollers could pass dry-shod. This portion of the valley belonged definitely to the McWhorters; Ira requested and received permission for the tree to be cut. It was a willow, hurt badly by lightning, and no great sacrifice in any event. He thought of kneeling to drink from the clean black water, he knew that this branch of Sweetwater would taste cold and leaf-mouldy, it would be a balm to mouth and tongue and throat and would pour slowly and darkly as if rinsing at a gentle course through his whole big body, into every extremity. He had risen before sunrise and worked long and well, and he needed a drink.

But better to try the spring beyond. Only a short way above the marshy plashy boundaries of the creek there stood clay and brown boulders exposed. . . . Here, he explained once to Lucy when he took her that way— Here is where the fairies live.

What kind of fairies?

Good ones, my dear. They are wet, very tiny, very green—

As big as me, Poppy?

Heavens, no. Miniature fairies of the damp sort, scarcely as big as your finger.

Where do they sleep?

Ah, there's that moss. Where do you think?

Yes, Poppy, I think they use the moss. And for table linen, too. Would they let me drink their water?

Assuredly. That's the reason they keep it running. Here, child, I'll make a cup of my hand. Beneath this rock, so. Now you bend down— take care, don't wet your boots and skirts— That's the way.

She faced him with plump pink face dripping, and said, I saw one, whilst I was drinking.

Where was he?

In the moss.

Alone he squatted now amid kindly memories and held out his hand. The water looked like a sheer fluted icicle. Ira had seen icicles long before, when he went to Washington City in winter. Water drenched his heavy hand, and curled along his wrist and tried to make its way up his sleeve, and he laughed and drew back his hand and shook it. This was the smallest, loveliest spring of several which he knew in these few square miles of domestic woodland. Especially the moss . . . his daughter was too grown-up to dream about fairies; she was twenty; the youth she loved had died of fever in the Yankee prison pen at Camp Douglas, Chicago, the winter before . . . or maybe she did dream secretly about fairies still. She owned a pretty mouth filled with all the young lady chatter and some of the young lady slang. Veronica would say impatiently, I declare, sometimes I believe that youngun has scarcely a wit in her noggin. But both the Claffeys were glad to boast Lucy as their own. She was dainty and valiant, she was skillful and kindly at nursing the sick be they white or black. Sick people followed her with their eyes. She would have made a noble wife for big Rob Lamar. But he was dead. So many were dead.

A chill came from darker gloom of pines and touched Ira's face and heart.

He shook his head, removed his hat, and—kneeling deeper and more painfully in the niche of stones and moss—he turned up his face beneath the steady pouring of the spring. He opened his mouth and drank deeply, swallowing steadily until he was satisfied.

Distantly sounded the slow talking of shod hooves on rock and hard-pan clay. Ira heard the approach as he was drying his face with a yellow bandana; he heard voices also, and a light metallic drag and jingle. With curiosity he examined the nearer paths to see who might be coming. Seldom did you meet hunters or planters in this quiet place; this section of the county was but sparsely settled— all the hunters gone to more dangerous hunting, some of the planters gone too.

A sorrel horse and a gray came in sight, moving cautiously down the steep trail from the north—from the direction of the empty Yeo-man plantation—and ridden by two young men. They appeared to be in uniform, at least as to pants and boots and hats, though one wore a jacket of checkered brown and drab denim. Behind them stumbled a youth in Confederate gray, bearing a surveyor's rod over his shoulder; and in the rear followed a tall ragged Negro who carried some sort of wooden satchel-box in his right hand and held a tripod and a looped linked chain in heavy coils upon his other shoulder. What's this, demanded Ira Claffey of himself in astonishment. Surveyors? Have the McWhorters sold out?

I want a drink, spoke the man in the checkered coat. He seemed to be in charge, for the little procession turned promptly along the declivity toward the spring. Ira walked to meet them.

Good day, gentlemen.

Good day to you.

The two horsemen dismounted. Both were officers or so Ira took them to be. Something about the undersized denim-jacketed fellow made Ira recoil instinctively if slightly as the man moved past him.

Look out you don't slip, Sid, said the other. The young private soldier and the slave were standing back, waiting to drink in their proper turns.

The unprepossessing man called Sid finished his refreshment and stood wiping his mouth on his sleeve. His jacket was smeared with clay, his boots greased reddishly with it. He had been walking in a marsh first; there was black muck higher on his legs.

You own this property? He was addressing Ira curtly.

No, sir. I believe we're standing on McWhorter land at the moment. My place begins yonder. He pointed to the fence barely visible among trees, south across the branch. He said, My name is Claffey. He offered his hand, but not eagerly.

Both officers shook hands with him. I'm Captain W. S. Winder— In belated respect to Ira's elder years he added Sir.

—This is Captain Boyce Charwick. He's from the topographical engineers.

Ira gave his grave smile. Are you looking up a new battleground? This would be rather remote from the lines.

Prison, said Winder.

A prison? Here?

It's possible. I'm charged with locating a site. We're considering several locations. This is one of them.

Ira had a thought of murderers and lunatics in chains. What sort of prison would that be?

A stockade to keep damn Yankee prisoners in, replied Charwick.

A stockade to keep God damn Yankee prisoners in, Captain Winder amended. They both laughed.

Ah, I see. But it's so far from—

Winder grimaced in a manner to show impatience or impertinence, Claffey could not be sure which. The captains climbed back into their saddles and stood waiting for the other two to drink—first the white boy, then the Negro.

It's a long way removed from the theatre of war, is it not?

My father, General John H. Winder, is Superintendent of Military Prisons. I have been authorized to seek a site for a new stockade. You've got railroad transportation here—

His hand swept and stabbed the horizon, pointing out things which Ira Claffey had known for years. He talked impolitely as if the planter were a child retarded in mind.

Excellent drainage. Bountiful supply of water; not that the Yankees are over-prone to bathe, or so I've heard.

Laughter.

I'm considering this area seriously because of the provender situation. You folks hereabouts are not tributary to Virginia when it comes to food. Self-sustaining, I'd say. Bountiful crops—or at least the areas where they could be raised. How was your own corn this year?

Fair, sir, said Claffey guardedly. Merely fair. Locally we received inundation at the wrong season. But— How on earth could you build sufficient structures to house—?

See these pines? How many million board feet of pine's around here, anyway? I didn't say anything about structures. We can take those trees and square them off, and slap them together, and build a fence around ten or twenty acres—a fence so high that the meanest living Yankee couldn't get over the top if he had an aerial balloon.

Laughter. Sid, you're a caution, said Captain Charwick.

Claffey stared. I was told that you are a topographical engineer. Do you agree, sir, that this location is ideal for a prison site?

Charwick said, his smile gone, Well, I agree in general theory with Captain Winder's observations. Of course I'm present strictly in an advisory capacity. His decision will be tailored by demands other than those of topography. He may be aware of military exigencies of which I know nothing—

Oh, thought Claffey, talk, talk, talk. I know your sort. We had mealy-mouths like yours when we were baking in the sun at Matamoras.

Captain Winder took up his reins. I want you to see the lay of the land on this southern ridge, Boyce. I went over it yesterday—

They were turning, the boy and the Negro waited in the path.

Where would you get your labor, to build such a large stockade?

Winder's rodent mouth puffed out as he wiped his teeth with his tongue. Mr. Claffey, sir, and he emphasized that address—Mr. Claffey, we can obtain the authority to impress all the labor we need. Tom Twitt's niggers, Bill Bump's niggers, your niggers, anybody's niggers. Also the authority to take your acres for our purpose—as much as we need.

Ira said coolly, I trust you'll require none of my acres. If my surviving son returns from the army, he'll need the land.

I take it you've lost a son? Young Winder set his boots tightly into his stirrups. My sincerest regrets, sir.

Two, said Ira. The youngest at Crampton's Gap, the eldest at Gettysburg.

Ah. Sad. A mere boy, I presume—a private soldier?

He was a major.

Winder looked disconcerted momentarily. He felt a stinging rebuke against his bumptiousness and cavalier attitude; it was apparent, yet he could not locate it, or discern in just what words and intonation it was phrased. He gave a kind of half salute. Captain Charwick touched his hat-brim. The Negro and the boy were already far up the slope with their burdens. The officers rode quickly away up the difficult steep, both riding effortlessly as if they had spent years in their saddles, as undoubtedly they had.

The party went into the woods. Claffey did not see them again after he crossed near the stile; he saw only the marks of their going. He saw traces where rails had been taken out beside the stile in order for horses to pass, but the rails had been restored carefully to

position again. Ira wondered whether, if these people had not chanced
to meet him at the spring near the Sweetwater branch, they might have
left rails lying after taking them down. Perhaps he was doing the
officers an injustice in the thought.

But he did not like their attitude. They seemed to bring a meanness
to war. There should be nobility about the business of risking life,
even the business of taking it. Why did we all respect more the memory
of the benevolent knight who died in battle—the profound and kingly
knight—more than the memory of the truculent, self-seeking warrior?
. . . The memory—or the legend? Which? . . . Both the godly knight
and the cruel one wagered the same; they wagered hopefully that
they would not need to lay their lives down; yet each took the same
hazard in the wagering, and one might fight as stoutly as the other,
and each would be just as dead as the other when the end came. It
was a thought to baffle him. Ira squinted his eyes shut and shook
his head like a horse shaking off flies; he always did that when he was
perplexed, when he was alone and there was no one to see him. He
had to guard against doing it before his family and his servants, for
he felt that simple dignity was an honest and important thing. Yet
somehow the shaking seemed to help.

He brooded his way back to the potato patches. It was now long
after nine o'clock. He had wasted a good hour and a half in his
wanderings and musings, and in conversing with the military party.
He considered it wasted, because for the first time in—when?—the
forest had not granted him the peace and food he sought. A prison,
here where always there had been the green pleasure of growth, or
water having its way with lichens—the blessing of gum, pine cones,
sly animals feeding, rare birds meeting their kind? Let them build
their prison someplace else, he'd have none of it. He knew the President, or had known him slightly seventeen years before. He should
go to Richmond (but it would cost a sight of cash, and cash was not
plentiful in these days) and utter a protest. He should take a firm
stand, if this supercilious young captain sought to preëmpt any of the
Claffey acres.

Oh, bother, bother. That Winder person said that they were merely
considering the site. No doubt they'll select another area, Lord knows
where.

He said farewell to the forest, and heard birds buzzing through it,
and had some thought of taking a shotgun soon and fetching a few
birds for the table. Claffey did not truly enjoy shooting birds (he
was an excellent shot; so all his boys had been) and he pitied the
blood and drooping which followed. But Veronica was like a child—
she beamed and giggled like Lucy herself—whenever he proffered
wildfowl. Black Naomi had a special blue earthenware dish in which
she cooked them. She used wine and onions—

Coffee and Jem had made great strides with the potatoes. A good two-thirds of the Brimstones were dug, and by noontime the hands would doubtless be ready to start in on the Hayti yams, which they preferred for the table, and which it was easier to raise as fare for the slaves because the Hayti yams were more prolific and they stored well. Common yams were the most prolific of all, but had rather a pumpkinish flavor. Ira couldn't abide growing them.

Coffee. Did you dig these?

Coffee was a long-armed, long-faced fellow with Indian blood apparent. Nossuh, Mastah, I use the hoe. That Jem there—he got the old potato hook. I done told him to look sharp.

Well, Jem, suppose you try the hoe instead. Potato hook's a tricky implement. You've hurt a few in this hill. Look there. And there, in the next. . . .

Real sorry, Mastah. They just jump up out of the earth and get themselves tore, fore I know what they's about.

Hear me, Jem. Do you use the hoe from now on, and give the hook to Coffee. And slow with the hoe. You'll need to eat the ones you bruise, and they don't keep long so. That you know.

Jem, wide and black and rubbery as to body, stood grinning weakly in an attitude of shame.

Caution, Jem, use caution. Hear me, now?

Mastah, I surely take care.

Gracious, thought Ira, I neglected to look into the pine straw situation. But there'll be sufficient, over on Little Sweetwater. We fetched none from there last year. . . . He continued to give the slaves detailed instructions. He had decided that they shouldn't get into the yams today. There was sun, and the crop would have to undergo a good drying for several hours before the piles were started. There were the floors of piles to be built, the trenches to be dug around the floors; then a few days of sustained drying should continue under pine straw only, before the piles were finally earthed up and barked up.

Ira went on toward the big house (oh Lord, if only he had paint) and stopped a moment at the implement shed, which he unlocked with a key selected from the hefty wad at his belt. He cleaned his budding knife and hung it in its groove. Then, locking up, he walked on around through the narrow carriageway, aiming for the west end of the gallery where he wished to examine some cold frames he'd built. But he was surprised to find a gig under the big oak, with an old black horse tied and eating oak leaves. At first Ira thought that the advent of this horse and rig must have something to do with the surveyors he encountered; they had so few callers these days. Then he recognized the horse as belonging to the Reverend Mr. Cato Dillard of Americus.

He heard a voice— Poppy, she said, and it was Lucy, rising drunkenly from the top step where she'd been sitting. She is grown suddenly

ill, thought Ira. An epidemic, perhaps? Some fever has struck? He
limped toward her and held out his arms as the girl came swaying
down the steps.

Oh, Poppy, and she nuzzled deep into his wide-flung coat. Poppy.
It's Badge.

Lucy— The minister's horse—

They wrote to him. A colonel did—and—a surgeon. They wrote to
him first. Reckoned it'd be easier on— On us.

Where's Mr. Dillard? Where's your mother, child? He shook her as
if he hated her.

She's on her bed. They came— It was an hour ago. The letters only
reached them last night. Mrs. Dillard is with Mother, and he's praying up there. He wished me to stay for prayers. I didn't wish to pray.

Still holding her in his arms, he waited and waited. Finally he
could command his voice and make it do what he wanted. He could
make it talk and sound like a human being, not like a beast's whine.
Lucy, where did it happen?

Some place up in Tennessee. Chick-a-something. He was hurt on
the twentieth of September, and we didn't know it, Poppy, we didn't
know it all this time, we were in utter ignorance. Why didn't they tell
us? You might have gone to him. So he died of his wounds, just as my
dear Rob died in that Yankee pen of his sickness.

. . . Lucy, are you certain that you don't wish to pray? I think—it
would—be—well—if we both went in to—prayers. Later Mr. Dillard
can hold a service for the hands.

It will do no good, said Lucy, but she came quivering along with
him. It never does any good. We should know that by now.

. . . And there sat in a window a certain young man . . . and as Paul
was long preaching, he sunk down with sleep, and fell down from the
third loft, and was taken up dead.

And Paul went down, and fell on him, and embracing him said,
Trouble not yourselves: for his life is in him.

Ah, it was not, life not in him in the slightest, but only abysmal decay and bad sight and odor, like the cross-bred pumpkin-gourd-
cucumbers in that unholy field yonder, nigh to the woods. He was the
last: Moses, the youngest, first; then Suthy, the eldest; now Badger,
the middle son. Get up from your mounds, you small fry behind that
old rusty fence, and join in lamentation, for we've only Lucy to help
us with the task of weeping.

The Yankees got Moses and Suthy. Yankees now destroy Badge.
They got him, with their many cannon and many men, and their
quick-shooting breech-loading rifles. Damn the Yankees. Damn them
forever, damn them to a hundred hells with their cannon and their
money and their blankets and their medicines. God—damn—the
Yankees. God damn the Yankees. God *damn* the Yankees. Amen.

II

Having shared the grief of the Claffeys for some hours, the Reverend
Mr. Cato Dillard at last handed his wife into the gig and prepared to
drive away. Grief was nothing new to Cato Dillard, whether he
suffered his own or witnessed it in that portion of humanity he considered to be within his charge; and he believed that all mankind he
had observed since leaving the seminary came within his charge.
Excepting, possibly, Roman Catholics. Sometimes he wasn't even too
certain about those. And, of recent years, Yankees. . . .

Veronica Claffey stared sightlessly at the canopy above her bed, and
lay unable to read her Bible or to respond to any prayer offered. Lucy
was in her own room, also, with the servant Ninny rubbing her ankles.
Ira Claffey attended the brief service to which the slaves had been
called. The black people's wail and chanting hung bitterly protracted
in the sunlight of early afternoon; the whites wished that the slaves
would not manufacture such sounds, but there was no way of hushing
them.

The servant Pet came with a withe basket containing corn bread,
fried chicken and a bottle of beer to refresh the Dillards on their drive
to Americus. Cato Dillard embraced his friend and then drove away
without looking back; it was better so.

He wished with recurrent regret that Ira Claffey was not averse to
metaphysical discussion, but Ira was averse to it. Ira was one of three
men among the parson's acquaintances who possessed sufficient scholarly background to indulge in such activity. Still Ira always changed
the subject as soon as Cato Dillard was well-embarked and as soon as
his tiny eyes burnt bright with intellectual zeal and as soon as his
eager voice thrummed with a new range and timbre of enthusiasm.
Ira's religion was of a gentle, affectionate, pantheistic variety, and he
refused stubbornly to be tricked into any exercise of theology.

I fear the beer may be flat, Ira said in parting. It's from the only
brewing which kept, and this year we can't spare the grain. What with
military levies and all.

Flat or not, it'll be tasty. Goodbye, my dear friend.

Goodbye, Mrs. Dillard. I can say but Thank You. Goodbye, Brother.

And the dry shivering handclasp saying more.

God bless you, Brother Ira. I'll pray daily.

Whatever benefit that may bring! Bitterness of the deep and stunning hurt.

I'll pray, Brother Ira.

And light wheels going away, and the gloom on all hearts.

Halfway down the lane with its magnolias on one side and its small oaks on the other, Cato turned to his wife and began to quote, So we say farewell to our lamented dead, and know only that we shall reassemble on that great day when all shall foregather—some from the East, and some from the West, some from the South— And it may even be that a few shall come from the North.

Muckle wish have I that any should come from the North. Effie Dillard was a Scotswoman. The words of her Rothesay youth came easily from her wide thin lips when she was stirred. She was wearing a faded frilled pink cap and now she lifted her straw bonnet and drew it on over the cap, which act would have seemed astonishing to a stranger. Mrs. Dillard had suffered fever many years before—had nearly died of it, and all her hair was lost. She wore caps, waking and sleeping. No one except a trusted servant had ever seen her without a cap, since she recovered. Not even the Reverend Mr. Dillard.

She was a bony, bent woman with knobs on her shoulders and a face like a yellow witch. Everyone in the region knew that she had a heart bigger than the area of Sumter County itself, and many traded on her accordingly. Her skin was marred by smallpox which she had acquired when nursing a brood of Negroes from whom the rest of humanity fled.

Effie, don't talk hatred.

I feel it. If I feel it I should utter it.

Thus purging your soul? The minister smiled a tired sly smile.

Aye. She gave him the ghost of her own smile.

Mr. Cato Dillard was plump and squat, and loose flesh squeezed out around his short neck in rolls. His hazel eyes lost themselves in chasms of veined wrinkles; they peeked out like twin squirrels in hiding. He was brilliantly far-sighted, literally as well as figuratively, and donned his spectacles only when working on his sermons or when reading tracts aloud to some blind or illiterate sufferer unable to read the tracts himself. He was sixty-six years old and still moved with the bounce of youth. The Dillards had no living children, but five of their eight grandchildren were serving in the army, all alive as yet.

Mr. Cato Dillard had one vanity: the tufts of luxuriant tingling curly silver, growing down past his ears on either side of his firm fat face, and so fluffy that the lightest breeze set them rippling.

Cate, she called him in private, and sometimes in public when she forgot. Now she cried, Cate! in a manner of alarm.

Is something wrong, my dear?

You've turned off the road. You're not bound for Americus. There's the railroad ahead.

Only bound down this side track on an errand. Briefly.

Where are we bound?

He wriggled guiltily. If you must know, we're bound for the Widow Tebbs' place.

Cate, are you daft?

The Cloth can be worn anywhere and remain unsullied. It is my Christian duty. And I might add—yours also, Effie.

Let me out of this gig, man. I'll not go.

You've been before.

On a fool's errand!

Effie, don't be difficult. She's a poor miserable creature, with no great happiness behind her, and only iniquity and grief to make up her present, and flames reaching ahead. But she's human, and I knew her grandfather well, and as a ruling elder he represented our congregation in the presbytery.

Scarlet is as scarlet does. What charity can you give her? I mean what charity would she accept? Neither The Word nor the practice thereof. She does not know the meaning of repentance.

Perhaps, at one time, neither did Mary Magdalene.

Ah. Touch pitch, I say.

Now, how often do you suppose The Saviour touched pitch? And how severely was He tarred?

Cate, you're daft.

But Mrs. Dillard gave no further remonstrance—only a reedy sigh now and then, as the little vehicle bumped down the miserable side road.

Over the railway tracks they rocked, the horse snorting when wheels grated on the rails: Blackie recognized the railroad and tossed his head at the notion of encountering a locomotive which always set him to spreading his legs and lifting wild ears. The Widow Tebbs' place was just beyond—a small house with a sloping roof like the tilt of a water-soaked visored cap. There was a ruined stable, a pig-pen, several miscellaneous sheds; and across a wide dirty yard stood a cubicle structure which had once served as a storage place for corn. That was when Dickwood Tebbs was alive. Nowadays it was fitted out with curtains, lamps, a reedy music box, and definitely a bed. In this building the Widow Tebbs did her entertaining. Her children referred to it as The Crib, as did Mrs. Tebbs' regular patrons. This collection of buildings was bounded by a fence of split palings, heavy with gourd vines, some sections leaning in and some sections leaning out. A few tattered specimens of poultry fled jabbering as the gig came closer.

To think you'd carry your own good wife to such a spot.

My dear, be benevolent and forgiving. Her eldest's just back from the battles, and he's wanting a foot. This is sad poverty, dire poverty.

When they halted before the sagging gate, they saw the flight of

something other than poultry: a small brown object which sped under
the house like a bunchy high-backed varmint. It was a child, a boy of
three or four, dressed in a loose skirt and shirt of filthy material. He
traveled on his hands and knees with a speed to baffle the eye. One
moment he was crouched, gazing fearfully at the approach of the gig;
the next he had streaked between the chunks of stone which supported
the old cottage, and had gone into darkness like a rabbit or a pig.

The Reverend Mr. Cato Dillard smiled. That would be her youngest.

Never knowing who his father is or was!

Doubtless none of them knows, save the eldest.

A flat-chested youth of thirteen came out on the stoop and stared
warily. Mr. Dillard said, Good afternoon, Floral.

The boy mumbled a reply. He had a head small for the skinny body
and long neck on which it was perched. His head was covered with
spiny golden hair, kept clipped raggedly close by his mother's shears.
He wore a dirty undershirt, and patched pantaloons were held around
his thin waist by a knotted cord.

Is your mother at home, Floral?

Yes, sir.

Then fetch her, please. And when you've done that, come down
here to the buggy. I've something for you.

The boy ducked through the door, there were mumblings inside and
then an exclamation of surprise, then Floral reappeared. He came
down the two steps and across the littered yard, walking gingerly and
seeking smooth places to set his bare left foot as he came.

What's ado here, Flory? Cato Dillard spoke with light jocularity
which it was difficult for him to muster, faced with the want and deg-
radation he witnessed, faced with the boy's wizened face and round
blank gray eyes. Did you hurt your foot?

Yes, sir.

How did that occur?

Stepped on a damn old nail in a board.

Hush that profanity, child, said Effie Dillard sharply. Now you
climb up here on the hub and show me your foot.

With agility, even if in some pain, Flory obeyed. Solemnly he presented the dirty sole of his foot to the woman's gaze. Effie took her
specs from her pocket, examined the wound, and gave an exclamation
of disgust. I'll be bound. That needs green ointment, and I must see
to it.

Will it hurt?

Never you mind about that. It's got proud flesh in it.

Yes, ma'am.

From his jacket pocket Cato Dillard drew a comfit-case of battered
silver; he had carried it since his youth. Solemnly he opened the lid
and revealed a hoard of lozenges. These are wintergreen, he said.

One for you, one for the little lad— What's his name, my boy? He went under the house.

That's Zoral.

Very well, one for Zoral. One for Laurel—

She ain't to home. She's over helping tend old Mrs. Bile. Both the niggers is sickly, and so's the old Mrs.

Save it for her. These are hard to come by.

Well I know. Flory sucked his lozenge with relish.

Where is Coral?

Coral wouldn't want no sugarplum. He just don't want nothing since he got himself wounded. Flory had a greedy eye on the lozenge offered for his elder brother.

He might fancy it. Where is he, bubby?

Took the shotgun and gone a-hunting.

What? On one foot?

I done whittled him out a crutch. Flory still eyed the lozenge. Had it all ready for him when the wagon set him down at the door. First thing he says was, I'll learn you to make gawk at my crippledness, and he took a swipe at me with the crutch. Coral's mean as sin.

The Widow Tebbs appeared on the stoop, noticeably unstayed but wearing a fringed shawl over an old blue poplin gown which had been obviously a hand-me-down and was too tight for her. Her ruddy hair was wound up in a mass of curl papers. Heavens, said Cato involuntarily, behold the Gorgon Medusa.

Don't you choose to light, Parson? And Ma'am? Her voice was high of key, nervous as a fledgling girl's voice . . . she had no great share of wits. Her soft chin was weak, sagging; her bright brown eyes kept up an incessant blinking. Her body bulged, but in keeping with its original construction. A walking fleshly altar to Eros, thought Cato. Nothing could be done with her or about her. Nothing, not from her maiden days which must have ended when she was ten.

Despite the fact that she had a son nearly seventeen years old, she was barely in her thirties. Marget Lumpkin she had been born, and her father once conducted a tannery in Americus. He drove his children from him by fiendish exercise of the most antique and ascetic religious profession. Marget, or Mag as she was more commonly called, was in trouble at fourteen, wife to a slovenly young farmer and mother of his child at fifteen. . . . She had a persistent pitiable fondness for color, whether in flowers or in ribbons; the rougher boys of the town in her young time knew for a literal truth that Mag would lay herself down for the mere gift of a brass button or a spool of crimson thread. Lumpkin was a respectable—even an honored—name throughout most of Georgia, but the poor girl had always loathed the sound of it, when meaner children teased her muddled little brain and called her Bumpkin. Hence she groped for some sort of beauty when she named her scrawny troop of children (three of them fathered by men other than her husband). She named them Coral, Laurel, Floral, Zoral. Dick Tebbs had been dead for ten years, but poor Mag was gone into whoredom long before he died; and he spent his last sullen sickly winters in cutting enough wood to keep The Crib warm while she did her entertaining.

Won't you light? The widow asked it a second time, as the Dillards sat in silence, pitying her. Effie Dillard's bark was savage at times, but she did not even know how to bite.

No, thank you, Sister Marget. We stopped by to offer a small gift; but it is a long homeward journey.

The Widow Tebbs brightened at the thought of a gift. Probably she thought of ribbons. She said, I do implore you not to call me Sister, Parson. Puts me in mind of Pa, and he was so cross all the while.

She came forward eagerly as she spoke, her soft red mouth spreading in a smile which enhanced her degenerate beauty.

Paint, said Mrs. Dillard, and lifted an accusing bony finger of her mitted hand.

Whereabouts?

On your face, woman. On your very lips.

Oh, no, ma'am. This is red off of a candy stick. I keep it special.

Effie groaned. Cato Dillard bent his head to conceal his own amusement; he knew that he was transgressing mildly in finding any glee in the situation, yet he could not help himself. He reached beneath the seat and brought out a solid weighty bag of soiled cotton cloth. Tis meal, he told the widow. A member of the congregation brought us a generous gift from his mill this week, and I'm sharing it with you, Marget.

Perhaps she would rather have had a wornout bonnet or the feathers or flowers from it, but Mag was grateful. Why, Parson, I give you thanks. Times are so hard with—

She was about to say, With so many menfolks gone to the army, but innate and unsuspected delicacy restrained her. Instead she said after hesitation, With things the way they be.

What about the boy's foot?

It's gone complete. Marget blinked more rapidly than ever, and tears were spilling. Poor little Coral—it was only his third big battle. He got a ball right through the foot, and them surgeons hacked it off. He said they held him down a-doing it. Always cutting. All a surgeon knows how to do.

Effie declared that they might be losing a second foot in the family unless precautions were taken about Flory. She produced a bottle of green ointment of her own manufacture, one of several medicines without which she would seldom travel abroad. She made Flory fetch a cup, and measured a portion of the medicine. Enthusiastically she recited the recipe while Flory listened with horror. Good refined turpentine and lard, also honey and beeswax; these had been melted together with a bit of finely pulverized verdigris stirred in. Did the widow have any beeswax? She reckoned there was some around, somewhere. . . . Well, Effie was determined to enter the house and prepare the poultice herself—or rather a little tent, stiffened with warm beeswax and worked into the oozing wound—but the widow said that her fire was cold and it would take time to build it up. Effie extracted a promise and had to be content with that. Flory still clung to the gig wheel and sucked on the second lozenge which he had wheedled out of the minister by mere exercise of longing in his pinched face.

While they were thus engaged, the whistle of a train sounded, and Blackie's ears arose and Blackie's feet spread apart, and Cato had to climb down and take Blackie's head and speak soothingly. The others watched the train come lurching, smoking past. The engineer managed a couple of extra whistle-toots when directly in front of the cottage; he knew the widow well, and always saluted her. There were a few soldiers guarding the burden cars—foodstuffs for the army, probably—and they waved and shouted pleasantries which could not be understood. The widow waved urgently in reply.

Just as last cinders were flying and while Blackie still snuffled, a thin youth progressed slowly around the corner of The Crib. He stopped when he saw the gig, then came on, looking at the ground beneath and ahead of him. He swung his body from side to side, pivoting on the homemade crutch, putting his right foot forward, hopping the pole of the crutch into a new position . . . thus he traveled. His pantleg flopped in rags around the stump where his left leg had been severed at the ankle. Coral did not resemble his mother in appearance, and bore no resemblance to the other children. His black hair was shaggy, his thick black brows pulled together in a hairy scowl, his cheeks were darkened with young untrimmed beard. In his right hand he carried a shotgun with a mended stock, and Cato Dillard rejoiced to see that a quail—no, two—hung suspended from Coral's belt.

I see you did well, my boy. Dillard spoke with enthusiasm as soon as Coral was within hearing.

Got two.

I never did hear that old gun at all, said Floral in surprise.

Well, it's an accomplishment, declared the minister. And working without a dog.

Coral glowered as if he'd expected the minister to say, Without a foot. He stopped near the steps and said guardedly, Old Zack got himself kilt whilst I was gone to— Just went to sleep on the tracks and let the cars run over him. Least that's what they tell me.

Coral, cried his mother, come down out the gate and make some nice manners to the parson and the Mrs.

No, said the youth. He moved painfully up the steps.

You got no call to be so mean, sonny. And they fetched meal for us; and Flory's saving you a candy.

Don't want no candy. He was gone into the cottage.

I told you so, said Flory, and popped Coral's designated winter-green into his own mouth. He's just poison mean.

You shut your trap, Flory. His mother struck at him but the boy dodged.

We must go. Dillard had climbed back into the gig. Marget, daughter, I merely want you to know that you are often in my prayers.

Thank you kindly, Parson, but I don't want to be in nobody's prayers. Had enough of prayers when I was little.

I speak now from the Larger Catechism: *We are by nature children of Wrath, bond slaves to Satan, and justly liable to all punishments in this world and that which is to come.* God bless you, Marget.

He began to turn Blackie away from the gate.

God bless you folks, too, and then Marget stopped in alarm at having been lured into saying it. She cried after them, I do thank you for the meal.

Save the poke, Effie Dillard yelled. Allow no one to make off with it. The dominie can pick it up one day.

Wait, the widow screamed. She sent Flory into the cottage to dump meal into a pan, and then he flew out again, waving the dusty sack in his hand. He hustled down the road at a limping gallop, and grinned shyly up at the pair when he handed them the bag. He breathed, Could I have just one more candy?

You're a little pig. Effie spoke severely. You should save some for your sister and your baby brother. Cate, do you give me that comfit-box. She counted out three more lozenges while her husband sighed. One for you, one for Sister, one for Brother. Mind, now.

Yes, ma'am.

And mind about that tent of green ointment, lest you be like poor Coral.

I'll mind. Ma can fix it, soon as we get a fire going.

They looked back at the house. Zoral was emerging from his den under the house but the widow seemed paying no attention to the child. She kept waving earnestly at the Dillards until they were gone across the railroad. She could not hear him, but the Reverend Mr. Cato Dillard concerned himself audibly with The Gospel According to Saint John.

Woman, where are those thine accusers? hath no man condemned thee?

Revelation comes later than yon, said his wife. *Mystery, Babylon the Great. The Mother of Harlots and Abominations of the Earth.*

Oh, Effie. I prefer The Gospel. *She said, No man, Lord. . . . Neither do I condemn thee.*

Back at the Tebbs house, Floral worked reluctantly for a time, fetching wood and kindling of pine splinters which his mother demanded. Coral was hunched on a stool by the table, plucking the first bird. He had put the shotgun on its pegs, and hung the shot flask and powder flask where they belonged. Flory went to take them down, and his brother spewed out a stream of profanity and struck with his crutch. You leave them things alone, God damn you, you little squeak.

Now, you youngsters—

Tain't your shotgun any more'n it's mine!

Tis, by God!

I used it whilst you was in the army. I got some ground doves and—

Ground doves! No wonder I'm shy a foot! That's the unluckiest thing a mortal can do: kill a ground dove. Any nigger in the county could of tolt you that. You hadn't no call to use the shotgun. Tis mine; because I'm the eldest and a gun is handed down from a father to his eldest.

God damn lie.

You touch my gun again and I'll beat the poop out of you.

Ah, you and your old crutch—

Coral hurled the crutch. It might have injured Flory but it only grazed his hip. Nevertheless the younger boy burst into squalls and hurried blindly out of the door, calling spitefully, You damn cripple! Crip, crip, crip, crip, crip, crip, cripple—! He tripped over Zoral below the stoop, and the stunted baby set up a bellowing. Mag flew to the rescue, calling loudly on the world to witness what troubles possessed her.

Floral retreated into woods behind the privy and solaced himself with a wad of pine gum. It occurred to him that if he carried a heavy club, and crept up silently on a covey of quail without disturbance, he might be able to get a bird for himself by flinging the club, much as Coral was forever hurling his crutch. Flory had tried unsuccessfully before with rocks, never with a club. He hunted around for a suitable bludgeon, found one, and tottered off among the trees. He played that the stick in his hands was a gun. Not just a shotgun, but a regular military musket. Maybe even a modern rifle. Maybe even a modern Henry rifle, a repeater with copper cartridges; he had seen such weapons carried by soldiers on several occasions when soldiers called upon his mother. Such weapons were captured from Yankees.

He played that he was killing a Yankee. Hold still there, you Yankee scum. You heard me. Don't move or I'll blow your guts out handsome. Hold right still, don't try to get away, you Yankee bastard! Look sharp; I warned you.

Flory lifted the stick to his shoulder. His face was contorted and he squeezed his eyes shut as he fired. *Poom.*

III

At this same hour in Paris a rain came blackly. It was mid-afternoon in Georgia, evening in the region near the old Medical College where the good Dr. Cordier had lectured hoarsely above his cadavers more than twenty years before. The good Dr. Cordier was long since in his tomb, but at a favorite café two of his former students now sat with wine. There was a tablecloth of flowered green, the crusty bread lay broken upon it, the big shiny casserole still stood on its seared frame above a burning lamp.

Dr. Bucheton reached over and selected a mushroom which had eluded him in gravy; he speared it with surgical precision, ate it, put down his fork and nodded across at his companion.

You see how it is, Henry. I not only take some pride in myself as a gourmet; I'm also a glutton. He patted the belly which stood out under his tight white waistcoat.

The bearded Henry Wirz said, I am a dyspeptic. He was a round-shouldered thin-faced man, past forty, sallow of skin, and with blood vessels apparent in his pale eyeballs which suggested constant pain, sleeplessness, a constriction of various forces clamoring for release. His French was spoken shrilly, almost explosively, with a pronounced German accent. Many people took him to be a Jew, but he was not a Jew. It was as if he sought to relieve the somber acids moving through his digestive system and in his leaden blood, by gauding himself in tints commonly worn only by younger men. His jacket was saffron, his shirt of checkered cambric, his stock of Stuart tartan silk. His right arm rested in a black sateen sling, and the arm was giving him misery this night; he kept groping across the tablecloth with the fingers of his left hand, and caressing and kneading the slim bandaged bulk within the sateen.

You still have the sulphate of morphia? In your lodgings?

The devil—yes. I have plenty. But I can't take too much of that stuff. Henry Wirz had something else in his lodgings in the Rue d'Assas: he had it hanging in the big wardrobe: a uniform of Confederate gray.

Be sure to reduce the dosage by degrees.

You don't have to tell me that. But you don't understand how it is with us in the Confederacy, Pierre. These things are unprocurable. The blockade is tighter all the time.

Dr. Bucheton nodded sympathetically, and filled Henry's wine glass, then his own. I don't pay much attention to what goes on over there. My dear friend, you'll forgive me when I state a simple if unpleasant professional fact. Between my own patients and what goes on at the hospital and my lectures at the school— Well, my wife tells the children not to run shrieking to their nurse that a strange impostor has forced his way into the house, on those rare occasions when I do appear. As for my mistress—

He shrugged. I should not beat her if she began to dally with a younger and more light-hearted man. It would be only justice if she did. Thus I cast my speeding eyes over the printed page, and I see that your Mr. Mason and your Mr. Slidell are still on this side of the Atlantic, and I wish them well, and I also would like to have you shipping to us cotton and rice and tobacco and other good things, but I don't want to go to war with the Americans about it. And I assume also that when the old friend of my student days appears, and lo and behold he is *Captain* Henry Wirz— I assume that he has possibly some business with Mr. Slidell in France? But I don't give it more thought than that. It's a physical and mental impossibility. Do you forgive me, Henry?

Wirz nodded. My arm is particularly troublesome tonight.

Come, I've just ordered cognac.

I have no head for cognac. You should remember.

Well, perhaps we should call it the poor man's sulphate of morphia or— Do you have cognac in the Confederate States, Henry?

Only what is left in a few people's cellars. Some we get from the Yankees. Damn this thing, Pierre. I think you injured the nerves when you removed the *sequestra*.

Hush, you very stupid fellow! The great Dr. Bucheton does not go about butchering nerves with his scalpel. Do you wish me to draw another diagram? Here, upon the tablecloth, give me your pencil—

Nonsense. I want no more of your diagrams. I want only for the pain to go away.

In time, Henry, in time. You must needs be patient. You've undergone a great deal of treatment—some of it very inept and messy, according to what I found when I got into that wrist of yours last Monday. This is merely Old Dame Nature's way of saying, My God, I've been stabbed, I've been raped, I've been slaughtered. Watch closely. The drainage has already decreased to a bare trickle. The efflorescence has decreased as well. And the seropurulent matter which came out of there! Where did you say you got this wound? In the battle of Louisiana?

No, no, no, Louisiana is my *home*. Or was. The wound I received in the fighting near Richmond, our capital. That was a year ago last summer. They called the place Seven Pines. God damn the Yankee who did this to me.

The fortunes of war, Henry. You know, I did some soldiering myself in '48. Have I yet told you about—?

Fortune of war or no fortune of war, may the good God damn the Yankee who did this to me. I say, Give him to me. Let me meet him face to face. Who are you, Yankee? Was it your fingers on the lanyard which did the wickedness? Show them to me; I will show you my hand, or my arm which you did such cruelty to; now show me, Yankee, your own evil hand which performed the act. So what is that hand like, and where is the Yankee? Is it a young man's hand—lively, tanned, hairy, a strong right hand? Or maybe the Yankee was left-handed?

Henry Wirz was speaking with such passion that Madame bent down from her smoky perch under the archway and gave him a searching look. An idle old waiter had drawn near, in alarm at having to deal with a foreign inebriate; a party of students and girls from the half-world had given up all conversation of their own and were united in attention.

Henry, said Bucheton in disquiet.

I tell you, I should like to meet that hand, and the man to whom it is attached! Ah—

No doubt you should, no doubt you should. Here, waiter, we'll both have another cognac. Immediately, if you please!

In his sudden outpouring of frenzy, Wirz had thudded his bandaged forearm against the table, and the act brought forth a single exclamation of agony. He sat silently, his glance turned down, the sweat standing like fragile pebbled topaz bulbs upon his high bony forehead.

Bucheton began chattering in rapid sequence punctuated by low laughter intended to be soothing. He spoke a string of gossip and reminiscence concerning their mutual student past. Not for one moment did he think that Wirz was imagining or magnifying the misery dancing amid the nerves of his right arm. Pierre Bucheton had seen the slivered radius and ulna exposed, and his own small bright tongs had tightened on crumbs of corroded bone which he found serrated amid the tissues of Henry Wirz. He was a companion of this patient a solid generation previously, but had not fallen in with him again until the current year. Ah, yes—in 1849 Henry had indeed sent him a letter; that was when Henry passed through Paris en route for America, his dead wife left behind beneath her slab in Zurich, his living children left with their grandparents. The note had reached Bucheton belatedly since he was gone with the army. So he had not encountered Wirz again until this modern time of 1863. He had never thought that Wirz would be one to bear adversity with the dignity which passes for serenity. Old Cordier and others had signalled their awareness that

Wirz was a talented youth—alert in the extreme, but too taut for his own well-being. His mind was an engraver's stone, ready to be saturated with the inks of acquired knowledge; but reasoning did not come to him with ease. There was no flavor of humor about him except the taste of humor which is found in most youths; maturity would dry it up—yes, and had.

Bucheton had been willing—even keen—to benefit Wirz with his skill and experience in surgery, and with no mention of a fee. Academically he regretted that Henry must suffer this persistent pain; but as a truth Bucheton had never suffered any great physical agony within his own experience; he had only seen others suffering. He knew that physical anguish was bad; he was sorry that it must occur. But he could dismiss it, since the ache did not lie within his own experience or within his own flesh.

A last draught of cognac?

No.

They went outside into a dark city fresh washed, but it was raining no longer. Bucheton's coachman hurried up to the next wide turning to bring the doctor's chaise. You'll squeeze in beside me, friend Henry, and I'll set you down at your lodgings.

I will walk through the night air. It is chilly, and a stroll may help to clear my poor head and make me forget this.

There are purse-snatchers about. We've been warned.

Even in this quiet area? Well, I have very little money.

They made their goodbyes, Wirz gave his thanks for the dinner, Bucheton cautioned him about the reduction of the sulphate of morphia dosage by measured degrees, he set a day and an hour when Wirz should appear for his next examination. He dared not insult the Herr Doktor Wirz by instructing him about dressings, though he longed to. But Wirz said that the young son of his *concierge* was a tractable youth, and had been taught to hold the basin and bind the ends of linen—so—and now and then got a franc for his trouble.

Bucheton embraced the captain perfunctorily, and then drove off in his chaise. Wirz strolled, rigidly round-shouldered, beyond the Boulevard St. Germain; he held his gold-headed walking stick gripped tightly in his left hand, and it was a heavy stick, and would offer punishment to any slovenly mendicant or possible footpad who approached him. Yes, be he pickpocket or ruffian, Wirz could lift the stick and bring it down hardily.

Be he a Yankee— The pale knuckles grew paler.

Through the cool glistening, Wirz walked homeward slowly. Later he crossed through a corner of the Luxembourg gardens, and two be-caped policemen strode toward him, bearing their batons, and one was carrying a lantern. The lantern was lifted, Captain Wirz spoke a salutation, the policemen gave him their respects and marched away.

His arm shriveled, grew cold, grew hot, grew fatter; it was at times made of iron; it was at times an elongated toad which squirmed; always it was an irritant, sometimes a beast.

—Very well. So if you'd undergone an amputation—

—But my hand. *Ach.* It is my hand which I need to retain— Condemn Bucheton and his smugness! If I'd but owned three hands I could have used two of them to operate on myself—

—But you have been your own surgeon at times. The first pink scraps, when they came near the surface; the older more recent bits, turned black as coal, and honey-combed— You worked in sweat, the bottle of whiskey beside you, the scalpel cleanly wiped, the tufts of lint soaking up the liquid— You worked methodically and well, and even on that night when you were home, and your wife was ill with the female curse, and Cora had the croup and was gagging with it— You worked as your own surgeon, with a Negro bug-eyed beside you—

—But still the leaping pain, the nerves like frogs in their jumping, the frogs bounding and saying, Let us out or we'll burst your skin.

—*Ja.* Frogs.

With discipline he sought to break his recollection away from the concern it held with his wound. Libby—he saw the desk, he put muster rolls into the narrow pigeon-holes when they had been checked, he heard the slam of guards' musket butts on the stones when they halted outside the door—not his door, the other door . . . sat outside the office of Mr. Seddon's deputy, he sat there during three whole forenoons and two and one-half afternoons, he sat motionless or nearly motionless, with his beard neatly brushed and his small gray cap held upon his knee like a bright-beaked bird he had trapped. Then he had his appointment. *Inspecting Officer of Prisons.* That sounded very well indeed.

Special Minister Plenipotentiary in Europe. That sounded even better. Of course he wasn't the only one, and also he was on leave of absence officially.

And why had they not made him a colonel? They had promised that he should be a colonel. Here he was now, doing a man-sized task with only boy-sized rank to wear. A captain!—no wonder he was treated like an errand boy. Actually he had never laid eyes on Mr. Slidell (though he pretended to Bucheton and others that he had). A secretary came into an anteroom on both occasions—once to accept the dispatches which Wirz had brought; the other time to give him an envelope of instructions.

His German was profound and scholarly, because he was native to Zurich and educated also in Berlin. His French was fairly secure, accent or no accent, because he had learned the language when very young; but he was twenty-seven years old before he began to speak more than a few words of English, and was handicapped further (as a

loyal Confederate he disliked to admit this) because he had spent
most of his thirteen or fourteen American years with the soft long
drawl of R-slighting of Southerners in his ears.

So perhaps that was the reason his promotion had been passed over
repeatedly? They thought that a man who talked like a Tam Tutchman
wasn't worthy of higher grade? What about that Prussian giant—what
was his name?—who worked for General Stuart? Wirz had heard him
laughing, bellowing delightedly, twisting up his whiskers; he stood
close to him once; and Von Borcke was unmistakably of field grade,
with his English nothing like so extensive as Henry's.

You had to know influential people, you had to know them well.
You had to know—

Ach, mein lieber Gott im Himmel! The arm.

He was walking, measured hurtful step by measured hurtful step,
on a stone-bordered path in the Luxembourg gardens, where he had
strolled so often when he was a youth; and one day he had even helped
two little boys with their sailing of boats, and a great breeze blew the
fountain spray loose from its jeweled column and spattered them thoroughly, and they all shrieked with laughter and so did young Henry
Wirz, and kindly he took off his shoes and stockings and rolled up his
dove-colored pantaloons, and he waded in to retrieve the two white
sailboats which the wind had tossed upon their beam-ends—

He was walking, grasping that slung arm which bred its torture, he
was walking in midnight amid the damp Luxembourg gardens; and it
did not seem real—walking in New Orleans would seem more real
nowadays, if only he could walk there; and in the Luxembourg gardens all of the Parisians turned out in full force each Sunday, except
for the thousands who went gabbling to the *Bois,* and all of them had
their dogs along with them. French dogs were a race apart: not like
American dogs, not like Southern American dogs, with their long ears
and jaunty scratching and their loose addiction to raccoons or brawling,
or their fondness for copulation in the open dusty roads. French dogs
marched in harness, they took tight little steps, they seemed to sniff in
French, they carried the pinned-up ears of one breed, the ruffles of
another, the hard-curled tails of still another heritage; they were indubitably French—they gestured with their strange tails as they met
and conversed—

The dogs. The Yankees were dogs. Oh, God. My arm—

Wirz walked there, and saw and felt no more than the barest impress of a fading past, hung like bleached wall paper against the facade
of the October night. What was more real was blackness of a late May
storm—*ja,* the night between May thirtieth and May thirty-first, it
was—and Blanchard's Brigade was moving up through steady pouring
rain, and the arm did not hurt at all because there had been no metal
entering to mutilate it. Come the next day, and the next . . . all plank

highways built up out of the marsh, and trees thick and dripping, and the uncertain scattered fire of skirmishers cutting through the forest where another brigade of Huger's Division was already making contact with the enemy—

Then came the smash of pain like a fist striking simultaneously his arm, his eyes, his nose, the soft thin hollow of his belly.

Go to the rear. And look out for those batteries moving up, and go stumbling off the corduroy while the great wheels draped with mud come skating past, and hold your arm and watch the blood run down between your fingers and— *Go to the rear.*

And never a moment, from that moment, divorced from the feel of the wickedness. Never a tingling second to escape it, never a long hour of waking to know that the throbbing was subdued. Only in sleep, only in blank blackness, with the bitter small brew of morphia to bring a void before you, and force you over the edge and into it.

Henry Wirz moved across wet and ancient stones. With his left hand he opened the iron gate; he went up to the steps and rang the bell for the *concierge*. A night-walker came past the fence, he heard the light conversation of her heels resounding under barren chestnut trees. She called with low fervor, Oh, *Monsieur,* one moment, please— He coughed and turned his thin face away. The *concierge* came muttering inside with a candle, chains were unfastened, the door swung.

One might then have gone far beyond Henry Wirz, through darkened bricks of the tall old house which once had been occupied by a marshal who died in Egypt, and over the soot and tiles beyond— One could have gone out in thought through the wastes of the *Bois de Meudon* where a suicide and a huddled hare and a softly wailing servant girl (newly and rudely taught a rite supposed to deal with affection) lay nearly in the same thicket— One could have swept on an instant past the spires of Versailles and over secret countryside where the River Eure rose in its initial brimming; and might have passed near Alencon in a twinkling, and given a blessing to old women who spent years with their lace and dangling shuttles; and sped across thrashing coasts of southernmost Brittany where the racket of nighttime winches was forgotten at Lorient and last lanterns were put out by the fog—

Away, away, going in thought or imagination above the long black swells, west and a little south, west and steadily bearing a little to the port dots of the compass, ignoring the marble which emerged from waves and was then sponged into spray by a fresh slapping of salt and was reconstructed into more jet and snowy marble far in the depth, and pushed up and out again to frighten the fishermen in their small plunging boats and to be seen by birds flying at night, except that none was flying—

And on past a Swedish vessel and a blockade runner which bore

no lights because Yankees were looking for her, even in these eternal
wildernesses of marble and salt which couldn't be measured easily
or plumbed; and on, in the single flaming of a thought, ignoring
lonely islands of the Atlantic and into the growing color which suggested a twilight and became finally a sunset and then a remnant of
late October afternoon in which coastal cities stood out boldly, and
where guards walked above the batteries of some forts which had
been attacked and some which would never be hit by any shells—

Above estuaries and over camps the fast wild thought might have
gone fleeting, born in a brain which truly had no power to bear it;
for this moment became a part of the future where a man can never
dwell, and where gods are merely invented, and where the new unseen sun gives off its roaring, and new unseen stars are intact.

The Fifth Maine Battery was bivouacked behind a knotty board
fence. When Portland Hyde and his friend Caldwell walked the
nearby lane at night they could see cooking fires showing pale red
in reflection above the fence, and raw living red through the cracks.
Now they moved in dusk, less than two months away from the winter
solstice; dusk or not, they did not care, for they carried a duck with
a fresh-wrung neck. Got him safe under your coat, Porty? You just
bet I have. Don't want no sentry putting down the law to me about
foraging. Yes, and then taking our duck for his own self. How do
you say we boil him? Twould be easier. Maybe so; but I just couldn't
stomach boiled duck. No, sir, I'd as lief toast him bit by bit on
a ramrod. I wish we had some peas; a pot of peas would go well along
with him. Well, why don't you wish you was to home, and having
Betty fetching in beans and biscuits? O laughter. . . .

Companies E and K of the Eleventh Vermont guarded a great pile
of earthworks and logworks outside Washington City. Here John
Appleby was freshly come on picket duty. He had retreated like a
smart soldier below a broken-off sycamore tree where he was cooped
safely from any wind or weather, and had a good sight at the road
in either direction whenever he felt in his bones that an officer or a
provost detail might be approaching. Mainly he thought about his
friend Adam Garrett, and how well things must be going with him.
Adam was recovered from his Gettysburg wound, which he had
received while serving with Stannard's Brigade. Now that the Sixteenth Vermont was mustered out, Adam had re-enlisted in the Eleventh
and was still at West Dummerston enjoying veteran's furlough.

Where was Adam? Maybe gone to take supper with the Smalls?
John groaned to himself, thinking of the Smalls and their big low
kitchen; well, yes, he'd liked Hallie Small too, but Adam always shone
up to the girls more successfully. Mrs. Small was noted for her fruit
pies all over the town of Dummerston, all the way from East Dummerston across the forest through Dummerston Center and down to

West Dummerston on the river. (Fact of the matter was, Adam Garrett was gone to a church supper on this evening. Next Tuesday he'd ride with his father to Brattleboro and take the cars, and head for Northern Virginia to join his new regiment and his old friend John Appleby. Time was when Adam never thought he'd get over talking about that piece of rib which was shot out of his side—he was so proud of it, and rejoiced in the realization that he wasn't actually killed, just hurt a mite. But lately he'd grown weary of telling the same story to the same rural garden-variety of ears. Nobody understood truly what he was talking about. He sat beneath a bower of bunting, and ladies bustled behind him with their big flat blackened pans of chicken pie, and he tried to see Hallie beyond the bunting, and prayed that she wasn't still mad because of that tiff they'd had when he caught Hepsy Clark and kissed her when they played Ruth and Jacob at the Jennings place— He said to old Deacon Root and young tongue-tied Mr. Willis and of course the minister, beaming gravely beyond— He said, Well, you see our regiment was on the left of those trees. There was a stone wall just ahead of us, but the stones was knocked loose and scattered. The Rebs give us one volley before they moved forward past the barn. I forgot to tell you there was a barn and farmhouse towards the Rebel lines from us—I mean, in between. He kept peering past the bearded listeners, trying to see Hallie. He caught a flurry of her plaid gown—)

Old Tom Gusset, Saddler, Ninth Ohio Cavalry, said to the sutler, That's a pretty price. Thirty cents currency for that one little tin? Look, old man, them preserves are strawberry and they got a little brandy in them, or so tis said. Would you guarantee that? Not me; I ain't guaranteeing nothing. How do I know it's true what it says on the label of the tin? Well, by cracky, if you don't know, who does? How much is that there tin marked quince and nut? That's dearer, partner. Thirty-five cents I got to get for that.

In a bleak ravine west of Chattanooga, a private of the Twenty-sixth Wisconsin said, Haltoogoesthere? Friends with the countersign. Advance singly and be recognized. Billy stood with his rifle directed on dim shapes moving among the trees, and he resented the added weight of the bayonet. What in the devil—? Oh, yes; the countersign was *Tippecanoe*. Advance singly, mister. You come one at a time. Advance with the countersign. . . . *Tippecanoe*. Hey, there, Billy— you sounded scared—I didn't recognize your voice. Gol damn it, I ain't scared, I'm just sick. Sick of what? Sick of beef dried on the hoof. Well, we may fare better, now that they've got rid of old Rosy Rosecrans. Think Pap Thomas will do better by us? I surely do— rumor has it that the first thing old Pap is going to do is open up a cracker line.

In a Richmond bedroom two great sagging wide-fleshed faces met and stared; one was cased in glass backed by crinkled quicksilver, and the quicksilver had flaked away from the mirror's back to make the imprisoned face more pocked, more scabbed, more seamed than it was in fact. Brigadier-General John Winder put up his pulpy fingers and inspected tenderly the bleeding notch which a razor had made in a ridge of loose skin beside his mouth (his mouth was a thin old scar, wide and long-healed and stitched together by mythical sutures; it was a fierce blue mouth). Amos, you black son of a bitch, what were you trying to do—murder me? A frightened slave in a frayed white jacket hovered behind Winder. Please, General, sir, I don't know what did happen. That old razor seem like it was nice and sharp when I strop it, but it just didn't glide tonight, sir, it just didn't glide. . . . Winder snarled in reply, saying no words, but he was a master of the snarl, his snarls spoke volumes of invective on complicated ugly subjects. Now he must appear at the President's table with a fresh-cut face. . . . You son of a bitch, go fetch a lump of alum! Don't stand there like a gawk, God damn it—*fetch!*

Aboard the United States sloop *Sea Sprite*, bumping on patrol beyond Mobile, a shaggy Irishman named Patrick was squatted in the head, doing his business at the same hour he always liked to perform it. On the same deck, at another place, another seaman was soliciting the youth whom Patrick adored.

I'll give you five dollars, Val, the man muttered—no, I'll make it six. Just think—six beautiful gold dollars.

I don't think you got six dollars.

Yes, I got them, right in this here sock. Hear them jingle? Val, if you'll wait till it's my watch below and—

I don't dast. He'd be mad; he'd maybe beat me black and blue.

Val, he won't know nothing about it, because he'll be on watch. I'll never tell, Val boy—you can trust old Sprit.

The boy backed slowly away, his ferret eyes gleaming with cupidity, his ferret head shaking. No, I don't dast.

Say ten, by God. I'll raise to ten; hain't got no more.

Well, for ten—

In the lines near Knoxville a boy from the Thirteenth Kentucky slid his rifle across a rock, elevated the sight slightly, and fired at a dark shape which had been drifting in front of him through the thickening mountain dusk. *Yipe*, and then swifter howls going away. I'll be blamed. Just one of those damn dogs again. Hey, Charley, what did you pop? Blame dog. Hey, listen, Charley, you got any crackers left? Got three. Give me one? If I crawl over? Thanks kindly.

Near the Rappahannock the woods were witches' woods where the One Hundred and Forty-eighth Pennsylvania crouched along a side road. Ennis, I noticed something. Well, what? It's the quarter-master; notice anything odd about it? No. Well, I did. Tonight's the first night he set up his tent right *in camp—not out with the wagon train.* Now, way it looks to me, we're stuck here for good. Might as well start work on a shebang tomorrow; I give my oath, I'd bet every shinplaster I got that we'll go into winter quarters right here. First time we've settled down since Bristoe Station. What do you say—about the shebang? There's whole loads of wood around, and if we get started before the rest pitch into it, we'll get first pick. By gum, Jake, I think you're maybe right. Get Balder and Timmelpennick and Douglas and Puffy; let's get after that wood *tonight.* Shake on it, Ennis, I'm with you.

A youth from a New York tenement who bore the name of Torrosian, a youth from the Catskills whose name was Plover, a youth named Mutterson whose mother was reputed to be the best cook in their Pennsylvania valley: Brewster's Brigade divided itself across a creek west of Warrenton, Virginia; pork was sizzling. Eric Torrosian tripped over a root and sent the coffee can spattering into the fire. Amid curses of some men and laughter of others he was sentenced to make up the wasted coffee grounds out of his own store. He had no more coffee in his knapsack, he had to walk a quarter of a mile to the sutler's cart, he went in resentment even though he recognized the justice of it.

At the headquarters of Major-General George H. Thomas in a corner of Tennessee, a tired bearded man leaned between his crutches and peered into a circle of lamplight where papers were spread. A man named Baldy Smith was explaining intently how he had prepared lumber for bridges. Did you establish a sawmill, General Smith? Yes, sir—cobbled one together—utilized an old engine we *borrowed* in the neighborhood. Building the pontoons right now for Bridge Number Three. In addition we're well progressed on a steamer for plying between here and Bridgeport—as soon as we achieve possession of the river. The man on the crutches said, Boat building? Have you a shipyard, General? Smith said, Oh, it's not much, but I think it should turn the trick. It's a scow made from planks we sawed in our mill—all well housed in—and the stern wheel is to be propelled by another steam engine we *borrowed* from a local factory. The man on crutches meditated; there was a tired smile under his brown beard. Seems to me you always were a good provider, even when we were Kay-dets at the Point. Don't think I've seen you since graduation, twenty years ago. Pleased to find you doing such outstanding work. . . . Smith looked at him earnestly. Thank you, sir. It's good to see you again, but I'm sorry to find you on crutches. Is that from the accident you suffered out West? . . . General Grant nodded. It was in August, when I went to New Orleans to talk to Banks. My horse fell. It's been pretty troublesome for over two months. By the by, I haven't notified General Halleck of my arrival here. Will one of your people please to take a message over to the telegrapher for me? . . .

Other crutches rapped across the rough planks of a prison hospital in central Virginia. An ugly beak-nosed man tossed on his pallet and mouthed, Why'n't you quit making all that racket? I was trying to sleep. . . . Oh, shut up, Chickamauga! Some fine day maybe that old hacked-off festered limb of yours will get well, and then you'll have some crutches of your own, and you can see how you like it. . . . Not far away, in a mire named Belle Isle, a New York City rough called Collins clamped his fingers around the throat of a sick Ohioan until there was no breath left in the man; then Collins went through the man's pockets and found the watch he sought, the watch wrapped in a dirty handkerchief with *Enoch from Louella* cross-stitched upon it.

Woods' Brigade of Osterhaus's Division of the Fifteenth Corps trailed along a road in northeastern Mississippi, marching still, they would march until after dark, and how long was it since the day they left Memphis? Willie Mann gave only automatic attention to demands of the march, the watching where to plant his feet, the watching to avoid ruts or rocks. He dreamed, as the last pink warmness of sun touched the heavy knapsack bulking on his shoulders, he dreamed of a girl named Katty. Right now, back home in Missouri, she might be putting a big pan of apples into the oven to bake for dessert that evening. Willie had eaten apples baked by Katty, and they were marvelous things: the scraped flakes of cinnamon bark toasted to black, the sugar changed to apple-nectar-syrup, the thick Alderney cream swirling slowly down through the hollow where the apple had been cored. . . . Beside Willie Mann a big-framed comrade was singing in a monotone as he strode. Titus Cherry couldn't carry a tune on a shovel, but he beguiled himself with song whenever they traveled as hard as they'd traveled this autumn day. The other boys didn't relish the sounds he made, but none of them was big enough to silence him . . . *what signifies the life of man if twere not for the lasses, oh? Green grow the rashes, oh, green grow the rashes, oh.* The tuneless rumble of Titus Cherry hung like a weight on the hearing of the rest, it seemed to retard them while they tramped. . . . On an adjacent road the Fifth Iowa Infantry trailed up a low slope where the Seventeenth Corps was pushing, and Eben Dolliver saw a bird he couldn't quite recognize: was it a jay? It didn't look like the jaybirds back home in Hamilton County—seemed to have more gray on it—it was over there in that scraggly oak—he wished he could leave the column, to see it at close range—maybe bluejays in northern Mississippi had more gray than Iowa birds would have at this season. Of course! he thought drolly. Confederate birds, Secesh jaybirds, they're bound to be gray. The man ahead of him snarled over his shoulder, Ebe, quit goosing me with your rifle butt. A butt in the butt, said someone else. A weak chuckle drifted up.

Pines, mountains, stones upon stones, the flat pocked farms below, the burned houses and disordered towns, the girl waving her kerchief, the crone spitting as the enemy passed, the armies squatting or moving, the oceans along margins where hunted craft and hunters went lurching as the wind of night rose. And scattered, dotted singly or by couples or by dozens from Texas to the White Mountains and down to the lead-speckled clefts of Tennessee once more, there labored a pulse and breathing of fifty thousand men whose fate bayed behind them—never seen, never heard, but driving them with the dedicated relentlessness of time itself, driving them toward a common destination.

The next morning before it was light, Ira Claffey walked in the woods with his grief.

IV

Often in early December the north wind beats thinly, steadily across the hillocks of Georgia; it comes like a sickle cutting unseen but felt, and the edge is rawly mean; and before dawn a woman should shiver from her nest (if an indulgent woman who could not presume to awaken her husband first to the task) and let her sleepy grasp go hunting charred billets piled in the corner. . . . The log sinks loosely, deeper and deeper among pink flakes after she has put it there, and for a minute or two there are no flames, only a sizzling. Then the resin has melted out, it pops and fries with a smell like cooking, there are spurts and explosions of crystallized juices as they burn to evaporation in a twinkling: the first solid flame is accomplished. Up it goes, crawls onto a splinter, hangs, droops, falls off, rises wider and more solidly. Its cousin flame joins it from the rear and over the top; the wide hot ruffle is a fringe and a high one, in seconds. The warmth comes out . . . it is good that the warmth comes, for that unseen sickle swings across every upland where the stalks have dried.

In this December darkness, Coffee's wife lifted and fired the small log.

She ran back, long-legg̀ed and monstrous in her rough short shirt; she rolled back the old comforters and plunged beneath them, and bundled them behind her muscular back and wadded them beneath her thin buttock. Her knees drew into the warm space behind Coffee's knees, her right arm slid around his hairy chest, her chin pressed close between his shoulders, and her own breath burnt in its regular strength beneath the covers, helping to warm them both.

Ung, said Coffee.

It's time, old man.

He was twenty-five years old, Pet was nineteen. Coffee could count to forty and a little past, which was often a convenience in his work, and he had learned proudly. Old Leander taught him. Pet could not count past the sum of her fingers, though sometimes she tried to add the sum of her toes; but this bothered her because she had lost one toe from the bite of a rat when she was small, and she could not quite understand why she never seemed to have as many toes as she had fingers. The bite of the rat came in that unhappy antiquity when

she and her mother belonged to Mr. Ganwood. It was a filthy plantation where they were owned, and there was never enough wood or
coverings or potatoes, seldom any meat except what the slaves stole
or hunted down; there was a whipping-morning for accumulated mis-
deeds every week—just before holiday, so that the slaves whipped
might have a chance to recover before they went into the fields again
. . . never any Christmas fit to speak of. Old Mr. Ganwood died a
smelly death in bed—slaves said that the Devil came and got him,
and certain slaves even declared awesomely that they had seen the
Devil coming: he wore a tall black hat, and had two hands with him
to fetch out the box in which old Mr. Ganwood was finally nailed.
Mr. Ganwood's hands were then parceled out at public auction, and
Pet and her mother Naomi became the property of Mr. Ira Claffey.
From then on (during the next fourteen years, except for privations
which occurred because of war) there was every sort of decent
generous allowance which you could name. The Claffeys always
made a wonderful Christmas for all their people, and they called
them people, and the people were pleased. And these very quilts
beneath which Pet now snuggled with her wedded husband, had
once covered white folks and made them warm; they were a trifle
frayed now, the green squares fading to yellow, the yellow squares
fading to white . . . this top quilt was warm, and had a softness.
　　Time, old man.
　　Ung.
　　Time.
　　How you know, old woman?
　　I just knows.
　　Coffee stirred, grunted, settled warm but lifelessly again. They
lay like a frieze taken down from the wall and placed flat upon the
solid roped bed. There were three of them, in this order: Pet, Coffee,
Sukey. Pet was married to Coffee when she was fifteen, and she had
lost three other children before they grew very large inside her. Each
time she had to stay abed for many days, and both the old and the
young mistress came to help attend her, and oversee just what Naomi
did for her daughter; and the young mistress made her drink of a tea
she herself had prepared. This was all very painful and dishearten-
ing, and in weakness Pet was certain that she cried enough tears
to fill the largest bucket in the kitchen. But now Sukey was an accomplished fact, and the child grinned all day long, and crawled
everywhere; she pulled herself up beside chairs, and grinned at the
old master and snatched at the finger which he presented with its
gold Masonic ring. Soon she would be walking.
　　How that child, you Coffee?
　　She all wet. He giggled sleepily. She wet but she sleeping. She
got me wet too.
　　Time, old man.

He yawned enormously. Still got time, and his big strong hand came hunting amusement. He began to struggle around to face her.

No, no, no! You be decent, man.

Still got time!

No, old man. No time now. Them chickens started in.

I don't hear them.

You listen, you hear them. Don't you come funning with me now. You come home tonight, I let you make fun then.

Oh, yes, old woman. I come home all tuckered out.

Sukey awakened and began to yell. Give her to me, you Coffee. Coffee gathered up the dripping child and helped her to crawl across his strong body until she whimpered happily at her mother's fat breast. Pet was built like a bean-pole, but she carried plenty of milk. The milk was rich, and Naomi said, Hi, just see that fat in it. Once Sukey was born she had never been sick a day in her little life.

Get out of there. You hear me?

The chickens were increasingly vocal; Coffee dared not ignore their summons any longer. He could hear the roosters in their high wailing whooping, all the way across the world. He guessed he could hear them away over at the Tebbs place, and in the scrawny village of Anderson itself. *Urr-a-urr-a-oo.*

Bell ain't spoke yet.

It'll speak, but don't you wait. You fly round, get your clothes, put on one more log, make yourself some count.

The bell spoke: pound, pound, pound. It hung in its gallows on the corner of Old Leander's cabin two cabins away from the home of Pet and Coffee, and it was one of Old Leander's proud tasks to ring the bell according to direction. He would beat it ferociously, then go hobbling back to bed. He had worked for a lifetime, he had toiled well and hard, he could sleep as late as he pleased. Nowadays however he spoke of Heaven with increasing frequency; he prayed hourly. He said that he had seen the three young masters in a dream, and they were dressed in raiment. The rest of the hands were impressed. They cried a little whenever Leander spoke of the young masters, and they too talked about raiment.

Alternately groaning and snorting, Coffee emerged from bed and put on the loose shirt and jeans which he had wadded under the foot of the bed. Wind cut through the few cabin-cracks and made even his strong frame shiver.

Where our shawl, woman?

On that peg with my frocksies.

He found the shawl, tied it around his shoulders, and padded away toward the door.

Don't you go making dirt by the door, you hear me? Old Mastah say everybody go down to the privy, else we get a plague.

Coffee mumbled that he had no intention of making dirt. However, the privy was a long way down the hind path, and cold made him squirm. It was dark, no one could see; all he wanted to make was water, and he went between the two small Walker's Yellow apple trees and made it. Around him rose the sounds of earliest morning, though still the night clung black; you could make out the blot of horizon in the east, you could separate the lighter darkness of sky from the darker darkness of earth, that was all. Jonas and Buncombe, his eldest child, were busy at the stables; Coffee could hear them talking to the horse and the mules. That little Buncombe was stepping around smartly these days; before long he would graduate on the rolls and be listed as half a hand. . . . Coffee put his fingers into both of the buckets on a split bench before the cabin door. Empty or practically so. He carried the pails to the nearest well, beyond the line of cabins on a rounding small hill above stockpens and stables. He put down the sweep, brought up water, filled the pails and carried them home. At the well he'd splashed water all over his face, and had rubbed his eyes and ears with his big wet thumbs. He was thoroughly awake at last.

Pet was up and gowned. She had put a second log into the fireplace and flames were merry; the room was cosier. Sukey sat squealing on the bed. Pet was digging around in the wide heaps of light loose ashes, hunting for yams she'd put there the night before. Coffee had reproved her a dozen times: he claimed that she was always getting the yams too close to the center, too near the logs, too near the actual burning. Well, she had done it again, but with only one yam. She lifted out the four—one charred nearly to a husk, one half raw, two excellently baked, and these two happened to be the biggest. She put them down on the table, and Coffee grabbed, and burnt his hand, and swore.

Don't you go a-cursing, old man.

Woman, I like to roast my fingers off!

Coffee, I don't favor no cursing. Dear Lord never favor cursing. Won't never rear this child mongst cursing.

Oh, hush you prattle, woman. He slapped at her playfully, and she assaulted him with the scorched forked stick she'd used for the yams.

Coffee said, pushing the muffled words out of his mouth while it was filled with potato— He said, I got to tote lunch for noontime.

You want me send a child down with your dinner? Coffee, we low on rations.

We eat too much. You burn too much our rations way! Old woman, know what we do today? We start working for the army.

Who all?

I told you once, I told you twice: me and Jem and Jonas. We all queesishunned.

What that mean?

Big soldier man, he come riding up and old Mastah go out to the
gate, and they talk right next me. Bet you old Mastah he mad through
and through. Soldier man say, I can't help that, Mr. Claffey, sir.
What it say here on this paper: how many hands you got for me?
Can't take no women; got to have men cut down trees and dig the
ground. So we all get queesishunned, what he say.

What that mean, though?

Just what he say. He say slack work now, won't make no hard
times, but old Mastah mad just same.

What you do? Whereabouts?

He say cut down trees, dig ground. Reckon over on Mr. Bile land
or mostly on McWhorter land; maybe some on our land.

Well, I got cold pone you fetch along.

Ain't we got no meat?

Well, I let you fetch one piece of pork with your pone. Tomorrow
Sunday, tomorrow blessed day, holiday, old man. You take your
club, go get us some rabbit.

Dad fetch, we do go through our rations! Bless the dear Lord you
get plenty snick-snack up in the big house.

No snick-snack like we used to get. White folks eat mighty plain
nowadays; old Mistess watch the platters, and she count and watch
careful, and she warn Naomi no waste, and she carry her keys right
on the belt of her gown, and she lock up all the time.

Get me my dinner-snack. Don't you hear Jem a-calling?

She wrapped a generous slab of pone and a smaller chunk of
greasy pork in clean corn-shucks, and Coffee put the bundle inside
his shirt. He tried to kiss Pet, she fought him off, the child shrieked,
and Coffee went fleeing. It was much lighter outside and before he
got to the tool shed he could see Jem and Jonas standing ready for
work ahead of him.

There was a slight ripple of excitement through their uneventful
lives at this thought of going to work for the army. Perhaps Coffee
was more steeped in melancholy than the other two, and thus he
had sought to keep up his own spirits by chatting with Pet while
they breakfasted. Behind his long ruddy-tinted face and within his
close-cropped skull Coffee had a brain which contained machinery
both for imagination and recollection. He remembered, he remembered. In the old days, and during a December week like this, they
would have had eighteen or twenty field hands picking cotton, maybe
four hands employed constantly at the gin, to say nothing of the
people bringing in corn, the people minding pigs, the people hauling
boards, the people weaving and making rope or mule-collars, the
people inevitably sick. These in addition to house-servants flying
round at the big house, or busy in dairy and wash house and store-

houses and kitchen. The Claffey place was something to behold, before the war.

After the unresolved campaigns of 1862, the drawn battles and tightening of the blockade, Ira Claffey had witnessed the *Mene, Mene, Tekel, Upharsin* in no uncertain characters. He sold his people right and left, and at great loss, for he would not separate families and would not sell to strangers unless he went personally to see where his sold-off people would be dwelling and under what conditions. In this late season of 1863 another year of protracted butchery and short commons had proved Ira's wisdom. The place could feed the Claffeys and the hands still remaining to them; that was about all it could do, after the military took their tithe.

Coffee might understand but dimly what his master had been about, and why; nevertheless he recalled autumns abounding in prosperity, autumns unperforated by worms of war and death.

He listened idly to the mumbling of Jem and Jonas while they waited for the master to appear.

One of the mules was sick with colic, and Jonas was reciting the remedy he desired to employ and the cure which would follow. It was something Old Leander had taught him when Jonas was young. Take a big plug of tobacco and cut off a slice maybe as thick as your little finger was long. Put the tobacco in cold water—about the size of that crockful, over there on the bench; then throw in four or five shovels of hot oak ashes, and let the mixture set awhile before you give it to the mule. Ask master or overseer to use his watch; ask him to tell you when fifteen minutes had passed. Then the solution was ready to use, and better not use more of it than a chunk bottle full at one time. It still had to be warm when you used it to drench the mule. Chances were that the mule would be well at once; but never let him near water for a good ten hours. If it were noon when you drenched him, you shouldn't let him drink till close to midnight. And never let him eat corn right afterward, nor do any more work that day.

Then old mule get well.

You drench that Devil mule like that?

I got tobacco waiting in the water. I got oak ash in my fire. When Mastah come I tell him about Devil; but I can't go work for old army and drench Devil mule same time. Can't be no two places same time.

A rear door of the big house was heard to open, and Ira Claffey appeared, followed by a setter who was partially paralyzed by the ills of old age, and dragged his rear quarters, sniffing himself into a succession of sneezes.

The Negroes watched with ready amusement. He think he young again, that Deuce. Think he go after partridge.

Claffey left the dog inside the house fence and prepared to latch the gate. Deuce vented a long shuddering whine, and held up his front paw. This was ritual of his, to gain attention, and never failed whether he approached black or white.

Poor Deuce, said Claffey, turning. Have you a thorn in your foot?

Whine, said Deuce, still holding out the paw.

What have you here? An old sand-spur?

Whine.

Claffey returned to the gate, reached through between the palings and pretended to extract a thorn from one of the crumbling split toe-pads. There, got it, he said. Deuce dropped his foot to the ground as if relieved of enormous trouble, and went capering about. The slaves laughed aloud, watching. Morning, Mastah.

Morning, Jem, Jonas, Coffee. I trust you said your prayers.

Jem and Jonas bobbed their heads vigorously, and after a guilty second Coffee nodded also, but in a lie. Ira Claffey looked at his watch, and Jonas stepped forward to tell him about Devil.

Very well, Jonas. I know about that drench. Leander used it for many years.

Yassah.

Have you oak ashes in your fireplace? Good—I'll drench Devil myself, and pen him away from food and water.

The slaves felt a great pride that they were owned by a master who did not stand helplessly, or labor among his fruit trees to no avail, or who did not spend the bulk of his time at whist or in lounging with liquor and no purpose. The dumb affection and faith they gave to Ira stemmed (much of it) from an awareness that he could do many of the same tasks they performed, and often do them better. In such an absolute monarchy, and in the shadow of such a monarch, there was the flourishing of a strange democratic pride; you had to see it and feel it and live it to know it, but it was there, and always exerting.

Claffey did the things an overseer would have done. He performed these tasks with reluctance because he did not approve the work laid out for his hands, demanded of them by their Government. He unlocked the door of the implement house and parceled out three axes and three spades which the slaves put across their shoulders. The tools had been well smithed to begin with; axe-helves and the handles of spades were of timber cured for the purpose. Ira gave to Jonas a whetstone and warned him not to lose it. Each tool had a *C* branded on it; Ira instructed the hands to guard the plantation property jealously. No telling what sort of raggle-taggle herds might have been assembled by the army folks who were impressing labor.

Ira Claffey took his people to the front gate. Daylight came clearly but no troops or workers appeared. He sent Coffee to the kitchen with instructions to fetch from Naomi a small pail of the burnt-grain brew which had to serve in these times, together with a cup and saucer for the master. He poured out his own cup and gave the rest to the people. They drank the hot stuff eagerly, smacking their lips in turn above the tin pail's rim.

Before they had finished, a disturbance moved along the lane from beyond the magnolias. There appeared a wagon drawn by two mules, the box heaped with miscellaneous axes, picks, mattocks, shovels. A bearded sergeant rode on the board beside the Negro driver, and a band of some two dozen blacks trailed behind, gabbling noisily. The rearmost file was closed by a fat youth of fifteen or thereabouts who burst fairly out of his shabby gray clothing, and who wore accoutrements and carried a musket slung from his shoulder.

The wagon halted in front of the gate. The sergeant took out a notebook and consulted it. . . . Mr. Claffey, sir?

Yes, Sergeant. I have three hands ready for you.

Says here you're supposed to have four.

So your impressing officer thought, but the fourth of my black people—full-grown males—is Old Leander, and he's in his dotage. I'll never send him.

Well, sir, right here it says, Mr. I. Claffey, four hands.

If there's any question about it, the officer may complain to me in person.

Might send the provost.

Let him.

Very well, sir.

Jem, Coffee and Jonas had been waiting with docility, grinning at friends from neighborhood plantations they saw before them, conversing in low tones. The sergeant swung round and called, You three nigs fall in with the others.

They stood, deeply puzzled.

Fall *in*, God damn it!

Don't curse my people, Sergeant. Ira Claffey spoke sharply. They're not accustomed to it. The sergeant means, Jonas, that you shall march along with the others.

Yes, Mastah.

They went, and Ira stood watching the procession as it traveled to the head of the lane and then turned north on a wood road past abandoned cotton fields. He closed his eyes, his head blurred quickly in its traditional shaking, he took a deep breath. Not enjoying the December breeze which continued to wield its knife, he strode off to drench his Devil mule.

The three Claffey Negroes went in docility with their fellows, and presently the sound of axe-strokes came spanking from a valley ahead. Halfway down the slope a man who seemed to be a soldier signalled

to the sergeant, and the wagon turned off to the left. This man wore
a fine overcoat of bright blue; it had a cape across the shoulders, and
instantly all the blacks coveted those gleaming brass buttons.

That Yankee coat for sure.

How you know, boy?

Count of blue. All them Yankee wear blue, blue, blue. Young
Mastah Badger tolt me.

But that gentleman ain't no Yankee gentleman. Old Mistuh Bile—
he got blue coat too, and he no Yankee.

That gentleman captivate he coat in the war, yes, boy.

They found in the throng people from nearby plantations and
smaller farms, people drawn from big places miles away, enormous
holdings which they had heard of in legendary fashion. There were
hands belonging to the Groovers, the Nickersons, the Rackleys, the
Vinings. A larger share of the impressed laborers were engaged in
carving out a narrow trench some five feet deep, cleaving down the
slope and passing disordered rails where old fences had been ruined.
The stile was pulled apart. Gangs dotted up the other slope, felling
pines ahead of the diggers; and one troop worked at nothing but
rolling fallen trunks aside, or heave-hoing with chains and oxen to
tear the roots and stumps loose. It was a fable of the circus which
the Claffey hands had never seen but hoped to witness before they
became as old as Old Leander. Something was going on in every
direction, and they found an added pepper of excitement in observing
the white youths who brought a show of force and urgency by
strolling about with their guns. Coffee felt his blood warming and
his pulse bounding.

What folks do here, you Jem?

White captain say they make jail.

Hi. Jail all over these here woods?

Jail for Yankees.

Hi. Reckon they got ten hundred dozen thousand Yankees cotched
already.

Yes, boy. They got ten hundred dozen villain nillain hundred
Yankees cotched.

You nigs get over here and line up for axes.

Mastah Captain, sir, we got our own axes. Old Mastah say we
keep them by us. They marked with the word, Mastah Captain. Old
Mastah say—

Ah, the hell with your Old Mastah! Step lively, over here by the
driver—

The driver was an impassive middle-aged creature named Scooper.
He belonged to Mrs. Barney Yeoman and was a power at the sawmill
when it was in operation. Also Scooper had local fame as the owner
of a vicious fighting-cock which had torn the feathers and throats

and bellies of all rivals in the region. The Claffey people had lost heavily to Scooper in the past . . . dimes and quarters too. They offered him no resentment; only respectful admiration. They assembled under his command, and Scooper put them in a squad of three; he knew that they were accustomed to toiling in unison and would do better so. With regret Coffee heard the order for them to deposit their shovels in the wagon bed to be drawn by other hands, but Scooper muttered that he would try to keep an eye on the implements.

These two pines here. Cut them down. Fell them over on this side.

The slaves cleared away the thin undergrowth, took their positions, and as chief axeman Jonas set pace and cadence. One, two, three; one, two, three; hink, hank, hunk; hink, henk, honk . . . blades tilted with power, evenly, deeply into fresh jeweled wood; the chips whirled out. . . . Hold up, you; I take a look; now stand back, I cut me a butt kerf. Hink, hink, hink, hink. That good, boy? It good, boy. Old tree lie right over here where Scooper say. Now we go again . . . hink, henk, hunk . . . already it seemed that the needled summit was quavering steadily, gracefully in knowledge of its own death. Behind the slaves another tree came roaring down, making the brown cones and dry needles fly amid dust, and all the people yelped and jumped and let their laughter rise.

Air did not grow much warmer but the workers did. Long since they had dispensed with wraps and hung them on the remains of the fence separating Bile and McWhorter land. Dumbly they were grateful that this clearing of forest did not take place necessarily in August . . . you could work up a mighty sweat, putting that old axe into the pine. But their muscles scarcely recognized the demand put upon them. There was always a demand upon their muscles, an order calling for bending, stooping, lifting, toting, kneeling, bearing, squatting, digging, heaping, covering, flailing. Jonas was thirty-eight or so, Jem perhaps the same age (nobody knew) and Coffee in his youngest prime. They were the sole male active survivors of a troop which once had thronged the cotton rows, cornfields, pig-pens, goober patches, wood brakes. Nowadays they performed any and every task, dreaming no further ahead than the cold potatoes of noon, hot potatoes of night, the boiled turnips, the tasty chew of pork, the picked game bones, the dog yelling that here were squirrels . . . dreaming certainly no further ahead than the next turkey gobble or Christmas gift or yielding of a giggling shiny body in a bed or down a fence-row.

Coffee and Jem stood aside, responding to Jonas's direction, and they watched his last quick heaving of the blade. Piny tendons grew taut, pulled, snapped . . . patch of shade tilted quickly off into space above their heads as Jonas leaped away. Then the hillside jumped beneath their feet, the mincing slam was in their ears.

Scooper, you want we cut him up?

No, cut-up gang do that. You take next one, like I bid you.

. . . Hink, hunk, honk. The heavy slicing once again, the designing of the kerf . . . cadence thrumming out to suggest a song.

Put old Yankee in?

Put old Yankee in the jail. How long?

Long, long, long! In the jail—

This here jail. Put old Yankee long, long, long. Put him in the jail.

Oh, how many do you say?

Six-teen-hun-dred-vill-ain-mill-ain-Yankee-in-the-jail.

The smash again, cones bounding like grenades, the cold good woods axed apart, and far away the buzzing of a stubborn and belated covey as they whizzed out of the forest; and did not know it, but they would never fly there again, they would never nest or hide or peek or feed or run, now that trees were coming down and stumps being wrenched and the long roots rending clay.

At noon the Claffey hands sprawled in solid sunlight, protected from wind by the bulk of a broken tree, warm as toast and with a few flies bothering them. Preparations for the stockade were more extensive than people of the countryside had dreamed. Parties of impressed laborers kept arriving all forenoon—also soldiers, with wagons containing ragged tent flies beneath which some of the workers would be housed temporarily. Labor was being brought from points as far as a day's journey distant; the Claffey people said, I wouldn't do it, reckon I'd run off, not sleep in these here woods but put for home and my own good bed. They saw a young captain master riding around on a sorrel horse; rumor said that also there were a major master and an old colonel master somewhere about, but none of the Claffey contingent saw them. Axe parties were kept toiling while the diggers had their nooning, in order to have progressed well ahead of the shovels. A certain grim if slatternly efficiency was now apparent in the whole enterprise.

When the first yells rose about nooning, the welcome fever spread visibly from gang to gang. The Claffeys saw the gang south of them putting their axes at rest and hunting their lunches; in turn they struck their own blades into logs and sought their jackets, or the corn-shuck parcels hung up somewhere; in turn the next gang to the north and east saw what they were doing, and followed suit. Someone had stolen Jem's corn pone, and Jem had nothing left but a jar of cooked rutabagas scorned by the thief. Generously Coffee and Jonas shared their own lunches with their fellow and partook of his ruta-bagas, changing about in employment of the old iron spoon. They were accustomed, at the Claffey place, to much more variety in the way of vegetables than most slaves ate; the plantation health was that much better in consequence. Old master had a green thumb—

two green thumbs—and just wait till those peaches and plums grew ripe again, and berries too. Watch for that lettuce and those onions and those okras when springtime came; yes, and collard greens or mustard, with pork.

You Jem, reckon they put Linkum in this jail?

They never cotch Linkum!

Take a powerful lot of soldiers cotch Linkum.

They is powerful lot of soldiers right here now in these woods.

They soldiers, they got guns, but they young. Take old soldier, lot of big majors like young Mastah Suthy, catch Linkum. Old Linkum he smart as old coon.

Old Linkum, he wear big blue coat like that Yankee coat soldier gentleman captivate from the Yankees.

Yes, boy, all buttons gold.

Never cotch Linkum, insisted Jem stubbornly.

You black little old turd, you not know Linkum.

Jem rose and glowered. Who you call black little old turd?

Scooper came round the crest of the fallen pine, snapping his fingers for them to get back on the job. They rose—not with too much alacrity; they knew Scooper well, and would have been astonished had he driven them as hard as he might drive a gang of strangers. Scooper was full of talk about what would be done with the pine trees, and the people listened with curiosity. Trunks would be trimmed to fit tightly each against the next, with branches and boles chopped clean; they would be set upright in the trench, with earth scraped back and beaten down to hold them solidly. They would be immovable, twenty feet tall, with a quarter of their length held in the ground; thus the fence they made would be a good fifteen feet in height, tall as the front gallery on a goodsized house. Jonas was the only one who understood readily the measurements and dimensions described by Scooper, but the slaves listened to his tale with interest. Jem had forgotten utterly his cross words exchanged with Coffee; they chuckled and nudged each other and said, No Yankee get across that big fence.

But old Linkum, said Jem. He get across.

Maybe he do that, agreed Scooper. He run up them post like bobcat.

The humorous thought of Lincoln running up the posts like a bobcat struck them with full force. They went back to finish felling the next tree in bright merriment. A corporal scolded them later and then they were comparatively silent, working with strong docility, doing what they were ordered to do and doing it well. Until near sunset the axe-strokes were snapping.

V

The next day, perhaps two hours after his hands were on the job, Ira Claffey appeared in a small two-wheeled cart, driving behind a brown mule and with little Buncombe, Jonas's son, beside him. Bun was only six years old but already Jonas had taught him to drive this mule, which was as tractable and dependable as a mule could be. After making inquiries Ira made his way down the slope and found the sergeant who was in charge of implement supply.

I wish to pick up my shovels, sir. My hands did not fetch them home last night.

Carelessly the sergeant declared his ignorance of the shovels, and was not choice about his language when he did it. Instantly Ira Claffey knocked him flat, and while the younger man lay amid the pine trash rubbing his jaw, Ira spoke calmly, describing his situation. There had been no requisition addressed to him about tools; merely he had been instructed verbally that he must equip his slaves for whatever work was demanded of them. Since his people were put in the chopping gang, he had requested that the unused portion of his property be returned. Such articles commanded a premium throughout the Confederacy, which fact Ira knew very well. He was unwilling for some Home Guardsman to profit from the sale or trade of those shovels.

There was every impress of honesty in Ira's statements; nor did the dull sergeant wish to encounter that fist again. Ira Claffey was distinguished in that community and the sergeant knew it. He had a loaded revolver in a holster on the wagon seat, but who would dare to use a weapon against a former member of the State Legislature, and the father of three dead sons, two of them officers? Grumpily he ordered the diggers to file by and present their spades for Claffey's inspection. One, marked plainly with the C brand, turned up within a couple of minutes; a second was found farther north, across the branch, but only after much searching. The third and last eluded them until a slave whispered that there was a spade with a broken handle in the wagon-box. It seemed that someone had tried to pry a big rock with the spade. Claffey put the shovels into his two-wheeled cart and took out a game bag, ammunition pouches, and a fine silver-

chased English fowling piece which had belonged to his elder
brother, Felton Claffey, and had been left to him in Felton's will.

Mastah, breathed the child shyly, you going take old Deuce?

No, Buncombe. Deuce is too badly paralyzed. His hind end hurts
him because he is old; he grows very tired.

Mastah, what you do for you dog?

I heard dogs up in the old pasture when I left the place; that's the
reason I went back for gun and ammunition. I think that pair from
the Yeoman place—what are their names? Twink and Wink?— They're
out hunting by their lonesome. I've shot over them before.

Mastah, said Bun with great conviction, reckon we folks ought to
have a new dog.

Well, Bun, if you find any good young dogs, free of charge, please
inform me.

Sir?

Let me know if you find any dogs—free.

Yes, Mastah, and the child grinned on his way, delighted beyond description at this first intrusting to himself of the two-wheeled cart for
a solitary errand. He drove the mule, whose name was Tiger, very
slowly all the way home. He listened with rapture to each thud and
crackling of the animal's slow pace, and yet with agony because each
step meant that they were a trifle nearer home. He thrilled to the
twitching of the reins, patched from scrap material as they were. Bun
sang, tunefully but singing no recognizable words, all the way home.

Ira Claffey heard the Yeoman dogs giving voice on distant uplands
after he had left the area where forest was in the process of being
spoilt. These pointers he sought were damaged through neglect—they
came from a line with good noses, and had undergone a certain amount
of proper schooling—but now a resident overseer and his family were
the only whites left on the Yeoman place, and the overseer did not
shoot. The pointers galloped in complete abandon; like mongrels they
scented and chased squirrels and varmints, they dug for little beasts in
burrows. Ira went through a pine grove where the hubbub from the
construction gangs (they were actually destruction gangs, and he
frowned at the thought) barely reached his ears. He saw a black-and-
white tail waving above the scrub; he whistled, and both dogs rushed
to him like rowdies. Wink would accept no discipline and finally
Claffey had to drive him off; the dog returned to his excavation of a
rabbit's tunnel. Twink, on the other hand, reverted handsomely to
better behavior when he became aware that Ira Claffey bore a shotgun.
He could not be depended upon, but at least he might give some hint
of birds waiting unseen ahead.

They hunted across one of the old cotton fields where now weeds
were romping, and raised only four ground doves, which Claffey would
not shoot because he had been reared in the superstition surrounding

them. . . . What other grief, he thought, could possibly befall? Well, I presume that if I were now to lose Lucy or—God forbid it—Veronica—

There was a trick of his imagination which recurred persistently; it had recurred, ever since the last ghastly news was brought by the Dillards. Ira kept seeing his sons around the place, he kept hearing their voices. Sometimes at home he would be in his tool shed, and it seemed that a corner of his vision caught the impression of young Moses going out the door. He was positive that sometimes, lying dry and wakeful in the middle of the night, he heard the faint ring of china from Sutherland's room as the young man got up and used his chamber pot. Ira did not believe in ghosts as such. But he thought that perhaps the actual impress of the boys' living had left a variety of sights, sounds and scents which had never been expended and were not dead, even though the boys were dead. He thought that all trees and shrubbery and walls and fences on the plantation might have absorbed the day-by-day activities of his sons, and still gave them forth, but faintly—as a roasted brick retained its heat long after it had been pinned up in flannel, and so afforded comfort to the cold feet of an invalid who needed warmth. And Ira needed this reassurance that his sons had once been part of a waking, busy scheme called Life; ah, he needed it.

He did not consciously imagine these figments of reappearance, but welcomed them when they befell. He could not share the knowledge with others; he had tried. He said to Veronica, Strangest thing, my dear. I was in the seed house looking up seed for top onions—you know, the tree onion: that's *Allium Cepa*, variety *viviparum*—because I thought it high time to start the onion beds. And distinctly I heard the house door open and close, and it seemed that Badger started down the path. I thought I heard him stumble across the little stones which border it—you know, walking heedlessly, rather floundering like the hobbledehoy that he is— That he was—

Veronica was racked with a fit of dry sobbing on the instant, and walked slowly out of the room with her hands pressed against her cheeks. It would never do to mention such things to her again. So he would never do it, not if he saw clearly all three boys ranged before the fireplace, toasting their parents with good humor, drinking strong drink from the small silver cups they'd had when they were babies.

In a prank which Veronica might have deemed cruel but which Ira thought beneficent, he saw the boys hunting beside him. He missed a fair shot at the first two quail which rose, because he was watching Badger and how the youngster carried his gun. Badger wore an old jacket of yellow tow which his mother had thought so disreputable that repeatedly she begged him to give it to a servant, but it was Badge's favorite. He wore also a powder-horn with a shiny brass plug or stopper, a powder-horn carried long ago by his grand-uncle Sutherland Claffey when Unk warred against the redcoats. The plug was a gem in sunlight and cast out little glistening daggers to stab the eyes.

Sometimes Badger was there, hunting, and sometimes the land was untenanted except for the pointer and the shadow which walked beneath Ira's own bulk. Sometimes he saw the other boys also, but today they were mistier than Badge, and Ira could not have recited what they wore nor what they said when birds went up and escaped their firing, or whether they got any birds at all. He saw them. . . .

He himself missed some more birds, finally got his eye back, and observed the feathers struck and buffed by fine shot, he watched the birds tumbling and felt sorry for them. He put nine quail into the game bag before he was tired. He could have shot many more if he'd had a proper dog; but the half-ruined Twink had done his best, and Ira praised him and gave him a biscuit from his pocket. He regretted the little speckled bodies still warm, dumped in a weight against his hip; he felt a gloom when he thought of blood on a beak, blood in a bright eye soon to be no longer bright. But death was walking the land with such enormous crushing strides that who was he to mourn this microscopic butchery? The birds would be a fair tribute to Ira's womenfolks; the women would know that he had thought of them with love, that he had tried to please.

As he returned slowly to his home at an hour approaching midday, the chorus of axes, shouts, songs, whistles, bellows and thuds came steadily louder, the nearer Ira approached to the Sweetwater branch and astounded hills hemming it. What ugliness—to know that there would soon be a prison adjacent to one's dooryard! He supposed that prisons were necessary, but the thought of this stockade pained him before it was even made. He counseled himself that he should be glad there was a prison—and in such a healthy area as this—for a prison meant that the young fellows who'd be placed in it were living still; they were not extinct as the Claffey boys were extinct, but they were breathing and able to walk around, even restrained by the fence of massacred pine trees. If there were no places of military detention it would mean that every individual who yielded to superior force was slaughtered when he yielded. That would be a massacre in truth.

But isn't all war a massacre?

Scarcely—not in the sense that we employ when we speak of Indians and massacres. It's not a complete wiping out. It is a knightly contest.

In what knightly fashion did your comrades the volunteers behave in Mexico?

That was a brutal and unprovoked war, although at the time I was comparatively young and did not understand. This is the War for Southern Independence. The Yankees call it a Rebellion. Indeed it is one: a Rebellion against a power whose authority is denied.

But you did not favor Secession.

Neither did Aleck Stephens. *Revolutions are much easier started than controlled, and the men that begin them seldom end them. . . . Human passions are like the winds—when aroused they sweep everything before them in their fury. The wise and the good who attempt to control them will themselves most likely become the victims.*

Georgia—

Sutherland died for Georgia. Badger died for Georgia. Moses died for Georgia. Rob Lamar died for Georgia—

The devil they did. They died for— They died—

That's it. The Alpha and the Omega. They died.

Yet in private philosophy unvoiced, unrecognized, chained in a dark place remotely in his belief, Ira knew that he was undervaluing his sons and perhaps undervaluing his own dreams. The legend must still be alive—the grave and powerful and courteous legend—it must be exalted somewhere, if so many young spirits had embraced it. And elder spirits as well. The legend must be shining, as the slain were shining in whatever realm they occupied. Ira wished doggedly that he could see the shining. But it seemed that he went home in the dark (midnight at high noon) and sounds from the region toward the northeast stunned him as he walked.

VI

In February the one black gown remaining to Lucy was worn shabby, pulled loose at many of its seams. She tried discussing this problem with her mother, but Veronica was treading farther and farther away from both husband and daughter. Often it was hard to win a response from her on any topic in the world. If you spoke of the boys, her face turned more haggard than ever and tears flowed. In speaking of black gowns Lucy had in fact spoken of the boys. Still addled with her own grief, the girl felt torture afresh as she saw her mother withdraw to her own room. Veronica slept alone, Ira Claffey had moved into Badger's old room. This began when he suffered a catarrhal attack during the Christmas season and wished to avoid infecting his wife. He had enjoyed no physical relationship with Veronica since the last black draught was given them to drink. It seemed expedient for them to continue dwelling apart.

Poppy, I must seek your advice.

What is it, my dear?

About my wardrobe. I tried discussing it with Mother but— You see, Poppy, my last black has gone by the board; and of course we daren't spend money on goods even could we find the proper goods at Mr. Campbell's.

But, Lucy, do you wish to remain in black?

For the time being I'd prefer it. At least until it's been a year since— I've the pale green silk—you know, the old one, my first silk when I was seventeen—and I'm positive it would take a strong black dye mighty well. I hadn't thought to dye a wool, though, for goodness knows how I'll feel about my wardrobe in the autumn; I might choose to remain in black, and then again I might not. Can't scarcely tell.

Her small tender laugh, the laugh he loved, but coming seldom nowadays.

Well, child, you can't wear silk daily.

Oh, about the house I don't mind—I've plenty of fixings for home use, unless we have callers. But when callers appear, or going to church, or just going to Americus— Now, I've the blue figured poplin I could dye; I've two cottons for summer wear which I'm sure would take it well—the blue sprigged on white, and the pink patterned walking gown we had made when I was at the Female Institute. You may remember it: all the girls were required to have them alike, and I surely never did like being all alike.

Ah. And now the uniform turns to black. For Georgians.

Father and daughter stood regarding each other mutely, and Lucy had paled at this observation which escaped him whether he wished it or no. She shrugged wearily, and he bent to kiss her on her high smooth forehead. I suppose there must be a great deal of black in other States. And at the North also, Poppy, she said in her soft voice.

Yes, yes. I've thought of that. He added hastily, Lucy child, I'd recommend the pink walking gown for the dye-vat, since it has an unhappy connotation of seminary days. I remember how miserable you were, forever begging to return home.

And at last you let me, like a dear sweet Poppy, and over Mother's protestations. I regret it deeply, but I never could keep up that old French, and I promised faithfully.

You're a dear good child, and you don't need French. All you need is to go on being Lucy.

Thank you, sir. And I'll take your advice about that little walking gown.

But who can do the trick for you? Ninny, Pet or Extra? Or does Naomi—?

Oh, you've forgotten what a remarkable dye-woman I did become in my very early youth. Before old Ruth died I learned heaps from her. I used to watch her by the hour—just plain fascinated by all the colors and the way things dripped. I wrote down some of her receipts on the blank leaves of Grandmamma's cook book. I've explored carefully: we've all the necessaries for black. I'll take Extra to do the dipping and fire-making; she's mighty slow, but she doesn't talk a body's arm off like the other wenches. I just never can compel Ninny to remain quiet.

Three pounds of sumac, lime water, half a pound of copperas, two and one-half pounds of logwood . . . Lucy assembled her materials. She ordered Extra to prepare kettles and tubs under shade of the wash shed and to build up fires there. She needed blue vitriol also, for the silk, and bichromate of potash for both dresses; she knit her brows above the scales as she weighed the portions with care.

Lucy's hair was not so fair as her mother's, it was nearer the color of honey in the comb, and of fine texture. Rob Lamar used to insist that it was not a natural growth, that no hair could be so fine, that Lucy had ordered it from a shop maybe in Paris, France, and then had it sewn to her scalp. She could cry no longer, no tears were left to her to expend on Rob and her brothers. Now Rob had been dead for some fourteen months; his wide-jawed face and merry straight gaze and pomaded hair were beginning to be confused, to fade in recollection. When she thought of him, which was at least hourly, he seemed always to be mounted and riding rapidly away from her—she could see his back, she could not see his face, he did not turn around to wave in the saddle, he kept riding.

She wore her delicate hair drawn straight up from her brows, and coiled high, knotted with narrow black velvet ribbons. She had not curled her hair for over a year, and wondered whether she should ever curl it again. Her brows were slightly darker than her hair, and they arched in high bent bows, and were luxuriant, as were her dark lashes. She was the only one in the family with brown eyes which were so dark as to be almost black; Grandmamma Sutherland's eyes, everyone said; eyes like Lucy's shone duskily, challengingly from the primitive portrait in the lower hall. Lucy's slim body was made for activity; she rode excellently, could fire a pistol without squeezing her eyes shut, had owned a better skill than her brothers when they played with bows and arrows. She learned to swim in the Gulf of Mexico when the family visited the Gulf coast when she was small, and she lamented that there was no place for her to swim at home, and lamented further because her mother refused her permission to bathe in the Flint River, partly because of water-snakes but mostly because ladies of the region did not bathe commonly in the Flint River.

While Lucy was still very young the exploits of Florence Nightingale were discussed in newspapers and magazines. Lucy burned to emulate the Englishwoman, and was discovered to have set up hospital in a bake house which had been damaged by fire and was not being used at the time. She had five unwilling small blacks for patients and was dosing them with her father's best brandy and Trask's Magnetic Ointment which she had prepared out of lard, raisins and fine cut tobacco. Her brothers dubbed her Florence Nightmare and applied the name until she stormed into tears; then they were contrite. A brother and a sister died as infants before Lucy was born, but she witnessed the arrival and eventual departure of two more little sisters during her childhood, and was stricken with the notion that if she had been grown-up and a capable nurse, the children might have lived. When her mother was ill Lucy tended her eagerly, banishing the wenches, banishing even old Ruth who was the wife of Leander and a skilled nurse in her own right.

There was no instruction in the art Lucy loved most, at the Americus Female Institute. An attempt was made to teach the young ladies French, religious history, geography, Use of the Globes, *Belles Lettres,* velvet and landscape painting. Lucy learned more of value at the plantation than she ever absorbed from this bewildering hodge-podge. From her father she drank of Keats, Wordsworth, Lord Byron and earlier poets such as Herrick, and could recite from their works at length. The Claffeys had a family game they played, quoting verse and the Bible, and Lucy excelled in this, and other members of the family delighted in hearing her recitations. She hated to sew, she loved to take off her shoes and stockings and run barefooted on the grass. Her father greeted her often in the morning with, *Hail to thee, blithe spirit! Bird thou never wert,* and her mother did also until blows of later bereavement were more than her mother could bear, and it was impossible for her to venture a pleasantry.

It grieved Lucy that she found no balm in prayer; privately she felt like a heretic about it. She spoke her prayers dutifully on retirement, and she had a small morning prayer which she almost always murmured on rising. But she had believed, simply and sincerely, that if she prayed intently enough she would keep her brothers—and later, Rob—protected from bullets. This had proved not to be true, and thus the act of prayer seemed of little consequence any longer. But Lucy did still believe in God as a personal Father, resembling considerably her own father but with whiskers similar to the Reverend Mr. Cato Dillard's. She saw him presiding in a gilt courthouse which rested on cumulus clouds—very high, and always in the west, and frequently lit fiery by sunsets—and the courthouse was populated chiefly by Claffeys, Arwoods, Sutherlands and their kin; and Rob Lamar's horse was tied outside at evening.

Innocently she maintained a deep-seated feeling (it was a feeling, it stemmed solely from emotion, it was not a conscious or deliberate reasoning) that there was a promise wider, warmer, kindlier, prettier than might be contained in the creed or practice of any established religion. At least of established Presbyterianism. She had been taught to regard Roman Catholics as misguided antiquarians, and she knew little of Oriental beliefs: she supposed that they were all barbarous if ornate. But this warm good life which suggested itself as a vague mixture of conduct and dream— It was both balm and provocation each time it affected Lucy. It was not solely the simple worship of Nature enjoyed by Ira Claffey and in no way conflicting with his faith. It was more personal and more feminine, an illusion of the world's sheer beauty mingled with sensuous and sensual delight.

She had supported dreams about Rob, beginning with the first touch and kiss he awarded her; but with Rob's long death (it took him months to die in her imagination) other men supplanted him, and most of these she had never met, and perhaps they did not exist. Babies were mingled in her hidden fancies, along with the act of love. Lucy did not know exactly how the act of love was performed—she had only wicked whispered girlish gossip to go by—but in lonely nights she lay charmed by the contemplation of her own body, excited nearly into fever. Somewhere there might still be a man's body constructed for the express purpose of gratifying her own . . . when she cooled she was crushed by the enormity of her sin, and prayed with moving lips and half-voiced sounds, seeking impossible perfection, swearing to the Saviour that she would never countenance such emotions again.

But the dreams persisted as she grew older and more lonely; in one breath she said that they were a product of Satan, inserted in her drowsy brain in order to disease her immortal soul; in the next breath she yielded lustfully, and went springing down long flowery avenues of the future—she scented blossoms never designated by any botanists, ate fruits beyond the ken of her father or any green-thumbed horticulturist, she counted the stars and knew each of their colored shafts as a light wielded by a friend. She tussled with chuckling dimpled boy and girl babies, lying naked among them on rich mattresses of violets (forever violets; her favorites; she wore them in their season) and waiting the muscular man who would step toward her, smiling and courteous but not to be restrained, out of tapestried shadows.

Inadvertently once she had come upon Moses and Badge and a group of their cronies, when they were all fifteen or thereabouts, splashing nude in Little Sweetwater. So she knew how young boys looked; she supposed that full-grown men must appear the same, but larger.

If she had possessed that intimate trusted friend whom girls in stories seemed often to have but whom she'd never valued, she would never have dared to tell the friend. And of course Lucy could not tell her father; although she had an inkling that he might understand better than most, and might not condemn her for her passion.

She drudged assuredly, bitterly, suffering the vanishment of her brothers, suffering a quasi-widowhood. Recurrently she tried to pray for particular guidance, but prayer as an unguent for burns seemed to have failed.

VII

Long since the mustering officer who assembled laborers for the stockade had yielded to entreaties of many small planters. He had released every slave (excepting trained carpenters) drawn from a plantation where there were less than five male hands; he had released half of all the rest. This left a crew of not more than forty hands still hewing fallen pines and planting them in the five-foot trench. Ira Claffey had never begged the return of Jem, Coffee and Jonas, but he welcomed them; now his hands were plowing and planting diligently, happy also at having hot rations prepared by their wives, no longer reduced to cold fare at noon. The ridges sustained a comparative silence; the chopping, the whoops of ox-drivers echoed only sporadically. A portion of the fence near the southwest corner remained to be set in place; the rest of the structure towered in a raw parallelogram enclosing seventeen or eighteen acres. A narrow strip at the south was Claffey land, the balance was requisitioned from the neighbors. Posts, so recently the trunks of living pines, had been coarsely stripped and squared to be planted tightly side by side. A dense odor of fresh gum occupied the air; it was sweet to smell; and blue smoke drifted by day from smouldering fires where stumps and roots were charring, and at night there was a devilish glow. Underbrush—there had been little of it to begin with—was scorched off. Less than twenty trees still lived within the area, most of these of little account as to size.

Ira's feet were drawn to the region on two or three occasions, but each time he walked away sick at heart. Beloved narrow deep valley where the branch of Sweetwater made its light music— This had been a place precious to him. He would have deplored the ruination on aesthetic grounds if it had been worked five counties away; but here, gashed on personal timberland, it ached like a sprain. Tight, tight, solid, solid, yellow, tanned, bleeding, the stockade stood, a savage excrescence fifteen feet in height. It marched its short side across the south (except for the gap still remaining), its long side stamped down the declivity through the creek and across it, and stamped up the hill to the north, and across the north once more, and back down the long east side. Better trained hands among the Negroes worked at putting up numerous sentry-boxes along the exterior; they worked under close supervision of uniformed soldiers, they were building ladders. More troops tenanted the neighborhood than ever before, and more came daily; they had cut a road beside the creek, a road leading up to the railway station. Disks of stumps stood up-ended every which way along the route, heavy with clay; ruddy roots curled like snakes and fingers.

Lucy said to Ira at their supper, You're somber, Poppy. She hoped to make a jest of it. More somber than at any time since the Mexican War.

He closed his eyes and shook his head, as she had known he would do. In her place at the table Veronica Claffey ate in rapt cold silence and refused to lift her gaze. Oh, said Ira, it's merely that I walked over there again and observed the destruction they've made and are making.

Lucy shuddered. I shan't go.

. . . But she did go at last for curiosity's sake, lifting skirts to climb above the tangle and the cruel rough places, her father putting out his hand to steady her as he limped beside. The blacks stared and lazed at their tasks, to see a woman there; soldiers stared also, admiring Lucy and thinking of girls at home, or perhaps many of them looked at her with desire as young men might.

She screamed softly when they approached the creek. Poppy! It's gone. Oh, oh, how dreadful! They killed it.

What, Lucy?

The spring. Our spring—where you used to fetch me for a drink when I was tiny— She turned away blindly. No, let us go back. I can't bear more, I just naturally can't.

Nearing the gateway where carpenters worked, she looked up at her father with angry eyes. Her eyes were wet above their blaze. Ira offered his handkerchief.

Poppy, where did it go? The spring—

Crushed down, Lucy. Tamped and dragged and beaten and stifled.

But what became of the water?

I imagine, with all that weight of earth forced over it when they dug the ditch and dragged the trees— It had to make a new way for itself. Likely the water seeps through behind rocks, far under all that weight of material, and finds its way down to the branch. Travels underground, you see.

What a pity. It was the fairy place, truly. Reckon you don't recall how I used to see them in the moss?

He made his grimace. Reckon I do, daughter.

It held a lovely flavor, that water. Didn't it?

Yes.

They walked homeward, they passed the place where black workmen scooped at strange angles of earth, where white soldiers in sweaty undershirts were toiling as well.

What are they making?

A fort, my dear. To guard the prison.

Oh, they've a cannon back there in the pines. They'll put it in the fort?

Doubtless. And more than that.

When they walked in their own lane, when noises of dragging and pounding and shoveling fell farther behind them, Lucy still wore her white face. Poppy, I've thought of something. Perhaps the Yankee who killed Suthy— The one who killed Mosey-Wosey— The one who killed Badge— And who captured my Rob. Perhaps they'll all be taken prisoner, perhaps they'll all be brought to the prison here.

Perhaps, Lucy, they're gone already. As the boys are gone. Perhaps they were slain in the same battles.

But it would be mighty strange if all of them—

In war, said Ira Claffey, seldom do you know whom you've slain. You fire, all fire, both sides fire their volleys, and singly. People are hit. You do not know. Artillery is anonymous also. It's better so.

There's nothing better about war, Poppy. Nothing *best*.

He turned and stood still and looked back, but thank God nothing of the evil could be seen from where they waited. However a smell came to Claffey's nostrils, and he glanced quickly at his daughter to see whether she too had sensed it. She gave no indication, but moved on, stroking the back of her hand with a magnolia leaf she had gathered, and she did not know why she had picked it up: an idle thing to do. The smell was one familiar to Ira Claffey but he could not recognize its source. It might have been that one of the plantation cats— there were several—had found its fate in being worried by a stray dog, and now lay beneath the bushes. A rank tangle hugged the fence, and bloated flesh might have been concealed there . . . or an unfortunate recollection of the bastard melons which had oozed their evil until the Negroes, at Ira's behest, got rid of them? Or a varmint of the woods? He did not know, but he detected stench for a time, and then lost it as he went to join Lucy, and to join her in dwelling on happier things if there were any way for them to do so.

VIII

Old Ruth had declared long ago that it was impossible to achieve a permanent black on cotton with less labor, but still it was incredible labor. Lucy estimated that the goods might weigh five pounds; hence she'd assembled three pounds of sumac, wood and bark together. This sumac had been boiled half an hour, then the goods had steeped overnight. Extra removed the cotton after breakfast and hung it on a rope to drip for an hour. Lucy added eight ounces of copperas to the sumac liquor, and ordered Extra to dip the goods for another hour.

We put it back in the lime water, Miss Lucy?

Yes, Extra, for fifteen minutes again. Did you make a new dye of logwood as I bade you?

On this other fire. It been a-boiling already.

How long?

I don't know, Miss Lucy. It just been a-boiling.

It should boil for an hour at least. Then the goods must be dipped for another three hours before I add potash.

They worked in the wash house, which was a shed with a roof but only two sides or parts of sides, and a great wide chimney arching above to accept the smoke. When gusts of spring breeze assailed the area, smoke was rejected by the chimney and came down to smart the eyes of girl and servant. Fires sizzled and spat beneath cranes in a row. Simultaneously Lucy was dyeing her silk, and that necessitated still another vat containing blue vitriol compound; the same logwood mixtures could be used for both, but would need to be diluted for the silk.

Extra was plump and slow-moving and had hips like a stall-fed animal. Her slab of wide-nostriled nose turned squarely up in the middle of her broad purplish face, and dripped with sweat; Lucy saw the sweat on Extra's nose, and it made her feel hotter than ever.

Extra, like Ninny, was a daughter of Old Leander—one of the eight daughters whom he had fathered and whom the dead Ruth had mothered—but the other six had all been sold along with their husbands and children, if any. Extra was married to Jonas, and they had two of the plantation's current four children: little bright Buncombe and four-year-old Gracious. Also Orphan Dick, a four-year-old boy, was tended by Extra. His parents had perished of galloping consumption during the first year of the war; but Orphan Dick was giggling

and spirited and strangely the mark of consumption did not seem to
be upon him; it might reveal itself later, Ira Claffey feared.

Lucy would be twenty-one during this year of 1864, Extra would be
twenty-three. As children they had played contentedly together; there
were few white girls of Lucy's generation among the neighbors. Pet
was closer to Lucy's age, but they were not so harmonious in disposition. Extra and Lucy had little shops in shade under the magnolia
rustle—shops well stocked with pine cones, acorns, bits of broken glass
which they said were jewels, and nosegays of seasonable flowers. Lucy
was the proprietor, and Extra came to buy, paying in currency of pebbles. Sometimes they could persuade adults or older children to patronize their store; then both became shopkeepers. When they tired of
such play, and in hotter days, they had a playhouse amid lower limbs
of an oak. The playhouse had been built for Sutherland originally in
1844, but by this time he considered himself too grown-up to enjoy it.
Lucy inherited the playhouse, and sometimes she and Extra would permit Moses, two years younger, to attend them there; mostly they did
not welcome him because he was a boy, he was too obstreperous, he
liked to pound and dance on the warped old planks. When they were
alone Lucy might set Extra to braiding flowery adornments. She would
say, Now, Extra, I shall read to you from my new book of verses which
Cousin Sally Sue sent for my Christmas book.

Yas, Miss Lucy.

Mind, you're to pay close heed. Should you like to commit some
verses to memory?

Do I got to, Miss Lucy?

No. But I daren't teach you to read—it's against the law, you see—
but I'd be very glad to help you commit a verse or two.

I don't want to, I guess, Miss Lucy, please.

Very well. I shall read to you. Mind.

> . . . *The Child is father of the Man;*
> *And I could wish my days to be*
> *Bound each to each by natural piety.*

Is that not beautiful, Extra?

Yas'm.

I'll read it again:

> *My heart leaps up when I behold*
> *A rainbow in the sky—*

We out of daisies, Miss Lucy. Better I go fetch more?

Go pick enough to finish the collar, and I shall wear it to tea.

She would sit dreaming over her book, the tree would speak to her,
her own voice would drift low to a murmur and then to silence . . .
she dreamed across the book and saw Extra—a dumpy, dutiful, black-

legged figure in faded yellow calico—tramping through weeds for more daisies to complete her fabrication.

Now, in adult state, slave and young mistress worked at preparing the black gowns for the young mistress. Extra toiled as seriously as she had when weaving flowers. Even her plump arms showed a dye not put there by the God who had designated her as a black. Lucy wore a pair of ancient kid gloves to protect herself, but be she ever so careful it was certain that her hands would absorb some of the color; there would be blotches; she would have to wear mitts or gloves if company came, until the color wore off.

Company came now. It was between ten and eleven in the morning, hot for middle February. The wash house reeked; this task should have been done in an earlier week tinged with frost. More chilly weather would arrive, but it was very bad luck that today the sun was wilfully unblemished by clouds. Cauldrons steamed. Lucy saw the beads drip from Extra's wide nose, and felt more perspiration growing amid roots of her own hair. She had bound her hair in a brown net, and had her skirts caught up, pinned in two places so that she would not trip as she moved in the combined chores of overseer and fellow-dyer.

Company appeared behind her: there was the clearing of a man's throat, an ahem and growl with which some stranger sought to announce his presence. There was no place for Lucy to flee. She felt supreme high-pitched feminine wrath that a man should creep close without warning. She faced him, her face looked boiled and baked, and she knew it; it was dreadful.

I'm sorry, Ma'am, to intrude upon you.

He wore a single spur, he must have been riding, probably he had tied his horse out in front. Naomi was in the kitchen, Ninny was doubtless above stairs, making beds belatedly . . . Ninny was slightly deaf, or pretended to be so habitually when the bell rang. (The Claffeys used to argue as to whether Ninny's deafness was actual or feigned; certainly it was periodic.) Pet, had Lucy but known it, was gone to the root cellar when the stranger rang, and Ira Claffey was gone to the fields. No one could have heard the bell except Veronica, and she was dedicated to a new and dreadful task: she searched wardrobes, presses, cupboards, shelves throughout the house, she hunted for any and all personal relics of the three fallen sons, and was putting them away—fabrics, china, wood and steel—in low chests in the room of Moses, the baby. Then, when they were filled and there was nothing more to put into them, the chests would be locked and shoved under Moses's bed. That was Veronica's plan; her husband and her daughter guessed at it, but said nothing. Ira looked for the boys' silver cups, and found them under infant flannels in one of the carved chests. He removed the cups and put them behind Scott on his own library shelf. Maybe in time Veronica might be cured of this burial passion, and again the cups could take their proud pathetic place in view.

I did try to ring, Ma'am, but there seemed to be nobody about.

I'm sorry no one heard the bell, sir. You see—we're dyeing—

He would think that she meant *dying!* He bowed. He spoke with the genial scratchy voice of an adolescent, though he appeared to be older than Suthy had been—perhaps he was near to thirty. Permit me to introduce myself, Ma'am. My name is Harrell Elkins. Have I the honor of addressing Miss Lucy Claffey?

She stood with hot face and soaked gloves, she edged behind a bench so that her hiked-up skirts mightn't be observed too readily. Mr. Elkins, sir, I'm Lucy. But, you see, we're engaged in dyeing and— If you would be so kind as to rest in the house, I'll have my servant escort you— I'll send to the field for Father—

He was in shabby gray uniform, there were dark blemishes where insignia had been removed. His old hat had faded nearly to green on the crown, and he held the brim in front of his middle with big pale hands on which a pink of very fresh sunburn was showing. He was a rangy man, with rounded shoulders detracting from his natural height; and his head was small for a man of six feet or thereabouts, and his ears stuck out, roundly, quizzically. He wore silver-rimmed spectacles; these glassy wafers attempted to conceal but could not conceal the dance of dark-blue-black eyes behind them. In no degree was Mr. Elkins handsome. In every degree he was a man peculiar to himself.

Miss Lucy, permit me. Do you recall that your brother Sutherland ever mentioned a Captain Elkins?

The steam from logwood and sumac and copperas blinded Lucy. Elkins thought that she was fainting. He stepped forward with strange animal grace and put his hand beneath the girl's elbow to steady her. He brought out a clean bandana and unfolded it. I'm sorry.

Thank you. It's only— Oh, that was mighty sudden. She tried to laugh, she made a sound, it wasn't laughter, it was a small cry. Of course. Captain Elkins! He called you Harry, didn't he?

Yes, Miss Lucy, people do.

You were not with him at—at Gettysburg?

Elkins shook his head. You see, I was with them both in the early days of the Sixteenth. I knew your youngest brother but slightly, since he was a private soldier and in another company; but I was near him when he died at Crampton's Gap. It was the same engagement in which Colonel Lamar lost his life.

She nodded limply. I—I was affianced to a distant cousin of Lieutenant-Colonel Jefferson Lamar.

Ah, yes. That would have been Rob?

Yes, Captain.

His eyes leaped with a spurt of life behind the lenses. Just Surgeon

Elkins now, Miss Lucy. I hadn't yet finished my medical studies when the war came, and I was determined on deeds of derring do. So I served as a soldier.

And you performed the deeds.

He chuckled. Mighty few, I fear.

Not according to the accounts we received from my brother, sir.

Miss Lucy, you're more than kind and I fear your brother was more than generous to his friends. But I stopped a few pieces of scrap-iron last spring, and thus was made unfit for further service in the field. That was some two months before Sutherland—died. Naught for me to do but resume my medical studies again; thus I've become a surgeon—very much of a neophyte.

Then you'll not be returning to the field?

I'd hoped for that, but our Government had other plans. For the moment I've been detailed to this region on what might appear to be a peculiar mission. I did welcome the assignment to this duty, for I've long wanted to call upon the Claffeys, if you'll pardon my saying so. . . .

At sunset, when Ira Claffey himself escorted his guest above stairs, he led the way down a short main hall, turned sharp right into the narrower passage which ran from east to west, and stopped at the second door on the right. With his hand upon the round white door-knob, Ira said, This was Sutherland's, and ushered Harrell Elkins inside. Elkins' saddle bags, with the waterproof roll containing his personal belongings, had already been fetched up by Ninny and stood upon a chair. There was nothing of Sutherland's in the room. Veronica had banished every young man's trinket and treasure to entombment.

His things are no longer here. Ira spoke in a manner of apology. His mother's put them all away. She has— Possibly you observed it, Harry. She has grown remote.

Elkins went to the front window and looked out at rows of trees fronting the lane. Then he moved to the smaller west window and glanced at plum-colored clouds and strips of glint between them. He turned. Thank you, Mr. Claffey, for calling me Harry. I was fond of your son. I fear I'm mighty shy, as a social individual, and have not made as many friends as some. Suth used to call me Cousin Harry.

We shall be glad to continue the designation, Coz.

I appreciate your welcome more than I can say.

Please to join me in the library at your convenience, Cousin Harry, and we'll taste a glass of wine.

Ira went down to the little library and found Lucy there before him. She was wearing her wornout black dress, but Ira squinted to observe that some one had been very busy with needle and thread, drawing the spread seams together so that the gown would serve. She wore also a pair of ancient black lace gloves: the dye had left its stain.

It would seem, said Ira, that you've taken especial pains with your hair.

She stared at him indignantly, as occurred seldom. Father!

I apologize, my dear. This is no occasion for levity. Nevertheless I'm glad he's come. Ira bent to unlock a cupboard, and drew out the glass decanters which he had not touched since the New Year.

Poppy, may I join you gentlemen?

What might your mother say?

Nothing. She merely bowed when I introduced Mr. Elkins to her. She bowed and said, Pray sit down, sir. Then she was out of the room in another minute, gone to Moses's room.

We'll be honored to have you. Now that I think of it, I wasn't awarded my morning kiss today.

You may have it belatedly. Lucy offered her face. When her father kissed her, she clutched his arms spasmodically, and whined.

Now, now.

Poppy, I think he knew my Rob! When he spoke of Crampton's Gap, he mentioned also Lieutenant-Colonel Lamar and how he died. I said that he was kin to the man I was to marry, and he said, That would be Rob. So he must have known him.

Ira thought about it for a moment. Likely that was at the University. Cousin Harry tells me that he served as assistant to the medical chemist there whilst pursuing his early medical studies.

You call him Cousin Harry? cried Lucy with disbelief.

He requested it. Daughter, remember that he and Suthy were struck by the same shell-burst at Chancellorsville. Though Suthy's was a minor wound.

Harrell Elkins appeared in the doorway, in obvious embarrassment because they were talking about him.

A small wood fire burned on the hearth; coolness possessed the later hours of the day. There had been no matches in that household for many months except homemade ones, and often the homemade matches would not strike. Lucy took a sliver of pine from an old glass vase standing handy, and brought fire from the hearth to wan leaning candles on the table. The light glared on Elkins' spectacles and made him appear as a monster with great orange eyes.

My daughter hoped that she might be allowed to join us, Coz.

I'm pleased. Harry Elkins' rough high voice was unsteady; but he spoke as if he meant what he said. You had a feeling that he might never speak other than a sincere belief, profound or trivial. He said, I trust that Mrs. Claffey is not indisposed, and then stood in shock at having said the wrong thing.

I believe she'll join us at dinner. Lucy, in honor of Cousin Harry's arrival, will you indulge along with us?

Thank you, yes, Poppy.

Ira reached behind the calfbound row of Sir Walter Scott and brought out three small silver cups. Lucy exclaimed; she was positive that her mother must have buried the cups in one of those dreadful chests, and Lucy was surprised but delighted to see that her father had recovered them.

These were the boys'. Lucy, do you take Moses's cup. I'll drink from Badger's. You, sir, Cousin Harry, may observe that the cup which I've handed to you bears the name of Sutherland.

Elkins peered closely at the little silver thing, the child's cup nearly concealed in his broad smooth steady hand. He saw the name, or did not see it: firelight and candlelight were tricky, and not much light of sunset remained to reflect into the room. A streak of water appeared on his slightly hollow cheek. Lucy turned her glance away, but she was glad that he had cried.

Ira Claffey poured dark sherry for all three, though Lucy's was but a token. I give you, he said, and then could not say the names. They drank, and when Cousin Harry Elkins put down his cup he said shrilly, scratchily but in reverence, God bless them all. Wherever they may be.

Lucy repeated it to herself when she was in her bed at ten. Wherever they may be, and she was pleased with Cousin Harry for saying those words and for thinking the thought. He was awkward, strained, almost self-consciously rustic as to habit; yet there was a benefit in being near him. In this single day of acquaintance she considered him as a kind of evangelical relative.

Between mellow yellowed sheets and under a woven blanket some two rods distant from the girl, Harrell Elkins stretched watching toward the ceiling, the ceiling which he could not even see without spectacles. He considered the six pairs of spectacles which he had toted to the army; and he had broken four pairs the first year, and how they cost, and where might one secure good magnifying spectacles now? This was the last pair of the six—here, on the stand beside Suth's bed—and it was remarkable that they had survived the burst at Chancellorsville; they needed only a bow repaired. A watchmaker did that while Harry was in the hospital—or rather, hospitals, since he had been in three.

He lay now savoring the sweetness of Ira Claffey and Lucy. He lay pitying the mother, and wishing that something might be done for her. Short of a general resurrection of the war's dead, he did not know of any act or treatment which might effect a change. He feared that Veronica Claffey must march without deviation toward the solemn retreat which awaited her: a retreat wherein people sat unspeaking in their rigid chairs, and did not listen to what others said, and took their meals alone, and when they smiled—rarely—it was as if to say, I know a secret but I shan't tell. It was terrible when they smiled. Harrell Elkins had seen them.

He felt drawn to Lucy and her father not alone because they were Suth Claffey's flesh and blood, but because they embraced him with a tenderness. All his life Harry had dreamt of warm companionship; he had not found it at college: only in the army, where the general scale of values resolved in his favor. Through young years he had walked in the discomfort of weakness, he had suffered varieties of scorn because he had a strange voice, because he was bookish, because he wore spectacles in a civilization where most young folks never wore them, because he could not see well enough to catch a swift ball or shoot a quail.

He could barely remember his mother. There was a faint recollection of a fleshy, frilled lap and the scent of cologne (it might have been a Sunday when she held him. He knew that she read from a book of Bible stories, and must have simplified them as she read). Also in memory he heard her saying to the cook, Do you let Master Harrell make thimble cookies if he wishes. Then no other memory except black nodding plumes, and his own shrieks because he did not understand death, he did not understand, he feared for his mother; who were all these people, and why did they hold their voices low and musty? His father was bitten by a rattlesnake while hunting, when Harrell Elkins was seven, and died two days later. Harry was reared, until ready for the academy, in the home of a second cousin whose ward he became. The cousin was a physician and surgeon, a cruel man, but brilliant and scientifically experimental by turns. Doctor Epps disliked Harry, whose funds he squandered to the possible enrichment of brokers in cotton and foodstuffs in distant Savannah. He devised strange punishments when the boy was driven to rebellion, when he did wicked things out of resentment at loneliness and immurement.

Once Harry dragged a load of loose cones and pine needles against the ell of the house, and tried to set the place on fire. Nothing burned except a wooden sill, since the structure was of brick. Servants caught the boy red-handed and gave him over to Doctor Epps. The doctor said that he must go to jail and be fettered, and live on bread and water. The jail was a barren windowless entry off the doctor's private sitting room; slats were nailed across the door, and Harry was incarcerated there, fettered with knotted hemp, and with a chamber pot and the traditional pallet of straw for furnishings. Bread and water were given him by the doctor, morning and evening. When Doctor Epps was at home, and not calling on patients or performing operations, he had his meals brought to him on a tray within sight and sound and smell of the child beyond the lattice. Doctor Epps was fond of boiled foods, and they smelt particularly pungent: Harry Elkins recalled the rich odors of ham and cabbage, pork and turnips, beef and onions. His cousin kept him in jail for five days, and then word got abroad through gossip among the slaves. The rector came to call, with fire in his old eyes, and Harry was released, counseled, prayed over, fed.

These were things which he might not tell the Claffeys now. He might tell them in time, if friendship grew as he petitioned that it would; he had told Suth a few of the incidents. It would have offended Harrell Elkins to know it, it would have wounded him immeasurably had he known that Sutherland Claffey's initial interest in him and attention to him were engendered first by a sense of the ridiculous and then by pity. Suth had written to his family: I dislike being a tale bearer, but then you must remember that young Moses and I are new at this task of soldiering, and shall wish to parade the story in completeness before your eyes. It is probable that I shall write to you more frequently than Moses, the idle scut. Of course his company is removed from mine by three companies, and we are separated by the rigid distinctions of rank and cast (sic!) but little birds tell tales now and then. I hear that he and another prankster of his ilk *borrowed* two of their officers' mounts, and went for a fine gallop yesterday. Tricks like that will land the youngster in durance vile, you may be certain; but I doubt they will get him shot by a firing squad! In my own company we have the most absurd *coterie* of individuals. Not that there are not splendid chaps as well, and those who will stand out gallantly when we face the enemy. Not in all the myths of the ancients have such *phantasmagoria* been assembled! In all my days at Oglethorpe I never saw the beat, in classroom or on campus. One *lieutenant* in particular— Ah, what a figure for legendry! It is said that he achieved his appointment because his late father was a classmate of the Hon. Gen. Howell Cobb at the U. some thirty years ago. The Yankees should see him: they would take off and flee, not a doubt of it. He is somewhere near my own age, but half bald already; he wears the ears of an ape; his voice squeaks like a warped windlass; and surmounting all this *manly beauty* he employs a great pair of specs—to make it easier for him to spy the foe, no doubt. His name is Elkins, and already to myself I call him Elky—you recall?— after the colt in the Rollo tale. Only yesterday I ordered him to engage his platoon in drill according to the time-honored Poinsett tactics. He had no sword to give him a manner of command; it seems that, lean of purse, he is still bargaining for sidearms. Upon my word, he appeared on the drill-ground with a grass *sickle* in his hand. The men were close to splitting. Elkins was immensely serious about the whole thing. . . .

Another letter, later. Your box arrived on a Saturday in fine order. Only the peaches were broken, and leaking rum along the way, no doubt to the satisfaction of sundry *baggage-handlers*. Nevertheless I salvaged them with content, and rinsed off the glass and mildew. Tell our loyal Naomi that her tin of *Federal Cake* made many mouths water and many hearts beat high. The sugar itself would have been a treat, since recently that commodity was lacking in our messes— why, I know not. Tell Naomi that henceforth, however, it must be dubbed *Confederate Cake*. Come evening, a few of the elect assembled in my narrow quarters to taste and to enjoy: those gentlemen around me with *chicken-guts* on their sleeves. Lucy will shrink, but that is merely soldier slang for the braid we officers wear. The redoubtable Lt. Elkins was in attendance. I must say, he is a saint as to good humor, never complaining, and always ready to crack a joke in his peculiar voice. It has come to my attention that the men respect him, and find comfort and perhaps inspiration in his dry sallies. . . .

Another letter. Elkins is a remarkably fine horseman, at least for the demands of a martial life. He is not spectacular in the saddle, he does not cut a fine figure, because of his odd posture; but he can take a horse anywhere. After our arduous *traverses* of the past week, several officers were complaining of saddle boils, chafing and the like. Including The Undersigned. Rob Lamar should be with us—there is a *Centaur* for you! But I must add that the *un-Centaur-like* Harry Elkins had no complaint of *mayhem at the hands of a horse,* and was fresh as the proverbial daisy. . . .

Another. It was our baptism of such concentrated fire. They were fairly focal upon us. With all that smoke and banging and—I regret to state—the sight of blood round about, many in the company might have felt like taking *French leave.* It seems in battle that sometimes there is a concentrated if brief period of silence—a vacation between the cannonading and musketry. In such a *holiday of silence* there spoke the easily recognizable accents of one Harry Elkins. He was remarking with a degree of pain that he wished the Yanks would cease throwing stones at us. In fact, dear parents and Lucy, what he said was not *stones* but another equally commonplace commodity in a stableyard where animals have been segregated for some time. You should have heard the men roar with laughter. It made matters indubitably easier for all concerned. . . .

. . . I have had to lecture Harry severely about exposing himself to enemy fire. He looked contrite, but finally faltered out with a statement that he was sure he was constantly more *scairt* than anyone else in the Confederate States Army, and that if he didn't consciously ignore the bullets snapping about him he might be guilty of some unfathomable act of cowardice. Furthermore, his opinion was that since a rank of infantrymen are compelled to stand up and attempt an advance in the face of withering fire, it behooves their officers to be nonchalant, even to the point of suicide, in disclaiming any attitude which might suggest that they were not invulnerable to *minié* balls.

I wonder if there is wisdom here?? Certainly food for thought. . . .

. . . He is so kind hearted. I feel that he is like a brother, now that Moses is no more, and Badge far away. Sunday night we had a fine talk by the fire. Harry told me of his ambitions as a physician and surgeon. Strangely he was instigated in these ambitions by the example of a relative who possessed experience and technical skill, but no Christian heart and soul. Harry declares that as a youth he swore that, since this relative was a *bad* doctor, he should grow up to be a *good* doctor. There is a strange and valuable salt flavoring his conversation; I enjoy it heartily. When this war is over we shall all be the patients, when necessary, of *Doctor Harry Elkins*. He says that he will give me physic without charge! . . .

. . . My own wound is a bagatelle: a mere splinter near the left elbow, which made me bleed *pints* and causes some pain, but will not disqualify me for full duty after a fortnight or so. But the thought of Harry occupies more attention. We are eager for word of him, and nothing is heard. His hemorrhage was severe: he was struck in the neck, at the base of his head, in the shoulder and chest. He kept insisting that no one should carry him to the rear; he was quite comfortable; no one must leave the firing line on his account. The last time I spoke to him he murmured something about, Give those Yanks a belting for me. They broke my specs. . . .

Harrell Elkins heard his own voice saying those words, now, as he sought sleep in Sutherland Claffey's old room. They had held that deep love which is disassociated from sex because of the nature of the lovers: they are men made for women, never men made for men. Abhorrent as decay itself was the notion that ever either of them could have loved physically one of his own fashioning, in intimacy. Elkins hoped wistfully that after long search he might find a woman who would (according to the Scriptural phrase he learned early) cleave unto him. The affection between himself and Suth was an attraction of opposites, solidified by peril into a union which only those who'd functioned together in equal peril might ever know.

Suth had known many women, although he was too much the well-taught young gentleman to discuss them. He was handsome, devoted to any phase of the patriotic career to which he had dedicated himself, pleased by his own accomplishments, a bit too vain for popular taste until the close song of bullets blew the swelling from his head. Fear of the death which was to come made him admirable at last, and so he remained to the end. In passing Sutherland Claffey was bewailed by his superior officers, envied in retrospect by subordinates, mourned by his men. He became the complete effigic pattern of a Crusader on a tombstone. So Harry Elkins thought of him now, resting in that sacred bed.

From the first moment of contact, from Lucy's primary flutter in

the wash house in front of dyeing-kettles, and from Ira's handclasp
and gentle knowing manner, and from the worshipful agony they
shared as they sipped from silver cups— From these and subsequent
sharings through the evening hours, Harry Elkins knew the Claffeys,
father and daughter, as new dignities and beauties to be respected.
In no degree could he have considered Lucy as a love for himself.
He dared not look at her romantically (not yet) even if he had admitted for an instant that he longed to. She belonged in sanctified
association with a dead lover, with her brothers' memory, and with
a father who was so obviously a man above most men, and with a
mother who suffered as a casualty of the conflict.

He thought, It was so good of them to take me in. He thought, It
was more than good of them to accept me as I scarce dared wish I
might be accepted. I am very fortunate. His twenty-five-year-old
body (not yet twenty-six, despite the scrubby hair and barren scalp
and the facial lines) relaxed in a baby's contentment. His arms slid
up across the pillow, his big fists were bent loosely, his fingers curved
in rest. He slept, but feeling in the last coverts of awareness that
some benevolence would be offered him.

In the middle of the night, Lucy Claffey walked and rolled once
more in that pagan dream wherein violets grew, laughing children
tumbled, the man come bare and heartily to claim her, to bear her
down among flowers while distant flutes were playing and the fallow
deer of legend were running past. The man was Harrell Elkins. She
roused herself from this sinful illusion with strength and in decided
horror. Never again, dear Lord, never, never, she prayed. Oh, that I
could be so carnal. Desperately she flung out her hand and found
the Shorter Catechism of her childhood, a thin brown tiny volume on
the round table by her bed. *What is forbidden in the seventh commandment? The seventh commandment forbiddeth all unchaste
thoughts, words, and actions.* She held it as a talisman until she slept
again deeply and her limp fingers fell away from the book. She was
inordinately silent at the breakfast table, and her father wondered
about it to no avail. He had been up early, showing Cousin Harry
about the place.

Lucy avoided being left in the room alone with Harrell Elkins;
that did not take much managing, since he was so shy of her. Soon after
they had breakfasted he asked for his horse, and little Buncombe led
the animal proudly to the front. Cousin Harry thanked them for their
hospitality, and rode toward the new stockade. It seemed that Ira
Claffey had invited him to be their guest while he proceeded on
duty in the region, and Harry accepted willingly. Lucy told herself
that she did not approve of the invitation, but Suthy would have
wished it, so she must say nothing. Never again, she swore, would
she dream such a dream.

IX

Eben Dolliver shouted at the guard in thickening darkness. What in thunder did you lam me for? Like to busted my head—

The guard called across the heads and shoulders of other prisoners jammed fast. I'll bust it sure enough if you don't shush.

I wasn't talking—

Somebody back in that corner of the car was talking. You heard me order you to cease.

You like to busted my head, repeated Eben in fury.

Again the guard drove his musket butt toward the obscure corner of the box car, but men squatted and ducked and the butt thudded against the wooden side. Keep quiet, Ebe, a boy whispered. He's mad. You'll but make him crosser.

The guard withdrew his weapon and again took up a station beside the closed door, speaking with fervor to a fellow guard about what he would do if the prisoners didn't shut up. The prisoners were talking about exchange, the all important subject, but the young guard believed that they shouldn't talk about exchange or anything else. He had been commanded to maintain order in the box car, and to his nervous taste maintaining order was synonymous with maintaining absolute silence. He was a frightened, fat, stupid youth, trembling at being shut into this small space with dozens of savage Yankees. No telling when they might spring at you, seize your musket, perhaps twist your arms and legs out of their sockets.

Certain of the prisoners were considering that very course. Sounds resolved into a disordered fluttering mutter, submerged by coughing, nose-blowing, a continual crunch of timbers as the car jerked into its couplings and again tried to pull loose from them, a chorus of clanking metal underneath. Woodsmoke from the antique engine drifted along the train's top and found its way through every aperture. People were half gagged by smoke, including the guards.

Pushed into a forward corner by weight of the mass on every downgrade, Eben Dolliver and his friends made queer plans and then abandoned them. How many's in here? I was third in, I watched the door and counted: we got forty-seven. With the guards? No, there's either four or five guards extra; I couldn't make out exactly. That makes fifty-one or fifty-two in all.

What I thought was we could pass the word around and have a signal. Somebody yell a signal. Then all at once we could climb on the guards and get their guns. Got enough to do it, weak as we are. Both doors locked on the outside. Couldn't get them open. We could wait, Charley. They're bound to open them in time. Then we'd have four or five muskets, and maybe even some knives or bayonets— Have they got bayonets on? One has. I seen him when he crawled in. Maybe we could bust out.

Eben Dolliver whispered, And get mowed down. They always got troops standing by with rifles ready-aimed, the second they sling the doors open. Wouldn't have a prayer.

Guess you're right. Well, it's better than Belle Isle. Hain't you droll? Least we could breathe on the Island. Can't breathe in here. After while maybe they'll stop, and march us out in the woods like they done the other nights.

The engine struggled slowly on a long upgrade. The load of smelly people fell gradually away from the front end of the car, displaced by the pull of gravity, and a mingling of pleas and curses and bitter chuckling rose from the herd now squeezed toward the rear. Members of the Moon Hotel mess dug their fingers into cracks and around interior braces of the forward end. Thus they clung in comparative ease for a time. Two of them found room enough to sit down.

Get stepped on down there, Kirke.

Don't care if I do. Good to stretch my limbs out. Gad.

They called themselves the Moon Hotel mess after a hotel conducted in Iowa by the father of one of the members. Nine in all had messed together on the Island: three were Iowans, one was from Indiana, one from eastern Kentucky, the rest from Michigan. Andrew Kirke had enlivened earlier days of starvation with detailed descriptions of the table set by his father. That was when they were in a primary stage of hunger, fascinated unduly by any consideration of food. As they dried and thinned (one died) on the limited diet of the Belle Isle winter, they found themselves losing interest in such fragrant illusions. No longer did they prompt Andrew to describe black pepper scattered on the surface of prairie chicken gravy. His favorite tale had concerned a political dinner during 1860, when plank tables were erected under cottonwoods in front of the Moon Hotel, and guests came all the way from Fort Dodge to join in the rally and to partake of Mr. Kirke's fare. Fried prairie chicken, two roast pigs, venison, platters of grilled pike; boiled potatoes, greens, hominy, green corn . . . Andrew had been fond of going into precious detail concerning the gravy. He said it had a brown film over the

top as it cooled, being well thickened with flour, but when you put
the spoon down through it the steam came drifting out, and the
skin of the gravy was broken, and hotter softer gravy was paler
underneath. Also Andy had a great deal to say about crab-apple
pickles, and sauerkraut made by the local German saloon-keeper.
Andrew was very fond of crab-apple pickles and plum butter; he said
that he dreamed often of these luxuries. By February the dreams had
fallen away, they no longer provoked in taunting routine, they no
longer comforted in sleep as a promise of what might be if ever the
men got themselves exchanged. (They did not refer to exchange in
the cynical sense, but in the hopeful one.) Rarely did the fancies of
food recur; then they came sharp and baking and quick, and left the
dreamer staggering.

The Moon Hotel mess promulgated certain rules; any person not
conforming would be banished. Everybody had to take exercise, they
had to walk about, it would help to keep their bodies and brains
alert. They must boil every spoonful of water they drank. A man
must keep himself as free from vermin as circumstances would permit. A lane lined by high boards ran from the Belle Isle pen down
to waters of the James; at night this lane was closed by a high gate,
but the gate was reopened each morning. Guards were on duty at
the river's edge: no chance for a prisoner to swim away, even if he
felt stout and bold enough to try it. But he could wash, and every
member of the Moon Hotel mess must wash daily. Above all no
despondent conversation was permitted. Members should talk, laugh,
jest openly about their situation. They had a debating society, although three or four of them did most of the talking. Andrew Kirke
could sing Irish ballads, Ebe Dolliver sang like a minstrel, most of
the others sang passably hymns or popular doggerel learned at school
and singing school. They sang almost nightly, even on the evening
after the morning when Sam Michols, Twentieth Michigan, was carried out dead. That night they sang, Rock of Ages, and, Glory, Glory
Hallelujah. They considered it a direct result of their discipline that
Sam was the only one they lost on the Island, and he had been
feverish to begin with.

Eben Dolliver referred to himself as middle-aged, meaning that he
was the precise middle individual, in age, of the original nine. Four
were older than he, four younger. Eben became twenty years old the
month before he was captured in the Chattanooga campaign. He had
marched four hundred miles with the Fifth Iowa, all the way from
Memphis to Chattanooga, to take part in that fight, and it was hard
lines to be captured in your first battle after such a wearing march.
The Fifth Iowa had marched upwards of two thousand miles in two
years; half the men of the regiment were already casualties; now they
were serving under their third colonel. At Chattanooga they took to

boats, and most of them had to find boats in the dark. They went floundering two-by-two on the edge of the Tennessee River, slipping in greasy wet places, barking their shins on stones they couldn't see, when a calm voice spoke through the November night. The speaker was so close that Eben Dolliver could almost have reached out and touched him.

Be prompt as you can, boys. There's room for thirty in a boat.

. . . Who was that, talking there on the bank?

Didn't you know? Austin tolt me he was here, overseeing us.

No. It wasn't Captain Byers—

Not Captain Byers's voice. Guess again.

The colonel?

Naw, naw, naw. Uncle Billy!

Get along, now! You mean Uncle Billy himself?

Sure enough.

It made you feel better inside, turning with slowness on the broad black cool water, expecting to have Rebel pickets start poking holes through you every foot of the way— It made you feel better to know that General Bill Sherman was right there alongside, taking at the moment the same risk you were taking.

Less than two days later, when the adjacent Army of the Cumberland ordered itself to take the top of Missionary Ridge after the commanders had only ordered it to take the bottom, Eben Dolliver was jumping over logs and rifle pits along with the rest of the Fifth Iowa. A lot of people started to scream warning ahead on the right—and there they were, seeming like more Secesh than Eben had ever seen at one time and in one place. They looked a lot meaner too. They were boiling and Rebel-yelling out of a tunnel which drilled the side of the mountain, and boiling up out of the railroad cut beside the tunnel. A few minutes later there was nothing to do but drop your gun and stick your hands up and waggle them desperately to attract attention so's you wouldn't get a hole through you. Looked like part of Company H was taken, and part of Company G, and some from A and B also. Only two or three fellows from C. Sixty-odd men gobbled by the Rebs in less time than a heifer'd take to switch her tail. And here they had thought they were winning a battle. Just went ahead too fast and too far. The Confederate artillery was already limbering up and streaking for the rear when they reached the artillery positions. Rebs marched them twenty-five miles that night to avoid their being freed by the Union advance. They were just about as dismal a gang of Hawkeyes as ever chewed biscuit.

They were marched and shipped by way of Bristol, Virginia, denuded of most of their possessions by guards before they reached Bristol. Ebe Dolliver had no blanket with him at the moment of his capture, but he was wearing an overcoat, which he peeled off as bidden to do. A couple of days later he got even. The prisoners were being hustled through icy mountains, and Ebe Dolliver spied a guard who didn't appear to be overly intelligent and who was wrapped in a crazy quilt. The quilt, a dirty one, was adorned with every color of the rainbow, but the material itself was tightly stitched, well stuffed, wearable. Hey, Johnny, what'd you say to selling your quilt for greenbacks? You can get another one from home. Yank, you all know we ain't lowed to have greenbacks. Look, nice and green, and Dolliver displayed his roll. How many dollars you reckon you got there, Yank? Thirty-five.

The quilt slid over to Eben's shoulder, and a lean hand extended for the money; the Iowan pressed the wad into the hand and moved away. Also the guard moved away, for he saw an officer approaching; he thrust the money into his pocket without looking at it. Two hours later the guards were changed, and Eben Dolliver never saw again the man he had victimized. The currency which had appeared so temptingly green was in reality wildcat currency, printed by Western stage companies and irresponsible and probably defunct banks. Masses of that scrip floated through the army, and became the joke and toy of soldiers; but Eben and his fellow Fifth Iowans talked the matter over and decided that the old guard wouldn't have known the difference even if he had looked at the bills. They doubted that he could read. Soon after they were captured, a Rebel said, All you Yanks that can write your names line up over here, and the entire group moved over. The Rebel officer was indignant because he thought they were making fun of him. To Eben's knowledge there had been one man in his company who couldn't read or write, and he was not captured. These ignorant Secesh just didn't realize what it was like to be raised in the North, especially in Iowa.

Wind cut across the mountains, and Ebe Dolliver was more than glad that he had acquired a quilt. Wintry wind blew them to Richmond and Belle Isle; they landed on the Island at the end of the first week of December. First thing they saw was a troop of armed guards dressed in blue, and some goose of a prisoner danced with loud cheers, smitten by the notion that Richmond had fallen to the Yankees and they were now among friends. Those blue-clad guards soon showed him how wrong he was, as they shoved him back into the file and threatened to fire. Next thing they saw was a line of twenty-two bodies—Dolliver counted—being carried out of camp feet first. It had been colder than usual during the night.

On the afternoon of February fourteenth the eight surviving members of the Moon Hotel mess were counted out of Belle Isle with exactly five hundred and ninety-two other prisoners. Wishful gossip in camp suggested that they were about to be exchanged, perhaps aboard a warship at some coastal port, but most of the wiser guessed the truth. They would be sent South, possibly to Savannah or Charleston. They hoped to go South because there they would find sunlight and maybe oranges and flowers; rivers would not be nearly frozen over as the James had been. The Moon Hotel mess had no business being numbered in this first contingent. Not a man of them was in the designated Hundreds. They flanked out, adroitly as imaginative and resourceful young men might do. Others—incompetents—sought to accompany them and were hustled and dragged away. You had to be sly about a thing like that. The foppish discipline of the Moon Hotel mess, once derided by people in adjacent tents, was showing its profit.

In this railroad train now, according to testimony of more talkative guards, they were being shipped to a prison called Camp Sumter. Yep, that's at Charleston, said some, recalling the first month of the Rebellion. Hope we get some decent shelter from rain. Hope the Rebs didn't blow down all them walls when they first fired on the Nationals there. Wiser folks knew that Camp Sumter and Fort Sumter must be two entirely different places. One night, while encamped beside the track, Dolliver and his friend Kirke had some conversation with a genial Rebel officer in command of the guards. This captain wore his left sleeve folded and pinned at the forearm; he said that he had encountered a chunk of red-hot shot at Sharpsburg. He said that he needed buttons for a new jacket which his wife was remodeling from the uniform of a friend who'd died. Dolliver traded four gilt metal buttons for four whittled from bone, which the Rebel was then wearing; he thought that he could get the bone ones sewn on sooner or later. In appreciation the Confederate disappeared for the better part of an hour and then came back and whispered, Sonny, here's some rations for you. He offered a little wooden pail containing thick stew—one of the most delicious substances Dolliver and Kirke had ever tasted in this life. It included potatoes, sweet potatoes, onions and a delicate meat which they thought might be squirrel or possum—it had a gamey flavor. Loyally they awakened the other six, and they ate the stew, turn and turn about, a spoonful at a time, until there wasn't a drop of grease left in the bucket. The captain had given them information also: he said that the Camp Sumter for which they were bound was in Georgia, not South Carolina, and was brand new—no prisoners had ever been kept there before. This was wonderful, for there would be no lice. Georgia in February would be Heaven compared to Virginia. The officer never came back for his bucket, so they took it along with them.

. . . Eben Dolliver's head ached where the gun butt had jabbed it. The skin of his scalp was broken, a trickle of blood stiffened his hair. Wonder the blow didn't crack his dome wide open! Throb or no throb, he made light of his injury: that was the manner of the

Moon Hotel mess—to make light of unpleasant things, after a primary
howl of distress. Also it was the manner of the Dolliver family, a
jovial set of millers (for five generations). Certain distant cousins were
lawyers and politicians, prominent in the new State of Iowa from its
inception. Eben's branch of the family was comparatively humble,
but open-handed and proud. His father had been responsible for organizing the first Campbellite church in the county when Eben was
a little shaver. Jotham Dolliver was a long-armed long-legged man
with a red beard which turned silver when he was still in his forties.
His booming untrained voice lifted continually above the mill's whine
. . . Joth Dolliver loved to chant of celestial hurricanes, far golden
rivers, forested shores, mansions in the sky . . . his joy was in the
rich illusion of Paradise as pictured by David and the Prophets, dripping with flame and jasper in The Book of the Revelation, solidified
in song by Isaac Watts and later poets. He practiced his benevolent
preachments through every waking moment, and communed pleasantly with his Creator when asleep. Never shrewd or tight-fisted in
the grasping fashion ascribed to millers, Joth kept his numerous family
on short commons because of his native improvidence, his native generosity. When a poor man came to mill, Joth was willing to grind his
grain for nothing. The family loved him as they would have loved a
prankish elder brother or a rollicking sheep dog, instead of as a father.
In straitened wartime hours when Eben Dolliver thought tearfully of
Home and its beauties, he recalled how his father towered at the
front of the one-room church, admired by the preacher (the greater
share of whose keep came from Joth) and leading in hymns; and
how the shrunken yellow-haired little mother, with seamed face and
big-knuckled warped hands and faded gray-and-pink shawl, would
look up at him with quicksilver in her glance as if to say, My Joth,
my dear Joth, how splendid you are, truly.

Dolliver's Mill stood on the west bank of the Boone River. Thickly
forested hills, seeming like young mountains to the gaze of prairie
dwellers, arose on the east side; but smaller hills on the west bank
of the river already stood denuded of timber, and white men had
lived in that country only a few years when Joth Dolliver moved up
from Poweshiek County.

Again and again the dam was torn out by crunching barges of ice
at the end of winter. Black walnut posts had to be re-established at
great expense and with grueling labor. Once, when Eben was thirteen,
the entire end of the mill was knifed away by towering shifting masses
of ice: it dropped into the ravenous river, and was swept off, and left
machinery and piles of flour sacks exposed to view. The Dolliver
family lined on the bank, watching the tragedy, weeping loudly—
weeping, every one of them, from the eighteen-months-old baby up

to mighty Joth. It was strange, but other men didn't cry, simply and naturally in the way of children, as Joth cried.

When very young it had seemed to Eben that his father was a normal man; and other fathers and neighboring men were not at all normal because one never saw them cry. Once Jotham rented a breaking plow, to open a breadth of raw prairie on a ridge across the road from his house (no sense in letting that fine land go to waste! Many days there was no grinding to be done at the mill, no one came with grists; Joth would be a farmer as well as a miller, and prosper at it) and little Eben ran after the big plow, trying to help. The plowshare ripped through a bumblebee's nest, and the next moment Jotham Dolliver was on the ground, rolling and bellowing. No, no—stay away, little Ebe, he was gasping between sobs. Oh, oh, oh, how it hurts, oh God, oh Lord forgive me for taking Thy name in vain, ow, ow, it hurts. Didn't know bumblebee stings could hurt like— Ow, ow! The unstung oxen stood and regarded him mildly. Eben jigged and wrung his hands; then he scooted to the house, bawling for his mother. She came to comfort her wailing husband, to plaster his swellings with cool mud.

Was Joth honestly a baby? Not so's you'd notice it.

The Campbellites joined with parent and somewhat snobbish Methodists—and with their fellow immersionists the Baptists—in organizing a camp meeting that same year. They chose the season after corn was too high for plowing and before small grain needed to be cut. In this brief period there might be only haying to interfere with an intense, informal period of devotion. Since Dolliver's Mill was more or less a gathering point for neighbors, and since the river offered charm for the young—they could wade in mud, catch crawdaddies, hunt for mussel shells while their elders listened to preaching—a platform was built in the walnut grove across from the mill. The idea appealed, socially as well as religiously, and people rode or drove or even walked from miles around. The grove held from a hundred to three hundred devotees at any given moment during the four-day session. Naturally all the ministers in southern Hamilton County took turns at preaching, together with various laymen (Joth Dolliver was one, to the pride of his family) who got up and exhorted.

This rural festivity, with sagging baskets of good things and with pretty girls bound to turn up, excited the interest of certain hulking youths who had a dangerous reputation throughout the community. Folks called them the Monger gang or the Monger tribe. There were two Monger brothers and a Monger cousin, with several cronies trailing along. Most other young fellows from respectable homes gave them a wide berth; they were said to go armed, the tricks they played were cruel and ugly, often they staggered drunkenly in public. Well, they came along to camp meeting on the second day and stood haw-hawing on the outskirts. Slowly their deviltry crept into the session and before long was close to disrupting it. They lounged, grinning contemptuously under the wide-brimmed black hats they all affected, and when hymns were tuned up the Monger gang made meeowings and calf-blattings under cover of the music. Old Reverend Grosscup went tiptoeing toward them and was heard to say, If you boys can't act civilized in true Christian fashion, we ask that you withdraw. They pretended not to have heard his quavering voice, but kept wink-ing at one another; they planned fresh mischief. Eben Dolliver could watch his father's face getting redder and redder, and he shivered to think what might happen . . . perhaps his father would order the riffraff away, and one of them would pull out a pistol and. . . .

One of the Mongers had a bottle of turpentine; a yellow dog trotted near. People at the back of the congregation could see what actually happened, the rest could only hear the outcry. Those young men caught the yellow dog and smeared turpentine on its rear. The creature rushed howling in circles, alternately bounding into the air and drag-ging its burning bottom across the grass in a frenzied attempt to allay the hurt. Joth Dolliver arose and called in a rough voice, Excuse me, Parson, and then forced his way back through the crowd.

The Mongers saw him coming. They stood in a tight group, waiting. The nearest fellow brought up a sly knee as Joth came close, but Joth stepped back quickly and caught the young man's leg with his two hands. He had tossed grain sacks about for thirty years. He turned this youth upside down in the air and dropped him on his head; folks nearest thought that the fellow's neck must be broken. Next thing Joth snatched the two biggest—Arney Monger and Benton Hakes— He caught them by their shirt collars, one by the back of his collar, one by the front. He flung them together, head against head, with all his strength, and both dropped to the ground. Arney Monger was rendered unconscious . . . you could hear the crack of those two skulls coming together, clear across the grove.

Bent Hakes got up on his haunches and reached for his clasp-knife, but before he could get it out of his pocket Joth Dolliver kicked him in the jaw. Bent shrieked to high heaven. His jaw was broken, and he gasped and struggled on the trodden-down grass, spitting out blood and teeth.

Sorry I was compelled to ruin you, Bent, but if it takes ruination to teach you Christian decency I'll work the ruin. Used to be the meanest rough-and-tumble man in Dubuque before I saw the New Light. I'll take you together or singly.

The Mongers were in full flight by this time, hustling toward the underbrush—all except the three on the ground. People gathered around them, and Doctor Dawson went to his wagon for his satchel.

People feared that the Monger gang might try to shoot Joth Dolliver from ambush, after that, but so far as was known they never attempted revenge—perhaps for fear of the lynching which might follow. One youth went to California that same year and was said to have been killed by the Comanches on his way back to Iowa. Well did Eben Dolliver know the fate of two others: Benton Hakes and Elston Monger. They died at Shiloh along with numerous others of the Thirteenth Iowa Infantry.

Watching his father deal out justice as he dealt it, Eben yearned for the day when he also would be grown and imposing in stature, and generally looked up to. But he grew only to average height by the time he was twenty. They had no accurate method of measuring in the prison pen, but he stood barefoot and back-to-back against Olin Claver from Michigan, and Olin had his growth long since— he was twenty-seven, and said that he stood five-feet-nine-and-a-quarter. They were of identical height. Eben had grown but an inch since he enlisted over two years before. He was pleased that from birth he had exhibited the reddish coloration of Joth Dolliver—reddish skin, reddish hair with a curly shine to it. Also he had his father's clear eager gray gaze, and usually through his childhood and teens Ebe's gaze wore the expression of a hungry youngster who has just been told that he may eat with the grown-up folks—he need not wait for second table. Joyfully he appreciated the commonplace and felt pity for those who could not. His laughter rang easily until he was weakened by captivity; still he laughed more readily than most.

His father's glee was found in song, his mother's in flowers. However demanding the cares of the family, Elizabeth Dolliver always snatched an hour to go gathering the first pasque flowers which blew like lavender bolls of cotton on breezy summits. She would cry in rapture, and sit by the furry little things with unheeded bees coming near— She actually talked to flowers, and her children smiled to see and hear her do it. There were six living children in 1861; three others had died. All had Biblical names: the living were Eben, Neri, Ruth, Jacob, Naomi, Jesse. All could sing. People used to stop their teams in the road to listen to the Dollivers. The first banker in the county seat cried in scornful envy, Guess I'd better go out and get myself a pile of debts and work my fingers to the bone, and not have a dime to show for it at the end of every year. Then maybe I could sing like those Dollivers. . . . Those Singing Dollivers, everyone said. When Ruth and Naomi were just knee-high to a bunny and a mouse, respectively, they were in demand to warble at patriotic or political functions. Three Cheers for the Red, White and Blue (Blue-blue-blue)— That was one of their mainstays in the way of secular songs, along with Robin Adair and Flow Gently, Sweet Afton. The boys had a quartet—Jesse joined it when he was only four—and they did noble

things with The Minstrel Boy, and Hail To the Chief, and Open Thy
Lattice, Love. But their father liked best to hear Land Of the Leal,
and of course he always joined in and drowned them out.

Song was born in Eben's heart, song thrilled in his ears from his
first moment of awareness; possibly that was why he was drawn to
the birds. As his mother worshipped bloodroots which came up leaf-
wrapped and pearly through poplar glades each spring, so her eldest
saw a charm in the first robin to appear—a charm and a lure which
he could not describe. In May, going out at daybreak to begin his
chores, the caroling from nearby heights of trees would turn Eben into
a statue. His father said, Come along there, Pillar of Salt. Come along,
Lot's Wife. Those are tuneful robins, but they won't put any mush on
the table.

Old Reverend Grosscup had a book called Our Feathered Friends,
With Copious Illustrations, and Eben borrowed the book so frequently
and kept it so long that finally Reverend Grosscup declared with
some heat, Well, I see nothing to do but to present the book to you,
Eben. Then you won't always be pestering me for the lend of it. He
wrote Eben's name on the smudged fly-leaf with a flourish and gave
him a little smack with his frail hand after the boy was holding the
volume to his heart.

Ebe went into the fish business when he was nine or so. An old
Indian, a Pottawatomie called John-John, used to come up the river
on solitary excursions with his gun and traps, and he would beg
for tea or sugar at Mrs. Dolliver's cabin door. John-John watched
young Eben trying to catch fish without success; he grunted and made
signs, begging twine from Joth Dolliver. They had to keep plenty of
twine at the mill, to tie and repair sacks. Well, that John-John sat
down and wove a beautiful fish net. In only one day he put it together. Then he borrowed an axe, and shaped a wooden block, and
into that wooden block he inserted four limber poles of willow. This
block John-John mounted on a post something like a well-sweep, and
the net was suspended to the four light springy poles. Above the mill
flume the Indian placed this apparatus, and showed Eben how to
lower the sweep until bending boughs of willow had spread the net
across the bottom of the flume. There John-John insisted on leaving
it stretched, though Eben was highly excited when he saw a large
pickerel come nosing through the shadows. John-John knew how
fish loved to swim away from sunlight, away from heated shallows,
and lie twitching contentedly in cool shade of the flume. More fish
came, more; Eben was fit to be tied. At last John-John let him throw
his weight on the exalted sweep, and release the willows from their
bending, and bring the net aloft, closing as it came. Little fish flopped
out through the wide mesh but big fellows were trapped securely.
Eben would always remember with a bounce of his heart: there were

three pickerel and two enormous pike in that first net-load. John-John said, Uh, good, and made signs to the boy that the fish trap was his for keeps.

In time the net grew rotten, the willows corroded because of their constant drowning at the flume's floor. But Eben could make other nets, he could cut more willow limbs. No one of his subsequent traps was as efficient as the one John-John had made, but they caught many fish. In certain seasons the mill ground day and night. Often there'd be a whole line of wagons whose owners waited their turn with grists. When the farmers were ready to head for home, they'd find Eben standing by. Wish some nice fresh fish to take home, Mr. Clark? Shouldn't you like to give your folks a treat of fine fresh bass, Mr. Hurst, sir? I got five beauties—just pulled them up—some are still kicking. The prices had to be low, for no one on the prairie owned much cash in those years. But five cents here, ten cents there, twenty-three cents one day, twenty-nine another: it added up. Eben kept his money in a cracked ginger jar. When he thought he had enough, he approached Mr. Corey, the watchmaker in Webster City, on one of those rare occasions when he accompanied Joth Dolliver behind a borrowed nag across more than a dozen miles of grass. Sir, have you by any chance't got a telescope for sale? No, bubby, but I got a catalogue with some pictures. It turned out that Eben didn't have enough money as yet; but Mr. Corey said that he would order the telescope, and keep it for Eben until he was ready to pay. Ebe bought it that fall in time to watch the birds moving south. That was why he had yearned for a telescope: it could bring a bird into his lap, he could count the feathers in a jay's tail, he could watch a distracted dainty warbler feeding the slob of a cowbird fledgling which she believed to be her own because he had been hatched in her small nest.

Eben Dolliver's fingers were cased only in flesh. It took years for them to wear the golden finish off the telescope's cheap brass, but they did wear it through. By the time he was sixteen you could see where his fingers clamped most often. The lenses were well ground nevertheless, and through them he won an intimacy with wrens which he would never have had without this device. His ambition outran all common sense. He read that nowadays, in cities, photographers had a splendid new method in their work, and could secure accurate likenesses on their wet plates of any object which remained still. If the object moved, of course the image was blurred. But take a brooding hen lark or a bobwhite. Sometimes she'd never flicked a feather or rolled her eye for as long as Eben observed her. Might it not be possible to take a picture of a brooding bird? But where might he find a modern machine for such photography, and how might he ever get together enough money to purchase it, and who might teach him to employ it? It would be more accurate than any artist's conception in Our Feathered Friends, With Copious Illustrations.

Other people might have spoken severely about Eben's addiction, except that he was known to be a stalwart worker. Joth Dolliver liked to say that he had two right hands. This one, attached by the arm to his shoulder— And that one. Over there. He meant Eben. Men chuckled when he said it, and Eben turned from tanned pink to beet red. It seemed a piddling sport, to most neighbors, when they discussed how Ebe put up a little shelf among plum trees next to the new-sided house, in winter, and begged scraps of gristle from his mother to place thereon for nuthatches and chickadees to eat. Also he learned that sunflower seeds were relished by birds, so each fall he worked among dry heads of rusty sunflowers, harvesting against the snowy season.

Strangers came to the mill—new people, usually, who had just taken up land in the vicinity—and they heard that Eben was by way of being an ornithologist. That's interesting, boy. Have you got a lot of them stuffed? Eben stared, horrified at the idea. He thought that he might be able to shoot a human being if Fate required it of him, but was positive that he could kill no bird. Some boys from the village of Homer came past the mill with a pocket rifle; they were shooting at kingfishers along the river; they said that the feathers would make a beautiful dressing for ladies' bonnets. Eben dove off the loading platform and attempted to impound the instrument of death, and got a trouncing for his pains; there were three of the boys, two of them huskier than he. But in the process he awarded two bloody noses to the victorious party, and they did not stalk kingfishers within his domain again. Honestly he thought that the birds were his, even on land not belonging to his father, even in thick timber which was the property of Bells and Bryans. He watched a yellow-breasted chat and thought, No one could make gold like that. No human, no mint in the world.

He was seventeen when cannon roared on a South Carolina shoreline and a call went up for volunteers. Eben and his father attended a rally at Homer where the Democrats broke down the Republican flagpole and Republicans dislodged the Democratic pole. The two poles were spliced together and raised on high in a new location, and the Colors went crinkling to the top. White-haired Beriah Seton, who had served in the War of 1812, stood up on a wagon seat and fired a pepper-box revolver at the sky. Men joined hands—a few women joined hands too, and a great many small boys. They circled slowly around the spliced poles, singing, Hail, Columbia, Happy Land.

Joth Dolliver was silent as they walked the five miles toward home under stars that evening. For Joth to be silent was to say that he was sick in bed.

What ails you, Pap?

Ebe, I was just trying to cipher out some way to go.

I'm going.

No you ain't.

Yes I am. You forget I'm practically man-grown. Seventeen.

Ebe, you'd have to have my permission, and I won't give it. Your Ma would be broken-hearted if I let you traipse to the army. I'm bigger'n more able than you, if I am past the age; and I'm a better scrapper. I can still lay you on your back. Do you reckon you could conduct the mill by your lonesome?

No I don't. Furthermore, there's that hundred and sixty-five dollars to be paid to Mr. Bell for the machinery you bought off him, and how'd I ever manage to pay that, come July first?

I know, Ebe . . . it beats me. But somehow I'm going. You ain't.

We'll see about that.

No we won't.

They stopped on the old Mesquakie trail through springtime thickets, and looked at each other in darkness. They laughed, and shook their heads in much the same manner, and then went on. Presently Eben struck up, Father And I Went Down To Camp. Joth joined with him. Elizabeth Dolliver and the younger children heard those voices among bare trees and spreading through the glades where hepaticas grew (hepaticas couldn't be seen in the dark, but they were there, ready to reveal silk on their stems when daylight came), long before Jotham and Eben struck their feet against the bridge's timbers. They fell silent, pausing there and listening to the rush of water across the dam. They stopped at the mill to see that everything was right; then they went home, and each lay awake for a time, planning.

Eben was the first to go. In mid-summer his father's sister fell sick in Marshall County, and wrote that she was having a hard time; could Dear Brother spare some cash? Her hands were crippled and she couldn't sew, and actually there was little in the house to eat. She had written to her married daughter in Kansas, but perhaps the letter had gone astray, for no word came. Jotham Dolliver dared not leave his mill; he was dressing both corn and wheat burrs against the next season, and had other repairs to make. Accordingly Ebe was dispatched with twelve dollars in currency—all that could be scraped up—and an old watch and snuff-box in his pocket which should be sold in Marshall-town and the money given to Aunt Esther. Stages cost too much; he walked part of the way, and was picked up by two movers in turn, so it didn't take him long to reach Marshalltown. There he sold watch and snuff-box for even more than the minimum which his parents had agreed that he should accept, and with delight he walked to a nearby village and presented the money to his aunt, trusting that it would see her through her disability until she was able to resume dressmaking once more. He spent the night on Aunt Esther's sofa, and at dawn was up and away, spyglass in hand, reveling in the activity of orioles and grosbeaks. Back in Marshalltown, he enlisted promptly in the Fifth Iowa Infantry, which was then being raised, giving his age as eighteen. This was a thing which explicitly he had promised his father that he would not do.

. . . Never have I uttered an untruth to you before, dear father, nor gone back on my word. But now I take up my pen for confeshin. I am bound to be a soldier and already am one in name. We were mustered in, here at Burlington, yesterday. I regret deeply that I was false to the vow you extrackted from me but trust you will forgive and forget. You are capuble of supporting the family whilst I am not. Hence it is My Stint not yours. Our Nation is in dire peril and if a nat's brain and a nat's fist may be of service, why, Uncle Samuel, here is your nat. Give my dearest love to Ma and remember me fondly to the girls and to Neri, Jake and Jess. Warn Neri not to attempt *crowbaticks* on the water gate as is his wont. I have my telescope along, and shall see many strange wildfowl in the Sunny South, so I hear. May the Heavenly Father keep and fend for thee. Y'r Affec'n't Son.

It was less than two years later, during the hundred-day siege of Vicksburg, when Eben received a letter from his father telling of the elder Dolliver's being commissioned as a lieutenant in Company G, Seventh Iowa Cavalry. A neighbor named Ennis, a man with some milling experience, was to look after operations at Dolliver's Mill; he agreed to pay Elizabeth Dolliver fifty per cent of the net profit. Jotham went out to Nebraska Territory, and one day, ten miles from Fort Cottonwood, he was shot down by a party of Cheyennes who tore off his silver scalp and built a hot fire between his legs so that he might not be able to procreate in the Next World. Had they known that he took pleasure in song, they would also have cut out his tongue, since he was the enemy of the Indians and they did not wish him to have pleasure.

. . . Miseries such as these roved through Ebe Dolliver's brain as he lay wrapped in his tattered quilt, in an open Georgia forest along the Southwestern Railroad. He did not know the details of his father's death; he knew only that he had been killed by Indians. The letter reached him shortly before the long march from Memphis to Chattanooga. Also there came news that Mr. Ennis was doing well with the mill, which relieved Ebe of certain worries concerning his mother, the girls, and Jake and Jesse. Neri had already run away to war, and was believed to be somewhere in Arkansas.

Ebe thought of his father, he thought of Indians, he thought of old John-John, he wondered whether John-John had ever killed and scalped a white man. Maybe he had, in some remote period when Pottawatomies warred against encroaching settlers . . . head hurt.

Blame that guard! There he was huddled against that tree over yonder past the nearest log fire. Like to crack him over his fat head with his own musket. Bet he'd never forget it.

Eben thought of the stew they'd been given, two nights before, and wished he had some now.

Suddenly he was sitting up, pushing himself up, holding himself up by his dirty hands spread against the ground. He had been lifted by a cry. There it was again . . . question and answer in the damp February sky, the sky holding no stars, no light. Only it held a mystic summons, a silver horning which might have been blown by the breath of ghosts or fairies. *Hear it?* he wanted to call to the guards and to the snoring, moaning, grunting herd of prisoners around him like swine in a wallow. Geese, ducks, elusive runaways, I know not. But they are birds of some sort, and they are going north, free and keen and shrilling about it as they have shrilled through the millennia. Oh, to be vaulting in empty blackness, to be flying with silent force as no others but the birds have gone. To unfasten from the throat that challenging whoop which is not a song, thin and far, and yet haunts as no other melody pealed. To understand the question asked, the answer awarded. . . .

Eben listened until the last hollering had left the limit of his hearing. Then he fell back and slept in peace, dreaming little but dreaming mainly of the mill and of a heron which kissed the willows as it soared.

X

What would it have been like in the old days at this same season? Ira Claffey tried to think. Not only the face and texture of the world had been altered, but also fundamental values underlying had been revised. It was difficult for him to envision the overseer's report which might have been handed him, say, in the late 1850's, if he had been absent, say, in Atlanta or Milledgeville. The corn land would have been ready for planting, but possibly sufficient manure would not have been hauled to cover it; some hands would haul manure for another fortnight. They would have been ridging up the land for cotton—perhaps fifty acres or more might be ridged up already. They would soon commence fencing. They would have finished rolling logs, perhaps? Usually the Claffeys were ready to plant as soon as anyone else in Sumter County, usually sooner. If the season weren't behindhand. . . . Ducks would soon commence laying.

What of the harness? Would it survive the rigors of planting, or shouldn't it be wise to set Putty and Shem to going over all the old harness? What of the twisted-cotton rope for plow-lines, the mule-collars constructed of sewn corn-husks? Would it be necessary to buy two or three new plows—cast plows, the Number Fifty size? Perhaps one of those rare but violent February deluges would have occurred, washing out the low place in the main road, taking out the oldest bridge on the road to Americus, forming gullies in the cornfield, washing out part of the slope where the slave quarters were built (the old quarters, far down the south ridge toward the main Sweetwater, and all standing empty except for birds and varmints, now in this February of 1864).

. . . Wind south, cloudy. One and one-half hands sick: Putty, Lake. Ten hands hauling manure. Eight hands still ridging cotton. Three hands in kitchen garden. Two hands still rolling logs. Ten and one-half hands repairing road after storm. Three hands mauling rails. Japeth building, Ruth spinning, Naomi and Pet cooking for hands; Leander and Jonas with stock; Triton minding the hogs. The fare would have been plain but ample for all, and there would be treats on holidays, on Sundays, and when Badge and Suthy came from Oglethorpe. The week before Christmas Ira Claffey always went to Americus to buy Christmas for the black people; always he needed at least two people to help him, and they went with a four-mule team when the roads were bad, for the wagon swayed heavily on its return trip.

His people worked hard and ate well and were housed snugly, but he did not pamper them to the point of abuse. If Nestor or Dudley misbehaved they would be punished, and knew it; but if they misbehaved frequently they knew that they would be sold; and so they were sold.

Ira Claffey was shocked speechless at the thought of a general abolition of slavery. He imagined hordes of illiterates trooping the highways with no roofs to lie beneath at night, with no one to buy food for them, with no money and without sufficient knowledge to buy sustenance for themselves. Worse than that, he saw them exploited as tools of unscrupulous white men who might fetter them in an industrial slavery in cities, where sun and comfort of wild places would be denied them.

When he was young he had walked through an area in New York (it was somewhere near the place called Five Points, and he had been cautioned to carry a pistol if he ventured there alone even in daylight) where besotted people white and black sprawled actually in the swill of the roadway, and wild eyes rolled in kinky heads thrust, slathering, cursing inarticulately, from windows. What terrors lay inside those crazy dwellings he could only guess. Twice he felt that he was being followed, but when he turned, stood, and put his hand in his pistol pocket the followers found business elsewhere. He did not have to defend himself, but he could find no defense for the wretchedness. In a box of offal and rotten vegetables which he stepped away to avoid, he saw—scarcely could he believe it. Stench or no stench, he forced himself to halt and look. It was the body of a child, a black child, apparently the result of an extremely premature birth. Such hideous exposure might never occur on any plantation he'd ever visited or heard of. He fled the slums and found refuge at his Broadway hotel, but it was long before he could bathe away this most evil recollection.

In the worst of his current imaginings, Ira had visions of Ninny, Naomi, little Bun, Coffee and the rest, being herded into mines or sweatshops and compelled to live in those tenements before which he'd shuddered. He did not see them or their descendants made respectable, dwelling in homes comparable to those of the whites, schooled, taught to work in trades or even in professions, making a satisfactory economic way as individuals and as a mass. He did not see how that transformation could be achieved in a thousand years, let alone a hundred. And the thought of black men given uniforms and arms and trained to make targets of the whites against whom they were marched— Ira ordered himself to slay this thought, never to entertain it, never to consider that the reality was even now in existence.

He worked among his cabbages, he sought for kinder musings as he held his trowel. Consider Cousin Harry. How good it was to have him about, how good to hear a young man's enthusiasm and prayer for the future. Harrell Elkins had humor and high hopes left to him; they had not drained away through his wounds or been expunged by peril and bereavement.

. . . These were Early York cabbages. Ira was choice of the delicate seedlings, he would not permit Jem, Jonas or Coffee to remove them from the glass frames where they'd stood over the winter. This task he must perform himself. Each time he touched one of the pale immature plants with its sheen, its blush of frost and dust, he thought of the mature plant which it might come to be in time: an oval head slightly heart-shaped, a short stem, all very firm and with a flavor to remember. If the cutworms didn't devour it first.

. . . Salt should have been sown in the prospective cabbage patch last autumn, but salt was hard to come by, like so many other things; it would have taken perhaps ten bushels or even more. But there was another way of guarding against cutworms; Old Leander taught it to Ira some twenty years before. Ira had had two of the hands at work on a dry day, throwing the ground into ridges and trenches: he'd cut some sticks to the exact length for them to measure with. The ridges were sixteen inches apart, the trenches seven inches deep. In the bottom of these furrows tender flaky young cabbages should be transplanted now—it was a moist day, a perfect day for the job. He would set the plants a foot apart. As soon as they were well rooted he would have the soil stirred gently about them; but the trenches should never be filled until all danger of worms was past.

. . . A benefit to have Cousin Harry at the plantation; his presence aided in exercise of Ira's own intelligence and Lucy's . . . Veronica was becoming a pale spectre who stalked, only a spectre. The horticulture which claimed Ira throughout his days could not occupy his thoughts at mealtime, his attention during evenings.

Except for the old wound, life had been good to Ira's body; he had treated his body sanely, had not drunk or eaten to excess, had been scrupulous about not over-indulging at the greasy banquets which many others of his persuasion fancied. He cherished still the sensual appetite of a much younger person, but there was left in the small circle of existence no object to serve as partner in his sporadic but tempting lusts. There had been two experiences wherein he sought to seduce Veronica into rapture; the first time, she repelled him by saying, I cannot, I cannot. Never in her life had she demonstrated refusal, even after her change occurred. (Ira thought that her change came about earlier than in most cases, and with fewer of the unpleasant symptoms, and was more abrupt.) But there must have been some dread protraction; not all the substance of her cold mania could be charged sensibly to the recurrent losses.

Still, a nail of anguish had been driven through her coil of white-blonde hair and into her skull, each time a child died. The four small children died; each time, that nail hammered in. Then the pause, then in rapid succession the great spikes marked Crampton's Gap, Gettysburg, Chickamauga. In delusion her husband turned his sad eye upon her and saw the seven nails bristled out like quills. No wonder that her expression was glazed, her tongue lying silent! Oh, my Veronica, such joy we manufactured between us, divine joy, brutal joy, every variety. It was a charm, and now it is gone, now it is gone.

The second time, he tried to persuade her with tender courting, but she lay like marble under his touch.

I cannot.

Don't say that again.

Because it is grief.

For God's sake, woman! It's not a grief, and never was.

Isn't that the way we begat our children?

Yes, but—

Our children are a grief. All but Lucy. Doubtless something will befall her too. You'll see.

Don't say it, Veronica. For God's sake don't speak the thought! We must think of Lucy as having a good life, a long life.

If I let— If I let you do It now, it would be as if— As if we were doing It again to get Suthy. To get poor little Arwood. To get Badge. Poor little Peggy. Moses. Lucy. Poor little—

Cease naming those names! You heard me! His coarse whisper was intense and frightening as a roar. Veronica sobbed, but she went on and spoke the other poor little names: Sally, Courtenay.

I'll leave you now. You want peace, and you want to be left alone. By God I'll leave you alone. You want to wallow amid the graves; go lie in them. You want to remain in love with the dead, you forget the living, you forget your own living.

I loved my children, Ira. Now all are dead except Lucy. Do you not pity me? Does the Creator not pity me? Perhaps—neither of you! The boys are gone, claimed by the earth. The boys—

Ira flew to his own room, he would not attempt this thing again. Let the juice dry in his body, let the green go from it as it went from cactus growing in unkempt untillable portions of the landscape. When cactus slabs died they turned disgustingly red, like rotten fruit. In extinction they were dry, papery, thin, discarded, bleached snakeskin. So let him, Ira Claffey, bleach.

But body and spirit refused to accept this dictum without a struggle, so at times he rolled sleeplessly, or put on his clothes at some unseemly hour and went pacing out of doors. The hoary Deuce rose from his deep drugged sleep of infirmity and, blinder each week than the week before, came nosing to Ira in the dark, cursed by imaginary sand-spurs. Ira knew that he should shoot Deuce, or perhaps put him to sleep with chloroform; still, there was no chloroform to be had, and as for the rifle—

Death, withdraw, cease reminding me that you are.

On one of these disconsolate strolls, at perhaps three o'clock of a cold morning, Ira went wrapped in the cape which had belonged to his father; his father had died in 1842, but the cape was still warm and wearable. Like some sad romantic being stepped from the tumult of Shakespeare he went cape-wrapped along the lane and came at length to the railroad, and the spot where ruts led to the house of the Widow Tebbs.

Poor Mag . . . even thought of her could come fairly to Ira in his extremity.

Fair, fair, she was more than fair; why, consider her: she was a glutton for It. What would she be like under the husks of her clothing, once those limp husks were removed? Why, she would be a pet, an adoring partner in the gayest crime of all: adultery.

She would be his fleshy little plaything—the welter of ruddy hair, the weak mouth wide with pleasure, the soft arms around him, thighs squeezing his own thighs.

Ira dropped his cape to the ground; too hot, too hot. Ah, could he ever permit himself to go up that doleful road, even sneaking in darkness? He picked up the cape once more, shook it, folded it across his arm, the while he was torn between seeking forgiveness and prayer and considering the spasm of excited debauchery which Mag might afford. Touch of his father's cape suggested the press where it had hung long among scent of camphor contained heavily by other garments there. There was his own military jacket with its epaulets turned dull by time, there were gowns of another day in which little Lucy had loved to swathe herself and then mince about with a fan. There was— He started, to think of it. A red silk wrapper which had belonged to an aunt. Veronica never chose to wear it, she did not approve of herself in red. What might not the gift of this wrapper to the Widow Tebbs provide for him? A devilish boy in Americus had made a rhyme about, Old Mag Lumpkin, I think she's nice, I gave her a ribband, she did It twice; that dull rhyme was recited in Ira's hearing years before, and he rejected it as unworthy of being blamed even on a child. He had not thought of it consciously since, but here it was, he thought of it.

If secretly he took the silk wrapper from the press no one would be the wiser. He could hide it somewhere—as he hid the cups from Veronica's grim collecting. And, when whips of ardor drove him at last to the Widow Tebbs' door, he'd have a present for her . . . am I weaker than old Deuce? Why dwell on this, why countenance the savage lurid yielding? I'm not twenty. I'm fifty. I'm old. I should be old. . . . I must be demented. What would Lucy think of me if she learned of the depravity of my plan? She would grow pale with the knowledge. What would Harrell Elkins think? He respects me sincerely; would I still command respect? Cato Dillard would mourn for me. My sons— If they saw, if they could see, if they do see and know—

At this moment of private torment, wavering still in the dull darkness of that road, Ira saw prickles of light ahead and across the tracks. Somebody opened a door, somebody came out. Later, as the muffled approach of feet grew louder, he realized that at least two somebodies were coming. He withdrew past the edge of the road and seated himself; he could not be observed against a mat of vines overhanging the fence and small trees there. Two shapes, men's shapes, formed in the road. Ira smelled tobacco.

She give you good treatment? Sounded like it.

I hope to shout. What did you pay?

She wanted a dollar, wanted a greenback sure enough. I says, Honey, I got nary a greenback, so she up and settled for five dollars Confed.

Identical what I give her. She sure did take the blaze out of my breeches.

Oh, she ripped and she tore—

They went on, singing not too loudly. Military personnel from the stockade camp. So this is the depth to which your passion has sunk you. You'd share with them, stand in line as men stood in line outside those squalid huts at Matamoras, you'd mingle yourself with hogs.

Are they more swinish than I? Where does the man end and the brute begin? Whom do I hear saying, Brute? Is it my own voice?

He returned to his house, petted Deuce, allowed the wheezing setter to climb the stair. This was a rare award and brought forth a wild waving of the rusty tail. Ira lifted Deuce to the high bed, Badger's old bed. At the foot of the bed Deuce curled gratefully, glorying in close contact with his master. With care Ira kept his feet to the left side, that he might not disturb the dog on top of the covers. Deuce went to rest in the early morning hours. When Ira awakened belatedly after seven o'clock, roused by sounds from below, the old dog was still curled as he had been hours before. Perhaps the heartworms had reached his gentle heart at last; he was fourteen. Ira had bought the pup especially for Suthy when the boy was ten, but forever Deuce regarded Ira as his one-and-only. Ira Claffey dressed quietly, in respect to the friend who lay upon his bed. Strangely he found a sweetness and warmth in this death, in the manner of its coming. Had he cried, Death, withdraw? It did not seem possible now, when one considered the gift and its healing permanent perfection. He carried the friend down to the library and placed him on the couch, covered with the old cloak; then he went to tell the others. Harrell Elkins said,

Poor creature. He must have perished of pure happiness at being allowed to sleep with you. Lucy went to the library and cried softly, lifting the cloak to stroke Deuce's white hair, thinking of her brothers as she did it. Poppy, maybe he can hunt with them now. In the Hereafter. He'll be so happy to have someone shoot over him again, to be able to go for birds. I declare, I love to think of it.

Of course you do, you dear sweet girl, girl with the tender heart, blithe spirit.

Veronica said, So he's gone too. I ask you to save his collar for me. I wish to put it with the other things.

Jem dug a grave in the pet cemetery not far from the family cemetery where a number of dogs, a parrot, a pony, and three especially favored cats were already ensconced. Ira and Lucy bore Deuce to his place, after they had breakfasted, and after Elkins was gone to the stockade; they were attended also by the three black children. Bun whispered to the others, Seed Old Mastah cry. Big tear on he face.

Harrell Elkins could not stand smiling tenderly through specs at the funeral scene. He thought that he should be on duty in the stockade region. He wriggled guiltily inside himself at realization that he was extending that duty beyond its demand. The task to which he had been ordered was vague but loaded with responsibility to the future.

Elkins was selected because he had two years of experience in the field as well as a medical degree. His orders read that he should examine carefully the new prison site, and set forth recommendations as to hospital facilities for an expected ratio of sick among a maximum of ten thousand prisoners. This entailed a study of climatic conditions, water, transportation, shelter. The diet of the prisoners was an unknown quantity; Harry assumed that they would receive the ordinary field ration of the Confederate soldier.

He applied himself seriously to the work, but by his third night in the Anderson community he recognized that there was little excuse for staying longer. At Milledgeville he had secured what crop and weather reports were available; from other sources he had scraped together figures on British campaigns in the Crimea and on illness incident to given numbers of troops in the Italian wars. He possessed also a lengthy report on hospitalization and the diet of prisoners at Dartmoor prison in England.

Superimposing this technical information on the structure of a firsthand study of a not-yet-completed-and-unoccupied stockade, he hoped to present a coherent report with attendant recommendations. *Surgeon H. Elkins will proceed to Camp Sumter, at the village of Anderson, in Sumter County—* No time limit was mentioned in his orders; paper work at most headquarters was performed sketchily these days. Harrell knew that he was naughty in drawing out his stay; this was the eighth morning he had risen at the Claffeys'.

XI

Veronica locked herself in her own room, to examine minutely a collection of beetles which Badger had gotten together when he was twelve or thereabouts. The beetles had been discovered atop a huge wardrobe in the boy's old room; wenches never dusted that surface—it was beyond their reach—and apparently the collection had been forgotten by Badger when he went away to college and later to the army. Beetles of various sizes and shapes were impaled on pins and the pins were thrust into a thin planed board. There were no differences in their coloration now: time and heat and tinier insects had had their way with the creatures. They were shells of shapes, more brittle than straw. Dead as he is dead, said Veronica to herself, playing over that dirge. Creatures smaller than they have long since made dust of their insides. So must similar creatures have made ruin of Badger's body e'er now.

At times she journeyed through her past—a limited past, on the whole, circumscribed by her own limitations as an individual. For years her body and her affection had been able to accompany Ira's, but never her mind. Intrinsically she was a selfish creature, not sufficiently elastic to examine herself; but taught the habit of kindliness toward others in her rearing and by example. In wartime the suffering of the South as a whole she deplored; never had it wounded her truly. She was not aware that in loving her offspring with such abandon she was loving herself. Her children, living, were important to her mainly because they were hers. Her children, dead, were a woe greater than the accumulated woes of all tribes, nations, peoples, places, centuries.

She thought, But I cannot leave them on this board. The pins will come loose. But if I should remove them—each beetle, singly, pin and all—I should be destroying the collection *per se,* as Badge put it together. So must it be wrapped for storage with everything else, but how, how, how? Cloth will not protect the delicate dry bugs. Jem is fair to middling as a carpenter; might I not have him build a little box? I shall try to make him understand. . . .

She saw seven children, assorted as to sex and age, set on pins in a row and labeled much as Badger had labeled these creatures—not Order, Family, Sub-family, Genus— But labeled with the names and pet names her children had worn. There was an empty pin, waiting for Lucy. I have a collection also, she told herself.

But the assemblage must be put away, it must be kept, retained in private, guarded. It will be— What is the term? I recall Doctor Kennebrew lecturing to us when I was at Miss Benham's. A study collection. Not displayed to the common view.

Secret, smelling of camphor, the more fragile things smelling of lavender amid camphor.

What is a scarab? A kind of beetle, to be sure. There is some association with mummies—

Instantly there rose before her the picture of seven mummies large and small, spaced in their colored coffins. There was a vacant mummy-case awaiting Lucy.

Doctor Kennebrew did not lecture about mummies. His bent was for zoology and botany. Someone else— It could have been Miss Benham herself who gave the lectures.

The pages of the *Southern Recorder* rustled at an 1830 breakfast table. It was always quiet at the Arwoods'. The servants were made to wear felt slippers as they moved about. In some slovenly households servants walked with their feet bare, but never at the Arwoods'. Bare feet made a slap-slap on the painted boards, slippers made a gliding sound.

Mr. Arwood. So Veronica's mother addressed her husband.

My dear.

Possibly have you discovered some notices concerning schools? As to the subject of our discussion on Sunday evening—

Ah, yes. One moment, my dear. Here it is. The issue of January second. Miss Benham, late Principal in several distinguished Female Institutions at the North, will reopen her Select School for Young Ladies in Milledgeville. . . .

Veronica was close to fourteen years in age. It was high time.

She remembered the winter school dress, the very next winter when she was close to fifteen. Miss Benham required her students to appear in what she termed Livery. The gown was of brown Circassian material, with a belt and tippet of the same. With these brown dresses the girls wore aprons of either black silk or of Holland cloth (Veronica's was of silk) and black leather shoes. They walked out as a troop of young Quakeresses.

Orthography. She remembered: the very name terrified her. So did Civic Knowledge and Statecraft. Some parents grumbled, that Miss Benham should instruct young ladies in such subjects. One would think, said old Judge Beatenbough at a dinner, that young ladies might be bound for the Senate.

Perhaps, said a lady timidly, Miss Benham is ahead of her time.

Ahead, Mrs. Rutland? Behind, by gracious! Portia's been gone some
centuries, has she not? Or, more likely, she never existed!

. . . Miss Veronica.

Yes, Miss Benham. And a curtsy.

Please to recite the statistics on Milledgeville.

Milledgeville, Baldwin County, is the capital of the State of Georgia.
According to the most recent census there are in Milledgeville a total
of one thousand five hundred and ninety-nine souls.

That is correct. How many white and black, Miss Veronica?

There are whites to the number of eight hundred and thirty-one,
blacks to the number of seven hundred and sixty-eight. There are attorneys to the number of twenty, there are—uh—eight physicians—

Six.

Six physicians, twenty-one merchants, nine innkeepers, two joiners,
six bootmakers, uh—six tailors—

Eight.

Eight tailors, four silversmiths—

(Veronica had no intention of going to the Senate, nor the desire
to go. She thought of herself as marrying eventually a man quite unlike her father; yet she knew that it was wrong in her to wish to marry
a man quite unlike her father. *Honor Thy Father.*)

Sixteen shopkeepers, five blacksmiths—

That will do, my dear. Well done, on the whole.

Eight children, seven dead. Not well done, my dear, on the whole.
But in the individual parts—

Like her daughter, Veronica had recurrent dreams, similar in general and sometimes identical in detail. They were not erotic dreams.
Thought that she had ever indulged in the act of copulation was increasingly repugnant to her, and thought of the variations of this art
which she and Ira had practiced (and which they did for entertain-
ment, for sinful pleasure, not in the doleful dedicated solemnity of
Begetting) was worse than repugnant. It outraged not only a code of
personal conduct but all religion, all philosophy, all virtue.

Her dream recurred not only when she slumbered, but with increas-
ing persistency when she was erect and seeming to be awake: saying,
Ninny, you neglected the vessel in the room where Mr. Dillard slept
on Tuesday night. It is smelling. Attend to that at once, do you hear?
Saying, Naomi, we shall have beaten biscuits to our luncheon. Saying,
So Deuce is dead. So he's gone too. I ask you to save his collar—

Her dream swept her into a flat bare neighborhood and along a
straight road lined with high stiff cedars or yews, very like the cy-
presses she'd seen in Europe when the Arwoods went abroad, a year
or two before Veronica met Ira Claffey. She walked and walked,
holding her shawl about her against an increasing chill, and soon she

met a stranger who said not a word, but pointed to the left with his stick. Obediently she turned to the left and passed through a gateway; sometimes she turned to look back at the stranger, sometimes not, but whenever she did look back he would be gone. Down a slight slope, turning to the right again . . . grass over which she wandered was cropped close, as if sheep had been keeping it down—or deer, in an English park . . . presently she reached a place made of white stone. It was not marble, it had not the sheen of marble; could it have been granite, was there white granite?

Come in.

But the iron door of the structure stood open already, she did not need to turn the knob.

Come in. It was a throaty voice, it might have been a man speaking, or more likely a contralto with a very deep voice, far in lower registers.

She glanced at the western sky. It was orange, the cedar-yew-cypresses inked black against the color.

Veronica went inside, after passing down three or four steps to reach the door. This building was half above ground, half buried. It seemed to continue indefinitely, reaching back into the hill which now appeared swelling above—

She went inside, and there the sarcophagi were spaced; but there were more than seven, many more than seven, they stretched on and on, on both sides of the room. And the voice echoed, echoed, echoed—the voice which had said, Come in—distantly through space of the room until it lost itself in a single *sostenuto* organ tone—

She went inside. Somebody, a stranger dressed in white (never a child of hers), sat up suddenly in one of the open coffins.

She came from her dream.

XII

On the evening of Wednesday, February twenty-fourth, they sat in
the library, playing a game. The three: Lucy, Ira, Cousin Harry.

They were continuing a gentle rite established a few days after
Harrell Elkins arrived. In conversation Ira quoted from The Bard; he
said: *For sweetest things turn sourest by their deeds; lilies that fester
smell far worse than weeds.* Instantly his daughter responded with,
We shall grow old apace, and die before we know our liberty.

She said, Shakespeare for you, Poppy.

Herrick for you.

They giggled, and Elkins was puzzled. I'm sorry, sir. . . . Lucy explained the pastime of rhymes and quotations which had been their
custom before the war, in family recreation.

I'm afraid I don't understand. That grating voice was become
strangely a joy to her hearing. Mr. Claffey said *weeds.* Shouldn't you
have begun with the letter S?

Oh, no, no. It's simple as simple can be. The next player begins with
the *first letter* of the *last word.* And you should be able to identify the
previous quotation, or it'll be a Black Mark.

I fear I would have many Black Marks.

Oh, come, sir. Come, Poppy. It'll be just like old times. Do let's try—

At first it was difficult, with the boys gathered close. Furthermore it
turned out that Cousin Harry was either martial or morbid in his selec-
tions, and very often both. He apologized. He said that when he was a
boy he had visions of himself as a soldier, but had never believed that
he would be one in fact. Strutting through the hours, harassed by self-
abnegation but determined to play alternately the part of Hector or
Patroclus, he had read brave chants before a glass, he had put on a
casque made of newspaper, had dragged his grandfather's sword.

. . . Very well. What was your last, Miss Lucy? Shyly he clung to
this formality.

She addressed him in comparative intimacy for the first time, and
her father grinned within to hear her. —*Before we know our liberty,*
Cousin Harry.

Liberty, liberty. Ah. . . . *Lightly they'll talk of the spirit that's gone,
and o'er his cold ashes upbraid him.*

There was silence. I give up, said Lucy. So do I, said Ira.

It's a quotation from Charles Wolfe. The Burial of Sir John Moore. It might be that I wasn't playing correctly?

No, no, Cousin Harry. You were quite correct. Poppy, it's your turn next, so you must accept the Black Mark.

Very well. The boys were still lounging close, but their shades were good-tempered and warming. *He is gone on the mountain, he is lost to the forest, like a summer-dried fountain when our need was the sorest.*

Oh, Poppy!

It's a Black Mark for you, Miss Lucy, cried Harrell Elkins gleefully. That's Sir Walter.

Raleigh or Scott?

Scott, you benighted wretch, said Ira. Thus they played willingly. Ira did not again stray into the cemeteries mourned over by Cousin Harry, but gave himself up almost completely to Shakespeare and the Psalms. Lucy roved among her favorites: Herrick, Wordsworth, Keats. Elkins would have been sonorous, but his tone was incapable of the designation, with *Ah! no;—the voices of the dead sound like a distant torrent's fall*, with, *My love is dead, gone to his death-bed, all under the willow tree*, with, *When the goodman mends his armor, and trims his helmet's plume.* Lucy looked at his earnest face, the round chunks of glass holding back the candlelight, the round ears standing out, and thought, He recites of heroes and is loath to admit that he is one. So were the boys, so was—Rob. But they are no longer in the flesh; and here we sit, playing at being the children they were.

Hours passed in concert were not all decked with such simplicity. They held conversation, often quite bitter, about the conduct of the war. Knowing that he could find trust in his faith and sympathy for his opinions, Elkins was outspokenly bitter against President Davis. Ira welcomed this expression of opinion as a man does when his own views are reflected, and presented perhaps with more authority than that with which he can present them.

If Fate had given us Stephens—

With that I'm not wholly in accord, Coz. I'm a respecter of Mr. Stephens, not a worshipper.

Nor am I, sir. But our President is scorned by many in the army. When General Toombs—

Oh, Poppy knows Mr. Toombs very well indeed, cried Lucy in interruption. And Mr. Stephens also—he's known him practically since boyhood.

Ira said in deprecation, Not since boyhood. It happened that in his youth he acted as tutor in a family with whom we were acquainted.

And Poppy pulled that brute of a Judge Cone off of poor sickly

Mr. Stephens when he sought to cut Mr. Stephens' heart out, at the Atlanta Hotel. Didn't you, Poppy?

Did you indeed, sir? Suth never told me.

Oh, said Ira, I happened to be standing near when the attack occurred. Several of us jumped to the rescue.

They were young, they were insistent, Ira had to relate each detail again. Lucy had heard the story more than once, she had heard it a dozen times; but always it gave her excitement and the kind of delicious horror contained in threatening fairy tales (since everything came out well in the end).

Harrell Elkins said meditatively, Hearing such an experience recounted by an eyewitness— It offers us obscure folk a kinship with the great.

No one might ever presume to term as obscure a gentleman who has commanded a company of the Sixteenth Georgia, Cousin Harry.

But, Lucy, I— Miss Lucy, it—

Thus he floundered, rustic and bashful, and Ira Claffey let him flounder, he spoke no word of rescue. He thought, Let him learn. He's a man. Let him admit it. In time I trust she'll teach him. Indeed he was a man, and Ira could not believe that in any face-to-face encounter Elkins would come off second best. He recalled how, on the third or fourth evening of his stay, Cousin Harry came from deep thought to ask, Sir, have you chanced to meet up with a Captain Winder? It's under his supervision that the stockade has been built.

Ira thought of the surveying party in long ago October. Captain Sid Winder. I'm afraid I don't care for him. If recollection serves, I met his father also, during the Mexican War. He was an extremely courageous man, unfortunately as ill-mannered as they come.

I met him today, said Harry. Captain Winder.

Ah?

Slowly the story came out. Elkins was interrupted by Lucy's coming into the room, and postponed the telling until her departure, since it was necessary for him to use profanity in quoting accurately.

. . . He said, Captain, will no barracks be constructed before the arrival of the first prisoners?

. . . Winder said, That's none of your damn business, Surgeon.

. . . Will you permit me to quote you verbatim in my report?

. . . We didn't build any barracks, I have no intention of building any barracks.

. . . Will any shelter of any sort whatsoever be erected?

. . . Not by me.

. . . Then why, for God's sake, did you cut down all the trees? At least trees within the area might have afforded a certain degree of shelter to the inmates, protecting them from the sun.

. . . Why protect them from the sun?

. . . Because direct exposure to the sun's rays, in this climate, and especially during the summer months, may cause a high degree of mortality.

. . . I hope it does, Surgeon, I hope it does. What the hell's the use of coddling a pen full of Yankees? I've got a pen here that ought to kill more God damn Yankees than you ever saw killed at the front.

Harrell Elkins arose from his chair and moved restlessly across the room. He stood looking out of the window, though it was dark, though panes shone back at him, though nothing could be seen.

What was your reply?

Oh, I asked him how many Yankees he had seen killed at the front.

And, Coz?

He said that he had a good notion to call me out. That he would call me out, if I weren't bespectacled.

And then?

Oh, I said that I wished that he would call me out, since as the challenged party the choice of weapons would rest with me. Informed him that I would select cavalry sabres at two paces.

What said he to that?

Oh, he kind of barked. He rode off.

For a moment Elkins and Claffey gazed blankly at each other; then their shouts arose. It was long since such lawless laughter had sounded within that room. Should it come to such a pretty pass, said Ira between gasps, I would be most proud to officiate in your behalf. In the kitchen servants heard the laughter and came creeping through the hall to listen closer, to wonder at the laughter, to grin and giggle in distant fellowship without knowing why. In Moses Claffey's old room Veronica heard the laughter. She arose, the candlelight making a nervous vulture of her shape upon the wall, and she crushed a pair of baby boots in her cold hands and said, not aloud, How *dare* they? In her own room Lucy heard the laughter and she sat with uplifted hair brush, smiling at herself in the mirror. She remembered how, when she was younger and before war overwhelmed them, it had seemed natural as life to have Ninny brushing her hair each night. But now Ninny, Extra, Pet and Naomi must do all the work of the house, which meant all cooking, baking, washing, sewing, mending, dyeing, weaving, spinning, soap-making, candle-making . . . the list stretched on. In these activities Lucy was mistress, driver and participant, much of the time. At night she slept as soundly as any of the black people, with as good reason to sleep. She brushed her own hair, one hundred strokes each night, even when she was really too tired to do it.

In a wine glass of water on her dressing table two violets posed for her. The violets were of different shape and color; one was much paler

than the other, and curled its petals, and was bluer. The other violet,
more purple, was of the crowfoot species.

Where on earth did you find them, Cousin Harry?

Twas inside the stockade, actually.

Seems like it's so early for them. Yet—no—Extra and I used often to
find them there, sometimes even in January. I do thank you.

I just happened to glance down—saw one first, then later the other
one. I recalled that you said violets were your favorite flower.

Surely they are.

I presume these are the last violets which will grow in Andersonville. When prisoners are put inside, the place will be trampled flat.

But it's Anderson, Cousin Harry, not Andersonville. The station was
named for Mr. John Anderson, of Savannah.

So I've heard. And the official designation of the new post is Camp
Sumter. But you know how troops are, Miss Lucy: forever applying
a special name to something or other. They call the depot village
Anderson, but they term the stockade Andersonville, to distinguish
it. . . . His rough voice sawed on, and Lucy turned the fragile violet
stems between her thumb and finger, and considered how she and
Rob Lamar had gone violet-picking three years ago. She could pick
twice as fast as could Rob—he was always hearing birds about, always
calling to his dog. But between the two of them they'd gathered so
many violets that her one hand could not enclose the stems.

No longer did they speak of Rob Lamar, she and Cousin Harry.
Elkins had known him barely, at college; he remembered going to a
pic-nic party where Rob also was a guest. Just that one pic-nic, said
Harry. I wasn't exactly what you might call a social butterfly. And
medical books and lectures do require a power of concentration.

But apparently there had been time for him to apply that power of
concentration to literature as well as to medicine. Cousin Harry could
grasp and identify more quotations than either Lucy or Ira when they
played their game. Thus far he was in the lead, with only nineteen
Black Marks against his name on the torn sheet of gilt-lined notepaper
they used as their scoring tab. Ira had twenty-six Black Marks, Lucy
thirty-eight.

By the evening of Wednesday, February twenty-fourth, Harrell
Elkins had left high-piled clods and blood-drenched claymores behind him. *She cannot fade, though thou hast not thy bliss, for ever
wilt thou love, and she be fair!* This he spoke with enthusiasm. Ira
Claffey found impish satisfaction in witnessing this slow fondness,
grown obviously out of proximity and sentimental tragedy. Cousin
Harry had announced that he must leave for Macon on the next day;
his work was finished, his reports and recommendations needed ampli-
fication and resort to other advices at headquarters. Lucy received

the news coolly; Ira observed her. She ate little at supper. When Pet took away her plate she mumbled in alarm, Miss Lucy, is you poorly?

I fear thy kisses, gentle maiden;
Thou needest not fear mine;
My spirit is too deeply laden
Ever to burden thine.

On this evening of Wednesday, February twenty-fourth (it was after nine o'clock), Elkins sprang up in the middle of Ira's deliberately wicked quotation of Shelley, crying, Beg pardon—looks like a fire! They joined him at the window: the entire valley to the north was colored brilliantly. The Biles' house was much farther beyond, the Yeoman house farther to the west, the McWhorters' farther to the east. Could the damp forest itself be burning, could the few sprawling houses of Anderson be alight?

In glow the three left the house and hurried west along the lane. Ira led sharply to the right on a footpath worked out by slaves going to and from the village. Years before, he had had his people build a crude bridge with a handrail across the little branch of Sweetwater and squashy ground surrounding it at this point. Looking ahead through the trees as they hastened, they could see that the newly carved-out road was become a sluice of ruddy light. It looked as if bonfires had been kindled for a gay homecoming (except that no one was coming home) or some such festivity (except that there was little to be gay about). Stumps, roots, branches, tops and needles: the debris of slain pines was heaped regularly to illuminate the road. These brush piles howled and crackled on high.

The snapping blazes revealed a train halted beside the Anderson depot; the train had been loaded with goblins, and several hundred goblins had trooped already from their box cars. Pine knots burned at intervals along the front and wispish lantern lights went scouting between ragged ranks, coming together again by twos and threes as if lightning bugs assembled for conference.

Next car, called a distant voice of authority. Count them as they come out, align them in ranks of fifty, two ranks deep, form them by Hundreds. Hold on! March those first eight men over here to complete this Hundred.

Many guards convened along the borders of the muddy road, and they were being ordered into position like posts of a loose fence stretching from fire to fire: one fire, three guards between like a short post and tall posts, next fire larger and farther away, five guards in between, next fire and three guards, more fires, more guards, the color of flames reflected as on splinters of broken looking glass by pine gum dry and icy on the stumps. Some of the guards had bayonets fixed to their weapons, others had not; there was a tingling gleam to the bayonets. Some of the guards wore blue and the blazes turned them to purple.

You men in this formation are First Squad, First Hundred. Repeat after me: First Squad, First Hundred. The ragged mumble following. You men in this formation are Second Squad, First Hundred. Repeat after me: Second Squad, First Hundred. Mumble, mumble in the manner of an extended groan. A thin mad voice soared, Hey, Johnny, how are the rations here?

Silence in the ranks! You men in this formation are Third Squad, First Hundred.

Something popped and burst in one of the fires, perhaps it was a bottle. Two guards approached the flames cautiously, they found nothing, they moved to their posts. You men in this formation are Second Squad, Second Hundred. Past trees and stumps the twin rows of blaze were spaced, curving slightly south, curving sharply north again all the way to the stockade.

Ira turned quickly at sound of a familiar voice. In a cluster his black people were grouped—all of them seemed gathered, even Old Leander and the children. Yes, all: Pet held the sleeping Sukey wrapped in her arms. A reek of orange touched their polished dark faces.

Mastah, please, Mastah. We come. . . .

Feared something was afire, said Jonas.

Mastah, is them Yankees over by them cars?

Ira cleared his throat. Yes, Coffee, I believe they are.

Look just like folks.

Mighty poor white trash, said the skinny voice of one of the wenches. There was a shiver of laughter.

A hand slid into the grip of Ira's hand, it was Lucy's hand, it trembled. Beyond her Harrell Elkins said, It's well that I was delayed until now. I can look them over tomorrow before I leave, and gain some notion of their general physical condition. It might affect my recommendations.

Yes, Ira heard himself saying, it might. But these prisoners are not newly captured?

I was informed that they were to come from Richmond.

Then there will be a difference in the physical condition of these, and in the condition of those who are brought here shortly after their capture?

Bound to be, sir. It was an inclement winter at Richmond, with severe mortality among the Northern prisoners. . . . Reminded speedily of the dead Rob Lamar, and how Rob must be pinned in Lucy's thought at this moment, Elkins felt chagrined.

Would these guards be the same troops who've been assigned here lately?

Twenty-sixth Alabama and Fifty-fifth Georgia. Or rather—remnants of those regiments. But I'm told that they'll soon be sent to the front, and some of the new Georgia Reserve regiments will be stationed here in their stead.

Orders shouted alongside the depot . . . goblins began to move. They straggled in a column of twos, guards hovering. Squarely through the avenue of flames they advanced, fifty couples, more guards, another fifty stumbling couples, more guards, the next shambling Hundred in their grotesque wedding march, the next. They were dressed in every variety of rags afforded by their own uniforms at the time of capture, every variety of garment flung out from Sanitary Commission barrels at Belle Isle, every variety bartered for, stolen, traded for, ripped from the dead. Pancake caps, slouched hats, citizens' hats, no hats at all, hair of the hatless looked like wads of leaves in oaks where crows had nested. Blue jacket, undershirt, a man wrapped in a shawl, another Indian shape with a blanket folded around him, more blue jackets and flannel shirts. (The Claffeys did not see him, he did not see them, he did not know them, they would never know him; but a youth named Eben Dolliver walked in his crazy quilt.) Some carried cloth-wrapped bundles, a few wore knapsacks on their backs, there were haversacks and rolls of bedding slung across the shoulders in Confederate style, one man carried a carpetbag, there were skillets and buckets hanging. The more mature were grizzled wildly in their beards . . . dirty crusted faces of sixteen-year-olds were pinched and squeezed. Oh thank Heaven, cried Ira Claffey in his heart, that Moses was never captured. He might have looked like one of these, like one of these; he might have been marched to one of those evil places of which I've heard, Yankee prison pens, Rock Island or Johnson's Island or Point Lookout.

. . . But if he had been captured, instead of shot in Maryland, he might be alive still.

. . . Are these alive? Walking, it is true—parading now before our gaze—but are they The Quick? Might not this be a procession of The Dead?

Few sounds did they make, they coughed, there were hawkings of those with maladies of the throat; one man kept bending out to blow his nose between his fingers. God damn it, he cried impatiently but recognizably, now I've tooted myself into a nosebleed again.

Hush up, Yank. You heard the order. No talking!

In all there were six Hundreds, although the final Hundred did not move with its full complement. There came a burst of steam, froth of sparks from the railroad engine; it jerked forward with the line of empty box cars, heading for Albany and foodstuffs which must be loaded. Driving wheels shivered and spun with racking clatter; no voice of guard or prisoner could be heard against the engine's riot.

Distantly on the fiery boulevard Yankees seemed fumbling in inde-
cision. There were delays outside the stockade gate, where names
were being checked, rolls written out. Flames wavered, expunged
them for a moment, brought the last batch into final glare and showed
them for what they were: insects disturbed in a sandy channel, progressing sluggishly as their own larvae.

With the train's departure, Ira could hear his Negroes returning in
an orderly drove across the branch. They were discussing the Yankees,
and had been sadly disappointed in the Yankees' appearance.

Harrell Elkins said, Did I tell you there's still a broad gap on one
side of the stockade? We've artillery mounted there.

Oh, Lucy cried, some may escape. They're such a desperate lot.

Never fear. A squad of guards remains on duty through every hour
of the twenty-four, and will until the gap is closed.

The torchlight procession has passed, said Ira. He led the way back
toward the plantation. He kept thinking, Why, they came too early!
I had not expected prisoners so soon. Lucy and Cousin Harry followed
slowly on the path, Cousin Harry helping Lucy in the dark. There
was not such strong light now; fires were burning down. But a deep-
ening glow could be seen from Claffey windows even after the three
people had said Goodnight and had gone to their rooms.

XIII

At nineteen years of age Edward Blamey was a corporal in the First Rhode Island Cavalry, and had been a captive since he was dismounted near Chancellorsville when his horse broke its leg. Edward was somewhat the worse for wear after an autumn and winter at Belle Isle, but his practiced eye still rolled keenly. Blamey had remarkable eyesight, inherited from generations of fishermen who put out daily past Point Judith, although he did not incline toward the sea.

The first morning after he'd arrived at Camp Sumter, he mounted a wedge of pine-root and clay which lay like the bulb of a giant's onion tossed aside. This was at a point of vantage on the northern summit, a few rods from the north fence, and Edward Blamey had a clear view of the whole interior. Most of the men were at work, rigging shelters out of the forest's wreckage left by axemen, but some were sitting in apathy, too tired or ill or depressed to join in this general pioneering. Groups gathered opposite the breach in the wall, staring at a brass cannon which glared back with its blank black muzzle.

Blamey's ancestors, who awarded him such vision, had been accustomed to gauging the activities of birds on distant waters and thus discovering shoals of fish they sought. In the cavalry, men used to amuse themselves by saying, Ed, I hain't got my spy-glasses handy. What are those critters doing on that road down yonder? Are they Federals or Johnnies? Or maybe a herd of muley cows? Ed Blamey could examine the tiny moving figures, and report that they constituted a foraging party of four men, driving in some rather sorry beeves. This he could do with his naked gray eyes narrowed to telescopic power. His comrades used to lay wagers as to whether he was right or wrong, but usually he was right. In this way he formed a perpetual diversion for himself—measuring distances, estimating numbers, evaluating faraway activities of troops or wagon trains. Most men would have needed field-glasses to do this; and Blamey's developed skill helped to win him two wide stripes.

As a cavalryman he had been compact as to stature, a spruce figure in spite of violently bowed legs that folks made jokes about. The spruceness was long since departed: Blamey appeared as a dried bean or nut, rattling in the husk of his short jacket and patched sodden pants. The big patch on the seat had come loose and flapped and sagged, every step that Ed Blamey took. No one of the people with whom he messed had needle or thread to repair the damage, and it annoyed Edward's dignity to have his grimy buttocks exposed to the world. Here his search could be pursued more widely and, he hoped, successfully. That was his main reason for climbing upon the hillock of stump: he wished to estimate the number of prisoners assembled in this new stockade, and pick out a likely group where men seemed better dressed and better supplied than the average; such a group might include a man with a housewife in his possession. That was Ed's chief compulsion; but also he knew that he would have done it if he'd needed no patch at all—merely for the challenge, merely from habit.

He stood breakfasting on part of the cornmeal mush he had saved from yesterday's ration. It had weighed nearly two pounds—a sizeable chunk of cold mush, and he hadn't eaten it all, because his mess still had some boiled sweet potatoes they'd purchased on the railroad. Ed Blamey assorted days in his mind. This was Saturday the twenty-seventh. Well, folks said that the first shipment had arrived on the twenty-fourth—five hundred and ninety-one strong. Those represented the six hundred who had been told off and marched out of Belle Isle on St. Valentine's day . . . there were rumors that they were to be sent to the North for exchange, and many men not included in this detachment tried to flank out with them, and were struck or—if unduly persistent—punished in other ways. Men yelled after the departing gang, Hey, give The Girl I Left Behind Me a pretty valentine for me! . . . Five hundred and ninety-one, they had reached this place: nine either died of disease en route, or were shot by guards in trying to escape from the cars. Two more detachments of three hundred each came on the twenty-sixth, one of these being Edward Blamey's crowd. The Rebs didn't seem able to handle more than a few hundred at one swoop. There was such a jumble of box cars coming south and troop trains going north, that the two groups had arrived within a few hours of each other. Officers commanding the guards hurried wildly about at the station, cursing. They said that rations had not been made available for such numbers. Some of the new men would have to go hungry, and they did go hungry, but they were accustomed to going hungry.

There must be nearly twelve hundred prisoners now penned inside this place. It was nothing like so crowded as Belle Isle, and Edward felt relief about that. His glance roved the fence. Somewhere above fifteen acres was the area contained. Later he would pace the length of the walls and then he'd know exactly. Of course that creek took up space, and obviously men and teams had trampled the adjacent sides into a mire when they were building the prison. A certain amount of uninhabitable space must thus be deducted from the whole. Blamey watched the creek, and stiffened with disgust: some people were squatted down, there, doing their business. Fine business indeed— didn't they realize that that was the only source of drinking water in the entire place? Well, he couldn't whip the lot of them (his spirit was dry, selfish and quiet; but he was impelled by the small man's demand for assertion) or he'd have gone down there and tried it. Doubtless guards or prison officials would put a stop to that dirty habit soon.

He thought of the James River, boiling coldly past the side of the Belle Isle camp, rushing foamy brown among its rocks. This creek wasn't much. Suppose it ran dry?

Edward Blamey thought to select the family engaged in building the most efficient-looking and best-equipped shelter of the lot. Over there, black figures tussling and heaving: it was beyond the creek valley on the south hilltop, and they were actually setting tall poles in the ground, and roofing them with what shone like India rubber blankets, fairly new ones. Men as well supplied as those men must have needles, thread, all such things. Ed Blamey chewed the last of his solidified mush and spat out a stray piece of unground cob. He slid down through the red twist of roots to the ground.

He called himself Number One, in slang he had picked up after joining the cavalry (which he and many of his companions still called *calvary* as they had when they were children) and one reason why he was in fair shape now was that he looked after Number One with care. At Belle Isle he had jeered and thrown clods like the rest when a few turncoats yielded to the inducements of Rebel emissaries, and marched out of the camp to accept food, clothing and liberty as Confederate States' soldiers. Ed's grim small conscience would not have permitted such deviation on his own part; at least his nervousness regarding The Wrath To Come would not have permitted it. But within limitation of a prisoner's existence Edward Blamey was adept at finding the dryest corner of any shebang, the freshest chunk of pork, the least weevily meal, the warmest spot by a winter fireside. His common expression, when anyone else touched an article belonging to him, was, That's mine. Take care. That's mine. He was not admired as generous or entertaining; still he kept himself as clean as possible, he would share his scrap of blanket if someone else offered a share in a waterproof in return; he would do his share in any task, but only his share. Here's Number One's chunk of kindling, he'd say, and put it down for the fire; but it would have taken much persuasion for him to go out and seek kindling for one of the invalids. He was not loved, he was accepted.

(Edward's father was treasurer of the Baptist Church at home in Rhode Island, and neighbors thought or pretended to think that the elder Blamey found certain unmentionable perquisites in his office.

This was untrue. Mr. Blamey's accounts could always be balanced to
the penny, and he was fond of asserting that they could be.)

On the south hill of the prison pen, Edward encountered the busy
batch of men he had observed from afar. Critically he paused to watch
their activity. A fine cabin was being constructed by their united efforts.
Slighter, weaker folks came lugging armloads of dry pine boughs for
stuffing chinks, more powerful men were disrupting roots and stumps,
dragging them into the outline of a primitive castle.

Dolan, you rat, said a deep vibrating voice. Blamey jumped to
hear it.

Hey? What did you say, Willie?

Dolan, you rat, that main pole's not resting proper. Put it deeper,
man—deeper. Make it stout.

Seated on a pile of blankets and overcoats, a mighty figure held his
huge arms folded across his chest. His head was oversized, covered on
top by scraggly ginger-colored hair, covered on the jowls and cheeks
by a scrubby ginger-colored beard. His eyes rolled large and white.
His arms were forest logs. My, my, said Ed Blamey in his thought, so
he's here too. Mosby the Raider! At Belle Isle he and Mosby had been
numbered in the same Hundred. The man's name actually was William
Collins, and he had earned the appellation of Mosby the Raider through
exertion of a piracy which might have caused the Confederate Mosby
to shudder, and surely would have filled him with loathing. Willie
Collins's philosophy was plain, abrupt: a weak man has no business
in this place nor in any place where physical force may rule. An invalid should die and be an invalid no longer. A strong man should be
strong to begin with, and should remain powerful. He cannot do that
unless he feed and shelter himself. I shall feed and shelter myself at
whatever expense of anguish by another. Is there a luxury, a dainty,
a pair of handmade boots, a Shetland shawl to be had? These I shall
have. Only a power greater than I can exert shall prevent me from
having them.

Edward Blamey had first observed William Collins in the ice of
December, in that week when many Belle Islanders limped on frozen
feet, making the same sound which Edward remembered his three-
year-old sister as making after she fell from a bag-swing and broke
her arm: a steady high keening like a fiddle string consistently tortured by rosin and horse-hair. You heard it everywhere, it lived in the
air, and on the earth where less heartened victims crouched, rocking
their shoulders and striking at their feet, trying to thaw them. Through
this sound came the blast of Willie Collins's rich voice saying, Take
them off, God damn it, you heard me. He had found a fellow prisoner
with feet the size of his own, and was forcing the prisoner to give up
his shoes. It seemed that Collins's own shoes had disappeared during
the night. The prisoner had huge feet but no other hugeness about

him; he was a rack of bones, his right arm hung idle from an old
wound. Collins twisted the prisoner's ear between thumb and finger,
forcing the man to the ground. There he stood over him, threatening
with the flat of his hand until the fellow untied his shoe-cords with his
one good hand and kicked off the shoes. Edward and others stared
glumly, but only one man tried to interfere. He was a sturdy Ken-
tuckian whom they called Dark And Bloody. Dark And Bloody plunged
suddenly toward the Irishman, caught hold of his arm and swung him
around. Before he could deliver the blow he'd aimed, Willie's foot
came up like a rock from a gunpowder blast and caught the Ken-
tuckian squarely in the crotch. One man fainted at sound of that
scream. After Willie Collins had paraded away in his stolen shoes,
people picked up the kicking figure from the ground and carried it,
twisting and blubbering, to the hospital. Folks said that Dark And
Bloody's testicles were mashed to a pulp and that the whole bottom
part of his belly was turning blue. Dark And Bloody, indeed. Few
people even thought of resisting Willie Collins after that. As would
be bound to occur, he gathered round him a mob of gentry of his own
persuasion: some were incompetents, mere chinless starvelings, but
they were feists who might hamstring a bull while a bolder dog had
him by the throat. Since dashing exploits of the partisan John Mosby
were common lore in that year, Collins was called Mosby. The name
stuck.

Loot was taken from all and sundry, either through open assault in
daylight or by sneak thievery at night. Loot could be traded, sold
to the guards in exchange for any comfort obtainable. Cash exchange,
the exchange of barter: it mattered not what machinery was employed
so long as stewpots bubbled and raw corn whiskey was delivered in
jugs. The more venal among the guards tolerated William Collins and
his gang because they were a source of knives, watches, scissors,
needles, buttons and clothing no longer commonly to be procured in
the South. Other guards looked upon Collins with disgust, and swore
to shoot him at the first opportunity. At Belle Isle Willie never went
near the boundary ditch in consequence. When a new prisoner had
been selected as a victim for search and seizure, and he chanced to
be a prisoner located near the ditch, Willie would send subordinates to
do the job.

In one whistling icy evening, a henchman named Tomcat O'Connor
was engaged in stripping the flannel shirt from a fifteen-year-old newcomer whom he had hammered into submission. The attack took place
close to the north ditch and came under observation of an old guard
whom folks called Father Time—a patriarchal mountaineer who never
swore at the inmates when ordering them about, but who misquoted
liberally from the Prophets instead. There was still light enough to

see, although lamps were winking on in Richmond and Manchester.
Father Time halted in his leisurely sentry's pace, took his unlit pipe
out of his mouth, lifted his musket and took painstaking aim. The report of his gun jarred nearer groups, and sent people crawling away
from their small fires. But Father Time wasn't shooting at random, as
depraved guards sometimes did: he was shooting at Tomcat O'Connor
and he was shooting to kill, and he did kill. Tomcat leaped high off
the ground when the ball broke through his chest; his arms shot out
to their fullest spread and he gave a loud gulp as he fell. The next
sound was a roar of laughter from Willie Collins as he stood safely
beside a crowded tent, half screened by his associates. Did you see
that Tomcat? he hallooed, pealing again with glee. Did you see him?
Faith, I thought he was trying to jump over the moon! Then, in a
lower tone, Barney, do you get over there like a brisk kiddie and go
through him, and fetch his clothes—soon twill be dark, and the guard
can't see to shoot you well.

So Edward Blamey had chanced to be counted into Belle Isle in the
same Hundred with this monster. Here at Camp Sumter or Andersonville or whatever they called the place, here, caged in a fresh stockade,
Ed Blamey was dully grateful that he was no longer in dangerous
proximity to an unprincipled force. . . . But he maintained a loathing
respect for the giant just the same. Mosby certainly did look out for
Number One in more than a fair way. You had to give him credit.

Willie sat in well-fed massiveness, boss and lord, the imperfect picture of a prisoner, the perfect figure of the New York City gangster
which it was said that he had been all his life. Ed Blamey knew nothing of New York except that it was a noisy and bewildering place to
travel through, and when he traveled through New York he had been
cheated by a motherly old Scotswoman who offered the boys chocolate fudges to taste. Aren't these fine fudges, dearie? and I'm letting
them go cheap: a shilling a box, and that's no much for fine sweeties,
is it, now? Everybody tasted the crumbs she gave out, and she sold
all the boxes she was carrying—twelve—as fast as the quarter-dollars
could be handed to her. Then she disappeared in the crowd, saying
she would be back soon with more sweeties. Edward Blamey was one
of those who bought; but when the boys opened their treats they
found that the boxes contained only bits of brick and shavings and no
fudges at all. New York also was said to be the home of the Plug
Uglies. Blamey rather supposed that Willie Collins had been a Plug
Ugly.

For now Willie owned a plug hat, and it rested on his knee, that
knee thewed as thickly as some men's trunks. He wore a long blouse
of blue, a plaid waistcoat, and a woolen tippet was tied around his
squat neck. A gold watch chain hung across his front, and he carried

a pair of officer's gauntlets stuck into his belt, and in his pockets he had two slung-shots which he might wield simultaneously when the need arose: these weapons he called his Neddies.

Also he was said to own dirks, and rumor armed him with a pistol. He took from his pocket a green silk handkerchief and, unwinding it, produced a thick sandwich of biscuit and meat which he chewed up in three or four bites. Oh, thought Ed Blamey, that was beef. How I'd like to have—

In front of Willie's kingly gaze the gang labored. This was still the winter season and night winds could stab you. The residence in construction was half a cave and half a fort: when the stout stump was torn out by chains and oxen it had left a hole, and this hole was utilized shrewdly in the construction design. Walls formed of wood and earth, the cavity enlarged and deepened, the sheets of rubber, the portions of canvas shingled aloft. If he dwelt here until summer Willie would have a tent constructed, for air and coolness; now he wished to be snug. Three of the men fabricated a mud chimney, as he had ordered them to do. Several of the company were apes close to Mosby the Raider in size and threat; but he had taken the measure of each as their resentfulness or ambition dictated, and at last they served consistently—if with occasional rebellion—the cause of Willie's enrichment and their own.

His ponderous head turned, his glance identified the gawking Blamey, his finger crooked. Ha.

Blamey did not stir; he supposed that Willie must be summoning a man beyond him. He looked back, there was no one else close.

Ha. You in the cavalry jacket. It's you I'm beckoning to.

Blamey approached with reluctance.

Come near me, Rubber Legs. God, a man could put a beer barrel betwixt them. Are you not from Belle Isle? It's in my own Hundred you were.

Ed Blamey nodded and made a sound.

What want you here?

This patch on my pants. I thought—maybe one of your men would own a needle and thread.

Ah, your ass is ragged, and that's the truth. Ho there, Lipsky. He summoned an undersized black-bearded man with a devilish face and one blind eye.

Lipsky can see to sew, for he was a tailor in his time. Lipsky, fetch you your tools and stitch this gentleman where he needs to be stitched. He wagged his rough boulder of a head while Lipsky sulked off to delve into a ragged bundle.

Once he tried to come at me with a knife, and I rubbed my thumb in his eye. That should teach him, hey?

Yes, chattered Edward Blamey, it ought to.

Speaking of eyes, I must needs speak with you.

Lipsky, the former tailor, unclean even among those droves of unclean and building a private stench wherever he moved, came up and prepared to thread a needle. So I can't sew pantaloons when a customer is wearing them, he moaned.

Be taking them off, Rubber Legs.

Blamey had little wish to remove his trousers but he obeyed. He stood in a shred of under-drawers while Lipsky arranged himself on a hummock and bent to the job.

Rubber Legs, they say you've the ogles of a hawk. Weren't you the one, now, who was forever spying out what went on near Libby? Sure, the fire in November! Every man of us saw the flames and people on roof-tops a-watching, but it was you who could spy how many there were, and could tell of the women you saw amongst them. Ah, it's good to be blessed with a brace of ogles such as yours. It should teach Lipsky a trick or two, should it not? Lipsky, you dirty sheeney, it's only one eye you've got for your sewing now, and why did you ever attempt to open up Willie Collins? So he rambled on while the tailor stitched, while Ed Blamey stood shaking, while other ruffians appraised Blamey's masculinity and were rude in their evaluation of it. Mosby the Raider pulled a second sandwich from his pocket and sat munching. He did not offer to share, but Blamey would never have offered to share had that been his own sandwich. Mosby talked on with his large mouth full, and crumbs of biscuit flew out each time he opened his lips on certain words.

And a multitude of his words were incomprehensible to the bowlegged young Rhode Islander—the argot of organized brawling throngs in whose ranks Willie Collins had slugged since he was a child. Sure, and there was another fire after the New Year, near to Libby, and you were telling all that went on. . . . It's little more than a fortnight since the Union cavalry, bless their barking irons, tried to capture Richmond and got themselves anointed for it; and the Rebs were pitching about on their forts and fetching up new cannon, and it was every motion you could see when they looked like mice to the rest of us. Ah, what a fine pair of gagers you're a-wearing in your head. May God damn you, Lipsky, bestir yourself with the gentleman's pants! Now, which of you kiddies has made off with Willie's flask of bingo? Nickey help me, I'll tear the wattles off your skulls if you've drunk it! He kept grubbing around among overcoats on which he lolled, and finally he gave a grunt of satisfaction and his hand brought up a brown glass bottle filled with some sort of liquor. Collins smirked at Edward Blamey and drew out the stopper with his teeth. The guards call it pine-top. It cost me a bean, and it would burn the gob out of most men; but to Willie it's like the milk from his dear mother's tits.

He spoke as if he could remember his dear mother, but he could not. He was brought from Ireland when a boy, by a father who died of what Willie called barrel fever in a Fourth Ward slum, in 1845.

Lipsky finished sewing the patch. It looked like it would last as long as the rest of the garment. This was the best tailoring which had ever been the fortune of Ed Blamey. He mumbled thanks to Lipsky, but the wretched fellow gave only a glare of his one good eye and put away needle and thread. Ah, you dead-ogled sheeney, roared Collins as the tailor passed him. He threw out his great platter of a hand in an attempted slap, but Lipsky dodged away. Willie Collins laughed, slid the brown bottle into his pocket, and again crooked his finger at Edward. Come, Rubber Legs. I've business with you. What's your name?

Ed finished knotting the cord which held up his pants. He forced himself to step closer to the giant, fearing that the slap thrown at Lipsky might now be directed at him.

What's your name?

Blamey.

Is it Delaney you say? I've a friend—

No, sir. Blamey.

Don't go to sirring me, or I'll tear the velvet out of your head. Collins is the name, you addle cove—Willie Collins!

Yes—Willie.

When did you come from Belle?

Got here a yesterday.

What's your Hundred?

Second Squad, Eighth Hundred.

And where do you dwell? Where do you come from? You look like a joskin from the hayseeds to me! Delaney, harken to Willie Collins. I've use for a pair of gagers like your own.

In that moment Edward Blamey thought wildly that Collins must be planning to gouge the eyes out of his head; he would have stumbled in flight, but Collins's hand had clamped on his jacket. Collins dragged him closer and explained his plan. This stockade enclosed a large area, far larger than Belle Isle. It was difficult to tell what was going on at one end of the pen when you stood at the other. Blamey should serve as a scout, an observer. He could tell when new prisoners were coming in at the gate, and which of those new prisoners possessed blankets or bundles, and where they went to domicile themselves. From far distances Blamey might be able to see whether men pulled watches from their pockets to look at the time; he might know which prisoner held a jackknife in his hand, and which only a bit of stick.

Cannily he might discover whether there were four men or fourteen gathered in a remote well-furnished shebang—whether the crowd was weak enough to be attacked, or strong enough to put up a dangerous defense. Ah, Willie would rather own eyes like Delaney's than the finest field-glass in the land!

It's on the best you'll be faring, along with these snafflers of mine. No more chicken shit, but fine sawney and stews, with a swig of pine-top to help it along. I've the best cooks in the land; you'll be my nose, man, my very nose! We're a jolly crew, a jolly crew, and so is Willie a jolly rabbit. You should hear the ditties I can sing. Ask any man from the Eighty-eighth Pennsylvania that I was captured along with. I've jumped a dozen bounties; and Willie Collins's pockets are lined forever, man, they're lined with beans. Ask any from the Seventy-second New York or the Hundred and Twenty-fifth New York or the Fourteenth Connecticut or the Hundred and Nineteenth Pennsylvania, for I've been in all of them; and they know my ditties. Should another man seek to take the brass from your pockets, you'll cry O Yes, O Yes, and my kiddies will be about you in a twinkling. And isn't that better than living on hog-fodder, and gadding the hoof? Sure, with me a fellow has everything he's needing except a ladybird.

Edward Blamey backed to the limit of his jacket's length and said No. It took courage for him to say this, but he did so through no conscious heroism. The peculiar mixture of promises, boasting and prophecy—the mingling of unfamiliar thieves' jargon with familiar slang of the army—left him puzzled and unnerved. His quick rejection of the offer was his father's rejection, Rhode Island's rejection, his elder brother's rejection, the rejection of the Baptist Church. The Wrath To Come was a flame kindled for robbers, adulterers, murderers, atheists; in time it would scorch Willie Collins and all like him. Ed Blamey did not wish to sizzle. The next instant he was jerked whirling, he was smacked by the bottom of Collins's shoe, he went through the air and landed on his face. Blamey got up and ran for his life. Blood began to ooze from a dozen small lacerations on his cheeks and forehead where tough roots had abraded him. Behind, he heard Mosby bellowing, I'll teach you to say No to Willie Collins! Edward Blamey fled to the north slope which now he knew he should never have left, and he promised himself that he would not go the South Side again.

When he came puffing up to the site of the previous night's encampment, he found acquaintances at work constructing a shebang. He had no special friends among them, but they asked about his injuries. Fell down, he said. Was up on a stump and a root busted under me. Later he warned that the Belle Isle raiders were present in force, and that it would be well for all their crowd to be armed

with clubs in case of an attack. Soon blood stopped running from
Blamey's abrasions; they were not deep but painful. He went to the
western edge of the stockade where the creek came in below the
high fence. A young guard peered down to watch him as Edward
Blamey bathed his face, but the guard did not offer to shoot nor did
he order Ed away. Apparently there was no observance of a deadline
here in this new place; and he mentioned it to his companions when
he returned to do his share (no more than his share) in preparing
shelter. No deadline? Just you wait, said a grim New Hampshireman,
they'll have one.

Edward contributed his lone two-thirds of a louse-ridden blanket
to the roofing of the shebang, he fetched boughs and poles for half
an hour. Then he went searching for a cudgel with which to fend
off possible raiders; he wanted a club heavy enough to drub a big
man's head and make him feel it. Any greenish pine he found would
be too awkward for convenience, and he roamed farther afield. Luck
attended him when he discovered a dressed length of hardwood
amid the litter on the ground. There was a rusty bolt or rivet hole
discernible at the broken end; this seemed to be the handle of a
spade or shovel which had been snapped when workmen were there.
Blamey observed that the letter C had been scorched into this handle
as if to mark it for identification. It was the tool he sought for a
weapon of defense, and he started back to the new shebang in an
emboldened mood.

During his search he had chanced upon a lone blue figure curled
in a hollow and partly sheltered by roots. The first time he passed he
did not bother to make further examination; that looked like a good
place to sleep, and Edward Blamey supposed that the man was sleeping there—it was out of the wind. But as he circled the hole on his
homeward trip he heard a wail and chattering. The figure moved, and
there was the sound of weak retching. Edward paused and looked
down. He could see foam on the man's mouth. Hi there, he said,
out of some sense of Christian duty. He remembered his father reading about the Levite who passed by on the other side. The man did
not move.

Hi, mister.

The curled-up man opened his eyes, they were glass, they saw
nothing, the eyes fell shut again.

Want something?

A weak voice said, Catherine.

What say?

The fellow wore a short cavalry jacket very like Edward's own,
but newer and cleaner; he could not have been long imprisoned, but
was about to be Exchanged. That was what they'd called it on the
Island—and probably in every other prison camp, North or South.

When someone died the others were apt to term him as Exchanged. When someone was shot by a guard they called him Paroled.

Hi, mister. What's your name?

The eyes failed to open, but the fellow shook quickly in spasm, and more fluid issued from his mouth. Swarner, he said.

What name did you say? Warner?

Swarner. J—H—Swarner.

Where from?

Second New York Ccccavalry. He managed to stutter the last word loose, but it was an almighty effort for him to do it.

You sick?

No.

Yes, you be. It was contrary to Edward's habit, but again he considered his father's favorite Chapter about the Good Samaritan (the moral of this text was cited often but practiced seldom by Mr. Blamey). Also his encounter with Willie Collins had stirred Edward into a recognition of Virtue as opposed to Wickedness. He supposed that he must be virtuous in the sight of God, if it would cost him nothing. He got down into the hole and bent over the huddled Swarner. Want some water, mister? I could fetch some.

No.

I hain't got any rations. You want rations?

No. Ccccatherine.

His attempted ministering thus unsuccessful, Edward climbed back out of the depression and walked to his shebang. Found a sick feller up yonder, he said casually to the others, but they gave little attention. They had seen many sick, many dying, many dead. In the middle of the afternoon they drew rations, and the food seemed munificent: nearly a quart of uncooked cornmeal, half a pound of beef, and a spoonful of salt per man. Mess Two still had five sweet potatoes left as well, and under the leadership of the New Hampshire sergeant—a mason by trade—a furnace of mud and sticks had been constructed. Ed Blamey and his family fed well, and they babbled about the improvement over conditions at Belle Isle. However, Ed still imagined that New York cavalryman bent like an abandoned cruller in his hole. Before dusk he turned his steps in that direction again, drawn as much by curiosity as by saintly intent. He came back from the east faster than he went.

Fellers, that man's dead as mackerel.

What man? Man you saw?

Said his name was Swarner.

Well, what do we do about it? Ain't he got no friends?

There don't seem to be nobody about.

The New Hampshireman, whose name was Colony, went back with Ed Blamey; so did the brothers Wingate, when they heard that the dead man was from York State. They were from Troy. The four men stood around and looked at the curved stiffening morsel in the fairly new and fairly clean jacket.

Got a good coat on him, said the youngest Wingate. I could use a coat like that.

Take it, said Colony. He'll never need it more.

Si Wingate slid down into the hole and, with some struggling, removed the jacket from the corpse. He climbed out, shook the garment violently, and turned out each pocket in turn. There was nothing in any of them except a half-gnawed turnip and, in the breast pocket, a letter worn to dirty tissue, a letter without an envelope. It was written in pencil and the penciling was blurred from much handling. Tup Wingate held the paper up to the fading light and spelled out a few words.

Seems to be from his sister, for she calls him Beloved Brother. Her name is Catherine. Hain't no address that I can see.

Take care with that coat, said Sergeant Colony darkly. Maybe he's dead of a plague.

No, looky there. He ain't broke out in any way.

He's too nigh to us for comfort, and if we leave him laying here he'll stink. Get a hold on him and we'll fetch him over to that nearest gate.

They went, carrying Swarner gingerly by his cold hands and rag-wrapped feet. As they approached the gate the adjacent guards called down a question from their sentry shacks.

He ain't from our mess. Don't know where he's from. We just come acrost him in a hole.

Well, Yank, put him next the gate. Somebody'll tote him out, the next time the gate's open.

They did as instructed and turned away through windy gloom. Then Edward Blamey owned an idea. He had a pencil in his pocket. Give me that there letter of his, Wingate, and the York State man handed it over. Blamey held the letter spread against a flat chip, and across the fading text he printed in big black capitals: *J. H. Swarner, 2 N Y Calvary.* He returned to the gate and stuffed the paper beneath the ragged trouser-band of the corpse where someone would be apt to see it. It was odd, but again it seemed that he could hear that weak stutter of, Ccccatherine.

The others were waiting silently, and they all walked back to their new shebang together. Scratches and cuts on Blamey's face were stiff and puffing; his entire face felt as if it were on fire. He wished that he were older and hairier, he wished that he had more beard than this dirty mouse-colored down which he still wore at nineteen. A beard would have protected his skin somewhat when Collins kicked him to the ground.

I wonder if he's the first to die in here? said Tup Wingate.

Colony said, Won't be the last, I'll warrant you that.

Next fellow dies, I trust he has some socks, said Si Wingate. I got great need of socks. This here jacket is a good fit.

Colony spoke again lugubriously. Won't be the last.

Oh, come now, Sarge. We victualed well today. This puts Belle Isle in the shade.

Ed Blamey walked in silence, feeling the hurt of his torn face, but feeling also immeasurably noble as compared to an ogre like Willie Collins. Once back in Rhode Island he would be bound to tell his father that he had assumed the role of Good Samaritan, or at least had tried to.

Won't be the last, repeated that dreary clipped voice.

XIV

Captain Oxford Puckett was in bed with the Widow Tebbs that evening when Floral answered their hallooing and stood outside the door of The Crib and responded with, Huh?

The widow said, Flory, Captain Ox has got a bottle of sorghum liquor in his saddle bag. Please to go fetch it.

Ox Puckett called out genially, I'll give you five cents.

Secesh, thought Floral resentfully. Can't buy much with that. Can't buy scarcely nothing. Nevertheless he ran off on the errand—running because he was a nervous child and liked to move rapidly, and could move rapidly now that his sore foot was healed. Also he knew that it filled his elder brother Coral with furious envy to see him loping. The feud between them was blind, unreasoning, intense, a feud almost to the death.

Oxford Puckett had known Mag Lumpkin from her infancy; he could remember her mother when she was large with child and the child was Mag. As a butcher's boy he had delivered meat to the Lumpkins. His father was the butcher, a savage hulk who kept a strip of tanned hide cut neatly into the shape of a paddle for the express purpose of beating his sons for trivial offenses. As fast as they grew tall enough the sons ran away from home; Oxford was the third to flee. He ran away to the army, and later served heroically in the campaign of invasion against Mexico City; he was given a sergeant's stripes in the field. After that the army was his life periodically, although he turned an unsuccessful hand at farming, butchering and harness-making between enlistments. He drank a great deal, but no one ever saw him when he could be described as drunk. He was a jovial round-shouldered little man, capable of extreme lewdness. Ox Puckett boasted calmly that he had practiced every sin in the decalogue of sexual crime at one time or another (he could not have employed such phraseology, however, in describing his wickedness, since he was poorly educated and had a limited vocabulary). Now in young middle age his silky beard and silkier hair were almost snow-white; his pale blue eyes shone like bits of bottle glass from a lined face the color of an old saddle. The beard concealed a chuckling sensual mouth and made him appear like some patriarch of religious pursuits. He had served wherever the Fifty-fifth Georgia served. His wiry abused body was marked with wounds received in two wars and also in brawls.

The captain and the woman lay resting. Mag giggled as she explored his scars with her loose hands.

Ow, lady.

Hurt you, honey? I'm sorry.

Got that from some damn Yankee at Cumberland Gap, and it was right slow to heal.

Ox, what's this here blue one down here next to your cock?

That's old. Got that at Chapultepec. Like to shot my manhood clean away.

Few's got more manhood than you, Ox Puckett. Well I know.

Reckon you ought to know if anybody does. How many men you reckon you've lain with, Mag, sweet?

Oh, I couldn't never calculate. You know I hain't got no head for figures and such. Maybe a hundred different ones in the course of a year . . . that was before the war. I guess so, honey. I've had a sight of folks a-loving me in my time.

Well, I'm a-going to love you again, right now.

Wait till Flory gets back with your liquor. I'd like a taste myself, if you'd be so kind; hain't swallowed a drop all week.

It's not much slouch of a drink. My, my, how I'd relish a canteen full of *mescal!* That'll put the Old Scratch in any man's breeches.

What did you call it, honey lamb?

Mescal. What folks drink down Mexico way. They make it out of cactus, so they say.

We got right smart of cactus here on my place.

Reckon it's a special kind they use. But this here other stuff— The boys over to the stockade call it pine-top. Sutler who sells it claims he puts a fresh rattlesnake head in every barrel, and it does taste like it, sure enough.

Flory returned with the bottle he'd found in Captain Ox's saddle bag, and tapped at the door.

Oh, hell. You'll have to go let him in, Mag.

Door hain't bolted. Fetch the bottle in, Flory.

There was no especial novelty in Flory's seeing his mother in bed with a man. He had seen her so ever since he could remember. As a very small child he had hidden in an empty barrel in The Crib, in order to peep out at operations carried on there. His mother saw the barrel head lifting and lowering; she caught him, and gave him a thrashing with the belt belonging to her customer of the moment. But in later pursuit of her vocation Mag became less sensitive to the scrutiny of watching eyes. Her daughter she would not permit to enter The Crib; some peculiar warped sense of delicacy kept her from allowing another female to observe her there; but both Coral and Floral had fetched and carried everything from peaches to firewood, more times than they could count. Sometimes the callers gave them gratuities, sometimes not.

Captain Puckett said, That's a good boy, bubby. Reach me my pants from yonder chair. When Flory brought the garment, the captain rolled over in bed and got out his purse. He extracted a good hard round Federal half-dime.

Godsakes, thank you, mister, said Flory.

You got some real live greenbacks in there, cried Mag.

No lie about that. Took exactly eleven dollars and sixty-three cents off of a Yankee this very day; and one of them green dollars is for you, Mag. What say you to that, hey?

Well, to tell the truth, Ox, I was suspecting you'd maybe give me a Yankee dollar. Or at least ten dollars Confed. It's so hard to get along nowadays; and since Coral come back from the fighting that makes another mouth to feed.

What I mean, lady, it's an *extra* dollar, all for you. Kind of a wedding present, on account of I'm happy to see you again.

You mean you'll give me two greenbacks?

Sure as hell don't mean nothing else.

Ox, you surely are a lamb. They don't come no better-natured than you.

Right now I feel like a red-hot lamb filled with hellfire. Christ, this pine-top hain't so bad! *Vamoose,* you small fry.

Flory said, Captain, sir?

Vamoose. It's foreign talk—it means to get to hell out of here. Same as *puk-a-chee.* But that's Sioux Injun talk.

Flory ran out into a dusk which grew colder by the minute. He hesitated wildly, swinging this way and that. At the house he had a piece of blanket which he wore tied across his shoulders for a coat— With this sudden chill in the air he'd like to have his blanket— But Laurel was at the house, and she'd ask him where he was bound, and she'd want to know where he got the money to spend at the village store, and she'd beg candy from him— Well, he might give her part of a stick— Coral he would never give a bite to, but of course Coral didn't like candy; all Coral wanted to do was snarl and curse, and clean that old shotgun, and tote it around in the fields as he staggered with his crutch—

His mind made up, Floral headed for the Anderson depot, coatless. There was one store in the place, consisting of a miserable collection of junk hawked to the public by a dirty old man named Uncle Arch Yeoman, no relation to the Yeomans who owned the sawmill. In other seasons Uncle Arch would have shut up shop long before this hour, but with the coming of two regiments or parts of two regiments on duty at the stockade he kept his door open until late at night. Uncle Arch was a reformed drunkard, a fanatical railer against The Curse of Drink, and he refused to peddle that commodity much desired by soldiers; but he kept candy, a few spices, grain coffee, vinegar, and a scanty supply of medicines. The troops visited his store frequently when off duty, so Floral Tebbs would not have to wait until tomorrow for his treat.

Floral had the candy associated with his mother in his mind. He could not read or write and could barely count; therefore the spelling meant nothing to him, and there was no difference in the sound. Horehound candy—he liked it better than peppermint or cinnamon sticks, or the wintergreen lozenges fed him by the Reverend Cato Dillard. Horehound candy . . . people said that his mother was a whore, he had heard the word applied to her often; he had heard coarsest conversation on the subject. The squared brown sticks, with a splintery dust of sugar on the outside . . . he thought of his mother whenever he rolled dissolving fragments in his mouth or, more frequently, when he hung about the store with not a penny in his clothes and could only glare worshipfully at the fly-specked jar where this delight was sealed.

He trotted down the railway track. At one point a portion of the distant stockade's interior was visible by day, and Floral halted in dimness to peer across the ravine . . . fires, little freckled winkings and glowings: that was all he could see now. He ran on. Lanterns hung high in Uncle Arch Yeoman's store, and soldiers lounged within the door or against the counters. Most of the soldiers seemed almighty old and tall to Flory, but some few of them were near to his own age . . . they always swaggered disdainfully when they knew that he was regarding them. In these few weeks since hordes of troops had camped down in the woods Flory had learned to avoid them except in some public place, such as the store, where the presence of grown men granted him a certain security from persecution.

He wormed his way through the gossiping crowd and confronted Uncle Arch across the counter where tobacco and candy were kept.

Well, what you want, Flory?

Five cents worth.

Horehound, same as usual? Five cents won't get you much. Maybe a teeny little hunk.

Floral opened his grubby hand and displayed the five-cent piece. Yankee money.

. . . Them Reserve regiments, a voice was saying behind him.

Flory, that's hard money for a fact. Uncle Arch began to rig a small poke of soiled newspaper, and he fumbled on the shelf for the sacred jar.

. . . Robbing the cradle and the grave, too.

. . . If'n Joe Brown comes around to rob *my* cradle back home. . . .

Uncle Arch's palsied hand dragged a few sticks of candy from the jar, and he began to crumple the poke.

More! demanded Floral. You give me that much for three cents tother time.

Times is hard hereabouts, Flory; prices have risen up. Well, reckon I can let you have one more little stick.

. . . Do tell. A man of seventy-seven? Pretty regiment that one will be.

. . . Georgia Reserves! Ought to call them *Pre*serves. Laughter.

Here you be, Flory. How's that wicked old whorehound, your Ma? Whorehounding about, same as ever, I reckon?

She's fine, said Floral, and began to burrow out of the store.

. . . And boys as young as thirteen, tis told.

. . . Sure enough. I knowed one that wasn't but twelve, and they took him.

. . . Drummer boy.

. . . No, sir, private soldier.

Floral Tebbs halted, bare feet frozen against the planks. For a few minutes he forgot even the treasure of brown sticks gripped in the newspaper bag. He had turned, he squatted down, he was listening, he wished he had a dozen ears. At last, when talk strayed to another topic, he slunk out into darkness. Now the sky was black, deadened by clouds; it was difficult to see the way until he reached the railroad. Then he ran on the rails, for they were scrubbed by wheels, they could be seen on even such a night. Floral ran lightly. Usually in this sport he was counting the number of paces he could take on a rail before losing his balance and needing to step to the ties; this night he did not count. The conversation of Uncle Arch's store roared back at him from raw fields, from pines and vines and roadway; he heard it all again; he battened on it. Not until he was halfway home did he open the paper and wedge candy into his mouth until he could scarcely move his jaws.

At the Tebbs house little Zoral, the baby, had whined himself to sleep in the bedroom; Zoral had been howling about something or other when Flory first left the place in response to the summons from The Crib. Coral crouched by the fireplace, popping corn in a skillet; it was his favorite evening occupation, but seldom would he share his corn with the rest, never with Floral. The sister, Laurel, was trying to stitch up a rent in her petticoat by light of a feeble rag lamp. She was a listless child of fifteen with a pinched sharp-featured face and eyes like a mink's. She ate clay continually in secret, though her mother tried to break her of the habit by frequent lashings of tongue and willow whip. Laurel's coarse carroty hair, untidy as it was, became a singular beauty in the dull glow of the primitive lamp.

What you got there, Flory? What you eating at?

Horehound.

Whereabouts you get it?

Uncle Arch's.

Whereabouts you get any money?

Captain Ox done give it to me for being valuable to him.

Coral said, Get some wood.

I ain't no nigger of your'n.

God damn it, tonight's your turn! I fetched it last night. Wish to God you had to tote wood on one leg like I got to.

Yes, said Laurel, tis your turn, Flory. Go get some wood like a good boy.

Well. . . . Generously he offered an entire stick of the brown candy to his sister, and she crushed it with her little teeth in rapture.

Reckon, said Flory, speaking casually from the doorway— Reckon I'll be going for a soldier.

Reckon you'll shit, said his brother.

Coral, you forget I'm a lady! came Laurel's thin moan. Ma won't tolerate no such talk from you. She'll give you a whipping if'n I tell her, crutch or no crutch. What makes you think they'd take you for a soldier, Flory?

Hope to shout they would. I heard them soldiers a-telling of it. Down to Uncle Arch's just now. Said they had them new regiments name of Georgia Reserves, and they'll take any number of boys my size. So I reckon I'll go.

Well, you get that wood first, dad blast you, cried Coral.

Intoxicated by notions of military accomplishment, Flory obeyed. He would not have responded to a just and deserved summons at any other time, but he was entranced by the thought that soon he might be marching and fighting in gray. No longer a child, no longer creeping in the guise of an outcast from even a portion of his own family. . . . Soldiers owned money. They must own it, else how could so many of them visit Flory's mother? She did not give her female valuables away: she sold them. (Had Floral but known it, he was contrived from a gift. His father had tried to sell Dr. Krieder's Ague Pills to Mrs. Dickwood Tebbs; his father had failed in the attempt simply because Mrs. Tebbs had no cash with which to buy pills, and said that she would rely on soot coffee, as most people did, for the ague. But she liked the blond limber-tongued young ignoramus who came soliciting her. He offered also a panacea for looseness of the bowels which he called Mother Felch's Blackberry Balm. . . . Blackberry?— repeated the woman. We got a sight of blackberries in our lane. Come nighttime I like to have myself a little stroll, and nibble at them blackberries. . . . Reckon you'll be strolling amongst them blackberries tonight? . . . Could be, mister. . . . She strolled, he was waiting, they rolled in illicit rapture. The salesman went drifting away with satchel and pack, with glib speech and limited jokes; he left the ripe seed which was Floral within her body.)

Flory had heard soldiers speak of chicken-guts. In time he'd have chicken-guts upon his sleeves.

Old pistols? No. A navy revolver, captivated off of the Yanks.

A horse. He'd never ridden a horse, but— He'd ridden a lame mule when they owned one. A horse—

We jumped them Yankees nigh side of the stream. They was shooting our asses off. I got turkey bumps all over my blame body.

Right oblique—hah!

Pre-sent—hah!

Rear, open order—hah!

Would they actually pay him eleven dollars a month? Even Secesh?

Flory brought in the wood, he brought in three armloads of wood. I declare to God, said his brother.

Floral Tebbs felt his way in darkness to the remains of the stable— half of the roof still hung there, but badly supported—and found that Captain Oxford Puckett's mule still chewed at old corn-shucks. Quietly Flory crept to the doorstep of The Crib. He hunched, entertaining fancies. At the house he'd gathered his section of blanket, he'd twisted the rag around him, it gave him as much warmth as he needed. The entrance to The Crib was on the south side and out of the wind. From within came muffled exclamations, the grunting of weight on bed-ropes, a faint light through cracks, and suddenly the caroling of the old music box. The instrument played well despite the grim treatment it had suffered. It had been kicked and dropped, ignored, wound up hour after hour, not oiled for years, oiled too lavishly and with the wrong sort of oil. The spiny cylinder turned slowly, and some of the spines were worn or broken away, but tunes had an elfin tinkle about them despite gaps and cluckings.

Inside the building, Captain Ox Puckett spoke loudly as if come to a sudden decision. Ma'am, you got all the smart out of my marbles. Reckon I'll head for that blame camp.

We drunk all the pine-top, honey?

Sure enough.

Oh, I do hope you come back to see me again.

Surely will, when the spirit starts a-working. Here's them two greenbacks, and I wish they was more, but also I got to live. Hain't many Yanks come in with cash in hand; the bulk is from Danville or Belle Isle, up Virginia way, and they got cleaned long ago.

Ox, bless you, I do love that extra greenback.

Fitten you should have it.

Floral listened to Captain Puckett getting into his clothes and stamping in his boots. Prompted by a vague shame, Floral arose and walked to a respectable distance. He stood, palpitating with illusions, until the door of The Crib opened and Puckett was revealed with the shine of candlelight on white beard and hair. He was creasing his old slouched hat, smoothing out the brim preparatory to wearing the hat.

Captain, sir, said Flory.

Ox Puckett squinted into the gloom. Sakes, Flory, is that you?

I want you should tell me something.

Come here to the door, you Flory.

The Widow Tebbs appeared behind the man, pulling a ragged beribboned wrapper around her. Flory, child, you ought to be abed.

It hain't late. Captain, I was scheming to go for a soldier.

Puckett laughed shrilly. God, you got the milk still wet on your mouth, bubby.

But I was down to Uncle Arch's and I heard them soldiers a-talking. They call it the Georgia Reserves; and tis said they'll take folks my size.

Ox Puckett said judiciously, Well, I know of four regiments of Reserves they're planning to muster, and maybe there's many more. But that hain't no life for a soldier: the lame and halt and blind. Course, you're just a mere child.

The widow cried, He hain't but twelve.

That's a no count lie, yelled Flory. You know well enough I'm growed to thirteen, nigh onto fourteen.

Looky here, Ox, said Mag fervently. What befell my eldest? Skun away to the army when he weren't more than fifteen, and now he's got to hop on a crutch for the rest of his days.

The bearded captain turned, leaned toward her, whispered something. Floral could not hear what he said.

Do tell? Just guard duty?

The captain whispered again.

And they do get paid?

Oh, like all armies. When and if.

But they get their provender?

Field rations. Keep soul and body in the same piece.

Floral stood ragged and wispy, barely within the vague spot of light which fell from the open door. With that cape of blanket hooded over his close-cropped head and around his weak shoulders it was hard to tell whether he was boy or girl. He was all of five feet tall. My, said his mother, Government must be hard up for soldiers if they'd take Flory.

Captain Ox Puckett fastened his belt buckle. You give forth a mouthful, lady. Where's the flower of the South? It got scythed down. We won't never have the Nation we had before. But if ever we're to whip them Yanks, the boys and old folks got to help. Take

my regiment or take them Alabama troops alongside us, measly as
they be: we got experience in the field. We could be used in the
field. Even a younger size of Flory could stand up on that parapet
over yonder and keep an eye on them prisoners so's they wouldn't
bust loose.

Well, I never.

You hear that, Ma? cried Flory in delight.

Yah, yah, yah, I heard. Now you cut for bed.

Captain Ox, please, sir. Do you know any generals?

Puckett put his heels together. Bubby, you can't serve in two wars
and not know some generals. More'n once I've stood as close to General Lee as I'm standing to you. And once I fit along of One-eyed
Jeff when you couldn't tell beans from musket balls count of the
powder smoke.

One-eyed Jeff?

President Jefferson Davis, if you like. Twas in Mexico.

Captain Ox, please, reckon you might fix it up for me to get in
the army?

Just in them Georgia Reserves, Flory.

But ain't they going to be a army?

Oh, kind of. Hell, I weren't much bigger'n you when first I went
hunting for a yard of skirmish line.

Well, I never, said the Widow Tebbs. Flory, you cut for bed like
I bid you.

Flory cut. Half the night he shivered restlessly beside the snoring
half-brother who hated him, and whom he hated. His thin brain
rattled with shots, bugle calls, orders, cannon rumblings, stirrup
squeakings, the clangor of bayonets. By God, he thought in a last
succumbing to weariness, I might even get to shoot a Yankee. . . .
Poom.

XV

In one of his several military capacities (in this case in the role of provost-marshal at Richmond) John Winder had spent most of the morning in preparation for the calling of a court martial and of inquiry. Also he had assailed verbally, with bellowing heard through four flimsy partitions, heard with fright by the five men and two women who waited his whim in the barren reception hall— He had assailed a Goochland County planter whose crime was not that of proven disloyalty but of anti-Secession sentiment uttered in his own neighborhood some three years before. The fact that the planter had since lost a son and a son-in-law at Cedar Mountain, and had had another Confederate soldier son crippled in a skirmish just before Second Manassas, did not serve as extenuation for his previous sin— not in General Winder's opinion.

Denied recourse to any code of chivalry, the unhappy Virginian was compelled to stand like a criminal before the desk of a Marylander and hear himself likened to spies, hirelings, Abolitionists, nigger-lovers, Lovejoys, Butlers and Thaddeus Stevenses, each epithet hurled with its dressing of profanity. The egg-smell of sulphur was in the air of that office and of adjacent corridors. The planter stumbled out, hurt and maddened, fortunate at not being ordered into prison for the evil he had committed: requesting a pass through the lines for a sister who was married to a Pennsylvanian and had long sought to leave the Confederacy and join her sickly elderly husband at the North.

Old J.H.W. is raring, whispered a one-legged corporal to a palsied sergeant.

Lordy, yes. You got those letters of appointment and assembly duly copied?

Right here, but I don't want to put my head through that door.

Better wait till he's calmed, Joey.

If ever!

John Winder was in no hurry for the letters of appointment and assembly. He had formed a habit through his sixty-four years of life; he preferred to sit brooding silently on whatever foul nest he'd constructed with the beak and claws of his hatred. He would warm those tough little orbs of wrath, let them hatch logical fledglings when again his rage needed reinforcement. He sat nearly motionless, glowering at the present, resentful of the future, distasteful of the past. His untidy gray hair dripped in strings below fat crooked ears, there were ink stains and stains of age upon his fat crooked fingers, the scars of consistent bitterness came down between his bulging eyes. The scar where Amos the slave had wounded him with a razor last October— It was whitely apparent on the pulp around his compressed mouth.

He had witnessed his own red blood turning to black in the year of 1814, when he was fourteen. The blood had been black ever since; he knew it, waking or sleeping; he felt it moving like pitch through the veins tangled throughout his big body. When his skin was pierced and blood ran, John Winder was invariably surprised to observe its crimson, for truly it was acrid black, he must be color blind—the world must be color blind not to know—his blood had been black since that day on the oyster bar in Somerset County not far from Rewston where John Winder was born.

What my father said, said Gay Chastain.

That old Winder was a coward? asked Freddy Darlington.

Father said he should be shot because he let the British take Washington.

Freddy was nigh to sixteen in age and nigh to eighteen in size, Gay Chastain was even heavier and more dangerous if not so old; what might Johnny Winder do about this? Not one thing. What could he do? Nothing. The slur was there, the tale of his father's inefficiency (at the best) or demoralization (considered possible in less charitable opinion) or downright cowardice and resulting deeds which named him as a traitor. It should not happen to you at fourteen, to have your father named as a traitor because he was held responsible for losing the fight at Bladensburg. It should not happen to you, it should not happen to a dog, not to the meanest slave in the parish, not to the most sluggish oyster crab, not to the wounded oyster eaten by the crab.

Johnny Winder stood rooted to the muddy bar, hammer in one hand, bucket in the other. It had all begun as a lark. He was glad that these elder youths had invited him to come oystering with them, for a lark like this might help him to forget the whispered odium newly attached to his father's name. They had fetched crab-cakes and biscuits, they had filched Tipsy Squire pudding from a suspicious brown tyrant who presided over the Chastain kitchen and larder, they had ridden far in their cart, had prided themselves on the size of the oysters they would break loose in a secret cove.

But in this moment wine was gone from the strong cool wind,

ragged waves of tidewater bit like rats at John Winder's wet boots.
He stood behind the shoreline thicket and heard his playmates turning themselves into torturers because they repeated some common
gossip, and thought that John was fifty rods to the windward instead
of prowling that same shaggy bar.

Attack them with his oyster knife, with his hammer? No, they
owned similar weapons, they were bigger than he, they were two.
Run home, fetch his double-barreled pistol, lie behind the oak at
Five Corners, shoot them down as they drove past on the homeward
trip (and probably wondering what had become of John even as the
round bullets flew through their young bodies)? One could not shoot
down the entire county, not shoot down the Nation, all the States.
(Or could one? Later he pondered. Ardently John Henry Winder
welcomed the advance of Secession forty-six years later, even before
his commission as a major in the Regular establishment had been
signed.)

Nothing could be as black, nothing had ever been blacker . . .
mud in empty shells, old housings of dead oysters, the mud was
squeezed into ink, almost it dyed the wet skin when it touched the
skin. He looked down through the smart of tears and saw cold jet
dripping from his fingertips . . . jet, jet, his blood had turned, oh
watch it dripping.

Somewhere between that awful island and the wilderness of low
mainland John Winder dropped his oyster bucket with its carefully
selected freight, and so the bucket must have been buried beneath
Chesapeake tides later. But still he gripped his hammer; he found the
small boat which belonged to Fred Darlington and which they'd used
for many an expedition, and he burst the boat's ribs, mauling away
in blind fury; it seemed that he owned the bull strength of the most
powerful blacksmith. He found Nap the pony tethered at a fence
corner where they'd left him, and Nap belonged to Johnny Winder
although the cart didn't. He unharnessed Nap, he rode him home
bareback, he left the others to guess, to grieve over the ruined boat,
to walk all the way to the nearest plantation and borrow a nag to
draw their deserted vehicle.

They sought John Winder later for questioning, they demanded
that he give an account of himself, that he pay for the boat, that he
apologize. Eventually he drew out his penknife. The Chastain youth
gave him a thrashing and threw the knife into the inlet nearby. John
Winder went home to load his pistol—his father found him, loading
the pistol. He was reprimanded, threatened with the lash, exhorted
to manly conduct, informed that an eventual court of inquiry would
most certainly exonerate his father when those orders issued to his
father by General Armstrong came to light. This prophecy was cor-

rect. General William Henry Winder was acquitted in the spring of 1815; he was reassigned to his command, but resigned promptly.

When John was a cadet at the Point three or four years later, he thought of that silly double-barreled pistol, and how he'd intended to take the lives of young Darlington and young Chastain because of their slurs; he thought of it when his father expressed to him a copy of the *Trials of the Mail Robbers, Hare, Alexander and Hare,* published in Baltimore with his father's pleas in behalf of the accused presented verbatim. *What is the* use *of dangerous weapons which can occasion* jeopardy *of life? . . . The use of dangerous weapons, to produce* duce *fear* of life *may be very different from the* use *of dangerous weapons, to put life in* jeopardy. *. . .* But certainly he, Johnny Winder, had intended to slay his quondam friends and thus get himself hanged triumphantly; he had not intended merely to frighten them. Ah, he would have accomplished his purpose if not restrained, for already his blood was black (he thought of the paint of oyster muck running down his hands) and it was a secret, naturally; but still it was odd that all might not see and understand.

Florida, Contreras, Churubusco, Mexico City. Consistently he exposed himself through those old campaigns. Twice came the brevets— once as major, once as lieutenant-colonel. No medals were offered, the brevet was sole recognition for a man who'd nerved himself to suicide when he was fourteen and had never recovered from the nerving. The National government became a composite demon. It was like the demons who beset an uncomfortable childhood . . . composed of moonlight, sycamore shade, mists, the shade of other trees, the distant thin light of stray stars which vied with the moon. Amid tangles of garden or driveway John Winder had glimpsed demons when he was small; they attended him, labeled Federal Government or National Interest, through a military career which covered forty-odd years (if a man subtracted the four years he'd spent as a resigned lieutenant, and added the years when he was a cadet).

Federal Government. Ogre. Tarred his father, pilloried him before the public gaze, drove the son into a studied heroism amid powder smoke when he would have been happier in flight, turned the son's blood to black.

John Winder had desired that children should be trained to scorn the National government as he scorned it, to loathe the Yankees as he loathed them, to crush all supporters of that Faith as one would snap the shell of a cockroach with his boot sole and feel the shell pop, feel gush and squirting, find happiness in the smear made so.

. . . His aide tiptoed into the office, making himself appear as insignificant as possible. This was not difficult since the aide was an insignificant man to begin with. Winder found a bully's satisfaction in towering beside insignificance.

Where is the list of officers eligible for the court martial and of inquiry?

The aide came hastening to lift a paperweight in the shape of a pink cat with two paws broken off. Once General Winder, in ordinary temper, had thrown that paperweight through a windowpane. Clerks scrambled into the street to recover it; the paws had been glued back but they would not stick for long.

Here is the list, sir.

What of the letters of appointment and assembly?

All copied, sir. I'll have them fetched—

Never mind now. I want the classification of charges!

I'll fetch it, sir.

Well, God damn it, hurry up! He had brooded on eggs of anger, they were ready to hatch, he could feel them cracking under the weight of his broad stagnant bottom.

Court would convene, a heart or two might be broken (that would be fair, if many hearts were mashed), the details relating to proceedings and sentences would be written up, the long confinement would commence. Let newspapers say what they would of him. He cared nothing for newspapers.

When, a furious editorial writer had demanded lately, will Richmond ever be rid of Old Winder?

Let them scream, spread their type, let them print, foam, froth, weep, clench their fists, gnash futile teeth.

He sat at the table of the President, he sat there frequently. John Winder might not be the most popular officer to enter the bar at the Spotswood Hotel, he might not be regarded too affectionately by fellow Episcopalians, meeowings might sound behind him in the street if there were a safe crowd about; but he wondered often if there was another brigadier who had the ear and unalterable patronage of Mr. Seddon and Mr. Davis as he held them. He knew that there was none. His curiosity on the subject was perfunctory, a judicious exploration of other political intrigue observed by him, resulting always in the fatuous knowledge that his position would not be changed until he desired it to be changed.

Brigadier-general, commander of the Department of Henrico, inspector-general of camps in the Richmond area, Supervisor of Prisons, provost-marshal-general of Richmond . . . in time, perhaps, Commissary-General of all prisoners held by the Confederacy? It would be a wise move on the part of the President to initiate this appointment, it would be a wise move for Mr. Seddon to expedite it. John Henry Winder would see to it that those same Yankees did not plague the Confederate nation further.

. . . In the 1820's weather was cold, the valley of the Hudson was a polar ice-cap, the Hudson was frozen tight. Students of the United

States Military Academy blew out white steam as they ran to their classrooms, they ran through heavy snow, there was a great deal of snow and it was impossible to clear it away.

Cadet Davis could be remembered mainly as a hobbledehoy with glinting eyes and abnormally large hands which always twitched (contrary to regulation) when the youth delivered a recitation in the presence of his tactical instructor.

His tactical instructor was a lieutenant named J. H. Winder.

Gentlemen, the Grecian army, at the period when the military art was in greatest perfection among the Greeks, was composed of infantry and cavalry. The former was made up of three different orders of soldiers. I shall request one of you to describe to us the three orders of Grecian infantry. Mr. Davis.

Huge hands gripping tightly, gripping nothing. Sir. Heavily armed were the *Oplitai*. They wore very complete defensive armor, and bore the *sarissa*. Macedonian pike—a formidable weapon about twenty-four feet in length. Light infantry were the *Psiloi;* no defensive armor; customarily they carried javelin, bow and sling. Intermediate between these two grades—

Not grades, Mr. Davis. Orders.

—Between these two orders— Thank you, sir. Between these two orders of infantry were the *Peltastae*. They wore a lighter defensive armor than the *Oplitai;* also bore a shorter pike.

Thank you, Mr. Davis.

. . . Thank you indeed, Mr. Davis. You will be Secretary of War when I am still a Regular captain, and you will not remember my skillful tactical instruction at the time, nor seek me out for well-deserved promotion, but— But that will be the fault of the Federal demon whom we both serve. When once we are no longer serving that demon— Thank you again, Mr. Davis.

The aide placed the classification of charges upon Winder's desk.

Who's outside?

The usual, sir.

Nothing usual about any of them. Except they're always a God damn nuisance. That man Betterson come back?

No, sir. Not yet, sir.

Tis just as well. Who's there?

Those two ladies again—Mrs. Polling and Mrs. Leftwich.

Yes, yes—son and husband in the calaboose. Son of a bitch ought to hang—feeding an escaped Yankee prisoner—

Doctor Kendrick—

He'll get no pass from me! Tell him to go way.

Yes, sir.

Tell him I'll place him under arrest next time he comes bothering!

Yes, sir. A Mr. Lee from over in Manchester—

Any kin to the general?

I don't think so, sir. He wants—

What mean you, Captain? *You don't think so!* Do you *know?*

No, sir. I didn't ask him, sir. I mean to say—

Anyway I'm too dratted busy. Tell him to go way.

A Mr. Buckland and a Mr. Prentice—they seem to be together, sir. Mr. Prentice has but one arm—I think he's a veteran, sir.

Did you ask him? Do you *know?* Why don't you present a few *facts,* God damn it?

And a Captain Wirz—

Who? Ah. With a beard?

Yes, sir. He's here in response to an order—

So he is. Send him in.

Henry Wirz had been sitting as he sat before in other offices, cap upon his knee, pained eyes darting inquisitively and disapprovingly over fellow petitioners in the anteroom. Once again he was in uniform; he had worn that uniform since he crept aboard the blockade runner in a French port, he had worn it for fear of capture by the Federals, he had no wish to be executed as a spy. The swollen right forearm was wound in its dirty black cloth, the thin face was set in the ice of longing. Wirz dreamed of freedom from hurt, he dreamed of rank and emoluments, he wished that his name were known, he prayed that one day his name would be known throughout the Confederate States. Captain Peschau came to bend down, put his pomaded head near Wirz's and to announce in a stage whisper which all might hear (and thus know that they were kept waiting, because Wirz had arrived later than the others), General'll see you now, Captain.

Danke— Thank you.

When Wirz stood alone before the wide cracked marble-topped table which served as one of Winder's desks, the general grunted and motioned toward a chair. He sat staring moodily at Wirz for at least twenty slow seconds after the captain had seated himself. Winder was applying deliberate discomfort, putting Wirz in his place, castigating him silently for wrongs which Henry Wirz could not identify or even recollect; yet he felt that he must have committed them, and hoped that he would not be stripped of his tiny rank.

Uh—Wirz.

Ja, mein General.

Worked for me before. . . .

Ja, sir. It was at Libby. Also in that Tuscaloosa.

Uh—long leave of absence—

Sir, in Europe I was. It is my arm. The wound I got from Seven Pines. But also I take dispatches and they name me Special Minister Plenipotentiary.

Uh—how's the arm?

The great pain I have. Sometimes it is so bad—

I'm no surgeon, said Winder harshly. Don't fret me with your ailments. It matters only that you're fit for duty or you're not. Are you fit?

Henry stiffened briskly and nodded his head many times. *Ja,* General Winder, I am fit.

Stop bobbing about.

Ja, sir!

After a time John Winder had softened his tone until it was near to a caress. Captain Wirz, do you bear any love for the Yankees?

Ach! Love?

I put a question to you. That same soft voice.

Is it I must now love the enemy? *Nein.* I hate them much!

Why, Captain?

Because— Why, because it is coercion! They invade the Sister States, they come with sword and fire, our rights they would trample—

And—your arm, Captain?

Ja, I tell you what they do to me! *Mein* General, I also was one surgeon before the war, and I tell you that my radius and ulna—

You wouldn't feel like—coddling Yankees?

What means this coddling, General?

Oh, treating them soft as silk. (His voice was softer than silk.) Babying them. Being—kind to them, Captain.

Kind? We must be stern. We must show them who is boss!

The thin mouth in the huge face began to curl lazily at its lined corners. John Henry Winder was cooing. Since you went abroad, Captain, we have constructed a new prison. My own son Sid was empowered to select the site and get the place in readiness; and it seems that he has performed his duties capably. It's in Sumter County, Georgia, near a little village called Anderson—

XVI

Dear *Cousin* Lucy, wrote Harrell Elkins, making a great gesture of his use of *Cousin* and underscoring the word in red ink as a pleasantry which he considered reckless. It is a weary hour, ten after ten by Grandfather Elkins' gold watch which is my sole fortune, if one excepts those acres at present untilled! I am weary to the point of desolation, yet find a comfort in projecting myself into the Claffey home and partaking of the company of those whom I cannot help but regard with fondness. May I be permitted to do so?

Why, you forward creature, thought Lucy in response to the mood. And then, stirred with secret guilt in remembering that Harrell Elkins now appeared consistently in her sensual dream, she could not drive him away although consciously she tried. She lowered the letter in her hand, closed her eyes, and reconstructed Rob Lamar. Far gone, far gone. She lifted the letter and absorbed Cousin Harry's polite inquiries as to her health, her father's health, his expressed hope that the condition of her mother had improved.

. . . You ask me to tell you of my work, yet it might be considered a repulsive task to any individual not of the medical persuasion. Lately I have traveled to one of our hospitals where hospital gangrene caused severe mortality. I assisted Dr. Joseph Jones in performing a series of *post mortems* and learned much. At his behest I wrote a preliminary report for the eyes of our Surgeon General; doubtless this will be promptly filed away; but how could one act upon it if he had the inclination to do so? Suppose I write—and I quote with pride: While the clots were absent in cases in which there were no inflammatory symptoms, their presence in other cases sustains the conclusion that hospital gangrene is a species of inflammation in which the fibrous element and coagulation of the blood are increased, even in those who are suffering from such condition of the blood, and from such diseases as are naturally accompanied with a decrease in the fibrous constituent. Suppose I write this (and I did). Is there any immediate and direct decrease in human suffering, is the ugliness alleviated? Are our men—more of them—returned in good fettle to their arduous hazard in the field? Not that it can be noticed! What may a scientist do but recommend? The practicalist, the Chief of Staff, the quartermaster, the commissariat: these and only these may expedite a reform. One fair shipload of drugs from the Continent of Europe would serve more purpose than a thousand such reports; and (gloomily) would serve more purpose than a thousand such men as write the reports. . . . On re-reading the foregoing I diagnose myself as suffering from a severe case of *cholera morbid,* if the pun may be excused.

. . . We fellows, when serving at the front, were accustomed to cracking raucous jokes in imitation of the orator who, secure in the certainty that age or physical disability or political expediency kept him from courting bullets, puffed forth his bombast: Would that I were only younger (or less corpulent or less generally bombproof)! How gladly would I shoulder a musket beside you brave lads, with what lightness of heart would I march at your side & & & et cetera. Well, be it said, dear *Cousin,* that now I find myself in that peculiar position which two years agone I would have scorned to High Heaven. Has your father need of a good overseer? Assuredly I could keep the black people contented and industrious; my very jocularities should turn the trick! May I apply to you for Good Character??

. . . Must have underestimated the Yankees in more ways than one. Now we approach the entering of the *Fourth Year* of conflict. At first it appears that we underestimated their *fighting* qualities. (I did, for one, and to my pain.) Next, their *staying* qualities. Over all, their *productive* capacity. Were we ever whipped, it should be a sad thing were we whipped by this ironclad blockade and (array me at strict Attention before the muzzles of a firing squad) by the blunderings of our Executive and his Fellow Cooks Spoiling the Broth. The adminis-tration of the Confederacy's military affairs approaches poltroonery! We had our opportunity, we had it on a round dozen occasions. No one might be allowed to act upon it. Now, after toiling for nearly three years, what is the sum? The lines in Virginia lie within a comfortable stroll of where they lay in 1861 (but there are little birds speaking of a vigorous onslaught soon to be entered upon by the Yanks, following the inevitable change in command). The ligatures of the blockade are shutting off our life's blood. The Federals control the Mississippi and its affluents. Thus the Department of the Trans-Mississippi must be written off, except for its nuisance value. Who owns New Orleans? The Federals. Who have swept not too triumphantly to the very door-step of Georgia (yet indeed they have swept)? The National army. Who have invaded boldly upon Florida soil, even though sent pack-ing at Olustee? The National army. *Cousin,* my lamentation is longer than Jeremiah's, and could get me a prison cell at best were it made public. Observe how I trust to your discretion?

. . . So there is naught to do but to proceed with one's task as faith-fully as one may. There is naught to do but close one's eyes to the in-fernal maneuverings of arm-chair busy-bodies who, to indulge slangily, rule the roost. I have applied repeatedly for a post of more activity; but there seems to be an especial pigeon-hole wherein my applications are stuffed, with passage pigeons flying nobly away with them from tother end. Daily (or rather nightly, when I am alone and seeking slumber) I recreate a panorama of Claffey acres, Claffey verandah, Claffey repasts, Claffey beauty & courage. See what selfish fruit your combined hospitality bore! Are there more violets in adjacent woodlands, *Cousin?* Or have you time for the seeking? I judge there must be none any longer within the confines of the prison pen itself, since it must be in an increasingly trampled condition.

Now it is past midnight, and the spirit weakens along with the flare of this inadequate lamp. Pray think of me kindly. I think of thee & thine with respect and admiration and with whatever degree of tenderness might be allowed. Y'r servant, *Cousin.* Harrell Elkins, Surgeon, P.A., C.S.

Lucy Claffey wrote to him, Would that I could offer better news of my mother, but I cannot. She has taken to having her meals above stairs; and, even worse, insists that her tray be brought not into her own room but into the room once occupied by the youngest, Moses, where also she keeps all objects pertaining to the memory of my brothers. In vain might I insist that her course is unhealthy and bound to destroy sanity. Such contention is useless: she has a will of iron, but a cold and unseeing will. Frequently she ventures forth in the evening, walking alone in her cloak if the air be chilly. Poppy attempted to accompany her at first; she would have none of it; then he ordered one of the wenches to accompany her, which Ninny does but ineffectually.

Enough of gloomy topics, Cousin Harry. What shall I tell you of those Claffey acres which you prize? I just fear I'm a poor interpreter of horticultural activities and always was. (Would that I might be allowed to be a nurse. Then should I meet you eventually in the tented field, no doubt?) Father is deeply concerned with asparagus at the present, and thus we have asparagus for dinner—as a topic of conversation, not as yet garnished with sour sauce. It seems that we are shy of salt, and not likely to obtain salt in quantity for some time to come, with the railroad so busy feeding both Lee's and Gen. Johnston's armies. The asparagus beds should have had a top-dressing of salt, two pounds to the square yard; hence Father is fretful about it. Mighty little do I understand, as well, about the production of beans which are now being planted or have been planted; but it appears that we have had such an awful lot of rain during March that the seed is liable to spoil without germinating! Land sakes. I do listen, and try to understand, for Poppy has no one else in whom to confide or to whom to complain! There is something about the pole beans which should have been planted simultaneously with the main crop of bush beans; but this he must explain when again he takes pen in hand &c.

Jem cut his foot severely, poor old black thing, on some instrument of endeavor—is it called a dibble?—and goes hobbling about. I really can't say that I wished for Jem to be hurt, for he is a good hand if he has no more wits than a duck; but it *did* give me a fair opportunity to indulge in what the boys used to call my Florence Nightmare tactics. Thus I have bathed his foot and tended him devotedly, and am rewarded by observing a good healthy uniting of his tissues in the laceration of that broad ebony foot. Once again, Surgeon, have you employment for me in the field?

. . . As an infrequent guest we welcome one Lieut. Col. Alexander Persons, now in command at this post.

(This statement was received with disquietude by Surgeon Elkins.)

. . . It seems that the command is divided, in theory, into three separate and distinct departments. I append this information for the interest of yourself as a military man. One officer in command of the *troops,* another in command of the *prison,* a third in command of the *post.* Colonel Persons is post commander; I think there is no prison officer on duty as yet, though he informs me that there are upwards of seven thousand Yankees in the pen at this writing, and a lot more to come. Land. What if they should get loose? Colonel Persons says it is needless to worry. He does not come often, since he is so hard put to, as he declares, make bricks without straw.

. . . The Rev. Mr. Cato Dillard, whom I called Uncle Dayto when I was small (and he insists that I apply the appellation still) was here with his wife for a night. Sakes. I do not mean that she is his wife *temporarily*—that could scarcely be, for they have scads of grandchildren—two lately dead in the army at the North, poor things. I mean that we were fortunate to have them as guests for one night, and Col. Persons came along to help eat the *pig.* Dearie me, the pig's name was Sec Stanton, and he was one of my favorites. Poppy said that he shouldn't be killed, now that the merc. rose to eighty-seven degrees the other day; but we were fresh out of meat, and Man must be served. (Also Woman. Naomi did a just heavenly fresh ham.) Do you enjoy theological—or is it metaphysical?—discussions, Coz? I just don't understand them, but beg leave to report, since my father will not *participate.* He says there is too much theology in the world, and not enough food to go round, and not enough honeysuckle, and too many tears. Well.

. . . While we award much learning and piety to men, we search the Scriptures, and bring every man's theory to this inspired test. That is Uncle Dayto speaking. Col. Persons: Every man's theory must differ. Rev. Cato Dillard: We accept or reject his theory, just as it may be in accord with, or differ from, God's revealed will. Mr. Ira Claffey: There's a nearly full moon; shall we adjourn to the gallery outside? Col. Alex Persons: I must return to the post. So many matters to claim my attention— Uncle Dayto Dillard: You have said that you did not believe in the doctrine of election because you did not understand it. But do you understand the mystery of Godliness—God manifest in the flesh? You agree that you believe that, and yet you accept it on the divine veracity. Col. Persons: Four hundred and fifty more Yankees due tonight, or so I was informed. I can't trust to the telegraph, sir. Mr. Ira Claffey: As I was saying awhile back, if you don't wash in the slips of the Hayti yam when you take them up in dry weather, it is of great advantage to grout them. Rev. Mr. Dillard: Can you not believe the doctrine of election simply because it is taught in the Bible, even though you do not understand it? Mrs. Effie Dillard: Cate, don't be an old blether. (She is Scotch.) Col. P.: What is *grout?* Mr. Claffey: That means to dip the yam slips into water thickened with rich earth— a thin mud, a muddy soup, I suppose you'd term it. It refreshes the slips, and gives them a thin coating of earth as a protection against the atmosphere. Rev. Dayto Dillard: If it be a doctrine of the Bible—and you cannot deny, according to your lights, that it is clearly taught— then you are *bound to believe it,* or make God a liar! Mrs. Effie Dillard: God's no liar, mon! Set a watch upon your lips. Uncle Dayto: Ah, we must have reverence enough for the perfections of His character to believe all that He has revealed, whether it comes in antagonism with our own previous opinions or not! Col. P.: Did they say four hundred and fifty Yanks, or was it five hundred? I must take leave, Mr. Claffey, and— Mr. Ira Claffey: Such a pleasant night. I'll walk a piece with you, Colonel. The Rev. Mr. Cato Dillard: Ah, tis a pity, Colonel, that I did not first meet you when you were a boy.

You will see, Cousin Harry, life at the Claffeys' is not sedentary these days.

(Damn Colonel Persons, remarked Surgeon Elkins honestly.)

. . . Trains come plunging with a regularity they did not exhibit in the piping times of Peace. Should I be at work on the west side of the house, I salute them through the window or through springtime foliage, and trust (when they bear to the North) that they are well loaded with viands for the armies. I know that I should reverence each sharp-pointed cow-catcher, each set of tall wheels, each funnel-shaped stack like an enormous weight above the cab & boiler and— What call you those round things? I shall go and ask Poppy. He says steam-dome. But they *do* make noise and ugliness, and soot blows far across the fields and (of this I am nearly positive) finds lodgment in the stray tresses of one Miss L. Claffey, and must needs be washed out.

. . . There is little more to relate, except the vagary of Nature herself, which as we know is a pattern and a repetition; yet each act of Nature seems new. I rise to the colored sunrise before six, and make my sad hymn of approval to the Creator as I dress myself. The field of onion tops is richly green; and above and beyond lie flat broken platters of mist hanging at various levels over the terrain—thin, solid, motionless. Somewhere (could it have been at the Female Institute, where I studied *useful and ornamental branches, including the French language*) I have witnessed such a beauty. Was it some strange print brought from the Orient? I know not. Friend *Coz,* I must up and be busy; the world's work is to be done, and I must do my share. These last lines are penned whilst I lie abed in the morning, but I am no lady of leisure. Breakfast odors soar aloft. Uncle Dayto is stopping by again this week; he and my father are soon to view the interior of the prison pen, as invited by Col. P. to do so. I presume they will stand upon one of the sentinels' platforms. Seven thousand ferocious Yankees? I should not call that a pleasant sight, nor should I desire to join the gentlemen in their junket had I been included in the invitation. Still it is no pastime for a lady, so they say. Will military exigencies prevail upon you to visit this region once again? I pray that they will. I have gathered no violets of late. With all wishes for your health & happiness, I remain, Y'r fond *Cousin,* Lucy C.

This letter lay in Cato Dillard's pocket, to be put into the mail by him later, when he stood crowded atop the stockade with Ira Claffey and Lieutenant-Colonel Persons. The Reverend Mr. Dillard and the post commander had many acquaintances in common in the Fort Valley region; Dillard had lived in that area where Macon, Houston and Crawford Counties pressed together. In whimsy the minister was constantly inquiring about the fishing in Mossy Creek, Bay Creek, Indian Creek—all the creeks adjacent to Fort Valley which he was sure that Persons should know now as well as he, Cato Dillard, had known them years before.

Ira stared at the prison and was in no mood to consider quiet streams and shiners flickering. He witnessed an ugliness which his worst imagination had balked at contriving. The last occasion when he'd gazed at the area was before those first scrawny columns moved in by firelight. Now he did not know how to term the nastiness. A rabbit warren, a den of rats tangling, chunky snakes upturned by a bottom-land plow? The free-piled stumps and brushy tangles were evaporated. A community of huts spread loosely over the slopes like warts, like protruding wounds with corners on them. Rags, brown pine boughs, blankets, sodden overcoats and oilskins: the earth festered with tunneling, cellaring, burrowing; materials were draped on sticks; and all space between was pimpled with moving humanity. Or name it inhumanity—

Shebangs, said Persons. That's the term the Yanks apply to their shelters.

How many men living in each one?

Any number you wish to name. Some live alone, many by twos or fours. The larger huts hold more.

Why are the men's faces so black? I thought in the first glimpse that you were holding all niggers.

Fat pine, said Persons. The smoke of their fires has darkened them.

How many thousand prisoners did you say?

Upwards of seven thousand, at the moment.

It appeared to Ira Claffey that there were not enough huts to furnish shelter for all.

You're correct in that assumption, sir. Many of the prisoners had no coats or blankets in the hour of their capture, or were robbed before entering the stockade, or afterward. They've had nothing to build with; thus they didn't build.

They sleep out, in complete exposure to the elements?

As you can see, no shelter was provided when the stockade was raised.

Ah, yes. I remember when Captain Winder was approached on that topic, and I recall his reply.

At this mention of Sid Winder the glance of Persons and the glance of Claffey met and held. The soldier recognized even more painfully than the citizen that there was a malignant connotation in the name of Winder as applied to individuals associated with this place. Both men had encountered the ruling genius—the father and cousin—and had formed their opinions of his character independently of whatever noisome reputation he possessed in the Confederate capital. Both knew the son. As for Cousin Dick (commonly believed to be General Winder's nephew because of disparity in age) only Persons was unfortunate enough to hold contact with him. Richard B. Winder was like his cousin a staff officer of the general's, and now wore the title of quartermaster of this expanding pest-hole. Lieutenant-Colonel Persons had been forced to stand by helplessly while Dick Winder superintended, in bored surly fashion, the construction of a bakery. The sheds stood on a slope above the creek immediately west of the stockade; Persons pointed out that its drainage would flow into the creek before the stream entered the pen; Captain R. B. Winder ignored the field officer as pointedly as the cousin of a commanding general might if he were particularly inept and selfish.

The quartermaster remarked to a subordinate within Persons' hearing, I have no orders to report to any quartermaster at all, no orders to report to any officer commanding troops in another capacity. I report directly to Richmond. I receive my instructions from Richmond.

In this application of nepotism even the headquarters of the Georgia Reserves at Macon were by-passed. Alexander Persons detested nepotism as any fair-minded man was compelled to detest it; and forced to nibble its rotten fruit in the discharge of his duties he grew particularly incensed. . . . Sidney Winder's levies of workmen, ignorant and unsupervised, had left lower reaches of the Sweetwater branch choked with felled trees and a mat of brush. The creek pushed sluggishly out from the east stockade, its normal insufficient velocity reduced to a trickle by this careless damming. When and if the bake house were ever completed, equipped and operating, what could be the result of its natural drainage and debris except to pollute to the saturation point a marsh already teeming with fecal matter and the hungrily copulating flies of spring?

I report directly to Richmond. I receive my instructions from Richmond. The weak voice bland and smug.

Sometimes Alex Persons came close to wishing that a bullet had found him at Cumberland Gap. Sometimes he wanted to scream to the dirty mendicants caged by the up-ended logs, I too am a prisoner. You think you know the entire story of restriction, do you? Each of us wears manacles, mine are not apparent, they are heavy, they chafe more than my ankles and my wrists, do you wear irons in your dreams as I am compelled to?

With the platform fairly sagging under their combined weight, the Reverend Mr. Cato Dillard stood as aloof from his friends as the meager plane would permit. But Cato was drained of all trivial talk about the Fort Valley community. Belatedly he saw the enormity of the thing below the fence; he was trying to justify it by poking for texts and muttering them softly. *Egypt is like a very fair heifer, but destruction cometh; it cometh out of the north.*

Did Cato think deeply and sadly about his two grandsons killed not long before? Ira Claffey could not know, but Ira felt for a moment that savage selfish brutality—the hideous latent desire of the bereaved to see other men drink the same juice.

Thus saith the Lord. Behold, a people cometh from the north country . . . they are cruel, and have no mercy . . . I will cause you to dwell in this place.

But why the devil without shelter, Brother Dillard? Ira put the question so sharply that it came as a rebuke as well as a profane echo to the Biblical murmurings.

Cato Dillard twisted his silky side-whiskers between nervous fingers. *Judge me, O God, and plead my cause against an ungodly nation.*

Persons cleared his throat. His handsome face had grown darkly intent as always when he stood aloft and examined the stockade and its people. About the question of shelter, Mr. Claffey. I've been hard after it since I came here, to no avail. Repeatedly the superintendent of the railroad has promised me a train; each time I thought I'd get eight or ten cars of lumber; thus far none has come through. I still have hopes.

Ira said, There are sawmills in this vicinity.

Certainly. I took that matter up with Macon.

Without result?

Persons said deliberately, It would not be becoming in me, as an officer, to discuss my superior officers, and with citizens. As a former soldier you must know that.

Colonel, you have my sympathy and my respect. But this pen is turning very rapidly into one vast latrine.

Into worse than that, sir.

What could be worse? The Reverend Mr. Dillard wished to know.

This place called Andersonville.

Persons continued, but still in the manner of changing a subject. The stockade . . . he pointed out where the last breach had been closed. Yes, those were new guns being put into position on the high southwest fort nearest the Claffey place. Captured from the Yankees in Florida, Persons declared with satisfaction. And fetched here to use in turn against the Yankees when and if an emergency arises. . . . The two box gates on the west; they worked efficiently; observe the rectangular stockade enclosing an area outside the actual stockade fence in each case; the outer gate could be opened, wagons driven inside, the outer gate closed, the inner gate opened. Thus the prisoners never had a possible access to the outer world at any given moment, thus they could never carry the gate in a rush by sheer mass of numbers. . . . Yes, the North Gate was used mainly for ingress, the South Gate for egress. Yes, those were more or less streets extending through the stockade's interior from each gate; it was essential that there be some cleared space for the distribution of rations, for the assembling of prisoners in formation. Therefore no prisoners were permitted to construct their shebangs within the area contained by those more or less streets . . . it was odd: the Yanks referred to the street opposite the South Gate as South Street, but the street opposite the North Gate was called by some Broadway and by others Main Street. Very odd indeed; you would think that they'd say North Street, but they didn't. Very odd lot, these Yankees . . . yes, many foreigners. Many roughs from the New York streets. Had the gentlemen witnessed any fist-fights since they stood atop the stockade? Well, watch . . . bound to see a fight sooner or later.

I've no wish to witness their wicked brawling, said Mr. Dillard in high disgust.

Persons touched his lips with a clean but frayed handkerchief. There was no way in which he might make these civilians appreciate the problems besetting him, so he would not try. Persons was accustomed to the stern indelible procedures essential to service in the field; he believed the things which were told to him—at first.

. . . A telegram came ticking: three hundred prisoners were due to arrive the next afternoon, and thus Persons arranged for their reception, and notified the quartermaster. . . . The train would not appear. It would not appear on the stated afternoon, nor during the next morning, nor the next afternoon. Rain would fall to soak the meal on carts where rations waited with no covering because no covering was available. Then, perhaps at eleven o'clock of the second night, and with more rain sweeping and with cold wind deadening the heaps of burning knots, not one train but three would arrive in the space of half an hour. Eleven hundred prisoners instead of three hundred (one engine had snapped a driving-rod above Macon, another train had been shunted to the Southwestern from the Savannah line; no one was expecting it, no telegram had been received).

Lieutenant-Colonel Alexander Persons grew pearly of face, his stomach hurt him, he wanted to belch but there seemed to be an obstruction. The pain went higher in his chest. His meticulous legal mind began to jerk from this subject to that; he thought he heard the snap of a leather whip lash, a thin whip lash like the tongue of a blue racer, curling and popping inside his skull.

Lieutenant, how soon can you procure rations for this new contingent?

Well, sir, reckon I got rations for six-seven hundred over to the tent, but I ain't got no transportation. Got two mules down sick, and a wheel just come off that old wagon. If Captain Winder—

Get your men out of bed, prepare five hundred more rations, I'll see that you have transportation. Mr. Ussery, fetch those two wagons that were hauling logs for the artillery revetments this afternoon.

Sir, I haven't got any drivers.

By God, Mr. Ussery, *find* some drivers! Drive a wagon down here yourself if necessary, then go and fetch the other.

. . . Colonel Persons, did you hear them whistles? Another train's halted down the track behind that one there; the sentry done tolt me.

Department of Georgia, Department of Georgia, and who was commanding the Georgia Reserves? Brigadier-General Howell Cobb. Or was Cobb now become a major-general? The Nation knew him better as a politician. Inspector General of Prisons, and who was that? Brigadier-General John H. Winder. Secretary of War, and who was he? Mr. James A. Seddon. Have you rations for these prisoners, Colonel? No. Why not? No one informed me that they were coming. How many wagons have you at the post? Four—no, I think five. Have you tools? No. Lumber? No. Is it night? Yes. Is it raining? Indeed, yes. Is there adequate drainage inside the stockade? Hold on a minute, old fellow, drainage for whom, drainage for what? Have the prisoners any shelter? No, no, no! But I didn't build the prison, I didn't lay it out, I didn't plan it, I didn't construct it, Sid Winder did that. *Directly after my command was captured at Cumberland Gap, I went to Richmond and reported directly to the Secretary of War for duty. He gave me instructions to report to General Winder. General Winder instructed me to report to Andersonville.*

Colonel Persons, I've had these men in formation for an hour. Do you want me to keep them standing here in the rain?

Well, what's the difference, Captain? There's no shelter for them inside the stockade.

But all our boys are soaked, sir, a-guarding them. I just thought if we turned them inside, our sentries wouldn't have to stand out here and—

What matters it, Captain Hamrick? You're soaked through. I'm soaked through, everybody's soaked through; and two more train loads to come. No, three: another just arrived—and from the south.

From the *south*, sir? Whereabouts?

Here's the escort officer's communication. Hold that lantern closer. Whom have we here? Ah, there seem to be above seven hundred . . . portions of the Seventh Connecticut, Forty-eighth New York, Forty-seventh New York, Seventh New Hampshire, One Hundred and Fifteenth New York . . . Sherman's Regular battery . . . Sherman, indeed! . . . here it says: Olustee, Florida. So that's where they were taken. But it says also: *colored* troops—from the Eighth United States and the Fifty-fourth New York. Damnation, Captain, we have no facilities for the retention of *colored* troops. *Colored* troops! What do they mean? What can we *do* with them?

Way I see it, Colonel Persons, sir, there's no such thing as a colored soldier. Now, if I had my way, I'd form my command into a series of firing squads and—

Ah, hush up, Captain Hamrick. We can put them to work. Appears to be some two hundred of them. Yes, yes—we shall put them to work outside, we have need of many hands. They could drive— But we have no teams for them to drive. They could fabricate— But we have no implements. They could build— But no lumber. Was that another train whistle?

Inside the stockade the newly arrived prisoners could not see where to go. They sat down in mud. They sat shivering. It was dark, they could not see. They huddled close together; but even so, the more energetic of the raiders found them in midnight and rain. A lament went up as a man was hit and his overcoat was taken from him, and a worse lament arose as another man felt gripping arms upon him in the streaming darkness, and struggled to resist: and so the rest of his captured company found him motionless in muck when gray light fell upon the place where he had resisted.

Fresh fish: that was the universal appellation for the newly arrived as it had been in some of the other pens. Look at them! Here's where you get your fresh fish! *Fresh* fish, *fresh* fish: *hooooot*, whistle, whistle; they come so cheap; who wants *fresh* fish? A dime a dozen, lady, a dime a dozen: herring, cod, mackerel and sticklebacks. Who'll buy, who'll buy, who'll buy *freshhhhh fishhhhh?* . . . The Olustee hundreds comprised the first large batch of unskinned victims who might be possessed of more than their usual complement of jewelry, buttons, blankets, shoes, tobacco and other useables or tradeables. Their scales had been scraped by Home Guards along the way but they had not been gutted. There would come more, there would come more.

Despite the withdrawal evinced by Lieutenant-Colonel Persons while he spoke of surface activities and refused to state the length to which he was plagued, Ira Claffey gave ear to the true complaint of the commander. Ira had not served as a soldier for many years, but he brought a quiet understanding to the soldier who stood beside him. Ira was not limited as many men, Ira could sense things beyond his experience. He knew that the entire Confederacy labored now in confusion and dismemberment. It was more than unlikely that the subordinate upon whom fell the responsibility of administering the affairs of a new prison in this remote spot should be given the equipment and personnel to serve his purpose; it was impossible. Engines would not run because irreplaceable parts fell away or because makeshift engineers were incompetent (the competent engineers were occupied with artillery at some crucial point). Fuel and food went astray, tires came off of wagons. Where is the quinine? There is no quinine. These muskets must be altered; we have no locks to fit; where are the locks? Stored in a warehouse? Who has the key, who has the manifest, the bill of lading? Someone knew, someone had these things, someone could tell; but he could not tell—he was dead at South Mountain, he was dead on the Chickahominy, he was dead at Fort Donelson.

. . . A new superintendent for the stockade, Persons was saying.

When?

This week. He comes directly under General Winder's office. I am to command the post only.

But is not the stockade a part of the post?

In geography only, not in the echelon of command. I wish, said Alexander Persons, scraping the inner surface of his heart as with a silver spoon, that I was back in the field with my regiment.

The new commander: who is he?

Some captain named Henry Wirz. He's a German or something of the sort, added Persons with obvious distaste. Mr. Claffey, sir, I'd just as soon not have his job. A goodly number of these prisoners were sick when they came in; many more sickened here; they're not getting the proper rations; I'd give them proper rations willingly, but I'm not the quartermaster and I haven't *got* proper rations for them. I don't consider even that my own men are properly fed! The meal is coarse and mouldy, the bacon's tainted—*when* we get bacon, and we don't get nearly enough. You ought to go up on that hill over yonder, past those pines.

Persons' hand shook as he pointed toward the north, east of the Bile property. His hand shook suddenly as if it had been employed as the instrument for spewing these words, as if he had torn loose the plaint, the volley of resentment and futility, by act of hand rather than by act of speech.

What would we find in the pines up there?

Graves, sir. We've carted off over two hundred already. . . . Turn the other way. Look at that dirty stream of water.

Once, said Ira, the stream was clean. I was accustomed to drink from it.

You wouldn't want to drink from it now. But the Yanks have to, unless they can dig wells deep enough to supply them.

Once there was a spring. Down here, almost directly below us. It was spoilt when they built the stockade.

I don't know anything about that, Mr. Claffey, sir. I didn't build the stockade. He added, as in a sudden dream, I have to keep telling myself that I didn't build it, that Captain Sid Winder did. There is another stream over south of your place—maybe a mile—?

Ira said, Little Sweetwater.

Is that the name? I thought this oozing marsh was Sweetwater. Though the prisoners call it Stockade Creek.

This was a branch.

Just the same, sir, that other creek is four or five times the size of this. It flows now perhaps twelve or fifteen feet wide and more than five feet deep in spots. I'm no engineer; preparing a legal brief is more in my line; but I'd estimate that the velocity of that other stream is possibly a mile an hour. Well, sir! Couldn't the stockade have been placed to include that stream instead of this one? I mentioned as much to Sid Winder. All other things were about equal: drainage, timberland, amount of clearing to be done—

What was Winder's response?

Rather vague. He declared that he had absolute authority in the selection of the site. I have understood from other sources that a site near Albany—a place infinitely superior to this—was under consideration also. But he selected this place. Damn it all, sir!

Persons wiped his forehead. I'm talking entirely too much. But, to sum it up, we've got prisoners with diarrhoea, prisoners showing signs of scurvy, prisoners dropsical, prisoners gangrenous. What we need here is a first-rate hospital; thus far I haven't been able to lay hold on any tents, much less lumber. . . . Do you wish to go below, gentlemen? I reckon you've seen enough.

Ira said, I saw no fights. The men were merely milling about. Idly, stupidly. . . .

That's all they have to do—mill about. You were fortunate in not observing any of those roughs pursuing their chosen vocation of robbery and mayhem. It goes on all the time.

Can't you stop it, Colonel? Ira was regretful that he had stated the question the moment it passed his lips, for Persons froze upon the ladder and looked down at him with scorn, while the sentry stood at a distance, waiting to resume his post.

How, sir? Appeal to their better instincts? Send armed guards among them? The kind of material I'm commanding here and now: old men and little boys, or dullards incapable of serving at the front? Send them inside with weapons and ammunition? It's bad enough to have to put people like that On Parapet.

Ira said, I'm sorry, Colonel. Then, when Persons stood beside him (the officer was breathing heavily, not because of the exertion of descent) Ira put his hand on his arm. He said, Obviously it's no fault of yours, and there's nothing you can do about it.

Yes, said Alexander Persons, I might be able to do something about it. If I had the wisdom of Solomon, the patience of Job, the courage of the Lion of Judah. How is that for Scriptural summation, Parson Dillard?

Cato told them, It was prophesied in the Book of Joel. *I will remove far off from you the northern army, and will drive him into a land barren and desolate.*

Brother Dillard preaches a very stern war, said Ira. But if he owned a tub of fresh collard greens and pork at this moment, he'd be inside distributing it to the hungry.

Dillard's face shone. A very fine notion, Brother Ira! Why shouldn't we do that at the first opportunity?

First off, said Persons, you should have to consult with Captain Wirz, the new commander of the stockade. And I assure you that he appears to be a gentleman of very short temper. He added in a low voice, He's ill. Suffering from an old wound.

The commander took leave of his guests and went rapidly away toward his headquarters tent where he knew that twenty problems, assorted but equally ugly, would be sitting like patients in a doctor's parlor; they would be aching, they would be waiting. In thought he saw the thin frantic face of Henry Wirz, and he recoiled from the thought: he had not liked that face in his first glimpse of it. This occurred during one of those hours of duplicated entanglement now traditional with the struggling Department of Georgia. Wirz appeared, bearing an order requiring him to assume command of the stockade. Simultaneously appeared a Major Griswold from some other direction, producing an order almost identical with Wirz's. Discreetly Lieutenant-Colonel Persons retired from the complication; he said merely, Gentlemen, you'll have to get your own orders straightened out. The matter's in abeyance, so far as I'm concerned. Wirz disappeared for ten or fifteen days, Griswold fussed about . . . at last came a telegraphed order which took the major away to some other station. Wirz reappeared, triumphant but more habitually irritable than ever. Alex Persons doubted not that the bearded little fussbudget had been all the way to Richmond to invoke the power of Winder's office. Strange business, he thought despondently. Who'd want a task like that? Thank the Eternal it's no chore of mine any longer. . . . Secretly he felt a stirring of pity for the caged scarecrows who had followed him, supplicating, each time he went inside. All he could do for them was to mention the bright probability of exchange, and Persons knew that he lied each time he used the word. So did most of the men; he knew that they spoke disgracefully of him the moment his back was turned. Remotely he forgave them. They reminded him—many of them—of his own Fifty-fifth Georgia boys he'd commanded earlier, and who were captured in the mountains, and must now be penned somewhere at the North. . . . Lieutenant-Colonel Alexander W. Persons discovered that he had a severe headache. The afternoon sun was too bright, it hurt his eyes. He went to his tent and found the row of lame halt problems waiting, just as he had known that they would wait, waiting in their home-cobbled bandages, smelling of their home-applied arnica. Gad.

Ira Claffey saw Cato Dillard set forth upon his way to Americus, provided with a lunch of boiled eggs and fresh lettuce sandwiches, but with no Mrs. Dillard beside him today. Once again she was nursing the sick somewhere. There seemed to be more sick than ever before. Many wounded soldiers were come home, unhappy families had been forced from their homes by Sherman's advance and now were compelled to hunt shelter with relatives in these out-of-the-way counties. Suppose that Georgia should turn into one vast poorhouse or hospital or similar charitable refuge, thought Ira (as the area termed Camp Sumter was turning into the latrine he had described)? He held a sudden impressive vision of beds, beds, beds, cots, cots, pallets, pallets laid out in rows, as he would arrange patches of vegetables, stretching from Bibb to Chattahoochee and south: Macon, Sumter, Dooly, Lee, Worth, Colquitt, name the counties, minister to burdens in the beds.

He went into the plantation's seed house and tried to concentrate the energy of his thought upon carrots. Carrot planting had been delayed by this and that. If he wanted a late crop the seeds should be put in before the middle of April; in his opinion they came up badly if you waited for warmer weather. He thought the carrot a remarkable plant, both from the point of food value and medicinally as well. He remembered carrot poultices which his grandmother had applied in those departed frontier days when Indian wars ruled the regions barely west of them, when he was young and saw imaginary Creeks lurking in each tangle of gum shoots, and heard with apprehension the tales of wagoners dragged from their seats and scalped in timberland roads. Carrots revived the thought of his youth; carrots would be a manner of refuge.

In neat rows in small paper bags, his seeds awaited him, ticketed first by year, then subdivided alphabetically. Let me cull out these few packets of '61 carrots; how did they ever come to be left? They should have been thrown away long ago; the seed will seldom germinate properly if more than two years old. Have we a sufficiency of the '63's? More than a sufficiency. Then throw out the '62's, all of them, along with the '61's; they would be uncertain, they would be a hazard. Thus into the refuse basket go the '61's (who died then?) and the '62's (Moses) and we shall plant the 1863's (Suthy, Badge) and they, the carrots, shall arise from the ground in this holy year of 1864—but not upon the Third Day—and who shall be The Departed in this holy year? Many Secessionists, no doubt; also many Northerners. Many Yanks in the nearby stockade. Colonel Persons said over two hundred were gone to their graves already. Granny, should you have used a carrot poultice for the nursing of these? Suppose you wished to give them butter (ah, who has butter except as a treat?): then you should use the carrots for butter coloring as you did in wild early days. Bend forward seriously in your cap and gray-fringed shawl and say to the servant (with her kinky hair tied with pink yarn to scare witches), as you did in the free remote wild early days: One will be enough, Rhody. We'll have perhaps eight pounds of butter in this lot and more than a single carrot might spoil the flavor. Grate it fine, grate it into *cold* water, Rhody; mind, I said grated *fine*. And Grandfather declared that one bushel of corn and one of carrots were worth more than two bushels of corn as feed for hogs. . . . But let the hogs run untrammeled for the most part, let them feed on mast, feed on acorns, let them rub snouts into the ground and trench it and roll the turf, hunting for other food they like. . . .

Always Ira Claffey prepared his carrot seed wisely according to rule: he had saved only the principal umbels; each head was cut as it turned brown, the seeds had been dried carefully in shade, rubbed out, and then dried further in the paper. . . . A carrot poultice. Had one been prepared for Lucy's young man when he lay giving up the ghost in Illinois? But indeed what disease, what hurt, required the use of this particular remedy? Ira could not remember. It was peculiar (as his hands tried to tremble, working with the seed bags, and he labored to keep those hands from trembling) to think that he could name the remedy but not the ailment. Starvation? Dirt? Incarceration? Was incarceration a recognized disease? Could a doctor turn away from a corpse and inscribe upon the needed record: this man died of a severe case of incarceration?

He thought that the prisoners within the stockade were not too crowded—not as yet—but they would become crowded past the point of mere discomfort if trains kept fetching them. But at the moment: seven thousand squatters on, say, fifteen acres of habitable ground. Not too deplorable. . . .

They occupied his attention as a combined wretched curiosity because they or their kindred had killed his sons. In this way they made their intimacy with Ira. His wife progressed into straitened madness, his daughter felt her young hopeful strength still asserting itself and so she might open ears and eyes to the possibility of love. For himself Ira could contemplate no longer a personal physical attachment which might affect his emotion and thus in turn color the activities of heart, intellect and dream which others typified as soul or spirit (indistinguishable to him: always they had been). Sometimes he thought that he was dried from the waist up, frozen from the waist down, saturated with morphia from ear to ear. Yet a strange awareness of humanity as a whole had come upon him and he dared not deny it; it had not lived in him before save as an abstraction. He'd found that in standing on that splintery post above the fence, with a piece of rotten canvas hanging from the sloped shake roof to give the guard partial protection from sun or driving rain— He'd found that he was identified closely with Lieutenant-Colonel Persons, closely with the youthful guard who came down to give them room, even more closely with the prisoners beyond. They began to appear as his problem and his pain solely because they were human, not because he knew them; he did not know them.

Again and again through weeks to come he would reappear on that sentinel's box, passed first by Persons and later in negligent fashion by subordinate officers of the guards because they knew Ira's face and learned that he lived next door, and sometimes drifted over to the plantation to receive a gift of fresh things from the garden. Lucy gave fried eggs to one lieutenant, milk to another, gingerbread to any of the younger enlisted men who visited briefly, shyly, but ready to talk eagerly of their mothers, sweethearts, hound dogs, if given half a chance. Illusions of his own dead children faded away from Ira Claffey. No longer did he see the boys hunting beside him nor did he hear them walking on path or stairway; and that was because his mind was still level, still sound; he had not gone astray with Veronica, his balance would not permit him to accompany her. For this he gave thanks in prayer even while he prayed for his truant wife. The convocation of young slain Claffeys was replaced by disordered anonymous Yankees . . . the one he saw crawling, laced doubled in the corset of scurvy, the one he saw crawling to the marsh with his unsoldered half canteen in hand . . . the Yankee he witnessed thumbing his nose arrogantly at Ira up on the parapet . . . the boy picking lice from his pubic hair, the freshly-arrived boy displaying a scrap of newspaper to others who crowded close, the boy who whanged away on a jews-harp, the two bearded men wrestling and slugging about something-or-other, the narrow-shouldered graybeard sliding his ragged trousers below his knees as he prepared for evacuation at the swamp's edge.

Sometimes in the middle of night, when pacing on desperate solitary rounds in his nightshirt, Ira fancied that he heard the warblers which had loved that tilted pine forest when it was a forest, the nocturnal animals which had lapped at the stream when it was a stream. But mostly he went prying among the present occupants. Had the graybeard died as yet? Who won the fight, and did one prisoner now own the other's pocket comb? What had those boys read about in the newspaper? A Rebel retreat, a brazen Northern lie? The musket shot rapped out, prisoners yelled in distance and midnight, fires of the outside camp shone hard through trees, a wagon rattled, an engine whistled, frogs hallooed in a steady stream of bird-like music along the low places of farther woodland (they had gone from regions closer at hand, the waters had become too dirty for them). Who fired the musket, and at whom, and did he hit him; and why did that dog bark? Did Ike or Johnny or Silas cry in his sleep, did Ike or Johnny or Silas find sleep?

More and more the power of Andersonville poured over Ira Claffey like a glistening dark tide; it was there, reaching around him, it was sticky (he thought of molasses leaking from a barrel but the tide was not sweet). . . . Once more to the stockade the next day, wondering, staring, absorbing increased terror of the thing. The mean strength in number of the prisoners rose to ten thousand during April, the graves were said to be over nine hundred.

One time the very cones were clean, unsaturated, untrodden. One time peaceful trunks stood warm and ruddy with sunset on them, purplish when you looked toward the sunset and watched their shadowy eastern sides. There was pure silence, the ground doves' cooing instead of the cooing which lorn invalids made. Wood of the stockade might have absorbed those wonders, wood of the stockade could never radiate them now. Wood of the stockade stood cut, hammered, malformed, mute in its resentment of the use to which it had been put. Once, said the night hovering above the increasing stench. Once.

XVII

When Henry Wirz arrived in March he rented a house owned and occupied in part by a man named Boss. It was a double house with scabby window frames, and on the side which was to be the Wirz habitat several of the outer shutters were missing. Mr. Boss offered but weak hope that these could be replaced by the time Elizabeth Wirz and the children arrived: where might he get shutters, where might he find a carpenter to make them, what of the hardware? In the rear yawned an abandoned cistern into which a gray cat had slipped to drowning a few days earlier, and now the cat's body floated like a striped bladder breaking the surface of dark seepage, and nobody'd even tried to get it out. This old cistern had been replaced by a more efficient one hollowed beneath the kitchen floor. There was no need for a disgusting spectacle, no excuse for it; Wirz's physician's soul revolted at the idea. The cavity might make a fit trap for an enemy but the gray cat had been nobody's enemy. Also Wirz feared that little Coralie might fall in as the cat had done. He requested assistance from Lieutenant-Colonel Persons and received it lamely (he felt that it was lamely, since he was sourly certain that Persons did not like him at first sight; God knew why). Shortly thereafter Wirz came riding in a wagon driven by a Negro and containing, besides Henry Wirz, another Negro and some tools and scrap lumber. He presided glowering and barking over the two blacks while they toted stones, shoveled earth, and finally turned the trap into a cylindrical morass less frightening. The cat's body was out of sight and out of smell. Scrap lumber served to construct a curb and platform ragged but efficient. Cora could not fall in. Susie and Cornelia were big enough not to endanger themselves heedlessly.

There. This was done. Had anyone ever said that he was not a good father, not a good stepfather? Who had said it? How dared they say it? They would not say it again. For Henry was a man who thought of his family even before he considered the interior of the double house or his own comfort, or which room would be shared by himself and his wife. Henry had wedded himself to the widowed Mrs. Wolfe in a Kentucky village near Louisville ten years previously. She possessed two children already whom Henry accepted as vague compensation for the boy and the girl he had left with their grand-parents in Switzerland. With dedication during those moments when he was not burning with the zeal to earn money and thus become rich, or to serve ardently the Confederacy and thus become a storied hero, he had worked at making Elizabeth Wolfe into a good Zurich *Hausfrau*. Sometimes an acid of indignation burned his stomach and told him that such labors were in vain.

The Major Griswold incident gave Captain Henry Wirz fresh self-confidence to the point of exuberance. His arm was no better, some-times he thought it worse; Bucheton's surgery in Paris had been useless, worse than useless because it caused additional hurt and in-convenience. Wirz should strike Bucheton from his list of friends (*ach,* where was that list and how long might it be?) and never consult with him personally or professionally again! It was as if the enormous quantities of sulphate of morphia absorbed by Wirz's body had built up a wall through which the drug's beneficence might no longer pene-trate; except that it leaked surprisingly through unperceived crannies at times. But exercise of such power as was decreed to him, knowl-edge that he owned prestige above and beyond his rank— They were neither food nor medicine but they were dazzlement. Aloof he could stand blinking at these brightnesses and feel no pain for a time. Griswold had been of field grade; but Wirz, the lowly captain, had managed to have Griswold sent packing and to another post. Wirz was bitter because allowed to wear no major's insignia, but delighted at his own immediate accomplishment. He would accomplish more. The demonstration should begin at once. As for General Winder, one must remember that Winder meted out promotions grudgingly. His own cousin, his own son—these were but captains, and after three years of war too. This was said to be the case because the elder Winder had been so long in securing his own promotion through lower echelons. It had taken him forty years to attain his majority in the Regular establishment. Well, let him permit Henry Wirz to administer this new stockade; let Henry Wirz be executive, reorganizer, jailer, shrewd schemer. He would do more for the Government in this capacity than the most vaunted leaders might do at the front. Then General John Winder should see who was worthy of field grade. *Ja.*

During that first night in the new house which soon would shelter his family, Wirz dwelt without furniture because the furniture had not yet been moved in. In austere extension of courtesy Persons had offered a tent to the newcomer for his convenience, but Henry Wirz wished to be withdrawn from the coughing and foot-pounding and challenging and rattling of camp life; he was no campaigner in the enviable sense; always he preferred to be withdrawn. He brought his blankets to the bare house, took silent supper with the Boss family, insisted on paying them— He could not understand why they pretended reluctance when he offered to pay them; food cost money; they were not in the restaurant business, but food cost money, you could not deny that.

Wirz sat cross-leggèd beside a candle on a box and worked out his plans in a manifold order book with a lead pencil. The book said *U.S.* and must have been captured, or perhaps preëmpted from some depot long before at the outset of the war. There was justice in the notion that now it was employed as a tool in the manipulation of Yankee prisoners.

. . . Thousands. Lieutenant-Colonel Persons had explained that the prisoners were divided into detachments of Thousands and subdivided into Hundreds, as was the case in other prisons. Ha, Thousands were too large, too unwieldy! Prisoners should never be unwieldy, they should be maneuvered as easily as one pushed dominoes. Ninety men were enough for a squad, a hundred men were too many. How many squads to be in a detachment? Henry Wirz pushed his scraggly dark brows together and peered through waving candlelight at the diagrams he had drawn, the numerals he had put down with neatness. Three squads per detachment—that was enough. Two hundred and seventy prisoners in the largest unit. It might make for more book-keeping but he, Wirz, would find somebody to keep the books. . . . The population of Camp Sumter must become more fluid, more malleable. He himself would make them more fluid and malleable.

If any voice were raised, if one person beneath his authority sought to resist reforms— *Ach!* Almost it would be a pleasure.

He worked with his left hand; he had learned to write with it, his right hand hurt him sorely. . . . Three squads per detachment, ninety men per squad. Should he term them squads? *Nein.* That gave him an idea, and the bilingual connotation caused Henry nearly to smile. They should be Nineties.

Prisoner, who are you? Sir, I am James Büttner, Third Detachment, Second Ninety— What mess? . . . Thirty men to a mess; that should be convenient for the quartermaster's purposes, convenient for Wirz's own, convenient for the men themselves (he did not wish to afford them any convenience truly). But the double series of threes would simplify things. Three Messes to a Ninety, three Nineties to a Detachment. Three Detachments to a— To a what? A regiment, a brigade? Leave it there. Let the area swarm with detachments, not with strictly military designations. It would be well for the prisoners to realize that they were no longer troops, they were prisoners. He would never refer to them as men, he would refer to them always as prisoners.

Prisoner, Attention! Speak up, Prisoner, tell me your name. Sir, I am James Büttner (*ja*, you traitor, James Büttner, with a German-sounding name!); Third Detachment, Second Ninety, First Mess. Perhaps it should be the other way around? Instruct him to say in order,

First Mess, Second Ninety, Third Detachment? Best to wait and see. He would tolerate no nonsense from prisoners. This they must get into their thick Yankee skulls at the very start. Suppose a prisoner did not speak correctly, did not reply in the prescribed manner? Then he should go supperless. Suppose that the prisoner continued to prove insolent, even so? . . . There were punishments. Chains could be forged. Wirz would cause stocks and whipping posts to be constructed; there should be arrangements for the bucking and gagging of mutineers; order should come from confusion. Confusion bred waste, expense, incompetence among the administrators. Everything here at Camp Sumter should be orderly. Promotions did not come about as a result of disorder. Henry Wirz blew out his candle and sought such sleep as his arm would permit him to find. It was not a good sleep.

Early he was awakened by children's talking and running about in the Boss premises. He arose, pleased that for the moment he did not have to dress his forearm amid uncomfortable surroundings. The bone infection healed and opened alternately; he had lost track of the number of times when flesh grew in scarred covering over the minced tissues, the number of times when inflammation redeveloped, swelled, heated, throbbed, puffed, to be relieved only by its own bursting forth through the taut thin surface or by the slash of an instrument which he or some other person wielded. Midway through the act of donning his clothes, Henry Wirz remained motionless for a full five seconds while a delightfully bitter thought overwhelmed him. Suppose that the Yankee artillerist who had hurt him was even now a prisoner within the stockade! What justice in that! . . . But how would he know, how could ever the prisoner confess his crime, how could ever the prisoner know that he had been guilty of that most heinous offense: the Maiming of Doctor Henry Wirz? Impossible. But still the creature might be there, one of those scrofulous pinched-faced gypsies he had observed when he peeked from a sentry station. As yet Henry had not entered the stockade proper, he had only observed. Today he would go inside; he would walk with keen deliberation, estimating necessary changes which must be brought about under his jurisdiction. It was good that he needed not to go with his forearm swathed; it had healed when last he was in Richmond, perhaps it would remain with dermis and epidermis intact for a time, torturing him slowly but not draining, not making yellow stains and smelling like bran.

Elizabeth had worked a new shirt for her husband. The day was fair (he glanced through the six-paned window with one broken pane) and thus he should not be forced to wear a jacket. He was an individual, he was no professional soldier (although he knew that he could offer wisdom, courage and efficiency beyond the ability of many professional soldiers) and as he sought to relieve the drabness of his being by use of bright colors when in citizen's attire, so he tried to vary the meanness, the uniformity of dun badly-dyed Confederate clothing. A few officers looked askance at him from time to time, but no one had ever lectured him for his lack of conformity. This was an army where few conformed or could conform. Uniform habiliments were scarce. In the field, men fought in red or tawny undershirts in summer, many of them were apt to be in Yankee overcoats when winter came. Officer X had a green velvet collar on his dress jacket because no gray velvet had been available when that jacket was stitched, Officer Y had a turned-down collar, Officer Z had a stiff standing collar. Officer Q wore the British vest he had worn when fighting for the Queen, and Officer P rode to inspect the pickets in a flat straw hat. Henry Wirz's reluctance to garb himself according to regulation was neither unique nor ununderstandable. If Elizabeth presented him with a beautiful calico shirt (*ach*, where had that woman gotten calico? She was clever at times) it was his own business; and he would wear the shirt because he liked new clothing and could not often come by it.

Actually it was not a shirt but a waist, a waist such as was worn by young boys, and it gave him a fleeting sense of extreme youth and energy to put it on. White pearl buttons adorned the bottom hem of the waist—Elizabeth had sewn them at the proper intervals—probably she had used an old wornout pair of his uniform pants to measure with. He pressed the staring pearl wafers through button holes and stretched his thin chest and tried to square his round shoulders. *Ja.* Very nice. She should receive from him a letter of thanks as soon as he had time to write it; but perhaps his duties would keep him from writing until Elizabeth and the children arrived.

He pulled on his boots with some trouble, reaching across with his left arm to drag at his right boot, not daring to stretch the tender right arm. He tied a black scarf about his neck and reached for his revolver belt. The new weapon was a pride. He had bought it while abroad after concentrated search amid the shops of Parisian gunsmiths. This revolver was in fine condition, though it was secondhand, and a special holster had been sewn to contain it. The cylinder itself was built of barrels, ten small barrels; and from the larger bore in the center of the cylinder a musket ball could be projected whenever one chose to pull the trigger which operated it. Do not fool with me, Yankees. No monkey business from you! . . . The acrid but pleasing scent of barley coffee came to his nostrils. Ha, this was a good day, his first day of duty at Camp Sumter. He wished that he might enjoy an egg, but Mr. Boss said that rats or mink or some such vermin had taken off the chickens. Doubtless he would be served corn pone and fried hog-meat, the common fare of these backwoods ignoramuses. Henry Wirz felt in his pocket for the silver dime which he must offer in payment, and went clumping to his breakfast.

. . . Yes, a very fair day; birds were straining with song as he rode toward the stockade half an hour later. This was a borrowed horse, a bad one because he was close to being fractious, and difficult to manage with but one arm and a half. Henry must procure another mount. He must speak to Captain Dick Winder at once, and convey the unpleasantly perfunctory greeting which General Winder had sent to Cousin Dick, and inquire after a sedate gray-white mare he had seen in the pine-pole paddock behind a kind of outhouse indicated as Winder's office, the previous day. The quartermaster was absent—a lounging sentry said with little respect, Well, Captain, sir, he's away someplace like he usually is. The sentry had spat tobacco juice dangerously close to Wirz's boot-toe. Discipline was needed sorely in these parts. He would instill it. Wirz pushed back his shoulders as he rode.

He called at Dick Winder's shack, could not find him, left word that he had called, and rode to the North Gate where he dismounted and tied his sore-flanked horse firmly to an adjacent railing from which all bark was already chewed. Henry Wirz would show this ragged hireling horde of Yankees that he was not afraid of them; he would go inside on foot, man to man (no, no—man to prisoner) and look them fiercely in their eyes. Wirz's own nervous pink-lidded eyes shone with fresh fire when he glanced at his shabby patent-leather boots. His boots would be dirtied by prisoners' filth but he would get a Negro to clean them for him. Yes, and he should have an orderly; he must have clerks; he concluded shrewdly that such might be found readily among the mass of Yankees. Errand boys, clerks, personal servants; he would make them walk chalk—no funny business from any of them; but if they volunteered to come Outside in response to his summons they would receive in turn many morsels of food not obtainable in the pen. Would he be justified in offering prisoners double rations if they came to serve him? Assuredly. No one could complain about that.

At the outer gate of the boxed-off rectangle the sentry did not recognize him as the new superintendent and refused to let him pass. Wirz shrieked, flew into the German which temper always made him spew, shaped the German into broken English once more— English interlarded generously with the oaths and obscenities which at least he could speak clearly. The sentry was unmoved: a stupid elderly fellow with lack-lustre eyes, split lip, stringy beard. Wirz brandished his orders under the fellow's nose; the fellow could not read, and Henry Wirz would make him sweat for this. He would write out a complaint to the lieutenant-colonel commanding! He—

Once on duty at this stockade you come, you dumb sentry you,

God damn you are my boss! I mean—son of a bitch—*I* am boss! It is
under my orders you come!

(*Ach,* why could he not speak the English better? It baffled him.
Elizabeth had tried to teach, even the little girls had tried to teach.
He knew that he was yelling like an idiot, and the recognition of this
fact made him but more enraged and yelling the louder. Lack of
facility at English had held up his promotion, lack of English—)

By God, I make you smell hell *oder* you let me in!

A coughing and apologetic Captain Hamrick was drawn to the
scene by Wirz's fuming; he identified the new superintendent of the
prison, the sentry accepted a furious tongue-lashing from Wirz which
seemed to draw no blood—perhaps the creature was deaf as well
as illiterate. Wirz passed through the enclosure, halting to survey
it critically although there was really nothing to see except log
walls, a broken wagon wheel leaning against the logs, and a bedraggled slave stretched at full length in the sun which by this time
was high enough to find the interior of the box: the black was either
sick or asleep or both. Well! In time there should be built a complete
second stockade rather than this mere border around each gate. What
was to prevent devilish Yankees from digging tunnels underneath a
single stockade? Then might they come squeezing through like fast-
bred rodents, emerging into freedom, ready to pillage the countryside
—burn houses and stores, corrupt the crops, ravish the women, seize
guns, shoot, shoot—ready to constitute a threat behind the Confederate
lines more appalling than that faced at the front. Certainly. A second
stockade should be constructed as soon as Wirz could wheedle such
security from the Winders.

He paused at the interior gate, quickly putting himself to rights
for the prisoners' eyes. His revolver hanging at his left side, ready
for his left hand . . . yes, fully capped, ready to spit. He made his
heavy gold watch chain hang true, and felt the forepiece of his cap,
and drew the cap jauntily to one side.

Going inside, sir? A pimply child at the inner gate put the nasal
question.

I am Captain Henry Wirz, commanding now this prison!

Just a second till I lift the bar, Captain, sir. The boy exerted skinny
arms under the wooden bar. Wirz helped him with his hand, together they worried the bar aloft and the wicket door scraped open.
Wirz stepped over the sill, wrinkling his sharp nose as an odor swept
to possess him. It smelled like an alley in one of those Parisian slums
where he had walked gingerly, not pitying the poor, but scorning
them for their filth, thinking that they should know better.

Wry-necked Smith was calling the roll. That was his regular task.
He was a Rebel sergeant on whom devolved many duties not too
complex but savoring of any ceremony which exemplified discipline.

He was a middle-aged man with a squeezed face, sandy mustache and goatee, and a perpetual frown of concentration. In Taliaferro County he had sought public office assiduously and was bound to be disappointed always on election day, but the next election found him undiscouraged. Smith was barely literate. He pronounced many names so remarkably that it was difficult for their owners to recognize them. Years before, on the way to a gin, driving a cart with his own bale of cotton atop, Smith had managed to upset the vehicle and was pinned beneath the load. His recovery amazed the Taliaferro County medical profession; but after that time his head was riveted around to the right; he could not turn it. When he wished to look in another direction he had to turn his whole body. At this late date the wastage of war had raked even this misshapen relic into the army, and soldiers of his company said that Wry-necked Smith was frozen permanently at Eyes Right: an officer had called the order, Smith had obeyed, and then the officer had forgotten to give the order of Front. Northern prisoners, as soldiers also, had come naturally to the same conclusion.

Wirz had never seen this sergeant before, and now regarded him with disfavor. His darting examination told him immediately that the prisoners were playing roots with the non-commissioned officer. It was an old trick; Wirz had seen them attempting it during his brief service in an Alabama prison and even at Richmond. They tried the trick but did not perform it successfully when Henry Wirz held the roll! It consisted, mainly, of making eighty-seven men, perhaps, seem to count as a hundred. Smith edged warily in front of the formation, moving a few steps at a time, moving to the right where his congealed gaze led him. Yankees responded to their names at one end of the rank, then ducked behind the bodies of their fellows and reappeared in line farther along, squeezing in, answering to the name of Johnson or Langley later as boldly as they had responded to Adams or Atherton earlier. One hundred rations were more to be desired by eighty-seven men than eighty-seven rations. And the game of roots could be played in divers other ways also: it was an aggravation to authorities, a positive swindle to the unalert.

By God, Sergeant!

Wry-necked Smith stepped promptly around to look at Henry Wirz.

These God damn Yankees, you watch them better!

Smith shifted his tobacco quid. Who're you?

Sergeant, it is now I command this stockade. Better you better watch all these damn Yankees. You watch them close! They come around behind, beating you every times!

A few prisoners hooted in the ranks, the rest watched apathetically, the rest were too tired to do more than that. For the most part only the young lean whipper-snappers in their teens had this dance and energy left to them. Ragged slouching ranks were of a sameness; there was such variety to torn attire or lack of it, such infinite variety in people's shapes and sizes that they seemed starved down into common face and form. Who had answered to the name of Lewis when previously he had answered to Gilmore? Wirz might not know; their uniformly tarred faces baffled him whether they wore hair or whether they didn't, whether they were scurvy-ridden and bent between sticks or whether they stood erect, whether they were well-fed raiders or waifs preyed upon by the raiders. Not knowing, feeling his way to absolute authority with caution, Henry Wirz let his patent-leather boots take him away.

He moved along Main Street toward the center of the stockade, holding his left hand upon the flap of his holster. His right forearm began to knock like the pulse of an aching tooth. Proximity to these devils had done that, *ja, ja.* The arm responded; the arm said, So these are the people who tore me, these are the inventors of my misery? *Throb, throb*—let me out, I am cased here in agony. Let me *out! Throb,* let me *out, throb, throb!* said the reeking suffering spirit fastened inside the arm, *let me see the Yankees.*

Wirz traveled almost blindly, moisture on his forehead, cold moisture on his stringy neck. He looked down: one boot-toe was befouled by excrement, fresh soft yellow human excrement; it had to be human, there were no dogs in the place. He said aloud, God damn shit, Yankees are shit— He kept walking.

A string of monsters great and small began to attach to him. They followed calculatingly, trying to evaluate this slight grizzled man, many recognizing immediately the power which he would hold over them, and wondering in the same breath how they might profit from it or avoid its impact. Since Wirz announced himself to Wry-necked Smith the word had gone coursing through mildewed formations and on and on . . . a limp word was spoken, a head was turned . . . group to group among the shebangs. Him? Yup, him. There he goes. What? Who? New commander. Where? Over there. Hey, leave us have a look . . . shoed feet, shoeless feet pattering in muck behind the solitary visitor in gray uniform trousers, the armed man in the calico waist. What is he, an errant boy for Persons? Hey, bubby, does your Ma know where you're at? Bet you a red cent he's got some sugarplums in that there pocket of his. Who? That's him . . . word was ahead of Henry Wirz now, people of the stockade were following in a drove, the news had spread faster than Wirz walked.

A dozen voices were blatting, their owners concealed behind huts or taking refuge back of their mates.

Hi, mister, where in tunket did you get that great big awful pistol? Will it shoot?

Beardy, don't shoot me!

Who's that specimen, anyways?

Wirz stood his ground, face twisted partly by pain and partly by desperate assertion. You hear to me, Yankees, you dumb damn prisoners! I am Captain Wirz. Now this stockade I command! You watch, you know what is good for you!

They seemed to have their faces corked like actors, they were hooligans from some weird treacherous minstrel troupe. Yah, sneered evil boys hiding behind other evil boys. Older ones or the more sickly (and all the sickly ones looked older than they were; so they were sick, they were fundamentally as vicious as the rest, but too weak to manifest their viciousness!) clung closer to Wirz. Some had actually the effrontery to touch the sleeve of his waist, and he drew back offended.

Captain. Please, Cap'n Wirz. . . .

You know anything about exchange?

Heard anything about exchange?

We're bound to get exchanged soon, aren't we, Captain?

They can't keep us here forever, can they?

We'll get exchanged, won't we, huh, Captain, please?

Ja, said Henry, who knew nothing whatsoever about the exchange or its stoppage—because he had been in Europe when that occurred— and who might not divine the resumption of exchange, because he owned no crystal ball nor knew how to use one. *Ja.* You all get exchanged pretty quick I guess.

He thought that he was being kind no matter how cruel he was in fact. These prisoners who clustered close were behaving like good children for the most part, and good children should be given peppermint sticks, horehound, barley sugar. This was barley sugar which he offered cheerfully, though it would turn to wormwood later. Bad children should be punished. That also would he do.

Several times during his march through this populated mire and during his businesslike return, he halted to examine the stockade from the prisoners' vantage. His glance bounded about like a mouse fallen into a slop-jar. Ha: one stockade only. So they *could* dig tunnels. Ha: Yankees swarmed tightly against the fence, some of them had even attached their jungly huts to the tall logs, seeking shelter from wind or sun. The most innocent shebang might mask fiendish preparations: elaborate ladders to be raised in the dead of night, a concerted rushing of the gate when ration carts entered or when a fresh draft of prisoners arrived or when— A deadline! There must be a deadline. And tomorrow—at once on paper, tomorrow in the fact—the personnel within the pen should be squadded over. The Thousands and Hundreds should disappear forever, supplanted by Detachments and Nineties.

With sycophants trailing Wirz returned to the North Gate. One fellow begged to go out to cut wood, another had written a letter which he wished mailed, another insisted that he was an officer—by rights a captain like Henry Wirz—and should no longer be confined here. Henry accepted the letter (which he neglected to mail for the petitioner, and which got mixed in with some old newspapers later on, and so was thrown out, and the prisoner's wife never heard from him again; never did she know that he died in Andersonville on June twenty-third, 1864, and was taken to the deadhouse without his name tied to his rags; so he became one of the Unknowns; but his wife and sons always thought that he had died gloriously if anonymously in the battle of Olustee). Henry said that there would be no wood-cutting at this time—later on, perhaps, and under heavy guard; he told the pretending officer to be off, to try no funny monkey business with him. He went to his new office, a rough plank shanty on the slope opposite the roadway below the large southwest fort. There, with considerable labor and recourse to the dictionary taken from his saddle bag, Wirz inscribed an advertisement to be tacked on the inside of the North Gate. He desired two prisoners, bilingual as to German and English preferably, with experience in the routine of military offices. Such men must give their paroles and could dwell outside the stockade. They would receive double rations; other emoluments were hinted at but not specifically promised. . . . Promptly there were five applicants for this seeming sinecure, and Wirz had them fetched outside later on. He interviewed them with increasing disappointment and finally made himself select his two. Neither of them did he consider to be of even average intelligence. (One was named Charles, the other Viggo—he was truly a Dane but he spoke German with a Schleswig accent. Charles was sickly, fated to die of a phagedenic ulcer within a few weeks. Viggo stole things to sell to the guards; Wirz caught him stealing soft soap, and had him turned back into the stockade.) They were but the forerunners of a host who would serve Wirz in his office or at and around his quarters, and some would serve efficiently. How many there would be Wirz himself could not guess, any more than he could have guessed how many prisoners would be confined there eventually.

That same day a guarded herd of Negroes found themselves sinking posts inside the stockade. Wirz's instructions to the youth in command were to drive small posts into the ground firmly so that some three or four feet of their length remained exposed; upon these posts would be nailed scantling strips to mark the deadline. Twenty feet inside the stockade, said Wirz, but the lieutenant was no surveyor and had not a good eye for measurements. At some points the deadline was established not more than sixteen feet from the fence, at others perhaps twenty-two. A howl arose from scores of unfortunates thus dispossessed. They had labored like insects to achieve their shelter; now treasured stakes were pulled out, pine lattice tossed aside; the men were told to take their blankets and coats and move. Furthermore the habitable area within the pen stood reduced by perhaps three acres. Indignation meetings were held, fists were waved, a few stones were thrown at guards.

Just let that Dutch son of a bitch show his face in here!

Deadline, hell. A Wisconsin man stepped angrily past the new posts and jeered up at the parapet, spreading his arms as he hallooed. Promptly several of the nearer guards began to aim their guns at him, and friends dragged the foolhardy man to safety. There was some doubt about whether Wirz meant business, whether the guards would really shoot. This doubt was dispelled quickly the next morning. Ironically the first victim was a German; the prisoners called him Sigel in derogatory reference to his crescent badge of the ill-fated Eleventh Corps. Exposure and illness had sent Sigel into the nodding ranks of the lunatics. Men called him the Old Clothes Man because he went jerking about in a kind of St. Vitus' dance, searching for stray rags or socks in the mud. Sigel observed a checkered scrap of cloth dropped probably by one of the blacks who had driven posts into place. Scantlings had been nailed already at this point, but a scantling meant nothing to the deranged wanderer, and he went pawing under the little barricade, white crescent corps badge and all. He was killed almost instantly by a handful of buckshot smashing through his chest. Prisoners screamed their hatred of the young guard who had fired, they drove him from his perch with mud and billets before he could reload. Another guard took his place. Later Wirz himself crept aloft to survey the situation . . . missiles flew again, obscenities smoked, the hatred was given freely and accepted just as willingly. The construction detail ran out of scantling before they had marked the entire deadline, and there would be dangerous gaps for a long time to come; wiser people tied cords at night, with tufts of rag to wave in warning, but always these cords were being stolen by other people.

The squadding over which began on the day of the death of Crazy Sigel was attended by a protracted insurrection. Henry Wirz was a fanatical believer in the Oriental philosophy of Go Thyself. If he depended on some other person's count, how could he establish the correctness of it? Imagine Wry-necked Smith charged with this task! Wirz was certain that half the private soldiers available to his purposes could not count to twenty without a mistake; he detected signs of unruliness among sergeants and the handful of commissioned officers subordinate to his command. Lieutenant-Colonel Persons himself had introduced the familiar system of Thousands and Hundreds. Through a smoked-up tent fly Wirz heard Alexander Persons denounce the projected Detachments and Nineties as purest fertilizer. *Ach,* was ever a prison superintendent so put upon, was ever a prison superintendent less coöperated with? So must he parade the prisoners and count them himself.

It took him hours to achieve the count, manifold order book in hand. By the time he had completed checking the Seventh Thousand, prisoners of the first detachments were out of formation and wandering all over the place. Bad children—they should be punished (what did he do to Cora when she was naughty? Send her to bed without her supper! So should he do with these!)—he was the man for the job, God damn.

Today for your badness no rations will come!

The howl which answered this announcement made Claffey slaves rise in alarm from their planting of a distant field, it brought men running out of Uncle Arch Yeoman's store.

This incident was unfortunate, but if it served to teach the prisoners to stay in line when they were ordered to, it should have served its purpose. One could not line up Thousands and tell them off into fresh Detachments unless orders were obeyed. In a melancholy drizzle next morning bayonets were fixed, the gate was swung, guards marched in with Wirz trotting in their midst as if he also were a prisoner.

Maybe you Yankees stay until dismissed, this day? he asked witheringly. . . . Once more he proceeded with his labored count, once more the sickly tired resentful beggarmen said, Oh, cowshit, and skulked from the ranks. Here was Henry Wirz, counting the new Detachment Twenty-three; and beyond him those vagabonds in the as-yet-uncounted Detachment Twenty-six were strolling down to the marsh because they claimed they had to do their business. Never could two hundred and seventy men need to do their business at once! Did they take him for a fool? They would learn the temper of the officer with whom they trifled!

Famished throngs swayed opposite the North Gate all that afternoon, watching with such hope that even sentries stared down to pity them. But no patched harness jingled, no wheels squeaked, no rabbit mules flicked their ears, no cornmeal was transported to its parceling out. Now forty-eight hours had passed since a bite of food had been issued. Only the acknowledged raiders had anything saved up for a rainy day, and even these joined in the din and grumble. Fierce youths who still had the litheness of willow and the verve of cats about them— They gathered in trembling groups, talk flew wildly.

Come along, old top, I'm with you: better off dead than starved!

If we get enough poles to batter with, we can bust out that little wicket door.

Certain—some of us are going to get shot, but the bulk will get through.

Harvey, I'll be right alongside you!

Let's every fellow grab a club and—

The gravel of these verbal torpedoes spread stinging; yet there was no leader, no supreme chemist to mix the desperation and hunger and rage, no one to shake the mixture and let it spurt. Far into hours of darkness the boys huddled and snarled; yet it was only a pathetic snarling, only a huddle.

Once more in early morning the Rebel fife squeaked its message of Roll Call. Once more came bayonets and the skinny bearded man, now so universally loathed, scooting in the shadow of their security. This day the prisoners' swollen feet seemed fastened to the ground with a mucilage of despair. They did not go ranging afield after they were first counted, they remained in ranks. Scores of them collapsed or sat down through sheer weakness; but they stayed, they did not drift, they were in the counted Thousands when the superintendent came back to make his final conversion into Detachments.

He rewarded them with their day's ration, but only that day's ration. (This he debated in his mind, after he was once back in the shed: might he not give them the meal for the two other days? *Nein:* too much all at once, it would make them sick, the incidence of mortality might rise abruptly. One day's rations: enough. They had earned this by good behavior. But their bad behavior of the two previous days had earned them exactly nothing save empty bellies. Like naughty children they must be brought to time, *ja.*) The toy mules came straining, the mess sergeants drew their meal, it was divided.

. . . He was but doing his duty, they must be aware of that. Since the squadding over was now complete, Henry Wirz had no thought that he needed longer a retinue of guards. The next morning he ventured into the stockade alone. Within minutes he came dodging out again, his unfired revolver shaking in his left hand, his calico waist dripping with mud and offal, his neck dirtied, his arms dirtied, his shoulder bruised where a rock had struck.

Gott, they were devils! But if he had emptied his weapon into the bodies of some, then the others would surely have torn him to pieces, no matter how many dropped to the guards' volley. He thought of a snake pit, thought of a lions' den. Prisoners seethed through his aching head all that day; he could not eat dinner, no longer did he have appetite; he wished he could drink but liquor made him sick; *ja,* even food made him sick, even the idea of food, for he was a dyspeptic. Prisoners jabbered and seethed in his dreams that night, he cried out hoarsely, he awakened the neighbors. Henry Wirz wished for his wife, for his family. He felt alone and misunderstood.

XVIII

Two older but not so hefty boys showed Willie Collins how to make a bully out of a dead rat and handfuls of shot. This was in 1843 when Willie was nine years old. A common play for boys in the Fourth Ward (and in regions equally depraved in other portions of the United States) was to attach a dead rat to a stout cord and whirl the rat over your head, or round and round beside you as you ran and shrieked. Live rats abounded, a dead rat was to be avoided only because of its putridity . . . you whirled the plummet, smaller children got out of the way, girl children ran screaming. You could have battles with other boys, biffing them with your rat until its tail broke off; then you had to tie the cord around the neck, and it did not swing so well; eventually the rat would be mashed apart, flogged out of all usefulness; then you had to get another dead rat, but there were plenty of those to be had.

The boys who taught a better trick to Willie were Danny Crogan and Gabriel Seek; one was white, the other colored but with red hair. Danny was dead at fourteen, his head splintered in a street fight. At sixteen red-headed Gabe was shot by a coachman who said that Gabe had raped his young daughter, and maybe Gabe had; but previously he bragged to friends that the girl gave herself to him, and she sneaked out to him a dinner bucket filled with delicious fried smelts almost every day.

Get you your rat, said Danny. Slit him open and take out the guts. . . . Get a fresh rat what ain't swoll up yet, said Gabe. Nail him to a board, scrape the skin so's it won't have much smell, so twill be good and soft. . . . Go you down to that tannery, end of Cherry Street; steal you a handful of the tan stuff and rub it on. . . . First thing you know, you got you a well-tanned rat. . . . It's then you sew him up. . . . First you got to put in them shot, said Gabriel Seek. . . . Och, sure: and it's tight you must stitch it, with the hide doubled, or the shot will leak. . . . Buckshot—that best. . . . Och, yes, said Danny Crogan. Go you down to Cowley the gunsmith, and he's got buckshot in the third keg from the door; and wait you till he's back at his bench with some crusher who's brought a pistol to him, and it's then you can snatch your buckshot and get away before he fibs you. . . . Stuff that rat full and sew him tight, said Gabe Seek, rolling his eyes.

Willie Collins listened, Willie Collins learned. Within a few days he had his rat ready, tanned at least well enough to suit him. But use stout cordage, he had been told. Rawhide is best; and tie it to the neck, for the tail would snap, it's that heavy.

Willie went out into the gloaming—it was autumn, and trees drifted their dry spicy leaves when you got where there were trees. Willie had been instructed to look for a hockey. There were many hockeys staggering in narrow passages close to the Gotham Court tenement where he dwelt; but these drunken men were half naked, and none of them might have so much as a hogg, a single ten-cent piece, in his rags. Willie traveled farther afield, swinging the heavy rat-pouch from time to time, to pretend that he was an innocent lad, playing innocently with a dead rat and that was the truth. He idled his way toward the East River. Nearby there survived a short row of prim mansions, their iron gates locked against incursions, holding red brick shoulders stiff against the loose hordes now spilling across Franklin Square where once George Washington had dwelt, where once John Hancock had walked.

A man moved toward Willie through the wan purple light. Most certainly he was a hockey; he was an elderly man, but he tottered as if he had swallowed an entire decanter of brandy before weaving on his homeward path. How was Willie Collins to know that Mr. Hans Van Auken, a long retired watchmaker, had suffered a stroke of paralysis the previous winter and could now walk only with difficulty? And would it have made any difference at all whether he was a hockey, fuddled with drink, or only an ancient with twitching limbs? Mr. Hans Van Auken leaned on his silver-headed cane, he wore a brushed beaver hat, his pantaloons were strapped neatly beneath his slippers. Had he seen danger approaching, he would have blown upon the shrill-noted whistle he carried on a ribbon around his neck, to alert policemen or servants or private watchmen, to send a thief scooting. But he saw no danger; he saw only a lad wheeling a dead rat round his head— Oh, poor lad from a poor home, and that was all he had to play with. Mr. Van Auken thought to give the lad a penny, and began to fumble in the lower left pocket of his waistcoat. A minute later he was dead. He died, he drained away unconsciously there on the cobbled sidewalk without a cry, without a whine, with the front of his fragile egg-shell skull crushed in, with several of his pockets turned out, and the treasured ebony walking stick gone from his dying grasp.

Two streets away Willie Collins thought suddenly about the walking stick. Were he seen carrying it, someone might know— He penetrated an alley, felt about until he found a narrow cranny between two jammed-up buildings. He put the silver head of the cane into this cranny and snapped it off. With the lump in his pocket, and still swinging his rat, he ran home to Gotham Court to see how well he had profited. He had profited to the extent of one gold watch, a few silver coins and coppers—and one gold eagle in the lot; and a beaded doeskin purse of Indian manufacture which Mr. Van Auken had carried as a precious souvenir sent by his son who traded with the Winnebagoes. This purse was found to contain twenty-eight American dollars, an English sovereign, and a promissory note for two hundred dollars drawn to Mr. Van Auken's favor and signed by a man named Cameron. (Since Willie could not read, this information escaped him and he put the note into the chamber pot.) Purse and money he put into his pocket along with the cane-head, and he was gloating over the watch by candlelight when rudely interrupted by Big Biddy.

Big Biddy was a gangling mulatto woman, deeply in love with Willie Collins's father when she was drunk—which was most of the time—and resenting him (because he was an Irishman, and white) when she was sober. Which was now.

A yack. Where you get that yack, Willie?

And wouldn't you like to know?

Give me that yack.

In a pig's ass I will.

She fell upon him, they fought, at nine years he might have been taken for twelve or older. Big Biddy had her hands full. (He had concealed his rat in a favorite hideaway, which was beneath a loose board under the pallet whereon Willie's father and Big Biddy slept commonly together or singly; otherwise Willie might have used the rat on her. They might look for purloined goods under the mound of rags which was Willie's, they had not wits enough to look under their own. . . . When their noisy ardor was spent, and when they were roaring with sleep, it was an easy matter to work the loose board out from beneath their couch.) At length, amid mutual buffetings and squawkings, Big Biddy was able to draw a fresh-filled gin bottle from the pocket of her red cloak, and she gave Willie such a bang on the head— but never breaking the bottle—that he went squealing down the stairs. The watch had fallen upon the bricks they used for a brazier in cold weather; when opened it proved to have the crystal broken and it would not run. But it was a gold-cased watch with the initials H.I.V.A. engraved elaborately. When Aloysius Collins came gasping in (you could hear his breathing as he approached, the grating wheeze of it, you could hear it from the bottom of the stairway) Big Biddy displayed her loot.

You black bludget, you. Where did you hoist it?

Kiddie had it, Al. She had drunk half the gin and was warming to him.

He's but a babe.

God damn, man, he had it.

Likely twas in the street he found it, muttered the gigantic decrepit Aloysius.

Yah, she sneered, disapproving of Willie because he had hurt her breast during the struggle. I bet you, man, he hoist it from some shop.

He's but a babe, ladybird, but a babe.

The next morning the elder Collins sold Mr. Van Auken's watch to a popshop proprietor for five dollars: he should have received much more, but he was stupid and quivering, and it seemed that wild animals were roosting above his bed when he awakened; he stood in need of liquor. During the day policemen came searching the stores of all the Uncles in the area, for the murder of Hans Van Auken had caused a great hue and cry . . . one of the dead man's sons was a rich merchant, another was a city official. They discovered the watch, Collins was pointed out as the man who'd sold it to the pawnshop proprietor, police came thundering into Gotham Court. But twenty men, including the proprietor of the Diving Bell (and the proprietor was well acquainted with the dead man's politician son) swore that Aloysius Collins had slept on a bench in the corner of the Diving Bell from five p.m. until long after the body of Hans Van Auken was discovered. Thus Collins's insistence that he had found the watch, broken in the street on his way home, could not be refuted. His wailing word was accepted as gospel in the end.

Al Collins could never have done it, anyway, declared the proprietor of the Diving Bell. He's a mighty man, but drink has took the pepper from him.

No one even thought of nine-year-old Willie. They said, Be off with you, when he came slinking around, when the police had his father in tow. They said, Away with you, you spalpeen. This is a sorry business.

Later, when the freed Aloysius was sufficiently sane, he beat half the life out of his son with a chair-leg.

Willie endured, although he screamed loud enough to awaken all of Gotham Court. He did not awaken all of Gotham Court; they were accustomed to screams. Willie had the money tucked safely away, and the head of the silver walking stick was hidden against a future emergency (he used it eventually to make a slung-shot which he lost in a fight) and he would savor sugarplums, oysters, fried cod, hot corn and any other dainty he chose—forever and a day, it seemed then. He was thunderstruck and delighted to learn that he had killed a man. He walked with puffed chest, he snarled at smaller children, he stood around with other colts in front of public houses on Water Street, watching men and prostitutes moving in and out, watching with glee the fights which always developed. Sometimes there would be several fights in the course of an hour, sometimes men were left for dead, sometimes they were dead.

It's myself who's kilt a man already, he told Gabriel Seek and Danny Crogan when he felt expansive.

You're not elderly enough to have hair in your crotch!

But I did. With my leaded rat, as you showed me.

And who did you give the nope to, kiddie?

Twas an old hockey.

Who you think you fool, Willie? . . . Ah, you're not elderly enough to—

And where are you after thinking I got all the brass I got?

Hoisting purses off of owls! cried Danny in great pride at his own humor. Willie grappled with him and they rolled in the street, gouging and biting, until some passing sailors thoughtfully kicked them apart and into flight.

At sixteen Willie Collins, grown already to some thirteen stone, drifted into river piracy with the Daybreak Boys, operating under the banner of Nick Saul and Billie Howlett. He was not yet nineteen, in 1853, when he stood in the Tombs yard and with interest watched Saul and Howlett drop from their scaffold. He did not wonder how it would feel to be hanged, he did not wonder about anything. A smarter slyer youth might plan the forays; he, Willie Collins, would carry them out. At least that portion of the work which fell to him commonly—the strong arm, the club on the skull, the kick in the groin, the arm around the neck until breathing stopped.

Wait till it's two o'clock, Willie.

Yes. Two.

Then get to Tanner's wharf; it should take you ten minutes. The watchman keeps a fire in an iron drum, to keep him warm. I think he'll be setting by the fire; if he's making his rounds he'll come back to it. Get him by the neck—take care he gives no yell, take care he has no chance to yell—and kick the fire into the river, drum and all. Then there'll be no glim.

That I'll do.

Mind, there must be no yelling.

He'll never yell, cove, that he'll not do.

. . . That he did not do.

It was said that a fellow named Slobbery Jim would take over command of the Daybreak Boys after Billie and Nick were hanged at the Tombs. But Willie Collins was not a favorite of Slobbery Jim. To begin with, the new captain was afraid of Willie, and still regarded him as even more stupid than he really was.

Willie drifted up into the Eighteenth Ward where he heard that pickings were easier, and so they proved to be. The system there was exceedingly simple, much more to Willie's liking and understanding than the devious split-second-timing incursions of the Daybreak Boys among docks and shipping. A man who called himself Paddy Delaney (he was built much as Willie was built, although he was not as large as Willie; and yet he was older, and more experienced) was Willie Collins's immediate superior. Take the corner of Twenty-ninth and Madison: that was all Willie had to do. Take the northeast corner— that was as good as any; and Saxey would have the northwest corner, and Cuban Cookie the southwest, and Skibbereen Mahone the southeast. If a well-dressed man approached in darkness— Well, take him and go through him. If there were two men together, as often happened, one of the other kiddies could step over from yonder corner.

They, and the roughs who worked with them, were known as the Honeymoon Gang—a satirical tribute to their cruelty. If a pedestrian strolling through the fog appeared to be well clad, and then, on close and violent examination, proved no fit subject for profitable keel-hauling, the Honeymooners would batter him to ribbons merely for the sport of the thing. Willie took to this stand-up-and-slam-a-man-down simplicity with gusto. The second week of his operations he was lucky enough to observe a lone gentleman in an opera cloak leaving a nearby cat-house from in front of which his untipped hackman had long since driven away in dudgeon. Willie put his hand over the stranger's bearded lips, carried him into a blind areaway and throttled him into insensibility. The man turned out to be a wealthy coffee merchant from Latin America; Willie could not know that; he knew only that he acquired over six hundred dollars in banknotes, to say nothing of jewelry. The newspapers cried that Juan Santa Maria Lopez, Esq., a visiting exporter, had been half-killed and was now under the care of surgeons at his lodgings, and had lost a fortune in jewelry to the roughs who attacked him. Juan Santa Maria Lopez affirmed that there were at least five men in the band who fell upon him.

I don't know who the other man was. Paddy Delaney sat with a cocked pistol in his hand. But let us be after seeing the sparks and the fawneys, you dirty buzzers, or I'll pop the bladder of one of you.

Saxey, Skibbereen and Cuban Cookie were loud in their protestations of ignorance of the affair, but it was not easy for Willie to lie with aplomb. Soon all four of them were arrayed against him, and that was too many, for Delaney and Skibbereen both approached him in size. He handed over a silk handkerchief containing the baubles, and gave up three dollars in currency which he swore by heaven and earth was all the money the foreigner had had upon him. In delight over emeralds Delaney did not press him further; but awarded Willie only a tenth share in the later proceeds as punishment. Willie never told about the six hundred dollars; in his mutton-headed musings he thought that he had out-smarted Patrick Delaney. He did not know that Delaney divvied up only a fraction of the money received for the jewelry. . . . The Honeymoon Gang waxed rich, then poorer as more police crowded that neighborhood in response to the agony of citizens. Some months later they were driven down into the Bowery by the intrepid Captain Walling and his Strong Arm Squad. It was merry while it lasted.

His giant's stature began to tell on Willie Collins, to make him a marked man. If a shorn and bleeding sheep complained to the authorities that he had been pounded by a robber of enormous height and girth, the police (or such of them as could be persuaded by bribery) went seeking Willie. Thus he was charged with crimes he did not commit . . . he had committed many . . . he did not know how many men he had killed before he entered wartime captivity, he supposed a dozen or so. Several times he was imprisoned; once he escaped, once he bought his way to freedom, the other times he served the brief terms to which he was sentenced. He thought of leaving New York but New York was home, he did not know where else to go. The body which had once been his bonanza was now a positive handicap. At rare intervals fortune sent a rich weakling into his grasp, and then he made sure that no evidence would be given against him. . . . Willie flaunted new duds in Barney Bright's Joy Mill where, according to the gilded sign outside, the mill ground out Joy, Joy, Nothing But Joy— and a little mayhem and venereal disease along with the Joy.

He lived—bellowing, pompous, frightening, thick-headed. He leaned on the rail of an excursion craft off Bedloe's Island and poked his shoulders and his whiskey bottle through the bunting in order to watch Albert Hicks, the high seas murderer, as Hicks fell through an open air gallows trap and struggled in strangulation. And if they ever come to hang me, howled Willie Collins, they'll have to hang me twice! A well-fleshed woman cooed beside him and wiggled her hip against him; she wore red gloves and red stockings; faith, and she wore little bells on her garters, the bells tinkled when she moved. Willie lived . . . he lived eventually with the Bowery Boys, he had fought alongside them when they raided the Dead Rabbits at the election polls back in 1856, but it did no good: Fernando Wood was reëlected anyway. But it was a fine fight. And again he had contended against the Dead Rabbits in the historic Bayard Street riot of the following summer; and could you guess the man he met there, slugging in the ranks of the Dead Rabbits with a paving stone in one hand and a shoemaker's awl in the other? Patrick Delaney it was, the erstwhile Honeymooner. They grappled in long anticipated rivalry . . . sure, and Willie was confident that Delaney died beneath the stamping of his brass-heeled boots. Willie lived!

For a fact Paddy Delaney did not die. The next time the monsters met, it was on Rebel soil with Rebel guards rimmed beyond them. It might have been that the two roughs were rocked in the same cradle in a Dublin slum, if anyone ever bothered to rock babies in Dublin slums: they embraced like grizzly bears, they wept and swore their loyalty, they drank what smuggled liquor was available and brayed for more. Ah, and I thought I had kilt you surely that day at the Bowery and Bayard. . . . Willie darling, it's me that was certain I was kilt; and months it took me to regain my strength, with half my ribs stove in.

Willie came to the sad pass of Confederate prison life through a series of misadventures. He emerged from another type of prison in New York after the war had begun. A turmoil of alternate patriotic demonstration and felonious interference was ruling the town. It was hard for Willie to turn a dollar or even a dime. Though they had a wary respect for Collins's proficiency the ruling gangsters held him to be bad luck and would have none of his services. He eked out an existence in Mulberry Bend, preying on the same sort of stumbling drunks and drugged seamen he had preyed on when he was a boy. In his late twenties Willie looked to be at least forty. The skin of his face and neck bore the coarse-seamed texture of middle age, there were stray shreds of glint in his ginger-colored beard, his hair-line receded. Soon he heard that he was being sought by the police again—something about a Norwegian cook who had been squeezed to death in a cellar, and the Norwegian ship's master had friends among the new Metropolitan Police. There was nothing for Willie to do but enlist, which he did quickly, and then deserted just as quickly, bounty money sewn in his drawers. In this way he went from regiment to regiment. It had never occurred to him that he might be sent into combat, but that was what happened after he joined the Eighty-eighth Pennsylvania, before he'd found opportunity to take his usual French Leave.

He had done well enough at Belle Isle but here at Andersonville he was doing even better. There were vastly more prisoners to provide the luxuries of existence both directly and indirectly. Day after day fresh drafts were pushed into the stockade: there were riches to be had, a plethora. For indeed there were no police to bother! Once more Willie was marked, towering above the rest, but his marking was as great a benefit to him here as it had been a handicap in the city streets. By April he needed not to stir hand or foot if he did not choose to move; he grew fat; but it would take a long while for his grotesque thews to become so wadded in corpulence that they would not serve him. He kept his own band well under control—not too many of them, but whittled down to comfortable size. There were a round dozen sluggers, also the cooks and housekeepers—two of these latter were homosexuals whose affection some of his men enjoyed, but Willie himself did not crave such peculiar ecstasies, his laughter burst at the very idea. There was Lipsky the tailor, and a few other scrofulous hangers-on who served for one purpose or another. Collins's Raiders were not the largest band in the stockade but they were feared above all others.

Collins's Raiders, Delaney's Raiders, Sarsfield's Raiders, Curtis's

Raiders. The name of Terence Sullivan was an imprecation; the names
of Heenan and Pete Bradley and Dick Allen conjured obscenities; you
shuddered as well when you thought of the Staleybridge Chicken or
the Harlem Infant, for these creatures had been pugilists and brought
their nasty experience like weapons into the stockade.

The population swelled steadily through March, train whistles
bleated at the station, the columns of rag-pickers toiled through the
ravine to the North Gate; they had picked enough rags in Virginia,
now they could pick them in Georgia. Stray infantry skirmish here,
stray cavalry encounter there—the gaping blue-clad flat-hatted seamen from an unhappy sloop, the battery men gathered in by the Rebs
when they were still limbering up to flee: all appeared. All had a certain small wealth in their pockets or on their backs or in the very
clothes which dressed them. The raiders took what they wished, and
were seldom disappointed. Their victims lost anything from their
buttons to their lives.

A hopeless teeming disorder was apparent in this polluted rectangle
from the very first. In tag-end days of February the initial thefts were
committed under cover of darkness or behind tumbled wafers of clay
and pine-roots: you knew that something bad was happening, it had
happened at Belle Isle and Danville, it had happened to some degree
in all the Virginia prisons, you didn't see it happening often, it happened out of sight, it was treacherous and to be feared.

What was the need of waiting for night? At first Willie Collins and
those like him had a notion that guards might shoot. They recalled
the death of Tomcat O'Connor, they saw no reason to die jumping as
he had died. But one morning John Sarsfield himself, with his minions,
was standing near the North Gate when a small detachment of Westerners (they included pickets gobbled up by a swift Confederate
movement in northwest Georgia) found themselves staring at Andersonville for the first time. These people had not been robbed of their
blankets. As did many folks from the West, they wore blanket rolls
in Confederate fashion, they carried no knapsacks. The blanket rolls
seemed bulky to Sarsfield's practiced gaze. He shouldered forward
and wrenched the roll away from the nearest prisoner. The man
hallooed, Sarsfield knocked him flat, the balance of the fresh fish
leaped toward Sarsfield, Sarsfield's Raiders swatted, stabbed, kicked.
This fight was over in less than a minute. Six of the Westerners lay
on the ground and the rest had fallen back into the watching throng—
several others shy of their blanket rolls, as was the first man. All of
the new-come prisoners were bleeding, two were unconscious. Sarsfield's Raiders were the richer by eleven blanket rolls filled with combs,
socks, extra shoes, Bibles (these could be bartered), gilt melaineotypes,
housewives, knives, eating utensils and name-it-if-you-like. The guards
on the parapet stations had not fired a shot; they watched idly or in

downright amusement; they said, Look at them Yanks a-fighting like a lot of dogs, just look.

Willie Collins and Pat Delaney lifted a leaf from Sarsfield's book. Sarsfield was intelligent; it was said that he had read law, had served three years in the army, had been wounded, his wound had healed, he had been promoted First Sergeant and later commissioned; his commission had arrived but he had not been mustered when he was captured. Hence he'd landed here with the enlisted men. Folks said that a bright fellow like Sarsfield had known all along that the guards would not fire. Or perhaps he had made a private agreement with the guards; and now guards might profit from each robbery occurring before their eyes and under the muzzles of their unfired muskets. No longer could the vice be relegated to darkness. It was here in daylight, stalking; it was an animal grown tall as the Methodist Church steeple back home, it was Force and Force only, it could and would maul you to a wet bloody rag if you lifted your fist in protest, or sometimes even if you lifted your voice.

A twenty-year-old named John L. Ransom, Ninth Michigan Cavalry, wrote in his diary: Colonel Persons commands the prison, and rides in and talks with the men. Is quite sociable, and says we are all to be exchanged in a few weeks. He was informed that such talk would not go down any longer. We have been fooled enough, and pay no attention to what they tell us.

John Ransom wrote in a sodden notebook that said *Pickell & Co., Commission Merchants. Chicago. Ills.,* on the cover in faded gilt letters. Get almost enough to eat, such as it is, but don't get it regularly; sometimes in the morning, and sometimes in the afternoon. Six hundred more prisoners came last night. . . . We have no shelter of any kind whatever. Eighteen or twenty die per day. Cold and damp nights. The dews wet things through completely, and by morning all nearly chilled. Wood getting scarce. On the outside it is a regular wilderness of pines . . . can just see the cars go by, which is the only sign of civilization in sight. Rebels all the while at work making the prison stronger. Very poor meal, and not so much today as formerly. . . . Prevailing conversation is food and exchange. A good deal of fighting going on among us. . . . Prison gradually filling up with forlorn looking creatures.

Johnny Ransom had a broken stub of pencil, and he chewed the pencil and made it smaller and found difficulty in writing with it; but he was determined to write a diary. Well, well, my birthday came six days ago, and how old do you think I am? Let me see. Appearances would seem to indicate that I am thirty or thereabouts, but as I was born on the twentieth day of March, 1843, I must now be just twenty-one years of age, this being the year 1864. Of age and six days over. I thought that when a man became of age, he generally became free and his own master as well. If this ain't a burlesque on that old time-honored custom, then carry me out—but not feet foremost. . . . The pine which we use in cooking is pitch pine, and a black smoke arises from it; consequently we are black as negroes. Prison gradually filling from day to day, and situation rather more unhealthy. . . . It is a sad sight to see men die so fast. New prisoners die the quickest. . . . It's a sickly dirty place. Seems as if the sun was not over a mile high, and has a particular grudge against us.

There was a dull man named Dawson who rose each day during that first month of the prison's existence and made his comment about the weather. If the sun came clear, ready to accumulate and radiate the fierce stout heat of a Georgia sun in spring, the dullard would declare, Well, Old Sol the Haymaker is going to get in his work on us again today. And if—as came about more often in March—the skies were cased with zinc and ready to leak or burst, Dawson called the skies and the day Old Boo. Well, Old Boo gets us again today. The terse keen wisdom of the ages can be recollected and quoted by a few; it is the dunces who conceive or incubate the old saws, the slang, the common parlance. Dawson stood daily and turned his bleared gaze upward, and spoke his piece. In no time at all most of the men capable of observing an anecdote were talking about Old Boo. Dawson fell sick, he died, he smelled badly, he was lugged away, no one cared much about him, he was not missed. Months later new prisoners would enter and soon would hear about Old Boo, and they would laugh about Old Boo and in time would shrink in their terror of Old Boo; and then like Dawson they would go down to death, blaming Old Boo; or if they were more fortunately tougher they might survive, and thus live to procreate, to have their children procreate, to sit one day in a rocking chair out on the shady grass under maple trees and tell their grandchildren about Old Boo; and then the grandchildren would go to bed, and cry out in the middle of the night with bad dreams, and when Mother came soothing they would say, He was going to get me, he was going to grab me. Who was going to grab you, dearie? Old Boo! Now, there is no such thing as Old Boo; I never heard of Old Boo; that's just silly. Say Now I Lay Me again, and go to sleep, and don't dream about Old Boo any more because there isn't any such thing.

Johnny Ransom took the wet stub out of his sore mouth and wrote painstakingly: Seems as if our government is at fault in not providing some way to get us out of here. The hot weather months must kill us all outright. Feel myself at times sick and feverish with no strength seemingly. . . . Raiders getting more bold as the situation grows worse. Often rob a man now of all he has, in public, making no attempt at concealment. In sticking up for the weaker party our mess gets into trouble nearly every day.

So indeed did the boys of John Ransom's mess; so did many others. But their resistance (heroic in starved slight youths who battled against a vast anonymous cruelty) was ineffectual. There was no concert in action, no assembling of a force sufficient to cope with well-fed enemies most of whom had practiced the arts of subjugation from infancy. Charity, Christianity, eagerness, righteousness: these were lame swords with which to be armed no matter what the Scriptures had to say on the subject. History had taught a million lessons, history would teach a million more; few might profit from the teaching. Angry and continually apprehensive, the prisoners said, If we all get together . . . take a hundred men, every man jack of them carrying a club; why, we ought to be able to— No one mustered the hundred, no one prepared the cudgels. Say, fellers, we'll make agreement with you folks in that Ohio tent; we'll swap protection with you. If any raiders tackle you, we'll join in; and you got to swear you'll side with us if we get jumped. How about them new folks yonder in the next shebang? Hellfire, twon't do no good to even ask them. Seventh New Hampshire, the whole boiling, and you know what that means: bounty jumpers who enlisted for the heavy pay. Not a true New Hampshireman in the lot, and I vow they'd turn tail in the first pinch.

The frantic disorder pertaining to housing—such as it was—and rations—such as were furnished— Disorder, crowding, the speedy rise of disease and resultant mortality: these ills worked for the raiders' benefit. One noon news came skimming through the mobs: smallpox— didn't you hear? It's rife. No, I didn't see the sick ones; but a boy from the next mess seen them: all blotched up and feverish, and itching like the Old Harry. Tis said the Rebs are going to vaccinate us. Well, by mighty, they'll have to cinch and hog-tie me before they'll get their rotten horse-piss into *my* arm! I seen a nigger man up in Virginia, and he lost his arm because of that damnable vaccination, and like to lost his life as well.

One day, urged by the bayonets of a seedy regiment marched inside for the purpose, the seven thousand men assembled in the stockade were walked to one side of the creek and made to return by slow files while the few contract surgeons scraped vaccine into their arms as they passed. Once beyond the surgeons, there was a growing rush to the marsh and boggy creek despite the fumes which now smoked above each turgid pool. People feared the vaccine more than they feared this noxious ooze—many of them did. They scrubbed madly at their abraided flesh, washing with mud and slime, trusting that they were expelling tainted medicament. There followed numerous cases of swelling and local putrefaction, with amputation and sometimes death as the logical result. Men who had bathed their vaccinations developed enormous sores, men who had not bathed their vaccinations developed enormous sores. There were as many theories about the sores as there

were sores; some believed that the vaccine had been adulterated deliberately with blood taken from syphilitic invalids. The surgeons
exhausted their store before half the men had been treated; the threat
of later vaccination was another of the clouds lying above the stockade.

It was a community demoralized in its inception, demoralized
through rapid growth, exploded into wreckage as each cap was det-
onated by a falling hammer: the cap of starvation . . . *bang!* and
more lives flame out . . . the cap of illness, the cap of chill at night
. . . *bang! Bang* . . . the dread of a beating, the water poisoned by
human filth . . . Godsakes, Piper, I dipped out a half-canteen of that
stuff and lifted it up to drink and— Godsakes, there was a turd floating
right under my nose! . . . The hammer of the rifle falling, the fresh
cap exploded spitefully . . . *bang* . . . the trigger pulled by an unseen
finger, by a finger far away, by a finger inert, by a finger fumbling.

In such a teetering confusion there were crops to be gathered by
savage simple people who knew but enough to strike a blow and had
the power to strike it. Willie Collins was happier in Andersonville
than he had ever been before. Other toughs emerged from their brutal
obscurity—a man in sailor's dress named Rickson, another alleged
sailor named Munn. They had been worms in the outer world; there
they stood in secret dread of manacles, a flogging, in dread of discipline itself. Here there was no discipline except such as the Goliaths
chose to inflict upon their subordinates. Among themselves they
brawled for fun, and to reassure themselves constantly as to their
status as chieftains. The handsome Munn scowled his ponderous way
among shebangs; weaker prisoners hurriedly freed a pathway for him.
The heavy-fisted Sarsfield commanded more power than he would
have commanded as the officer he never became in fact. Charley
Curtis reminded some prisoners of the orangutans pictured in books
of travel . . . low-browed, massive, his voice was a grunt, he had a
trick of tearing the ear off any victim who offered resistance.

Sentries clucked at their stations. By God, Holley, I'm damned if
them Yanks don't just beat the devil.

Sure enough. Like a pack of wolves.

Holley, I hain't never seen a pack of wolves; but if'n they're as
mean-tempered and all gone filthy as these Yankees I sure as hell
don't want to!

. . . Ah, Delaney, and it's over to my own headquarters you must
come immediately; and wait till you see what I've got to treat you
with. Pine-top, man? Never! It's a bottle of the finest brandy I've
tasted since first I joined up. Devil knows where the guard at Station
Thirty got it. A fine pocketknife I gave him for it, with four blades
and a bone handle. It's from a fresh Marylander I took it— Ah, you
would have split a gut! Nickey snatch the lot of us if he didn't make
to jab me with it when I asked him for the knife politely. Sure, and

there he lies yonder; hark you to the noise he's making still; his jaw went to pieces like a teacup when I tapped him.

Hymns receded from the hearing of a bowlegged Rhode Islander named Edward Blamey; he could not hear his father reading aloud: *Therefore I say unto you, Take no thought for your life, what ye shall eat, or what ye shall drink; nor yet for your body, what ye shall put on. Is not the life more than meat, and the body than raiment? Behold the fowls of the air—*

So regularly that it became a commonplace, a frightened-looking young officer in a shabby dun-colored jacket appeared within the stockade on muleback; he rode from point to point, rattling off his memorized screed whenever he thought there was an audience sufficient, and receiving invariably the same vociferous response.

. . . Your Government has cruelly abandoned you, as you can now see, for it makes no attempt to release you and refuses all our offers of a fair exchange of prisoners, North and South. Since your capture you must have become increasingly aware that the Southern Confederacy will soon succeed in achieving its complete and undisputed independence. The Southern Confederacy now offers you an opportunity to enter its service. You will be taken out of this uncomfortable spot, you will receive bounteous rations and adequate apparel; you will be given an attractive bounty, and, at the conclusion of hostilities, you will receive a land warrant establishing your right to—

Aw, go fuck a duck.

Got any of those bounteous rations along with you now?

Why, your adequate apparel hain't much better'n my own.

Where's my farm going to be, with that land warrant and all? I don't want no farm in Texas. Got a nice farm in hell?

Who the devil told you I wanted to be galvanized?

Now and then a lone man—sometimes two or three at a time (comrades who had talked it over and decided that they would dishonor themselves before they would die; but they were few)—slipped to the gate in dark. They asked to speak to an officer, they mumbled the words, the guards had no respect for them and they knew it, they felt a fierce hot breath of living Unionists down their spines, they felt a fierce cold breath of Unionists who were dead.

Some men wondered why, above all, the professional bounty jumpers and roughs did not take advantage of an opportunity to crawl out of this obnoxious slough. But the more discerning might understand easily; within these precincts there was prosperity for the rapacious. Unless driven frantic by the need for women, few of them cared to enlist as Confederates; they saw the Rebel sentries ill-housed, ill-fed, ill-equipped; where was the profit? As galvanized Rebels they would be suspect for a long time, and might not enjoy the freedom awarded to ordinary enlistees. They would have no eminence, they would be regarded suspiciously, accepted by their mates with a grudge. As ordinary Outsiders who had given their parole, even though they did not take the oath as Secessionists, they might not leave the region of the stockade under penalty of being shot. Women? . . . Sometimes you overheard officers joking about an obliging widow who lived nearby. Where were women, what were women when one considered food and drink and other comfort to be secured through bestiality and—later—barter? The more articulate thugs muttered about frying pans and fires; the less articulate thugs said nothing, but proceeded with their program of theft and murder in sullen dedication.

Edward Blamey recognized that Number One was doing poorly by himself. His grandmother used to make the best beach plum preserves anyone had ever tasted; Ed Blamey dreamed nightly about beach plum preserves; he saw himself ladling out the winy richness into a saucer, he felt himself spooning up the preserves and swallowing with love . . . his grandmother fried a chicken the day he went to visit her. With his three-tined black-handled fork and with his sharp black-handled knife he worked steaming white meat free from the little bones, and ate chicken with beach plum treasure spread thereon; there were sage and onion dressing, boiled potatoes, chicken gravy . . . he said, Grandmother, guess I'm feeding like a hog, but I do want to ask you for another saucerful. He heard his grandmother chuckle, complimented to the point of endearment; and then he awoke and knew that he dwelt in steadily increasing filth, that he owned a small amount of rough corn-meal-cob-meal in which black bugs were crawling; that was all he owned, he had no salt; he had a raw place on his right shin which pained and worried him; the shebang leaked badly, and water came around you with awful freshness, awful chill until the faint heat of even one's own weak body warmed it, but the bodily heat could not warm it enough. The gums of Ed Blamey's mouth were touchy, his teeth loosened in their sockets. . . . *Eat, or what ye shall drink; nor yet for your body.* . . . The Wrath To Come was less effectual, it moved shapeless beyond this horizon of up-ended logs, it moved far past the sentries, the sentries were more of a plague than The Wrath To Come. Suppose he was jostled in a crowd, as some prisoners had been jostled when clawing for rations, and so was jostled against the deadline until some half-brained guard thought that he was trying to escape, and shot him through the head? His father wouldn't want him to die . . . Edward, you got to look out for Number One; if you don't, who will? His elder brother wouldn't wish him to die of bleeding toothless gums with which fabrications of coarse cornmeal could not be chewed. There was a rumor that some day, somehow, bread would be baked Outside and issued to the prisoners instead of meal. But Ed would not be able to chew corn bread if his teeth were gone.

The Baptist Church would never demand that he die. Oh, certainly—
die in battle, die in a charge, have a bullet rip his rags, have a hot
bulb of grapeshot take the top from his skull. But not to decay by
inches and parts of inches . . . folks at home, all of Rhode Island;
nobody demanding that he die as men now died near him; no idols or
human patterns of the past exacting an assurance that he must spoil
here while some people were stout and gay and able, living in plenty.

No one had said a word about this smelly eventuality when he
joined the cavalry. At least, he couldn't remember that they had. *With
the garlands of victory around her, when so proudly she bore her
brave crew . . . the shrine of each patriot's devotion, a world offers
homage to thee.* Good enough for singing on the Fourth of July
when everybody crowded on the green, and Judge J. T. Day stood
up on the bandstand and talked about hosannahs of filial devotion arising even unto the blue Empyrean; and the Daughters of
the King Sunday School class had decided to serve a public dinner
for the appalling sum of twenty cents per person in order to raise
money for the new Baptistry (the old Baptistry leaked down into the
cellar), and that meant more chicken and dressing and other sorts
of preserves besides beach plum, and apple butter and coconut cakes;
and Edward Blamey and some of his friends had stuffed a toy cannon with powder and wadded newspapers, and they touched it off
right in the middle of Judge J. T. Day's speech, and then they ran
like whiteheads when they saw the constable coming . . . ran long
and lightly and youthfully with their pockets filled with torpedoes
and Chinese crackers and squibs . . . *three cheers for the Red, White
and Blue!*

No. Scarcely. You didn't feel like cheering for the Red, White and
Blue when your teeth were coming out, or threatening to come out,
and when your shebang leaked dolefully (By Mighty, said the scarecrow Sergeant Colony, we got more rain than roof) and when Si
Wingate whined with fever for three days and nights and was then
carried to join a row of fat-eyed motionless people near the gate, and
when Tup Wingate squatted in agony with his ragged pants pulled
down and bloody stool dripping from his haunches.

Got to look after Number One. Well—

Weavers, malleable iron workers, machinists, railroad men, printers,
tanners, shoemakers—oh, above all shoemakers in this nearly shoeless
domain!—Rebel emissaries appeared, guarded, every day or two. Any
millers, saw or grist? Oh, shoemakers. . . . Who'd like to work in
Macon? All you got to do, Yank, is sign this here little old piece of
paper; make your mark if you can't sign. Yes, sir, Yank, I got a
golden opportunity for you: any man who knows the cobbler's trade!
Nice boarding place, good bed to sleep in, that old lady sets a fine
table, and wages on top of it. You boys *are* tight run here, sure enough.

But I reckon you can see which way the cat's jumping now. Just chew
on it, Yank; don't need to make up your mind today; I'll be back
a Friday, and I'll tell that old lady to put on a mess of pork and
turnips against your coming. . . .

Aw, dry up.

That old lady got any *young* ladies with her, mister?

Any *young* ladies in that good bed you was talking about?

I hate turnips! Tell her to cook some nice green peas instead.

Can't read nor cipher, so *you* make my mark for me—great *big* mark.

Hey. Go stick a weasel up your ass. Right beside the cobbler's
bench, Mister Monkey!

The bulk of the men knew that in cutting shoe-leather or in reaming
bolts or in tanning hides or in mixing mortar or in baking bricks for
anyone in this bleak hated region, they would be fighting for the
Bonnie Blue Flag (where was it? They had never seen the enemy
with a Bonnie Blue Flag; they had seen him with the diagonal cross
and stars on his red battle flag) as surely as if they rode with Forrest
or marched in Hood's columns. The bulk of the men resisted these
commercial missionaries as they resisted the gangling lieutenant with
his claptrap chatter about Adequate Apparel and Conclusion of
Hostilities.

The bulk of the men, again. . . . There was the silent haggard louse-
ridden harness-maker from Indiana; people in his mess referred to
him as Fort Wayne; he disappeared one day, and folks said that they
had seen him near the South Gate; and other folks said later that they
had heard Fort Wayne was gone to Albany to fashion the tug-straps
which were his specialty. His mess argued about it.

A parole is just a parole, after all. What difference whether you're
paroled to work Outside, taking care of mules, or whether you're
paroled to work in Albany?

Plenty difference!

Bet your life. One way you're just here at the stockade, same as if
you were on the Inside. Other way, you're helping the Reb artillery
to shoot your own God damn brother.

Well, Fort Wayne had three kids to home.

Do tell. I got *four*.

A Pittsburgh printer vanished, so did a stationary engineman from
Schenectady: one was said to be working in Macon, the other in
Savannah. . . . No one knew. The men were gone; not many of them
went; perhaps seven or eight went in March out of the whole stockade.
More than seven thousand others stayed and drank the water or
didn't drink it, and popped the lice like popcorn from their frayed
jacket seams when they held the jackets over blazing pine scraps. The
pine scraps were fewer now, you couldn't just pick them up, you had
to bargain for them. A lean Scandinavian corporal called Nellie Bly

because his name was Nels—he cut his wrist deliberately with a piece of tin and died quietly at sunrise, saying nothing. Adoniram Kempley insisted on taking off what remained of his clothes and sitting naked on the edge of the marsh, day and night; he said that he was waiting for somebody, he would not utter the name of the person he was waiting for; he perished within the week. An artilleryman they called Indian Giver was throttled in broad daylight by one of Curtis's Raiders because he refused to part with his pocket comb. Paul Hexley tore his heel on a crumpled cooking pan, and soon he had no heel, nor any foot to have a heel on; soon he had no life. An undersized sixteen-year-old musician called Wabash huddled around, unable to play the fife with which he had entertained his fellows earlier. His gums looked like spongy rotten plums, they thrust oozing far out of his mouth, his lips spread back to let the gums protrude, it looked as if he were holding a bit or a gag in his mouth, a bit or a gag heavy and purplish and artificial.

That's scurvy, said Edward Blamey, and I got a touch of it. He lay alternately perspiring and shivering until the eastern sky grew murky instead of Stygian above obtruding sentry stations. Then he took silent terrified leave of companions who did not even sniff, who thought that he might have gone to the sinks. He crossed Stockade Creek and crouched down within a pole's length of the unearthly root-and-oilcloth-and-log-and-blanket structure known as Collins's Castle on the South Side. Later he was challenged by hangers-on; he stood with docility while they ripped out his pockets and found nothing except an uneven set of small flat grayish stones which he used to play checkers with, with Sergeant Colony. The roughs threw the stones away, biffed Edward Blamey until his ear rang and seemed deafened; they swaggered off toward the gate. After nine o'clock in the morning Willie Collins emerged from his castle, a furry half-naked trunk, the walking trunk of a ginger-colored tree, yelling for someone named Donner: where the hell was that meat he was after frying? Edward Blamey went to the ruffian's side at once. He could not feel his feet touching the ground in their broken-soled shoes. But still The Wrath To Come was a long way off, he could not hear its roaring.

Member me, Willie?

Agh. . . . The giant rolled his red-rimmed eyes, yawned, snorted. What want ye with Willie Collins?

I got a sharp pair of eyes. You called them ogles . . . made me a kind of proposition. Member?

That I do. Inside with you, Rubber Legs. He took Edward Blamey into the wide cave above ground, the cave half in the ground, and it was warm inside, whatever uncertain springtime chill and wetness ruled elsewhere, and it smelled of fried food and vomit and dirty males and liquor, and oh Heavenly Father it smelled of food, and oh

Heavenly Father there was a fire beaming on the baked mud hearth, and oh Heavenly Father don't send The Wrath To Come.

Look you. There's a shebang yonder, name of Parker House. Artillerymen, so tis said.

Nigh the North Gate, Willie? I think I know it.

That you must. Striped blankets on the roof? Twould be the one. Watch you well this day, and run to me the first minute there's not more than two—mark you, kiddie, I said *two*—of the Sams inside. We've tried them before; they're hell on wheels; but they've greenbacks buried there. Mark well, or I'll tear the velvet from your head! Not more than *two*.

Willie . . . what's velvet?

Your red tongue, you addle cove! I'll rip it out of your throat with these fingers if there's more than two men in that shebang when we hit the place.

He gave Edward Blamey some fried potatoes and onions, gave him half a cup of pine-top on which the Rhode Islander choked, but which coursed like fury through him. Ed Blamey wandered idly afield, selected a vantage point, watched with care. The Boston men might never dream that he was observing them. He counted carefully: there were six about the place. Two went away, another left later . . . he couldn't be certain . . . by noon there were but two about? Suddenly he saw three men standing in front, talking; then one picked his way toward the North Gate; the other two went back inside the Parker House. Blamey shot himself into the presence of Willie Collins like a misshapen bowlegged projectile. Five minutes later the yells had gone aloft. Raiders! had been cried to no effect, for the other partners in the Parker House could not reach the scene in time. A thatch was torn aside, a tin can of currency was gathered up, blankets were pulled from the roof. One of the two defenders lay gulping spasmodically, holding his abdomen where kicks had smashed his bowels; the other defender lay unconscious, his head cracked, bystanders had heard the bone crack when he was clubbed.

Edward Blamey drank deeply of pine-top that night, trying to forget the thing that had happened, the thing which he had brought about. Och, what a pair of ogles! cried Willie Collins. And there was a hundred and twenty-nine dollars in that wad! Cookie, break open another box of biscuit for our friend Delaney, and where's that cheese, and what came of that tin of mushroom pickles? Sure and I feel a song coming on.

In Athol there lived a man named Jerry Lanagan—

Is it a song you can sing me, Delaney? A good melody to tickle the heart—

No, said Edward Blamey, I can't. Can't sing a note.

XIX

One bright morning at the end of April late sleepers awoke to find both South Street and Main Street tenanted by recumbent bodies on which fresh sun shone brightly blue, from which fresh sun tore spasms of gilt where buttons spangled or where patent-leather chevrons reflected. Hundreds of new prisoners had been herded in through both gates during the night, and they bedded in those streets because they had nowhere else to sleep and feared to go wallowing in the dark.

Well, by God, these are the freshest fish that ever got hooked.

Fresh fish, hell! Looks like the Rebs gobbled up a brigade of major-generals.

Looky. Silk chevrons on some.

Patent-leather. . . .

Looky that gang. Got feathers in their hats, I swear.

Hey, there, Yank! If you be a Yank. What you from?

A man roused slowly as if he had drunk himself to sleep on liquor, as if his head puffed and rang, as if he saw rats gnawing close. He gazed at the blackened hairy skeletons a-crowding. Huh?

I said, What you from?

Hundred and Third Pennsylvania.

Where you get grabbed?

Huh?

Whereabouts were you captured?

Oh. Plymouth, North Carolina.

Plymouth? You must be Pilgrim Fathers for certain. Hey, Pee-leg, come take a look at these Pilgrim Fathers!

The term Plymouth Pilgrims would cling to them throughout their captivity; it would be a short captivity for many. They awakened in the pit squarely beneath a privy used by devils, the shock numbed and dumbed them, the devils' evacuations poured over them, they were mired, they were suffocated, they drowned, they died.

For most their war had been a light and easy war until the seventeenth of April. These regiments dwelt at quiet if important forts along the coast all the way from Fortress Monroe to Beaufort, and good food came in on supply ships, and the quarters of such garrisons were dry and clean. On a Sunday you might attend services at

Grace Church. . . . Off duty, a man could lie along old pilings and
whip a line around his wrist, and toss the plummet and baited hook
out into shifting water, and prepare for a stripèd fish to flap and
lunge and delight him. . . . The Eighty-fifth New York, the One
Hundred and First Pennsylvania, the One Hundred and Third Pennsylvania: every man waited contentedly for boats to bear the regiments
northward. It would be a lark, sailing for home on a veteran's furlough. Instead came a powerful ram called the *Albemarle,* and three
brigades of troops attacking by land. Cannon thudded from the forts,
the *Albemarle* ripped past unscathed and sent the *Southfield* rolling
into the sea and pounded the *Miami* into flight. Federal troops on
land held out for two more days, then they surrendered to what
seemed like a million polite North Carolinians who did not even
search their knapsacks.

Looky, Charley, at them bureaus.

I swan. Member when I was a new recruit, I packed one of them
big bureaus off to the front. How it like to gauled the shoulders off
of me. Hey, Yank, what you got in your bureau? Got any spare
crackers to swap?

I'll warrant you he's got everything but the kitchen stove.

He'll have that under that big feathered hat of his.

You actually tried to fight a battle in rigging like that? No wonder
you got grabbed.

The newcomers explained haltingly that since they stood in momentary expectancy of sailing north from Plymouth, they were wearing their best new uniforms at the time the Confederate onslaught
began; after that they had no chance to change, they never even
thought of changing their clothes. They fought from the seventeenth
until the twentieth of April and then were captured in finery. Along
with the veterans' brigade were the Sixteenth Connecticut Infantry,
the Twenty-fourth New York Independent Battery, a company of the
Twelfth New York Cavalry, and two batteries of Massachusetts heavy
artillery. Two-thirds of these captives arrived on this day; the rest
reached Andersonville on May third. Not a man of them had ever
envisioned a place like Andersonville in his ugliest imaginings. The
immensity of smell, the shrunken limbs, the pot bellies of the dropsical,
the oozing mouths of the scurvy-ridden— Blackened masses of faces
which pressed close with hungry eyes staring— The bundles of lousy
hair bristling out, wads of lousy beards a-stringing—

There they sat with freighted knapsacks, the heavy oblongs with
good rolled blankets atop, and stuffed with every civilized comfort
known to the easy regime of garrison troops—troops who'd never
marched a thousand miles or (many of them) even a hundred miles—
There they sat, with sun glittering on their niceness. They could not
arise from the ground.

How in tarnation did they ever get in here with all that truck? It's
a sight for sore eyes.

You know the answer to that one. Guarded by Regular troops instead of these chicken-shit Home Guards!

Hey, Corp. You with the fancy mustache. Swap you two good
blanket poles for that canteen? You got to have blanket poles or else
you got no shebang to dwell in. Come along, old top, I'll show you
what I mean—

They moved in stricken daze, their eyes saw things, the brains behind them would not believe. Raiders began swooping down, the
moment individuals were separated from the mass which might have
given protection—and did, for wiser ones, for a time.

Wiser and more resilient than many of his fellows loomed a broad-
shouldered young man of twenty-three with a well-trimmed mane of
black hair and ears wide and outstanding. His mouth was full-lipped,
his brown eyes brooding and thick-lidded, and he had the Semitic
nose fancied by cruel cartoonists and seldom seen in fact. His name
was Nathan Dreyfoos. He was well at home in the world although
never had he thought to find himself domiciled in a roost such as
this. Born in Boston, he had spent most of his life abroad, traveling
from country to country with his father and mother, taught by English
tutors the while. His father was a purchasing agent for merchants in
eastern American cities, buying everything from tweeds to olive oil,
and back again to watches and Parisian perfumery and Bavarian
china and Flemish glass. Nathan was tri-lingual as to English, French
and Spanish, speaking also subordinate dialects of the latter language.
He spoke a good deal of Yiddish and some German, Italian and
Swedish. He owned no ambition in life except to worship the better
elements of the past and (in some vague manner as yet undecided) to
acquaint people with lessons and glories of the past, to the eventual
comfort and enrichment of humanity.

Abroad when the war began, Nathan Dreyfoos felt no upsurge of
nationalism. His parents were barely removed by one generation from
their separate European backgrounds, and thus had returned easily to
Continental attitude and thought. The young man heard about the
burst of civil warfare with disquietude and regret, because wars inflicted miseries, and he was benevolent of heart and did not wish
to have miseries inflicted. He liked Boston, New York, Philadelphia; he
grew momentarily and remotely saddened at thinking of Bostonians,
New Yorkers, Philadelphians being slain in battle. He liked Charleston and New Orleans; was it not a horrid thing that people from
South Carolina and Louisiana must now die or be mutilated? He
would have felt a personal concern of infinitely greater depth if he
had learned that in Madrid they were raising an army to invade
France, or that the Dutch were assembling a navy to sail against
England.

When again he walked an American street he strolled in citizen's clothing tailored by Desborough. One evening he stood sipping wine in the public room of the Astor House when two young officers of the Eighty-fifth New York moved close to him and, having absorbed more drink than their heads could carry, felt it incumbent upon them to discuss in clear ringing tones the worthlessness of well-dressed stay-at-homes who permitted braver men to go out and do their fighting for them.

Present company excepted, said Lieutenant Corley elaborately.

Oh, yes, indeed, said Lieutenant Stevenson. As a matter of fact, my dear Tom, I've heard that our Hebrew brethren are disinclined to violence of any kind. A fellow couldn't hold them responsible. . . .

I beg your pardon, said Nathan Dreyfoos, but they pretended not to hear him, although most men in the place were turning to watch. Nathan paid for his wine, and stepped into the street. He had not long to wait in the reflected glare of gas. Soon the lieutenants appeared, flushed and talkative, bound for another bar-room. Politely Nathan invited them to step back inside and apologize to the company there—not so much for the insults directed at him personally as for the remarks about Hebrews. Corley, the broadest and longest, said that he would see Nathan in hell first. Very well, said Nathan Dreyfoos, let us go. By way of this alley.

In the alley he flattened Corley with his first blow, and Stevenson rushed upon him. Stevenson struck the cobblestones while Corley was rising and thus it went for a time, amid yells of servants and guests pouring from the Astor House. The two officers were alternately smashed and toppled, while Nathan received no damage except to his attire. Mr. Halliburton, his favorite tutor, was a Cantabrian athlete with not-too-thwarted ambitions as a pugilist. Once Mr. Halliburton cracked Nathan's jawbone; then the guilty pair had to connive to keep this dark secret from the senior Dreyfooses. Nathan was a seasoned expert at boxing as well as a seasoned expert at fencing, and felt regret at what he was doing now. Yet, in some disquieting manner, this performance seemed called for. A policeman put a cautious hand on the young man's shoulder while he was bending over the bleeding and amazed Lieutenant Corley, and told him that he was under arrest for brawling in public. Nonsense, said Nathan, and gave the policeman a five-dollar bill. With his arm around Corley and with Stevenson stumbling sore-faced against his right side, Nathan led the way to his own quarters upstairs, and of course they were handsome quarters. A doctor came with plasters, a mumbling Negro carried off the officers' clothing to be repaired; more wine appeared, together with cold beef and chicken. The gentleman talked long. Corley and Stevenson spent the balance of the night in Nathan's big bed and Nathan slept on the sofa. In this way the Eighty-fifth New

York gained a somewhat poetic linguist who insisted on enlisting as a private soldier because he feared the responsibility of command.

. . . But, damn it, my dear boy! Your father must know heaps of men with influence, and you just heard what Tom said about *his* father and the senator. There's bound to be a vacancy soon and—

Now, listen, old chap. I'm acquainted with Colonel Fardella *personally,* not just as a subordinate company officer. When once he hears that you can speak Italian—

In France, said Nathan, my best friend was my father's coachman. But a fellow of culture and—

In Spain, Nathan told them, Olmedo the gardener was my best friend. I knew poor people, I knew a charcoal burner in the hills, I knew bandits. I am very much at ease with such people.

Oh, damn it, Dreyfoos! We've got no charcoal burners, and not too many gardeners or coachmen, I'll wager that. Our men are mostly young chaps, boys from good Christian homes— Beg pardon—

Blessed are ye, when men shall revile you, and persecute you. . . . Nathan smiled at Lieutenant Stevenson and put a hand on his throbbing arm. In Málaga I was accustomed to playing my violin for the monks. And I know the Beatitudes of your Faith. And I do come from a good home. I could be harmonious with the men in your command.

He served under First Lieutenant Corley and Second Lieutenant Stevenson and was promoted by rapid degrees to the rank of sergeant, with the approval of those surrounding him. In the attack on Plymouth both Corley and Stevenson were killed—the former by a shell from the *Albemarle,* the latter by a stray musket ball half an hour before the Unionists surrendered. During the days which followed his capture, Nathan walked with a heavy heart. He was disconsolate at losing his friends, yet he thought they had died for a sound purpose. That long ago night, in the Astor House, the ebullient youths grew articulate in stress of emotion following their thrashing. They had persuaded Nathan that since he turned out to be historically minded, he must look at the present conflict in the historical sense. The Nation had been founded in bitter conflict, and had achieved to world importance through further conflict and through its own crowding growth to the West. Broken in half, the impact of America on the world and on the future would be lessened; the United States and the Confederate States would resolve into puny second-rate powers. It was so throughout history . . . look at the federations which made strength; look at Grecian history, Roman, western European.

The Union *must* survive! cried the blond young Corley, with his bruised mouth full of chicken.

And, as a born American, it is your strict duty to aid in that survival!

But I love the South of this country as well as the North.

Do you suppose that General George H. Thomas, for example, does not love Virginia? He was born in Virginia, Virginia is his mother State! Why is General Thomas fighting for the Union? Because he recognizes the necessity of resistance against armed rebellion! The Nation is bigger than any one State or group of States, Friend Nathan. *It is historically demanded that this Nation survive as a single entity.* If you go to the army, as you are *obliged* to go to the army, you will be fighting—not as a renegade American returned to these shores, not as a native Bostonian, not for the State of Massachusetts. You will be fighting for the greatest, noblest commonwealth which ever gave a benefit to mankind: the single, Federal commonwealth of sister States, the United States of America!

Cracky, Tom, cried Salem Stevenson. I can't wait for this war to be over, so's you can hang out your shingle and strike for the Albany assembly!

Corley was duly modest. Well, I used to twist a mean verb, as they say, when I was on the debating panel at the Academy.

Stevenson mounted stiffly to a gilt-tasseled chair and, champagne glass in hand, demanded to know of Nathan whether he had ever seen Daniel Webster in the flesh. He, Stevenson, had.

When my eyes shall be turned to behold for the last time the sun in heaven, may I not see him shining on the broken and dishonored fragments of a once-glorious Nation . . . on a land rent with civil feuds and drenched, it may be, in fraternal blood—

Toby the floor-waiter knocked softly at the door. If the gentlemen could kindly be a mite more quiet. Lady in Number Twelve she feeling poorly. And it's nigh to four o'clock.

They talked more softly, but still they talked earnestly. Nathan was forced to admit that his grandparents on both sides had been immigrants because they sought the opportunity and safety which America afforded. He was forced to admit that his father had advanced in a fashion impossible in most other countries . . . was this not, then, a debt which he owed to the Federal Union and which he must pay by offering his own body and spirit? Stirred to intimacy, Nathan now told how his grandfather Margolis's father and mother had been beaten to death and hurled into the flames of their own house, while the baby which was Grandfather Margolis lay covered by straw nearby and thus escaped extermination in that *pogrom.* His new friends (the heedless Jew-baiters of a few hours before) paled at the description and clucked in sympathy.

These memories returned with blinding force during the heartbreak of defeat and surrender, during the pain of being transported as a chattel of war. Because he was accustomed to travel and acutely sensitive to each impression, Nathan did not dwell, however, in a stricken doze. Automatically his mind said, This is new. This I have not seen before. This I will remember. . . . The enemy's reserve pickets marching us forth. They say this village is Jamesville. The last was Foster's Mills. . . . Why this desolation, why the white and fire-marked chimneys of houses no longer standing? The damage must have been done by our Union troops when they raided to Whitehall. . . . Our guards say they are from the Thirty-fifth North Carolina. A very decent set of fellows; and civil war becomes increasingly dreadful when I realize that it was they or their brothers-in-arms who killed my friends the two lieutenants, without whose instigation I would not have come to fight in the first place. . . . Suppose my father and I had sailed to New Orleans (and we might have done so, but for the blockade) instead of to New York? Then I might have met some Southerners and been insulted by them, and might have whipped them in the same way; and then, over wine and meat, might have been persuaded that their Cause was the Cause truly just, and so might have found myself wearing their uniform. . . . No, no, impossible! Because a civil war proves in its very waging that it is the nastiest business afoot; and it is to prevent for all time the recurrence of such strife that we thinking Union troops are willing to endure. Corley and Stevenson are now wiped off the slate, along with so many thousands of others. Perhaps the damp sponge of Fate is waiting to rub out my own name. If so, I am willing to let it be rubbed, because I came earnestly into this situation. I am confident that the North will prevail; I am assured that, eventually, the forces of dissolution will crumble; I know in my heart and soul that one day both sections of this Country will again be forged together, never more to be split.

The great lamentation of the future will be concerned only with the fact that, by and large, the most energetic and high-minded youths of all these States involved were the ones who perished; and most of them were too young to leave their seed behind them. It will be a long weakness for the united Nation of the future. The soul which might have written the compelling opera went winging at Manassas Junction. The hand which might have sculptured a shape fairer than *Moses* was shot off on the Chickahominy. The brain which could have managed the richest agronomy of all time was drilled by a conoidal bullet at Stone's River. The hearts which might have beat with the rhythm of philanthropist and priest and educator . . . O wicked Gettysburg, O doleful Vicksburg, O thrice lewd Fredericksburg!

> *Lang wull his lady look*
> *Frae the castle doon,*
> *E'er she see the Earl o' Murray*
> *Come soonding through the toon.*

. . . Good old Halliburton, and the ballads he sang before the fire-place; and Mother chording on that ancient gilt spinet in the corner, and candle flames bowing in obeisance to the legendry, and the warm sea touched with stars at the foot of our lawn. Will ever I see them again? Will ever I know the future?

O sad maimed Future! Where is your prime inventor? The ocean covered him with barnacles when the *Monitor* went down. Where is the saint whose scalpel or microscope was intended to still the scream of cancer? We Federals spattered his skull at Missionary Ridge. O long discordant Future drowned in tears, as now my soul is drowning! Where is the President whose power and nobility might have led a healed Nation to world-enfolding glory? The fever took him at Rock Island, in Arkansas, in Libby Prison, at Fort Delaware. He wore blue, he wore butternut. He drew a lanyard, he tore the paper of a cartridge with his teeth, he galloped behind John Morgan, he rode to meet the lead on that last charge of Farnsworth's in a Pennsylvania glen. Minister and explorer, balloonist and poet, botanist and judge, geologist and astronomer and man with songs to sing . . . they are clavicles under leaves at Perryville, ribs and phalanges in the soil of Iuka, they are a bone at Seven Pines, a bone at Antietam, bones in battles yet to be sweated, they are in the soil instead of walking, the moss has them.

So Nathan Dreyfoos had mourned, seeking adjustment to new situation and recent tragedy . . . a town called Williamston, the prisoners resting in a pine grove, guards lounging about and some of them flirting with girls who came tripping fearfully in the crowd scampering to see the Yankees. The village postmaster, fat and old and pink-faced, came trotting up with his leather pouch like an amiable Saint Nick; he promised to mail letters for any of the prisoners who wished to write to the folks at home. Yes, sir, boys, them letters'll be sent through your lines at the first opportunity. Don't thank me, boys—glad to do it—my own Andy got took by your fellows up in Maryland and he's still a prisoner of war; but once't in a while we get a letter from him. Nathan Dreyfoos blinked away the tears which came suddenly, and smiled down at Saint Nick. I hope he's keeping well, sir. Oh, yes, Sergeant, tolerable, tolerable.

Nathan wrote hastily on half a sheet of paper, he gave the rest of his paper away to boys who had none. Dear Father and Mother, I trust this will reach you with the assurance that I am unwounded and in fine fettle. But there is sad news: Plymouth has fallen to the enemy and those of us who were not killed were taken prisoner. My friends Stevenson and Corley are among the dead. I do not know where we will be imprisoned; some say at Charleston or Savannah. If all our warders are as gentlemanly as our present guards and as the kind person who has promised to mail this, then shall we be well treated indeed. Please advise Halliburton of my situation; I think he is still at the Embassy in Paris— People in gray began ordering the prisoners

into column; there was not time to write more; he scribbled, Y'r Devoted Son Nathan, and Saint Nick took the letters away in his pouch,
and girls' shrill voices began to sing in the grove, *Hurrah, Hurrah, for
Southern Rights, Hurrah,* and the marching prisoners answered with
a roaring *We'll hang Jeff Davis to a sour apple tree,* until they were
silenced by the guards. Tramp, march, stride, the long shadows on the
dust, the long dusty blue column in rising dust, the dogs coming out
to yap, the Negroes staring and laughing.

They had some sickness that night; the Rebels put up a tent for the
sick; the prisoners slept in a void something like bliss. At least nobody
is a-prosecuting us, said one serious countryman from up the Hudson;
and most of the others knew that he meant to say persecuting, and that
was a joke, and they made much of the joke. They were filled with
crackers and raw pork, and knew that they had nothing to fear from
captors who would put up a tent to shield sufferers from the night.

They lost their charitable North Carolinians at Hamilton the next
day. A new band of Confederates succeeded them, but still there was
no brutality; still appeared the nightly ration of black-eyed peas, meal
and bacon. . . . The twenty-fourth was a Sunday, and before the
prisoners were formed in column for the march to Tarboro a throng
of them got together for prayers and Bible reading. They sang, Sweet
Hour of Prayer, and Nathan hummed along with the rest for he did
not know the words. . . . Should I chant *Kol Nidre* for them? I fear
that I do not know that, either. Ah, my poor violin, neglected in its
case in New York. Or is it in New York? Father said that he would
keep it safe. I wonder where it is.

The train at Tarboro, and striking the main road at Rocky Mount,
and rattling on into the South to meet a warmer spring. . . . Now the
men were weary of singing; there was a good deal of arguing and one
fight in Nathan's box car, a disturbance which he quelled with haste.
Their guards were from the Twenty-eighth Georgia and a very stern
officer of the guard—a captain named Johnson—ordered the doors
closed at dusk. Then there was mashing and pressing and squeezing
and jerking through the long noisy night. A drummer boy wept that
he was being smothered.

And I bet you wish you were home with your mother, Tyke.

Yes, God damn it, I do!

Well, so do I. So does every last man of us. So quit bawling, Tyke.
It won't help none.

All right, Corporal Reeves. Sniffle, snuffle. I'll quih-hit—

Pikeville, Goldsborough, Wilmington with its lean blockade runners
lying silver gray by the docks. There was some firing out at sea, the
prisoners crowded hopefully against their ferryboat's rail and soon were
rewarded by observing the return of a steamer which had tried to
run the blockade. Yeh, yeh, yeh, the men yelled. Try again, Johnny—

better luck next time!—but the crew of the steamer could not hear them, and a few sailors waved affably, and shouted jocular insults across the water, or appeared to be shouting them. . . . The new train had platform cars. Various men whispered about jumping off and striking for the woods, but the armed Georgians beside them looked as if they could shoot so no one made the attempt. Younger prisoners waved and hooted at the people, black and white, in every village which the train went smoking through. Cinders came back to sting their eyes, and sometimes glowing flakes were lashed out of the air to sting and burn; but still it was better than being crushed in box cars. . . . In Charleston the ropy beards of Spanish moss swayed dreamily, the flowers were magenta and pink and gold; in Charleston an old Negro came up to the cars with a bucket of hot fried shrimps to sell and his bucket was emptied in a twinkling.

Look at those women. Picking peas in their garden.

Man alive! Wait'll I write Pa about that. Up home I don't think he'll have the peas scarcely planted.

They changed trains again at Savannah and only thirty-five men were put into each box car. There was room to stretch out. It was good to lie down, even though the cars did seem to run on square wheels, even though grit came flying in all night and the sound of hammers deafened a fellow's ears. The next day they stopped in a wilderness where there was a shack marked Station Number Thirteen, and here the prisoners were marched to an adjacent stream and permitted to wash.

. . . I'll be beat, Lewis. You know, my brother Lafe was in a prison pen in Virginia, up until he got exchanged, and he said they never had a chance to wash. So they got lice all over themselves. This is pie. If this keeps up we won't be doing badly at all.

. . . And, Sim, look at the rations they're issuing, up ahead. Looks like soft tack and fresh pork. And beans. By gum, so tis!

. . . Well, if this be a sample, bring on your hippypotymus. Georgia for me!

That night they were marched into the Andersonville stockade; and so they woke up staring, and they could not believe, they could not believe.

Nathan Dreyfoos said, It was too good to last.

But, Sarge, they can't mean to *keep* us here.

Look at the other prisoners, Allen.

But they must have made a mistake. Maybe they sent us to the wrong place. Maybe this is a *punishment* camp. Eh, Sarge? Oh, for God's sake, Sarge, please do ask the guards if there hain't been a mistake! A man can't *live* in a place like this.

A great many of them don't, said one of the blackened hairy creatures who stood watching and listening.

What say?

A great many of them don't.

The boy who had been pleading with Nathan Dreyfoos buried his head in his arms and began to blubber.

Nathan sat quietly in the bright stinking sunshine for a while, trying to decide what to say to Private Allen. At last he put his arm around the boy's shaking shoulders and said, Don't do that if you can help it, Allen. Weeping is the easiest but the worst thing that any of us can do here.

Yyyyeh.

You still have your strength. We have arrived at this ugly place in splendid condition. Instead of indulging in tears, we must keep our spirits up and our wits alive. There may be some way out.

Yyyyeh, Sarge.

Perhaps you can escape. Perhaps many of us can.

The man who had said, A great many of them don't, moved off slowly through the crowd. He thought of Nathan, He talks like an officer, but is only a sergeant like me. He oughtn't to delude himself about escape. . . . Oh, well, I used to try to escape, myself. Eventually I learned that it was wiser to devote myself to the science of living here, living as well as possible and as long as possible. . . . I wonder what that big Jew has got in his big knapsack? Maybe we can make a swap.

The man's name was Seneca MacBean, and he came from Galena, Illinois. He was long a prisoner, shrewd in experience with mankind before he became a prisoner, shrewder now a thousand fold. MacBean had served with the Eighth Illinois Cavalry until that storied afternoon of July first, 1863, when dismounted troopers of Gamble's Brigade went stringing east from a certain bullet-pocked seminary building, still firing their carbines if they had any rounds left to fire. In the town beyond they ran down this street and that, hunting for a way to safety, darting across backyards, trampling the rhubarb and onion tops and moss roses. Eventually the way behind them was barred by panting gangs of strangers in sweat-drenched gray shirts and undershirts, and the way ahead was thronged with other sweaty people who advanced on them meaningly with muskets at the ready.

Drop that carbine, Yank.

One man tried to get away by climbing a brick wall, and several guns banged, and the man fell into a tangle of tomato vines. This is *futility*, said Seneca MacBean, imagining that he was setting the word in Italic antique boldface; it was an odd trick, emphasizing words in that manner, but he was a printer by trade; he had been a printer's devil at ten. He called to those of his men who were near, ordering them not to resist. Forms all locked up, he said. We've gone to press, gentlemen. The cavalrymen did not know exactly what he meant by

this, but the example of Sergeant MacBean was unmistakable: he
had dropped his carbine, and was holding up a yellow bandana in
lieu of a white flag. . . . At Belle Isle he tried to escape by swimming
the James River but was picked up by Home Guards on the Richmond
side and returned to the Island. Here at Andersonville he had tried
to escape by tunneling, along with a great many others; some dogs
scouted him out, less than an hour after he left the tunnel. Seneca
MacBean was resting, exhausted, on a cypress knee in the nearby
swamp. My tongue, he told his friends later, was hanging longer than
the dogs'. He spent a week in the stocks, which he endured stoically,
and was then marched back into the pen.

Wirz remembered him well, because of his height (his rangy body
towered four inches over six feet) and the circumstances. So, Henry
Wirz would say each time he encountered the bony Illinoisan, Maybe
you want you should go back in the stocks, *nein?*

No thanks, Captain.

Then no more tunnels you make, you bad sergeant, you!

Nope. I won't.

MacBean sustained himself at Andersonville by conducting a laundry. He had two wooden buckets which he cared for lovingly in order
to keep them from springing leaks. He had no soap, but ashes and
sand served. He'd made himself a scrubbing board, buying the end of
a wide planed plank of hardwood, and this piece of plank he had
grooved diligently. It did not work as well as his grandmother's well-
remembered scrubbing board, back home at the shady end of Bench
Street, but it worked.

Often he thought of his grandmother; he could see her scrubbing
under a morning-glory arbor as she had scrubbed when he was small—
when his grandfather lost his job, when Gran MacBean took in washings, when Seneca MacBean drew those same washings—pressed beautifully by Gran's hot irons—back to the tall homes of the Campbells or
Gratiots or Kittoes on his squeaky-wheeled wagon, or sometimes in
winter on his sled.

Senny, did your Gran say how much it was, this time?

Yes'm. She said she guessed a shilling.

Wait till I get my purse. . . . Here it is, in fractional currency. Count
it carefully. Or can you count, yet?

Yes'm. I can count to a hundred.

What are you sniffing at, Senny? Those muffins Ellen is baking for
tea?

Yes'm.

You shall have one. Ellen, fetch a strawberry muffin for the Mac-
Bean child. Fetch two. . . . And little Mrs. Gratiot smiled down at him,
and he thought that she was beautiful.

It had been a good childhood, marred only by trivial matters like poverty, like being an orphan, like having a grandfather who often lay on his bed for days at a time . . . mumble, mumble, mumble, sometimes in English, sometimes in the Gaelic which John MacBean couldn't recollect when he was sober. Then, at the age of fifty-nine, John Mac-Bean signed The Pledge. I've never gone back on my word, he told the plain-faced woman who loved him devotedly. No more do I intend to go back on this word I've given now. He did not go back on his word; he never took another drink, and repeatedly counseled Seneca never to take The First Drink.

It was drink that took that fine handsome father of yours, laddie, and, in a way, it was drink that took the fair young mother who bore you, for she had not the will or strength to survive. Never take The First Drink.

Seneca did not, until he was seventeen. Then, while working across the big river in Dubuque, he fell in with a riotous crowd of Irishmen, and attended a pic-nic where the whiskey called forty-rod was flowing. He took The First Drink, the second, the third and more. He became furiously drunk, scrapped with the Irish, thrashed several of them, was himself thrashed by the survivors. He throbbed to wakefulness in the middle of the night, pounded, aching, black-eyed, scratched. He lay abandoned in that same horrid grove, lying in his own vomit.

He washed in the first stream he came to, and tottered back to his lodging house where he wrote out a pledge for himself and signed it with a quivering hand. In the morning he looked at that pledge and could scarcely make out his own signature, so he signed it again. Like his grandfather and the other storied MacBeans whom he had never seen but of whom he had heard much, Sen MacBean did not go back on his word. He owned immeasurable strength. Sometimes he felt that he needed all of it, to keep going in Andersonville.

Seneca was proud of his sign and pleased often by his own humor. In early March, when there was still an abundance of forest trash all over the place, he had amused himself by hunting for curly splinters, chips and other morsels of pine wood or roots which had dried into the shape of letters. At first he tried merely to assemble an alphabet; then he got the idea of a sign to advertise his laundry. He had assisted another man periodically in washing the prisoners' clothes at Belle Isle; but now the other man was dead, so Sen went into business for himself. He pulled little nails out of a pair of wornout boots which he acquired, and tacked the rustic letters on a branch suspended above his hut. Since Illinoisans were often called Suckers, he had a name ready-made for this concern. *Sucker Laundry & Cleaning Co.* read the sign, *S. MacBean, Prop.* Only the *k*, two *a*'s, the *b* and one *p* (and the & sign) had needed to be cobbled together a bit. The rest of the letters were natural, just as he had found them, and Seneca MacBean was

fond of pointing this out. In time he met a few fellow printers, and
they had discussions as to the type style of the various letters—Gothic,
Tudor black, German text, and so on.

He prospered if anyone could be said to prosper in the stockade.
The more intelligent and resourceful prisoners recognized that cleanliness would aid in their survival; scrubbing would allay the activities
of vermin; it was as simple as that. But few owned the facilities for
even an attempt at washing their clothes, and many did not own the
strength to try. Seneca MacBean accepted any currency, for he could
barter away things which he did not need. Except corn bread (later)—
he would not accept that. He would take wood, clothing, buckles, vegetables, bones, pieces of string, buttons, fragments of reading matter—
any and every object—in payment for his services. His arms and
shoulders were powerful, even after the Belle Isle winter. He ate sparingly, he ate not to allay his hunger for that was impossible; but he
ate only those materials which he thought would be good for him; if
he thought that something might make him sick he would not feed on
it, no matter how hungry he was. He drank only water from wells dug
on the higher ground of the North Side; this he received as laundering
pay from the proprietors of the wells. He weighed in the neighborhood
of a hundred and eighty pounds at the time of his capture, went down
to perhaps a hundred and fifty on Belle Isle; now at Andersonville he
managed to hold this weight very well, it even seemed that he had put
on a few pounds, or was he dreaming?

Collins's Raiders had begun operations the moment they entered the
stockade; Sarsfield's Raiders and Curtis's Raiders and the rest were not
far behind with thefts and incursions. If there was any man whom
Willie Collins feared that man was Seneca MacBean. Collins never
attacked Seneca, and discouraged those of his herd who suggested it.
The man named Tomcat O'Connor, who was shot by Father Time on
Belle Isle— He was a former member of the Daybreak Boys in New
York City, who found as much delight as actual profit in overhauling
a weaker man. A few days after he reached the Island, O'Connor attempted to remove from Seneca MacBean's finger the old seal ring
which had belonged to John MacBean's father's father, in Glasgow.
Perhaps Tomcat outweighed Seneca by twenty-five or thirty pounds.
A starved assemblage actually left the ration wagon to watch the beating which MacBean awarded to Tomcat O'Connor.

People screamed, Kill him, kill him! You should have killed him.
You could have killed him—

Yes, I think so, said Seneca, and licked his raw knuckles. Along with
the raiders he recognized that this was a violent world, and violence
was a necessary adjunct to reaching a desired end. The difference was
that the gangsters and he had different conceptions of what might

constitute a desired end. They were selfish and avaricious; Sen was not. He enjoyed serenity, but (like so many Scots before him) he was willing to engage in conflict to attain serenity. *We shall have Peace if we must fight for it* was a philosophy jested about through the generations, but to Seneca MacBean this seemed not incongruous.

The morning when the Plymouth Pilgrims arrived he was halfway back to his shebang when consideration prompted him to halt and then to retrace his steps. He found the big Jew at the same place where he had seen him first, except that now he was standing with knapsack and blanket roll at his feet, gazing curiously toward the South Side. A hullabaloo ascended over there; it sounded and looked like a riot. Morning, said Sen MacBean, and told the stranger his name and regiment, and held out his hand.

Nathan Dreyfoos responded in kind, but when he released Mac-Bean's hand he looked down at it and smiled. I cannot understand why your hands are comparatively so clean and—

And the rest of me dirty? That's the result of my laundry business. Scrubbing for hours, every day. But it does crack my hands and make them sore. Tell me, Sergeant, have you been squadded yet?

Last night before they turned us into—this place. I'm Thirty-ninth Detachment, Second Ninety, Third Mess.

But you've got no quarters as yet?

No. They said— The Rebel sergeant's words were, Pick out a place.

It's getting increasingly difficult to pick a good one. How'd you like to come over to my shebang, and see how we live here?

A fresh series of yells and shrieks issued from the South Side, and Nathan Dreyfoos jerked his head. What's going on, over there?

Raiders. Probably attacking some of you new men.

Raiders? Nathan would learn in another hour that three boys of his regiment had strayed incautiously near the headquarters of Charley Curtis. When attacked these boys screamed for help and several more of the Eighty-fifth New York went to their assistance. The battle ended—if such battles could be said to ever end—with three of the Pilgrims kicked and clubbed into insensibility . . . one had a fractured skull, and died four days later. The rest had their jackets and shirts literally torn from their backs, and of course all of them lost their knapsacks.

They are gangsters, robbers, said MacBean. The majority of them come from the slums of New York. Come along. I'll show you my shebang.

Thank you. I'd best stay with my men, here. Do you mean that the Confederates do nothing to ameliorate this situation? They allow hoodlums to go unpunished?

Friend, said Seneca, you've got a lot to learn about this place. You fetch the people of your squad together, and bid them sit on their knapsacks. Get at least six or eight together, and bid them keep to-gether. What have you got in the way of arms?

Nathan looked his astonishment. But all our weapons were taken from us when we surrendered.

All, mister? What's in these bureaus? Knives, forks— You got any scissors amongst you? Any Barlow knives? Even a spoon; you can break off the bowl, sharpen the end on a stone: it makes one of the meanest weapons alive because you carry it concealed in your hand. . . .

Nathan went with Seneca MacBean to the northwest central portion of the area, not far above Main Street where they had met. MacBean lectured him all the way there. He said frankly that he had been struck by Nathan's size and physical makeup, and by the manner in which he addressed Private Allen.

You have qualities of leadership, Dreyfoos.

Thank you, but I fail to see what good— In a place like this—

Too few retained those qualities. Some had them before they came in, and lost them immediately or gradually. I want to see you retain your strength; hence my special interest in you, and overtures on your behalf. This business of these raiders: they're all over the place, grow-ing worse and worse by the day. First off, it was sneak thievery at night. Then jostling and hustling by daylight. It's getting so bad that couple of them will walk up to a man and knock him flat, right in plain sight, and take what he's got. Only way a man can survive is to keep big enough and mean enough for them not to tackle. But the bulk of the prisoners aren't big enough to begin with . . . some of those pests are regular giants, and they muster anywhere from a dozen to four dozen helpers and hangers-on apiece.

Nathan meditated on this. Then the only way to overpower them would be by concerted action.

I guess you'll get along, said MacBean. He exhibited the new she-bang into which he had been compelled to move when the hospital was set up in the northeast corner. Oh, he said, we had a fancy domi-cile to begin with. Snug as a bug. Then they got the notion of a hos-pital on that very site, and we were condemned out of there.

Could you not move your house?

No, twas pine. All too dry to stand moving; the tufts fell to pieces. Of course this wood which you see now—ridgepole, front poles and so on—all came from there.

Where will we newcomers get wood for our poles?

Buy it. You can buy anything here. From the guards, from other prisoners, from that skinflint sutler. If you have no money you will pay in kind, so to speak; it's barter, but still it's buying and selling.

Do you have any poles to spare, Sergeant?

MacBean lowered his voice. Got four beauties hid underneath that trash there. They belonged to my comrade, fellow name of Lawrence, also from the Eighth Cavalry. He died this month and I was his sole heir.

How many have died this month?

Close to seven hundred by actual count.

Out of how many prisoners?

We might have numbered ten thousand before you folks arrived.

Nathan said something in another language.

What say?

Never mind, Sergeant. It is difficult to— Ah. I should like very much to buy your poles so that we may rig our blankets and overcoats. I'll offer you— He thought for a moment. You mentioned scissors. I have a beautiful pair. I won them in a game of bluff, he added with a grin.

Mister, said Seneca slowly, I'll take you on that. No—hold on—on second thought, you keep ownership of the scissors, and give me something else. Here's a proposition: how'd you like to be a barber? Shears, even little ladies' needlework shears like they have sometimes in a housewife— They're awful hard to come by, in here. A haircut is equally hard to come by. Suppose you set up shop as a barber right here alongside my laundry. That will give you various benefits: you can win a small income—food, bits of this and that to bargain with. It'll all help. Mind what I said about a man retaining his qualities of leadership! *And* his power to take care of himself!

But the rations which they give you aren't—?

You'll see. Wait till this afternoon. Nothing but that damnable corn-meal, I'll be bound. Our mess hasn't tasted meat in nine days—I've counted. A little salt once; extra peas on two occasions. But they were pretty wormy. I warn you, Dreyfoos, you'll go downhill unless you take extra special precautions.

I thank you for the advice. I'll be a barber although I've never been one. Will it be difficult to learn the trade?

Don't think so. Never tried it—but then I never was in the laundry business before—except as a delivery boy, back home. I suppose it's just a case of clip, clip and more clip. If a man gets clipped close enough it helps with the bugs. Beards, same way. I haven't got trimmed for some time—too busy washing. So I'll be your first customer. And mind to warn your men away from that deadline. Don't even step close to it. The Twenty-sixth Alabama guards aren't too bad, but those damn Georgians would rather shoot than eat.

XX

Sometimes General Howell Cobb, one-time cabinet officer and now serving as commander of the Department of Georgia and of the reserve troops, wondered why circumstance had ever compelled him to assume a charge which demanded so much and paid so little. Emolument was nothing. One could not set a cash value on service to one's Country but there should be a clean spiritual benefit accruing. Howell Cobb received no pence of this sort to put in the purse of his soul. He was a big man with a mane (sometimes in dreams he saw himself stepping about in a toga; and sometimes—worse—he was uncomfortably aware that he resembled a rustic auctioneer with a loud voice whom he had known as a boy). His most important immediate duty as he saw it was the raising, arming, equipping and training of Georgia Reserves. This was not even making bricks without straw, it was making bricks without clay. He had seen the first railroad trains go through Macon, bearing off-scourings of Belle Isle and other Virginia garbage heaps. He thought that even this starved and ragged human material would have served better in construction than the scrappings allotted to him. He stood with thick pompous face set, he stood with lowered hat-brim, and reviewed in solemn gaze and more solemn spirit the worth-less ranks which formed his regiments. Blank-eyed little boys with oozing noses; shambling uncouth illiterates better cast as village idiots in this dreadful drama; hollow-cheeked doddering bearded relics who stood with trousers wet, their prostate glands turned to jelly by age. His worry was such that it could admit but little space for considera-tion of Yankees penned by a pine wall he had never seen—Yankees stalking in a Winder-contrived cage, Yankees Winder-fed, Yankees guarded by a Winder-appointed minion.

Nevertheless someone in Richmond was hearing groans and ghost-stories, and orders could not be ignored when they arrived over the signature of the adjutant-general. Howell Cobb brushed his locks, had his servant pack a satchel, and traveled the sixty miles to Camp Sumter accompanied by his chief surgeon and whatever other staff officers might be spared from headquarters. Wednesday, May fourth, was a fine fair day. In this dressing of warm spring sunlight the stock-ade did not appear so ugly as General Cobb's active imaginings had

painted it. Henry Wirz, panicked into flutter by the influx of braid
and crusted stars, pranced nervously on the left of the mighty slow-
treading statesman as the little party toured the prison with guards
lounging ahead and behind.

A general break was the first bugaboo which must be laid, and
Cobb devoted his attention to this chore. Wirz prayed for battery after
battery of artillery to be placed here and there; but General Cobb
assumed wisely that the four pieces of cannon now in position could
rake the pen handsomely if need arose. He inquired into the state of
ordnance, the quantity of grape available for quick reloading; he
thought the supplies ample, and said as much in a report which he
began to indite within a few hours after his return to Macon.

*Headquarters Georgia Reserves, Macon, Georgia, May 5, 1864
General: Under your orders to inform myself of the condition of the
prison at Andersonville, with a view of furnishing from the reserve
corps the necessary guard for its protection and safety . . .* ha. His
service in the field had not been lengthy, but he felt at least that exposure to enemy fire had made a veteran of him promptly, completely.
O curling scraps of down on cheeks of jaundiced hobbledehoys; O sodden pants of the agèd; O nitwit cropper able better to handle a hoe
than a musket, and bound to chop out the corn, in your foolishness,
and leave the chickweed! *There are now in the prison about twelve
thousand prisoners, in an area of less than eighteen acres, with a stockade around it about fifteen feet high. I presume the character of the
prison is well understood at Richmond, and therefore give no description of it.* Might one be able to box or bottle a smell? Even a small
phial of smell? How shrewd it might be to ship off a well-packed box,
the squat glass medical tube wrapped in cotton to prevent breakage,
the label traced in an indecipherable script used by surgeons in jotting
down their requirements: Contents, 10 cubic centimeters Smell, Andersonville, Camp Sumter, Sumter Co., Ga., May 4, 1864. By the Eternal,
sir, it would cause a sensation in those pothersome offices with their
rows of meddling clerks, their snidish field grade officers who built a
supercilious wall between High Command and Reality! The unpack-
ing, the group around the desk, the peeking and wondering, the
stopper withdrawn, the stench bursting out of its concentration, the
panic to follow. . . .

Howell Cobb's massive face did not bulge in a smile, but he felt an
awful smile shaping inside him. He went on writing.

*I took the liberty of making several suggestions for rendering the
prison more secure; and if the tools could be had, I would recommend
that the entire prison grounds should be surrounded by fortifications,
which could be put up by the troops, whose health would be promoted by the employment.* Health—a pretty word, a worthless one under the circumstances. What was health among troops? Health was a

singing of the blood, a bellowing of energy to be released in horseplay, high jinks, conflict, the mass surge and peril and murder of a campaign. Health was a chicken roasted on a ramrod, a bayonet jammed between the ribs of a hireling, a fist-fight on an embrasure, a thumbing of the nose. Health was sacrifice, dash, shooting coolly or in frenzy, health was a Rebel yell which went aloft until it seemed that unknown stars must seize and hold it . . . contain it to be given back to future heroic generations when future heroic generations might need to hear the sound, to tell babies in their cradles to listen for that long hoot and be inspired by it when once again the drums came beating. Health was the lusty war fought by vigorous youths with braided muscles on their bones, with God's own good hot butter husbanded in their testicles. Where were the healthy? Name the spots in no necessary order of geography or chronology: Fair Oaks, Corinth, Vicksburg, Sharpsburg, Gettysburg, now many other *burgs?*—Gaines's Mill, Mechanicsville, Manassas, Pittsburg Landing. Take your spade, historian, and go to digging. You might unearth Leonidas, Varus, King Harald; or at least anonymous Jakes and Johnnies who were cast proudly in their mold. Assuredly you could not dig up these spindle-shanked Antiques and Horribles who comprised the command of Howell Cobb.

He sighed, he wished for a long just peace, and himself rising in the Senate to a Point of Order. He wrote.

The most important change is the one suggested in the accompanying report of my chief surgeon, Dr. Eldridge, that is, the erection of hospital buildings outside the prison. Upon that point there cannot be two opinions among intelligent men. It ought to be done at once, and such is the opinion of every sensible man who has examined the prison.

Here was himself, who had practiced the usage of words with dignity and color throughout his adult life, who thought that language was tonic and decoration— Prison, prison, prison; prisoners, prisoners, prisoners. Had he not a synonym in his cartouche of verbiage? What did you call a prisoner except a prisoner? What did you call a prison except a prison? Might you term Andersonville anything other than Andersonville? Call it mire, muck, sink, morass, dump, dung, cesspool, chamber pot, hog-wallow, cow-pie? Somewhere there must be proper synonyms . . . they did not come readily.

Wirz had said, General, I tell you I am a physician! Those sick should not be so many among the well ones.

I presume, Captain Wirz, that you have done what you could.

Always I do. *Himmel,* at night I keep thinking, What should I do?

I observe that you have made some attempt to provide shelter for the sick in that northeast area—

Tent flies we got, and some—what you call it?—canvas. But to make the hospital, must I have many men move from their huts. *Ach,* they make my head hurt when they yell from it! And so many more men without shelter it has now become; so, so many more sick we have. General, better I was a colonel, this should not be!

It is not a matter of your rank, Captain. It is simply a case of our possessing neither tools nor materials, nor sufficient personnel.

And such a bunch of guards, they are bad and foolish. Much trouble have I got from them, as also from these damn Yankees.

The prison is already too much crowded, and no additional prisoners should be sent there until it can be enlarged. The effect of increasing the number within the present area must be a terrific increase of sickness and death during the summer months. Prison, prisoner, increasing, increase . . . what had befallen his vaunted claim to the majesty of words spoken or set down in ink?

Poor Alexander Persons. A good just capable dependable man in peacetime—and, thus far, in wartime, though he seemed overcritical of superiors. It gave Howell Cobb a wrench to see Persons placed in such a position. (It gave Howell Cobb an even more severe wrench to observe the position in which he himself had been placed.) Wirz was a blundering snapping sputtering little wretch; but at least he stood devoted with a whole soul to the task of superintending prisoners; he was busy at the job; you could see that he was busy at it, he was not playing checkers in a tent nor swimming in sorghum whiskey. Where could you find another Persons, another Wirz? Oh, you might replace the other, you could never replace the one. But Henry Wirz was a direct appointee of Winder; and in essence Howell Cobb would be impugning Winder's ability if he so much as suggested a criticism of Wirz.

I understand that an order has been given for enlarging the prison. If it was possible to make another prison it would be much better, for I doubt very much whether the water will be sufficient for the accommodation of the increased number of prisoners. Prison, prison; much better, I doubt very much; should it be If It Were Possible or If It Was Possible? Suddenly Cobb had grown weary of words.

He recalled smell and faces. Sharply, sharply. Might one not box up a face and send it to that same Richmond office to be looked at, to be regarded with horror?

The general management of the prison under Colonel Persons is good, and he manifests a laudable desire to discharge his duties in the most efficient manner. There, that takes care of Alex Persons. *The duties of the inside command are admirably performed by Captain Wirz—*

Howell Cobb's tired sense went wool-gathering for a time . . . he recognized at last that his sense was vote-gathering, in retrospect or in dreamy ambition . . . vote-gathering must be really wool-gathering when a man had military responsibility ravaging him.

—Whose place it would be difficult to fill. There, that takes care of

the little German-Swiss captain. *I take the liberty of enclosing a copy of Dr. Eldridge's report.* Oh, he should have said Surgeon Eldridge instead of Dr. Eldridge, but what in damnation was the difference! *I am, General, very respectfully yours, &c., Howell Cobb, Major-General Commanding.*

He penned his own endorsement, and told his adjutant to have the thing sent along with the enclosure of Eldridge's report. He wondered what other endorsements these papers would bear eventually. *Received A. & I. G.O., May 21, 1864. A. & I. G.O. Received May 26, 1864.* The best, the speediest of military mails were slower than lame blind mules these days. He thought of Richmond, and labored in the thought under that increased lethargy and blank doubt which overwhelmed any good mind when it considered Richmond and the pale clerks and ambitious limited majors skittering about like white rats denned in a cracker box. To whom might General Cooper pass along this report if indeed he chose to pass it along? To what generals, to what gentlemen in rumpled linen suits, to what musing bespectacled bigwigs in shabby frock coats—bigwigs more interested in the portraits for which they might be sitting than in the flow of life represented by neat stacks of mail arranged in square little islands on their desks, in front of yawning pigeon holes? Howell Cobb had seen such gentlemen and such islands of mail, and knew the amazing depth of a pigeon hole. A pigeon hole was not a well; a well was of lesser depth, and so was a vertical mine-shaft with its steam windlasses lowering. A pigeon hole went straight down to China, and papers fluttered out at the other end, and the Chinese picked them up and squeaked and clacked at the strange symbols, and burned them later in censers before their idols with due ceremony. Already Secretary Seddon's endorsement had become traditional. There were carping children who told tales out of school. *Noted.* That meant that he had read the contents, or at least had cast his weak gaze across the lines. *File* or *filed.* That meant that the report should be filed or had been filed, personally. *J.A.S.* That meant James A. Seddon, Secretary of War. It was more efficient to employ initials than a signature, it took less time and required less effort.

Well, Eldridge's accompanying report would make good reading for someone, sometime, somewhere, if anyone should bother to read it, if it should not be awarded the mere cursory scratch of those three initials. *I found the prisoners, in my opinion, too much crowded for the promotion or even continuance of their present health, particularly during the approaching summer months. . . . At present their shelters consist of such as they can make of the boughs of trees, poles, &c., covered with dirt. The few tents they have are occupied as a hospital . . . very many of them suffering from chronic diarrhoea combined with the scorbutic disposition, with extreme emaciation as the consequence.*

Extreme emaciation. Howell Cobb looked down at his own fist,

clenched like a solid creased pillow upon his desk. Might not many of
those skeletal creatures have once worn the flesh which now dressed
his bones? Might they not, like he, have worn even too much flesh?
Likely.

The hospital being within the enclosure, it has been found imprac-
ticable to administer such diet and give them such attention as they
require, as unless constantly watched, such diet as is prepared for them
is stolen and eaten by the other prisoners.

Thieves, said Howell Cobb in response to his surgeon's elucidation.
Roughs. Hooligans. Why, Captain Wirz had told him—

Enemies of my Country. Brutes to be restrained. Monsters to suffer
durance, fiends to be boarded in their cell. Pray to Almighty God that
the necessity for grapeshot should not arise, but once it does arise let
the lanyard be quick, the cap in instantaneous flash, let the powder be
dry as toast, let the mass of balls go flying.

He sighed, he put thought of his and Eldridge's reports as far away
from him as his thick mental arm could reach. Let him now go back
to the dread task of building bricks without— Without anything.

By long lamplight, until very late at night that same week, Henry
Wirz worked at preparing his own report. This was directed not to
General Cooper, the adjutant-general, but to Major Thomas Turner in
Richmond. Wirz had been instructed by Winder's office that Turner
was next superior in the echelon of that command. A direct appeal to
General Winder would have suited Wirz much better, but he feared
that any attempt on his part to skip echelons would defeat its own
purpose promptly.

By this time he had acquired a more tolerable military family, being
rid of both the ailing Charles and the light-fingered Viggo. He hoped
with all his heart that the report would be free from grammatical
errors, and the necessity for this he enjoined constantly upon his clerks.
The clerks went to bed at eleven o'clock that night, but Henry Wirz
stayed awake until nearly twelve; and continually he peeked at the
final copy.

. . . The number of prisoners on the 1st day of April was		7,160
I received up to today, from various sources		5,787
I received today, recaptured		7
Total		12,954
The number of dead from the 1st of April to 8th of May is	728	
The number of escaped from the 1st of April to the 8th of May is . .	13	741
Leaving on hand		12,213

. . . I am here in a very unpleasant position, growing out of the rank which I now hold, and suggest the propriety of being promoted. Having the full control of the prison, and consequently of the daily prison guard, the orders which I have to give are very often not obeyed with the promptness the occasion requires, and I am of opinion that it emanates from the reluctance of obeying an officer who holds the same rank as they do. My duties are manifold, and require all my time in daytime, and very often part of the night. . . .

H. Wirz,
Captain Commanding Prison.

His small harried heart would have shivered with anticipation could it have known how favorable would be the endorsements to come. Wirz was open to just damnation on almost any charge conceivable but the sorest prisoner within the stockade could never call him lazy. He owned a virtue commonly respected: its name was diligence.

Strangely enough another man named Turner was now active in the life of Henry Wirz. Argument raked persistently between them as to whether a stipulated price amounted to thirty dollars or to thirty-five. The stipulated price was the standard amount on the head of a runaway Yankee. Wesley Turner was a master of hounds; previously he had worn gray, but now he operated in civilian capacity as a professional Yankee hunter. The dogs were most of them ordinary foxhounds or coon dogs with good noses; also the hunter mustered three vicious snapping creatures of mixed breed: perhaps they were a cross between the mastiff and the bull terrier—no one could tell for a certainty. These were known as catch-dogs; they were worthless at a scent, but would race along with the hounds. They served splendidly for scaring, treeing and sometimes tearing escapees (runaway Yankees were not called Escapees but Escapes, in prison slang).

Armed with pistol and horn, Turner rode his mule on a circuit outside the stockade early each morning; dogs sniffed and snorted ahead and behind. Often they trailed a guard or a Negro instead of a Yankee, and brought up yelling among tents of the Georgia regiment, among the Alabamans. Their master tried to beat sense into their heads with a long pole; soldiers stood jeering to watch him. Many of these youths had heard guns fired in anger, some had been wounded, a few had even been captured early in the war, to be exchanged later (fortunate prisoners, in a day when the process of exchange existed still). They had little respect for the man on muleback and no respect at all for Wirz; all who served at the stockade stations were disgruntled at coming under Henry's command during their tour of duty. As soldiers they recognized the obligation of any man to escape if he could manage it. The more depraved of the lot were trigger-happy, and boasted of Yankees they had shot at the deadline; however they saw nothing outlandish in the effort of a Northerner to tunnel out, flank out, or even to leap on the back of a guard while scratching through the forest with a wood-detail. In all justice they knew that they would have tried the same trick were the situation reversed. Dogs were an ignominy, a bullet was more to the point. The very baying of trail-dogs suggested that a black man had fled rather than a white.

My Daddy used to keep a catch-dog. Big brindled bastard.

Whereabouts was this, Nucky?

Wayne County. If a nigger walked off, man who owned the nigger might have hounds, but mostly they never owned no catch-dogs. Use to hire Buster from my Daddy, and Daddy'd have to go along to handle Buster, and times he'd take me along with him. Old Bus he trailed a damn nigger in the brush along Goose Creek— What I mean to say, them hounds did the trailing, but Bus was right in there with them, and when he come up to that nigger he just gave that nigger sut! Like to tore all the hide off one of his legs. God, you ought to heard that nigger holler.

Leastways he was a nigger.

Nigger ain't got no damn right to put for freedom!

But these here greasy mechanics ain't no niggers.

God damn, boy, some of them is!

But not the white ones. What I mean, a soldier is a soldier, I mean a white soldier. How'd you feel to have a catch-dog coming for you, like you was black? Nucky, I'd sure enough taste piss in my mouth fore I'd like to be niggerfied in such fashion.

That fucking Dutch captain! He's white-livered for sure.

Liver so white that chalk'd make a black mark on it.

God damn, sure enough.

Nevertheless Wesley Turner's pack of hounds was feared with reason by every prisoner who possessed the boldness and energy to attempt flight. If roll call disclosed that new Escapes were loose, or if a tunnel was discovered, or if the guards noted any peculiar activity among Outsiders— In any situations such as these Wirz shrieked for Wes Turner; the horn tooted, hound voices soared, catch-dogs growled and galloped. Through springtime only thirteen men managed to avoid being overhauled, as noted in the superintendent's report; and four of these were among the seven picked up by patrols in farther regions and fetched back to Andersonville. (The other three unfortunates had fled from a railroad train near Savannah and were brought to Andersonville because it was the prison nearest their point of recapture. Out of the frying pan into the fire, they said when once they stood inside the gate. None of them would survive the summer.)

Wes Turner was richer by nearly one thousand dollars Secesh before the first week of May. He increased his pack in consequence, and traded for a Colt's revolver to replace his old smooth-bore pistol.

Look a here, Captain. I never got no pay for them last two.

Ja, ja, ja, you was paid!

I never was paid, and I lost old Trip out of it. One of them damn Yankees had a knife, and he cut old Trip bad when Trip come up to him. I had to shoot him, by God.

The Yankee you should shoot instead!

Well, I did beat the poop out of him. But you never paid me for him, nor for the one I took over behind Widow Tebbs's place.

Ja, I show you on the book. You are bad, you Wes Turner, come always to bleed me for money. You think maybe the army is made from money, *nein?* Maybe I am made from money? Benny, it is you show this bad Turner in the book. . . . Here you see it, *mit* your own eyes!

Look a here, Captain Wirz, you know I can't read.

Benny can read, and now you he will show. Benny, you God damn Yankee, you show him!

First May, 1864. Paid to W. Turner sixty dollars, two prisoners recaptured.

So what you say to that, hah?

Well, it should a been seventy dollars. First off you promised me thirty-five dollars apiece, and then when I come to claim my rightful money you said thirty dollars—

Get from my office out, you Wes! Son of a bitch—

Don't you dare call me no son of a bitch, you little Dutch bastard!

Ja, I call you son of a bitch. Never do you call me one bastard!

Ahh—

Ahhhh, also! Now get out once!

Thus they contended with the meaningless futile insult of the weak and surly and suspicious.

A brilliant idea for the discouraging of tunnels had occurred to Wirz. He planned to put it into effect as soon as enough spades could be secured. His notion of a second, outer stockade must remain in abeyance for the time being, since the labor would be monumental; but he thought that a deep ditch might be dug without too much trouble. Prisoners (Negroes taken at Olustee) could do the excavating, since all his offers of double rations and other blandishments were refused scornfully by the bulk of the whites. But Negroes were an element apart. Neither he nor his superiors countenanced the assumption that they were bona fide military prisoners. He thought of them as wicked slaves who not only planned that nightmare, a slave insurrection, but who had actually participated in such an attempt. Most of the black captives from the Florida campaign had been preëmpted for outside duty as wagon-drivers, grave-diggers and the like. These creatures he would set to digging as soon as he could put spades in their hands. Whenever an engine squawked at the

Anderson Station he set a youth flying to see whether the long-desired shovels might have arrived along with a new batch of prisoners. Sid Winder told him scornfully that he had experienced little difficulty in requisitioning necessary tools when the stockade was built, but there was a sudden paucity of spades when Wirz sent a detail abroad to seek such necessaries from nearby plantations and smaller farms. His status was understood throughout the neighborhood. People told the would-be requisitioners that Wirz was merely in command of the pen and had no authority to levy on the countryside for anything; only military engineers had such authority. Since this was uncomfortably the truth, Henry Wirz was forced to content himself with the hope of coöperation from headquarters at Macon; General Cobb had promised to do what he could. . . . A ditch, a very deep ditch. Guards should patrol it day and night. How deep would Yankees have to dig in order to avoid projecting their tunnels into that ditch? Very deep; and this they could not do, they were not all coal-miners.

Wirz worked zealously, feverishly at devising punishments for the insubordinate, and once the strap of punishment was prepared he wielded it with gusto. He arranged a row of foot stocks and another of spread-eagle stocks wherein men were locked to stand with their arms extended. (This latter colony caused him private discomfort, since when fastened therein a Yankee bore an unpleasant resemblance to Christ on the Cross. Henry considered himself a good Catholic, although he was not a good Catholic; in secret he felt that he had been guilty of profaning a symbolic sacredness; yet like an Oriental he would lose face if his orders were rescinded and the spread-eagle stocks taken down.) He conferred lengthily with smiths at the camp, and the result was a complicated series of chains and balls among which sinners could be manacled in a double rank and soon were. Trying to escape was a crime, so was complaining about the rations, so was the act of insulting a Confederate soldier or even remonstrating with him. The application of these tortures depended upon the superintendent's mood. Thus prisoners were puzzled and terrified by his capriciousness since Henry was a slave to moods. Sometimes a Yankee amused him in the manner of his attempt to break loose or in the manner of his recapture; then Wirz might greet him tolerantly, almost affectionately, and turn him back Inside with barely a slap on the wrist. Sometimes (mornings after his right arm had kept him awake were especially evil) a prisoner might offend him merely by way of address, solely by the earnestness of supplication. Then chains were fastened on, then the divided stock-arms were locked firmly.

I teach you to tell me bacon is bad.

Captain, for God's sake—

Son of a bitch Yankee, I teach you. Here you stay two days.

You dirty Dutch shit-heel, if I had a gun—
Now you stay one week!

True, he regarded his own punitive measures as painful and ugly, but pain and ugliness must be the lot of all vile humanity who walked in such filth, who planned to escape in order to burn munitions and ravish tender Southern girls, who had been so cruel in their warfare as to inflict a hurt which went throbbing through the years. . . . Devils who hurled mud at him . . . he would show them.

. . . The other Turner, the Richmond Turner, endorsed Wirz's report of May eighth with flattering alacrity. He wrote: *Captain Henry Wirz, commanding prison, reports in reference to the general condition of the prison, and suggests the propriety of increased rank being given him. . . . Respectfully forwarded, recommended. Thos. P. Turner, Major Commanding.*

General Winder in turn added his cramped agreement: *Approved and respectfully forwarded. Captain Wirz has proved himself to be a very diligent and efficient officer, whose superior in commanding prisoners and incident duties I know not.*

But the insignia of field grade shimmered only in a worthless future. There was no new metallic sheen on Wirz's jacket. Winder did not promote him, he only wrote the words Approved and Forwarded, he wrote words of praise. A simpering clerk in a remote office pinned the report to a sheaf of others and placed the pile under a paperweight to curl. Promotion would be awarded this hysterical tyrant only when he had no prison left to command; it would come as the accolade of a hopeless and disheveled Confederacy.

Under his consciousness Henry Wirz thought of the prisoners as animals, although he was not sure what sort of animals. They varied their coats and colors and shapes from time to time; some days they had hoofs, some days claws, some days they were stripèd, some days shaggy as bison. Monkeys they appeared to be when they were picking lice, fabled more ferocious apes when they fought in torment, herds of two-legged domestic beasts (but unfriendly, apt to burst through rails and perhaps trample children) when they were marshalled about in a squadding. Finally one night while in bed Henry had a recollective illusion. It was part memory, part dream and nightmare.

He was very young, perhaps eight years old, and had journeyed with his parents from Zurich to Bern to visit his grandmother. He had heard about Bern and the bears there, kept traditionally in their pit. It was the thing to do, to take children to see the bears; all children of Bern were taken so, and thus the little visiting Henry was escorted to this zoo in his turn.

He had not expected that the bears would be so large, and there was a growing feud between the two great males; perhaps the mating season approached. They growled horribly, slapped at each other, one bit the other on the shoulder and a scream arose. Keepers came with long poles and separated the combatants; one was driven into his den and made to remain behind a grating. At this roaring fearful confusion the throng of children gazed wide-eyed, and some little girls hid their faces in their aprons. Henry had no apron, but he could never have hidden his face had he possessed an apron, for his glaring dark eyes were nailed against the bear pit; he could not look in any other direction, frightened as he was. A few other children were led away, Henry could not be dragged.

At last when comparative peace reigned among the fierce brown animals, he saw that people were tossing carrots over the ledge. Two bears, trained to expectancy by long association, sat down with fuzzy legs spread and opened their mouths to catch the morsels. One, a mother bear, had a trick of making cumbersome gestures with her paw, indicating her mouth, indicating that she wished more carrots.

There was a vendor with a pushcart nearby, and Henry begged a few sous. He went to the cart, bought a bunch of carrots, and returned to the feeding. One by one he tossed the small tapering vegetables (they were clean, they were crisp, almost he wished to eat them himself but it was better to feed the bears; the carrots were of a delicate pinkish orange, they were beautiful). Not once did the bear miss, though Henry Wirz's aim was far from accurate . . . the bear weaved on her haunches, she leaned far out, she swayed from side to side. As the bright morsel flew, seeming to go past her, her jaws would snap and No More Carrot.

This trivial recollection, half dreamed in the night, resolved the identity of the Andersonville prisoners for Wirz into a common dark hairy form. They were bears, they seemed very stupid but they could bite and rend, worse perhaps than African lions.

A few days later he was in his splinter-new office, checking a roll of arrivals which Ben Dilley, one of his Yankee clerks, had put before him. He was eating a lunch at the same time. He had bacon sandwiches and a thin bundle of well-scrubbed carrots, also a canteen of weak elderberry wine. Wirz had eaten his two sandwiches and had drunk most of the wine, and was snapping carrots between his prominent front teeth. The clerk jumped each time that Wirz bit— it sounded like a cap snapping—and then would come the fast grinding sound as Henry Wirz chewed, opening his mouth under his beard.

Suddenly the report of a sentinel's gun popped through the air, and there was yelling in the pen. Wirz sent Benny to see what had happened, to find out about the shooting.

Ben came back. Prisoner, sir, he said.

Is he dead?

No, sir, he's kind of kicking around. Guess it went through his thigh.

I go see, said Henry Wirz.

He went to the nearest sentry station, climbed, and looked down. The wounded man was lying well inside the deadline at the edge of the marsh, and seemed wallowing in pain but making very little noise.

You shoot him? Wirz demanded of the wan-faced guard.

Huh-uh. Twas Tom Luckey over yonder, and the boy pointed.

The superintendent called across thirty yards to the next station where the sentry had just finished reloading. For why you shoot?

He was scooping up water clean inside the line, Captain.

Then it is good you shoot. . . . Wirz spoke to the staring prisoners below, whose permanent anger was always so obviously intensified by such occurrences (they came more frequently all the time). Some from you son of a bitch Yankees get that Yankee who was wounded. From out the deadline take him; I let you move him.

The victim's friends sprang into the fatal area promptly and lifted the youth from slime in which he writhed. They carried him across the narrow footbridge and up the hill toward the South Gate, planning apparently to have him ready for examination should any of the stockade surgeons appear. Wirz turned from watching the departure and studied the mass of wild dark faces upturned below, and felt their hatred sweep through him, and he fired back his own silent hate. They were bears . . . here he stood with carrots again, he had come up with the things in his hand, he had not realized that he was carrying them.

Before he knew what he was doing, Wirz had shifted the five remaining small carrots to his weak right hand, and his left hand went over to feel for a single vegetable and to toss it out and far.

There was a scramble, more faces turned up; there sounded profanity, scattered insults, a scatter of laughter. Again Wirz threw a carrot. Bern, he said in his soul. It was long ago, I was so little. *Ja,* they are bears.

Fresh carrots were seen seldom in that place except by raiders who might purchase them from guards. (It was against the rules, of course; but much trading went on every night, much buying and selling, and often even in the daytime. Wirz would have been powerless to stop the practice even had he cared to.) Hands groped, waved, snatched at space, the bears were grabbing and fighting, bears were growling as in that ancient pit in Switzerland. One at a time Henry Wirz threw the rest of the carrots and saw them vanish into turmoil. Wirz turned away and descended the ladder carefully; he had no wish to fall, to fall and hurt his arm. Bears, he kept saying to himself.

XXI

Chickamauga possessed almost no beard at all; he said that it was because of a disease he had suffered when young. It was at Chickamauga that he was wounded (the same battle in which Badger Claffey received fatal wounds); it was at Chickamauga that he was captured; in the hospital he had talked incessantly about these experiences, so the name clung to him. But also he was called by a variety of other names. Poll Parrot, Pretty Polly and Fortune Teller were some of the designations applied to him—this last because he carried a deck of ragged dirty cards in his pocket, and would tell your fortune for one dollar Confed. If he liked you he would give you a very good fortune indeed; he would say that he saw you alive, well, returned safely to Michigan or Massachusetts, sitting down to dumplings and chicken-pie, the admired of a beautiful young woman, and rich too. But if you had offended him in some way (and many people did offend Chickamauga daily, and well did he merit offense) he would see all sorts of dreadful things in your future. His protruding eyes, green as peas, would glow devilishly as he related his advice. Keep away from water, and did anyone in your family ever die of dropsy, or was anybody in your family ever burned to death—I don't know for sure, but it says right here in these cards that someone in your family got burned to death or maybe will get burned to death . . . these things he saw for you. His head was bald, and people had a joke and said that his head was perhaps the only place where Chickamauga was balled. Some people said that Chickamauga's true name was Hubbard, some said Hulburt; some said he was from the Ninety-sixth Illinois, some said the Thirty-eighth. If you asked him he would try to tell you, but he had the sort of deformed lip which made it impossible for him to enunciate with complete clarity. The sobriquet of Poll Parrot was apt also; you had only to look at his nose. Chickamauga talked to anyone, everyone, jabbering on in every waking moment; and when he slept his mouth fell open, and his snoring was the grunt of a hog. It seemed often that he did not sleep at all, but went crutching nervously throughout the stockade even by night, and thus was as well known to folks on the North Side as on the island in the marsh. He wore a pair of Rebel pants, and the right trouser leg, empty throughout the greater part of its length, was turned up and pinned by several large thorns. The smell of his breath might have been an emetic. It was difficult to believe that he had come to exist through the natural process of conception and birth and growth; it was as if he were a changeling from a Grimm tale, delivered by a troop of elves, and wicked elves at that. It was impossible to believe that anyone had ever loved him, and yet somewhere sometime someone must have kissed his horrid face and held him tenderly.

Chickamauga had learned early in life that benefits might accrue to him if he curried favor in high places, so he came to know Henry Wirz very soon after his draft of prisoners was sent down from Richmond. Wirz, thinking about it distastefully, came to the conclusion that he must have seen Chickamauga the very first time that he, Wirz, came into the stockade. Always that wheedling hare-lipped murmur, high in the mouth and throat of the cripple . . . we don't get enough to eat, and Captain, if I tell you when someone is going to escape, and prove it too, will you let me have a piece of meat?— not jackass, but real honest to God meat; and, Captain, I heard some fellows talking, and I think they're digging of a tunnel, and I think I know where it is, and if I find out just where that tunnel is, will you let me go Outside and pick berries? Look, I won't try to Take Leave, I couldn't try to Take Leave, I've only got one leg, and I couldn't very well run away with these here crutches.

Wirz disliked Chickamauga as he disliked most people except his wife and little Cora; also the weird Poll Parrot face was a Yankee face. But Henry recognized the necessity for having spies and informers within the stockade, and since Chickamauga's half-mad babblings were looked upon as the outpourings of an idiot child by the prisoners, it was possible that they might speak unguardedly in his presence. Wirz did give the one-legged man small favors from time to time. Maybe the prisoners thought that it was out of pity, but few of the prisoners believed that Henry Wirz had any pity in his heart. Henry Wirz did have. He had pity for himself.

Chickamauga prayed constantly to be taken Outside, but the Outsiders must be able-bodied in order to perform work demanded of them; and once he was put on Wirz's list of informers he might as well have ceased praying to go out, except that he was granted two brief sumach berry excursions with the wood gang. From these sorties he returned more voluble than ever, carrying extra berries in half of a broken wooden bucket. The first time he set up shop on Broadway and sold his berries (one at a time, for the most part, but some customers had sufficient means to buy a dozen) at a sublime price. Sumach berries, dried on the bush or not, were a recognized antiscorbutic and thus valued highly by the prisoners, who ascribed all sorts of tonic values to the bitter fruit.

After the second trip Chickamauga made the mistake of going into business on South Street and that was near the haunts of the raiders. A foot came out slyly and hooked itself around one of Poll Parrot's crutches, the crutch was jerked from under the bald man's weight, he went sprawling. Of course when he arose the berries were halfway to the sinks; people pointed out the thieves, but what might this plundered salesman do against raiders? Naturally he sought each day to find favor with them just as he did with Wirz; he followed the chiefs, wheedling and lying and offering information about fresh fish who were reputed to own enormous bankrolls or gold watches. He went capering after Collins or Sarsfield or Delaney, after any and all of them, until the epithet of Brown Nose was added to the weight of those other names he bore already. But the raiders who stole the berries were young boys, mere hangers-on, ambitious ruffians who strove to emulate their lords. Willie Collins laughed when Chickamauga came complaining. He said that the berries were all eaten, and why hadn't Chickamauga brought some to him, to Willie Collins? This the cripple planned to do, next time he went Out, but he didn't go Out again.

When the Plymouth Pilgrims appeared the raiders came into luxuriant funds; they enjoyed banquets of pork, rice, milk, green vegetables, they even had coffee and army crackers at times. Bundles of canteens filled with pine-top were smuggled in dusk to the conical tent which now rose alongside the headquarters near South Street. They sang, bellowing through night hours, singing off-key and sometimes ending up with a free-for-all, a battle royal among the chiefs. They owned strength enough to fight, for their board was better set than it had been when they were campaigning; the food was excellently cooked (why not? They had kettles, iron skillets, plenty of wood) for they'd found trained cooks among the horde of New Yorkers who clung in satellite formation around them; and one skilled cook had been impressed bodily, captured and kidnapped and retained in slavery, mourned as dead by his Philadelphia comrades on the North Side.

Liquor bubbled, voices grated into the night.

> In Athol there lived a man named Jerry Lanagan;
> He battered away till he hadn't a pound.
> His father he died, and he made him a man again;
> Left him a farm of ten acres of ground.

Estimates of the wealth brought in by the Plymouth Pilgrims ran as high as one hundred thousand dollars in greenbacks; probably the actual amount was but a fraction of that sum. Nevertheless in hands of the raiders the Pilgrims were bunnies gripped by hounds. The raiders soon had most of the money . . . thus they had eatables, they had potables, they had prime and power.

> *It's of a fierce highwayman my story I will tell:*
> *His name was Willie Brennan and in Ireland he did dwell,*
> *He rob-bed from the rich and he gave unto the poor,*
> *And all the folk did call him Willie Brennan On The Moor.*

Somebody was persistently singing John Brennan instead of Willie. Who the hell is singing John? Tis Willie—

Hell it is. It's John.

God damn you, tis myself will show you! Willie!

Thwack and tussle, and burbled shouts and hootings, and people nearby crawling away because they feared that guards might fire.

Willie Collins's voice roaring out, Hold up, you shitty spalpeens! I'll clout the skulls of both of you.

Clout them he did, and then there was only a snarl and moaning.

I'll teach you, you bastards. When you sing it you'll never sing John. Nor Willie Brennan. Willie Collins! Me! Do you hear? Me—Willie Collins! For isn't that the thing I do—a-robbing from the rich and a-giving to the poor?

Dread laughter in darkness.

Sing it, devil suck it, as I bid you.

> *It's of a fierce highwayman my story I will tell:*
> *His name was Willie Collins and in Ireland he did dwell—*

In New York he did dwell—

In Andersonville he did dwell—

In the stockade he did dwell.

Laughter, with Willie's booming the highest.

Chickamauga was fascinated by these monsters as pimps and mendicants forever are fascinated by might and especially by the might of the cruel; but they would have little of him. They did not fancy his bad breath, his snoring, his split-lip chatter. Even Lipsky the tailor knocked him out of his path, threw his crutches aside and delighted in observing him as he crawled to get them. Furthermore the leaders feared that in his approach to idiocy he might apprise intended victims that raiders were at hand, and so they'd meet with no success in stripping the victims. They drove Chickamauga from their neighborhood more frequently than they welcomed him. They welcomed him only when a credulous superstition was ascendant in the drunken state, and they wished their fortunes to be told.

Chickamauga cringed at what he hoped was a safe distance, trusting to be summoned.

Poll, you devil. Pretty Polly, come you here.

He would jerk along eagerly.

Polly, do you tell my fortune. Have you your broads?

Yes, yes, yes, got my cards. What will you give me?

I'll give you the toe of my boot if you don't hasten—

Yes, yes, but you want a good fortune. A real good fortune? Give me a bowl of them beans and bacon— Give me a big bowl and I'll tell you a great big fine fortune— Give me—

Ah, hush your jawing. Here, Cookie, fetch the bastard a bowl of that kitchen physic. Hurry up, God damn you.

They stood, begrudging the Fortune Teller even this moment of good faring, while he spooned the stew with a trembling hand.

And, please, Willie— Please, Willie— Just one little drink of sorghum whiskey— Just one swallow—

I've no bingo for the likes of you.

But I'll give you the best fortune I ever gave—

Give him a slop of bingo, Willie, to hush his guff.

Ah . . . that bottle there. Damn you, Cookie, never pour too much. Don't be wasting of it on the likes of him. . . . Now, then, hustle with that fortune before I snitchel your ugly conk.

The thick soiled cards spread on a barrel head, the mumbling and scowling as Chickamauga bent above, and moved the cards in a pattern, and rejected some, and shook out others. He was nearsighted, and had secured a gift of spectacles while in the hospital, but the spectacles were long since broken.

Hurry up, you addle cove.

I see you going out of here.

Exchange?

I can't tell. Maybe exchange.

And how soon would that be? Speak up, you vampire.

I think it's July, cried the Fortune Teller in triumph. Yes, yes, it's July. You go out of here—

And to where am I going? To another stockade? I'll fib the living—

No, no, please, Willie— Not another stockade! I see you going— I see you wearing citizen's clothes! Beautiful, beautiful citizen's clothes. You are sitting in a great big gilded dining room—it's a lobster palace. You got a pretty lady with you. You got—you got champagne! And beefsteak! And strawberries! You got—

Ah, enough of your—

You mustn't hurt a fortune teller, Willie, wailed Chickamauga in fear but in severity. That's very bad luck. Don't you dare hit me again—

Well, it's not me that will club you. Willie Collins laughed richly; he liked the idea of himself with a pretty lady in a lobster palace. Now, tell me, Poll— What's the hair that lady's got upon her head?

Golden.

Golden? Why—

Yes, sir—lovely golden hair, and she's got a red hat with a pink feather on it—

With what? You vampire, speak up like a man! Don't you come at Willie Collins a-spitting and a-clacking like a bludget.

Pink feathers! What I said. Pretty pink feathers on her red hat—and curly yellow hair—

Doubtless a whore from a goosing slum on Water Street.

This was said by someone behind Collins, and Willie whirled, waving his club. His friends scattered, laughing uproariously, but bound to keep away from that angry club. Unable to select a particular target at the moment, Willie turned back and kicked the barrel and sent the cards fluttering. Chickamauga sought to elude him, but fell over his own crutch, and Willie Collins gave him stripes to turn his bottom black-and-blue. You ugly pigeon, you've sought to plague me. Don't you know that I like them with brown hair? I hate all women with yellow hair, indeed I do, for one of them gave me the Venus curse when I was a lad. Get out of this and don't you never be coming back! *Whack.*

No, no! Willie—

Get—*whack*—out— *Whack.*

No—oh God—

Chickamauga was now in pain, and would be for days, but he was hurt by these blows no worse than already he had been hurt by repeated woundings of life itself which offered no caress to him, only blows, blows, blows; and he did not know how to earn a caress from anyone. He crawled to his crutches and went weeping away, helped along by a few charitable persons who had been watching the scene, and who perhaps risked the wrath of Willie by ministering to the wretch. Chickamauga did not again seek the company of the raiders; his playing cards were lost; Collins had trampled them into the mud.

About the time of the arrival of the elegantly garbed prisoners from North Carolina, the quantity of rations began to decline; the quality had been non-existent for a long while. Men estimated as to whether they were getting one-quarter or one-third as much food as they needed to keep them going. To augment his slim pickings, Chickamauga could now be seen peeking and prying with double energy; he was bent on gathering some small detail concerning an escape plan which he might sell to Wirz or to the Officer of the Day. Even his insipid reason assured him that he must have accurate identifiable evidence; no mere rumor would suffice. On the morning of May second, when the first load of pone came rocking into the stockade behind its sorry mules, there was a concerted rush by a band—not of raiders, but of ordinary prisoners who had aligned themselves for the purpose. The cart was swept clean in an instant, and all over the vicinity men could be seen, darting or creeping off with two, three, four flat loaves clutched to their bodies . . . in some cases other prisoners hustled after them, bent on robbing the robbers. The cart-driver scratched his woolly head, the guard picked up the musket which had been knocked from his grasp. With two sergeants comprising this detail they drove back out to make their report. Guards on the parapet stood threatening, but mercifully no one was fired upon except one foolish man who went clambering past the deadline near the sink, seeking a scrap of stolen pone which had tumbled there. He was shot dead, shot through the head.

Wirz shrieked when the news came. An edict was pronounced at once, delivered to prisoners at both gates, and spread rapidly by word and shouting until the population was apprised wholly: no further rations would be delivered that day in punishment for the offense. Wirz was so righteously indignant that for once he forgot all about the necessity for personal guards. Revolver on his belt and holster unfastened, he came through the South Gate wicket . . . he had been awake all night with his arm, and stepdaughter Susie (his family was now arrived) had an illness and whinnied with it. Henry Wirz sent about among surgeons as soon as he reached his office that morning, seeking for sulphate of morphia, but the surgeons had none to give him.

He stood, teeth bared under his beard, cursing the ring of scarecrows who threatened and jeered.

By God, I find who stole that bread. Who stole bread? You, fellow there—tall— Did you steal bread?

A slow shake of the head.

By God damn, I find out.

Behind the nearer rank facing him, other voices ranted. Oh, shut up, you dirty Dutchman. Kill the son of a bitch. Take his pistol away from him!

He was getting nowhere with this crowd, so he turned with precision on toe and heel and started in the opposite direction, advancing toward a portion of the encircling throng who resembled the ones he'd just faced with a quality identical in appearance: they had the same thin blackened frames, the same clumps of matted hair and beard, the same rags, the same shedding of humanity.

A stone sang past his head. Wirz turned and drew his revolver. Two wads of mud struck him from the rear, one on the rump, one near his collar. Again he whirled.

I teach you to throw mud at me!

Teach us, teach us, you Dutch son of a bitch! Go ahead, old boy, teach us! What?—with that fucking pistol of yours? Yah, yah, yah, yah, yah—

His voice pressed thin and shrill from a shaking throat. I wish I find out—

Buck and gag the bastard! Let's buck and gag him!

—Wish I find out who says to me such insulting words, I kill the damn Yankee, soon as I eat my supper!

Hear, hear! Aw, listen, Hartley, the poor little critter never had his supper. Hard lines, old fellow, hard lines—

Mud flew toward Henry Wirz. He shut pained eyes and tried to squeeze the trigger of his revolver as he aimed it; he could not squeeze the trigger, the hammer hadn't been pulled to cock, he tried to cock the hammer, his twitching thumb knocked off a percussion cap. What would befall if he stood unarmed before these fiends?— oh death, oh beating and pain and death and lynching—suppose they got hold of his arm—his *right* arm—

He turned and ran violently toward the wicket gate, trying to jam the revolver into its holster as he ran, ducking his head to avoid stones. Voice from the parapet: Hey, open up that little door down there for the captain. And then the wicket swinging, and his own boots bumping the ledge as he clambered through, and mud striking the gate, and the prisoners howling as if they had done a brave thing. What was brave about that? Why should they exult? They were thousands against one, and he was a wounded man, and he had been aching all hours of the night—

He rubbed sweat from his forehead. I want a squad, he ordered. I want I should have two squads with muskets loaded and fixture of bayonets. Then I go back inside, I find those thieves who stole bread from the wagon.

Chickamauga was neither a witness to this event nor a participant in it. Chickamauga was skulking far over on the North Side close to the western border of the stockade. He had reason to think that several tunnels were being constructed, and Henry Wirz was driven wild by the threat of tunnels, and hoisted into glee when he could find a tunnel and break it in. Wirz would pay well for the news, granted it were correct, or at least he should pay well if he had justice about him. Sometimes Chickamauga doubted lugubriously and correctly that there was any justice in anything. But he held some small clues and itched to find more.

That night the Fortune Teller went to the sinks to relieve himself— not through any sense of sanitation or natural tidiness, but because he had learned that he would be pummeled if he grew careless near the habitations of other men. Diarrhoeic prisoners might be forgiven their lapses by the charitable—not Chickamauga. Sometimes he cried, to himself or to others—it did not matter—because he thought that no one ever forgave him for anything.

So he was at the sinks. In twilight he might have been mistaken for a stump, though by this time there was no visible portion of a stump left in the area. All stumps had been splintered apart by the population's knives, forks, bits of tin, sharp stones, or even their own fingernails. The digging up of subterranean roots was in progress, to continue through the summer. But since Chickamauga squatted motionless on his one good leg, half supporting a portion of his weight by means of his leg-stump and a trusty crutch, there was nothing about him to cause alarm.

The man who came and stood nearest him did not indicate by word or gesture that he saw the mutilated figure amid shadows and spongy mats of excrement. If Chickamauga was not a stump then he was a rock, a harmless ghost, a blot before night-seeking eyes, an ink-blot spotted on a copybook of the past, a grease-stain on the muster roll of the future.

The man stood quietly, he did not squat, he might have been taking a leak. But at nighttime no one bothered to go far in order to leak; all the earth was becoming rapidly saturated with those poisons which sick men exude, and it wasn't worth a fight (except in the more fastidious messes, and most of these people would live longer because of their care) to challenge a man when he leaked close to you. There was no sound of urine spraying. What could the man be a-doing? Chickamauga watched, he could not see.

For perhaps three unyielding minutes the man stood there, and as he faded off another figure came to take his place. The watching cripple could not be satisfied as to just what went on—his nearsightedness provoked him—but it seemed that the men made some slight contact . . . maybe it was a word they exchanged. Then the second man took the place of the first, or stood a few feet to the left of where the first man had stood. As in the initial case there was no stream of water. Only a dry trickle or so it seemed. Chickamauga had the ears of an owl; he could hear much, especially at night.

He hoisted up his ragged Confederate pants and crutched to a more comfortable post of observation after the second man departed. He waited, he waited and listened and observed as adroitly as he could, he crouched on watch for another hour or two. The life of the pen continued to make itself felt and heard with that groaning, hacking, contending crystallization which lost all variety because it had too much variety, and so came into a sameness like a single musical note played with monotony and forever . . . half-hourly reports of the guards, the boy who came creeping to the sinks soaked in tears and kept sobbing repeatedly for Aunt Ida and saying again, Aunt Ida, if I could only see you, if I could only see you and old Fan and the pups, Aunt Ida . . . *hulp, look out! Raiders!* (This very distantly.) Station Number Three, eight-thirty o'clock and all's well. Aw, go fuck a duck . . . the mumble, mumble of how many thousand voices, dressed underneath with individual gagging, individual bursts of wind, noise of the fight which may have meant death to some boy weaker than the monsters who bore him down . . . Station Number Four, nine o'clock and alllllls welllll. Station Number Four, nine o'clock and Jeff Davis just buggered himself. And the very earth which was earth no longer, but instead a wet blanket of fecal matter laid across the rounded ribs of the sad punctured world—this apology for earth made its own conversation around Chickamauga; the unseen pools bubbled and stank, the bubbles came out of them as if forced by slow bellows underneath, and worms were working in that slime, or phantom snakes or toads. The bubbles popped, swallowed themselves, the smell came thickening.

But there was living going on, quite near the sentry Poll Parrot whose name may have been Herbert or Hurlburt or Hulburd or Hubbard, and what matter what it was? Or what mattered now whether it was the Thirty-eighth Illinois or the Ninety-sixth Illinois that he came from? Sometimes he thought that he had forgotten all; sometimes he was confident that he remembered clearly, even back unto the day when he was drafted and left the steam and boiling water and floating bits of food in that restaurant kitchen where he washed dishes on Madison Street in Chicago. He had washed dishes in Michigan and in Toronto and Milwaukee too.

There was living going on, a brief dwelling and visiting marked by men who came and went repeatedly. By judging their shapes against the night he thought that identical figures stood near him again and again. They didn't leak, there wasn't any water about the business they did, they only let go with a dry trickle.

At last, puzzled but still suspicious, Chickamauga went up the slope to his lonely shebang made of pine bark and portions of an overcoat. As often occurred, someone else had preëmpted his sleeping space. This interloper was an invalid on his last legs, or rather on his last raw wounds and swellings. He offered no resistance when Chickamauga spanked him cruelly with a crutch and drove him away to weep and die without shelter above. (The man was dead, with his head turned on one side and syrup congealed from his mouth, when Chickamauga saw him the next morning. . . . By gum, you won't come stealing my bed no more.)

The cripple pondered concerning those figures moving in darkness near the sinks, he pondered as well as his lame brain would let him, but he could not understand. He thought with self-recognized slyness that he would go and investigate further at dawn, as soon as it was light enough to see, but before daily activity of the camp had destroyed whatever revealing evidence might exist. Then he settled himself beneath mouldy rags and dreamed of food.

Since he was a boy he had toiled in proximity to food and in proximity to big coal and wood ranges; he had heard and seen and smelt cookery, he had scraped away pungent food left on many plates and platters, he had saved the best of these leftovers for himself, and so he'd dined almost daily on the best. Sometimes the stuff was of a nature which might not bear reheating, but still it was of the very best. He had eaten veal chops with mushroom ketchup, he had eaten *Hasenpfeffer* along with rich dumplings speckled with caraway . . . oh, a fat lobster claw, dripping with butter and drenched in lemon juice . . . peach cobbler . . . just at this moment he thought of *Königsberger Klops* and that dish also he had rejoiced in, in the last German restaurant where he worked. He could not pronounce the name recognizably. His fellow kitchen employees teased him through the hours, trying to get him to say *Königsberger Klops,* but they were always teasing him. They said that he said *Whaneywhagger whop.* He thought of food.

Sometimes there was a falsehood about the dawn. Some of the dawns were honest, murky as old dishwater, draining gradually lighter to reveal the jagged parapet, guards on high, the insane panorama of those masses of huts and sagging shelters, the scrawny wretches who stalked. Other mornings were honest in the fog they brought, for fog made the place the nightmare landscape which it was—fog accentuated nearer angles and ugliness, it turned the inhabitants into those visible apes they'd become in spirit. Chickamauga snored through his beaked nose and dreamed that he was being held down while people sawed his leg, as actually they had held him, with whiskey dashed into his mouth; he dreamed of this particular past and awoke yelling. Winking and shivering in cold he eyed the sky. This was surely the most dishonest dawn ever climbing up. It had a gentle yellow pinkness, and mockingbirds and redbirds were piping with spirit beyond the fence. In such an approaching sunrise one should be forever a child, and have a rosy street to scurry down on the way to work, with no one else abroad except an occasional stomping laborer or a night watchman turning his steps toward the warm breakfast awaiting. Chickamauga had known such sunrises, years before he became cut apart and confined.

He got up hurriedly, shivering in his trunk and three stiff extremities as he tried to stretch himself for the task of exploration. He clawed round in his pockets and found some bits of corn-and-pea bread and gobbled them. On his way down the slope he discovered the dead man whom he had beaten; so he searched the dead man's clothing and found more pone: two ragged rocks of it which the dead man had been unable to eat because his teeth had fallen out from scurvy, or most of them had. Chickamauga found a stub of red pencil less than an inch long, barely big enough to write with, and a fold of dirty paper covered with scribbling. Chickamauga could read quite well, but he was uninterested, so he tossed the paper aside . . . probably a last love note or a last Will & Testament, and who cared about that?

Something firm and flat, sewed within the lining of the corpse's gummy blue jacket (it was a cavalry jacket, short, with some of the seed-shaped buttons still attached down the front, and—Chickamauga bent closer, squinting through colored dimness—yes, there were a few stray threads still clinging to the shoulders, enough pattern of thread knobs to mark the shape of a bent rectangle on each shoulder. So the man had been an officer, one of those strangely dedicated beings who chose to accompany their men rather than go to an officers' prison; and so he must have torn off his shoulder straps before his rank was noted, and he must have given his name as Silas Fassett, Private, Co. G, Eighth Michigan Cavalry; and so he must have come here with his men, and he must have watched them all die off or else he would not have been alone and untended, worming about for a place to lie in and a place to die in, and finding both while his bones still throbbed from the punishment of Chickamauga's blows).

Chickamauga brushed aside the assembled lice and tore open the rotten jacket lining. He brought the flat object out, he snorted with excitement as he ripped shreds of decayed dun-colored silk which wrapped it. It was an ambrotype, a double ambrotype in a frame folding face to face. Cheeks and ribbons of the females therein had been tinted pink and yellow. From the left-hand frame smiled a young girl with bunched-up black curls, and in the right-hand frame that same young girl, a bit more grown up and certainly more than a bit more serious, held a fat stout-legged baby on her plaid lap, and both of them stared directly into your eyes and deep beyond them. They would have stared directly into Chickamauga's soul if he'd possessed more than a shred of one. He dug the woman and baby out of their frames, wondering earnestly if the frames could be gold, but probably they were only of brass and gilt. Nevertheless he'd rub the thing up; and when he set up shop to market it, he would do so on Main Street in order to escape the raiders' attention if possible. He threw the ambrotypes away and went off toward the sinks, pausing occasionally to polish the frame upon his rags. . . . He threw the ambrotypes away, and the one of the mother and child would be unheeded, trodden deeply into muck before an hour had passed, never being recovered, going to demolishment in time. But the picture of the mother before she was a mother—this would be picked up by a lonely youth, Opie Brandel, Co. E, Nineteenth Maine Infantry, and Opie would love and cherish her until he died in June; he would pretend that she was his girl, when in reality he had no girl because he was shy and hoarse-voiced and toadlike; he would call her Ellen because once he had loved from distance a Sunday School teacher named Miss Ellen; he would take her out, when he lay alone at night and when he felt strong enough, and he would turn her small face close to his own hairy one, and he would whisper, Ellen; and sometimes moonlight would find her there with him, and they would be quite alone, and there would be love between them.

Chickamauga ventured near the sinks. His crutch-marks had long since disappeared in slime, but he moved here and there until he was confident that he had found the exact spot where he squatted the evening before, and thus could select the place where mysterious men had appeared to do a mysterious errand. Here it was and . . . ah . . . other places nearby. He balanced his weight on his leg and poked about with one crutch. . . . It would all sink down and disappear during the day, but these traces were unmistakable. Clay and sand, that's what it was—clay and sand, and occasional shreds of brown wet roots too slender for use as firewood . . . a few pebbles. Earth, dirt, soil. Those men had fetched quantities of sandy soil in their pockets or in bags, and had stood sifting it into the bog so as to escape detection.

Who was digging that tunnel, and where was the mouth of it? Under a folded blanket and secreted planks or a lattice of brush, most likely—under the ragged roof of somebody's shebang. Well, there were so many huts. Yes, and so many tunnels or attempted tunnels. His split mouth grinned, thinking of how the men would swear if they knew that he, Poll Parrot, knew their secret already or at least a portion of it. He knew that they were digging the tunnel, and they thought that neither he nor anybody else except the loyal workers themselves knew that they were digging a tunnel. And in time Wirz would know about it, too; and Wirz would give him at least jackass meat, or maybe even currency, or salt which he could trade, or a chance to go Outside for sumach berries. Shrewdly Chickamauga sifted a little of the brown-yellow-sand-clay into his pocket for a specimen, and then he went away: there was nothing more to be done here just now.

That day, after his Ninety had received their rations (each prisoner was given a quarter loaf of corn bread, weighing possibly six ounces, and a piece of smelly pork weighing a little less) and after he had eaten his, and had eaten the portions taken from the dead cavalry-man's pocket—after dining so, he crouched on Main Street and held up his ambrotype frame for sale. Soon a man came by who had been a jeweler when he was a citizen; when Chickamauga begged him to, the jeweler examined the frame and hefted it lightly in his thin hand, and scratched with a bent fingernail. It was, he said, merely gilded brass, just as the vendor feared. Well, the brass could be broken apart to serve for little tools or implements if no one needed it to frame pictures in.

Here's where you get a nice daguerreotype frame, cried Chickamauga. Step this way, gentlemen, and see a fine frame, beautifully gilded, fit to put pictures of your loved ones in. He would have tried to pass it off as solid gold but knew that he could find no takers; also he might attract Collins, John Sarsfield or their ilk. Best to admit that the thing was merely gilded brass. Step up and see, step up and see. . . . Other voices contended against his: men selling rice, men offering tobacco, men with buttons to sell, and boiled potatoes; a man with a ragged *Harper's Weekly* to let, another with a New Testament for sale. Right this way, a beautiful gilded frame to put your loved ones in.

A tall well-built youth with every look of fresh fish about him stopped to examine the merchandise. Chickamauga was excited. This man might be laden with currency.

What did you say this was?

Ambrotype frame! Beautiful! You got a picture to put in it—?

I can't understand you, so quit trying to make me understand. The youth opened the frame, closed it again. How much?

Five dollars currency. Five dollars greenbacks.

The boy laughed, threw the frame at him, turned to go.

Wait, wait! Chickamauga was desperate. This was the first person who'd shown any interest. How much will you pay?

Fifty cents Yank.

Fifty cents Yank? For this fine gilt—?

The customer started away through the crowd, but Chickamauga hastened after him. Wait, wait, mister. Give me seventy-five. Seventy-five. He kept repeating it until he was sure that he was understood.

Look here, Old Clatterpuss. I'm a watchmaker by trade, and I can do some tinkering whilst I'm in this prison pen. Got a few of my tools and— I could use that brass, but I'd have to cut it up—

In the end they compromised on seven dollars Confed, and now it was Chickamauga himself who went shopping. He bought nine small onions with one of the dollars, and a pinch of salt for fifty cents Confed extra, and later he traded two of the onions for a bit of raw meat and bone which the vendor insisted was veal but which was probably dog. He went back to his shebang and cooked a stew in the battered stewpan he'd stolen two weeks earlier, using pine splinters he'd brought from the outside on his last berry trip. Once he bothered to look down the hill to see whether the dead cavalryman was still there; he was, but neighbors were complaining; soon some of the more able-bodied neighbors would carry him away. Chickamauga finished his stew with relish.

He spent on the whole a peaceful and satisfying day. He watched two fights from a safe distance, he saw a wounded man bleeding after he'd been stabbed, he stood in a circle of other rubbernecks and observed a priest from Outside administering Last Rites to a consumptive old man; for a time he followed the priest on his rounds. Wirz appeared in the sentry-box at Station Number Nineteen, accompanied by another Confederate officer with a gray beard, and was roundly screamed at by the inmates. A prisoner was shot and killed near the deadline of the east stockade; the guard insisted that he'd tried to cross the deadline; other prisoners said the victim hadn't tried to cross—that he had been jostled. The guard was ordered out of the sentry-box afterward; there was a rumor that he was a patriarch eighty years of age, and how had his eyesight been good enough to enable him to shoot so accurately? Chickamauga attended also a prayer service conducted by an exhorter of the Methodist faith. He attempted to join in hymns because he enjoyed singing, but no one would ever let him sing—he made such a harsh noise—and this time was no exception. The prisoners manhandled him, hustled him, pushed him away, while the exhorter called warnings and quoted Christ in a loud voice. Vaguely Chickamauga felt a kinship with Christ, for He too had been pounded and scorned.

On the whole however it was a good sunny day, beginning with his discovery of the ambrotype frame in the dead man's jacket, and on through his examination of guilty sand deposited near the sinks, and on through all the rest. The events proceeded as on many other days, but sun shone for hours, a pleasant relief from the chill soaked skies which had clung recently.

That night he posted himself on a route where he might detect the sand-distributors passing, but rain swept down to drive him to cover. The next day Chickamauga shook with the ague for hours and lay miserably in his shebang; he took down the remnants of overcoat to wind around him. He still had currency, and bribed a neighbor to fetch rations. The man brought corn bread and a cup of coffee made from roasted okra seeds; Chickamauga paid more currency to have the coffee heated up. Gradually he regained sufficient strength and initiative to resume his detective operations.

On the night of Tuesday, May tenth, he followed the sand-carriers to the door of their shebang. It took him several hours to accomplish this feat, but Chickamauga felt that luck was with him, and relayed himself, as it were, from man to man through the sleeping, waking, growling, snoring, praying, gasping populace. The shebang was a large one, solidly made—there was even one whole rubber blanket incorporated in the roof. It was tenanted by a mess of Westerners, most of them Iowans. This information Chickamauga pumped from not-too-close neighbors the following morning, by means which seemed to him shrewd.

That morning Chickamauga was at the South Gate long before even the orderlies had arrived to examine prisoners who pleaded for hospitalization. He did not wish to meet the orderlies; he sought Captain Henry Wirz himself. When Chickamauga could get a sentry to heed him, he was stunned by the news that Wirz was sick abed. He moped about . . . should he approach the Officer of the Day or should he not? Wirz might pay better. He wanted to be certain that Wirz knew the source of the information which would be whispered, so that he might appreciate Chickamauga in the future; Chickamauga had no currency, but maybe the Officer of the Day was also flat of purse; certainly some food should be forthcoming; Chickamauga had fasted the day before; he suffered diarrhoea following his ague, and feared to eat corn bread because it irritated his intestines; how could he wait for Wirz and the next day? Perhaps someone else would stumble upon this tunnel project in the meantime and retail the information to guards, and Chickamauga's hopes would be dashed because he had delayed. It was this latter consideration which kept him hanging there, and finally sent him bounding toward the officer, the moment that familiar soiled red sash came in view.

Please, Lieutenant— Please—

What's ado? The Officer of the Day happened to be a plump oyster-eyed man named Gholson, resentful at serving as a lieutenant in middle age when people with half his years were sometimes captains, majors, even colonels.

Outside, whispered Chickamauga, bending close with wretched breath.

The lieutenant drew back in disgust. What the hell do you want to go Outside for?

I got some information. He had to repeat it two or three times before the officer made out what he meant. I don't want to talk in front of all these prisoners. Please—Outside—

The lieutenant turned pompously, called up to the parapet to have the wicket opened; and, squeezing his gray shape through, he beckoned for Chickamauga to follow. At that moment a shower of rain came down; it had been threatening since daylight, and the Officer of the Day directed the cripple to follow him under doubtful shelter of the nearest sentry-platform. Here they stood screened from all eyes, with outer gates of the protective cubicle closed firmly beyond them.

What do you know? The officer turned down the brim of his old yellow hat.

Chickamauga had no hat or cap. Water pearled on his bald head and pinched beardless face, it dripped from his bent nose. Please, will you pay cash? Cash?

Gholson put his hand in his pocket, then took it out again. He said, lying obviously, Left my purse in my quarters. I hain't got no cash to pay you. Speak up.

Please, sir, just a little something to eat. Maybe you could get hold of some meat?

Meat. Everybody dreamed about meat.

You stay here. As a gesture the lieutenant unsnapped the flap of his holster, and then walked over to the outer gate and knocked loudly, calling for someone named Sipes. The wicket opened, a face appeared, and Chickamauga stood chilled and dripping but watching eagerly.

Sipes, send up to the kitchens for a dish of them nigger-peas. And a spoon. Make it lively—I hain't got all day.

Big dish, Lieutenant?

A can full will do.

In the background Chickamauga jiggled on his crutch, eyes swelling out as he thought of hot peas.

There was a degree of shelter beside the outer gate, for rain was driving from the west. The fat Gholson lounged there while leisurely he cut a chew from his tobacco plug, put the plug and pocketknife away, and began to roll the fresh chew about in his mouth. He called through moist brown lips, You better have that information, crip. I'm wasting a sight of time.

Presently the wicket reopened and a small mess tin and a spoon were handed through to Gholson. The lieutenant signalled to Chickamauga, and the man came hopping across. Actually the nigger-peas were still warm, even in cold rain, and there were a few fragments of bacon in them. The lieutenant handed the treasure to the informer, saying, Just like the Planters' Hotel in Charleston. You even got a spoon. What do you know? You can talk while you're eating.

Chickamauga tried to talk while he was eating, but the officer soon stopped him. You cow-mouth bastard, I can't make you out. Eat them peas, and then talk, and talk sense or you'll go in the stocks.

Nothing had ever seemed so wonderful since the last dream of *Königsberger Klops*. Well, and he spooned up the last tasty drop of sauce, I know where there's a tunnel.

He told all, he gave a clear description of the Westerners' shebang.

Reckon I know that one. They got them a rubber blanket on the roof?

Yes, yes! Rubber blanket—

Chickamauga tried, again without success, to beg currency; then he asked for more peas or for an Outside pass with the next wood squad, but was refused. He began to cry. The lieutenant gave him a fair-sized piece of tobacco cut from his plug. Chickamauga did not chew or smoke, but this would be excellent for barter. He was ushered back into the stockade and went in, feeling that in some way he had been cheated. But Wirz might still let him go for berries when Wirz heard the tidings; anyway, another tunnel would be dug sooner or later. The memory of those heavenly peas lingered in his mind and on his tongue.

About forty-five minutes later a file of twelve guards followed Lieutenant Gholson into the pen. Ten of the men carried guns with bayonets fixed, and the lieutenant had his revolver out and cocked, carried dangerously in his hand. One of the men lugged a shovel and one a pick-axe. Gholson had no inclination toward the circuitous; he led his little army to the guilty shebang as directly as the crazy unsystematic arrangement of huts would allow.

The Westerners were lined up. Five had been caught at home, but two others escaped because they happened to be away. The five said that they were the only dwellers in that place; this they would still affirm, even in torture of stocks and balls-and-chains. They did not admit that people from adjacent shebangs had also helped in the digging (this was true of course). Away the prisoners were marched, to be put into a chain-gang. Wirz regarded a prisoner's attempt to escape not as a duty, a military obligation to his own cause, but as a fiendish effort to visit murder and rapine upon an innocent countryside. The shovel man and pick-axe man remained behind with Gholson still in command, breaking the ground around the tunnel's entrance, and filling in the hole. A hundred silent neighbors stood and glowered. Others went about their ordinary affairs in an elaborately casual manner, fearing to be associated in any demonstration of sympathy or resentment. The tunnel itself was well-made and well-executed ... it was rumored that the leader in the enterprise had engineering experience. The tunnel began with a vertical shaft, shored up in its more crumbly portions, and other people could only guess at its depth before the horizontal passageway began. As was usual, the opening had been concealed by a blanket near which a couple of men were forever lounging during daytimes.

Chickamauga kept away from the immediate neighborhood while the arrest and destruction took place. He ambled along Main Street, seeking the best possible rate of exchange for his tobacco, and he said, What do you know about that? when people discussed the tunnel and pointed to the little squad of prisoners being marched Outside for punishment.

Chickamauga made finally a handsome bargain in which he paid his tobacco as rent for a deck of cards; he would be allowed to keep the cards for twenty-four hours, but was instructed not to lose so much as a single card under penalty of having his parrot's nose mashed flat. With these tools so necessary to the fortune teller's trade, he went about through the afternoon with satisfaction and profit. He devised fortunes for a few cents here, half a spoonful of salt there. He encountered a prosperous newcomer who delighted in hearing that positively he would be exchanged within either three days, three weeks or three months (could it have been three years? the man worried later) and he paid Chickamauga with a wooden plate filled with freshly fried potatoes of which the newcomer had a supply. After delighting in these viands and others, Chickamauga turned in and slept until sunset when the sky was clearing.

He returned to Main Street, trusting to earn a supper by means of his art, and was calling for clients along the muddy strand when a hand fell upon his shoulder. He turned and looked into the narrowed eyes of a seventeen-year-old stripling whose muscles had not yet fallen into threads. Two other men, older but equally grim, were with the prisoner.

We're from the Fifth Iowa, he said sternly to Chickamauga. You're the one who give our friends away.

No, I ain't!

Hell you ain't. You were all around there early today, asking questions about who lived in that tent—

No, I wasn't! You let me lone—

Hell you wasn't. Didn't you say he was, Ebe?

Yes. One of the other men had moved around behind the cripple to bar his escape. I saw him and heard him.

The tall youth struck Chickamauga on the mouth and knocked him against Eben Dolliver; he would have fallen if Eben had not been there, and he lost his crutches. He tottered forward on his left leg as Dolliver shoved him away. The youth punched Chickamauga twice more—in the belly, and he doubled forward; then on the side of the jaw. The victim tried to scream but could make only guttural growlings and gaspings, for his breath had been nearly knocked out of him. He stretched his length in the greasy mud, he tried to roll away from punishment. The youth wore shoes, or apologies for them; and with these shoes he kicked Chickamauga in the ribs four or five times.

Stop killing that poor cripple, cried a shocked voice.

Try and stop me. He got our friends on the chain-gang!

The youth awarded several more kicks, and so did the man beside him. Ebe Dolliver did not kick, but he approved the treatment, shocking as it might have seemed to him when first he was captured. They went away and left Chickamauga, who began to sob stupidly as soon as he had enough wind.

Some kind men were nearby, and they stood appalled at witnessing what seemed to them such unprovoked viciousness, yet they were not strong enough to interfere. They helped Chickamauga to stand up, they wiped blood from his mouth; one prisoner who professed to a knowledge of anatomy felt along the unhappy creature's ribs and assured him that they were not broken—only bruised. These benefac-

tors even offered him a jacket at the edge of their shebang where he
rested for a time. But it was growing dark, and there was not room
for him there. People were settling down, tightly packed in spoon
fashion, to spend another May night and to pray for August. (In July
they would pray for November, in February they would pray for
June.) Chickamauga could hobble, though stiffly. He traveled to his
own shebang.

A stranger was there, and he was more powerful than Chickamauga,
crutches and all.

This here's my shebang.

Do tell. It's mine now.

I'll larrup you with this crutch—

I don't know half what you're saying, but I've moved in here and
I'm going to stay.

Chickamauga begged and cajoled, he asked for people in nearby
shelters to aid him in expelling the intruder, but deaf ears were turned
to him: he had won no regard from any by his previous conduct.
Justly or not, this claim-jumper was going to stay. It was very chilly
for a spring night. Chickamauga suggested that it would be warmer
for two of them than for one; so the man agreed to share his stolen
couch with the true owner. They lay together, shuddering . . . the
other man had been drinking, and where had he got liquor? After an
hour or two he became nauseated, and staggered off in search of water.
He did not return, probably because he was unfamiliar with the lay
of the land and could not find his way. Chickamauga took down the
wisp of overcoat and wrapped it around himself. He could not sleep
for a long time, his ribs hurt him terribly. Sniveling and mourning, he
fell asleep and dreamed about his father. He was a little boy again,
his father was drunk and chasing him with a strap. Chickamauga
awakened in tears, but slept later and dreamed no more.

Morning came with sun, but it was misery for the lame man to haul
himself up on his left foot. Knives were thrust into his side, a hammer
had mauled his jaw and left it out of shape. But he hungered. He took
stock of his stores . . . only salt, and not more than a few cents' worth.
However, no one of the playing cards had been lost when he was
beaten the previous evening, and thus he might hope to earn a breakfast at even this early hour. Fearing the Fifth Iowa boys more than he
now feared the New Yorkers, he picked his way past the sinks over to
South Street and solicited for an hour or two without success. His
voice worn shabby by repetition of his slogan, Chickamauga was
squatted alongside a temporarily deserted shebang when two men
passed; they were not strangers, they were men he knew.

News traveled like birds in that community, and a rumor flapped its
wings. The men were talking close at hand as they dawdled painfully

along . . . one was bent forward with scurvy. They did not see Chickamauga beside them, though he could have reached out and touched them with his crutch.

Hear about the cripple?

Heard he give away about a tunnel on the North Side—

So he did; he told Wirz. Well, one of them Iowa boys was shot last night on the Outside, trying to Take Leave from the chain-gang. You know that fellow they call Big Mizzoo: he just tolt me; and he had it that them Iowa boys are hunting all over hell and high water for old Poll Parrot, and I reckon they'll make him sweat. The men moved on, their voices weaker in the camp's noise.

Wirz, Wirz. Wirz was the only hope now. Drooling, perspiring between his shiverings, Chickamauga set out for the South Gate as fast as he could travel. He had only twenty rods to go. As he approached the deadline and dead-row he saw a wagon drive in belatedly for a load of bodies, and Henry Wirz rode behind the wagon on his gray horse. With an armed guard near, the wagon guard, Wirz did not feel menaced and alone.

Wirz recognized an essential nastiness in this mutilated gabbler and dreaded encountering him, despite the various traitorous services Chickamauga had performed. Gentle and tired with age, the white-gray mare shied away from the figure which came humping. Wirz, an awkward but determined horseman, brought the beast under control with strong use of the bit.

Get away, you— You frighten my horse!

Captain, please, please, Captain, I want to go Outside.

It is nonsense. Why you go Outside?

This was a dilemma. Had the lieutenant told the captain of Chickamauga's recent service to them? If Chickamauga mentioned it now, it would come as an assertion of guilt to all ears listening nearby.

Because—there's bad men here. They beat me last night. Captain, they beat me! I didn't do nothing bad. They—

Such stories I do not wish to hear. Go away, you damn Yankee!

The boys—the men—they made up lies about me! They—they hit me and knocked me down and kicked me— God's sake, Captain Wirz, they'll kill me unless you take me Outside!

Now you get away from my horse.

Chickamauga tottered forward, hand straining for a grasp on the stirrup. Wirz kicked out with his boot, he drove him off. You damn fool son of a bitch, you get away from my horse or my pistol I take and shoot you dead!

Men were close, herded close to the deadline, and many as always had petitions for their keeper. Aw, get out of that, Poll Parrot, somebody yelled. The Flying Dutchman don't want you.

Outside! Captain, please—they'll kill me—

Wirz took the mare past him, and Chickamauga toppled fairly against the scantling which ran on deadline poles. Tears were spurting afresh . . . oh, not again, he wailed within his soul. Not to be hit and kicked again, kicked until I die of it.

. . . The deadline! He said either My God or Mother—those closest could not tell which words he uttered, or whether it was only a discordant mumble of M-sounds. Chickamauga adjusted his crutches, bent down deliberately and placed his hand on the scantling. In a tumbling tilting maneuver he got his crutches over the scantling, and used them as vaulting poles to hop his left leg across. He stood poised on forbidden ground.

You damn fool son of a bitch, get out from that deadline! the superintendent screamed.

Chickamauga faced him. No, I won't, he said more distinctly than he said most things. Not unless you take me Outside.

Wirz swore in German and drew his revolver. Come out, or I kill you dead.

Then kill me, God damn it.

Light was spreading behind Chickamauga's tight-shut eyes, light was battering with a sound against his brain. That's what you want to do, a voice rang at him, and not a voice from any human. It said, Stay. It said, They'll never dare shoot you. They'll let you go Outside.

He spoke again, with something close to clarity, I won't come out unless you promise—

Wirz took aim, then lowered the weapon. He turned his thin bearded face upward and began to berate the sentry. My job is to keep these damn Yankees, never to shoot them, you lazy, you! Your job it is to do that. That Yankee is inside the deadline. Shoot him!

The sentry was a sixteen-year-old from the Twenty-sixth Alabama named Ben Drawhorn. Had he been one of the Fifty-fifth Georgia, Chickamauga would have been dead in a twinkling; but the Alabamans were schooled to hold their fire better than the Georgians. Ben held his old Queen Anne musket, it was loaded with buckshot, the muzzle went from side to side and up and down in an extravagant circle.

I can't shoot that man, Captain—

I fix you, you bad sentinel, you! Now (to the prisoners closest to Chickamauga) you get that damn cripple out from that deadline! You I will not shoot! Wirz put away his revolver.

Promptly fellow prisoners dragged Chickamauga back to safer territory despite his struggles and strident protestation. Wirz was at the gate, he was beating and hallooing to have the portal swung, and slowly the hinges began to squeal. Wirz rode out with intent to discipline the reluctant boy on the parapet, the private who had disobeyed an order from a captain.

Look at that bastard.

A solitary voice said it, and then there came a dozen concerted yells mingled with laughter. Chickamauga had crept back inside the dead-line, once hands released him, and while all attention was directed to the exit of Henry Wirz.

Again the white-faced boy lifted his Queen's-arm. It was one of the ancient pieces altered for percussion. His act, as well as the hullabaloo within the stockade, told Wirz what had happened.

He screamed beyond the wall. If that damn bitch cripple is again in the deadline— Shoot him! Shoot, damn you, like I command you shoot!

Chickamauga was a good three yards within the line. No man could reach him to draw him out without exposing himself to that musket.

People understood him to say with stubbornness, I want to go Out-side. There's some bad folks—

Young Ben Drawhorn stood with open mouth and bowed shoulders, but he was aiming the musket. He pulled the trigger. The cap did not explode.

God damn you! They heard Wirz's boots clumping on the ladder outside. I come up there and show you—

The explosion of the powder charge interrupted his cry. Ben Draw-horn had re-cocked his musket and this time the cap did not misfire. The buckshot tore Chickamauga's lower jaw into a loose red spray and went deep inside him, to rest in his breast somewhere. He fell, jaw-less, blood spurting wide. Up on the sentry's platform Ben Draw-horn dropped the musket and staggered back with both hands forced against his face, covering his eyes, but if he exclaimed no one heard him. Wirz soon appeared beside him on the box; he scarcely glanced down at the fallen Chickamauga, but instead began a violent accusa-tion of the silently sobbing boy.

Someone called up, Can we carry him out? and Wirz told them to go ahead. They picked up Chickamauga and bore him off a little way, and then put him down to die. Though he could not speak without that lower jaw, his tongue was still active, and waved violently as he tried to talk. People wondered later what he would have liked to have said. On the whole there was little regret at his passing, but men laughed about that stoutly wagging red tongue in its crimson nest. It haunted some of the more sensitive in their sleep and for long.

XXII

It had been early in May that Ebe Dolliver, the Iowa bird-lover, first munched a ration of cooked bread. This came about a day or two after certain men were detailed to go Outside as bakers. The prisoners looked for a grand improvement in their rations as a result, but did not find it. As the novelty of a loaf instead of loose meal wore off, they realized that cobs were being ground along with the corn, and that the resulting cake was nearly as hard as hickory and scratched a man's bowels to the quick as material passed through. People complained in communication to folks Outside, and the reply came back that the Outside men's job was not to grind the corn, only to mix paste and bake the pones. In grinding quantities sufficient (or insufficient) to feed twelve thousand prisoners many cobs found their way among the kernels through accident, more through carelessness on the part of stupid blacks and shiftless whites, and still more through deliberate criminal neglect. From being a wealth and a much-sought-after currency, which the bread was at first, it changed to garbage. People went around with the stuff in their pockets, offering to trade; there were few takers among the old prisoners, but some among new ones until they became prison-wise.

You began to find slabs of uneaten corn pone among personal effects of the dead. Soon you began to see chunks of the stuff lying outside doors of shebangs—unwanted, cast aside. Wood was a treasure compared to bread, for you could cook other things over wood if you could secure other things to cook. The character of the morass along Stockade Creek changed in color; it was no longer composed solely of feces and organic slime; there was now a brownish yellowish crust, a flotsam of corn bread in every stage of spongy decay. Great metallic flies, frightening in burnished brassy armor, whirled above with a humming louder than bees. Some few prisoners might have had bowels of iron: they ate the stuff stoically, it did not rake their insides, the blood did not appear.

In revulsion from this stony ration, Eben Dolliver considered meat. Adjusted to the protraction of his starving, he did not beguile himself with discussion of Moon Hotel dinners and the like—with thoughts of his mother's marble cake, fresh baked hermits, apple salad. Meat

appeared as a medicine in his ideal, meat might have been bottled or
put into pills, it might have rested in huge ornamented jars, well
stoppered, on the shelves of some apothecary. Ebe tried to count the
varieties of meat he had known, and sometimes in the middle of the
night he thought of a new variety to add to his list. He tried to make
up a hundred sorts of flesh which he had eaten in his young life, and
was well on his way toward that goal. At first he said only pork, beef,
lamb and the like, but soon recognized how different they were. Bacon
was quite another thing from sausage, ham hocks were not to be confused with pork chops. Yet all came from the same beast. Eben argued
with himself in detached philosophy on the subject, and at last yielded
to his own importuning. Every variety of pork should be counted, and
so with other products of other beasts. A catfish was not like a bass,
nor was a wild goose like a tame chicken.

(Strangely he had never objected to killing chickens, and had killed
many at his mother's behest. He did not think of poultry as being
birds: they were filthy and cannibalistic in their habits, they did not
sing a dainty song, they did not enliven the hazel brush with miraculous flashes of blue and rose. They were wedded to the dirty ground
where they fed, and he loathed their squawking; he was willing to
kill them, for they were not a free wild glory which lifted him.)

The Moon Hotel mess clustered still in brotherhood, they tried to
keep to their rules. Their effort at bathing was become a sorry thing.
Hull of Michigan and Mendenhall of Pennsylvania were gone into
scurvy: the linings of their mouths puffed and spotted, cords hurting
in their legs. Still they made an attempt to speak cheerfully, to join in
weak choruses. Everyone had heard the stories and anecdotes of the
rest over and over again; yet now and then a man thought of something new to tell.

Mendenhall thought suddenly of a neighbor of his, a fat bachelor
who did not have all his reason and was the butt of jokes. The man's
name was Johnny Jober; tales of Johnny, told in Mendenhall's best
Pennsylvania German style, enlivened the mess for days. The boys
would say, Let's hear it again, Mendy. Tell about Chonny Yober and
how he put the shingles on his roof upside down. I like to split over
that one. So Mendenhall would gather strength and tell again . . . the
neighbor sat in his wagon and called to Johnny on the roof and said,
Hey, ain't it you put on them shingles ass backward? And how Johnny
sat and gazed at the whole of that shed roof he'd shingled, starting
at the ridgepole instead of along the eaves, and how he burst into tears
and how he said—

People lay in shade of the shebang, tittering at these fine new stories of Chonny Yober, the stronger men breaking out with guffaws at
the proper time. Other prisoners arose and came near, staring mutely,
as if wondering what all the laughter was about, and yet not really

caring. They drifted away slowly to be replaced by other mute watchers. The shuttle of this vagabond audience wove itself back and forth, flies hummed and bit, the blistering yellow stench of May sun was high. A wave of heat stole up to distort the looming fence and sentry stations, to turn them watery.

Often Ebe Dolliver drifted loose in thought from broken accents of Mendenhall's recounting; he went off alone in his mind to dream of meat. Once, at play in the woods, he and little Neri had killed a groundhog; they had butchered the creature and cooked it over a small fire, trying to live like wild men or outlaws in hiding. Had he counted the groundhog among his meats? He thought he had; maybe not. That would make eighty-three varieties of flesh, if he hadn't counted groundhog previously. Eighty-two, eighty-three. . . . Had he counted the last buffalo killed in their section when he was a little tad? Roll Brewer gave a chunk of the meat to Joth Dolliver as he came past the mill. Ebe remembered how they gathered round when the roast was removed from the baking pan—rare lean meat looked like gigantic rare beef but more orange in color; the fat was yellower than beef fat. . . .

Forever, in time, he wandered to the birds. When wearied of enumerating medicinal meats, Eben found ease in following a ground-robin. He had heard that towhee was also a name for this bird, perhaps a name given by the aborigines. Black-white-and-bay, the industrious little folk scratched their way among old leaves in a silent place. Eben had lain motionless and watched their coming . . . sometimes walking like hens upon the ground, but prettier and more delicate than hens . . . no sound but the watery trill of a fly-catcher hidden in some ravine, no other sound except light wind making poplars tremble their coins of leaves in pride, and the *ink, cheerink* made by ground-robins themselves as they gossiped.

Again he saw his first indigo bunting. . . . He sat on a special hill said to have been once a place of massacre; larks rose and descended and rose with spirit again, giving out their long fluting . . . more of them, more out in the grass, they played pipes across the boundary where an ear could still hear them; and then the ear lost strength to pick up their piping, but somehow a sleepy brain knew that they were practicing by multitudes in remoter pastures . . . their sound was a wonder, a promise of brave simple measures to be rippled Up Yonder . . . *or if on joyful wing, cleaving the sky . . . sun, moon and stars forgot, upward I fly.*

He examined a catbird's ragged nest, he saw the lettuce tint of eggs contained therein. (They looked like candied eggs in a grocery store jar.) He'd bound a handkerchief across his mouth, not to taint the catbird's eggs so the mother would refuse to return; it told that one must do that in Our Feathered Friends, With Copious Illustra-

tions. . . . Male redwings, polished like shoe leather with soot from
the pot rubbed into it, redwings so black that they were silver in
the morning as they swayed on reeds around a prairie slough. Their
Quaker wives, wearing The Garb, more modest than sparrows. . . .

When Eben arrived at Andersonville there was still activity among
the tousle of mutilated pine. He'd explored past stumps that first
day, observing how the gum oozed from every cut. It had turned
white, crystallized, flaky; he chewed some, but he wasn't accustomed
to it—too much taste of turpentine, so he spat it out. Small birds,
some he knew, some he'd never seen before— They took wing, streaked
away through air before Eben as he walked. Come back, stay with
us, he said in his heart, with the enchantment of eerie high-going
larger birds still fresh in memory—the unidentified northbound tribes
he'd heard two nights previously. But the birds would not stay,
prisoners frightened them, they went to live in less disturbed areas
beyond the rectangular fence.

Through the remainder of springtime Eben heard their mating
tunes, their early salute, one light instrument's sound imposed on the
trickle of a hundred others, many of them different. But now in May
it was hot summer, a Georgia summer. Birds sang less, they sang
little. If he'd had his precious telescope he might have spotted them
and fetched them nigh to him again: there were many places on the
North Side where you could see the outside fort at the southwest
corner, and woods beyond that. On the South Side, near the South
Gate, you could look across the fence where it dived toward the
creek; you could see past the pine-roofed deadhouse, see smoke spilling up from the bake house, see guards and Outsiders trailing about
their work, mule teams moving. Sometimes, oh sometimes, there
shafted a blade of gold, an agate of whirring slate and white, the
red speck which was a redbird. That was all Eben could see of gods
and goddesses. His telescope had been stolen out of his knapsack in
front of Vicksburg; never had he found the thief.

Eben Dolliver knew that his body had changed, but he did not
feel an alteration of his spirit; only it seemed easier nowadays for his
spirit to separate from the body and go hiking into underbrush which
his corporeal shape was restrained from entering. Bell's Woods,
Bryan's Woods, the single towering hill far north of Dolliver's Mill
which settlers called Mount Washington: Ebe could visit those places
in turn or simultaneously as impulse directed. In those places he
discovered painted buntings he had never glimpsed, the groove-
billed ani of which he'd only read, mockingbirds he'd seen during
his first Andersonville week on the one happy day when they were
sent Outside under guard with axes in their hands. . . . Flights of
passenger pigeons came to impress the Iowa groves with uncountable
numbers when they roosted; but peculiarly they wore no longer the

dove and peach colors of orthodox pigeons—they were as tropical immigrants, with blazing crests and the plumes of peacocks.

Eben sat with skeletal hands around his knobby knees, sat in shade furnished partially by the crazy quilt he'd cheated away from the Rebel, a quilt no longer crazy but patterned with dun in varying degrees. Exposed skin of his lank frame was pigmented with the pitch from burning oily wood, hardened in, baked in: it could not have been scrubbed away by soap of whatever strength; Eben would have needed to be flayed in order to be cleaned. His mop of pink hair hung stiff with dirt and twisted in a curl at the nape of his neck. His meager beard was a lichen spread over the weathered grime of his face. This was the afternoon of May twenty-fourth, a Tuesday.

Within a few minutes the more active prisoners went wild. They leaped into the air, they found stones to throw, and threw them, and the stones came down and struck other prisoners to their grief. They began capering with lengths of board or dry pine torn from walls of their shebangs; with these improvised cudgels they battered at space above their heads. Now and then there was uplifted a howl of triumph, and several men converged, scrambling on the ground, snatching at something; and then one man would rise, the obvious victor, waving something in his hand.

Birds had come. They were swallows, a multitude, planing low in any direction, giving out irascible cries. They came like bats past the guards loafing on the stockade's rim and made the guards jump as wind of their passing brushed the guards' faces. One swallow came alone, a dozen swept in a different direction to intercept his flight . . . now they spread and teetered in point-winged circles, so numerous in a given space that they must have broken themselves to bits and hatched a dozen new birds from each whirring fragment. High, aloft, squeaking, their pale swift breasts turned dark as their wings against the low motionless sun; then down to fairly comb the earth, and crowds gesticulating there and trying to kill them, and killing some. The birds' wings clapped like limber scissors, their split tails were sharp as if drawn by pen and ink, the plumage of breasts and bellies was pearl when they came close, low. It was one of those convocations to which swallows are addicted under seasonable conditions; but no man might know why they had herded into this ugly place, and the swallows did not know.

The stockade became a trap holding them in its grip. To the swallows it appeared that the sky was not sky—a favorable avenue, an uninterrupted lake wherein they might soar to any independence they desired. The sky was the lid of the trap, it seemed pressing down on them, they resisted its pressure with new squealings, and swarmed up to burst through it and were forced back to earth again by some compulsion impervious as the screening of a cage. With speed of insects they cut here and there, up, down, across, behind. Never did swallows halt to roost atop the huts; they rubbed the angles of huts, disturbed the hot motionless air, you felt it blowing this way and that as if fans were wielded. By how many scores, how many hundreds, how many thousands, did they appear? Were they as numerous as the tramps who grabbed at them? They seemed more numerous.

Killing birds, said Eben Dolliver aloud. They're trying to kill birds. He heard a boy's voice speak from distance. Give me that there pocket rifle. You got no business shooting kingfishers. Another boy saying, Just try and take it from me. Joth Dolliver saying mildly from the mill door, Now, Ebe, don't you try to pick a fight.

Killing birds.

Again they were bats, their wings were pointed like the wings of bats, perhaps in fact they were bats deployed from some awful cavern of history, and dressed in disguise of feathers to tempt these people into wickedness. It sounded as an Indian fight must have sounded; men voiced their stuttering chorus of yaps and yelps, the swallows burbled their own cries. Two huts away from him, Eben saw a tall man bounding up and down, a jacket spread between his hands. He was trying to batter the birds with his jacket, trying to swaddle them with the cloth; even as Eben looked the man swaddled one. He wadded the garment around the bird, made a ball of it, he killed the swallow by crushing the jacket-wad beneath his feet. Then he sank down on his knees, and when he arose half a minute later with a grin on his hairy face there was bright blood on his chin. Raw? said Kirke behind Eben. Not for me, mister. If I got one I'd pluck it and toast it on a fire.

Why, declared Eben, once more aloud, they're meat.

Meat might be concentrated in pills and potions, it was tonic. The doctor said, Now you go straight home and take a dose of meat. Swallow down a big dose of blood, hot blood. It's the anodyne you stand in need of. . . . Had ever he thought that birds wore flesh beneath their down? Never before had they done so, now they must be wearing it. For all those thousands of years since they left off being snakes (this he believed; early in 1861 he had read a borrowed copy of Darwin, mostly in secret since his father did not approve) they had dressed their bones with thistledown instead of tissue, and doubtless the bones were leaf green, fragile as new maple leaves.

Myrtle warbler shy and peeking, goldfinch bold upon the milkweed plant, the fleeting dust of rust which blew when fox sparrows shot themselves across a road in spring . . . what was that soul bubbling its wet poetry from solitude of the dry brush pile? Call it angel, call it brown thrasher, call it heartbreak, call it God's blessing. Call it meat.

Call it a swallow.

Eben Dolliver pulled out the heavy stick which anchored his comforter to the shebang's roof in daytime, and could be drawn loose when the quilt was needed for a blanket. Hey, Ebe, take it easy; trying to tear down the whole roof? He emerged into open bird-haunted space, and a flight of the frantic things went up and away from him, and raced like moths toward the marsh, and new stragglers came flipping above. He waved his club this way and that, he beat it in a circle. Many other prisoners had been making desperate attempts at capture since the swallows first swarmed, and had not managed to strike a single specimen, but they did not own the luck of Eben. At the fifth or sixth ferocious smash of his stick there was a light thud, and something bounced on the ground like a crumple of blue-black-pale-gray paper blown by a wind. Other pirating hands tried to snatch it, but Eben plunged at full length, he fell on the bird and crushed it with chest and arms. He wrung its neck as he arose. Vaguely he heard surviving swallows condemning him with tiny words as he pushed his jaws, as he sucked, as he spat out feathers.

XXIII

An unbearable announcement was made in the Claffey household some time around the end of May or the first of June. When Lucy thought of it drearily, afterward, she could remember the season, not the date. It was just before the Big Rains began. There had been heavy rainfall in March, the weather improved generally during April, May was mostly hot with some unseasonably cold nights . . . ah, yes, the unbearable announcement was made perhaps during the first few days of June. Lucy counted rains that month as the unsheltered prisoners beyond the surviving fringe of pines counted them. It rained during twenty-four of the thirty June days that year. It rained on twenty successive days.

Her mother— Before the Big Rains—

The thing began with the misdeed of a white cat designated as Columbus. Lucy had named the creature thus because of his exploring propensities in kittenhood. He was always crawling about somewhere and getting stuck, and then sending out piercing yowls for assistance. He climbed high into trees, and ladders had to be brought; he entombed himself for two days within an unused chimney; once he crept into the west wall of the library and strips of siding had to be removed in order to rescue Columbus. The blacks could not pronounce the kitten's name—mostly they spoke of him as Cumbus, and the Claffeys fell into the habit. Having now attained great size and some age, Cumbus had left off dangerous explorations. He'd turned half wild, he prowled savagely in the woods, whipped or assaulted other cats frequently, and only approached the kitchen to steal. He was a powerful animal, built like a wrestler, pink scars showing all over his white head, green-eyed and selfish.

Ira Claffey brought a hat filled with mushrooms from the woods, and Lucy clapped her hands. These were a favorite of theirs; Ira had identified them as *Russulas,* unmistakable with broad caps of lavender-rose, short stems, gills delicate as the flesh of a nicely cooked fish. They had a tender nutty flavor when prepared with care, they were tastier far than the common agarics which Ira used to grow on trays in a dark shed, before the war, when he had time to spare for such nonsense.

Poppy, I declare they're remarkable. Regular honey lambs. Where did you find them?

Among oaks above Little Sweetwater. Shall we have a pie?

I'll take them out to Naomi myself, and I'll most certainly count them so's there'll be no foolishness; I'll warn Naomi that all—yes, sir, Poppy, fifteen of them—had better be in that little pie! We'll be just as selfish as selfish can be, and eat that whole pie our own selves.

Ira said with anticipation, Twill be the best thing I've eaten since the Mexican War.

Course it will. With scads of gravy under the crust, and just a mite of onion.

I've fresh chervil and marjoram! Chervil in the third row of the kitchen garden, and marjoram in a pot on the shelf yonder.

Well, Poppy, not too much, or you'll sacrifice the woodsy taste. I'll snip just a teentsie bit with my shears and give it to Naomi in a poke. What a pity—

She stopped speaking on the instant, hurt by thought of the silent woman who remained mainly above stairs. A pity, she repeated, that Mother nor the boys never liked mushrooms.

No, they did not. She does not. Father and daughter held a brief merciful silence between them. Automatically they both began to look toward the ceiling and then away quickly again, neither wishing the other to realize how they had responded.

The mushroom pie came pungent and brown-crusted from the big oven in proper season for dinner, but at that moment Coffee and Jem turned up a den of small snakes in the south pasture lot, and the resulting squalls sent Ira to the scene to make sure that no one had been bitten and that the snakes were destroyed. During this interval the treasured pie waited on a kitchen table, half covered with a padded tea-cosy to keep it warm, sending its odor far. Lucy heard a combined clatter, thud and shrieking from the kitchen; she groaned and wondered What Now? She was going to investigate, but Extra came lumbering into the house to offer a report, her rolling eyes wet with tears of joy, black face shining . . . gulping for breath between yells as she tried to talk and could not manage it.

What is it, Extra?

Miss—Luce—yah—

What is it?

That—Cumbus cat—

Lucy was standing at the foot of the front stairway. Extra writhed and gesticulated before her.

Extra, do wait until you can talk.

Yah! That Cumbus cat—

It came out that Cumbus had been drawn to the kitchen by gravy scents. Unnoticed by servants he had leaped upon the table with thievish intent, and in his approach to the pie he had somehow upset a leaning platter. The platter smashed against a pitcher, other pots and pans had gone tumbling; the terrified cat jumped for the window but instead had landed in a tub of warm water— The chronology of this misadventure was confused by the narrator's gasps and cries of delight. From the recounting emerged a picture of a bandit righteously punished by immersion, soaring off between cabins as if Old Satan were after him.

Old Satan, Miss Lucy! That old cat, that what he think—

Well, Extra, thank you for telling me, and I'm very glad our pie was saved—

Ira had reëntered the house by this time and stood quizzically regarding his daughter and the black woman. A sound from above drew their combined attention to the head of the staircase. Veronica stood thin and stiff in her shabby mourning-dress, and the icy indignation of her expression was a glare.

Please—daughter—Ira—Extra. Above all— *Extra!* She spoke the slave woman's name with guttural rage.

Lucy could not move. Ira took a step or two on the stairs. He said rapidly, My dear, what—?

You're making too much *noise*. You'll wake the *children*. We must have quiet in this house. They're *asleep*.

The mushroom pie went mainly uneaten that day; Lucy gave the remains, which were really the bulk of the pie, to the blacks. She thought, I am weary of staring dumbly. How long must we stare, how long must we be dumb, why can we not expunge this cloud which swelters and strangles us, takes away all air, takes away even the desire to breathe air? She was so young that she felt blind fury at injustice, she wanted to reorganize the scheme of birth and life and death (she thought not of reorganizing the scheme of procreation, but had she suffered a wound while loving she would have wished to alter this process too, because of wrath).

Soon it was learned that the children dwelt in Moses's old room; Ira had feared that was where they would be domiciled. It was not clear whether all the other Claffey children were there or only the boys who'd died in the war. Perhaps little Arwood, Peggy, Sally and Courtenay slumbered in the same chests with Suthy's knitted boots, Badger's brown plaid cambric dress, Moses's unblemished New Testament & Psalms which he was awarded for committing to memory one hundred and one verses of the Scriptures, most of which he promptly forgot. Did the children sleep rosy and in health, did they choke with the diphtheria which had claimed two, did they complain with whimpers that the surviving family and slaves walked too heavily, spoke too loudly? They might not complain about laughter, there would be little laughter for them to complain about. At first Ira was afraid to go into that room. He muttered to his daughter, By God, my child, I can't go. At last Lucy, braver in this hour than he, visited the ghastly chamber while her mother walked abroad with the mystified Ninny trudging dutifully behind. To Lucy's relief she found no little beds made up. These she had feared she would find, she had entertained visions of her mother arranging a row of spectral pallets. It was good to observe— No, there could be nothing good about it; but it was helpful to know that the dead young warriors occupied couches which were simple illusion, not actual linen and feathers and ticking.

Sometimes Veronica spoke of The Boys, more often it was The Children. *Shh.* This to a Pet or a Ninny who banged about while scrubbing the floor. You must work more quietly; I do not wish them waked. *Shh.*

Out across the yard in the kitchen Naomi blubbered about it.

Miss Lucy. Is Mistess gone *crazy?*

Hush, Naomi.

But she know the boys dead at the North. She know it! She know they not little babies in that room up there!

Now, Naomi. The middle-aged slave sobbed, hot and perspiring and smelly, against the white girl's slenderness; Lucy stroked the broad damp back with her hands; it seemed that she was reaching out through distance to touch Naomi. Now, Naomi, it's only that— My mother is ill, we hope she will be better soon. She is ill.

Suddenly the enormity of the cruel cycle weighted Lucy, it crushed and tore her inside and out. She said, louder and louder, She's not crazy, you fool thing! Ill—do you hear me? Ill! Her straining hands came up and crumpled Naomi's gown at the shoulders, and her pinch must have caught patches of the Negress's skin in its compression, for Naomi struggled and cried, hurt in body as well as in her bewildered soul. Upstairs in the house Veronica stiffened at hearing Jonas bawl at his mule in the lane outside. She went to the window, looked down to where Jonas must be working, but she could not see him for the trees. She put a cool finger against her lips. *Shh.*

XXIV

The relationship between himself and Seneca MacBean worked to the immediate benefit of Nathan Dreyfoos and those close to him, but also it was a grain of reassurance for the rawboned printer from Galena. A strength like the strength Nathan had to offer (and would retain in considerable degree if he followed the direction of a more seasoned man) was another stud in the bludgeon which Seneca Mac-Bean planned to fashion for wielding at some future date. Nathan had manual dexterity—Sen was not surprised when he heard that Dreyfoos could play the fiddle—and as a barber he was a success promptly, although at first he worked too slowly to make much profit. . . . Food, MacBean urged him, that was the thing. Try to get food first of all. Rice, barley, root vegetables, bones, salt: a stew was the thing. He knew; he lived mainly on stews, and he was keeping his grip. If a man couldn't pay in food, try for some article which you might barter for food. Nathan Dreyfoos was a willing pupil in the grim curriculum of stockade erudition, and he emerged with other talents peculiar to himself.

For example, Sen smiled when he noticed the hook-nosed sergeant's activity during periods when there were no customers for haircuts. He would look up from his scrubbing and wringing, to see Nathan toying with one of the tent poles he had bought. The pole was of hickory—light, smooth, tough, springy. Seriously with his penknife Dreyfoos was working one end of the pole into a short sharp point. Well, Seneca thought, he'll learn in time. Learn that it doesn't pay a man to twiddle himself by mere whittling—not in here. Too many other things to do: assemble firewood, swap, build a fire, cook, keep the vermin down. He was bitterly amused further when he saw Nathan toasting the sharpened end of the pole over a fire. What's he doing—pretending he's got a sausage on a stick at a pic-nic?

Not long afterward two of the worst characters in camp sauntered near—a pair of sailors named Bill Rickson and Al Munn. Close behind drifted a group of six or eight, the inevitable pack of hyenas.

Hi, Sergeant. Come here. We'd like to talk swap.

Don't move, said Seneca in a low voice. They carry brass knucks.

But Dreyfoos was advancing on the sailors, the slim tent pole similar to a cane in his hand.

Like to swap them scissors off of you. Now, I got a gold watch that—

A club came out of a pant-leg, another out of a sleeve. Blows were aimed and delivered on empty space. Munn bellowed and clapped his hand to his side where his sailor's blouse was ripped and his flesh torn. Rickson bored forward silently, wheeling his club; then he stopped, then he began to give ground. That pointed pole was everywhere, threatening his belly, jabbing at his throat, whipping right, left, up, down, in, out. It raked his hairy arm, the club flew. Munn circled, crouching, arms swinging wide, to take Nathan in the rear, but Seneca MacBean was there by that time, doubling his fists.

Oh, come out of it, Billy. Munn moved away, not looking back, examining his skinned side as he went.

The valiant cohorts had already disappeared, and people were crawling out of the shade of their shebangs to observe. Two or three rocks flew. One very nearly struck Nathan instead of striking the man for whom it was intended. The silent Rickson, now without a club, joined Munn in retreat. He stopped to rip a post from a shebang which he passed, tried its strength in his arms, the post snapped like a candy stick.

Hell, Billy, come along with you.

They went away; folks gazed wide-eyed. Usually an encounter with raiders ended in a manner different from this.

Nathan Dreyfoos stood watching the sailors as they pushed their way down the slope. Will they come back?

Not in daylight. It'd pay to be on the lookout at night; they might try to cut your throat for revenge. Sen MacBean slapped Nathan heartily on the buttock. To think I thought you were frittering your time in idle whittling. *Always whittle from yourself and then you'll never cut yourself.* What you call that thing—a spear?

Only a pointed stick.

How you handled it.

Well, you see, Seneca, I began the study of fencing when I was eleven.

Ever fight in the prize ring?

Never. But I have experience in boxing.

Dreyfoos, it'll take time but— Let's get back to work. I've got a pair of dirty pants half washed, and the owner has naught to hide his nakedness until I dry them. Now I think you'll get more customers to your barbering. Why? Because they'll feel safe from the raiders, merely being near you. By gum. MacBean brayed with one of his nasal peals of laughter. You handled that weapon (he called it weepon) like I'd handle a line gauge.

Nathan Dreyfoos messed apart from Sen MacBean and slept apart from him as well. He felt his obligation to the boys of the Eighty-fifth, though some of them were intractable, many would not be buoyed up . . . they had a fierce mistaken notion that their discipline ended with their imprisonment, and they only snarled at Nathan and others who attempted to set them to rights. But most daytime hours were passed at the combination laundry and barber shop. It grew to be a center of community interest, a meeting place and gossip mart. Nathan wore his knapsack to work each day, and carried off to his own shebang such articles as he had acquired for pay during the day. His ration of corn pone he broke up and put into the eternal stews. Every two or three days he had to spend some hours on shopping tours, bargaining his way along Main Street or to the sutler's shack, trading off rawhide shoe-laces or shirt buttons or tobacco for vegetables, sometimes even for meat. At times he went calmly to South Street, which was definitely raider territory, but always he carried his homemade spear. He was attacked once more in daylight; after that the raiders looked the other way. The thought of night did not worry Nathan Dreyfoos severely. Ten of them slept in a wide shebang made of their coats and blankets, and it was a rule that at least five must remain at home at all times, day or night, armed with knives, spoon daggers and clubs. Sarsfield's Raiders made an attack there one afternoon; the five housekeepers fought savagely until others of their regiment could lend a hand. Sarsfield got only one poncho for his pains, and it was announced that one of his men had been stabbed in the belly by Private Allen, the boy who had burst into tears the morning he landed in the stockade (it was rumored that the man died later as a result, but perhaps that was but a rumor).

Way I look at it, said Seneca MacBean. Oh, there's heroisms and heroisms, but more than heroism is going to be necessary to clean up this mess. It's like you've said and like I've thought: concerted action.

Often I do not understand you, Sen. Your speech . . . you speak much of the time with the—forgive me—rural dialect of so many Americans. You employ army slang and colloquial words. The average boy in my company would not use words like *concerted*. Or *overture*.

Seneca studied this. Well, my father was a schoolmaster but he died before I was born. My formal education was poorly come by. But I'm a printer, and my grandfather was a printer before me. Printers get to know language. We're faced with words, editorial-wise and otherwise, which we mightn't face were we mechanics. . . . No, Brother Nathan, to proceed as I was going: concerted action is the only answer. Discipline, organization. I've friends who feel the same way, and one of them is a better organizer than I could be. That's Key, from the Sixteenth Cavalry—fellow who was just in here awhile ago, fetching this old blue shirt. He's also a Sucker, from Bloomington. Big courageous-looking man, isn't he? I warrant you he'll *be* courageous too, if the time ever comes. And take that fellow who looks like a red Indian—comes from the Sixty-seventh Illinois Infantry—you cut his hair a-yesterday—

They call him Limber Jim.

Limber Jim—that's he. And Ned Carrigan from Chicago. And Johnny McElroy—he's little but he's determined. They'll all fight, and fight well, but it means organization and thought and planning. It means a campaign to be mapped out, and troops to be selected and raised and mustered.

Nathan Dreyfoos gave his slow wide smile. It seems that you people are relying chiefly on your fellow Illinoisans. Can this be partisanship?

No, exploded MacBean sharply. And then . . . after a pause . . . well, could be. Now, take you. You're Eighty-fifth New York, but mighty un-New Yorkish. I suppose your life abroad has given you a kind of universalness.

Universality.

Thankee. Where's my sand bucket? Ah . . . trouble is, we *ought* to rely on Westerners. I'm one, I understand them, they understand me. Most of your New Yorkers—saving the raiders—and Pennsylvanians— They stick by themselves. Even the New Jersey boys tend to cleave together, and dog bite the man on the outside. Did you ever see anything like the way Massachusetts folks hang tight? And so with most of New England. Now, Michiganders are something like them—but I'd say humanized. Westernized New Englanders? Is that what you'd call them? They talk much the same way. Say *I be* instead of *I am*. But they're more awake, more Western.

Nathan Dreyfoos felt a lack and ignorance. This is my country. I was born in it; Corley and Stevenson taught me that I must attempt to live for it and die for it. Yet I know so little about it. He said, It must be like the difference between Catalonians and Madrilenos and Andalucians.

I don't know any of them, but it's doubtless the same. Take the people from Ohio, Indiana, Illinois, Iowa, Kansas—some of the Minnesotans—there aren't too many—and some of the Missourians too. Cut off the same bolt of goods. Sometimes you'd think that if one studied McGuffey they all studied McGuffey. If one studied Ray's Arithmetic they all studied Ray's Arithmetic. They think—

MacBean hunted for the word. They respond alike, he said.

—If we need police, and we do need police—

—I'm not condemning Easterners solely because they're from the East. A lot of Easterners could help, and a lot of them probably will help us out, if we get started—

—I've talked with Limber Jim, and Key, and you. Haven't talked to the others, but Key's been sizing everybody up. In due time—

—There's dire need of police right now. But Jerusalem wasn't built in a day.

Rome.

Thankee, Brother Nathan. Rome.

The friendship grew like a seedling in a frame under glass under strong sun; it might have been manured by the manure of Andersonville, which was everywhere. The metaphor occurred to both men, separately and singly (it was inescapable) but neither would have defamed the friendship by citing it.

It was an attraction and trust of opposites, a mutual reliance on men identical in faith and sanity. The straitened horizon of Galena and Chicago and the few other towns where Seneca MacBean's fingers had streaked from upper case to lower case— It stretched to include the picturesque cities where he had never walked and probably never would walk. The young man who'd had no roots to let down into the soil of his birth found himself anchored increasingly, attached by invisible tentacles to loam of the Middle West which he had never trodden or dug or scented.

MacBean had had no confidant in his life, except his grandmother, his grandfather, and one young woman whom he'd adored in Chicago a year or two before the war. (She was frail, her heart hurt her. Her mother worked on occasion, part time, folding printed sheets in the shop where Seneca slugged the galleys. Generously and thoughtfully the elder woman invited the lonely young man to Sunday tea in rooms which she and her daughter Phoebe occupied. After that he was there each evening, and in time contributed to their support. There came a cold sleety morning when a little boy pounded on Sen MacBean's door at his lodging house and presented a note which read *Dear Friend Seneca. Can you come to me at once. Phoebe has died in her sleep.*)

Sen became garrulous at times, talked of his ambitions in civil life, said that he'd like nothing better than to be the editor of a small town newspaper. . . . Bet you I'd raise the fur along their spines. Always something which needs correction in any town: sidewalks, sewage, corrupt officials, or maybe a new railroad or canal. A newspaper editor never need look far for a stone on which to grind his axe. . . .

How did he come to join the cavalry?

That was an oddment. It began when he was a little boy, dragging those willow baskets of washings along the even east-and-west streets of Galena or—much worse—up and down the nearly vertical north-and-south streets of Galena. There was an older boy named Clovis Tibbetts and he had a black pony with a red saddle. The sight of this pony drove Seneca into fits of jealousy, quiet spasms of envy. In solitary imaginings he owned not a pony but a horse; the horse was as high as a house, and not merely black but black and white; the red saddle was crusted with gems on the saddle-bow. (I guess, said Seneca, that the stirrups were solid gold.) But this was mere wishful illusion: no creature except a rat ever dwelt in the MacBean stable during Sen's boyhood, no nervous fairy hoofs twinkled along the driveway. (I didn't want to *be* Clovis Tibbetts, he said. I just wanted a pony—or a horse—as good as his or better'n his.) Acutely he recalled one hot afternoon when he was lonely, he had nothing to do, he had no work to do, no one to play with; his grandfather snored in a stupor; his grandmother was ironing clothes. Gran, he said, I wish—

What do you wish, lad?

Wish (he whispered it) I had a pony.

What would you do with a pony, laddie?

I'd ride it.

She said brightly that she would prepare a pony for him. He must remain inside the house, he must not peep out until she gave the word. He waited, his throat dry, his breath coming fast; he hid himself in a closet so that he might not be tempted to disobey her command. When at last she chirruped from the lawn outside he came dashing. . . . What magic was here? She had said that she would fix a pony for him. Did she know a neighbor from whom a pony might be borrowed? Had she—? It was a pain and jabbing but— Had she *borrowed Clovis Tibbetts' pony?*

The woman had done her best. She had rolled a cask from the woodshed—a decrepit wooden barrel which had been salvaged from somewhere and was to serve as kindling. On this cask she had folded a makeshift saddle made from a shawl, and she had attached reins of faded ribbon. Now, lad, she said, bestride your pony, and ride far far away. Ride to the ends of the earth. . . . Sen nodded, he thanked Gran in a murmur, he waited until she was gone back to her work, and then reluctantly he climbed astride the barrel. It did not look like a horse, it did not smell as a horse smelled, it was a miserable makeshift, it did not feel between his legs as a horse must feel.

And damn, he said. Soon I looked up—might have heard a noise out in front, along Bench Street—and there he was. Riding past. Clovis Tibbetts on his pony. Red saddle and all. Right then was when I joined the cavalry.

Ah, yes. I understand. I have never been poor—I might be a wiser man had I been poor. But I understand.

Never rode a horse until I was grown, except— Oh, once in a while, bareback to water, on somebody's farm. But I had the notion.

I know. Anyone who's had dreams would know.

Then I was working away off, hell to yonder, when they fired on

Fort Sumter. The paper I worked for was edited by a man who hated
Abolitionists, and he declared that only Abolitionists were rattling
the sword. Maybe I had absorbed some of his teachings—you know,
putting his notions into type. He had a fine style with words, somewhat like Thomas Carlyle. And equally opinionated! So it took me
a while to make up my mind.

. . . Funny what this prison life does to a body, Brother Nathan.
I never told anyone about that heretofore, except one lady. But this
awful place makes a man talk at times. And dream.

Nathan said, A man escapes in his dreams. I go far, even though
I have not been here long.

Well, I can guess what you mean. Paris, Rome, England—all those
lands where you've been. But take care you don't go too far. Man
can't live sole alone on dreams.

I shan't go too far.

Not far enough to lose those qualities of leadership. They'll be
needed. You'll be needed.

No, I shall not go too far.

Seneca MacBean said that he had a hero who demonstrated qualities of leadership. . . . Perhaps from the time his young fingers first
plucked type Sen MacBean had been possessed of a desire to tell
his own story in his own way. Between the ens and ems of his occupation had risen the legendary skill of the campfire yarn-spinner,
the cracker-barrel raconteur. He loved a good story for the story's
own sake, and told stories well; but when his own emotion or experience was involved he could rise to a simple dramatic height.
He chewed the words with wide jaws, there was slyness in his eyes
as he talked, he seemed meditating between sentences; yet the pauses
were urgent in their very silence. Any listener would wait with eager
ears and soul, his attention would not wander until the nasal Western voice carried along the narrative and made it march and shine in
the telling.

So Sen had a hero. At home they called the man Cap, because
one time he had been a captain in the army. He was not at all the
embattled swordsman of antiquity, like the Gillies MacBean described by Seneca's grandfather. John MacBean said that forever
any youth should be proud to wear the name of MacBean; the youth
had only to think of Gillies. Gillies MacBean stood alone in some
old Highland war, to guard a breach through which the enemy must
advance. He fought until he became a martial saint; at last he was
killed; the dead lay piled. Gillies MacBean was the subject of a lament
which the wrinkled Scottish printer could recall only in part: *And
each day the eyes of thy young son before, shall the plaid be unfolded,
unsheathed the claymore.*

So be proud to be a MacBean, ye ken.

Yes, Grandfather.

Say, Aye!

Aye!—and then his grandfather would chuckle.

But the man called Cap, said Seneca, was styled differently. He remembered seeing him, the day Cap first came to town, progressing slowly off the boat which tied downtown at the wharf on Fever Creek; the wife came first, in charge of her little family, and Cap followed, carrying two kitchen chairs in his hands. He had failed in business since leaving the army (he drank himself out of his commission) and was being more or less pensioned by his father. His two brothers ran a business, and Cap was destined to help them, and people hoped he'd make a go of it. But the brothers were sharper than tacks. Cap was not.

Take a farmer: he'd come into the store to trade for some harness, and Cap would help him to select the harness, while the brothers watched suspiciously.

Farmer'd say, How much is this here harness?

Cap'd say, Let's see. Here's the tag. Twenty-five dollars.

Farmer'd steam and blow up. This here set? Twenty-five dollars? Why, by mighty, it hain't *worth* twenty-five dollars!

And Cap'd examine the harness all over, critically. Then he'd shake his head and say, Guess you're right. Doesn't look like twenty-five dollars worth to me, either.

And then those brothers would be fit to be tied.

Time the war busted out, Cap was eager to join up again, and they had a local militia company called the Jo Daviess Guards. But the folks in town held their own notions about who should be officering that company, and Cap wasn't included in their speculations. They held an election, but Cap wasn't elected; somebody else would command. Well . . . he couldn't carry liquor, and once he'd been compelled to resign from the army, and a man who had no brains for harness-selling probably wouldn't have any brains for commanding a company. With his tongue unhinged by a glass or two, Cap told a few of his friends that he'd written to Washington, written to the War Department. He said that he had been educated at the National expense and now thought he ought to repay his debt to the Nation; in his own opinion he was fit to command as much as a regiment. But no reply came. Some clerk had scorned the letter and filed it away.

Well, Seneca MacBean was back in town, called by his grandfather's last illness, the day that the Jo Daviess Guards marched to the train. They looked pretty fine, for green troops; they had a power of sparkle to them, and the young officers looked imposing. Then a few folks started to laugh. What did they see? Here came old Cap, walking or marching or whatever you want to call it, along the street.

He was keeping pace with the Jo Daviess Guards, bound and determined to follow them at least as far as Springfield where troops were rendezvousing. There he trod along in his shabby citizen's clothes and faded hat, carrying a limp carpetbag in his hand. Quite a sight. No wonder the folks laughed and nudged one another.

My hero, said Seneca MacBean. What you might call Qualities of Leadership, in upper case.

Where is Cap now?

Some weeks ago I heard that he'd been given command of all the armies of the United States. Man by the name of Grant.

XXV

The first few days of Floral Tebbs's military experience had been marked by wide-spread festivity: the planning thereof, the excited contemplation thereof, the celebration itself. The Twenty-sixth Alabama was about to leave for the front and a majority of veterans in those ranks looked forward to departure with hysterical relief. They did not care how many Yankees shot at them in far hills where soon they would reëncounter the enemy. Battle would be a delight in comparison to the stench and monotony of this duty at Andersonville. Georgia Reserves would relieve them here, Georgia Reserves would go On Picket and On Parapet instead of the Alabamans. Good enough for them.

Flory Tebbs wished that he also might be bound for fields of glory, but still the primary appurtenances of soldier life were thrilling. Contemplation of the altered musket issued to him sent him into a blissful daze. He loved to touch the cracked walnut of the old stock, even though he forgot and left his piece leaning outside to rust against a tent-rope the first night, and was cursed by his sergeant. The sergeant was a pimply mentally retarded youth named Sinkfield whose chief accomplishment before this war seemed to have been in the killing of little pigs at an Atlanta slaughter-house. Sergeant Sinkfield was fond of reciting the death throes of little pigs and could imitate their squeals to dread perfection. After enduring a shove, slap and verbal blasting from this bestripèd hulk, Flory took to polishing his musket with sandpaper which he and two new cronies stole from an ordnance chest left untended at the big star fort. The musket barrel accumulated no more rust, it was abraided until it hurt the eyes in sunlight, it gleamed beneath the stars.

When not trooping through one of their disordered drills or digging fresh trenches for latrines, the raw Reserves were set to clearing a space on level ground among the pines near the road to Anderson Station. This area was dragged, pounded, wet down, stamped again, swept clean. It was to serve as a dance floor. Everyone prayed that no rain would fall on the thirteenth of the month. No rain came. Throughout the countryside folks made a holiday, and black people thronged to watch. The string band played for hours; The Girl I Left

Behind Me seemed the only rendition on which fiddles, banjos and the two guitars could get together properly, but there was better music offered in solo by various musicians. Dust crawled in a cloud from the clay floor. Over to the east beyond the uneven palisade and sentry shacks Yanks stood in droves, watching the merrymaking across that low place where the stockade dipped over the creek. They stood upon high ground on one side, the celebrants were upon distant high ground on the other side, they could see. It seemed funny to have Yanks watching you while you danced.

Floral Tebbs did not dance; he did not know how to dance any more than he knew how to read, and he did not like to have girls near him. The detail of unlucky guards who had drawn Parapet lounged on their platforms, peering toward this unprecedented frolic, paying more attention to the gaiety than to the Yanks they were set to watch. Thus no one was shot at the deadline during those hours, and sly bold prisoners took advantage of the opportunity to steal wood and comparatively uncontaminated water from the danger side of the scantlings.

Laurel Tebbs, her little witch's face afire with excitement, was whirled from hand to hand, from group to group. The gross Sergeant Sinkfield attended her persistently, hugging her thin body against his oversized body whenever he found a chance. Laurel wore an old purple gown of her mother's, gathered in wads at the waist to take up the slack of extra goods; she had done this alteration herself, and it was not wholly successful; but the color was bright, her petticoats were mended, she had scrubbed and pressed them, they showed when she swung and skipped, men found them enticing no matter how bare and brown and bony the scarred limbs which twisted beneath the folds. Laurel had upset a pot of boiling water over her feet and ankles when she was tiny. Plentiful scars still showed, mottled, pink, creamy amid the tan.

Flory regarded his sister with disgust, and stalked away to the pit where bodies of two foraged half-wild hogs were basted slowly above barbecue coals. Just look at my younger, cried the Widow Tebbs to Captain Ox Puckett as they bounced to the end of the line. Going along over there. He does make quite a soldier.

Flory? He won't never make no soldier.

But he is one. In that little Yankee jacket too big for him—

Honey, these here Reserves is slime. Just pure slime.

Ox Puckett, how dast you? Flory hain't no slime!

Oh, no, not him specially. What I mean: no fit drill, no fit discipline. The non-coms is quarter-witted and slothful, and anybody knows that non-coms are the backbone of the military. Leave us pray to God there don't come no general rising of the Yanks! These here Reserves would cut for it—I don't care how snipsish is the jacket Flory's a-wearing! . . . Come along, let's get into this new set. But let me kick off these boots first and go sock-footed.

Coral Tebbs attended the pic-nic, after declaring with oaths that he would die sooner than go. He spent some time glowering at dancers from a distance; later he accepted a gourd half filled with pine-top and was drawn into conversation by two of the Alabamans who happened to have been in the battle at South Mountain back in '62. The conversation became animated, rowdy; the pic-nic was ignored by Coral and nearly ignored by the others; little points of fire burned in Coral's black gaze. He drank more pine-top and later became sick at his stomach, and threw up behind a tree. The Alabamans had seemed suddenly like comrades, and he had had no comrade in a long time. Now the Alabama boys (comrades: what were their names? Loopy and Cox) would be going to the front, and he could not go to the front. He could not go anywhere much. He fumbled his head-aching way toward home long before the pic-nic was done. Uncle Arch Yeoman saw him reeling; he came out of his store and smelled liquor, and upbraided Coral, and offered him a Temperance tract.

God damn you, said Coral, I don't want no Temperance track. Go wipe your ass with it! He pressed the paper into a ball and threw it at Uncle Arch, and went on toward the Tebbs place, whimpering to himself, blowing his nose with his fingers as he traveled.

His brother Flory had found also boon companions in a manner which suggested that they might be more or less permanently welded in partnership, since they were members of Flory's new mess and slept beside him. Both were from Chatham County and had known each other before they came to serve. One was a tall starveling who'd spent early years at a Poor Farm, the other a runaway apprentice who declared that his father was executed early in the war for murdering his lieutenant. This latter youth, Irby Flincher, became Flory's favored compatriot because they were nearly of the same size although Irby was three years older than Flory. Times when they stood unclad Flory took pains to conceal his nakedness from the others because he had no hair and the other elder boys had hair. In anguish Floral inspected himself and petitioned the Almighty to grant him hair, and by June was rewarded in observing a few limp sprouts of blondish texture above his rudimentary organs. . . . Irby Flincher had a trick of giggling privately with the other member of this triumvirate whose name was Mackey Nall. They talked of corn-holing, browning and other mysteries unknown to Floral Tebbs.

Floral was beaten up several times during the early weeks of soldiering. He was whipped by Sergeant Sinkfield, by Corporal Woodall, by a loutish private from up in Bibb. Once he attempted to run away to the Tebbs place and scream his trials to the widow; but fleeter people fetched him back. Sinkfield talked of bucking and gagging, but Flory was sentenced finally to march back and forth on picket duty with a Yankee knapsack on his back—a knapsack filled with bricks. It appeared that he was turned to be a whipping boy, being one of the smallest and perhaps the youngest in his command.

One night he and Irby Flincher got into a discussion about which should sleep under a new leak sprung in their rotten tent, and Irby attempted to enforce his demands. Flory had come to the end of his rope. He shrilled, I don't give the shit off'n a tomcat if your Daddy *was* a killer, and very nearly gouged out one of Irby's large brown eyes in the resulting struggle. Irby shrieked for help, Mackey came to help him, Floral Tebbs bit the lobe from Mackey Nall's right ear. After that he was termed a devil-festered little runt, and respected accordingly. Within a few days he and Irby and Mackey were friends again, and swaggered together off duty.

Irby said, You know them bricks.

What bricks, Sojer?

Like old Stinkfield-Sinkfield compelled you to tote for punishment. Member where they come from? From nigh that bake house.

God damn, I don't hanker to carry no more bricks.

But I got a good idea come to mind. Let's get down back of them stumps where no one can't see nor hear us, and I'll tell you what.

Together the three squatted in hiding and Irby explained his plan. They were bothered by mud in their tent; water rose out of the trench beyond the canvas whenever new rains came pelting. Well, sir. There were plenty bricks over next to that bake house where apparently old Dick Winder planned to build a new oven. Well, sir. There wasn't any guard set over them bricks. . . . Irby Flincher's eyes were huge and pale-rimmed and luminous—they looked like the eyes of Holy folk in Bible pictures—they shone with wistful brilliance when he talked feverishly.

Sojers, we can crawl over there one at a time in the dark. No guards about, specially if it's raining pitchforks and nigger-babies. Make a tolerable platform, raise our beds out of the mud.

But twould be hard sleeping.

Ain't hard sleeping better than wet sleeping, Sojer?

Spose the quartermaster cotches us?

Oh, he couldn't cotch the pox! Where do you reckon he got them boards from—build himself a fine new office and quarters? Some of that same lumber Colonel Persons got to make barracks for the Yanks in the stockade!

Hell, it hain't fitten them Yanks should have barracks and us have none.

Reckon we'll have barracks fore long. So I heard tell. But meanwhile—

They made private creeping sorties, the bricks were transferred laboriously. Their other tentmate (an asthmatic Millerite with brown fangs who warned the three little ruffians to prepare for an eventual reappearance of Christ on earth) threatened to disclose their thievery unless they toted some bricks for him too. They whispered about a possible accident which might ensue; they had heard of such executions awarded to soldiers who made themselves obnoxious . . . a loaded gun might go off suddenly, unexpectedly. But none of them had yet whetted his savagery to the edge of cold-blooded murder: they liked to talk about it, that was all. They fetched bricks for old Ducky Duckworth, they had a dry and well-paved tent. There was never any official inspection of the tents . . . it was expected that barracks would be constructed soon, and so in time they were constructed. Meanwhile no one appeared to have missed the stolen bricks, and the three robbers prided themselves.

Together or singly they stole other things. The post adjutant owned a slab shack to which only he had the key, and rumor claimed that the shack was stuffed with good things to be sold at fancy prices to prison sutlers. Floral Tebbs watched sharply whenever he passed this structure on a slight incline above the road. He observed that it was set on posts, but that a very small person—one of his size or Irby's—might snake his way between the squat pilings and perhaps gain entry from beneath. Boards had been nailed tightly to the sleepers, ambition was thwarted to begin with. Later Flory discovered by candlelight, and with Mackey and Irby lying along the ground outside to shield the candle's flare— He discovered that one of the sleepers was worm-eaten. You could practically push the nails out with your fingers, or at least with a claw-hammer if one might be filched. In time this too was accomplished, and, under cover of the trampling and barking of a thousand new prisoners arriving in one night, the nails were dispensed with. Irby and Flory got into the adjutant's shack and passed things out to Mackey Nall beneath the floor. They made several raids before an investigation disclosed the nature and manner of this burglary, though not the perpetrators thereof; then the floor was rebuilt and a guard was stationed at the building twenty-four hours a day. Nevertheless the scrawny freebooters had made off with red pepper, honey, salt, saleratus, half a bushel of onions worth sixty dollars Secesh per bushel, an entire box of tobacco worth twenty-two fifty; and to crown their achievement they had drained away several quarts of precious sorghum from a vast barrel which was believed to be worth the startling sum of three hundred and twenty-five dollars—not Secesh, but in greenbacks.

But what's that there saleratus good for? (They had secreted their spoils in loose underbrush beyond the guards' sinks.)

Sell it to the Yanks, old Poop Brain.

What they want with it?

Oh, they use it for bread and truck. Maybe biscuits. Medicine.

What you get for it?

Buttons with hens on them, if not cold cash.

The brass buttons on Flory's jacket had been removed before the garment was handed to him, his own buttons were mere disks of wood. He longed for eagle-shine, he longed for the gleam of minted stars. Dog my cats, Sojer. How many buttons ought I to make a Yank give me?

Say a jacket-full for a teeny little sack. Don't you fret—they'll get the buttons if you got the other stuff.

That night they swung to a new shifting of the guards. Flory found himself On Parapet at sundown. He'd called his squealing eight o'clock and all's well . . . his half-after-eight, his nine o'clock and all's well . . . he heard taunts flung up because of his childhood and the baby squawk of his voice. He itched to kill a Yankee as he had itched long; yet he was afraid to fire his musket because old Ducky warned him that the kick would knock him off the platform and break his neck for him. Flory had never fired the musket; they had no gunnery range, no targets; he wondered if truly the kick was worse than the kick of Coral's shotgun. He had no idea how to begin negotiating with prisoners, but presently he became aware that something odd was going on at the next station. Several prisoners huddled near the deadline in the dark. A good-sized moon was rising in the east. Soon it would be light enough to see what was happening. But when the moon preened itself in unattainable yellow splendor the Yanks were vanished.

Flory looked down across the newly excavated ditch on the outside. No sergeants in sight, no details moving about. The coast was clear. He called to the guard at Station Number Thirty-eight (a mere acquaintance, a nearsighted older man who ignored Flory usually); he called, trying to make his treble seem gruff and casual. What'd you get over there, Johnson?

Pair of shears, bub. I swear, won't the old lady be proud.

What kind of shears?

Sewing shears sure enough.

What you have to give for them, Johnson?

Bub, quit calling my name out loud. . . . I give some salt.

Sakes. Where you get that old salt?

Well, where you think, you little fart? I ain't telling nobody. Now you shut up—quit your yelling at me fore we get in trouble.

This warning caused Flory to fall silent. Soon he lost himself in a child's musings, the eternal Wish I Had of the scrawny and ill-favored. He dreamed of horehound candy (he would buy a quantity when he was paid) and favorite foods which he had tasted infrequently and thus considered rare, and he dreamed of foods he had heard about

but had never seen or smelled, and of other delicacies of which he
had never even heard . . . what were they? Off in delectable space
somewhere beyond the buzz, the murmur, the squawling, the reek of
this prison . . . great hot platters of tempting meats and colored fruits.

He wished he owned a pistol such as was owned by this officer and
that. A gun was all right; he had been taught how to load his musket,
how to cap it, how to draw the charge. But there was something especially man-grown about the idea of a holster rubbing beside your leg
as you moved. Flory liked the flap of a revolver holster, he liked the
way it curved and fastened down, he liked the feel and solidity and
promise of guarding leather, the way it became polished by rubbing
and by sweat (he had never worn a holster, he could but imagine).
He had lost much of his curiosity about Yanks, knowing them with
intimacy now when they congregated below him. But Flory had been
told that there was money to be made out of them, profit to be gained;
he desired money and profit. He did not know how to begin a transaction, he was afraid that the Yanks would laugh at him. Floral Tebbs
hated to be laughed at, and yet he was laughed at frequently.

His imaginings were limited by primitive inexperience. He was an
infant and an illiterate, but some illiterates had absorbed the stimula-
tion of profound emotion and thus were above the beasts. Flory was
not. He was a beast, although a weak and confused little animal and
thus proportionately dangerous. He did not know exactly what occupied the thought and attention of the branded scoundrels whom he
had been set to watch. If he considered that they had secret pulsations
and agonies such as lacerated him, it was only to ascribe to them a
concerted wickedness: they would like to get out, and rove horned
and prankish through the unprotected landscape. He must give none
of them an opportunity to do this.

(Within ten rods of Flory's sentry-box an ex-miner and an ex-baggage-handler and an ex-mule-driver and an ex-book-agent-who-longed-
to-be-a-writer-of-novels huddled together in their rags busy with lice.
They were wrapped by the tape of common knowledge, common
tragedy. They had been comrades in the Forty-fifth Ohio, and already
had watched numerous of their friends die, and these men also would
die. The other three listened while the book-agent told of scuppernong
grapes. He had traveled through gulfside wildernesses a few years before the war, and that was how he'd come to know scuppernongs.
Three shriveled fuzzy skull-faces pressed near him and low moonlight touched them when they turned, and the blanched brains behind
the faces played, each in its own fashion, with imagined joy of fruit
juices, fruit crystals, the power contained in thin skins and rich pulp
of a peculiar sort they had never tasted and now never would taste.
The book-agent said that the grapes crawled on truant vines in wild
places where you'd never think to find them. You drove along the

forest road in a buggy or a wagon, and the driver stopped suddenly, and you said or he said, Here they be. You reached out and pressed the bulbous things into your mouth. They were salt and sugar and sustenance, deep purple purity and grace, tang and promise. You rolled an invisible morsel of their taste around on your tongue, and it struck the roof of your mouth and it occupied your soul and you could think of nothing else. Here it was: spice and fragrance and power. It was like the moment when you were with a hearty woman and she yielded with her drive and delicacy, and you yielded unto her your whip-snapping and private bitter concentrated flogging, and here it was and this was it, the summation of bountiful flavor. Your body lived and died and was revivified as you absorbed.)

Floral did not know how he might have appeared to the prisoners, or how his fellows might have appeared. It was impossible that it might occur to him to wonder how the prisoners thought of him and other Reserves. He did not realize that after the moon ascended farther, wafer-thin above the stockade, guard shacks along the eastern parapet became small haunted houses with death dwelling in them. The shaggy figures of guards stood motionless or rarely moving, but always with menace in their silhouetting; so he himself, not yet fourteen, was a menace. The guards said to the Yankees in essence between their throat-hawkings and tobacco-spittings, Try to get past us. Only try. We have bullets and powder, the musket barrels to contain velocity and expend it against you. We're up here On Parapet; you ain't; you're down below. We got our eyes on you. Just try it, Fourth Pennsylvania and Fourth Vermont and Fourth Kentucky and Fourth Iowa. Try it, Thirteenth U.S. Infantry and Cole's Cavalry and Michiganders and folks from Wisconsin in the Iron Brigade. Try to get past us.

Night and day, in sunlight and smell, or in moonlight or in darkness and increased and concentrated smell . . . we got our muzzles ready and the percussion caps ready on tubes at tother end, and the squeeze of powder and balls jammed in between. We loaf up here, excused by too old age or too young age from feeling any feeling but a blind unreasoning unreckoning undiscerning hatred. We loaf on our planks, we are bored, we cry the reports of the hours and half hours. Somebody starts off on the stroke of twelve or of seven or of two or of whatever hour of the night, and middling thereafter, and the calls drone from lair to lair along the fence. Post Sixteen, ten o'clock and all's well, or we yell for fun, Post Thirty-three, ten o'clock and here's your mule. Maybe some other members of our far-flung regiment are laughing their livers out along the rim, or maybe they aren't paying any attention at all, and wouldn't have sense enough to pay heed if they had the waking ears to pay heed. Just try to get past this stockade, just try to get past the deadline in shadows, Tenth Connecticut and Pennsylvania Lancers and Twenty-second Indiana and Pennsylvania

Bucktails and folks from out West, from Crocker's Brigade and such. Just try it; all we ask, or sometimes we won't even wait to ask; just try. We got the muskets loaded and we ain't asleep by any chance. We got the fire ready, Chicago Board of Trade Battery and Second Maryland and Minnesota Indians and any God damn niggers that claim they're soldiers like white men, even Yankees, and haven't been sent to a labor detail in the burying trenches yet. Just try it. In stench of wormy black, in clarity of the thing in the sky, we linger amid haunted houses on the fence, and we dare you. You will die if you take the dare.

Hi, Reb.

Flory jumped from his vague blank retreat and looked down. He had thought it was a post, it wasn't a post, it was too wide for a post, and that post he'd thought it was (the toughened remains of a small pine from which prisoners ripped the last splinters) had disappeared under erosion of fingernails and homemade knives sometime previously.

Reb. Hi, Guard!

With shuddering hands Floral Tebbs slid his musket barrel across the fence.

Take care, don't shoot me, you damn fool.

Yank—get—away—from that—deadline. Flory spoke the words thinly with a mouth near to blubbering.

Hah. Thought you was the guard we call Little Tattnall. He's usually on this post.

Flory's jellied finger went inside the trigger guard. The Yankee stood close to death, he didn't know how close he stood. Flory's stage-whisper came down to him. Little Tattnall's took sick. They give me this post.

You might do. Be a sport, kiddie. Raise that gun barrel a trifle. . . .

He was safe, after all—he was up on the fence—no Yankee could jump fifteen feet into the air, although sometimes Flory imagined that a Yankee could. Flory tilted the musket toward the moon.

Thanks, kiddie. What I need is soda.

Who're you?

Kid, I'm Donner. You ought to know—Willie Collins's cookie?

Flory had heard of Willie Collins since the first time he went On Parapet. Collins had been pointed out to him, he had seen the giant, had watched him slugging and bossing.

You understand? Soda. You Rebs call it saleratus.

Flory shuffled loosely on his perch. I got some.

This was a miracle, the Yank asking him for saleratus; and all the time that twisted paper had been lying squeezed in his jeans' pocket.

Guess you didn't follow me. Little Reb, what's your name?

Flory.

Well, Flory, Willie wants some York biscuits. I got everything else—

sufficient flour and butter and sugar, got the milk souring. But we need soda. Saleratus.

I—got some.

Devil suck it, here's luck! You know what I mean, now? Sal— Saleratus.

How much you got?

Nigh onto a pocket full.

I'll be sucked. What you want for it? Greenback?

Flory spewed the low words in a stream. No I want buttons with hens on them.

Give you two dollars in good currency.

No. Buttons with hens on them.

You fool little Reb, I'll give you a bean, a gold piece.

Want buttons with hens—

The man named Donner swore softly and went stalking off until he was mingled in the noisy pattern of moonlight and tilted shebang roofs, until he could not be seen moving, could not be separated from the wide-spread garbage dump with its fire-flickers and bird sounds. A few minutes later the cry of *Raiders!* was raised near the creekside. There was a feeling that a few people ran toward the spot and many more went tottering away. More minutes elapsed, Donner returned. The light swept increasingly brighter, increasingly shadows flattened as the moon sailed. Flory could see that the cook held a loose dark patch in his hand.

I got here a jacket with them buttons on it.

Dddon't need no jacket, Yank. Just buttons—

Brown your God damn nose, I hain't got nothing to cut buttons off with! Should I pull them off twould likely bust them little gilt loops. Kiddie, you got a string?

Flory had no twine, he had not thought to bring a length of it.

I'll hurl it up. You catch. Donner wadded the garment and tossed it high. It fluttered and fell short within the deadline. Casually the big Donner stepped across the deadline and picked up the jacket. Johnson, the guard at the next station toward the north, and the guard at the next station toward the south— Both were watching, neither bothered to lift his gun. They were more accustomed to such transactions than was Floral Tebbs, but Flory would grow accustomed. Donner weighted the jacket with a wad of mud, wrapped it with care, threw it high. It came hard and hurtfully against Flory's face with a button bruising his eyelid when it struck. His calico hat was knocked from his head, but he held the jacket, he had it in his arms, he had buttons with proud eagles threatening amid circles of stars, those were the glory he sought.

Well, kiddie, I'm waiting. Toss the soda.

Flory tossed it and Donner caught the poke easily in one hand. He said nothing more but strolled into the tangle of huts and population; and Willie Collins would have his York biscuits the next morning, with butter and jam and rashers of fresh bacon.

In the huge conical tent draped beside Collins's winter castle, Donner leered through the firelight at Edward Blamey. Rubber Legs, you did a fair deed.

What?

Member that freshie you sighted this afternoon with the artillery jacket on him? I was hard put to find some buttons just now, to buy soda for these biscuits. Damn if I didn't mind that artillery jacket then and there.

Edward Blamey remembered. He was moved into that overcoat shebang, this side of the sinks, wa'n't he?

Hah, he's still there. Little squirt—he weren't more'n sixteen and skinny too—he tried to give me trouble.

Cookie looked critically at his big right fist and saw that there was blood drying. He wiped the blood on his trousers. He quoted gaily to Ed Blamey before he turned to his wooden trough, to begin raising the biscuit dough— He quoted, If you don't believe I'm a butcher, just smell of me boots.

Ed Blamey reached for his bottle of pine-top.

On the sentry platform Floral Tebbs stroked buttons of the stolen jacket, and considered how they would shine even more delightfully in the sun if tomorrow became one of the rare fair days of this month, if indeed the sun shone. He would rub buttons, they would be alive with golden fire, people who had no such buttons would look their envy.

Fifty rods away a gaunt Jewish sergeant of the Eighty-fifth New York (but still powerful, holding control of himself, not straying too far no matter how many similar moons he had worshipped above other lands) sat with big hands clasped across his ragged knees, worshipping this moon. Suddenly Nathan Dreyfoos realized that he had been craving the moon and the silent simplicity and clear freedom which it represented more than he had craved any delight or fulfillment during the twenty-three years through which he'd lived. He had forgotten that brothers-in-arms and brothers who had once borne arms alongside him had suffered and hungered and desired in the same manner. He had been selfish, insensitive to their need. He thought of the dead Corley, the dead Stevenson—he had neglected their memory utterly. He was blanketed with shame. In weakness he prayed to moonlight and to the Almighty God or Monster who made that moonlight, he prayed: Oh, give these other survivors the same release and independence, afford them the same ability to go kiting beyond the stockade, grant it more quickly and more firmly than you grant it to me!

He begged this; but it was as if some caterpillar of voracious falsity crawled active beneath the stalk of his benevolence—a larva who fed on the stem, and awarded rottenness before it could be recognized by his soul (but recognized only by the small portion which begged). Please me first, give me escape in the first moment you can manage it, I care not for the rest, find me a way out, leave me free, Devil take the others.

XXVI

Sometimes it seemed to Henry Wirz that his brain was made of rubber, it was a rubber sack filled with stones, it stretched to paleness as more stones were necessarily introduced and as the weight grew. Stones were labeled Hospital, Crowding, Incompetence of Guards, Poison Swamp, labeled with many other unpleasant names and reminders. In constant screaming temper Wirz bounded from desk to stockade to headquarters, back again to the office of the quartermaster, thence to the quarters of the surly Dick Winder, back on horseback to the stockade to mete out a new punishment or to make a new observation. If it were possible for him to loathe the prisoners more each hour of his life he loathed them so. But his trained physician's attitude could not countenance the filth of these creatures without wishing to exorcise it merely on the grounds that it was filth. A row of sinks—these he'd built (they were totally inadequate, and this he knew; but they were placed on the lowest ground within the pen for purposes of drainage; and half the sick were too sick to use them, to muster strength to creep or stagger to the sinks; and he ran out of lumber). A bridge across the creek—this he'd managed to have constructed (but it was too narrow, it sagged: again the shortage of lumber and tools). A shoring of the creekside, a fumbling attempt to deepen the stream and thus increase its flow . . . this hopeless effort was achieved amid shrieks. Almost before his eyes Henry saw planks of the shoring melt away, split for tent poles, hacked into bits for firewood. His shivering hands were tied, the entreaties he sent to higher echelons were lost or filed. Who cared? Not the Winders.

By God, I get that damn hospital out of there once.

Odds seemed at times insurmountable but he toiled with frenzy, he hated the sight of those few tent flies packed in the northeast corner, hated the sight and clamor and stink of invalids motionless or gesticulating. In heat of late May he would have rested with pride if rest were ever a state to be attained by Henry Wirz (but it was not). He saw the tent flies sprouting in a new location, and outside the pen at last. He'd procured more tents, lumber to build bunks (not enough lumber, not enough bunks) and had even built a portion of a separate fence around the establishment. It was not a good hospital. At least it was outside the main stockade. Outside, *ja* . . . he kept telling himself that it was better, better. Rotten tent flies, a considerable number of small A tents, a limited number of wall tents scraped from some camp farther at the North and dumped off a flat car one rainy day along with the sodden supply of A tents. . . . This collection of awning rose on a few acres of land east of the star fort, east also of the surgeons' offices. The ground was higher than the areas immediately adjacent, and sloped toward the southeast, but marshes sent up their aroma on two sides. A small stream, one of the many branches amid those valleys, ran through a corner of the hospital enclosure. Quickly this became a thing of reek and evil.

This was the place where Ira Claffey's black people had dumped their loads of bastard melons months before. A more noisome cargo of decay was now dumped here on the twenty-third and twenty-fourth of May. After that many people were carried out daily on carts, and more came to take their places, puffing, drooling, hullooing; they were lugged in blankets or on makeshift stretchers, they were carried in the arms of stronger men.

Still it was better. It was outside the stockade. Outside! Much better, *ja.*

Four patients were jammed into each of the A tents, eight patients in the wall tents; under common flies lay as many as could be crowded together—six or eight men—sometimes more, under the larger flies. Bunks had been made by driving forks of saplings into the soil and placing scraps of planking—or, more frequently, pine poles—across them. But— Not enough bunks. The sick lay on the ground, some had pine straw, some had no pine straw. If Henry Wirz had been able to devote a greater share of his time to this task he would have seen to it that all had pine straw to lie in. He was a very busy man. He had to be many places at once.

Captain Winder, I tell you now, it is again I make request for you to— Requisition for spades and axes! It is I must have a larger prison, God damn!

Oh, that's all very well, to speak of implements; and I got them last year and I presume I can get them again; but these damn planters won't coöperate. All of them want to keep their niggers at home. They raise hell all the way from Macon to Milledgeville every time I try to get hold of a few niggers.

By God, mine own niggers I got. Prisoners I got, nigger prisoners. In the carload I got them!

Well, wouldn't that be forced labor? Contrary to the Rules of War? Next time I have communication with my father I'll—

I tell you, you Sid Winder, those picks and spades and axes, those I got to have. God damn, I blow them Rules of War up somebody's ass, I tell you!

Sid Winder had been manicuring his nails with his penknife. After Wirz left he saw a great bluebottle fly upon the barrelhead beside him, and tried to impale the fly with his knife blade, and missed. He thought, Little bastard of a Swiss squirt. I don't understand how the old man tolerates him. But we surely are killing off a lot of damn Yankees here. Everybody's got to do his share. Sid Winder thought of Harrell Elkins, thought of him with undying hatred and with a fear which he could never quite put down . . . cavalry sabers at two paces.

Wirz hacked fiercely at the problem, and eventually he secured his coveted tools. Once more the chant of black voices moaned among trees, this time due north of the existing stockade. Once more resin dripped, chips spun, shaggy tops came crashing.

Oh, he gone up there. Never come back again.

Where you say he gone?

Ooohhh. . . .

Work went forward with speed surpassing far the laggardly construction of the original stockade. Only some ten acres were to be enclosed, the ground was mainly flat, there was no creek to be crossed, no gates to be made. Simply it was an extension of the rectangle by about six hundred feet. Main Street and South Street would still serve as arteries for traffic and commerce. It was told lugubriously Inside that the raiders would undoubtedly preëmpt the fresh space for themselves—it would not be saturated with slime, it would be higher, more healthful, farther away from effluvium of the marsh. In fact the raiders had no intention of moving. Why should they move? They had their castles, their pavilion, they had all the room they wanted; as for effluvium, most of them had been born in it. Faster, faster sounded the click of axes, drone of the diggers, sharp cries of overseers beyond the north wall. Henry Wirz was no lounging Sid Winder. He drove unceasingly.

Where you say he gone?

Ooohhh, ooohhhh, way up there above.

He gone up there, up in the sky. Never come back no more.

Ooohhh. . . .

A strange calm, comparative silence came in the middle of June: heavy work was done. Now was essential only the final touch on ladders and sentry stations. On the evening of June eighteenth there came the sound of digging and prying. The more energetic prisoners gathered outside the deadline to gape up at shacks on the north rim. There were no longer any guards on those platforms. A portion of the fence began to sway, first one log toppled, then three or four others were pried and they fell thunderously. That's enough, a voice called outside. Big enough hole for them to get through.

Provident prisoners had taken up already their dirty bundles of personal belongings, their cooking tins; they rolled the fabric of she-

bangs and were treasuring the poles. Men seeped gingerly across the
abandoned deadline at first, but soon a minor riot ensued as more
and more sought to force their way through the aperture, to make
claims on new holdings in the clean area. There were more than
twenty-two thousand people in the place on this day, and if these
twenty-two thousand were distributed evenly throughout the old acres
and the new there would be an end to unbearable swarming. But—
Hold on. What of the future? How many more trains would come
wrenching to the Anderson depot? It was rumored that all prisoners
held by the eastern States of the Confederacy might be concentrated
in this one place. For how long would pressure be relaxed? Oh, dear
Lord above, it would tighten, it would tighten.

By the hour of darkness the bulk of migration was concluded. In
human and animal fashion grass had appeared greener on the other
side (it was greener, it would not be for many hours; by the next day
there would be no grass) and more folks stampeded into the north
enclosure than could be accommodated. Many late arrivals limped
back to their old haunts in disgust, and in turn found their original
quarters occupied by men who had moved up from marshy regions;
there were fights throughout the wet moonlit hours. Henry Wirz rode
home pleased with himself. They had said that it was impossible to
move the hospital outside; the hospital was now outside. They had
said that it was impossible to enlarge the stockade; the stockade had
been enlarged. His immediate project was for the removal of the old
fence. Seven hundred and eighty feet of palisading, each log twenty
feet in length . . . dried out; and the buried ends would not have been
long enough in the earth to decay. What might not he build with this
treasure? A separate punishment stockade—he had thought of that,
he had planned for that with what amounted to affection. And bridges
and trestles. On the morrow he would cry for wagons, wagons. Should
he not obtain wagons from some source or other the logs could easily
be snaked out at the ends of chains, hauled by mules. If worst came
to worst he might harness gangs of Negroes together and have them
pull the logs.

Chastised into performance by tightening of narcotic energy, he
was back at the stockade soon after sunrise on the morning of June
nineteenth. He climbed fussing to a new sentry station north of the
corner of the old stockade. At first he became sick at his stomach and
tottered dizzily; then he began to rave, literally, until frothy spittle
flew from his beard. The fence was gone. The old fence was gone.
The solid palisade was vanished as if giants had leaned down from
the sky and plucked the pines like toothpicks. It was not merely that
the old line of stockading had been dug up or knocked down: *there
were simply no logs in sight.*

Who, who, who? That damn Sid Winder? That damn Dick Winder?

That damn colonel commanding the post? No one had authority to do this thing. The lumber was his, his—it belonged to Henry Wirz, he had plans for using it— He stood gasping for breath at last, German curses still lingering in echo— He would find curses in English when— When he had more strength— He would go to General Winder in person— His property had been stolen. A seven-hundred-and-eighty-foot line of logs twenty feet tall. Someone had taken his logs.

Prisoners, sir, the old guard was saying weakly behind him.

Vas? What you say, guard?

I said, Captain, twas the prisoners as done it.

Them damn logs? *Mein* logs? Them damn Yankees? Son of a bitch—

Yes sir, Captain. We heard them a-doing it. All night long. But nobody'd give us any orders to fire. And they wasn't inside the deadline—not much, anyways—

Yankees. They had taken his fence, with their bare hands they had taken it, picked it apart with striving fingernails, scraped it to nothingness with puny primitive tools. Firewood, flooring, roofing: it bloomed about the fuming area. As Henry's vision cleared, he could look down and recognize split pine posts here and there, the rows of newly splintered material.

They do that, he croaked again, not daring to believe.

Yes, Captain, they did so, sure as white blossoms make little apples.

He crept down the ladder, his head was aching. Twenty-two thousand three hundred sixty-two Yankees. Was that the last report he had drawn up? No, no, he could not recollect. Twenty-two thousand Yankees, each had eight fingers and two thumbs . . . *ach, ja,* some had been amputated; but there were more than twenty-two thousand prisoners, and so— Call it two hundred and twenty thousand fingers. He closed his eyes and he could see the mass of those clawing twitching curling fierce fingers like a nest of worms as big as a house— As big as— As big as the Louvre? Not that big.

He was so beaten by his loss that he could perform little work that day. He was very nearly gentle with the people who worked in his office. He gave his errand boy part of his lunch brought from home. Wirz muttered that he had no appetite. He rode home early and in a near stupor. He went to bed at dusk and lay staring up at the low ceiling, and said *Nein, nein* when Elizabeth offered chicken broth. Two hundred and twenty thousand fingers pulling his logs apart.

Papa, said little Coralie when she came barefoot and in her nightdress, Please, Papa, can I get in bed with you?

Ja, Liebchen, he said after a moment or two, when the knowledge of her request reached through befuddlement. He held up the covering with his left hand, and the child giggled and hunched with pleasure, snuggling close to his side.

Shall you sing me the song, *Mein Vater?*

He liked to have her call him Father in German, he had taught her
to do so. In his cracked nasal voice, but softly, softly, he began to
sing a little song which a kind old lady had sung to him first in 1826
when he was but four. He wished that it were 1826 now, he wished
that he were but four. Cora lay still as a mouse, her gentle apprecia-
tive breathing reached his ears.

XXVII

Laurel Tebbs came in shyness to the Claffey plantation, seeking the loan of a thimble. I did have one, she said in her high-pitched voice. Her voice was a whine suggesting some kind of animal inheritance, an inheritance from an animal whipped too frequently for its own good, and fearing more blows. Did have one, silver one what belonged to Granny or so twas said; but Zoral he kept a-playing with it, dropping it down a crack; and then I'd have to give him a lick and make him crawl under the house after it; and one day he couldn't find it no way, nor could I, though I went under the house my own self; and I surely hated to do that, count of the dead chickens and rats he's always a-dragging under there. Reckon maybe he dropped it down— She lowered her tone, faced with the delicacy of Lucy's presence. Down the privy.

Lucy said, I'm sorry it was lost.

Coral he was kind enough to make me a thimble out'n a big acorn; but that split in two today; and I was part way through sewing myself a gown, and I hain't got no other gown fit to put on, cepting this one, and the purple one used to belong to Ma. That's for dress-up.

Lucy said, Come into the house, child, and let me look about. She addressed Laurel thus naturally, not realizing that the girl was fifteen, thinking of her still as the shrunken bag-of-bones she'd always been, peering from behind fences and weed-brakes at the doings of the Claffeys and their people.

Laurel's father was a frightened Americus widower who had the devil's own time trying to support his five children on meager returns from his occupation as cooper. Mr. Marion Padgett was hopelessly pale, his kinky hair was orange, his sad small face was spattered with orange freckles and so were his hands and wiry arms. When he made a statement of a fact it sounded like a question, for every sentence ended with a rising inflection which said, Excuse me, was it all right for me to say this, to say anything at all? His children sounded the same way, even when speaking to one another. Marion Padgett hovered over them ceaselessly, putting clothes to soak at ungodly hours of the morning, running from his workbench to take a boiler from the fire, putting down his hammer to take up a soup ladle. He was fortunate in that the children never needed discipline or punishment, they were all too wan and apologetic to fight even among themselves. The Padgetts trotted to the Methodist church each Sunday like a covey of starved red-headed warblers, but mainly silent warblers who did not know how to warble. One day in 1848 a bearded stranger with a tall beaver hat marched into the cooperage which stood in the same yard as the Padgett cottage. It appeared that Marion's sister had died in Charleston, and her husband had preceded her to the grave by only five days. There were no children, no other relatives, no heirs but Francis Marion Padgett. The property consisted of a house and furniture and some jewelry of value, together with a large lot on Meeting Street and five well-trained Negroes, and forty-two hundred dollars in cash. Marion Padgett spat the nails out of his mouth and wandered in a daze. His children wept to see him go, and he was deaf to the stranger who hastened for a time at his side saying, But, sir, where are you going—? Damn it, sir! Mr. Padgett, I request that you pay some heed to what I am saying— Come back to your house, sir! Your children are in tears! Eventually the lawyer had to return to the cooperage alone, and he parceled the children out to neighbors, and sat in a nearby inn awaiting Marion's return, in dudgeon. He had to wait three days.

Reports drifted back of a Marion Padgett who wandered from one seller of brandy to another seller of brandy. Mistrusting any orthodox depository, he carried always what few funds he had about him in a chamois-skin bag tied to the belt which held up his pantaloons. Through rigorous saving and self-denial and child-denial he had accumulated thirty-seven dollars against a mortgage payment of forty dollars, plus the quarter's interest which must be paid soon. Reports drifted of a Marion Padgett who hired a horse and chaise and was seen driving madly over rough roads in the adjacent wilderness. In time he arrived at the Tebbs place. Thus he fathered Laurel. (There was always some doubt about this in the Widow Tebbs's mind, since it chanced that she had entertained two other red-headed gentlemen in that same week. Well, she said, my little girl does look a sight like that Marion, and I knowed him when I was scarce more'n a infant myself; but I reckon she looks a sight like one of the others, too. And I weren't yet a widow then, and— But it's been quite a time since; and all them doses of gunpowder never did do no good at all. She had a vague thought of puppies and kittens. The child cried, and Mag picked her up and cuddled her. She thought briefly of Marion Padgett, now said to be living in distant luxury. She thought once more of Marion, then he strayed from her simple mind, he returned seldom.)

This was an especially hot day, and Lucy was conscious of the strong odor of Laurel Tebbs as the round-shouldered little creature moved beside her. She said sharply, Miss, have you bathed yourself of late? as she might have said it to one of her own servants, and then felt that she had been heedless and cruel, and was ashamed.

Nome, spoke the languid voice. It's so hard to bring up water from our well, and Coral he's always off to the forest, and Flory's gone to the army, and Zoral's but a babe. Ma she's always a-entertaining or a-sleeping. I just can't scarcely pull that big sweep, hain't got the power.

Then you shall go over to Little Sweetwater, said Lucy brightly. For I have some rose oil which I pressed, and I shall give you a bit of that, and it's no earthly good, of course, if you're not freshly scrubbed. And I shall give you a square of Windsor for your own.

Miss Lucy, whined Laurel, I'd be plumb scairt to go naked in the creek. Too many sojers about.

Then go far up the creek, the big creek, where there's no one.

That I'll do, if'n you say I got to. Please, what's Windsor?

Tis a toilet soap I've made myself, and scented with caraway, and it's just the best! Except for variegated toilet soap, and I used to make that too, with Extra shaving the bar-soap fine; but we've no longer any Chinese blue and only a teentsie bit of Chinese vermilion.

This conversation occurred in the hall and on the stairs, and Laurel now stood with her hostess in Lucy's chamber. Oh, just lots of pretties, she said without envy. She was accustomed to seeing silver and portraits, certain elements of grandeur although decayed grandeur, when she helped at the Biles'. But she had never entered a dainty young lady's room before.

Lucy searched though work-basket, work-table, drawers, appraising her stock of thimbles. She thought that she owned four but could find only three. One of these had belonged to Great-aunt Mary Flo; Lucy remembered this woman as a waspish invalid in a scarlet silk dressing gown; she cherished no particularly pleasant memories of Great-aunt Mary Flo. And the thimble was too narrow for her own finger now that she was grown.

This you may have.

For to keep?

Certainly, for your own. Mind and don't let Baby Brother get his paws on it.

Reckon I can hide it from him. The girl smiled in wan delight. Didn't figure to come a-begging. Twas just for the lend; but I do thank you, Miss Lucy.

Now for rose oil and the Windsor! Lucy found the oil on her washstand shelf and poured a trifle into an empty pill-flask which had been saved with care. Here's the toilet soap in my cupboard. And—

Critically she inspected the stringy hair of the child beside her; actually she expected to see vermin, but did not find any; she spread the hair with her fingers with disgust but also in explorative curiosity.

She was very curious about fellow human beings—wondering privately how they ate, cared for their bodies, washed or did not wash, felt, thought, lived, died. Certain influences in her rearing cried that this was unwomanly, and Lucy had pride as a woman, she did not wish to be unwomanly although often she knew that she was unladylike in the generally accepted sense, and felt impish about it.

Such a lovely color to your hair, Laurel. It's like a wild orange, and I remember how Uncle Felton fetched a sack of them.

Hain't never ate no orange. Ma says they're good to suck but mighty puckerish.

But pretty hair should be tended—I suppose it's like the oranges themselves—they must need sun and rain, and your hair needs soap and water.

Well, I did wash it with soap but it like to burnt the hide off my head. And it got all stiff as weeds.

You had no fit shampoo, I fancy. Lucy scribbled a note at her desk and rang for one of the blacks; after some time there was a response. Ninny looked injured at finding Laurel Tebbs in the young mistress's bed chamber; she stood in a silently sneering attitude, firm in conviction that the young mistress was demeaning herself.

Do you go, Ninny, to my father. He is in the seed house or store shed, and do you give him this note.

In this way Laurel was endowed further with a vial of Lucy's own shampoo contrived of aqua ammonia, salts of tartar, and alcohol flavored with bergamot. Lucy instructed the girl how to mix the potion with rainwater, and how to rub it through her hair into her scalp until the lather had gone down, then how to lave it out in the clearness of the creek or in more rainwater. Laurel promised faithfully. By this time she was enamored to the point of idolatry. Lucy whirled before her eyes in a froth of the room's pretties.

Is them your brothers what got kilt, Miss Lucy?

Not this one, child. Tis a miniature of my father when once he was a soldier too. But this daguerreotype, here, and the two ambrotypes yonder. Those were my brothers.

Surely is a pity. . . . My brother Coral, surgeons cut the foot off'n him.

I have seen him since, poor lad, with his crutch.

You got—? Laurel whispered it, and could not look at the young woman as she whispered. Got yourself a fellow?

Lucy did not speak for a moment. . . . I fear not. There is a friend, a gentleman who writes letters sometimes. But— She busied herself in emptying a basket of woven bull-grass, and this too would be a gift for Laurel; the girl could carry home her bottles, soap and thimble. Child, have you a—fellow?

Kind of. He sure did pull me round when we danced, when them

Alabama sojers was a-leaving. And he held me tight against himself, she managed to breathe in confidence. A few minutes later she was running down the lane with the speed of a field-mouse, her scarred legs flashing under tags of calico. The spring of extreme youth was in her frame, appreciation for the gifts was foaming, the certainty that she must follow Lucy Claffey's injunctions (and the sooner the better) was a delight intense enough to be named as a pain. Laurel bubbled to herself shrill bits of worship which she felt might be profanity, yet not the obscenity which she heard spoken often by Coral and Floral. Mercy God, she cried with pulpy pale lips, Mercy God, damn, hell, Jesus, damn hell, Mercy God. She stopped once shortly near the railroad, for a train approached, and she scarcely saw or heard the engine until she was beside the track. Boys rode on some of the platform cars or sat in box car doorways. They shouted, whistled, pretended to shoot Laurel with their guns, but she gave no heed. She had taken the tiny phial containing rose oil from the basket, and had withdrawn the glass stopper and was drinking in the odor with long rewarding sniffs. When the train had gone Laurel fled homeward, her sunbonnet spreading wide soiled wings above her shoulders where it had fallen.

Old Mrs. Bile taught Laurel to sew when the girl was eleven, and thus her thin fingers could fly about the business of it. Coral had caught a string of catfish that morning, and the widow fried balls of cornmeal to go with them. There were turnip greens and pork as well, but Laurel declined all invitations to join her family at table. The rest ate eagerly, greasily, washing down their feast with quantities of okra coffee. Zoral gagged on a fish-bone and choked himself into purple regurgitation before his mother could extract the bone. Through this excitement Laurel did not lift her head from her work, she did not leave her bench and basket. Her gown was finished before two o'clock, fashioned from pieces of calico sent by Effie Dillard. Waist and skirt did not match—the one was of a green pattern, the other of gray—but to Laurel they were measureless beauty and pride. What you a-doing there, Sissy? inquired Captain Ox Puckett when he came stamping in. By Ned, ain't you a regular little Betsy Ross, like they claim stitched a flag for General Jackson or somebody! Soon Ox and the Widow Tebbs had retired to The Crib, Coral was asleep on his bed, and Zoral was a train growling back and forth in front of a chicken-coop depot. Laurel crammed her new gown into the bull-grass basket and carried off soap, shampoo and rose oil which Lucy had given her. She took also two torn towels, reasonably clean, and some scraps of underclothing. Not even to Lucy could she have expressed her desire to be fresh and scented and neatly put together, in body and hair and dress alike. Passion was in her, her eyes snapped with it as she darted across the field behind the old Rambo homestead next door and sought upper reaches of Little Sweetwater.

In a shallow calm pool among willows she whitened the water; frogs leaped away, crayfish scuttled to safety. No one came to spy upon Laurel's nakedness, although she blushed in this fearful solitude, made small squeals when she found a leech upon her leg, felt malarial fever through her limbs at every crow-call. Once she was scrubbed and dried the rose oil made aromatic madness on her skin and in her hair. Why had she not fetched her mother's looking glass? Oh, to gaze upon herself, to see whether her bright hair was the damp loose cloud of ecstasy which she believed it to be when her hands went through it and let it fall and then strayed aloft wonderingly again . . . an idea came to her, in the end. With skirt held high she waded to a dark untroubled place beneath a cypress, and stood motionless, not breathing until the water was cleared, unrippled; then the girl bent forward, squatting, and saw her own thin wild face wavering up at her, and saw the hair . . . oh, Mercy Jesus, God, hell. . . . Oh, Miss Lucy, lady, I do thank you for them soaps and the potion.

That evening Captain Ox was long since departed; but another mule was tethered, and a lamp burned in The Crib and was then put out at the caller's request. Zoral slept in a wet place of his own making. Coral had gone crutching off to Uncle Arch's, empowered to buy navy plug, meal, and a stick of red candy for his mother's use. The late lopsided moon had not yet risen, nor would rise for hours; but starlight yielded golden brownness to enrich each tuft of nearby trees. Laurel Tebbs sat on the step, leaning her shoulder against a post. My, she had the unspoken thought, it surely does stink bad. That there prison pen yonder. Them Yankees must be powerful dirty, dirtier than ever I been in my born days. She thought of Little Sweetwater, and how savage and lonely must be the region where she had bathed; perhaps dangerous wild beasts were prowling beside the very pool wherein she had splashed—formless ferocious wild beasts— she trembled before the notion of their stealth and blackness. She thought of the shampoo, the cake of Windsor worn to a flake; she thought of the rose oil, and scrambled up to bring her bottle out of hiding. She had concealed the bottle within an old clock (the clock did not run, it stood dusty on a high shelf, it was a good place to hide her thimble or any other treasure which might be coveted by Zoral). There was still a spoonful or two of oil in the flask, and the girl resumed her place on the step and held the bottle to her nostril, and believed that the stockade's vapor could not reach past this immediate fragrance. Presently a dark shape detached itself from hollowness of the roadway, seemed to halt indecisively, then drifted forward. It was a man who tripped over the crude two-wheeled cart which Mag had prevailed upon Coral to build for the baby; the man swore heatedly and then came closer. Laurel stood up. Ma ain't in the house, she said automatically. She's over'n The Crib, she's got a caller.

The man laughed. Honey, I never did come to see your old lady. Come to see you.

She roasted quickly in the heat of her own flesh. Now, you look a here, Sergeant! I'm but a girl. It's my Ma who does the entertaining.

Sinkfield came up to the step and stood with hands on his wide stuffed hips. Sakes, honey child, I wouldn't want no truck with your old lady. I like young ladies, like you. Member how we danced at the pic-nic?

Hain't no pic-nic going on tonight.

Look what I brung you, and he brought forth a crumple of paper. Brown sugar. What they call maple sugar, manufactured away at the North. Ain't that nobby?

Laurel tossed her head, and brushed her wiry hair with her hands, then smoothed it against her scalp once more. Oh, she said, I don't much care for sugar no way.

Took it off a Yank that I went through at the depot. Thinks I, Well, now I wonder who'd like this? Thinks I, Bet I know who'd like it. That pretty little Laurel Tebbs, that's who. So reckon I'll just mog along that way, once't I get off duty and get myself a pass. His big hand reached out to touch her knee, Laurel slapped the hand. Sinkfield laughed, he took his hand away. Aw, come along now, honey. Just please to take one bite.

Well, she said, I will try it.

Sinkfield lounged against the post, he seemed to tower tall above Laurel, although he was not truly tall, he was only heavy and loutish. She pressed the stopper of her rose oil bottle into place, put the bottle in her lap, and explored the wad of newspaper which the sergeant had pressed upon her. She liked the odor which came up, she examined the flat lump and few granules which had broken loose. She tasted cautiously.

Now, ain't that fine, Laurel?

Oh, it don't taste like much.

Ah, you know it does.

No, it don't neither, she snapped.

Aw, does so.

Well, she said, twill do for Zoral.

Who's that?

My baby brother. Baby half-brother, mean to say. We're all halves.

That Flory just a half-brother also?

Uh-huh.

Little snot.

I'll have Ma take a stick to you, you go saying bad words front of me!

Why, snot hain't a bad word, it's just what comes out of your nose. And I do have a task, keeping Flory in line. But he's really scairt of me, so I fetch him up sharp. Never had to thrash him but a couple of times.

Officers and sergeants and such— They ain't *sposed* to hit the boys under them. I heard Captain Ox say so.

Sinkfield grasped the girl's hand and tried to draw her to her feet, but she exclaimed and held back, and with her left hand hugged the paper of sugar and the bottle into her skirts.

Laurel, honey, less you and me take a little walk—

Her heart was thudding like a hard fist knocking at a door, nok, nok, nok, nok, nok. No, I don't want to. Look out there, you'll spill my ssssugar, and her voice also was a slippery entity and seemed to writhe out of management. She twisted her hand loose from the sweaty grasp.

Well, less put it away somewheres.

Well, I—

Just a little bitty walk, honey?

Well . . . you got any sulphur matches, Sergeant? Please to strike a light for me, so's I can see where to put my sugar. She retreated into the house and Sinkfield groped after her. He lighted the match, Laurel brought a candle (in times of comparative plenty they used lamps and candles in this house, they did not have to use grease-lights). She put the rose oil into the clock, the sugar into a dusty pitcher. She stood, short rapid breathing hurting her chest, heart breaking itself apart inside her. She stood with slightly lowered head, gazing at Sinkfield through the flickers of tawny light, conscious of an indefinite limitless power which she now held. She thought that she should like to use that power to hurt Sergeant Sinkfield, she wished that his face was not so broken into pink and yellow rash; but if she hurt him severely he might not come back again, he might never dance with her again, he might never pull her tightly against his overgrown body again.

You want—? Her voice shook with the excitement ruling the room and the lout and herself. Want a drink of wwwater?

He grinned. I don't need no water, honey. He came around the corner of the table, and Laurel retreated before him.

Want a peach? We got some.

Why ain't you just like a little peach your own self! That pretty peachy hair and— He had her hand again, he had both hands; she laughed shrilly, without reason. She shook her head and felt the loose clean hair whipping. Again it must be like a loose cloud, a lovely scented cloud; she wished she could see herself in a mirror.

Laurel, listen—

Whwhwhat?

Less take that little old walk.

Reckon Ma might give me a whipping.

Pshaw, she won't know nothing about it. Just a little bitty walk.

Well, if'n I do go—

Ah, strength was in her, strength of mules and horses and cruel spring winds a-twisting, power of red blood flowing in rivers, power of engines and staring stars. You know I ain't but fifteen. We got to stay in earshot of the house, now you mind that.

Sure we will, honey.

And— And you got to promise you won't hit Flory no more.

Why, sure I won't if you ask it. Little snot like him—

Ser*geant!* And you got to swear you'll stop a-saying that word. If'n I go. For a walk. Just a— A little way. Real close to home.

Sure enough, honey, I'll do anything you say. He drew her out into the broken wilderness of tan light and umber shade.

Within one hour she had returned to the house, and alone, alternately running a few steps, driving her bruised pelvic region into the motion of flight; but it would pain her severely, and cause her to move more slowly, and then she would walk as one entranced. One sleeve was torn nearly loose from the new-stitched gown and fluttered as a light wind came to toss it. Certain sundered tissues scraped rawly each step that Laurel took, hot moisture oozed, her ragged drawers were stained with it. Had she said she'd go for a walk? Yes, she had said— She had said, We got to stay nigh the house, but he had drawn her on and on, across the railroad and beyond a fence into a bushy corner of the Claffey acres (which site he had selected previously with an eye to solitude and convenience; the grass was long there, no houses stood near). The unidentified power which had coursed in Laurel's frame and spirit was frozen solid, it was no longer a power, it was ice and wail and terror. She heard a mushy voice battering her ears as later the big dry rod had slain her maidenhood. I'm just the funniest feller. She heard her own treble drawling, How so? . . . Count of the jokes I make, and tricks. I just keep them boys at the camps a-laughing all the while. You mind what my name is: I told you at the pic-nic: tis Jester. Jester Johnson Sinkfield. And what Jester means is a feller doing stunts and jokes. You got a funny-bone, Laurel? Less see— And the clumsy hand digging her side, her own protestation resounding. . . . You ever see a little pig hung up by his hind legs a-squealing? Funniest thing you ever did see! Twas my task at the slaughter-house up Atlanta way; I took care of the little ones, and didn't they just rip. Way you do is first tie their legs, like this. No, no, honey, I hain't a-going to tie your legs together; here, give me your hands; no, give me both hands; we'll play like you was a baby pig, just the prettiest little baby pig, and like your hands was his hind legs; here, I'll use this big handkerchief; and I'll tie them tight, see? Like this; ah, that's good. Ho, ho! Well, look at little Laurel, and I got your hands tied tight. Yes, by God, so I have. And you ain't a-going to squeal, are you? Cause you don't know how—and cause I'm going to take this other nice clean handkerchief *and stick it in your mouth,* by God, I'm going to stuff it in, ah, that's better, ain't it better, honey, because you can't squeal no way, and now I got you, Laurel, *get this damn dress out of the way,* and by God, hot damn, holy Jesus H. Christ, I'm a-going to stuff something else in somewhere, ah, aha, aha, *aha—* And her own cry gagged to a mumble, a mumble and shudder turned back by the fabric in her mouth and rolled angrily in reverse to poison the very soul which had sent it forth.

XXVIII

Ought to call them the Black Brigade or the Dark Avengers or something similar, said Seneca MacBean. He was going over the list of secret Regulators in his mind. He knew a man who'd dug for gold in California (well, he knew several such men, but none of them had ever found much gold) and that man spoke of this new contingent, organized so slowly, quietly, solidly, as Vigilantes. That sounded foreign to MacBean's ears, so he always used the term Regulators. He would have called them The Blacks or The Darks—he had heard of the Scots Greys—because so many were black-locked. It wasn't just the pitch which stained their faces; they were dark to begin with. Take Bill Rowe, Michigander from the Ninth Cavalry. Very swarthy as to hue. Take the fellow everybody called Limber Jim, from the Sixty-seventh Illinois. Looked like an Indian, and maybe he did have Indian blood. Well, there were even some full-blooded Indians on this team! Take Nathan Dreyfoos, take himself: both black as to hair. And take the ruling genius of the lot: he was a printer like Sen MacBean, but from Bloomington instead of from Galena; his name was Leroy Key and he was a sergeant in the Sixteenth Cavalry. Fully as dangerous to toy with as MacBean, Key had a talent for organization and planning which matched Sen's, and an outright executive capacity far exceeding the Galenan's.

Lord smiled on us when he sent Key here, said Seneca.

Key has the manner of a colonel.

And he'll *be* better than a colonel, mark my words!

I have a new recruit, Sen. I spoke to him again this morning, and he'll be at the meeting tonight. Certainly he will be accepted and sworn.

Name?

His name is Hill, a sergeant from the Hundredth Ohio Volunteers. Extremely broad shoulders and the mildest manner in the world. But—

Sen MacBean slapped the board with the tattered drawers he was washing. Don't need to tell me. I wonder I never thought of Hill before! Just goes to show how stupid I can grow. Why, when we hit

Belle Isle there was a bully name of Jack Oliver, Nineteenth Indiana.
Had everything pretty much his own way until one day he got to
picking on an old man in A.R.'s mess. I mean Hill—that's his initials
—A.R.

MacBean paused for a time as if he were considering what style
of type to use to set A.R. Hill's name and initials.

A.R. says to this bully, Mister, I don't think that's a nice way to
talk to an old man. Talking slowly, the way he does, kind of spelling
out the words like a chorister would line a hymn. Up jumps Oliver
with, Maybe you want to take it up? Well, mister, says Hill, I don't
go around hunting trouble, but I generally take care of all that's sent
me. . . . Oh, you should have seen it, Nate. A.R. went around that
fellow like a cooper round a barrel. Oliver's front teeth were out, his
ribs busted, his face looked like it had been run through a job press.
He was what you might call better mannered after that.

Nathan nodded but he was still seeking recruits. Is Oliver now in
Andersonville? Is he one of the Raiders? If not, possibly we could
enlist him.

Nope. Scurvy. He's a sorry picture now. I saw him tother day
going along Main Street. His cords had pulled in on him and he had
to travel on all fours. Pitiful sight.

Six new recruits were accepted into the band at the assembly that
night. Sergeant Key'd worked cleverly at organizing a screen of
singers and religious exhorters. These pickets were trustworthy men
who approved heartily the plan for concerted action against the
raiders, but who would be prevented by age or infirmity or small
stature from taking active part in any pitched battle. A sergeant
named Waddell, whose home was in Kenton, Ohio, had founded a
prayer meeting late in May, and from the devout boys and elders who
had been regular attendants Key could levy with no fear of betrayal.
As dusk came down the communicants assembled according to pre-
arranged plan beyond Main Street but not too close to the north
fence. There were a number of ordained ministers among the prisoners, and some one of these discoursed fervently, turn and turn about.
There was a bearded lay preacher named Frank Ives who served
his stint. . . . Brothers, I will take as my text this evening Romans
Fourteen, Twelve. *So then every one of us shall give account of himself to God.*

Hymns arose simultaneously from other circles nearby.

> *My heavenly home is bright and fair,*
> *No pain nor woe can enter there;*
> *Its glittering towers the sun outshine—*
> *That heavenly mansion shall be mine.*

All hail the power of Jesus' name!
Let angels prostrate fall;
Bring forth the royal diadem—

Tho' ev'ry prospect pleases
And only man is vile—

Come, Thou Fount of every blessing—

Behind this mask of humanity and psalmody the canny destruction was in planning. The band of Regulators crouched in tight concentric circles; a few sentries walked their beats on the outskirts while Key stood tall before serious eyes watching him. It was impossible to keep raiders or their spies from knowing that something unusual and foreboding was in progress, but at least it was hoped that specific information—the personnel, equipment and tactics to be employed—might be kept from the enemy.

Key's sober nasal Illinois voice droned calmly under cover of sacred choruses.

I'm going home to die no more,
To die no more, to die no more,
I'm going home to die no more.

Bring forth the royal diadem,
And crown Him Lord of all.

Tune my heart to sing Thy grace—

Armament was the chief problem; that, and coöperation from Rebel authorities. A fear was voiced that when warfare commenced actually on a decisive scale, Wirz would make good his threat to sweep the stockade with canister. His jumping nerves might cry that here rose Insurrection, here came Riot, now the Yankees were trying to storm the gates as he had feared.

We must figure out some plan for apprising our jailers in advance.

Key, that ain't no good. Too many spies among the Paroles outside, and they'd get word to Curtis or Collins or Sarsfield or somebody in the twinkling of an eye.

That's correct, Goody. There would necessarily be the briefest of intervals between the apprisal of our intentions, and the actual attack.

But spose the Rebs refused us permission?

I don't think they would, Ned. Mike Hoare, you got anything to say on the subject?

Hoare was a slim powerful man from Jackson, Michigan, who had been captured during Dahlgren's abortive raid against Richmond. He spoke, feelingly and to the point, on the subject of armament. In battle they would be going against a horde possessed of knives, slung-shots, brass knuckles, probably some pistols. God was usually on the side with the heaviest artillery. Well. . . .

O that with yonder sacred throng
We at His feet may fall!

It took more nighttime meetings, and shrewd manipulation and bargainings by day, to equip even squad leaders with anything like decent arms. The men were determined that no more of them should commingle with that yonder sacred throng than became absolutely necessary, but that as many raiders as resisted should commingle. The Sucker Laundry and its adjacent barber shop served as a mar-ket-place where owners of weapons or incipient weapons might be questioned judiciously and persuaded to part with these essentials when bribed by community resources. MacBean and Dreyfoos gave liberally of their world's goods to this cause, and MacBean was effec-tive as a missionary enlisting financial support. In this manner nearly two dozen makeshift knives and eight real knives were secured, to-gether with two lead-filled billies and many improvised slung-shots; leaders worked at improvising more. But clubs would prove most effective when the army took the field, and it was lack of these imple-ments which perplexed Key and his lieutenants. Long ago the few trees left standing in the area had been torn apart, the very roots had been excavated piecemeal and burned, every remainder of the old north boundary had vanished as if eaten by ants. Few tent poles could be found which were tough enough to serve.

Face the music, said Sen MacBean. Pine just doesn't make a good solid club. Maybe a green branch, properly cut and peeled; the rest's too brittle and splintery.

Nathan said, I should have made more pointed lances or rapiers last spring when still they could be had.

Certainly, you ought. But no use crying over spilt milk. Maybe we can take enough clubs away from the toughs before they bowl us over?

No firearms came to light during a first cautious census by the Regulators. On the hot morning of July second it became known that a shriveled little Italian of the Forty-eighth New York had died in his shebang during the night. Nathan Dreyfoos was called to the scene to act as interpreter during a debate which ensued between neighbors and fellow Forty-eighth New Yorkers. The neighbors sought to have the corpse removed immediately, the comrades wished to wait until a priest named Father Peter Whelan appeared on his rounds; he came inside nearly every day. Nathan spoke only a little Italian, but by resorting to French and Spanish he managed to persuade the survivors to convey the body to the deadline and await Father Whelan there.

The Forty-eighth New York was known commonly as the Dead Ducks or Lost Ducks (their official designation was *Les Enfants Perdus*) and it was said that every nation in Europe was represented in their ranks, and wags insisted that no two of them could speak the same language. Nathan looked down at the dirty corpse still dressed in its short-tailed jacket and kilt-like nether garment, he looked down at this morsel come so far from some olive-grown hill to give itself to Georgia soil, he pitied the morsel. In helping other lank paupers to lift their dead he felt a lump against the sunken chest and found, to his delight and astonishment, that the little man had been possessed of a small revolver of German manufacture. Apparently *L'Enfant* had never felt called upon to use or even brandish the weapon since he entered the stockade; his companions expressed obvious wonder at this discovery. Despite their shrieks, Nathan appropriated the revolver in true raider fashion and carried it away with him, as well as nine rounds of ammunition and a box of caps.

I felt that the greater good would be served, Seneca.

Course you're right. Isn't that what they call the End justifying the Means?

We could use it. Some one of us. Perhaps Key?

Key it should be. I happen to know that he shoots passing well with a pistol. You know how the bulk of us cavalrymen are, with a hand-gun: passing bad. But I was told that Key won a pig one time in a pistol match when he was with the Sixteenth. And those other Dead Ducks don't deserve such a prize. Only interesting thing I ever knew that bunch of riffraff to do was to capture and cook and eat a snake they found in the bog, last spring. Brother Nathan, did you ever eat cooked snake? No? Not even in Europe?

I have eaten eels.

Mister, to think I've got you for a comrade!

Nathan traded a haircut for some rancid grease and with this substance he scrubbed off rust which had formed, and took the stiffness out of the weapon's mechanism. Soon he had action restored to a serviceable state, and presented the revolver to Leroy Key whose firm face broke into a grin when he saw it.

Before nine o'clock that night three figures rose out of gloom beside Key's hillside shebang. The Illinois sergeant heard his name spoken.

Need to see you, Sarge. Talk with you.

The Illinoisan's first thought was, They've heard about the revolver. They mean to take it away from me.

He knew that these evening callers were not Regulators; a Regulator would have given the password on approaching the chief's tent at night; this countersign was changed daily, and on this day the countersign was *Sangamon,* and no one had said *Sangamon.*

Sergeant Key stepped out into the putrid disorder, into poultry sounds and far-worse-than-poultry smells which saturated the dusk and seemed always worse when you left the kindness of your own lodging. . . . Even rags stretched between you and the sky seemed to afford a comfort, a guardianship.

He could not have remained inside; they would have sought him out, he would have been stabbed or bludgeoned as he lay.

To the gaze of these three emissaries who squinted their challenge he seemed to stand weaponless.

He said later that he thought one of them was Mosby the Raider's man Dolan; he was almost certain that it was Dolan; he could not identify the other two.

Will you listen, Key? We people on the South Side have been hearing things.

What did you hear?

Talk of police and such.

You did?

They had been sent to kill him. Their bosses were most of them not brainy men, but they knew enough to squelch an uprising (it amounted to an uprising against authority, since from the beginning the raiders had been the supreme power operating in Andersonville) by cutting off its head. Who had talked, who had carried information? No use figuring that out, you couldn't figure it out. Too many cooks stirring this particular kettle of broth.

Is it true? They asked it naively.

Yep, said the Bloomington printer.

A tiny fire was burning some twenty yards away; it was strong enough to make a glint on the knife which showed in the hand of the nearest man. The others moved in closer, Key heard the rasp as a club or billy was drawn from under a belt. He flung up his right hand holding the fortuitous revolver, and clicked back the hammer as he lifted it. He would have fired on the instant, but felt that he must wait almost until the men were upon him. He dreaded missing one of the dusky shapes and shooting some innocent person in a hut beyond. The metallic sharp *kack* was as good as a bullet except that it did not kill. The raiders' committee fell back before the sound so rapidly that it seemed they must have anticipated Key's gesture. They ran off like cattle blundering; one of them crashed into and through a shebang, there were grunts, wails, sounds of ripping, the sound of entanglement, the sound of a big man wrenching himself loose from fabric and then thudding away after other creatures who galloped in ruthless retreat.

On the fence a nervous guard fired at the sky, you could tell from the direction of the painted flash that his musket was pointed upward as he fired. Key stood listening and deciding what to do.

He thought that he had given sufficient discouragement to these individuals, but more might creep up on him later. He hated the event more than he hated peril to himself: it was forcing the Regulators' hand. They were by no means ready for an engagement. But from now on none of them would be safe from murder under cover of darkness, nor would they be safe in daylight unless they clung together. Key released the hammer of his gun, put the revolver inside his belted jacket, and went in search of Nathan Dreyfoos. He owed his life to the present of the revolver on that day.

He called softly outside Dreyfoos's hut, and the lame voice of Private Allen said, No, he's not here.

Where's he at, son?

Gone over to MacBean's place.

In the region of the Sucker Laundry & Cleaning Co. several dark shapes were motionless as stumps while Sergeant Key approached, then detached themselves from the ground to greet him as they recognized his figure. There were MacBean, Dreyfoos, a long-armed man from the One Hundred and Eleventh Illinois known as Egypt, and Ned Carrigan from Chicago. Carrigan was a jolly youngster of enormous frame who had fought in the ring and admitted reluctantly that he had killed another pugilist with one blow during a prize fight held in a hay barn near St. Louis. Had he emerged from another environment Carrigan might have been one of the raiders; as it was he stood ready to march in phalanx with fellow Westerners.

What you doing, boys?

Talking things over.

Where's Brother Nathan? That was what Seneca MacBean called Dreyfoos continually, and Key had adopted the address.

I am here, Sergeant Key.

Key felt through darkness, found Nathan's hand, shook it with spirit. That pistol saved me, Brother Nathan.

The others pushed closer around him as he told of the experience, and there was a general cluck-clucking. Glad you're sound, Key. But that surely is a poser.

A restlessness rose within the stockade on this night, and through regions close around. It affected the mass of the living. The raiders (such as were sufficiently sensitive to recognize the thing, to feel) ascribed this uncertain tingling to the fact that a definite organization was being formed to controvert them. Key and MacBean and Limber Jim and Nathan Dreyfoos and the rest— They ascribed their nervousness to the indisputable evidence that now their enemies had knowledge of the Westerners' plan, and the hand of the Regulators might be forced to bring about calamity. The flame-spit of a sentry's gun, fired from the parapet when hoodlums ran away from Leroy Key and his revolver, had never initiated this quivering but had underlined it, punctuated it, emphasized it, shown that it was there. Camp Sumter with its thousands and the pen controlled by Camp Sumter were become a loose black jelly on the saucer of Georgia.

A boy named Dolliver felt the tremor and he thought of blackbirds. They dwelt in wavering tribes amid prairie sloughs, they clung festooned on reeds and made amiable metallic sounds; but something occurred suddenly to disturb them, and you might not descry the signal given, you might not identify the messenger. He flew in without your seeing him . . . or he could have been a hungry animal approaching soft-footed, wet-footed, intending to feed on blackbirds. He could have been a snake winding there, intending to feed on blackbirds' eggs. Whatever the peril, the redwings flocked up above grasses, glint of jewelry came off their shininess, the small throats rang with what they were saying and fearing.

A man who hailed from farther on the plains, and like the Indians had crept in a coyote's skin in order to approach buffalo herds closely, thought of buffalo as Eben Dolliver relied on birds for comparison. Where were this man's comrades of the Eighth Kansas, where were Williams and Gensarde and Freeman? Dead they were, dead during the month past. Where was Weidman? He was here, he was close, and he would not die until October. But the erstwhile buffalo hunter did not linger for long, dwelling on the tragedy of his friends, thinking of how they had rotted or were rotting, and how he himself was putrefying while still he could walk and talk. He sensed the drift of the night, sensed its peculiar qualm. In comparison he thought of a herd, and could smell fairly the bitter dusty buffalo, the oily perfume shed by kinky manes. He could feel the plain shaking like a drumhead merely because so many creatures stood and moved upon it. They were feeding quietly . . . then a surge reached them and alarm was conveyed to thick brains within the mountainous skulls. Heads lifted, eyes rolled, hoofs touched the ground, refused the ground, there was a telegraph wire stretched under dry earth, a message was tapped there. Was it arrow or bullet or wolf which would come? There was a fright not yet become a true fright (call it rumor spoken silently from cow to cow, call it legend never dignified as fact). A message reeked in the unseen telegraph wire. Which bull might read it, who could read the code? Was this disaster, or merely mosquitoes, or sharp seeds of the spear grass itching their moulting hides? Might one become reassured in time and thus stand ready to munch, chew a cud, lift a tail, let the dung go splashing? The Kansan believed vaguely that such a herd was around him. He was one member of it. In his dream he wore horns bent upon his head.

And also this was the ominous swaying and bawling of cattle who felt a storm on the way. It was sleepy clucking of poultry on lime-smeared perches (perhaps a weasel slunk like a rapid worm, skimming, twisting amid the stones on which the poultry shed was built. The weasel was trying to find a way in).

A wounded veteran of the Seven Days—one of the few such veterans now serving with the Reserves—sniffed suspiciously on the platform of Station Number Thirty-nine. He rolled his quid into his cheek, spat across the jagged chopped pine, called to a fellow guard in darkness thirty yards away.

What you say, Pokey?

Didn't say nothing. Thought you said something.

Didn't say nothing myself until now. But hain't something funny going on?

Somebody down there by the deadline?

Can't see nothing. Too blame dark. But it feels like they was up to something.

Feels that way.

Station Number One, eleven o'clock and alllls wellll. Station Number Two, eleven o'clock and alllls wellll. Station Number Three . . . repeated yell, voice to voice, boy to man, man to boy, boy to boy, boy to man, man to very old man, going along the rim in yapped solo and chorus, overlapping, muttered, squealed, neglected by two guards who were asleep, finished within a minute or two, seldom derided and interrupted by prisoners in this unsubstantial night.

Men who knew cities felt the tremor of a crowd which might turn into a mob and go to breaking windows and upsetting freight cars to loot them. They thought of a mob not yet a mob, yet ready to spring into a mob if the stone were hurled or the oath were cried.

There was a Turk who had worked in a zoological garden; he understood wild animals; he knew that there were nights when lions walked unceasingly, when mothers carried their cubs into farthest corners and lay licking them, when big fierce faces rubbed against the bars. He knew that there were nights when a rumbling growl came without a reason which could be guessed, yet the growl sounded and was coughed and grunted from cage to cage. No lightning trickled above the horizon, no storm approached across the peasantry beyond the town; but electricity occupied the air. Animals smelled stronger on such a night, and this was such a night, Andersonville smelled stronger now.

MacBean said, Going to turn in, Brother Nathan?

Somehow I am not sleepy.

Lieutenant Davis, Wirz's deputy, swung sock-footed legs off his hot bed and groped around for his boots. The officer who shared Davis's quarters mumbled, Going to check the Posts?

Reckon I'll take a look around.

Not time for regular check, is it?

No, but I just can't sleep no way.

And there was a man who had spent much of his youth in fishing for mullet. He recalled the glassiness of pools amid mangrove islands, and how on a still day there might be no mullet; then suddenly the treasure would be leaping, drove after drove plunging up out of the water, throwing themselves with curve and flip, thousands of pounds of mullet racing under shallowness which had been quiescent and now so quickly was torn. In this man's thought the prison was a bay and prisoners were fish. What might occur to set them into antics beneath the salty surface, ripping out with their burnished heads, arching in long thrusts of purplish silver, high and wet, jumping by hundreds, the sun sharp upon them? Something in secret avenues of shell and sands, something moving fiercely; a summons and threat among mullet; there was something. . . .

Now, the mayor he knew Brennan. And, I think, says he,
Your name is Willie Brennan, ha? You must come along with me—

Devil suck you, Sarsfield! Tis Willie Collins, never Brennan.

Way I heard twas Brennan.

Och, nay, never! It's myself who trained my kiddies to sing it different. Give heed:

Your name is Willie Collins, ha? You must come along with me—

Oh, Collins on the moor, Collins on the moor!

Fuck Willie Collins! Laughter, laughter. . . .

Now what rat has thieved my bottle of bingo? Hand it over, or I'll tear the wattles—

They were gathered in and around the tall conical tent of Mosby the Raider (seldom called Mosby at this late day, called Willie Collins by most). The roll was a roll of the damned and damnable, the rich, the blind uncaring cruel, the selfish, the powerful, the exalted of this place. The sailors Munn and Rickson, Patrick Delaney of the Dead Rabbits, Curtis with brick-red brow and brick-thick bone above the brow, John Sarsfield the renegade hero from the One Hundred and Forty-fourth New York: these were the leaders. If a roll of colossi had been called they would have answered Here; Willie Collins would have roared his response along with theirs. Turbulence possessed them, they drew together, drank pine-top, sent underlings with loot to the deadline to bargain for more. They said, These greenbacks are enough, and be after telling that snot of a guard I'll never pay more for a gallon; and he's to let it down in buckets with no leak to them.

In Athol there lived a man named Jerry Lanagan;
He battered away till he hadn't a pound—

Their cohorts sat or lay, attendants encircling the captains. The cooks cooked late, a smell of fried meat came up to vie with the wide mat of ordinary stench (and other prisoners watched this convention of monsters from a distance they hoped was safe; on scenting the meat and watching the orange reek of flames they thought of Hell. The meat of sinners was burning). Edward Blamey had learned to drink unmeasured quantities of sorghum whiskey. He was become the first drunkard in uncounted generations of stiff New Englanders, Old Englanders, Norman French. His eyeballs were laced with pink veins like silken thread tangled on oystery whiteness, but his fantastic vision still served . . . excepting in nighttime, then it did not need to serve. One of the homosexuals crawled close to importune him. This fellow had been hounding Edward Blamey for some time. Edward kicked out with a strong sound stolen boot, the homosexual screamed like a frightened spinster and told Edward that he was perfectly horrid. Where was The Wrath To Come? Out yonder—oh, out yonder—stalking through the spread of tremulous hours. The Wrath To Come was kept at bay, Willie Collins could keep it at bay forever. Edward Blamey grunted, belched, rolled over on his blanket, rested his untidy head on a bent elbow, slept immediately. But he had a nightmare wherein the leaky baptistry of his Rhode Island boyhood was filled with pine-top, and Willie Collins said, Delaney, you rubber-legged louse, it's you must drink it up. Edward Blamey set to work laboriously to remove planks which formed a lid above the immersion tank; first he had to shove back the old oak pulpit, and that was a job; next he had to roll the faded greenish carpet, with its worn place where the preacher always stood; next he had to lift the planks one at a time. And when he had raised the last plank, and peered down into a dim splashing interior, there sat his own father, totally naked, bathing himself in raw burning whiskey. Mr. Blamey rolled his cold narrow gaze toward the frightened son crouched above him and said, *But if thine eye be evil—*

Edward awoke yelling. No one paid attention to him. The leaders were drunker than ever, they were boasting what they'd do if any self-appointed police came against them.

By God! That joskin Key. I'll tear his pecker off.

And the other—?

MacBean? Also a printer.

Take him at the back, Johnny boy. I'll take him in the front, same time.

Ah, but give me a chance at that Jew-boy, the Plymouth Pilgrim, him with the pointed stick!

Hell, you had your chance, and he beat you out!

Why, you son of a bitch, I'll— So he beat me, did he? Why—

Pass that canteen my way—

Coarse laughter, the bellow bursting out, uncaged cats sitting large and two-legged, the hoot and lashing of them.

> *Now, Brennan is an outlaw, all on some mountain high.*
> *With infantry and cavalry to take him they did try.*
> *But he laughed at them and he scorned at them—*

Ha, and what are you saying there? *Collins,* you bastards. *Collins! Collins* is an outlaw, all on some mountain high—

Oh, it's Collins on the moor—

Bold gay and undaunted—

He batter'd away till he hadn't a pound—

Take your God damn hand off my—

Edward Blamey slept again, he slept a better sleep for a time; then he saw his father, but it was not the face of his father after all; it was the body of his father, but the face was the face of a fellow Rhode Islander whom Edward had observed in June, digging a hole and secreting something therein. Acting on this observation, raiders circled promptly to dig up the hole again and take what it contained. It contained a tiny miniature painting of the boy's mother (his branch of this Rhode Island family was well-to-do) in a gold frame set with pearls. The boy strove to defend his property with his life, and so he did until his life was taken from him along with the miniature in its frame. Edward Blamey saw his face, somehow it was the same face, both before and after what occurred; and how could that be when a two-hundred-pound man had stood upon that face and stamped it with cavalry boots?

> *Oh, it's Collins on the moor, Collins on the moor!*
> *Bold, gay and undaunted stood young Collins—*

Other men did not think of buffalo or blackbirds or mullet or city crowds in this midnight, because they had no knowledge of these creatures; but there was a quiet boy from a quiet shore who thought of seabirds he had seen when he walked the coast at evening. Gulls roosted far out on an island little more than a shoal, for the sea was calmer than usual and there was dry space for them to roost upon. They settled in white and dark and golden throngs as the last sun caught them (the boy thought of angel throngs). He looked away from the sea and island and sitting gulls, and progressed homeward along the shore path . . . it was like a moorland of his ancestors' past, with wraiths to be avoided if one traveled when the fog came in. The boy walked on, carrying his heavy wooden tool-kit slung by a wide strap over his shoulder, for at seventeen he was close to being an expert at his craft, and had been repairing a dory that afternoon. Again he looked to the east, and there they were, there they were, rising. Some matter had caused dissent or alarm among the gulls, they boiled up like masses of dark leaves flung in October. Sun was down and hidden, no longer were the seabirds colored or angelic with natural cream or ivory. They flaked in a storm-cloud of black fragments, whirled in a peevish choir, their penetrating squall came across the crush of waves on rocks. Oh, what had caused this uneasiness and hurled them into the wind again? Something, something.

The devout man named Frank Ives said, Sleep's impossible. Are you awake, Brother Ellicott?

Yes, Brother Ives. So're Berwick and Harper.

Dunlop, over there? Are you awake, Brother Dunlop?

Brother Dunlop squeezed the swollen fingers of his left hand with the unswollen (yet soon to be swollen, soon to be decayed) fingers of his right hand. I'm here. Shall we pray?

I had been thinking that we might read in response. Been thinking of Second Corinthians, also First Thessalonians.

We got sufficient light, Brother Ives?

Private Harper said eagerly, I've a lot of pine splinters left, wrapped in my jacket.

Pass them over. Ah, there's still a coal or two.

I'll blow, said Ellicott. Soon there was flame showing, soon there was enough light to read by and would be for some time if splinters were fed into the blaze with care. The men of this shebang pushed in a wad around the bright tiny wavering flare, and Frank Ives turned to Page Sixty-three of his ragged Hymnal, whereon one of his favorite Readings was printed. Move your head a little, Brother. No—this side—put it under Alex's arm. Now we can all see.

I know Corinthians and Thessalonians practically by heart, all four books of them, said young Percival Berwick. Don't need to see. Read away, Brother.

For all things are for your sakes, that the grace, being multiplied through the many, may cause the thanksgiving to abound unto the glory of God.

Chant of response, tuned in that lower octave used by congregations, the same sound as in a Mass, the same faith as in a Mass, the faith to make gangrene of secondary importance, faith to make a soul exult and feel that it was hung on an accompanying Cross, and would soon be with Someone in Paradise. *Wherefore we faint not; but though our outward man is decaying, yet our inward man is renewed day by day.*

The starving Frank Ives read serenely, *For our light affliction, which is for the moment, worketh for us more and more exceedingly an eternal weight of glory.*

Low concerted murmur of the response, the S-sounds laving as it were read in the village churches most of these people had known before they came to endure Andersonville. *While we look not at the things which are seen, but at the things which are not seen: for the things which are seen are temporal; but the things which are not seen are eternal.*

Their neighbors—some of them—had cat-called before, then had grown tired of jeering when they learned that they could not affect the radiant purpose of these consistently practicing Christians. Neighbors tolerated songs and services, or else paid no attention; some neighbors died, some moved away; one was now a convert and living in this shebang. He was Dunlop, the man with the gangrened hand. He would speak Salvation as long as breath was left to him, with the ardor which only newly made zealots may know.

Outside the fence a patterned scrap of brown light moved reluctantly along the hard-trodden path communicating from sentry station to sentry station. In some instances Lieutenant Davis went to the trouble of swinging his heavy body up the ladder-rungs and standing beside the guard for a while, staring down at the interior, rubbing his chin whiskers as he gazed. Then down the ladder again, and on to the next station, carrying his tinkling lantern, walking with the flap of his holster unbuttoned and often letting his hand slide around the revolver butt to find reassurance. Close, so close to the angry beasts, close to storied crocodiles. They were lying in their mud only a couple of rods away. They could do anything. Think how they had melted away that old north fence on the night of June eighteenth. If they could nibble a pine wall—timbers twenty feet tall, including the portion dug out of the ground, and extending seven hundred and eighty feet from east wall to west wall— If they could chew that to vanishment in a single night, what might they not now effect if they chose? Look sharp, there, his heavy voice drawled to the perched sentries in those instances where he felt too weary to climb. Hear me, now. You watch sharp, you hear?

Yes, sir.

You see anything queer, anything different?

Well, sir, they seem to be doing an awful lot of circulating.

What you mean, there, circulating?

Kind of keep moving about.

And at Post Number Forty he would hoist himself up the ladder again. He was a coarse lustful young man more or less popular with the troops he commanded, and hated not too cordially by the prisoners. When he became brutal he was brutal only through lack of feeling and not in a calculated fashion. He was the sort of man who might have found delight in the act of rape, if lured to commit it through a girl's petting; and then he would have felt sorry afterward, and

would have begged abject pardon . . . he would have brought the
girl later some ugly but (to him) expensive gift. His small pale eyes
protruded abnormally, his mouth was loose, he should have worn a
full beard instead of chin whiskers to conceal his weakness from the
world. He was not above taking bribes; on the other hand he declared
loudly that it was a shame and a sin to see how these God damn
Yankees were compelled to live. Man couldn't keep no self-respect
whilst living like a hog, no sir. Secretly he was very much afraid of
the Yankees, especially afraid of the lean silent ones. Thus he swaggered, talked loudly whenever he entered the stockade, glared when
Yanks came up to him with their petitions, pushed his eyes even
farther out of his head and stood scowling while he listened, but he
did listen. Often he granted the prisoners' requests. Yes, he would ask
Captain Wirz to release Willis Lowell, citizen teamster, from the
stocks—Lowell had been there three days, that was sufficient punishment for his offense. Yes, he would permit three men from the
Eleventh Kentucky Cavalry to go outside and pick berries—they had
a touch of scurvy, but still only a touch, berries might save their lives.
No, emphatically, he would not demand that Lucas Rensem, Fifteenth
Missouri, be put into the hospital—that was solely up to the stockade
surgeons, he could not go around interfering with stockade surgeons
in their performance of their duties (besides, it would have been too
much trouble for Lieutenant Davis).

He insisted that he had a bad heart, he could not perform any
heavy work, any task too arduous. He took refuge in his disability the
moment trouble loomed. Lieutenant Davis hated and feared trouble
of any kind. He declared repeatedly that he was an easy-going man
and he liked people to be easy-going. When Wirz screamed at him
(as he screamed at anyone and everyone except his small daughter
when he was in the mood to scream—which was every hour, and with
increasing frequency)— When Wirz screamed at him, Lieutenant
Davis's fat face sagged in offended alarm, and he put a fat hand on
the breast of his tight-fitting gray jacket and cried in an injured tone,
Captain Wirz, sir, now you quit abusing me; I'll enter complaint to
the colonel; mind, now, I got a bad heart—

Ach, you and your bad heart! Also a bad brain you got!

Captain, mind, now— I ain't a-fooling. Surgeon said I got a greatly
enlarged heart, and can't suffer such abuse no way. I warn you, I'll
just fall out!

It is I wish you *would* fall out!

Just keep on like that if you want a corpse on your hands! Gluey
tears seeped in Davis's eyes.

What a fat lazy corpse I would have once.

He was lazy in truth, but also he held a certain addiction to duty
(again, if the duty were obvious and apparent to all, and if any lapse

on his part would be apparent to all). The threatening magic of these hours had drawn him from his cot, sent him patrolling, hauled him up to several of the platforms.

He went aloft for the last time at the southwest corner, breathing heavily from his mile-long journey and the climbings and descents. Davis eyed the high-blazing raider fires with resentment, and listened to the Brennan On the Moor, Collins On the Moor song and imprecations accompanying. Now you just bet they're a-whooping it up.

Sure are, Lieutenant.

If twas solely them burglars from New York— He said this much aloud, and then realized that he should not reveal his perturbation to the round-shouldered child who leaned on his musket beside him. Davis descended, contemplating responsibility on every rung of the ladder, fearing as always that the ladder might break, feeling inexpressible relief when again he stood on the ground, and yet feeling a persecuted sadness that any momentous decision must be his. If he called Wirz from bed, and Wirz decided that nothing was wrong with the stockade's population, Wirz would make him sweat for it. But if some conflict did develop during the remainder of the night, if the dreaded outbreak did occur, if twenty-five thousand brutes and cripples pushed against one of those gates, hammering even only with their heads and their fists— If they built a stairway of the dead, if they piled up only a thousand dead men and then twenty-four thousand living men mounted on their bodies to flow over the stockade in a filthy tide, as all had feared that they were capable of doing—

Davis heard the One o'clock and all's well begin to wail along the parapet as his feet took the path toward headquarters. That cry decided him. There were several hours of darkness remaining; he could not shudder through those hours single-handed. Now he wished for Henry Wirz longingly. Even if Wirz cursed him, brandished his fists under Davis's little knob of a nose, told him that he would see to it that Davis got no leave for six months at least— It would be near to a comfort.

The superintendent's office was closed and dark and locked. Davis's lantern revealed the sentry stretched on a bench at the right-hand side of the door with several hound puppies intertwined on his chest.

Wake up there, you. By God, you ought to be court-martialed and shot, and that sure is the truth. I got a great mind to—

Lieutenant, sir, I ain't asleep. No, sir. Just laying here playing with the pups— Puppies flew, the sentinel got up stiffly, white-haired and shaking, and reached for his gun. You got to remember that I'm an old man, nigh on to seventy, and I do get tuckered a-standing up.

Where's Red Cap? He round here somewheres?

Sleeping inside the shack, Mister Lieutenant.

Say, Sir, you old goat.

Yes, sir. Sir!

Davis slapped on the closed door with his flabby palm and bawled,
Whah-ye! Red Cap! This yell of his was the lieutenant's traditional
signal for order, for attention; it was a summoning and a prelude.
The more sprightly among the prisoners used to imitate Davis's cry
very much to his wrath, but the fomentation of a Davis rage was not
to be feared like a Wirz rage. Some believed that in bawling, Whah-
ye! the man was in fact calling, Where are ye? Others said that it was
a corruption of the time-honored Oyez uttered by a bailiff. In any
case it attracted immediate compliance, and now Red Cap arose from
his pallet and answered at the door. He slid the big bolt and peered
out, his tousled hair spun gold in the lantern flickers. He had been a
drummer boy with Company I, Tenth West Virginia Infantry and was
fourteen years old at the time of his capture. Wirz took him Outside
as personal orderly and messenger; there was something faunal and
winning about the boy. It may have been that Henry Wirz thought
to save him from those deviates who slunk among the raiders or followed their sailor protectors like mincing bitches. The youth's name
was Ransom Powell, but prisoners and Rebels alike called him Little
Red Cap, and they pictured the home he came from as a kind and
lovely place, with a mother who wore pink aprons, baked pans of
spicy gingerbread, and taught Little Red Cap his prayers. His face
shone eternally for he was well fed, he starved not, and in his favored
position he could do much for less fortunate comrades. Little Red Cap
smuggled everything from hopeful tidings to pork ribs and onions
whenever an errand took him back into the stockade.

Want you to go seek the captain, boy.

Yes, sir. Want I should ride? Course the captain took the Old Gray
Mare home with him.

I reckon you do have to ride, you little Yankee limb! Can't walk all
that way, and I want Captain Wirz bad, and I want you to hustle!
You take my own Mouse mule.

Quickly the boy filled and lighted another lantern and put on his
tiny shoes . . . small shoes indeed on his small feet, they might have
been cobbled by elves, they were solid patches. In rare good humor
Wirz had promised the boy boots, but thus far no boots could be
found small enough to fit him. Ransom Powell clapped upon his head
the crimson peaked cap with its tarnished gilt lace which had given
him his name. Davis watched the freckled light go bobbing down to
the pen where Mouse was kept; soon the lantern was blown out, and
Davis could hear the shrill eager voice of Red Cap ordering Mouse
into speed on the narrow road, and could hear him switching the
mule's flank, and it sounded as if Mouse were bucking in resistance.
Dimly it seemed to Davis that even a domestic animal might feel the
tautness of this hour. Davis sat heavily on the step and felt the pres-

sure of apprehension wrapping him like an overcoat unwelcome in July.

He growled at the sentry. Old Man, you get up there and walk your beat like you're sposed to. Don't you know nothing? Joe Brown ought to feed you to the hogs!

. . . Later he grew too nervous to sit idly, and went slouching off to the South Gate, and listened to the guttural hum and wailing of that terrifying herd beyond the up-ended logs; and then he thought that he was too tired to stand listening longer, and he thought that his heart was swelling large and painful within his ribs. Some day twill bust, he thought drearily. Just like a bottle busting in a fire. . . .

Davis considered that Wirz was long overdue when at last Wirz arrived; indeed the captain was long overdue, for he had been operating on his forearm when Little Red Cap arrived at the Boss house. He had been picking out scraps of honeycombed bone with a steel knitting needle. Henry Wirz cursed Little Red Cap vehemently (this was not unprecedented but it was unusual. Like many another of the most savage of his type, Wirz had a genuine fondness for children. He remembered his own childhood with nostalgia, thought that he had been happy then, cried sometimes when he thought of Paul and Louisa Emily left perforce with their grandparents in Switzerland. *Ja*, so tall they had grown by this time; and it was nearly a year since he had seen them. Nowadays he was impatient with his stepdaughters because they were of awkward and seemingly unmanageable age; they had been sweet tiny creatures when first he knew them, but now their skirts were long, the girls were flighty, unpredictable, openly disobedient at times. Coralie was still wistful and birdlike, she was only nine-and-a-half, not quite nine-and-a-half).

So God damn you, you bad Little Red Cap, you!

Captain, please sir, I couldn't help it. Lieutenant Davis ordered me to come fetch you—

Nothing you know why I should be fetched? God damn, did you *ask? Nein!* So all the way to that damn stockade I must worry, worry, worry. Now, you bad Red Cap, this strip of linen you hold here. . . . Nah—*here* you hold it, I hold it *here.* Now you wind it once. *Ja*—son of a bitch—I tell you—not *once* only around the arm. Wind, wind, *wind!* Sweat gleamed on Henry's thin forehead, fell from his sharp nose, made wet places on the thickening bandage. The pressure on the tangled tissues became a steady ache; yet it was a benefit; frogs in the arm kept piping as always, Let me out, let me *out,* and the bandage would keep those frogs in check.

Seneca MacBean said one day to Nathan Dreyfoos, after a particularly lively encounter with the superintendent, You know, Brother Nathan, Wirz is the most even-tempered man I ever saw in my life. He's always foaming mad.

So he was foaming mad as he rode through threatening woods toward the pen, and little Ranny Powell wisely and cheerfully fell farther back into darkness, pretending that Mouse would go no faster. So Wirz was foaming mad when he encountered the unhappy Davis in thick hot smell (Andersonville seemed to smell worse in the night than in the daytime, and how could that be?). True to the lieutenant's lugubrious prophecy, Henry swore that he would grant no leave to any subordinate so derelict in his duties. . . .

For why you call me from *mein* house? All the nights I got to work too, all the daytimes too? You say nobody is shot, nobody is making escaping, *oder* they not set fire to the fence, *ja?* So what are you good for, you damn Davis?

Captain, now you quit. You know I got a weak heart and—

Ja, a fat ass you got also, lazybones!

All right, by God! Just you go up on some of them sentry stations. I bet you never heard them act like this afore, not so's you could notice it. . . .

The captain went blaspheming to the southwest corner of the prison and climbed to the same platform where Davis had stood before him. He came down so quickly that the aggrieved exhausted young officer was frightened anew. Why you not call me more quicker? *Gott,* I think those bears they try to force the gate!

Captain, they ain't tried, yet. But they make so much noise and—

Kind of act so funny, all over the place, and—

Now you get the Officer of the Day, you have him get two guards on every station. Not *one,* God damn son of a bitch, get *two* on every station! How you say— Double these no good guards! Now I go over to the fort, I get that battery commander from his bed out!

The battery commander on the star fort was not in his blankets or on them; he was sitting unsteadily on the earth fort above the rude fascines, smoking his pipe. He was nearly as glad to see Wirz as Davis had been. He declared that he had not slept all night. The guns were already shotted up.

And fuses in those touch-holes you got?

No, the fuses had not been inserted. He was always fearful of an accident. . . .

Better accidents we have than Yankees break out maybe!

Well, he couldn't insert fuses without an order. . . . And, listen to me, you damn Switzer, you don't rank over me, and don't go giving me no orders.

One order you get from the colonel, and that damn quick! Wirz went fuming away, and decided also that he would ask that an order be issued to have every piece of artillery manned completely until daylight, and that the gunners not only have the fuses inserted in the touch-holes but that they be standing literally with lanyards in their hands. Thus at a second's signal the stockade could be raked. Momentarily Henry Wirz closed his strained sore eyes as he rode. Not with those eyes but with the lenses of memory he saw once more that tussle in the pit at Bern, and stood frosted in terror at sight of it. Oh, the bears. . . .

But there was no plan for a sundering of the barrier, no intention for a mass swarming. The weird impatience could not be chained to a fact unless there existed some cloud of precognition, which spilled to affect nearly every man of the region and shiver him into alarm. Far beyond fancied cities and blackbirds' swales and upland prairies where the buffalo pawed and Arapahoes were tented— Thousands of miles away, that restive spirit might have risen like a wind with no one to say its origin. It seemed to come from the top of the world and perhaps from airless space beyond the top of the world—the restiveness of time itself which will not be quiet or comforted, but travels unceasingly. And where, a few more wise and humble men thought, does time begin? And what shall be the ending, and shall there be one?

XXIX

Implacably the sun came up steamed and polished. Ready to fry you, said the sun. Yes, yes, this day you shall fry; forty or fifty of you shall be carried off on the sizzled tray of the day when the day is through; the last grease shall be cooked from those forty or fifty; declare them to be cracklings; put them into the loaf of the soil, and I shall bake the whole loaf anew on the next day.

Old Sol's going to get us again, prisoners said. Hell, I'd ruther have Old Boo get me. Hell you would; you cried your ass off in the rain, all of June.

Among pine barrens north of the Anderson depot a locomotive halted, steam was down, there was no wood left on the fuel tender. Cars bumped to a halt and three Negroes descended with their axes from the tender. A rail fence little more than a relic yielded to their blows, but there were only a few panels of fencing left there; then they had to attack a scorched fallen tree. In less than an hour's time the tender was loaded once more, steam was up, the line of decrepit box cars dragged toward Anderson, axles rattling and trusses loose and clanking.

Three hundred and fifty-two strained embittered Unionists were counted from the cars. A majority were native to the mountains of western Virginia, and thus were objects of particular scorn to guards who refused to admit the existence of the new State of West Virginia (those who had heard of it. Little Red Cap was accepted and favored because of his youth and charm and handsome vitality. At the worst the Secessionists put him down as a misguided child, they did not think of him as a traitor to his State).

Duly enrolled as prisoners, the West Virginians began to file in through the North Gate. Edward Blamey blinked away his alcoholic tears, spotted the vanguard, evalued their rolls and haversacks, reported to his master. Collins's Raiders were thus the first into the fray, but other bands were not far behind. They descended upon the newcomers with ferocity unmatched. It was as if they were driven by an impulse which had not ruled the raiders when they slugged merely through cupidity, merely through the craving to exert their strength. The night of unrest had tempered them with beastliness. Haversacks flew from hand to hand and were distributed through the air, jackets were ripped, buttons flew, sleeves were pulled out. In earlier months there had been a pretense of innocence, a masquerading as humans on the part of the raiders. That was when incursions were limited to nighttime; and later the bulk of them might lounge or stroll or play chuck-a-luck, elaborately aloof from strife when six hooligans descended on, say, two Westerners who happened to own a poncho. But in this sharp hot morning the evil element rose in an unrestrained body, they were a single baboon. There were a few stray calls of *Raiders!* from more knowledgeable prisoners who fled the area; then a hush lay over the two or three thousand people who stood near at hand, backing off, pressed together in ragged watching ranks, an audience who had paid their admission in the coin of long starvation, the coin of sickness and penury.

Raider forces whirled around the West Virginians like the outer wheel of a corn-sheller cranked by Furies; and each newcomer was a cob to be expelled from the inner mass, to be hurled out, minute by minute, with all his kernels wrenched off. A hand was grasped, an arm was jerked, a bloody bewildered youth staggered free; he collapsed to feel the pounding throbbing draining swelling of his smashed nose, to wonder at scratches seared along his naked ribs, to wonder why he lived barefoot and in his under-drawers, to wonder why and how he lived at all. A quarter of an hour earlier he had been a man, an entity defeated and captured, but still a man with a name and with masculine pride.

He had been Miller Sprouse, Sixth West Virginia Cavalry, age eighteen, a brown-eyed brown-haired brown-faced person with small hard freckled fists and owning better-than-ordinary skill with a carbine. Here he was, captured, but guards on the train had been—most of them—wounded veterans missing a hand or an eye or an ear here and there; and thus they had been stern but decent. Miller Sprouse owned a good uniform, shabby but clean, and he had a rubber raincoat rolled around his blanket, he had a canteen, a spoon, fork, pocketknife, soap, a comb; he had a well-equipped housewife, a diary in which he scribbled painfully a few misspelled lines each day (this was an especial promise made to a girl named Tildy Freeborn; and when he came home they would be married and would raise corn, melons and younguns on a small farm on Beasley Run; and his father had said that Miller could pay him for the farm, so much per year, depending on how crops did. He was to help his father and Tildy's father mine coal during cold weather). Miller Sprouse had sixteen dollars and fifty-seven cents in currency; the Rebel guards had taken nothing except his cap and the old silver watch which wound with a key, and the key had been lost. He had his health, his identity, he had high hopes of escape; folks said that Andersonville was just a place with a fence around it, and surely that would be more promising than imprisonment in a tobacco warehouse or an abandoned factory in a city; you ought to be able to dig a hole and crawl out, or something.

Then suddenly a gate closed. They were crowded into a cubicle; they said, Hell, this is a little bitty prison, and people laughed about it. Then another gate opened ahead, and they passed into unavoidable unbreathable smell like all the untended privies in all the United States put together; it smelled also like dead skunks or polecats before birds got at them and cleaned them up; it smelled also like Grandpa Abbott smelled when he was dying of that there throat-cancer. A roar and a howl, and thousands and thousands of hairy shaggy black-faced devils swaying all around the place, and then lifted another roar with a different sound. Suddenly he thought that Paul Handland and Scott McConkey were fighting, just ahead of him; but no, they were fighting with two or three strangers, great big fellows. Something hit young Miller Sprouse on the side of the head, and he saw stars, and through the stars he saw a wide scarred face like a monkey's face (he had seen a monkey once in a circus)—that was how the face looked, except much larger. A hand twisted across his shoulder and jerked on Miller's blanket roll; he said, By Gol, and he punched and twisted and gulped. Something struck him in the belly, it felt like a cannon-ball driven against him. He was on the ground, gasping for breath, unable to find any breath in the mass of struggling bodies. Hands fought over him, his jacket was twisted, they like to pulled his arms out of the sockets as they pulled that jacket off; his shoes were gone, his trousers hauled from his kicking legs; he was propelled, shunted, flung; he landed painfully on dirty ground again; he was peeled, shucked, shelled; why was he here, where was he, what had happened, what was his name, he was half naked, marred, bruised. Still he couldn't get his breath, it seemed that his ribs were cracked, he could scarcely lift his left arm, one eye was closing, why, what, when, how, what had happened, why?

Seneca MacBean said, It's the beat.

Nathan Dreyfoos took his brooding gaze from the scene and looked a question.

I say it's the beatingest!

Leroy Key nodded. Worst yet. What you think, Brother Nathan?

Nathan thought, This is the repetition of history before our eyes. There comes no answer from philosophy, religion, morality. There is but one answer to a manifestation of brute strength; that is a manifestation of greater brute strength.

Aloud he said, Have we the strength?

That's as may be. Think so, Seneca?

Beyond him the silent Limber Jim scowled his half-breed scowl.

Key swallowed. Shall we put it to a vote? If we try now, and get whipped— That'd be the end.

Mister. The halting voice of the mighty Ohioan, A. R. Hill. There ain't no need to vote. Them roughs have really put it to us.

Get clubs, somebody said.

Anyhow we'll make a try for it. Come on, Brother Nathan.

Key, MacBean and Dreyfoos moved toward the North Gate. The struggle was done, it had been completed with incredible speed. The last of the raiders trailed triumphantly toward the South Side, waving trophies. Feists and hyenas loped ahead, bound to explore the haversacks they'd taken; Willie Collins and Pat Delaney strolled almost benignly in the rear. Willie was counting greenbacks, Delaney drinking from a bottle. A howling began on the South Side in the vicinity of the raiders' pavilion; there ensued a private tussle, men came crowding and pushing and punching, to see. A collection of obscene cards had been found in a pocket of one of the stolen jackets. They were of the sort vended by unscrupulous sutlers—made in Germany, it was said, and colored gaily. They depicted mass orgies in which men and women copulated on sofas, beds, tables, even on the floor. The ungodly had leered at them before, but all old cards were long since defaced or lost or handled into ruin; these were bright, they were new and trim; the boy who'd owned them crouched moaning at the end of Main Street, spitting out blood and splintered teeth. His fellows sat weeping or cursing, stripped to the hide.

Little groups of kindly intentioned prisoners assembled to do what they could, to offer sips of water, bits of corn pone. This was the most flagrant assault which had ever occurred, and affecting by far the greatest number, and was pursued with swiftness beyond imagination. The bulk of the helpless Yankees appeared stunned by it.

They were stunned further a moment later at the latest pronouncement of the prison superintendent. Almost simultaneously news was posted at both North and South Gates. A general wail ensued: Wirz said that no rations would be issued that day. He hinted that he might not issue any more rations until the prisoners had seen to it that no such disgraceful episodes would be repeated.

Puts it up to us with a vengeance, said Seneca.

Actually, Nathan told him, we would seem to have Wirz on our side.

Key started toward the deadline but MacBean pulled him back. Key, you got folks to go home to. I have none. Deadline's an infernal jumpy business, with all these trundle-bed soldiers so nervous on the trigger. He pushed fairly up to the scantling and was greeted by a gun muzzle from Station Number Eight. We need to speak to Captain Wirz, he called to the calico hat behind the gun.

He ain't here, Yyyank. Get off'n that deadline!

I'll get, but you get Wirz.

I'll ask the sergeant when he comes round. Get back, you. Hear me?

I hear you, but you get Captain Wirz.

They waited in staring sun for more than twenty minutes, but after a time Nathan believed that he heard the guard talking with someone on the path outside. They hoped for the best, they knew that spies were watching them, they prayed only that raiders, emboldened by their morning's feat, might not charge in mass attack upon Regulators or suspected Regulators before the ranks were filled. Presently the wicket in the North Gate squealed open and the plump face of Lieutenant Davis appeared.

Whah-ye!

We don't want you, Lieutenant. We want your boss. The three moved toward the wicket.

What you want to see him about? He's busy.

Tis important.

A matter of life and death, said Nathan Dreyfoos.

All of that, said Key.

Davis's puffy little eyes looked their alarm. I'll let the three of you into the enclosure here; but you better be sure it's important or the captain will make you smoke.

Course, said MacBean, settling his long shape in shade of the palisade— Course we're correct. Whole prison's a matter of life and death.

Death, mainly.

If we prevail, said Nathan, it will become a matter of life for some who otherwise would have died.

Blame you for a philosopher, Brother Nathan.

A very childish one.

They relaxed in the gift of shade. There was no real shade within the prison except in the best-constructed shebangs. Here, in this cubicle surrounding the North Gate, a fifteen-foot height of logs built a barrier against the scorch and would until the sun reached its zenith; in that same hour the western end of the cubicle would begin to furnish shade. Davis had gone, but he left one armed guard beside the outer gate. Suddenly this guard jumped aside almost guiltily as the outer wicket was jerked open. Henry Wirz tripped across the sill. He wore his calico waist with no collar—there was a naked collar-button showing below his Adam's apple—and the waist was wet with perspiration, and he bore his arm in its black sling. The three prisoners got up quickly and moved to meet the smaller man. He stood with thin hot face lifted toward them, beard stringy and damp, angry eyes jumping.

Captain Wirz, sir, said Leroy Key.

To me you come to beg rations? *Nein.* I have said it, it will be so: no rations you get today!

We're not here to beg for rations.

You I know not. Him—pointing to Nathan—I know not. You—to MacBean—I know. Speak it out once, you bad sergeant. *Was gibt's?* You want you should go in the stocks again?

Not so's you could notice it. What we want is clubs.

For why you should get clubs, God damn?

To handle those raiders.

Wirz swore in German, then in English. To the surprise of the others Nathan Dreyfoos began to speak laboriously in German. Almost no words of German had passed his lips in several years; still, there was the similarity to Yiddish, and he was getting on tolerably when Wirz interrupted him with a sharp gesture.

Parlez-vous français?

Oui, Monsieur le Capitaine.

The conversation was continued and concluded in French, at which Nathan was more proficient than Wirz. Still the linguistic barrier fenced them apart from the rest of mankind at this moment; Henry Wirz felt inferior when compelled to speak in English, as he was compelled to speak it through most of his waking hours. His inferiority begat an underlying resentment to sustain the heap of his other resentments. This was sensed by Nathan Dreyfoos, it was the reason he had attempted German.

Leroy Key, capable commander though he was, might not have obtained the promise of armament. Wirz would have been dyed in suspicion because of the Bloomington printer's essential American qualities, his essential Yankeeness. Seneca MacBean would not have persuaded Wirz to furnish clubs: already MacBean had tried to escape, he might be planning some new trick when he appeared with an artless request for Rebel coöperation.

But Dreyfoos was recognizable to the superintendent as a European whatever his nativity. Wirz held the ancient Teutonic-Swiss distrust of Jews; and as they talked he became hurtfully aware of the tall young man's culture; Nathan's fund of culture exceeded Wirz's obviously. Nevertheless this employment of French brought back student days, young days, better days. It suggested old Doctor Cordier and Bucheton and Jacques and Annette and Mimi and Louis Modave (young things, gone, some dead, Bucheton scorned but still representative of youth and freedom) and other boys and girls of the past who danced together and drank together and worked together and made love as in a careless mural depicting some opera. In the long ago, when Henry Wirz spoke chiefly in French, his arm had not pained him, it had not been pierced by hot iron and made into a draining hurt. Fate had not then compelled him to superintend the mess of muck and vagabonds which now he was called to boss. Each flowing nasal phrase, spoken and heard, was redolent of a past superior to this baking hour with sunshine flaring and hordes of human vultures to be detested for their dirtiness as Henry detested slum-dwellers because of their poverty.

Nathan spoke briefly but impressively of the Regulators. He pointed out that they were mainly non-commissioned officers, men accustomed to discharging responsibility. If given the help of Confederates they might conceivably bring about an orderly regime within the stockade which had not abided before. Prisoners existing in a city ruled by surly barbarians were assuredly less tractable than prisoners existing without the dread of robbery, kicks, strangulation: was that not plain to see? If the raiders were put down a better authority might prevail, and certain worries of Andersonville's supervisors would be lessened or even vanished. This made sense to Wirz, no matter what fright he had endured throughout the previous night. Promptly Nathan won the promise of clubs.

He won more than that. There had been fear that clubs might be torn from hands of those who wielded them, as happened so often in brawls. Therefore Nathan asked that each club be provided with a loop of hemp or rawhide, as in a policeman's billy club. Henry Wirz nodded and believed that he could furnish these thongs.

Time was of the essence. Wirz said that he would order a company of Reserves to the Yeomans' sawmill at once. The sawmill, though not now in operation, had spawned a large trash heap. Quantities of seasoned hardwood of odd sizes and lengths could be found there.

And additional rope, Nathan insisted. With which to tie our prisoners.

This I give you.

When it comes to that, said MacBean, where we going to put the bastards on trial?

Key requested, Might we use one of these gate cubicles for a place of detention, maybe a court room?

Was—?

Nathan explained in French. Again Wirz agreed on grounds of practicality. But he said that they must not take too long about the trial of their prisoners; they must be quick, efficient.

Got to be quick and efficient about the whole blame business.

They thanked Wirz for his coöperation and trusted secretly that no vagary would cause him to change his mind. They returned to the stockade to assemble squads of Regulators.

Had it not been for a broken grindstone, Ira Claffey might not have been forewarned of the encounter which was to take place, he would not have witnessed it.

It was share and share alike in these times of stringency: the grindstone at the Yeoman place had been broken beyond repair several months earlier, and in this week the big shining Scooper had appeared with a cart, to borrow the Claffey grindstone and sharpen Mrs. Barney Yeoman's hoes, knives, axes, other implements. Now he came driving to return the stone, and Jonas and Jem lifted it from the cart. In shadows of the implement shed Ira heard the deep-voiced conversation of the slaves, punctuated as always by their falsetto laughter. Scooper was guiding his mule down the lane when Ira walked out to see that the grindstone was undamaged and had been returned to its proper situation under the low roof built to shelter it.

Big doings, Mastah!

What say, Jonas?

With them Yankees. They going fight!

It came out that a party of soldiers had visited the Yeoman sawmill to seek for hardwood fragments in trash heaps, fragments which, according to information furnished by Scooper, were to be made into bludgeons. Scooper had sworn that this was true: he had seen it with his own eyes. No telling what those Yankees might do next. The soldiers were cutting the cudgels to size, and fastening a loop to each club.

He say all them Yankees set to kill each other today, Mastah.

Save us folks the trouble, said Jem with patriotic virtue.

Ira told the black men, I think Scooper must be mistaken. Do you get on with your rebuilding of that fence. He returned to his work in the shed, cataloguing seeds which had been dried from the choicest of the earlier vegetable crops. But Ira could not rid himself of the bizarre notion which the hands' conversation had evoked. At last he put his pencil down, locked the shed, and started deliberately toward the stockade. Tension of the night now lay over the sunburnt region as an implacable silence. Ira quickened his pace. When he had passed the star fort and looked back to see cannoneers at their posts he forced himself to go even faster. Sentry shacks loomed: two of the Georgia Reserves instead of one stood on every platform, and Ira identified officers ganged at those stations nearest the gates. At the post by the south corner the fat figure of Lieutenant Davis, wearing his familiar ragged straw hat, went toiling up the ladder. At the next post were two guards. Ira mounted to the platform and looked into the shrunken face of Floral Tebbs. A bearded Reserve with frightened eyes stood behind the boy.

What's ado, Flory?

Them prisoners, Mr. Claffey, sir. Just you look.

Beyond the marsh, where the slope piled steeply toward the north, the hillside had become a mosaic. This was a mosaic composed of Yankee faces by the thousands. The prisoners congregated, raw shoulder to raw shoulder, thin belly crowded above thin buttocks; if they were toys, and had been placed so by many busy children, they could not have been packed more securely. Above each mat of tangled hair was a portion of another countenance. Some way speedily, without plan or reckoning, those mobs had managed to sort themselves for observation. There was no hill, no bare mud to be seen, no she-

bangs—nothing but this studding of fierce small faces. Here was their
amphitheatre: they had found it, were employing it.

Denizens of the southern area had drawn back, squeezing perilously
near the deadline in a crescent; it was a crescent which lapped from
both ends into the battle array of the raiders. Ira had heard of raiders,
as who had not, yet he was unable to single the beasts out, designate
them as such. He saw only that the core of the throng—massing near
the conical tent close to South Street—was composed of men in prime,
men of stature, some wearing better garments than Ira wore. He
wondered who might dare to come against them. Then, picking their
way up the slope from creek and bridge and marsh, he saw a column
of men deploying with military precision into a wider rank, becoming
a sickle blade as they reached the top of the hill. He thrilled to observe
that many of these prisoners were of a stature comparable to the hoodlums at the summit.

There had been a tactical error on the part of the raiders, in their
not pushing ahead to resist volunteers approaching from the north.
The cat-walk and its approaches were narrow; they could have been
held indefinitely. Forces attempting to move by flanks through the
adjacent mire would have been bogged down in the most literal
fashion. But the raiders' supreme self-confidence was born justifiably
of a thousand successes speckled with a scant dust of failures. Their
assault on the West Virginians that morning had strengthened belief
in their own invulnerability.

Key instructed his lieutenants, Proceed with all caution, approach
in silence. Then, at the first stroke of encounter, drive with every
ounce you've got.

The raiders were expending precious breath on obscenities and
threats. Man for man, no matter how ample their diet of recent
months, they were inferior in condition to the Westerners now
breathing in their faces— Westerners who came without a word to say.
(No orders were cried. Their plan had been dinned into every man's
brain.) The raiders were soaked in pine-top, they'd caroused throughout the night into this day.

The front rank of the attacking force feinted toward the right, then
veered obliquely to the center where the most gigantic of their
enemies were grouped, and their supporting flanks veered accordingly.

Brother Nathan, said Seneca, I'll think of Clovis Tibbets on that
pony. I'll make like I was pulling him off of it.

(So was Michael Hoare now gathering strength to expend against
a neighborhood bully who had pounded a beloved younger playmate,
while little Mike Hoare sat up in bed, tremulous with scarlet fever,
and watched through a window. The bully moved away from town
before Mike was grown to a size which might have permitted revenge.
The fact that he had not revenged himself was bitterness for years.

. . . So was Bill Rowe about to smite an officer who had hounded him when first he joined the cavalry. . . . Dad Sanders told himself that here stood the rich Methodist who had extracted the life's savings of a gentle relative who sickened and died under the strain. . . . Key himself was lifting a club against a boss who had wounded him particularly. . . . Consciously, or deeply unperceived and yet present, the same notion instilled a flaming fury in the souls of other men, Egypt and Sergeant Goody and Ned Johnson alike. Tom Larkin said that here stood the neighbor who poisoned his dog; A. R. Hill was about to encounter the schoolmaster who had beaten Hill's tongue-tied chum with a strap. . . . Nathan Dreyfoos saw a squat Spaniard with the face of a Moor, he had watched this man stoning a puppy to death in a slum by the sea when he, Nathan, was too small to do more than scream; so grown with skill and power he could find the Malagüenan again. Ned Carrigan was hitting against death; death itself had been a monster ever since the day he killed unwittingly a grinning rock-faced pugilist with whom he had been drinking jolly beers two nights before. . . . Limber Jim, the sinewy man from the Sixty-seventh Illinois who looked like a Sioux, did not have to tax his imagination; this was well, since he had almost no imagination. He grunted within himself. He picked out the huge gingery shape of Willie Collins. Limber Jim knew that Willie Collins or one of his gang had killed his, Limber Jim's, brother.)

They wore the visors of desperation but they were not blinded by the visors. Their desperation rose from the knowledge that this was The Moment, they had primed for it, The Moment would not come again. If they failed in the first onslaught they would fail in the second. If they failed for an instant they would fail for all time. Their line would be broken, individuals would be wrenched from it—as witness, again, the West Virginians of that morning—and individually they would be tackled until they were stamped to ribbons on the ground or gargled their bloody way back down the hill. They thought of weaker comrades who were here now, they thought of the weak and disconsolate to be tossed into this place next month. The same mayhem which had ruled before would terrorize throughout a heartless future. There was only one thing to do; they said it again in their hearts: win quickly, win decisively, crush the head of every constrictor before its coils twisted in the fatal pulling.

Help one another to win, feel no obligation of pity or quarter. If a comrade staggered an enemy with his blow, and the raider came weaving toward you, and you had the split second to do it, you were to stagger him again. Forget decency and Christianity, because decency and Christianity themselves had absolved you of any necessity to observe them. The bite would be here, the kick in the crotch, the pressing out of the eyeball, the tearing of the nostrils, the champ of your teeth to rip the muscle from an arm before the enemy's fangs went into your own. Win this first battle, in truth it would be the last.

The issue was decided more speedily than any Regulator could have dreamed. Vaguely some sensed that the climax of their endeavor had not yet come: it would come only when the most formidable of the raiders were put to death. By the massing and delivering of disciplined strength they achieved a victory which might have been achieved long before, had they put themselves to the test.

They dealt first with the core and spine of the gangs; the extremities and supports fell magically from the huge leaders with each blow put down. To gallery gods like Ira Claffey and the Reserves, watching from the platforms, there was only a roaring tangle, with lines swaying for two or three minutes; then a breakage, a sloughing off of defenders.

In microcosm the assault had its history in the experience of Willie Collins. He stood grumbling and scornful, bleared hot gaze trying to single out the largest and most contemptible of the joskins, as he called them. It was a term of opprobrium: joskin meant a rube, an oaf, a bumpkin untried and without danger in him. So these joskins had approached, and even while Willie Collins was aiming his fists at the pressing serious individuals who dared to challenge, a club sang against the base of his skull, it made loose explosions of silver within his head. A youth from Wisconsin—one of the smaller agile Regulators, who had been ordered merely to prevent spectators from joining the raiders if he could— This seventeen-year-old countryman (a German, a young dairyman, a joskin if you please) had filtered his way behind Willie. He struck with the whole force of his young arms and body. Collins turned with a howl. Even as he turned a heel drove into the soft place above his left hip-bone and dented his bowels. Collins swung back, slamming out the hairy freckled rocks which were his fists. He mashed down two men, one was a man of his own gang, Willie was confused. A longer club hurtled from somewhere into his right eyesocket and half the world turned to blood. Even while he struck down two more men, others were diving beneath his fists. Another kick in his groin . . . the welter of his own people seemed turned against him, impeding him, they got in the way, they got in the way. His left eye observed the blank face of Limber Jim. Shrieking he tried to reach that face; but there was a small body diving between his legs, a larger body contending for the possession of his right leg. The next instant the horizon of close-riding figures descended with a jerk. Willie's head went back; he was down, more feet danced upon his face, more feet beat his belly with staccato blows. He entertained a ruling perplexity of Why, How now, This is not the way it should be, What am I doing on the ground? He is dancing on me. . . . The bastards fear me. Faith, I'm greater than they. Hammer stroke. A wooden stick forced past his spread lips and breaking off some of his teeth and wounding his tongue, he could taste the bitter sap in that piston of wood. Something was wrapping his left wrist. He tried to utter the rallying cry, O Yes, O Yes, as he had yelled it in New York; but the sole of a boot trod his left eye and closed it, another boot crushed into his stomach. His left arm was jerked out and to the left and twisted. A dozen hands were on his legs, prying—and now the right wrist— What was that, a rope? Wrench, wrench, wrench; the noose brought the two thick wrists together and wrapped them, no matter how he strained. Willie could only say, Agh, agh.

Sarsfield also was down. Patrick Delaney had flattened a row in front of him before his shin was cracked by a kick, and so he staggered; then whiteness burst inside his skull, he heard nothing more, he went into deepness. Many raiders began to break and run.

Flying in appalled retreat was the bowlegged figure of Edward Blamey. The favorite weapon which he had fetched with him when he came to subsist with Willie Collins, in the spring: he had it still, he'd tried to use it to advantage. But an Ohio quarryman rose in front of him, and Edward Blamey could not resist a man of such size. He turned and ran. He fell into a shallow well; the next thing he knew, people were dragging him out and tying him. One of them damn sailors, he heard someone crowing. It was an error understandable. Edward Blamey had long since thrown away his cavalry rags and was garbed in stolen navy blouse and bell-bottomed trousers. Now, what of The Wrath To Come?

Hangers-on went skulking toward the marsh; but people who might have sheltered them before out of terror of their masters were now shrieking, Here's one, that little bastard, went down that way. Throngs of lightweight Regulators spread in successful pursuit.

It was an object lesson for all time; yet man might never learn that a wickedness must be singled out and struck if it is to be done away with. Man would keep on equivocating, searching himself for a sore. He would declare to internal rottenness here and there, would declare that there was no concentration of sin among the enemy merely because he had discovered a wrong within his own structure. The lesson was reiterated during those intense minutes; yet it would be ignored and forgotten. The pulsing organs of raider vitality were separated from their body abruptly. People saw that the body could not survive. In bruised awe they offered thanks to their Spook of battles. Forty or fifty chief offenders were tied and dragged toward the gate. A hundred more could be hunted down and singled for trial during the afternoon and day to follow.

Twas easy, someone gasped later to Seneca MacBean.

MacBean sponged at a flap of skin torn from his stubbly cheek, and grinned crookedly. No, mister, twasn't easy. But if the world ever saw concerted action it witnessed it right here today.

XXX

The Claffeys sat upon the gallery in rocking chairs moved out into the dusk when hot rain stopped and the sky dried slightly and pale stars appeared. There was a boon in that the wind blew from the southwest for a time. Wind came lightly but with persistence, and kept the prison's smell away as if the wind were a strong bold hand held steadily at arm's length, palm outward, restraining the stockade and that murmur more apparent at night than in the day.

Lucy held a mended blue fan which had been a prize won for accomplishment in ball room deportment when she attended the Institute, and her father was armed with a Macon newspaper with which he might fan himself; but it was unnecessary to employ these fans more than languidly until the wind changed.

It changed, it shifted to the east, then bore farther from the north. Smell walked the trees in a cloud and swept across the open veranda among short squared primitive posts which supported the upper gallery. Now the fans switched steadily.

Poppy, shouldn't I have the wenches make a smudge?

It all depends. Whether you wish to be smoke-dried or whether you wish to breathe—this.

Reckon I'd rather have smoke in my eyes, said Lucy with a nervous giggle. She lifted a copper camel-bell which Uncle Felton had brought from Egypt before she could remember, and rang it. She waited, rang again, waited, rang, rang, rang.

From loneliness at the far end of the gallery Veronica called a warning in her weak dried voice. I just got them to sleep, she complained.

Mother, I'm merely summoning the wenches.

But you'll wake the children.

Ninny came shuffling. Lucy sighed, it would profit nothing to upbraid Ninny for tardiness, Ninny would pretend that her feelings were hurt because the young mistress did not recognize her deafness and excuse her because of it.

Do you make a smudge, Ninny.

Yas'm. In that old kettle?

Did Jonas cut fresh evergreens today as I bid him?

Yas'm.

Wet the boughs thoroughly, dip them in water before you pile them on the coals. And do you put the kettle over there, Ninny, this side the jonquil bed, for the smoke to reach us.

Presently two dark figures lurked in the gloom, the glow of fresh coals went aloft, Ninny and Pet were lined against the glow. Each was a sorceress, you could imagine that they assembled ingredients for a potion.

Round about the cauldron go, said Ira. *Gall of goat and slips of yew sliver'd in the moon's eclipse, nose of Turk and Tartar's lips.* He left off quoting Macbeth abruptly as he realized that the next was *finger of birth-strangled babe,* and neither he nor Lucy cared to mention babes, birth-strangled or otherwise. Wet greenery was pressed into the kettle, spice of cedar swept the Claffeys. They waved the thickest smoke away but still it was wreathing close, protecting them, building a wall to keep out Andersonville. The black women went away.

Poppy, I heard Mrs. Yeoman's Scooper talking with our hands.

And?

He was telling them that the smell reaches all the way to Aunt Ella May Piggott's place when wind is right.

When the wind is wrong, Lucy.

Her laugh a phantom. Ah, certainly. When the wind is wrong.

Ira measured distances in his mind. At least two miles.

All of that. Well.

Smell fought to get through the aromatic cedar. Sometimes it wormed past the clouded drift, sometimes it accompanied the smoke, riding on top of it, crawling beneath slyly. The smell was crafty, it found a way . . . wall of smoke was rifted, leaky. Smell said, Do not forget *me.* Do not forget *us. I* will not—*we* will not—permit you to forget.

Poppy, is it— Is it the Dead?

Partially, I suppose. Although they're so far in the other direction. But mostly the marsh and its filth, and the Yankees themselves.

How many have died by now?

Thousands, tis said.

I overheard you speaking with Uncle Dato, Poppy.

Ah, I regret that.

· About—the hogs— In the cemetery—

Such things are bound to happen. I mean—when burials are so shallowly and carelessly made. In any event, more earth is used now. They're—deeper. Lucy, shall we speak of other matters?

Mean little drafts, guerrilla breezes, they hovered close to the ground, went aloft suddenly, took smoke high, reduced it to no value. Ira went down and moved the hot kettle with a stick, shifting it into a position he thought more favorable. Soon the wind worked capriciously once more, Andersonville was upon the gallery, the gallery was within the stockade.

Lucy strangled. We must go into the house, Poppy. Oh, this is the worst yet! And close all windows tightly.

Daughter, it's too blamed hot!

Yes, yes— Poppy! I've just recollected: I've still some Balm of a Thousand Flowers. I'll go fetch.

Her limp-skirted figure fluttered away against the gleam of one low lamp inside and Ira heard her speeding on the stairs. He got up heavily and pushed through the heat and smoke and night and smell, making his way to Veronica, hoping that a share of smoke traveled to her thickly enough to do some good. She too was in a rocking chair, but she sat bolt upright, she did not rock, the claws of her hands were bent tight under the old silk shawl. She ate very little nowadays. She must have raised her eyes to look at Ira although she did not move her head. She whispered, At least that youngun is not clattering her bell.

Of course not, my dear.

See that you walk with care. This old gallery pounds so.

Certainly. I came to see if the cedar smoke reaches you.

Veronica drew a long breath with intense and lingering satisfaction. I like it, Ira.

He said brightly, So do I. Evergreen smoke is one of the pleasantest things. Somehow it causes one to think of holidays and good times, does it not?

She said, Noooo, said it softly and drawn out like the plaint of some animal. Not the evergreen smoke, Ira. The other. The Yellow Smell.

He was cast, cast in his shabby rough but dignified clothing, he was metal poured and cooled. His body was a portion of the statue that he made inside his garb. The spirit which dwelt in that body was molded also (might it ever again walk abroad, witness beauty and thrill to suffocation to it, be proud, be generous, might it know the fierce satisfaction of suffering?) and the spirit was the skeletal structure which a great and awful Molder had strung together to hold his illusion together; so by some accident in a foundry the original skeleton was part of the finished bronze.

Not solely a statue . . . he was a group. He was Laocoön with serpents wrapping him.

Yellow smell, my dear? Smell has no color. He said it because silence knocked at his ears—this nearer silence, separated by leagues from the crooning of the stockade.

I like it. It's Them.

She said again, They smell because it hurts Them. So. I want Them to be hurt. A chuckle crawled beneath the stilted calm of her tone.

Why? Oh, why? And he was not certain whether he spoke the scream of query aloud or whether it rose only within him, and was unvoiced; yet she found question or answer to his communication as often she had found them when sane.

They killed Moses.

My dear. It's a war. People are—

They killed Sutherland.

Veronica, you hear me? People are killed in wars. They take risks. It—it finds them—

Killed my Badger—

Hush up, you— You idiot! You idiot woman! Didn't you yourself just insist that the children were safe, safe asleep upstairs, I shouldn't walk heavily on this gallery? You know they're there— They're asleep upstairs! You said so—

O smell. Well he knew it, he had known it longer than anyone else. He found it when the first cross-bred vines tangled under a fence and dragged their rotting fruit shaped like skulls, and he sent a slave to rid the region of their presence. He'd smelled it—unidentified, unticketed but still noticed—in the long ago when he and his daughter journeyed to their plantation from the incompletely fenced area and he wondered: was it a dog, was it a worried cat, what was the nuisance which lay gassy?

Course they're asleep.

She agreed to this austerely and did not seem to be aware that he had named her an idiot; or, if she were aware of it, did not resent it.

Ira knew for the first time that there were two notions and knowledges claiming Veronica's belief simultaneously. There was no rhyme or reason to this. Veronica was a youngish mother still, of child-bearing age, haughtily maternal. She owned a troop of boy-and-girl children possibly all of the same size. This unseen litter she tended with selfish devotion. They were dead but they were alive, she saw that they were fed but offered no bottles or breasts or mugs or spoonfuls; they wailed when they were sick and Veronica soothed them, changed their napkins, did the nursing stint herself, would not let old Ruth do it if old Ruth were about.

And, in identical moments and treading in a quite different avenue of fancy, she was the bereaved lioness whose cubs had been slaughtered . . . yet crueler far than a lioness, not only willing to perform more slaughter in revenge but willing—nay, eager—to brood on an awfulness and call it a Love.

She tittered about it. She said again, I like it. It's Them. Surely it must hurt Them when They smell like that.

Some of this she spoke aloud . . . the rest seethed inside her and only bubbled out in laughter.

Lucy was close, Lucy stood beside her father and her skirts were brushing him. He stumbled away and bruised his shoulder hard upon the nearest column; this alone kept him from falling off the gallery onto plants and rocks beneath—because he could not see, the night loomed black as a student's slate, he could not see through it. Lucy held a bowl in which she'd mixed her Balm of a Thousand Flowers cologne with water. In this bowl three of her small pocket handkerchiefs were saturated and should be wrung out: one for her mother, one for herself, one for Ira. They had done this a few other times when the stink overwhelmed them. Lucy thought that her cologne was all gone, used up, and then she remembered another older bottle in her cupboard with a small quantity of cologne remaining in it. They might make masks through which to breathe and thus be able to remain on the porch in comparative coolness. The night was so stifling. In the house it would be worse.

This was the first occasion when Veronica rejected the aid, the boon, the ministration.

Mother, Lucy insisted again, but the woman waved her off.

Tis a pleasing scent. Tis—attar—

Surely it is pleasing. But let me spread the cloth over your face. See—it's all wet—and cool—

With dread strength her mother pushed the hand away. My dear young lady! Don't be insistent. Don't be impudent—

Mother—

Gifts should never be forced by the giver! Mind, now. I worked it once in cross-stitch. Twas something like that. Twas a motto—

But, Mother, if you insist on breathing that noxious scent you'll be ill. Cousin Harry warned by letter that the very air must be laden with miasma. And—and the effluvia of so many who are sick—

Dying, said Veronica. Dead. Better dead.

Her thin iron hand and arm swept up and out, hurling the bowl from Lucy's clutch. It was a heavy vessel, not fragile, it did not break immediately. There came a loud splash on the gallery's floor, then no sound but the bowl's rolling as it made small thunder across the hollow boards (Ira thought of skulls again, he thought of a skull rolling) and then for a portion of time, the part of a second, there was silence as the bowl went through space; then it struck the ornamental ridge of stones bordering a flower bed. The smash said, This is termination. Something definite has happened. Something is over and done with.

Balm of a Thousand Flowers rose up to vie with the stockade's smell and the faint odor of charred cedar lingering, to be defeated first by the other, and soon they were both defeated by the one. Andersonville towered and struck, almost you could see it in the night, it slapped as the hand of Veronica had slapped the bowl gone to atoms.

Lucy found her father and sank her head against his arm. Veronica Claffey sat motionless, no longer giving forth her laugh. That was one kindness in a life grown dank otherwise.

Lucy whispered, Question Forty-two.

Ah, in the Shorter Catechism? You learned it all so well. You were a good child, you've always been a good child.

The sum of the ten commandments is, To love the Lord our God with all our heart, with all our soul, with all our strength, and with all our mind; and our neighbor as ourselves. Poppy, I did. I tried to. With emphasis upon the neighbor part—

My dear, in loving thy neighbor you are also loving God. That's apparent within the Scriptures. And outside them.

I tell you, I tried!

Good child.

Don't call me blithe spirit, Poppy. I'll never be again.

Yes, yes, you'll—

Never! Poppy, I want to— I want to *damn God.*

Oh, poor Lucy. Poor—

What did you do, to deserve this? What did I do? What did *she* do? Nothing at all, my dear. It's—but a misery—

Is not all life, as it's come to us? Oh, dear God, let me damn God! Let me damn Him and damn Him and damn Him—

Now the weeping came with a puppy's cry, and Ira stood holding the girl as she sagged. Behind them Veronica told Lucy to use caution. Never waken little Arwood, she said. Troubled with colic as he is.

XXXI

Sometimes Our Dear Lord (or was it Our Lady?) let Father Peter Whelan dream, and did not cause him to repeat endlessly in ritual the offices he managed through waking hours. Sometimes Our Dear Lord made him a boy again, running through dim beech woods in County Meath. Our Dear Lord allowed him to go for an evening stroll, as when he was in the seminary, and he heard cosy laughter of Terry Shanahan ahead of him and the solemn grunt of red-faced John Gilligan waddling black-cassocked close behind, the solemn voice of John Gilligan declaring that primroses were worldly objects and so not to be admired, since admiration might lead to worship, and thus would be committed a transgression of the soul if not of the flesh. Sometimes. Only sometimes.

Father Peter Whelan was a very old man, aging a year each day he served in Andersonville. He had come to Andersonville from Savannah on the sixteenth of June, bearing in his hand and in his intelligence the same Roman Ritual which Benedict the Fourteenth authorized nearly one hundred and forty years before. When he slept he was an effigy, except that no effigy wore so many facial lines, compressed into the texture of woven fabric, perhaps coarse linen, perhaps fine lace. When Father Whelan slept he seemed to be dead. There was the smallest possible respiration of his thin chest, his gray hands were folded across his body, he lay motionless upon his back, the wide thin firm lips did not twitch.

Only bright watery blue of his eyes made Father Whelan live when he opened his eyes; still, the prisoners never saw him asleep, they did not know that he went into death when he slept. When they saw him it was to observe him prowling without rest, papery under weight of an old umbrella with broken bows, an umbrella faded, mildewed, hit by the steady sun; but the umbrella became a symbol of strength which amounted to audacity in one so frail, so old.

Haley Ladden was dying, Haley knew that he was dying, his breath was a long hard rattle. Priest— Father. His imaginings twitched off to Dubuque and he named Father Whelan as Father Jackson whom he had known when he was a little boy.

No, no, me son. I'm Father Whelan.

Not—same priest—here—awhile back?

In May, me son? Twas Father Hamilton from Macon. I'm Father Whelan. Sip of this water now, me boy.

A surgeon would have said that Haley Ladden was close to total blindness from extravasation of blood as well as from fluid in the posterior parts of his eyes. A surgeon would have said, His ulcers have assumed a phagedenic appearance and extend over a large extent of surface, and present irritable, jagged, and everted edges, and are destroying the dead tissues down to the bone. Except that no surgeon had observed Haley Ladden because he had no friends to carry him to the gate for examination; and when Haley had been able to totter in that direction supported by his own limbs and canes he had not been able to get within fifty yards of the gate.

How old are you, me boy?

Don't know. Nnnnnnn. Sseventeen. . . .

And where was your home?

Dubuque . . . Ioway. . . .

And are you a Catholic, me boy?

Yehhhhh. . . .

Oremus. Domine Deus, qui per Apostolum tuum Jacobum locutus es: Infirmatur quis in vobis? Inducat presbyteros Ecclesiae, et orent super eum, ungentes eum oleo in nomine Domini—

Ernst Kamphoefner was dying, Ernst did not know that he was dying; instead he would be paroled, and his captain and the village grocer and a girl named Anna had just called on him to tell him so; they said, Pack your plunder, boy; home we go maybe tomorrow, and forget all about what happened to the Seventy-fourth Pennsylvania nearly a year ago—

Here, me son. Let me wipe your poor mouth; and taste the cup of cool water I bring you.

Ja. . . .

And what is your name, me poor lad? And where do you come from?

Anna, she was by me. The parole I got now. *Ja,* I go home. Ernst Kamphoefner writhed and thought that he was standing, thought that he was walking off between Anna and Captain Dromke; but he was only lifting his head a trifle; more of the evil liquid poured from his mouth; and a surgeon would have said— What would a surgeon have said?

Ah, I know that you're a good Catholic, me brave boy, for you've got the Holy Cross around your neck. Taste another sip of the water I've brought you.

Ja. . . .

Tattered umbrella building its shade upon them, the bone handle of it thrust into oozing ground. *Et oratio fidei salvabit infirmum, et*

*alleviabit eum Dominus: et si in peccatis sit, remittentur ei: cura,
quaesumus. Redemptor noster—*

A surgeon would have said, In cases of ulceration of the mucous
membrane of the intestinal canal, the fibrous element of the blood is
increased. Bill Skelly would have said, Ah, I fear to die, Father, for
I've sinned— How I've sinned— But Bill Skelly could not speak; only
his great swollen eyes could roll wildly, watching the seamed austere
but gentle face pushing close above. *Gratia Sancti Spiritus languores
istius infirmi, ejusque sana vulnera, et dimitte peccata, atque dolores
cunctos mentis et corporis ab eo expelle—*

Eyes, ears, nostrils, mouth, hands, feet. The smell of oil upon the
cotton, little wads going into the bashed tin cup, the dab of corn
bread rubbed upon Father Whelan's thumb; fire reaching for these
remnants once Father Whelan was finished with them. Oh, were other
deeper more dangerous fires reaching for Tim and Jackie and Barney
and Olin and Fritz and Owen and the rest? He must hasten, he must
tread far and pray long, he must not let the flames sear the young pale
souls which had been caged within rotting ribs and horny skin, but
which would soon be freed. They must go shrived if they were to be
freed.

Violet stole hanging on the tall frame, that frame wasted by age and
by the giving out of unmeasured pity . . . sun coming through a split
in the umbrella's top to blaze upon the violet stole and try to fade it.
Et ne nos inducas in tentationem

Hoarse mumble of response made by Father Whelan himself, because the dying boy could not speak the words. *Sed libera nos a malo.*

Salvum fac servum tuum.

Mumble running down into a whisper. *Deus meus, sperantem in te.*

Some might have thought that the bishop should never have sent
so elderly a man to labor amid agonies, but to Peter Whelan this was
the accolade supreme: ardently he had dreamed of martyrdom, this
was martyrdom, it was a reward scarce to be expected while he remained upon Earth. He went about his tingling earnest creepings
nerved by bitterness of the task. He felt a pride; pride was sin, he
recognized this sin in himself, he was abject, he prayed with humility
again. *Refresh the soul which Thou hast created, that being bettered
by Thy chastisements, he may feel himself saved by Thy healing.*

Are you a Catholic, me son?

Mais oui.

Ah. And what might be your name?

Please. André Fromentin.

Ah, I've never the French to help you—the vernacular—and I pray
daily that the good bishop may see fit to send Father Clavereul from
Savannah, for he's French and could warm your soul with his speech,
me boy.

Please— *Monsieur le Curé.* We get exchange, *non?*

Now, me boy, concern yourself with affairs of the spirit, concern yourself with God.

But, you hear—? Those officers, of *la Confédération.* We get exchange, very quick now, *non?*

Me son, those are temporal affairs, I have no knowledge of them. Truly it's enough, and it's essential, that you heed only the word of God, the love and law of the Mother Church.

But, *Monsieur le—*

There were so many of them, too many of them. More and more Father Whelan found it necessary to employ the short form for Extreme Unction, the short form for the Apostolic Blessing. A demented man rambled in confession and recited all manner of lewdness, another demented youth begged to partake of Communion (it turned out that he was a Campbellite, not a Roman Catholic; that was the form of Communion he sought). Father Whelan turned his wet blue gaze toward the depot when, once out of the stockade, he set out on a tiring homeward march. Perhaps others would be sent to aid— Not him, he wanted no aid, he asked for none. But to aid those dear lads yonder, whose souls were crying for blessings, who might sputter and yell in pits and lakes of The Damned if the Rites were not available. *Ego, facultate mihi ab Apostolica Sede tributa, indulgentiam plenariam et remissionem omnium peccatorum tibi concedo, et benedico te.* Oh, let the poor child be strengthened to resist all temptations of the Devil and to die happily in the Lord! Eyes, ears, nostrils, mouth, hands, feet? Nay, no time for that—the gagging sounds in the throat, the eyeballs are glue— Quick swipe of oil on the forehead only, a hasty jumble, Latin falling over Latin with recklessness to beat the fiends, to exorcise them permanently. *Per istam sanctam Unctionem, indulgeat tibi Dominus quidquid deliquisti. Amen.* And now the boy is dead, but— kiss the Holy Cross— He died in the Lord, he died happily in the Lord!

Perform only the essentials, the skeleton rite established by Christ. Give the Sacrament without additional prayers ordained by the Church. It is a sadness but— Give it, give it— Quickly—

If Father Clavereul should be sent to help the prisoners Peter Whelan would kneel in thanks. There had been some talk of sending also Father John Kirby from Augusta. And— Ah, the Jesuit from over Mobile way, Father Hosannah— He spoke three or four languages, perhaps more. Perhaps in time Bishop Verot himself might appear; he had hinted as much; and with him might come the vicar-general, Father Dufan. These were a hope, they could be sought in prayer. They might never be secured but they could be prayed after.

O Lord, hear my prayer.

And let my cry come unto thee.

During those weeks when Father Whelan was on the point of taking up his burden and did take it up, Andersonville suffered the loss of another benignant influence and was afflicted with a baleful one. Lieutenant-Colonel Persons was relieved of his command: the creased spongy face of John Winder pushed above the Georgia horizon. It was an added cruelty that General Winder should arrive to assume personal control at the very moment when Alexander Persons had finally achieved some success in his long hunt for lumber. Rolling stock was at a premium but Persons possessed the grave stubborn spirit which does not recognize defeat. He knew but to apply and receive a rejection, make a new application, find it rejected or ignored, apply again. The first train which he won was composed of nine carloads of lumber, the second—weeks later—of six, the third held eight cars. Lumber was being unloaded from Persons' sixth train on the afternoon when General Winder and his little party descended upon the graveled platform of Anderson Station. Persons had gathered fifty-one carloads of lumber in all. Long yellow planks lay stacked in an orderly little city and sent up their fresh clean odor to vie with the stockade's efflux. Then disaster stamped down from a newly-arrived train, the meaty face came pressing.

As I remember it, Colonel Persons, you were the first officer to suggest that the hospital be taken out of the local stockade.

No, sir, that's scarcely correct. Captain Wirz came to me, urging the removal.

What was your reply?

I told him, sir, that I had no authority to effect the transfer.

And then you addressed a communication to me in Richmond?

Yes, sir, that is correct. I asked for permission to take the hospital outside.

Can you recall the reply?

As I recall it, General, the permission was denied.

I presume you have copies of the correspondence in your files, Colonel Persons?

Sir, I retain all copies as instructed.

If you chose to refresh your memory you would find that permission was most definitely denied. I don't forget things like this, God damn it!

The general choked with rage and walked up and down the platform for a time, muttering to himself; you could see his jowls twitching spasmodically, his face growing dark, then lightening gradually as a new thought came to him. He halted, turned, and crooked a finger at Persons, who moved forward in obedience to the silent summons but was consumed with a fury to match Winder's.

You acted on your own recognizance, didn't you? Did anyone try to persuade you to ignore the fact that I'd declined to give you permission for the removal? Did Wirz persuade you?

It would be incorrect, General, to say that he did. We were both of the same mind about it. When permission was refused or declined or however the general wishes to state it, Captain Wirz remonstrated with me.

What did you tell Captain Wirz?

I told him to proceed with the hospital's removal.

Upon whose authority, then?

I told Captain Wirz that I would take full responsibility.

Bare-faced disobedience! And, by God, you're positively smug about it!

Persons thought, still in a rage by no means blind— He thought, as a hundred other military men had thought, as a thousand civilians had thought while Winder served as provost-marshal— He thought, If you were my own age, sir! If you didn't have those dratted stars wreathed upon your collar! How I'd like to knot my fist and push it into your doughy phiz! How I'd like to stand up to you with a pistol!

He said, speaking with a pained deliberation which would have revealed to his intimates that he was very near to physical assault, age or no age, rank or no rank— It occurred to me, sir, that if the general were here in person, on the ground and possessed of firsthand evidence as to the necessities, the general would very likely revise his opinion. Since I held this belief, I gave Captain Wirz instructions accordingly. I repeat, sir, that I assume full responsibility.

Winder growled meaningly, The general is now here, he's on the ground, by Jesus Christ. I'm going to get you out of here so fast your head'll spin!

Persons said nothing, he dared not speak.

The entire system is being reorganized, d'you hear? I shall be in sole command of all prisons east of the Mississippi. That's General Cooper's plan, and it meets with Mr. Seddon's approval and with President Davis's approval, by God!

Persons' throat and mouth and lips were chalk. I have seen no orders from the I.G. to that effect, sir.

So you haven't. But it's in the offing, and I'm giving it to you directly from the horse's mouth, Colonel. Do you think for one moment that you field grade officers, supposedly occupied with your duties in the field, know everything that goes on in Richmond? In a pig's ass you do!

Respectfully, General Winder, I am bound to call your attention to the Article of War which states that superiors of every grade are forbidden to injure those under them by tyrannical or capricious conduct, or by abusive language. . . . I shall instruct an officer to extend to you and your party the courtesies of my post. Until I am relieved, sir. Persons saluted, ground his heel into the platform, walked away.

He was on the point of throwing up, he hoped that he could control his palpitating stomach until he was out of sight.

Winder bellowed after him, Very well, Colonel, the hospital's outside and it shall remain outside; we've no people to spare for the task of mopping up milk that other men have spilt! I'm here, I'm on the ground, but I tell you that I'll never set foot inside that damned stockade, I'll not sully my boots with Yankee scum!

His military family stood clustered fawningly behind him; Captain Peschau cluck-clucked his tongue, shook his head, and spoke in deprecation of Lieutenant-Colonel Persons to the others.

. . . Find himself commanding Fort Shit on Ass-hole Creek.

. . . Find himself a captain, you mean!

. . . Shouldn't be a bit surprised. Just look at old J.H.W. He's in a slather.

. . . Well, walk softly, Major.

. . . Soft as silk, Jack my boy.

Alex Persons had gone so far as to prepare plans for the barracks which he hoped to erect within the enclosure, working until all hours at night with one Lieutenant Wright of the Fifty-fifth who owned some engineering experience. Sid Winder would have been the logical officer for this task, but Persons knew better than to broach his plan to any of the Winders. With Wright he had labored to secure the maximum amount of effective shelter at a minimum expenditure of planks. So a master drawing had been made, and copies traced through impression paper. Reports were being drawn on the quantity of tools and labor available, some of the lumber had actually been carried as far as the North Gate. Persons strode, defeated and ill, past aromatic stacks of sawed pine. His hope, his accumulated treasure . . . now it would be stolen. He knew what would happen to the lumber after he was sent packing (and it did happen thus). Forty or fifty structures growing over the trampled hillsides, but not within Andersonville. No shelter for the prisoners, but offices and quarters for General Winder, Cousin Dick Winder—dear Cousin Dick!—and Sid Winder. A hospital for the guards, perhaps—they had nothing but tents, but better tents than the Yankees had. Perhaps more barracks for the officers of the Georgia Reserves. Sutlers' shacks— Reserves would floor their tents with precious boards, they would shade their canvas with more precious boards— Agh.

Lieutenant-Colonel Persons stumbled behind a tree and was sick in fact. Cold sweat stood out, his temples were pounding him to death. He halted at a nearby well with its leaky tub, washed his face, then went on to headquarters.

He didn't like Wirz, he didn't see how anyone could ever like Wirz; but he had grown to admire the sickly man's zeal. Every frenzied blundering attempt of Wirz at providing better facilities had met with Persons' approbation. Persons had loaned his best men to aid Wirz in the hospital's removal, in the shoring of the ugly stream. Lieutenant Wright himself had volunteered to supervise the stockade's extension. Paroled prisoners and black labor had done the trick, and would have done this trick of barracks-building if allowed to proceed. Alex Persons understood the whole truth at last. Henry Wirz was a frothing little ferret, a martinet of a repulsive sort, but at least his brain was oozing with ideas and some of the ideas were good ones. He was not impelled by humanitarian motives but by a desire for efficiency; had he been provided with the means he might have superintended a cleanly prison if a cruel one. Obviously he wished revenge, but at the same time he was given seriously to stewardship (his own version of stewardship).

General Winder wished to kill as many of the prisoners as he could. It was as simple as that.

Now he would kill them in increasing droves. Persons had seen those reports assembled with so much cursing and fussing. Wirz was always brandishing reports under his nose. He could not recall the exact figures, of course, but he did remember round numbers. The mean strength in March was about seventy-five hundred, the deaths about three hundred. Mean strength in April ten thousand, deaths six hundred. Mean strength in May fifteen thousand, deaths seven hundred. Morbidly he had asked Lieutenant Wright to count marked graves in the cemetery (there were believed to be many unmarked, because of the carelessness surrounding burial) and Wright had reported fifteen hundred and eighty-two marked graves. Alex Persons presumed that the mean strength of prisoners might rise as high as twenty-two or twenty-three thousand when figures for all of June were summed up; that would mean an additional twelve or thirteen hundred dead. What would be the value of prisoners' barracks in summer? Alex Persons was a Georgian; he knew very well what the value of shade would be. Once he had put a thermometer out in the June sun and the temperature was marked at one hundred and twenty-nine degrees Fahrenheit. In winter he had witnessed as much as twenty-two degrees of frost. The hospital would never have been removed from the stockade unless he, Persons, had exceeded his authority—had, in fact, deliberately disobeyed an opinion if not an order. And now he would be whipped away from this command, the barracks would never be built. Winder would toast Yankees throughout the summer as surely as if he held them impaled on a ramrod above a camp blaze. And, next winter— If it were an especially cold winter— And often in Georgia an especially cold winter followed an especially hot summer, as this was growing to be—

Lieutenant-Colonel Persons thought that his removal from this command would save his life, but it would rob him of an opportunity to save whatever dignity was left to the Confederate States Government insofar as Andersonville was concerned.

He performed courtesy chores for the general and his party, and then left the post in charge of Major Flournoy. His own head was on the chopping block, he had put it there himself, the blade would come down today, tomorrow, next day, it didn't matter.

He rode to the Claffey plantation, he hadn't the strength to walk there. He found Ira among peach trees, and Ira offered him a green peach.

That's all I'd need, Mr. Claffey, sir! Already I've been nauseated today. I mean that truly.

Ira looked at Persons' face, and picked up his implements promptly. We shall go into the house, Colonel. Why not lie awhile on the sofa in my library?

I fear I'd take permanent possession of it.

They did go into the house. Persons sat with a glass of blackberry wine.

One of my daughter's many triumphs, Colonel. And most settling to the stomach.

Persons sat hunched on the sofa. Soon he was pouring out the Winder story. I speak to you, sir, because I must speak to someone. You're a citizen, and I'd probably be churched if it came out that I was blabbing. But— Oh, devil take us. I'm going to be churched anyway!

He sipped the wine and said presently in a calmer tone, You have patience and tolerance, Mr. Claffey. And you have been a soldier.

I did know Mr. Davis, said Ira. It was during the Mexican War.

Twould mean nothing. That senile wretch has the President's ear, or so everybody says.

Will this change in command result in immediate deterioration of the local situation? Ira laughed dryly. You see, I'm trying to speak in military parlance.

Persons told him, biting off his words: It will mean this, sir. No individual of whatever rank will have the right to interfere with General John H. Winder in any shape, form or fashion. This order will give him absolute dominion and control over every Yankee prisoner east of the Mississippi—and of course that's where most of them are. The extended engagements now being fought above Atlanta and below Richmond— You can understand that, Mr. Claffey. The bulk of all Yanks captured by us during the progress of these campaigns, which campaigns I pray will be terminated by the success of our arms—

Amen, sir!

The bulk of the captured Yanks will land *here*. That old monster has planned it so, else he'd not be sending all these trainloads. I've exceeded my authority—he calls it bare-faced mutiny—and I shall be flogged or broken for it. So farewell, Mr. Claffey, and bless you for your hospitality.

He stood up, and Ira took his arm and walked with Persons to his horse.

Persons went but Winder stayed. And in his dedication Father Peter Whelan stayed. Peter Whelan dwelt sparely in an unpainted shack nearly a mile from Andersonville. His stove was a charred hollow stump at the door with a half-burned-out grating spread over the top and blackened stones to hold his little kettle in place. There was an open frieze of sky and pines showing around the edges of the roof where shakes had peeled; when rains came there fell steady leakage all along the ridgepole. There was no door, only a gaping doorway and a half of a cedar log for a step. Father Whelan's army blanket was spread over a compressed mound of pine straw and oak leaves. Rats came to visit him at night but they did not offer to bite; he'd hoped that the persuasion of Saint Francis of Assisi might rule these small creatures away from their natural savagery, and it did rule. Father Whelan wore a coat of faded blue linen, and this jacket was busy with lice throughout its seams. He tried to keep the lice in check, burning them off over a flame as he had seen the Yankees do, but it was only a gesture. There were too many hovels into which he must crawl, too many shivering skeletons beside whom he must crouch or even lie to hear their mutterings. Lice lived in every beard, every squirming tuft of hair. Father Hamilton had warned him about vermin after the Macon priest made his explorative visits during May. Indeed, said Father Hamilton, it's such a filthy place. The men huddled together, crawling with filth. Ah, hear me—I went in there wearing my white coat, and I'd not been there but one quarter of an hour at the most, when a guard kindly drew my attention to the condition of my coat. It was fairly alive. I had to take my coat off and leave it with the guard, and perform my religious duties in my shirt sleeves, the place was that filthy.

Och, the poor boys!

But you're an old man, Father Whelan. Do you think you can bear with it?

If Bishop Verot should send me— Ah, no. If Our Lord should send me—

I fear you'll but sicken and die.

Jesus, Mary and Joseph, may I sleep and rest in peace in your holy company.

Henry Wirz showed not the slightest objection to providing Peter Whelan with a pass to visit stockade or hospital as he chose; perhaps he might have objected had Whelan been a minister of the Protestant faith. (Thus far only one Protestant had evinced a desire to enter Andersonville to preach; and he was a die-hard Secessionist who preached Secession intermingled with Christianity, and came near to being thrown out bodily by the prisoners.) Henry Wirz placed the leaky shack at the priest's disposal and saw that rations were issued to him by the guards' commissary. Other than that Wirz did not seek the venerable Father's company; he felt that Whelan was disgusted if not appalled by boorish profanity, and since Captain Wirz might not conduct his superintendency of the prison without employing boorish and worse than boorish profanity—

The old priest. You got him a place to sleep, *ja?*

Yes sir, Captain. Sergeant Prather fixed him up tolerable in that old shanty over past the sawmill.

Every day inside among the Yankees he goes?

Yes sir, Captain. I just seen that old bumbershoot of his a-flapping along the road. Generally he gets inside by nine o'clock, don't come out till nigh onto dark.

The Church had a power greater than the power of all armies of all countries and all centuries put together; partly because its equipment and tendons and the valves of its bejeweled heart were disciplined, but mostly because it was the Church. (When Henry Wirz thought of the Church, which was seldom, he thought of a certain dark portal in Bern where columns of midgets and saints and beasts with gargoyle faces marched unendingly toward some sort of doom; medieval craftsmen had made them march that way, and so they frightened a little boy worse than the Bern bears.) Naked Christians stood with bellies exposed to tigers' claws in Rome, they quailed at a subterranean roar which came up from dens in Italica (then they saw a light shining). A prelate was squeezed into an iron basket, and to and fro he swung above the coals; and so many thousands of fires had cooked other flesh through the ages (yea, there were fires in Smithfield as well). The poisoned wine, the small hidden dagger, the ring with the needle's prick, the solemn walling-away . . . road of rocks bruised by sandaled feet or multitudes of feet which wore no sandals . . . heavy fall the pikes of Cromwell's men, down comes the axe. . . .

Father Whelan lay like that same effigy again in hot darkness, rude-shirted and bitten by bugs; he lay in temporary death; there was no one to see him unless saints peered through split shakes of the shed's roof. Sometimes he ran as a youth in beech woods again— There was a path which went to old Brigid Shachlin's house, and she would roll a hot potato from the ashes to thank him for the fish he'd fetched her—

The Church was greater than sun, moon and stars; because God had made these, but the Church was God's extension in time.

Quid petis ab Ecclesia Dei? Fidem. What to ask, indeed, of the Church of God? Faith, nothing but faith. *Was begehrst du von der Kirche Gottes? Den Glauben.* (As learned by Henry Wirz, as learned by the boy named Ernst Kamphoefner who now lay Exchanged in a ditch to the north— Why, his illusion had been correct; there was Exchange, he was now at the North with a vengeance.) *Que demandez-vous à l'Eglise de Dieu?* Respond, André Fromentin, and say *La foi.* Ah, if Father Hosannah came from Spring Hill College— the Jesuit school— He could speak many languages, not merely the Latin and the English and the Gaelic like Father Peter Whelan. He could Baptize any converted soldier of the polyglot Forty-eighth New York, and in the vernacular; he could Baptize a Bohemian. *Co žádáš od Církve Boží? Viru.* He could Baptize a Pole. *Czego żadasz od Kościola Bożego? Wiary.* The Church was taller than MacCillicuddy's Reeks, taller than the Rocky Mountains were said to be; because God made the mountains, and God founded the Church, and the Church was God's action extended from eternity into time. . . .

Pilgrims went barefoot to Lourdes, pilgrims crawled on stairways, they crawled up hard brown rocky hills to pray to the Virgin of Guadalupe, the *Virgen de la Cabeza.* Lame pilgrims crawled the gray-green rocky cone of Puig above Pollensa and planned to leave their crutches at the top. The servant girl wept in the Confessional. The beggar stole silver from the poor box and thus he became a thief instead of a beggar; but he could be forgiven, he could do a penance, not necessarily was he deeded to the flames. The sickly child in Seville—sickly, but with a face like a rock-rose—shivered and danced when *pasos* went swaying past, when drums rolled hard, when gypsies wailed from the balconies. *¿Qué pides de la Iglesia de Dios? La fe.* The Church was more majestic than blue sky or dun sky or black sky, for God had made the sky of whatever color. *Che cosa chiedi dalla Chiesa di Dio? La Fede.* The old Italian was trodden to death by a crowd pressing forward to see the Pope.

Through endless dusty muddy decades nuns went walking to beg, nuns lifted the heavy stinking sick, nuns put gruel into sagging mouths of the idiots they tended, nuns unwound the swelling abraiding bandage and put on the newer sweeter kinder bandage, nuns sponged the soiled buttocks, nuns changed the bed. The monsignor stole the orphans' money, the cardinal employed the assassin, the priest seduced the sniveling young lunatic put into his care. The Church was greater than any force or inhuman beauty dreamed or named by man or men because the Church was above these wickednesses. The knife of perfidy could not disembowel the Church, worms of jealousy could not gnaw its structure, the powder of hypocrisy could not explode to shatter its columns. *What doth faith bring thee to? Life everlasting.*

In the morning Father Peter Whelan arose again. He prayed. He washed himself at a wooden bucket, and shaved in cold water, and cooked a bowl of mush and another of peas; then he was fed sufficiently until night. He rid himself of as many lice as he could. He walked the long hard hot distance to Andersonville, walking in broken shoes which he himself had tried to sew together, walking under the ruin of his umbrella. *Salvum fac servum tuum.* Sun hurled itself against him, against the prisoners; the thick stench came to meet and claim. He would not come dragging out through that gate until dusk; another day would have passed, he would be a year older. Still he would serve.

XXXII

Johnny Ransom, the twenty-one-year-old from the Ninth Michigan Cavalry, scrawled his scrawl. The farther advanced the summer, the death rate increases, until they die off by scores. I walk around to see friends of a few days ago and am told, Dead. Men stand it nobly and are apparently ordinarily well, when all at once they go. Like a horse, that will stand up until he drops dead. . . . Was ever before in this world anything so terrible happening? Many entirely naked. . . . Sores afflict us now, and The Lord only knows what next. Scurvy and scurvy sores, dropsy, not the least thing to eat that can be called fit for any one, much less a sick man, water that to drink is poison, no shelter. . . .

He knew whereof he wrote when it came to scurvy. Johnny Ransom was barely able to walk; he had been unable to participate in the raider fight however much he applauded the Regulators.

He wrote: A new prisoner fainted away on his entrance to Andersonville and is now crazy, a raving maniac. That is how our condition affected him. My pants are the worse for wear from repeated washings, my shirt sleeveless and feet stockingless; have a red cap without any front piece; shoes by some hocus-pocus are not mates, one considerable larger than the other. Wonder what they would think if I should suddenly appear on the streets in Jackson in this garb. Would be a circus; side show and all. The Glorious Fourth of July. How shall we celebrate? Know of no way except to pound on the bake tin, which I shall do.

In fact it was the Glorious Fourth of July, and raiders knelt in subjugation. Solemnly the bent scurvy-racked Johnny Ransom beat upon his bake tin.

He wrote: The men taken outside yesterday are under rebel guard and will be punished. The men are thoroughly aroused, and now that the matter has been taken in hand, it will be followed up to the letter. Other arrests are being made today, and occasionally a big fight. Little Terry, whom they could not find yesterday, was today taken. Fought like a little tiger, but had to go. Limber Jim is a brick, and should be made a Major General if he ever reaches our lines. . . . The writer hereof does no fighting, being on the sick list. The excite-

ment of looking on is almost too much for me. Can hardly arrest the
big graybacks crawling around.

John Ransom was loved and tended by a mighty Indian from Minnesota named Baptiste, called Bateese by all. You get well soon, said
Bateese. He brought to Johnny the potato parings which his industry
had purchased. Like Seneca MacBean the Indian conducted a laundry
of sorts, and said that he had no time to fight, must wash. But he
would grunt his approval when he saw the worst of the raiders suspended by ropes.

The young diarist traced his words with slow devotion: Have taken
to rubbing my limbs . . . badly swollen. One of my teeth came out
a few days ago, and all are loose. Mouth very sore. Bateese says, We
get away yet. Works around and is always busy. If any news, he
merely listens and doesn't say a word. Even he is in poor health, but
never mentions it. An acquaintance of his says he own a good farm in
Minnesota. Asked him if he was married—says: Oh, yes. Any children?
Oh, yes. . . . Is very different from Indians in general. Some of them
here are despisable cowards—worse than the negro. Probably one
hundred negroes are here. Not so tough as the whites.

Stub pencil fell from weakened fingers, the hurting head came forward and lay on Johnny Ransom's arm; Johnny dreamed of the Pepys
whom he had read avidly and strove to emulate. He dreamed that he
would survive agonies to come, and in some fine fair future hour
would journey through that gate. His diary, his precious stained
scrubby notebooks saying *Ledger* and *Day Book* and *Cash Receipts*
and *Pickell & Co.*— These would accompany him.

He stood in the office of a publisher, the publisher was portly and
sagacious. What cash down payment would it be necessary for us to
put forth, Mr. Ransom, in order to secure the highly estimable privilege of printing your remarkable diary? By Heaven, young man,
what a ghastly experience you have passed through—and yet, memorable, memorable indeed. And to think that you are one of the few
survivors! Yet the vast American public should no longer be denied
the cultural advantage which will redound and we are prepared to lay
a goodly sum on the line, Mr. Ransom, a goodly sum.

The publisher toyed with his thick gold watch chain, the fraternal
emblem dangling there was diamond-encrusted. So if you would
venture to suggest an appropriate sum, to serve as binder for our
agreement—?

Frankly, sir, I'd thought in terms of one thousand dollars.

One thousand dollars? Perfectly preposterous, young man, pre-
*poster*rrruss!

But, sir, I—

It would amount to an insult to my professional integrity, Mr.
Ransom! A thousand dollars? Humph, I'll pay you a hundred.

But, sir, one hundred dollars—

I didn't mean one hundred dollars! I meant one hundred *thousand* dollars! Beamingly the publisher opened his desk, scratched around here and there, and then began to toss small bags filled with gold coins, to toss them at John Ransom. John dodged and ducked, the plummets fell faster, one struck him in the eye and he yelled with the grief of it. A horse-fly had bitten him on the right eyelid. He sat awake and scorching in the dry bath of the shebang. Bateese came near to feel the back of Johnny's neck, to feel fever there, to say, I bring water.

July 5, wrote the young man a day later. Court is in session outside and raiders being tried by our own men. Wirtz—

(Never could he spell this name correctly.)

—Has done one good thing, but it's a question whether he is entitled to any credit, as he had to be threatened with a break before he would assist us. Rations again today. I am quite bad off with my diseases, but still there are so many thousands so much worse off that I do not complain much, or try not to however.

Boiling hot, camp reeking with filth . . . men dying off. . . . Have more mementoes than I can carry, from those who have died, to be given to their friends at home. At least a dozen have given me letters, pictures &c., to take North. Hope I shan't have to turn them over to some one else. . . . Rebel visitors . . . look at us from a distance. It is said the stench keeps all away who have no business here and can keep away.

(All except Ira Claffey, who appeared on a sentry platform daily. Guards begged tobacco from him, he tried to remember to carry a plug at all times; though often he would forget, he used tobacco so rarely himself. He looked down and saw Newgate, Bedlam, and camps where he had heard that Spanish torturers herded the rebellious in colonies of New Spain. He watched the pen where Andy Jackson had suffered and sickened when he was a boy, when the spunky Andrew refused to clean a British officer's boots. He observed the misery of Seminoles, saw Osceola dying in filth and stony pride. Here was an inclusion of every indignity and deprivation which a captor might visit upon those he'd shackled. Shackles? So identified: Ira saw the chain gangs dragging as he walked back to his plantation. He marvelled how Henry Wirz could sleep at night, he did not know that often Henry Wirz never slept.)

At the end of the week, first decisions of the court trying the raiders were written out on a sheet torn from the manifold order book (captured: a Federal manifold order book) which had been donated by Wirz for judicial purposes. This paper was posted upon the South Gate. Many crowded there to read it; the news spread far within minutes, and was the signal for congratulatory hullabaloo.

Willie Collins, Patrick Delaney, John Sarsfield, Charles Curtis and
the sailors Munn and Rickson had been sentenced to be hanged by
the neck until dead. Seventeen other men were sentenced to floggings,
buckings and to the stocks or chain gang for various terms.

The court's deliberations were still proceeding when Henry Wirz
sent for Leroy Key and Seneca MacBean. The two were conveyed to
his office under guard.

The Gate pen I got to have back!

Captain, you told us we could have it to keep our prisoners in,
to use for the trial—

Ja, how many days you have it now?

Key still objected, MacBean said nothing. Seneca had deplored the
leisurely garrulous aspect of the trial; he thought that it was a mistake
to lean over backward in selecting a court of thirteen sergeants, all
of whom were recent arrivals at Andersonville. He supposed that this
was a weakness inherent in American institutions; he called it creaky
justice. It had worked to the Nation's detriment many times before,
and no doubt would until the end of time. Those new-come sergeants
had no true conception of what occurred within the stockade during
raider-ridden months. They had but academic secondhand knowledge
of the fear which had gripped, hands which had gripped, the rup-
turings and burstings and fracturings so commonplace. MacBean
would have been perfectly willing to place any and all of the captured
roughs before the muzzles of a firing squad. He would have been willing, if not eager, to stand with that squad. But the dubious chimera
of fair play fogged the scene. Cogitations and ramblings of witnesses
and counsels alike had long since passed the point of practicality.

You God damn Yankees got lead in your ass, Wirz was screaming.
All day you take to tell one man you hang him, one more day you
take to tell one more man! Maybe a year you take for the rest, hah?
Gott, I must use my gate. Those damn prisoners I put back Inside!

Wirz granted but an hour's grace, and said that he would turn the
remaining prisoners back into the stockade, using bayonets if necessary. The Illinoisans were dismissed with a few more execrations, but
MacBean lingered, even when a guard jerked at his sleeve.

You go when I tell you, you bad sergeant! *Oder* you also I put in
the stocks!

Captain, one thing: we've got to have some wood. Planks, timbers,
plenty of ropes—

For why should I give you those things, God damn?

Can't hang the guilty folks on thin air. We can't make a gallows out
of our shebang poles.

All you damn Yankees thirst for blood!

MacBean stood grinning with saturnine calm, and let Wirz brandish
his fist until the arm tired and the fist fell. He saw fierce darting pain

in the captain's face, and was annoyed to find himself pitying Wirz. Resolutely he put the pity down.

Going to be a good fellow, Captain, and give us a nice sound gallows? We got hundreds of qualified carpenters who'd be willing to work without pay—

He won the promise of adequate materials for the execution, to be delivered—on loan, not as a gift—within the stockade on Monday morning. Wirz had shrieked that the hanging should occur the very next day. MacBean pointed out that the next day was Sunday, and thousands of prisoners might object to a sextuple execution on the Sabbath. It wouldn't matter to him, he said.

But you might get a riot, Captain.

At that dread word the superintendent winced and agreed that Monday would be best. MacBean went back to the cubicle, provoking guards to rage by his sauntering, and found that the six condemned hooligans had been placed in stocks to await their death. Key adjourned court permanently. The seventeen men already sentenced were herded off to punishment; but more than a hundred others still sat with bound hands (the feet of the more recalcitrant were also bound).

Can't turn them back inside, MacBean told Key, without taking off those ties. They'd be torn to death instanter.

The innocent along with the guilty?

Hells bells, they're all guilty.

Word of the intended repatriation of untried, unconvicted raiders had seeped into the pen; prisoners were roaring. Many, who had been reluctant to assist the Regulators until tide of battle turned in their favor, were now vociferous in declaring their hatred of the accused. They brandished cudgels, declared that they would pound the accused to a pulp the moment they appeared.

A hasty trip through the wicket convinced Key that the danger was real and not fancied. He sent another appeal to Wirz but it fell upon deaf ears. Several squads of guards with fixed bayonets entered the enclosure through its outer gate, and Key shrugged hopelessly.

I don't like it, Seneca.

Don't like it too well myself, but what's a feller to do? Let's you and I haste back inside for keeps.

There was not time to marshal the Regulators. They were scattered over the entire stockade, and had it been possible to marshal them, nothing could have resulted except the burden of perpetual guarding and tending. Swarms of the furious came milling as Key and MacBean stepped through the narrow portal.

Make them run the gantlet, said MacBean in inspiration.

This notion was accepted with roaring enthusiasm. To the end of his life Seneca would believe sincerely that he had saved many lives in this way, although what was the purpose in saving lives such as these? It was apparent that when those hated men were shoved individually through the door they would be mobbed as fast as they appeared. . . . A gantlet was something else: it appealed to a sporting instinct however savage. It suggested in its very form an Indian tradition that if a man managed to flee under a lengthy rain of blows, and survived them, he would achieve to some asylum.

Before the first unhappy New Yorker was shoved through the wicket, a vengeful population had formed a lane for the man's reception. Hundreds of others rushed to extend the course of punishment. The first New Yorker through the gate was an undersized long-armed man called Monk Galloway, ticketed appropriately because of the length of his dangling arms, the flatness of his bald dome, the jut of jaw and scrolling of face. He had trailed with the Roach Guards through a number of street brawls. He knew Willie Collins by sight, if Willie did not know him, before either of them ever heard of Andersonville. Monk was afraid of Willie, and thus had joined the gang captained by Curtis. He was not large, but a dangerous fighter: a man who delighted in cries and blanchings of his victims; then his eyes shone hot, his breath puffed short, spasmodic. Had he come to trial, Monk Galloway might not have been hanged but would have been condemned to a chain gang.

A guard's weapon prodded him, he stepped across the bottom plank. Immediately someone kicked him in the thigh; a club was swung at his head, the blow missed. Holding arms lifted and bent for protection he was propelled down the line by a succession of swats and punches. He fell beneath howls and punishment, leaped up and closed in a tussle with the nearest men. A club snapped against his right ear, already corrugated with scars of old feuds; when he was torn out of this grip and hammered on to the next, he bled at ears and at the nose, his eyes protruded with gleaming fear of death. Any individual of the herd assailing him, he felt that he could have handled alone—in many cases two or three of them together. But neither were they now fellow prisoners nor a flock of bleating creatures to be snapped at by wolves of his species. They were turned into gesticulating Indians, cannibals. They could have been weaker than cats; still the blows would have fallen, there were too many of them.

A new chorus of shouts rang at the gate, another and larger man was hustled. His name was Myles Crickland, his home had been a lumber camp in Michigan. He'd never stolen so much as a dime, and never whipped a smaller man for gain, until he came to Andersonville. But while being shipped he had fallen in with John Sarsfield. Crickland had not wished to starve any more than Edward Blamey wished to starve: he lent size and ferocity to the Sarsfield cause. The same prisoner who'd aimed the initial cudgel stroke at Galloway now

whirled his club at the target of the Michigander's head; this time
the blow did not miss. The dazed lumberman faltered in a blind circle, his weight carried him completely through one pouncing screaming line before he fell. He could have been pounded to death then
and there, but another raider was forced into the arena, attention was
distracted. Crickland fell to his knees, fell further. His length stretched
across the ground, his shoulders shook as he blubbered. Three contorted youths stood above him, alternately kicking with bare feet and
jabbing with poles wrenched from some nearby shebang. . . .

The third man was one Ross from Boston; the fourth a stupid
longshoreman, middle-aged, who'd supported the banner of Patrick
Delaney. A voice yelled, I think he killed one of our boys, and Ross
ran away from that voice. He pushed his bulk down the lane with
lurching strides until he was tripped and fell to be stomped upon.
Old Cleary made rough agonized progress behind him; most of Cleary's
clothes were torn off before he'd gone as far as Ross. . . .

So they came: Murphy, Rae, Billings, Apgar, a dozen more, to
receive hackings and thwackings, to be swatted, bloodied . . . beasts
of prey turned miraculously into dogs, to accept that cruelty visited
upon homeless animals, to know—for the first time, perhaps—what it
was to sustain the attack of wretches who gave quarter only when
distracted by a new victim.

The eleventh man through the gate was Edward Blamey. Seemingly his legs were more bowed than ever, since he wore a sailor's
clothing. In an instant boys were yelling, Look out! Look out, he's
got a knife! Certainly Edward Blamey had a knife. In looking after
Number One he'd kept gold pieces sewn in the collar of his blouse,
and with a gold piece had bought a butcher knife from the venal
Mackey Nall, unperceived by Regulators who also guarded. How Ed
Blamey had concealed that knife: whether in blouse or sleeve, how
he had hidden it when his hands were tied, no one might ever know.
The blade flashed in Edward Blamey's freed hand, files of prisoners
scattered before him. He went tearing away down the slope; but all
The Wrath to Come which had been preached and which he had
dreaded, cried at his heels.

Blamey had never been a fast runner. Desperation gave him speed.
He fled squarely through one shebang, tried to rush through another
and was staggered by the collision. He went to the left . . . no, that
way lay the deadline; he held a swift vision of guards lifting their
guns above him. He raced back to the east. A small group stood in
his path, he yelled, knifed at them, did not strike anyone. The men
jumped apart, then joined the pack baying on Ed Blamey's trail.

A lone man watched his rapid approach. His name was Lynn, a
solemn farmer from Indiana who had been in the stockade only since
the first of the month; he had not been set upon by raiders on his

arrival; his uniform was fairly new and fairly clean. Lynn had bull strength left to him. He'd been busy this day, had helped to carry two dead bodies to the habitat of the dead, and was rewarded with the common premium of being allowed to go Outside with a wood detail. His own wood was secured in the shape of a long rail of pine; once the rail had been part of a Claffey fence. Lynn returned through the North Gate. He lugged his pine pole all the way to the shebang he shared with friends on the southern slope, and had been wondering what to do with his prize . . . whether to seek help in cutting it up, whether to sell all or only part of this wooden treasure. He must consult with friends, and they were not at home. He stood as if once more armed and with the Union forces, holding his rifle at Present Arms; actually he held the tall rail straight into the air.

Edward Blamey might not have seen this man; again, he might have seen him and decided flashingly to run the risk. His rubber-legged stride carried him directly in front of Farmer Lynn, and when Ed was two leaps distant the rail began to speed in lowering. It came down rapidly. It had been vertical, it went through its portion of an arc. The sound rapped clear as it struck squarely atop Edward Blamey's bare head. The knife flew. Blamey never thought again, there was no waking mind surviving to reason or repent. The Wrath overtook him. He did not know that Number One was dying, did not know when Number One died.

XXXIII

Lord, have mercy on us.
Christ, have mercy on us.
Lord, have mercy on us.

Death On A Pale Horse: people described Henry Wirz so, because of course he rode the old gray-white mare and wore his one suit of white duck.

More and more was Wirz departing from prescribed military usage in his habit and attire. One might have thought that John Winder would upbraid him for these lapses and bring about a reformation. The fact was that the old general paid little attention; but rarely did awareness of slip-shod deportment penetrate the toughening hide which wrapped that senile brain. The guards were slovens, their officers slovens. Sid Winder wore a plaid shirt and a straw hat; Cousin Dick was neater than he, but still he wore red knit galluses. The general himself had streaks of egg and fat upon his tunic, he belched heavily after eating, he ate prodigiously, you could hear him belch if you were standing in the yard outside his quarters. On a single occasion was it observed that his tantrum rose from recognizing that the Swiss captain was not up-to-snuff. An edict had come from Richmond forbidding anyone to issue an order for transportation except on the orders of chiefs of bureaus, or commanders of Armies and Departments. Wirz complained that this dictate locked up the post decisively and hampered him in discharging his duties. He appeared before John Winder with a request that the general obtain an order which would make him, Wirz, an exception and would allow him to issue transportation at least in Winder's name if not merely above his own signature. No one else was in the room with the two, but Captain Peschau sat at an improvised desk on the outside stoop, and two sentries lounged near. They heard a familiar bellow, a wail which stemmed apparently from physical anguish. They heard John Winder roaring, God damn it, can't you grant me the courtesy of appearing *in uniform?* Henry Wirz emerged trotting, with his face ashy; lips trembled under his beard as he muttered, as he ran. It was believed that old J.H.W. had emphasized criticism by grasping the captain's arm, his wounded arm. On this day Wirz wore the bright-piped calico waist, pearl buttons and all; but he had worn it many times before in the general's presence without engendering annoyance. Peschau decided uncomfortably that General Winder had eaten too much pork again. Peschau wondered how soon he himself would stand to endure a verbal thrashing. He watched Henry Wirz retreating on horseback after his usual struggle to hoist that round-shouldered tormented body into the saddle. Peschau thought that he should not wish Wirz's job—not for a fortune in greenbacks, a fortune in gold; not for all the flimsy banknotes which ever poured from Confederate presses.

Death on a white horse, Death on a pale horse, Death warmed over, Death cooled off. So the prisoners typified Henry during this forenoon of July eleventh, when he headed a procession into the stockade.

Holy Mary, pray for them.

All ye holy Angels and Archangels, pray for them.

Holy Abel, pray for them.

All ye choirs of the just, pray for them.

Several thousand new prisoners had arrived since the first of the month, and it was rumored that the raider element might thus be heavily reinforced; there were the usual complement of ex-Bowery Boys, ex-Atlantic Guards, ex-Dead Rabbits in all drafts of Northerners who'd served with the Army of the Potomac and had been captured during the campaign against Richmond. Leroy Key was taking no chances with gangs: when it grew light enough to see, in the Monday dawn, he mustered Regulators and sent each detail to its task.

Early came the scream of ungreased wheels. A wagon rocked slowly through the South Gate rather than the North which was the more common portal of ingress. With an eye to drama and emphasis, the southern hill had been selected for a gallows site. The wagon contained beams, posts, planks, together with a keg of tools and a huge coil of precious rope. Volunteer carpenters set to work promptly inside a hollow square of Regulators whose clubs were ready to discourage any attempt at interference. Willie Collins's castle and the conical tent, which had served as unofficial headquarters for the raider chiefs, were but a few rods distant (beneath the latter shelter one could see disordered heaps of dirt where prisoners had dug, looking for buried treasure—some said that they had dug successfully, some said that they found skeletons of anonymous murdered men—as soon as the ringleaders were bound and hauled away on July third). The frame was of simple construction but would serve to hang six giants, or so its designers believed. They'd drawn a rude sketch the day before, and MacBean relayed the plan to Wirz so that proper materials might be secured. Two posts were set into the ground and a heavy beam secured across their tops. Within this structure, at about the height of a man's head, two wide planks met in the middle—their outer ends resting on cleats nailed against the side posts, their inner ends supported by braces pierced with holes in which ropes were tied.

Get the idee, Archibald?

Not quite.

See, they'll put them fellers on top of the planks, make them stand there. See them ropes coming down from the top brace? Each of them ropes will be noosed around a feller's neck. That's what them sailors are doing now—making nooses. Then, when they get the condemned all noosed up and ready to go, and when the boss gives the word, some folks will jerk on them other ropes down beneath—

And the braces will be ripped out, and the two planks fall, and them sons of bitches will join the Heavenly Choir!

What choir did you say?

Oh, they'll be in hell alongside Judas Priest and Captain Kidd and my own fatherinlaw!

Holy Abraham, pray for them.

St. John the Baptist, pray for them.

St. Joseph, pray for them.

All ye holy Patriarchs and Prophets, pray for them.

Sun rose hotter, people said that this would be the hottest day yet suffered. The great glaring mass of sun seemed concentrated as in a locomotive's head-lamp, burning against the fresh gallows on the South Hill. The mosaic on the northern slope began to shape and tighten long before carpenters completed their task; boys selected vantage points and sat to watch, but soon they were forced to stand as other vagrants came crowding, there was not space in which to sit. They stood wearily, stared, jostled. For pity sakes quit sticking me with your elbow. Who, me? I ain't sticking you—blame arm's too weak to stick anybody, Charley. Yes, and know what your legs look like? So I do: two darning needles with pumpkin seeds stuck on the bottom of them. O laughter, it is food and tonic; the brave have it, the brave drink of it and give it back to those in need. . . . A singing-school teacher from Danbury lay motionless in a shebang beyond Main Street or Broadway or whatever you wished to call the distant sluice; his heart pushed lazily inside his ribs, shuddered, bubbled for a moment, went on beating reluctantly again; the songster from Danbury did not know that anyone was about to be hanged, he did not have an illusion to stimulate or hurt him, he knew nothing, felt nothing. A Delaware oysterman lay motionless near the east deadline, he lay in no shebang but exposed fully to the sun, he had no shebang, not a friend to carry him to thin shelter, soon he would need no shebang, his back was a water blister, his bony arms were blisters; under raw ribs the heart twitched gamely, fluttered—why, in that very moment it stopped, it ceased while we stood observant! A thousand men lay or huddled in a thousand far-flung places and did not care about a hanging; did not care who was hanged or why; but more than twenty thousand others plastered slope and ridge with their staring, their press.

Carpenters built a rough stair at the south end of the gallows; there were several cleats nailed across runners; they built their ladder stoutly, the condemned were heavy men.

St. Peter, pray for them.

St. Paul, pray for them.

St. Andrew, pray for them.

St. John, pray for them.

All ye holy Apostles and Evangelists, pray for them.

Where ground tilted upward beyond the southwest corner of the stockade, where guns of the star fort threatened the stockade's interior, citizens and slaves of the county stood waiting. Women white and brown held their children up, they told their children to watch. Long before sunrise carts had been a-rumble on the road from Americus, mules stalked piny ways from the high region to the west, old men trudged out of damp lonely settlements along the Flint River. To begin with, a cordon of Reserves had lined with their bayonets, ordered to keep the populace in check, to hold them back from space directly in front of the cannon. There was room, it was pointed out, for all to see.

Just stand over there past the end of them rifle pits. You can see tolerable well.

Few people will assemble to watch a man living, most will congregate to watch him die.

The region immediately under the muzzles was higher, the view broader there, you could grasp a wider panorama of the interior. Bit by bit, moment after moment, the throng of ragged farmers, blacks and children came edging. Reserves were not trained to this task, their officers had ascended to sentry stations; they began to disperse and mingle with the very crowd they'd been set to restrain.

On the hill to the immediate north, across the Sweetwater branch, there was an area below the guards' camps where more than a glimpse of the fascinating interior might be obtained across the stockade's dip through the ravine. Here also humanity clustered—hangers-on of the Reserves, homeless servants who'd wandered from raided plantations in Alabama and northwest Georgia, who'd starved their way along the railroad line and here were impressed to serve as wood-choppers or grave-diggers. They massed, wondering, giggling.

They going put Yankees on that thing.

Yes, boy, sometime you hang a man—he fall down—old rope just pull he head square off—smick, smack—clean off he body.

Yi!

Ma, what's they a-doing yonder?

Them Yankees are going to *kill* each other.

Why, Ma?

Cause Yankees is bad.

How they going to kill each other, Ma?

Now you just shut your trap, and watch.

All ye holy Disciples of our Lord, pray for them.

All ye holy Innocents, pray for them.

St. Stephen, pray for them.

St. Lawrence, pray for them.

All ye holy Martyrs, pray for them.

Six assistant hangmen had been selected by lot from the ranks of Regulators and stood close together, watched with round eyes by prisoners nearest them; they were ready for their task with meal sacks and cords, the two youngest sought to minimize the strain of the hour by clowning. They tussled, wrestling, they did not fall to the ground, it was a sham battle, each was trying to force his meal sack over the other boy's head. Key said testily, Come along, come along, you'll get plenty of action in a few minutes; and they permitted the rebuke to turn them more sedate, as if deliberately they had sought rebuke.

An audible murmur drifted from outside the stockade, it spread in a quiet but distinguishable wave, born in throats and on the lips of the hundreds who grouped in two galleries on God's side of the fence, not on the Devil's; and it fell across the jagged parapet and rolled slowly through and over observant thousands within the pen.

Must be coming. Must be fetching them now.

Can't fetch them too soon to suit me.

That God damn bruiser of a Curtis like to killed me when he took my watch.

Well, he did kill one of our Twenty-second Connecticut boys.

You see him do it?

Don't you wherrit yourself: he done it.

The South Gate squawked open and crunched against posts set to receive its weight, the parade came in. Death On A Pale Horse rode ahead, and close behind the mare walked Father Peter Whelan wearing his soiled violet stole. The six condemned giants swaggered together, moving between double files of Rebel guards; Willie Collins's laugh echoed booming, he was laughing at something Delaney had said. There were no wan Floral Tebbses and Irby Flinchers bearing arms alongside the raiders; ranks of the Reserves had been combed to select a handful of veterans available for this chore. The guards had been ordered to shoot at the first sign of a break. These shaggy gray- and blue-clad men walked ready to fire, their hands lay across the locks of their guns.

Sure, you bandogs, and it's men like us you think you can fright with your twaddle of hanging?

Let's jump the bastards, Paddy!

Wait till we're rid of these guards.

St. Sylvester, pray for them.

St. Gregory, pray for them.

St. Augustine, pray for them.

All ye holy Bishops and Confessors, pray for them.

Swarms of black-faced Yankees split and fell away from the cautious advance of Wirz's mare, they did not wish to be stepped upon. Wirz traveled toward the gallows as directly as terrain and assortment of huts would allow; he bent past the mare's neck, watching for wells or dangerous pits, he had no desire to be thrown. Father Whelan followed Wirz on foot. He had washed his old jacket and it was still wet from the washing, so he came in his patched shirt. A smelly breeze lifted from somewhere to sway the ragged hems of his stole; prisoners looked with interest at the pretty color, the pretty violet. Nowhere else within the stockade was there violet. There were so few bright colors to be seen except often the color of blood. Father Whelan carried his umbrella beneath his arm, he did not have it spread, fractured bones of the umbrella thrust out and dangled. The Ritual was clasped in the priest's withered hand, his Crucifix was detected by glaring sun.

Wirz turned, motioned, jabbered an almost unintelligible order. Three or four Reserves moved forward hastily to open a wider path with their bayonets, and around the gallows area the hollow square of Regulators broke in obedience to Leroy Key's command. Make way, hurry up, so's we'll get them inside. The procession came to a halt. Wirz nudged his mare to one side, the square tightened once more in additional security. Seneca MacBean was horrified to see that the raiders walked unbound; this was a most stupid oversight on the part of Confederate authorities. He muttered softly about it, and with Dreyfoos, Corrigan and Limber Jim he stepped closer. Ready with your clubs, boys, minute those guards go out.

Prisoners!

Wirz's voice cut the fetid air, and as usual a few people on the outskirts began to mock his accent.

To you now I return these men, good as I got them. You say you try them yourself, you find them guilty. Nothing do I have to do with this—it is you, you prisoners.

The porcelain face of Henry Wirz was more drawn and gleaming than ever; he kept pausing in his speech, hunting for proper words. Those closest could see his pointed pink tongue coming out to moisten his lips under the ravelled beard.

Now to you I commit these men. Of everything with them I am washing my hands! Do to them what you wish, for it is you—you prisoners—who find them guilty.

He hesitated for another second, scowling, perspiring.

May *Gott* have mercy on them *und* you prisoners.

His wiry nervous voice went high. Guards, About—*Face!*

Lines swung into position with the click and thud of shoes and weapons.

Forward—*March!*

They went toward the gate. The square of Regulators squeezed closer, smaller, no longer a square, it was become a twisted circle under force of compression from the outside.

St. Benedict, pray for them.

St. Francis, pray for them.

St. Camillus, pray for them.

St. John of God, pray for them.

All ye holy Monks and Hermits, pray for them.

The manner of Wirz as much as the speech he uttered had its quick effect upon the six condemned. They looked at one another, they looked into hard faces of the Westerners who approached them cautiously but grimly. Had this been a threat, a kind of malignant jest? They'd sneered at the sentence when it was pronounced, boasted mutually of what they would do to the first person who put a hand on them, what they would do to the last person. They'd marched for long in the chain-mail of their established wickedness, bragged of their established wickedness; most of them had known little besides wickedness; they ate of it, drank of it, embraced and made love to a quaking rotting harlot called Wickedness. For what reason did there exist weaker mortals except to serve as foils, targets, scullions, spies?

Were they come to an End? They had never come to an End before. Their seizure and the comedy of court and trial were but a trivial interlude. Organ grinders had brought a Jocko or two to Andersonville in order to entertain them. Soon the monkey tricks would be finished, and somehow— In some way— By swindle, bribery— Through blow or cutting or strangulation the roughs would win back to the peerage they'd enjoyed, grown fat in, continued bloody-handed in.

Sarsfield gazed in disbelief at the gallows. His soldier's eye took in the crude but solid construction, his criminal's eye saw the nooses and rolled away from them and then came back to congeal.

He brayed, You don't really mean to hang us up there?

That seems to be about the size of it.

They might roar now, at least all except Rickson were howling; yet they'd had their fun before. They had taken joy in tormenting Father Whelan. From the moment word reached him that the six were condemned to death, the priest burned with ardor. Never was such challenge offered him before! To Peter Whelan, the Devil was an entity as real as himself, real as Wirz or the last boy he'd shrived. The Devil had maintained strict possession of these six souls, obviously, through their lifetime. What a triumph for the Church could Whelan loose

those tight slimy tentacles, cause them to unwrap, extract the bruised
suffering souls and wash them to purity! Examination disclosed that
all except the close-mouthed Rickson had, in dim forgotten childhood,
partaken of some semblance of Catholicism, or admitted to a Catholic
inheritance however remote. Sincerely the priest hoped to bring them
to admission of guilt. This admission might be achieved properly only
if the men recited transgressions in detail and came eventually to repent. Because of their mutual imprisonment in the stocks, the privacy
of a Confessional might not be observed; but Peter Whelan would do
his best. . . . None of the six could believe that they were to die, and
this ceremony became a sport.

Collins, man, you must go to confession. Our Lord is beseeching
you to go.

Faith, I'll be going.

I want you to make a good confession.

Sure, and Willie rolled puffy blood-traced eyes at Delaney and
Munn in stocks beyond him.

When did you make your last worthy confession, Collins?

Twas in my mother's belly.

The others guffawed.

Sins you shall confess in a good confession are the sins you have
committed since your last worthy confession; but I'm praying, me
son, that you will make a general confession.

What the hell might a general confession be?

Tis every sin of your entire past life you must confess, or at least the
sins you may remember most clearly.

And why must I be doing this?

You are about to die, me son. They tell me that you've been found
guilty— Oh, how I hate the word! Of *murder*. And you shall be executed, you shall be put to death for *murder*. I am but a humble servant
of the Church; still I'm striving to engender contrition in your poor
soul. I'm striving to loosen the grip of the Devil; he's had his claws
upon you for so long, that he has.

What should I be after telling you, priest?

Call me Father, me son.

What should I be after telling you, Father? and Willie Collins
winked so enormously that you could very nearly hear the snap of his
eyelid.

Recite your past sins, and try to feel as much real sorrow as you're
capable of feeling.

Well— There was a priest in New York—

And was he the one who heard your last confession?

Shit, never! He was the one I killed!

May God have mercy on your soul—

Sure, I cracked his throat with this very hand! And after he lay dreaming, I tied him to the top of his altar. And then— I set fire to the church! What a pretty blaze it made!

Delaney twisted his head in the adjoining stocks. Willie, lad. Was that before or after you were raping of the nun?

St. Mary Magdalen, pray for them.

St. Lucy, pray for them.

All ye holy Virgins and Widows, pray for them.

All ye holy Saints of God, make intercession for them.

Confronted actually with a machine erected for the express purpose of wrenching their lives away, they felt that they had been tricked. Their unanimous reaction was a rage the more blinding because of its complete futility. How now, how now? They stood without a tie of restraint upon them—now they should lift their hands, they must grasp and tear—let feet and elbows go flailing into the rank of blank-visaged men pressing close.

But— But—

The joskin called Key stood beyond their reach, he stood— Nickey snatch the lot of us! He stood with a revolver in his hand! And that black Indian of a Limber Jim stood with a bowie knife exposed. A bullet could reach or a steel blade slice before a man might crack more than a head or two; and here formed a hundred or two hundred of the damnable police with hate freezing their faces.

Howl no longer, thought Willie Collins, as his whole awareness and minor intelligence went draining into his boots. Howl no more.

He gave a shivering gulp. Thick tears began to ooze. His voice was shaking, humble. He called through the almost visible spume of threats and curses, Be quiet, you bastards!

Strangely they became quiet. Their terrified calm went spreading like a cloud's shadow through the population around them, and raced over the stockade as a moving representation of that same cloud, a brown silent formless wraith darkening the hill it passed across. The pen was more quiet than it had been, day or night, from the moment the first prisoners passed through the gate in that distant torch-lit February. At one end of the world sounded a locomotive's whistle, at the other end of the world crows made their wah-wah-wah; slopes of staring people were unspeaking and uncalling in between. At last Willie Collins and the rest might seek the very help they had derided.

Be still, lads. Willie added, with that pitiful dignity achieved by the brutal when they have fallen, Let the priest speak for us.

Ah, prisoners, cried Peter Whelan. Soldiers, if you like. Hear me now, please to give ear to me words. Can you not find forgiveness in your hearts? Have you no pity and no mercy? Remember our dear Lord who died upon the Cross to save us all from shame and sin! What would our Lord say, think you now, if He were standing among us at this moment, with His dear face aglow with inner mercy, with

the light of compassion shining from His dear eyes? Would He ask for
blood? Nay, nay— He would be beseeching you to spare the lives of
these, your fellow men—

No, said one flat voice in the nearer crowd.

Be merciful, spare them, O Lord!
Be merciful, deliver them, O Lord!
Be merciful, deliver them, O Lord!
From Thy Anger, deliver them, O Lord!
From the danger of death, deliver them, O Lord!

The dry shivering voice continued its plea. What will it profit you
if you demand now the death of these six miserable men? Sure, they're
sinners. But aren't we all, does not each of us here on earth have his
faults, are we not mortal as these poor condemned men are mortal?
Oh, lads, prisoners, men of the North— Will this gallows bring back
from the grave the boys who've been done to death? Never. Can this
gallows expunge, lads, the miseries which have been done, the pain
that's been inflicted? Never, never. A gallows cannot make, it can
only mar. Search your hearts, now, lads— And find pity for these
miserable sinners— And find mercy again in your hearts, for surely
you shall find God when you find mercy— Spare them, lads!

No, that same single voice came biting.

Ferocious hating brothers of the lone boy (whoever might he be?
And perhaps his mother or sweetheart or Sunday School teacher had
said many times, Luke is the tender one. Just see how gently he
handles Tab's kittens. He's such a gentle lad, wouldn't harm a flea)
put their cry up against his, and supported him a thousand fold and
supported him ten thousand fold. Peter Whelan's supplication went
drowning. No. No. *No.* The short grunting yells thudded as if a master
chorister stood with ferule uplifted, beating rhythm. No. No. No. No.
No!

Hang them, rose the high-pitched hoot of a mountain boy who'd
been stripped at the North Gate eight days before. Hang them, by
Mighty! Haaaang them.

Hang them, said posts of the fence. Haaaang them, said every sentinel's platform. The gallows cried, Haaaang them; each beam and
timber implored a choking. You could see that lacy face of old Peter
Whelan turned in agony. (He was more miserable than he would be
at any moment until he dragged himself out of the gate for the last
time, in October.) His lips were moving, his jaws went up and down,
but no man standing at his elbow could have heard him now.

From an ill end, deliver them, O Lord!
From the pains of hell, deliver them, O Lord!
From all evil, deliver them, O Lord!
From the power of the devil, deliver them, O Lord!

No, no, no, no, *no!* Never deliver them, let them strangle and stretch. Let the long jarring fall snap their necks, let nooses crunch, let the men's breath fail, let them die hard. Never deliver them, O Lord. Hang them, hang them, haaaang them!

Henry Wirz had reached his office some minutes before, but the wide slamming chant brought him out immediately, he stood bewildered on the step. What were those prisoners up to? Bears, what message do you growl?

Was gibt's?

Said the clerk who stood behind him, speaking in German— Captain, it is the prisoners, all calling together. They demand that the big men be hanged.

Why don't they get on with it, then?

Charles Curtis stood at the right of the file against whom the implacable demand of Hang them, Hang them, was cried. His gorilla shape was shortest in stature of any of the condemned. When honest (but dull and brutal to those about him) he had wielded a tamping-bar on the railroad in Providence. There was trouble because he struck a fellow workman with that same tamping-bar; his fist would have been nearly as lethal. Curtis decamped to Boston, found employment on the docks, found opportunities for profitable banditry. Again the police chased him, this time to Brooklyn, where he and a partner went buccaneering in a stolen boat through several lucrative seasons. In time they quarreled over the use and abuse of an anguished housemaid, a Scandinavian immigrant whom they'd kidnapped and lugged to a deserted wharf. Curtis's partner was found floating a day or two later, minus a portion of his skull; Charles Curtis sought seclusion in a battery of the Fifth Rhode Island Artillery. He was believed to have killed at least a dozen men with his own hands while in Andersonville, and to have been responsible for the murder of many others in his role as gang leader. But still he did not wish to hang, and now roared that he would not hang. Other Fifth Rhode Island artillerymen would sink to their doom in the mire of this place: Doyle would die in August, Calvin would die in September, Fay in August, Garvey in August, Sisson in August, Eaton in October; even at this moment one William Wallace lay in final stupor; and all were comrades, some from Charles Curtis's own battery. Not one of them but would have prayed to see him swinging. Still he did not wish to hang. I'd ruther die this way, his thick harsh voice came bursting. With arms folded across his face he dove into the line of Regulators.

His weight and force and suddenness flung their bodies away on either side of him, and two men went flat and his feet came down upon them as he plunged. Some idiot shrieked that Curtis held a weapon. He's got a knife, got a gun, look out, he's got— A mass of crowding prisoners outside the ranks of policemen scattered in terror. Curtis made rapid progress down the slope, he did not need to fling people away, they flung themselves in fear. A string of Regulators sped yelling a few rods behind. Get him! That's Curtis! Stop him, you down there! and the emphasis of their hollering cancelled the chorused litany which was still being called on the northern slope.

To the taut mind of Henry Wirz this commotion suggested but one thing: a prison break. It had been so long a dread that now, in coming (he thought it coming, he thought it in progress) it was nearly welcome. Gus, he screamed, tell the battery commander— When Gus the clerk lingered useless, dumb and rooted to planks whereon they stood, Wirz himself leaped from the stoop with a jar which racked him and went flurrying up the hill toward the star fort. He extracted his revolver from its holster as he ran, nearly dropped the weapon, he tried to cock it as he ran. Fire! soared his anguished cry, slender and shrill as the voice of a child at play, a child playing Indian. Fire! Son of a bitch! Why do you not fy-urrrr? . . . All soaked and gasping he stumbled past an embrasure, fighting through a tangle of country people and slaves who pushed first one way, then another; they did not know where to run, they felt that they must run somewhere.

The battery's commander glared in disgust. Gol damn, Captain Wirz, can't you see nothing? Those prisoners are running away from the fence, not towards it—

They try to break loose—

Naw, naw, *naw.* The artilleryman reached for Wirz's arm, clutched the right arm which was of course the wrong arm. Wirz howled. The artilleryman managed to turn the hysterical superintendent around, he tried to soothe him. Anyway, how the hell would I dare pull a lanyard with all these niggers and youngers and old folks too, square in front of my guns? Them Reserves ain't worth shit.

Henry Wirz bullied the Georgia Reserves back to their task. They came with shamed faces from sentry platforms, came out of the crowd itself. Responding to their brandishing of bayonets and threat of muskets, citizens and blacks allowed themselves to be folded away from the cannon. Guns could fire now were it necessary, but no necessity lived. People within the pen were become more static; they thronged to watch the capture of Charles Curtis, who'd halted mired to his middle in the slough of feces and maggots.

Regulators halted their pursuit at the margin of the swamp when they saw how speedily the Rhode Islander's excursion into freedom was halted. Well, here he is. A voice sang it from somewhere in the rear, as such voices always sing. Who in hell's going to go into all them worms and turds after him?

Without a word Nathan Dreyfoos waded to the task. He thought, In some fashion I can cleanse myself later. Someone must fetch the beast or he'll never come. At least I am strong enough to resist him in turn if he resists.

For some time Nathan had been reduced to the wearing of sandals carved and stitched by himself; but with the overthrowing of the raiders he was well-shod from Patrick Delaney's private hoard of boots. In amusement he felt now that it grieved him more to insert these new (to him) beloved shoes in the sickening bog than it did to know that ooze was working steadily higher on his torn pants and pasting putridity against his skin—skin perhaps not too clean, but at least pure, purer than the slow-foaming lake of drainage human and inhuman. A line came to his fancy: *Not all the perfumes of Arabia*— He felt young pardonable pride in knowing that others behind him were admiring the fortitude he displayed.

Curtis stood gasping in an attitude of defense, arms half bent, fists but half clenched. No, Nathan told him in a low voice, you will not die here. You shall hang; you have been sentenced; you shall hang.

Nathan pushed his long left arm forward, but holding the hickory club ready in his right hand, until he felt and saw his fingers grow around the open collar of Charles Curtis's flannel shirt. Bulbous green eyes stared into his own eyes with no hatred which Nathan Dreyfoos might detect; first he saw a fear and then a yielding, a blankness. He thought to himself, I have hypnotized him, or else he has hypnotized himself through his very flight—and how foolish it was! and where could he have fled to?—

Come, Nathan commanded in a stronger voice.

Curtis moved with him humbly, almost as if pleased to return. But his heavy breathing was a frog's grunt; his breath came quicker and quicker, he shook visibly with each labored respiration.

Want— Want a drink—

You shall have water.

Not— Not this—

There is water waiting you. At the gallows.

A certain amount of whistling exultation rose protractedly out of the thousands who observed; there were a few hands which spatted in applause; for the most part the inhabitants watched in silence. His hands holding Curtis's wrists behind his back (Nathan heard his tutor's suave voice out of the past: I say, old chap, shall we wrestle today?) the captor brought the condemned man up to more solid earth. First their brown shining dripping thighs were visible, then knees and lower limbs; maggots dropped along with the breakage of muck reluctant to be severed. Once Nathan slid and tripped, but the rock of Curtis's body kept him from falling.

The Rhode Islander continued with painful gasping. Give me— Drink—

Yes, you'll get water—

There was a tangle of Regulators on the margin; Nathan delivered his prize into this clump. Then he staggered toward even firmer ground; he did not realize it, but he was breathing almost with the force and noise of the man he'd caught. His mouth hung open, sweat drenched down from his bony face, dripped from the high point of his beaked nose; but his eyes were luminous with triumph. People gave him plenty of room because of the pudding which clung to his clothes. Curtis was dragged up the south side of the ravine, but Dreyfoos made his way along an avenue which opened before him to the west. He saw the creek gurgling under and around the posts, heard it gurgling. When he'd come fairly against the deadline he looked up at the sentry station with smiling appeal.

Let me—go inside—if you please. In the stream—

Yank, get away—!

Please! I wish— Only to—stand in the creek? The water's comparatively—clear—within the deadline. My legs—are plastered with—

The little sentinel gabbled a threat, but someone pushed him out of the way, and the plump chin-whiskered face of Lieutenant Davis looked down in excitement amounting to anguish. Nobody's to fire at this Yank, he said distinctly. Pass it to them other stations, hear me? The word went along the fence, called to each guard within range. Don't fire, don't fire at that big Yank. All right, tall feller, said Davis to Nathan. I've done got you covered with my own pistol, so's you can get inside that deadline and clean yourself off. *If* you can! Gratefully Nathan obeyed. The swarm of nearer prisoners watched with envy. Numerous men had been shot at that point, trying to scoop cleaner water from beyond the deadline. Nathan splashed and scrubbed with his hands.

On the hill Seneca MacBean told Limber Jim, Well, that ought to help a little. But if we all club together, we can buy better water from some of the wells. Kind of think we owe it to Brother Nathan. He'd present an awful problem to the Sucker Laundry and Cleaning Company right now.

What about Curtis? asked someone.

Lived dirty, can die dirty, said Limber Jim.

Limber Jim felt satisfaction in the knowledge that only one raider had sought to follow the runaway Curtis. That was Patrick Delaney: he'd taken a tentative step or two and then Limber Jim was in front of him with uplifted knife. Delaney backed away and allowed himself to be tied as the others were now tied, as the wretched smelling Curtis would be tied whenever he got up from the step where he had collapsed.

He sat for five or ten minutes, he sat on the bottom rung of the rough stair on which the six must ascend to execution. His legs had crumpled inside their dreadful coating. Give me drink, he kept saying, over and over. The charitable bucket turned toward him with each request. He drank with sputtering gulps, pushed the pail from him, gasped, belched, water ran from his beard and from the corners of his mouth. His eyes were fat as clams. It was as if he saw nothing but the bucket, wanted nothing but water.

Through Thy nativity, deliver them, O Lord!

Through Thy cross and passion, deliver them, O Lord!

Now indeed would Willie Collins kiss the object so foreign to his thick lips. He was not to die taunting; for the first time he knew that he was about to die, and in a fashion in which he'd never believed that he would die. Along with Curtis and the rest he drowned himself in water. Gossiping wonder rose from nearest crowds, those who could see the thirst of this grotesque clan and hear their petition and swallowing. Already one—twas Rickson, people whispered—had filled his belly until it was bursting . . . he threw up, threw up water and whatever else was inside him. Regulators jumped out of the way. Yet a minute or two afterward Rickson was beckoning to the boys with pails. Several of them kept trotting back and forth to supply this inordinate demand.

Sergeant Key, please— Them Clevelanders said to tell you they want to know who's going to pay for all this water.

Too bad, said Key. But their well is nearest.

Tell them Clevelanders, came the drawl of Seneca MacBean, that the Good Lord will reward them in His own good time. And no funny business, or I'll be over there directly and drop them down their own well.

A suggestion was made: Give them Mosby's watch. Reckon he'd ruther have water than his watch.

MacBean went to speak to the giant. Father Whelan was busy with Delaney beside him, and Seneca was compelled to push next to the priest; he apologized at disturbing him. Peter Whelan did not even hear him. His lined face was blue with effort, his wide firm mouth had become a blur, the soul within him must be blurring as it labored— embracing the doomed with one spiritual arm, jogging the Devil away with the other. Sen MacBean came back with a gold watch chain hanging over his finger.

Says he gave the watch to a guard outside, hoping to have his bonds cut loose, but I assume the guard didn't dast. Anyway here's the chain to it.

Mister. The slow-spoken question of A. R. Hill. Is that chain made of little oak leaves kind of hanging together?

Yep.

Than I guess twould be Martin's chain. Willie Collins took it off of him whilst we were at Belle Isle.

Know the heirs?

That I do.

Give them avaricious well-owners maybe a link apiece? Twould more than pay for the water; and you take the rest to the heirs, should you ever survive to get back to Ohio.

That I will. Hill put the chain in his pocket.

Through Thy death and burial, deliver them, O Lord!

Through Thy glorious resurrection, deliver them, O Lord!

Through Thy admirable ascension, deliver them, O Lord!

On the platform of distant Station Number Thirty-three, Ira Claffey spoke to the Reverend Mr. Dillard.

(Cato Dillard had come early from Americus with some idea of visiting the six hoodlums and praying over them. Ira explained to his friend that he'd heard the men were all Catholics and thus would not desire Presbyterian attention. Cato breakfasted lengthily at the Claffey house, could not make up his mind whether any good purpose would be served if he witnessed the hanging; he said that he had never seen anyone die except in bed. He believed that the gravity and horror of the thing might be reflected valuably in future sermons wherein he should describe certain penalties awaiting the unregenerate. Ira Claffey himself had intended all along to watch the execution were it possible. Lucy shivered away from him, and did not understand, and spoke indignantly of Morbid Curiosity. Ira had seen a man hanged long before, in Mexico—a man put to death for a criminal assault upon a child. He had approved that sentence and was glad to witness the dealing out of punishment—as now, he believed, he would be glad to observe the final agony of these rogues. Had it fallen to him to be a hangman in such a case, he would not have cringed, he would have done the work. He thought that a man might not know how to be gentle toward recipients who needed gentleness, did he not know how to be savage with the proper targets for savagery. He thought his a just and honorable code. Secretly he believed it should be followed internationally, but doubted that it ever would be. Thus, after toilsome examination of their separate philosophies in the matter, the two gentlemen arrived in the vicinity to find the roughs already marched inside; and it was cried that one of them had broken away in flight but was recaptured. Every station near the scene was weighted with spectators past the point of safety. Officers and men hung upon the ladders. Ira and the minister were compelled to walk the stockade's path to the far east wall. Accompanying Ducky Duckworth on Station Thirty-three roosted a corporal who came often to the Claffeys' for garden truck. This youth took the guard's musket and sent the frightened sputtering ancient down the ladder, to his immense relief. The two citizens climbed up and gazed at gallows and thick knots of humanity corded there, they saw the infinity of paupers who looked on.)

I have Sutherland's field-glasses by me, Brother Dillard.

Ah, I saw. Captain Poe fetched them to you, after—?

After Gettysburg. Watch closely—they're like twin spy-glasses—each tube must be adjusted of itself, to suit the eye.

Cato Dillard stood with white whiskers pushed by the mild breeze, and had much difficulty in adjusting the glasses to suit his vision. Ah . . . *The wicked are like the troubled sea, when it cannot rest, whose waters cast up mire and dirt.* And the priest proceeds with his pagan rites!

You know, Brother, doubtless he feels sincerely that our rites are the pagan ones.

Them there Catholics, said Corporal Yount. They bow down to wood and stone. Yes, sir, they worship idols. My own brother he went into a Catholic church one time, at the North, and he seen the idols with his own eyes.

Caught in the circle of vision, never knowing or caring whether men put a stare on him or not, Peter Whelan toiled with eyes, ears, lips, hands and the opening and pressing out of his own honest soul. In this fierce moment recollection cried for blessings on a group of serious men in the Rome of long ago, who had made it possible for him to award these poor creatures an apostolic blessing. In his youth— When first he entered the Church— No, it could not have been done then. As a young man Peter Whelan had been taught the clear theology of the time: the sacrament of Extreme Unction could not be given to those who stood in danger of death from a purely external cause. So it stood even today. But in Father Whelan's young time there was no clear theology about the last blessing. Bishop Miter announced his belief that the apostolic blessing could be given only when Extreme Unction could also be given, Cardinal Cassock said Nay—he felt that the blessing might be awarded to even those in danger of death from external cause. So the argument abounded, it had abounded for a long time. Peter Whelan's memory went back to a chilly night in front of a welcome fire—why, it was in 1841; he was still in Ireland; he sat before Father Monell's peat—and the eager voices spoke on every side.

. . . Very definitely. Twas announced by the Sacred Congregation of Propaganda.

. . . And what was the question submitted?

. . . Truth is, it concerned a condemned criminal.

. . . You mean to tell me, Father, that the Sacred Congregation declares the last blessing can be given on the same day that a man dies?

. . . Sure and I do. How grateful all the condemned, of the present day and the future as well, should be for this leniency! Blessings be upon the Sacred Congregation of Propaganda! Sacrament of Extreme Unction or no Sacrament of Extreme Unction—

Oh, Father—

Yes, man.

Twas a hockey. I broke his head with a rat. I was but a child—
What are you saying, Collins?
A drunken man. He was that elderly! I killed him, Father, killed
him dead—
And do you truly and fervently repent of that crime?
Father, I do, I do—
And all your multitude of other sins?
Och! But it was never true about me slaying the priest. Nor about
the nun, Father—
I'm endeavoring to awaken in the poor soul of you as much real
sorrow for your past sins as you are capable of feeling.
I repent, Father! Truly, truly, truly I do.
Through the grace of the Holy Ghost, the Comforter, deliver them,
O Lord!
In the day of judgment, deliver them, O Lord!
And which are you again, you poor miserable creature?
Name's Munn.
Yes, indeed, I get you mixed, lads. And Munn, me boy—for it's not
more than two and twenty you can be— Ah, Munn. Name your sins
and be contrite. Feel the sorrow of them!
There—there was a boy. Cabin boy.
And when was this?
When first I served aboard the *Kitty Cat*. But—we were in dry-dock—
Did you commit murder, Munn?
Twasn't that. My watch below and— He was there. Weren't no
others about. He—he was little. Kind of a pretty little boy. Not more'n
twelve or thereabouts. So I tied him up and pulled down his pants—
He did yell and cry! I put it up— Up his—
Time is fleeting, you poor miserable Munn. Do you truly repent of
your abominable sins, me boy?
Oh, Father— I do, I do repent!
We sinners, beseech Thee, hear us.
That Thou spare them, we beseech Thee, hear us.
Lord, have mercy on us. Christ, have mercy on us. Lord, have mercy
on us.
Leroy Key had been glancing at his watch again and again. Now
he stood with watch in hand, and nodded, and made a clicking
sound toward the hangmen who were grouped close behind the condemned and seemed so slight in comparison. Those designated as
actual executioners were two named Harris and Payne; at Key's signal
they moved toward ropes which lay coiled neatly on opposite sides
of the scaffold. A grimy youth with caked pinkish hair (he came from
Hamilton County, Iowa—his name was Dolliver) put a cautious hand
at Willie Collins's back and poked him several times, and finally
pushed Willie into motion. Willie blubbered whole-heartedly, his

vision was so watered with tears that his blundering feet had difficulty in negotiating the ladder's steps. Eben Dolliver helped him to
climb. First step, said the young man, pushing the hulk along. . . .
Next step . . . now the third. . . . Next one. Take care, he said, it's
wider. . . . Now up you go, onto the planks. Dolliver prodded Collins
along the braced boards to the farthermost noose. Willie went with
the docility of an agèd blind dog. Eben Dolliver took him by his
rigid elbow and made him turn to face the east, as others were being
made to turn, close beside one another, bound arms pressed close,
their thighs pressed close. There they were lined in another minute or
two: Collins, the reeking Curtis, Munn, Delaney, John Sarsfield,
William Rickson; and Rickson was the only one who made no sound.
Father Whelan had offered the Crucifix even to this Unbeliever, but
Rickson turned away with an annoyed jerk of his head. Whelan
sought to follow the parade of the dozen men up the ladder, but
Sen MacBean restrained him. Sighing audibly, the old priest moved to
the east of the scaffold and opened his precious little book. He began
with *Adjutorium in nomine Domini. Qui fecit caelum et terram,* but
soon realized that little time remained; he must seek a shorter form.
He began again: *Ego, facultate mihi ab Apostolica Sede tributa—*

Three minutes to talk, said Key. If any of you want to talk. You'll
go at eleven o'clock.

All were talking except the iron-jawed Rickson. John Sarsfield's
voice rose above the rest; he was telling of his being wounded in the
field, of his life being blameless before he came to Andersonville.
Munn said, Four months ago, when I came here, I'd never stole a
dollar in my life. I—I got a mother and two sisters in New York— And
this made Willie Collins think of a wife and child who had been
merely incidental in his life and whom he had deserted calmly. Boys,
he wailed, don't hang me! Spare my life, boys, for I've a wife and
child at home—

*Indulgentiam plenariam et remissionem omnium peccatorum tibi
concedo.*

Aw, said Paddy Delaney, shut your jaw, Willie Collins. You'll never
be getting the governor's stiff. If I had to live on the rations the
rest of you live on— Faith, I'd rather hang! Only if a man were to
steal would he get enough to eat in this damn place.

Peter Whelan looked up at him in admonishment. Me son, did you
not truly repent of your crimes? Concern yourself with God.

Father, I've got this watch in my pocket—pants pocket, I can't
reach it with my hands tied— But I see Pete Donnelly a-standing
below; and Pete, tis in my pocket on the right side; so you shall have
the watch after I'm gone—

Two minutes, said Key, looking closely at his own watch. Payne
and Harris had uncoiled the ropes attached to the two stout braces

beneath the planks, and stood in soldierly fashion with the ropes' ends in their hands.

Pete Donnelly, there's this ring upon my finger; has a fine jewel in it, and be after giving it to Pete Bradley, him that was once a jaw cove at the City College—

Father Whelan interrupted his reading with increased sternness. Me son! Let go these matters of Here On Earth, temporal matters. Turn your attention to the things of Heaven!

But, Father, I've got to dispose of my property.

In nomine Patris, et Filii, et Spiritus Sancti. Amen.

Crows in faraway woods said, Wah-wah-wah. Sun came boiling and baking, people on the sentry platforms and ladders were motionless, the crowds on the two outside slopes were near to being motionless, the thousands of clustered prisoners were more near to being motionless than they had ever been before, the mosaic of faces beyond the marsh seemed to glisten and fry in the sun.

The thin hands of Eben Dolliver widened the noose, preparing it for Willie Collins; he had to reach far and up to spread the noose for Willie Collins. Slowly he worked the heavy rope over Collins's puffing trembling face and began to tighten it around the immense neck. Other hands toiled with other nooses. Voices of the five talkative condemned were a busy convocation of guinea-fowl. At the outbreak of the Rebellion I enlisted and served three years with the army thinking that my mother and sisters will hear of this makes me wish I'd neh-heh-hever been born oh lads be after finding mercy for me as the priest told you and Pete I've a few beans in my watch pocket, and distribute them to the kiddies. . . .

Amid babbling of the rest came the thick dull mutter of Charles Curtis: I don't give a fuck. Get ahead with the job. Don't take all day about it.

Per sacrosancta humanae reparationis mysteria remittat tibi omnipotens Deus omnes praesentis et futurae vitae poenas—

One minute, said Leroy Key, never lifting his head from the watch held close to his gaze. It had been his father's watch, presented to Key as a talisman when he went off to war; and Key's father had been opposed firmly to capital punishment. Leroy Key wondered what his father would think if he knew of the necessary use to which this watch was now put.

A meal sack went over the head of Rickson, a sack masked the face of John Sarsfield, muffling his voice. But continually that voice hurried with its explanation, boast, extenuation. Bad company it was, bad company—first off, the only thing I stole was rations. Sacks were drawn to cover the heads of the other four, and as with Sarsfield their murmurings went down proportionately in volume. Don't lay it on so thick, boys were yelling impatiently in nearby ranks of watchers.

You're a God damn villain, Munn, and you know it! That bastard
Sarsfield killed a fellow used to live in our shebang! Willie Mosby,
you dirty— Yeh, he took Paster's blanket when he was laying sick to
death. Get ready to hang, you noisy sons of bitches!

　　. . . *Paradisi portas aperiat, et ad gaudia sempiterna perducat. Amen.*

Time's up, said Key.

The vast chant had begun behind him, in front of him, sun burned
hard, the hillside larded with its thousands was shaking, heat waves
rippled, the pound of ten thousand voices and more became a steady
beat of drums. *Hang* them. *Hang* them. *Hang* them. Four function-
aries jumped from the scaffold more or less nimbly, two of them went
down the ladder with caution. Sergeant Key looked questioningly at
the executioners. They had the ropes ready . . . Payne nodded in
reply. Key looked to see that the assistants were well away from the
gallows, and they were. He held his hand high, pulled it down sharply.
Payne and Harris dug their heels into the ground simultaneously and
flung themselves back, toward the east and the west; the braces flew at
them, planks came banging down. Men standing closest could hear
the combined thud and snap as six huge face-swaddled bodies
dropped, those in the center speeding down a fraction of a second
before those at the ends . . . there was a suggestion of a V in the
shape of the descending mass. Willie Collins's great feet struck the
ground with a double thud: his rope was shorn in two.

The other five raiders gyrated slowly, some of them were struggling.
Certain of the watchers thought of fowls hung outside a poulterer's.
In an instant Munn and Delaney were without motion except for
the dangling, the gradual heave and twitching of weights and ropes
subjected to sudden shock. The necks of Curtis and Rickson and
Sarsfield had not snapped. They died of strangulation, waggling
their corded legs, gesticulating with their corded hands and arms in
a strange leisure. Sarsfield died more ruggedly than the others. His
knees came striving up; almost they touched his chin; he jerked his
legs down once more.

Lookit that vein in his neck, said a low voice.

Thought twas going to bust.

He's still kicking.

Guess they didn't get that thing tight enough around his throat to
begin with.

Most attention was centered on the tumbled shape of Willie Collins.
Leroy Key and several others swore the slow powerful oaths of men
who do not curse frequently or fluently. Eben Dolliver stood appalled,
overcome by the belief that this accident had occurred through some
neglect of his own. In no way might he be blamed. The Confederates
had searched high and low to find sufficient rope; some of it was
old, long exposed to the weather in some other more prosaic use;

and the section employed to build Collins's noose was rotten in its hempen core.

Take off the sack, said Key. Already it was stained with blood, and Willie's lips were pushing against the wet bright red surface. A shiny fly came with burnished buzzing intent, prisoners batted away other diving flies as they lifted the huge man's head, drew off the sack, and worked the noose loose. Willie's face was the color of cigar ashes. Blood came steadily from his nose and mouth, some people thought that it was issuing from his big ears also; boys would say later that Willie was bleeding from the eyes. Give us that bucket, called Seneca MacBean. A pail of water was brought forward, and MacBean dashed its contents over the waxy face. Blood ran away in pink rivulets, but fresher darker blood reappeared insistently. Father Whelan recited a private prayer for Willie, and held the Crucifix close. *Kyrie, eleison. Christe, eleison. Kyrie, eleison. Pater noster—* His old anguished voice slid to a whisper. *Et ne nos inducas in tentationem—*

They drew Willie into a sitting position. Men supported his shoulders and bleeding head while other hands worked furiously at preparing a fresh noose. His eyes were protruding from their sockets until it seemed they would burst forth and roll like crab apples on the ground. He said, Agh, agh. And then, Agh, where ammmm I? and drew the low words out lengthily. Ammm I innnn theee otherrr worrrld?

Soon see where you are, bastard, Limber Jim told him.

Och, boys, I've never hurted you—

Kilt my brother, said Limber Jim softly.

Willie twisted his sore neck, his head lolled back. As through waves of heat he must have seen the gallows turned to milk, and milky men standing aloft, making milky frenzy of the milky rope. For the sake and love of God! Do not be putting me up there again. God has spared my life, has he not, now? Father— Priest— Tell them, tell them! God meant that you should be merciful to me, indeed He did—

Rope's ready.

Hope you got it strong enough this time.

Hell, twould hold a dozen of him. Twould hang Wirz himself, and the laughter rippled as people thought of the meager round-shouldered despised captain.

Sed libera nos a malo. Salvum fac servum tuum—

Fffather, tell them— Father—!

Be putting your mind with God, me boy. Peter Whelan knew sadly that he could gain nothing by pleading again with these grim avengers. Repeat, son. Repeat the words: *O my God, who putteth his trust in thee—*

Och— My—God—who putteth—his—trust—in— Father! *Father!*

O Lord, hear my prayer—
Och, Lord—hear my—prayer—

Hands spread around Willie Collins as they had spread on July third when he was kicked and beaten. Hands and arms held him, he was being carried, lugged like a great sack of booty. He heard the priest intoning, seemingly far below him: *And let my cry come unto Thee.* Willie struggled dutifully to repeat the words as bidden, yet he could say nothing more. A hasty vision occurred as cloth was pulled over his face again, as cloth covered the sun and diffused its royal glare. Something about a boat decked in bunting, and a woman's hip rubbing his own hip, and a man—that name? Was it Hicks?—dropping from his perch on Bedloe's Island. Said the bellow of Willie Collins through the years, And if they ever come to hang me, they'll have to hang me twice! In anguish he wished to speak to the audience before him and explain a variety of things. He wished to tell of his father, of Big Biddy, of turmoil in the long-forgotten Gotham Court. Something tightened against his windpipe. He was free in space. A cricket's voice said *tik* in his ear.

XXXIV

Lucy wrote. Dear Coz: Yours of July the 4th rec'd. and contents noted duly, with especial attention devoted to the illustration which was executed with a flourish remarkable in one professedly so weary. We did enjoy the row of Yankees sitting on the great Chinese cracker, with Mr. Lincoln's tall hat in prominence! What an excellent fashion in which to dispose of those grand nuisances at the North! You did not identify the rather furtive figure shown setting a torch to the fuse. Who in the entire Christian domain wears spectacles as large as those? Twould be someone very proud of his spectacles, or else ashamed of them. Tut. You would not know, because you do not wear spectacles. Or do you? I can't scarcely recollect.

Hereabouts the Yankees have no Chinese crackers, nor crackers of any kind, poor things. Dare I consider them as Poor Things? But charity should still be Christian virtue in an embittered age such as the one in which we dwell. Therefore, Miss L. Claffey, be virtuous and call them Poor Things! Poppy goes perpetually to watch. Wild horses could not drag me, though I hear that many ladies have been. Twas told that recently a bevy of simpering *beauties* from Americus or some nearby community ascended in daintiness to the guards' little stations, assisted gallantly up the ladders by eager officers; and from their lofty situation they amused themselves by sprightly comments made to the prisoners; asking them how many niggers they owned at the North, Shouldn't they like to have currant cakes baked for them? —*et cetera*. Had I been one of the unfortunates thus goaded, I should have hurled mud balls at Their Sweetnesses. Father became surly when he heard of the event. But still he himself insists on going to the pen each day, though not to taunt the captives. He says the mere thought of the place keeps him disturbed of nights. I conclude tis the unpleasant odor which causes me to lie restless.

But even amid such squalor there can arise amusement at times. For instance, immediately following the execution (which I recited to you in some detail. Second-handedly, of course: I fear that my letter must have gone astray, and trust that eventually it shall turn up) the bodies of those executed were cut down, and preparations made to convey them to the graveyard. While this was being done, the *gal-*

lows itself just naturally melted away! Wood is very hard to come by over there; the sight of those fine posts and boards was more than the wood-starved populace could bear. My father watched, he said it was a sight: Tom going off with a length of rope, Dick and Harry scuttling with a rafter betwixt them. There were no guards inside the enclosure at the time, so the light-fingered *gentry* made off safely with their plunder. Tis understood that the prison's superintendent became apoplectic at the news.

I have met him barely: a glum bearded gentleman of *foreign* extraction. Some time since, Poppy thought that it would be an attention for me to call upon the Captain's wife, so newly come amongst us. They dwell at the Boss place (one side, since it is a double house), and there I rode upon our tallest mule, ensconced upon my dearly-belovèd-but-seldom-used-nowadays saddle. With Jem stepping beside in the role of groom! I invited Mrs. Wirz to take tea at some future time, but she has never availed herself of the invitation. The two elder children—I understand that they are the progeny of a previous union on the part of the lady—are named Susie and Cornelia, and are quite young ladies. The only child of Captain Wirz and Mrs. Wirz is little Coralie. Is that not a pretty name? She is nine or thereabouts: a gay and bubbling creature with extremely fair skin. Proudly she displayed her treasures, much impressed especially by a necklace her father fetched her from abroad. The elder half-sisters speak of and to her tenderly as Baby Sister. The child was having her hair combed and curled when first I saw her. Twas sweet to see that fair head between her mammy's knees. The child said, with that definite air with which some infants impart nonsense, My Daddy is a Catholic, my Mother is a Methodist, but *I* shall be a Baptist when I am a grown-up lady! I felt that I should attempt to persuade her into our Presbyterian fold; but had no such dramatics as *immersion* to offer. Later we talked of horses and riding. Her big eyes gleamed as I described the fashion in which my brothers used to cavort, the fences they used to jump.

I observe that I have said little of the mother. She is short, small-boned, a bit inclined to plumpness. Her voice is affable; poor thing, they have so little space in the small half of that double house, and it must be a trial. One of the elder girls possesses also a beautiful voice. I heard her singing in the garden. Mrs. W. set out her best to serve me what passes for *Java* nowadays (but her wench could not make miracles out of crusts or okra, as can Naomi): an Austrian china coffee set complete with pitchers, very lovely, purple flowers on white. As I said, she has never returned my call, but I do not think it rude. She has much to claim her time. The husband appeared before I left. He is grave, almost to the point of glowering, he seemed; but, poor man, he suffers from an old wound, and his arm was slung, and Poppy says tis often carried thus. He is commended to the tender mercies of the Old Scratch by guards and Yankees alike. Still, I should not be surprised but that he does the best he can, and with so little in the way of supplies or food available. I should not say food: tis sickening to watch the munificence of our garden go to waste beneath the sun. Even after our black people have eaten their fill. Poppy plants so much and tends with such care that we are surfeited with green things. One day I loaded the wenches with baskets of turnips and lettuces, and set out to play Lady Bountiful—even to Yankees. We were turned back by the guards, who said that we must have a pass. I knew not how to obtain one. I reported the matter to my father that evening, and thought that he would be highly indignant; but he only smiled his patient smile and said something about dipping the Nile with a sieve.

They do make *beer,* those Yankees. Now I shall offer you the formula, in the event that you may wish to tipple likewise. They mix cornmeal in water, and beg or buy some sorghum from the youths who guard them. This concoction is set out in the boiling sun to brew or ferment. Perish the thought! I should not wish to be a brewer, nor even to taste. On the other hand, Poppy declares that the mixture is good for them. Might it possibly delay the effects of scurvy from which so many are said to be suffering? What say you to this, out of your lore of medical wisdom? Please, Surgeon, do not prescribe such a dose for your ailing *Cousin!*

Enough of such jesting. Now to a sadder report: my mother's health concerns us greatly. We are powerless to cope with the situation. More and more through recent weeks has she ignored the plate put before her. I have tried broths, jellies, egg-nogs and the like, have racked my brain to no avail. She appears to be starving; it is self-induced. Were she to take a fever, the end would be near. But in her demented state she is deaf to any plea or argument put against her. Weep for me, Cousin Harry. I am so very tired of weeping for myself. . . .

Elkins wrote: Dear Cousin Lucy, Your letter of recent date has crystallized an intention in my mind. I have requested an assignment to duty at Camp Sumter. I cannot guarantee that I shall get it. Vaguely have I told myself, in viewing repeatedly those reports relating to shocking inadequacies at the stockade, that I would be serving our Nation far better in that situation than I might in Macon or Savannah. Sometimes there is naught upon my desk in the way of a paper. On other occasions you might dig far beneath the heaps ere you unearthed a veritable caricature of a surgeon who finds fewer and fewer *hairs* to scratch upon his head each day. As you know, I earnestly desired further duty in the field, and this was not to be. Were I at Camp Sumter, I might feel that I fought somewhere along a line of battle, even though my task entailed saving a few lives among the very human beings whom once I strove to destroy. Humanity seems crying aloud, and who is there to listen? Certainly not those dullards up Richmond way! Report and file, report and file: *that is all ye know on earth, and all ye need to know.* Our poor and admired Keats! Would he not have had a quicker wastage had he dwelt in that City Upon Your Doorstep, Coz?

But now I am impelled to add another motive, and that is to be of service to you and yours, who have been so generous, more than generous, in the friendship afforded me. I am not worthy of the name *soldier* in so putting my own desires above whatever orders have been issued or may be issued. But let us observe, my dear Lucy—

She read the line again and again. The first time he has addressed me so. . . .

—I am but one of mankind, proportionately selfish. I witness selfishness demonstrated in variety each day that I live; even did I see it so when engaged in the field. Now I am not a *soldier;* I am a surgeon accompanying the military, and subservient to military command. My intelligence is puny at best, I confess. But at night, in or out of my slumbers, I hear a voice saying, Go to Camp Sumter. An angel ordering me about? Could that be? I know not. Angel or fiend. But I have applied as I described to you *ante,* and shall be in inner turmoil from now on. There is this to be said, also: they are so woefully understaffed, and it is so difficult to procure even the most indolent of the contract surgeons for duty at Anderson, that someone might observe, Huzza! Have we here an imbecile who actually desires to go there? By Heaven, he shall go!

Lucy wrote: Your most recent dispatch has Poppy and me agog. Frankly I dread to inform you that not even your tender offices would aid my poor mother now. She is sinking, all skin and bone she is, and with such a stare. We try to force her physically to take nourishment. Grief, what a time. And the weather hotter and hotter. May I say primly that twould be a comfort and a pleasure to Poppy and myself to know that your kind person was at hand, not merely the kindness of your thoughts? Poppy is so concerned with the desperate condition of those prisoners. It occupies him night and day. Fairly does he walk the floor. I read to him the portion of your letter describing your intent. He struck his hands together and spoke something in this wise: I have seen the hospital, and am aware that no individual might cope with the situation. There are too many lacks, too many needs. But surely it would be better for those suffering youths, and better thus in the sight of God, if at least one man of strong purpose were to be on duty at the hospital.

Oh dear, I have made a botch of trying to convey the tenor of his thought. But at least, Coz, he hopes that you will be ordered here. And so, I confess with all maidenly decorum, do I. Now must I scamper off. Pet has the toothache, and I am to pull it. Your old room—Suthy's room—is awaiting you. Surely twill not be necessary for you to sleep yonder in that squalid place? No, unnecessary—I know that much—I see various of the surgeons lounging past in the lane, and hear their talk. They dwell elsewhere. Many I fear are very much *elsewhere* much of the time. . . .

Elkins did not appear until late in the month, and when he did arrive he was accompanied by a soldierly person named Chandler. They had become acquainted briefly at the Macon headquarters. When at last Harrell Elkins boarded the car which would jolt him sixty miles to the south, he found Colonel Chandler sitting with luggage beside him.

Elkins possessed and exuded the power and sweetness of the simple man who has suffered. Colonel Chandler might have been withdrawn, almost austere, confronted with a person more pretentious. Elkins's shape, appearance, voice, attitude made him a butt for the ignorant or unheeding; but identified him as trustworthy promptly to the experienced and discerning.

The two men bumped along through the hours, side by side on the scratched wooden bench with three militiamen and a wounded home-going corporal chattering distantly at the forward end of the car. Colonel Chandler was a graduate of the United States Military Academy. Like so many devoted to his cause he had felt that the Confederacy (like its army) was the repository of the best brains and abilities extant. He had never attempted to evaluate the economic factors, in fact was not too keenly aware of their existence, until repeated thudding defeats of 1863 made him aware. Now he saw his new proud Country prostrate before Northern assaults, armored only by its armies. The Confederacy was weaponed no longer with hope, only with determination. To most men Chandler would have voiced his opinion never; to a few he would have spoken directly if satirically. To Elkins, through the seven tiring laggardly hours, he opened his heart. The men were stronger friends when they got down from the ugly car at the Anderson station than many people would have been after an extended sea voyage. Harrell Elkins begged the colonel to accompany him to the Claffeys'—he knew that he would have been welcome. The colonel said No, he must get about his business. The assistant adjutant and inspector-general, Colonel R. H. Chilton, had ordered him to make a thorough examination of conditions at the prison, and to prepare a report as soon as was expedient.

Which report, came the grating voice of Elkins, who was no longer tempted by the illusion of justice, will be filed in the nearest chamber pot?

I fear as much. Nevertheless, what does one do?

Proceed according to the orders at hand!

Harry took up his residence at the Claffey place once more. Chandler went to live beyond the Sweetwater branch, where he was shrugged at by Henry Wirz (behind his back) and scorned by the Winders.

Harry had built his return to this region into an accomplishment: a savoring of all that was reassuring or noble. In common with those who dream too pleasurably in advance of an event, he suffered a letting down. His later warmness with Lucy had been constructed on paper; now, confronted with each other, the two young people remained aloof. But Ira offered affection and hospitality . . . Elkins felt himself received properly. Nevertheless there was a weakness, a lack of fulfillment here. The plague of Veronica's insanity pervaded the household as did the odor of Andersonville. Harry sat by the woman's bedside, was horrified but not too surprised at her shrinkage. He recognized fever, he felt the age-old perplexity of the physician who observes shadows of death merging, and feels that there is necessity in the approaching death; yet has sworn to hold it off as long as he may. In the end Elkins could recommend nothing but the hope that gruel and milk and soft eggs might be forced between the wooden jaws. He hoped the sufferer might be deluded into coöperation with those who would help her. Then he went to the prison hospital, he turned ghastly when he saw the prison hospital. He stayed for an afternoon and the following night; he slept heavily the next day, and was returned to the hospital before sunset.

XXXV

They tortured Veronica through the night, cooking her on the griddle of her bed. Veronica wished to be free of the griddle and of Them. Who They were she did not know, but They were many; some were white, some colored, They had hands and voices, They did annoying things like sponging the shred which was her body, putting spoons to her lips. She would set her jaws, spill the contents of the spoons, laugh because she had tricked Them again.

Ninny, rouse yourself.

The servant grunted, sighed, rolled her head against the padded chair-back.

Ninny. I'm speaking to you! Rouse softly.

Eyes opened at last, the kinky head shook. Yas, Miss Lucy.

Lucy whispered intently, I'm falling asleep myself, watching so. It is after one by the clock, so I must snatch an hour's sleep or I'll be fit for nothing. Hear me now: the master is with Jem, doctoring the Blackberry cow again, trying to save her. Should he come into the house he is not to watch by my mother's bed, but also must rest. Hear?

Yas'm.

You can't tell time, mused Lucy unhappily. (She had tried to teach Ninny to tell time, she had taught Extra when they were small; Ninny could not be taught.) Do you come over here to the clock, Ninny. Now, watch with care. This large hand moves faster than the small one. It will go slowly around—like this—and will pass the small hand; then when it reaches *here,* you are to come to my room and awaken me. Understand?

Yas'm, whispered the black woman, bored and frightened by the soft ticking wooden clock.

Veronica heard low conversation, heard it unheeded. I won't, she told herself stubbornly. Definitely I shall not. They cannot compel me. She lay with eyes closed, dry lips hanging apart and revealing a protrusion of her small beautiful teeth.

Later there was no sound in the room but that conversational clock and the easy snoring of the slave who again had fallen asleep a few minutes after Lucy left. Through coarse cloth fastened across open windows in lieu of mosquito netting came the vile odor and an audible medley of birds or children. . . . Her children? No. Safe. Asleep and must not be routed out. They're gone to war. In the ground. The taller are dead. Nay, it is the smaller ones who are dead. Indeed, yes, Mrs. Ladshaw, Sutherland is still at Oglethorpe but this is his final year, commencement will occur in July. Moses has gone boating on the Flint with the McWhorters. Arwood lies sickly again, we fear for him.

She was ruled not only by craft of the demented but also by slyness of the cooked and dying. A deep resounding voice said, Come in, so she must respond to it as always. She'd heard the voice often in recent hours but, when she attempted to leave the pan in which she lay parching, certain creatures restrained her.

Miss Veronica, you must pretend to be tractable, pretend that you are submissive. With quiet leer and calm you must accept the heat over which They are baking you, even though you stick to the pan.

You are crying before a cupboard, you have shuddered down into a pile. This gown belonged to Baby Peggy, you have your face buried in it. . . . Move spectrally, or They'll put you back into the skillet and build blazes higher.

Remotely birds and children made incessant mild tumult, closer at hand the Yellow Smell walked. It surrounded the bed as if curtains were drawn to hold it in; but curtains were not drawn. Veronica had her eyes opened at last (hard scheming burning eyes) and could see that it was true: curtains were caught up. She could look past the foot of the bed and see that solemn clock on its table, and the frizzled head of a servant lolling. Snoring again, said Veronica. Abominable sound. She should be broken of the habit, but how?

Please to recite the statistics concerning Macon, Miss Veronica.

Macon, Bibb County, has a population of two thousand, six hundred and thirty-five souls, according to the census of 1830. Of these there are whites to the number of one thousand, four hundred and fifty-two; blacks to the number of one thousand, one hundred and eighty-three.

Correct, Miss Veronica. Well done.

Had she said Well Done On the Whole, had Miss Benham said something about beetles? No, she spoke of sarcophagi.

There was a vacant mummy-case awaiting Lucy.

Come in . . . deep voice echoing through the hill. The stranger pointed with his cane. Best to tread in the direction indicated.

She slid from bed, making no noise as she went but the light whisper of skin-and-bone gliding over a sheet and out from under another sheet, stealthy murmur of sheets folded to allow her to pass from their prisoning. Her white hair clung heated on her shoulders, fire in her shoulders must set it to crackling. At least the bed, the griddle, claimed its suffering prey no longer. She was free but frying. She found annoyance in this realization—snarled about it, drawing back lips until the full pearliness of her teeth shone. Even this sound did not rouse Ninny. Veronica swept from the room, holding up the long crushed muslin of her gown daintily. She paced over shadowy air of the hall, walked on a cushion of air. . . . Ah, who'd left that candle at the head of the stair? It might cause a conflagration: she'd extinguish the candle. *Puff.*

There was a pool . . . spring . . . pool where slippery green frogs were captured by the boys. Always a cool pool. Could she find that pool she would lave herself in it, splash her face, wash off the scorching, expunge patterned streaks which the grid must have branded upon her.

Stay, twas a pan.

But wash off the burning.

Quietly, quietly down the stair, hands pressing the rail, bare foot after bare foot seeking the next lower step; how many feet did she possess? As many as a caterpillar owned, and each pair of delicate adhesive feet cushioned on a single segment. But, Badger, child— you are to fetch no more live worms into the house! I know, I know— twill make a butterfly in time—but do you go to your father, and he can grant you space for your treasures in one of the sheds—all for your own. Shall you call it the Claffey Museum? Ah, indeed, a Museum of World-Wide Wonders? A splendid designation; and I shall be delighted to view it when you have your specimens in place.

Empty pin, waiting for Lucy.

Quietly, quietly—turning of the knob after the bolt is drawn— quietly, quietly. They shall not hear me and pursue, I shan't let Them pursue. It is incredible, but They might harm the children as They've sought to harm me.

Come in.

There was a star above stolid black heat, more stars yonder . . . tilt your head wisely and observe the combined low lamp of stars. They'll guide you to pool and coolness. Softly, easily, walking on empty cotton of the air, feeling nothing, nothing underfoot.

O heat, dry up my brains! tears seven times salt, burn out the sense and virtue of mine eye! So said Ophelia, so said Ira Claffey in the game they played. Your turn is next and you must identify it, so name the hour and minute of Shakespeare: easy to do so, since Ira has used that quotation frequently in the past. Now, then: *eye,* and your own line must begin with an E. Inculcate lessons for the children, since they sit rapt and listening. *Even a child is known by his doings, whether his work be pure, and whether it be right.* There, younguns— tis Proverbs, Twenty, Eleven—but I'll not tell you. The burden is yours, the guess and reckoning and bickering are yours also. A raw

cold wet evening outside, and Christmas approaches—what a time
that will be for all!—and the eldest boys home from school, and Moses
shall enter when he is sixteen. Now they are rioting, the two eldest
demanding more of the peach cider. Lucy, daughter, do not guzzle it;
of course tis not fermented—but a trifle at the most: Ira has reassured
me—but drink demurely, my daughter, drink demurely. Mere sips,
the token of jollity, the barest token.

O heat, dry up my brains! There is too much heat, too persisting
and head-twirling heat, so find the dark pool with dispatch . . . leaf
mould making a cup above the soil, tiny scrolls of plants which swim
and grow in their swimming, and Ira declared them to be algae. Un-
glimpsed, naturally, in this darkness and faint lamp of stars. But find
the pool for its clamminess. The heat shall fade.

Halt, rang the changing voice of a young boy. Halt! Who goes
there? His voice was a chicken-cry when he spoke so abruptly, he had
the throat of a rooster.

What is a picket? I heard Them talking of pickets when They had
me trapped in the pan. Once indeed there was mention of a war. . . .
I have called, Mrs. Ladshaw, to pay my respects to you and to your
husband, to offer what sympathy we may. We heard that your noble
son gave a splendid account of himself before—before—

Someone else!

Yankees killed Moses. Yankees killed Suthy. Yankees killed my—
my— Sally and Courtenay. They were but infants; the Yankees took
them to the army and so they too—

Halt!

Sudden scratch of orange in the night, the singing and rush of
some narrow pointed force close at hand.

Veronica continued walking the thick piled mass of dark air, her
feet were unhurt by the pillow they trod. How strange that one foot
should feel as if it were cut by a scrap of thrown-away metal or a
splinter of wood, when her feet were swimming her forward to the
pool and touching nothing, nothing.

Godsakes, Allie. What was that?

Me. Shot at something.

I heard you give a challenge. Who—?

Just seen something white. It kept a-moving and truly scairt the
piss out of me.

Think you hit anything?

Didn't hear no yell. Must have missed.

Better reload, cause the Captain of the Guard will—

I'm reloading right now. They any white mules around here?

I seen a gray one tother day. Might have been that, but I don't see
how you could have missed a mule.

Sure as hell I did miss. Else I kilt him dead.

Heat, dry up my brains. For the sake of pity do not keep pounding them. Do not continue your scourging, Heat. Above all do not continue your ringing of bells and pushing of coals within me; and do not continue your dryness, dryness, dryness, my hands are dry.

Explosion of that gunpowder, contained within a musket barrel and booming free on the slope east of the Claffey house, brought Lucy upright in bed. Oh, blame, she thought, probably another guard has shot another prisoner. I'm positive it was a shot which disturbed me, seems I can sense its echoing, echoing. Is it too late, have I overslept, did Ninny fail to obey orders? Or perhaps Poppy has come into the house at last and sits nodding by that bed yonder— Poor thing, he should be asleep. Poor Poppy, he must sleep— In light gown and wrapper she trotted along the hall, and a moment later was cuffing Ninny savagely.

You black *wretch.* You— Where *is* she, where *is* she?

Ninny blubbered, Mistess, I done know! She—she gone from her bed—

Run, get my father. Hear me? *Run!* Lucy swung the palm of her hand, her hand grazed Ninny's hair and ear, the servant howled and went rushing. Through night below the rear windows Lucy could hear Ninny groaning her rapid way past cabins toward the cow shed, her cries of Mastah, *Massstah* growing more prolonged and growing in volume. Lucy ran from room to room, she lighted a candle here, a candle there, lighted a lamp. She dropped down to look into threatening space below each bed in turn. Even Harrell Elkins's bed; it had not been made since he slept in it; she saw the creases his male body had put upon the sheet. . . . There were no closets in the house. Houses like the Claffeys' were never built with closets; but Lucy banged open doors of every wardrobe which might have contained the shape of her mother, that desiccated form gone to eighty pounds or less. She held a frantic notion that her mother might have sought to immure herself in one of those chests dedicated to the dead children; she beat fists against the chests; they were locked. Veronica was not above stairs. As Lucy sped down into the lower hall she heard Ira Claffey open the rear door with a crash. She floundered to meet him.

She's gone, Poppy!

Not in one of the other bedrooms?

No, no, I've searched all. That shiftless wench was dozing, and Mother left her bed— Poppy, Poppy! I should never have lain *down!*

Together they hunted hastily through lower rooms, then in disorder realized that which they should have noticed all along: the front door stood open to the night. Ira fetched a lantern from the rear stoop. She may have gone over to The Pines, child. He said that, not wishing to mention the family burying-ground. Often they spoke of their cemetery as The Pines.

I'll go see, said Ira.

Let Ninny rouse the hands!

But she's suffering hysterics because you struck her, child— I reckon you've never struck her before. Jem is fussing with her. Do you clothe yourself at once.

Ira hunted with no result among the graves; he'd thought that surely he would find Veronica there. He went to the blacks' cemetery, even to the pets'. Rouse up, old Deuce, and aid me in seeking your mistress, and he thought for a moment that Deuce came wagging. When he returned to the house Lucy had put on shoes and stockings, and a shawl over her wrapper. Already she had called Jonas and Coffee. Jem came lumbering a moment later. Ira told them off to the search. He warned the slaves about stopping in their tracks if challenged by pickets, and explained what they must say.

Lucy, you shall go with me. I can't let you explore by yourself, not with these vagabond troops about. Though we should surely cover more ground if you— We'll go toward the stockade.

Can't you fetch Coz from the hospital, Poppy?

How could he aid, other than to seek as we are seeking? If we do not find your mother promptly I'll appeal to the Officer of the Day.

One slave poked west toward the railroad, another (Jonas, the most trustworthy) moved among trees which screened the rifle pits and fort. They were told to cry, Mistress, Mistress, as they wandered. Also the black women were recruited; Orphan Dick wept along with Ninny, he did not know why. The women were ordered to investigate orchard and shrubbery, areas close to cabins and sheds. They went crying Mistess, Missstess. It was a strange fluting and rumble of calling voices spread farther and farther apart, muting in lonely black distance, small lights poking wan fluttering holes in the curtain of blackness, curtain of heat and decay.

Veronica Claffey discovered her pool. It had altered . . . oho, no frogs? Badger then shall have none to place in spirits, in glass jars within his Museum of World-Wide Wonders. Elsewhere he must collect his frogs. Veronica waded toward the pool, the earth grew spongier, looser, her bare torn feet began to slip through feather beds of air whereon she strolled, her feet began to splash. It was difficult to draw her feet free from ooze and plashing, they sucked deeply, something drew her feet down and mired them. This, she decided, is whence it cometh. The Yellow Smell. For it is here, and They must be here because it comes from Them. They make it.

They were a far different They from Those who'd baked her on the bed, on the griddle iron. They were Yankees.

Grid, pan, skillet?

A spider?

Come in.

Will you walk into my parlor, said the spider to the fly. This she began to sing in a crusty sharp tone. *Tis the prettiest little parlor that ever you did spy.*

But although wetness smelled, although Veronica struggled amid reek, she struggled in comparative coolness. The marsh was soft . . . pool lay beneath, the pool would comfort her could she but reach it. *O heat,* a remembered voice was quoting. Assuredly heat would dry up her brains did she not lave and lave and lave. A slow gurgle sounded; why, the pool was moving. The collection of moisture would be treated serenely with moss and water bugs as she'd dreamed it; and Veronica Arwood was too wise a girl to be afraid of water bugs. Just skitter you hand, Mis Ronny, said Mammy Pen. Just skitter, skitter with you hand, child. Then all them bug they go a-fleeing.

Deep in the bog she squatted and began to skitter, and thought that bugs skated off from her disturbance.

. . . Halt!

I've halted, we're halted.

Who goes there?

Mr. Claffey from the plantation. We're hunting for Mrs. Claffey— she's stricken with fever—ill—wandering somewhere.

Is it Mr. Claffey sure enough?

Here, I'm holding the light on my face.

Why, Mr. Claffey, we hain't seen nobody.

Hold on there, Jeff, Allie done shot at something, while back.

Good God, did you—?

Yes, sir, I fired at something sure enough, but don't reckon I hit nothing.

What was it, what did you see?

Just something white kept a-moving even when I'd challenged.

Where? Which way?

Right down that way, sir. On that path winds around there, going over south side the hospital.

In time Ira found the woman. His lantern picked out her fragile figure now not so white, crouched in muck and painted with muck, the wide-spread slime of the hospital's drainage. He waded in, lifted the muttering creature, carried her out. So dry hot on that spider, she said distinctly. Shall need to drink more. The stuff dripped from her chin, plastered her night-dress, her babbling mouth was anointed with it. Ira strode lamely, carrying Veronica to her bed. Lucy scampered gasping ahead, she began to call to the black women before she entered the dooryard.

Come in.

Veronica went down those several steps as she had gone in fancy so many times. Smaller tombs within this larger edifice were open, and someone dressed in white lay within each marble shell. Or was it marble, was it granite? Off into nethermost reaches the bell-stroke of that voice resounded, and above outer roofs a sky must be painted mystically, yews or cedars must be black against retreating sunset.

Someone dressed in white sat up suddenly in one of the coffins.

A swathed arm stretched, grave-wrapped finger pointed, indicating the destination toward which Veronica must venture. In this instance she did not come from her dream. She thought of some great truth which she should announce, she should call it back to people behind her. Then she heard children running and laughing ahead, and began to laugh, herself, and to run toward the children.

XXXVI

John Winder stood with Henry Wirz on a sentry platform. John Winder did not see the bears witnessed by Henry Wirz; he saw scum, a marsh under the scum, pollywogs in the marsh. They were too thick, the marsh could not support their life, it was fated that many would die. Perhaps the survivors, if sufficiently cannabalistic, could sustain themselves directly by feasting on dead pollywogs. Or indirectly, as by swallowing fruits to be reared in a forest of growth which the dead creatures had manured.

I have not yet seen your most recent return, Captain.

General, that Gus Gleich he is sick. *Ach,* so much trouble I have with my office! And that Gus Moesner, he is good for the work, but with the English he is not so good. Slow he goes, *ja.* Tomorrow I present the return of prisoners to date.

Approximately . . . Captain?

Sir, it is maybe twenty-nine thousand now.

Because Winder was older in his mind than in his years, and sometimes worse than senile in his addiction to a crusty past, he sent Cadet Davis to the board again. Winder, aged perhaps twenty-seven, sat behind his small desk on a raised platform, and the cadets of this section sat before him, lining the sides of the long form—six on the left, five on the right, now that Mr. Davis had vacated his chair. Mr. Davis stood beside the easel which held the board, and gripped a pointer in one of his knotted bony young hands—the hand nearest the board, as prescribed.

Elementary tactical combinations of the Greeks were very simple, but they were methodical. An army corps was composed of—

The pointer found the long printed word at the top.

A *Tetraphalangarchia.*

Sprightly young Mr. Wayland at the lower end of the form wished to make a joke about this, you could see mischief peppered in his eyes, you could see his naughty soul fairly writhing for release within his rigid body; but he had a dangerous weight of demerits already, and the tactical instructor's hard eye was upon him.

This consisted of sixteen thousand, three hundred and forty-five *oplitai.*

The pointer moved.

An *Epitagma,* numbering eight thousand, one hundred and ninety-two *psiloi;* also an *Epitagma* of cavalry numbering four thousand and ninety-six men.

Might you explain to the section, Mr. Davis, the composition of the grand phalanx.

Yes, sir. Thank you, sir.

The tip of the pointer went walking. *Tetraphalangarchia,* four. *Phalanxes,* sixteen. *Chiliarchiae,* sixty-four. *Syntagmata,* two hundred and fifty-six.

. . . But in Andersonville these scraps of mouthing, hobbling, gurgling debris were neither Greeks nor Romans. Said old John Winder, They are Yankees, they are Nationalists; they must be treated so.

He cried at Henry Wirz, and so unexpectedly that Wirz's nerves gave a leap— He cried, I haven't yet set foot in this damnable place, nor do I intend to!

Ja, General. It is not good you do so. You they would attack!

Ah, I'm not afraid of the sons of bitches! Are *you* afraid?

No, no!

Ah, you fear them.

Sir, they are very bad. Like bears in Bern.

Where in hell's that?

Sir— I mean— General Winder, so many we have now; not more should be sent by me here.

God damn it, *you* don't send them.

I mean— *To* me at this stockade. They should not send more.

Winder made his stiff heavy way down the ladder, the ladder sagged and groaned under his weight. Flory Tebbs, displaced from the platform by the coming of these officers, stood bug-eyed and expected the ladder to smash and the general to fall with it. But to Flory's disappointment the ladder did not break.

Winder returned slowly up the hill to his office, breathing heavily as he went (he felt somehow that the prisoners had made him short of breath and he blamed them accordingly). Late that afternoon, when Wirz's delayed regular return was placed before him, he meditated upon it and then addressed himself with testiness to the adjutant and inspector-general, General Cooper.

Your indorsement on the letter of S. B. Davis, relating to the strength of the guard at this post, contains a very severe censure—

Winder sat for a time with the penholder shaking in front of his thin mouth. He wanted to chew the penholder, for thought, but he might press that infected tooth again. In old age he was trying to break himself of biting penholders.

—Which I am sure would not have been made if you had a clear comprehension of this post, of its wants and its difficulties. Reflect for

a moment; twenty-nine thousand two hundred and one prisoners of
war, many of them desperate characters—

Just how desperate, Cooper might never know. If Cooper could
have stood upon that platform, if Cooper could have seen the lanceless
Oplitai— God damn it! If Cooper could have seen squirming pollywogs in the marsh—

—A post a mile long by half a mile wide, the stockade for prisoners
within one hundred and sixty yards of a mile in circumference, numer-
ous avenues leading to the post to be guarded, public property to be
cared for, guards for working parties—

He did bite the penholder at last. The jolt from that savage tooth-
nerve went like a knife through his upper jaw and splintered the top
of his head. He wrote on, as soon as his vision cleared. The ink was
hot, the ink bitter, the ink black, black as John Winder's own blood
had been for nearly fifty years.

You speak in your indorsement of placing the prisoners properly.
I do not exactly comprehend what is intended by it. I know of but one
way to place them, and that is to put them into the stockade.

He thought, And remember me to the President, devil burn you.

Again he retreated to the Hudson, he retreated into a classroom of
1827, a classroom of early 1828. . . . Did Mr. Davis have his pointer
in hand? Had he advanced to the blackboard? Yes. Did the *Tetrarchiae*
still number one thousand and twenty-four, the *Lochoi* or files, four
thousand and ninety-six *Enomitiae* of four men each? Did Mr. Davis
remember? John Winder remembered.

Perhaps ten days later, at two o'clock in the morning, Elizabeth
Wirz roused up to see a dull brown bird on the ceiling above her and
on wall and windows. This bird was the shadow of her husband
Henry as he bent above and beside a stub of candle, extending his
arm in a nest of rags and lint.

Husband, are you picking again? Her high-pitched voice was soft
with sleep.

Gott, it is that I must pick. Almost it kills me, Ilse! He called her
that often, it being an affectionate diminutive of Elizabeth with which
he was familiar; also a favorite neighbor of his Zurich childhood had
been named Ilse; the name had a connotation of warmth.

Elizabeth put on the nightcap which had come off while she slept,
and in her wrapper went to help her husband. He had some surgical
instruments in a pan, and had been trying without success to relieve
the congestion of his old wound by establishing drainage. He cursed,
not directly at his wife, but he cursed civilization around her, behind
her, ahead of her. He complained that his left hand trembled with the
pain engendered by his right arm: so he was making a botch. Fur-
rowed hide of his forearm was a stubble field of angry corrugations—
there were marks of old openings and old healings, there were long

fresh ridges of cherry red drilled unevenly amid silvery scar tissue.
Kinky black hair grew in disorderly patches, it did not grow upon
scar tissue.

Will never I be rid of this?

You said you did not wish it amputated, said the little woman sadly.

Nein, rather would I be dead. He indicated an area which he
wished to have sliced with his scalpel, and afterward he wished the
incision deepened by use of a sharp probe. Elizabeth had performed
this surgery for him several times before but once she fell in a faint
while doing it. This was the first time Henry Wirz had made such a
request of her since the day when she fainted.

You are giddy? he asked anxiously.

No, husband. I'll try the scalpel, as you bid. She tittered, trying to
comfort him: My, I'm such a baby, Henry. And you, poor thing, suffering eternally—

He gasped, Ilse, do not scrape. It is sharp. Now you cut. Cut deep!
The incision was made, the jiggling probe poked in. The woman felt
a roaring in her ears. She shook her head and gritted her teeth, continuing with the task. There issued forth a secretion, but not in the
quantity that Henry wished, and no flakes of separated bone came
with it. Wirz thought that adjacent to the mutilated radius and ulna
there was a reservoir of fluid which might later come pouring through
the avenue made for it, and so pulsation and hotness would diminish,
and so he might sleep again.

Bandage was constructed, linen was wound once more, the candle
extinguished. The man and the woman got back upon the bed. Soon
Elizabeth was breathing regularly in sleep. Henry's mind went jerking.

He was concerned with a chain gang. Twelve men had been
shackled in this particular gang, ironed by the smith at Wirz's command. It was a creditable job: Captain John Heath, a commissary
officer, superintended the blacksmith at the task and saw that all was
well. The men thus confined were dangerous. All had tried to escape,
two of them had attacked guards, one had tried to escape twice. Now
he would not escape again or even try to! Each man had a chain and
a shackle around each ankle, the chain leading forward to the man
ahead of him; with legs so shackled, the prisoners could step but
eight or ten inches at a time, and mechanically all were forced to keep
in step. Each owned a small iron ball which he had to lift and carry
in his hand when he moved, and there was a much larger ball chained
to every group of four. By combined pulling of the gang the larger
balls could be dragged.

At the present a problem intruded. One of the prisoners came down
with diarrhoea in its most violent form, and Henry Wirz did not know
what to do about this. The final plea brought to him when he left the
prison at the end of the previous day had been a complaint of the well

prisoners fastened to the sick one. At first they'd tried going along with him to the sink, whenever he had to Go Out; but he had to Go Out all the time. The Yankees fastened to him declared that it was ruthless to compel them—the well, the comparatively unsick—to share the groanings and splashings of a diarrhoeic prisoner. They did not wish to spend all their time at the sink. Nor did they wish to be sprayed with juices of the sick man when his explosions overcame him suddenly, unavoidably.

What was Captain Wirz to do about this? Also they were always complaining that the chain gang and stocks were inhuman. Henry responded cuttingly, jeeringly, asking them if they had ever heard of civil prisons and punishments awarded therein.

If you be good once—model prisoners—in those stocks you should not be, in this chain gang!

That made sense to Henry Wirz, why did it not make sense to the prisoners? Because they were bears. Because most of them had not the wits of bears. Could they not understand why they were being punished?

Him with the diarrhoea: he was something to think about. As a physician, Henry deplored the sight or knowledge of men compelled to associate with the ordure of the sick. That was the reason he'd sought to move heaven and earth, that was the reason he'd managed to have the hospital taken outside the stockade months before. But as prison superintendent he must maintain discipline. Once committed to an act he should not falter, for any change would be interpreted promptly as a demonstration of weakness. The prisoners must not believe him weak. Suppose he yielded to their importuning and allowed the diarrhoeic Yankee to be separated from the others? They would feel that they had won a victory. They were not victors, they were prisoners. How should he decide? His arm hurt him so.

A hot wind came from the northwest, suggesting a shower to follow, and blowing before it the smell of Andersonville which had penetrated across dark low hills even as far as the Boss house. Pine branches were soughing, cardboard leaves of magnolia racketed. So, upon the high hurtful fence laced around a valley of sleep which he fought to enter— Perched on this indeterminate palisade, Henry Wirz had the notion that he was hearing waves, hearing a sea creasing under the bow of a blockade runner. Again an officer said to him, I'm sorry, Captain, we think the Yanks are chasing us, we've got to get up more speed, we've got to lighten ship. That's the reason those sailors are dumping out the cabin furniture. That chest of yours, Captain—

It was a handsome chest, carved—purchased in an old shop near the Seine, said to be of Italian origin. He was fetching it as a present to Elizabeth. It had not cost much, but his wife would think it beautiful.

Your chest's got to go, Captain. That's the order: every heavy object overboard that can be spared.

He did not protest for long, he saw the sense of the thing. They must lighten ship, so he must contribute his mite. He had no wish to be overhauled by a Federal cruiser. Only after the handsome old black cube (black as ebony, perhaps it was ebony) had gone tumbling into spray, heaved across the bulwark by two brawny sailors— Only after some small objects had scattered in the wind did Henry Wirz strike his right hand across his left and leap and sicken with the pain of it, and call himself a *Verfluchter Hund*. His chess set! The beautiful figures, the knights with ornate manes— How could he have done such a thing? Oh, old yellow ivory. He had left the chess set packed in the heavy carved chest. He could have taken pieces out and stowed them in his clothing one by one. He had loved chess when he was young; often he'd promised that he would teach Elizabeth to play; so when he saw this ivory set offered (the Jew who sold it declared upon his faith that it was stolen; thus he would let it go cheap, and to a foreigner, because he feared the police) Henry had envisioned contented hours when he sat beside his wife and taught her—first, the principle of the thing—later perhaps she might understand some fine points as well. Such relaxation it would be for him after a demanding day. Now the Atlantic had it.

Wind faltered, no rain came, magnolia leaves thrashed less noisily. Still Henry Wirz was not asleep: he ranged along that boundary which it seemed he could not pass.

A doll for Cora: that had been saved. It was in his big leather pouch (he was not requested to throw the leather pouch overboard). Also there were gloves for his stepdaughters, bottles of perfumery to be appreciated by Elizabeth, lockets for the older girls. Small things, old things, mostly second-hand, shopped for, bargained for with zeal. Henry Wirz had so little money, and the plantation he'd owned in Louisiana was gobbled by invading Federal troops during the Vicksburg campaign. He had managed to buy also a coral necklace for his small daughter: a coral necklace naturally, since her name was Coralie.

He passed into the haunted fen of sleep. He fastened the coral necklace around Cora's miniature neck. But, *Gott,* he found that he was fastening instead a metallic collar; from it would depend an iron ball, Cora would have a struggle to lift the ponderous orb whenever she moved.

He told himself, Now will I employ the sulphate of morphia. He had only one dose left, he did not know how soon he should be able to obtain more. The situation as to drugs and medicines was growing worse and worse.

Elizabeth awakened and found his shadow brooding. She hoisted herself on her elbow with a moan of sympathy and alarm. Oh, poor husband! Henry, can you not sleep at all?

Now maybe I get some sleep, he said heavily. He stumbled back to the bed, forgetting to put out the candle; so his round-shouldered parched body shone like a shadowgraph against candlelight, a desiccated body draped in false folds of the voluminous nightshirt.

Elizabeth, tomorrow to Augusta I go. I get things put together, I leave that damn Davis in charge. Maybe I am gone a week, maybe more.

But, Henry, why up to Augusta?

It is for the sake of *mein* arm, Ilse. I hear this week there is that Surgeon Greenaway in Augusta, and better he is with bones, better nor that damn Bucheton. I talk with one colonel, and he show me where he was wounded, and a bad wound from the scars; it is that Surgeon Greenaway fix him, and now he is well. In the arm, like me, but with him it is the left arm. He show me: his fist he clinch—clanch— how you say? *Himmel,* he punch a bag of meal with his fist, he punch hard, this I could not do! So now I ask leave. I go—tomorrow, next day—I report sick—

Husband, you didn't put out the candle.

Now I have my morphia I put him out. So.

No longer did the big bird flap his wings or crouch or move, there was only darkness, and wind growing.

XXXVII

The report which Colonel Chandler inscribed was conceived and projected with earnest intelligence and in contempt of human weakness, human blundering. Hatred he must put aside, hatred would render his pen insecure and detract from cogency. But he sat so astounded that he could not even write the dateline without error. *Andersonville, July 5, 1864.* It was August, and he wrote July; he did not realize his mistake, not even when he'd finished the report and sealed it. July had been a weary crowded month; in various tasks which he was ordered to perform, Chandler had written *July* a dozen times daily, thus he wrote the word of the wrong month now. *Having, in obedience to instructions of the 25th ultimo, carefully inspected the prison for Federal prisoners of war and post at this place, I respectfully submit the following report.* He went on to describe the dimensions of the pen, the deadline. He erred in his calculation as to the number of square feet available to each prisoner, and then discussed the stockade's creek. *Excepting the edges of this stream, the soil is sandy and easily drained, but from 30 to 50 yards on each side of it the ground is a muddy marsh, totally unfit for occupation, and having been constantly used as a sink since the prison was first established, it is now in a shocking condition and cannot fail to breed pestilence.*

He despised what he'd found here—disorganization, frailty, deliberate intent—because it reflected upon the Confederacy which he had embraced and which he had served with heart and body. He saw the Confederate lake which might have been pure (fed as it was by noble patriotic springs), muddied. He sat with ink upon his fingers, keen gaze turned against sheets of paper before him. He was aware of an awful truth while his pen scratched dutifully: the bravery of a Nation's men may resist the attack of outsiders, but what defense can be managed against creeping diseases within? Guard your legs with leggings (snakes cannot bite through them), glove your hands, helmet your head, wrap your belly and vitals to keep out cold . . . or even put armor outside to withstand blades and bullets. But an unseen worm will find its way down your gullet and make nuisance inside you until you sicken and fail; what will you drink for purge or tonic?

As Alexander Persons had put his own good head upon the block, so Chandler was laying himself open to censure with every curl of script, every indited comma. There were too many people of grade superior to his who would not countenance implied criticism. Yet Colonel Chilton had instructed him to make this inspection; by the eternal God he would set down exactly what he had seen.

He mentioned the efforts of Henry Wirz, his attempts to construct sluice and sinks, he told why this had not been done successfully. *No shelter whatever, nor material for constructing any has been provided by the prison authorities, and the ground being entirely bare of trees, none is within reach of the prisoners, nor has it been possible, from the overcrowded state of the enclosure, to arrange the camp with any system. Each man has been permitted to protect himself as best he can, stretching his blanket, or whatever he may have, above him on such sticks as he can procure, thatches of pine or whatever his ingenuity may suggest and his cleverness supply. Of other shelter there is and has been none.*

He discussed Nineties and Detachments. *But one Confederate States officer, Captain Wirz, is assigned to the supervision and control of the whole.* He spoke of the turmoil which had prevailed, and mentioned the sentencing and hanging of raiders as it had been described to him. He told of the absence of medical attendants within the stockade, and the parade which went creeping to the South Gate each morning, and the squeeze ensuing. *The hospital accommodations are so limited that though the beds (so-called) have all or nearly all two occupants each, large numbers who would otherwise be received are necessarily sent back to the stockade. Many—twenty yesterday— are carted out daily, who have died from unknown causes, and whom the medical officers have never seen.*

The face of John Winder seemed staring fixedly at Colonel Chandler across the field desk, the colonel's hand began to quiver. Desperately he sought to master vibration, to control his pen as he recounted the final horror observed that day. It was strange to entertain the apparition of Winder now, since the old general could not have been directly responsible for this particular wickedness—only indirectly responsible, only indirectly. *The dead are hauled out daily by the wagonload and buried without coffins, their hands in many instances being first mutilated with an axe in the removal of any finger rings they may have.*

Control was vanished. Chandler let the pen slide, and arose and went to the tent's door and lifted the rotten canvas and felt it tear bedraggledly under its own soiled weight as he held the folds. He peered out through stench and heard the faint voices of guards crying from the stockade's rim. Low in the west a bent flake of moon was receding and would soon be gone.

The colonel mastered his nervousness after a while and returned to discuss the condition of the hospital, the sick, the utter confusion of the medical staff. Most of this latter knowledge had been gained necessarily from second-hand sources; he was wary of it. But he put down a statistical summary: *the rate of death has been steadily increased from 37 4-10 per mil. during the month of March last to 62 7-10 per mil. in July.*

He wrote for nearly another hour, summing his recommendations and suggesting prisons in two additional localities which had been mentioned to him by General Winder before his exchange with Winder became acid. *In conclusion I beg leave to recommend that no more prisoners be sent to this already overcrowded prison. . . . Since my inspection was made, over 1,300 prisoners have been added to the number specified in the reports herewith.*

He felt his mind straying, it could not sustain him. He wanted to tell all, he had not told all. He began to worry about the uncertainty of his sources, especially with regard to hospital and surgeons. He must walk in the night and speak with someone—perhaps even have a glass of comfort, perform some selfish act in order to soothe the grating of his nerves. He thought of his assistant who had followed him to Andersonville, Major Hall; the mere fact that Hall was a direct subordinate ruled him out. There was another man whom he felt he could trust, this man he should seek.

Colonel Chandler did not wish to leave his report and the attendant papers lying about. He did not yet wish to lock his field desk, he might have a use for it later tonight. He folded the sheets carefully and put them into the pocket of his threadbare linen shirt. He took hat and sidearms and walked toward the Claffey place. Three times he was challenged, three times he identified himself and went past pickets. He was in no way confident that Harrell Elkins would be at the Claffey house or that he would be awake. But Elkins had gone on duty at four o'clock that morning, had slaved for twelve hours, had enjoyed whatever broken naps his frayed weariness permitted. Now he sat upon the gallery with Lucy.

Elkins said something about their not being gods, but they would offer the guest nectar in any event.

I should be glad to taste nectar. Colonel Chandler saw a white pitcher in the gloom. Elkins had gone promptly to fetch another tumbler; Chandler did not know what they meant by nectar, he was too strained to speculate.

Lucy explained, Tis from the Toccoa apples. A relative brought us slips from Habersham County long ago; but Poppy declares they don't flourish here as in those hills yonder.

I should think not. Colonel Chandler thought of ravines where the Chattahoochee rose.

But my father has a green thumb, so they do bear. The apples are just past ripe, and I direct Naomi to stew them with honey when honey can be had. We press out all the juice and express a kind of sauce, sir, and we've always called it nectar. I hope you'll think it's just the best. Tis mixed with cold spring water, so please to drink deeply and healthily. She added, when Harry came with the glass, I had some difficulty with Surgeon Elkins. She gave a little laugh which suggested a depth of other emotion.

Has the surgeon been ungallant, Ma'am? Has he been annoying you?

Truly he has. He refused to drink apple nectar at first; said he didn't thirst for it.

Frankly, Miss Lucy, he has no good taste.

The girl's voice shook. He would not drink it because the Yankee prisoners had none.

Elkins shifted his heavy feet and uttered a bleat of remonstrance.

Colonel Chandler lifted the glass in his hand and held it to vague light which came from inside the front room. My own victuals have choked me since I came here. Nevertheless I forced myself to eat them, and— To Elkins— Nevertheless you should force yourself to drink nectar.

Lucy thought that the visitor must have appeared for a purpose. If you gentlemen will excuse me, please. They arose, Lucy went rustling away.

So it stuck in your craw? Chandler felt an angry tendency to coarseness. The men seated themselves again.

You know how women are, Harry told him—Elkins, the man who knew so little about how women were. Perhaps I might mind the hospital less if it didn't accompany me perforce when I'd left it. Can I be of service, sir?

I have intruded upon you and the young lady.

Scarcely the place or season for romantic chit-chat, Colonel. The surroundings are not conducive to romance.

Mr. Claffey has retired?

He is abed and with either Shakespeare or the Apostle Paul. He asserts that he finds a refuge of almost equal character in the historic plays or in the admonitions to the people of Corinth. Mr. Claffey goes so far as to say that this is damaging to his religious stability.

Since we are alone, Surgeon, may we have a candle?

The candle was brought and stood leaning under its flame, attacked by tiger moths. By this light Chandler examined his papers. If you will be so kind as to confirm certain details I'll be in your debt. Let me see— I took my ratio of deaths directly from the report of the chief surgeon, Dr. White. We'll not bother with that.

To be frank, said Harry, I assisted Surgeon White in the report's preparation.

I'd guessed as much. Is it correct that such original hospital arrangements as were suggested were intended only for the accommodation of the supposed ratio of sick to a total population of ten thousand men?

That is correct.

Do you know how many prisoners were on hand, in camp and hospital, on the first of July?

Elkins's voice scratched. I was not present at that time, as you know, but I recall seeing a return recently. Something over twenty-six thousand on hand on the first of July.

And how many new prisoners were received during the month?

Something over seven thousand.

Making a total above thirty-three thousand, then. How many died during July?

Above seventeen hundred.

Would you guess as to how many are sick within the stockade, untended?

Impossible to state.

Now then, of the medical officers: how many hold commissions?

But ten hold commissions, sir. Most of the others are detailed from the militia. As for myself, I sought this duty because I was driven by the need.

Elkins stood up nervously and struck his hands together. I might admit also to more personal and selfish reasons for wishing Andersonville duty, but let that pass. Since I am ticketed as unfit for service in the field, I felt justified in trying to manipulate myself into a sphere where my conscience would assure me that I was needed. As a former officer I should be reluctant to state that many of our surgeons have accepted positions here to avoid service in the ranks. But, by God, sir, I do say it!

I know the type, said Chandler. They'll relinquish their contracts as soon as the present emergency exists no more and the militia is disbanded. Pray sit down, Elkins. You've been working long and hard—too long and too hard, I fear.

Harrell sank back into his chair. He said dryly, But little injury would result when those contracts are relinquished. The men who hold them are generally very inefficient. Many of them only visit the post once a day, at Sick Call. They bestow but little attention on those under their care.

What is your opinion as to the management and police of the general hospital grounds?

As good as the limited means will allow.

What are the facilities?

There is a necessity for at least three times the number of tents and amount of bedding on hand at this time.

What of medicines?

The supply is wholly inadequate. Frequently there is no supply of medicines. Great delays are experienced in the filling of requisitions.

Chandler folded his papers, put them away, pinched out the candle in order to discourage insects. Both he and Elkins had become oblivious to the hurt of mosquitoes. Hordes droned day and night, sometimes in visible clouds, again they were blown away by a wind. The two men sat in silence for so long that Harrell Elkins fell asleep and was roused by his own head snapping forward. He came awake to see the colonel's dark shape poised on the edge of the gallery, his back to Elkins. The young surgeon had a vague sleepy thought about some seeker for self-destruction teetering on the edge of an abyss.

Chandler was speaking of the past, something about his youthful days at West Point, and Elkins tried to send his attention hounding on the heels of Chandler's conversation, so that the visitor would not be aware of this lapse into slumber.

Walked the same paths in his time that I did in mine, said Colonel Chandler. And so, of course, did Grant and Sherman and most of the leading Yankees. They're enemies now, but I do not hold them to be arch-fiends. This old wretch seems to fit the description. I could not speak in this fashion to a subordinate or a superior; but you, sir, are a doctor—however young—and doctors must be father confessors to all.

Elkins managed to say, A portion of the responsibility which we must assume with the Hippocratic Oath.

Gad, sir, that man is completely indifferent to the welfare of the prisoners! He's undisposed to do anything to alleviate their sufferings. When I remonstrated with him I received only foul language in reply; when I spoke of the great mortality existing among the prisoners, and pointed out to him that the sickly season was coming on, and that sickness must necessarily increase unless something was done for the prisoners' relief—the swamp, for instance, drained; proper food furnished them, and in better quantity; and other sanitary suggestions which I made to him— He replied that he thought it was better to let half of them die than to take care of the men.

Elkins said, I have encountered the son, never encountered the father.

Major Hall had spoken to him previously. I'd suggested that he present some recommendations to the general whilst I was otherwise engaged. The major returned to me white of face; when he reported the fury and the obscenity employed, I could not well believe him, though I do trust Major Hall. I thought it incredible, thought that he must be mistaken! No, says Hall, he not only used those words once, but twice. Well, my friend, as I have just stated, subsequently General Winder made use of the same expressions to me.

Chandler took up the belt and sword and pistol which he had put aside when he sat down. I trust that you will forgive me, Surgeon. I'm better for the gift of Miss Claffey's nectar, and for your patience.

My work here is concluded—if there can be any conclusion to such an effort—and I shall be proceeding to the headquarters of the Army of Tennessee.

Their hands squeezed, the colonel wished Elkins success in his labors and cautioned him about wearing himself to the bone. He sent respects and sympathy to the Claffeys, then walked away across the black lane. Harrell Elkins was fast asleep in his chair before Chandler had reached the first picket.

It was almost lewd, thought the colonel, that he should now be entertaining memories of long-ago days at the Academy. Yet he presumed that it was because an illusion of idealistic service had been projected to youths there. At present, in observing the ideal trampled so cruelly and the service debased, he turned for comfort to thought of surroundings where this dream, now mutilated, had been born. Had John Winder been human when younger? Had he stolen bread-and-butter and hidden it in his leather bell cap, as Chandler had done when he was a cadet? Had he joined in a bread-and-butter feast after Taps in the old South Barracks? Had he gone illicitly to Benny Havens' and plunged his hot face into a mug of beer bought on credit?

> When you and I and Benny, and all the others, too,
> Are called before the Final Board, our course in life to view.
> May we never 'fess on any point; but straight be told to go,
> And join the army of the blest, at Benny Havens', oh!

In his tent Chandler relighted his lantern and stepped upon the path he had longed and yet feared to tread. He wrote a supplemental report to Colonel Chilton. In a small way he thought he would have been harming his own conception of the military ideal to which he was sworn if he did not do so. It was as if the flag had been befouled by Winder. He, Chandler, might not be able to scrub the colored folds clean again; but he wanted to own his soul, even if he were shorn of rank in the process.

My duty requires me respectfully to recommend a change in the officer in command of the post, Brigadier-General J. H. Winder, and the substitution in his place of some one who unites both energy and good judgment with some feeling of humanity and consideration for the welfare and comfort (so far as is consistent with their safekeeping) of the vast number of unfortunates placed under his control; some one who at least will not advocate deliberately and in cold blood the propriety of leaving them in their present condition until their number has been sufficiently reduced by death to make the present arrangement suffice for their accommodation; who will not consider it a matter of self-laudation and boasting that he has never been inside of the stockade, a place the horrors of which it is difficult to describe, and which is a disgrace to civilization. . . .

XXXVIII

The young old friends from West Dummerston, Vermont—Adam Garrett and John Appleby—had taken up tenancy together on a portion of the crowded terrain commonly designated as the Island. Their green past was fled. Nowadays the fact that they had a halfway decent shebang (even though the Island lay surrounded by putrid bogs, and thus its inhabitants were named the Leper Colony) was more important than a remembrance that once, side by side, they'd walked to the covered bridge across the West River, and extended their fishing poles, also side by side. It was more important to Adam Garrett that he had been able to barter for a handful of dried beans, than that he had been wounded at Gettysburg when he served previously with the Sixteenth. It was more important to John Appleby that he brought home a fair mess of roots to repay laborious hours of digging, than that he had served under the admired Colonel James M. Warner, an actual graduate of the United States Military Academy . . . few of the Volunteer Regiments could claim such a commander! Camp Bradley at Brattleboro, with Hallie Small and Hephzibah Clark fetching loaded baskets on visitors' day: that was forgotten. So were forgotten old Austrian muskets put into the excited hands of awkward country boys. John forgot the filth of Cliffburne barracks since now he dwelt in an ocean of filth which would have made Cliffburne spotless in comparison.

The youths remembered only that they were both captured at the abortive Weldon Road battle southwest of Petersburg, in the early evening of June twenty-third.

Their principal friends on the Island, since so many of the Eleventh Vermont boys lay dead, were two artillerymen from Battery E of the Fifth Maine. One was sick, one was in comparatively good health. The Maine boys lived in a dugout adjoining. Sometimes in early days of captivity the four New Englanders argued vociferously as they cited the advantages of their respective States. Sometimes they came close to blows; then in the end, being good Christian village boys with a bounce of humor, they shook hands and said that it was a pity there weren't some New Hampshiremen in between to act as a buffer.

Through blinding heat, with mosquitoes keening thicker each night, they neglected rivalries and ignored the remembrance of Maine and Vermont. Might there be parents and clear-eyed tawny-haired girls who mourned them as Departed, or who had heard the truth of their capture and prayed for prison doors to be swung? Appleby had raked hay on his father's three mowings terraced above the gentle valley of the West River, Garrett had unpacked boots and weighed out sugar and sacked salt in his father's store. Portland Hyde had ridden logs in a river: he was a lumberman and proud of it; and the man Caldwell boasted earlier of how many cows he'd milked night and morning since he was knee-high to a cow. At last it mattered not what they had been, where they came from, what orderly dreams they'd once held. Congregationalism mattered not, nor did the fact that Hyde's mother had been a Quaker and his father was not a Quaker, but still his mother insisted on talking Plain in their home. . . . Andersonville reduced them to a single pattern: they were stamped out of that pattern by the enormous heavy die of confinement, like a row of four toy tin wretches holding hands.

Late one day the lumberman Hyde died of dropsy as the sun was draining down behind the fence. Adam Garrett and John Appleby tossed a penny to see which should go with Caldwell, carrying Hyde down to the dead row. Appleby lost—or won, depending upon how you looked at it: Caldwell had agreed to give Hyde's shirt to the man who helped him. It was not so much the weight of the body as the awkward task of handling a tall object like Portland Hyde, who weighed perhaps ninety pounds at death (exclusive of the fluid in him) but was still six feet and three inches in length. His flannel shirt was not good for much—tatters, mainly—but it had three large buttons on it. John Appleby planned to wash the shirt in a broth of ashes and get rid of most of the lice for a time at least.

Caldwell came over and said, He's gone. He ain't got a breath in him, and they all crept back to take a look at Hyde. The lumberman lay flat on his back with brown eyes protruding, and late flies settling stubbornly around the eyes, and moving in and out of the open mouth.

If there was some way to prick him and get rid of all that there dropsy water, he'd be simpler to carry. This was Appleby's idea.

I could use my penknife, Adam Garrett suggested.

Not on Porty, Caldwell cried, bristling. He may be gone to meet his Maker, but no one's to put a blade in him.

Hellfire. I was jesting.

I calculate we should hold a service. Porty was a good church man.

Garrett told John, Fetch your Scriptures.

John's Scriptures consisted only of Matthew with part of Mark and the last two pages of Malachi. He had them rolled around a bit of stick and tied with yarn, and covered with a piece of stained linen.

Handling the flimsy leaves with care, he thumbed until he found the verses he sought.

. . . He is not here: for he is risen, as he said. Come, see the place where the Lord lay.

And go quickly, and tell his disciples that he is risen from the dead; and, behold, he goeth before you into Galilee; there shall you see him: lo, I have told you.

A few people came from surrounding shelters and watched apathetically; they stood with rough hair fuzzy against the pink sunset. A neighboring New Yorker called out, If I see him I hope he's not still sick. God, how he stunk. Hope you take him out of here tonight, Hay Rube.

I'll Hay Rube you, next time you get within reach of my club! Caldwell threw a stone which had braced the main pole of his shelter; he missed the New Yorker, but the little crowd dodged and scattered, and went back home.

Leave us repeat the Lord's Prayer.

Garrett felt that this service was miserable and inadequate, whatever the intention. They mumbled through the Lord's Prayer, and tied the dead man's big toes together with a bit of hemp. Then the Vermonters tossed their penny.

Caldwell stood musingly as he flicked lice out of his beard. Guess I'll pack up and move. Moving day for me. Or moving night.

Where to?

Member there was four fellows from our battery living over on the North Side? They come down to see us last month. Well, I hear that two are still alive. You know how it goes: man doesn't like to live alone.

He worked Hyde's body aside until he could remove the bark from their storehouse. They had some rice, a packet of dirty stationery imprinted with eagles and goddesses, a wad of soft soap in a rag, two pencils, a suspender strap, a few other odds and ends.

Caldwell wrote on a torn envelope, *Portland Hyde Battery E Fifth Maine Artillery* and with another strand of hemp string they tied this paper around Hyde's ear.

I'll bind these oddments up in the blanket, and Caldwell did so, folding the ragged edges tightly together so that nothing might be lost. With a last length of tent cord he tied the pack over his shoulder, and turned to shake hands with Adam. Drop in if you get up our way. It's in the furthest northwest corner, right past the last big well. They got two gray army blankets on top, and old pine boughs around the edges. It's about the biggest shebang in the neighborhood.

You'll still have to draw rations with your old Ninety, Adam warned him.

But I can dwell happier up there with my Maine friends. Maybe I can flank into their Ninety one way or another.

And get put in the stocks?

It'd be worth a try. Come along, Jim Along Johnny.

They lifted Hyde, Hyde made a belching noise; Caldwell had him by the feet, Johnny by the hands. We won't take off his shirt and drawers till we get him to the gate. They carried the corpse into the gloom.

Garrett cried while they were picking their way down the slope of the Island, Hi, Caldwell. Tent poles—

You can have them, Adam. More than I can fetch now. I don't want to come all the way back. His words floated faintly up the incline where tiny fires were glowing, with apes crouched above the colored flames, blowing in turn to keep the fire climbing through damp bits of splintered roots. For another minute or two Garrett could watch the two vertical shapes with that horizontal thing swaying between them; he lost them against deeper blackness of the marsh.

Adam wrenched up the four tent posts which had supported the blanket roof above that abandoned hole. He brought also the stones piled for extra bracing. Air smelled better already, with Hyde carried away. The New Yorker had been right . . . it was just the way he said it.

John came home half an hour later, picking his way stubbornly among shelters, and being roundly cursed when he stepped too close to any person or fire. You could follow his course up the low slope of the Island merely by listening to the oaths following as he moved.

He did some cursing on his own account after he reached home. That plaguèd God damn bitchy dropsy! Hope to high hell and hellfire I never get it! Scurvy's bad enough, but— Adam, I vow, I stopped down there in the creek and washed my hand a dozen times. Even them maggots smelt clean by comparison.

What was it? Dropsy— You mean Portland Hyde?

Damn, twas his hand. I mean the skin. We'd got his drawers and shirt off of him, and then we took hold to give him a heave across that little fence. I vow! The skin come loose from his hand like it was rotten cloth or something. Just peeled loose like a big glove. There he was in the row, and there I stood, a-holding onto the skin of his hand where it come loose on me. I like to puked my gizzard out.

Garrett muttered.

What say?

I said, Glad that I lost that penny toss. You can have the blame shirt and welcome.

I got it right here. Them three buttons will come handy, though one is split. What say? Want to turn in? Want some rations first?

They decided to eat half the piece of pone they were saving, and reserve the other half for morning. They still had one onion, but it was keeping well; they had agreed to save the onion for soup, in order to flavor the next meat ration when and if it was forthcoming. Mosquitoes hummed thickly while the men ate. They lay down, spooned closely; each covered his head with an old leg-of-drawers.

Garrett slept well, or at least better than usual; he dreamed of ferns. He tried to think of Hallie before he drifted into slumber; but rapidly she was joining the remote company of people in his past whom he could never reassemble, by voice or figment of face, no matter how earnestly he attempted to conjure them. He dreamed about a ravine of ferns below Black Mountain; it was summer, and there was agreeable coolness, and he walked through the bank of ferns. A woodpecker went down in long slicing flight from one tree and soared quickly up against another dead trunk, and clutched, hammering. Garrett didn't know what kind of woodpecker it was. But he saw the ferns clearly, and someone said something about blackberries in plenty.

Bam. Pam. Two shots woke them up . . . among mosquitoes . . . after midnight. The shots sounded like muskets but of different bore. There was a faint yell, whether the cry of the victim or a hoot of derision they did not know. A few voices called out the persistent litany of, Give the Rebel son of a bitch a furlough, then there was such silence as ruled—the wasting, crowded silence of mumbles and wails and snarls and hog-callings which went on forever, latticed like a visible structure beneath the stars.

With sunrise the vast population began to own a dimension of activity as well as sound, with men kindling fires anew, men beginning to bargain for food, men beginning to fight and tussle, men squatting at the sinks, men foraging for water in the marsh, men unable or unwilling to reach the sinks and squatting along the swamp's borders instead. Johnny was first out of the shelter, but he returned promptly and pushed his head back under the sagging overcoat with an expression of incredulity akin to amusement on his blackened face.

I swear, Adam. Damndest neighbors we got.

Adam Garrett joined him on hands and knees, and together they stared amazed at the transformation adjoining. When they went to sleep the night before, the dwelling-place which Hyde had relinquished through death and which Caldwell had given up as a matter of choice— The depression was a depression only, with no shred or twig to mark it. Now new poles had been put up, and a canvas cover which was close to being clean and white flaunted in the early breeze. The cover hung nearly to the ground on their side, but when currents of air twitched it, figures could be seen snuggled together in the scooped-out pit.

Did you hear anybody move in? No more did I.

Freshest fish in the ocean, I'll be bound. See how clean that cloth is, Johnny?

I'm going over. Appleby went away while Adam was still stretching and rubbing his eyes.

John came back soon, babbling with gossip. It's sailors, he announced in the gasping muted mumble with which they commonly maintained privacy when privacy was desired. . . . Two of them. Great big hairy fellow, big and fresh and strong, got meat all over his bones. Big old fellow, could be maybe of the age of thirty-five or forty. The other one is puny—just a boy fourteen or so. They're newly took by the Rebs—only last week, or so I make it out. But the old chap is some kind of foreigner; I can scarcely catch a word he utters.

Garrett's brother-in-law had served in the marines, and he remembered talk of weird doings aboard ships. John. That sounds like a seaman and his chicken.

Chicken? What in tunket is a chicken?

A little boy. Cabin boy, most likely. He belongs to the big man, and that chap takes care of him and loves him. He pulled Appleby's head closer to his, and lowered his voice to a bare whisper, and told more.

I never heard the beat of it! Appleby cried out in horror. Never heard the—

Mister, you've heard of corn-holing, hain't you?

Oh, yes. But just imagine. On a National gunboat or warship! You'd think the officers—

I didn't say *all* the sailors. I just said some of them.

They soon heard it related that not one but three or four sailors had been accompanied by their chickens when the latest draft of fresh fish arrived. The Vermonters were busy with Hyde's obsequies, and did not notice excitement at the North Gate which had attended incoming squads. For the seamen had, for the most part, retained their sea-bags. This came about because they were guarded by a detachment of infantry newly removed from some position of coastal defense, now journeying north to aid in the resistance above Atlanta.

John cried indignantly, Just their damn good fortune! If they'd drawn a company of these volunteer Home Guards! I vow, it takes militia to comb you over.

The huge sailor domiciled in the Caldwell-Hyde hole told them about it later, when they could understand his speech more ably. He said that he had a razor, he carried it folded in his sleeve, and he could flip it out, opened and threatening, in a manner to strike terror. After the incoming prisoners got off the cars at Anderson, and were standing in uneven ranks waiting to be counted again and marched to the stockade, two Reserves did in fact descend on him and demand his sea-bag, and the boy's. The razor whistled close, the Reserves fell back, cocking their muskets. A voice snapped at them, an officer's voice, and the Reserves were ordered away before they had a chance to fire. A few of the forty-odd navy men in the detachment lost their possessions, but most kept them intact. It was lucky for them that they arrived after the breaking of the raiders instead of before. People guessed that they wouldn't have gotten halfway across the stockade with those bulging canvas bags.

The mighty sailor had slit his own bag to make this fresh canopy, since he owned no blanket or overcoat. He and the boy had short-cut pea jackets however; these they used for bedding. The big man was Irish, speaking an almost unintelligible collection of syllables which he tumbled round and round, deep in his thick throat. When he gave his name, to Garrett's ears it seemed to be Paydrog. Hence they called him Pay, and the other neighbors did too. He was a shambling, round-shouldered giant with a rim of cinnamon-colored brush shaped carefully down the boundaries of his cheeks and across his chin. Soon he gave up shaving, and used the razor for other purposes; then the razor was stolen from Pay one afternoon. He bellowed for a solid hour but it did no good: the razor did not reappear. Likely one of the New Yorkers got it.

They called the little boy Chickie at first, but Pay showed resentment; it seemed that the term was for use only by the adoring partner, or in the third person. The boy was named Valentine, and he had been born near the wharves of the Delaware River at Camden, New Jersey, and had gone to sea when he was twelve or thereabouts. Val sported a spoiled, simpering little face, a mouth which could smirk out of all proportion to its puffy pink fatness, and polished eyes reminding Adam of nothing so much as the eyes of a trapped garter-snake. Val could curse—and did, hourly—in a manner to put any of the raiders to shame. But Pay he addressed in cooing accents to drive the neighbors mad. Val seemed trying to imitate a mourning-dove.

Or a honey-bee, said Appleby in hate.

They do live high. Whilst you were digging roots this afternoon, and whilst I was on guard, they cooked up a stew—I mean, Pay cooked it. It had salt, too; he'd been down and made a barter opposite Stockade Creek. Had salt, onions, potatoes, some of that there Rebel vegetable—what you call it, all squashy—?

Okra.

That's the one. And two beef bones— reckon they're mule, though— and a big piece of tripe.

Tripe! Come along, I don't like being played for a fool.

Well, they had it. I set out there, and so did the New Yorkers, and that old saddler from Ohio. We set around on our marrowbones and watched them, and we could smell pretty good, too. They finished everything in that big pot, or pretty near, and Pay says to the lad,

Did he want more? No, no, says Val, and made that silly face he's always making.

What did they do with what was left?

Pay give it a heave. You heard me. He flung it out.

Well, why didn't you—? *You* can go dig roots tomorrow.

I calculate to.

Then Garrett felt that he had had enough sport with his friend, and lovingly he produced the two bones he'd salvaged. There was gristle along the sides, the marrow would be intact for they had not been cut open, and there was actually a wad of lean meat and glutinous fat around the end of one bone. The New Yorkers made a dive, he said, but this little Vermont apple-knocker got there first.

The two flat hats, bobbing about next door, became a familiar spectacle, just as other familiar spectacles had existed before in the same locality during the tenancy of the Maine artillerymen, just as further familiar spectacles would in time supersede this one if the same eyes were there to witness. The flat hats bore in printed letters the words *Sea Sprite* but one day the bristly Irishman was not wearing his hat. He had sold it to a guard for brown sugar, a little envelope of brown sugar. Val had a sweet tooth.

The big sailor's store of money ran out quickly. Then, article by article, Pay hawked away his fortune. He bartered extra pairs of blue pantaloons for meat, his extra pairs of socks . . . he sold his sailor blouses, he sold tough linen thread, big hanks of waxed cord, many of his needles. He'd had something to do with the sails aboard that sloop on which he and the chicken were captured. In time he even sold the gold-beaded Rosary that hung around his own neck. Val was the possessor of a fine wardrobe—little white sailor suits trimmed in blue, little blue sailor suits trimmed in white. These costumes had been hand-sewn for him, lovingly, by his protector. Not a stitch of the chicken's possessions would Pay offer for barter—not until dire necessity on Val's part forced him to it. Then he disposed of them to some of the elder guards who bought the clothing for their children; he sold them for rice, turnips, a half-rotten melon, rancid bacon, anything he could get. Of course he was cheated roundly.

He had lost weight from the start, rapidly and visibly, as biggest men always did. It was as if a bony structure melted away beneath the stout countenance and let the exhausted cheeks and other features fall loosely, as they were a mask grown limp and hung upon a curtain rod. Folds of flesh around his neck drooped like cloth, then tightened up in a turkey's wattles. The beard, no longer shaped, straggled out in tusks and horns. The ruddy skin became black as a miner's . . . Pay spent hours with his head pushed down in pine smoke, blowing at reluctant flames of his cooking smudge.

Also he washed Val's clothes stubbornly, hunting for less pestilential pools of the morass, prospecting here and there, and finally going to work with ashes and muddy water—wringing, rinsing, twisting, pummeling sodden cloth with a stick and with his fists—striving to keep Val the mincing blue-and-white dainty thing he'd been before. The neighbors, most of them, were beyond the point of catcalls and ribaldry about this; they only stared in a manner of bored impudence and disbelief. Pay himself was far beyond the practice of sodomy or any other misshapen act, but he proceeded in a pattern long established: he owned an affection, it had come to rule him, he was selfless, savagely devoted.

The silver-haired Ohio saddler, whose name was Tom Gusset, did a brisk trade in the repair of leather goods. He had managed to keep some of his knives, awls and the like, when he came in. Each day he set up shop, now near the North Gate, now near the South, and cried his skills aloud. He would cobble a strap or a shoe or a leather cartouche flap—he could do such things soundly and speedily with the aptness which lived still in his fingers—but he worked only for currency or for some victual he fancied. One day there was excitement when a batch of freshies came in from some fort in the Carolinas, and one of them had smuggled a packet of candy: gaudy, viscous sticks striped with red and white. Promptly the candy was distributed to the four winds; the newcomer needed a blanket, a cooking can, things more imperative than candy. Gusset acquired one stick; it was stared at and coveted by all. The saddler limited himself to a half-inch at a time. After two days there was still a sizeable stub remaining.

However, he found that the heat of his body was melting the sweetness as he carried it about in his clothing. Privately he dug a storage den, and buried the precious colored fragment. He'd put it in a chunk of hollow cane which he owned, and plugged up the ends. The chicken must have seen where the treasure was put away, though no one knew it at the time.

The next afternoon Garrett was root-digging and Appleby housekeeping, when an explosion occurred in the Ohio quarters. Previously a fight had begun, across the swamp on the slope of the North Side, and most of the stay-at-homes were down there watching the fight. Three angry skeletons were engaged in a battle royal over ownership of an old boot; literally they sought to club or gouge one another to the death. Then came the outburst closer at hand, and Johnny looked out to see Val in full flight, with the old saddler loping after him.

He told Adam, You should of seen it. Didn't know that old rooster could move so spry. He had a big belt in his hand, and he was wheeling it like all possessed. The youngster legged it like the Old Harry was after him. He'd dropped the candy prompt when Gusset spied

him in the act of thieving, but Gusset was bound to teach him manners. I calculate the chicken would of got away scot-free, but he was
tripped by Pay's own shelter-rope. That strap buckle sung out like
it was a bullet, and it bit a piece out of his bottom. Should of heard
him yip.

Garrett scratched the filth of his beard. Don't like that. Was it a
big piece the buckle took out?

Well, he had blood on his bottom. He went dancing away, still yelling like possessed, and hanging on to his ass with both hands. But
I could see blood on his little white cookie. Right side.

Take any kind of scratch or cut. Even a blister. Remember Green-
berry? That was the way he went, from just a blister on the palm of
his hand. Remember how that arm busted open, all the way up to the
elbow?

Don't talk about it.

Reckon Pay will take it out on Old Ohio's hide.

Reckon he wanted to, but he couldn't find him. Gusset knew what
was in the wind, and he moved off the Island before Pay come home.
Likely he's joined some other Ohioans he knows, one place or another.

Appleby came closer to whisper, Pay's got Val under the shelter,
bathing his hind end. Heard him say he'd kiss it and make it well.

It would take Jesus of Nazareth to make that well.

Johnny was shocked. That's sacrilege.

I know, but ain't it true?

Remorselessly the spoilage began; Adam Garrett's prophecy came
true and more than true. The wound was puffed and swollen at first,
then increasingly discolored (this was what the Irishman told his
neighbors later, after he had come, leaking tears, begging them to
help). Val fretted day and night, he had to lie on his left side, then
on his stomach . . . Pay bathed the wound, the bathing hurt, Val
cursed him with shrill hysterical fluency.

Johnny, that's a bad luck shebang, most certain.

Where?

The old Maine hole. First them other miseries, now the chicken.

Gad. I wish he'd stop his whining.

You'd whine the same way, with one side of your bottom swolled
up and turning blue.

He oughtn't to have tried to steal. Thou Shalt Not Steal.

Everybody steals around here.

I wouldn't.

Reckon we both might come to it in time.

There he goes, squealing again. Just like a porker at a butchering.

The Vermont neighbors advised hospital, so did the New Yorkers,
but Pay stood dumb and tearful and merely shook his awful head.

They'd never be letting me care for him in the hospital, now would they?

Not likely that they would.

Sure, I'll care for him myself. Ah, Chickie, Chickie, it's the fine good broth I'm making for you now, do you hear, do you hear me, little Chickie?

In these days he began to sell Val's clothing from the sea-bag which had been sacrosanct before. He would bribe a neighbor to sit by the shelter door and keep an eye on things while he went to market. No longer did he fall in for rations, he refused to take that much time away from the nursing of Val. He sold the once-delicate uniforms which he had constructed, the two silk handkerchiefs, at last the small bright shoes. He'd sold his own shoes long before; he was barefoot; he cut one toe half off by stepping on a sharp broken cooking pan of tin. This injury did not try to close itself up as the boy's did; it stood open, draining constantly, but soon stuffed with worms. Pay was in pain along with his chicken, but never did he complain of his own hurt.

Little cans of stew bubbled constantly, the slices of fair raw vegetable were presented, they were pressed upon Val; he'd have none of them. He suffered a night of delirium and hootings. John had looked at the buttock that day when the Irishman tried to dress it, and the entire adjacent area of the thin small body was polluted, discolored, sending out a stench. It was as if the boy wore a great black pillow stitched against his frame from his knee to the middle of his back, and it was splitting wide.

No, no, no hospital, mates—they'd never be letting me tend him. . . .

Another steaming, frying, boiling, stewing afternoon, when the whole marsh crawled and lifted and sank in its maggoty tides. People went down beneath the heat, they went flat in permanent submission. As the Vermonters sat weak in sweat beneath the shelter, Garrett pointed out to John that four different dead-parties were wending toward the dead row at one and the same time. . . . Watch them, he said. Four, all at once't. Over there—just beyond that blue overcoat shebang.

I see them.

And there's two chaps— I'm certain they're carrying a dead one— yes, they are—right by that well where all them folks are haggling. And over there, above the sink-path. And just down here. . . . They dropped him. Fellow with a piece of blanket tied around him like a skirt. Now they're picking him up again. Four all at once't.

I see another. There, towards the North Gate. That'd make five.

Another evening of Val's clear-voiced agonies, but in the protracted hotness of the night his crying was muted; at last he sounded more like a crippled kitten than a pig about to be butchered. By morning he was giving no utterance at all. Pay fought to jam food into the blackened horny little mouth, but Val could not swallow; soup welled up and rose like water in a spring, and ran away down the emaciated face. Pay took the boy up in his arms and sat rocking back and forth, muttering in Gaelic. It must have been Gaelic, no one could understand what he said.

About three in the afternoon they heard a thin roar from the Irishman, and folks came to peer. Pay had the body wrapped in his arms, and he kept patting and slapping the shoulders crazily; but even his frenzy could put no heat in a shape which was cooling implacably, or limpness in a body which stiffened in that bent attitude into which it had been pressed.

Well, now he'll have to carry him down to the row.

Says he won't.

He'll have to.

Says he wants to bury him here where he can lie on his grave.

There's a hundred men hereabouts who'll say they're not going to dwell above a corpse. Anyway, they'd stop rations for the whole camp. You know that.

Might as well have corpses around as what we got. Couldn't smell much worse, now could they?

I vow, no.

The New Yorkers were moved to a kind of pity; they persuaded Pay to take the little body down to the line. Come, they said, we'll help.

Ah, none except myself shall carry him.

Tie his toes together. Here, I'll do it. . . . Very well, come along with you, Irish. It's hotter than hell today. He'll be swolled up before nightfall. You got to get rid of him.

Something told Garrett, Best go and watch. The final certain summation of tragedy would now occur; he felt it in his scorched and weary bones. Bring your Scriptures, Johnny.

But them fellers are Catholics. Holy Romans, next to being heathens.

Adam asked Pay if he wanted to hear some Scriptures read, or a prayer. . . . A Protestant prayer? Never.

They had difficulty in learning the dead boy's name; but from Pay's mutterings they decided that Valentine Connell must be correct, and they wrote it on a scrap of paper, along with U.S. Navy and buttoned the scrap on the chicken's blouse.

Get along, Irish, the New Yorkers were insisting.

Sun burned hard against Pay all the way down to the marsh. Adam and Appleby followed at a slight distance. Pay carried the half-curled body just as he'd held it in his arms all day—bare legs caught up over his right upper-arms, left forearm supporting the blue-bloused back.

The hairy claws of hands which had slapped and stroked were motionless.

He carried him, without once adjusting the burden or moving his hands or arms, all the way to the dead row; there he put Valentine down. He placed him on his right flank where the wound was out of sight. Then slowly Pay stripped off his own ragged verminous blouse and spread it above the shrunken yellow face. He stood back, gasping audibly; there were no tears to come.

Put him down without a screech, muttered Appleby. Never thought he would.

Watch, said Adam. I got a feeling.

The fence was a swimming mountain of tan, tall and close through oily heat waves. Standing near the scantlings of the deadline which ruled behind the dead row itself, it seemed that you could hear the very pop of resin as it cooked from upright logs.

A young guard stood directly above them, leaning under the low sloping square of his roof. He held his musket poised idly across his chest. He stiffened and seemed to grow taller in an instant.

Watch this, said Adam again.

Hellfire, no. I'm getting out of the way.

The throng of prisoners who stood nearest the dead row began to step back, pushing backward with hasty steps, jostling and using their elbows. The crowd split, widened. Pay had put both his hands on the rail.

Yank. Take care, called the guard.

The Irishman bent down and slid one shoulder under the scantling. There came a warning whistle from the guard at the next station toward the right, the last station next to the gate. Up above, the nearest guard had his musket butt at his shoulder, but his hands were trembling and the gun barrel moved in a loose circle.

Get out of that, Yank.

The scattering of prisoners became a stampede. Even scurvy-ridden ones who sat closest, waiting for a first blessed shadow of the stockade to cool them when the sun went low enough— Even these cripples were hobbling and rolling and lurching away like stiff ungainly gnomes.

The guard directly above could not bring himself to pull the trigger. Pay stood erect inside the deadline and walked two steps toward the stockade. Guards at the right and left stations fired almost simultaneously.

Thirty days, thirty days, the prisoners were howling. Give the Rebel sons of bitches a furlough. Pay lurched when the balls went through him; he turned slowly and started back toward the deadline. Then he toppled forward, and the force of even his desiccated body snapped the scantling when he fell.

XXXIX

There were times when sound of thirty thousand people assailed the senses more terribly than might have been imagined by one who was not there to hear them. Since the overthrow of the raiders the stockade was well-policed by Regulators, operating under command of the slow-spoken A. R. Hill of the One Hundredth Ohio Volunteer Infantry. Few civilian communities of comparable size could have boasted an equal passiveness and freedom from violent crime. But there were bound to ensue rivalry, fuss, abrasion. Men contended in a mere bickering or in a tussle to the death. Waldo took umbrage because Ned snored against the back of his head when they were pushed together at night, Amos claimed that Hez had stolen the bacon rind which Amos had bought on South Street the day before. A young agnostic, reared in an intensely Protestant environment (but who now shunned any established religion, and was darkly contemptuous of Catholics)— He called Herrity or Hanrahan a mackerel snapper or a Pope's child. Thus the private war which might be fought merely with words, more likely with fists and feet, not too rarely with slung-shots or hickory staves. Herman said that he had heard that a friend had told him (a friend who had it on good authority) that the whole Twenty-fourth Michigan Infantry was made up of bounty men; and Guy from the Twenty-fourth Michigan rose up to affirm that not a man in his regiment had received so much as a dollar in State or County money, and anyone who said he had was a lying son of a bitch.

Oh. Does that mean that I'm a son of a bitch?

You heard me.

Thus the ear torn off, the bitten nose, the kicked belly, the friends of both taking up the conflict, fists and feet and clubs mixed, the cries of, Keep your damn fighting over in your own territory. Don't come busting up our shebang or we'll beat the poop out of you.

Aw, shut up. Aw, hush your jaw. Aw, hush your gab. Aw, pound salt up your butt. Aw, bugger your brother. The talk of struggle . . . niceties worn off, the demons in every individual appearing unskinned (if he had such evil dwelling within him, and most men did have). The noise the men made.

The argument which resounded pointlessly, the sick red rheumy eye a-glowering. Any man who reads a word Charles Darwin has written is destined for Hell. Who said that? I did. Think you're a preacher or such-like? Think you're God? I didn't claim I was God; but it says clearly in the Scriptures that— Who are you, to interpret the Scriptures to me? Now, listen, Columbus Ohio, don't get gay. Take your hand off my arm. The devil I will. The devil you won't. *Whack. Thwack. Crack.* Come along, fellers, you'll spoil the mess! Hey, come aid me, he's too big for me to handle . . . looky here, Columbus Ohio, pick on somebody your own size. Well, you're my size and— The noise of strife: the men made it. Forever they constructed a contention if one did not exist naturally.

Thirty thousand men, so many making noises. The hullooing of the crazy, the whimpering of the bruised, the chop of knife or broken hatchet against a precious length of stovewood, the yell of the man offering five onions for sale, the quivering laughter of two friends who met suddenly at the North Gate (and each had supposed the other dead, and before winter both would be dead), the guard calling across to another guard, the bumping of wagon wheels at the South Gate, the wail like a cheer, the cheer identical with the voice of agony, the very small sound such as a canteen dropped, a stick snapped in two, wind broken from a body. The sound of Andersonville.

Nathan Dreyfoos told himself, Thirty thousand men might form a city of very fair size. But in a city of very fair size they would be spread far, some would be in homes, some in offices, others would be walking the streets, others would be down at the docks, others asleep in the park. Here the area is estimated at some twenty-nine acres, but that does not take into consideration that there is a deadline space twenty feet wide, or thereabouts, lining all four walls. How many acres should be subtracted to account for the deadline space? Two acres? The stockade is now said to measure, by engineers who have paced it, approximately sixteen hundred and twenty feet in length, and approximately seven hundred and eighty feet in width. Within the available rectangle, how many acres should be subtracted for the marsh? I am no engineer. Three acres less? Four acres? And the two streets must be kept unobstructed, so that wagons may drive in.

Let us say that our rectangle contains at least twenty acres of habitable space in which we may dwell—perhaps a trifle more. That would be a population of fifteen hundred men per acre. How many square feet in an acre? I know that there are six hundred and forty acres in one square mile, but how many square feet in—? I am no mathematician.

I am more fortunate than many people here, because I have patience, imagination, and recollections to stay me. My body may suffer, it has fallen away, it may fall into nothingness and I shall go into nothingness along with it. But my mental health is superb, my spirit was never better. It is strong, quiet. I muster my humor with a shrug when need be. I have known many quiet places, and now I may go to them, released to ride where I list in my cart or on my *mulo*, seeing warm gray mountains saluting the milky blue sky, seeing poppies, hearing a woman cry to her child, *Mah-ree-ah!* in the village below my feet.

Nathan Dreyfoos possessed a reservoir of pictures, perhaps he had more beauty stowed away than almost any other prisoner in the place. At will he could go to Suffolk or to Rome. There was the Swedish naval base; Karlskrona was the name; he could go there whenever he chose. Did Karlskrona have as large a population as Andersonville? He was positive that it had not. . . . He could go to Málaga. Málaga had many more people in it than did Andersonville.

But he did not want more people, so now he would leave. He would get into his *burrito* cart, the fine strong cart he'd had when he was eight or nine. But then his father insisted that José accompany him, unless he were to drive within restricted limits of the beach behind the big house . . . no, no! Better was the time when they'd come back to Spain again—Nathan recollected: he was fifteen at the time. That was when his father permitted him to go alone into the mountains. Nathan had begged endlessly that he be allowed to go, and alone; finally Solomon Dreyfoos weakened.

My son, there are bandits.

Father, I'm not afraid. Six feet one—

Yes, yes, yes, six feet one, and skinny as this pen in my hand!

Now, Father, did you ever know, personally, a man who was attacked by bandits on the road where I will go?

So which is the road on which you will go? You would go to Granada?

I thought I had rather go to Ronda; I've been to Granada by coach. I should like to go west to Marbella or Estepona. According to the maps, there are fine roads leading across the mountains to Ronda, by way of Ojen or Gaucín—

Fine roads? They're nothing of the kind. I was there, years ago, when you were small. Don Juan Huelín and I— A miserable road, very long, very winding, very steep, going no place at all, huge stones rattling down the cliffs, going no place whatsoever, our carriage nearly upset— Ah, I think it *did* upset! A wheel came off and—

Father. Did you meet any bandits?

I'm telling you, my son, there were bandits all about!

Did you meet any?

Go away, go away, don't twit me, I'm a busy man. Go get yourself hit over the head by bandits. No ransom will they get from me!

Nathan, don't tell your mother that you contemplate anything so dangerous. Such a worry it should be for her.

But I've already told Mother. She thinks it's splendid.

Well, well, well, Mr. Halliburton says that you have done so fine in your studies. I promised you should have a treat if he gave a good report on your work for the recent months. Now it's late in July: a holiday you shall have. Oh, my poor son, going to the mountains with bandits—!

Nathan flew up the wide winding marble staircase from the ground floor of the house, where his father's office was located; he sprang up that staircase three steps at a time, and found his mother working at needlepoint in the high cool sitting room. She tortured her eyes to build the thing, but she was not happy unless she put in four or five hours of work daily. . . . She was creative: she wrote simple little rhymes about children and pets and gardens, and many of these had been published in newspapers and magazines. The money which she received in small amounts for her efforts was kept in a purse of blue brocade, especially to give to beggars or to nuns who came soliciting alms.

Nathan's mother had been Rose Margolis. She was brought together with Solomon Dreyfoos by a marriage broker in Boston when she was twenty-four and Solomon was forty-three. The match was made in Boston but little Nathan considered that it might have been made in Heaven. Never did he hear his parents exchange a word of doubt, rivalry or recrimination. They must have been solid in devotion from the day of their wedding. Rose was big-boned, homely, and had grown very fat by the time she was in her middle thirties; Sol Dreyfoos appeared to become more spare and stooped, if more energetic, each year of his life. He was nervous but dependable—a haggard black-eyed man with a little string of whiskers which looked false.

Nathan was an only child, but he wished that he had brothers and sisters by the dozen; it would have been such fun when they traveled, which was aggressively, constantly. Solomon's business took him to England and France, back across the Atlantic to Boston, Philadelphia, New York again; perhaps back across the Atlantic to France again; by boat to Spain; thence by boat to Genoa or Naples; back to Boston in the autumn once more. We, said Solomon, are the Wandering Jews. He said it often, he said it to Nathan when Nate was three, and Sol was holding him up at the rail of a fast mail ship, listening to fog horns announcing that Liverpool was near and the fast mail would become slow mail if the fog didn't lift.

. . . Went springing up those stairs, his brooding eyes alight, his wide loose-lipped mouth at a grin. His mother pushed down her specs and beamed at him, her plump hands came away from the frame whereon she was effecting seriously a collection of marble columns, bedizened ponies, incredibly lean and pink greyhounds, and a peasant population provided with baskets of fruit and vegetables. Sometimes she worked for a week on one figure, sometimes for a fortnight on another; when she was in a mood to work on flowers she could not work on knights and ladies. Therefore the assemblage of figures seemed suffering from ulceration at various colorful points, some looked like lepers, some were skeletal; but Rose could see far beyond this incompleteness, she could see the thing of beauty which would emerge.

What are you going to do with it, Rose? And what shall you do with it in the end, Madame? Is this destined for a museum, Señora? Oh, no, and her smooth contented laugh rippled, the sound which to Nathan was the most comforting music in the world (when he needed to be comforted, which was seldom: the world was so kind to him, so violent and mean to many other boys he saw). Oh, no. I just thought maybe it would make A Nice Present To Give Someone. She always said that, whether she worked at lace or embroidery: A Nice Present To Give Someone. Rose loved to give things away—personal things, toiled over. At this rate it would be a long while before her latest needlepoint became A Nice Present; she had begun it in Holland early in 1854, and here it was July, 1856. Of course she worked on other things from time to time, and she had written a sonata in between, to say nothing of seven poems entitled respectively, Humility, The Happy Lambs, I Tread the Path, To My Kitten, Trust, On A Sleeping Baby, The Bobbins. Five of these had been accepted by editors and published, and now reposed in the album for which Rose had worked covers decorated with silver wire stitching, and which bore the imposing title, The Works Of Mrs. R. M. Dreyfoos.

Sol Dreyfoos thought the album a magnificent thing, and was eternally fetching it out to show to callers. Each poem or musical achievement of his wife's filled him with admiration. Always he said that he did not think he understood it completely (an old purchasing agent like himself—nothing but figures in his head—nothing but francs and dollar-signs and pounds sterling!) but that it was very beautiful. Secretly he was alarmed to see how little his wife's creations brought when they were sold; Sol wondered how composers and poets got along; he had heard that they didn't, that many of them starved.

. . . Mother, Mother!

Hm. You are smiling so hard I know you have great news.

Mother, he's going to permit me—

Now, I am glad! That is his business, Nathan; it is a father's business, not the business of a mother, to decide such things. But for your sake I am so glad he decided that you are to go. Nathan, come and look. I have finished my bananas.

Yes—they're wonderful. They're like gold—

Bananas, real bananas, are like gold—

Mother, I've been considering. I think I'll buy Tomás from the gardener.

Buy Tomás? I thought you planned to borrow a mule if—

But, you see, then I should feel that Tomás was *mine*. He's a splendid donkey, young enough not to tire, but splendidly disciplined. Nor does he bite or kick. Olmedo loads him with rock, halfway up to the old Gibralfaro, and brings him down with it—two great panniers, heavy as can be. Back and forth, all the day through, up and down. And still Tomás is ready for more. I've ridden him at sunset after he'd toiled like a slave, and he was fairly ready to canter—

Hm. That will take your savings.

But it would be such a lark, *ma chère maman,* to know that he was mine. I should feel like an emperor—like one of your people stepped from that needlepoint frame. Hills, valleys, vistas, *las montañas, las colinas*—all mine, all mine, spread before my gaze as if I were king of the entire landscape—

Ah, young ambition! Nate, you should not wish to be a king.

Of course not. I don't wish to be one truly. But—you know the feeling I mean—

Ja, ja, ja, the feeling of possession. It brings security, and that is what we seek. But what would you do with Tomás after you're coming back from your jaunt in the mountains? Where would you stable him? We have no room in our stable.

Tomás isn't very large and he's *very* good tempered. I should think that Carlos might make room for him somewhere.

But Carlos says that horses do not like to be stabled with *mulos.* And who would feed and water poor Tomás? You should have to pay one of the servants; and you know how your father bids you not to be extravagant because you are a rich man's son.

Well, *es verdad.* I suppose you're right, Mother, as usual. Very well. I'll *rent* Tomás from the gardener!

That is my wise son. When shall you depart on your adventure?

Oh, not until Monday. Hang it all—I promised the monks I'd bring my fiddle and play for those old blind people on Sunday. They said it would be a joy to them.

Nathan, you play very well. I wish your dear grandfather had lived longer so that you might have heard him play—

I did hear him, when I was a little tad. Twice, in Boston.

But then you were too young to appreciate. I had hoped so that you would take up the violin in the way he did. But that means work, work, work, practice, practice, practice, the livelong day.

Ha. Precious chance I've had for that, living here and there as we do—

But, Nathan, you don't truly *like* to practice.

I know it, hang it all. But I don't play too badly as it is. And at least Mr. Halliburton says I've done well with my studies. He must have praised me to Father, or I'd never be permitted to go.

Nathan, he did praise you to your father; I heard him do so. And I think that Mr. Halliburton is the very best tutor we have found for you, ever. Should you like to invite him to go back to America in the fall, with us, after we leave England?

Oh, *Madre!* He's a hundred times pleasanter than that old Revere, and a thousand times more intelligent than Cuff was. That would be simply ripping!

Very well, I myself shall speak to your father about it. We will see. It will be expensive—the passage—but— Nathan, one thing. When you ride to the mountains, you must forget who you are. You must be dressed very simply—almost like—

I know—like a peasant—in rough clothes!

You speak almost perfect Andaluz, or so I hear the servants say. So I am not worried about— And you are tall and strong, you can run foot-races, you are a fine fencer. So I shall not worry about— But, my son, there *are* bandits in those mountains. Many.

But I'll travel like a poor chap, I'll put up only at the cheaper inns.

Well, God go with thee.

She looked at him after he had kissed her and was gone prancing away to dicker with the gardener— She looked at him as he left the room, and before she adjusted her specs again— She looked at him lovingly and thought, Life has been and is being too easy for my son. But what can one do? Should I want him to starve as I starved when I was a little girl, when my own father could not get work in the cafés? Should I want him to tramp the roads with a peddler's pack on his back, as dear Solomon did when he was of the same age? But Nathan does not seem cut out for a merchant. He does not seem cut out for anything except to be a dear sweet son! And he is kind of heart. Thank God!

Nathan's impulse was to buy beautiful accoutrements for Tomás; indeed this was nominated in his agreement with Olmedo. Reluctantly he decided that new harness must wait until his return: the crimson-and-purple halter, the embroidered bands of heavy stitched fabric to bind Tomás's chunky body, to pass below his efficient fly-batting tail— These might attract envy and cupidity along the road, they would most certainly attract attention. Accordingly the boy set forth with a newly curried Tomás but with the old patched stained furniture. One basket carried the few necessaries which Nathan allowed himself in the way of clothing and toilet articles, another held bread, cheese and wine against emergencies. He was armed with a damascene clasp-knife from Toledo and a rusty double-barreled pistol bought in

Sheffield when he was twelve; his father warned him to keep this armament out of sight. He had also his long-saved hoard of money concealed in an old innocent-looking loaf of bread, together with a bottle of saleratus to be used in case of snakebite, and a volume of Lord Byron. The entire household gathered in the courtyard to wish Nathan godspeed and to criticize his appearance . . . his legs were so long that they nearly touched the ground. Solomon Dreyfoos said that if Tomás grew weary Nathan must pick the donkey up and carry him. Olmedo the gardener embraced first Tomás, then Nathan, then Tomás again; this would be the first time Olmedo and Tomás had ever been separated since Tomás was a colt and was first acquired. Olmedo's dark tinny cheek quivered at thought of it, and the tears ran and split amid his wrinkles. He always called Nathan *Hombre!*—which pleased Nathan exceedingly. The *camereras* waved their aprons, and mule and rider picked their way through the gate out into busy Málaga with its towering carts and moving black boulders of oxen. In this way Nathan rode into one of the most rewarding experiences of his young life, and he had been trained and had been shown the way to find a reward in almost any experience.

. . . Soldier, is the sun staring meanly? Does it burn your eyeballs and crack your lips? Retreat into the cave.

The steps had been formed as early as the Fourth Century A.D., or so an earnest and archeologically-inclined old priest believed . . . Nathan Dreyfoos and the priest crawled there together, Nathan going first across the slanted fissured crumbling stair, the priest following with cassock belted up, his bony legs arching down, his sandals seeking a safe hold on the surface. Down through fig boughs and blackberry vines, down through shadows where fat grass-green lizards held up their gargoyle heads in alarm and then scooted away. Down to the altars thirty meters below. Roofs of both chapels had fallen in—an earthquake was believed to have shaken the huge squared blocks apart, some hundreds of years since—and thin silky moss waved like miniature fields of wheat on the rich slimed slabs. No other people, no spectators, no ghosts . . . the priest knelt before the damp seeping altar with its defaced fresco depicting San Jorge above; he prayed briefly. Nathan Dreyfoos stood with straw hat in his hand, watching, listening to the flutter of birds in fig branches far overhead, the increasing flutter of speedy little bats in stalagmited caverns beyond San Jorge's ruined altar. Sun was low behind the mountains, soon it would be evening, Nathan's watch said that it was almost seven o'clock . . . but coolness coming from these fissures was never implacable, never born of decay. Something lived deep in the blackness, and that thing which lived was not a Fright, it was gentle and dignified, golden as a candle flame.

My son, you do not pray.

Often I pray, but I do not kneel here. I am a Jew.

But many Catholics in Spain are Jews, or were Jews. Why, what of the Jewish bishop of Burgos? What of the great artist Gil de Siloé—?

I know.

Some of our best Catholics are—

I know.

In your house, do your father and mother keep the Jewish holidays, the dietary laws of the Jews?

My father says that we are all children of the world at large, thank God—not children of a given Church or creed. He does not keep the prescribed laws, but he respects those who do. He respects all men who adhere to that in which they believe.

Then there was nothing in your training to prevent your kneeling with me here and now, young man!

Nathan said after some thought, My body remained standing but my soul knelt.

They crept back up the steps, stung by blackberry barbs.

I appreciate your guiding me to the cave, *Señor Cure*, said Nathan. Will you accept this small offering for the poor of your parish?

The mountains tawny as lions, their hide like the hide of elephants, their shape like a herd of oxen asleep, and blue light coming up behind them as if a great cool lamp were sending it . . . Tomás brayed in greeting at seeing his friend reappear. This time he brayed exactly fifteen times; Nathan counted—*aww, eeeh, aww*—fifteen times, and the most that Tomás had ever brayed was seventeen.

Can I reach the next village before dark?

No, no, no, my son, you'll be an hour short; and it is death to wander in the blackness of these mountains when you do not know the path. I have a bed to spare, but it is now given over to a Carthusian who broke his leg while crossing the hills, and some shepherds found him and brought him to me. Juan Solivellas takes travelers into his house. Go past the church ramp, then turn right at the first street beyond. His house is on the seventh step below; go with care on that old Moorish ramp: the cobble stones are in bad condition, the sewer is broken in. A red gate leads to his courtyard; and you'll see the stable beyond the well, and the house itself is on the left. You may smell the olive oil before you get there, the women may be cooking *churos*.

. . . In Andersonville there were no *churos*, no paste squeezed in long tubular sections, swirling in steaming oil, stirred round and round into concentric patterns with a hot smooth stick, giggled at by naughty boys who made the obvious jokes about their appearance . . . lifted from olives' fat at last, to drain and dry. O joy and warmth and crispness—joy of fat and brownness, joy of taste, taste, taste as your teeth went through and your tongue played and your soul sprang out to thank the beaming cooks.

The life of Nathan Dreyfoos had been rich as olive oil, rich as golden circlets manufactured therein. It grieved him that other men might not possess the variation of a past to comfort them. He felt that (except in cases of the very young) it was the people of enforced limitation who went down quickest. Had Evatt known nothing except a brindled cow, a milking stool, a street with elms? These were not to be had in Andersonville. They were not to be had in the army either; but it was one thing to live as a human, to march and contend as a human with other proud humans beside you; and it was another thing to be a black starved worm among black starved worms. Had Percival known nothing except a lexicon and a row of students? Had Hank known nothing except receding water and the clams he dug upon the flats? . . . Ah, the prisoners bent, they faded, they crawled—ah, they ceased their crawling, began to caterwaul; soon came the cessation of their cry. Even in the oven of this August, Nathan felt himself invulnerable. He could not be drained, cooked, panicked. Always there bloomed stanch memory of various beauties. Far away, but beauties still. The fence was fifteen feet high, the imagined mountains taller.

XL

Eric Torrosian said, My mind's made up.

His friend Malachi Plover said, I wouldn't try it.

But I've made up my mind. I'm going to try it.

Hell of a way to flank out. I couldn't never do it. I'd get a gripe in my insides and just whoop them up.

Eric Torrosian had worked with his father up and down the city of New York, carrying bundles of rugs and trying to sell them from house to house. His mother, who was a German, insisted that he should attend school instead; and she and her Armenian husband engaged in conflicts over the matter and supported a grinding persistent feud between them. Sometimes the mother triumphed: Eric was sent to sit behind a desk at Mr. Gottfried Ringel's day school where the rooms were always too cold in winter and too hot in summer, and where the washroom smelled like poison. For such instruction as was awarded her son, Mrs. Torrosian had to pay two dollars per month. The father beat the air with his hands and wailed that the price was exorbitant. But Anna wanted her son to be a lawyer and this was the first step.

Eric didn't get to take more than the first step. His father managed to remove him from school periodically on various pretexts, and finally had sufficient excuse for a permanent cessation of Eric's school days. Henry Torrosian slipped on a flight of icy steps and rolled all the way to the bottom, not well cushioned by his pack of rugs. After that he was unable to carry bundles, and Eric had to go along as pack-horse, else there would have been nothing for them to eat. Eric pleaded with his father to get a pushcart, but the old man demanded, How would I get a pushcart up and down stairs?

You could leave the cart, and carry up one rug at a time to customers.

And have my stock stolen? You are a devil.

No, Father. You could get a little boy. You could give him a dime to watch the cart and keep thieves away.

You are a lazy devil. So I've got that many dimes? Come along with you, and mind you don't crush that packet of new laces.

This went on until Eric was sixteen, nearly seventeen, and one day he was walking alone on Broadway, on his way to pick up an express package, and he was attracted by a sign stating the large bounty offered to men who would enlist in the newest regiment being raised. He went into the tobacco store which served as recruiting headquarters, with two desks and a flag and a brilliantly-uniformed captain and an almost-as-brilliantly-uniformed sergeant and a not-too-brilliantly-uniformed pair of privates, accompanied by several neighborhood idlers who were not enlistees: they said that they were merely chewing the fat. One was a bearded old doctor whose hands shivered with palsy; but he guided Eric Torrosian into the back room among tobacco kegs and told him to take off his shirt. He pounded Eric's thin chest and cupped his hairy ear against Eric's ribs, listening. Also he whispered that Eric must unbutton his pants; he would see if he had any visible symptoms of syphilis. The entire examination took about three minutes, though they told him that a surgeon would look him over later. The old doctor, or so he claimed to be, begged the boy for a chew of tobacco, and, when he had none to give, the man said that a few cents in currency would be just as welcome; then the doctor could buy his own chew. Eric gave him a three-cent-piece and the doctor thanked him effusively. He propelled the boy into the front room, punching him alternately in the back and in the buttocks as he moved close behind him. He said, Captain O'Connor, I give you my word—a fine specimen of young manhood. A fine, fine specimen. This was the first time anyone had ever called Eric a fine specimen of manhood or even of boyhood, and he was proportionately pleased. He gave his age as eighteen and signed the roll. He was eager for the bounty, but they told him that the money could not be paid until he reported for duty at an uptown armory; that is, the State and Special bounties might be paid then. The National bounty would not be forthcoming until a certain amount of red tape had been untied.

Eric was sent home to get his personal belongings, and was warned to report at the armory not later than seven o'clock that night. Also he was given a ticket good for dinner and supper and breakfast at an eating-house near the armory, and the sergeant presented him with a paper nosegay of red-white-and-blue flowers to put in his button hole. Those soldiers laughed after he was outside, or as he was going out; he heard what they said; they knew well that Eric was not eighteen; in fact, one of them didn't think that Eric was even sixteen. He guessed his age as fifteen, which infuriated the boy, and made him consider going back inside and giving that soldier a piece of his mind. But he didn't go.

Instead he picked up the express package and took it home, where his father was mending the fringe on a mottled rug which had been chewed by rats somewhere in transit. Henry Torrosian was sitting cross-leggèd on the big wide work table shoved against the window to gain light. This alone prevented him from stabbing Eric with his needle when Eric gave the news. Anna burst into dreadful lamentation and cried and prayed in German, and when she could be understood she demanded that Henry go immediately to the recruiters and inform them that Eric was only sixteen, and couldn't go to the army.

You do that and I'll run away.

Where would you run to?

I'd walk, I'd catch rides on freight wagons. I'd get a job as a prentice in Philadelphia or Boston or somewheres. You'd never find me.

He spoke the truth, for he had planned to run away if they scotched his military plans.

Ai. Now by my own son I am deserted. My back is lame, boy. How can I carry carpetings up and down stairways?

Get a cart, get a boy, like I said. Then he played his trump card. He said that he would share his bounties with them. Was it one hundred dollars from the Government, fifty dollars from the State of New York, fifty dollars Special Bounty? Eric was not certain as to the amount but he would give his parents half the accrual.

Soon his father had put on his black beaver hat—he'd worn that same hat ever since Eric could remember, and long before Eric could remember; he mended it himself— Henry put on his black beaver hat and went to bargain for a used pushcart. Anna hung through the window, calling to neighbor women in the four-story building opposite, telling them that her bold son had enlisted and would soon go to fight Rebels; when the war was over he would return—as an officer, most likely—and then he would become a lawyer.

Eventually Eric and thirty-three other recruits were transferred, from the regiment in which they had originally enlisted, to the ranks of the One Hundred and Twentieth New York. Eric was a serious-minded youth with syrupy eyes, a mound of coarse black hair, hollow cheeks and thick, wide lips. No one picked on him because of his youth; firstly, there were many other fifteen- or sixteen- or seventeen-year-olds in the One Hundred and Twentieth New York; secondly, he had grown up in a neighborhood where one must maul or be mauled in a fight, and he had learned aptly several delicate tricks of mayhem. He served with no complaint and liked the life better than life at home, although a cannonade always frightened him, it made him turn sheet-white and shaking; still he trotted along with his musket as the others trotted, grunting and mumbling when he caught enough breath to do so. One day in May it was unbearably hot, and the Virginia woods were afire, and folks said that wounded men were being burned to death in the woods up ahead: if you listened closely you could hear them screaming. Eric listened but he couldn't hear the shrieks—too many cannon in the distance. What he did observe, however, was a broken tiny farmhouse barely visible through trees on the right, and he made out the remains of a wooden well-curb out in back. Even a ruined well might hold water, and he and Malachi Plover and a big youth named Kennedy discussed the problem in low tones. This task called for one man to climb down into the well, one to pass canteens back and forth, one to remain on guard. On a farm of that kind, a mere wasted shell of a farm, most likely there would be no rope remaining on the windlass or else the windlass wouldn't work. Every canteen in their company was dry as a bone; the regiment had sprawled in those woods for a long time. Eric Torrosian talked to his sergeant. The sergeant said that he didn't dare give him any Hitch Up And Go Ahead; their orders were to remain where they were, until ordered to move forward or back; but the sergeant guessed that the One Hundred and Twentieth would be lying right there on their lame asses the rest of that day. He handed over his own canteen to Eric and so did others. The sergeant turned his back and pretended not to witness their departure.

There were a few bullets whining through the forest from time to time and whacking into trees, and a few men in the regiment had been hit by this overflow of fire, so the boys kept low. Malachi and Eric left their muskets and other equipment behind; they were bedecked with canteens until they could barely crawl, and they wondered how they'd ever make the return when those canteens were filled—if they were filled. Kennedy crawled behind; they warned him to keep his musket off cock, they didn't want to be shot. In the shelter of the stripped old cottage and out-houses they scurried to the well, and Eric saw water shining at the bottom. Kennedy found an old wagon tongue lying in the grass, and they employed it as a kind of ladder . . . Eric crawled down, and Malachi passed him the canteens two at a time, dangling from extended straps taken from other canteens. It was cool and wonderful at the bottom of this mossy, slimy shaft; there were frogs and maybe lizards slipping about; the water was muddy as soon as he'd stirred it up, but it was water.

Suddenly in woods nearby a crashing wave of gunfire broke out in a string of sound like Chinese crackers at a celebration, and son of a bitch if you couldn't hear the Rebs a-hollering. Let's get, cried Malachi, and his face loomed patched with shadow, an inhuman face as he bent over the well-curbing. A piece of the rotten wood broke beneath his weight, and damp dust and splinters and punk came down all over Eric Torrosian's upturned face, and fairly blinded him. He wouldn't bother with those last two canteens— Yes, surely he would; maybe one was *his*; so he wound the straps around his neck and went pawing and wrenching up the wagon tongue, trying to shinny up rapidly, tearing his clothes as he went. His left eye pained him, and it had dust in it and it stung and watered. When he got to the top and tumbled out on the ground the other canteens were lying there, just the way Plover had dumped them when he took flight. Malachi Plover was halfway to the fence, but he was looking back as he ran, and he beckoned wildly at Eric when the boy appeared. Kennedy was a couple of rods ahead of Plover, and Eric saw him turn, halt, lift his gun and fire, and he heard the ball tear the air past him. There was a loud *bum, bum, bum* of answering fire from the other side of the little farm. By this time Eric had dropped to the ground and so had Plover. They both saw Kennedy: he threw his arms out widely—his musket flew one way, something else from his right hand flew in the other direction, and he seemed to jump high and fall backward as if the wind had been knocked out of him by a boxer's blow. Back among trees the flags of the One Hundred and Twentieth were being hastened to safety, and the entire regiment was seeking safety too; the boys couldn't see hide nor hair of anybody, except for those bobbing wads of Colors. (When the regimental Colors were presented, they were presented by a rather pretty spinster sister of one of the field officers who said charmingly, These Colors are warranted not to run! Hah. Eric thought of her now—straw bonnet and black lace mitts and all.)

He stood up and held up his hands, for Rebels were all around him. A tall fellow with seasoned sunburnt face pointed to the doorway with a revolver in his hand and said, Yank, go over and set down on that stoop. Go on, youngster, move—move e'er I put a chunk of lead through you! So Eric went to the step of the ruined house and sat down. Presently an armed soldier brought Malachi Plover to sit beside him, and Malachi said that Kennedy was dead, stone dead. He had been pierced by at least five bullets. Malachi gave the news stupidly, and Eric received the news just as stupidly. They sat and looked at grassy ground before them, and now and then stole glances at the Rebels who guarded them. It seemed odd to see gray and tan and brownish dust-colored figures standing erect so close at hand. The only ones they'd seen previously, close at hand, had been lying mute.

In this manner Eric Torrosian was captured, and no enemy so much as touched an article of his belongings that first night. But the second day following, when the guardianship of seventy-two prisoners was taken over by irregular troops behind the lines, he was stripped of watch, pocketknife, new shoes and all such sundries. He saw what was happening to the column and managed to put slabs of currency inside both cheeks, for recently he had been paid. Hence the villains got only his small change. He talked oddly, with those folds of money bulking between his teeth and the wet flesh of his mouth's inner lining, but since the Rebels didn't know how he talked at other times they discerned nothing suspicious in his responses. His cheeks appeared smooth instead of hollow, and the Rebels didn't know that he was naturally hollow-cheeked. He saved twenty-nine dollars in greenbacks which would be about three hundred dollars Confed. It gagged him when finally he removed the money, and he vomited copiously, but at least he had the money; and it helped to keep him and Malachi alive after they reached Andersonville, and it fed them en route. Malachi's money was stolen.

They arrived at Andersonville in a pouring rain, and waded through mud all the way from the cars to the stockade.

They landed in a shebang with three fellows also from the Second Brigade of the Fourth Division of the Second Corps, who had been captured in the Virginia woods too. The other fellows said it was true about the wounded being burned to death in the forest fire; one man had been wounded himself, and, temporarily weakened from loss of blood, he had to lie there and listen to the squeals and *yaaah* and Mother, have mercy, shoot me for *Goddddssake*. Finally he summoned enough strength to drag himself out of the fire's course and into some smoking rubble where a blaze had swept already. The man's name was Toby Mutterson and Toby bragged that he had been a hero and had pulled out another man as well, but he didn't know what happened to the other man finally. Toby's clothing was pretty well scorched as he lay amid those soft embers, and he exhibited the holes and raw brown fibers to prove his tale. He said that his blood-soaked condition might have saved his life; and the bleeding had stopped, praise be, and didn't start up again. He was wounded in the fleshy part of his thigh, but the bone wasn't broken.

Toby did not thrive at Andersonville because worms got into his wound promptly, and the authorities wouldn't let him into the hospital because he made the mistake of walking down to the gate surgeons to apply for admittance, instead of being carried. He jerked and whined in his sleep, and then his wound would hurt him so badly that he'd get up and limp around outside the shebang and blunder against neighboring shebangs or step upon sleeping men, and would be cursed and pummeled. Someone told him that ground oak ashes would expel the maggots from his wound, and he begged Eric to buy oak ashes for him. Finally Eric found an old man among the guards who said that he could burn some oak and fetch the ashes for ten dollars Confed. When the twelve o'clock round of calls issued from the stockade's rim that night, Eric must be lying in wait in blackness, just next to the deadline in front of the old guard's booth. The guard would toss down a cord with a stone attached to the end, and Eric should fasten his currency to the cord; the guard would pull it up, and then he would toss out the cord a second time with the packet of ground-up ashes attached. . . . Faithfully Eric followed instructions; he crouched amid shadows and heard the yells go out, and the answering growls of prisoners. A guard would start in and call, Station Number Three, twelve o'clock and all's well, and immediately the prisoners would start yapping, Twelve o'clock and, Mister, here's your mule, and other things less polite. Station Number Five, twelve o'clock and all's well, and the whoop to confound all guards and all enemies, Station Number Five, twelve o'clock and go diddle your grandma.

The stone fell down, Eric found the cord by fumbling and raking with both hands; here was the rock, and a long end of string for tying; he knotted the folded one-dollar U.S. greenback into place and jerked the cord hard to signify that the money was ready. It went scraping and tapping up the wall, and after a few minutes there was another thud, and Eric Torrosian clawed round until he found the string and the precious solid little envelope tied to it. He took the packet and ran back to the shebang as fast as he could go, which wasn't very fast. Oh, thanks, thanks, thanks, you're a real sport, Eric; give me that stuff, so's I can start getting rid of them old cutworms; Eric, I swear that when we get out of here and get North, you come to Pennsylvania and my mother will take good care of you; cook you the best pork ribs you ever tasted, and shoo-fly pies and truck; and you can lie abed on a featherbed all morning if you want to. Come on, let's open the paper up. . . . They were out of pine splinters, they had no light, so Toby Mutterson had to anoint his wound in the dark. Pretty soon he began to howl like all possessed. Oh, God, it's killing me, help me get that stuff out of there, and he went plunging around, rolling and gargling in the dark, and asking for somebody to pour water in his wound. But you say you don't want swamp water, and that's all we got. It'll just give you more worms. Ow, ow, ahhhh, I don't care what God damn water you use; the hell with clean wells and well rights, the God damn hell with clean water; wash it, wash it out, it's killlling me. And people from other shebangs hallooing, For Christ sake, quit that noise, you crazy poop. . . . So they used swamp water, and washed out Mutterson's lively wound; Eric guessed that he and Malachi sponged the wound a dozen times with a scrap of rag. Toby would howl every time they touched the suppurating hole, but after numerous swabbings he subsided into a quieter whimpering. At dawn they woke up and looked; here were the remains of the packet. No oak ashes. Salt. That was it: just plain coarse salt.

Eric went to the old guard's station late that day when the old man came back on duty, and he stood below and assailed him. The old man said, Sonny, I couldn't find no oak like I said I could. I lowed salt would do tolerable well. Eric kept crying epithets which had sunk early into his memory, but the bearded guard stood looking earnestly beyond Eric and pretending that he was deaf. Just about dusk Eric came back, and this time he had a stone. It was a fine stone, round and brownish and hard, and it was half as big as a goodsized apple. He watched his chance, and when the guard (a skinny patriarch he stood against the pale yellow western sky) was looking the other way, Eric flung the stone. He had taken careful aim, and as a small boy he had thrown stones in numerous street fights and hurled them accurately, but he missed the guard's head by a few inches. The old man must have been astonished when he heard that whirring past his ear. He caught up his piece and fired into the stockade; in the dimness below there was a great scurrying and terror, but apparently no one was hit. The next day Eric saw a little throng around a shack of rags and pine bark, and people were pointing. He went over for a look, but naturally did not confess that it was he who threw the stone to provoke the guard. From the looks of that pine bark the musket had been loaded with buck-and-ball: maybe one of the old Sixty-nines from Harper's Ferry. They took three buckshot and one heavy ball as a standard load. The charge passed just beneath the roof-tree, out the other side, and into earth beyond. Six men spooned together in that shack, and not one of them hit. Eric felt better. But Toby Mutterson was carried to the hospital the next Sunday, and they heard within the week that he was dead. Almost nobody ever came back from the hospital.

Eric went down to the old guard's station and waited for him to appear. He wanted to have the satisfaction of telling him that he had killed Toby with that salt, although Eric's conscience assured him that Toby would have died anyway sooner or later. Pretty soon the guard was changed, but it wasn't the graybeard who came; it was a gaunt child. His gun was bigger than he was by far and maybe weighed more. Hey there, guard, where's the old man used to be at this station? The boy was frightened—it seemed to be his first time on duty—for he jumped in surprise when Eric addressed him. Go way, Yank. We can't speak to prisoners. Oh, don't be a dunce; be a good fellow; all the guards talk to prisoners. Come on, where's the old man? The boy looked around cautiously and then leaned his small shaggy head across the rim. He's dead, Yank. Just died today. . . . What do you mean, dead? How did he die? . . . Just had a fit and died; just fell in a fit after eating. . . . That seemed queer. It seemed almost that Toby had come back like an avenging angel and taken the old man away with him.

Well, Eric Torrosian had made up his mind, and he wasn't going to die like either of them; neither with worms and bad blood like Toby, nor in a sudden fit like the old man. He refused to shrink into slow wastage as he saw so many others doing. He was going to flank out of there, and it seemed that there was one way in which it might be done. He would flank out with the dead.

He hated and feared the dead, as most people always have, and sometimes when he looked at the long horrid row of them he questioned himself concerning his reason for this detestation. In actuality their ugliness was no worse than that of the living, except perhaps in those cases where the eyes had congealed open. Somehow those eyes

made Eric think of grapes he used to see in fruit-stalls off the Bowery—
grapes that were a little squashed—shed of their skins but still bulbous.

The living around him were ugly and he himself was ugly. A man
died, and Malachi Plover helped to carry him to the dead row, so
Plover and another fellow took what was left in the dead man's
pockets. Among other things the dead man had a mirror: a round flat
wafer, tin on one side and looking glass on the other. It had been
broken, perhaps long before, but two stiff shreds of the silvered glass
remained stuck in the frame, and they were big enough for you to
see yourself in, with the slash of the break cutting across your face
and making a scar which didn't exist. Eric Torrosian regarded himself with fright when he looked in that mirror; he looked like dead
people. Being swarthy as to coloration and cursed with a stiff black
beard, he thought that by this time (more than three months a prisoner) he looked like his own father. But Henry Torrosian's beard
was combed gently, and his hair was clipped by his wife's scissors;
when he could afford it he brushed cologne into his beard and linen
to make himself more agreeable to lady customers. Eric had no cologne
and no shears. His beard was grown into a mass and swarmed with
lice; his hair, always lengthy, was black disordered sedge. Thin by
the determination of his own nature (and—he disliked recognizing
the thought but the knowledge was there: he was thinned by ex-
cessive masturbation during his early teens. He had heard that masturbation would drive him insane, and he had bad dreams in which
he saw himself insane and roaring) he had fallen away as a filthy
ghost since he entered this stockade. Maybe he weighed ten stone
when he came in; he doubted that he weighed seven stone now.

He could pass as a dead man if he could remain quiet, and could
endure without a sound the persecutions to which he would be subjected in handling.

Therefore, the second evening after he said, My mind's made up,
he was sewn into a blanket by Malachi. It was a mere shred of
blanket, a pattern of holes held together by shoddy scraps, a spider-
web, a leaf chewed by bugs. Once in a while you saw a dead man
bundled in such wrapping, although more frequently they were carried down in their pants or drawers, and very often nude. It appeared
that no one would bother to rip the worthless remnant from Eric's
body. Eric reached out and shook hands all round with his comrades,
and then Malachi Plover stitched the upper part of the rags in two
or three more places. No trouble about breathing; the holes took care
of that. Malachi and a Pennsylvanian (a companion of the dead
Mutterson whom they called Dutchy) lugged Eric to the dead row
and whispered Goodbye before they put him down. The wagon
wouldn't come in until dawn, it was feared, and Eric would have to
lie in the mute flat rank all night. Sometimes the wagon did appear

in the evening, and the dead were lifted on, twenty-five or thereabouts to the load. Eric had instructed the boys to put him down
somewhere near the farther end of a section of twenty-five—say number twenty-three or twenty-four. That way he would be almost certain to be placed on top of the load. But more bodies had been deposited since they spied out the situation, and Eric was actually
number twenty-five, but he did not know it. His friends feared for
his life. Maybe the blacks who took him away would carry only
twenty-three or twenty-four as the first cargo, and Eric would find
himself at the bottom of the next load under hundreds and hundreds
of pounds of bodies. Well, there was no help for it—he had demanded
that they aid him in this attempt, so Goodbye, old fellow, and I'm
glad I ain't laying there instead of you. They went away.

Slowly Eric Torrosian relaxed the few thin muscles remaining to
him, which he had drawn taut to simulate the stiffness of a corpse.
He dared not actually move his limbs while there was any daylight
left, else a passerby might pay heed or a guard peer down and detect
him. He lay in overpowering stench, for the man next to him had died
of gangrene. This smell affected him, and at last he coughed involuntarily, and then gagged from trying to quell the coughing fit;
thus he vomited. Not a soul heard him. Too many similar sounds in
the area beyond that strip of scantling which ruled the dead from
the living.

Another corpse was dumped at his right side. . . . Shadows deepened beyond Eric's blanket holes, the general brownness of twilight
came down; this did not take long to occur, for it was late when the
others fetched him. But it seemed as long again as all the days which
had passed since he was captured. He thought of bursting from his
rough shroud and crawling out of there—giving up the whole miserable effort—and then he heard a howl of gate-hinges and felt the
damp earth shake beneath an approach of heavy wheels. The dead
wagon, it was the dead wagon.

Negroes' voices talked to a guard, bodies were hoisted.·

Hey, wait there. This one he got pretty good pants.

You nigs step lively. Take them pants off outside, not here! I want
my supper.

They grumbled between themselves, but went on with the loading.

Said the guard, You got a full load. They were in the act of lifting
the thing next to Eric. It was dark. Eric began to tighten his arms
and legs and neck muscles and back muscles, he began to stiffen his
toes and fingers.

Ain't but two more to go, Mastah Guard.

Oh. Step lively. . . .

Big paws grasped Eric's upturned naked feet and dragged him
forward. More big paws went scraping under his shoulders and sank

hurtfully into his armpits; yea, he was rigid, he was rigid, they were tormenting him, he bit his tongue, it seemed that he must squeak, cry out, confound them into thinking he had come alive, get rid of their clasping, he'd never thought that they'd try to tear a corpse apart. *Hoy*. They swung him back and forth. *Hoy*, they said together on the second swing; and *hoy!* they cried in unison at the termination of the third swing, and he went sailing. Let go my stiffness, he thought in terror as he rose through the air, and then his head struck the head of a corpse atop the load; it struck a fraction of a second before his feet came down on the pile. Eric was knocked senseless. Just one quick burst of light, a sound to go with it. Nothing after that.

When he recovered consciousness he was in the deadhouse and his face was bloody, and he didn't know where he was, but he was in the deadhouse. Could a man bleed after death, if his nose had been smashed? Eric had bled; he thought for a time that he was dead; maybe he was dead; he was cold, he had never been so cold before, the cold was through and all around him, it emanated from the cold dead, the earth was cold underneath, the air was cold above, Eric was cold, the dead were cold, all the world cold, all the world dead.

If ever he walked in the world of men again, he would tell that world how the dead smelled. They smelled like a dog run over by a beer wagon, and it crawled into a narrow space between two houses just off Houston Street, and there it lay whimpering unheard and unsought and unwanted for a day or two, rotting even before the rot of unliving flesh began. Eric went into that place after a ball he had tried to catch but had missed, and so he smelled the dog four days after it died, and he had to pick up the grimy ball lying beside the grimy dog. These Andersonville dead smelled like that. They were the reek of privies and corruption found in oozing drain-pipes, they were the garbage box, the neglected fallen greasy flakes in gutters of fish markets, they were the greasy water put into an old bottle and stoppered and left in the sun (the boys whom Eric knew used to make bombshells like that, to throw at each other in warfare of their gangs; they called the bottles stink-bombs). The dead were old vomit, old bandages, old pus. They had no decency about them, they thought they were sainted and needed not to yield to manners required of men who were not dead. The dead breathed decay from lungs no longer breathing, and their lung cavities were putrid but they were cold. They had no fire or flame or query or statement about them; they lay grinning in beards and hayrick hair, their tongues were thrust out sometimes, their mouths were split open and tongueless sometimes, the fluid ran from their mouths sometimes, the fluid ran from other orifices of their bodies sometimes, the breath of their death went into soil on which they lay, and colored the cold air on

either side of them, and it ascended in a noxious weighty metallic
cloud above them, and the cloud was cold, and the people who made
it were doughy and cold, and they were dead.

Baleful in their silent mockery of him, it was as if the very silence
which they created laughed along with their smaller individual
silences. No more to do a thing any child or man-grown object had
ever desired or earned—never to make the sound or speak the word or
hear the sound; never, never to dream. In weak and stricken dread of
this motionless herd, Eric Torrosian reconstructed their lives in the
same fashion in which his own life had been poured: he shaped their
existences so. Never to taste furry red wine from a stone bottle, never
to eat an egg (ah, he had been fond of hens' eggs) and never to eat
the pickled herons' eggs which he had tasted once. . . .

The long Springfield with its proud eagle on the lock: never to
clean it again, never to bite off the cartridge paper, never to abraid
fingers with the crisp fine sandpaper bent as a polishing cloth. Nor
to march, nor to suck boiling brown coffee from a blackened tin
cup. Nor to fight in a street fight, and roll across stones, and drive
your elbow against another's belly, and hear him yip in his hot
squirming as you fought. All these things the corpses had renounced,
and Eric loathed them for it, because in silent conclave they were
censuring him for even remembering such events, and for wishing
to relive them. . . . Never to walk a street and see white-tanned-
stoutly-patched sails rising at the end of the street between brick
buildings, and to hasten, hasten for fear of missing closer sight of
the ship as it pushed the Hudson waters aside. Never to make torn
wisps of wastepaper into a ball for a kitten to play with, never to
watch the kitten propelled upward by invisible springs in its feet,
to see it somersault delightedly with the paper wad caught between
mossy-striped paws. Never to rub a dog's warm ribs until you found
the Magic Place, and then, when you had found the Magic Place
and while you were scratching it rapidly, you'd see the dog's foot
beat mechanically in air as if he too were scratching the Place, and
so you laughed and called it Magic. These matters were not agreeable
to the dead. They scorned these matters, and gave out, in one solid
and crippling stench, the verdict of their disapproval.

They refused also, these dead, to ever more carry great bales of
rugs upon their shoulders, to ever more gaze past the bright curtains
of eating-house windows and envy the well-to-do who sat before their
porter and oysters, their beer and bread and pigeon breasts and
lemonade and cod.

To heave rocks at sparrows shooting past, to be afraid of a priest
because he might lecture or thump you, to hear a woman's voice
teaching softly beside the warm stove, and with waxy smell of candles

in your nose— To hear the woman's voice buried in the long ago, separated from this moment by trivial and crabbèd years, but coming out stronger as the scent of candles continued—

To hear her teaching, *Zu Betlehem geboren*—

Your voice. *Zu Betlehem geboren*—

Ist uns ein Kindelein—

Your voice. *Ist uns ein Kindelein.*

The dead would have none of it, never, never. They would abolish all treasure great and small, they would abolish pleasure, and assuredly they would abolish the rite of pain. They had voted to do so.

To read a tale and feel your fancy drift, to walk with Little John, to draw a stronger bow than Friar Tuck himself, to be bored with Rollo and his cousin James, to wheel the thick blade of Marmion . . . they said No, they said, We will not do it, they said, We decline and refuse. Sternly. Forever. And they said also, We renounce the right to creep into rich houses, rug-laden and awed, and sit small and dusky and self-effacing on a bench in the hall while the old man is explaining about rugs to a rich dame in her parlor, and to marvel at polished mirrors and embossed walls with purple ladies playing tag under green trees.

Nor would the dead approve of rioting over a dumping ground, and bringing up forgotten wealth from beneath the layers of soaked straw and barrel-staves. Clock weights they would not discover, nor the pestle minus its mortar, nor the brass false teeth so colorfully green in corrosion, nor the torn corset nor the horse-collar with a rat's nest inside and baby rats peeping. . . . Nor would the dead countenance a solid click of billiard balls, smells of cigar smoke, the rich ferocious male laughter, the small voice saying, Paper, sir? Paper? . . . Click of billiard balls, the odor of peanuts being chewed, broadcloth buttocks bulging up beside green tables, the deep hearty frightening male laughter.

Gone always, gone completely, never to be tolerated. The dreams lonely but enfolding . . . waking at night with nothing but your youth and the creamy lust of youth to keep you company . . . ah, vision . . . ladies appearing again, with the satin rustle in which they always tread, the imagined French scents in which they've dipped themselves, the delicate foot protruding coyly cased in its shiny slipper . . . and what is this? You are privileged: she has accepted you, this golden creature here, here, *here,* she has flung over all standard of deportment, she has gone wicked, she is a pure woman but also a strumpet; invitingly she draws up her gown to reveal the delicacy underneath, she is begging you to roll and tussle and lose yourself for eternity in the lacy lake of her female state . . . power of her prettiness rules you in hidden imagined rapture until once more you are weak and exhausted, and you lie spent, and no doubt will be a maniac soon, barred, groveling in a cage.

The illusions of Eric Torrosian flared for minutes only, but they were numerous, they ruled him hard. Leaden, chill and stiff as sticks, the dead knew secrets but the secrets were secrets concerning a business of rot and dripping.

From them now he would run away. Eric climbed to his feet. The deadhouse . . . he was beyond the stockade, he was in the deadhouse made of pine boughs, he'd heard of the place, now he would go retching out. He had no blanket to cover him longer; even those skimpy tatters had been taken from him by Negroes while he lay insensible, and in their ignorance they thought he was dead.

He went staggering into the night and walked directly in front of a terrified guard. The man lifted his piece, fired, shot Eric Torrosian through the chest. At that close range the musket's charge tore a great chunk out of the boy's heart and it dangled behind his broken rib as he fell.

Eric did not witness pine flames which burned above his glazing eyes, nor hear the speculations voiced. A record of the event was noted down, and Eric Torrosian was carried back into the deadhouse, where he was welcomed by chuckling unvoiced, unheard, but still the chuckling was there; and the ground was cold, cold, cold, and now everyone in the place was dead, and soon Eric also was as cold as the others, an accepted member of their fraternity.

XLI

Willie Mann was determined not to drink water; drink water he would not, unless personally God awarded it to him as from rainclouds, as from dew condensing. People said, Rain is in the air, sometimes; and those were the times when Willie Mann heard them, and tried to pretend that he didn't hear the people because they might take advantage of his idea, which was somehow to suck rain out of the air before it broke loose in form of orthodox globules to be wasted, spraying or hammering against soil which could never absorb or appreciate rain, against men who were only chilled or killed by its coming.

Willie Mann, Twenty-ninth Missouri Volunteers, came into the stockade shortly before the six raiders were hanged. Thus he witnessed a big man breaking free from a mass, a core of blackened faces and striving thin arms half naked and half ragged; he saw that man plunging at a loose long pace all the way down the slope and into the marsh next to the Island. Willie saw what that marsh was made of; in his innocence he had not dreamed of its construction when first he arrived; he thought that the bad smell came sole alone from those bodies which supported those faces which stared and yelled and called him and his fellows fresh fish. He thought with tears spreading inside to drown him—he thought that these eviscerated cannibals or whatever they were— He thought that they were jeering and taunting; whereas mainly they were giving him a rowdy grim welcome filled with curiosity and a certain envy because he had not been compelled to suffer as they had suffered. But now he would suffer.

The stench had been their stench, in Willie's first diagnosis, but a bulk of it was the stench of Stockade Creek and ooze surrounding. He gazed, he couldn't believe it, after Curtis ran away and plunged until he was mired waist-deep, and Nathan Dreyfoos waded in after him. Also, when Willie Mann heard that the tallest of the condemned was named Willie Collins it brought a dread kinship with the captured ringleader. He tried to tell himself that there must be hundreds of Willies walled in here, and so he should not be absurd about it; but that night he dreamed fiercely of the monster . . . gallows stood on the southern hill's shoulder, and when planks were knocked loose and when (never tell Katty or Ma what happened then!)— When at last all six stretched shapes hung gyrating leisurely from their ropes, there seemed a dark completeness, a finality to the course of his initiation. Willie Mann was now a full-fledged prisoner with a parched tongue. One of the executed men had, in his unknowing way, helped to parch that tongue by once trying to walk on substance unsuited to man's support. He was not Jesus, not even an exaggerated cartoon of a wicked overgrown Jesus born in a sinkhole instead of in a manger; so he had tried to walk upon the stuff, and had gone down. Willie Mann wandered once more to stare at the place.

He witnessed prisoners floundering or creeping—senior prisoners of vast stockade experience but apparently with no sensitivity. He saw them with their cups and chunks of broken canteen material. They sought water and found it. It was putrid thick ink, and they called it water. It was the oil of corruption, the wine from dying human bowels, the lively acid of iniquity, and they dared to call it water. It was a soup rising from wet invisible wells drilled by the Devil himself, and stewed out of festering meatbones and rotting bits of cloth, corncobs, abandoned corn bread, the fresh tanned floating strings of firm healthy excrement which came borne on narrow tide from habitations of guards outside the jagged fence, the watery yellow slime drained from dysenteric hordes inside the jagged fence. A million million million worms worked in its borders, a black frosting of insects clung above and busy. These debased fellows of Willie Mann's were willing to voice the evilest lie of all, and say Water.

Maybe they had never known true water, but Willie had. To begin with, the well of his family on the edge of the tiny Missouri village where he was born— This well was famous in the neighborhood. It served four families including the Manns, and Willie's father said that the more the well was used the better he liked it. Doctor Zachary Mann was a slender solemn fellow with a sparse beard and mild brown inquiring eyes. His dappled mare Annette and his pale duster and his chaise with tall mended wheels: all were familiar to the entire northern end of the county and in southerly regions of the county above. When Doctor went to some farmhouse and found three or four children staring with fever (maybe one might be dead before he arrived) Doctor Zach Mann lingered eventually at the farm well. He noted the site where it was dug, he brought up water and held it to the light in a glass, he sniffed, sometimes he tasted wryly and spat the water out again and rinsed his mouth with some liquid carried in his own satchel. People said that Doctor Zach was foolish on the subject of water; but no one of the eight Mann children died in infancy. In this case it seemed that the shoemaker's children had shoes.

Willie's elder brother Sam had been killed at Wilson's Creek or else in a skirmish immediately preceding the battle—no one knew which, or could find out for certain—so Willie begged to go to the war in a manner of vengeance. Not until you're eighteen, said Doctor. You got your mother to see after, if Annette should be scairt by the cars and run away with me.

Of course fat Annette had never run away in the thirteen years of her life, and probably never would run away; but the doctor was a determined father, and he extracted his promise. Willie did not know how to deceive because he had never been taught nor had he suffered the example.

The week before his eighteenth birthday—that was the same week they heard the news about Vicksburg—recruiters came to the county seat, and Willie begged to go to the courthouse and sign the roll.

You're not eighteen. You promised—

But I'll be eighteen a Sunday.

Wait till then.

Want me to leg it all the way to Saint Louis and maybe join up with a batch of foreigners?

Doctor debated in his mind, and at last arose from the tattered sofa (Linda Moberly's baby had been slow, and it took all night, and they nearly lost both the baby and Linda, but everything seemed all right now). He told Willie to hitch up Annette and not say anything to Ma. Silently they drove the five miles to the courthouse, Doctor dozing beside his one surviving son. When they pulled up along the shiny hitch-rail with its little strings of horse-hair caught in the polish of horses' rubbing, Doctor opened his eyes alertly as if he hadn't been asleep actually any of the time.

Well, sonny, go in and sign.

Willie came back, pale-faced and beaming—he came down from the courthouse three steps at a time, and nearly landed on top of old Mr. Cull Calaise, who remembered Indian attacks on that very spot, and had actually shaken hands with Daniel Boone though he always spoke of him as Colonel Boone.

Did you sign, sonny?

Yup. But it's all right, Pa—I mean about me being eighteen. I hain't got to report until a Monday, and I'll be eighteen by then.

They drove home slowly; on the way Doctor stopped to dress the stump of Mr. Rector's finger at the cottage by the sawmill; and he stopped also to peek in at the exhausted Linda Moberly and her baby girl. When he came out he said, Sonny, I don't want you ever to take up doctoring.

Don't reckon I will. Rather be a soldier or work on a railroad. But why?

Might vaunt yourself pridefully, and get puffed up.

How so, Pa?

Hard to explain. Way a doctor gets to feel sometimes. Not maybe like God, but like the dear Lord's little finger.

Up over the next green hills the weary Annette took them along, making hungry sounds inside her round empty belly, making louder sounds from her rear. They passed the abandoned Gentry house . . . Mr. Dolph Gentry had Rebel tendencies, and had left the county long before. They passed their next-door neighbors, the Garshows; and also Paul and Silas Garshow were wearing gray, and were said to be off fighting in General Sterling Price's army somewhere. It was funny and awful how the neighborhood was split up, and so were a lot of other neighborhoods in Missouri.

Anyway, I got old Garshow to move his well.

What say, Pa?

There—you can see it gainst the west.

He pointed with his whip. That's the new well: fine high curb, and observe where she stands. Under that cottonwood, high and convenient. But down the slope's where they had the old well; just lazy because twas a low spot, and they figured twas easier to reach water so. Tweren't more than six foot deep, I swear. And just go up amongst them cedars sometime—when you come home from the fighting, I mean—and count them graves. Seven Garshows and five of the in-laws, the Teddlers.

All from a rotten well, Pa? Could that be?

Could be.

First off that night, after they had broken the news to Ma and the five girls (Addie was newly married and moved away) Willie went along the edge of the oatfield behind the barn, he went in thin plum-purple light of a hot evening in Missouri (although he had never seen evenings in any place other than Missouri at that time). He went to call upon Miss Katrine Fiedenbruster.

The Fiedenbrusters had moved to the region only four or five years previously; they had come from Germany by way of St. Louis where Jake Fiedenbruster had been a thrifty shoemaker, but now he wanted to be a farmer and was one. The kids at school made fun of the little Fiedenbrusters because at first they spoke only a few words of English and those badly . . . it was during the winter term. Willie was not yet fourteen at the time, and very slight; but he was muscular from hard work, and also he liked to wrestle with his big brother Sam. Well, he was coming home through soggy snow, and he heard shrieks ahead. He looked and saw all the little Fieden-brusters running and crying and yelling in German. It turned out that big Ame Moberly had ambushed them, and Ame wasn't merely playing Indian: this was a real devilish ambush he had arranged. In advance he'd prepared ammunition consisting of snowballs soaked and then frozen; the missiles were stony and dangerous. He'd hidden

behind the low crab-apple trees at the corner, and when the contingent of foreigners came by in their blue knitted woolen winter caps
and scarfs, he up and opened fire. It was a mean business—snow-
balling girls, especially with frozen balls—but Ame did have a mean
streak in him. (No more, though: he was killed in the attack on Fort
Donelson.)

All of a sudden it came over Willie: what would his father have
done?—truly he worshipped his father. Well, he figured that Doctor
would have lit into Amos Moberly, so that was what Willie did
now. Ame was whooping and dancing and running after the wailing
Germans, and then stopping to heave another accurate snowball, and
then he'd yell, Why don't you talk *decent?* and then another ball
and another shriek. Then Willie hit him like a cat off a limb; they were
in the snow. Standing up, using fists solely, Ame might have thrashed
Willie to a jelly, but on the ground the slighter boy held an advantage, after all those tussles with tall Sam. It was a bitter fight, however—gouge and punch and twist and choke. At least Ame was bent
on choking in defense. But Willie brought his boot up against Ame's
belly, good and solid; after that there was no fight left in the bigger
boy—nor any wind, either.

The Fiedenbrusters stood like a gallery, watching, fearing, ap-
preciating the virtues of their savior. Finally when Ame got his
breath back, he went off homeward across the old stubble field, refusing to look back because he was ashamed of being beaten, and
even more ashamed at his own crying. He wouldn't speak to Willie
for weeks and weeks; but at last they became moderately friendly
at a church supper in the spring; and certainly Amos never plagued
the Fiedenbrusters again.

The day after the fight, Willie found a pink-streaked winter apple
in his lunch bucket, and his mother hadn't put it there: he'd watched
her preparing his and his sisters' lunches, while he leaped with impatience for fear Teacher would catch them with the tardy bell.
Next day, some spicy heart-shaped cookies of a kind he'd never seen
or tasted before. He saw Katrine Fiedenbruster watching him, and
then her face turned red when she saw that he saw her watching
him; she turned away quickly. But next day, more soft gingery cookies. It would have been easy for her to slip things into his lunch
bucket undetected. All the buckets and baskets stood in a row on
the long bench in the cloak room. . . . Willie realized suddenly how
very pretty Katrine Fiedenbruster really was. Her skin was creamy
white, her little cheeks were round as cookies but soft as fresh-stirred
candy, her neck reminded him of ice cream. Suddenly he thought
that he would like to eat Katrine Fiedenbruster—actually eat her up,
and how good she would taste—and then he was overcome with embarrassment at having entertained such a thought . . . and he thought

of other things that he would like to do to and with her; his face
flamed behind his McGuffey . . . he made a botch of lessons on that
day. But he made a great to-do about shoveling slush off the path
for old Mr. Spriggs, after school, and his sisters went home without
him, prepared to tell Ma how Willie had declared in geography class
that Prussia was the capital of Russia. The Fiedenbruster tribe went
home without Katrine, because she was the eldest girl and now partook of a special fifteen-minute lesson in English which Mr. Spriggs
awarded because for some reason he declared that she was a noble
little Dutchwoman, and pinched her cheeks and made them even
pinker.

Willie scraped and scraped. When finally Teacher came out with
his cane and surveyed the results, he said, William, you may not
anticipate a brilliant career as a scholar—not after today's blots and
witlessness—but I vow you could make a living with a shovel.

Teacher locked up the schoolhouse and thumped Willie's head
with his stiff old finger, and turned west along the road toward
where he boarded with the Pattersons. But Willie and the noble
little Dutchwoman had to go east.

She walked fast, Willie walked faster, soon he was up with her and
walking at speed fairly beside her, but she kept her hot face turned
away.

Katrine. . . .

She seemed fearing to reply, and why should she hide her face in
the folds of knitted blue?

Katrine. Let me carry your books.

Nein.

Why not, eh?

Cause—

Let me carry your stuff.

Nein. Mineself I—carry—

Katrine, listen here. He snatched her free hand, and stopped her,
and held her as a prisoner; she faced him with damp reddened soft
face and blue eyes like silver.

You put them cookies in my bucket—

Nein, she breathed, but of course she breathed a lie.

Yes you did. What kind of cookies are they?

Boy and girl, they stood alone in the slushy road, and nobody was
about—no Teacher, no brothers or sisters or schoolmates, no rigs or
teams—nothing there but February wind and a crow calling, and a
pervading cold consciousness of spring to come.

Lebkuchen, she whispered.

What? Them cookies? Is that what they're called?

Ja.

She did not resist when he took her books and little willow basket.

They made an awkward if not heavy burden along with his own things. In utter silence the children walked the way to a lane which bordered the Mann farm on the west, for the Fiedenbrusters lived down that lane on the old Carrington place. Katrine thanked him in the thinnest of whispers, and dared not meet his glance when she did it.

Willie stopped, halfway to his home, and stood looking across the field at that gray-shawled, blue-topped little figure a-hastening, and then she turned to look at him, and thus again each saw the other looking.

She was his girl, in this modern grown-up time; he was her fellow. They had belonged to each other, in pure and solemn devotion, from the very first.

Five times he had managed to kiss her. But only in kissing games, when other folks were looking on and laughing. And only on the cheek, because she'd try to hide away from him— She would seem to fight him. But not too hard—

This night the plum light was intense around him and around the white house of the Fiedenbrusters, and the strong glow went up as if from prairie fires beyond a row of cottonwoods, and a chorus of whip-poor-wills challenged steadily from black hollows of Beverly's Timber. Oh God, please God, to be alone with her, to be alone in Beverly's Timber or any place else in this spooky nighttime wonderland, but to be alone—

They roosted on a small porch and on the steps, the Fiedenbrusters. Papa and Mamma sat in the two rocking chairs received as premiums. Katrine and Wempkie, her next youngest sister, had sold bluing and vanilla throughout the neighborhood in their spare time; the rockers were their own accomplishment, and they were proportionately proud, but tonight they sat on stools. The girls had put down their mending, because now it was too dark to see properly, and they had taken up their knitting because they could knit ably, by touch, in the half-dark. All the girls could—even Marta and little Lena.

Jacob and Fritz were gone to the army. Henry and Lou were giggling out behind the plum trees—smoking grapevine, they were, and they became terrified and heavy with guilt when Willie Mann came upon them. Peter and Buck chased fireflies around the yard in this rare dusky moment of playtime, and the toddler, Link, was staggering after them.

Good evening.

To you good evening, Willie Mann.

The party on the stoop and steps loomed before him in dark solidity; they were a unit, a strong sedate family unit. How could he ever pry Katty loose from them?

He burst out with his tidings. I signed the roll today. Pa drove me to the courthouse. I'll be eighteen Sunday.

Katty upset the work basket on her lap. Scissors and thimbles and a darning ball and things tumbled all over the stoop planks, and some things rolled down into the lily bed below. Willie had no matches; Willie did not smoke. Mrs. Fiedenbruster sent one of the girls into the house, and she came back with a small block of sulphur matches. Willie took the matches from her, and scouted amid tapering lily leaves until Katty's lost property was restored. He straightened to find big Jake, the father, standing beside him, a mighty post of hewn manhood in dead brown darkness when the last match sputtered out.

Jake Fiedenbruster shook Willie's hand. This is good. Now you are a man, like my Jake and Frederick are men, like your brother was a man. When do you go?

I reckon we go next week. They aimed to raise a company, but the recruiting captain said they'd never get that many in these parts— too many folks already gone to war. Ben Carrington's signed, and Hudson Moberly and both the Pittridge boys.

Ja, das ist gut. It is bad, but it is good. Were it not for *die Kinder* I too should go.

The girls sat motionless on their stools and on the steps, and Katrine seemed to exude a deeper silence than the others, and Mrs. Fiedenbruster rocked heavily in the chair too small for her fat body, and the chair protested with squeaks. Down at the gate the boys still cavorted after lightning-bugs, making few sounds in order to keep from frightening the bugs.

It was late—far too dark to lure Katty from her family circle by this time. They would say that it was dark, her family would not permit her to walk down the road with him; that much was certain. But he would not have to leave for several days and—

After he was in the army, especially after he became a prisoner, he liked to think of that night. Mostly he thought about an afternoon before he went away, and what had happened then. But he chose also to consider the firefly evening (*chose* was scarcely it: memories pushed over him and fed him and choked him with their color and scent and shadow, whenever he was not occupied by the immediate urgencies of war).

No longer did the town band blat forth its resounding Hail Columbia or Benny Havens, Oh! Two trumpeters were dead of smallpox in Kentucky, the piccolo would roll its sweet trills no longer when operated by the breath of big Tad Wheeling because big Tad Wheeling's breath was taken from him by grapeshot. Most of the drummers were scattered and drumming still, but drumming at remote guard-mounts in remote places. No band—but throngs of people on the cindered platform, waiting for the cars to come; sisters to weep, mothers to weep and squeeze you desperately, fathers struggling to seem calm and unweeping, little brothers torn between wide-eyed fear for your lives and the ecstasy of envy. Everyone stood with bowed heads, after the engine pulsed to its hot and blowing stop, while Reverend Collins spoke his prayer. Baskets of lunch, the sacks and satchels, the umbrella Hud Moberly's mother made him take along (how they would play with that, on the cars, and brandish it out of the window at other towns until the sergeant shouted them down).

Katty. Jewels and weapons in her bright wet blue eyes, the knowledge of what had already passed between them, the knowledge of her fragrance and softness and tenderness striking him like intoxication. Mother—ah, yes, one loved a mother—Willie loved his mother. Father—ah, Doctor was a father to be respected, to give the charm of calm manliness, to receive it back as his natural due. Sisters? Willie put his arms around the lot of them, or tried to, and patted them as a choice sprigged calico bouquet. But—Katty—

Finally, people had the decency to let him stand apart from them, to stand with Katty alone, looking directly into her face. She was not a tall girl, but she was nearly as tall as Willie.

Look what I bring to you, and she gave him a package. It seemed to be a bottle, sewn up in clean muslin and insulated against breakage with wads of paper inside the cloth.

Katty. . . .

You do not ask me, but it is lemonade.

Katty, I. . . .

Loaf sugar, one pound. In a trance she recited the formula. Citric acid, one-half ounce: this I buy from Mr. Partridge in his store. Also lemon essence. In a mortar I mix it, and it is all very dry. You should be sure to keep the bottle tight all the while.

Katty, you'll write to me and let me know if. . . .

Then, when it is your lemonade you want, I have here this tablespoon for you to measure. Not heaping, not flat, but round—so. That will make it proper. *Ach,* the amount of water I did not tell you: one half-pint. But maybe you like it not so strong; then more water you should use. Be sure to use pure and cold water.

Yes, yes, pure and cold— Katty—

The whistle blasted, steam blew on high, wet spatters came down. The boys went fleeting up the steps into the car, the sergeant was already aboard, Allen Pittridge was waving Willie's bundle at him and screaming, Come on, Will, I got your plunder—

He kissed her, and all her folks were staring; long he mashed his face on hers, his lips grown fast around hers, and all his folks were staring too, and all the other folks were staring, the world was staring.

Then he was in the moving car, and smoke went alongside to mask the people stumbling and waving and trying to sing, smoke lifted to disclose old Mr. Cull Calise waving his flask at the train and quacking an invocation: Give 'em hell, boys. Scalp 'em, scalp 'em!

Glory, glory, hallelujah. Glory, glory, hallelujah. Glory, Glory—

So the knowledge that he must absorb nothing but purest liquid was a lesson set first by Doctor, learned fervently by Willie Mann, and endorsed by Katty in the final adjuration she gave him. Pure cold water from pure cold wells and springs. In this way Willie learned to go without water; he went without water when he had to—and often when he didn't, because he was over-zealous and his comrades thought him possessed of a mania. Privately he recognized that indeed he was possessed of a mania, but believed that it would sustain him. At first he was inclined to grow costive. This tendency he disciplined sternly by muscular exercise of his own abdominal area, by rubbings and proddings and twistings and bendings. Eventually he was convinced that his body needed only the moisture brought to it in mouthfuls of ordinary foods, though he drank boiled coffee along with other boys, and reveled in sweet milk whenever it might be bought or begged.

He survived the rigorous and disappointing earliest months of soldier life; he survived two transfers, the first frightening skirmish, the first utterly terrifying pitched battle; he survived four later battles, and various bang-bangs of desultory musket fire from rocks and woodlands (he refused to dignify these as skirmishes, because not an enemy was in sight). People caught scarlet fever in the winter of 1863–4; Willie Mann did not catch it. People caught mumps—fifteen boys in his company had the mumps at one time, and the mumps went down on four of the boys, and one boy died—of mumps and respiratory complications and gosh-knows-what. Willie Mann had had the mumps when he was nine; he did not catch the disease now. People died of pneumonia, intermittent fever, remittent fever, camp fever. Willie Mann suffered no fever whatsoever. He had grown half an inch since he enlisted. He was five-feet-seven and weighed one hundred and thirty-eight pounds. His round tan-colored eyes were solid and all-seeing. His tan-colored hair grew wavy and thick, and twisted in a tuft like a queue at the nape of his neck. He was more wiry than ever, and still liked to wrestle; and one of the bigger corporals was a wrestler too, and taught Willie many new holds. Willie Mann read a Chapter nearly every day, as he had promised his mother that he would do; he failed to perform this rite only in times of fighting, or in times of marching when actually he fell asleep between strides and pitched to the ground or tumbled against the man ahead of him. Willie owned deep-driven lines on either side of his little-boy's mouth, and nets of spidery lines around the outer corners of his eyesockets.

He kept his body as clean as he could, and he dreamed of Katty Fiedenbruster. He carried his little Bible in his left breast pocket, confident that it would stop any bullet which sought his heart, and he had a letter from Katty folded in that Bible which letter would most certainly amplify the defense of the Bible, and he dreamed of Katty always while sleeping and whenever he could while waking.

Her lemonade was, while it lasted, a chalky treasure to be jeered at by his fellows, and promptly to be begged by them. He would remember always: hot, hot, and hollyhocks drooping on their roadside spikes, and dust twirling ahead sometimes diagonally across the road from southwest to northeast, the way cyclones blew. Sun made shivers out of remote windbreaks of cottonwood and sawed-off willows, and when the green regiment lay gasping at rest on swales along the floury roadside they could hear roosters wailing about the heat on distant small farms. Roosters talked with their mid-afternoon midsummer crowing, wan and hot and limp: it was not the inspiriting cry they uttered at dawn. Squad by squad, Willie's company was allowed to approach the nearest well. The widow who lived on that place had given her permission when the lieutenant asked her, and the boys were cautioned not to step on nasturtium beds, and to treat the old gate kindly. Forcibly imprisoned within the house, a shaggy shepherd dog uttered his barks in regular pounding cadence, without let or variety. *Owgh. Owgh. Owgh. Owgh,* until you thought you'd go crazy with barking and hotness and dust and solid sun.

Then was the time for Willie Mann to produce that bottle which Katty had given him, and the spoon to go with it. He measured cannily: the rounded spoonful, as she had directed. What in tarnation, Will? What you got there? Medicine? A physic? He shook his head and tried to look wise, and succeeded only in looking smug. The others sensed his smugness; they made uncouth remarks about the stuff he was stirring into his can of water and—soon—the stuff he was drinking. Oh, but that was a good deep clear cool well; his father would have approved.

But Tite Cherry and Rom Hillburner were his especial chums, and they had respect for Willie and knew that he wasn't a dunce; neither was he an invalid in need of salts and powders. They hung back and begged quietly for a taste. After plain water, Katty Fiedenbruster's gift seemed a nectar. The word got around. Consistently thereafter Willie was importuned each time the squad descended on a well . . . he set his jaw, and shrugged: to think he'd ever toyed with the notion that the powdered lemonade might last through an entire campaign! But a man couldn't be niggardly with his campmates—especially not when he and Tite and Rom and Rom's brother Reem all messed closely together. Remus Hillburner was a natural born forager; if he couldn't beg a basket luncheon from bonneted ladies in some village he could manage to subtract a tender pullet from one of those same ladies' hen-coops. Once he came back into camp with a corned leg of beef, and where had he stolen that? Reem stood in fine favor with the lieu-tenant, and even the cross-grained sergeant regarded him with a tenderly appraising eye. Pity that he had to die of fever that winter.

Tite Cherry and the Hillburner brothers and a few others had their share of the deliciousness proffered by Katty; probably more than their share, for Willie was generous to a fault. The day he emptied the bottle, and smashed it against a brick wall in sacred ceremony so that nothing else would ever be contained therein— That day he thought to himself, Hard lines from now on. Oh, I'll drink; but maybe Katty's lemonade powder took away a lot of the sickness I might have found in those wells along the roads, and now I got to show caution. So he did, though often his dry innards coiled like snakes at the sight of his fellows plunging their faces into dark streams which edged through dirty towns—rioting around some broken-down open well or cistern with a privy on one side of it and a hog-pen on the other, and manure piles rotting close.

In arid moments like those he thought of Doctor, and somehow he managed to live and to train himself into Going Without. The disci-pline Willie wielded over himself was not so bad, in all likelihood, as the discipline which Doctor had had to muster. In rare intimacies Willie had learned the whole story, bit by bit: the bestial father, the blows and tortures and eventual flight, the busy lordly doctor whose garden-digger and stable-boy the senior Mann became, the medical books borrowed secretly—*thieved* would be more like it—and read by light of a tin lantern until the weary body fell off the bench and the weary brain hummed with a demons' litany of discutients, femurs, carminatives, and tartareous adhesions. The Latin learned so slowly, the trip to a strange city on borrowed money, the waiting-on-table, the long lectures listened to by tired ears, the shoveling-of-coal, the first cadaver to excite the spirit—

Doubtless his father was more of an ideal and symbol to Willie Mann than the National Flag; definitely more of an ideal and symbol than a vague thought of the President and the Congress and the en-graved unfinished dome of the National Capitol. So what would Doctor say if he knew about Willie and Katrine? What would Doctor say— what would Doctor *do*—if—?

Hard lines, waiting to hear. Oh, hard lines.

The letter came finally, and gave to Willie a release and a freedom and vigor he did not well deserve, and knew that he did not well deserve.

It was not the only letter she wrote to him, but it was the only one which reached him until the spring of 1864.

It was after the Evening of Fireflies, and word had come that the soldier boys should prepare to depart on Wednesday. Sunday the skies wept at thought of their going. The Fiedenbrusters attended one church, the Manns another, so there was not even a glimpse of Katty to be caught in the wet of noon. In afternoon Willie put an old piece of blanket over his head in lieu of mackintosh, and walked to the Fiedenbruster place where things were dismal in the extreme. The two youngest boys were sick abed with whooping-cough and you could hear them whooping like animals or Indians or something as you sat in the sitting room. Wempkie and Marta insisted on keeping their elders company, and Katrine was indignant about this, and spoke shortly to her sisters and her face became colored as always when she was angry. She sat and looked out of the little window and Willie thought she was mad at him. He suggested Authors—the Fieden-bruster girls owned a set of the cards, each card decorated with im-posing pictures of Dickens and Wordsworth and Shakespeare and folks like that; if Marta asked Wempkie for Love's Labour's Lost, Number Two, and Wempkie didn't have it, then when it came your turn you could say, Marta, do you happen to have Midsummer Night's Dream, Number Two? Sometimes Authors was a jolly business; but Mrs. Fiedenbruster wouldn't let them play on this day because it was Sun-day. She said, No, *mein Kinder,* hickory nuts you can crack.

Katty said pettishly, *Ach,* Mamma, it won't do no good. All last year's nuts, and dried up. Not fit to eat.

It was dull indeed; the drizzle kept up outside. Jake Fiedenbruster slumbered noisily on the sofa in the kitchen-dining room with a red handkerchief over his bearded face; and the other children read Sun-day School books around the kitchen table . . . those were all they were allowed to read. Willie went home early, and was cross with his sisters; and back at the other house Katty covered herself with a comforter on her bed and Wempkie's, and cried. He couldn't know that, of course, but she told him later.

Monday dawned as prettily painted as Sunday had been the tone of zinc. Willie went out to do his chores (only two more mornings would he do them) and he was so charged with life and strength that he roared martial songs at the top of his voice while he loped about with forks and pails. *We leave our plows and workshops,* sang Willie Mann or more properly chanted Willie Mann with sublime disregard of pitch because he could never carry a tune on a shovel, *our wives and children dear, with hearts too full for utterance, and but a silent tear.*

His mother heard him, and thought of how the dead Samuel had once sung, with more melody, and she lay crying as she looked at bright light making gilt out of the slanted walls across from her.

His father heard him, and snorted, half in his sleep and half awake. Not quite a silent tear, observed Doctor in a mumble.

But Willie's mother thought of the dead Sam, and of Willie's departure day-after-tomorrow, and she cried steadily if silently. Doctor was lying on his back with yellow hairs of his beard intertwined with darker curlier hairs of his chest where his nightshirt hung open, and he realized that his wife was crying and why she was crying. He struggled round in bed until he could put both arms around Minnie; so she cried, so he tended and soothed her by saying nothing but by holding her close.

We dare not look behind us, roared the youth at the stable, *but steadfastly before. We are coming, Father Abraham, three hundred thousand more.* Morning glories were candies of pink and blue where they crawled on the trellis against the privy wall, warming wider and wider although the sun was not yet high; nasturtiums were orange and gold butter spread on the green bread of the lawn beside the well-curb; the tiger cat named Victoria sat on the wooden walk with legs cocked wide, and scrubbed herself with a harsh pink tongue. *We are coming, we are coming, our Union to restore—* Florence had built up the kitchen fire, and smoke smelled sweet; it promised toast and eggs and fried salt pork to come, to say nothing of the best red cherry preserves ever made.

Willie thought of the holiday to be his as soon as morning chores were done, because soon he was going to the war. He thought of Beverly's Timber, and the crawling of Beverly's Creek, and the wide brown hole where first he had learned to swim, and where catfish hung dreaming outside the porticos of limestone where in earlier summer they made their nests and guarded their eggs. He thought of hazel thickets he had known in frosty fall; and now in July the grass would turn its tall length flat and lie in springy windrows like little glades of Nature's featherbeds stretching from bunch of brush to bunch of brush.

. . . Would you like to go there with me?

. . . *Ja.*

So that was the way he dreamed it. Within the hour after breakfast he stood at the Fiedenbruster kitchen door with his old stained straw hat in his hand . . . aw, Katty. Please ask your Ma. We could have a splendid pic-nic party: just you and me. You won't have to fix anything—I'd fetch all the sandwiches and truck, and we got half a hen left from Sunday dinner in the cooler. And a jar of Ma's grapejuice. I'll bait your hook and everything; you won't have to touch a worm.

My mother might not let me go. Alone in the woods—with a young man. *Nein,* she might not—

Dog my cats, I'll ask her myself! He shooed Katty aside with enthusiasm, and found Mrs. Fiedenbruster in the buttery, lifting a damp cloth filled with white curds. There he asked her. The old clock spoke persistently on its shelf above the sink—the clock brought from Bavaria with such care, and it had monkeys and vines and rose petals painted on the front. The rooms were strangely silent, except for that clock, for all the rest of the Fiedenbrusters worked in field or garden save for the ailing little boys, and they dozed.

The mother pushed her specs down on her round nose and peered intently over them. I do not know. Katty is so young a girl— But you are a good boy, Willie. And you go to war. Maybe you get killed, *nein?* She took up a corner of her wide blue apron to touch the honest wetness in her eyes.

Mutter, that you should not say!

But it could be. *Ja,* Katrine, you may go for pic-nic by Willie Mann. Across the road you must go, and through the long cornfield. I do not wish the neighbors should see you go—two, alone. And Willie, you take good care of *mein Katchen?*

Course I will.

No female Fiedenbruster dared permit a boy to prepare the luncheon to be carried to Beverly's Timber or anywhere else, so Katty was a long while about cutting and wrapping the food, and would have been an even longer while about fixing her curls and getting into her fresh checked gingham. But her mother hastened her up. Mrs. Fiedenbruster deemed it wise that the other children should be unaware of this rustic festivity. They might be allowed to think that Katty had been permitted to spend the day at the Mann house, with Willie and his sisters; *ja,* that was what they could think. Jacob she might tell, Jacob she might not tell: she would decide later . . . come, come, little daughter, away with thee before the girls come from the garden in; and at the gate thy Willie is already with fishing poles. . . .

Corn waited to conceal them, corn was a wilderness with its sharp-edged bent swords of leaves, and the new silk a beauty at the tip of every heartening ear. Solemnly the girl and the boy moved down the long damp corn-row; it was a task; if Katty moved first the leaves chafed at her hands and face; if Willie went ahead the long leaves whipped back and spatted Katty; but they made their way, the corn smelled youthfully rich and filled with strong green juice; they made their way.

He took down two rails of Mr. Beverly's fence, so that he might aid Katty across with a minimum of skirt-hoisting, and then with care he replaced the rails—set them solidly back into their notches.

It is beautiful, Willie. Here I have never been.

Not in Beverly's Timber? Don't you folks ever come over here to fish or—?

By the creek at the bridge I have been. That is all. But with you I will not be afraid.

Well, what in— What could you be feart of?

She looked up shyly, then the brown lashes came down. Maybe bears.

Naw! Haven't been no bears in these parts for years and years.

Maybe a—wolf? Maybe wildcats? (There was still a touch of v in her w's; it sounded nearly like *volf* and *vildcats*, and Willie loved her for it . . . he loved her for many things.)

He remembered the two lines going loose into Beverly's Creek, and the way those lines broke at angles beneath the surface. The stream was brown and pale but you could see to a certain depth in the holes, and you could make out wide-headed shadows of catfish as they came to investigate the twin baits, and rejected them, but clung near, watching still, waving their limp feelers in derision. He remembered the unhappy turtle which did indeed bite hard on Katty's bait, and so she squealed and fetched it up: she was so excited that she kept talking in German (that was the language the Fiedenbrusters used at home, naturally enough); and part of her hair came down while she was cavorting and exclaiming and waving her pole about. The turtle marched grimly over grass, trying to go back to his deep home; and now Katty was deploring all fishing and fishermen.

Ach, and he has that cruel hook. In his poor mouth! *Ach,* Willie, it is so cruel. I cannot bear to see.

Naw, naw. It won't hurt him a speck. Here, I'll cut him loose.

Ach, the knife! It must hurt him so— She buried her face in her hands.

. . . All done, Kat. See, he's loose. Just look at them legs wiggle when I hold him up.

But he has the bleeding, Willie!

Just a trifle. His mouth is as hard as a rock—it'll well up in no time at all. Want to put him back in the creek, yourself? No? I'll put him in. In you go, Turt. Farewell, Turt.

He remembered great iridescent butterflies which whisked above a damp spot far in Beverly's Timber—the small black-and-orange-and-white butterflies which sat tasting the shallow pool, and shot up when you came too close . . . they wheeled and sped faster than flies . . . and a strange tiny bird of purplish blue beyond, the shyest of the shy, and making soft his song before they alarmed him with their coming.

Willie. Worshipping whisper, the quiet curls and peachy skin and smell of her so close . . . his breath clogged in his chest. Willie, so beautiful a bird. What name?

Dog my cats, Katty, I don't know. Never saw it before. Twasn't a bluebird.

Nein. He was even much more beautiful. Maybe a fairy bird?

They laughed about it, they wandered on, a groundhog raced heavily to his burrow, the girl yelled about it, and clutched Willie tightly and said that she had known there would be bears.

He remembered the sunny place, the deep ravine where a basswood had been undermined and had fallen across the thinning stream;

thus it left a hole in the dark green roof, and sun beat through to stamp this one circle of hot gold amid the shadows. He remembered the willow basket placed between them, the red-bordered cloth which Katrine produced and spread: the pickles with cloves clinging to them, the ivory of hard-boiled eggs, the slices of dark cured ham and corned beef, bread-and-butter sandwiches, the jug of milk.

(Within the stockade men dreamt of food until the very dreams slew them as surely as bullets. It was this luncheon which Willie Mann dreamed of.)

The luncheon, the solitude, the laughter of the creek, the peewee songs, solid piling clouds hiding the sun at last.

It started with gingerbread. She offered gingerbread and then took it back roguishly and said, *Nein*, already you have eaten too much.

But—I—want—that—gingerbread!

Nein. She was on her feet, flying away from him . . . oh girl, oh goddess, oh the temptation in retreat and running, oh always in illusion the dear figure rushing away; and the hardihood of the male to pursue, the hardihood to effect the capture, to press the twisting arms tightly, to stumble, to sprawl together, to continue the embrace.

They had never kissed like this, their mouths had never touched before; they were alone, oh God the solitude, oh Katty, oh God the taste and smell of you, oh the hot ferocious breath of you, and breathing together with a gasping. . . .

She would cry softly, *Nein*, but when he sought to manage some denial and sought to drag his face from hers— Their mouths grew together again. And soon there was all the dainty majesty of her bosom revealed and touched and explored and slathered and warm with his kissing—

Nein. Ach, Gott— Not *mein* gown, Willie— It is wrong we do this! *Ach*, Willie— *Küss' mich, küss' mich, küss' mich*—

Long he heard the tender gasp and whisper of her maidenly protestation, long he surmounted all objection which propriety had taught the two of them. Virgin boy and virgin girl, their tears and exclamation of desire and fright and conscience and terror and sheer abandoned delight were commingled throughout their uniting. Somewhere beyond the ferocity which ruled them, there stood a vast disapproving congregation composed of parents, brothers, sisters, Reverend Collins, Reverend Mueller, Sunday School teachers, aunts, Jesus, neighbors, teachers, Disciples, Apostles, the county sheriff, God the Father.

In a later hour Willie was impelled to blubber when he stood alone in the forest where she had sent him. He heard the splashing of water; there at the brookside she must be striving to repair the damage to herself and to her costume; and when he returned it was to see her hastily hiding a small damp bundle in the willow basket.

She sat in grass, he sat near her; she was calmer than he as she did up her hair, working knowingly by touch for she had no looking glass.

Wretchedly he importuned her, and she looked at him calmly. You think I am a bad girl?

Naw! Katty, I made you do It.

So we have done It. It is as if always I knew that we would.

Katty, do you think—?

What do I think, *mein* Willie?

Do you think—? Mightn't—? Maybe now you'll have—a baby?

Ja. That could be.

Hi. He sat higher and stared at her. Let's get married. I'll marry you, Katty. We could get wed tomorrow.

Nein. Mein Vater und meine Mutter— They would say I am too young. I am only sixteen until October. If I say I should be wed to you, then they know that we have done It. My mother she was wed to my father at eighteen was the age. Always she has said her daughters must wait until also they are eighteen.

But if you— If—a baby—

Then so, a baby I will have. When back you come from the army, then we can be wed.

He urged, he pleaded and begged and cajoled . . . she repeated that she was too young. Again they lay in each other's arms, but there was a sainted seriousness in their touching; and again they stared at close mysterious range, and seemed worlds apart, and never the youth and the girl who entered Beverly's Timber light-heartedly with their fishing poles and basket of lunch.

I guess somebody ought to horsewhip me. Or maybe shoot me. I promised your mother—

Quietly she placed her firm little finger on his lips. Talk no more, Willie. You are full of the talk. Some day we shall be older.

There was a noticeable sadness in the depth of her eyes and the depth of her tone; yet she was serene, she had courage, she had an amiable wisdom, and here she was fifteen months younger than Willie Mann. A burden seemed placed now upon her fine slender shoulders, and he marveled confusedly at the way she managed it: the weight she carried seemed not labeled as Guilt but as Womanhood. In vague wonderment the boy ascribed her strength to the discipline in which she had been reared and also to the heritage awarded to Katrine by generations of good-hearted peasants with limited but sturdy minds. . . . Katty was his forever; and she seemed much older than he; strangely she seemed like his mother.

Nevertheless he fretted constantly, once he was away from her and coping with the first dread impersonal complications of soldier life. He lost weight, gave sharp retorts to his companions when they joked at him, was sullen if tractable beneath the scrutiny of his sergeant.

Aloof on his sweat-soaked blanket at night, he envisioned all manner of complaints, disasters, social disgraces. Katty had a baby and the baby was born dead. Katty died in childbirth. Katty had a baby, and the baby was an idiot, waving foolish arms and legs and grunting like a pig. The neighbors drew in their skirts when Katty passed. Katty's father tied her in the woodshed as soon as he learned that she was pregnant, and beat her daily with a thick willow switch; and he walked up and down the road with his cowhide whip coiled in his huge hand, watching for Willie to return from the army so that Jake Fiedenbruster could savor the glee of thrashing Willie to a pulp. Sometimes these imaginings took the form of distinct colorful dreams and nightmares. Titus Cherry said, What in time ails you, Willie? You were groaning and growling in your sleep like my little brother when he et too many gooseberry tarts.

My dear friend, she addressed him timidly at long last, and that was the letter he carried folded in his Bible. (The Rebels did not take his Bible from him when he was captured; and sometimes he thought it was better for him than food; but the mere thought of locusts and honey made his mouth water.) My dear friend, I take my pen in hand to write that I hope you are well. Often I think of you and wish to see you. One letter from you I rec'd. but it is not wise that you should speak so freely of such matters, setting the words down in pencil and paper; for suppose my mother or my father should have chanced to read it?? Quickly I put it in the stove! But I write to inform you that no more such worries should be entertained in your thoughts. I have waited long in order to make certain; two months have elapsed and now I am certain that there is no fear. Willie, I am young and know very little of such matters! But I am sure now and you may be sure and free in your heart. By that I do not mean that you should be free enough to seek for another friend! For you are mine, Willie, and I am thine. And I am trying to remember the verses which Teacher set for us upon the big slate, but it is something about a vine entwining, and maybe about a stump. Oh, my Willie, the tears are flowing freely as I think of thee, and some have fallen upon this letter paper. Is it not handsome, with the Flag and spirit of Our Fair United Country standing side by side, and all in beautiful colors?? It is dear, costing five cents for each pretty sheet and envelope, but I paid for it with some of my berry money. May the Heavenly Father bless and keep thee safely, my dear friend Willie. Now I have covered all the little paper. The mother is calling to me to pare a pumpkin for the pies. Always I am thine, heart's dearest. Katrine Christine Ernestine Fiedenbruster.

There were other letters later, but none rang with the joy of this. As he wore it to a thin tinted rag, rereading and rereading, Willie thought that he heard the brown polished music box playing—a small music box which the Germans had brought from the Old Country along with their clock and the ugly silhouettes of two grandmothers and two grandfathers.

Now Willie could hop like a young frog in springtime. He was the life of the squad, sometimes the most bounding, least trammeled spirit in the column. No task was too arduous, no march too wearying, no shellfire too filled with threat. Remus Hillburner perished of his fever, Romulus Hillburner was shot through the knee and sent home to walk stiff-legged through the balance of his years, Titus Cherry was creased on the head by a bouncing piece of solid shot: they left him for dead, with blood pooling in his eyesockets, and then when they went back to fetch his body Tite wasn't there at all; and he came walking into camp that night with his scalp stiffening and painful where some old Rebel granny had kindly sewed it up with linen thread. Within the month Titus was well again, sound as a nut, and his mass of long black hair covered the huge scar. . . . Willie Mann suffered neither wound nor sickness, and was promoted to fourth corporal. The delighted Katty jigged and squeaked when she received the news, and that very day she wrote a letter to Willie with the word *Corporal* underscored with red crayon in the address, but the letter never reached Willie.

It was that same June day that three boys in torn brown shirts descended upon Willie from a cleft in Georgia rocks, and called him a Yankee son of a bitch, and told him to stick his bayoneted musket in the ground or they would blow his guts out of his ass. Willie's musket was empty, and his companions were scampering in retreat for the moment. He had no wish for his guts to be blown through any aperture whatsoever, so the bayonet sank quickly into earth. The boys (two of them appeared even younger than he) took all his accoutrements, along with his pocketknife and old silver watch, and the twenty-one cents in currency he had in his pocket. They snatched his knapsack and pawed through it, but they took nothing except the little blue housewife his sisters had sewn hastily for him before his departure. And later one of the boys came around with a shamed face and said, Yank, I reckon that was stealing, and stealing is a sin in the sight of the Almighty, and he gave the housewife back to Willie. Willie rather expected to have his watch returned also, and asked for it boldly; but another Rebel who now possessed it suffered no squirmings of conscience.

Along with other strays Willie was guarded rudely in various tanyards, schoolhouses, sawmill enclosures, cotton gin enclosures, and periodically on the cars. He arrived at Andersonville along with three hundred and fourteen fellow prisoners, only one of whom he had known by face but not by name when he was a recruit. This person, whose name was Dundridge, was no fit companion for anyone, be he man-at-arms or prisoner. One day Willie's ration disappeared while he rushed to answer a call of nature; he was almost sure that Dundridge took it and gobbled it, but he had no evidence. . . . Willie owned a capacious tin cup, fine to drink out of, fine to boil coffee in, or even stew or mush. Well, the cup disappeared also; and a day or so later Dundridge made a great to-do about a cup he had bought from a guard. Somehow secretly Dundridge had scoured off all the black, and he had twisted the handle to make it look different, but Willie snatched the cup and looked inside on the bottom. There it was: the crude symbol composed of W and M which Willie had scratched with his bayonet point long ago. Dundridge denied, protested and finally threatened; which vociferations Willie halted by means of the old-fashioned hip throw, and he banged Dundridge's head against the ground until a guard bruised his bottom with a musket butt and said, If you're such a smart scrapper, little Yank, why didn't you scrap harder and not get cotched? Dundridge and Willie remained distinctly aloof. In the hospital at Andersonville, Dundridge died, and his death was recorded as being due to marasmus—a wasting of flesh without fever or obvious disease. When Willie Mann heard of his demise he did not feel regretful in the least: he regretted only that so many others had to die. With an angry mustering of fanatic quality he was determined that he himself should not die.

If he had known more about the business of being a prisoner (he would learn) he would have recognized that he was of the type to last long. He was a knobby tanned streak of lean, such as you might extract from a bacon slice. He had youth, no extra weight, elasticity, a good humor, he did not require much food for sustenance, he had taught himself to drink very little water and now he would drink even less.

He held lengthy private conversations with his father, conversations in which he supplied the dialogue for both; yet if Doctor had been dropped into the stockade from a gas balloon his questions and comments would have been no more characteristic.

Sonny, tell me about that Dundridge.

Well, I know a fellow works Outside every now and again, and he was fetching pine boughs to the hospital. He heard it from another fellow from our Ninety—I mean from our mess. Said he died of marasmus.

Hain't no such disease in my book. Oh, I know the term; but it's employed to cover a multitude of sins. Did he have fever?

Not a grain, when he was sick here.

Flesh seem to fall away?

Reckon that's how you'd describe it. Didn't slough off—wasn't nary a sore on him. Teeth didn't come out, neither. Take that Canadian—the one they call Frenchy in that A-tent shebang over there. You can pull his teeth out betwixt your two fingers if you're game to try. I've seen him win money on it.

Dropsical?

Not so you'd notice. Entirely unpuffed-up.

Scurvy?

No trace. I kept three raw potatoes for days, and Dundridge saw they were there, but he never touched one. And he was a born thief.

Any signs of catarrhal affection, pleuritis, oedema, anasarca, ascites, hydrothorax or anaemia?

He just died.

I say twas water. What well did he use, this fellow Dundridge?

Pa. Come take a walk with me alongside that marsh. . . .

Willie was born to hardihood, for all his small size; Titus Cherry was not, for all his impressive bulk. Cherry wore a cap which would drop down on most other people's ears. He had a mane of hair black as a crow's back at midnight in the dark of the moon, and thick rounded eyebrows of the same material. His pale green eyes were slightly crossed, one of them was always looking off somewhere over the mountains. Once he rowed with Sergeant Buford about fatigue duty which Tite felt he hadn't deserved; one word led to another, and finally Tite said slowly, Well, I'll say no more. Dasn't make any proper argument with you—the kind I'm honing to make—long as you got them stripes on your sleeve. Buford was a gingery man who stood nearly as tall as Cherry and had served six years with Regulars in the Indian country. Also it was rumored that he was experienced in the prize ring. He said to Tite Cherry, If it's stripes that's bothering you, bub, they're easy taken off. So the two of them walked down behind the quartermaster's wagons and a grove which shielded them; they went with half the company following and making bets. Sergeant Buford took off his jacket, stripes and all, and began to roll up the sleeves on his tough freckled arms. Tite Cherry just stood observing the sergeant and kind of smiling at him while his left eye searched upper regions of the trees. Then, without removing his own jacket, he stolled over to the tailboard of one of the wagons. There stood a barrel of flour, all filled up, top nailed on solid. Usually it took four men to load or unload one of those barrels—two in the wagon, two on the ground. Tite dropped the tailboard on its chains and—standing beside it, with everyone watching with their jaws hanging open—he put his right arm halfway around that barrel and began to pull . . . pulled the barrel right over to the edge and past. Holding the barrel tight against his body and staggering only a little, he eased that barrel to the ground with scarcely a jar.

Everybody made a sound. The sergeant touched his lips with his tongue. Bub, can you put her back?

Reckon I can. But I'd have to use both arms.

Don't rupture your belly, bub.

Shan't.

. . . And all eyes still on him as he bent his knees and brought his body low, keeping his huge feet close together. He put both arms around that barrel and suddenly pushed himself erect and brought the barrel up against his chest. He slammed it back in the wagon and the whole wagon shook, loaded as it was. Tite turned around to face the crowd; he was laughing. Flour dust was on his black hair and his dark face, and tears or sweat ran down through the dust and left tracks.

Sergeant, I could break you in two.

By cracky, said Buford. (He was a model churchman; never swore.) I'm beat if you couldn't. Ain't but one thing to do. He offered his hard freckled hand, and it disappeared in Tite's dark hairy grasp, and they stood chuckling. Other folks went up to slap the flour barrel and to see if any two of them could move it, but they couldn't.

Willie Mann had been less than ten days in Andersonville when one morning he stood by the North Gate watching some fresh fish come in. Rebel sergeants were leading newly-instituted Nineties into various areas, designating these areas as places for them to settle themselves; which was all very well, except that by this time practically every square inch of habitable ground was already taken up by pioneer squatters, so there were bound to be fights. Suddenly a mighty black-and-blue shape loomed out at Willie, and he went scrambling past the populace to throw his arms around Titus Cherry.

Tite stared long, down into Willie's face. He said, You're mighty poor. Just skin and bone.

I never had much more than skin and bones, Tite. When'd they get you?

Twas a Friday. I was out a-foraging with Linton and MacCarrick. They tried to cut for it, and both got shot. I gave myself up. He said these things in a tired awed voice, not the genial rumble of the Tite Cherry whom Willie had known as a fellow campaigner. Both eyes seemed peering distantly into the sky; it was as if Titus had had one crossed eye before, now he had both of them crossed. This place, he said, this place. What is it?

Hell, Tite. They call it Camp Sumter. Andersonville. You had any rations today?

Not since yesterday. They gave us cowpeas when we were on the cars, and a little bit of mule.

Come along to our shebang. I got some corn bread saved.

So he had, but when he offered it to Tite the big chap squeezed his eyes shut and made a gesture of refusal.

Oh, come on. It hain't too bad. Just coarse and dry—no salt.

It's all dirty and got cobs ground in it. I'll go without.

Someone might have struck him a heavy blow with a fence-rail, the moment Tite entered at the gate. That was the way he acted—dazed and disbelieving. He appeared to be telling himself, This is not true, this will fade away. He answered the questions Willie put to him about the Twenty-ninth Missouri, and whether they had thought Willie dead, and whether Titus knew whether Willie had been reported as killed— He answered questions dutifully, sleepily, as if there were some secret Other Person whom he had to consult before he could come up with the answers. In between times he would turn his majestic head from side to side, taking in the stockade and its people and its stench and its noises—rejecting the whole business and probably assuring himself that he would wake up soon.

Going Without was one thing for a little shaver like Willie, and quite another thing for Titus. . . . There wasn't room for him in the shebang where Willie dwelt, though Willie tried to have his friend included, no matter which Ninety he was in. At nightfall Tite went down the hill to bunk with the fresh fish with whom he'd arrived, and to contribute his blouse as partial covering for a new shebang. He did everything demanded of him with docility, yet his thoughts seemed far away. Willie had not been long enough in the stockade to have observed intimately such cases; yet there were many. The hatchet of horror lay waiting for certain men the moment they stepped through the North Gate; it came up invisibly and struck them between the eyes, its blade went deep, the hatchet fractured their skulls and the will and the purpose and the reason lurking inside; everything was splintered, they could not put the pieces together again; so they died, so Titus Cherry died.

He would not eat. Willie ranted at him, cursed him, knelt and prayed beside him. He talked of Duty, parents, Tite's little brother who would long to see him return— He spoke deliriously of good times they would have, back in Missouri together— He should go to Canton and join Tite and Tite's people; Tite should come to visit him— They'd spread long tables out-of-doors under the wild grape arbor, they'd invite all the Fiedenbrusters and Moberlys, doughnuts and roast beef and baked apples and roasting ears would be theirs.

But in the meantime you got to feed on something, Tite. Can't exist solely on air. Bad as these rations be, you got to relish them.

Know what I saw, Will, know what I saw?

Oh, don't tell me that again!

It was down below there towards the sinks. Two men a-squatting with that running-off-of-the-bowels. And this other man—he was crippled—

Tite, you got to think of other matters! You got to keep your mind healthy. I tell you, it goes on all the time— I've seen it, everybody's seen it, tain't anything new!

He crawled right along behind them. Soon as one would get through with his business, he'd move along and then get the feeling and go to squatting again. This cripple would dig in his business. He was getting chunks of stuff—corn bread and it looked like potatoes—that the other man had et. Went right through him, never even changed color. And Willie, Willie, he was—

Oh, God alive! All right—say it, it ain't anything new— He was eating the stuff. Because he was hungry! Tite, you got to eat. I tell you, you got to. Not *that*. You don't—

Picking it out of all that loose business. I saw him. Little pieces of bread and— He was crawling along, eating it—

Or sometimes it was dead bodies which bothered him more, as his fever and lassitude grew intense; but usually it was a scene such as he had witnessed near the sinks. Flesh hung on him like loose clothing, his sagging hollow cheeks were pink and later yellow beneath the grime. He slept, sat, walked, later tottered alone. The sinks fascinated him, and the marsh beside the sinks, and he sat for long periods staring, with wide gummy lips moving soundlessly under his raw black beard.

Willie had little left to sell, but now he sold the housewife with its needles, pins, coils of thread, scissors, brass thimble, buttons. He bought meat, vegetables and rice, cooking them for Titus in his big tin cup, to have each offering declined as the first corn bread had been declined. . . . The meat was dog or cat, the rice had worms, the vegetables were poisoned by the Rebs. (This was later, when Tite's mind as well as his vision began to sweep to far and absurd places.) One cupful of stew he managed to upset and waste when he swept out a gaunt hand to gesture refusal. . . . Willie was a philosopher. He had been fond of Titus, he had loved him as much as any other comrade, as much as he had loved Rom Hillburner; he squeezed out tears for Titus, but he wolfed the other food as fast as Tite turned it away.

When Titus Cherry could stand no longer but lay jerking on his sodden blanket and recognizing no one, Willie prevailed upon two men from his shebang to help him carry Tite to the surgeons at the gate. First morning there was a dreadful press, and they couldn't even lug Tite through to be noted; the cries of That's All, No More, No More, Wait Until Tomorrow— These cries arose only fifteen minutes or so after they had fetched him. The other men growled about it; through his starvation Tite held only a fraction of the weight he'd owned when campaigning, but still the burden was nothing to be ignored by sickly men. Next morning Willie scratched amid his few effects and came up with a broken pocket comb and two iron staples which had fallen from the ration cart one day and which Willie had picked up quickly. The staples might be used as implements of some sort; he had hoped to keep the comb, because he could rid himself of many vermin with that; but nothing counted at this time but getting Titus to the hospital (though few people recovered strength in the hospital. The vast majority of them died as soon as they were lugged there. Still the thought of Hospital was a poultice to apply against whatever brotherly affection remained to Willie Mann). He offered these articles to the same men who'd helped him carry Tite on the previous day; one refused, one accepted the staples, and Willie enlisted a man from Tite's own mess through payment of the comb. They started very early, and thus got Tite through the gate and into a stall. There one orderly prescribed Dose Number Three, which was for scorbutus and all wrong; then a surgeon came by and shook his head, and tagged Titus Cherry for Hospital. He died there on a plank two or three days later, unconscious but mumbling until near the end.

I won't die, said Willie. God damn. I won't. Pa, I won't die. Katty (now the sheerest of visions, vague and papery), I won't die. Won't drink the water neither.

He chewed dryly, he chewed with his sore jaws, he chewed the bitter woody bread, chewed beans and the worms which dwelt in them. Part of the shebang where he lived was formed from a square of oilcloth which Willie had retained in his knapsack on capture. The first young Confederates did not preëmpt it, and—later, obeying some fortunate instinct—Willie put the oilcloth inside his shirt. So he brought it into the stockade, and it was impermeable at first, though the oiled part began to flake off under the burning sun. But August developed with recurrent fierce rains, many of them occurring at night; old-timers said it had been like that in June when it rained twenty days straight—some said it rained twenty-four days in June. Since early spring the earth of Georgia had held no thirst.

The loose soil was soaked, swollen past saturation. Occasionally it rejected a fresh onrush, and in one afternoon of early August its rejection was violent. Hour after hour a downpour thrummed on woodland, stockade; it pounded the dripping huddled masses of mankind within pine-stalked limits. Trickles ran down north slope and south, they widened into cascades; the stolid marsh became a lake pocked with infinite stabbings, the slow-crawling creek became a torrent. Yellow tide frothed and clung against those posts which were driven near the commonly-oozing streamlet. The tall logs had been high and dry before, now they were laved. Laving became a battering, each pole weakened in its socket. Deeply those trunks had been imbedded, but water weighted through the coarse ground; its constant pushing stroke could not be resisted.

First a single log of the eastern palisade swayed (benefit accomplished for a space: a portion of the accumulated sewage would be swept out of the stockade down the flat valley. But soon it would be replaced by new seepage) and the massive length of wood leaned hard against another beside it. The combined heaviness of the two was enough to urge a third post from its socket. So it went: in minutes a dozen thick jack-straws had tumbled and splashed. There was a gap in the stockade.

On high ground immediately west of this aperture, men rose from drenched hovels in disbelief. No wall, they cried in the rain, not believing it. Look at that hole! Promptly they came swarming from this same high ground, which was called the Island because ordinarily a pond of fetid ooze twisted to the north of it, and an equal morass curved to the south. Look at that hole! Stockade's gone!

They leaped swearing and screeching, some swam in the force of the cascade, others were running on the banks. Hundreds of prisoners on the twin slopes also had observed this catastrophe which might prove to be a release to all the thwarted and unkempt, so they came jumping.

Not a shot was fired by any guard. Some people thought later that the drilling rain had dampened their enemies' powder charges and caps, as it had cooled the prisoners' will to burst free. A wise battle-toughened sergeant cried an order, and frightened Reserves came tumbling from their shacks. The word was passed along, and quickly, around the south boundary. It reached the earthen fort and the camp to the southwest beyond and the camp to the northwest opposite the North Gate. Squads, companies, guards not On Parapet came to mill at the breach, urged by those few officers alert to the danger involved, urged by the babbling Lieutenant Davis.

Henry Wirz was not on duty. He was gone to Augusta, reported sick, the surgeon pecked at his arm. But among frantic subordinates left to discharge the duties he had laid out there were enough to form a nucleus of strength. They marshalled quaking boys, coughing gray-beards, they held them along the boundaries of the raw river and formed them there with guns level, bayonets fixed.

Skies kept melting and falling, the hose of mettlesome gods was directed down. On one side of the gap scarecrow Yankees congregated, on the other side herded scarecrow hobbledehoys and patriarchs—but with the impact of weapons. No boy tried to gallop past them or sought to pierce the tide and swim to freedom beneath its crest. Reinforcements trotted through the dark rain until prisoners gazed across the breach into a solidity of muzzles and steel. Philosophers said wearily, It couldn't be. Twas too lucky to happen. They turned back to whatever shelter they had left, whatever other shelter they could find or imagine. In time the storm ceased its pounding. Within a night and a day laborers had made the stockade as solid as it was before, and no flash flood of equal proportions came again.

In such thudding storms Willie Mann claimed the right to adjust his portion of tent-patching to his needs. In darkness he would lie with the broken oilcloth funneled toward his mouth, and rainwater would drip or pour, depending on the amount and velocity of rain— It would be directed into Willie's open mouth. Thus he drank. These periodic dilutions were accomplished amid snarls and resentments of his tentmates . . . if you weren't such a plaguèd young fool, and bound to sop up rainwater, we could all be laying fairly snug. . . . After discussion and prevailing acrimony during saner hours, it was agreed that Eph Bainbridge's overcoat should be extended to help cover the gap left by Willie's oilcloth, and that Willie should betake himself into other regions—clear away from the shebang, over against the deadline, and that he should lie unsheltered—when again he chose to absorb the gift of the rain. He did not tell his mates how bad the rain tasted. It was tainted with the prison's effluvia as it came down; effluvia seemed to lie like a mattress above the thirty-odd thousand men and their reek. By the time the rain had dashed down to proximity with the crowded trampled earth it was noxious with retchings and throat-clearings and smells of disordered digestions, with the taint of corpses which had been more dead than alive when they were alive.

How many gallons less had he drunk in this year of 1864 than he had drunk in the year of 1863? There was no way of estimating. He saw a spreading fountain somewhere off in the past or the future, such a fountain as was pictured in the Versailles of their one European travel book at home; and that fountain, with foamy push and laving, represented the canteens and cups and reservoirs which Willie had not poured down his hard-surfaced throat. He thought that his throat was made of old harness, he thought that his throat was sunburnt and peeling as his bony face was peeling and burnt. Desperately he worked at manipulating the scrawny portion of his trunk which hung flat beneath the hoops of his ribs; it wouldn't do to grow costive, there were no physics to be had, and he was one inmate for whom diarrhoea held little threat—he'd only had a touch of it twice, both times mildly. When he witnessed his own feces he thought that a rabbit must have been halting there instead of Willie Mann.

. . . Thunder tussled in the southwest and a deluge burst upon the soaked stockade shortly before midnight. Clouds had gloomed and pressed low as if challenging the slivers atop the fence to rip them open; so in time they were ripped. Willie lay half submerged in a pool, close to the deadline on the steep north slope. Oilcloth covered the upper portion of his body, and stiffly he held his thin elbows immobile and pressed his palms up to tilt the long-punished fabric. The ill-favored ill-flavored storm distributed its substance into his mouth, flowing over cracks in his lips, filling cracks inside his mouth which felt like the cracks in a plaster wall.

Lightning had been gashing since the storm broke, but suddenly a thrust came close enough to singe the hair in any man's nostrils. Willie's ears popped; he thought that he had been struck and torn and melted by the blaze (vaguely he recalled a farmer back home who'd had the watch melted in his pocket and the nails melted in his boots when he was struck). For a while Willie could see nothing but the rough ball of fire which had seemed to bounce on earth beside him, he could smell nothing but scorched brimstone and sulphur and storied chemicals. Prisoners hallooed in the nearer shebangs, and wanted to know who had been hit. Maybe no one had been hit, but you would have thought that a dozen people had been tossed and carved by the lightning's lash, the crash of bursting cannon.

Willie felt cold all along his side. He was drenched, he had been drenched before, but this was a strange and different coldness. Had lightning tapped the blood from his body, was his blood chill instead of warm? He flung out his right hand. There was a bubbling, a running in the mud.

Willie Mann rose up on shaking knees. The next glare told him the truth . . . a stream, a small stream of clear water was coming his way, flowing desperately toward and around him. Another flare: he could see it rising in lather and bubbles from muck within the dead-line space, carrying chunks of clay, swirls of mud, carrying scraps of bark and even pebbles on its crest. It wasn't the rain . . . this was colder than rain, by God it was clearer than rain. He could see it in repeated explosions of the crazy sky. It was a little brook, a spring, it was coming out of the ground.

He fell forward, burying his face in the flow, draining mouthful after mouthful, trying to condemn his stony throat to a banquet of swallowing. This was something to drown in, he would drown in it. Then he rose, supporting himself on trembling hands as he screamed with all his strength, Water! Fresh water! It's a spring! He did not distribute these tidings with any notion of sharing a treat with the rank and file of fellow men; it was only that he had to voice the discovery, bellow it above cracking thunder in order to reassure himself that it was true.

Within a matter of seconds there were fifty men tumbled around him, guzzling like spooks shed by the bursting night; and more scores came shoving on top of them.

Previous moisture had been nothing but the muck of obscenity; now there was Grace. How did it taste? It was Doctor's water and Katty's advised water: pure and cool and clear. It tasted as a forest pool where none but clean russet-coated beasts assembled to drink,

and where unspoiled Indians bowed to drink and pray. It was the
spring found by Daniel Boone when Boone came tramping in youth,
prime, or frosty age. It tasted of simple and pretty things: violets, and
taffy, and winter making pine-tree patterns on a thin sharp window
pane. It was Beverly's Creek with crawdads scuttling, and the blue-
purple-sky-colored bird being delicate in woodsy air overhead, the
miniature bird the virgin boy and virgin girl had seen and heard, the
bird without a name. It was the well at Grandpappy's house, where
butter and cheese hung in a damp sack, and sometimes fresh little
wild strawberries were put down there to keep them cool. O water,
O bittersweet the cleanliness; it carried its own spice, not the meager
drip of disconsolate rainfall; but you could taste the clarity of this
stuff for all the rain which smashed upon it. The stream grew wider,
it came in free panic seeping under the sagging timber of the deadline,
it flowed and talked of Church and Christ Himself, it rippled of
Home. Lightning reeked persistently, lightning was like fragrant
lilacs in the bubbling reflection. Water, water, fresh water here, a
hundred dollars a drink! Yells lost the restriction of words, all yells
united in a single persistent whooping blast; and cripples tried to
share as well, but many of them were knocked down or aside as the
rush went on. Guards crouched under the slanting roofs of their
sentry stations, they did not like to step out in the rain; some men
feared that guards might shoot into the scrambling mass, and already
weaker individuals were being shoved fairly across the deadline, and
the deadline broke, but still the guards held their fire. *He clave the
rocks in the wilderness, and gave them drink. . . .* Clear and cool
and pure, as the saintly Doctor and the saintly Katty had ordered.

   . . . Tasted of ferns, and wake-robins which opened early and pale
when blackbirds were teetering on new green reeds and making their
chink sounds . . . O springtime when bees came swarming, and sap
had climbed clear up into the bundles of new maple seeds. Dear
water—it might have been released by thunder's pulsation or the
spear-thrust of lightning itself, and already a dozen prisoners announced staunchly that they had witnessed the very bolt which drilled
the ground. It might have been released by the heaviness of saturation of soaked sandy soil . . . all those torrents of June, these new
freshets of ugly August uniting to disturb the hard-tamped anchorage
of a hillside where every tree had been felled, where a ditch had
been spaded out, where roughly squared pine trunks had been
socketed, where an ancient sweet spring had been hidden and trodden
into muteness.

   It was the deep round narrow haunted cistern at home, where you
busied yourself with rope and bucket on washday, filling the family
tubs before you took yourself off to school; yes, that wine from the
cistern was rainwater, but not the rainwater of Andersonville funneled

from rotten blankets, from draped overcoats with the taste of forgotten blood and forgotten piss in them . . . ah, so long tanked among dark buried limestone and cistern lining that the water awarded itself the flavor of a native spring, nor did it smell like rainwater longer.

Knowing nothing of this magic breaking forth, Ira Claffey stirred on his bed beyond the stockade and the southwest hill. He emerged from a dream about one of his dead sons, and was aware of lightning's brilliance and protracted thunder. He might have heard (he did not hear, at this time) a child speaking from memory. Lucy it was.

. . . Where do they sleep?

. . . Ah, there's that moss. Where do you think?

. . . And for table linen too. Would they let me drink their water?

. . . Assuredly. That's the reason they keep it running. Here, child, I'll make a cup of my hand . . . miniature fairies of the damp sort, scarcely as big as your finger.

. . . I saw one, whilst I was drinking.

It was not frozen, it was not ice, it was running loose in a summer night in Georgia, yet it had the perfume of icicles. You were a little boy again, and there came an exceptionally heavy snow to swaddle the roofs, and then a quick thaw, and then a freeze again. They hung in tapering clubs at the corner of the house where the slope of the rear portion met the slope of the front. Icicles were a menace, and Doctor said to knock them down with a pole; so you knocked them down, and it was sport. But the tiniest stilettos of all, the baby daggers on the summer kitchen eave—these you did not set to falling and crashing. These you broke off and carried in your red mitten until the hairs of yarn grew crimson against the icicles, and you sucked the icicles as you walked; they tasted crisp and of winter.

It was a fresh apple, this water, a harvest apple eaten before it was quite ripe, but still a softer apple than the one Katty had hidden in your lunch bucket. It was feast and comfort for a good elderly dog named Ben. Here, old fellow, you're panting at a great rate— and you're so warm in that heavy coat of yours— Here's the pan. And lap, lap, lap eternally after you had set the pan of clear water before him; lap, lap, lap, lap with a long tongue as pink as boiled meat; and the gratitude he offered when he came to sink his muzzle upon your knee. . . .

O wild grapes with their tan, O inner bark of slippery elm, O tang and tendril of sorrel growing crisp: these tastes were there. High on a shaded hillside in Beverly's Timber the winding gully cut its course, and there stood an elm in serenity—not a slippery elm, but one of another kind—with a great bared root outthrust, and the root had grown bark upon it like the trunk of the tree. Scored deeply across this mighty root, a little stream came down. Sometimes it dried to nothingness in late summer when no rains fell, but usually it was there, in winter it might be frozen, usually it was there, a baby waterfall across the root, a fall three inches wide and perhaps a foot long in the falling. It had built the dark depression by its own persistence over the bulk of that elm root, and when you were small you could lie at length beside the resulting pool and put your face beneath the hollowed root and let the waterfall wash your face and drown your mouth. Even slim Willie had grown too tall, by the time he was thirteen, to fit into the gully and force his face under the vertical pouring, but he remembered the wet clear drowning. So he remembered it this night.

As Willie Mann remembered, a thousand other men remembered beneficent drinks they had had; but not all of them were capable of entertaining the poetry Willie entertained; very few were capable of entertaining it. Something said in their souls, Water has come, it's here, it has burst from the hill, look out for that deadline, and when they'd scrambled and fought to absorb their share and more than their share, there might have been the briefest flash of recollection: a horse-trough in which a youth bathed his hot head, the welcome bitterness of cool beer in a riverside saloon, a natural flowing well where sulphur and other ingredients formed corded flowers and patterns beneath the foam, a lonely cave where stalactites dripped.

But it was Willie's water, he called it his own, he was the first prisoner to detect and taste it. For a time he lay recumbent beneath the scuffle, alternately sucking through the short tube he made of his lips, or plowing his entire face into the current. Then, as the rush and crush and fight developed to a point of actual danger—as men wailed and swore and caught weaker men by the arms or legs and dragged them away, bound to usurp their places— Willie had been kicked enough. He staggered off to a safe distance with water splashing inside him as if he carried a tin pail within his tight-drawn skin. He lay down and belched; a small portion of the water arose with belching and trickled from the corners of his mouth . . . but he had Gone Without, he had Gone Without for a very long time, and now he had drunk his rich reward and soon would drink again.

The riot continued. Lightning snapped at gradually decreasing intervals, but the flashes were quaking longer as the storm moved on. Wide-spread electricity revealed every filament of the scene with clear exactness: there was the stockade towering with the nearest sentry shack cut sharp on an impressive green-lilac sky—you could even see the shakes of the sentry-shack roof which had curled like leaves in a summer sun—you could see the guard and count his whiskers and see him spit. Then blackness ruled, hurting the eyes; groans and yells and admiration of the miracle continued; then another extensive glaring quivering, and closer at hand you witnessed the tufted heads, the bald heads, the tangle of ragged shapes bending, squirming, elbowing, beating about, making a herding as beasts should never herd—bound to drink, bound to drink the good water for which Providence exacted not one red cent; and no one else could put a price upon it, for it issued from beyond the deadline.

Wirz was gone, Wirz was sick abed. But the next day Lieutenant Davis looked down from the parapet and ordered a sluice to be built, conducting the flow past the deadline into camp. Make it long enough, he ordered. I don't want that gang busting them posts and scantlings down. Davis knew that if there was too much shooting by the guards at this particular point there would be some sort of investigation; Davis hated investigations chiefly because of the paper work entailed. It was no skin off his behind: there were plenty of springs outside the stockade to supply the Confederates amply, and so no need to conduct the new little stream in a westerly direction, through the fence itself. Davis would never have spent the effort or the attention necessary to drill a deep well for the prisoners; but since the storm had dug one the prisoners could have the use of it. Furthermore, there would now be less incentive for people to sink deep wells; thus opportunities for tunneling would be decreased.

A. R. Hill and his police brought about a form of discipline that day; the discipline continued tolerably. At any hour you could look that way and see two extensive lines of prisoners shambling along, moving by degrees toward the sluice and filling their cups, their cans, their broken canteens, their leaky kettles. Some who owned no such equipment merely stood in line, waiting for the treat of drinking from their dirty hands; and then they returned to the end of the line and gradually progressed springwards again for another drink; it was something to do.

Providence Spring, they called it universally. Many were the sermons recited by worshipping lay parsons who spoke their pieces throughout the stockade whenever and wherever a congregation might be assembled. They ascribed the phenomenon to direct interference by Celestial engineers, and more than one man swore that he had seen angels at the spot. Only the most hard-bitten heretics stood on the outskirts, heckling and desiring to know why God hadn't acted sooner, before their comrades died from drinking the maggoty reek of the marsh. By and large the flow was accepted as evidence that the One Above had not forgotten the stockade and the people in it, no matter how many generals and exchange commissioners had chosen apparently to forget.

Willie Mann read his soiled Bible with new energy, and was very near to becoming one of those same lay preachers. But he did not sermonize, he only read aloud from the Book to any friends who would listen. He thrilled at each reference to springs or brooks or just plain water which he might find, and he found them in the Psalms, but of course the seventeenth chapter of Exodus was his favorite text at the time, along with Numbers, Twenty. Sometimes Revelations. A mean scarecrow sauntered past and halted to jibe at him. Willie glowered in a rush of returning strength. It seemed that his bones jangled together when he moved, that his young muscles had shriveled from ropes to threads; but he rushed upon the profane scoffing heathen and hurled him flat in the mud. His congregation cheered him derisively. Willie went on reading aloud.

They shall hunger no more, neither thirst any more; neither shall the sun light on them, nor any heat.

For the Lamb which is in the midst of the throne shall feed them, and shall lead them unto living fountains of waters; and God shall wipe away all tears from their eyes.

More sharply, more eagerly distinct than in weeks, Katty moved through the Biblical incidents which came to his attention in reading. She wore Hebraic robes and trod the wilderness. Willie regarded Providence Spring as a portent . . . had he suffered doubts before, had he doubted when he watched Titus Cherry die? Now he knew. He would return to Missouri, he would walk once more in the timber, he would wed Katty, they would have flocks of children. They would have a deep well, clear and pure; and on August days the children would petition him for cool drinks, and so as soon as they were big enough he would train them to operate the well-sweep or maybe the windlass—he didn't know just what sort of machinery he would have. But he heard the water trickling . . . it was there for him to drink, for all men to drink.

Guards talked about it outside, and so Ira Claffey came to hear of the spring. He listened with wonder, he heard his sons chatting and drinking there, he heard the voice of small Lucy, heard his own voice. . . . Here, child, I'll make a cup of my hand. Beneath this rock, so. Now you bend down—take care, don't wet your boots and skirts— That's the way.

XLII

Cato Dillard searched his conscience and found himself remiss. In first years of the war he had made a kind of game out of discovering Biblical support for the Secessionist cause. When Prophets discussed people of the North he knew of course that they referred to historic or fabled Hebraic wars. The Prophets were not cognizant of Abolitionists, or of greasy mechanics from urban New York and Pennsylvania who must now be considered as supporting the Republicans and Abolitionists, no matter how much they might differ in private theory. Cato Dillard was far too intelligent to believe so.

But still it was a game and titillating; it taxed his powers of research and application. Always he shone before a challenge.

Effie Dillard labeled the Southern cause as Right, and the Northern cause as Wrong. She prayed nightly that Lincoln would be packed out of his White House, and that Washington City, New York City, Philadelphia and Chicago might know the triumphant tread of gray columns. She let it go at that, she was too busy in the application of her flouncing ardent Christianity to waste hours in poking after a reassuring Text.

Both the old people suffered anguish as their grandsons were destroyed (five were gone by this August of 1864—and all in the past eight months: two dead of disease, two of wounds, one killed in a Hood's cavalry skirmish) and then they found comfort in the stout draught of Faith. They believed that a general family pic-nic of Dillards and their descendants would ensue during that sunny afternoon following Resurrection Morn.

In early months Cato had thought of conflict within Andersonville just as he'd typified it in speech: brawling. His witnessing of the raiders' execution, and subsequent examination of the motives involved, shattered this opinion. The men had died attended by an officer of the Catholic church; they were Catholics; surely the priest would have refused his services in the mere conclusion of a brawl. Ira assured the Reverend Mr. Dillard that those hanged had been sentenced by a Yankee court, defended by Yankee lawyers, prosecuted by Yankee lawyers or men serving as such. So Redeemed Yankees had sentenced Unredeemed Yankees to the worst penalty on earth . . . naturally there were worse penalties in the Hereafter . . . it was disquieting to think that, by law of averages, there must be many elect Presbyterians milling within the stockade . . . religionists conducted services, Cato himself had heard their songs arise.

He besought the Scriptures again to relieve his confusion.

Now, thou son of man, wilt thou judge, wilt thou judge the bloody city? . . . Cato read Ezekiel, on through all the talk of whoredoms and abominations which never ceased to offend him; because he was pure, had remained pure through his life, taught purity to his children, trusted in turn that they had passed this limpid inheritance on to the next generation. *And Aholah played the harlot . . . and she doted on her lovers, on the Assyrians her neighbors . . . which were clothed with blue, captains and rulers, all of them desirable young men, horsemen riding upon horses.* Yankee cavalry, beyond a doubt.

Mr. Dillard sighed, thudded his Bible shut, opened it again on the Gospels instead of the Prophets. Always he had imagined St. Mark as owning a voice firm but gentle, and especially gentle as he recounted the exploits and recited the words of the Gentlest Man. Cato Dillard's own father had possessed such a voice, such a spirit.

> *. . . So is the kingdom of God, as if a man should cast seed into the ground;*
> *And should sleep, and rise night and day, and the seed should spring and grow up, he knoweth not how.*

Cato Dillard lifted his gaze from the fine-lettered page, and snuffed his candle, and sat pillowed up in darkness beside his slumbering wife. He looked across sharp patches of moonlight on the old carpet, and through the window into moonlight washing warmly his own garden.

> *For the earth bringeth forth fruit of herself; first the blade, then the ear, after that the full corn in the ear.*

This is a desert place, came the words of that later Chapter, *and now the time is far passed.* Andersonville? It could be, could be. *They have nothing to eat.* And what had the Master said to that? *He answered and said unto them, Give ye them to eat.*

Effie, said Cato in the dawn, what of our green corn?

Yon patch is past roasting, dry in the husk. We've a bit left in rows past the woodshed.

Where might we get green corn in any quantity, roasting ears still soft and green?

Effie ceased her tinkling into the slop-jar, slid the cover into place (the knitted cap over the pottery cover prevented any clanking, there was only the dull *koom* of the jar's closing) and adjusted her skirts carefully before she stepped from behind a little screen of woven

bull-grass which modesty dictated should be placed in its three unsteady sections to shield the commode.

From Brother Ira Claffey, man! He plants long, he plants late as
well as early; his maize will no be dried to crispness yet—not all, to
be sure. But what want you with green corn?

Roasting ears, said Cato. He slid his spotted old legs out of bed
and removed his nightcap.

For whom?

Yankee prisoners.

Cate, you're daft.

He replied with that geniality coming easily to those who feel that
they have arrived at righteous decision, Were I daft as often you've
described me to be, woman, I'd have populated a dozen crazy-houses
e'er now.

But what want yon Yankees with green corn?

They'd wish to eat it, don't you believe?

But— Cate— Would it be fair to our own grandchildren? Our brave
boys in the field—?

Have you never become acquainted with the Sixth Chapter of the
Gospel According To St. Mark?

Away with you. Those were—Disciples—

Five thousand Disciples? he asked archly.

Twas a congregation of The Just.

He mused pleasantly as he pulled on his stockings. Not only corn
in roasting. But also root vegetables: we've turnips in plenty, carrots,
beets—

Yon cabbages are rising into seed and waste, cried Effie in spite of
herself.

Enthusiastically Cato wrote to Ira Claffey, telling him of his plan
and inviting Ira's assistance and generosity. The minister had not been
informed of Lucy's little march with wenches and baskets, and her
inability to reach the stockade. He thought, as many well-intentioned
people have often thought, that he had conceived of a particularly
glossy charity—a bounteous impulse instigated by God, no doubt, but
still a personal mercy. He wrote: *If a brother or sister be naked, and
destitute of daily food*— The General Epistle of James eludes me for
the moment, Brother Ira. Puss is asleep upon my Bible, and I shall
not disturb her, since she may be dropping kits before nightfall. Last
time she had them in the drawer containing my *drawers* and stockings! But what think you of the proposal? Neighbor Stancil has
promised the lend of his big wagon, with a four-mule team; and he a
Methodist! The Dennards, Lindsays and Nunns all express themselves
as willing to give; and I should think a few bushels might also be got
from the Lockridges and others, perhaps more than a mere few
bushels; they might donate plenteously. Have you green corn enough

and to spare? What of your cabbages and the general collard situation? I have set Buff to pulling turnips that they may be scrubbed.
A further suggestion comes from Mrs. McCrary: her own dear child
languished last year on an isle at the North, without sufficient coverings for his poor body; and she has sat with me, and we have explored
God's opinion, or have attempted. Since the lad is now among The
Blest (but they did have shelter; he died in a barracks, twas said)
the lady has possessed an overpowering intent to find favor Aloft by
exhibiting true Christian mercy to his enemies. She is assembling his
entire stock of shirts, jackets, pantaloons and the like, to be offered
to destitute Northrons. As we have observed, there is prevailing ragged-
ness at Anderson, in some cases amounting to nakedness and resulting
indecency. Poor as we have become in this struggle for Independence,
and to repel invading hordes, I should think a goodly supply of
serviceable clothing might be gotten together if each gave his mite.
I myself am contributing boots—which pinch me, I admit, but might
not pinch some shoe-less Yankee. *But the wisdom that is from above
is first pure, then peaceable, gentle, and easy to be intreated, full of
mercy and good fruits, without partiality, and without hypocrisy.* Mrs.
Dillard goes flying about, attempting to collect medicines; and such
a small stock can be assembled; and she dare not rob her own closet
too grievously, since her attention is demanded by many ailing persons
now and again. But boots, potions, turnips, green corn, undershirts
or melons: all seem of value, all I should believe would be received
thankfully by the lads there, misguided into cruelty though they have
been. Now, dear Brother, what of the military who are in command?
Will they see fit to admit of our charity? I grow alarmed at considering what has come to me of the superintendent and the general commanding: both obstreperously and insistently profane, tis said. I have
not heard that either is addicted to The Bottle, but that they take a
particular delight in cursing; and also this is reported of the troops
under them. However, I should think that if we were to seek *not
permission in advance,* but were to appear bag and baggage and
basket, they would be bound to accept our small offering for the unfortunates *perforce.* Since many of the items are spoilable. Ah, also:
Mr. Marshall has promised a pig. Though I had to fling Testament at
him for an hour to get it! The pig must be butchered promptly before
our departure. One cannot speculate as to the weather; but I should
hazard an opinion that, all things being equal, and you receiving no
advices to the contrary, our little caravan might arrive by Friday mid-
day. If not on Friday, look to see us on Saturday. Mrs. Dillard is bound
to come on for the distribution, and shall be accompanied by a few
other ladies, I make little doubt. Do not feel that you must *feed* them,
Brother, or the rest of us; but we shall pay our respects, and hope to
gather up your own donation. Word has reached us of the miraculous

spring bursting forth there. Could it be the same spring where you were wont to wander, and where we have sat many times; and where I told you of the Highland Presbyterians at Darien; and where in turn you told me of the so-called Dorchester Puritans, your own kinfolk in Liberty County, of more than a century since? *Behold, I will stand before thee there upon the rock in Horeb; and thou shalt smite the rock, and there shall come water out of it, that the people may drink.* Puss is still upon the Bible, but I need no reference. As a mere child I was enamored of Exodus, and all the dramatic events therein, and the building of the tabernacle, and what was a cubit? Theology should be awarded early to a youth, that he remember; but often I was naughty and put aside my Catechism, and loved to watch the Hebrews at their fights. Ah, me. My pen has been trailing about; but should that not be the privilege of an old man's pen? I wish it were yam time. Then we might assemble a quantity. Perhaps we can perform further philanthropy in the autumn. I have neglected to tell you that Neighbor Pace (Baptist) is giving carrots; and little Neddy Hinchley has just made an errand to inform me that his mother will contribute what fruit is left to her in all this hotness. Sakes, as your Lucy would say, what a scorcher is today! Heaven be praised that our dear Sister Veronica is no longer called upon to endure Earthly miseries; but sleeps, knowing no misfortune, and in fully justified hope, I am convinced, of a Glorious Resurrection. I pray for you daily, Brother, and please to include me in your prayers. Until the oncoming of our charitable migration, then. In Brotherly Faith & Hope, Yrs, C. Dillard.

Post Script. Will wonders never cease? I must have been inspired, truly, in getting my plot a-going. This missive was folded, I was seeking for wax to seal it, when appeared Mrs. Banister from across the way. You know her: an Episcopalian. She'd come for a Seidlitz powder, if Mrs. Dillard possessed any. (She did not.) Am informed by Mrs. Banister that General J. Winder is a *Communicant.* Their church here in Americus is new in organization; and the rector observed that he had seen General Winder, when in Richmond, partaking of the Holy Eucharist. They have been busy recently selecting their vestrymen and church wardens; and *Gen. Winder was named to be a warden.* Now certainly we have nothing to fear. A church warden could never refuse us permission. The tales borne to me of his profane utterances must have been made up out of whole cloth. Or were in error, since both names begin with a W; and only the Switzer must have been the sinner. C.P.D.

This letter was carried to Anderson on the cars next morning, and lay for three days in an old salt box at Uncle Arch Yeoman's, where mail intended for citizens of the community was left until neighbors or slaves distributed it. Jonas brought the letter in to Ira while the Claffeys were at breakfast with Harrell Elkins. The project was discussed with animation. Cousin Harry, so often gone into taciturnity these days and so often oblivious of them both, sat with spectacles shining . . . Lucy had the sly thought that the glass lenses were burnished by inner blaze stoked by brain and heart. Oh, and how he does need a joy, she thought. Would that I might afford it for him! He sees hospital, thinks hospital, will recognize nothing but hospital and wrongs contained there.

Cousin Harry talked constantly, with spirit; he'd interrupted Ira's reading several times with approving comments, with further suggestions. Now that the letter was put next to Ira's plate, Elkins discoursed on vinegar.

They appear to have forgotten it. Few other adjuncts to the diet could be more efficacious in treatment of scurvy. If you could get word to those Americus folks, they might fetch some barrels of it.

Our own supply is limited, said Lucy.

Elkins stared at her, watery eyes flicking rapidly in magnification. Surely you're mistaken, Cousin Lucy. You have that great cask on the roofed gallery beside your kitchen—

But it diminishes so rapidly.

However could we use much vinegar? asked her father. Solely for salads, and a trifle for spicing. Daughter, have you been making pickles in quantity?

Not I, not in this heat. And most of your gherkins were burnt by the sun, Poppy. But still there's less and less vinegar each day.

Have some of the black people developed a thirst?

I've detected no such addiction, said Lucy. She was replying directly to her father, but looking directly at Harrell, who sat with smooth face reddened and who made a great business of picking a muffin to pieces.

Lucy lifted her voice slightly, meaningly. It is as if some person came by day or night with a flask, opened the bung, and drew off vinegar.

For a moment the implied accusation and the expression of guilt held Ira perplexed, and he regarded the younger pair with amazement. Then, as the surgeon put his big hand to his forehead and concealed his face, Ira began to chuckle. Merriment spread among the three; Lucy collapsed in giggles; Elkins's shoulders were shaking, though it seemed that he might have been moved by sobs as well as by mirth; in fact he was close to sobbing.

Have you the tell-tale bottle about you? asked the girl.

Still refusing to face her, Elkins put his other hand down into his pocket and brought the flask forth. His voice shook as he confessed. A very small bottle, you see. A mere brandy flask.

Ring for more coffee, my dear, said Ira. Then, to Harry: Did you think we'd refuse you, Cousin?

Elkins removed his spectacles, wiped his eyes (He is almost comely, thought Lucy, without those great glaring things. I wish that I could see him more often thus) and managed to compose himself for confession. It was only— The first time the thought occurred to me— You see, none of you were about. I observed Naomi at the keg, filling a cruet, so of course I knew that it contained vinegar— I didn't wish to trouble anyone.

Have your depredations been confined solely to vinegar? asked Ira.

Elkins stared owlishly. Why do you ask that, sir?

Now that I'm put in mind of it, Jem complained that something had been at the cauliflowers.

But you have an over-supply of garden truck.

Not of cauliflowers. We're far from the seacoast, and enough salt's not be be had for preparing the beds. Just how have you been conveying cauliflowers to the hospital, Cousin Harry?

I put them in my pockets. And in corners of my medical kit.

What—whole cauliflowers?

You do appear right bulgy at times, said Lucy.

Not whole cauliflowers. I separate the small flowers, the segments— You see, sir, and Cousin Lucy— I've had no wish to run afoul of guards or of the Chief Surgeon. My small benevolence—the result of petty thievery—might not meet with his approbation.

Naomi had appeared with a steaming pot of grain coffee, to fill their cups, and had been interested and amazed. Miss Lucy, that Mastah Harry, he always asking me for bones.

Just leftovers, said Elkins weakly.

And he make me save potato parings.

Ira shook his head. But we've so many other things. Much has gone to waste, all through the summer.

I—I had no wish to bother you. And I feared to tote a basket. Twould have aroused suspicion, perhaps resentment.

He sipped the last of his coffee with rapid swallowing, he said that he must be up and away. He pushed back his chair, arose and spoke a thanks for the meal, bowed, and went into the hallway where his kit lay upon a chair. He cried a last goodbye through the open door and turned toward the outside gallery. He was halfway down the steps when the light tap of shoes sounded behind him, and he turned quickly. Lucy walked upon the gallery, she was coming toward him. The young man stood motionless, it was almost as if he knew what to expect; he saw her intent, and stood graven; he wished solemnly, he wished in his entire being to share with her; yet he felt wearily that the wrongs of the world and of this particular day and this particular portion of the world were overwhelming them; he dared yield to nothing but the demand of a task he had set for himself.

Lucy spoke two words— Dear Harry, she said. She bent forward and flung her arms around his neck and kissed him long on the mouth.

Do you mean love? he asked, when their faces were apart.

Twas for your great heart, Harry. I understand so well why Sutherland loved you.

But do you mean love? For a critter like me?

I don't know what I mean, she said softly. I but wished to—award you— Perhaps a kiss from me is nothing—

Elkins pushed her from him rudely. No, no, he mumbled (and it was odd, but she thought of a squirrel; he reminded her of a squirrel, a great baldish squirrel a-muttering). He said, I can't bear it. We can't— Not in this! There's so much filth and screaming. You should hear the gangrenous! No, no, you should not, I couldn't bear for you to hear them—

But I do, Coz.

You do? Where? Here?

All the way up here, she said with stoicism. I hear them screaming. My ears are keen.

May God damn the people who brought on this war. Elkins spoke in a whisper. He went away down the lane toward the first rifle pits, satchel swinging back and forth in accompaniment to his lunging pace. Lucy stood watching, and then tears washed him from her vision.

At the breakfast table Ira sat with a shred of bacon suspended on his fork, sat motionless and musing, unaware of the tenderness and hurt of this contact on the gallery. He was scarcely aware that Lucy had left the room. He considered his old friend the Reverend Mr. Dillard, and how native sweetness had transcended dry dictates put forth in the Directory for Worship. Very clearly did Ira recall an adjuration to the sick—was it in Chapter Twelve? Thirty-five years earlier Ira Claffey had hoped to become a minister, he had studied with diligence; but eventually saw himself standing before a frosty barrier over which he had no wish to scramble. What would a Presbyterian minister say to the wretched of Andersonville if he felt himself bound by the Directory? *He shall instruct the sick out of the Scriptures, that diseases arise not out of the ground, nor do they come by chance; but that they are directed and sent by a wise and holy God, either for correction of sin, for the trial of grace, for improvement in religion, or for other important ends. . . .* What wise and holy God had constucted the stockade? Was his name Winder? What sin had been performed by the Northerners? The sin of being Northern? Moses Claffey was born in 1845. . . . Let us select a Moses from Indiana or Vermont. He did not die at Crampton's Gap; at the age of eighteen or nineteen he finds himself in Andersonville, he lies in the hospital and is tended by Cousin Harry; or perhaps he is less fortunate, he is tended by a contract surgeon. Did not the disease of the Northern Moses rise from a putrid kennel in which he was compelled to crouch? Did it not come from the chance which fetched him into captivity in the first place? Oh, wise and holy God, I bless thee for correcting the sin of this Yankee youngun! I beseech thee to award him an additional and increasing trial of grace. Pray to improve his religion; he whimpers and gapes because you have removed his teeth, puffed his gums, fattened his tongue, put the poison in his belly and his blood. . . . And final admonition to you, you cringing Federal Moses: See that you do not despise God's chastening hand, see that you do not faint under God's rebukes! . . .

Lucy had gone to cool her face. Now she returned to the room, she came in slowly. Ira did not even look at her; he was lost in disgust at the prim and calloused, lost in admiration of a man who could rise above what fusty pettiness he'd been taught.

Your elderly Uncle Cato Dillard, said Ira. He's a man.

Yes, Poppy.

Daughter, I swear it: with each review of certain pages—in recollection, naturally—I approach agnosticism.

Yes, Poppy.

And he had thought to find her shocked. His eyes came up under wiry brows now turning whitish, and he saw that some fresh wrong had been visited upon the one great Love remaining to him.

But— Heed me. The thought of Mr. Dillard can expunge a variety of sins, it can draw a rusty nail from a wound—

Yes, Poppy.

Because he is *good,* so good that he is beyond precepts set forth by creaking meddlesome little minds.

Yes. . . .

My dear, about the vinegar. Did you catch Harry *in flagrante delicto?*

Her wan voice . . . Twas in the dawn. I looked from my room and saw him. Lucy's laughter rattled mechanically. There he was, crouched down, making a most serious business of filling his flask.

Then immediately we should go into the business of manufacturing it! Possibly Coz can fathom a method for smuggling it by the quart; he's a gentleman of resource. Have we another full barrel at hand?

In the pantry shed.

Then instruct Naomi to tap the fresh barrel, and we shall use the other for mothering. Have the wenches roll two casks beneath the roof—sugar casks would do nicely—and use a proportion of one gallon of sorghum to, say, eleven gallons of clear rainwater. Portion the current vinegar, remaining in what we should now call Coz's keg, into the other barrels, to supply the mother. Within the month, if the stuff keeps working and doesn't die, we should have fresh vinegar in quantity.

Ira considered, and then added a question. Have we any gauze or other coarse woven material, fly-proof, among the household supplies?

Not an inch. All used up, long since.

Then take it from the windows of an empty room.

Nnnone there, and he looked up in anguish to see her crying. Lucy made a strong successful effort to control her voice. I took down the last, months ago. I even took the material from the windows of Mother's room after—she— To make repairs. The only chambers with anything resembling a mosquito-bar are your room, mine and—Cousin Harry's.

Ira thought in annoyance that if the young people were married the gauze might be taken from one room or the other. He felt a rising impatience with Harrell Elkins. Then take it from my room. We must have it washed and dried with care, to cover the open barrels, to keep out flies. As our good Dr. Chase says, vinegar is an industrious fellow but he does need air in sufficiency.

I shall take it from my own windows, said Lucy stubbornly.

Damn it, you shan't, cried Ira in full testiness. He was appalled, he had not been driven to such expression of wrath with Lucy since she was fourteen, and sulked because he would not buy her a phaeton. He got up, stamped to his room, pulled down the cloth from both windows. By this time he was enraged with himself because he had become enraged. Below stairs he heard Lucy ordering the black women about, and soon came the rumpus of barrels being brought to the kitchen gallery. Ira descended grumpily, gave over the gauze to Extra for washing, and mumbled an apology to an ashen daughter who ignored him; he could not blame her for ignoring him. Ira was especially patient with the hands that day, fearing that his unsettled condition might cause him to display an additional sharpness to creatures wholly in his power. He still remembered, after forty years, his fright and disgust at witnessing a neighbor abuse an old horse solely because he, the neighbor, had achieved low score in a shooting-match.

Ira turned deliberately from contemplation of the stockade and its problems, and from any thought of Lucy and her grief (he did not fathom the exact nature of her grief, but was positive that it concerned Harry). He tried to soothe his spirit by renewed admiration of the generous Mr. Dillard, and this in turn led to his reflecting on Americus and its people. Ira had known the town well in years when business took him there, when his plantation was itself a business and not a region of weeds surrounding an orchard, a cornfield and a few garden-patches from which a living might be eked out for a handful of whites and blacks. When Cato wrote of Nunns, Dennards, McCrarys and the like, he was fanning a memory.

Eventually that day Ira Claffey worked in a daze. . . . Veronica was young and sane, a lovely morsel to tempt him with her eyes and slimness of her waist and conversation of her skirts . . . the children bounded noisily; they had to be hushed, but their eyes were gay and their cheeks ruddy: the surviving children . . . again Suthy broke his arm in falling from a chinaberry tree when he was four; again Badger shot his turkey through the head at one hundred yards at least—oh, lucky shot, and how he swelled about it . . . again Ira had a slave whipped—which one? was it that expensive sullen blacksmith called Caliph?—for beating his wife . . . again he persuaded Veronica to indulge in brandy—the only time; he could never persuade her to touch brandy again—and he seduced her accordingly, and what a seduction: he remembered her frenzy and bleatings; but the next day she was pickled in remorse perhaps because she had been pickled in brandy, more likely because of what she'd done in bed; twas often so; no wonder that the first thing she put aside, as she went into lunacy, was lust . . . again, in somber and quieter illusion, he chipped the stones for his babies' graves, so little time elapsing between the making of those small slabs. . . .

Thus he returned in thought to Americus. At least a portion of its inhabitants were not uncomprehending, unaware of that grotesque pen yonder and the pathetic bounty being assembled for its occupants . . . Dennards, McCrarys, Lindsays: there were many on the hill. The hill was shaded by oaks and cedars, and the monument of young Mr. Hudson, with its fine urn atop, was easily the handsomest. *In Memory of Leander M. Hudson. Born Feb. 22nd 1823. Died Nov. 21st 1851. A native Georgian and a resident of the town of Oglethorpe. He breathed his last among strangers where he now lies. Habitually active and energetic, he sprang to the duties of life, but looked beyond them to the rewards of Heaven.* Well, well, so should we all; and a year ago I would have sworn that I was serene in considering the rewards of Heaven; but what is this shaft sticking out from my breastplate? has an arrow come through? and what is the name upon it? Damnable stockade—you've taken my belief from me—

Oh, not yet, not yet; but the struggle is on—

Jem.

Yas, Mastah.

That end's not braced properly; those small stones will roll in the first freshet. Coffee, come to help. Do the two of you work that stump beneath the cross-piece to support it whilst you remove the stones. . . . Now then, see that boulder over there? Go dig it out, and roll it here to hold the cross-piece. Twill last out a hundred storms.

To the junior members of an orphaned family, he was a noble, generous and devoted brother, and to the suffering poor a prompt, liberal and benevolent benefactor.

Take lesson from the existence of young Mr. Hudson, and let us at

once be prompt, liberal and benevolent. Indeed we are so. This bridge
has been unsteady since the great rain of a week or two ago, and only
carts could cross it safely. That wagon of Mr. Stancil's would have gone
through it like a hog through a cucumber frame. And tomorrow is
Friday, and if the fair weather holds, the wagon will come creaking
this way with its freight of kindliness; and we must haste, haste to
assemble the baskets of our own contribution. Turn out, all hands,
to feed the guests; there are grown to be some thirty-two thousand
of them. How many might Mr. Stancil's wagon feed?

Ira stood, overseeing the Negroes as they toiled in the gush and mud
of Little Sweetwater; he stood muddied, and nursing one finger which
had been squeezed between logs of the bridge; he stood stricken out
of all reverie by recognition of the futility of this enterprise. Let the
loaves remain in the baskets, tell the little boy to run away home with
his fishes. Cato Dillard, you wear no beard, you were not born in
Bethlehem, there is no Aura about you. . . . But, stay. Tis a gesture,
but not idle. If a single Yankee Moses is kept from starvation, the deed
is worth the doing.

Returned to the plantation, he gave the hands a brief recess and
urged them to put on dry things. Still wishing to avoid Lucy, he went
to the burying ground and sat for a while beside the freshest grave.
Several weeks had passed . . . he did not like to think of what was
happening to the body packed in that homemade coffin; yet more dreadful was the recalling of what had happened to the mind and body
when they were extant. The war killed her, Ira thought, as surely as
if a Union sharpshooter squeezed his trigger.

And she was far out of his life before she died; so that was tragedy
piled upon tragedy. He wondered if ever he would marry again, he
wondered even if he would lie with a woman, ever again. He thought
of Mrs. Lou Ella Mickley, often he thought of her. When Ira was
much younger he had served two terms in the Legislature, but refused to run for a third term. He refused also to be a candidate for
Congress; he'd found that honestly he loathed the trading, back-biting
and double-dealing upon which many politicians thrived. It was during his freshman season at Milledgeville that he met Mrs. Mickley at
a dinner. She had been widowed at twenty-one, and was a woman of
means—chubby, brown-eyed, curly of hair—who kept no maiden aunt
or other relative dwelling in chaperonage, and was completely oblivious to gossip which shafted around her until even the gossipers wearied
of it, and selected other targets. Soon she and Ira became lovers. His
relations with Veronica were unfavorable during much of that period,
for he found himself aggravated by Veronica's selfishness and indrawn,
Arwoodish ways. Not yet had he adjusted himself to the fact that she
lacked certain virtues which in blindness and early passion he had
awarded her. Never was there the delighted madness in his coming

together with Lou Ella Mickley which ruled him when he was with
his wife; yet they had their raptures, he profited from her serenity,
they built pleasant childish humors between them, he thought her
sage and valuable in most opinion about State and National affairs. The
inevitable quarrel occurred when Ira announced that he would not
run for a third term. She asked him why; he said honestly and artlessly that he did not wish to spend so much time away from his family.
Family, family, family—you think nothing of *me*, care nothing for me—
who am I? I'm a Nobody—I have cast aside all thought of womanly
reputation because of *you*— She became the complete picture of the
Other Woman Who Loves the Married Man, through all ages, nationali-
ties, codes. . . . It seemed that the bruising of her reputation was less
than fatal to Lou Ella Mickley. Within two years she married a vigorous bachelor senator, a rice-grower from the tidewater region; his name
was Febresen, and he went off in 1862 to command a brigade. Promptly
he was shot dead at Second Manassas. Ira had seen the lovely Widow
Febresen just once since then; it was in the spring of 1863, when last
he was in Milledgeville. He stopped at a crossing to let a carriage
pass; he was looking, not at the lady who drove, but at the rubbery
little groom in patched livery, sitting pompously up behind; and then
the carriage slowed, he heard his name spoken. Ira, was all she said.
Her hair was almost white—prematurely so, for she could not be much
past forty. The bright brown eyes shone at him, then filled with tears.
Ira had removed his hat, he was bowing, he moved toward the vehicle;
then she had spoken to her horse and was driving rapidly away. She
left an impression of daintiness and vivacity, as always. She left a
memory, but it was not enough for him, probably not enough for her.
He tried to envision Lou Ella as living here with him at the plantation,
war or no war. He could not see her so.

    . . . What if the malignant miracle should occur, and Sherman
should take Atlanta? Any disaster might follow; blue columns might
sweep even to Milledgeville. Possibly I'd best persuade Lucy to invite
the widowed Mrs. Febresen to come to us, here and now. . . .

    Wretched fellow! Sitting by your wife's grave, her frail unhappy
mortality gone so recently into seclusion— Gad, man, what ails you?

    Tis that monstrosity past the lane and fort and pits and barricades.
It unsettles us all, unsteadies the world.

    Now he resolved to make some sort of explanation to Lucy for his
churlishness of the morning, perhaps to comfort her by finding the
specific source of complaint, by offering a balm—he did not know what
unguent it would be. Ira set the men to searching corn-rows for those
ears which were still in the milk. He hunted through the house for
Lucy, and found her at last below the front gallery. Little Gracious,
the five-year-old daughter of Jonas and Extra, was propped against a

pillar. The child's brown foot extended over the porch's edge; there was a basin in which the foot had been washed. Lucy stood in the lily bed, holding Gracious's tiny ankle in one hand while probing with a needle. The child made not a sound though her cheeks were varnished with tears.

She has picked up a sliver, said Lucy.

Shall I aid you?

I've most of it out, now. Gracious is being a soldier, and naturally soldiers do not shriek or squirm. And she is to receive a pink ribbon for her hair.

The last of the splinter was drawn out, the wound anointed with salve; Gracious had her pink ribbon, and went hopping off to parade it before her mother. Dear Lucy, said Ira gently. The girl looked up at him, then turned away blinded. Ira slumped on the step, and opened his arms. Lucy fell against him and sobbed for a time, she made inarticulate sounds in weeping, as if she were trying to tell a lonely story and could not.

You'll get no pink ribbon from me, Florence Nightmare.

Gggive it to little Gggracious, she gasped in the hysteria of laughter accompanying her wail.

No, to the Widow Tebbs!

. . . She could laugh more authentically at last, and sat away from her father. He offered his handkerchief, she mopped her flushed face with it, he suggested that she blow her nose, she blew her nose loudly. Her fine-spun hair was straggling. Ira brought a square mirror from the hall, that she might see to bind her hair properly again. They sat together on the gallery stair with the Andersonville smell intense, the Andersonville hum rising like the buzz of a rookery.

Twas here, Poppy.

Here?

On these steps, after he'd breakfasted. Just as he was leaving. I followed him here, I kissed him, I was the aggressor.

And—he—?

She said that her life was become a forlorn trial. She had not expected it to be such a trial, once her mother was relieved from the confusion which ruled her and ruled them all.

Is it right to wish people dead, Lucy asked. Is it ever right? For I wished her dead, I did, I did.

Good God, girl, so did I.

And I'd thought there would be some— Some peace in existence, some comfort for us, even in this ghastly war and with this ghastly pen— But no, no; twas worse than ever. He returned here, he shouldn't have returned. He says nothing at all. He comes home with that hospital stench hanging about him, he sleeps so long and with such exhaustion. He's thinner by far. His jacket fell open this morning; I saw the holes in his old belt, where the tongue of the buckle went through. There was the deep crease in the—the shabby leather, where he used to wear his buckle. I could see it, that little old crease. And now he wears it two holes farther along. And he wasn't plump to begin with, Poppy, truly I've never seen him plump. And such little bits of food he eats. Grief! And his abstraction is so intense—it's as if he were off in Macon or some such place. But I know where he dwells in his fancy, and always. It's over there. Oh, Poppy! No longer do we play our game—not even when Harry is supposed to be taking his ease. Ease? Grief, he knows not the word! One night we sat here on the gallery, and you were abed; you said you wished to read, but I know your notion was to leave us alone, and I—I did appreciate it, darling Poppy. But he would say nothing, do nothing! I gave a quote or two, to tempt him on. And silence, always silence. I fetched a pitcher of our nectar, and offered it, and he— He said, The folks in the hospital have no nectar. I bristled up and said I knew that well enough—I said they came to fight us, to invade, and this was the fate they found— And that—that Southern boys died at the North, as well— He drank the nectar then, but not as if he liked it. And then Colonel Chandler came, so I trotted off. But in the hall I heard them speaking. And Harry said a few words about, twas scarcely the proper time for romantic chit-chat; that was what he said, I'll never forget it. Romantic chit-chat! And I was only trying to be kind to him, to—to aid him—trying to make him rest his bones and—and his soul. I teased him about the vinegar, Poppy. Was that wrong of me? And then I fled after him, and kissed him; I'd never done such a thing before—not even to poor Rob—though law knows that *he* was forever after me, pursuing, trying to snatch a kiss—

Do you love Cousin Harry as much as you loved Rob, my dear?

Much—much—what is much? How much love is there in the world, how much can a girl give? How would I know? How would any girl know, any woman? Cause I'm a woman, now, Poppy—I was scarcely a woman then. At least—before Rob died. And—and all the boys. But we've had this dreadful thing come upon us, and then— Mother— Sakes, I know I'm speaking mighty disjointedly, scarcely making any sense at all, perhaps making no sense! But this is a different kind of love I feel now, because I'm older, and we've been through *plain hell*— oh, I know I shouldn't mention the Bad Place—just like a man might— Scarcely ladylike! If the folks at the Institute could hear me now!

Ira asked softly, How did Coz behave when you kissed him?

Just stood here like a stick, just like a plain old stick! Then he says, Do you mean love? My goodness, what did he think I meant? Oh, I told him he had such a great heart and—and I could understand why

Suthy was fond of him. And then he says something about himself being an old critter, or something. And I said I reckoned my kisses didn't amount to much. And then he gave me a shove, Poppy—he just shunted me away from him. He just as much as told me there could be no love in his life, no love for me, not with that awful stockade and hospital around!

Poppy, she said much more quietly a little later. I don't believe he's right. Do you? Shouldn't love be bigger than—? And embrace more than just—? I mean, whether there were a stockade and a hospital or not? Or even a war. Seems like there've always been wars going on, one place or another. And boys dying in them. But people still managed to love one another.

A time to mourn and a time to dance. . . .

I wonder, Poppy.

You see, Lucy, men don't love as women love, my dear child; and the sooner you get that into your pretty little head, the better. But you never will, because you're a woman. And women go on forever, trying to see— It's like that looking glass in your lap. Women look into the glass and expect to find their own love mirrored; sometimes they delude themselves into thinking that they do see it; but actually they never do, never do. Men aren't capable of giving Woman Love— they can give but Man Love. And tis never enough, Lucy, never enough. Especially in the sensitive.

She muttered, Heavens knows I'm sensitive enough. I'm just a little old sensitive plant.

Forever, Ira told her, people speak of woman's intuition. But men have intuition also; perhaps they may call it by another name. They say that they observe, evaluate, study the evidence, arrive at conclusions—and half the time tis only intuition! And I'm equally as sensitive as you.

He spoke deliberately. Coz was enchanted by you from the very first moment of his arrival.

I can't believe that, Poppy.

Then continue being maidenly!

He kissed her hair and went away. It was better to go now. He had planted a seed, she announced that she rejected it; that meant nothing, the seed was there, it would grow.

The rest of the day Ira continued with preparations. He was proud of his vegetables, he saw that baskets were filled liberally. He found a boy's satisfaction in contemplating how Cato Dillard's eyes would bulge when he saw this store: pungent roots all scrubbed, carrots glowing orange, turnips with purple scalps, rippled wrapping of cabbages, the grainy opulence of fat squashes.

. . . How many people would these feed?

. . . Oh, quite a number.

. . . But, stay, what have we here? What populations stand milling, awaiting invitation to sit down at our table?

Ira took down his atlas and learned that they were planning to invite to feast the entire population of Columbus, Ohio; or the entire population of Kansas City, Missouri; or of Utica, New York; or of Wilmington, Delaware; or (this was closer to home, it jolted him) Savannah, Georgia.

Granted that permission would not be denied, he wondered how the good things might be divided and distributed. Many times Ira had watched the issuing of rations within the pen; he did not know how they were issued at the hospital; he must ask Cousin Harry about that.

He had stood, garbed with pity that stiffened into a coat of horror, and watched wagons entering the stockade, wheels screaming, drawn by miniature mules (they were mules with sores; and those were the same wagons in which he'd seen The Dead carted away).

. . . Wagons had their guards. The guards stood watching at the headquarters of each Detachment as that Detachment's portion was dumped upon the ground: mostly the long hard cards of corn bread, sometimes a portion of old bacon . . . and Ira had seen that bake house: he knew how the mixture was tempered with flies before the slabs were baked. Recently there had been stock peas on occasion, stewed to a mush. Watching through his binoculars, Ira could observe that some masses of the peas appeared half cooked, other masses were burned to blackness. Of course there would be no salt. . . .

So they entered: four-mule teams, a Negro riding on the nigh wheel mule of each team, the complement of four or five guards joining each wagon as it entered.

. . . Third Detachment sergeants?

The sergeants of the three Nineties stepped forward. Here we be. Third Detachment rations.

Dry goods boxes dumped, the sound of shovels scraping. Food was ladled upon the ground. The wagon rattled on to headquarters of the Fourth Detachment, and left the three squad sergeants dividing seriously.

. . . Three Nineties in each Detachment, three Messes in each Ninety.

A prisoner stood with his back to the apportioned piles. Behind him a shaggy man put out a finger to indicate each pile in turn.

Who gets this?

Second Mess.

Who gets this?

First Mess.

Who gets this?

. . . Already the Third Mess sergeant was claiming the remaining pile.

So it would go in the Messes. One piece of bread about half the size of a brick, for each man—his ration for a day—and sometimes a piece of meat as large as two of his fingers, sometimes a wad of mush or stewed cowpeas such as he could hold in one hand.

Who gets this?

Number Nine.

Who gets this?

Number Fourteen.

Who gets this?

Number Five.

Ah, lucky Thompson! That was the biggest pile. . . .

Hell, he can't eat it, Bruce. Jaws won't work. . . .

Ira arose earlier than usual on Friday. It was a fair day, so he directed that the vegetables be fetched from the shed where they had been locked up to guard against thievery. There was a rough platform of planks in the side yard; Ira decreed that the baskets should be piled there, with room for Mr. Stancil's wagon to back and turn.

The gaunt Harry Elkins came down to observe the arrangement with interest. Harry went to fill his vinegar bottle, he went off to the hospital with pockets stuffed with parsnips and onions. Ira watched him depart. Come what may, he thought, there are a few vegetables which will in fact go down the gullets of the sick.

Ira lived in the high humor of a kindly man doing a kindly deed, and well aware of it. He admitted as much to Lucy when they breakfasted.

Poppy, I've been thinking. What about the chests upstairs?

(No one had touched them since Veronica's death.)

Would it pain you to open them, Daughter?

Everything hurts, she said. But I was so distraught yesterday that the notion didn't occur to me. . . . There's so many things of the boys'. Do you agree with me that it would be Christian in us to offer them?

Ira thought of jackets in which his boys had strolled and hunted, he thought of precious boots left behind them when they went a-soldiering. He considered Moses's cambric shirts, fluffy rolls of well-darned home-knit stockings. Let us give some, Lucy—not all. In our little neighborhood we're now the sole family who can manage a charity. So many people are impoverished; also we know not what our own needs will be in the future.

He smiled. I may be reduced to wearing Badger's jeans. Although I fear I'd split them apart! And what of Cousin Harry? His old military clothing is worn thin.

Then will you help me to select, Poppy?

After I've parceled work to the hands.

There were delays. A farrowing sow accounted for much of the delay; then it was discovered that Old Leander was sick abed and must be tended. . . . A fence was down: rails stolen by Georgia Reserves or by paroled Yankee prisoners detailed on a wood squad.

It was close to high noon before the clothing chests were closed and shoved to their places again. A sad dreadful illusion of Veronica Claffey was locked inside each chest. Shoes and clothing had scarcely been prepared for distribution, along with the freight of vegetables, when the Americus procession ambled down the lane from the west. It consisted of three vehicles: the Dillards ahead in their gig, followed by a carriage containing three ladies of Americus; also young Dr. Pace, with empty sleeve pinned against his coat. He had been struck by a piece of solid shot in 1862. The Stancil wagon brought up the rear. A cluster of Negro boys were riding and driving and making great festivity out of the whole matter . . . some were singing as they came.

(What would it have been like in the old days? Ira wondered . . . August date, mention of a fair morning in the journal, mention of wind east or northeast. Who would have been confined, expecting her baby? How many hands would have been at the gin? . . . No, no, too early, no one would have been at the gin, they would not have started picking cotton yet; not nearly. But how many would have been pulling fodder, how many hauling leaves for manure, how many would have been out with their ploughs? Oh, let dark voices chant a soft chant . . . let simple recollections invoke the day I gave them a treat, and all unexpected . . . the time we killed a small beef and gave the black folks dinner, all because Badger'd won a race! And also I gave them a little bacon, and some syrup to go with it.)

Cries and compliments arose from the Americus contingent when they saw the outlay of the Claffeys. Cato Dillard beamed, his tufts of white whisker were frothy. *So they did eat,* he declared, *and were filled: and they took up of the broken meat that was left seven baskets.*

I doubt, Ira told him, that there will be any broken meat or loaves or digestibles to be taken up on this occasion.

He asked in a whisper, while slaves were stowing this additional treasure aboard the Stancil wagon, Have you received any news to indicate that your sanguine hope is justified?

The minister's chunky face was a wrinkling smile. We need no further word, Brother Ira! General Winder is a communicant of the church, as I advised you.

We might run into a stumbling block in the shape of subordinates.

Surely he will be able to override them!

Perhaps the general is not here? He goes away at times on other duties, or so I am told.

Twould be no fatal delay! Most of these things will keep, except for the hog; and that we could take to the hospital.

In some fashion Ira felt his own anticipation diminishing in proportion to the Reverend Mr. Dillard's enthusiasm. Ira thought now that he should have taken the bull by the horns, he should have made judicious inquiries in advance. Well, no help for it: they were committed, they must be off to deliver. Lucy would not accompany them. She should remain at home to oversee a dinner for all.

Ira climbed aboard the wagon and stood in the rear, green corn ears sliding around his legs. The little parade jolted west on the lane once more, but with the wagon ahead. Ira pointed out to the driver: this road intersecting at the right . . . turn back on it, past the next intersection . . . swing left. He thought it wise to aim first for Wirz's headquarters, although gossip had it that the superintendent was absent. Also that road was closest to the stockade's entrance. There might be no need for journeying across the railroad to the Winder house.

Wagon advanced, gig and carriage followed on behind. As they approached the south camps, pickets stepped into the road to halt them. Ira Claffey got down to confer. Senior among these pickets was an elderly sergeant who came often to the Claffey place for garden truck.

Ira sought to bribe him with cabbages.

Mr. Claffey, sir, *you* could pass—no trouble bout that. But I can't let all these other folks through. And this here wagon . . . I got to send for the Officer of the Day. Maybe he'll admit you all past these posts.

The Officer of the Day never arrived. Instead came a chaise driven by a frightened gray-clad youth, and with General Winder's sagging face pressed out of it.

What the God damn hell's happening here?

Again Ira swung down from the big wagon. Sir, he said, there are some ladies in our party. . . .

I don't give a good God damn how many ladies there are! Tell them to go way! What are you people up to?

General Winder, we have here a load of green things, together with some clothing, to be distributed to needy prisoners. This is a contribution from the people of Americus.

Where do you think you're proceeding, and by whose authority?

Cato Dillard came from his gig, the wounded Dr. Pace followed with dignity. General, said Dillard, I have learned that you are warden of the newly-established Episcopal church in Americus.

I'm no such thing!

They named you to be one, sir.

What's that got to do with a wagon load of corn?

Not only corn: we are laden with fresh vegetables—a great variety of them. People have denuded their closets, sir, to furnish some clothing for the sick and ragged.

Winder climbed out of the chaise, grunting with the effort. He stood with folded arms, scowling first at the trio before him, then at slaves who watched white-eyed on their wagon perches. He stepped to the edge of the narrow road, and glared at the women in vehicles behind. He turned back.

You mean to tell me that you people are fetching these things to the prisoners? Not to the Confederate guards?

Cato told him, I have observed that the prisoners are in dire need.

Turn around, cried John Winder explosively. Go way! Drive back! Get out of here!

Dillard's voice was shaking; Ira knew that the quaver did not come from fear. General Winder, this is a gift, offered free out of hand. Please to let us pass.

I'll see you in hell first. You're a damn Yankee sympathizer, and so are all the rest of you!

The quiet sickly Dr. Pace had crept forward until there were but inches between his face and the old general's. Do you know where I left my arm, sir? In the Valley of Virginia.

I don't give a hoot in hell where you left your arm! I wish that all damn Yankee sympathizers—and every God damn Yankee prisoner too—were all in hell together!

Ira Claffey closed his eyes for a moment. He was biting his lips, finally he could speak. I do not believe, sir, that it is any evidence of Union sympathies to exhibit humanity. Nor do the rest of these people. Nor the ladies behind. . . . All of us have been bereaved by the war. Some still have young relatives at the front.

Winder howled, I know you, Mr. Claffey! You live right over there. You're always poking round—up on the sentry shacks. I've seen you with my own eyes. Well, by God, you'll poke no longer! I'll see to that.

He went waddling back to his chaise and stood muttering under his breath. Then he turned once again. You talk humanity, you citizens. There's no humanity about it. When you bring this stuff up here, it's intended as a slur upon the Confederate States' Government. And, by God—also an undercover attack on *me!*

Winder got into the chaise, then thrust his face out for a last cry. I'd as lief the damn Yankees would die here as anywhere else! By God, upon the whole, I don't know that it's not better for them. Now you folks vamoose!

Dr. Pace had turned back toward the carriage, his face chalked by this encounter. Cato Dillard was making strange breathless sounds, Ira did not know whether he was weeping or praying.

Ira gritted his teeth in final effort. He approached Winder's vehicle.

One final request. The provisions are here, they're in the wagon; we shall promise to make no further attempt to convey things to the prisoners. But since these provisions have already come thus far, will you allow them to be taken inside the stockade, and distributed?

The pulpy face pushed toward him again. Not the first damn morsel shall go in! I only wish that I could issue an order to confiscate these goods. I haven't authority to do that; but I have got the power to prevent any damn Yankee prisoner from having them. By God, they shan't get them!

He yelled to pickets while the chaise was being turned: You heard me! You're not to let these folks move an inch further toward the stockade. . . .

Mr. Dillard and Ira went to rejoin the others. Some of the women were crying, Mrs. McCrary had her head on Mrs. Lindsay's shoulder. For him to say that I was a Yankee sympathizer! she sobbed. Mrs. Effie Dillard sat with fury of the Covenanters frozen in her pocked face. Her rage was so great that she could not yet begin to spout; presently she would spout.

Someone touched Ira's sleeve hesitantly. It was the old sergeant of the guards.

Mr. Claffey, sir. Wistfully. Since you can't take them things in to the Yanks, would you mind terrible if us folks got a little of the truck? Rations are mighty poor in these parts. Always have been.

. . . Clothing they took back with them, the vegetables and meat they gave to the guards.

XLIII

Old Tom Gusset, Saddler, Ninth Ohio Cavalry, lingered far past the time which might have been allotted regularly to men of fifty-eight in Andersonville. His enforced retreat to a den filled with fellow Ohioans, when he fled from the wrath of the Irishman called Pay, wrought no change for the better. These were people from the Forty-fifth Volunteer Infantry, they were dying fast. Tom took the place made vacant by the demise of the ex-mule-driver, but the ex-miner and the ex-baggage-handler were in final disgusting stages of scurvy. The gums of the latter were sloughing away, he spat out wads of rotten membranes, it was feared that he swallowed other wads when he grew too weak to expel them. Only the ex-book-agent-who-longed-to-be-a-writer-of-novels was in fair shape, perhaps because he was slight and elastic to begin with. Once again this was an object lesson in the waning of the mighty athlete, the survival of the stringy and undersized.

Soon Tom Gusset let his implements lie idle, he lost ambition, he had no taste for the puny rations which his industry might have purchased. He did not wish to repair boots or straps, he said that he was too busy or too tired when customers approached. The ex-book-agent, one Woolstock, counseled and warned. Woolstock had imagination, together with a great affection for the human race and an ardent interest therein. He knew that apathy was as destructive as any of the identifiable diseases which erased the population like a sponge in the Devil's own hand. Indeed he had manufactured this metaphor and made use of it, but Tom Gusset was not impressed.

Use your tools, old fellow! Don't just sit.

Wooly, I feel too sickly.

You'll really be sickly, too, if you don't perk up.

Don't feel like perking.

Think of your folks at home, Tom. Think of the glorious day of return, think of banners flying in the wind, and ladies strewing garlands, and—

Hell, young fellow. I'm old and I'm plain tired.

Tom had been vigorous previously, had done a young man's job in a young man's army, had held his own with people less than half his age. Now he sat and stared. Strangely he seemed suffering from no scurvy; diarrhoea did not wreck him; if he endured gripings he did not complain about them. He shook with no coughing, his eyes did not blaze, malarial fever did not shiver his frame. But suddenly he was become a vessel so empty that it seemed that vessel could never have contained the sauce of abounding life. Since he would not work he acquired no extra necessaries such as rice, salt, beans or bones. If he had owned any more candy he would not have had the energy to bottle it safely in a length of hollow cane. Certainly he would not have had the strength to chase a fleet young thief among the shebangs, punishing him (and thus killing him eventually; killing the shaggy Pay as well) with a belt buckle.

Woolstock quit uttering invocations because Gusset would not heed them, and soon did not even hear. Gusset ate less and less of the gnarly brick of corn bread which came his way each day. At last he ate none at all, he did not rise from the ground. The treasured implements of his saddler's career were stolen, and he did not care. The miner died, the baggage-handler died. Woolstock himself nursed a scratch on his arm and feared gangrene, and quickly saw and felt and smelled gangrene developing, and knew in last brilliant agonizing that now he too was doomed.

New prisoners, horrified and frantic at what they found here, shoved into the shebang and occupied mud where the Ohioans had suffered. Oh, they were new, not yet emasculated, they pitied Tom Gusset, thought it ghastly that a man nearing sixty should be in that place, thought it ghastly that anyone should be there, thought it a diabolical conspiracy on the part of the Confederacy, and on the part of the Union as well, that there should be such a place. They gave Tom Gusset his ration, they scraped away other mouldering rations which he had abandoned, they began to bet on how long he could live without food.

In fact he lived a surprisingly long time . . . day by day he shrank. It was discovered that he was dwelling in Ohio. He was living with his first wife, Lennie, who had died in early middle age after bearing Tom nine children. His second wife, Ada, was a vicious little shrew hated by her entire neighborhood. Tom had left his harness shop and joined the cavalry in order to get away from Ada. Not even in final insanity could he wish to rejoin Ada, but Lennie became a warm, good-scented vision. Of course he saw her always beaming at the end of the supper table, or rising to whisk more muffins from the oven. Little faces turned admiringly toward Tom all along the board. Olinthus boasted of the groundhog he had dug up, Eva and Leora giggled about a hair-pulling which had ensued at their Sunday School pic-nic, Willis begged to go and spend the night at a favorite cousin's. Tom Gusset, proud of his family, proud of his pink-cheeked wife and also proud of himself, spooned up the meat and gravy which his toil had provided.

Tommy boy, he'd say to his eldest, you better take some more pigeon pie.

God, said newcomers in the shebang, there the old bastard goes again. This time it's pigeon pie.

Now, Eva, don't say you don't like bean porridge. You know your Ma makes the best! It's from Granny LeMay's own receipt.

Artie, help yourself to another chunk of squash and please to pass the plate.

Think I'll take a little more of that hot slaw, Hiram. But help yourself first. Right in front of you.

The prisoners screamed, God damn you, old man, dry up!

He sat in mud, his thinning fingers no longer skilled and active, but frittering about with splinters, garbage, or even with rolls of mud which they took up and wadded. The splinters were Scotch scones, the garbage became tasty buttered onions with plenty of salt and pepper on them, the mud was cream pie.

Lowell boy, do have another fish ball. And Maudie's plate is nearly empty. Pass her some more of that boiled tongue and some of them parsnips.

Help yourself to another nice baked potato, Hiram.

The prisoners tried to stop their ears. I swear, they cried, if he don't cease that craziness I'll go crazy too. I swear, they cried, I got a notion to lam him over the head with this pole. Finish the old relic off! . . . Oh, leave him be, Mansfield. He's old, he hain't got long. . . .

He had far too long insofar as these new prisoners were concerned. Ain't this nice tenderloin, Linthus? Do take that last piece for yourself; now, hush, the rest of you—Linthus is titled to it, he split all them kindlings for his Ma while Hiram and Artie snuck away to play ball. Lowell, don't take that cold rusk; Ma is bringing some hot ones right now—better for you hot. Leora, you and Maudie got to toss a penny to see which one wipes the dishes. Here, I got two pennies right here in my pants; I'll give each of you a bright new cent, and you can match. Don't know how to match? Well, Pa'll show you. Watch careful.

I tell you, Lennie, you've baked some mighty good nut loaves in your time, but I never saw the beat of this one. Tommy boy, you spread that butter thick on your nut bread, for Granny always said there wasn't nothing like butter to put flesh on young bones. Eva, pass your saucer and I'll ladle you some more of these fine stewed cherries.

Nathan Dreyfoos strayed deliberately into remembered satisfactions with his good mind; old Tom Gusset strayed on whatever scraps of wounded fancy could still support him. The house rose before and around him, the small light green house overflowing with Gussets, the house which had supplanted the log house of Tom's father (the house of squared logs had been moved back to serve as woodshed, dairy, cob house, general domestic repository. The children gave shows there; the minister thought it wrong for them to engage in theatricals; Tom Gusset shook his finger at the Reverend Mr. Sifert and said that his children could give all the blame shows they wanted to).

Gol damn, cried out one new prisoner in the shebang, think I ain't lonesome for my own wife and folks? Think I don't wish I was back in Frenchtown with Amy and Lily and Byron? Why the devil have I got to listen to this, night and day?

Oh, hang onto yourself, Melvin. He ain't got long.

Day after day Artie was offered his asparagus, Leora her buttered onions, Tommy boy his ham. Tom Gusset had been declared killed in battle through some misinformation by an alleged eye-witness. The evil-tongued Ada sold his harness shop and settled down to live comfortably in the old green house—peeking from behind curtains at the two young girls across the way, poisoning dogs, throwing boiling water at cats (which managed fortunately to elude her), shrieking at children to stay out of her yard. Naturally none of her stepchildren or stepgrandchildren ever came to see her. Thus the news that Olinthus was killed near Atlanta and that Hiram was captured and sent to a pen in Tyler, Texas— These griefs brought her no grief. . . . The silver hair and beard of her husband crawled with lice, the prisoners declared that he had a gallon of lice on him if he had a gill, he seemed thinner than paper, you could actually see his bones through transparent begrimed hide. His raw voice cackled without let, his eyes saw fairest and dearest forms, his shrunken nostrils smelled them out of the past.

He tried to get up a while ago and just couldn't.

That's what I been waiting for! He tried to resist us before, but I don't think he can resist us now.

Hospital! Good idee.

Next morning old Tom Gusset was carried to the South Gate; they carried him there before dawn so that the press would not be too great, so that they would not hear the No More Today, No More Today blasting hope that they would be rid of this nuisance once and for all.

Their luck took them to Contract Surgeon Number Six, one of the most humane and resolute of the eleven contract surgeons working at the gate. When the Yankees brought up Tom Gusset in their turn, this surgeon, a bearded little wren named Crumbley whose home was in Albany, had already sent to the hospital the three patients whom he was empowered to assign there on this day. For some mysterious reason there had been but thirty-four hospital deaths since the previous day; hence ten of the contract surgeons might each designate three prisoners—and the eleventh, four—to fill the vacancies. Dr. Crumbley begged the attention of another surgeon whose allotted vacancies were not used up, and as a result Tom was carried into a wall tent and placed with seven other patients. Four of these were in the two beds, or rather shelves with which the place was furnished; the rest lay upon the ground in trodden pine straw saturated with qualities unmentionable. From this low couch Tom's dramatization of recreated joys reached any ears willing to listen.

This was a rich and beautiful way in which to die. For he had no recognition of pain, stench, wail or ordure. He dwelt in an established past which was as good to his demented soul as was the cold compress to the feverish, the oven-baked flannel to the chilled. He dwelt in that content without chronology, he needed none. His conscious brain was ruptured, his cracked voice talked ahead. Tell you what I'll do, Mr. Lloyd—your boy Fred has owed me for them collars nearly two years now. Now, if you'll pay both bills—yours and his—today, I'll let you have that buggy whip at cost—just what it cost me. Thank you very much, Mr. Lloyd—you have been a good customer for years, but I just can't carry a heavy load of old Accounts Due. Yes, you bet— Thank you, Mr. Lloyd. Good day to you.

A ghoul crept in at night to rob the dead and the sick too; he stepped upon Tom Gusset's hand and broke the weakened bones, but Tom did not mind the crushing, not for long. He gave one bleat, and then muttered about it for a time, and then was beaming in his village again. Eva, you are a mighty good little currant picker! Ma told me about it, and it was a good thing you got them before the birds did, and I'm going to give you a dime all for your very own. May basket night? I thought I smelt taffy when I came in. How many baskets are you going to hang, Maudie? Eight? Ain't that more'n last year? And last year you got ten hung to *you*. Looks like you're a very popular young miss with your feller scholars!

A boy young enough to be Tom Gusset's grandchild lay beside him. He was mainly unconscious (this was good, since his lower bowel was in shreds, and some of these shreds protruded from his body), but at times he emitted little owlish cries. Queerly enough Tom was aware of these sounds, and ascribed them to a June dusk when his children marched purposefully along the street and he and Lennie sat on the bench he had built under the ivy. Screech owl, they call that one, dearie. Funny they call it screech. It's just as soft as the cooing of a squab. I do like to set and listen to it. I suppose he's calling to his mate. Listen to them kids—that's Willie's voice—guess he's captain of his side. Listen to them signals. *Danger*, he's calling. *Danger!* Bet that means the other side is getting further and further away. It's an old trick—we kids used to do it when we was little. Cept we called it Old Wolf, the best I can recall, instead of Run-

Sheep-Run. There they go pelting off. Listen at them! *Run, Sheep, Run!* Old Wolf's going to get you!

We were lucky, Lennie. Think how our own kids all got through the diphtheria all right, and the Billingses lost two.

You know what I'd like, right here on this scrapple. Some of that sweet pepper hash. Well, I must be getting blind—didn't see it on the table, and here it was right in front of me all the time. Try some, Lowell, do. It just spices up this good scrapple to perfection. Yes, yes, that's Granny LeMay's old receipt also. . . .

First complaint I ever had, Mr. Conrad, that my workmanship was unsound! Sure, I can see it's broke, tore squarely in two. But it wouldn't tear like that unless you'd put undue strain on it. Ain't any journeyman harness-maker in the world could make a tug that bad out of such good leather. And I ain't no journeyman—I'm a master, as any other person in this community will bear witness. Fact is, Mr. Conrad, I think these two busted ends parted company *during* the runaway, and not before. Couldn't have been a busted whiffle-tree on that there ancient vehicle of yours that caused it, now could it? . . . Lennie, he looked like he could have gone through the floor. Don't know when anything has struck me so funny. He just slid out of the shop—you know, kind of mumbled something—and then skedaddled. I just set there and laughed till I shook.

Tom Gusset's vocal machinery was pulled apart by undue strain, as his good sound harness had been pulled. On the next day you would have had to bend close to his ghost's face to hear him speak (except that no one would have wished to bend close to such crawling ugliness, and there was no one to bend close). Lennie, dearie, don't turn your face away. Ain't nothing to be ashamed about. Everybody does it—married folks—and now we're married. Wasn't it funny, way they tied all them old shoes and pots and things on behind the rig? My, what a racket that made until we'd outdistanced them all, and I could get down and pull that blame stuff off of there. Lennie, dearie, let me kiss you again. You know what? That's a real pretty night-dress you got on. All that stuff around the top—what you call it? Yoke? Sounds like twas meant for oxen, now doesn't it? Cept you ain't no ox. You're just the sweetest prettiest little thing that ever. . . .

Artie, said the wispy raw voice, do have some more beans. Best you ever tasted, I'll be bound.

Tom spoke in this way until there was no mechanism left for speech, no germ to sustain the flower of life. Eventually mules took him away, he lay at the bottom of the load. Twas funny, said one of the black men who'd shoveled earth over him by indifferent spadefuls. They all smell pretty bad. Seem for a moment that this old one didn't smell so bad. Seem like I smell a nice place, with good things cooking.

How you talk, Jeff. Ain't no good things cooking round here.

XLIV

Lucy cuddled upon an old cushion beside the gallery pillar. She gazed, not at Elkins and her father above and beyond her, but into dusk which seemed to flow and falter with a visible tide of sound and smell.

She asked, Have you spoken to any of your superiors about this matter?

I have made verbal suggestions to the Chief Surgeon.

From his own portion of dusk, Ira spoke. What did you tell him, Coz?

Asked him why the army didn't send us all away!

Harry Elkins thudded his tired boots upon the porch. I said that it was useless for surgeons to exert effort, when the patients were starved down to begin with. If the prisoners were receiving the vegetables which they should have—and if the prisoners had more room— at least half of them could be saved. They need the right kind of diet, more than they need medicines.

Did you tell him about General Winder—?

Indeed I told him! I said that it would be possible to have a large supply of green things brought from this plantation alone. I know that I was not presuming on your generosity, Cousin Claffey: I said that things were spoiling in your garden, I said that you would send him vegetables without charge. They were going to waste, doing nobody any good. . . . If he would connive with me to have them admitted to the hospital, lives might be saved. He observed that he would like to have the garden stuff; then turned off and spoke no more about it.

He feared the wrath of Winder, Coz.

He did—and does.

Elkins got up, pulled from his chair by the extremity which overpowered him increasingly. I wrote a report, with recommendations. Entirely unsolicited. Should you like to hear it?

I'll ring and have a light fetched, said Ira.

Sakes, I can fetch a light while we're still striving to enlist the attention of Ninny or Pet! Lucy brought a shielded candle from a nearer room. By this small light Harrell Elkins knelt with papers spread upon his knee. His spectacles were silvered, his face looked like hardened leftover dough.

Lucy thought, It rules him. What chance will he ever have to own a softness? The thing is too big, too stern and vengeful. Harry must succumb beneath it, thus must I succumb. . . .

Elkins's voice was grinding out the words: And to ascertain and report the causes of disease and mortality among the prisoners, and the means necessary to prevent the same, I respectfully submit the following. Causes of disease and mortality. One: The large number of prisoners crowded together. Two: Entire absence of vegetables as diet, so necessary in the prevention of scurvy. Three: The want of barracks to shelter prisoners from sun and rain. Four: Inadequate supply of wood and pure water. Five: Badly cooked food. Six: Filthy condition of prisoners and prison generally. Seven: Morbific emanations from the branch or ravine passing through the prison, the condition of which cannot be better explained than by naming it a morass of human excrement. . . .

There must be a fair place. . . . Again Lucy's youth served her in struggling against resignation. She would not accept this ordeal as a mode of life—never, never. It was not for this that women carried babies in their bodies and endured the torment of expelling them. It was not for this that an orb was set in the sky, and pin-holes and studding of stars gave suggestion of great glories, layer on layer, in regions outside the system of planets. Not for this did a purple bud rise gently out of compression against its stalk, and spread to make the rippled foil of a violet. Not for this did water set stones to grinding, nor did owls call, nor did warm rain spread and soak the ground. Not for this did tiny creatures work within the soil. . . .

Elkins read on. Preventative measures are suggested as follows. One: The removal immediately from the prison of not less than fifteen thousand prisoners. Two: The detailing On Parole of a number of Yankees sufficient to cultivate the necessary supply of vegetables; until this can be carried into practical operation I suggest the appointment of agents along the railroad line, to purchase and forward a supply of vegetables. Three: Immediate erection of barracks within the stockade, for shelter. Four: Let squads of prisoners proceed with axes, under adequate guard, to secure sufficient wood for their purposes, in thick forests nearby; and let proper wells be dug to supply the deficiency of water. A single bubbling spring, pure though it may be, cannot serve properly thirty-three thousand men. Five: Divide prisoners into squads, place each squad under a sergeant, furnish the necessary quantity of soap—which can be manufactured by prisoners themselves, working, again, under guard—and hold these sergeants responsible for the personal cleanliness of each squad. Six: Supply the prisoners with clothing at the expense of the Confederate

States' Government; and if our Government be unable to do so, candidly admit our inability, and call upon the Federal Government to send clothing. Seven: There should be a daily inspection of bake houses and baking procedures. Eight: Cover over with sand the entire morass within the pen, not less than six inches deep. Board the stream or watercourse, and confine the men—also the Georgia Reserves outside the stockade—to the use of their sinks. Make the penalty for disobedience inescapable and severe.

. . . Why, my dear Harry, cried Lucy's crippled appealing fancy, you are up betimes.

My dear, did you not know when I left our bed?

I was sleeping so soundly that I scarcely heard you go. Then later I moved my limb, and the place where you had lain was still warm. But you were gone from it.

And were you alarmed, love?

No, I felt that you must have gone to call on old Mr. Bile.

So I did. Ah, the fruition of a lengthy peaceful life! It is a rest which cometh after the three-quarter century mark. I tell you, dear, there is a saintliness about the old. I would best describe it as the imminence of heaven.

Harry *darling*. Surely you must have encountered some of the old who were unsaintly in the extreme! I knew one such woman: twas a great-aunt: a regular little witch she was.

Ha-ha. And so have I encountered such, dear Lucy. But what of the Reverend Mr. Cato Dillard? Is he not nigh to sainthood?

Oh yes, Harry, Uncle Dayto is, of course; and some of the young are sainted too; but just *listen* to our own younguns.

What are they screaming about?

Rapture, beloved Harry, pure rapture! Their mammy has them at breakfast out amongst the plum trees. She has set up the little blue table which Jonas made for them, and she's lugged chairs. Ira and Suthy are having a fight, pelting each other with handfuls of plum blossoms; the girls are shrieking in protest. But come along with you, dear, you've been a mighty while without your breakfast.

To be frank, I could eat a horse.

No necessity for that. And certainly not one of *our* horses. . . . Naomi, you may bring the biscuits. Have you kept the sausages hot? And remember that the Doctor prefers his eggs basted over the top; but lightly, Naomi, very lightly, and peppered to a turn. . . . And—oh, Harry—I have a gift for you. Tis all your own; no one must touch it but you. The children have their own, but this is my dear Harry's jar. *Gooseberry jam*, my love, and what fun I had a-making it for you. . . .

Sheets of paper crinkled on Elkins's knee. A moth struck the candle flame, whirled, scorched. The candle sputtered lightly, flame resumed its small steady towering.

The dry voice kept growling. One: For the hospital I recommend that the tents be floored with planks; if planks cannot be had, with puncheons; and if this be impossible, then with pine straw, to be changed frequently. Two: There is an inadequate supply of stool boxes. It is recommended that the number be increased, and that the orderlies be required to remove them as soon as used; and before returning them, see that they are well washed and limed. Three: Diet for the sick is repulsive. They must be supplied with the necessary quantity of meat broth, with vegetables. Four: Surgeons should be required to visit hospital patients not less than twice a day.

Finally, I cannot too strongly recommend the necessity for the appointment of an efficient medical officer to the exclusive duty of inspecting daily the hospital and cooking facilities, requiring of him daily reports of their condition to headquarters.

I have the honor to remain, Sir, very respectfully. . . .

His words trailed away. Elkins rose, slapped the papers against his thigh, then smoothed them carefully.

Lucy drifted back from her private fairyland. Once again the prison smell was in her nostrils . . . and this was the present, it was 1864, they were upon the gallery, these things had happened, were happening, would happen.

Ira inquired, Coz, to whom did you make this report? To Chief Surgeon White?

I felt that it would be futile. Nor did I address Acting Assistant Surgeon Watkins. What power has he?

I thought that possibly you might have addressed Colonel Thurlow?

Merely does he command the Post, replacing your friend Lieutenant-Colonel Persons. What could he do? And as you know, Surgeon-General Moore is at Richmond, and has received many other reports heretofore.

Ira said dryly, I take it that there would be no point in addressing Brigadier-General John H. Winder.

No point whatsoever.

Then whom—?

This is not a copy, said Harrell Elkins, speaking not only to Ira and Lucy Claffey, but to swaddling stench and noise of the night—to the stockade's denizens, to corpses in earth on the hill—speaking to all people within the Southern Confederacy, to all within the Northern States.

This is not a copy. It is the original report. I would not waste time, sir, in sending a hopeless plea to Mr. Seddon, or even to President Davis.

One after the other, he held sheets to the candle flame; let the blaze broaden, let paper burn down to his fingers, let the flakes fall. Almighty God, please to note and file, said Harry.

Lucy caught her breath, her face went down into her hands. She wept quietly until Ira was gone. Then there came a wonder. She found herself in Elkins's arms; this was no dream; she found herself in his arms; but only for a moment. Firmly he said that he must go on duty.

XLV

Judah Hansom was one of many men who tried to escape from the prison through a tunnel. He was twenty-six years old, and had a thinnish face with small sad green eyes. His mouse-brown hair was mostly gone—premature baldness was said to have run in his mother's family—and his slanting forehead carried branded transverse lines which might have grooved the brow of a much older man. But Judah's shoulders were broad out of proportion to his medium height, and his great arms might have come swinging from a jungle. When a citizen he had been in fact a farmer, but first and foremost he liked to think of himself as a woodman—rather, a woodman before whom no trees should be spared unless especially desirable for shade, fruit or nuts.

Judah Hansom did not tell his comrades how much he dreaded lonely darkness below the earth's foul crust. A silent person by habit, he had never grown sufficiently articulate to voice other than commonplace utterances. The few people who had known him, and the further few who had been sufficiently interested to assay his nature for themselves, typified him as phlegmatic and unfeeling. He needed space around him in order to settle into security. When Judah worked through the first strength of his youth he gained more than pride as he saw the forest dissolve, yard by yard and stick by stick, under the clamor of his axe, under the assault of axes of his fellow workmen. He felt a private comfort, an exalted assurance, because he was achieving space; he was building it. Sometimes wide long vistas opened after trees lay toppled and the tops were stripped; he could stand sweaty, even when there was snow about, and soak his muscles and spirit in the blue boon of limitless distances surrounding him. He could look over the nearest ridge and see other feathered rolls of hills go inching toward the Adirondacks and always fading in shade, growing looser as to texture and detail, until they brought up unyielding against the mountain wall.

Knowing little except the ritual of helve and blade and forest silences, Judah found his God easily. He was devout after the manner of unimaginative men who have known little of human complication and the resulting perplexity. Moreover he had lived in civilian affairs as a practiced coward in that he avoided constantly, deliberately any situation which might bring him ill, any force against which he might not cope readily and with the assurance of victory. A town . . . he hated towns because there the trains champed and blew sparks from their cumbrous funneled stacks, there the teams tried to run him down, there strangers jostled and talked loudly of people and matters beyond his experience. He stood away from towns. Women and girls . . . they appalled him with their rustling and cackling, with constant reminder in every tone and gesture and mood that they were of a different pattern physically and yet were somehow glad and impudent about it. In that remote farmhouse called home there was only Aunt Annie, and she wore freckled blue calico caps, with a slatted bonnet literally bigger than a half-bushel measure when she worked in the garden; she had a scant black mustache turning gray, and clumped in heavy plain-toed slippers when she walked about the kitchen; she did not seem like other women, she could be endured because she never giggled and was fully as dour as Judah Hansom's father, her brother . . . it was just that she refused to wring a chicken's neck, and couldn't abide snakes, and you must never mention privies in her presence.

At a church or neighborhood sociable Judah squirmed in a corner on the most uncomfortable chair he could find, if the party were a small one; or he stood in a doorway and stared suspiciously from behind draped flags or corn-shucks if the party were large, a real merry-making. He mumbled Thankee when the hostess or her daughters offered a plate of pie and a mug of coffee. He went home early.

From the time he was sixteen or seventeen he feared that all women might wish to marry him because of the land—it totaled over six hundred acres—which his father owned. His father was niggardly, and bound to have Judah earn his salt, as Elijah Hansom expressed it. Judah developed craft with the axe very early, and had left school and was hiring out as a woodcutter at the age of fourteen. He did not mind hard work, he had never minded it; he preferred it to any sort of ease he knew (he had known very little ease of the body) because the Hansoms believed that there was a virtue in pain and discomfort. In another time, another civilization, the Hansoms might have squatted on pillars in order to bring about their own saintliness or to emphasize it to the rest of mankind.

But they did not court death, despite their eagerness to torture themselves. They wanted to live long and toil determinedly and reap what they were fond of hearing the preacher describe as a Bounteous Harvest. Whenever the preacher mentioned a Bounteous Harvest the elder Hansom reacted in thought to his six hundred and twenty-four acres, his livestock, the mortgages he held and which yielded him, under pressure applied, a steady and substantial interest. He thought of the three hundred and ninety-three double eagles and the small sack of silver coins locked in an iron box under the chicken house floor (the chickens would fuss and squawk if anyone came in there at night and started to dig) and which box only Elijah Hansom himself knew was buried. He had not yet informed his son Judah about the box, which had been brought from New Hampshire in a wagon before Judah was born. He planned to tell Judah in time. He thought of the lesser amount of cash placed to his credit in the Bindale Commercial Savings Bank, for convenience sake, and of the still lesser amount kept on the highest pantry shelf in a broken coffee-mill, and which of course Judah and Aunt Annie knew was there, although they never mentioned it. These comprised his Bounteous Harvest; it was to accumulations such as these that Reverend Burgess referred. Son Judah considered Bounteous Harvests in identical terms, although his own harvest was comparatively skimpy as yet.

They did not court death; death interfered with Bounteous Harvests unless death appeared as boon and release to an invalid. Take Elijah Hansom's wife Clementine: she died when Judah was two, and had not left her bed since Judah was born. It was a great relief to Elijah Hansom when Clementine was Gathered To Her Reward (Reverend Burgess preached a sonorous funeral sermon) because he had to hire a woman to look after her for thirteen months, until Annie could be prevailed upon to come and live with them. Disgusted neighbors who had bold tongues and who did not owe Mr. Hansom any money said that poor Clementine was brought to premature labor and consequent disaster through overwork and short commons. Mrs. Calkins went over there only two days before the skinny infant was delivered into Granny Ballentine's hands— She went to buy a set of eggs. Lo and behold, there was Clementine Hansom putting up currant jam, and the kitchen hotter than Tophet, and right behind her on the table were fifteen quarts of beans she had already put up—Mrs. Calkins counted. She said, Sakes a mercy, Clemmy, let them currants spoil. Oh, no, says Clementine, and she looked like a wrung-out dishrag, poor little body. If I let anything spoil, Lijah would make me rue the day. It's not the canning that I mind, really, because I can set down part of the time. But I hate picking berries so. Twas awful hot out there in the sun around them bushes, out of the shade. . . . Well, you saw what happened.

The Hansoms did not court death, but usually death seemed to find them without much trouble and without much warning. Judah's great-grandfather was killed instantly at the battle of Bennington. His grandfather, also named Judah Hansom, slipped on the ice while crossing a river in his old age, and lay peacefully unconscious until the end. Elijah, the one who fathered young Judah in York State, perished in 1860 through wrath at hearing of the nomination of Abraham Lincoln. Elijah said that the Democrats were bound to be defeated, come November, and all the ragtag and bobtail of Creation would ride into office on that quarter-witted monkey's shoulders or through his appointments. They would frisk in public offices like rats in a cheese-keg, they would squander public funds, their relatives would feed from the public trough; there might be a war, and certainly banks would close—not that Elijah had ever trusted banks. Nor had he yet brought himself to inform his son Jude about the hoard beneath the dirt floor of the chicken shed, which was basted generously in extreme secrecy every six months or so. By this time the iron box contained more than nine thousand dollars.

Elijah Hansom said that rats in public office would hold what he called High Carnival as soon as that lantern-jawed baboon was inaugurated. He was so mad that he would have beaten a wife if he'd had one, or Son Judah if Judah hadn't been too big for him to tackle. Well, he couldn't whip his sister Annie, so he decided to go out and cut down a tree. There was a maple at the corner of the woodshed, diseased and ugly; habitually it cluttered the yard with fallen branches, and one big live branch was scraping at the kitchen roof and threatening to dislodge shingles. The maple appeared as Lije Hansom's enemy, so he touched up his axe, and Annie heard him say that he was going to level that blame tree if it was the last thing he ever did. It was the last thing he ever did. Later it was decided that the grass was wet on that slope, and the man must have slipped in striding away from the trunk when it tipped. Aunt Annie heard the tree go down, but she heard no further remarks from her brother, and two hours later she went out to feed the hens. She saw the fallen maple, and saw something black-checked and reddish alongside the trunk. The black-checked material turned out to be Lijah's shirt, and the red turned out to be—

It took nine neighbors to turn the trunk off of Lijah Hansom, and Judah didn't know a thing about the whole business (he had driven to the lumber market in Bindale with a load of seasoned posts; the load weighed so much that he had to use oxen) until he was halfway home, late that afternoon. Then he met that squint-eyed little muskrat of a Benny Ballentine, and the Ballentines didn't like the Hansoms any more because Elijah had brought foreclosure proceedings against their nephew. No reason for them to act mean about it: Mr. Hansom asked only that which was his in the best judgment of God and man. Well, little Benny Ballentine looked Judah squarely in the eye and said, Howdy do, orphant. Judah thought, Tosh, that's a funny thing for him to say. Calculate he's trying to get gay with me, and maybe seeks a hiding. Except that Judah was mild of manner, and never brawled with the neighbor men; he hadn't been in a fight since he was eleven, and then he lost; but now he was too powerful for any of them to wish to tackle him. . . . When he passed the Petrie place, Sally Petrie ran out waving her apron, and she told him.

(The iron box reposed beneath chicken-droppings, while Judah Hansom dwelt in Andersonville. It would remain there indefinitely. No one ever found it. The chicken shed would burn down, much later, and bushes would grow on the site.)

Well, Judah was twenty-two when his father died, and twenty-four when he went into the army, and nobody expected him to go. Everybody thought that he would hire a substitute if the draft wheel turned against him. Strangely, it was that same squinting Benny Ballentine who really set the knapsack on Judah's back and the bayonet hanging at his belt. Benny went away with the first troops raised at Bindale . . . spunky little rat for sure. His father said admiringly in Wilkins's store, By mighty, my Benny hain't afraid of God, man, nor the Devil. When this was repeated back to Benny he grinned and squeezed his eyelids even tighter, and he said in his high-pitched voice that he was truly afraid of God and the Devil, but he hadn't yet met any man that he was afraid of. He doubted that the Rebels were any worse than Hulk Allen at the livery barn; and once Hulk Allen had knocked Benny flat with one slap of his big hand . . . when Benny got up he was holding a bottle with a broken neck, and he took off half of Hulk Allen's right cheek before the livery barn folks could tear him loose from the big fellow. So Benny went to war, and got himself shot through the chest at Big Bethel, Virginia, and he came home coughing. He kept coughing all the time. His mother said that although the wound had healed on the outside, front and back, it didn't seem to have cured itself in Benny's vitals. He had to keep a pan by his bed at night, to cough into, and sometimes he raised blood. It was silent at night under the high black-trunked maples on that cool road beyond the single business block of Bindale, and if you walked home late, like from prayer meeting on a Wednesday, you could hear only two sounds: the sound of your own feet on the hollow wooden sidewalk, and the sound of Benny Ballentine, hacking away on his bed past the white picket fence and the white lilacs and within the walls of the little white house.

Well, Judah stopped at the smith's to pick up two wagon wheels for which Mr. Whiteman had forged new tires. Jude, said hairy old Mr. Whiteman, whose son and son-in-law had both been killed in the ranks of the Forty-second New York at Ball's Bluff— Jude, I heard tell you was going for a soldier.

Mr. Whiteman was always saying that, every time Judah came around, and it was a provoking thing to say, because Judah had no intention of becoming a soldier. Judah preferred not to patronize Mr. Whiteman as a result; but he would have had to drive all the way to Herkimer otherwise, for Mr. Whiteman was the only blacksmith in Bindale since Uncle Delhi Lawrence died.

Even before Judah could open his mouth and ask, Where did you hear that?— Before Judah Hansom could say a word, up spoke Benny. He was sitting close to the forge because he had chills much of the time, and he wore his blue overcoat even when other folks had their sleeves rolled up against the springtime sun.

Not him, chirped Benny Ballentine. Might get shot.

Usually they were a talkative group, there at the smith's—the lame and old and idle. But now they didn't utter anything, and just went on chewing their tobacco and playing with nails. Judah felt his face go red as the forge. He didn't dare to look at Benny. From the re-membered influence of his father, Judah had absorbed the notion that the war was somehow brought on by a group of capricious politi-cal bosses whose dupe Lincoln was. No sane person ought to sup-port the war in any way because it might eventually ruin the country; banks would close, prices paid for lumber would go down, people wouldn't be able to pay their interest.

Might get shot.

He could hear that echoing tartly as he drove to the farm, he could hear it from afar in the protestation of sheep which his two hired men, and temporary assistants in the shape of three young boys, were dipping. The ewes seemed quacking in the nasal tone of Benny Bal-lentine. There had promised to be a great deal of money in sheep, for markets needed more and more wool, now that no cotton was forthcoming. Judah acquired a promising flock, pastured on hills cleared by his own axe. This day the smell of the dip nauseated him, and he regretted ever having bought the flock. Baaaa. Might get shot. Baaaa.

All night long he heard the sheep and he heard Benny, and as soon as he finished choring in the morning he sat down on the wash bench and made a list of things which he must do that day. His eggs grew cold upon his plate, his cakes steamed no longer, Aunt Annie called in vain. Judah saw his hired men disposed for the day, and then he hitched up and drove to Herkimer. The bank had been open only forty-five minutes when he got there. Jude did some business at the bank, and then he went to Mr. Endicott's office and made his will. He left five hundred dollars to the Congregational church, five hun-dred dollars to the one surviving cousin in New Hampshire (this cousin he had never seen, but he did it from a sense of family duty) and he provided for Aunt Annie through whatever years might remain to her. He supposed vaguely that you might term the rest of his prop-erty to be a backlog. Lawyer Endicott kept taking off his specs and putting them on again, and then losing them amid the papers on his desk. Obviously he thought that Jude Hansom was crazy, and maybe Jude was. Baaaa. Might get shot.

Judah drove directly—not home, but to the village of Bindale. It was an hour past dinner time when he walked into Mr. Whiteman's smithy. Benny Ballentine been here? No, Ben don't usually appear before mid-afternoon.

Judah didn't go to the Ballentine house because he wanted to tell Benny right there at the blacksmith's, right in front of that same crowd, right in the middle of the hot smells and tobacco juice and horse smells and scorched parings of the hooves, and fumes and heat. He had some business to do at the local bank and with a couple of folks whose property was mortgaged to him, so he went and did it. He hadn't eaten a bite all that day, and began to feel weak although he wasn't truly hungry. He went into Wilkins's and bought some crackers and cheese and salted codfish, and sat in his buggy beside the free-flowing town trough while he ate. It was shady there under the elms, and it was a good place to eat a luncheon however belated. He could drink from the wet-moss-draped old pipe, drinking from the stream before it fell into the stone trough below. Providently Judah always carried a nose-bag under the buggy seat, and he had brought along oats for Molly . . . she tossed the nose-bag contentedly while Judah munched as if it were a duty, and it was one.

About three-thirty Judah Hansom had done everything which he must do, so he went back to Whiteman's. He dropped Molly's block on the ground and snapped the catch against her bridle; this was merely a gesture, since Molly was docile and wouldn't have stirred unless too badly fly-bitten. Judah walked inside the smithy and found Mr. Whiteman busy shoeing Reverend Hathaway Burgess's old horse. The Reverend himself was there, chewing stick cinnamon instead of tobacco, and there were the regulars: Captain Mattice, Grandpa Corning, Lame Peter Jones (he was the only Negro in the community, and insisted that his father had once belonged to a British general) and a couple of little boys. And Benny Ballentine. Benny was sitting on a flat-bed wheelbarrow; of course he wore his army coat clinging around him. Everybody stared when Judah came in and walked to confront Benny. Mr. Whiteman dropped the horse's hoof to the cindery ground with a thud. The forge sent out its cherry-colored glow, and surprisingly the scorched odors were appetizing.

Judah turned around to Reverend Burgess and said, I left five hundred to the Congregationalists, and then he turned back to Benny.

I provided for my relatives. You'll get the backlog.

What?

I just call it the backlog. It's the bulk—what Mr. Endicott calls the residue. Pa's place—my place—the farm and all. It goes to you, in case; and I calculated you might wish to know.

Benny's mouth was open, and he had a sudden coughing fit. No one else could speak a word; they were gagged with amazement. Reverend Burgess went and got a dipper of water from the bucket and put his arm around Benny Ballentine's shoulders, and offered the dipper. Benny sipped some of the water and got control of his fit.

He asked of Judah, What in conscience are you talking about?

I made my will today. Might get shot.

He went out of the smithy, unsnapped the catch from Molly's bridle, picked up the block and tossed it into the buggy, got in and drove home. He arranged with the eldest hired man to bring his wife from Bindale and to live at the farm with Aunt Annie and to farm the place on a moderate share; but all disbursements and receipts were to be handled by Mr. Endicott at his office. . . . Aunt Annie said nothing, in her usual fashion. She cooked an especially fine supper for Judah; she went out to the garden and pulled a big dish of radishes, because Jude was fond of them, as also he was fond of chicken pie, and she had that, with plenty of mashed potatoes; she gave him also cold roast lamb, flint pickles, and opened her last jar of quince preserves. They ate in silence, they and the two hired men; but this was not the dull ordinary silence of people who are too tired physically to talk, and honestly have little in common to give them mutual pleasure or annoyance, and who do not even bother to speculate about where some neighbor was bound when he drove past that day. It was a silence laden with emotion and a sense of change, desperation, hazard, alteration, and some fear.

Judah ate well, however, and when he got upstairs to his room he was so stuffed that he couldn't even read his Bible. He lay back across his bed, and the world whirled high and far and speedily; he thought he heard a tree coming down, he thought he heard his father speak gruffly. He awakened hours later to find the lamp chimney burned black, and a horrid odor of coal-oil filling the chamber. He tiptoed down the stair, washed at the bench, and went upstairs with another lamp newly filled. He packed his satchel, being in much doubt as to what he should take. He thought of taking his favorite axe, but decided against it; they would have plenty of axes in the army, but perhaps he might be given no opportunity to use one. He packed his Testament. Judah felt slightly annoyed at finding how few things he owned or even wished to take with him; he even put in one of the Rollo books he had been given when he was a little boy. His Bounteous Harvest at the moment seemed to have run mainly to land, sheep, mortgages and cold cash. He was taking but fifty dollars with him— Mr. Endicott could send more, when and if he needed more, but Judah understood that everything was furnished in the army—you didn't have to pay for your food—maybe you had to pay for your uniform, or did you? It was a puzzle. He packed an extra pair of pants, and four more handkerchiefs.

Aunt Annie heard Judah moving about in his chamber, so she rose earlier than usual; the hired men, in accord, began their chores in the murk of dawn. One would need to drive Judah to Herkimer,

and thus some hours would be lost from the work-day; it was best to
be early birds. Aunt Annie cooked her usual platters of ham and eggs,
and stood in dark gingham by the stove, cooking flapjacks as long
as there was need for more.

Jas Wilkins said, Want me to hitch up Molly?

Judah nodded. I'll be ready in a trice.

Aunt Annie came and sat at the other end of the table, glad to
be removed from the wood-range and its heat. They were alone in
the long kitchen when Judah arose. She looked up at him, teacup
in hand, and her small black eyes held a light.

You know, Jude, I'm nigh onto seventy. I was elder than your Pa.

Judah stood behind his chair.

Know who was president when I was born? George Washington.

Since Benny Ballentine had so strongly altered Judah's life, or
maybe even taken it away from him, Judah was conscious of new
emotions. He didn't like these feelings. An almighty thickness swelled
in his chest and throat, his heart beat hard.

Never said nothing about it before, but if I'd been young and not
a female, I'd have gone to fight e'er now.

Uh. Why?

Count of the Union. I mind Lijah used to fume about politicians,
but the Union's bigger than any of them. Bigger than any one man,
anywhere. It's got to be fit for.

Maybe so.

What was it altered your intentions, boy?

Uh . . . a fellow said something. Made out that I was scared of
getting shot.

Ain't you?

I calculate nobody ever wants to get shot. Except maybe a crazy
man.

But you're going. I mind my own Pa, your grandpa, talking about
Grandpa Elza Hansom. That was his father. He got kilt at Bennington when they was fighting the redcoats. Had his face to the foe when
he fell. You got plenty stockings in your satchel? I mind Pa always
held that a soldier needs fresh stockings more frequent than most
folks.

These were more words than she had spoken to Judah or to anyone
else in the past month.

Before Judah got into the buggy and took up the reins beside
Jas Wilkins, Aunt Annie came out on the low porch. She shook hands
with Judah, and gave him a parcel wrapped in store paper. Here's a
luncheon to do you on the way. I put in a bottle of tea. It'll be cold,
but it'll help to wash it down.

Thankee. Clumsily, hastily, the first time he had ever done it in his
life, quite without intention or expectation, Judah kissed her hairy

wrinkled face. He scraped the off wheel against the gate when they drove out, because he was embarrassed and annoyed with himself for yielding to such display.

He traveled from Herkimer to Albany; there he saw soldiers in the station, and asked them where he should go to enlist, and was directed properly. Five days later he was delighted to find that he should wear the crossed axes of a pioneer; he knew nothing of soldier life—except what Aunt Annie had told him about frequent changes of socks—but axes and other tools he understood very well indeed. Judah was helping to construct a log bridge in northwestern Georgia, more than two years after he enlisted, when a power of hoofbeats drummed on the pioneers' hearing, and they were captured before they could fire more than half a dozen rounds.

He spent blank appalling days after his arrival at Andersonville. As with so many of the incoming prisoners, Judah had no appetite and believed that God had forsaken him. Then his native tenacity and resource began a slow but growing assertion. He examined the lay of the land adjacent to the shebang which he shared with four other pioneers of his regiment, and decided after due deliberation that a tunnel was feasible. What Judah sought was freedom for freedom's own sake. He was actuated by no particularly noble patriotic motive; Aunt Annie had died of a stroke, the previous January; he had no person to return to—no person with whom he was deeply concerned, unless it might be Benny Ballentine. If Benny had coughed his life away by this time, no one had taken the trouble to inform Judah. Judah was driven by no strong intention of revenge; not necessarily did he despise Rebels and wish to kill them, although in fact he had killed two—one by mashing his head with a piece of railroad iron. He yearned for peace, quiet, woodland space. This must have been a nice piece of woods, right here, before this dratted stockade was built. . . . Also Jude deplored the stench, the pushing bickering mass. Except for the constant presence of smells of sweat and smells of manure (and sheep-dip) his had been a cleanly life before he entered the army, and cleaner than most lives after he was in the army. He wanted to smell again the juices of trees after he had cut them. He held the clear odor of sap and crushed leaves mingled with his ideas of Paradise. People said that the streets Up Yonder were golden, the walls of alabaster, but Judah was convinced that there were a lot of woods and hills as well, else no one should wish to go there.

He and the other York State people pooled their resources and prepared to dig. They had some half-canteens and cups, but there were no shovels anywhere about. Judah decided that serviceable little spades might be whittled out of hard wood, and he roamed ceaselessly, hunting for the right sort of wood to purchase. He possessed thirty-six dollars in greenbacks which he had concealed inside the split covers of his pocket Testament shortly after being captured. A Reb took the Testament, leafed through it, gave it back to Jude and never observed where the covers had been sliced and stuck together again. Also some of his companions had a little money. With luck they discovered a Marylander who owned a hoe, or the remains of one: the handle was only about eight inches long, the rusty blade was split in two places; still it was a tool. The Marylander was ridden with scurvy, and perishing for vegetables. They offered six dollars Federal, he held out for ten; finally they bought the hoe for seven dollars, and acquired two thin dried shakes which seemed made of some sort of hard wood—Judah had never seen that kind of wood before. Now they needed to buy or rent or borrow a knife for whittling the shakes into spades, and they owned no knife. Rumor had it that one of the men in that shebang over next to the dead-line—the one with a piece of oilcloth forming part of the roof— One of those men was said to own a good knife. Judah went over there, and all the occupants were gone bartering or root-digging except for the lone housekeeper who sat reading a stained and ragged Bible. He was a stringy little chap, not much bigger than Benny Ballentine at home. No, he didn't own a knife, but it was true that one of his household did; the man would be coming back before long, so the little fellow bade Judah to sit down and wait. He reckoned that a bargain might be struck.

Want to hear a Chapter?

Don't mind. What are you on?

I just finished Nehemiah.

Hard going.

It is for certain, with all the children of Benjamin, and Levites and things. I read it through when I was just a little shaver, but now I swore to take her all the way through again. You a Baptist, by any chance?

Congregationalist.

And Jesus answering said unto him, Suffer it to be so now: for thus it becometh us to fulfil all righteousness.

Don't need to go preaching immersion, little chap. Not to me!

Well, I'll start on Esther.

Good enough. I only got the New Testament by me.

The youth began reading in a shrill wiry voice, and Judah Hansom sat in stinking shade, listening, with all the vast growl of the stockade muted somehow by heat, muted more in this mid-afternoon than at most other hours. The little chap's name was Willie Mann, and he was a Missourian. Willie liked the part about the beds of gold and silver and the colored pavement, and especially he seemed to like the part about the wine served in vessels of gold, for he read that verse twice in a row.

Ever drink any wine, Mister?

Judah said, Had an aunt used to make it out of cherries. But she said it wasn't an intoxicant. Tasted pretty good.

Ma made grapejuice, but it wouldn't keep none too well. I know some German folks that make beer at home. . . .

Willie returned again to Esther, and then once more he and Judah fell to talking. Willie told about Providence Spring and how it had started up, right on top of him, when God seemed to smite the hill. Judah had heard about this miracle, and under the watchful eyes of police he had stood in line twice daily for water since his arrival.

He said, I know where there's a dry well.

Where at?

Right in the corner of our shebang.

How deep is she?

Calculate it might go to twelve foot or so. Hain't no water in the bottom.

You know, said Willie Mann, a sight of tunnels have been dug from some of those wells.

They sat in considerate silence for a while, both thinking hard. Wirz had made good his threat to build a second stockade in order to discourage tunneling, and now in August the second stockade was a fact. Outsiders reported that it stood at a distance of perhaps one hundred and twenty feet, rimming completely the interior pen. Folks who had seen the fence said that it was not as high as the stockade proper, but still an effective deterrent to escape. Many believed, considering the Federal advance upon Atlanta, that this new work was as much a structure for defense as well as for restraint.

That there well, said Judah Hansom. Not too far from the deadline.

I know. But a hundred and twenty feet farther to go than earlier. Few boys have done much tunneling since July. Little profit in it.

So I hear. Do you know anybody who ever made it to the Outside?

Oh, I knew one fellow went out with that bunch of Buckeyes— guess twas a fortnight ago—but the dogs got him. But some have made it, folks do say. Course the Rebs found most of the tunnels and busted them in.

Judah said, Think your tentmate would part with his knife?

Not likely, but he'd rent it for a dollar, or so he has done before.

Mind speaking to him about it? How big is the knife?

A Barlow, about so big. Got two good blades on it still, and he keeps it well whet.

In this way their friendship began. Within a week Willie Mann was committed solidly to the task of excavation, and he kept at it with a passion exceeded only by the burrowing of Judah Hansom.

Judah ached for trees and blue space, Willie had Katrine pictured in rosy soft flesh before him when he dug in loneliest depths. Most of the others worked with comparative apathy, and did not send out so much dirt, and could not stay underground as long as these two. Judah and Willie were more able-bodied than others of the group, although Willie was plagued by encroaching illness. He had loose teeth, one came out, his limbs hurt him, his mouth was sore perpetually. He kept the faithful large tin cup as a thing sacred to himself, to drink from, to feed from; he would not lend it or share from it because he feared in conscience that he might infect others.

The twelve-foot well had been dug by earlier inmates solely as a well and not as a preparation for escape. It went straight down and ended in a floor of caked clay. It had gone dry on the opening of Providence Spring, but Willie could remember when the fetid seepage of it sold for five or ten cents per cup. He had never consumed any of the water because there were too many sick in that hut above, but now they were all dead (or carried to the hospital, and thus probably dead). He remembered these things within the hour after Judah Hansom first came calling, for the knife. You knew things in this stockade, you recognized men or incidents of the moment; then, under the blanketing of days and nights and listlessness and dissolution, they were gone, scarcely a portion of memory, never a portion of recognized history. The past drifted from you because it was nearly identical with the present, and would be a stencil from which the future might be printed.

Seven men worked at the tunnel, the rest of the shebang dwellers crouched uncaring up above. There were Judah, four of his fellow York State men, Willie and a tentmate of his. They used the hand-carved spades, the hoe, canteen halves, and a utensil made from twisted stovepipe. Each had special tools which he preferred, but there was room for only one man at a time to toil at the face of the tunnel. On the bottom of the perpendicular shaft which had formed the old well, the tunnel began. It ran at right angles to the stockade with a slight downward trend. People hoped that it would clear safely the region of Providence Spring, for now rocks could be seen when you peered down into the clear pushing water. Levering stones of any size would be beyond the prisoners' power. It was concluded that at a distance of sixty feet from the tunnel's commencement the passage would have extended to the line of inner stockade posts; eventually it would rise gradually like a long straight hollow blacksnake extending toward freedom.

The symbolism of the snake occurred to Judah as he shoved his shoulders through the orifice, and thrust his long arms in alternate attack against packed earth. He had devised a system of working with the two whittled-out wooden spades. They were rather like bent paddles with sharpened edges. He would dig-dig, dig-dig . . . a downward and backward shaving of the soil, until a harvest of loose dirt lay before his face . . . he could rest his chin on it, and particles got into his mouth and nose if he didn't take care. Then with the hoe which he had dragged along with him, he would work the loose earth under his body until he could surmount the pile of it and shave deeper into solidity ahead.

He thought of that blacksnake . . . tunnel inching forward. He thought of his father, of Aunt Annie, and more often of Benny Ballentine. . . . Might get shot. Well, he hadn't gotten shot, and now probably wouldn't get shot unless he were careless about the deadline. Baaaa. He did not prefer dying here, either, as he watched ungainly hosts weaken and starve and slough their manhood away. If he were bitten by catch-dogs outside and finally bled to death, it would be preferable to puffing with dropsy. Judah's body was transforming itself into a loose pulp inside his caked hide, and he wondered how many pounds of weight he was losing each day.

It had been agreed that no man should be compelled to lie cutting away at the penetration of the tunnel for more than one hour at a time. None of the party owned a watch, but a sun-dial of sorts had been rigged up with pebbles and splinters, although someone was always stumbling over it and spoiling it. This served moderately well as a reminder to the men above, but only on sunny days. Other days they had to guess at the time. When they were digging at night, it was simple; then guards signaled from their stations on the half hour. Night or day, it made no difference to the creature who mined below. All was empty earthiness, the raw earthiness of the grave. The world was composed of nothing but soil, and you could not see it—it had no color, there was no light, there was not even true blackness after you had once immersed yourself in the ground, because somehow it seemed that you needed the suggestion of associated light in order to recognize blackness. This color, this formlessness, this silence declaiming—you could recognize nothing except the feel of your implements, the sound of breathing and labor, the pumping of your heart, the drifting march of people and distorted events which came as a nightmare troop. You dug.

. . . Muskrat. That was the creature Judah'd always considered Benny Ballentine to be, but nowadays he couldn't be too sure. More like a squirrel.

The right-hand wooden shovel had a notch in its crude handle, and that notch hurt Judah's hand halfway up his first finger, and it rubbed it, and maybe made a blister; he must change paddles and hold that paddle in his left hand.

Mr. Endicott owned a letter press with a big iron wheel to work it, and once when Judah was little he went to Mr. Endicott's office

with Pa, and he kept wanting to play with that letter press, so finally
they said, Very well, bubby, go ahead. He liked to smashed his little
hand in it; oh, how he did bellow; but Pa said it would teach him
a trick or two. Maybe so. He never more wanted to play with letter
presses.

And earth coming back around his chin, and he could lift his
matted bearded chin and kind of nudge the soil back under his
Adam's apple against his ragged breast; then he would have to grunt,
and put down his spades, and lift himself on one arm, and get the
hoe and work the loose earth farther back from the face.

O silence. The pressure of lurking solid tons above, every pound
a threat. O pressure and squeeze and no clarity of vision. Sand in
eyes, burning, and the moisture oozing from eyelids. Bad air draining
from the crude noisy world upstairs, and impregnating soil it touched
as it passed with its taint, and flowing gradually through the hard-
won cleft until it oozed across Judah Hansom's sour body, drifted
through the itching hair, the itching hair of his peeling scalp, the
itching fungus of his beard, and found its way into those caked
nostrils with which he still drew the breath of life (it smelled like
the breath of decay).

He served more than his stint; so did Willie Mann. Each held
his private reason for making perpetual sacrifice as he went worming
a rod or nearly a rod beneath the populous sty on the surface. A
man they called Old Bush—and a fellow pioneer of Judah he was—
Old Bush said he couldn't breathe for long down there; he didn't
know how the others breathed, he thought that they must be half
mole or ground-puppy. He said he nearly smothered the last time he
crept below. Now, fellers, you know I hain't no shirker; Old Bush
has always tried to play fair and square, hain't he? . . . sat with
pained legs bent beneath him, gluey tears coming down from his
harsh pink-lidded eyes . . . tried to do my share. I want to get Outside
just as bad as the next feller, but I can't stomach that chore thout
no air.

Judah served Old Bush's shift, Willie Mann served Lew Ammons's
turn when Lew lay crippled with cords taut as fishlines in his legs . . .
a big fish pulling at those cords, and what was the big fish's name? Ah.

Judah recognized that he must have committed some unpardon-
able sin, and was now engaged in a fruitless attempt at expiation. He
searched his past for the sin. He could not find it. Had he ever made
unto himself a graven image? Well, if you could call a pumpkin
head . . . he carved one of those when he was nine or so, and held
it up to the window to frighten Aunt Annie, but she paid little heed.
Had he taken the name of the Lord his God in vain? Only when a
chip flew into his eye, or when—

Remember the Sabbath day . . . six days shalt thou labour . . .

dutifully, willingly, piously he had bowed to these injunctions. He had honored a father in whom there was almost nothing to love. Why this restraint and tightening of lands and seas and antiquities? All Creation past and all Creation of the moment built into a box of clay, sand, pebbles, moistures, for the unique purpose of caging a Judah Hansom who had never liked to stand within a closet with the door shut, who felt manacled when he entered a room as small as the kitchen pantry, who had wept at crawling into the oat-chest in the barn when ordered there on an errand. Had he borne false witness, had he stolen? Nay, nay . . . oh, tarts and cream when he was small; he had stolen the prize Red Antwerp raspberries after being instructed not to touch them. Aunt Annie whipped him with a lilac switch. Had he committed adultery? Oh, Heavenly Father, he had not so much as kissed a girl when the rest were playing Spin-the-Platter; he'd just pretended to kiss Lydia Ruggles—he sort of pushed his face down past her cheek against her neck, and his face was a fiery furnace, and once again he was the first to leave the merrymaking.

Had he coveted? Well, once he saw a giant in Seth Howe's Circus, and the giant had such mighty legs and arms that Judah wished the giant's legs and arms were his own. Perhaps that was coveting.

He had worked hard and long. He had been frugal, he had prayed, he had eaten bread earned by the sweat of his brow; frequently he had fed tramps when his father wasn't around; in the army he had stayed awake many nights to nurse the sick, to help nurse the wounded, because he thought that God expected him to do these things, and he had done his full share of marching and hewing on the days following, no matter how sleepy he felt. He had slapped his own face to keep himself awake, he had given himself a bloody nose with a careless slap, and thus recognized himself as a martyr.

How long must this tunnel be, how long could a hollow blacksnake grow to be? Judah put back his hand and felt for the knotted length of rags and string which they used for their reckoning. It was like the dirty tail of a kite: there was one big knot tied every three feet, so that it could be felt in the lonely dungeon where no light ever fell. His hand found the nearest knot and pulled the strand tight against the peg to which it was anchored at the tunnel's beginning. . . . He'd scratched out another foot and a half, at least, since he came in.

Dark, dark, dark. The dread, the stifling, the granules in the mouth, the ache of ill-nourished arms which seemed mouldering away even as they were employed. Judah Hansom lay pressed in a vise of the ground. The Adirondacks tumbled all the way down from York State to heap themselves on Rebel ground in Georgia, to effect extinction, the worst extinction if one of the quickest, the extinction of the squeeze, the extinction of the stamp and mashing.

A light snapped ice-white, glaring behind his eyes even as his tired
paw hunted for the hoe.

That was it: the truth.

Now it was revealed.

He saw, he saw—he had reasoned it out.

Deadfalls. Traps made of logs. He'd made them often in the woods
in winter, balancing heavy logs, trimming triggers and notches deftly
so they'd never slip. How many creatures had he crushed beneath
those logs? Pine martens, weasels galore, even a lynx . . . he'd sold the
furs, he'd made money out of them; never should he have slain
those animals, not in that way. Not with deadfalls. For this must be
the wickedness because of which he was now commanded to be a
lonely beetle.

The stockade of Andersonville was a deadfall log, balanced prettily
above him, ready to drop.

Willie Mann crawled to relieve him, Willie closed his hand on
Judah's scabby ankle, and the perspiration was flowing anew.

Hey, Jude. Muffled voice booming stuffily.

Like I was under a deadfall.

What say?

Maybe a backlog. Like I told Benny . . . twould all be his, and now
Aunt Annie's gone too.

Hey, what you talking about?

Oh.

I got a drink for you. I got the canteen and bucket and bootlegs.
Here you be. I'll pass some up to you, and start filling back here.
My, you done a sight. Lots of dirt.

Willie, I thought twas Eri's turn down here.

He's got running-off-of-the-bowels again. I'd rather do his chore
myself than have him stinking everything up like he did the other day.

What time is it?

Six and after, hot as blazes still. Guard just shot a fellow in front
of the Twenty-third station, clear over at the northeast corner. Everybody's yelling about it. Wirz came up to the station.

Oh. Who'd he shoot?

They say it was a Michigander, I don't know who. Here, I got water
in your own cup. Harris fetched the bucket from the spring, and
we all had a good swig. Sorry, but I reckon I spilt half of it a-crawling in.

Thankee.

Now I'll get out to the well with these bootlegs, and you can back
out after me. We'll pass them up. Eri is holding the cord, if he hain't
gone to the sink. Somebody's got the cord.

Air was shut off for awhile. I thought I was going to stifle. What
happened?

Oh, couple of strangers came by, hunting for a man named Kennedy they thought was in your regiment. We were all sitting in front of the well, but we eased the overcoat across it just to be safe. They stayed about five minutes, but none of your comrades knew the man they wanted to find. Know him, Jude?

No. Could be he got captured after we did. It seemed longer'n five minutes.

Judah was shivering as he hitched himself out into the shaft and began to beat damply suspicious fresh dirt from his rags. They always did that before climbing to the top again. Thus far they believed that they had escaped the detection of informers. They were sly about their disposal of the dirt they hoisted up.

Judah was shivering, but it was the idea of the trap, the deadfall, the log pitching down, the tumbling Adirondacks, the power of a million tons of Georgia land coming down on him like a boulder squashing a grasshopper— It was this terror that ruled him. Willie Mann crawled to his job at the blacksnake's head, and Judah Hansom went up to join tribes who had at least light if they did not have freedom.

As had occurred throughout all the long hot months, heat bred a fury. It was in a pattern so repetitious as to be unworthy of note. First, the sunset swaddled with dun metallic clouds, lightning twitching sickly behind them. Then a distant sound of lonely caravans, caravans traveling with heavy loaded wagons, and their trip was pursued down a pike of corduroy construction, hollow, hollow underneath . . . great wheels a-rumble, the ravine and slopes of the stockade unsteadied by rumbling. Then the beckoning of wind above the fence, the beckoning changing to power and malignancy, scooping lower in whirls and whorls, papers and ashes caught in the wind's scope while thirty thousand rough male termagants began yelling with tonic of the wind which brought decent air to them for a moment (during most sunlit days no breeze moved between the walls, the stolid smell went aloft unbroken). They looked to props and fastenings of their huts, they hung onto scraps of overcoat, jacket, blanket, pine boughs; they hung onto their scraps of roofing material; but every now and then a chunk of clay-daubed chimney was blown free, or a loose leaf of Bible or a ragged leg-of-drawers went kiting on high, and showed black as a bat against the evening glare. Then, usually, rain hit them. Sometimes rain barely touched, and then lifted to assault another region; but more often it lingered to whip the people here. Guards turned up their ragged collars and hunched beneath sharp-sloped roofs of the sentry stations, but those high shacks offered little protection: soon the guards were as drenched as the men they watched.

To Judah, Willie, Old Bush, Eri, Lew and the rest, as they grubbed sporadically in turn—or to Judah and Willie as the responsibility of labor at their little mine's face came more and more to the two of them—freshet or tempest or cyclonic garbage flapping above could make no difference.

We grope for the wall like the blind, and we grope as if we had no eyes: we stumble at noon day as in the night; we are in desolate places as dead men.

That was Isaiah, and the Missourian and the York Stater had mourned like doves and roared like bears, each in his time; they knew Isaiah; the verse recurred to them separately in their struggles.

But Job persisted more strenuously with Judah, for Judah's bleak past life had been tinctured with the illusion of Job. He had thought it a compliment to any man to say, He has the patience of Job, and secretly had hoped that such compliment might in time be paid to himself.

Let that day be darkness; let not God regard it from above, neither let the light shine upon it.

Willie Mann had a grimness behind him, but there was music ahead. Judah had a grimness behind him and a grimness to go to. But still he thought of hills leading off to lakes and summits above West Canada Creek, he thought of the sound of a grindstone, he heard loons on one of those lakes, he felt his axe-blade sink cleanly into damp dressed wood, he saw the polished designs traced by God on a new chip as it lay prettily like a great coin.

Pelting through night the rain protracted, making gum of ground which had been gum before, recently, and would be gum consecutively again. Earth loosened, it was soaked sponge which amid the hours lost its spongy quality and dissolved into a paste as loose as cow manure. Dawn came gray, cooler than the dawn of yesterday; clouds were still soaked and soaking; at five-thirty o'clock, as time was told by the few watches still remaining to those hordes, no true light was discernible . . . clouds roosting above the eastern fence . . . barest hint of morning, perhaps imagined. At the bottom of the perpendicular shaft, knotted rags tightened once more in measurement, a new knot was counted.

Willie Mann came up with triumph in his shrunken face. He rubbed the colored spittle from his lips with a caked little hand, and his eyes were like pale brown buttons. Cracky, Jude. We ought to be under the stockade by now! Well past the deadline, at least.

How far do you make her?

Sixty-six feet, by cracky. Allowing for the curve in the slope, that'd bring her nigh the stockade or past.

Judah and Willie had saved their rations of bacon to eat for strength in the new day. Now they sat at the edge of the shebang, munching without more words for a while. The other York State men were spooned behind them (the rain had been unseasonably cold after the seasonable scorcher on the previous day, and men sought one another's warmth). Over in Willie's own shebang his comrades were still tented silently, none stirring. Close at hand Old Bush drove oxen in his sleep, as he did now with increasing fanaticism. Ho, he chirped, Bright . . . gee . . . he spoke to Bright more often than he did to the other ox of the team; apparently Bright had given him more trouble at home . . . gee, Bright!

Old Bush don't sound able to go down, Jude.

Wouldn't keep digging for more'n ten minutes if he did go. Tain't his turn, anyway. Whose chore is it?

Willie pointed. Lew Ammons's. But I reckon he's over in our shebang all twisted up. He's got the scurvy badly. I trust I don't get it that badly.

They chewed the last pulp of raw pork; it was called bacon, it was nothing like bacon except that now and then you found brownish gristles of lean amid the curdled fat. You hunted it over for worms, and pulled out those worms you could see; then you shut your eyes and popped the pork into your mouth, and chewed and chewed to get it down, and it hurt to chew if your mouth was getting the way Willie's mouth was getting.

Judah rose up on his haunches. I'll go down.

No, no. You did one spell at six, another around ten.

That was only part of an hour whilst you went to the sink.

Then you did a full hour in the middle of the night. Two or three o'clock.

Finished up at three.

Jude, you're doing a lion's share and more than a lion's share. There isn't any call for you to dig the whole tunnel.

Judah set his wide thin jaw. I feel rested like.

I'll go down myself.

What in tunket! You just finished your chore.

What about Eri?

Not till he gets over that looseness, if he ever does.

You can go for half an hour, said Willie with finality. Just let me take a breathing spell, and I'll be down to spell you.

William, we got to keep digging while we got our strength. If we tarry too long, we won't never get out.

I know. And I'm bound to get out.

So'm I.

That's why we're killing ourselves, Jude. But his fierce small face was grinning. We'll make it, comrade. Just think of that: sixty-six feet!

Judah Hansom made his way into the tunnel and set to work. He moved the last disturbed earth left by Willie; he filled two bootlegs with it, and then he fell to with his twin spades, shaving at the tunnel's

face. He felt again, as perpetually, the dread of small space, close
walls and roof, the pressure coming about him.

Let darkness and the shadow of death stain it; let a cloud dwell
upon it; let the blackness of the day terrify it.

In the York State shebang, not in his own hut, Willie Mann
stretched his brief narrow length and rested his cheek against his
bony arm. Katty, are you there, are you somewhere? *Ja.* He liked to
imagine that he heard her replying to him thus in a whisper; but he
had forgotten what her whisper sounded like; he knew that she would
often say *Ja* or *Nein,* but he couldn't remember how she sounded
when she said it.

Considerable disturbance began growing, over around the deadline and stockade to the west, and now the dawn was strong enough
for one to see the pen in all directions, to see filmy figures moving
in a thin slow shuttling mass among planes and angles of the shelters.
It seemed to Willie that he had heard, remotely, some sort of thud
and squeaking—the squeal of wood on wood as if one heavy timber
trembled in sliding across another.

Considerable disturbance. Of course the prisoners always made a
noise, but this was a noise of wonder and speculation; a good many
men seemed peering and pointing. Willie braced himself on his
elbows to watch. Suddenly he got up and ran toward his own shebang
as fast as his sore joints would let him.

Lo, let that night be solitary, let no joyful voice come therein.

There came the Adirondacks, rolling upon Judah Hansom. The
deadfall log was made of mountains, and he was the pine marten
beneath. He recalled lovely golden tones of a fresh-killed frozen
marten's thick fur when he lifted the log which had crushed it.

Let the stars of the twilight thereof be dark; let it look for light,
but have none; neither let it see the dawning of the day.

Judah in confusion observed a clear portrait, in memory, of Benny
Ballentine. The portrait was clearer than a miniature painting, clearer
than any type of photograph now prepared by modern methods:
ambrotype, daguerreotype, wet-plate photograph, any modern thing
he'd ever seen. Might get shot. But I didn't, Benny, didn't, never did
get shot. What? Judah Hansom tried to speak to himself. What is
this? What happened? In spite of the fears he'd hoarded, he was
surprised to desperation . . . he heard his axe clanging as he stroked
it, he heard a raven in fine fair winter woods ahead.

For now should I have lain still and been quiet. I should have
slept: then had I been at rest.

Shoving dangerously near to the deadline, Willie Mann and lame
Lew Ammons and a growing congregation from that section— All
stood gazing up at the stockade. Two posts had pitched down and
in—it was at a point perhaps a rod past the nearest sentry station—

and rapidly sentry stations were thronged with more than their usual complement of guards. The two posts had dropped a yard or more, and the third, the tilted one, had dropped at least that far. No one of that immediate crowd except Willie and Lew knew exactly what had happened; but it would not take the guards long to decide, and then of course they would come hunting for the tunnel's mouth.

How high is our tunnel roof, Willie?

A yard and more.

Who was down there, Willie?

Jude. I should have been.

Why, you barely finished. . . .

Lew! Let loose of me, get your claws out of my hide! I'm going down the well, and see—

Twon't do no good.

Or as an hidden untimely birth I had not been; as infants which never saw light.

Willie went scrambling down the old well shaft, he lost his hold and fell the last several feet, landing on his face and knocking out two of his loosened front teeth. He went back into the tunnel as far as he could crawl, and with bleeding mouth he called Jude, Jude, Jude, until more earth came sliding around him as if responding to his cry. He had to snake backward out of there, rapidly, in order to avoid those developing cave-ins. He examined the ragged rope with his hand, on the way out, counting knots; he might have missed one or two. He told his companions, once he was come up to the surface, that he had been able to penetrate the tunnel only to a distance of approximately forty or forty-five feet. Beyond that point the ground had settled, and directly beneath the stockade it must have settled more quickly and tightly than anywhere else. What would one of those pine logs weigh? Maybe a foot to a foot-and-a-half in diameter; and they were said to be twenty feet in length, though but fifteen feet in height showed above the ground.

There the wicked cease from troubling; and there the weary be at rest.

There the prisoners rest together.

Willie Mann and Eri Gaines went down into the well and, working with the speed born of acute necessity, managed to close up the mouth of the tunnel. It was not an especially good job, and would not have defied close scrutiny. Still, the guards never found it. They were too incompetent, too old, too young, too impatient, they moved too rapidly about their search. Eri Gaines would die in Andersonville, Willie Mann would not, Lew Ammons would die in Andersonville, Old Bush would die in Andersonville, Willie Mann would not. Benny Ballentine would live to be eighty-six.

XLVI

. . . Soldier, do you hunger, are you sickened by the bitter fare they give you, the bitter fare withheld? Would you dine again on fresh plucked quail and baked potato? Sit down and place the wooden trencher across your knees, and—mind! the potatoes are very hot, they can burn your fingers; and the birds are scarcely cooler. . . .

So once more Nathan Dreyfoos strayed from Andersonville, and higher, higher he was riding: no more Moorish towns streaked in white along the precipices, no more farms. Stony watercourses (all dry as toast because the upper snows were long since gone, and so the water of snows' melting was gone) enfolded each its treasure of pink and green, the dry hills squeezed their pink and green, the pink oozed luxuriantly from watercourse crevices as if the hand of the hills had pressed it from a tube, and its name was oleanders. A billion oleander blooms to tickle the soul . . . how long, asked the boy, have they grown here? Did Carthaginians plant them, did Phoenicians scatter the seeds? Nay, magpies and nightingales must have let the treasure fall from their beaks when this wild portion of the planet was still cooling.

Out into the path the squat charcoal burner marched, and held up his hand in a manner of defiance, halting Nathan, halting the little *mulo* in his tracks.

Good afternoon.

Good afternoon, friend.

Please, do you have wine with you? My bottle is dry. My wife should have brought me wine yesterday, but she did not appear. I have been drinking water but I fear to become ill because of the water.

That is not true. The water in these mountains is pure. I have been drinking of it for two days.

Ha. You are young. I have thirty-one years, and I have health because I drink much wine.

Friend, I have two liters of wine with me, and I am happy to share with you. Nathan reached into the basket hanging behind him and brought forth a hide bottle which bulged like the udder of an unmilked goat. The eyes of the charcoal burner gleamed with joy, and blackened corners of his mouth twisted, and his sooty eyebrows went on high. God will reward you, he said. He tipped the bottle above his open mouth and the lovely purple stream spurted. He drank, swallow, swallow, long swallow, pause, long swallow, swallow, swallow, swallow. He lowered the bottle, not so bulging now, and said, Ah, in a rapture which echoed along the splintered chasms above.

You dwell here alone?

Through many days. It is necessary, because I am a charcoal burner, and must keep the fires going, and distribute the wood, and remove the *carbón* when it is charred. My wife lives with her father on the road to Gaucín; she cannot live with me here in my hut, because the place is too high for her. You know—women, with their infirmities? Or do you know? You are very young. How many years have you?

Only fifteen.

You are tall, *hombre*—taller than I, by far, and I am twice thy age. May I be permitted to have more wine?

Yes, yes, yes—please.

Again the thin pretty stream curving, the open mouth receiving. The urine of the gods, said the charcoal burner, and he and Nathan laughed at the ancient jest.

Man, what name have you?

Natán. And you?

I am called Pepe. José Romera and Mancera, but of course I am called Pepe. Natán, can you shoot a gun?

Yes, I have skill with guns.

Can you kill birds?

I have killed many birds. In France, doves; also here in Spain. In Scotland I have shot many grouse. In the United States of America I have killed many birds of the name of wild ducks—some are called mallards, some are called teal.

Is that a jest? You have traveled in many nations, and you are so young?

Nathan Dreyfoos felt uncomfortably ashamed, and felt also a sudden discomfort which did not stem from shame. Perhaps Pepe was acquainted with bandits, and would tell them that in these mountains and on this path there traveled a youth who had ranged far and wide through the world, and whose parents must be wealthy without doubt and able to pay a large ransom.

But he felt also that he must not lie to Pepe. He had been taught that there was an infallible virtue in truth for its own sake. Solomon Dreyfoos said that even in business it was not necessary to lie. There were wiser and more diplomatic ways to avoid offending, or to convey an intended meaning; a man should cultivate these methods, and not burden his conscience with untruths. Nathan could not recall himself as telling fibs—not since he was six or seven, and stole comfits and barley-sugar, and denied it, and got a thrashing.

He said, My friend, it is a strange story, too long a story to be related now. But I swear it by the head of my mother.

Natán, I have a gun, also powder and shot. In this upper valley are many *cordonices* but my eyes give me pain and I cannot see as well as I could when I was younger. Perhaps it is because I have filled my eyes with smoke for so many years, as a charcoal burner. I grow weary of baked potatoes. Do you like baked potatoes?

Yes, very much. Especially with salt and butter.

Salt I have, but no butter. But how should you like to dine on baked potatoes, dinner after dinner, luncheon after luncheon? Also for breakfast? I have bread and oil; but my bread is growing dry as a rock; my wife was to bring me fresh bread, and I pray that she is not sick. Natán, why should you not take my gun and shoot some quail? Can you afford to spend the time? I have wasted powder and shot, many times; as I informed you, my eyes are bad. It is early for quail, but certainly the chicks are now large enough to take care of themselves. Please?

For reply Nathan brought his mule off the track and past the smouldering charcoal kilns, and up to the very door of Pepe's hut. It was the usual habitation of shepherds or herdsmen in lonely places —a conical wigwam thatched with pine, floored and based with stones, softened with a thick bed of dry grasses.

Where is your gun? Where is a good spot for Tomás to graze?

I have my gun in my hut, wrapped in a blanket. It has rust but it will serve. Is Tomás the name of your mule? He is a handsome animal. See—below here, immediately beyond those large rocks, there is still some grass—some of the grass is still green or partly green.

I shall remove the saddle.

Natán, allow me to assist you.

. . . High he went along the scar of a stream no longer a stream. He could actually hear birds piping ahead of him. The gun was a smooth-bore flintlock, very old, it had a loose stock, it would not do to load it with a heavy charge. It would be necessary to kill the quail at close range, he would need to shoot quickly as they rose. The gun's lock had proved rusty and stiff, but Pepe used olive oil, working it into the mechanism with his thumb, holding the weapon aloft, turning it, oiling through gravity. Nathan examined the flint, didn't approve of it, requested a fresh flint, which was found. He donned an ammunition belt—a kind of antique bandolier, dry and smelly, with pouches for shot, powder and a special fine priming powder. Nathan rubbed this latter substance in his palm, and sniffed it. Where had such powder ever come from; how had the lonely charcoal burner acquired it? It was fine, silvery, beautifully blended, crushed to infinitesimal particles, finer than the finest English powder; surely it would explode with a flash, instanter.

High he went, there were plants like sage, plants like heather, surely they were sage and heather. Clumps of cobalt live-forever flowers tufted underfoot, the afternoon sun glinted on scraps of marble, two eagles swung challengingly. The first quail came flurrying up with a light roar; Nathan lifted his gun but did not shoot. He wished to grow accustomed to the feel of the weapon, to grow accustomed to the buzzing of quail's wings and the sight of their feathers whirling, their wings blurring. Another bird, more birds . . . next time he would fire. Two feathery little bombshells went bursting up in a single second, and Nathan took the left-hand *cordoniz* of the brace; he longed for his own double-barrel. The fancy powder burnt with the flame of a star, the charge roared with a sullen gasp in the rusty barrel, the shot flew out, the bird came down. Nathan reloaded laboriously before he went to pick up his prize, and it was well that he did so: another bird flew out before he reached the dead one. In Scotland he had known an old gillie who called such a lonely lingering refusing-to-fly-until-the-last-possible-moment bird a *jouck* or *jouk* or *joock*—anyway it was rhymed with *book* or *look*. The jouck died in midair and fell near the other. Far down the glen Tomás brayed in annoyance each time the gun was fired. Nathan wasted but two charges on empty air; also he wounded one bird slightly, crippling it until the poor thing went hobbling into the shrubbery and he had to run after it and dispatch it with a stick. Otherwise he shot to perfection, and came back an hour later, glorying in splashes of oleander pink which burst from creased valleys far below. He lifted his voice in a homemade *flamenco*. His new friend Pepe replied in kind; he sang with a voice far more musical than Nathan's; he confessed that he sang assiduously, beguiling his loneliness all day long and sometimes in nighttimes when he thought of his young wife. He sang now a *saeta* completely out of season. He sang that it was a long and dolorous road which Our Lord was compelled to walk . . . oh, dear Lord, the nails in his hands . . . so heavy the Cross. Pepe had drunk more of the wine and—wineless for two preceding days—was growing slightly tipsy. He had put several fat new potatoes to roast in the ashes of his kiln, and displayed proudly to Nathan a bottle of oil which he said was the best to be had in Andalucia . . . it was refined in Coín, highly refined . . . members of the royal family sent all the way from Madrid and Aranjuez for this same oil.

Nathan came apparently empty-handed, except for the gun from which he now drew the charge for safety's sake.

What? No fortune? No quail? I thought you were an expert.

See, *hombre!* For a trick Nathan had tied the dead birds to a cord slung down the middle of his back. He lifted the loop over his head and twirled the feathery burden to the ground in front of the startled charcoal burner. See. Ten birds. Sufficient? Roast them all and eat all you please, and keep some of them to eat cold at your next *comida!*

Nathan had eaten nothing since early morning except cheese and a wad from a loaf of bread (he preferred crusts to the insides of the loaves, and had eaten the crust from this loaf the day before). He sat on a rock with long arms bent around his knees, watching Pepe at his cookery. It seemed that Pepe could cook birds as well as *carbón*. Pepe had made a long spit of peeled wood and on this spit the quail were impaled, roosting and roasting in a solemn headless gutted row. Someone else must come past this lonely place now and again, for Pepe admitted that he could not shoot birds, yet he had the crotched posts for his spit already cut, old and blackened; and crevices had been prepared to receive them. Yes, someone else came to that place and secured quail.

My friend, you have some other person who provides *cordonices* for your kitchen?

Pepe turned swiftly. His face was so baked by the heat and so dirtied by his occupation that Nathan could not estimate the expression accurately; yet he was certain that Pepe gave him a look of intense suspicion.

No, young sir. No one.

But the posts for the spit? They were prepared.

Oh, once I had a partner. That was long ago. He is dead, he died beneath an avalanche. See? Over on that next mountain. Under that great loose mass of gray stones, he is lying there somewhere, very deep down; it was impossible to dig him out. No, no, *hombre*, this is a lonely place! No one comes.

. . . But now, he cried in another hour, waving a quail breast aloft, this is indeed my afternoon of fortune. You have brought me good fortune, Natán! See: look down at the cleft where the path curves, where the clumps of mullein are growing. Do you not see her? My wife! See, she comes with one basket on her head and another on her arm. She is late in coming, which means that she will spend the night with me. Thanks to God.

Her name was Angelita. She had blue eyes, narrow but dancing, and tumbled brown hair which did not appear too clean. She was nearly as brown as the original Moors who must have been numbered thickly among her ancestors. Her tough legs, her round hips swung with a flourish beneath the layers of colored Andalucian skirts, and caused Nathan much aching later when he lay in bed, in a distant village, and thought of Pepe and Pepe's wife, and how they must be united in that wigwam.

. . . Does the ugliness corrode you, soldier? Would you escape its burning and stain? Then drift once more where holly oaks and stripped cork oaks put down their shade.

He'd spent two days in Ronda. For hours he'd leaned on the bridge across the chasm, staring down at specks which were swallows and pigeons, at larger slower blacker specks which he supposed were crows or rooks. Gypsy children hung about to importune him for money each time he stirred, but he was deaf to their whining and had ears only for the loose rumble of the shrunken stream far below. He wondered how it would have been had he lain as a prisoner in that jail so close at hand—hearing the shrillness of swallows, the hollow eternal vesper song of the river, yet walled away, fettered tight, unable to participate in the beauties of the gorge . . . how would it be, to be a prisoner? Oh, he lamented, that there must be any prisoners, anywhere, in any time.

On the second day following, Nathan became in fact a prisoner— at least he was taken in charge by others, he was commanded to do a thing he had not planned to do. It came about as Tomás paced sedately up a narrow path, a connecting link between the road which led from Ronda to the Cuevas de Becerro and the road which led from Ronda to Burgo. A peasant had told Nathan about this track, he had drawn a map in the dust with a stick. Many miles of traveling would be saved, and the path led through wild and beautiful country (all the country roundabout was wild, it was beautiful . . . a few late poppies shed brilliant blood in the valleys, bees lived above thistles as dainty as orchids). But the peasant had been incorrect about the feasibility of the path for a traveler on muleback. Good enough for black goats with their stiff wiry legs, but a trial for a tall youth whose own knees were scraped by jutting rocks along a dozen keyhole passages. Nathan had to dismount and let Tomás follow him through rising crannies, and for a time he had to carry the baskets, for they were fairly torn from the mule's trappings by the narrowness of the way. Still it was a fair adventure. Once they routed out a wolf which galloped off disdainfully, twice Nathan saw spool-spindled horns of the ibex gleaming on some upper shelf. Over the crest of this range the road turned wider once more, and again Nathan was able to ride.

He sang discordantly, he wished he had his violin. He could not make pleasant music with his voice but the sheer enthusiasm of living youth made him roar. He sang Mendelssohn, sang airs for which there were no words, he invented ohs and ahs and roodle-doodles to support the strain. The path wound down through a gradually widening gorge, and Nathan could see a sparse flock of sheep feeding where grass began once more, and two motionless dots which were the shepherds, watching. Why two shepherds for a mere eight or ten sheep? And there leaped no dog to challenge him as he approached. Nathan left off singing as he approached, and was about to call a greeting when he was treated to an abominable surprise: one of the shepherds reached down behind a boulder and came up with a blunderbuss—truly, one of those bell-barreled relics which you saw in museums. He waved this weapon in Nathan's general direction and ordered him to dismount.

Why do you threaten me with that ugly gun? Is it because I'm such a bad singer?

Bad singer, good singer, it matters not. Get down from that mule! Examine his pockets, Tello.

Nathan stood with his hands in the air, frightened but managing to keep smiling. The armed shepherd was a sour-faced fellow of middle age; he had greasy iron-gray hair curling to the collar of his patched blue jacket. The other man resembled him—perhaps a son or a much younger brother—but was less forbidding in appearance, and wore a yellowish smock. He had been eating food laden with garlic, his breath nearly suffocated Nathan, who liked garlic well enough but not in such nauseous doses.

Behold, he has a pistol, brother. Unloaded.

Take it from him nevertheless.

And a splendid knife.

Take it. And money?

A few coppers only.

He must have more, perhaps concealed. We'll find out later. The Wolf will soon discover whether he has money or no. Young man, where are you bound?

To Burgo, said Nathan, thinking it best to name the nearer town rather than Málaga.

Is your home in Burgo? And what a magnificent mule we have here!

We have no mule, Nathan cried. The mule does not belong to me; he belongs to a friend; his name is Tomás, and back to that friend Tomás goes.

Not if I give you a dose of stones from this weapon of death, *bobo*. I do not believe that it will shoot.

You'll soon find out if you attempt to flee. Now, march! We go to *El Lobo*. You have heard of him, no doubt.

Is he the wolf I frightened on the trail some kilometers distant? Nathan was terrified, but still he insisted on jeering at his captors. He felt that it was essential for him to put up a bold front. The wolf ran like a *cabrito* the moment I appeared. Will your precious *Lobo* do the same?

You'll see. March! Tello, lead the mule.

Despite his fright, Nathan wondered about the sheep, and whether they would be left to the mercies of predatory beasts. He did not wonder for long. The elder bandit—for such these must be—slid two fingers into his mouth and emitted a whistle as piercing as the blast of a French locomotive. A little boy came bounding down the slope before they'd taken many steps; he did not stare in surprise at Nathan and Tomás, for he had watched the whole performance from his perch on the walls of an ancient fold. He was a ragged dwarfish creature with squinting brown eyes.

Rafaelito, the sheep are in your charge.

Yes, uncle. The boy whipped a sling from his rags and went to assume his duty.

If you harm me or the mule, declared Nathan, soldiers will come into this region and give you a taste of bayonets.

Soldiers? I laugh at the word. *El Lobo* is ruler here.

He'll learn whether he is ruler or whether Queen Isabella is ruler, once those soldiers appear.

I spit at the word. The iron-gray bandit spat. Now you shall march. *Siléncio!*

They prodded Nathan Dreyfoos along for nearly two miles on a side path which might have been fit for kids; it seemed to Nathan that certainly the track was not suited to the travel of adult goats. He slipped and stumbled, Tomás stumbled, the bandits carried Tomás's baskets, the bandits walked cat-footed with the elder man ahead and the younger behind. Finally they reached a chasm choked with bouquets of oleander. The elder man grunted and unfastened the black scarf tied around his neck. This smelly kerchief he folded into small compass and bound tightly across the upper part of Nathan's face. The men took him, one by each arm, and going thus blindfolded he found it easier to travel than before, because the men were practically carrying him. He could not guess where they went: it must have been across a wide field above the chasm's brink . . . throughout most of the journey there was room for the three of them to move abreast, and Tomás squirmed dutifully behind—Nathan could hear him coming. *Urrro,* said Tello again and again, urging the mule. In time Nathan felt a coolness as of shadows, and the captors altered their positions: one was ahead of him, guiding, with Nathan's hands on his shoulders; the other had his hands on the boy's hips. Nathan brushed a raw cliffside, first with one shoulder, then with the other. He lurched, and might have fallen if the bandits had not supported him. Surely they went through the narrowest defile in those mountains. A hand ripped the cloth away from his eyes and he stood blinking. Here was a region of yellow precipices, shallow caves curling darkly beneath the overhang, caves oiled with the woodsmoke of centuries. Hannibal's soldiers might have slept there, and a thousand herdsmen had bedded away from the rain, delighting in the comfort of their fires through the ages which followed.

El Lobo and four of his men were lunching off eggs and roast veal, and where had they got hen's eggs in such a weird place? *El Lobo* was perhaps thirty-five or forty years of age—tall for an Andalucian, not as tall as Nathan. His tanned well-chiseled face carried the marks of smallpox spread thickly, and when he grinned he displayed wide-spaced brownish teeth which were near the size of tushes: doubtless those fangs had given him his name. His blue eyes were intelligent and piercing, but somehow there was madness in his manner. The gods have glowered on me, thought Nathan with dreary humor. Father was right about the bandits, and now they will knock me on the head; and no one will ever know where or how I vanished in these hills.

El Lobo was dressed in baggy black pantaloons and sash and a silk shirt which had once been red but was faded to pink across the shoulders, and discolored otherwise by the ravages of perspiration. He wiped egg off his mouth and arose leisurely to survey the new arrivals. Rocks made the table, rocks made the stove and cellar, and they were paved and upholstered by a collection of colorful and very dirty blankets.

El Lobo sauntered forward with a crust of hot veal in his hand. He stopped immediately in front of Nathan, examined him from head to foot, then offered the meat.

Thank you, said Nathan. I am not hungry.

Because of fear?

I suppose you are The Wolf.

Thus I am called. What name have you?

Natán.

The Wolf stared, rolled up his eyes, and clapped a hand to his close-cropped head. Nátan, Natán, he repeated. Of all travelers who might have chosen to pass this way, to think that it should be you! Why, Natán, your home is in Málaga. And this animal is Tomás. Where did you sleep on Thursday night? At the small inn conducted by Angel Matas and Dorado, the inn known as the House of Gold. You feasted on chicken, cucumbers and *manzanilla.* You paid in gold coin, and it was difficult for Señor Matas to provide the change. Oh, Natán, you have broken my heart today!

How is it that you know these things? asked Nathan.

I know everything which occurs within this region. I have friends, and the news is carried to me promptly. If this were not true I should have been hanged long ago. Even so I was caught and imprisoned—long ago—and have no wish to be caught and imprisoned again. Observe these scars on my wrists. And—here—on my legs. Those came from fetters. Never again shall I be fettered.

He dropped his greasy hands on the surprised boy's shoulders and called him *hombre.*

Nathan inquired dizzily, Why do you greet me in such a manner of friendship? Is this a false thing?

No, no, it is true. You are a friend of the husband of my sister.

It is impossible.

No, no, it is true. How many birds did you shoot for Pepe with his old gun? My sister tells that you are a polite youth with excellent manners, and probably have great wealth in your family, for you have traveled to the ends of the earth. And you gave Pepe your wine, freely, when he said that he had thirst.

This conversation was accompanied by a chorus of exclamation and repetition on the part of the other men clustered around them. He shot birds for Pepe. Pepe cannot see to shoot. Yes, probably great wealth in his family. Very tall for a boy. Pepe said that he had but fifteen years.

Antonio, you and Tello are idiots. Did you not know these things? Could you not recognize Natán from the description?

Antonio, of the greasy iron-gray hair and blue jacket, mumbled something or other.

Antonio, how often have I said that you were an idiot?

Very many times.

¿Es verdad? Now everyone was laughing, and The Wolf had his arm around Nathan. Nathan felt himself enfolded in their primitive childish circle; it was a good and simple warmth he felt; he was still enough of a boy to linger joyfully with the notion of playing bandit.

Suppose, he said, that it were true that my family had wealth. Would you keep me as a captive until much money was paid?

Ah, I have a number of friends who are men with fortunes. I have taken them to hunt the ibex. I did not keep them as captives. No, Natán, you are a friend of my sister's husband and thus you are a friend of mine. Come and enjoy some veal and wine. I fear that the eggs are all devoured. The veal is roasted beautifully; and it was stolen from the herd of Don Miguel Sagasta and Arias, but butchered only yesterday.

At last Nathan knew the identity of that other marksman who fetched quail, sometimes, for the larder of the charcoal burner. . . .

Why, he asked over the veal, does Pepe not give up his work as charcoal burner, and come to live this free-and-easy life with you?

He has fear. Once the soldiers took him and tortured him, hoping to discover where they might seize me. Pepe did not tell them, for the very good reason that he did not know. He does not know, at this moment. He would rather blacken himself with carbón, he declares, than risk his neck as we outlaws do. Oh well, one day they may shoot me; but never again shall I be lodged in a dungeon.

Antonio and Tello went back to their sheep, but Nathan remained with The Wolf. Nathan lived blissfully through the dream of that afternoon and the long evening following, and the night. There was a wide moon in this week. A sentinel was on duty each hour through the night, and perhaps more sentinels were posted nearer to the roads.

The men took turns at sentry duty, in the manner of soldiers and with almost no bickering. It was hard for Nathan to sleep; he did not rest well, but he did not really wish to sleep at all; he wanted to stay awake, and glory in the enormous blue and silver myth which moonlight made of this region. Valley and shallow caves lost their entity as an actual part of the world's surface—they became legend, along with the storied tinkle of goat bells somewhere in hills below, the wolves which howled on upper pinnacles, the gem made by a lounging sentinel overlooking the crack in the boulders which was the door to this mountain closet. The sentinel stirred, he moved his musket, it took fire from the moon and became a diamond wand, again it was a black stick and part of his bulk as he sat blanket-wrapped against the coolness. One sentinel had a big pipe and perpetually he smoked dried mullein leaves as a treatment for his cough. His pipe would glow and sputter when he came down to put a twig in the low broad fire and light the pipe, the strange tonic odor of charring mullein would penetrate deeply into the nostrils of Nathan Dreyfoos. And with it would come the smell of baked meat, the scent of the campfire itself, the rough sour scent of old perspiration in old stained blankets. Over all— the dry pervading smell of dry Spain itself, Spain and its mountains, the rocks long lived-over, lived-among. . . . I am alone in the hills, sleeping with a gang of outlaws. It will be a memory for me when I am old, so old that I cannot bestride a *burro* but must sit sideways like a woman. What a memory, what a joy. It is more potent than the oldest brandy, the richest wine from Jerez.

They arose at dawn, they ate soon after sunrise, they ate the raw flat ham of the hills, long slices razor-thin. They drank their hot brew of scorched brown oats, and filled their mouths with bread, and laughed. The men were joking with *El Lobo* about some feat of villainy planned for that day; again it concerned Don Miguel Sagasta or some relative of his who did not appear to enjoy the bandits' favor. But Nathan could make nothing of their jests; they seemed to speak in a kind of code, and with sly references which he couldn't follow.

Must you be on your way so soon? asked The Wolf pointedly, and Nathan knew that his visit was to terminate at once.

Tomás was unhobbled and brought from his grazing, and harnessed for the road. Ceremonially *El Lobo* handed back the knife and pistol which Tello had taken from Nathan.

Don't fasten his baskets, ordered The Wolf. The way is too narrow. You, Joselito, and you, Pedro, shall carry the baskets and guide Natán to the outer world. Be sure that his blindfold is tight.

Embraces were exchanged.

I have a small gift for you, my friend The Wolf.

Ha, in most times I select my own gifts. From the purses of callers, or the purses of their relatives. I trust it is not a watch or a ring? I have many, and it is difficult to dispose of them. But I am happy that you have a gift for me, Natán.

It is this: a small penknife. I bought it in Paris several years ago. It does not look like much but— Now, do as I do. Hold it up to the light, and apply your eye to this tiny hole. What see you?

El Lobo bayed with delight. A beautiful woman! And without clothing. And all in color!

The men clustered eagerly to view in their turns.

Natán, this is a hard life for women. I have a woman friend, I have had many others, but they cannot dwell in these chambers of rock for long. It makes them complain, and also their presence causes much dissension among the men. But this woman you have just given me— Ah, she can delight me when I am lonely. Has she a name?

I have never given her one.

Then I shall give her one. I'll call her Belita. I like that name, and never have I had a friend named Belita. There, there, Belita, rest snugly in thy private little pocket.

Adiós. Until a little while.

No, no, Natán. Farewell for ever. I feel that we shall never meet again, but I shall remember thee.

Nathan and Tomás were escorted to the road where he had been taken in charge by the shepherds, but neither they nor their few sheep were in sight. He said goodbye to Pedro and Joselito, and they stood watching as he moved down the long crooked trace, and he waved back at them many times, and they at him.

(*El Lobo* spoke the truth; he and Nathan were not to meet again. In 1859 Nathan read an account of Spanish bandits, in a British magazine. It mentioned *El Lobo,* and told how he had been captured when he visited Ronda in disguise. He was put into a cell while the authorities wrangled about whether or not he should be condemned to death. They wrangled long, and The Wolf was suffering from consumption. He died in his cell. Nathan was pained to learn of this, but he was able to divorce his own recollection of the bandit from the hateful, coughing, damp, expectorating misery of the picture conjured up. He saw *El Lobo* always, in his mind's eye, presiding over rude lunches by hillside fires; he saw him enriched by moonlight, and listening to the wail of his brother wolves even as he slept.)

Being young and thus inclined toward rebellion, sometimes Nathan Dreyfoos doubted the existence of God, and very often he doubted the benevolence of God. But there were no moments of question or refusal as he progressed slowly eastward and southward through the mountains, hearing far away the mule song, seeing new eagles, marveling eventually at wind playing with loose grain on threshing floors near the villages, knowing that the last range of coastal hills would be

roasted brutally by dry summer by the time he arrived there; yet he
could carry highland poppies, gay blue straw flowers, the chocolate
limbs of stripped cork oaks (curved with promise like the legs and
arms of beautiful brown women)— He could carry with him whatever
beauties he chose; a sad or an ugly thing he should ignore, he should
leave behind him.

Men of a village walked out to meet him sternly as he reached the
outskirts; he dismounted and removed his hat while they paced in
close-packed ragged column, for a flat black box was borne on the
shoulders of several. They were bound for the white-walled cemetery
on the next windy ridge. The coffin was a small one; it was a child
who had died. Now that was a sad thing, and should be left behind
. . . never carry it consciously; let the very awareness of death die;
abandon it in the hills or wherever else it occurs to provoke.

He passed a troop of gypsies, and one of their women had a wet
reddish horror instead of a nose, she was dying of this cancer, and
had stuffed a rag into it, and her black eyes, once perhaps as lively as
Nathan's own— Her eyes stared and said, This is a horror, I am it,
I am the horror, do you see me, how could you avoid seeing the
horror which I am? Her claw came out for the coin he gave; and
Nathan thought in momentary agony of the Jew whom most of the
Jews rejected, and why had not He chosen to walk Andalucia with
His healing ways a good eighteen hundred years after He walked
Palestine? This was ugliness; forget it, let the hills forget.

Nathan thought of his own mother's voice saying, God go with thee,
and thought of the gentle perfection of her soul; and a great fountain
of love for mankind and pity for mankind spouted up within him
. . . take the beauties along, basket loads of them, bury the miseries
beneath clay willing to receive them.

Here and there he found shrines, some no longer in use, unoccu-
pied by Crosses; others wearing small flowers which the peasants had
left, and an old woman in black and two sunny freckled little girls
knelt in front of one shrine. Nathan thought of the cave of the two
altars, and how the felt of moss was blanketing those fallen rocks, cut
and squared and beveled so long before. . . . How many sandaled
feet had walked this road, how many bare feet, and for how long a
time? How many mules had gone tinkling in file, how many whips had
snapped, how many weapons of steel had been lugged by the armies,
the retainers, the bandits, the youngest soldiers whooping a song of
adventure? Each hill was dignified by its own antiquity . . . yes, yes,
so it must be throughout the whole Mediterranean area. Sometime he
should go to the land of the Moors, sometime to Egypt, sometime to
Greece and the land of the Turks. He knew that in all those regions
he would find that same impress of centuries to reassure him. It
should have been frightening—the visible evidence, the reminder that

human beings had been in love or warring hereabouts for thousands of years—but it was not. It was heartening.

At fifteen Nathan was growing tall of spirit as already he had grown lengthy of body. He must study more and more, he must ask Mr. Halliburton to lay out an intensive course of reading, so that he could immerse himself in the great ocean of the past. The common truth now occurred to him for the first time (as in the first discovery of all common truths, it seemed very uncommon indeed, strictly personal, strictly his own attainment in thought): that there was no protection against the ills of the present day, no shield against dangers of the future so infallible as the wisdom which arises from a knowledge of the past. This was true, true! Nathan sang discordantly in celebration of this remarkable thought. So he rode on, singing. Would he serve the world as a philosopher or as an antiquarian? He didn't know, it didn't matter, he would learn and serve.

The sun came hotter each day as he neared Málaga. He had bought Tomás a hat of heavy straw, with slits for his ears to stick through. Nathan decided to ask his mother, with her artistic skill, to draw a pen sketch of Tomás thus decked out, and he could keep it always. In Coín, the bandit areas now far behind, he went shopping. Coín was a bustling town, despite its distance from the sea, and there were many shops; Coín was the second largest city in the province, according to the Atlas of Spain put out by Bachiller. Here Nathan found the woven harness on which he'd set his heart; delighted by ornate medallions and colored tassels he permitted himself extravagance which would have brought a perfunctory groan from Solomon Dreyfoos; but Olmedo the gardener would be proud as a duke. And Tomás—he tossed his head, he brayed seventeen times as soon as the new adornment was put upon him. Nathan bought colored sandals for the *camereras,* a trinket for each of the other servants, a medal of St. Christopher for his tutor, a work basket for his mother, a pill-box of chased silver, very old but with the soft glory of antiquity when it was polished afresh, for his father. On a stifling Sunday evening, just when strolling soldiers and sailors began packing the avenue to smile at girls and whisper compliments if they got a chance, Nathan rode into the courtyard in front of the huge house which they rented from Don Carlos Alessandri. He was home at last, he had wandered for weeks, he had known that he would find delight and the beginnings of maturity in his traveling. He had found them.

These treasures, invested through years, brought to Nathan a perpetual income—an appanage which could not be withheld from him by any lord chamberlain of the future. It accrued in Andersonville when sorely needed.

. . . Soldier, does stench arise in waves? There's honeysuckle tangling on a broken tower above the pale sea. Go and find it.

XLVII

Commonly the Federals believed that a month's furlough was the mandatory prize given to any guard who shot a prisoner. They did not realize how silly this was in its essence. They did not realize that if this were true the mortality from gunshot wounds would have ascended to fantastic heights and that not half the guards would have been left On Parapet, they would have been off enjoying furloughs. A majority of smaller boys among the Reserves were homesick to the point of hysteria, so were many old men. Also the sentry shacks were infested often with nit-brained incompetents who had been rejected by recruiters until this season of Georgia's downfall, and who grew as murderous under one sort of influence as they might have grown tractable under another.

Sharing crowded miseries were several hundred citizens who had been gathered up along with the military during raids and Yankee defeats. Most of these citizens were teamsters employed by the National Government; there were sutlers, some topographical engineers, a few male nurses, a few telegraph operators. One of the latter was shot and killed by Private Mackey Nall of the Fourth Georgia Reserves, late in July. The victim was a nearsighted man named Loughran, a native of Cincinnati, whose specs had been broken before ever he was counted Inside. Loughran's distorted vision could not estimate the fatal breadth of the deadline area, not when a section of scantling had been stolen during the night. Just after sunrise he blundered along the barrier. Mackey Nall screwed his face into a wad and shut his eyes as he fired. Citizen Loughran was dragged away with a ball in his backbone and he died in pain a few hours later, spared the longer pain of a hacking death from the consumption which had thinned him to a mere paring of humanity. Mackey Nall said, I blooded this weapon sure enough, when they stacked their arms on coming Off Parapet. Irby Flincher and Flory Tebbs both felt the tremor of curiosity and envy. How did it feel, to shoot a Yank?

By Jesus, Sojers, did you listen to him holler?

We heard him holler but—

A Yankee ain't but chicken-shit neath my feet! Reckon they all deserve killing.

Flory and Irby wished to know if Captain Wirz had been cross when he interrogated Mackey.

Oh, he wasn't mean about it no way. Just says, Was that prisoner past the deadline, and I said he sure as hell was. Then he says, God damn Yankees ought to stay away from the deadline, or something like that. You know how he talks, foreign like. Can't tell much about what he is speaking, saving when he cusses. Course, that's most of the time.

Some weeks later a dancing skeleton, clad only in dirty drawers which draped his nether portions, trotted within the region surveyed by Irby Flincher, trotted in ever widening circles. Scurvy-bent Yankees fell back to make space for his gyrations. His gray elf-locks waved, he waved great thin hands limply, bending them at the wrists, the hands flapped on high as he held his stiff arms aloft. This wild man's leapings carried him on a course wider and wider, bound to include the deadline if he continued to travel so. Irby cocked his musket. First one voice, then another, then more, took up the warning in a litany of pleas. Don't shoot, hey, don't shoot! He's crazy. Hey, guard, don't shoot, he's crazy, that's a *crazy man. Guard!* Irby lifted the heavy gun and sighted ahead of the crazy man, sighted at the deadline where he thought the man would strike, he waited for the victim to pass beneath his muzzle. The wild man danced ahead, a prisoner grabbed one of his arms, he spun twice around before he broke loose from the Yankee holding him, and then he came on, flapping his hands like fins. Don't shoot! Hey, that fellow's crazy! So Mackey Nall thinks he's Big Injun Chief, was the only thing in Irby's mind. Now you just bet I'll show that Mackey. His buck-and-ball gouged the Yank's ribby chest, front and back; there flew a smoky red spatter.

Oh, you son of a bitch! You son of a bitching little—

Thirty days for you, thirty *days,* you coward!

Give the little fart a furlough!

Joe Brown's Pets! Trundle-bed poops—

You'd break your neck running if anyone ever busted a cap behind you, you knee-high piss-ant!

They're all piss-ants. Think of shooting a crazy man that way!

That's old Weinlund from New Jersey, isn't it?

Yep, deader'n hell. That little cuss up there just shot him!

Only one of the other nearby guards was enraged by this abuse to the point of firing, and his charge made a harmless splash in the marsh beyond. Irby Flincher tried to reload his musket. His body was shaking worse than he had feared it might, he was spilling powder right and left. His jaws ground out the words, Mother-fucking old Yankee mudsills. . . .

That night Nall said, So you went and done it too.

Them was my orders: shoot to kill. I sure as hell kilt.

Their tentmate Duckworth read them a lecture, rambling and vague, based mainly upon Thou Shall Not Kill, but the children gave him little attention. They were bent on putting their equipment to rights in case the sergeant appeared, they were bent on feeding themselves and then proceeding to Uncle Arch Yeoman's store where they might barter some of their stolen sorghum for tobacco (they had sold all of their stolen tobacco to Yanks, except what portion they themselves had chewed).

If Thou Shalt Not Kill, old whiskers, what you a-doing up on that fence with a musket?

I never did want to come to be a soldier no way. I'm of a religious persuasion. They just took and fetched me! The old man let the asthma rock him, shook his tousled head, held his Bible closer to firelight. He could not read the Bible actually; yet lines of text stimulated his memory; his wife could read, he thought of her reading, he thought of verses he had learned or partially learned, they were mixed up, they were addled as his mind was addled. And now his wife was dead, many months dead. Oily tears ran in his wrinkles.

Floral Tebbs felt once more the weakness of the unaccomplished. Irby and Mackey invited him to accompany them through yellow-smelling twilight to Uncle Arch's, but there was a carelessness in the manner of their invitation. It was as if, Oh, shall we ask him? Oh, he might as well come along. Usually when the path to the road narrowed, one of the three had to fall back or go ahead, only two could walk abreast. Usually it was Floral and Irby Flincher who walked abreast, but now it was Irby and Mackey Nall. They Belonged, Flory Tebbs did not Belong. They had each Shot A Mudsill. He had not Shot A Mudsill.

. . . Got me a Yank today, cried Irby with nervous glee, and all the faces came closer through pocked light of tin lanterns. Men with beards, men with mustaches, men with heavy mannish voices— They treated Irby Flincher as a full-fledged adult, as one of note.

Where you shoot that Yankee—in the head or in the body?

Kill him quick, or did he flutter much?

There was a dark-faced young man from Savannah who was said to be of Spanish or French extraction, and who had certainly spent a great deal of time in prison before the drafters got him, for he could tell you every detail of a city prison's interior, sleeping arrangements, menu. I got me two already, declared Looey Blooey, which was what they called him. Always I aim for body, not the head. They wag their heads and you might miss.

I sure didn't miss today! Again attention swung toward Irby Flincher.

Uncle Arch doled out tobacco in payment for the sorghum. Them

Yankees steep themselves in wine, he said. Natural born drunkards, and let that be the fate of every drunkard! Oh, I know that some of you military people are engaged in liquor traffic, and as engagers in that traffic you are equally guilty as if them same drops of devil's brew had passed your own lips—

Uncle Arch, cried Irby, where'd a feller be apt to make the raise of a canteen of pine-top around here?

Now you get out from my place, you Irby!—I don't care how many Yanks you done kilt. I got my cattle-whip for protection, and I'll sure take it to you—

Aw, Uncle Arch, I was a-funning.

There hain't no fun in the sight of children with empty bellies, in the sight of women a-selling their virtue along city streets where them saloons are! Irby, you pay heed: doubtless twas the Almighty's own hand that pressed that trigger, not yourn. For them Yankees send ships to tropic ports, and just load them with nothing but rum. Look not upon the wine when tis red in your cup, and them are the words of our dear Lord. But them Yankees look upon the wine, and they sop it up like beasts, that they do.

Someone wished to know, Well, what about Jesus Christ, when He done changed that water into wine, like it says?

Heed me, you all! Twasn't no wine like people got today. Twas a special kind, kind of Bible wine, twouldn't fuddle a man's wits. Kind of grapejuice and tweren't wicked to drink it. But this here wine them Yankees have a-brewed and are a-drinking of, in this day and age— And brandy-peaches too! I mind the day a bunch of Yanks was marching past my little place here, bound for the stockade, and one of them actually had the evil intent to ask me did I have any peaches-in-brandy to sell, and he waved a greenback in my face. Little Irby, you're a good boy, and so is Mackey there, for you were avengers tried and true! If I wasn't so tight run I'd give you each a stick of candy. As tis, I'll give you one stick, and you can divide betwixt the two of you.

Here tis—cinnamon candy. He sniffed. . . . No, this one's a peppermint stick.

Shoot to kill when you got to shoot. Them rum-pots are one and all traffickers with Satan. I hear they got them a round thousand saloons in the great City of New York alone.

Uncle Arch Yeoman's opinion of the Yankees' drinking proclivities was formed during the raiders' heyday; he had not bothered to re-adjust it. The bulk of prisoners still sane, and with hopes and imagination still active, were much more concerned about the progress of Sherman's army than they were with bartering for pine-top.

A great many fresh fish had come in after the fierce engagements of late July; those battles were indecisive. A spindly but tough young prisoner named John McElroy declared tersely to fellow Illinoisans: Anything short of an absolute success is a disguised defeat. There was a general nodding of heads over this. Leroy Key and Seneca MacBean felt the same way; thus shrewder prisoners refused to entertain an extravagant notion that they might be freed at any moment. They heard of the defeat of Stoneman and his cavalry, they twisted their lips. They heard of the defeat of Union infantry at Etowah Creek; they spat, their silence was a snarl of acceptance of the inevitable. A few maltreated Rebel newspapers found their way Inside; the columns proved conclusively that Sherman's failure was already become history. Prisoners heard later that Sherman had raised the siege of Atlanta and fallen back to the Chattahoochee River. From that moment even men and boys who'd owned the most ardent spirit sat in bitterness.

Through dusk of earliest September, Floral Tebbs walked a beat immediately outside the headquarters of the post commander. While he was there certain momentous tidings penetrated to even his stunted intelligence. He heard a dispatch being read aloud and commented upon. Flory had no idea what Atlanta was like. It was a place. Savannah, Macon, Richmond, Washington, Americus, Albany, Milledgeville: these also were places, he had heard of them. The Government was there, he supposed, in any or all of those places. He had no idea what Sherman was like or how many troops fought under his command . . . Sherman was a Yankee. Flory supposed vaguely that Sherman commanded all the Yankees in the world (in this way there was a confusion of Sherman with Lincoln) but on overhearing the conversation of officers, and finally paying heed to it, Flory stood aware that Sherman was in Atlanta.

He brooded over this. He said nothing to comrades later, when they were eating bread and bacon, and trying to boil crust coffee in a leaky pail. Flory desisted from spreading the news at this point chiefly because he feared that the rest would not believe him—being jealous, as is humanly common, of the individual who possesses factual information unpossessed by others. Nevertheless Flory desired to cry disaster from his own private housetop. But he would want no one to press him for details, since he was not sure whether Atlanta was the most important city in Georgia or not. He was not sure where Georgia began and ended. He was not sure whether or not Atlanta might be the capital of the whole Confederate States and possibly some Yankee States as well.

Some people had talked jokingly of Sherman's having a tail. Some said that General Sherman had hoofs on his feet, that he galloped on all fours, bore sharp spreading horns, raped every Southern woman he came upon. Some said that he was a Negro in disguise. This might lend credence to the legend of wholesale rape, since all blacks were believed to be lusting secretly after white women (had Flory been certain just what lust might be, and how the deed of rape was practiced, he would have been more comfortable).

After the meager supper there came a change of guards On Parapet; Flory was told off to Post Number Four. He climbed to the platform and stood shivering and a little feverish with a cold which had been irking him. He dreamed of a vast Atlanta studded with domed buildings such as he had seen in the few magazine and newspaper illustrations which came his way, in the fewer books he'd ever peeped into. Through this cartooned ornate metropolis rioted columns of armed Yankees, and at their head loped the rapacious Sherman with six pistols on his belt and a knife clamped in his fangs. Yankees were bursting buildings apart, playing ball with babies tossed from bayonet to bayonet. . . .

The eight o'clock call came droning from stations beyond. It was relayed immediately from Station Number Three on Flory's right. Station Number Three, the guard called, eight o'clock and all's well. Flory stood with feet apart, frail hands clenched around his musket barrel. He put a special agony into the news he squawked abroad: Station Number Four, eight o'clock, and Atlanta's gone to hell!

Bewilderment of the next sentinel on platform Number Five (he was so astonished by Flory's squeal that he failed to respond vocally) went unheeded in the hubbub which burst beyond the deadline. It was as if Floral had jerked the cork out of a bottle from which acid froth, invisible but sputtering, fumed high.

Did you hear that, did you hear that? The guard called it! Yep, I heard. Hell, you can't trust those snot-nosed brats. But— Heard it . . . Atlanta's gone to hell! Must mean Atlanta's fallen to the Federals. . . . Weak cheer here, louder stronger yip in another direction. A deeper manlier yell spread from a hundred nearer shebangs and scraped-out pits, it blended up, spreading wider. It seemed that the entire aggregation, the compressed city-full of depraved tramps, was roaring. Flory might not know it, but he instigated numerous prayers— many spoken, many unvoiced, some pronounced formally and accompanied by hymns, by such people as Frank Ives and his devout circle.

(And by a man named Boston Corbett, who had been captured in Virginia and who entered the stockade on July twelfth. Boston Corbett was as staunch a patriot as he was a religionist. He prayed hourly that he would survive this ordeal because he wished to go on serving the Nation. He did not know that he would survive this ordeal, but he would survive it; again he would walk in blue uniform instead of this sloven's attire which dressed him now; and in a future hour a man would slay the President, and Boston Corbett would slay the man who slew the President. He would become a subject of fame, contradiction, praise, censure, envy, perplexity, abuse. He would stand serene in the same faith which prescribed a Holy prayer when he heard of Atlanta's fall.)

Guards were more suspicious than the men they guarded. Many refused to believe this news until they had checked with sergeants when sergeants appeared on their next rounds . . . even until sergeants checked with officers and came back to report between tobacco spurtings, yep, twas true: the story was all around the camps. Sherman had pounded into Atlanta. The Reserves might be manning these local embrasures any day now. The news was in such general circulation by the time Floral Tebbs came off duty that men forgot the fact that he had been the first to cry those tidings aloud; he was disappointed, tried to brag shrilly, was ignored.

The next day Flory's contingent was ordered On Picket instead of On Parapet; they spent doleful hours shifting about in the rain. It was customary for Sergeant Jester Sinkfield to seek the driest spot possible under these conditions; he apportioned duties to his men, and then went to sleep in the smokehouse on the Bile property, where he had cowed the black caretakers into submission. Once he was vanished the pickets knew that they would be safe from observation for many hours. They left the road and scooted for the trees. Flory, as junior of the lot, was made to walk through rain to a point of roadside vantage every now and then, in case an officer should decide to ride in that direction. Mackey and Irby had been told off into another detail. All of these fellow pickets in this detachment were taller, stouter, older, rougher than Flory Tebbs. Chill of the thick steady rain, slippery clay underfoot, the motionless dripping pines all spooky, and seeming lifeless in their very height and aloofness— These evils increased Flory's sensation of futility, of Not Belonging. He had not felt like this since first he was enlisted, he had not felt like this after gouging and biting his companions and winning the accolade of devil-festered little runt. If a stray Yankee had appeared before him on this day, Flory would have shot the Yankee instanter.

Flory, you go take a look.

Ah, I just took one.

No, I reckon not, not in an hour surely. Officer comes along and we get tromped on in a hurry. Now you go!

So once more down the path, once more scrambling on a short cut to the road's edge and the curve of the hill . . . wet and spineless, knowing he had no spine, not even wishing that he had one. God damn it to hell, those guards On Picket over next the depot got all the hats, fast as any prisoners got off the cars; and nowadays fewer and fewer Northerners came with hats. Here was this saturated ruin of quilted calico dripping its hated streams down Flory's neck, down his front. No longer was there a decent hat within the stockade which

might be traded for; they were gone; if you were a baby guard you
wore the calico monstrosity which had been given you by the Government, you could get no other. Twice Flory had attempted to steal felt
hats from fellow Reserves; once he was detected in the act of thievery,
once afterward. He got a beating on both occasions. Anybody could
whip Floral Tebbs except Irby and Mackey Nall; and now, since they
were exalted beyond him by their recent accomplishments, he feared
that they would try to whip him again. Flory's nose was running, the
steady bathing of the rain did not help his nose at all. He mourned
wordlessly, he wiped his nose on the cuff of his jacket where he had
wiped it before.

Got to do it. Got to.

There would be no peace or security for him on earth unless he did.
Whom should he shoot? Where? When?

Next time he went On Parapet—

Donner? Donner was the cook of the late Willie Collins. He it was
who'd fetched, in payment for saleratus, the buttons with hens on
them which now adorned Flory's makeshift uniform. Donner had not
died with the ringleaders, he had been sentenced to the chain gang,
had served his sentence, was now become a sniveling beggar, lethar-
gic, dropsical. Once he had been savage, surly, once he had overawed
the other prisoners, had preyed upon weak ones. Now he tottered
toward his doom unwashed, unfed, unfeared, unloved. Sometimes his
wheezing voice reached to the hearing of Floral Tebbs when Flory
stood on his platform. Hi . . . guard . . . member me? Donner? Man
who got you those buttons . . . you member . . . with eagles, like
you wanted? Please . . . give me . . . give me. . . .

Yank, said Flory haughtily, what you got to trade?

Me? I got . . . nothing . . . please . . . give me a gristly bone,
maybe? Or you got . . . lard, like?

Can't make no trade less you got something to trade.

Got . . . maybe . . . bacon? One day . . . seen you eating a
chunk of pork up there. . . .

Now, listen, you old greasy mechanic you— Get away from here
fore I take a pot-shot at you!

The brim of the quilted hat was folded under clogging rainfall, it
was like an old woman's sunbonnet, heavier than any old woman's
sunbonnet, more grotesque. Distantly Flory heard the creaking of
wagons on an adjacent road beyond the trees, the creaking of wagons
being hauled up the hill with their loads of dead bodies. Rain seemed
thinner now, you could hear things, you couldn't hear the mutter of
Andersonville and it seemed good to get loose from it; but you observed the faraway snap of a whip, you heard the driver ordering his
team, Now you boys walk off on your tails!

—Donner. Why not shoot Donner, next time he came doddering around?

—Shoot somebody.

—Some damn Yankee, some old bastard Yankee.

—Or just fire at random, maybe somebody would get hit? If Captain Wirz demanded to know why Flory had fired, he could say, Twas an accident. That old hammer just cotched on my clothes, sir. It did.

No! For the other boys had fired deliberately, they had aimed at specific individuals, had picked them out in their sights. They had stood like soldiers defending a barricade (and certainly they were in an act of defense, as sworn to serve. They were defending Georgia against the horde of hated savages within that fence). Mackey and Irby had done a studied purposeful thing; each of them had; they won praise for it. Floral Tebbs might never hold up his head beneath its sagging soaked drippings of calico, he might never claim to be a man until his finger squeezed the trigger and the charge split the air and split an enemy's body. . . .

What you see this time, Flory?

Never saw nothing. Heard some wagons yonder.

Must have been on the graveyard road.

By Jesus God, Norrel, I did think I smelt something for sure!

Hain't you ever been On Picket hereabouts before, Barty? You ought to been here on a hot day like a couple weeks since. By God, them damn Yanks did stink meaner than a bucket of turds.

You know, they ought to plant them deeper.

Sure ought. You hear how them hogs got to rooting?

How I would hate to have a hog of mine feeding off'n Yanks. Twould poison the fat on his back for sure.

O laughter, and rain renewing again, and wind beginning to stroke the treetops; the clay slippery as lard beneath your sorry shoes when you walked on it; and awareness of long shallow trenches beyond the pines, and the thought of what lay compressed there.

The storm developed, beat, lifted, went away. Pickets straggled back to their proper station. They lounged, chewing quids until Sergeant Sinkfield appeared headachy and sullen because he had slept too long. Everyone's spirits, except the spirits of Flory Tebbs, rose when they had marched back to camp. Under a dripping tent fly sat that rarest of his species in any army—a paymaster. Several delighted old men assisted him in counting out that portion of the Confederacy's substance which might accrue to this command according to whatever records were kept in the frightened town of Macon.

Major Lonny. The good-natured voice of the colonel. (The colonel was thirty years old. His voice held a drawling yet spirited quality. A pigeon-toed barefooted Afric in a gray jacket with gilt buttons—

This proud small servant, whose name was Little Jolly, led the colonel
to his desk, led him home, led him to the water closet. There had been
a flash, a popping, a quick searing like boiling milk being poured
over the colonel's eyeballs— That happened more than one year
before, when Captain Charles Whitlow Overcash of the Eleventh
Georgia led his company across the Emmetsburg Road in Adams
County, Pennsylvania; and now he was promoted, he served in the
Georgia Reserves. Aha.) Major Lonny, I think it would be wise for
you to take this money at once and pay our troops now on duty at
Camp Sumter. Most of them have not been paid since May or June.
The general declares (Colonel Overcash laughed lightly, always he
laughed easily and lightly; he was glad to be alive, he had not expected to remain alive) that we are not in funds, shouldn't spare a
farthing for soldiers' pay, and so on. But he has finally left the matter
to my own discretion; and I am informed that additional disciplinary
problems will face the commanders of these units unless the men
have, very soon, something to chink together in their pockets. Excuse
me, Major—did I say chink? Rather I meant something to wad and
squeeze together in their pockets. General Sherman might greet us
across the breakfast board some fine morning; and it's better that the
troops should have this prettily printed currency than that Sherman
should. Goodness sakes, Major Lonny, Sherman doesn't need the
money! Why, he must be independently wealthy by now—he and all
of his bummers. My own Uncle Billy—*not* Uncle Billy Sherman,
most emphatically—has a nice place up in Floyd County. I mean to
say, sir, he *had* a fine place. And he's standing there in trepidation,
watching the bummers go by with all the livestock, the few remaining
head of livestock which the niggers declared they had hidden safe
away in the woods, and naturally they hadn't. Uncle Billy is fearing
for the safety of his house, when up rides a good-looking Yankee on
horseback and says, quick as scat, Insure your house for fifty dollars.
Yes or no? . . . I'm afraid the answer must be No, says Uncle Billy,
for I haven't fifty dollars handy. Got thirty? says the Yank. You know
how they are—very deft at business, most definitely shrewd, able to
drive a bargain; unlike we lazy Southrons. Haven't got thirty, says my
unfortunate Uncle Billy. I am the proud possessor of sixteen dollars
Confederate, and one handsome gold watch, a lady's watch, designed
for dangling on her pretty bosom, but now reposing in my vest pocket,
sir; and formerly it belonged to my Aunt Jonnie Lee. Will that suffice,
Mister Insurance Broker? Entirely adequate, says the Yank. You may
now consider your house as fully covered by insurance. Well, that
Yank posted two armed men at the front gate and two at the rear,
until the bummers were gone from there; and thus they did not burn
the house of my Uncle Billy, although they burnt the Izards' and the
Witherspoons' and the Foxworths', who were apparently improvident

folk with straitened vision which did not permit them to see the wisdom of such a transaction, sir. Ah, where was I, Major Lonny? Digressing again, I fear. Digression is the curse of my life, sir. You will take this cash, proceed to Andersonville, and pay through the last day of the month just past. All ranks. That is an order. My adjutant will provide you with travel orders and, of course, the rolls. I think they are very long rolls indeed. That is a pun, Major, a gentle one. *Long Roll,* you see. I must repeat that to my wife this evening. Little Jolly, where are you?

I's here, said the tiny voice from the floor beside him.

Little Jolly, what are you doing?

I's playing with them big glass marbles you done give me, Mastah Colonel Charley, sir.

At long taw or short taw, Little Jolly?

Sir?

Merely a jest, Little Jolly. The terminology of marbles. That will be all, Major Lonny.

. . . And soon the colonel knew that it was growing late, other people were leaving, he heard the jingle of sword chains, he heard goodbyes given at the end of another work-day, heard feet going out. And soon the black child led him through a door, down three steps, along a cool place where he could feel coolness, down six more steps, across a place, down five more steps; then the colonel felt bricks under his shoes. . . . Horse smell, the voice of Benjamin who served as coachman, the metal step, the metal rail to grasp, the squeak and settling of the decrepit vehicle under the colonel's tall strong weight. Soon the colonel was at home, soon his daughters came to him. He played with their curly hair and he said, It's Patsy.

No, I'm Ginny.

Nothing of the kind, Miss. Possibly you are Linda?

Ha, ha, ha, and gleeful shrieks coming up around him, as if he stood in the middle of a pleasant-smelling and pleasant-sounding bouquet of little girl shrieks. Ha, ha, ha, oh Daddy, we swapped, we changed, Ginny and I changed our ribbons, and Mother did Linda's hair in *pigtails* just to tease you, Daddy.

Then the smell of meat and corn gems, and roasting ears also, and pungent taste of boiled greens, and ripe melons, and hot crust coffee. And chatter, and Sue reading the news to him, and there was so little of good in the news; yet somehow it seemed like good news even when it was bad. Later the yawning, and the saying that tomorrow was another day; and soon the long trip to the chamber, and preparation for retiring. The mutual prayer. At last the lying down in dark together . . . strange way which the blind seem to have, of detecting the difference between daylight and dark.

Sue, pet, is there a moon?

Tis a very new moon. . . .

Captain Sue, I thought as much. Captain Sue, have you employed those horrid curl-papers again?

No, sir, I was under strict orders not to do so.

Delighted to know that you obeyed orders. You may be permitted to approach the Colonel . . . indeed, you may be permitted to approach even closer . . . ah, that's better.

Her body shaking suddenly, her grief wetting his naked arm, her hot wild young wet grief.

Sue . . . after a time . . . don't.

Charley— I—can't—

Is it because I'm—? You said you wouldn't, again.

Tisn't! No, no— Oh, Charley, what if they should come *here?* To Macon? What would they do to *you?* To—to the girls? To—me?

I think we'd all be safe, my dear. Very safe indeed. There are some decent people among them.

And tears to come, and soothing and exploration and then the easy bliss . . . increasing power of bliss, the burning gasping glee of bliss, the ease, the wiping away of hurts of war or any other hurts. Colonel Charles Whitlow Overcash went to sleep.

Major Lonny, acting as paymaster, went to Andersonville.

For some hours the poverty-stricken Reserves edged past the extemporized office consisting of a broken field desk cobbled together by the addition of one leg which wouldn't fold, consisting also of several barrels turned on end— They presented themselves, smooth-chinned or bald-headed, bearded dreamer or young dunce, to the paymaster's extemporized family. They signed for their money or made their marks; there were more marks than names, for some of the signatures were little more than marks although the individuals insisted that they could write, and read too. Fragile scrip was put into their hands, more than three thousand folds of it, when all was done. This distribution had begun when Floral Tebbs and his party were On Picket and was completed by lantern light; thus all contingents of the guards On Picket and On Parapet had an opportunity to draw their pay, excepting those unhappy individuals in the guardhouse. (In the latter cases commanders signed for the men; some of the men would never see their money.) Flory had fifty-two dollars Confed in his pocket. It didn't remain in his pocket for long. He kept taking the money out and looking at it.

You going to wear that money out, you Flory, fore you get a chance to spend it. This from the gangling Mackey, who was scarcely less excited about his own pay.

Aw.

Flory had never owned fifty-two dollars in any kind of currency before; almost he had never owned fifty-two cents. He should have received fifty-four dollars for a part of May, for June, July and August. (Early in June the rate of pay for infantrymen was raised from eleven to eighteen dollars per month.) But fines stood against his name: on two occasions he had been fined one dollar for misuse or abuse of Government equipment. Now he wished that he had been better behaved.

Think I know where, said Mackey in concealed excitement.

Ask that there tall what-you-call-him, said Irby Flincher. You know, Sojer, from Company D. Jim Waller—that's his name. He went there recent, and knows where to go.

Think we could find it in the dark?

Maybe steal a lantern. Twill be dead dark soon. But let's ask that feller Waller.

They spoke in riddles, and Flory Tebbs might not know what was going on, although he clung to his comrades. He talked boastfully of cleaning out Uncle Arch Yeoman's candy jars, and maybe the tobacco box as well; he complained with the others that they were not paid nearly enough, the Government ought to allow them more money now that the purchasing power of Confed had shrunken so badly. He talked of buying a bottle of pine-top, or maybe only half a canteen of it. But Irby Flincher and Mackey Nall continued to dwell apart from him, he could not reach them, they whispered at times, they laughed loudly about some joke in which Flory was not asked to share.

Ah, said old Duckworth, man might know what you was up to. Get off with some idle young strumpet, and act like Sodom and Gomorrah!

Flory wondered who Sodom and Gomorrah might be; certainly they were not in Company E; they might, like the man Waller, be members of Company D.

Duckworth preached at them, but received only nose-thumbings from the unregenerate. Best you should give the bulk of your substance to the Lord, and prepare yourselves for His coming! For He's a-coming, make no doubt of that. And where will you be when we all get called to the Judgment Seat, lined up maybe like we done today in front that paymaster?

Aw, go lay an egg, you old Duck.

Boys, I give no care how you revile me and spit upon me. For well I know I'm Saved; but when the flames of the Devil start a-reaching and a-grabbing after you, then will you regret! Great shall be the lamentation of you all, with wailing and gnashing of teeth!

Irby gnashed his teeth, Mackey combed through his lore of obscenity which was vast though hackneyed. Floral followed the other boys when they left the tent; he fought to hold back tears; he was scorned, undesired, he had not Shot A Mudsill. But, by God, next time he went On Parapet. . . .

Look who's a-coming, said one of them, and they turned and stood challengingly in the gloom. What you want, Flory?

Where you bound, fellers? What's ado?

Hell, Irby, we're done in.

Naw, let him come along.

Bet he couldn't even get it up, and they both laughed loudly.

I could, when I was his age.

Well, bet on it. Bet you a dollar?

Bet! So we might as well take him with us, so's we can see. You got your pay in your pants, Flory?

Got it, cried Flory. He slapped his pocket. Now, please to tell me where we're bound? To Uncle Arch's?

Naw, naw, naw, not to Uncle Arch's. Mackey tried to mimic Flory's treble. And twill cost you at least five dollars Confed, or so tis said. First we're going over here to Company D to find that man Waller.

Irby Flincher added in a whisper, Then we got to get us a lantern, cause we don't know the way around outside the post too well. And we got to get past the sentries.

Ho, cried Flory, hain't no trick to that! Reckon I know every coon-trot in this country.

Lanterns were guarded jealously, people were forbidden to remove them from any tent or shack where such illumination was permitted. But Flory Tebbs thought suddenly of the paymaster. That major, he whispered to his companions; and they stood to listen with what amounted almost to respect. Major Lonny had not yet left the camp, they had seen him strolling past with other officers while they cooked their evening meal. There was no northbound train expected during the evening, and if a southbound train arrived with fresh prisoners at this late hour it couldn't depart until all the prisoners had been counted from it. Hence the paymaster must be spending the night, hence a tent must have been made available.

While Irby Flincher sought Private Waller, Flory and Mackey hunted out the paymaster's tent (there was such a tent, indeed) after questioning only a few people. It was called the Visitors' Tent, and stood slightly northeast of their own camp, among pines near the path which led to the soup house. The sentry guarding this region was stationed even farther to the northeast. Flory and Mackey snaked silently among the trees and came up to the Visitors' Tent from the rear, and saw no shadow walking on dirty dark canvas. A faint light glowed. Mackey made cat sounds, then growled like a dog. Nothing moved in the tent. Flory went under the rear canvas and, sure enough the paymaster must be in residence, for there was his desk dumped in the corner, complete with the mended leg sticking up and straps buckled tightly. Flory thought of currency, vast slabs of it, still to be paid to other troops; but doubtless those scabby black bags were now well-guarded at the commander's headquarters. He blew out the lantern, he and Mackey carried it away in triumph, and met Irby Flincher at a pre-arranged rendezvous in the ravine below the fort.

We got to watch sharp. Sentries on the depot road.

Well I know! Stood there often my own self.

You tell me, said Flory, what direction we're bound?

Over towards the car tracks, then left.

Flory had learned Right and Left since he joined the Fourth Reserves; he had never been absolutely certain just which was his right hand, and his left, before. Such designations were not applied at the Widow Tebbs's house. One said, Under there. No, tother side. One said, It hain't on the shelf next that corn. It's nigh that rag lamp alongside the string of dried pumpkin.

Flory said, Left? Then we got to get past the depot and past them quartermaster's offices and stores.

And car tracks go smack betwixt them buildings and the guards' hospital, so's there's bound to be sentries.

Just you leave that to me, said Flory pridefully. He led the way through sloping woodland toward the northeast fork of the Sweetwater branch, but avoided a swamp which spread between the three small forks. They skipped across the ooze and continued west up a fourth miniature fork which began at a slow-rising spring amid hummocks near the railroad. They crossed the tracks and circled warily south and west beyond General Winder's quarters; there were lights burning in the quarters, a dog barked protractedly but the dog did not come close.

You taking us plumb to Alabama, Flory?

Now just you watch. Well do I know this region. Hellfire, Sojers, I was raised here!

He could not guess their destination, or what excitement awaited; it was enough that he moved respected and depended upon. He hadn't shot a prisoner yet, but he would shoot one perhaps tomorrow. Meanwhile he seemed to have regained the stature which he had assumed when he fought his friends, when he bit off a portion of Mackey's ear. He fancied that possibly some of the other older guards had decided to buy a pig with their riches; and Irby and Mackey were invited to partake of this delight at some secret wilderness barbecue, because of their prowess in killing prisoners. Yes, that could be the answer to this puzzle, easily. The bed of fire glowing a welcome, scorched dripping body of the pig held up on its spit, scent of burnt hair and cracklings newly made, the bottles of liquor handed round. Well, pine-top gagged him and burnt his little throat, but once more he might try to drink it. He was a man and a half, by God. Or would be.

Now he ain't a-guiding us to Alabama, Irby. We must be halfway
to Egypt or somewheres.

Jesus Mighty!

What is it?

God damn stump. I like to broke my leg! Flory, you get us out this
here forest or I'll kick your balls off.

Light the lantern, Sojer.

No, too many guards yonder. Flory, you—

Them lights ahead, said Floral Tebbs, ought to be that quartermaster place. We get around there safe, we can come square out on
the railroad.

I think the little bastard's right.

Sure as death I am right.

They were not challenged, no sentinels walked near, they left stores
and offices behind them and floundered through vines until they could
creep into a low ditch and then up to ties and rails beyond. Reckon
I guided you in the right fashion, cried Flory triumphantly.

Reckon you did. Waller says it's just down the tracks past here,
then take first road to the right. He says usual you see a lamp a-burn-
ing in the house.

Flory stopped so abruptly that the others bumped him. They swore,
stepped aside, looked at him through vague damp starlight, for the
slice of moon was fallen below the trees. Where we a-going? He
added, Sojers, but the word became a gulp and a grunt.

He's scairt.

I said he was too blame small. Couldn't get it up—

Flory, they wanted to know, and spoke jeeringly between their
giggles. Flory, did you ever poke a girl?

His voice was shaking. Whwhwhat's that?

You know. Give her a good poking, where it does the most good.

No, I never, he managed to confess through puny bewilderment.
Never did.

Aw-haw! I win my dollar.

But—where we—going to do it? Whwhwhat girl?

Oh, she ain't exactly a girl, guess she's a growed-up lady with kids
and truck, but Waller says she does take a good poking and likes it
right well. Hell, that's where lots the growed-men guards go. Even
officers as well.

There's a nigger wench along that road up northwest of the depot,
said Mackey. But they say this white lady is better. But you better
have that five-dollar shinplaster handy. I still think I'll win that dollar
off'n Irby, sure enough.

They started down the tracks. Flory stood fastened to mud and
gravel between the ties. After a few minutes he could not make out
the slight shapes which were his companions, going on ahead with the

tinkling lantern, seeking the lane which led to the Widow Tebbs'. Flory trembled in momentary spasm, a taste of his supper came into his throat. He had a wish to put his head upon his mother's lap and cry and cry and cry. Sometimes he had done that, when he was little, when he was hurt; he had done that when he was bitten by a stray dog, he had done it when he was watching workmen on this railroad and a stone flew from under a pick and hit him on the cheek. When he was hurt, his mother had been kind to him, often. She'd say, Now, you hain't kilt. Just stop that bawling, baby boy, cause twon't get you no place. You want bread-and-lasses? Well, I'm a-going to fix you some right now, and she had been tender if coarse-spoken when her flabby hands lifted her apron or petticoat and wiped his face.

Irby and Mackey were gone ahead into the night. It was not far to the side lane. Once they seemed to halt, as if waiting for Flory. They moved on after calling some taunt intended for his ears. Flory turned toward the north. For a time he tried his old trick of walking on the rail but he kept falling off. He trudged on, and then there were men with guns immediately ahead of him. He toppled into the ditch and lay motionless until the men had vanished. It could have been that these were sentries patrolling the area of stores and offices. No lights in any of the buildings by this time. Even Uncle Arch's store was dark when Flory reached the depot's vicinity. He walked wearily into camp, slipping past guards who were probably asleep. Before he reached the wall tent which was Home he could hear old Duckworth's snores.

Mackey Nall was not so fortunate. When later he and Irby Flincher tried to creep to camp they were challenged. Irby made his escape among trees, but Mackey was seized and a pass was demanded of him. He had no pass; thus he was marched to the guardhouse. . . . Irby crawled into the tent as silently as he could, a few minutes later, and when Flory coughed the other boy could tell by the manner of his coughing that Flory was awake.

You little prick, muttered Irby.

Just bet I ain't. Want me to come over and rub your eye out like I nearly done afore?

Leastways you never have got you a Yank, and I did, by Jesus God.

Irby. Did you—? Whereabouts is Mackey?

He got cotched and jailed. I damn near did too.

Irby, did you—do that—? Poking that lady—?

Hell, we never got no chance. Blame yard was just full of folks a-waiting their turns.

The bulk of their company drew Parapet the next morning and marched straggling along the gummy road toward the east, and deployed by uneven files down the path which led from station ladder to station ladder. When he had climbed in his turn Flory found himself on the platform of Station Number Forty-one, and saw that Irby was a few rods distant on Number Forty-two. Irby Flincher's inherent viciousness had resolved itself into a combined hatred of Yankees, superior officers, comrades. Honestly Irby could have told no one which he loathed the most (because in fact he despised himself most of all; and thus like all who find themselves despicable he turned the weapon of revulsion out and away, waved it blindly, brandished it at God and Nature) but he seemed declaring in each twitch of his moody eyes or his blobber-lip that Flory was less worthy than dung, less to be admired than a maggot. Irby's studied contempt reached along ninety feet of jagged post-tops even when it was unvoiced. When it was voiced it took the form of rusty barbs, fish-hooks twisted through Flory's skin.

—Whyn't you hold your gun proper?

—Hey, you Flory! Lost me a dollar, you did!

—Shouldn't never have bet you could get it up.

Sergeant Sinkfield, swaggering in the path on a round of inspection, looked up and told Irby to shut his trap. This rebuke administered to his tormentor should have delighted Floral Tebbs but he was plunged too deeply into the pitch of despair. His nostrils were raw and dripping, his soul was sodden as the mat of motionless gray clouds overhead, he had had no appetite for breakfast. He gazed stupidly at hobbling currents of prisoners, unable to sense their demented activity or inquire about it, unable to ask a question of himself.

A fresh rumor of exchange had come into the stockade, it had been peddled by Little Red Cap. Promptly this rumor gave birth to many little rumors and they were waved, hugged, embroidered, waved hysterically again, as if no such gossip had ever been voiced to be accepted by the credulous, to poison them in time. New (and therefore vigorous) prisoners talked together volubly, slapped one another on the back, pumped one another by the hand, spoke of Akron and Fort Dodge and Mattoon and New Haven. Surviving veterans (therefore they were cynical men) who had managed to retain a fair portion of their strength, swallowed momentarily beneficent pills of legend which brought—momentarily again—vitality into frames and minds long clutched by the drug of cynicism. Their eyes shone despite any discipline they tried to impose in order to keep their eyes from shining; they went with briskness to shebangs of friends; they said, Have you heard? Well, I don't believe it— But— Thought I'd tell you— Somebody heard Wirz talking in his office— Ten detachments going out right away. No, seven. No, six. It was a letter to General Winder from the Rebel war department. Everybody who can walk, going to Savannah. No, Charleston. Paroled. No, exchanged. Going to take them on boats to Maryland. They're going to remove all the sick. No, it's just us well ones. Have you heard—? Did you hear about—?

Men who were in the early stages of crippling illness arose and walked as if a gentle Stranger had strolled among their couches of rags and earth and had said, Walk; you can take up your bed if you want to, you can leave it behind. But— Arise and walk. Boys who lay infecting the spirits of the rest with slow or hasty decay— These boys got up on their haunches, they tried to stand and they could not stand but still they tried to stand. Ten detachments going out tonight! No, tomorrow. No, I got it from a feller who got it from a guard. Got it from a baker, got it from Lieutenant Davis, got it from— Going to take out all the cases that have to be carried and take them on a ship to New York— Take them to Philadelphia. Paroled. No, exchanged. Six detachments to be counted out, day after tomorrow.

Going to make an exchange at New Berne, North Carolina! Make an exchange at Norfolk. Cooking extra rations for eight detachments to take along on the cars. Sherman's got too close. Sherman's ten miles away, only thirty miles away, Sherman's only a hundred miles away. Sherman sent a flag of truce and told the sons of bitches that he'd execute every Rebel citizen behind his lines if the Rebs open on this stockade with those damn guns. Lincoln sent a telegram to Richmond and told the Rebs that if they open on this stockade he'll have artillery open on the prison at Rock Island, the prison in Chicago, Sandusky, Elmira, Point Lookout. . . . Five detachments going out tonight, twelve detachments going out tomorrow.

Boys who were crawling got up and hobbled on scurvy-tightened limbs, boys who were motionless began to crawl. It could have been that the dead already deposited in the dead row began to roll away from it . . . there seemed motion and flexing among stiff meager bodies on the hill yonder even as shovels tamped them down. It's true, it's honest. They're going to nail up a notice this afternoon on the North Gate! A Rebel general's coming inside to make the announcement. Two detachments going out every day from now on. Going North on the cars, going North on ships, going to Florida, going to New Orleans. All the sick, all the well.

Alice had been forgotten, Mother had faded into infinity, Etta had become too misty to be remembered, Sister Kate had become meaningless; so had Father, so had Brother Rufus, so had Shep, so had Muggins the cat. So had Home faded, so had ginger cake and cucumber pickles and the thud of the village fire gong and the bubbling laughter of a certain child. Amazingly these glories reappeared as the rumor went firing to the Island in the marsh, as it went banging against the far north wall, bouncing back to be reflected from the old raider area near South Street. Home became not only a long neglected, long vanished prettiness; it became a certainty, alive, resounding, tinted, embellished, you could taste and smell it. Prisoners gathered by dozens where before they had stood by twos and threes. Now they were pushing by hundreds in the wide rutted streets. A man went mad suddenly and ripped the blanket which was the roof of his solitary hovel, he said that he would need it no more; a boy went mad and sailed his precious half-canteen at a guard. Someone cried that an official notice had been posted on the inside of the North Gate, and throngs went loping or tottering to see the notice for themselves; although the gate had not been opened, no Reb of importance or unimportance had come Inside, no notice had been nailed.

To this trotting and outcry the ears of Floral Tebbs might have been sealed, his eyes stared unseeing. He did not comprehend or even observe. A waif conceived in misery, born in misery, chewing misery for a ration, he appeared to shrink within himself while his scrawny structure remained immovable. He was blighted before he began, yet this blight was unrecognizable and so could not be cured; he felt the blight but could not name it. Bruise of stone, no meal in a lean season, dog bite, nail in his foot, Coral's crutch lamming into his back, nose running now, Sinkfield's wide hand slapping and slapping, bellyache from eating green peaches, wet and weak in the rain, not enough cover on a cold night, no pennies for candy when he craved pennies for candy: these had made his life, a life marred in the making. It seemed that his slight rubbery soul left his body with the explorative dash of a rat emerging from its hole—uncertain dash toward the chicken coop, dash toward the swill barrel—ha, is that a step, a threatening sound, a smell? Then dart to the burrow again and hide. But while his soul was free and vibrating aimlessly it looked back and saw Flory's shape upon the sentry station, and noted with disgust how bedraggled was that shape, how leaking the nostrils and hacking the cough, how filthy the hat and coat sleeve . . . ha! Into the rat hole again. Tattered rat soul scooting into tattered rat body.

Irby Flincher twisting every device for torture.

—Hey, you Flory. Want to go a-poking tonight?

—Fraid to get grabbed by the sentries like old Mackey.

—Hell, yes. Reckon you're scairt of your own farts.

—No guts. Never will have.

—Hain't got guts enough to shoot a Yankee.

The voice of some unknown ancestor lifted in strength from the past, rang out from an unknown unmarked grave (or perhaps it was a genteel grave with a good name on it, guarded by marble) and spoke one word to Flory, and he heard. The word was *Assert*. He did not know this word, had never used it, but it commanded him and he obeyed.

His bony pallid left hand tightened around the wood and metal of musket barrel and stock. He lifted steadily with his left hand, and his bony pallid right hand slid down to clamp below the gun's lock. He strained upward with both hands and tilted the barrel until the butt was at his right shoulder; then he pressed it back, tighter and tighter, until he held notion that he was grinding flesh and little sinews there. Pick out a big one, he told himself. By God, yes, biggest damn Yankee in sight. Now his left hand was far forward, the first finger of his right hand curling past the trigger guard. His thumb wrenched on high to heave against the hammer, he saw the cap exposed on the tube, saw the open rear sight. Slice of the front sight moved into its groove in gentle and orderly fashion. Twin sights strolled here and there, settling first on one man, then on another; and Irby Flincher was hullooing from Station Number Forty-two and another guard was hullooing from Station Number Forty. Also prisoners had seen Flory aiming the gun, and they began to run, to duck and dodge. A tall dark-haired prisoner, a very tall very dark-haired prisoner, turned quickly from the group with which he had been conversing and stood rooted in one fatal fractional second of immobility. The sights were roosting on his face, and he was not more than thirty yards away, in a bee-line, in line of bore and line of sight. *Poom.*

XLVIII

Oh, ho, ho, ho. Flory was halfway down the ladder when his arms dissolved, seemed to lose connection with his trunk; he fell the rest of the way, he lit on his side but with those useless arms stretched above his head, and so he did not break one of those loose useless arms. His cheek was mashed against the butt of the gun which had drifted from his hands while still he wavered upon the platform and thus he arose with blood upon him. He did not understand, he did not know that it was his own blood, he thought it was blood from the tall prisoner which gushed to that supreme height as thrown by the nozzle of a hose (once he had seen Mr. Claffey spraying fruit trees—the hose stretched out, and two slaves worked the handles of a pump which brought solution from a tank upon a wagon, and another slave dragged at the hose, and the masked Mr. Claffey himself held the nozzle, directing poison against trees. The masked Mr. Claffey was terrifying, utterly. Floral cut for home).

As now he ran.

Yells of other guards, the demons' yells from within the pen, were no deterrent; they were a wind propelling him. He blew before it like a wisp of cotton blowing, forgotten cotton spilled from cart or picking bag in the earlier childhood of Floral Tebbs when cotton was raised in those parts . . . but the long white wisp would soon find lodgment against a weed, Floral lodged nowhere.

Palisades were behind him, rifle pits were behind, the star fort loomed on the left. Someone grabbed at Flory's arm but he tore his arm away. Hey there, Sojer! Bubby, what the devil—? His calico hat was gone. Drip from his nose ran over his blubbering mouth and tasted salty, and went dripping off his chin. Sheds and tents of the south camps lay to the right, a detail of guards marched in the narrow road directly ahead. The boy swung blindly and darted between tents, and then the long shape of the guards' hospital was before him, and the railroad stretched behind it; soon Flory's feet found the ties although he could not feel his feet striking anything, not even when they blundered against the rail and when they were tripped by the rail and when he fell across the rail, and then arose and went jogging.

He did not feel his body striking the railroad track when he fell, he did not feel himself getting up and running on. *Oh, ho, ho, ho, ho.*

Close after him bayed every wolf of which he'd ever heard, close crept every rattlesnake and mad dog and varmint of fact or fancy. The tall Yankee trotted in the pack, shooting out his blood at every pace; and there were Irby Flincher, Sergeant Sinkfield, ghosts from a graveyard, gators from the marshes. Woogums trotted there.

When he was very small he'd played with some of the blacks from the Claffey and Bile plantations. Long since they'd all been sold away —Hector and Isaiah and fat brown Brutus and the rest—but terrors they'd contrived were here pursuing, skeletal hands were reaching.

We not go no further down this way, Mass Flory.

Nossuh! Not down them dead trees, all that black water—

Huh, nig? Why not?

Woogums get us sure.

Huh, nig? What's Woogums?

Close they pushed together and the smell of their color was around him as he listened, and as he cried loud scorn and said that there were no such critters as Woogums in the swamp.

. . . Yes, boy! The truth, yes, it the truth, Mass Flory! Woogums all live down there, I hear growed niggers tell bout Woogums— And my old lady, she belong Mistuh Ganwood fore she belong Mistuh Ira Claffey, we both belong Mistuh Ganwood, and she say I not never go down them bog ways, for Woogums get me sure. All the Ganwood niggers tell bout Woogums. They got eyes red like coals' fire, and big long teeth like bobcat, and they hands they come from the grave, all bone, just bone.

. . . Old Woogum he come in cabin at night, he get real hungry, and he like eat baby— Baby girl he like pretty well, but baby boy he relish lot more! He like white meat pretty well, like black meat better! Old Woogums they live in hollow tree yonder, and they got big cave place back behind all that black water; big storehouse like place, all just smack full dead children they keep for they dinner. Woogums they howl in the nighttime, sometime howl all night long. Well, I hear Woogums howl in the daytime too, you Brutus. You hear me, Hec—

. . . Woogums got long nail on they dead bone finger like great big cat claw, and they reach right through and rip out you belly. Hi, that truth! And old Woogum he all gray like death. Death gray color. They keep old buzzard in cage for have cage-bird, and they teach old buzzard how sing like lark.

And Woogums teach old buzzard how howl, too! Like Woogums.

And Woogums grow real tall—

Yes, boy. Yi! And make himself small like mouse, so he get in your cabin; then he get big again. And he eat you, he *pick your bones.*

Out of the dreariness of six long years the mysterious voices talked in Flory's memory; so there were Woogums behind him now, along with the Yankee whom he'd shot, and the other masses of mad Yankees whom he'd guarded . . . ghosts his half-sister had told him about . . . every terror which could creep or dance or gnash its teeth. *Oh, ho, ho, ho, ho.* It would seem that he had no breath left for sobbing, no breath left to feed his body while he ran; yet he sobbed still, he ran.

Ma, he tried to shriek as he staggered into the dooryard past leaning vine-draped palings. Ma . . . he made but a drawn-out M sound, a Mmmmmm, a mumble barely heard. Zoral had gathered mule-apples left by some mule belonging to a customer, and this dung was upon the step. Again Floral slipped and fell. Again he did not feel the hurt; he bobbed up, gasping, went through space, struck the side of the open door with his shoulder. He staggered back against the door and it crashed shut under the impact. Then Flory was in the bedroom. Laurel was not there, Coral was not there, the Widow Tebbs was not there (oh, faintly, distantly tinkled the music box; she was in The Crib). Flory rolled under the wide disordered bed and pushed his way through lint until he lay against the wall, he lay shivering, trying to draw more tightly against the wall. His foot jerked out spasmodically and upset the chamber pot. His ears listened to liquid go trickling away, draining down through cracks of the floor. At last it quit dripping. His ears heard nothing, there was nothing for them to hear but that frenzied explosion of the musket and the squawk of death following.

After a long while there did come another sound: a scratching at the outer door of the cottage, was it wolf, Yank, or Woogum? Something was coming, some small shape approached the bed, trot, trot, trot. No word was spoken through otherwise unyielding silences, no bay went up, there was no snarl of threat or upbraiding. A tiny hand lifted the hanging bedclothing draped over the edge, and Zoral squatted there. He peeped in at his half-brother, and the half-brother turned his head and saw him.

You get out of here, you Zoral, was the thought which crawled in Flory's mind, but he could not speak. Beady eyes looked into Flory's; then the queer pinched face grinned. In that grin was awful understanding—the age-old wisdom of the dwarf, the cretin.

XLIX

Flory was carried back to the camps and put in jail—not for the slaying of the prisoner, but for deserting his post. There had been so many other crimes of similar nature that the stockade did not buzz for long about this topic, though the victim was well known. The stockade buzzed night and day about the matter of exchange. With official stoppage of exchange long before, the weaker people had given up hope, the very strongest had felt their hopes watered, thinned to vanishing. No one was in possession of all the facts, many were in possession of no facts at all. Yet they hated ruthlessly and with catholicity of hate. Alike they hated General Benjamin Butler, General Ulysses Grant and Colonel Robert Ould, the Confederate agent for exchange.

A tale which had survived more than two years of war centered around Howell Cobb, who was quoted as refusing to exchange prisoners on a man-for-man basis, when General Wool suggested it. Accordingly Cobb became despicable. . . . President Davis was said to have written to General Lee in discussing difficulties in the application of the cartel: *Scarcely had that cartel been signed when the military authorities of the United States commenced to practise changing the character of the war from such as becomes civilized nations into a campaign of indiscriminate robbery and murder.*

So we're robbers and murderers, are we?

God damn right. That's why they treat us so. They got us shoved into this one big shit-house, just to keep reminding us that we *are* robbers and murderers!

Charlie, what would you do to that son of a bitch Davis, if you could get your hands on him?

I wish you boys would quit your cursing. *Thou Shalt Not Curse.*

It don't say that in the Bible.

It says not to take the name of the Lord thy God in vain!

Well, Estes, I never did cuss, fore I joined up. Tried not to, out of respect for my mother. Guess I never did cuss much till I came to Andersonville. But, by God, this stink-pot— And when I think of boys I know at home, like Harley Tatham and that slob of a Jewett—

Never did join up, wouldn't be drafted, hired substitutes— And now they're walking around, big as life, walking down Prospect Street, maybe taking girls for a buggy ride, going on pic-nics to Strawberry Point— Here I sit in this— Know what I'd do to Jeff Davis if I could catch him?

Hang him to a sour apple tree?

By God, yes. By his balls!

For my part, I'd like to hang that God damn Stanton from the same limb.

Why, Shroder?

Why? Cause way back two three years ago he cut loose with that General Order to arrest all disloyal male citizens within our lines!

That wasn't the fault of Stanton—

Hell it wasn't—

I *do* wish you boys would cease your blasphemy—

Listen, Estes, the word hell ain't blasphemous—

Well, I do wish—

It was the fault of that damn old Dutch Steinwehr. He arrested some citizens up in Virginia and told them they was going to be put to death. No wonder the Rebs got mad.

Cracky, I remember that! The Rebs said we had violated all the rules of warfare; said we were on a campaign of robbery and murder against unarmed citizens and peaceful tillers of the soil. Or something like that—

If you truly want to know who's at fault: tis all on account of the niggers. Never should have put them in uniform in the first place!

Wirz is real hard on niggers. Up there at the graveyard. Georgie Hudson went out on wood-detail tother day, and they went nigh the cemetery. Wirz was having two of the niggers whipped. Georgie said they fair to beat the Jesus out of them; said you could hear them yelling halfway back to the stockade—

God damn Wirz to hell. He's as bad as General Steinwehr.

Two rotten apples off the same Dutch limb!

Wirz ain't really German: he's a damn Switzer—

I *do* wish you boys—

This was a reflection of general opinion. The exchange of Negro troops had been a problem insurmountable. The Confederates declared that many of the colored soldiers were former slaves (as indeed they were), and armed by the Yankees. Thus the Yankees were, in effect, inciting an insurrection against the civil populace of the South. White officers commanding those black troops were held to be beyond the protection of any military law, and should be punished according to State laws. . . .

That damn Ben Butler. It all started with him—

How do you mean?

You know what happened when he was commanding over in New Orleans: he hung a citizen, said he had been pulling down a National flag—

The hell with the National flag! I'd like to pull the damn thing down myself.

That's treason!

If this be treason, make the most of it.

Yes. *Give me liberty or give me death.*

Likely you'll get death.

You'll get liberty when you die.

Yep. Exchanged.

Yep. *Paroled!*

Get shot by that little snot up there on the fence.

You can take all the Stantons and Jeff Davises you want, and hang them on a sour apple tree. Hang them any way you choose; but just give *me* Grant!

That drunken worthless poop! Enoch, wouldn't I just like to get my hands on him! At least before they rot off. . . .

What's Grant got to do with it?

Twas in all the papers up North. Didn't you see me talking to them fresh fish that came in yesterday? One of them was from the Thirty-first, same as me. He had it on good authority: Colonel Ould—that's the Rebel agent—agreed to a man-for-man exchange a while back, and Grant positively refused. He wept a few crocodile tears; he said it was soooo hard on our men down here in Andersonville, not to exchange them; but it wouldn't be fair to the rest of the dear boys who were left in the ranks still to fight. Just imagine that!

It's God's own truth—or the Devil's. Grant pointed out that every Johnny held by the North would become an active soldier against us, the moment he got exchanged.

And us?

We're worthless, we're dirt.

That drunken skunk!

You know he *was* drunk at Shiloh. That's why the Rebs ran all over us.

Grant said that if they exchanged the Rebs held by the North, it would probably defeat Bill Sherman.

Bill Sherman! He couldn't get us into a scrape that old Pap Thomas couldn't get us out of. . . .

As I just said, Joel, we're not worth blowing up. Not worth the powder and shot to do it! Just look at you and me and the rest: sick, rotten, starved, hungry, bowels running loose, teeth falling out— Oh, wouldn't we just make soldiers once again!

Hell, I couldn't carry a musket fifty foot, let alone my knapsack and forty rounds.

Certain we're worthless. We're poison! Just let us set here in our own filth until we're mildewed—

I'm mildewed already, by God.

If you boys will only stop—

They felt the deadly justice of their universal opinion.

It was to an encampment such as this that Henry Wirz had returned at the end of August. Wirz came thinner, more probed, more scraped and drained. The right arm burned and leaked as it had never burned and leaked before. The surgeon Greenaway was no miracle man.

Wirz accepted records kept by Lieutenant Davis and the clerks, and tried to make sense out of them in his regular report.

Consolidated Return for Confederate States Military Prison, Camp Sumter, Andersonville, Georgia, for the Month of August, 1864.

Prisoners on hand 1st of August, 1864:

In camp	29,985	
In hospital	1,693	31,678

Received from various places during

August	3,078	
Recaptured	4	3,082

Total		34,760

Died during the month of August	2,993	
Sent to other parts	23	
Exchanged	21	
Escaped	30	3,067

Remaining on hand		31,693

Of which there are on the 31st of August:

In camp	29,473	
In hospital	2,220	31,693

The same complaint has been made again against the carelessness and insufficiency of the guard of the thirty prisoners. . . . Perhaps twenty-five more escaped during the month, but were taken up by the dogs before the daily return was made out, and for that reason they are not on the list of escaped nor recaptured.

That only four were recaptured is owing to the fact that neither the guard nor the officers of the guard reported a man escaped. The roll-call in the morning showed the man missing, but he was too far gone to be tracked. As we have no general court-martial here, all such offenses go unpunished, or nearly so.

The worthlessness of the guard forces is on the increase day by day.

H. Wirz,
Captain Commanding Prison.

In Augusta, however, and during the journey south, Wirz had felt that his load might be lightened soon. It was this belief, expressed incautiously to subordinates, which caused the rumors to gush. For several days Henry Wirz had received no orders, no directive of any kind to support this opinion. Nothing in the world could have pleased him more than the withdrawal of the vast plaguing mass. After the fall of Atlanta he was hopelessly certain that a removal could not be accomplished. Yankee columns would go fanning out from the city and slice the railroads, surely. . . . But less than forty-eight hours after the Atlanta news came, Wirz was summoned to Winder's headquarters.

The old general lay on a sagging sofa which had been requisitioned for his purposes from somewhere or other. He lay there frequently nowadays. He did not lift his head from the cushion when Wirz came in and saluted with his left hand. He did not return the salute or invite the superintendent to sit down.

Captain—

Ja, mein General?

Shut the door!

Wirz closed the door and returned to stand beside the sofa, while Winder rambled hoarsely. The general seemed to be excruciatingly tired; he had been traveling; probably now he dwelt in dread of capture by Sherman's cavalry.

We've got to get these God damn prisoners out of here.

Where, sir, do you take them?

Savannah, Charleston—maybe even up to Florence. I had another stockade built at Millen. Designation: Camp Lawton. Not ready for them yet, no facilities—

Wirz wondered drearily what facilities had ever been provided at Andersonville.

Can't bother with the sick; take the well ones. God damn sick can die here as easily as anywhere else. We'll fill up detachments with only those able to walk. Get them out of here as fast as cars are available to carry them out. Use open cars, flat cars—any type—just so they've got wheels on them. Trouble is, half the God damn bastards will go leaping off the cars and running wild all over the countryside. They'll try to join Sherman; and that's just what we don't want. That's where you come in, Captain Wirz. I want you to impress upon these prisoners that they are to be *exchanged* immediately. A good share of them have their time expired anyway, and won't try to join Sherman if they think they're going to be exchanged and sent to the North.

But, *mein* General— Where do they get exchange?

God damn it, I didn't say that they were to *be exchanged!* I said that you were to *tell them that they would be exchanged!* Can't you get that through your thick Swiss skull? You are to *tell* them that there is to be a *general exchange.* Tell them that vessels are waiting in the harbor. Instruct your subordinates to talk exchange, exchange, exchange, where the prisoners will hear it. Drop rumors where they'll do the most good. I don't want these black-hearted Federal sons of bitches to cut for it. I don't want them loose. At least there are some thousands of them over there in the pines that aren't going to trouble anybody further!

Wirz repeated: *Ja.* So I am to tell them they get exchange. But truly they do not get exchange. Then they do not run away.

That's the ticket, Captain. Transportation officer thinks he can get me two or three trains by tomorrow—day after tomorrow at the latest. How many would you say are able to travel?

Upwards from two thousand prisoners we have already by the hospital. In camp maybe thirty thousand we have. Wirz considered slowly. Maybe half from those— No, maybe twenty thousand from those. They could walk—they could walk to the cars.

Then publish that information immediately!

A laugh like a growl sounded deep below the seamed bulging face, deep within old tissues.

I'd like to see their faces when they walk into Camp Lawton, instead of aboard a ship! By God, maybe I will be there to see their faces! Twould be worth the journey.

He dreamed aloud: I am considering removing my headquarters as far as Florence. . . . God damn Sherman. God damn all the Yankees; but God damn Cump Sherman the most. I wish I'd had him in my class at the Point. I'd have made him sweat! But of course he was there years after my time. . . .

Winder hoisted himself suddenly into a sitting position and glared at Wirz as if he had just discovered him in the room. Well, what are you lingering for? Get out, and to the business! Carry out my orders to the letter. I've got to see to it that Sherman isn't reinforced by any prisoners that might be halfway considered as able-bodied. Get along with you. . . .

Ja, mein General. Wirz got along.

Faithfully he drew up an order, and copies were passed along to Wry-necked Smith and the other roll-call sergeants. On the evening of the sixth of September, squads were assembled within the stockade. Wirz's order was read aloud.

Prisoners: I am instructed by General Winder to inform you that a general exchange has been agreed upon. Twenty thousand men will be exchanged immediately at Savannah, where your vessels are now waiting for you. Detachments from One to Ten will prepare to leave early tomorrow morning.

It can't be true.

God. Can't be *true*.

And will I go back, and will I find a pale blue sky in spring—the spring day which meant the most to me, though this is next to autumn now, the heat is cooling. And will I go back into that day, or go ahead to it? . . . Somehow be exchanged, get home, make my way to the day again, and springtime clinging around the day. When that ribbon-blue sky is covered by thin motionless film: more a suggestion of clouds than clouds in fact . . . my shadow elongated, when the sun hangs low, to five times its normal length. I know—I've paced it off. I'm little, I'm but five feet tall; but my shadow was twenty-five feet long on all that fresh grass . . . fresh grass tender as fine minced salad under old weeds. And larks talkative beyond us; frogs in Garnett's marsh trying to talk comfort; a solitary crow reiterating some annoyance a hundred times. And peach blooms, breath-taking in their cream and candied pinkish flesh: fluffy, close-packed, strung out along the twigs and thinner branches . . . broom straw blazing, polished tan like tin, letting the low sun burn it up . . . haze like Indian smoke, a springtime haze, all over the horizon.

God, God, it isn't *true*.

Through all the raw yelling.

. . . But if it were true— What a soldier I would be! Oh, what a cavalryman I would be again! Just take me back, up in that Tennessee valley, and see how fast I travel when the bugle starts to blat Assembly! The orderlies wouldn't have to wear out their patience, trying to get the laggards to fall in for Roll Call. Gad, how glad I'd be for stable duty! And when they blew the Water Call, how glad I'd be to mount my horse and ride him! Let them sound a million Guards or Drills when I get back! Why, great damnation, there'd be music in the Surgeon's Call! *Come—get—your—q-u-i-n-i-n-e. Come, get your quinine; it'll make you sad; it'll make you sick. Come, come.* Let them play Reveille, then Assembly, then Boots and Saddles; let the gunners go to hitching up, let the buglers signal Forward. Let the wheels roll, let me hear Right Turn, Left Turn, as batteries roll away. I'll never be a lazy coffee-cooler again. What a soldier I will be!

Oh, God, I don't *believe* it.

You mean to tell me—God, or Holy Ghost, or Somebody—that all those rumors have come to life and built a thing we can believe? Why, I see Alice now— I'd forgotten her for so long. And Mother comes back in my mind, and Etta is standing here, and Sister Kate has come to have a meaning. Father does mean something now, and so does Brother Rufus. So does Shep; I can even tolerate Muggins the cat! I can taste the ginger cake and cucumber pickles—taste them on my tongue, and I can hear that fire gong a-thudding, and I can hear the laughter of a certain child. . . .

You mean to say there's a *world* within the world?

There's cider to drink?

There's Chicago smoke to smell, instead of these pine smudgings?

You mean to say I can stand with Ma in front of St.-Mark's-In-The-Bouwerie once more, and look up at that facade with its trees and animals a-feeding, and feel good holy thoughts? That I can run my fingernail through moss above old Peter Stuyvesant, and think all sorts of grave and holy thoughts about the past? That now there can be a past, because there is a future?

God, God, oh God Almighty!

Slap me on my sore back, Willie.

Punch me in my sore belly, Herbert.

Swat me on my sore arm, Augustus.

We're a-going home.

You mean to tell me there can be that slough beside the Mississippi, and great big channel cats a-waiting there? That I can walk to Hazel Green, that I can work the dasher churn for Auntie? Mean to say there's hazel nuts in Wilder's brush? You mean to say there's that cold clear good driving honest clean wind coming in across Lake Huron? You mean to tell me there's fresh respectable snow atop the Alleghenies, and we can go a-sledding? Oh, how glad I'll be to cut the wood, to clean the old cow's stable. How glad I'll be to wrench the flinty dry corn ears and thud them up against the bang-board. . . .

How glad I'll be to climb the stairs to Sweet's. And let's see— What'll I have? Why, Uncle Amos—thank you kindly, Unk. I'll take a glass of ale—maybe two glasses, or more, if you give the word. And let's see now: well, these are Long Island oysters, but— Yes, that'll be fine. Thank you, Uncle Amos. And I wouldn't be surprised but what I could eat a dozen, right along with you. . . . Here's the nice fresh lemon juice, and there's pepper sauce in the flask. Yes, thank you. And I'd like to grind off just a few flakes of this good black pepper. A dozen of the oysters, then! No—don't think I'd fancy flounder; but I'll take the broiled halibut, if you don't mind. Broiled halibut? That's good: just the way I like it, in that little crockery baking dish; and kind of sputtering and talking as the darkey brings it to us. And boiled potatoes, too. Yes, I'll take some slaw along with it. And all the good fish market smells coming through the window, and sounds of wheels a-rumbling, and masts a-sticking up along the waterfront like great big weeds, and beer-barrels being rolled across the sidewalk, and—

But tis true, by jumping Jesus Christ!

Well, let me tell you first: twill be good to be back with the boys! If you know anything about the Army of the Cumberland, you remember that we've got just about as good a record as any regiment that trains around Pap Thomas. And you know him: he don't allow no slouches near him! You can bet five hundred dollars to a cent on that. And then offer to give back the cent if you win! Ours is Jim Steedman's old regiment. You know him: you've all heard of old Chickamauga Jim. You remember how he throwed his division—seven thousand fresh men—into the Rebel flank on that second day at Chickamauga. Hell's bells! he made Longstreet wish he'd stayed on the Rappahannock. Hell's bells! he made Longstreet wish he'd never tried to get up any little sociable with a gang of Westerners! If I do say it myself: we've got as good a crowd of boys as ever ate a chunk of sow belly. We got all the grunters and weak sisters fanned out the first year; and since then we've been on a real business basis. . . . No, no, we weren't licked, we never were licked! The way I got caught was when we left camp one night and went out about five miles to an old cotton press. A nigger told us there were a lot of nice smoked hams hidden there, and we found them all right, and hitched up a team to take them into camp. Hadn't seen no Johnny signs anywhere, so we set our guns down to help load the meat. And right then a company of Reb cavalry popped up out of the woods and flung themselves on top of us before we could say Scat. You see, they'd heard about the hams, too.

Tis true.

We're going.

That's official!

You heard the Rebel's reading of the orders.

There will be a smell and blush of haws upon the hillside, if I can but survive to reach the hillside. . . .

Brother, I believe a brief service should be held.

A service should be held indeed; but I should say not necessarily *brief*, Brother Frank!

And now Brother Boston has prayed.

And now we shall read: *The wilderness of the solitary place shall be glad for them; and the desert shall rejoice, and blossom as the rose. . . .* And the sound and rumble of response, the muted chant of response, congregational response, all in a lower worshipful key. *It shall blossom abundantly, and rejoice even with joy and singing.*

*. . . And the ransomed of the Lord shall return, and come to Zion
with songs and everlasting joy upon their heads: they shall obtain joy
and gladness, and sorrow and sighing shall flee away.*

The first detachments were marched out of the stockade on September seventh. Ira Claffey was busy with his Negroes constructing a log bridge across a branch of Little Sweetwater at the farther boundary of the plantation where August storms had left destruction. So he did not see the prisoners go, he did not know that any were leaving definitely, he had heard only rumors.

At midnight his light slumber was disturbed by an unprecedented screaming of engine whistles at the Anderson station, where the side track switch was jammed; a train waiting there could not enter upon the main line until repairs were effected. Ira went to his window. The valley glowed red with those same baleful flames which had shone in February, though tonight flames were fewer. It was one thing to guard prisoners being fetched into Andersonville, quite another thing to watch and guard them on their way to be Exchanged. . . .

Ira put on his clothes and hung a shawl around his shoulders; the night was unseasonably chilly. He went through woods and past the south camps and stood close to watch the exodus, then moved nearer the South Gate.

Some of these were the identical goblins who had marched in their Belle Isle rags half a year earlier. Their rags were worse now: many Yankees were nearly naked, their grimy skeletal limbs were sticks. Ira wished to cry a hosanna because these people were being taken away, yet he could only grieve at their plight. He did not know the men and boys, he did not know their names. They were enemies reduced beyond the point of enmity because suffering made men brothers, and made brutes into men to be pitied. Undoubtedly there were raiders, or their one-time sycophants, in the halting collapsing throng. Starvation they'd shared with the rest. It divested them of monstrosity.

. . . Here marched Eben Dolliver, with one other survivor of the Moon Hotel mess. Here walked the sergeant named Colony, who had once been a member of the same household in which the dead Edward Blamey was numbered. The Wingate brothers lay on the hill toward the north. . . .

A queer shape moved in torchlit gloom beside Ira, and he saw that it was the Confederate sergeant with the twisted neck, whom often Ira had observed on duty.

How many are they taking, Sergeant?

Reckon bout ten detachments left already, Mister. Reckon there's about seven coming out tonight. They're only letting the well ones go.

Would you call these prisoners well?

Leastways they can walk. They won't let no crawlers go. Nobody that has to be carried.

. . . Here moved the wraith named Private Allen who had shared the shebang with Nathan Dreyfoos; and Tyke, the drummer boy who had wept in a crowded box car last spring. There were the Vermonters, Garrett and Appleby, and somewhere ahead of them staggered their neighbor from Maine. In the herd was a soldier named Malachi Plover, and another named Willie Mann (one day, before many months had passed, Willie would press his clipped scarred head into the pink cambric lap of Katrine Christine Ernestine Fiedenbruster). . . .

The boy who'd kept a diary, John Ransom, was just coming through the gate. Ira did not know him, he knew none of them, yet his heart went out. He thought, Only the well may go, that lad is unwell, he can scarcely walk. Actually he can't walk: that big Indian is holding him. The edged voice of an officer clipped through the shadows: Hold on there. Wait! That man can't walk. He can't go Out—

Such a press of smelly bodies crowding. The officer ran for a few steps on the outskirts of the column, gesticulating. He turned, seeking a guard. The shaggy-haired Indian leered in pine knots' flare, his hard face grinned, his teeth shone. Yes, yes, he walk all right, he go. Still he had his arm wrapped around the sagging bent scurvy-ridden puppet whom he loved and carried. Other prisoners bawled and muttered, they seemed shaking in mass hysteria, a disbelieving delight . . . more pushed out through the gate. The officer had to run back to his post again, he could not prevent this violation.

. . . Here were numbers of the Regulators who had crushed raider bands. Some of them walked crying, there were prayers being said. A weak voice was heard: Annapolis, here we come . . . hellfire, Ned, probably just go to another stockade . . . can't be as bad as this one. . . .

Their weakness claimed Ira Claffey and made him their relative. He turned and limped into darkness. He stumbled against a stump, stumbled again over exposed roots. He could not see because of his tears. Behind him the angular form of the Galena printer, Seneca MacBean, was just strolling through the gate. His friend Nathan Dreyfoos was not with him. The horrid thing which had been Nathan Dreyfoos lay wormy beneath a yard of loose soil on that distant hilltop. The shot fired by Floral Tebbs had drilled his gracious brain.

L

About two o'clock in a white night Ira Claffey was awakened by a persistent pounding at the front door on the gallery below his room. Seldom had he been routed out at unearthly hours except as a prelude to catastrophe. There was the time the quarters burned at the McWhorter place, the time a black child was snake-bitten while walking in her sleep, the time Uncle Arch Yeoman's simple-minded daughter put her right hand into the hot stove because she had stolen money from her father's purse with that right hand, and she recollected a Biblical injunction she'd heard preached. Veronica Claffey walked to doom in nighttime. The news of Moses Claffey's death had come at night. Also a train was wrecked at night on the line north of Anderson with several people killed and many injured. Ira took up no robe but hurried down in his nightshirt. Apprehensively he drew back the two bolts.

Coral Tebbs was poised outside the door, dark eyes glistening in the candle's flame. Nowadays he traveled on two crutches; long ago he had shaped a rude crutch himself to match the one whittled out by Flory.

Mr. Claffey, sir. It's Laurel.

What say, my boy? Ah—your half-sister—

She's took bad. The old lady asked me would I traipse over here and seek that there surgeon.

I fear he's at the prison hospital.

What about Miss Lucy, sir? Hain't she good at tending the sick?

Come into the house, Coral. I'll fetch my daughter. What seems to ail your sister?

Reckon it's a kind of fever. She's clean out of her wits, and talks foolish like. Seems like she's griped in the belly or something. She just keeps a-clutching and a-moaning. Ma's scairt to death.

Ira went up to Lucy; her door was not latched; he tapped and then opened the door and called softly until Lucy sat up in response. He gave her the message and then went down and sent Coral on his way; the lame boy would travel slowly. Ira dressed quickly, and sipped cold okra coffee until Lucy appeared, gowned. She had brought down some necessaries which she fancied might be of use. Most of the things were packed already in a basket which stood always above her wash-stand, ready for emergencies; this was her Florence Nightmare basket, it was traditional in the household. Ira carried the basket as they trudged through moonlight to the Tebbs cottage. They spoke of the moon, of its aloofness, of the drama inherent in its very placidity because of the marvels it had witnessed for so long.

On such a night as this, said Ira.

I know, I know. Did I ever tell you, Poppy? Once I ran away in the moonlight, and no one ever knew that I had gone. I rose—well, I reckon you can guess: to use the vessel—and then I looked out. The night was just plain mad—like this—cream all over everywhere. So I snuck, Poppy, just plain snuck. Mother would have perished.

How did you get out?

Remember the magnolia which used to grow beside my window, and it grew sickly, and you took it down?

Climbing down trees in your night-rail. Ha.

I did get scratched a teentsie. Then I ran and ran and ran. Accompanied by Deuce. Met with no disaster whatsoever, but I felt *wild*. Oh, might the Lord make me young again!

You crone, said Ira. They walked on in silence, chuckling a little, and then growing more serious as the Tebbs place could be seen directly ahead with lights burning in the two rooms; they thought of the sick girl waiting there.

Whatever can be the matter with that child, Poppy?

I trust it's nothing catching.

Don't be selfish and cruel, sir. Poppy, does her mother— Does she still— I mean, do all those men—?

All the time, said Ira shortly. He shuddered within, thinking of how his disturbed lust had nearly sent him into the widow's bed many months before. Am I dried, he thought, dried up and old before my time? At least I feel that I'm commanding myself better than I did. The long sadness has been a disciplining factor.

Coral was just entering the dooryard ahead of them, and the Widow Tebbs hurried out to the stoop on hearing their approach. She was fully dressed, twisting her hands in her apron, her plump face sticky with tears. Did you fetch the surgeon, sonny? Oh, she's bad took—my poor little Laurel—

Ira explained that Harrell Elkins was at the prison hospital. Lucy took her basket and sped into the room beyond, with Mag following her. Before she closed the door Ira had a glimpse of Laurel's face in the low lamplight; she was discolored, her abnormally thin face seemed now abnormally bloated, her lips hung apart, she gave forth alternate grunts and whinnyings.

Coral dragged out a chair for Ira and sat across the table from him.

Mr. Claffey, sir. You got a chaw tobacco on you?

I'm sorry, Coral. I use tobacco but infrequently, and have none now. Sometimes I enjoy a pipe. Ever smoke a pipe?

Little bit, when I was soldiering. Ruther chew.

How does Floral get on with his soldiering?

Little cuss, said Coral. He shot a Yankee, killed him dead. He hadn't no call to go firing like that. God knows I hate Yankees—got good reason to hate them—but I wouldn't go around blasting right and left the way he done.

Oh, he was too young to go for a soldier!

Well, he hain't got sense enough to bell a buzzard. Ma says Flory's daddy was easy-tongued as they come—just a real charmer, so she says—but Flory hain't got cat sense. He's in the calaboose; been there ever since the day he shot the damn Yankee, and I reckon he'll be there sixty days. They come over here and fetched him back, a squad of them.

Coral tittered scornfully. He was under Ma's bed, and little Zoral he pointed him out to the squad.

Where is Baby Zoral now?

Coral jerked his elbow toward the door. Asleep in that old hen-coop out there. Ma said she couldn't have him sleeping in yonder, with Laurel laying sickly, and I was fetched if I'd have him sleeping alongside of me, count of he wets the bed so bad. So he's got a kind of bed in the old chicken-coop. Reckon he likes it tolerable.

Through this conversation there had sounded a murmur of voices in the room beyond, punctuated—to Ira's pain and fears—by the wailing of the sick girl. The door opened and Lucy appeared with her face paler than it had been. Poppy. May I speak with you? Outside.

They went into the wonderland of moonlight which could enrich every object, which enriched even the tumbled dooryard and made each grotesquerie a prettiness.

Oh, Poppy. It's dreadful! You must go for Cousin Harry.

Child, Coz can't be two places at once; he'll feel that the sick need him over there, as indeed they do, and he'll be distraught. Nevertheless I'll try to fetch him. What ails Laurel?

That woman— The widow told me most artlessly. She's such a simpleton! Poppy, I dislike to speak of such matters to you, but know that I'll be forgiven. The girl—Laurel—was going to have a baby. Her mother discovered this when some time had elapsed since the girl asked for— These are womanly matters. But for—cloths. Well, the widow undertook to interrupt the pregnancy; she employed a wooden knitting needle, of all things. And this is the result.

Ira exclaimed sharply and hurried toward the lane, but turned back before he had reached the corner. Lucy, do you go inside and do whatever you can—doubtless there's little you can do—until I get hold of Harry. But Laurel will require constant nursing, constant attendance, if indeed she survives until morning. There's a train at the depot, disgorging prisoners or perhaps taking them to Blackshears—the Lord knows. I mean to send a note to Americus for Mrs. Dillard, by the engine-driver. I've no writing materials in my pockets.

Lucy flew into the cottage. Coral obliged by finding a stub of pencil in the old clock, and a torn envelope of patriotic pattern. (This relic had been discarded by some visitor of Mag's, and depicted an embattled female Confederacy, complete with helmet, sword and flowing robes, who had just given the quietus to a writhing dragon. Mag said, That's right pretty, and pinned the thing upon the wall as a picture to admire; but Coral hated it always and was glad to be rid of it. Coral said that war was no business for a woman; if there was dragon-killing to be done then let the menfolks go do it.) Ira put these things in his shirt pocket and fairly ran toward the tracks; he feared that the train might have started already, possibly he could flag it down. But no, the light still glared dully; the train motionless, it turned out that a gang of blacks was wooding-up the engine's tender. Ira could not actually run because of the tendon which had fastened itself to the femur of his leg, but he hopped along, perspiring, and made very good time. It was odd, he thought . . . now the smell of Andersonville was thick as smoke, yet he and Lucy had forgotten it when they were moving at slower pace through the moon's beauty. It took but the suggestion of an evil and a stink to bring increased evil, more persistent stink.

He found an amiable bearded engineer who was glad to be of service when he heard that a girl was stricken. It was expected that the train would reach Americus in an hour and a half, and Ira had no longer a fast horse on the plantation—nothing but mules and two feeble pensioners.

Are there not ordinarily some niggers about the depot at Americus, even in nighttime?

Sure to be, Mister. There's the wood gang, and usually some of their pickaninnies.

Then give one of them this note I'm scribbling and—here, this bit of currency—and send him to Parson Dillard's with all haste!

Ira crossed the branch and went up through spectral light and shadow to his home. Twice he was challenged by sentries—there were many more of them about since Atlanta fell—but he had no trouble getting past; he was known by sight to practically all the guards except a few recruits newly come.

He awakened Jonas and told him to hitch a mule to a cart. Ira's wounded leg was plaguing him because of unaccustomed exertion, and also he could imagine Elkins's weariness (but it was a steady exhaustion which the younger man would never admit in so many words). Ira started east along what was left of the lane. At this spot once he had scented decay and had held a fear indefinable . . . the battering of a lifetime had slugged against him and his since then. . . . Bordering wild shrubbery was gone, the area was gashed by a thousand heavy wheel-rollings, the lane ended in an embankment with rifle pits strung beside. Out of milk and mist ahead came a lone figure with skull face ashine: if a child had seen it the child would have run squawking. This spook was Surgeon Elkins who had given the shreds of strength remaining to him and was now ordered to bed by the surgeon commanding.

Violets, said Harry distinctly.

Ira Claffey reached through the pale light and put his big hand around Elkins's arm, and shook him slightly. Did you say violets?

I thought of them, not far from here, said the rough high voice. Twas the first time I visited the stockade region. I picked two, for Lucy.

Ah, violets no longer. Naught but exhalations.

The surgeon yielded himself to Ira's support for a moment only, as if he wanted to be a little boy again, to let an adult take over his charge. Then he pulled loose and straightened his shoulders even while he shrugged them, as he were saying, Come, come, I'm well again, I'm adult, strong once more, I'm still a man.

I dislike to add to your burdens, Coz. But would you be able to come to the bedside of a sick child? A young girl, daughter of our neighbor, the Tebbs woman—

Surely. Did you know that there were two kinds of miasma identified by medical writers?

They were nearing the Claffey gate, and Ira could hear crying wheels of the cart as Jonas brought it up from the stables. He said, The girl is in a desperate condition. I've sent to Americus for Mrs. Effie—

Mrs. Prod-Pry! Forever with a question—

You should be flattered, Cousin Harry. Ira tried to laugh about it. She's vastly respectful of your erudition, and means to learn whatever you can teach her—

I shall teach her, said Elkins as they halted at the gate. Two miasmas thus identified. The *kino* and the *ideo*. One consists of exhalations from the human body in a state of disease, the other of exhalations from vegetable decompositions and saturations generally.

Jonas came driving up and leaped from the cart. Bad night air, Mastah. He was firm in the belief that night air was more dangerous than day air, stockade or no stockade.

Then get to your cabin before you catch your death, Jonas. You in your shirt-tail. The slave hastened off, a tatterdemalion under the serene moon. Ira demanded abruptly of Harrell Elkins whether he felt capable of approaching this new responsibility. You, he said, poor thing, with your babble of violets and miasmas.

That was mere relaxation. Harry tried to be spry as an athlete when he pulled his awkward body into the car. Pay strict heed to the professor, sir. *Kino* and *ideo:* we have both varieties at the hospital, together with a few not yet ticketed by those who research into the matter. But I shall ticket them. Now, then, and he lifted his gaunt glassy face to the white light above. Tell me of the patient, sir.

She's fourteen or so. It seems she was in the family way and her mother sought to abort her.

Elkins growled a curse. He swore but seldom, and then it always came as a shock; it was like seeing a parson cut a buck-and-wing behind his pulpit. Is there severe hemorrhage?

I'm not aware. Daughter Lucy is with her. Laurel would appear to be unconscious or in delirium. I believe she's very weak, and in acute pain.

A pox on all abortionists! Good grief, sir, have I my medical kit with me? Harry looked about wildly.

You're clutching it in your hand, said Ira weakly.

He had grave doubts about Elkins's ability to deal with this dangerous baffling case, rubbed to a rag as he was, chanting absurdities. But once arrived at the cottage Harrell Elkins became all physician; you would not have known the depth of his depletion unless you'd looked intently into his bony face. The questions he asked of the widow and Lucy were terse, searching, sane. Elkins opened his kit and withdrew tiny flasks containing his store of drugs, holding them with care to the light as he read the labels, holding them with a hand no longer sunburnt—a wide bony hand that was pale and seemed frail and yet remained unshaking. Have you salt and common loaf sugar? he asked of Mag.

The widow was in such a twitter that she scarcely knew. Yes, she did own salt . . . twas in a box . . . now, where was that salt-box . . . reckoned there was a mite of sugar on the shelf. . . .

I'll go see, whispered Lucy.

No, have your father and the lad make a search. Elkins lowered his voice. And get this woman out of here.

I'm to stay?

I fear I shall need your help. His spectacles were opaque, frightening as he looked down at the girl. In a most intimate way, Madam. He had not addressed her in such fashion since the long ago day of his first arrival.

Coral was of much more help than his mother. Small quantities of salt and sugar were discovered, a pint of soft water was put to simmer upon the fire. The Widow Tebbs huddled, banished to the porch where she mourned for a time and then fell asleep and snored loudly.

Thank Heaven, said Harry Elkins, as if Lucy understood the drugs he mentioned, and their use. I've still a bit of white vitriol in my kit. And sugar of lead—I shall need to scrape the bottle. Attend me, please.

He put into her hands a miniature mortar and pestle. This contains alum. Please to pulverize it finely.

He had rubbed the patient with fever liniment, and was applying cold compresses. Such a paucity of needfuls, Lucy heard him muttering. Always a paucity. Damn it, here's a muslin pillowcase, appears fairly clean. Sacrifice, and she heard the tearing of the muslin. When she looked at Elkins again he was bending tenderly over the smelly moaning invalid with a fresh moist compress. Is the alum well pulverized, Madam? he inquired without turning.

Tis to a powder, sir.

Do you fetch the pot of water that's simmering.

She brought the steaming pot and watched with respect as Elkins stirred in his materials—salt, sugar, the alum she'd powdered, the drugs he'd measured. She found mysterious satisfaction in the steam which rose from the compound, in its whiteness, its odor. Lucy regarded Laurel Tebbs with that affection which a kind person gives to fledglings fallen from their nests, to starved stray dogs and cats. Laurel was a pathetic beast which had been treated cruelly, Lucy agonized with her in sympathy, she hoped that Laurel would not die. But momentarily also she might forget danger and delirium, and see beauty wrought between herself and Harrell Elkins: they had combined to make medicine, she had squeezed the pestle, she was helping him to help another.

Return this to the fire, please.

When she came back he had drawn a syringe from his bag and was inspecting it critically. You know— His abrasive voice seemed to speak from a sad vague past. My uncle was a surgeon, as I've told you. A wicked man, I believe, but I recall some of his theories and adhere to them whenever possible. He believed in professional cleanliness, he thought that disease might be spread by untidiness. I'm but a beginner. But I feel discomfort unless I've washed my instruments— again, whenever possible. Tis impossible to keep them clean over there—

Lucy knew the place he meant when he spoke the last two words.

Take this syringe and cleanse it in a basin. Give it a scrubbing.

In this way they toiled until the window was gray, until the moon sank toward western woods and lost its brightness. Coral slept on his bed, Ira Claffey slept at the table with his head on his arms, the widow had risen and gone to The Crib to resume her slumbers. Once, in the last hour of night, surgeon and nurse heard voices outside; they paid no heed, they were working. Ira told his daughter later, smiling behind his hand, that one of the middle-aged officers from the Reserves had appeared, a man whom Ira knew slightly.

He was more than astonished to find me in the cottage. I fear he was somewhat the worse for drink. The Widow Tebbs sent him packing.

Poppy. If you please!

Well, my dear, I thought it amusing.

Reckon I don't. I find it disgusting!

Yet peculiarly she found no disgust in her experience with Elkins as they bent above the skinny misery in the bedroom. She had never thought to share an intimacy, even a second-handed intimacy, with any man unless she were married to him. She knew that women as nurses went about bathing the sick; they bathed men, but only their hands and faces, perhaps they bathed their hairy chests a mite; male nurses did the rest. She had not believed that in this night or in any night she would be lifting the limbs of another female, opening those limbs, striving to preserve immobility in the sufferer while the man beside her manipulated his syringe, his sponges and compresses. The possibility had never even entered her mind. She was close to being appalled at discovering her lack of abashment.

We are faced with a variety of complications.

Yes, sir.

On the one hand it's essential that we reduce the fever, and in doing so must reduce the pain suffered by the patient; on the other hand there's been butchery; we must treat the local situation— As now.

Yes, sir.

Sometimes Laurel was silent, sometimes she snarled or cried out recognizable pleas, sometimes she tossed her arms wildly while wailing; it was difficult to tend her. Sometimes she made so much noise that Lucy could scarcely hear what Elkins was saying.

. . . Necessary to . . . more quietly . . . you see, I must hold the syringe . . . injection . . . regular female syringe would be preferable but . . . none . . . into the vagina for at least. . . .

The Dillards came driving up behind Blackie two hours after daylight. Laurel was still alive although Elkins had feared that she would die with the sunrise; she'd weakened terribly. But deep within the girl's scrambled inheritance there was a will to live, there was power to be invoked—that tonic contained in bodies and souls of some of the weakest, some of the most wasted.

Effie Dillard bustled furiously to her task, ragged starched cap-frill standing out like sunrays above her pocked yellow face. She took one look at Harrell Elkins and ordered him home. Clean white cloths appeared magically, rough towels were drying and warming in front of the fire. Be off with you, Surgeon, or you'll be lying sickly as this unhappy lass! She set the amazed Coral to picking the chicken she had rushed to decapitate before leaving Americus. If only I can get a wee swallow of broth down the child's throat. Away with you, Surgeon! The dominie can help me as he's helped before. Cousin Harry and the Claffeys rode off in the cart.

Before Harrell Elkins went up to bed he stood gazing fixedly at the bedraggled Lucy. Florence Nightmare, he said, indulging in the family jest as his beloved Sutherland had done often.

Mrs. Dillard fetched everything from febrifuge to Peckham's Cough Balsam, from emenagogue tincture to female laxative and anodyne pills. She must have cleared two shelves of her medicine closet. She shared the concern of Elkins: it appeared that she would lose her patient about four o'clock of the first afternoon. She worked in frenzy to stimulate the child's heart action and circulation. She reported, when Cousin Harry was able to look in the next morning, that Laurel was mending. Harry did not share this hopeful opinion. But when the girl lived still, two days following, he asked Mrs. Dillard what witches' remedies she had employed.

A spicy friendship grew between the voluble Scotswoman and the weary young zealot. They made dreadful jokes about live chickens split with an axe and laid upon a sufferer's wound, about black cats killed in the dark of the moon. When Elkins and Lucy arrived at the cottage in company, they came laden with provisions which Lucy had selected; but Harrell declared the rusks to be English worm cakes, the fresh bacon to be toad ointment. For sprains, strains, lame-back, rheumatism And So Forth, he recommended it. Obtain good-sized live toads, four in number. He described the process. Put into boiling water and cook until very soft. Then take out and boil the water down to one-half pint, and add fresh butter, one pound; and simmer together, and at the last add tincture of arnica. Lucy squealed and covered her ears, Mrs. Dillard regarded Elkins with studied malevolence. Well enough for you to scoff and jeer at wiser elder minds, young man! But I had yon toad ointment from a physician of the old school, and with it I cured two women of caked breasts. She added in meditation, Some folk might think it cruel to the poor toadies. But you could no kill them quicker.

Cato Dillard spent two nights at the Claffeys' and then returned to Americus to keep an engagement with the ruling elder. But Effie remained at the Tebbs place for more than three weeks, sleeping on a sofa which black people brought from the Claffey house, sleeping close to her patient so that she could be alert at the first groan from Laurel. Mag was allowed to occupy the bed in the front room (but only after Coral had been commanded to beat the mattress in hot sunlight for an hour, and after fresh bedclothing had been put upon it). Coral was billeted in The Crib with Zoral; Effie Dillard demanded that he burn the chicken-coop which served previously as Zoral's kennel. Coral undertook to obey, but Zoral witnessed the preparations and set up such a screaming that Coral took pity and dragged the coop behind the ruined stable where Zoral might dwell in it when so minded. The Widow Tebbs's professional life was at a standstill. She sulked because of this, once she had recovered from fright over her daughter, and once she recognized that the girl was recovering, that friends had saved her.

Mrs. Effie preached a violent sermon on the subject of abortion until the widow was in tears. Then Mrs. Effie offered her Georgia version of cockaleekie, and spice cake baked between bedside labors. She won Coral's heart with vinegar pies and with the gift of a miniature brass pocket pistol which had belonged to Effie's own father. Immediately thereafter she sentenced Coral to scrub the front room's floor and to help her in wiping down walls.

She scolded about the state of affairs under the house, and declared that she would fetch one of her own Negroes from Americus some fine day to rake that smelly mess.

Coral said, Taint that which smells mostly. Reckon it's the stockade yonder.

You're daft, lad! A reek arises through the very cracks in the floor. Think you I've no nose upon my face to smell with?

Reckon it's on account of that blame little Zoral. He's fetched by the sight of a dead critter. Always pulling them under the house to play with. Plays like they're a train and he's a engine-driver.

Then I'll work him a poke of yarn balls, the poor mannie, and he shall sport with those.

Reckon Zoral he wouldn't fancy no such pretty-plays. What he likes most is a dead bat. He hain't never had but one, less twas when I was off to the war.

On the second day of her stay she found time to scrub Zoral in a tub of hot water and to clip his shaggy hair. His yells were heard past the boundary of the Claffey plantation. She levied upon Lucy for clothing. Sundry items were extracted from the funereal chests packed by Veronica Claffey; Lucy saw no sense in hoarding all those things, neither did her father. Zoral was provided with under-drawers for the first time in his life, which article of clothing held fascination for him: he was always lifting the skirt of an ancient plaid dress once worn by Sutherland Claffey, and bending over to look at his own drawers. He received a wide-brimmed red straw hat which had belonged to Lucy. The hat vanished, only to reappear later on the head of a very young Reserve private who strolled past the house.

Effie was out of the cottage in a flash. Young man, you've stolen yon hat from the bairn!

Didn't steal nothing, lady. He sold it to me for a polecat I done shot over here on the railroad. We made a trade.

But the bairn's an innocent! Scarce can he speak an intelligible word!

Well, he made out that he wanted my polecat, and he kind of grinned, and he give me the hat. I was tickled a-getting it, for I had none.

Effie's sense of justice compelled her to lecture the youth on his sin in taking advantage of a simple-minded infant, her benevolence compelled her to provide him with a paper of sorghum candy.

Two barrels of whiting had been discovered in one of Ira Claffey's sheds, so from Ira the minister's wife begged a few pounds of this material. She asked her husband to stop by the glue-works at Americus before he drove north on his next visit. Here were essentials for the manufacture of whitewash. Mrs. Dillard presented Coral with the bullet mould and powder flask which should have accompanied the brass pistol. Submitting to this bribery, he worked without resentment at mixing a wash for rooms in the cottage. Even Zoral was taught to carry water in assistance, though he spilled half the water each time in mounting the steps, and managed to fall into whitewash when the vat was full, thus entailing more work for Mrs. Effie, more laundering of Zoral, more roars. Very soon the widow sat sewing carpet-rags in a freshly whitened front room (later she was made to shape the circular rag-rugs themselves: she manufactured two, lumpy and uneven, to present additional hazard to Coral and his crutches. One rug was variegated rosily, the other blue and white. Mag thought them beautiful) and Laurel pursued her convalescence in a freshly whitened bedroom.

Twas sin of the flesh, lass. You're fortunate that God let you live, that you weren't punished by the Deil!

Ma said she'd just have to use that there needle on me, count of I hadn't come round. It hurt terrible, Ma'am.

Tis not that evil to which I refer. I refer to the carnal deed in the first place.

I didn't want to do it; he done it to me. And I was scairt to tell Ma for fear she'd take a stick to me.

Ah, I fear you attempted to emulate your wicked mother!

Don't know what you mean, Ma'am. I wasn't trying to do nothing to Ma. She weren't even here in the cottage when't happened.

I mean you wished to do wicked things, lass. With men, as she does. Which is why she's scarlet! Who was the man?

Twas Sergeant Sinkfield. He said twas just a game we was a-playing like when he worked— With little pigs— Laurel rolled over and buried her face in the pillow, she wept savagely and would tell no more. The alarmed Effie Dillard soothed her gently, blamed herself, blamed some unknown sergeant, blamed the Widow Tebbs. She lured Laurel into sipping a glass of her best scuppernong wine, and sat to read aloud somewhat incongruously from an old copy of the *Temperance Songster.*

> *Come, all ye merry maidens,*
> *Miss Lucy or Miss Poll,*
> *Come pass around the paper,*
> *You're sure to sign them all!*

. . . Cate, the lass shall come to dwell with us.

I feared you'd suggest that, Effie.

And why do you say feared?

For we're old. Punished by age, by the adversities which have befallen our beloved State. Flogged by bereavement. . . .

I'll no leave her here to suffer and to sin!

Then she shall come as you wish.

Such a help as she'll be to me, Cate! I'll teach her to sew, to work my caps. And to read and write: she shall make copies of your sermons before you muddy them up with lead pencil, man. . . .

Laurel's pinched face brightened and beamed at the prospect. She had never been to Americus, she thought it quite a city. There were said to be great glass spheres of colored liquid at the druggist's, and a tin roof on the Masonic Hall or some such place. Coral affirmed that there was an entire case in Kinnett's store filled with nothing but candy, or had been when he last saw the town. Mrs. Roach's carriage was believed to have red wheels. It was told that Judge Ladshaw had a pet monkey which would eat goobers and throw the shells in your face.

And you'll be taught to knit, and be taught the Shorter Catechism. And you're no to greet about it!

Nome.

And I'll clothe you decently as a God-fearing lass should be clothed; and not one soul in the place knows of your trouble, so you're no to cast sheep's eyes at the men.

Nome.

In this way you shall be lifted out of iniquity and in time shall stand Redeemed.

Mag said, Just think on it. My little girl, going clean to Americus and getting new gowns. And maybe a bonnet of her own. Well, I never. Don't you go a-getting yourself in a family way again, Laurel, hear me? You like to died of it.

Twenty-three days after her arrival at the Tebbs cottage, Effie Dillard set out with Laurel for Americus. Only Mag saw them off; tears ran at the thought of her daughter going far away, and for so long—how long? But there was the winning thought that—perhaps—

on this very night— If word got around— She might prevail upon Coral to visit Uncle Arch's and remark casually that Mrs. Dillard was no longer in residence at the Tebbs place. I hain't lain with a man for such a while, she thought. I'm nigh dead rusted.

Coral was hunting, Zoral crouched in his hen coop behind the stable. Mag waved happily if tearfully from the stoop. You get holt of any extra ribbons you save them for your Ma, she called. Or glass buttons, like. Blackie drew the two-seated buggy down the lane; the gig would not have been sufficient for the three of them, since Cato Dillard waited at the Claffeys. As wheels lurched over the railway a detail of shabby gray-and-blue jacketed Reserves trailed into the lane from the left. They had guns and wore equipment, they were bound for sentry duty perhaps, bound somewhere.

In the socket beside Mrs. Dillard's right knee sprouted a buggy whip which had never been used. It boasted a long braided lash with a streamer of red silk, though the streamer had now faded through pink nearly to white. This handsome object had been presented to Cato Dillard by its fabricator, who was a member of Cato's flock. The Reverend Mr. Dillard would never have struck Blackie with the thing, not for all the world, but he disliked to offend one of his congregation and so carried the whip displayed.

Mis Dillard, Ma'am, said Laurel's limp voice. Would you please to pull up a second?

Even as Effie drew upon the reins, the girl leaned forward and across her lap and, to Effie Dillard's paralysis, extracted the whip from its socket. Blackie stopped, wheels stopped. A whiny questioning voice requested, Sergeant? A dozen boys turned, and with them turned the bloated pimply face of Sergeant Jester Sinkfield. Laurel shut her eyes tightly and her knuckles turned to white bone; she struck with the force of both arms. She had not much force to muster in her slow-recovering body, yet it seemed she must have been awarded strength from some outer reservoir beyond the reckoning of men. The lash was narrow, limber, tightly braided. It opened up Jester Sinkfield's face across the right cheek and into the chin, it sliced his lips in half. No wound like that would ever mend except as a scar. The bellow of spurting agony sent Blackie forward with a lunge, though the wild-faced Mrs. Dillard tried to hold him.

It's all right, Ma'am, said Laurel. Reckon we can drive on.

LI

Ira Claffey received a letter from Lieutenant-Colonel Persons which saddened but did not surprise him.

You may be interested to know, wrote Persons after polite preliminaries, that I am no longer in any position to assist in a reduction of the horror on your doorstep! This came about because of a proceeding to enjoin the authorities from further continuing the prison there at Andersonville. Observe how the legalistic mind seeks to take up the weapons to which it has been trained. In the character of counsel, I drew a bill for an injunction to abate the nuisance. What makes it a nuisance? You should be well aware, and are. The graveyard makes it a nuisance—the military works, fortifications, wretched personnel, etc., make it a nuisance to you property holders there—and the stockade generally is a nuisance, from the intolerable stench, the effluvia, the malaria that it gives out, and things of that sort. After I drew the bill I went to see the judge of the district court. I read my bill to him and asked him for the injunction. He said that he would appoint a day on which he would hear the argument in chambers. This general suggestion of secrecy should have given suspicion and caused me to lose heart, but still I was consumed with fervor. So the judge appointed a day; I made preparations for trial and was about in the act of going to present the argument, when I received an official communication from General Howell Cobb.

Harrell Elkins, to whom Ira was reading this letter, slapped his hands against the table.

General Cobb asked me if that bill was to be charged to me—the bill against my own Government, was the way he termed it. In reply to his communication, I wrote him that indeed I had drawn the bill, and that it could be charged to me. He replied, through his adjutant-general, Major Harrit, that he deemed it inconsistent with my duty as a Confederate officer, to appear in a case like that, presenting, as General Cobb declared, a bill against my Government. The tenor of his communication was unmistakable: it was obvious that I would be treated by court martial or something of that sort. I said to General Cobb that if he deemed what I had done in the matter unofficerlike, I would leave the case. He said that he did deem it that way, and would be glad if I would retire without being driven.

. . . The authorities are responsible. I cannot say who. The great blunder has been the concentration of so many men at one place, without proper preparations. Again and again the authorities were notified of the fact, but to no advantage. I think some of the higher officials are responsible; but who they are I cannot say. A stockade with supposed accommodations for not more than ten thousand prisoners, and there were nearly forty thousand prisoners sent to it! Captain Wirz cannot be blamed for that. No man on earth could have abated the rigors of Andersonville, except the man who wielded the power. I do not know that man. General Winder was in advance of me, and several others are in advance of him. Who is responsible I cannot say. . . .

Poor man, said Ira, poor man. He looked across the table at Elkins. Poor Cousin Harry, he said.

Poor prisoners, said Elkins. Poor Nation.

Ira thought with increased bitterness that it was a very poor Nation. He felt as he might have felt had he possessed an affectionate, vigorous, beautiful sweetheart, and seen her take to drink or narcotics, and thus deteriorate. It seemed that there was some one thing which he should do personally; but he was not aware what it might be, no search seemed to give the answer. Once, in a borderland between waking and sleeping, it even occurred to Ira that he might calmly assassinate General Winder—turn his back on religion and morality, take the law into his own hands, cry that he was invoking a higher law. He sat up in bed, shocked yet still playing with the possibility. But who might then follow Winder? A worse Winder, no doubt; if such there could be.

The population of the stockade was diminished greatly; to what extent it was difficult to tell. There was still a capacity load of some twenty-five hundred sick in the hospital. A list of figures came to Elkins's attention; he copied them down and presented them to Ira without comment. From February twenty-fourth to September twenty-first, there had been recorded nine thousand, four hundred and seventy-nine deaths.

Nearly one-third of the entire number confined, said Harry. My experience leads me to presume that also there were a great many unrecorded deaths.

It was apparent from advices and from observation that Henry Wirz lived in concentrated terror of a prison break, even with the great lessening of the pen's population. He fussed about at the star fort, the thought of Kilpatrick's cavalry hung like a saber above. He was continually fetching orders to the battery's commander regarding ammunition and the alerting of personnel. At any time, if Yankees on the interior gathered in a mob, Wirz demanded that the cannon should open fire. All through September and into October ragged throngs were herded to the station as rapidly as transportation was made available. No longer could they be considered as tractable, because word of Winder's duplicity had inevitably trickled back to Andersonville. There were more attempts to escape than before. Few people had any desire to be removed to Millen or Florence or Charleston, or to be carried south to Blackshears—any of those places might be worse. Since they had been hoodwinked, and since actually no exchange was in effect, men went plunging off the trains at every trip. Many were shot, or were mutilated in the process of their tumbling. A few got away into lonely underbrush and dragged out starved existence until eventually they were picked up by rustic Home Guards. Only a handful were successful in eluding those armed bands who rode piny forest ways in persistent patrol. The region was filled with straggling refugees from upper counties of the State . . . also there were many runaway slaves . . . every dirty-faced vagabond was suspect as an escaped Yankee prisoner, aching to cut a throat. Wirz bristled beside columns of outgoing Federals, revolver ready in his hand. Sometimes he fired the revolver; it was told that he had killed several prisoners; also it was affirmed that he had killed no one, had shot in the air, or had not even drawn his weapon.

Uncertainties of these cooler drying weeks twisted like stray dust-devils through the countryside. Paroles were sundered right and left; sick boys stumbled in the swamps, vanished there. Hounds of Wes Turner, reinforced by a pack tended by another oaf named Ben Harris, went hollering day and night. Wirz yelled, paid out currency to Harris and Turner, fought with them about price per head and numbers of individuals recaptured. Wirz yelled, his arm yelled back at him, he perspired until his clothing was soaked. Wirz caught cold, went riding again in a fever; he meted out stocks-and-chain-gang penalties for the most minor infractions. Wirz yelled. . . .

In a certain lone glade surrounded by tall trees, shovels sank and turned. The naked bodies were rolled, pushed down. Flimsy records were kept. An effort had been made, on the part of stockade prisoners and hospital attendants alike, to record names and regiments of the dead, dates of their dying; but many scraps of paper were torn from corpses in handling. A slab of split pine grew at the head of each grave. But they were not individual graves, they were populous trenches, they had been filled with cold fruit, each appeared to be lined by a single fence, grave-slabs were the palings of the fence. A marker read: Vork C (that was the name of the thing underneath) 5 Mich (that was the regiment) K (the company) Sept 22 (the date). Slabs said, Unknown, Unknown. A slab said, Waiter G 9 Minn H Sept 9. Scrawled penciling: Brewer J S 6 New York B Oct 2. Rough wood with splinters sticking out on the edges: Lickley P 1 New York Cav E Oct 5. Or Hoagler N C 39 Ind E Oct 8. Or Ballinger Geo 87

Penn D Oct 9. Or Unknown, Unknown, Unknown. There were four-teen Joneses and twelve Johnsons from New York State alone, had any-one cared to go stalking and peering and counting, collecting Joneses and Johnsons. Tossed clay made a wide hummocked quilt from edge of forest to edge of forest. Negroes on duty with the burial detail tried to desert in droves. They were dragged back, tied across stumps or logs; whips popped, the shrieks came up. Wirz trotted fiercely to the scene and said, *Ja,* him I know, that tall one. Three times he has tried for escape! Five hundred lashes he must have! Perhaps the flogger took pity and gave only two hundred lashes after Wirz's back was turned.

Within the stockade Wirz had achieved an autumnal triumph: several long open sheds, built again on the North Side near where the first flimsy hospital had existed. Beneath these sheds many of the stockade's sick might be placed; at least they were out of the rain. There were not beds enough, room enough for the sick in the main hospital. Wirz thought that he should be praised for this accomplish-ment . . . no one praised him. General Winder grunted, growled, de-parted in a northerly direction. . . . There was space enough now: people reconstructed more commodious shebangs, using rags and twigs, the very louse-ridden earth which had been yielded by com-paratively stronger departing throngs. Those were detachments newly told off, containing again only men able to walk.

Inner acres were studded with slow-moving bent figures, no longer a press, but creeping loosely, widely, wandering hunched, wandering forever in a search for scraps of abandoned valuables . . . half-canteen here, a button there, a belt buckle which might be rubbed up and traded to a guard for a collard stalk. It was a poorhouse half denuded, but still the smell rose festering. Winter was on the way, soon the air would be colder, thinner, rarer in a hint of sleet to come.

Another visitor appeared at the Claffey house, escorted one after-noon by Cousin Harry, whose lined face beamed at satisfaction in again meeting with an admired friend. Dr. Joseph Jones had become medical chemist at Augusta while the young civilian Harrell Elkins studied there; Harry was privileged to work as his assistant for a time. During the previous spring exigencies of war had pushed them into contact again, when Cousin Harry toiled in exploration of hospital gangrene. Jones was a brilliant and observing man, some years Harry's elder, but essentially much more the scientist than the soldier. Never-theless he had served for six months as a private in the ranks during the earlier part of the war. Now belatedly the Confederacy exhibited a tendency to make use of his erudition. . . . Jones declared that he was flabbergasted by Andersonville. He had heard merely of unusual mortality among the Federal prisoners; he had never dreamed of the nature of drainage, water supply and food supply. He had never dreamed that no shelter whatsoever was afforded. He said, I am so appalled by what I see here that I find myself at a loss for words.

This was at an evening meal shared by the three men. (Lucy had withdrawn in order to give them full scope in discussion.)

Another report? asked Ira. Reports have been made to every section of command in the past, and were met with identical silence.

In my innocence I had thought in terms of fevers, said Dr. Jones. In August I had an opportunity to visit Richmond and suggested to Surgeon-General S. P. Moore that conditions at Andersonville might be worth a minute investigation. Indeed! Little did I think that—I was told nothing, nothing! Believe me, sir, not a word was breathed of this horror. I considered only that a large body of men from the Northern portion of the United States, suddenly transported to a warmer Southern climate, and confined upon a small portion of land, would furnish an excellent field for the investigation of the relations of typhus, typhoid and malarial fevers. I received my orders, proceeded here, and walked into—this.

You should have seen the stockade during that same August, Elkins told him. Since then a great many of the Federals have been removed elsewhere.

How many are now confined, Harry?

Perhaps fifteen thousand, all told, stockade and hospital. However, numerous detachments are still being sent forth. It is hoped that the total may be reduced to at least eight thousand or thereabouts by the first of next month.

Have conditions at the hospital been in any way ameliorated by these withdrawals?

Not in the slightest, sir. We are tight run—never tighter than now. There's not an inch of space remaining within the hospital itself. In fact our task has been increased and intensified by these outgoing detachments.

Why on Earth—?

Because many of these prisoners were cared for to some degree by their comrades. The comrades were ordered away and were forbidden to carry the sick along with them. There was a certain amount of subterfuge, naturally; some of the sick did go along with the well. But the greater number were left in what amounted to abandonment. Therefore the increase in the ratio of reported sickness and resulting mortality.

Dr. Jones had produced his Richmond orders, with which Surgeon Isaiah White, in charge of the hospital, was duly impressed. In this way Jones was able to have Elkins transferred from other duties temporarily to serve as his assistant, both in post mortem examinations and the rough draft of his report. The two men drove themselves mercilessly through all hours of daylight in first-hand exploration. At night papers were unrolled upon the Claffey dining table. The plantation's stock of candles suffered, and Lucy was at her wits' end to see that more candles were manufactured immediately. The two surgeons correlated their notes. In tired voices suggestions were made, there was mutual criticism of style and content.

I can't say merely a pile of human excrement, Harry. It does not convey the enormity of the thing; we *must* convey it.

Let us see . . . say, filthy quagmire of human excrements.

Yes, much better.

Alive with working maggots, Elkins added.

More impressive still. And hideously correct!

Lucy tapped at the edge of the open door: would the gentlemen take coffee now? They would indeed. Ninny was sent with the old Bavarian china pot, the chipped delicate cups. Grain coffee was poured, a smidgin of precious cane syrup stirred in.

Where will you go, sir, when you have concluded your investigation here?

Jones said, Doubtless to hospitals connected with the Army of Tennessee, and shall probably be there until November. For the eventual preparation of the final draft, I must await the reception of answers to numerous other inquiries I've made. . . .

Diarrhoea, dysentery, scurvy, and hospital gangrene were the diseases which have been the main cause of this extraordinary mortality. The origin and character of the hospital gangrene which prevailed to so remarkable a degree and with such fatal effects amongst the Federal prisoners, engaged my most serious and earnest consideration. More than 30,000 men, crowded upon twenty-seven acres of land, with little or no shelter from the intense heat of a Southern summer, or from the rain and from the dew of night, with coarse corn bread from which the husk had not been removed, with but scant supplies of fresh meat and vegetables, with little or no attention to hygiene, with festering masses of filth at the very doors of their rude dens and tents, with the greater portion of the banks of the stream flowing through the stockade a filthy quagmire of human excrements alive with working maggots, generated by their own filthy exhalations and excretions, an atmosphere that so deteriorated and contaminated their solids and fluids that the slightest scratch and even the bites of small insects were in some cases followed by such rapid and extensive gangrene as to destroy extremities and even life itself. . . .

Let's see, Harry. Where is August?

August, August. There August lies yonder, under the saucer.

. . . August: fifty-three cases and fifty-three deaths recorded as marasmus.

That was the terminology.

But surely this large number of deaths must have been due to some

other morbid state than slow wasting? If they were due to improper
and insufficient food, they should have been classified accordingly.

In our hospital, said Harry Elkins slowly, there have been peculiar
notions regarding statement of the causes of death.

But, Harry, if due to diarrhoea, dysentery or scurvy, the classification should in like manner have been explicit!

I suggest, sir, that you incorporate that query in your report.

Elkins hoisted his thinning body into a bent but standing position,
and beat his hand on the table in a fashion now grown characteristic.
Let us take, for example, *vulnus sclopeticum*. A great many deaths
have been entered as due to that cause. I am referring to prisoners
shot by guards. As you are well aware, sir, that is the technical name
for a gunshot wound! Even stranger recordings have been made. I
found, when ordered to assemble certain previous reports which had
been made at best in fragmentary fashion, that on the eleventh of July,
six men died of *asphyxia*. I was very curious about this. . . . Had the
men smothered in their sleep? They had not. It was merely that they
were hanged by the neck until dead. Those were the raiders executed
by their fellow prisoners. An amusing circumstance, do you not think?
He cackled.

Pray sit down, said Joseph Jones sadly. Where were we? Ah, yes:
August again. What was the mortality of mean strength, sick and well,
in August?

Nine and nine-hundredths per cent.

What was the first month—February or March?

The first prisoners came in a few days before the end of February.
Thus the first figures available for a complete month are for March.

And the rate then?

Three and eleven-hundredths per cent of mean strength for March.

Then the rate of mortality has very nearly tripled, for the prisoners
as a whole?

That does not approach the rate of hospital mortality, sir.

Ah, I'm well aware of that. But let me have the sum of deaths for
September eighteenth. I believe you said that would astound me.

Here it is: one hundred and twenty-seven.

In *one day?*

Correct, sir.

My eyes are swimming, confronted with numerals. Let us put
numerals by for a time. . . . Now: have you seen my preliminary description concerning the hospital itself?

They hunted for the papers, found them at last jammed into a worn
saddle bag which served as Doctor Jones's literary kit.

The patients and attendants . . . are crowded into this confined
space and are but poorly supplied with old and ragged tents. Large
numbers of them are without any bunks in the tents, and lie upon the

*ground, ofttimes without even a blanket. No beds or straw appeared
to have been furnished. The tents extend to within a few yards of the
small stream, the eastern portion of which, as we have before said, is
used as a privy and is loaded with excrements; and I observed a large
pile of corn bread, bones, and filth of all kinds, thirty feet in diameter
and several feet in height, swarming with myriads of flies, in a vacant
space near the pots used for cooking. Millions of flies swarmed over
everything and covered the faces of the sleeping patients, and crawled
down their open mouths, and deposited their maggots in the gangrenous wounds of the living, and in the mouths of the dead. Mosquitoes in
great numbers also infested the tents, and many of the patients were
so stung by these pestiferous insects, that they resembled those suffering with a slight attack of measles.*

Harry, lad, you've fallen asleep.

Why— So I did, so I did. My apologies—

Ira Claffey wondered without much confidence whether this third
effort of a dedicated Confederate would turn the trick. Some people
held three to be a lucky number . . . the third time was the charm . . .
old saws of that nature. Persons, Chandler, Jones. Would demands of
other duties allow Jones to complete his report? Would a sudden
onrush of Federals from Atlanta preclude the completion? If the report
were completed, what of its reception at Richmond? . . . Harrell
Elkins shared Ira's fears, yet he toiled with angry enthusiasm. Joseph
Jones made certain that the statistics which he carried away with him
were as accurate as might be, despite slovenly bookkeeping at original
sources. He turned to the prose body of his report only when eyes and
brain refused to accept another statistic. Thus those at the Claffey
house might have little idea as to the shape this report would assume
eventually, the damning quality of the utterance. Only an occasional
summary relating to a specific fault stood out in something like acceptable form; these Surgeon Jones read to his angrily-impressed small
audience the night before his departure. Jones held that there should
be nothing secret in his document. He hoped indeed that it would be
published in all directions. He felt that he was violating no confidential
rule, where his Nation or his superiors were concerned, in including
sympathetic citizens in the last candlelit session.

*This gigantic mass of human misery calls loudly for relief, not only
for the sake of suffering humanity, but also on account of our own
brave soldiers now captives in the hands of the Federal government.
Strict justice to the gallant men of the Confederate armies, who have
been or who may be so unfortunate as to be compelled to surrender
in battle, demands that the Confederate government should adopt
that course which will best secure their health and comfort in captivity; or at least leave their enemies without a shadow of an excuse*

for any violation of the rules of civilized warfare in the treatment of prisoners.

It was still October when Dr. Jones went away. As he had foreseen, he was ordered to the hospitals with the Army of Tennessee. Harrell Elkins returned to miscellaneous overwork, the disorganized routine of hospital and stockade gate. He had a special corner of an outbuilding wherein he strove to rid himself of lice and fleas before reëntering the Claffey house after each tour of duty. Despite his best intention, vermin did accompany him. Lucy prowled with coal oil, hunting the sly tiny villains.

She observed that her father was growing more and more detached as the autumn lengthened into November. Ira shirked self-appointed garden tasks . . . sometimes the Negroes were left with nothing to do because no work had been laid out for them. Ira went often with his gun to the uplands but brought back few birds. Sometimes he brought no birds at all—the weapon was unsmudged, had not been fired. I wonder if he thinks he sees the boys, as he murmured that once he saw them a year since? cried Lucy to herself. I wonder. . . .

Ira routed his daughter from her bed one evening, when Elkins was asleep, when a small fire burned on the library hearth. Ira made Lucy don a comforter and sit before this fire.

I am going. Today I decided that I must go. I cannot dwell in harmony with myself unless I try.

Go where?

To Richmond—where else? Did I not tell you what was my thought?

Poppy, you've said nothing. Sakes! Nothing at all. You've gone poking sometimes with your gun, sometimes without it. I declare, I've tried to think what ailed you, and could never decide. I knew it must have to do with the prison. You've changed in such a way since Surgeon Jones was here.

Ira sat staring at the fire, his chin on his fists. Beg pardon for any withdrawal; it was a matter I had to thrash out. But viewing those three men—all doing their best to secure a reformation—our friend Alex Persons; then Chandler; Jones at the last. Indeed we've heard nothing from Jones, there's been no alteration of circumstances. Conditions grow worse steadily at the approach of winter. You've heard Coz say so, and his opinion is to be trusted above others. Gad, it seems the others might have offered their reports as Coz offered his: wafted into flame, directed upwards to the Almighty!

No, no, he cried, and stood up to wave his fists. It cannot continue like this. I'll not let it continue!

But, Poppy— All the way to Richmond? And it's just a trial, traveling these days. Everyone tells that. And such a sight of cash. Poppy, have we—? Do you have sufficient funds?

I shall draw money out of my box, come what may. Daughter, as

you know, I was acquainted with President Davis many years ago.
But still I knew him, and he knew me. What is a commander? A man
with subordinates, many of them appointed directly by that commander. Somewhere along the line of subordinates sits the official who
individually might rectify the present, who might benefit the future—
I know too well that past months cannot be rectified. Perhaps I was
appointed by Fate, because of this acquaintanceship with the Chief
Executive! It may be that I have disregarded impassioned summons
heretofore. I have been sluggardly, Lucy—weak and sluggardly. A man
may not feel he has done everything he can do—not until he has *done*
everything he *can* do.

Then God speed you, Poppy.

Lucy. In a tone of equal tenderness. I cannot leave you alone—not
with a man in the house to whom in fact we are not related.

She sat in silence.

Early the next morning Ira set out for Americus. There was a fairly
good horse left on the Yeoman place, he borrowed that horse. He conferred with Effie Dillard. She came somewhat reluctantly to the plantation on the following day, leaving a long list of admonitions to Laurel
Tebbs: tasks which Laurel must perform, comforts and duties essential
to the well-being of the Reverend Mr. Cato Dillard.

A grievance, she told her husband.

No grievance, Effie. It's kindness which you must award to friends.

Aye, we dare risk no scandal where our dear lass Lucy is concerned!
Bear with it all, Cate. You shall be in my prayers nightly, husband,
and in my thoughts each hour.

At the Claffey place Ira was immersed in his own preparations. Lucy
stood behind a curtain and watched the round-shouldered Harry striding off to the hospital. Suddenly her cheeks grew hot, she closed her
eyes and spread her hands against her cheeks.

LII

Fire swept Atlanta on the night of November fifteenth, and rumor held that Sherman was driving on Augusta. Because the entire Southwestern railway line had been taken over by the military, Ira Claffey was compelled to apply for a pass before boarding a train. Permission was granted readily: another contingent labored here since the departure of Winder and his flock. Wirz and Colonel Thurlow survived, together with some members of the surgical staff. Commissary and quartermaster's departments were administered by new people, so was the office of transportation. The transportation officer was a plaintive little grub who had been shot through the throat and could not raise his voice above a whisper. He whispered thanks to Ira. . . . Quantities of yams, cabbages, onions, pumpkins from the Claffey plantation found their way to the officers' mess. Some people considered it possible that Wirz might have given permission for such fare to be carried into stockade and hospital also, had he not feared the slug of a fist thrusting down from Florence or Camp Lawton.

About four o'clock in the afternoon Ira took leave of Lucy and Mrs. Dillard; Harry Elkins was on duty at the hospital. Ira walked to Anderson Station carrying his own carpetbag; there was no meanness about this nowadays; his hands were at work getting winter wood, he did not wish to take one hand from his task. Ira sat on the tailboard of a collapsed wagon almost until dusk: the train had been long delayed between Albany and Americus.

There were other delays to be incurred north of Anderson. A rail sprang from ties, it had to be spiked into place. An engine crew was become a track maintenance crew in these times. . . . In darkness the head-lamp would not operate, it was burned out. For such emergencies an old-fashioned dolly was carried aboard the wood tender; but it lay buried under pine lengths, so there must ensue unloading before the flat little car could be dragged out and secured in front of the engine. Knots were set aflame, the engine sparked mournfully at a mule's pace as if it shoved a gay bonfire unwillingly. Pine flames leaned back against the shield, red glow stole ahead, cars grated, creaked, shoved together in couplings, pulled apart in couplings. The train crept, its ruddy fingers of light closing slowly on the rope of track. Interiors

thickened with the smell of woodsmoke and deep-dyed sweat, together
with smell of the place where some passenger had been sick. The door
of a corner privy banged back and forth; it could not be secured and
kept from banging; the wooden privy box shifted and smelled. A bench
was built along each side of the car and across the ends, another bench
ran down the middle. On this slept, end to end, several youthful
soldiers dragged from some port farther south. They were being sent
up-State to serve as reinforcements . . . from a hundred other posts
such elements were drawn. Reinforcements, reinforcements, said slow
rough wheels chewing the rails. Sherman's left Atlanta . . . Sherman's
out of Atlanta. . . .

Ira Claffey rested in a front corner of the car, as far from the privy
smell as possible. But the bench was narrow, he could not stretch safely
upon it as thin boys did. He tried to pillow his head on his bag, tried to
secure himself against the tenacious hammering of patched equipment.
It was gray sunrise before they reached Macon, and they did not leave
Macon on the Georgia Central for many hours. Lucy had prepared a
basket of corn sticks, pickled pork, and biscuit sandwiches spread
with sorghum, along with an old brandy bottle filled with grain coffee.
The five freckled mossy-necked boys in the car had no food. They explained to Ira Claffey that they had been told to draw rations; but
rations were refused because of some technicality. Ira divided his store
of meat and bread into six portions as equally as possible. Also during
the eternity of waiting outside Macon, a stout Negress came along the
track offering fish for sale. Ira treated the soldiers to fried catfish.

He thought that he had seen refugees before . . . truly he had not
seen them. Oh, there had been visible evidence of distant battles,
wickedness of distant campaigns. Stupid frightened black people
inched along the railway, along the road past the Claffey plantation.
Some of the Negro men had been impressed—captured, as it were—
and set to menial tasks in the Andersonville cemetery or around the
camps. It was whispered through the neighborhood that some of the
more comely Negresses were persuaded to linger for a time, to afford
pleasure for men in a tent outside the picket lines. Ira's own pickaninnies had come from play along a weedy fence, fetching a stray child in
verminous rags. Scarcely could you tell the sex of the critter. The hair
was kinked, the body neglected, eyes rolled frantically. Only children
of its own size could have lured it to the plantation. Lucy gave orders
that the thing should be scrubbed and fed. It turned out to be a little
girl. Lucy named her Dryad, since she was found in the woods, and for
nearly a week the black children enjoyed their new playmate; until
Dryad quarreled with little Gracious and ran off, declaring that she
was going home to her Mammy. Ira ordered the hands to go searching.
They never found her, nor did she return to the plantation again. They
heard nothing more of the child. It was feared that she might have

been drowned in Little Sweetwater, or perhaps went down into a bog.
. . . Yes, he had seen black people drifting, and some whites. He
was accustomed to ragged nomads who glared suspiciously, whose lean
yellow faces gave forth little except suspicion and colder resentment.
He had seen them in their camps, had watched against their thefts, had
given them food in every case when they came to beg. Their starved
dogs skulked along with them, forever it seemed that the dogs traveled
on three legs.

But here in the Macon region tumbled hordes who had been shunted
out of Atlanta and smaller towns in the northwest region where Union
brigades came growling and firing. Along the side track sentries were
disposed solely for the purpose of restraining these confused tribes.
Ira stood in the car door, observing with pity, and hearing reiteration
of the guards: no citizen dared board this train without displaying a
pass for self and family. This rule was honored in the breach, and Ira
surmised that there had been some bribes as well. Benches and floors
filled up with strident women, squalling babies, madcap older children
who wrestled and ran, making holiday and war dance out of the whole
miserable matter.

There came the tall judge with face like dry paper. His eyes were
pink-rimmed, he twisted his skinny beard, said that he had had two
sons and three grandsons in the army. But all were dead, sir. All were
dead . . . and the Yankees had taken over his house, sir, and flung
him out to wander and starve, sir. There came a spinster seamstress
dragging her mother along. The fat old lady scolded and palpitated;
she said that her head was spinning, and where were those aromatic
salts, Letty John—where were those salts? There came the small shy
pretty woman, large with child, trying to manage two covered baskets
and two little boys who owned their mother's cool brown eyes and
soft voice and fuzzy brown hair. The woman said that her husband
was serving under General Hampton, and wasn't this just the beat?
. . . A slobbery fat man, drunk and threatening; he claimed that the
Yankees had killed his hogs. He swore that he had escaped barely with
his life, and was confident that his wife was ravished by invaders. But
he had run off without her; it appeared that he had not waited to see
what had befallen her; perhaps he could not bear to witness her
ravished condition. . . .

There was the nine-year-old boy who had been separated from
grandparents with whom he traveled. He wore a miniature gray uniform with ragged braid on it. He was naughty, he stamped and
screeched, slapped at smaller children, yelled that he was hungry. Ira
offered him some biscuit and sorghum, but the boy snarled that he
didn't want any of that old nigger food: he wanted spice cake. . . .
Two meek maidens of teen age; they were not twins, but were dressed
in similar shawls and gowns, almost identical bonnets. One of them

was doubled with abdominal cramps. She cried quietly, could not refrain from holding her hand against her middle, she buried her face against her sister as she cried. . . .

A grinning servant with a face like crumpled black tin. He said that he was taking care of The Doctor. Yes, sir, he was taking care of The Doctor. And the doctor was every day of eighty, and carried an ear trumpet, and stared hopelessly out of eyes on which the film of cataracts showed. The servant said his own name was Jack and he had belonged to the doctor for forty-four years. He said that he knew his numbers, he could cipher well. It was in 1820 that the doctor bought him, bought him in North Carolina. That was before they moved down here, and—he lowered his voice mysteriously the doctor wasn't deaf then; but he was very deaf now. No sir, old Jack wasn't going to stay to home. He knew what would happen if he fell into hands of the Yankees: he would be worked to death on fortifications, or else would be put out right smack in front of all those soldiers; right in front of the line of battle he would be put, to absorb shot directed at the Yankees. Or else he would be sent to Cuba and sold. And he knew well enough what the Yankees did to old women and young children: they would be drowned like blind puppies or cats. No, sir, he was getting out of there. The Doctor didn't want to come, but he had done persuaded The Doctor. Yes sir, he had done persuaded him. They were going to Savannah, that's where they were going.

Wounded soldiers in the throng . . . boys with bandages. . . . A loud-voiced young woman with brilliantly red cheeks and coils of brassy hair straggling. She made much of rustling her patched silk gown, she giggled when the young soldiers talked to her. She laughed as the ignorant and light-brained laugh. Her laughter went up in a shriek, she could not laugh without shrieking. The shriek would start on a high note, it sounded like ungreased axles of the train itself, it held a protracted *eeeh* at high pitch, it died down only to spout again when something else was said. . . . A very new baby wailed cease-lessly. It said *lah* at regular intervals. Ira began to count the *lahs*. He counted to two hundred with scarce a break, then wearied of counting and became insensitive to the sound . . . heard no more of it, though the hungry mite wailed on, was silenced briefly at its mother's breast, refused the breast, continued *lah*ing.

There sat a small Jewish tailor with fat small wife. The woman cried a little, touching her eyes with a folded cambric handkerchief, but she made no sound. At last she opened a willow basket, brought out lunch: some strange crackery compound, and homemade cheese. The old couple munched stoically. They said that their son and his wife had elected to remain at home. The son had lost his arm in the war. He said that he had no fear of the Yankees, had often traded tobacco for coffee. Actually he had traded with the Yankees when they were

fighting at the North! But Mamma here— She would not wait. She
thinks the Yankees would kill her. I do not believe it so, but that is
what she thinks. But this is not so bad. It is bad, but it is not so bad.
When I was a lad— That was many years ago—it was in the Old
Country. I remember I fled with my parents, for soldiers were to kill
us, and it was cold, much colder than now. . . .

Eventually the car was crammed to suffocation, though some of
these runaways grew restless because the train did not move. They
pushed their way out, left the car, went perhaps into some other car
or back into the town. Once a woman shrieked, Yankee cavalry! There
they are! and there was a great pushing and punching as everyone
struggled to see. But no Yankee cavalry could be found on the landscape—only some Negro boys leading several head of mules.

Once again in afternoon the rusty splintery worm crawled its course.
Engine puffed and shuddered, greaseless axles screamed like caged
demons above tortured boxes, loose metal banged and thudded, steam
and smoke went coughing. May we get to Savannah, Sherman is loose,
Sherman is loose, Sherman is coming. Sherman has left Atlanta, gulp,
Sherman has left Atlanta, gulp, Sherman is loose, gasp, Sherman's
coming, gasp. In its soiled pink shawl the baby cried. Rustling in soiled
silken skirts, the girl with brassy locks still squealed, boy soldiers said
funny things to her.

In late afternoon the train stopped dead with a grinding lurch which
sent the passengers into convulsions. The jolt was so severe that Ira
Claffey supposed a driving-rod must have lashed up into the engine,
or that the engine had upset and cars rammed it. Ira was hurled
against old Jack on the side bench. He got free from the caterwauling
mass of citizens, and carried his carpetbag to the door. . . . It's a
wreck! Children clamoring. Ma, we're in a wreck!

The car was upright, there rose no sound of flames, no demonstration
of serious injury. I don't believe it's a wreck, said Ira. Now everybody
hush!

He pushed open the rickety door and peered out and forward along
the left side of the train. Soldier boys ganged around him to peer also,
they pushed their heads past Ira, over and under the arm with which
he braced himself. The train was halted on a curve, the engineer was
getting down, several Negroes had hopped off the tender. Two officers
from another car hastened toward the engine.

We ain't allowed to get out, sir, said a youth. We got to stay aboard,
less we're ordered to get down.

See if you can quiet these women and children, Ira told him and the
other boys. I'll attempt to satisfy our curiosity. He swung from the
car, still carrying his bag; it would not do to leave it behind.

The engine-driver stood at the front, rubbing sooty hands against
his flanks. Two Confederate officers were with him, and were joined

by bearded citizens. Come all the way from Albany, an old man said, just to run into this! The engine was smashed into a barricade of logs and ties. Smaller logs had been sent flying, one had been hurled like a spear to bury itself in the side of the embankment. The train stood in a cut rounding the lower portion of a hill. Heavier substance of the barricade remained, crushed under forward wheels or surmounting the cow-catcher. Two wheels at the left side were pushed from the U-shaped track. We hain't got the power, the engineer said sourly, to lever them back.

Who would have done this? Ira asked.

One officer unfastened a revolver holster and fingered the butt of his weapon. Could be Sherman's folks have got this far. I heard last night they was headed nigh.

You might be captured, Major.

The old major declared emphatically, That's just the rub. But my orders were to take this train. Naught arrived to countermand them.

Ira Claffey pointed. A wisp of smoke blew above trees perhaps one hundred rods to the northwest. It was the light forerunner of a thicker column—twisting, congealing, darkening to black as it climbed.

By Mercy, said the engine-driver. Could be those damn bummers!

I thought twas customary for them to destroy railroads, rather than build barricades.

Hell, mister. They'd do anything!

A younger officer exclaimed nervously. Now that they had moved past the engine other fires loomed ahead, the horizon was layered with smoke.

Reckon I'll take to the woods, the wrinkled major said decisively. Got no wish to be snatched up by Yanks.

Ira walked back beside the cars, trying to decide a wise course. If Yankees had penetrated this region (it was apparent that they had; or at least some accompanying bands of straggling raiders must have done so) they might shoot anyone who seemed anxious to conceal himself. He thought that under these conditions the woodland offered little sanctuary. He considered it unlikely that the frightened freight of refugees would come to harm. He recalled what papers he was carrying. Papers should prove his identity, give evidence that he was not a Confederate soldier in citizen's clothing. Ira reached his own car and spoke one low word to faces studding the doorway. Sherman. Three of the boys came down like jumping jacks, weaponless, not even pausing to secure haversacks. Two others went back for their equipment, then they sprang down as well. One youngster sprinted up the embankment immediately, filling his shoes with ashes as he climbed, and disappeared over the edge. The others stood debating, while there ensued a gush of women and old people and children from the cars. Ira walked away from the train, south around the extremity of the curve, until he was out of sight. He should strike for a road, any road. He had not gone out of earshot, however. A series of yells rose behind him—staccato whoops of challenge or triumph. He walked steadily, glancing occasionally over his shoulder to see if he was being followed. Later he heard shots. He hoped that no one had been hurt, he trusted that the shots were fired merely for intimidation, or in a celebrating spirit. No one pursued him. If a bushwhacking gang was raiding the train they must have come up too late to see his departure.

Ira came to a creek where rails were supported by a trestle; he slid down and crouched beneath the trestle. He had with him nearly three thousand dollars in Confederate currency . . . he did not know how long it would take him to reach Richmond, how long to return. He carried also a letter from Americus authorizing him to draw a draft as necessary. Now he thought it wise to destroy this letter: the practice of holding for ransom might exist. He tore the letter into scraps and scattered them on the water. He left one hundred and eighty dollars in odd certificates, rolled this money and thrust it into his pocket. He was dressed very nearly in his best; no one would believe him if he professed to be penniless. The bulk of the money, together with his watch, he put into his wallet. He disrobed partially and, constructing a belt of handkerchief strings, bound the wallet against his inner thigh. In the carpetbag Ira carried only clothing and a few toilet articles. Again he thought it better not to be empty-handed on meeting freebooters. He put the razor case into his coat pocket, the razor might serve as a weapon. Reclothed, he ascended to the railway, crossed the trestle, found a wagon road a few hundred yards to the south. There were no vehicles in sight—no pedestrians, no animals, not a figure moving.

The train had halted but a few miles beyond Macon if one judged correctly the speed and the time elapsed. Possibly Northern troops were in Macon already or would be immediately. If Macon were captured, Milledgeville also must have been captured, or would be captured soon, or besieged. The reduction of an important military point such as Macon, the reduction of the State capital itself—to be accompanied by wastage and looting—would consume time. If Ira traveled rapidly across country toward Savannah he might reach that port before Yankees did. He thought of counties to the east, reviewing geography involved. He must get across the Oconee. Traveling southeast by way of Reidsville he might keep to the right of the Federal advance, and thus escape stragglers. Perhaps he would still be able to journey by boat from Savannah or by rail from Savannah to Charleston. . . . A horse. Wilkinson County had not yet been raided: he might be able to buy a mount and travel long, and next day trade his horse for a fresh one. . . . How far is Savannah? Perhaps a hundred and fifty miles as the crow flies? . . . Ira was embarked upon a sacred course. His conscience had sent him into this hazard, his conscience must sustain him.

Sun came through low haze and turned the rutted clay road to a brassy streak. Ira halted, looked to the west, flattened his hand, held it out at arm's length with wrist against the horizon. The sun would set in little more than an hour. He resumed his plodding. The way swung slightly to the north, then back south of east. There came a rise, he topped it, he stood on a slight ridge. . . . No smoke ahead, but several separate trunks of smoke twisted at the left. He envisioned them as outskirts of a forest which might thicken. He must avoid that forest, not be tangled in it, not be lost.

Ira saw himself in Richmond, signing for a room at the Spotswood Hotel. Halls were filled with belted officers in gray, with citizens shouldering. Streets were a press and torrent . . . horses bringing down their hoofs, army wagons a-jumble. There were beggars and armless veterans . . . Ira imagined one young man with both legs gone; the fellow pushed himself upon a wheeled platform as Ira had seen another beggar do in a Northern city long ago. This legless man had a cake of solid wood strapped to each hand: with these slabs as motive power he drew himself ahead, bumping, straining on his low cart. These things Ira saw . . . perhaps prostitutes sauntering at entrances of small lanes, the Capitol rising beyond.

He stood eventually in the presence of Mr. Seddon. He had never seen Mr. Seddon, but a friend told him that the Secretary wore habitually a black skull cap. Appropriately beneath that cap his face was a dry corpse-face bereft of vitality. Eyes were pits, the voice mouldered as it spoke. . . . There loomed a repository in the shape of a burial casket, with glass where the face of a dead person might be seen. Therein was contained no body: only the mass of reports sent by inspecting officers and angry surgeons. Pleas of good men like Persons and Chandler and Jones . . . you could witness those reports through glass, each rolled into a little rod, tied tightly with red tape, scratched with chicken tracks which said that those reports had been Noted By Secretary Seddon And Then Filed Away.

No, doubtless he would never stand before James Seddon, he could but try to reach Mr. Seddon's presence. Guards, underlings would hold him back. He would stand instead before some other desk, be greeted tonelessly by a slit-eyed subordinate, be told to go away, just as General Winder had ordered the people of Americus to go away with their vegetables.

Sir, as I have described to you, the place is a menace and disgrace.

But upwards of twenty thousand prisoners have already been removed, Mr. Claffey!

Some of them have been returned, because there seemed no safe place to hold them, either at Savannah or at Blackshears. True, the crowded conditions have lessened, but smell continues. And disease. A higher percentage of hospital patients go to death each day, because they constituted originally the sick and crippled, the unable-to-travel, the weaklings, the rotting outcasts.

Mr. Claffey, the Secretary is engaged. He cannot possibly see you.

Then I shall presume to address myself to President Davis. I knew him— It was during the Mexican War—

Blank formless visage, still formless, still blank, still repellent . . . somehow wearing a supercilious smile. The President knew many people during the late War with Mexico, Mr. Claffey! I doubt that he would recall you. I doubt that he would recall your name.

Then I shall go to—

To whom?

Surgeon Elkins addressed himself in appeal to the Almighty God. Can I not do the same?

God will not see you. He is engaged.

In desperation of anguish. . . .

Oh, please to hear me, please to assist! I plead not solely on behalf of the miserable Yankees who whine and vomit in those several acres of so-called hospital between the creeks! I plead on behalf of my three sons who died boldly, died with honor. I plead on behalf of our dear new Nation, on behalf of whatever tradition shall be suffered to exist when once we have gained the—the—victory, the—unchallenged independence we seek. What matters a chivalrous Lee if we have a Winder? What matters the sacrifice of a Hood, if we have a Captain Wirz? What matters the competence of a Johnston or the spiritual strength of a sickly Stephens, if we have at home only the incompetence of venal surgeons, incompetence of a Seddon, frailty and futility of a sickly Seddon?

You are near to provoking me into issuing an order for your arrest, Mr. Claffey! You are presumptuous, stubborn, ignorant of necessities of war. Go way!

Then nothing can be done?

Nothing. Go way!

I prophesy with all the terrible ardor I can muster: this will be a stench in the nostrils of history.

Those are not my nostrils, nor the nostrils of any living soldier or office-holder. How can I be held responsible, you upstart? Who can be held responsible?

If an individual, it is difficult for me to name him.

Ira Claffey felt the doom of his hope. Still he must progress, win through to Richmond. He felt that Sherman's entire army was on his flank . . . beloved Creator, I must turn that flank. He limped on. How could a mere carpetbag grow so heavy?

Ahead appeared a house and outbuildings on the north side of the road. It was a substantial house; but as Ira came closer he could see that the steps were in bad repair, some windows were broken, there was a scurrying which occurred among outbuildings at the rear. He heard the whinny of a horse. Then, past the next clump of leafless trees, he saw three horses standing riderless in front of the dwelling. Saddles were empty but there were odd-shaped baskets and bundles tied to the saddles. Some hurly-burly was in progress within the farmhouse. Voices raised . . . Ira heard suddenly a scream that started as a squeak, a moan rising in pitch until it pierced walls and roof. The yell was accompanied by a dragging banging sound. Murder, he thought. That is the sound of murder. He dropped his carpetbag at the gate and hurried along a graveled path littered with debris and chicken droppings. He went up five steps to the gallery, felt a board break beneath his weight; he did not fall. The door was a double door, giving on an open hallway which passed directly through the house; a door stood open at the other end. No person was in sight. There were pans, utensils, implements hung along the passageway. A tall chest of drawers stood against one wall, and bundles of seed corn dried from the roof. Banging sound and the continuing shriek filled the first room on the right; Ira blundered there. The scene struck him swiftly: a mussed bed, a gray-haired woman—perhaps an invalid—who sat stiffly in a small rocking chair and held her hands over her eyes as she wailed. A medium-sized man was bending in front of another bureau there. He had pulled out all the drawers and was rummaging, dipping both hands into masses of clothing, bundles of letters. A rag doll was tossed aside, tossed over the man's shoulder, the doll fell at Ira's feet as he entered. The man swung around, straightened. His hand went to his hip as if reaching for a weapon. Ira struck him on the side of the jaw; the man sprawled and lay grunting. His face was stubbly, the beard grown out an inch. Plunging, two other men came across the corridor from some opposite room. Ira whirled, ready with his fists, then he dropped his fists. He saw the muzzle of a carbine. One man was tall, clean-shaven, the other squat. Yes, both carried carbines. Ira thought swiftly that he would be shot, he stood anticipating the blow of bullets against his body. These men were in blue or half in blue. Still they did not look like soldiers.

Where the hell did you come from, Mister?

Ira stood thinking of the combined charge of those carbines, still expecting it.

You belong here?

I was passing.

Passing?

Passing by. I heard screams.

Look at Terry, said the taller man. Lowering his carbine, he came past Ira as if he did not exist. Hi, Terry! What you doing on the floor?

Son of a bitch hit me.

Why, Mister, said the taller man. His hair clung matted, straggling under his shapeless colorless hat, dirty silver at the temples. He must be nearly as old as Ira. Mister, you like to killed our partner here. You could get shot for that!

The old lady in the chair had quieted down. She'd lowered her hands, hands bounced up and down upon her dirty aproned lap, her jaws kept twitching spasmodically, her pale eyes gyrated in knots of wrinkles, she appeared to be having a fit.

The man called Terry raised into a sitting position. He sat feeling his face. By God, where'd I put my pistol? I'm going to kill that son of a bitch!

Yes, said the taller older man mockingly, you kill him, we're like to be hung. Come on, Terry, get the rocks out of your ass. Let's move along.

He took Terry's hand and pulled the man to his feet. Terry staggered back against the rifled bureau.

Mr. Secesh, the taller fellow addressed Ira, you got any money?

I have a little money.

Then we'll just take that.

Ira reached for his pocket.

No, no! Right pants pocket? I'll just take that myself. Keep your gun on his head, Lester, he directed the man in the door. For Christ sake don't shoot me if you got to pull trigger. Swiftly his hairy hands slapped around Ira's breast and flanks, feeling for a pistol, but he did not touch the inside of the thigh. One hand struck the razor case in Ira's coat pocket. The razor was produced, the man put it in his own pocket. That'll be for Terry, he said. He needs a good shave—don't you, Terry boy? He found the fold of Ira's bills, counted swiftly, pocketed the money. By all appearances he was the commander; yet his blue coat, torn at one shoulder, bore no insignia of rank. Lester, he ordered the squat fellow with the carbine, go take a look-see. And you, Mister Secesh—he motioned with his own weapon. Go over and set down on that sofy. There was a couch behind. Ira backed off, sat down in obedience. From outside sounded the inarticulate yap of Lester. Then he came stumbling to the door. Critter soldiers, he said breathlessly. Despite his blue jacket he must not be a Yankee born and bred: not if he said critter soldiers.

Whereabouts?—

Two three fields yonder—

They galloping?—

Sort of poking along. We got time to get—

Then let's get! Stay where you be, Mister!—

The rough-bearded Terry had already moved speedily if uncertainly into the passage, and Ira could hear him, with Lester, crossing the gallery, descending the steps. There was a wrenching of rotten wood, the sound of someone falling, a spout of curses and simultaneous laughter from the man who had not fallen. You keep setting, the tall man directed Ira Claffey. He pointed his carbine once more in Ira's general direction. Glad you had some currency on you, even Secesh. Our luck's been skinny all the day. I swear that these folks haven't got nothing to bite or break. Then he was gone; you could hear pull of leather as the men mounted . . . quickly the diminishing sound of galloping. Ira stood at the cobwebby eastern window and watched the party moving with speed along the clay road, disappearing behind a bank of chinaberries which might or might not shield another house. He turned to the old lady who had not left her chair, who still sat shuddering. It's all right, Madam. He doubted if she heard or understood him. There was a scratching in the passageway. He stepped to the door and found two Negro girls, aged perhaps nine and eleven, who shrank away from him and then went scurrying toward the rear. They wore crude gowns made of sacking, they looked like miniature witches in panic, they began yelping in the rear yard. Ira recognized a jangle of buckles or weapons, a muddle of hoofs outside. He stepped to the gallery, and counted: six cavalrymen in the mixed blue-gray so common nowadays among Confederates, yet gray predominated. These were no bushwhackers—not in the way they sat their horses, not in the way they were poised. They filed through a gate from the western field. Only one man drew a revolver, though all were gazing curiously at the stranger who made his way down the ruined steps and walked to meet them.

Your house? asked a soldier.

No. I was on the road. The Yankees stopped our train.

We saw it, said another. We was watching from the woods. Reckon you hain't no Yankee?

I come from Sumter County. Ira told briefly of the occurrence at this farmhouse. All six cavalrymen rested quietly, gazing down without comment, unimpressed. Just bummers, they said. Same old story, happens all the while. Did you say that the old lady was hurted?

I doubt they laid a hand on her. But she seems hysterical, shocked and frightened half to death.

Which way did you say them bummers went?

Due ahead, east. They were galloping: I fear you'd have a hard time catching up. What is your organization, gentlemen?

We're with Joe Wheeler, said one with tarnished stripes of a sergeant. Then, to another— What you say, Lilly? Less pick ourselves a bummer or two for supper. They rode away.

Ira Claffey reclaimed his carpetbag. He found that he was covered with sweat in spite of chill raw air which blew with increasing sharpness. The hazy sun was hiding behind western pines. Ira heard someone at the house, he turned to see. An extremely tall Negress stood above the steps, facing him belligerently. Her skirts were pinned up raggedly above spindly shanks, she had a faded red cloth tied around her head, two of the corners stood up from the knot like erect ears of some animal. Her hands were on her hips, though one hand gripped a wooden potato masher.

You go long, she ordered Ira distinctly. Done you bother round here, bother Miss Gracie no more!

Ira grinned. He went along the road to the east, following the little band of Wheeler's cavalry who were trotting, then loping, who soon disappeared over the ridge. There stood a new column of black smoke in the north; Ira fancied that he could see flames at the base of it; a large structure must be burning beyond those empty fields. He turned to look back at the ramshackle farmhouse. The angular black woman had come down from the porch and stood in the road, a stiff threat against the fading sunlight. She turned and went back to the gallery.

Ira marveled, as he had marveled earlier, at the peculiar casual quality of war. He had a baffled curiosity concerning smaller events which accompanied warfare, offshoots of the cruel parent plant. He wondered how men might ever conceive tapestries and paintings which they created, presumably to portray battles. He had never traveled abroad, had seen but a few great paintings; yet those he had seen—or engravings in books—never suggested the fact of war. Ira remembered the first man he ever saw struck by a bullet. A column of troops, cooking inside thick blue uniforms, wearing jackets and shirts open at the neck (some mutineers against authority, some bold seekers after comfort, had actually taken their jackets off and flung them away)— The column straggled into the pitted street of a Mexican village, stumbling over red-dusted stones. He remembered a white church on an eminence beyond; he remembered women in black costumes who ran toward that church, some carrying babies, herding children ahead of them. He remembered that some of the children were naked, they looked like sprites. Then a party of guerrillas, or citizens acting as guerrillas, fired from roof-tops ahead. There was a patter of balls pocking into various individuals of the troops or scraping on hard-baked earth and stones, squealing in ricochet. A young man directly ahead of Ira was struck. He was blowing his nose at the moment of impact, blowing his nose into a dirty handkerchief turned brown by grime of the march. The man made a sound like *gah,* he swung out his right hand holding the handkerchief, brought it back again. Adjacent people scattered; orders were being shouted, officers were trying to deploy men off that fatal road, to have them take shelter behind rocks. The man with the handkerchief (Ira couldn't remember his name for a certainty; he thought that it was Bradley) had gone down on one knee in a kneeling posture. His musket, which he had been carrying slung, fell from his shoulder and lay with its barrel across the foot bent behind him. Then he finished blowing his nose. Ira and two others had halted to give him aid. The soldier wiped his nose carefully, and all the time he accomplished this rite, a wet place was spreading down from the hole in his coat. A button turned red, then drops fell from the button and a polished fly buzzed close. The man fell forward and a little to one side. When they turned him over it was amazing to see that he had a mystic grin on his face, as if he were delighted at the whole occurrence.

Oh, Ira cried, it is casual, casual. War and death in war are un-studied, never built in rigid pattern as once I believed that they would be.

So it went forever: a colonel directing troops in battle, his jaw swollen with toothache; the straggler shot behind a fence whilst in the act of evacuation; a bottle lying on the battlefield, a bottle with no label, containing some dark liquid, the neck trimmed off neatly by a bullet . . . still the bulk of the bottle was unshattered. The casualness of war . . . thing without duplication; no several shots ever sounded quite alike, hills gave back different echoes. The song of war was never sung twice in the same way.

As Ira Claffey went on helplessly and hopelessly, with twilight following him and then overtaking him, he perceived the same dis-ordered uncertain quality which had been in his thought. He thought that fog rose to the north and east. It was strange to have fog and smoke mingled, resembling a wall of bad weather rising to threaten. Then he began to smell the fog: it was not fog, it was thick dust. There had been no rain in these parts, fields and roads were un-seasonably parched.

What might so disturb the dust?

Vast numbers of wheels and hoofs.

It seemed that he heard them: wide-flung rumble and pushing and treading beyond the ridges.

On an instant he felt earth trembling under his feet, responding to a drumming from behind. He turned and stepped across a ditch for safety's sake. Out of dimness and dust a throng of blue cavalrymen bore down upon him. No Confederates, these: solidly in blue, and a veteran aspect to them, even at first glimpse. There galloped fifty or sixty men in the group. What was the strength of a troop or a squadron? —Ira could not recollect. They poured past, only a few streaked faces turned to regard him. What was a man, a citizen standing beside a fence with a carpetbag in his hand? They had seen many such figures. Then darkening dust was so thick that Ira could not see where the riders had gone. He wondered if they would overtake the half-dozen of Wheeler's men, he wondered if they were seeking them.

He went on aimlessly, grieved by growing awareness that invaders were all around him, ahead of him. He would never reach Savannah, never reach Richmond. Dear Lord, I started too late. I should have gone earlier; but had not dreamt that I could do a particle of good until desperation drove me to believe it. Murky landscape was turned pinkish. As Ira walked he began to identify individual stronger glows which gave forth a solid color: large fires, two to the left, one directly ahead and seeming low and wide as if a valley were lit, another fire ahead and slightly to the right.

Night tightened. Ira passed a stand of forest, mostly oaks—he could see the points of leaves clinging to the starkness, revealed easily against illumination beyond. He passed the last of the trees and stood where the road dipped. Yes, it was a valley. A house was burning, there seemed to be other embers beyond. A figure moved beside the crackling house, some other figures were motionless. Flames burst and stung; it sounded like a vast popping of corn; fleet somersaulting embers made unholy pyrotechnics above the blast. As Ira came near he heard the sound of crying as if dogs howled there. Closer he came limping to the yard fence. There was too much heat, he could not approach the actual blaze nor could the victims whose home was spouting aloft. A woman and a girl—mother and daughter—stood clutched in each other's arms. Tears seemed fairly boiling on their faces, yet they did not dare turn from this ascending horror; they stood hypnotized as they wept. The woman was comely; but her hair was coming down, her wet round cheeks were varnished in reflection; she was young, perhaps not much above thirty. The daughter was old enough to have her skirts long, but she had not put up her brownish hair: it was a mane around her shoulders, and one small ribbon was gilded by glow. The hair became a lovely thing in that light.

A man spoke beside Ira. By God, I never burned that bridge. I never. And look what they done to me!

A few things had been dragged out, but only a few: a barrel had been rolled, a clock stood on the barrel; there were two chairs, a kettle with tongs sticking out, a pile of bed-clothing, a bonnet, a lantern: Ira saw these things. Now a black-and-white cat rushed frantically across the hot open ground, leaped up on the fence beside the two men, gave them a look of fury, spilled herself down into darkness of the road.

Leastways, said the farmer, we got the kittens out. We forgot them; then my girl went back and fetched the basket, and blame near got herself burned up a-doing it. Strangely he gave a weak giggle. First off I thought you was neighbor Barfield from beyond the ridge; now I see you ain't. You ain't one of them bummers? and suddenly he loomed at Ira and lifted his hands as if ready to throttle.

I'm from Sumter County. Claffey's my name.

Name is Keeling, said the bushy-bearded man—a tall fellow, extremely spare of body. Somehow Ira thought of an Andersonville prisoner, and wondered what the resemblance might be. I'm Jim

Keeling, said the man again. Always played fair with the Yanks, and reckoned maybe they'd play fair with me if they headed this way. But it didn't come out like that, as you can see. He turned and yelled, Minnie, you and the girl get away from that, now. Sparks liable to set your gowns afire!

Neither the woman nor the girl answered or moved. They were rooted and clutching, still crying.

You got a chaw on you? asked Keeling. No? Well, the surgeons done told me I shouldn't chew tobacco neither, count of my digestion. But it's something to do. . . . He told his story to Ira as flames kept howling. He had been drafted more than two years previously. His wife and the girl and an old grandfather tried to work the farm while he was gone, but now the grandfather was dead. Good thing he didn't live to see this! He'd of had a fit and fell in it. For he built this very house, mostly with his own hands. Well.

Jim Keeling served finally with the Forty-ninth Georgia and had been wounded in Virginia the previous summer. . . . Twas a spent ball, but it nigh knocked the breath out of me. Ever since twas healed, I've had great difficulty keeping my food down. That's how come I lost so many pounds: don't weigh two-thirds my natural self now.

Shortly before sunset the bridge beside that house had been set afire. None of the Keelings saw who started the blaze, they saw no one running from the scene. It was just that suddenly they heard and smelled and saw the fire, and ran into their yard to watch the bridge burning. . . . This ain't exactly a turnpike through here, mister; but it's a good road and I spose valued by the Yanks accordingly. After that bridge fell through, just a while ago, a whole kit and boiling of Yankee cavalry come into this here very yard.

I think I saw them, said Ira. They passed me, beyond that hill. At least fifty of them.

Could have been—they looked like five hundred to me. They said I'd burned that bridge to hold up the Yank advance, and I told them, by God I never. Well, they said I ought to have kept from doing it whoever he was who done it. They said I was big enough; and then they found my gun and they says, See, you could have kept anybody from burning that bridge. So they broke my gun, smashed it gainst the fireplace. I couldn't do nothing to repel them; they was far too many for me. Anyway I'm sickly, as I tolt you. Well. The officer, he said twas retaliation: that was the word he used. Said he'd been ordered to perform such duty, and by that time some of his men had took my sow, and blooded her, and had her up on a horse, like the horse was carrying double. Don't reckon they took much else. But it don't matter now—everything's burning, cept the little bit we got out. They just marched us from the house and cut some sticks of pine from my wood pile and went to torching right and left. When they had her well alight, they rode off. Then we run to get what we could; but, as you see, twasn't much.

It seemed odd to Ira that the Federals had left the low stable and other outbuildings untouched; perhaps they were pressed for time. Thus far a light but steady north wind had turned the drift of flames and embers away from the sheds; but now, as the roof of the house went in with a bright crash, a shift occurred. Blazing little birds traveled to the southeast and still more easterly, settling in profusion upon the sheds. Simultaneously with Keeling, Ira saw this danger, the wife and daughter saw it as well. All went hastening past the furnace. Before they reached the stable new tongues were showing on the dried shakes.

I got a couple buckets here, mister, shouted Keeling. Help us fetch water from the creek!

Ira cried, I've a bad knee; but help me to get up there!

A cart stood near; Ira and the younger man pushed it with desperate strength against the stable. Ira managed to mount from cart to roof, with Keeling shoving at his legs. The man could not help much . . . Ira tore his own clothing . . . in another moment he had scrambled among the jeering flames. He yelled for a broom which he had seen lying in the yard; Keeling passed it to him while the young girl came laboring from the creek, spilling water from two wooden pails. Ira beat savagely with the broom, other naughty embers were flurrying down. Between water and poundings, the flames soon went out.

Best that your womenfolks splash water on those shed roofs too, Ira gasped. . . . So the danger passed as the main body of blaze went lower. They moved like actors on an orange-lighted stage. The area of illumination included the road, where now several horsemen could be seen halted, watching the affair. The stable was saved. . . . Ira had more difficulty getting down than he'd had ascending, until Keeling got his wits about him and fetched a homemade ladder from among his fruit trees. Ira walked across the dooryard toward the road, to find that the watchers were a youngish Federal major accompanied by three soldiers.

It's too bad, said the major.

You should know. Bitterly. Your people did this.

Your house? asked the major.

Ira smelled burning of wool, he found where his coat sleeve was charring, he slapped at this tiny destruction. Not my house. It belongs —or did belong—to the man approaching there—a former soldier, wounded into the bargain.

Jim Keeling came up with no fear and shook his fist at the Northerners; the major's horse shied. You blue-bellied devils, said Jim Keeling. Burnt the roof right off the heads of my family! Does a man's heart good to see you Yanks warring against women and girls!

The Unionist motioned toward the ruined bridge beyond, where posts were glowing still. What of the bridge?

I never put hand to it! But I wish your damn Sherman had stood here and heard my wife and daughter a-crying. We should of marched into the North, God damn it! Would of trained you God damn Yanks how to act decent.

Major Hitchcock, sir! cried one of the privates. You want us to arrest this man? He's abusive.

By no means, Chris. His house has just been burnt; I don't blame him for being abusive, not in the slightest. The frightened cat raced across the roadway once more, and the major's horse began to dance. He brought the animal under control and pulled over against the fence. He asked calmly of Ira, Have any troops passed this way, sir? At the moment I'm looking for some people from Illinois.

Obviously they've passed. They were cavalry.

No, no, and at this closer range Ira could see that Major Hitchcock's face held a great weariness, there was solemn grief in his face. No, I'm seeking infantry. Perhaps they're on the next road north.

He addressed himself directly to Jim Keeling. A word with you, Friend Southerner.

I got no good words for you, said Keeling. And I'm no friend.

I wish to say this: the fortunes of war held your army mainly away from the North; but at least you made no bones about burning Chambersburg, Pennsylvania. And we've had you people planting mines in the roads ahead of us. Citizens—making war! Some of our boys have been killed by those mines, some had their feet blown off. We've discovered you Georgians burning forage and corn along our route. Therefore General Sherman has ordered that houses will be burnt and cotton gins will be burnt to keep them company. Back on Buffalo Creek we found a bridge in ashes. The adjacent house was destroyed. I must admit that I felt impelled to argue with the general about this, and I'll tell you exactly what he said. He said: Let the enemy look to his own people. If the Southerners find that their burning of bridges only destroys their own houses, they'll soon stop it.

His face was tinted to bright copper by diminishing flames. Major Hitchcock closed his eyes in concentration, then leaned toward the people in the yard. He spoke earnestly. That is General Sherman's belief, I heard him say it. He said: In war everything is right that prevents anything. He said that he feels there's nothing to do but to make war so terrible that when peace comes it will *last*.

There was something in his speech. . . . Where were you born? Ira asked. . . . Hitchcock smiled. Alabama. But my parents had come from the North. Oh yes, I was reared in Missouri and in Tennessee, but educated at Yale. I do have, as you might understand, a strong sympathy for the Southern people. Also I hold unalterable devotion to the Union cause. Now we must be on our way. Good evening. And you, he said to the tall thin Keeling— I am sorry for your loss; but I fear it had to be. Abruptly he rode toward the creek, soldiers clattering after him. The Georgians could hear them splashing through the stream, then they vanished.

Ira spent the night beside the embers. It was unhappily warm there, an open refuge from November's chill. The Keelings took the bed-clothing which had escaped destruction and bedded down in the stable. Jim Keeling said that he owned plenty of clean corn-shucks, they were not uncomfortable. The people offered to share their meager supply with Ira, in appreciation for help he had given them, but he refused. He was affected deeply by their gratitude. The man insisted on bringing a piece of canvas, and with this Ira made a rude tent to keep off winds. He lay within the folds, watching the play of light from ruins which still fried. He thought that he was safer here than he might be along avenues traveled by dangerous bands who clung alongside the Federal advance. Men would see that destruction had occurred already; obviously the place was stripped, they would pass by.

There came disturbances through the night: horses passed, men talked; they stopped to discuss the lingering blaze, went on. Once two wagons came also, with hullabaloo about their fording the stream. Soon after sunrise a frightened elderly couple appeared with a basket. These were the Jarells from down the road, and feared to come sooner . . . they had seen the blaze, knew that the Keeling place must have burned, there was nothing else to burn at that point. Mr. Jarell said that his own place had been visited by foragers who took nothing except chickens. They said that Mrs. Keeling and her daughter must sleep in their house for the time being. It appeared that they were distant cousins of the wounded veteran; Ira heard talk about Aunt Mame and Cousin Neddy. The Jarells had fetched bread and side meat . . . Ira ate but sparingly. An extra mouth was a dreadful thing in times like these.

Ira went into the privy and extracted a thousand dollars Confederate from his hoard. He insisted that Jim Keeling should accept this as a loan—to be paid back, without interest, when and if. It may be worth nothing at all, now that the Yanks are come, Ira told the haggard man. Again it may be the only currency in circulation for some time. Do with it as you can. Keeling cried openly.

After Ira stopped to play with the rescued kittens in their basket— with the mother cat no longer terrified but buzzing contentedly as the kittens fed—he went away. He smiled grimly. Literally he did not know which way to turn. From conversation which he'd heard, and rumor reaching the Jarells during the night, he judged that the bulk of the Federal army trod paths to the north and east. There was no point any longer in even considering Savannah.

Freebooters had passed but more might be trailing. A man might remain in danger as long as he remained in this region . . . all people would be in danger. Ira wondered if a talon of the blue iron hand reached toward Andersonville. He might come home to find his own house in ashes; but at least thousands of the prisoners still incarcerated were too weak to do much revengeful harm. Most of the Reserves could not fight, they would run away. He thought of hasty feet trampling in his hall, big shoes pounding the stair, drawers jerked out, tables upset. In his imaginings a hooting bandit dressed himself in Ira's Mexican War uniform and went parading. Ira Claffey thought about his black people. Most of all Lucy was in his thoughts. But he felt that Mrs. Effie Dillard could cope with almost any band of raiders. Also Cousin Harry would be at hand. . . . No, he found no real worry, none worth entertaining. Resolutely he put the unhappy panorama out of his mind.

Beyond the next hill he was confronted by a party of terror-stricken citizens, driving a few head of sheep and a white cow about to come fresh. There were dogs trotting, and children, and an old man being pushed in a hand-cart. They just gave us sut! cried an old woman. My son-in-law, he'd made thirty-two hundred gallons of syrup; twas more than he had casks for, so he'd sunk a tank in the ground, buried it deep, and if those Yanks didn't come along yesterday and help themselves to the whole! . . . They ruint my flower garden, cried a younger woman. They took Pa's watch! screamed a child. Oh, mister, they all cried. You better turn round and go back tother way. . . . Wouldn't even wait for me to give them the keys to the bureau, cried the woman who'd lamented the loss of her garden. They just smashed in the drawers with musket butts. . . . They shot Jed! cried a little boy, as Ira continued doggedly on his way. He speculated drearily who Jed might have been: dog or pig or tomcat, he did not suppose that Jed was a person.

He went on and met the mass of the Union army's right wing: rank and file and furbelow. Long afterward, Ira learned that there had been sixty-odd thousand men in the punishing hordes which slammed from Atlanta to Savannah; but on sight he thought that there were millions. The next northwest-to-southeast road was crammed as he had seen a small hallway in Milledgeville crammed during legislative session. There was not space enough in the road for the people. They would have shoved fences aside but the fences were gone: smoking patches showed where rails burned during the night. At the first intersection a foraging party assembled with their loot. A group of boys stood guarding a heap of smoked hams—a heap which might have filled one of the Claffey wardrobes to capacity and then some. The boys were laughing, not especially in arrogance, but seemingly with sheer spookish joy of living and of plundering. Always Ira would remember one: a hard-faced youngster of seventeen or thereabouts, who stood arrogantly with a cob pipe turned upside down in his mouth, as he would guard it against a rain; but it was not raining now. Whenever in after years someone said Sherman, or Sherman's Invasion, or Sherman's March to the Sea, he would think of that lean boy . . . freckled, beardless, shock-headed, with upside-down pipe. A big wagon came banging, and the boys yelled a question at the wagoner. Thirty-ninth Iowa? The wagoner nodded. He did not pull his four-horse team to a stand. It was impossible for anyone to halt in the road: too many people came swarming on their course. As the wagon continued, the group of youths labored after it with armloads of the hams. They pushed hams up across the tailboard, unseen hands received them apparently, hams vanished into the black-draped interior. Back and forth the soldiers went, hurrying through a distance of perhaps thirty rods before the meat was all put aboard. Them Iowa boys must have found themselves a big butcher, said someone behind Ira Claffey; but he could not even turn to see who was talking, he was agape.

There rode on good horses a noisy herd of wenches (all young, perhaps the youngest was fourteen) dressed in gowns of colored silk stolen undoubtedly from some wealthy house. Crimson and gold of their disheveled costuming fairly hurt the eyes. They were headed by a pompous fat Negro bestriding a dappled stallion; he rode bareback, he kept turning to the chattering mounted bevy behind, holding out his hand, saying sharply, Keep up, you all, keep up, stay together! He wore a gilt-piped coat hanging open, unbuttoned, and a beaver hat too small for his head. Ira supposed the fellow was some officer's servant who had gathered this harem.

Ira stood at the edge of a clump of trees and blackberry vines; still he carried his carpetbag: it had endured through vicissitudes since the train was stopped. But now he felt the bag wrenched from his grasp. A clumsy young man had stepped out of the lounging files, twisted the carpetbag away, and was going off with it coolly. A voice sang sharply, Hi! with an inquiring lift to the cry. A young lieutenant on a bay kicked his horse into a trot along the edge of the field and overtook the robber. He retrieved the carpetbag, whirled his horse, came back to Ira. Here, mister, and he leaned down to deliver the bag. Better drop it out of sight behind that brush. Some of these folks have got the itch, they'll steal anything in sight! He was gone before Ira could thank him.

He tossed the bag behind him into a weed patch. He would have liked to have sat on his haunches. His stiff knee would not permit this, but a little farther on there was a stump; there he sat for a time. Regiments, cattle, black wanderers, wagons from which corn and parlor chairs spilled down, more lounging tough companies—the crowd kept flowing. Ira thought of a celebration he'd seen in New

York, with Broadway thronged between its shop fronts, brass bands
hallooing. Here there were no bands, although he did see a bass drum
carried atop a chaise. It was as if the earth had erupted in the northwest and spewed a strange concentrated lava of people, brown and
white, to come rolling down these sluiceways. A Negro woman skipped
there, young, waving long bony arms, trying to make screams although
her voice was worn from previous screaming. Tildy, cried another
black woman, overtaking her and tugging her to the side. Now you
quit crying for that baby! He's safe with Jesus. . . . In the wwwater,
the other woman kept blubbering. In that old wwwater. Got push
off that old bridge. All these soldier folks they push my baby. . . .

More troops coming, herds of ragged blacks keeping them company. Zachary Clark, a voice yelled. Oh, Zach, where are you? and
a big laugh sounded ahead, a curly head turned. Zachary Clark was
a Yankee soldier, an older man, his ringlets were silver, his fleshy
face beamed. Right up here, he called in response. Come along,
Archie! . . . What you carrying, Zach? . . . Ladies' pants. . . . And so
he was: a queer double bag made from voluminous drawers with
each leg tied at the bottom. This strange receptable rode atop his
right shoulder, his rifle was slung on his left. . . . What you got in
them pants, Zach? Hey, Bob! . . . there was running of feet to catch
up with him. . . . I bet you'd just like to know! Voices drifted off into
the pounding, striding, hoofing, wheel-turning.

Smoke and dust lay in a compress high over the road and beyond
it . . . would Georgia ever rise again? Smudge of the Keelings' house
had been but a firefly. Ira thought drearily of what Major Hitchcock,
the tired-faced Yankee, had said the night before. Hitchcock spoke of
burning cotton gins. Oh, would we have ruined the simple economy
of the North, if we instead had made a march? Say that we had gone
the length of Indiana. Would we have put their corn into ashes? Perhaps, perhaps. . . . No, no, we would never have done so. I, at least,
have a pretention to decency. So have people like Cato Dillard, so
has even the crippled Coral Tebbs—a hard warped pride. So have
men like the unfortunate Keeling. But would we have done this,
what homes might we have looted? In Indiana are no slaves for us
to turn loose, but— Ira thought of the vicious Winder. He treated us
so. How might he have treated Yankees at the North? Ira got up
from his stump, went back and gathered up the carpetbag. Now he
did not even care if it were taken from him. So much else had been
taken from everyone.

A silver shine came bobbing along the road: yes, it was a helmet, a
souvenir perhaps from Napoleonic times. God knew how it had ever
come to Georgia. But a boy found it, in press or cupboard, so now he
wore it gaily, the old horse-hair plume blew in the wind. *Mooooo* said
the cows, great buffalo herds of them, they dropped their dung as

they traveled. A thousand feet of men came to tread and skate in
slime behind them, wagon wheels came to crease the dung.

But these people were not mere bummers: bummers drifted far
on the outskirts of the march. These men were plunderers, they were
arsonists, but first they were soldiers. They had the stringy tough
weathered look of veterans, they were of the West, there was a
pioneer hunter's quality to their marching. They carried blankets
rolled, their rifles were well rubbed; very few wore the bulky knapsacks, their haversacks swung as Confederate haversacks swung. Ira
thought of what their units might be: Thirty-second Missouri, Ninth
Iowa, One Hundred and Eleventh Illinois, Nineteenth Wisconsin,
Thirtieth Iowa . . . they looked as if they had risen out of tall grass
and unkempt woods. . . . Have we sufficient force to stand against
them? Will they be turned back before they reach Savannah? Never,
thought Ira. Our power is drained; we cannot halt them, scarcely im-
pede their youthful brutal Western force. Miner, trapper, lumberman,
and miner's son and trapper's son and lumberman's son: they come,
they possess somehow the quality of Indians, you expect them to
whoop as Indians do, some of them whoop so.

Ira Claffey suffered the depression of one who looks at bad weather
and knows that he may not restrain it. . . . You cannot subdue a tornado; this shaggy twisting wind has sprung from beyond the horizon.
Its thunder is heard, lightning has knived us already, rain comes
smashing, our roof is gone.

He was haunted by the absurd delusion that if his sons had been
allowed to survive, they might have kept this rabble out of Georgia.
But if his sons had been born beside the upper Mississippi, instead
of in the county where they were born, they would have helped to
make the rabble. He turned and started south stubbornly, resolved
to watch no more. He had seen enough, seen too much. These invaders took everything, burned everything, they cut their swath toward
the coast. Now Ira Claffey was marooned, and so was Andersonville
marooned, unless wild cavalry had gone pushing there. Behind him
the jumble of individual identifiable sounds resolved into a low roar,
the call and flapping of a million birds. There they traveled, cutting
landscape at his back: Forty-seventh Ohio and Fifteenth Michigan and
Twelfth Indiana and Fourth Iowa; they'd gathered up the very soil
of Georgia, folded it around them, were wearing it as uniforms. . . .
Later that day, Ira managed to buy a dinner of sorts, and also a very
sorry mule. He rode the mule down into Dooly County where the
mule died. Ira walked the rest of the way home.

LIII

. . . We go the gate again, Surgeon Crumbley. What is your news from Albany? A letter on Thursday, to be sure? I am glad, sir, that Mrs. Crumbley is mending. It must be an ordeal for you to serve so far away during her illness. . . . Paregoric? Fortunate that it was available. I wish that we might have some at this point.

. . . No, no, Surgeon White established no particular pens for any of us today. I observed no such notation on the Duty List. Take any pen you choose—they'll all be filled. There remains but to prescribe formulas and numbers as has been the custom. How many have you on your list? Mine runs up to thirty-odd: Number One is prescribed to serve for diarrhoea; Number Two for dysentery; Number Three for scorbutus, and so on. Is it in accord with your notions of medical procedure to take the discretion entirely away from the prescribing physician himself? I objected to this in my first assignment to such duty, as did you. I felt that I could not prescribe properly for my patients. I looked upon it as utter quackery! Quite so, Surgeon Crumbley. I discovered that the diseases from which our patients were suffering stemmed from want of the proper kind of dieting, remedies, etc. To begin with, I was convinced that I could have done more—indeed yes, I know I could—with proper dieting, than I could have with the medicines available. When first I came here—it must have been for two whole days, not more—I examined each new case, made my diagnosis, wrote out my prescription accordingly. I found that the medicines had not been supplied. I asked the reason, and they informed me that I was not to practice in that way: I must practice according to the numbers and formulas presented. I told them: I know nothing of such formulas and numbers, and care nothing for them. And, gentlemen, I refuse to practice in any such way! . . . What's more, I went my round, diagnosed the cases again, made out a prescription for each case. It was extremely laborious; there were many under my charge, as you will understand, Surgeon Crumbley, as you have had under your charge. I sent up the prescriptions, and once again they were refused. I said to my clerk—a Yankee prisoner, no less, and On Parole, but with some claim to a background embracing pharmacopoeia—I said, What ho, Yank? . . . Surgeon Elkins, he told me, it is quite useless for you to make out such prescriptions.

It would appear that there is a blockade.

It would appear that if President Davis himself were suffering from the pip, perhaps he might be served.

Might the Secretary of War be served properly? Might General Winder? Let us say that is a moot question.

As I recall now, you were overjoyed, Surgeon Crumbley, when a bottle of paregoric was found—a medicament to relieve your wife—in the recesses of some friend's closet in Albany.

Let us not seek narcotic for our senses, sir. Twill be unavailable.

For diarrhoea? Red pepper, and decoctions of blackberry root and of pine leaves.

For coughs and lung diseases? A decoction of wild cherry bark.

For chills and fever? A decoction of dogwood bark.

If fever patients seem to crave especially something sour, let us dose them with the weak acid made by fermenting a small quantity of meal in a barrel of water. Vinegar? My flask is empty, I regret to say. My vinegar is a tiny vial of fresh water sprayed into the Sahara sands.

Let us consider gangrenous sores. Ha, ha—here is the specific: peanut oil, no less! May we hope that the hospital orderlies do not steal it for a slosh in which to sop their corn bread! Dear, dear—why be picayunish about the matter? Gangrenous patients will die anyway; the hospital orderlies might live, and not eventually join their fellows amid pine straw, amid oozing holes where stumbling sick have let go their bowels, amid pools where stumbling sick have let go their bladders. What fun if the hospital orderlies were to be tricked—damn Yankees anyway, and Paroles, what's more—and let them have a ration of castor oil instead! What a lark!

How many are you empowered to admit today, Surgeon Crumbley? Five patients? The same for myself, sir. So we shall stand in our rude pens at the gate and observe the flow, the crawling and the carried. . . . My, my, here is a grand ulcer, to be sure: at least four inches in diameter, on the calf of the leg. . . . What have we here? Necrosis of the jaw. Hold still, patient. Keep him still, friends of the patient; hold the patient, let me make an examination with my fingers. . . . Huzza! Necrosis indeed. A piece of bone nearly an inch long came out attached to my finger.

. . . It is my opinion that the diarrhoea commonly observed hereabouts is an attendant symptom of scurvy, not to be confused with the ordinary camp diarrhoea observed in our own army.

. . . Generally there is an enervation of the nervous system. It runs down in consequence of the dietary condition. Naturally the nervous system must sink under such pressure. I observe the effect manifested in idiocy, dementia and other mental weaknesses.

. . . Yes, yes, I should expect that morally such abject circumstances would produce deep humiliation and resignation. However, the effect seems otherwise: the moral attitude of the prisoners declines, men seem to abandon themselves. The well will steal from the sick, the sick will steal from the dead. Why, by God, it has come under my observation that the sick will nerve themselves to remarkable accomplishments, and steal from the *well!*

. . . That man with the bucket in his mouth, gripping the bail of the bucket as a dog would hold a bone? I have seen him frequently. He crawls for his rations.

. . . Surgeon Crumbley, have you observed the deadhouse in the hospital lately? When first I went there, there were boards forming a shed. Goodness sake—but the boards disappeared. I presume that they were stolen by those inmates of the hospital able to crawl. Lately the dead have lain with no shelter whatsoever, until wagons and mules and niggers came to cart them away.

. . . Did you observe that patient bearing the name of Clayton? Yes, yes, carried away just now . . . but you should have heard him exclaiming how he was put upon! He had a good stout belt—buckle and all—and he contended that the orderly fancied the belt. He said that he woke up; his arm was open and raw, as you remember, and he declared—it was in the night—that the orderly was rubbing gangrenous fluid into his sore. The belt, you see. What matter now? A false accusation, perhaps . . . naturally, yes: the orderly was a Yankee as well.

. . . For the treatment of wounds, ulcers, etc., we have literally nothing except water. The wards, some of them, are filled with gangrene, and we are compelled to fold our arms and look quietly upon its ravages, not even having stimulants to support the system under its depressing influences.

. . . Ulcers are produced from the slightest causes imaginable. A pin scratch, a prick of a splinter, a pustula, an abrasion, or even a mosquito bite are sufficient causes for their production. The surface presents a large ash-colored or greenish-yellow slough, and emits a very offensive odor. After the slough is removed by appropriate treatment, the parts beneath show but little tendency to granulate. Occasionally, however, apparently healthy granulations spring up and progress finely for a time, and again fall into sloughing, and thus, by an alternate process of slough and phagedenic ulceration, large portions of the affected member or large masses of the body are destroyed. In this condition gangrene usually sets in, and if not speedily arrested soon puts an end to the poor sufferer's existence.

. . . On examining the roster I find that twenty-four medical officers are charged to the hospital, and yet but twelve are on duty. The rest either by order of General Brown (at their own request) are off on sick leave or leave of indulgence. In order to attend to the wants of the sick and wounded, not less than thirty efficient medical officers should be on duty in the hospital.

. . . The corn bread received from the bakery, being made up without sifting, is wholly unfit for the use of the sick, and often, as in the last twenty-four hours, upon examination, the inner portion is found to be practically raw. . . . The corn bread cannot be eaten by many, for to do so would be to increase the diseases of the bowels, from which a large majority are suffering, and it is therefore thrown away. All then that is received by way of subsistence is two ounces of boiled beef and a half pint of rice soup per day, and under these circumstances all the skill that can be brought to bear upon their cases by the medical officers will avail nothing.

. . . Surgeon I. H. White, chief surgeon post, informed me that timely requisitions have been made on the quartermaster's department for the necessary materials to make the sick and wounded comfortable, but thus far he has been unable to procure scarcely anything.

. . . Feeling we have done our whole duty, both in the eyes of God and man, we leave the matter to rest with those whose duty it was to furnish supplies and build up a hospital that might have reflected credit on the Government and saved the lives of thousands of our race. . . .

Harrell Elkins believed truly that he had done his duty in the eyes of God and man. But he had not done all his duty; his work would end only with the termination of the hospital, with the last death there, the last removal. He went home in the dark. He had served an hour and a half past his time. Scarcely had he seen Lucy since Ira Claffey left. Harry did not allow himself to think of her when he was at work; but he could not keep her out of his thoughts at other times—especially in those many occasions when he was too tense for sleep, when he could not relax, when he lay taut as a ramrod, feeling thin and hard as a ramrod. Mrs. Effie buzzed about, but discerned soon that the young man was actually too worn to engage in professional discussion. She recognized that Elkins had toil and nuisance thrown in his face in a quantity beyond her accumulated experience. She thought that she might derive benefit from him in the future, if the cyclone of foreseen defeat did not tear him away from this region.

Harry remembered a period of shellfire when missiles came down and burst interminably. He had thought then, along with the rest of the troops, Won't it ever stop? I'm so weary of it. Can't they ever stop firing those shells? Can there be anything else in existence beyond this constant crouching, waiting, fearing, jarring? . . . So battle recurred to him now, in the form of hospital and stockade gate. Will it ever cease? Nay, never. It cannot, cannot, will not, never will cease.

November wind hit him and it was dark, dark; the surface of the lane was so ruptured that he stumbled even though he knew the way. He reached an open area of lawn behind a fence at the corner of the Claffey orchard. A lantern was being carried to the rear shed where Elkins always stopped to brush and examine his clothing. Someone had been watching, someone had made out his approach and was ready with the lantern (for the supply of oil was low: one could not leave a lantern hanging alight indefinitely, one took care, one saved and saved). He went up the drive and into the shed corner. There the lantern waited, hung on its peg; but hands which had carried it and hung it were gone away. He thought he knew whose hands. He took off his jacket, shivering in cold. He shook the jacket, worked over his shirt with the brush he kept in this shed, brushed the jacket, brushed his pants. He felt an itch. He closed the shed door, removed his shoes, took off his pants and shook them violently, turned them inside out, examined the frayed seams. He killed four graybacks, he could find no more. A flea went hopping into space. Harry wiped his shoes with a rag, and then dressed once more and carried the lantern into the rear hall of the house. Reflected gleam of candlelight drifted from the library ahead. He blew out the flame, put the utensil on its shelf, and went hesitatingly to the library door.

You are late, Cousin. Lucy was curled at the end of the sofa in folds of a faded shawl, she held a book.

Yes, late, he said. What have you been reading?

Keats.

I wish that I were not too weary to play the Poetry Game with you.

She came to meet him in the doorway, her voice telling a secret. We are alone.

Alone?

Our neighbor, old Mrs. Bile, is said to be dying. She's been poorly for a long time, and Mrs. Effie was sent for. Jonas took her to the Bile place and fetched back a note saying that Mrs. Bile's condition was grave. Thus Mrs. Dillard must needs spend the night.

Do you think that I might be of service over there?

I doubt it, Harry. She is very old, very frail. I presume twould be merely a case of rest and quiet—mild stimulants perhaps.

Should you be there yourself, Lucy?

She had lowered her face but lifted it quickly. I thought that you would need me, she said.

Suddenly he could not breathe.

No Game for you, sir. No tug and pull upon that tired brain! I had Naomi put by a few necessaries before she went to the quarters. She's left a fire, so now I shall prepare your supper.

Somehow I feel especially soiled tonight. A weak chuckle caught in his throat.

Your pitcher is filled, I trust. But I'll just bring some hot water, Cousin. The large kettle is on—

You will not tote water for me, said Harry firmly. He followed her out to the kitchen. She went ahead, carrying a candle, holding her hand to shield the flame.

Do you go scrub now, she told him when she had filled the pitcher. I'll make ready, and serve you in style upon a tray.

With an apple in my mouth and sausages about my neck?

He heard her quiet, Most assuredly, coming after him. In his room Harry Elkins stood upon the mat and bathed. He owned some clean clothes, for he had been given most of Sutherland's. Certain garments had been a trifle tight for him before, they were tight no longer. The trousers were now too loose. He belted them tightly, put on slippers and jacket, arranged his maroon stock. Maroon might have done for Sutherland Claffey; Harry thought that in his own case maroon was absurd; but still it was the only such scarf he owned. He went down into the library. Lucy had put his supper tray upon a table, and stood rubbing her thumbs against her first fingers in a display of nervousness quite adolescent. Through strained silence Harry could actually hear the pressure and squeezing of flesh upon flesh. Later he could not recall exactly what was said. He remembered an overpowering sense of isolation, and then recognition of a long tortured defeat: it was as if Ira Claffey directed the thought to him across chilly dark miles which separated them. He had a notion that Lucy spoke of ham and warmed-up biscuits, he was not sure. Rising out of knowledge that the two of them were alone, sole alone, alone in the house, alone and unwatched and unguarded, there shafted suddenly an enormous desire. The candle was behind Lucy, so light which shone from it made transparent delicacy around the outer surface of her hair . . . candlelight limned her figure, made it dark and solitary and haloed. Why should stockade and hospital diminish into oblivion now? They had refused to diminish before. Harry's weariness gave desperation, desperation gave strength. He started to say, The morning you kissed me, the other time I held you in my arms. . . . He was shocked at the harshness of his own voice. He could say nothing more, he whirled Lucy against him. God, God, he heard her gasping, before her mouth was smothered by his. The two of them pushed against the table, wrapped close: over went the candle upon the tray, there was a flash and sizzling, the light went out, there was faintest smell rising from an edge of ham newly scorched.

. . . And my darling, my darling Harry, I've never before, as you know, because it's sinful. It's— I shouldn't ask you if you have— No, no, I daren't ask.

But Lucy, I—haven't.

Never before?

Never.

They were in his room; somehow each felt that it would be an additional wickedness to have gone to hers.

Soon as we're married, Lucy whispered, lifting herself up to peer closely at him in gloom— We shall move in here, shan't we? Somehow, my room— It was always mine, my maiden room. Actually this is larger—

He drew her face down into the hair of his chest. You know, he said, and well aware that simple frankness was ridiculous— This is adultery. We've committed adultery, are committing it.

She breathed, Yes, yes, Harry. Will we burn in Hell?

Myself, perhaps yes. No one could burn you, no power of fiends.

But—the Bible— Uncle Dayto, and sermons— All the prayers I've uttered and other folks have uttered. Oh I declare, we're so wicked, aren't we? . . . Why didn't you love me before? Why didn't you let me know that you loved me?

You know.

No, my darling, I don't, I don't. Tis the same old hospital, same old horrid stockade, the same nasty knowledge of men dying, dying, dying, watching them die, smelling them die. It must have been the same today for you.

Harry told her, Not the same now. Suddenly I felt that I must turn to you.

Darling.

There was only their struggle and rapid breathing for a time.

Afterward he was the first to speak. Should you wish to play the Game? he asked.

Yes, yes, yes. . . .

I shall let you into the secret without a Black Mark. Proverbs, Fifth Chapter: *Rejoice with the wife of thy youth. Let her be as the loving hind and pleasant roe; let her breasts satisfy thee at all times; and be thou ravished always with her love.*

Lucy began to whimper. But I'm not your wife, you see.

Do you suppose the Lord will forgive us for being a bit hasty, Lucy? Possibly we could do penance as Catholics do. Just for the sake of a few days?

My love, twill be weeks. There are the banns.

Something else, said Harry. First Corinthians, somewhere or other: *But if they cannot contain, let them marry.* So we shall, Lucy.

She repeated, We shall. And presently she asked as they lay side by side gazing up into dark, What would Suthy think?

He would shoot me, beyond doubt.

He cannot shoot you now.

Again they were silent for a long while, until timidly Lucy began to trace the pattern of his eyebrows with her finger. In turn she pushed down the weary crumpled eyelids and let her hand pass smoothly and coolly over the closed eyes. So odd to see you close, even in dark, without your specs. Harry, you must know I'm very wicked. I suffer lust. Harry, I—I've dreamed of you.

So have I dreamed of you.

In this way they broke the dignity of rearing, cut through the veil of morality in which both had been draped. They were shocked to discover that they did not feel at all depressed about it. They kept reiterating that they should be sunk in remorse, should be praying for forgiveness. The staunch pure code forever applied—and especially in Lucy's case—seemed a shriveled broken hedge behind them. They had crashed through it, had cavorted in Eden.

I wonder, said Harry, when the Fall will occur, Cousin?

Dear Harry, you must call me Cousin no longer. Soon you will say Wife, soon say Mrs. Elkins, Ma'am. She tittered at the thought; then relaxed wide awake and glowing, a little sore in intimate portions; but enriched by joy. She believed that her joy would be perpetual.

Old Mrs. Bile died the next morning, and Mrs. Dillard was driven back to the Claffeys' at noon by a Bile nephew. Effie's mind was filled with recollections of a peaceful passing; she thought of agéd death as a release from all sin and pain, a glorification to be envied; she continued in busy thought, concerning herself also with Heaven, and the notion of her own children and grandchildren revelling there. In this mood she scarcely recollected that Lucy and Harrell Elkins had spent a night to threaten chastity. She presumed that she knew a gentleman when she saw one, and a lady as well. She knew that no gentleman such as Elkins would presume to dishonor a pure young lady, that no pure young lady such as Lucy would presume to desire to be dishonored.

The footsore Ira came trudging up with the dusk—thwarted, charged with dread weight of the invasion he had witnessed, dread knowledge that he had started for Richmond too late. . . . Twould have done no good in the end, Poppy, Lucy soothed him. And God let you come back to us safely through all dangers. When they sat alone later, with Mrs. Effie sleeping, and Elkins not yet come from the hospital, Ira saw the new Lucy. He recognized much, almost he guessed and could imagine more.

His stubbled face broke into a smile. My dear, you appear comely, especially comely.

She came flying, running across the room, dropped down, buried her face in his lap, hugged his legs convulsively.

Is it Cousin Harry?

The fair head nodded violently.

I take it he's declared himself?

Again the furious nodding.

Now, how dared he do so? He has not spoken to me.

Her head was motionless, her face burning against him.

But do you wish me to forgive him?

Once more the nodding, more rapidly than ever.

Are you happy, my dear?

Oh, Poppy, she mumbled.

In that event I shall embrace Cousin Harry with fatherly affection when he appears, and we shall take a glass of wine together.

They did in fact do this; but Elkins suffered the guilt which he had not suffered when lying with Lucy. He spilled his silver cup of wine— Sutherland's cup—before it was half empty, temporarily miserable. He thought that he should confess the enormity of his sin. Almost he struggled to speak awful words, to ask forgiveness of this wronged father; then the whole wide picture of agony near which and in which they had lived, rose before him. It was a persuasive mural in which life and death were elementals and essentials—not the practice of morality or of social or religious custom. He thought, Come, come, don't be a child about this matter. He and Ira shook hands fervently on separating. Harry went to his room and slept with more bliss than he had known in sleep since first he sought duty at Andersonville.

The Reverend Mr. Cato Dillard took delight in publishing the banns according to elderly Scottish procedure; this practice was approved by the presbytery. Cato almost regretted that he might not cry Lucy and Harry indefinitely; but rules said that they were to be cried on three successive Sundays, and that was enough; so he made the most of it. The Dillards approved contentedly of the match. Effie foresaw pleasant future episodes wherein Harrell Elkins might instruct her in medicinal procedures. Even so she rankled a little when she recalled his sport about toad ointment. . . . Cato Dillard gave opinion that each of the young pair was an excellent Christmas present to give to the other, albeit a trifle in advance of the season. Banns were cried on the twenty-seventh of November, on the fourth and eleventh of December. Cousin Harry entered a plea for a wedding on the twelfth, but Lucy said that they must wait until Wednesday the fourteenth. That was her mother's birthday. It would give her the feeling that her mother was somehow part of this solemn joy, that Veronica Claffey was no longer a forlorn shrunken monster to be shuddered away from in thought.

The Dillards arrived at the plantation Tuesday evening, accompanied by Laurel Tebbs, who had acquired the art of blushing whenever spoken to. She carried with pride a puckered bag of black silk,

complete with drawstrings. This feminine delight had been given her
by one of the neighboring Dennards of Americus, who found it among
the effects of a recently deceased aunt. It now contained a pocket
handkerchief actually dampened with cologne, and a square looking
glass which said on the back: *Compliments of Beglois & Sons, Cotton
Brokers, Savannah, Ga.* These things were Laurel's personal property,
she would not have parted with them under any circumstances. She
had also a pill-box containing seven imitation garnet buttons which
had come off an old gown of Mrs. Effie's, and were a present to
Laurel's mother. Laurel was driven in style to the Tebbs place. Mrs.
Dillard refused to allow her to spend the night there: she was sure
that the widow must have retrogressed since October, she said that
someone would call for Laurel at eight. . . . With Laurel safely bedded
in Moses Claffey's old room, the rest stayed round the fire a while.
Cato Dillard quoted liberally from the Directory For Worship.

Marriage is of a public nature.

In her heart Lucy did not agree: she thought it rather a private affair.

The welfare of civil society, said Mr. Dillard, fraying his whisker
tufts between his fingers as he beamed, *the happiness of families and
the credit of religion are deeply interested in it.*

Well they should be, his wife agreed.

*Therefore, the purpose of marriage ought to be sufficiently published
a proper time previously to the solemnization of it.*

I think that it has been sufficiently published in our case, Cousin
Harry murmured sleepily. Three mortal Sundays.

*It is enjoined on all ministers to be careful that, in this matter, they
neither transgress the laws of God nor the laws of the community.*

Cate, said Effie Dillard, you *are* an old blether! Away to
bed with you. Away to bed with all of us.

The wedding day dawned gray, murky, raw. There were to be few
guests, there were few whom the Claffeys wanted for wedding guests.
Elkins had been given leave of indulgence from his hospital duties for
two days; he would not request more leave, though Lucy begged. He
said stubbornly that he would not be happy for longer, he would be
thinking of his patients, of what he might do for them. Of the fellow
surgeons he invited only Dr. Crumbley, that slight brown-faced man
with whom he had worked long, and who labored with earnestness
approaching his own—not enforced by external strictness, but of the
soul. Two loads of Americus Presbyterians came driving up in mid-
forenoon. These were not people rooted deeply in affections of the
Claffeys: they were merely people whom the Claffeys had known for
long, and so a strong association was imagined if not practiced. Two
of the younger women had gone to the Female Institute along with
Lucy. There ensued a certain amount of embracing and tearful cooing

. . . these social appurtenances were vague, meaningless. Lucy could observe them, they did not strike deep. She looked beyond the people, saw Harry's luminous eyes smiling within their glass.

That is all ye need to know, she misquoted gently when they were near each other again, ignoring the tangle of conversation.

Truth is beauty, said Harry. God bless you.

Bless you!

He did that when He brought me to you.

Shortly before the ceremony was to commence, the party received recruits. Ira it was who looked first through the window and saw them approaching: the stuffed rounded figure of a woman in ragged fringed shawl and broken-feathered bonnet, a woman dragging a small child in a cart which squeaked . . . the sullen black-haired youth teetering on crutches behind. The Tebbses! Ira whispered. Whom have we to thank for this?

Lucy peeked with him at the window. I make no doubt, Poppy, that we have our dear Harry to thank. Remember his ministration to the girl? . . . She hurried out on the gallery.

Miss Lucy, crowed Mag, we done heard about your going to get married! We do thank you, and the surgeon too, count of you all done so much for poor little Laurel. We hain't got much to offer, but I made a wreath: wedding wreath, kind of. Twould be good for Christmas greens as well. . . . You Zoral! Let go that now!

She snatched up a wreath which the boy had been plucking at. It was quite handsomely made, of dark holly with pine cones attached; the cones were tied with fragments of old ribbons.

And Coral—he went and shot you a coon. They're right good roasted now. Zoral, you yield up that coon, baby boy—tain't yourn, belongs to Miss Lucy! Zoral screamed and struck when she took the dead raccoon from him.

You're much too kind and, oh so thoughtful, Lucy cried. I just naturally love roast coon! And such a pretty wreath! I declare, we've had no time to think of Christmas greens. . . . Ira came to make sure that Coral could negotiate the steps on his crutches. The three were escorted inside to become a portion of the Dearly Beloved Assembled.

LIV

The first memory which Meriwether Kinsman held was of a crooning. The song was played by a bird which adhered to topmost twigs
of a vase-shaped elm which grew against a corner of the Kinsman
cottage. The cottage was small, old, white-painted. The elm had
grown large during years since the house was built, and swelling of
its gray seamed trunk actually had pushed the cottage askew. Lichens
were thick upon shingles and on the north side of the elm's trunk—
it was hard to tell where trunk left off and shingles began. In this
tree, almost a part of the house, the brownish-gray bird gave its fluting. A bird not only gray . . . tints of peach and blue . . . this was a
mourning-dove which sang, although Meriwether Kinsman did not
know its name, would not know it for years. The bird made promise
of peace and strength intermingled; it blew upon an instrument, a
wet wooden instrument. The boy was very young at the time, indeed
it was his first memory. He was in bed, a ragged colored comforter
over him. He remembered . . . he had been playing with the squares
of material in the old crazy quilt. He bent and folded the cover in
small hands, trying to match red with red, lilac with lilac. Then
warbling came from on high.

What is it? he thought. Oh, what is it?

He was in his trundle bed, the quilt had been cut down to size. He
rolled over the low edge of bed and ran to the open window, he
pushed his tufted yellow head out of the open window, and looked
up . . . space between the leaves, Merry could see all the way to the
elm's top because one branch had been broken in a recent storm.
There lived the bird in earliest morning serenity against light sky.
There it fifed its rich low tone. So it was his first memory. So Merry
Kinsman would go fifing into Eternity.

His mother was a widow, a bakeress, proud of telling how she was
forty-two years old when her son Meriwether was born; she had not
expected that she would ever have a child. Merry's father died when
the boy was a baby, died because he was drunk and caught his
clothing ablaze in the middle of the night when he sought to prepare
an oven fire. Promptly Mrs. Kinsman took over the full task of baking
in which she had merely assisted before. The child's next memories
were of yeast and flour and dough—always dough—and great heat.

And awareness also that in summer the Kinsmans had more money than in winter, because many wives of the village refused to bake themselves along with their bread; although they preferred to make their own bread in cooler weather.

Merry went to school only until he was eleven. Then Mr. Adams, the miller at the edge of town, refused to let Mrs. Kinsman have any more meal or flour until her debt was paid, and Merry went to help at the mill. . . . There were sacks of grain stored in an upper story of the mill, and the sour-faced Mr. Adams instructed Merry to fetch the grain down to a lower floor, to pile sacks near the hopper. After dragging down only one of the lubberly sacks, and falling on the stairs and nearly breaking his back, the boy began to speculate upon some other method. The water gate was closed, the mill was not turning, Mr. Adams had gone to vote. Merry rigged a competent trough out of smooth-sawn planks and extended this trough on a slope from the upper story to the lower. He arranged an open sack at the bottom end, and began pouring grain into the trough above. By this means the entire burden was conveyed soon to its proper destination. Merry ran down to cord up each bag again when it was filled. Miller Adams returned at the moment the child was tightening the last sack in triumph. He did not praise Merry for his ingenuity. He said that the boy had demonstrated how lazy he was, and Mr. Adams would tolerate no lazybones about the place. He slapped Merry, to make him remember; then ordered him to drag all the sacks up the stair to their original position, and bring them down again, as he had been told to do in the first place. He said that this was a lesson which Meriwether Kinsman would not forget. It was in fact a good lesson: it taught Merry to avoid fiends in human form, such as Mr. Adams, whenever he could.

Mr. Adams was a part of America . . . Merry preferred to forget that portion of America. He thought that America should be constituted of men and objects deserving of veneration. Some children worshipped guns which hung in their homes, and guns were a good thing, they were part of the Nation, a sustaining part; but Merry had something which he adored more. Toby Rambler bragged about his father's rifle with its tawny maple stock, and stars and crescents of brass; and in Micah Jones's house there was a Queen's-arm above the fireplace. But neither these boys nor others owned a fife, and Merry Kinsman had a fife. It had belonged to Aaron Briggs, his mother's father.

He found the fife several years before—he was seven at the time, he was hunting peppermints. His mother had bought him peppermints as a Christmas treat. They were delectable wafers, odd as to shape, but bearing the same pink beauty and same pink taste. She said that Merry must not eat them all at once, he must save some for a rainy

day. Well, a January thaw had set in, and this was a rainy day, with
dark water drilling steadily into big pocked drifts around the cottage.
Mrs. Kinsman was busy over pies, and no one restrained Merry as he
explored for mints. Several high shelves hung on brackets in a corner
of the parlor, and Merry had observed that often things were put up
there to be kept out of his reach. He labored to put a smaller chair
upon a larger chair, and then a hassock atop this structure. By such
means he could clamber aloft, his seven-year-old eyes and fingers
might proceed with their examining. He did not find the mints but
he found something else. It was a stained tube of pale brown wood
with a peculiarly-shaped hole cut near one end, and six smaller holes
piercing the tube farther down. Rims of metal were inlaid at either
end of the thing. It was a fascinating object, he did not know what
it could be. It seemed that one might play upon it . . . he tried to
blow in the end but no sound issued.

Merry teetered on his crazy structure for too long. The hassock
began to slide. Merry came down abruptly, chairs and all, in noise and
pain. He howled, but the strange implement was unhurt in his hand.
His mother rushed to see that he was not killed, then she gave him a
spanking. Often she spanked him when still she had flour on her big
angular hands; often his breeches were white on the seat, a fresh
spanking would dust flour into the air like smoke. Merry roared until
punishment was concluded, then forgot it promptly in wonder of the
thing he had found.

Ma, what is this?

Tis Pa's fife.

What's a fife?

It makes music. My Pa—your Grandpa—played that when he was
fighting gainst the British.

I want to play music on it, Ma.

Well, I don't know how. But you can play *with* the fife, if you mind
and keep it careful.

She did indicate the one hole which should be blown upon, but
Merry could not sound a note. He had a strange sensation that some
utter beauty, some almost religious joy was being withheld from him.
Was there no one in the neighborhood, or perhaps in all of Pennsylvania or in America or in the World—no one to show him how? It
seemed that there was no one.

The next summer an event of patriotic interest was celebrated in
a grove beside the Susquehanna. (Ah, he loved the sound of the
river's name, he loved all those names: Wyalusing, Towanda, Mehoo-
pany, Meshoppen. Lovely places, he had heard of them, their Indian
sound sent a prickle through his being, they had the accent of America; so did Tunkhannock and Wyoming and Minooka. He thought of
feathers and paint, and moccasins made from deer's hide; he thought

of birch bark, arrows whistling, a gobbling yell going up. He thought
of Grandma Rummer's house on the edge of the village across from
the mill. It was the oldest house in town: there were logs under
modern siding, and the original door still hung upon its great hand-
forged hinges, a door low and narrow—tall men had to stoop—but
thick, strengthened with iron. There was a deep triangular gash
driven into this thick wood, and children were fond of gathering on
the step and poking their fingers into the cut. Everyone knew the
story. Indians had come speeding along that road, long ago . . . just
before dawn, it was said, of an autumn day. A tall Indian with a
hideous face dashed up the path to the Rummer house and tried to
push open the door. When the door would not budge he yelled, he
struck with his hatchet. Here was the mark to prove it. Did the
Indian run away, did someone shoot him as he threatened on the
doorstep? No one knew, least of all Grandma Rummer. She was deaf,
aging. . . . Oh, yes, children, she'd say, in answer to questions. Twas
in Grandpa's time, but he's long dead. Twas when he was young.
That's just where that red Indian hit with his tomahawk. And then
the townsfolk banded together and drove the villains off, and I've
heard tell some was killed on both sides. . . . This was something to
think about, in autumn, in mornings when mists of night still made
their curving pattern above the shining Susquehanna. Oh, there were
other towns of which men spoke: a place called Blackwalnut, a place
called Sugar Run; there were Luther's Mills and Eagle's Mere and
Greene's Landing. They were not Indian names; but somehow they
sounded like Indians, like America.)

His mother might not attend the patriotic celebration; but she said
that Merry could go along with the Rambler family, and she provided him with crullers and pies. Merry might trade with other children, and thus come in for his share of chicken and salad and cold
spiced beef. His mother gave him a half-dime. He could buy lemonade
if it were being sold.

He rioted round the grove with other boys. Life was not a pic-nic
for Meriwether Kinsman; indeed he had seen little of pic-nics, so he
enjoyed this one utterly. . . . A cannon which some young men had
dragged there . . . when it went off, it sounded like the hills along the
Susquehanna falling apart. With throbbing ears and starting eyes
Merry Kinsman peered through smoke to see whether indeed the
hills were blown apart.

But greater delectation lay ahead, it came marching. Distantly
above squall and chatter in the grove sounded a high-pitched round-
throated wailing. This wailing was sustained by a grumble: old
voices of the past talking together in slamming monotone, talking of
wars, talking of something native and peculiar to the landscape on
which people stood and stared. A rude platform had been erected to

hold speakers and other dignitaries; but the program was not yet
commenced, and Merry Kinsman and a troop of other boys trampled
on yellow planks, cutting capers. He was on the platform when he
heard the distant piping and spasm of drums which came along. Then
he was in air, floating through air as he leaped from the platform,
floating through space as he ran toward the cart path which wound
from the main road into this oak and chestnut wood. A homely procession appeared. People said, My, just look at the old soldiers! There
were seven of the old soldiers, marching with a few younger men in
blue uniforms. The old soldiers were not in uniform, although Uncle
Dan Ellis was among them, and he wore a strange-shaped cap which
Merry had never seen him wear in his butcher's shop. Judge Ephraim
Knowles was one of the old soldiers; truly he was not so old: there
was not a glint of gray in his hair, his luxuriant brown beard bristled
with challenge. Seven of the old soldiers walking together . . . they
had fought the British, their noses had sniffed powder smoke. Uncle
Dan Ellis was glad to show any child the place where a portion of his
ear had been shot away, and where an old blue-silver streak raked
behind his ear, where thin graying hair would not grow.

More wonderful than their presence, more wonderful than their
momentary exultation and enduring fame, was the music coming along
with them. A tall man with cottony white hair—a stranger—sustained
in his hands a fife very much like the one which Merry had found
upon that high shelf at home. It spoke with the crying of hawks, high
wild lift of an eagle's shriek. There were two small drums muttering
in accompaniment, one larger drum booming at intervals in uninterrupted cannonade; but Merry had eyes and ears only for the fife, for
the fierce-eyed man who played it. The tune was ragged, savage. The
old man played it over and over, and Merry Kinsman ran before him,
looking up and back. He trotted backward most of the time. Once he
fell, in a muddy place where the cart path turned; he got up, trotted
on, keeping pace ahead of the martial music. The tune began with a
slow and ponderous threat in lower registers. You thought of horses,
war horses, parading off somewhere, going in cumbrous decision to
engage in a battle. The great decisive powerful horses wore trappings
of leather and brass; dragoons bestrode them. Solid shot flew but
they kept coming. Above the storm, hawks and eagles began to soar.
They were over the trees, far over powder smoke, they carried glinting banners in their beaks. They said, Here we are: ferocious, untrammeled . . . the Conestoga wagons rumble in roads beneath . . .
muskets are being charged and fired, bayonets find the blood of invaders. But here we are, high and fluting! We have power not possessed by more orchestral flutes, we carry a shot-riddled flag held in
many beaks. Our tanned wings are wheeling . . . we are America, embattled America. High, proud, far and high!

Certainly other tunes were played that day; Merry could not remember them. He hummed and whistled and burbled the initial chant, the thing which pierced and tooted ahead of the little throng as they came to display themselves, to be proud with the pride which only soldiers feel, which only men may feel who have risked themselves in a war. The tune had been conceived in such pride and spoke of it. All the way home the boy whistled the tune. He ran into the house whistling it. His mother came, floury as always, cloth tied over her hair, apron dusty. She said, Why, Merry, child. You back so soon? Still he kept trying to rebuild the new tune (which was in fact so old a tune) and imagining that sunburnt drumheads were vibrating alongside him, that the boom of artillery arose.

Child, what are you whistling? What is that song? Her face seemed whitening under smudges of wheat flour.

He cried, They played it at the grove. Uncle Dan Ellis was there and all them old soldiers, and young ones that fit the Mexicans, and— They was an old gentleman with white hair, Ma, and he had a fife thing like—like this.

He ran to find the fife of chocolate-colored wood, to show it to her.

But that tune, child—what is it?

I don't know. His tough small lips began building the delicious sounds once more.

His mother sat down on a stool and began to cry. Pa used to play that, she said between sobs. I don't know the name, but it's mighty old. A martial tune like when he was fighting gainst the redcoats. Pa used to play that.

The boy was haunted throughout the night by weird important melodies, haunted especially by the Tune Which Pa Used To Play. Amid fifing and drum-beats he thought that Indians were running loose, he was being chased by a black bear. In a later dream he shot that same bear with an antique weapon. He had graduated from trundle bed to full-sized cot. . . . He left this cot as a fugitive might have stolen, for fear his mother would not wish him out of bed: she might declare that he should be in bed because it was night, because little boys belonged in bed. He went through darkness until his hand closed upon the favored thing, he took it back into bed with him. Eventually he returned to sleep while lying on the fife, and had another dream approaching nightmare in which his chest was impaled by an Iroquois arrow.

In the morning, since there was no school at this season, he could run errands. First off he was sent to the grocer's shop with a basket of cookies, bearing a note addressed to Mr. Yunke the proprietor. The Widow Kinsman hoped to trade these cookies for cherries from which to make pies. Mr. Yunke had no cherries left this late in the season; he kept the cookies to sell, on shares, or to serve as credit against some future purchase. He gave Meriwether another note to this effect.

Merry did not deliver it, not immediately. Instead he ran to Uncle Dan Ellis's butcher shop and found the elderly man in his ice shed. There meat was kept through the summer. In winter time Uncle Dan and his sons and his daughters' husbands cut ice for future needs, and dragged great chunks of it to the village on an ox-sled. It always smelled cool in the shed. Ice was covered with sawdust, and sometimes in summer Uncle Dan could be persuaded to sell chunks. People made cold drinks; root beer was the favorite.

Uncle Dan was trimming a leg of lamb, his knobby scarred hands directing the sharp knife keenly, surely.

Uncle Dan. Who was that old man? That old soldier?

What say, bubby?

He played that thing yesterday. At the rally, before all them gentlemen started to make speeches. He played the fife—

Oh. Name is Parker. Mr. Abijah Parker. Dwells over to Crow Corners.

Crow Corners was a weary way: six miles. Merry Kinsman went there on that same day. He carried his grandfather's fife. He walked through dust all the way to Church Hollow, then a farmer came along with a team and gave him a ride. At Crow Corners he inquired shyly for the tall cotton-haired Mr. Parker, and was directed to a barnlike structure behind an apple orchard where Abijah Parker pursued his trade of wheelwright. Merry Kinsman could hear ringing tools before he reached the place. Mr. Parker was working alone, pounding a rim upon a hub.

. . . The tune, he said, was called Jefferson and Liberty. Oh yes, twas old; it went all the way back to the Revolution. That was not the war in which Abijah Parker served, but his own father had been a soldier under General John Sullivan. Oh yes, young boy, it was a mighty old tune. And some there were who called it Paul Revere's Ride, but Mr. Parker and his fellow musicians had always called it Jefferson and Liberty. And some there were who called it The Gobby O, he didn't quite know why. He said that sometimes musicians referred to their fifes as gob-sticks; again, he didn't know why.

He told Merry Kinsman about the Saranac. Planking had been taken up from a bridge, there were just runners of the bridge, and British tried to cross on those runners. They were brave, young boy! They were brave, they kept a-coming. Mr. Parker believed that some officer should have stopped them but maybe their officers were killed by the first volley. And us Americans behind ramparts on the other side—we made up our minds not to let them British get across, so they never even got to the middle of the bridge. They kept running on them three lines of stringers. They were soldiers, they obeyed, they just kept a-coming. And there wasn't nobody left to give an order to halt. Twas sickening work, young boy. Sickening! Folks talk about the bloody Saranac, and that was the reason: all them bodies gushing out their blood, fast as they fell into that water, turning the stream to red. Twas sad, because war is sad business.

Sun came through apple leaves and lay kindly on the hair of the old man, the gold hair of the child.

Mr. Abijah Parker did not offer to resume his labor with the wheel hub. He and Merry Kinsman sat upon the step beside other leaning wheels against the wall of the building . . . wheels like those had carried wagons forward, had borne supplies, had lugged people into wilderness . . . larger thicker wheels supported the cannon. . . .

His own fife was put away, doubtless on a shelf or in a bureau in the neat brown house beyond; but Mr. Parker held Aaron Briggs's fife. His firm tapering knowledgeable fingers pressed tightly over six holes and rose and rippled as tunes rippled and rolled. This one, he said; we played it. Funny . . . you said your Grandpa was a fifer too, and this here cocoa-wood was his; but I reckon we never met, though I've met many a good fifer in my time, and drummers too. This is the old Eighteen-twelve Stop March. We played it frequent.

His beardless lips caressed the hole into which he must blow. There came a great wisdom thus early to the boy beside him. Merry could see clearly things which he had never seen and might never see. He could have an understanding of matters which factually he might never understand or even witness. But it was as if he held familiarity with them now. . . . You thought not only of guns: you thought of implements, you thought of cauldrons in which maple sap boiled, you thought of late winter woodlands where sap froze to an icicle at the tip of every spout hammered into a maple tree.

This one, he said. We played it. Tis called Charley Over the Water, and maybe was made up about the Bonnie Prince himself. I've heard tell my mother came from Scotland. . . . You thought of bagpipes. You had never seen bagpipes, did not know how they were shaped; nor did you know a claymore, but you saw the blade flashing, and heard young men rushing through heather, and you did not know what heather was, nor how purple it bloomed in August.

This one, said Abijah Parker, is the Cuckoo's Nest. . . . That one I played just then? Tis named the Jaybird. And so you thought of birds again: the gentle bird who'd fifed low-toned for you in first awareness, high on the elm. And hawks once more. All were American birds, flying high.

Another Stop March. Now, notice how I watch my stops. The Old Seventy-six, and I reckon folks played it in the Revolution, when they was fighting Hessians not far away from here. . . . Here's another six-eight, he said. They name it Tattered Jack.

He tried to show Meriwether Kinsman how to spread his fingers
among the holes; but Merry's hand was so tiny that his fingers would
not reach. This way, Mr. Parker said. Now you take your left hand—
so. You put it out in front, put the thumb at the back to help hold.
The three middle fingers on the first three holes—so. Now your right
hand: it goes down here, and with the thumb to hold the fife likewise. Three middle fingers, bottom three holes. All closed tight for the
first note. When you want to take a high octave, you hold up this highest finger. Makes the tone clearer so. Otherwise it's kind of graty.

This one, he said. Two-four, of course. We called it Gilderoy.
Reckon it's about a kind of fable. . . . And this, he said. Two-four
as well. We called it Adam Bell's March, and it goes clear back. Now
this, said Abijah Parker, and his fingers were limber—you would not
have known that they were elderly fingers, that joints were stiffening
as joints of the aged must. They were so fluid, notes which sped were
fluid and oily. . . . Called that one the Turkey Gobbler. So you
thought of turkeys running wild, their burnished necks metallic in
the woods, spurred feet fleeing. You heard the rifle sound: a man in
buckskin clothes had shot a turkey, shot him dead. . . . Haste To The
Wedding, said old Mr. Parker. You thought of a frontier wedding,
people dancing as fiddles whined.

Abijah Parker's bent little wife came out on the cottage stoop and
cried, Hoo-hoo. That, he said, was the signal for dinner. Mother
doesn't know we've got company to set down with us, he told Merry
Kinsman. But she'll have plenty to eat. Always does. I always did
like to set a good table, and somehow managed to do so. He took
Merry by the hand and led him to wash at a bench beside the well.
Soon the three of them sat at table in the narrow kitchen with its
crooked floor, and a bright new step-stove gleaming hotly, squarely
in front of the wide fireplace. Mrs. Parker said in a hushed mousy
voice, Little boy, and she bowed her head, and then she lifted her
eyes again and said, Father, warningly. Old Abijah bowed his head,
and Merry bowed his; but he kept stealing glances at this great man.
He could not refrain from watching. Abijah Parker had his eyes
squeezed shut, his brows were tufted, icy, his forehead cragged. For
what we are about to receive, the old man muttered, hold us to be
thankful, dear Lord, and love and keep us all. Amen. There were
tiny new potatoes boiled in pink jackets; creamed peas, a great bowl
of lettuce, a jar crammed with thin young onions, green tops spreading to form a bouquet . . . slice after slice of pungent ham, sliced
thinly, with a sugary crust to it; a platter of eggs basted until their
tops were white, freckled with pepper. There was berry pie, a big
yellow pitcher of milk, pickles and jellies such as Merry had never
tasted before. He would dream of them often. In fact he would sit

at that table again and again, until the day of hushed voices, the day when, grown a mite taller but still skinny, he would be conducted into the front parlor to see a black coffin placed across chairs. . . .

They said that it was a weary way for young feet to travel. Best to wait by the gate until a neighbor came. The first who passed were only farmers headed for a mile or two beyond, and they drove slow oxen. But soon appeared a swirl of hot dust, with the dappled neck of a big gelding reaching up out of dust, bright wheels flashing, sun flashing on spokes. It was Squire Hart, no less, and he was going all the way to Merry Kinsman's village. So Merry was hoisted up beside the fat squire, who talked unceasingly of things of which the boy had no comprehension. He remembered later that *litigation* was a favorite word of Squire Hart's. All he could do was to sit in blissful daze, listening to those remembered bright notes rolling through the orchard . . . imagined columns of rough soldiers tramping. The Jaybird . . . Adam Bell's March, Tattered Jack; above all, Jefferson and Liberty. He heard them, he heard them when he was set down at the Widow Kinsman's gate; he heard tunes crying above and beyond his own lament as the willow switch struck sharply against his little legs and bottom; heard glorious music after he was put to bed without any supper. But he had his fife. He held Grandpa's fife gripped in damp hands . . . useless fife. His infant fingers could not spread to cover the holes.

. . . Joe Jew came by. As always that was an event of first importance. Merry's mother was removing cakes with her long-handled paddle, she was out at her oven which abutted on the roofed back porch. The boy ran to carry good news.

Ma! Ma, it's Joe Jew! He's stopping at the gate.

Everyone in the region knew this peddler; he had traveled those roads for years. His ill-tempered brown pony, his jolting wagon with oilcloth top and sides: this vehicle was a peripatetic treasure house. No wonder children clustered hopefully at the tailboard in every village. Sometimes Joe Jew was in a generous mood, he passed out sugarplums; sometimes he was grumpy, he pretended not to see the children. His name was Joseph Iscowitz, and people knew him all the way up to Binghamton and over to Elmira in York State. Twice a year the Widow Kinsman stocked up on spices, flavorings and fruit color; necessarily she bought things like these from Joe Jew because of the paucity of such stock for sale locally. . . . Wonderful cases, all secured by straps, hanging in the wagon; and any one of them could be carried by its strap over the little man's shoulder as he made his hunched way to the front door.

First off he fetched his case of spices and candies. Mrs. Kinsman selected for her needs, and brought the ginger jar in which she kept her change.

But I want you should see my threads. Such a beautiful new stock I got, Mrs. Kinsman! . . . He could call her by name: that was a trick of his trade; Joe Jew had the names of thousands of customers salted within his curly head. He could say, Well, well, and look at little Hannah. My, how she is growing!

Smart time I have for fancy sewing, said the widow. I can scarcely catch an hour to do the mending for Merry and me.

Joe Jew insisted, he gave Merry a somewhat crushed caramel to show that his heart was in the right place. He fetched the case containing needles, scissors, yarn and such trifles. As always, the child was fascinated by rich colors, delightful purples and crimsons and tans of tinted thread. Still a packet of pins was all that the widow felt that she should afford. She looked wistfully at other items, but shook her head with discipline.

As Joe Jew was closing the case and sighing—as he always did, no matter how much people bought—there was a light thud. Some shiny black object rolled on the old carpet.

Wrong case, said Joe Jew. Now how did that get in here? He picked up the thing.

Instantly Merry Kinsman's eyes were alight. Oh, please— Oh, Mr. Joe Jew. It's a kind of fife!

No fife, said the peddler. No, little boy, they call this a penny whistle. But the price is a dime.

A tin whistle . . . actually it was not composed of tin: it was made of some heavier metal, perhaps lead. Probably made in the same mould with hundreds of others. . . . Ma! cried Meriwether Kinsman, dancing as he waved the thing in his hand.

You've got along thus far without a whistle, Merry. Guess you can get along still.

But, Ma, *look*. It's just like a fife, cept—see—you blow in the end. It's got six holes, like a fife. Look, Ma, they're real close together! I can reach them with my fingers. I can't reach the holes on Grandpa's fife until I get growed.

The little boy, he loves the whistle, said Joe Jew, wheedling. It would be nice were you to buy it for him?

Can't afford it.

Oh, Ma!

Can't afford it, said the widow sternly. She ushered Joe Jew out of the house and went back to her oven. Merry collapsed on the step in tears.

Joe Jew clambered up into his driver's seat with some difficulty, since he had been more or less crippled for years (some said that the pony ran away with him) and he clucked to brown Sadie. Wheels started to turn; then Joe Jew pulled on his reins and said Whoa. Little boy, you come here.

Merry ran to the edge of the road, wondering.

Tell your Mamma I would settle for apple turnovers.

Merry rushed shrieking through the cottage, then his heart sank into his bare feet as his mother informed him that her stock of apple turnovers was spoken for; he must carry the basket over to Mrs. Doctor Neely's within the hour. But, she said, relenting, I would be willing to give him a sack of cinnamon buns. Last baking didn't sell too well. She made a sack out of newspaper, because manufactured paper sacks were expensive, and Merry carried this poke filled with a dozen buns to the peddler.

Well, said Joe Jew, shrugging. A good apple turnover would be so much better; but I am next door to a beggar, so I cannot be a chooser, and no dinner did I have this noon. Nothing but work, work, work, peddle, peddle, peddle! He complained for a moment more; but he accepted the parcel of buns, and passed the wonderful whistle down to the boy. Merry did not even see him drive away, he did not realize that Joe Jew was gone. He stood graven, caressing the magic tube. He tried to remember what Mr. Abijah Parker had told him; he tried to remember how Mr. Parker's fingers looked on the fife, how he held it. This was different; but it was the same, because there were six holes. And anyone who could learn to play on such a whistle could, Merry was sure, learn to play upon a fife. He sat again on the step, no longer in collapse. He remembered . . . six holes . . . all closed for the first note. Then lift this third finger of the right hand for the next note. Now—up with the second finger as well . . . now up with the first finger. Loose shrill notes crawled softly if uncertainly. Soon Merry was playing the scale. It would not be long . . . oh, mercy and delight . . . it didn't sound like a fife: the music was thinner, more bird-like. But the same tunes could be played, and in the same way.

The next time he could win permission and beg a ride over to Crow Corners to sit at the feet of his idol, Merry was discomfited to find that Abijah Parker rather sniffed at the whistle. Oh, that's not much, the veteran said. Sounds like a sparrow. I mind seeing a gypsy or something, playing such a little toot as this, time I was in Philadelphia. Walked right along the street, squeaking away on it. Had a tin cup hanging on his belt. I guess he expected folks to give him pennies; but I didn't give him none; I couldn't abide the infernal noise he was a-making.

Said Merry Kinsman shyly, I can learn the proper tunes. Then, when my hands get big enough to reach acrost the holes on Grandpa's fife— Well, then I'd know the tunes, wouldn't I, Uncle Bijah?

(Now they had grown to this intimacy.)

Well, maybe that makes sense. I guess you could. You know, I hadn't come across no one else, except for drummers of course, who

really cared about my fifing. Not for years and years, not till you
come along. Now, set real quiet and I'll play a six-eight for you—an
easy one. Oh, Lassie, Art Thou Sleeping Yet—I'll teach you how.

Through the next hawking, eagling, rolling years he taught him.
Oh, yes: The Raw Recruit. Oh, yes: The Huntsman Hornpipe. Oh,
yes: Granny Will Your Dog Bite? It was as if rough shrilling voices
of a hundred deerskin melodists had lain compressed within the tube
which Merry Kinsman learned to play; only his weaving fingers
might let them loose. When at eleven he was forced to servitude under
Miller Adams, it was tragedy worse than the punishment he received
in his grain sack episode, far worse than slaps or slavery . . . it was
molten agony poured within his being . . . Mr. Adams would *not*
tolerate his whistle at the mill. Mr. Adams told him to take that
wretched thing home and never bring it back, or he'd fling it clean
over the mill race into the Susquehanna. He said that only idle boys
would sit around, blowing on a thing like that. (In fact, for Mr.
Adams's money, no one except idle folk make any music at all. He
held fiddlers in especial scorn, and would not let his daughters go
into any home where fiddling and jigging were permitted. Therefore,
as so often occurs, both daughters managed to get into trouble, and
had to be married; and neither was happy in her enforced matrimony.)

Merry was small for his age: a towhead whose hair deepened only
slightly in color as he grew older. His eyes were large, solemn, gray
as the river on a cloudy day; but his hands and feet were large out
of proportion. He could play Grandpa's fife instead of the tin whistle,
by the time he was twelve.

Visits to Abijah Parker were few and far between. Winter time
was the only chance usually; and it was a grave chore to get across
those six miles through drifts. But Merry did go plodding. Once a
storm struck when he was halfway home. Drifts were higher than his
head, white hard salt of snow ripped and stung his eyes, worse than
the dust of the mill might sting them. Merry Kinsman lost his way, he
came near to perishing, he lost a mitten. The right side of his face
froze, fingers were frozen on his right hand. It was with difficulty
that he was thawed when at last he stumbled upon a house occupied
by an old German couple. Still the thawing was not accomplished
properly; Merry's fingers swelled and grew discolored, one of them
split open. It was thought later that the finger might have to be cut
off, and what would that have done to his fifing? But the finger was
saved, eventually Merry could use it. Few boys could have been as
thankful for anything in the world, as was Meriwether Kinsman for
this fortune.

When the war broke out (or, as Uncle Dan Ellis always put it, when
the army broke out) Merry longed to go and serve as a fifer. He
knew for a certainty that already, even at his tender age, he was a

better fifer than might be found among musicians of an entire army corps. Uncle Bijah had said as much. But the Widow Kinsman was not well, she had dizzy spells, sometimes she had to sit down and rest her head upon the bread board. When Joe Jew came by that year, Mrs. Kinsman invested heavily in several remedies which the peddler offered and recommended with enthusiasm; but none of them seemed to help her a great deal.

Merry dreamed almost nightly of cannon fire, the long roll of drums. He dreamed of himself shrilling out garrison calls, winning applause and praise for his skill, as well as for his bravery in thundering battles. He dreamed . . . still he dared not run away and leave his mother. One benefit came, because he was old enough now, at thirteen, to take over a great many baker's tasks: he was allowed to give up his work under the hated Adams.

Mr. Adams flew into rage. He said that Mrs. Kinsman still owed him money; he said that Merry hadn't worked off all the debt as yet; he threatened to sue in a court of law, but nothing came of his bluster. Mr. Adams threatened also that he might refuse to sell any flour at all to Mrs. Kinsman. Merry thought that Adams would reconsider if he, Merry, came with cash in hand.

Good morning, Mr. Adams. I come for some white flour.

Oh. How much you want, Merry?

Two two-dollar sacks.

You won't be able to carry them.

I brung the little wagon that I use when I'm peddling bread and stuff about town. I can haul it all right.

Well, let's see the color of your money.

Carefully Merry counted hard-won dimes and half-dimes, quarter-dollars, broad pennies. He counted coins into Mr. Adams's palm. He knew that the sum was correct, he had counted it at home.

Hain't but three dollars ninety-eight that I can see.

Yes, sir, four dollars!

But the miller had to go through the pile three times before he admitted that the amount was correct. He took out his purse, dumped in the change, dropped the purse back into a deep pocket in the skirts of his white dusty coat. Now, he said, that'll go on the debt your Ma still owes me.

Merry gaped. Oh, the man was so tall, so cruel, he was a giant. He could handle a sack of wheat as if it were a rag doll. He stood there in his grim adult state. He was rich: he owned a farm, he owned two houses in town. And Merry was poor, he was only thirteen, going on fourteen; and skinny.

You mean— He gulped again. You won't give me my flour? Ma's got to have it.

You tell your Ma I'll sell her all the flour she wants, soon as she settles up with me. I figure she still owes me better than seven dollars. Money doesn't grow on trees.

Indeed it did not, and no one knew that fact better than Merry Kinsman. His shocked voice rattled in remonstrance: Mr. Adams! You said you'd credit us a dollar a week, for the time I put in here. We figured it honest, and—leaving out the seasons when you was closed up, and that time you said you didn't need me, you couldn't use me for about five months—and leaving out the time I was sick with my hand— Well, Ma says the debt *is* paid. And more.

Seven dollars and thirty-five cents to go, said Mr. Adams.

Merry wondered what Uncle Bijah Parker would have done at the same age. Abijah had been only a few years older than Merry when he fought the redcoats. With clarity Merry Kinsman saw immediately just what Abijah Parker would have done. Merry walked steadily to the corner where stood Mr. Adams's desk, closed up to keep out as much mill dust as possible; and he knew what stood in that corner behind the desk. Mr. Adams had a persistent fear of two enemies: a rat and a thief. The one would ruin his grain, the other might put a knife to his throat and make off with his money. Mr. Adams considered a loaded shotgun good insurance against either threat. Merry jerked the old tablecloth which hung over the weapon to protect it; flour flew in a cloud. When the cloud settled sufficiently, Mr. Adams was looking into the twin barrels of his own gun. Merry had cocked both hammers.

My little wagon's just outside the door, said Merry.

You young devil. Put down that gun!

You're just a highway robber, said Merry. I come to buy flour, you took my money and then said you wouldn't give me no flour. That's just plain robbery, and robbers ought to get shot. So you take two sacks of flour and put them on my little wagon your own self, or I'll let go with both barrels.

You—you— You're a murderer! You—

Tain't murder to protect yourself against robbers. That's what you always say. That's why you keep this here shotgun loaded, and warned me not to touch it. Mr. Adams, you load that flour, or I'll shoot you here and now.

There was no more dust floating. The miller could see clearly the boy's cold gray gaze, see his finger close to the triggers. Sweating and gasping, Mr. Adams stumbled about the business of loading sacks on the homemade cart with its strong but sagging wheels.

Now, said Merry Kinsman, I've took the caps off both tumblers. That's just so you won't shoot me, Mr. Adams, and maybe claim I stole your flour.

The bearded miller looked down at the boy in utter terror. Never in his life had anyone ever pointed a gun at this man, and told him that he would be shot if he didn't do thus and so; and sincerely he knew that the youth had been ready and willing to kill him.

What do you think the constable'll say, when I tell him that you threatened me with my own gun?

He won't say a thing, sir, cause you ain't going to tell him. Of course Merry was correct again: he knew that Mr. Adams would not tell anything, could not tell anything. He knew that Mr. Adams would never try that trick again, for fear that Merry might kill him in some fashion afterward, whether Mr. Adams's shotgun was put away safely or whether it wasn't. Merry went home with the flour. He held his head up, held his gaze up, he thought the drums were rolling around and behind him. He could hear the scream of Abijah Parker's fife, climbing to the last exultant cheer of Jefferson and Liberty.

One day in the summer of 1862, when Merry was fourteen, Mrs. Kinsman fell flat amid a shower of bread loaves. Merry had been up early to prepare the fire, and was out wielding a hay fork in Mr. McMurchie's field. Thus he did not discover his mother; it remained for customers to do that when they came to the house. A little girl was sent running to the McMurchie place. . . .

The afternoon following his mother's funeral, Merry Kinsman wandered near the warped wharves stretching out across mud flats as the river shrank to its late summer level. He would have liked to have gone fishing; he had even gone to the woodshed and examined a willow pole which he had not had time to ply in two years at least (because there was so little time for him to enjoy the sports of other boys). The fishing line wound about the dry willow was frayed in several places, as if mice had chewed it. So no fishing.

Merry's grief for his mother's departure was not so much grief as a shattering and displacement; and, as people have often mused, the sadness of death was not a sadness at reviewing a death, but a sadness at reviewing the misfortunes of a life. Merry's emotions had stormed as he sat staring silently into space, not hearing prayers and the polite sniffling of neighbor women. His mother had had so little! She was stern . . . truly it was not her fault . . . poverty at times very nearly squeezed her into the shape of a termagant. She had looked longingly at pretty things offered in the cases of Joe Jew, she had not been able to buy them. Merry had seen her eyes brighten, as indeed his own eyes brightened, at seeing beautiful tight little rolls: purple thread, scarlet thread, thread of pea-green. And there were lengths of flowered new calico, itching to be sewn, itching to be made into frilled gay aprons. So must his mother have wished to wear happy aprons of bright-patterned calico, instead of workaday aprons made roughly from flour sacking. . . . There were those gleaming embroidery scissors, snapped temptingly by Joe Jew, and sun starred up from the steel surfaces as he snipped the scissors back and forth. They cost sixty cents, she could not buy them.

But some peace came to Merry later, when they put the Widow Kinsman into the ground, because now she would be in recollection and literally a part of American soil which bold men had enriched. Some of the bold men were her forebears. Merry thought that it would have been appropriate if fifes and drums fluted and banged above her mound, because she was the daughter and the grand-daughter and the wife of soldiers. Would ever she be the mother of a soldier? . . . He heard her tight thin voice say, Merry, what tune is that? Pa used to play that. He contrived a scene wherein she was being welcomed by a conclave of Briggses and Kinsmans and their kind . . . bony men in three-cornered hats, frontier women in bonnets. Also there seemed to be a few Indians coming out of the woods, with baskets of fish or popcorn, as they had come to the Pilgrim Fathers. Distantly, persistently fifes blended. They were playing Oh, Lassie, Art Thou Sleeping Yet? . . . drums grumbled with spirit. Why, of course that was Uncle Bijah playing—Mr. Abijah Parker. He had been gone nearly a year . . . Mrs. Kinsman would sit on a cabin step beside him, and say, My own Pa—Aaron Briggs—used to play that. Did you know him when you was at the Saranac?

Meriwether Kinsman poked beside the Susquehanna. He had no desire to go back to the house: it was gloomy, with the minister and Squire Hart and several other people sitting around and talking about Merry. Mr. Rothrup held the mortgage on the house . . . there was the question of who should serve as guardian for Merry, and to whom, perhaps, he should be bound. Someone suggested, Better bind him out to Enoch Adams, since he already knows the mill work. When informed of this, Mr. Adams declared, with a cry which sounded almost like an oath, that he would never take Merry. Then they talked of Farmer McMurchie. He was nothing like so mean as Mr. Adams, but still short-tempered and plagued by rheumatism. His wife had a reputation as a disgusting cook, an incompetent housekeeper.

. . . Sun approaching the nearest hill to the west, the Susquehanna glinted. A flat small barge stopped and anchored at some distance, and its crew of two young men were pulling toward the shore in their skiff.

Hey there, they said to Merry Kinsman. Where can a feller buy tobacco around here?

At the grocer's.

Where's that?

He told them, he pointed up past the first brick house and shading elms. He asked the young men where they were bound.

Harrisburg, they said. That was more than one hundred and fifty miles down the river. It was the State capital . . . oh, how he longed to go there.

We're taking a load of stuff to sell, in the barge, they said, and told him that they were cousins. First we'll sell the load, then the barge and this here skiff. Then we'll join.

Join what?

Why, the army, of course. A great log gate swung open, smoke of battle drifted in . . . or maybe it was the door of Grandma Rummer's house swinging, tomahawk dent and all. . . .

How much would you gentleman charge, to take a passenger along to Harrisburg with you?

How much you got?

There was more talk; it did not take long. Merry went scooting to the grocer's, carrying currency which the young men had given him to buy a pound of tobacco fine cut for the pipe. With this package he hurried home. Mr. Rothrup's horse was still tied outside, still the people were settling Merry's fate. He entered through the back door, hunted out a basket, filled it with what food supplies he could assemble quickly. He observed how cold and dark the oven looked; he wondered who, if anyone, would be baking there again. Merry put the covered basket on the bench behind the woodshed. He emptied jingling contents of the ginger jar into his own pocket, and uncrumpled a few wads of paper currency. His mother had been saving against the mortgage interest. He was lucky to be facing the world with a few dollars, rather than with empty purse.

Merry presented himself in the hot parlor, where all tried to treat him kindly.

The minister put his arm around the boy's shoulder. Merry, lad. We have now decided that you shall go to the McMurchies. That would be better than the Poor House, wouldn't it? Ah yes—far, far better. And twould be so sad and lonely for you to stay here in the night again, so Mr. Rothrup will drive you out to the farm directly, if you'll but get your things together.

Merry bowed his head as if in assent. He could not trust himself to speak. Suddenly he felt impatient with himself for scheming to trick these well-intentioned people, yet trick them he must.

He went upstairs and made a bundle. There wasn't much which he needed to take, there was not much which he could take. He gathered a few keepsakes from the dresser . . . silhouettes of his mother and father when they were young. He took Grandpa Briggs's watch, which the widow would not consider selling in direst season. He slid his fife down into those inner loops of his jacket which Merry's mother had sewn according to specifications. Softly he tore the mosquito-bar from a window above the kitchen roof and went across the roof and down the apple tree—a route he had traveled often since he was six or thereabouts. With basket and bundle he thought of himself as the traditional fugitive of caricature. He thought that he should have had a stick over his shoulder, and the bundle swinging

from the end. He climbed across a stone fence and circled through
the weedy orchard behind the Striver house. He met only Rudy
Banton, who carried a string of suckers; and Rudy Banton was peculiar in the head—he cared only about hunting or fishing, and could
not talk plain: it made little difference, meeting him. Once on the
river road, Merry hurried to Darwin's Bend, which he had indicated
when he spoke with those strangers at the landing. Sure enough
there was the barge, anchored off shore—one young man sitting in it,
the other concealed in his skiff among drooping willows. A few minutes later Merry was aboard the larger craft; they drifted down the
Susquehanna, shadows of hills covered them.

The cousins were named Norton, and they came from Towanda,
where their fathers were in partnership, owning a forge. . . . Our line
is iron. Born to it. They showed Merry some of the materials included
in their cargo: grilles and hinges and such. These they would sell in
Harrisburg—part would satisfy certain orders, the rest would have
to go on the open market. Merry nodded as if he knew as much about
hand-wrought iron as he did about the home baking business.

We're Paul and Silas, the cousins told him. Everybody knows the
Nortons, up Towanda way. Born in the same week.

No, said Silas. Nine days apart. Remember that, Paul: I'm still your
elder.

And went to the same church and same school, and our fathers
are brothers, and what's more than that, our mothers are first cousins.
How do you like that, hey? Thicker than thieves, aren't we, Si?

Thicker than fleas, Paul. Yes sir, Mr. Meriwether Kinsman: they
don't come any thicker than we two. Just like two fingers on your
hand. . . . Why, what are you a-fingering of? What you got there?
. . . Well, I swan, it's a fife. Can you play it? . . .

There were obstructions, rapids to be encountered and traveled
past. Some of it was heavy work—loading and unloading the barge,
beating paths through weeds, lugging ironware. The light tiny skiff
was an eggshell: Paul Norton could hike it up on one wide shoulder
and carry the thing. But they had a set of rollers on which the barge
must be hauled when it was necessary to land it; and Merry's job
was to lift out the rear roller as soon as it was exposed by the boat's
progression, then carry the thing to the front and insert it there, and
repeat successively. There were nights when his body, unaccustomed
to such concentrated exertion, ached steadily like a sore tooth. He
thought his arms and legs would fall off. But the Cousins Norton
praised him for his willingness and, later, aptitude. Merry loved this.
Scarcely had he ever been praised by anyone—except Uncle Bijah,
when at last Merry mastered the rapid intricacies of a freakish tune
called Hell On The Wabash. . . . There were long days, comfortable
and lazy, when they dropped smoothly in wide easy current, with

only a pole to be thrust down now and then. It was fun to trail a fish-line over the side. Soon they had more fish than they could eat, but the Nortons said, Keep fishing, Merry; we can trade for garden truck. The cousins smoked great pipes with curved stems, smoked them perpetually. They said they had cut their pipes from the same block of cherry root, had sent away to the city for proper amber stems, and naturally the two pipes were just alike. Paul and Silas squabbled good-humoredly sometimes; one claimed that the other had taken his pipe—he could tell by the taste of the spit therein.

What's this place? they'd call to a man on shore.

Shickshinny.

And what do you call that, over there?

Mocanaqua.

. . . Drifting down, down the gentle river. Oh, mister, what lies over beyond there?

That, friends, is the great and aggressive city of Wapwallopen.

. . . Farther, farther against the sun: Hey, stranger, what's this place?

Berwick to be sure.

And yonder?

Oh, acrost and up the road you'd come to Nescopeck.

It seemed sometimes as if Indians were all around them in canoes. That week there rode a moon, comforting, serene. Merry watched the great silver whiteness as it freed its surface from eastern hills and pushed higher, higher in clarity . . . half asleep on a blanket he contemplated the moon. Maybe Paradise was up there. Now his mother was there . . . Uncle Bijah played his fife on the moon . . . that was where the gathering of linsey-woolsey Americans was taking place . . . tufts of willow shadowed on a sandbar ahead. Ah, red Indians, Merry thought, advancing in their birch-bark boats. A night bird cried in the sky.

They cooked on the barge; they had a box which they would fill with sand, they could build their small fire. It was fun to cook on a boat. Tender fish would curl and sizzle, salt fat perfume of frying would drift. There were other adventures: Silas Norton encountered a cross bull when he was cutting through a pasture to trade for eggs at a farmhouse. And all three of the voyagers—the broad-shouldered brown-haired cousins, and the skinny blond Merry—were chased out of an orchard by a watchful farmer, when they thought to appropriate a few apples of the Early Harvest variety.

Hey, boy, what's this river flowing in, here on the right?

The Juniata, mister.

Then they could sing and put their hearts in it . . . *Wild roved an Indian maid, bright Alforata . . . where sweep the waters of the blue Juniata. . . .* Spires of Harrisburg rose before them, there must be a parting. It would take the Nortons some days to dispose of their wares,

before they would be ready to enlist. Merry Kinsman could not afford
to sit idly; he felt that he dared not spend money at a tavern, because
he had so little money with him, so little in the world. Actually he
did not care about money, because it seemed now that the mapled
world of America belonged to him completely, and the Susquehanna
as well, and the fabled fabric of the Juniata. Generously the Nortons
offered him a share in proceeds, if he would help them with their
delivering and haggling. But Merry said No. He knew that they did
this purely out of kindness, and he would be cutting into their profits;
he would not really be able to assist, he would have to be shown and
told what to do. His strong slender hand disappeared repeatedly in
the huge grip of the Nortons. He was presented with a gift to remember them by (as if he needed reminder!): a pipe which the
cousins bought for Merry on arriving at Harrisburg. He had admired
their manner of smoking pipes, had enjoyed the scent of tobacco, said
bashfully that he might wish to try, himself. He felt grown and manly
with this untried pipe and a paper of tobacco in his shirt pocket.

After leaving the Nortons he inquired of a few bearded soldiers,
asking where he might find the recruiters.

What for? Does your Pa want to join? and there was laughter.

They told him: they said that the best thing for Merry to do was
to go out to Camp Curtin. That was a long hot walk but eventually
Merry found himself standing under a tent fly. A sergeant with a red
face and sunburn peeling all over it— The sergeant said, What might
your name be?

Meriwether Kinsman.

Good enough name, but I reckon the ranks of the Boys' Brigade
are full up. Again that laughter from the idle and clustering. How old
might you be, Meriwether?

Fourteen.

That would be a trick! Is your family hot after you—or maybe the
uncle you ran away from?

Sergeant Glisson, ordered a vigorous young captain who had just
come stooping under the fly, don't you go to signing up any children!
Just mean trouble for us later on. He frowned at Merry accusingly.

Sir, said Merry. Here's the point: there ain't no one chasing me.
There ain't nobody *to* chase me, there ain't no one knows where I've
gone; I've got no one. He told how he had left the village the very
afternoon of his mother's funeral, and who was there now to transport
him back up the Susquehanna? Who would want to, anyway, and
why? It was so obvious that he was telling the truth that the young
captain relented, he put his hand on Merry's sleeve. Glisson, he said,
could be that they have need of another drummer in the tiger band.
Can you rattle a drumstick, bub?

No, sir, I can do better than that.

Out came the fife. Merry Kinsman played Jefferson and Liberty as he had never played it before; he played it as Abijah Parker might have played it when homespun columns were approaching the Saranac River. Before he finished, the captain was smiling and twisting his thick black mustache with approval. His black eyes danced; and two boys behind the sergeant were beating out a drum accompaniment on cracker boxes.

Oh, go and get our Principal Musician! cried Sergeant Glisson in delight. Go long, one of you, and fetch him. What's his name, what's that new chief musician—Cassidy? Tell him we've got a fine addition to his Sheepskin Battery!

That day Merry Kinsman was sworn in. His age was put down on the rolls as eighteen; that was the practice. Later he encountered a good many boys two or three years older than he; but Merry was said to be the youngest in the regiment, and he was the smallest of all the fifers. In no time at all, after he had learned the strains for regimental and camp duties, he was accounted also the best. Shortly before they prepared to depart for Cockeysville, Maryland, a new company came moving up to take its place alongside Merry Kinsman's company, and there rose a combined roar of recognition. There stood Paul and Silas Norton, side by side in a rank. It was a stout friendship, a valuable one, but all too short. The cousins went out of life together as they had entered life and faced it. Both were killed at Chancellorsville, next May.

. . . Reveille, Second Camp, Third Camp . . . many bars away the fifes silent, drums rolling. Slow Scotch . . . again the roll. The Austrian, and roll, roll. Quick Dutch, The Hessian, Quick Scotch, roll, roll, roll. Drumsticks were like dry bones of the past become hot fresh bones of the present. Sometimes Merry Kinsman thought his fife was the child of the drums, sometimes he thought his fifes fathered the drums. . . . Peas Upon A Trencher. How merry the tooting of the brisk two-four . . . how surprised he was to learn that there was one call for breakfast, an entirely different call for supper. How naked and piercing the notes poured from under his fingers: the Surgeon's Call (Quinine Call, the boys named it) and a dozen different Guard Mounts, and Assembly and Retreat and Tattoo! He wished that Uncle Bijah was there to hear him spraying out the Single Drag. Maybe Uncle Bijah was there.

In ranks of the drum corps (one drummer and one fifer from each of the ten companies, with a regimental bass drummer thrown in) he met musicians of a dozen different communities. Two or three older men had traveled far and learned a lot. All Take Tea, The Squirrel Hunters, Biddy Oats, On the Road To Boston . . . many more he heard for the first time. He learned them. Here's a new one, the Principal Musician said, and here's the way she goes: *When we go down to*

*Washington, when we go down to Washington, I was shot five times
in the ankle bone, and once at Manassas Junction. . . .*

This is a hard one, son, said a tall fifer with a whiskey breath. (Yet
somehow he reminded Merry of Uncle Bijah.) A clog, and tis hard
to do. We call it the Corn Cob. . . . And this here one. His hand went
down through firelight and lifted a tin cup: stolen whiskey mixed with
water therein. Old Tupley was becoming drunk again, but still he
could fife, he said that he could fife better when drunk than when
sober, but Merry decided early that this was not true. Now we're
heading into another six-eight, Tupley said. One maybe you never
heard before. Tis called, Go To the Devil and Shake Yourself.

Meriwether Kinsman drank deeply of Tupley's lore. He did not
drink whiskey, he only smoked his pipe and listened, but the tunes
squirted into his memory and nothing could dislodge them. It was
heartbreaking to participate in the final tragedy surrounding Tupley,
but duty decreed that Merry must. During the same battle in which the
cousins Norton lost their lives, Tupley disappeared. He was supposed
to carry stretchers, he carried none; he was required to assist at a
field hospital, he was not there. Later a sergeant discovered the old
fellow drunk and quaking. He had hidden himself in a thicket behind
an oak tree, had pulled leaves over his head in an effort to conceal
himself. He was dragged out, arrested, confined. After the Northern
army crossed a flooded Rappahannock in retreat—after the broken
regiment was bedded down in a camp, Tupley was drummed out by
the very musicians who once had respected his skill. It was a sad day,
but they played, they obeyed orders. Shattered companies lined up,
musicians massed . . . poor Tupley, coat hanging open, face like a
mussel shell, beard dripping with drool as he passed in disgrace with
big signs hung upon him, signs saying *Coward* front and back. The
Rogues' March shrilled. War was not all a pic-nic, though Merry found
it a better pic-nic than most until he was captured.

The Sheepskin Battery became a hospital brigade in every battle.
Drums were left behind, fifes put aside. Musicians went out hunting
amid thickets and haycocks, hunting for the fallen, and some of them
were killed doing this. Merry himself was nicked in the side on the
second day of Gettysburg; blood came freely although the wound did
not hurt much. He was frightened. Still he recognized that at last
he was one of the elect: he had Shed Blood for His Country. . . . He
climbed a wall. The countryside was thick with smoke, thicker with
noise; but Merry ducked his head, and was bound and determined to
go over that wall because someone yelled that young Brinkoff of Company C had tumbled wounded behind it. Merry Kinsman did not find
Brinkoff; he found instead a party of crouching men in gray who
glared at him, poked guns at him. One of them marshalled him away
through mats of smoke to where other lugubrious captives were

herded behind a barn. You hurt bad, Baby Yank? asked a Rebel. He ripped Merry's shirt when Merry lifted his torn jacket, he examined the wound. Hell, ain't nothing wrong with you that a good piece of sticking plaster wouldn't cure! Just set here and don't move till the firing stops, else you'll get shot by your own men! That night Merry was taken to the rear of the Rebel lines with others. So he became a captive and remained a captive through the long winter at Belle Isle, and then was taken to Andersonville.

He celebrated his sixteenth birthday by watching the raider chiefs fall and dangle. Because of extreme youth and litheness, he remained in fair shape until August, then went downhill rapidly. Of the several members of his regiment who survived in the stockade at this time, there was only one with whom he had been fairly well acquainted previously: a youth somewhat older than himself, named Stricker. Stricker was captured in the same battle which made Merry Kinsman a prisoner. Stricker had but one hand, he could render little aid to Merry after scurvy began to bend and shrink him. Merry tried to flank out with detachments removed in September, but failed. He was knocked down by Henry Wirz, who became hysterical at seeing invalids trying to pretend that they were sound. Merry Kinsman was turned back Inside and languished alone, since Stricker had become a Parole at the hospital (and later would become a patient).

Merry had recollection of being carried somewhere in a blanket. At this time he was thinking, as he usually thought, of his lost fife. It had remained in his possession through Belle Isle; there he played it to the diversion of fellow prisoners. Also to the pleasure of the Belle Isle superintendent, Lieutenant Boisseau, who often asked Merry to strike up a tune, and once had him to dinner. Lieutenant Boisseau frequently fed Belle Isle prisoners who caught his fancy; but such a thing was unheard of at Andersonville, except among favored Paroles detailed directly under Wirz.

Merry's fife was taken from him by a guard while they journeyed south from the Richmond-Manchester area, so he arrived at Camp Sumter fifeless. Here he met up with a young fellow of his own age who had managed to retain his fife. Occasionally the boy lent it to Merry, but only occasionally, since it turned out that Wabash Davey was jealous because Meriwether Kinsman could play more skillfully than he. Finally the condition of Wabash Davey's mouth was such that he could no longer build a tune. Merry now sought to bargain for the abandoned instrument, but had practically nothing to offer, and Wabash sat upon his fife—a dog in a manger. After he died his mates in the shebang held the fife for a high price. One morning the thing was reported as stolen; at least it disappeared. If some raider had taken it and found that he could make no music, he might have thrown the fife into the marsh. . . . Merry encountered also several musicians,

most of them drummers, minus their instruments; during their season
of comparative strength they sat in fury whenever they heard bleating
across the stockade's rim. There was a single fifer who played camp
duties for the Georgia Reserves. He could play but one tune: The
Bonnie Blue Flag, and that badly. It was The Bonnie Blue Flag for
Guard Mount, Reveille, Mess Call, everything. Federal musicians
cursed until severally they lost interest. One by one they died. Only
two of the little group straggled out in the autumn, when able
prisoners were removed. A freemasonry had held them together because it was the habit of many soldiers to regard musicians patroniz-
ingly or even with scorn. The term Sheepskin Battery was somehow
derisive when applied by others. But in their own cult fifers and
drummers were proud of the name.

. . . Stronger people carried him in a blanket, bent double with
scurvy as he was, gums puffed into a wad. On this day, so early in
the morning, there loomed a vacancy; Merry Kinsman was conveyed
to the hospital. Some attempt had been made to separate types of
cases, but exigency decreed that often the gangrenous would lie
among scorbutics or those suffering from diarrhoea. Merry emerged
from a spell of sodden unconsciousness to listen to wailing on one side
of him, to feel the loose splashings of his left-hand neighbor shooting
warm against his leg. A face swam above him often during the icy
weather . . . he shivered and shook with cold. The face said, Lad,
I've brought you a scrap of blanket. Hands pressed the fabric around
him, Merry was weakly grateful. Face was attached to the body of a
surgeon. Face wore great spectacles. Face brought to him sips of
diluted vinegar with a bit of salt added. Once Face even brought him
a trickle of some burning fluid which he said was whiskey . . . Merry
Kinsman remembered that once there had been an old whiskey
drinker named Tupley who was drummed out of camp. . . .

Face said, Here is a bit of raw potato. It would be good for you—
raw sweet potato—if you can but get it down. Merry tried to gnaw the
fragment, but another of his teeth came out and the contact hurt his
mouth. He gave up with a groan. . . . Face had a knife, the knife
scraped and scraped: you could hear the dragging sound of that blade
on hard substance of potato. Shredded filaments were injected into
Merry's mouth; in this fashion he could swallow them. There came
a noble keen spicy taste. He hoped that his eyes, though deeply receded in a swollen countenance, could look appreciation.

Once he saw something else clearly. The face had withdrawn
mistily, had become a bread board. That bread board stood upon a
shelf in the Widow Kinsman's kitchen. The old German lady, who
tended Merry when his hand was frozen, had given it to Mrs. Kinsman.
It was carved of pale wood—a perfect circle. It was really a plate to
be put upon the table, with little flowers and vines growing in carved

wood around the edge. The cut-out letters read: *Gib uns heute unser täglich Brod,* and that meant give us our daily bread, or something of the sort. It was the only German which Merry knew. He associated it in his mind because the wooden bread plate was round and the surgeon's wafers of glass before his eyes were round. It was odd to think of scraped sweet potato as being daily bread.

Merry became alert in imagination during his last hours. Because he had poetry in his nature, and the simple selfless courage sometimes evinced by good children who have a love of life, he could depart from personal tragedy and forget utterly the strain which disease put upon his carcass. He saw himself as a symbol of a proud manner of living. . . . Fifes were good, he thought, because of what they taught and the way they sounded. There needed to be no other reason for the existence of such music. . . . It did not occur to him that other boys in other lands had felt the same about their lands. Meriwether Kinsman's honor and his faith were one with those of an Iroquois or a Delaware: he thought that his Nation was the best, that was all there was to it. It was the best because it was the best. Also because it abounded, or had abounded, in moose and wild turkeys, in mountainous wagons rumbling west, in long rifles to guard the wagons.

In this time the world turned into a picture which Merry thought someone should paint, he felt that it would be painted in the future. Perhaps even now somewhere there wandered a young veteran like himself who ached with the same vague unreasonable impractical dream which had occupied Merry Kinsman since first he stood, jumped and ran within that Pennsylvania grove, since first he heard fifes and drums. It was a dream unfounded in necessity (he hated the idea of necessity because necessity had ruled his childhood) and would pay a penny to no one (he hated the idea of pennies because men like Mr. Adams were always counting them). His dream took the form of marching men, old and young, who hammered drumheads and blew upon a fife. One was of the stamp of the dearly recalled Abijah Parker; he was the tallest. There was blood upon a bandage, bright blood shed willingly as Merry had shed his driblets of blood above the soil of his native Pennsylvania. There was smoke of cannon, men came through it. Dead and dying were upon the ground, wreckage of war littered the earth, bullets made their harsh quick *raahhhh,* screaming off into terrible space. Somewhere sometime an artist might paint this picture; never could he paint the sound; other men and boys would have to fight in other wars, in order to pick up the sound again. Will ever our dear fifes be silent? Merry Kinsman wondered . . . somehow weakly he feared that they would be. Brass bands, he thought. Too many folks like their noise; and also there are the music boxes. . . .

But in distance were desert places and fabled mountains, so still the eagles and the hawks would cling to wild free air. They would hang high, wide of wing, angry of beak, ready to assault any force which came to threaten America. But— Why, he thought, I sought to destroy Americans by bolstering an attack with my melodies! And now, in captivity, Americans have destroyed *me*. I would weep at this awful knowledge, but somehow am too weak to weep. They have destroyed me—Southerners have killed me dead—Southerners, but still Americans. And how many bullets did the One Hundred and Forty-eighth Pennsylvania put into Southerners' skins? Too many, he thought, too many; so they have taken revenge.

He lay quietly, hearing nothing of the mutter and squeal beneath that canvas and sagging scraps of pine, until the surgeon came again.

So you're still with us, the queer voice came down to Merry's ears.

Yes. He could let a whisper steal from his rotting mouth. He wanted to add something about, I'm still here but shan't be for long, but could not find the words, could not summon strength to send forth the words. He felt that familiar solution of vinegar and salt wetting the great black mass of tissue from which his teeth had fallen out. Trickle found its way into his throat, there was a taste, he swallowed, it tasted good. Oh, how good it tasted. Chore name? he asked. It was his way of saying, What is your name? and it was strange to think that he had never asked before, he had never considered that Face might have a name.

My name, lad? Elkins. The surgeon floated away.

Merry Kinsman stood motionless upon a formless plane. Now, he thought, I am removed from the earth, am here with the eagles. He looked down and saw a crowded mass of filthy skeletons, young and old—most of them were young skeletons—with blackened hide drawn tight, hide still trying to cover the bones and not always succeeding, for some of the bones had broken through the hide, and were oozing and raw. Up with the eagles, he said. He heard a rush and snap of their wings. He looked down and saw the surgeon return, saw his own shape lying, saw the surgeon bending, saw him straighten and turn and summon an orderly. Together surgeon and orderly picked up the wisp of Merry Kinsman, a piece of canvas was slid beneath; they carried the wisp out from under the sagging canopy; later two other ragged orderlies carried it still farther; but the watching Merry had lost interest, was turned away, did not care where they carried it.

Jefferson and Liberty, said the unmistakable voice of Abijah Parker beside him.

I hain't forgotten!

Six-eight! The drums'll catch us.

Merry's fife was pressed into his hands, his hands were grown strong again. Uncle Bijah played the first three notes alone, then Merry joined him. They strode off together through the smoke, drums thudding and booming beside and behind them.

LV

Late in the autumn of 1864, John Winder had established his head-quarters at Millen, Georgia, rather than at Florence, South Carolina. His new title of commissary-general of all prisoners east of the Mississippi brought with it a complete assumption of command, giving him full latitude. As he had told Henry Wirz in early September, the designation of the new prison at Millen was Camp Lawton. Here the superintendent, a lieutenant named Boyce, held some misguided notion that Yankees could make pretension to the estate of Man. In vain did General Winder attempt to dispel this idea: Boyce was a gentleman. John Winder would have loved to remove him, but literally there was not another officer to take the post.

Mortality at Camp Lawton was enormous despite improved internal conditions. Prisoners died of wounds, they died because Andersonville had wounded them. . . . Within the stockade nothing was known concerning Sherman's advance. No fresh fish came to carry news; no fish had come excepting unfresh fish from Andersonville. Winder established grotesque but effective penalties, forbidding the circulation of gossip on the Sherman situation to any of the prisoners. Therefore they were not hard to handle when, at three o'clock of a drizzly morning in late November, the first detachments were routed out and herded to the cars. Within a day or two the entire living population of the stockade had been removed to Savannah. At first it was thought that they could be left there with safety. This was not to be: Sherman aimed at Savannah.

General Winder traveled up to South Carolina as speedily as possible. There, with the Florence superintendent, he arranged for eventual reception of Andersonville-Millen prisoners. Without difficulty he infected red-headed Lieutenant Barrett with his own viciousness. This was simple to accomplish: Barrett had practiced cruel arts since he was a child.

Barrett's latest exhibition of native tolerance and charity concerned a rumored tunnel. The tunnel could not be found, but Barrett was convinced that it was there. General Winder filled his subordinate's ears with mumblings concerning successful tunnels at Andersonville, by which means allegedly hordes of Yankees had crept forth to despoil the Confederacy. Barrett ordered all rations withheld from the stockade's population until the tunnel-makers should voluntarily give themselves up to justice. After several days of enforced starvation (during which many of the more sickly were released from pangs by the most obvious means) sturdier Unionists banded together and selected four tunnel-makers by lot. In the interests of community survival these four marched to the gate and were delivered to the tenderness of the red-haired Lieutenant Barrett. His charity was exemplified promptly: he hung them by their thumbs for only two hours. He might have kept them hanging for five hours, but after two hours even he had become wearied of their yells.

Like Andersonville the prison at Florence was a parallelogram composed of pine trunks. Prisoners declared that the Confederates were the God damnedest people to go around standing logs on end. Fifteen acres of ground were enclosed by the palisade, including the inevitable creek, swamp, deadline area. No sentry stations bloomed atop the fence: there were only platforms for cannon at four corners. Earth had been shoveled against the outside of the pen in a high embankment; along this elevation guards walked their posts, beating a deep path into the mound. It had been difficult for John Winder to hoist himself to the eyries of Andersonville. Here there were easy twisting trails by which he might ascend. So he could stand, top of the stockade breast-high against his thick body . . . he could rest stained hands on the axed ends of logs, and peer down at the seething shivering herd.

Sir. They resemble a bunch of rats, don't they?

A slippery sucking voice had spoken beside him. The general twisted his head, glowered. Who're you?

Excuse me, sir! I'm afraid I shouldn't have intruded on your thoughts. I apologize humbly.

. . . He had the manner of a pawnbroker. Or he was a man with something to sell . . . you did not know what he was selling . . . manner of a pawnbroker. Or else the manner of the weakling who approaches a pawnbroker, trusting to receive more than the pledging of the trophy is worth, knowing that he will never redeem it . . . perhaps he has stolen it. . . .

Here was the man who would bring John Winder to his end.

He was Sammons Kight, native to the Florence region. His miserly father and elder brother kept this incompetent on short fare. Sam Kight was forty-one, he looked older. His shoulders slumped, arms were limp, his belly jutted under the shabby long gray winter coat.

God damn it! Can't you answer with civility? I said—who *are* you?

Captain Kight, sir. Excuse me—I assist your adjutant—

Without saluting or assuming the semblance of military posture, Kight removed his crushed felt hat. You could see his bald tight scalp glistening even in steady wind of February. Tendrils of brown hair lay brushed silkily across his bald head, brushed laboriously. Kight had a flat nose with hollow fuzzy nostrils; he wore a shaggy mustache; his mouth and chin disappeared beneath the mustache. He wore greasy spectacles, glasses cut into flat ellipses within brass frames; the window caging the right eye had been shattered, glued together again.

Captain Kight was married to a wisp of a woman whose father had married her off to him because of his own father's wealth. None of the wealth had come their way. This woman drudged through cares of a numerous household aided only by two bungling Negresses, one of whom was quarter-witted. Rooms of their cavernous home were encrusted with religious mottoes. Bible reading occurred night and morning, Grace was spoken before each meal, Thanks rendered afterward. Agony rose from the Kight place on Sunday afternoons when one child or another was discovered in some activity deemed detrimental to the Sabbath, and was flayed accordingly. Mr. Sammons Kight held an office in the Baptist church, he was superintendent of the Sunday School. He respected the term *Loving Kindness* which he mumbled as a single word. He droned it long, pushed out his small lips under brindled hair whenever he spoke the term.

What you want with me? Hey?

Nothing, General Winder. . . . Nothing at all. . . . I was off duty . . . merely looking . . . at the prisoners.

Kight put his life into his throat.

General, allow me a question? One can see that most of them are villains—shockingly depraved— And yet— Would it be possible for the Word of God to lighten their souls?

He went on eagerly: A service of prayer, perhaps even a sermon attuned to their needs? I would be willing to volunteer! I know of others who—

No God in any of their souls! They haven't *got* any souls! Now you go way!

Yes, General. Yes, yes. Of course—

The captain went gliding along the sentries' path. . . . He had seen Winder many times across the breadth of a room. He had risen, bowed, smirked, had been ignored. Nevertheless he felt fearfully that something was now accomplished. Winder at least knew who he was.

Meat supply dwindled in the Kight family. It was decided to do a certain amount of butchering in mid-winter to supplement sides and hams still remaining from the first butchering of the season. Accordingly six hogs were chased and roped in woodland adjoining the country homestead of Sam Kight's father. A single carcass fell to the share of Sammons Kight.

Even this was enough to awaken excitement in his spindly children when they heard the good news.

Mr. Kight, asked his wife drearily, Is your Pa giving us a whole hog, sure enough?

So he says. Sam drank dregs of grain coffee.

I am glad! All the little ones have just been a-begging and a-begging. We're so shy of meat these days.

A great hope had risen within Sam Kight—a brilliant idea with which he was toying. Through natural inclination and sad experience he had grown to accept the truth: value and importance could not be gained in this world without the coöperation, even the benevolence, of higher stronger authority. Sammons Kight was mightily afraid of God, he believed that other men awarded veneration to God solely because also they were terrified by Him. In turn Sam was afraid of his father. Early in life he had learned that his father would award him no benefit unless he was pleased with him . . . to this office of giving pleasure Sam obtained but rarely.

He had hoped to be a minister. His father would not hear of it. Ministers earned but little money. . . . Sam studied long, he'd studied earnestly if ineffectually for the Law. He had failed each time he was examined. Old Kight roared, thrust him into the small ironmongery which he owned in Florence. Sammons had undertaken later to manage a tobacco farm belonging to his brother. He failed with one crop after another. Until this last winter of the war he failed at everything he undertook, except his superintendency of the Sunday School (in that also he would have been accounted a failure, had anyone been willing to consult the children). In 1862 Sam marched off to war, racked by ordeals awaiting him . . . he fell sick, lay near death. Eventually he was sent home, discharged as an invalid. Now in this fourth winter he was delighted to be addressed as Captain. The bottom of the barrel had been scraped. Sammons Kight was one of the scrapings.

But suppose he reached a higher situation in the military establishment? Suppose he was awarded field grade? . . . Captains were a dime a dozen. There were even captains who could barely read! And he, Sam Kight, had read Law for a time in the office of a man who later went to the Confederate Congress!

Suppose he were to be made a major? Generals had it in their power to award promotions. Suppose that Sam Kight pleased General Winder? He had scarcely been able to please anybody. . . .

As kindling for fire of his plan he could assemble only a few shreds of conversation: laughing and rather scornful conversation which passed between the adjutant and Winder's son, when one day that worthy sat beside the adjutant's desk.

But if the statement which he had heard were true . . . Sam became inattentive to clerical duties, he snapped at his children when they were restless during evening Bible reading at home (he was quartered in his own house, there was no other place for him). Later

he took little Ocie into a bed chamber and whipped him with his belt:
Ocie had sneezed repeatedly during the long prayer which followed
Bible reading. Kight intoned a new prayer over the moaning child,
put on his belt, went to the kitchen shanty to inspect a hog's carcass
which hung outside the door. It had been fetched, drawn but not
quartered, from the senior Kight's homestead that evening. Sam put
his pale hand upon the pebbled clammy hide, he inspected the
chopped ends of ribs, he thought of General Winder. He looked at
scrubbed cloven hoofs, he thought of the Devil, he thought also of
General Winder, he thought of pickled pig's-feet.

Captain Sam Kight was up betimes the next day, giving orders to a
reluctant wife. He badgered her into acceptance of a task far beyond
her strength and beyond the abilities of the two wenches.

He was nervous through the morning, blotting reports which he
copied. His hands shook. He dropped a sand-filled bottle which they
used as a paper-weight, and broke it . . . the adjutant spoke biting
words. With his own hands Sammons Kight swept up the glass and
sand; he did not ask a subordinate to do it, though there were two
corporals in the office.

Early he had requested an audience with General Winder. The
desired permission was slow in coming: Winder wanted to know why
the damn captain didn't talk to the adjutant instead, about whatever
it was he wanted to talk about. Having progressed through echelons,
it was nearly noon when at last Sam was permitted to tap his transparent knuckles against the old man's door, and to be growled at
after he had entered and closed the door.

John Winder sat upon the sofa which had been brought by train all
the way from Andersonville (there might not be a sofa available
in Florence). The general was dosing himself with Harlem oil. This
mixture, composed of flowers of sulphur boiled in cottonseed oil, with
amber and turpentine added, was accounted to be of great value in
strengthening the stomach and kidneys, stimulating liver and lungs,
quieting asthmatic complaints and palpitations, dispelling shortness of
breath. The formula had been given to the general by a subordinate
named Gwenn, who called it Welch medicamentum. Colonel Llewel-
lyn Gwenn was alarmed at symptoms displayed by his superior.
Winder started out with a dose of ten drops, now he took twenty-five.
His thick breath could be heard.

Damn it, Captain, what you want?

Excuse me, sir. I—I have an invitation—

Invitation? Winder snorted, swallowed down the spoonful of drops,
sputtered, wiped his sagging mouth with the back of his hand. From
whom?

From myself, sir.

The devil! What kind of invitation do you want to give me?

Sir, it has come to my attention that you are very fond of fresh pork. Where the devil did you hear that?

Sir, it was—your son—the captain— I chanced to overhear him speaking with Major Crawley—

John Winder said decisively, after belching over the Harlem oil: Hell, yes, I do like fresh pork. Who doesn't? Precious little we've got around here these days.

But, General, a whole hog has come into my possession, and—

Twelve officers, including the trembling Kight, sat down to a pork banquet in the Kight dining room. It was a mid-day meal: Winder insisted that he could accept only if the meal were served at noon on Wednesday, February the eighth. He had to go over to Columbia on the afternoon train.

The drawn-faced Mrs. Kight managed briefly to greet her husband's guests, to be presented to the general; then she staggered back to the kitchen. She had been up most of the night, overseeing groaning black women in the preparation of sausage. Mrs. Kight had done the bulk of the work herself. . . . Penny, the dullard slave, managed to chop up a portion of the best loin, instead of scraps set aside for the purpose. . . . Nevertheless the other loin was roasted. There were patties and chops . . . the roast was garnished with strips of side meat. Appetizers of pickle were ready on the table, with several bottles of tart wine and two bottles of spirits which the desperate Sam had wheedled from his brother in exchange for the Kight mantel clock. There were two bowls of sweet potato pudding, mounds of corn sticks on platters. A private plate of sausages was put before General Winder. The old man gobbled rapidly, never looking at his host, talking only to the aide who sat at his left hand. . . . The general drank but little. He said that he must have a clear head for multitudinous tasks awaiting him.

Scorched and oily smells of roast and fried meat drifted up the staircase to torture a throng of wan children huddling above stairs. The children wondered what was being done with the bones; they wished that the soldiers would leave quickly; the children would like to put their hands on those bent chewed ribs before the wenches got at them. . . .

Less than an hour after they'd trooped in through the unpainted double doors, the guests took their departure. Soon General Winder and his military family stood upon the railway platform, awaiting transportation.

That was a meal, sir, said Captain Peschau.

Too damn greasy. That captain's niggers don't know how to cook. . . . Sammons Kight was not present to hear these words: he was in his house, praying actually and idiotically for a promotion which never came.

Captain Peschau said something or other to the general; the other officers were standing at a distance; later Peschau could not remember exactly what it was that he said. He thought he heard a responsive grunt. It was a strange response. Peschau turned quickly to look at his commander.

The platform of the Florence station was composed of cinders and gravel, tamped down between old splintery ties; it was one of those wide ties upon which Winder beat his swollen face as he fell. Peschau saw him sagging, Peschau tried to hold him, Peschau was a slight man, he could not support the weight. The old man's bulk draped the aide's straining shoulder, swept his arm aside, pitched loose. Other people exclaimed, came diving. They turned John Winder on his back. Eyes glared out of a face slaty blue. People kept exclaiming, crying to the general. They kept calling, General *Winder*, again and again, as men might try to awaken a sleeper.

Cashmyer's tent, said someone.

He referred to the nearby abode of Philip Cashmyer, John Winder's detective officer.

Ralphie, run for the surgeon!

Ralphie was running already.

Five pairs of hands slid beneath the great chunk. Two hands slid under each of the old man's thighs, two hands were straining up under each of his shoulders. Another pair of hands supported the mighty drooping head and helped to support the shoulders as well.

The officers went laboring toward a tent beyond the station. The detective came rushing to hold up the tent fly and admit them. As gently as possible they put the general upon the single cot, saw it sag deeply, weight straining the cords; they heard the crunch of cords against wood. . . . John Winder was breathing. . . . The surgeon came at a dog-trot. A ring of idle ragged troops gathered at a safe distance from the tent.

Inside the tent John Winder gazed at the canvas roof with eyes unmoving, bulbous. Presently he gave an explosive belch; there drooled a trickle from one corner of the open mouth; the massive head swung slightly to one side. The black blood was turning blacker. . . . A little later the surgeon pushed down the crusty eyelids and weighted them with Federal coins.

When Andersonville learned of this demise, they were quick to supply the last words spoken by John Winder (although in fact he was not granted the dramatic gesture of a last utterance): My faith is in Christ. I expect to be saved! Wirz, cut down the Yankees' rations!

Two railroads—the North Eastern, and the Wilmington and Manchester—formed a junction at that insignificant village of Florence. In a gray wintry swamp not far from the intersection of iron paths, straggles of moss clung to empty branches. This was not the luxuriant Spanish moss of more southerly regions: it was a brittle neglected

fuzz, a last relic of sub-tropics. It dangled dried and feeble on emaciated boughs, dark as the stuffing of a carriage cushion. Amongst these
tatters roosted a convocation of vultures. Solemn in silence they
wadded on higher boughs. They had lunched to repletion (as had
the officers in the Kight house) but a consumptive cow had been
their fare. The buzzards squatted, waiting for a new death, or for
the discovery of an older death.

Suddenly they moved, shifting position, some moved to outer limbs.
Their wide heavy wings stretched when they hopped; there was the
scraping of feathers as they shifted and then draped scalloped black
shawls about their bodies again. A raw wrinkled neck twisted, a
hooked beak went out and drew back into immobility. It was almost
as if another of their kind had come, unseen yet detected, to dwell
among them.

LVI

Coral Tebbs slid his shotgun through the drying leaves, resting its weight in a low crotch of a sweet-gum sapling. He bent lower to sight. The hawk was still there: that was its favorite perch on the stub of a high dead cypress branch. You could tell that it was the hawk's favorite perch, for even at such a distance (he estimated that it might be ten rods) the accumulation of droppings showed like whitewash on a lower limb. The hawk bent forward, disturbed its wings as if for flight, then folded back onto the stub again. Old chicken stealer, thought Coral. I've come a weary way, crutches sticking in soft ground long the edge of this here marsh. Wonder how many other one-footed folks ever try to leg it through woods like these, crutches and all? . . . Chicken stealer! I'm going to spoil your guts.

He had been waiting over two hours for the hawk to return to its perch, and now the hawk had come back, and Coral's bony finger sank slowly against the trigger.

Powder exploded, the boom hurt, the butt crunched into the youth's shoulder. A dust—feathers?—blew loose from the bird. The hawk went forward into space, wings half lifted again, but wings bent under, wings bent under.

Got you, you son of a bitch, cried Coral in his heart with hate like glee. Birdshot'd never carry up there, but a mite of buckshot done the trick. That's a right heavy animal, he thought in continuation, as he heard the body go plunging through cypress twigs and heard stringy streamers of moss ripped loose and saw them waving. Then came a light damp mingled thud and splash as the hawk landed at the edge of some shallow pool which Coral could not see.

He put his dark brows together and rubbed his hairy chin with a speculative hand. Well, now. Hawk must be a hundred and fifty foot over yonder and all sorts of brush and vines in between.

But damn if he wasn't going to get that hawk, if he had to crawl to do it. He'd have a sorry time, hoisting his crutches and wriggling his one sound limb over all those logs and tangles but— By God, he meant to take that hawk home. Tote it all the way home, and maybe his mother would like to have a couple nice big hawk-wing fans for next summer instead of the regular turkey-wing fans that most folks had. Tote it home, dump it down on the stoop and say, Here's one robber ain't going to make off with no more of our fries. Cripple or no cripple! And wouldn't that puny little dragged-out Flory be fetched? Sick at heart, poison sick with the jealousy, Flory would be. Flory couldn't have got this hawk first shot or hundredth.

Coral took a bearing on the hawk's vacant perch, perceiving where the area directly beneath it must lie in the thicket ahead. Tough work, a-crawling and a-climbing, and he'd have to leave the shotgun right here. No help for it; but he could always use a crutch on a snake if he met one. Coral reloaded the gun and hung it in a tree. Then he hitched his way along the damp cypress log and pushed through a layer of vines, looking back constantly to keep to the bee-line he had established. Thorns bit him, but Coral only cursed in spirit monotonously and proceeded on his cautious stubborn path. He fell when his crutches caught on a root; then he cursed aloud. He swore at root, crutches, swamp, hawk, the winter sun overhead; he swore at his own clumsiness, at the Yankees who'd riddled his foot, at the surgeons who had cut it off. He went on, breathing heavily; and from ahead sounded a faint plashing as if some wild animal were molested by his approach. Oh, damn to hell, why hadn't he toted that gun along, somehow or other? Here he might meet up with something else to shoot, and he would have no gun, and—

At last he panted beneath the half dead tree. Surely this was the place—it was open, a small glade higher and drier than the surrounding thickets—yet no hawk could be seen. Yes, yes, here were white spatters of dung on some sodden old cypress knees; this was the place, it had to be. But no hawk.

What was that sound he'd observed as he came? Surely not the beating lunging flopping noise a big bird would make if, not killed as dead as Coral had thought, the creature were still trying to take flight or struggle off through the woods. Then, immediately before his gaze, Coral Tebbs saw footprints in the mould, and those footprints were filling slowly with water.

All right, God damn it, he heard a strange strained churlish voice; it was fearful to recognize that voice as his own. He'd just passed another tupelo tree, and now he found himself backing against that tree, small as it was. All right, God damn you, he said again to the gloom. Got a knife here.

So he had, one made at home, and in a scabbard of his own construction. He'd sewn the bent fold of old leather with toil through several evenings; it contained the honed blade of a butcher knife which, had he but known it, once graced the kitchen of his grandfather Lumpkin. Coral had made a handle for that knife by wrapping the rusty spike with strings of rawhide.

Got a knife here. Come out them bushes, mister.

Sprouts and vines and moss were motionless, then they twitched, then the twitching died and they were motionless again.

Telling you for the last time, come out them bushes.

A figure arose to confront him. It was such a spook as might have sent any field Negro of the region scuttling. It was a spook somewhat smaller than Coral Tebbs, nearly beardless, with a crusted blackened skull for a face, and dressed in scarecrow shreds of flannel and jeans. Coral could not recognize immediately this starveling for what the thing really was. He had never stood aloft on a sentry's perch, rimmed on the stockade; his condition precluded any climbing of ladders. True, he had lurked to watch wagonloads of bodies go past, but usually the dead were naked; often they were bloated, before or after death.

By God, said Coral, that's my hawk you got in your hand.

Sure enough. The creature had the hawk, and the hawk hung limp-winged and bloody.

What you doing with my hawk that I just shot off'n this cypress?

The figure tumbled loosely out of the vines and went down among twisting knees of the swamp: it was half a sitting down, half a falling down. The thing wore a mouldy cap with a corroded clover leaf on the top of it; you could see that the clover leaf had once been red, but the visor of the cap was gone. The thing still held the hawk.

What was you going to do with my bird, you?

Faint weak voice whispered, Eat it.

Well, I hope to shit, said Coral Tebbs. Son of a bitch if you hain't a damn Yankee!

Yes.

God blast your measly soul to hell!

Guess He's nearly done so.

What you say?

Nearly blasted my soul to hell already.

You got loose from that pen over yonder! Well, I'm going to turn you in.

Go ahead.

Reckon I'll get a reward, too. You got ary weapon about you?

Naw.

What might be your name? You are a measly rat for certain.

Name's Stricker.

What?

Naz Stricker.

What?

Nazareth Stricker.

That's a hell of a name. God damn Yankee name. Where you from?

Hundred and Forty-eighth Pennsylvania.

You mean to say you damn Yankees'll eat a hawk? Hawk ain't fit.

I'd eat anything, said Naz Stricker.

I did hear them trail-dogs in the night. Never did hear the catch-dogs a-barking. Reckon twas you they was after.

The Yankee swayed, seemed about to fall flat, then caught himself and remained in a hunched sitting position.

Coral Tebbs swung his crutches and his leg, moving closer. What's that red dingus on your cap, you?

I don't know.

You don't know? Guess you damn Yankees don't know nothing. Worse'n a pack of niggers.

Yes . . . do know. It's—clover leaf. That means Second Corps. Red because we were First Division of the Second Corps. . . .

What division was that?

Naz Stricker considered dreamily. The battle was a long time ago, a lifetime ago. Caldwell's, he said.

When Coral lay on old dry blood-blackened straw in a wagon, while a column of wounded pitched and screamed and muddied up and down the racking Maryland hills, he had seen prisoners marching alongside, unwounded ones. At Anderson Station he had, many times, watched ranks of fresh prisoners being formed into squads while Wirz danced and mouthed at them. Thus he had seen many Yankees close at hand. He had felt the venom fly from his own eyes, it was as if the Yankees must feel it also, spraying over their skin and burning as it sprayed. Put the sons of bitches in the pen; let them stink; let them yell; shoot the first bastard who comes nigh the deadline. If he'd received a lighter wound with no amputation resulting— Oh, he'd learned that there were plenty of them, wounded Confederate veterans who were considered unfit for further duty in the field; yet they had been accepted to help fill up new ranks of the Georgia Reserves. They were guarding Yanks, and a thousand times Coral Tebbs had wished that he might stand among the guards. Bet he'd show those blue-bellies who was boss . . . how he'd show them! A thousand times he had looked at Flory, with his thin little-girl voice with scarce a rasp in it— Looked at Flory prancing to show Ma what a swell he was as a soldier, all togged out in Yankee jacket and Yankee breeches too big for him, and a big calico hat sinking over his ears— Looked at Flory and thought, Devil beat the ass off of me. Look at that: he can pack a musket, and go on guard, and all I can do is crutch myself through the brush— Looked at Flory and hated Flory's guts, silently or aloud.

You going to come along of me.

The Yankee's eyes were shut.

Want I should bust your head with this here crutch?

Go ahead, came the whisper. Bust it.

Hold up your hands, God damn you! So's I can see you hain't got a weapon.

The hawk slid into muck below the cypress knees. The ragamuffin's right hand came wavering up; the left hand came wavering up, except that there was no left hand. Nothing but a tattered sleeve and what appeared to be a grimy bone sticking out of tatters.

Coral made a sound. Oh, by God, his soul was saying, oh, by God, and yet he could not speak a word which sounded like a word.

The escaped prisoner's arms fell back beside him.

Yank. The harsh sound of the word hurt the throat of Coral Tebbs as if that throat were scraped by a dull knife. Yank, what you got there? What befell you? Your hand—

They—took it off. Right at—the wrist.

Who took it off?

Rebel surgeons.

Where'd you get hit?

I was damn near—back home. Just a few counties away—up in Pennsylvania. Twas at—Gettysburg.

A red glare swept Coral's gaze. For a moment he could not see the shriveled youth in rags before him, could not see the shriveled face or the foolish visorless cap, could not see the rotten embroidery of the red clover leaf; nor could he see the barred wings of the hawk he'd shot, or gloom pervading there in loneliness.

What day? . . . God damn it, I *asked* you. What day of the battle?

Second day, I guess it was. Right by that—wheatfield.

Oh, by God. We come against you! I was with the Fifty-third Georgia. I'll be buggered with a cob!

The Yankee sat without moving. Then shudders began to disturb his body as if he suffered an attack of ague. His lips were jelly; he hadn't lost all his teeth, you could hear some of his teeth clattering against each other as he shook.

Look at what you done to my foot! Coral swung his leg forward. Think you're the only one got hit? I'd rather be shy a hand like you than shy a foot like I am!

This shrunken scarecrow spook could be made to say nothing, he could not be made to look up. Coral tore a crutch from beneath his right arm and wrapped his hand around the stem of it. By God, I'm going to bust you . . . but the cudgel remained suspended in air. Coral's breath was burning out of his lungs in blasts, and saliva trickled from the corners of his open mouth. Slowly he lowered the crutch. At last he slid it into his armpit again.

Yank. Come on. Going to take you in!

The boy tried to arise; he seemed to try to arise; again he slid back among cypress knobs.

Catch-dogs ought to have got you and that's a fact. How come they never got you last night?

I held—to—wet places. And used—pepper.

Pepper? Where'd you get pepper?

Bought—it—from a guard.

Come on, you Yank!

Feebly the Northerner shook his head. Can't do it.

You can't move? You claim you can't move?

Naw. Can't—move.

Then I got to knife you or blow the damn head off'n you.

Now fierce tiny blue eyes glinted up from dark sockets of the skull. Blow—damn—head off me? What with?

Why, dad blast it, I got a shotgun back in them bushes! What'd you think I shot that hawk with, anyway? Here—give me my hawk.

The Yankee didn't move, so Coral steadied himself and employed a crutch to work the muddied hawk forward into his own possession. He tied the weight of it to the cord looped around his neck; yes, it was heavier than anyone might imagine. It was remarkable, how a hawk could look so light and cloudy, wheeling above trees; yet it seemed to weigh as much as a fox when you were carrying it.

—Can't make up my mind, said Coral.

—Can't you make reply? Didn't you hear me tell you I couldn't make up my mind?

—Whether to stick you with this here knife.

—Shotgun's back yonder. Couldn't see you from there, count of all the brush. So I'd have to clamber all the way back here.

—By God. Dirty damn Yankee! Not fit to waste a charge of powder on.

—Yank, what was that name you give me?

—Oh. Nazareth Stricker! Chicken-shit name for certain.

Coral Tebbs toiled back through the canopy of gum branches and stickery vines. In two minutes the mute crouching ragged figure of Naz Stricker was masked from his sight. If Coral had breathed in trumpet blasts before, he was breathing in engine blasts by the time he reached the tree where hung his shotgun.

He owned the loose extravagant imagination common to many primitive people who have dwelt as outcasts, who have dwelt in lonely places. His hates were simple, unreasonable, intense; in time perhaps he might grow to love with as little reason and with as great an intensity. . . . He pictured the Yankee, Nazareth Stricker (somehow it sounded like Bible talk) as struck by his shotgun pellets, bursted and ripped as Coral had seen other boys bursted beside him. Good enough for him; there was nothing good for a Yankee except killing. Pennsylvania . . . so that's where he came from. Funny place,

peopled by a herd of foreigners who couldn't even talk like white
folks. Coral remembered standing with other shaggy dusty hungry
boys outside the door of a brick farmhouse; he recalled the barn which
stood beyond; damndest looking stable or what-do-you-want-to-call-it
he ever saw. Stable was about as big as a county courthouse, and it
stood on a hillside, and part of it was built straight out in the air, and
there were cows standing underneath the built-out portion and feeding
there (not for long: the foragers herded them away) and there
were queer round signs and symbols painted on the barn in color . . .
Lieutenant Anglin talked to Captain Tyree, and Coral overheard the
lieutenant saying that those queer arrangements had something to do
with the Evil Eye. What Evil Eye? Bunch of God damn foreigners and
hirelings, like most of the Yankees. . . . He stood there with others,
and two fat pink-faced women gazed out at them with swollen eyes
gleaming in terror.

Lady. You got some bread to spare us?

Ja. Bread we got. Today was baking.

Meat. You got any meat?

Ja. Pickled pork we got—

Got any beef?

Nein. The beef is all.

Cakes? somebody shouted behind Coral.

Ja. Crullers we got. Today was baking.

Well, the damn Yankee womenfolks could cook like sin. Coral and
the rest made themselves a meal, they made themselves a meal under
peach trees until they like to popped their bellies open. . . . He saw
Naz Stricker as coming from such a house. Except Naz Stricker could
talk straighter talk than the rest of those hirelings at the North . . .
shooting was too good for him. Because he came from a pinkish-
reddish-brick house, and there was the springhouse yonder where
were spread wide pans of milk with cream rising slowly, and Coral
remembered how he stood with a tin pan of milk held in his quivering
hot hands . . . he drank slowly and tenderly and continually until
the friend next to him—fellow name of Jo Coppedge—said, Look, Cory,
this here's the way to do it. Jo Coppedge put down the pan he was
holding, put it on the damp cool stones, and lifted from inside his
shirt a big wedge of solid cherry pie, and using that pie as a utensil
Jo Coppedge skimmed slowly across the surface of the milk in the
pan, he pushed the dripping chunk of thick rosy-crusty pie all the way
across the pan. When he took it out it was coated with golden cream,
it was dripping with rich cream, and Jo bit deeply into pie and cream,
pushed his hot thin dusty face into the mass of pie and cream, and
his brown eyes rolled bright above the thick paint he had thus put
upon his face, and he said, Oh, Mister! . . . Damn Yankee hirelings
. . . shooting too good for them . . . not worth wasting powder and

shot . . . Jo Coppedge got killed right in front of that same wheat-field that Coral and the Yank were speaking of.

Nrrrrwhuck.

Dad blast it, *Jo!* Coral reached down and lifted Jo's arm, and gave it a jerk, and then let go, and the arm fell back. The sound of *nrrrrwhuck,* the sound of the bullet's whacking, it resounded in Coral's ears even after the bullet had passed through Jo Coppedge's face and had broken through the softness of his brain and had splintered scraps out of the bones of his head and had gone crooning tenderly into space beyond, and had left the cream of Jo's brain a-dripping . . . white-yellow of cream, red of the cherries, *nrrrrwhuck,* dad blast it, *Jo!* Captain Tyree waving his pistol, pointing his pistol, he was crying an order, but there was too much noise, you couldn't hear a word. *Whoooooo,* said the Fifty-third Georgia and began to stumble forward, and Coral Tebbs was moving with the rest, firing and loading, ram-ming down another charge, firing into smoke, seeing no Yankees to shoot at, but squeezing the trigger into smoke, until someone dropped a big rock on his left foot and ankle, and it felt numb after the first blow—it felt as if the rock were still lying on top of his foot and ankle, pressing off all feeling. A voice boomed against his ear, saying something about The Rear; so he started picking his smoky way backward, away from the thicker lower newer smoke, using his gun and another gun he had picked up, using the two guns for canes, and he kept putting his wounded foot down upon the earth, taking regular steps with it, but he couldn't feel the ground underneath it each time he pressed it on the ground. . . .

Coral Tebbs took his shotgun from the tree, examined it with a crafty smile playing under tufts of silky black beard which grew longer and less silky, week by week, in weeks when he neglected to shave with his father's old razor. He cocked the shotgun, looked at the swamp from which he'd emerged, thought of Naz Stricker sodden and weak and helpless (all Yankees should be sodden and weak and helpless) and then thought, What a weary way, back through all them logs and brambles, and my crutches sucking down into the marsh the while. He thought of Naz Stricker throwing his arms wide and going over backward or forward as lead wrenched through his body at high speed. He thought, Wish every Yankee in this here world had the shit shot out of him.

It would be a long way, back through those tangles.

Coral Tebbs hated Naz Stricker on principle, and hated him also because he came from Pennsylvania and probably came from a fine brick house, and probably had eaten cherry pie and thick cream all his life. Those foreign Yankees had every damn thing in the world: big houses, and barns built out into the air, and factories to make things, and buttons and shoes and blankets, and medicine if they got

sick . . . had everything they needed, except good powder. Secesh
powder was a hell of a lot better than Yankee powder . . . Coral had
heard that it was foreign, the powder in his own cartridges—heard that
it came from England or France or Africa or some such far-off place.
Once, in a hospital, he lay for two days on a pallet right betwixt two
Yankees . . . he wouldn't talk to them, but he heard their talk. They
talked about gunpowder, and how the dirt was so bad in their powder
—regular black dirt, right out of the soil, they said, and manufactured
so by some thieving contractor in a factory— The dirt was so bad that
half the time you couldn't fire at all. Never knew whether your gun
was going to shoot or not. He guessed they were laying it on mighty
thick, just for his benefit, because they knew he was Secesh. But finally
they got taken away to a prison hospital, and then there were just
Secesh alongside. That talk about the powder haunted Coral's mind.
Finally he asked an older man—a corporal, he was, from the Twelfth
South Carolina, and also wounded at Gettysburg— Asked him if twere
so. Hell, yes, said the South Carolinian. Once't I was out on the field,
a-seeking my young brother after we'd had a mean scrap, and I run
smack into a clan of Yankees. Reckon you can believe that I laid low
and pretended I was one of the dead. Well, boy, them Yankees wasn't
looking for wounded. No, sir, boy, twas powder they was a-seeking.
Confederate powder, out of the pouches of us Confederates. They'd
open up a pouch, say, Hell, he ain't got none, he's done fired all his
cartridges, or words of that nature, and then go on looking for more.
I was scairt piss-less they'd come grubbing around for my own pouch,
but finally they went tother way.

Ever find your brother, Corporal?

Surely did. He was deader'n hell, and puffed up already. . . .

Slowly Coral Tebbs held his thumb against the hammer, retaining it
against pressure of his forefinger applied to the trigger. Slowly he
put the hammer down upon the cap.

If he had killed any Yankees in that battle he couldn't know, but
certainly he had fired his rifle until it fried his fingers to touch it, so
he'd sent a lot of balls flying. If he had killed any Yankees in that
battle they were the last ones he'd ever get to kill, on account of his
foot being cut off . . . not even fit to serve as a guard on the stockade,
like that vile little freak of a Flory. If he didn't go back and shoot Naz
Stricker now, he might not have another chance to do it. Because
Naz Stricker might run away before he, Coral Tebbs, got back. . . .
Oh, reckon not. Too tuckered.

—Come back with some guards from the stockade.

—Not Flory. That'd be a feather in the little stinker's cap that he'd
flaunt and pride himself on forever.

—Heard something about a reward.

*—You mean to say you damn Yankees'll eat a hawk? . . . I'd eat any-
thing. . . . They—took it off. Right at—the wrist.*

Twenty-five dollars reward? Maybe thirty? What was it folks said
about Turner and Harris getting so much a head for every escaped
prisoner that their dogs ran down?

—Twas thirty. That was what folks said, down at Uncle Arch Yeoman's store. Thirty dollars a head. Course, that would be Secesh.

—Why, by Jesus. Here was home. He'd come all this way, toting
that hawk, and it was a weary way.

Coral stood examining the house and The Crib and the whole area
with suspicion. Couldn't see a mule under the trees. Ma might be entertaining, but he considered it unlikely. She had entertained through
practically the entire night; now it was nigh onto noontime, and
doubtless she would be asleep. What with Flory messing with the
soldiers, and Laurel gone to the Dillards', the Tebbs family was
surely eating high on the hog these days. Coral suspected that his
mother was suffering in some degree from the Venus' curse, for he had
seen her dosing herself out of mysterious bottles. But always she was
in good humor; it didn't seem to interfere with her entertaining of
visitors. With all the troops in the neighborhood (far less than in
previous months, after that big batch of Yanks was taken away in September—but still hundreds and hundreds of those Georgia Reserves)
and with citizens traveling in droves, to get away from Bill Sherman—
Sure enough! High on the hog. Two less mouths to feed: just Ma and
himself and the baby—and the old lady had a sight of shinplasters
which he had seen, and he reckoned that she had more tucked away
that he hadn't seen. Once in awhile she even gave him money without
his asking for it. She said, Coral, sonny, I do feel so shameful bad
bout that foot of your'n. Now you take this currency, and go you down
to Uncle Arch's and buy yourself a nice plug tobacco.

Coral rolled his chew in his mouth and thought about it. Suddenly
he found himself wondering whether that damn Yankee, Naz Stricker,
chewed tobacco. Stricker hadn't asked him for any—hadn't said, like
most folks you encountered, What's the chance for a chaw? Give
me a chaw. Lend me a chaw. Hain't had a chaw all the day.

I'd eat anything.

There was something about that damn Yankee that was important—
yes, sir, damn important. Coral's brows squeezed together as he tried
to consider what that important element might be, as he pegged and
swung his way toward the house with the hawk bumping against him
(and he reckoned he'd be chafed sadly from the continual bounce,
bounce of the dead hawk). In solitary cogitation of the solitary way
he went, Coral had acquired a habit of searching for whys and where-
fores. He pried silently, constantly for reasons. The reasons he found

were seldom the right ones, the purposes he ascribed were often bizarre, the motives and imagined results were apt to be fantastic. His lonely speculations exceeded the limits of his intelligence, but there was no one to tell him that he might be wrong. He kept pondering.

He froze suddenly, he was motionless for a second or two; an astonished grin widened his mouth. If both hands had not been occupied with crutches and with retaining the shotgun on its homemade sling, he would have slapped himself across his ribby chest. He had found the answer.

Naz Stricker was the first person he had talked to, since he came home, who had lost a foot or a hand in battle! And, by Jesus God, he got wounded on July the second, nigh that same wheatfield where he, Coral, felt his own left foot and ankle crushed and going numb.

—Long way off.

—Like a nigger song. Oh, long, long, long, long way.

—Course, they did give Coral a lot of whiskey before they started cutting. They said, Boy, get yourself drunk fast. They had a big barrel of Pennsylvania whiskey, and it was good whiskey, and you could hear a little firing in the distance, but it was nighttime—there wasn't much firing.

—Would the Secesh surgeons give whiskey to a Yank when they were going to go to slicing and chopping? Well, by God. He ought to ask the Yank about that.

—Boy, get yourself drunk fast. The dipper coming closer, someone holding the dipper, whiskey splashing and Coral swallowing and gagging, and the whiskey burnt like coal oil and it gagged him, and moths and other critters were going like fiends against the big bright lanterns hanging under the tent fly up above . . . surgeon said, Where'll we go on this one, Luce? Articulating surface? Right above the nodule. Single flap or double flap? . . . Farther up. Single; he's got the hide to spare . . . *ahhhh!* And that was his own first fierce scream, coming back to ruin his ears, coming back sometimes in the middle of the night to be echoed again by his own throat, to make the baby wake up and yell in sympathy, to make that rotten little Flory say, Aw, shut your trap and try to act like white folks, you.

—Long way off, Gettysburg place.

—Naz Stricker said that he lived not far away from there.

—But what about the whiskey? Hell no, you could bet on it. Good whiskey was too scarce all over the South; they'd not go to wasting it on some damn Yankee.

—But that was in Pennsylvania, where Stricker got shot, where he got captured. Well, they had plenty whiskey there—wagonloads of it. Stole it in that town yonder, name of Chambersburg—great big kind

of warehouse chock full of it. They called it Monongahela or some such
foreign name; said they could read it right off'n the barrel label.

—Ought to ask the Yank about that.

Coral Tebbs moved beneath a stunted magnolia tree which twitched
its hard papery leaves next to the stoop. Zoral was playing beside the
step, playing with a small dead chicken from which a mink had sucked
the blood . . . minks got a chance't of chickens nowadays. Coral had sat
up two nights with a lantern, trying to intercept the enemy, but always
he nodded and went to sleep . . . maybe minks were too smart for
him. Zoral wore a jacket which the widow had hacked out of a Federal
blanket, with the broad stripe showing, and he had a string tied
around the chicken's neck, and he was dragging the chick after him,
making train noises. He paid no attention to his half-brother Coral,
sometimes he paid no attention to anyone, sometimes not even to his
mother. The Widow Tebbs insisted that Zoral had had brain fever
when he was just a mite, and like to died of it. Coral regarded this
disgusting baby and his disgusting sport with equal disgust, then went
jigging up onto the stoop and into the house. His shotgun caught
against the tilted post and nearly threw him backward; he cursed in
loud fury, and awakened his mother in the bedroom where she slept
(she had slept with Laurel when Laurel was at home, and Zoral occupied the foot of their bed) when she was not at The Crib.

What you do, Coral?

Nothing.

What you cussing about?

Nnnnn.

Where you been, Coral?

A-hunting.

What you get?

God damn bastard of a chicken hawk.

Oh, Coral. Such language as you use the while!

Well, look who's a-talking! Maybe you got religion like old Grandad-
Blow-His-Bottom-Out that you tolt me about?

No, I hain't got no religion; but I like gentlemanly ways. When
menfolks come to me to be entertained, I always ask them, if they be
strangers, Will you please act like a gentleman and not cuss?

Well, I got that damn hawk, and I reckon he's the one took so many
of our fries.

Where you get him, Coral?

Swamp back of the hill.

Well, I reckon too that he's the one, and I do thank you, sonny. You
want to go purchase yourself a plug tobacco?

I still got some.

His mother was in the bedroom, and he could not see her, and suddenly for a special reason he was glad that there was no one else in that one room which served as dining room, kitchen, sitting room, and Coral's bedroom. He dumped the bruised dead hawk upon the hearth and stood looking at it, and for some strange reason mirth came to him. Mirth came so seldom. Coral said loudly, God damn Yankee chicken hawk. He batted the hawk into the cold fireplace with his crutch.

—Like what they call a lodge.

—Freemasons?

—He guessed his daddy hadn't been a Freemason, but he'd heard that his grandfather Tebbs was one.

—Jo Coppedge used to say, When I get growed I'm going to get to be a Mason, sure enough. You can go anywhere and do anything, and you got somebody to help you out. Take Yanks: Suppose you get yourself captured, and you say to a Yank— You give him that secret sign or utter them secret words. Then you got a friend for life.

—A lodge which only those who are shy a hand or a foot can belong to.

—Secret words?

—Secret sign? Tain't so secret. Sign is: you got a leg that comes down, and suddenly there ain't no foot on the end of it. Sign is: you got an arm that just ends short off. Like that damn Yankee Naz Stricker.

Even while he stood in contemplation of the disordered table and shelves, Coral heard his mother snoring in the next room. She snored like a man. The more finicky of her customers had complained about her snoring when sometimes the customer and the Widow Tebbs both fell asleep after their encounter, and then the customer was rudely awakened by the growling roar beside him. Coral had heard Captain Oxford Puckett laughing in The Crib. Hi, Mag, put the lid on it. You sound like a battery of brass Napoleons firing at will.

But now the hoarse throbbing from the next room spelled security for Coral's endeavors. The wicked grin twitched on his thin bearded face. Wouldn't Flory's jaw fall off if he knew about this? Flory would plain fart. Opportunity to catch a Yankee—maybe to shoot him— Opportunity to get thirty dollars, even Secesh! It seemed to Coral that he was visiting a personal spite on Floral by the procedure which he planned. There was nothing in this world which he might enjoy more.

Well, toting the stuff was a problem. But soon his eye roved to his old army haversack, hanging on a peg beside the chimney. It was burdened with dust, soot, scraps of crumbled plaster accumulating during the months which had elapsed since the ministrations of Mrs. Dillard. A Yankee sack, a small one; he'd picked it up in 1863 in the woods near that place—what they call it? It was a hard word to say—

Chan-cell-ors-ville. It said *U.S.* but half the belts and canteens and buckles and equipment in the Confederacy said *U.S.* Coral reached up, got the sack, opened it, expelled some mummified remains which turned out to be those of a mouse, and shook the sack vigorously. There.

Fried pork? Hell yes, there was a lot left on that platter. It was good; nice pink stripes in it, and fried just right, even though twas cold. Liberally Coral helped himself to the slabs. Black-eyed peas? Hell yes, a regular hopping John. The mass of peas in the huge brown bowl was studded generously with chunks of hog jowl. (Strangely as occurs, the Widow Tebbs, in her slatternly ways and in her slovenly ignorance, was an excellent cook. If one did not inquire too closely into sanitary conditions. When times were hard, times were hard. But times weren't hard, at present, not for the widow. The menfolks liked a snack, many of them, afterward . . . they'd say, Missis, I could relish a plate of fried potatoes right now. Got any bacon handy? Maybe piece of pie, maybe cup of nice cold milk? I'll pay extry.)

Coral found a torn Macon *Telegraph* and wrapped a mass of peas and hog jowl in that. Cold potatoes—sure enough. Chunk of pone—the Widow Tebbs's pone was always crisp and well salted—when she had meal, when she had salt. Apple pie. Nearly half the pie left, and let Ma think that he'd eaten it all. I declare, she'd say. Coral, you going to eat me out of house and home.

Out in the yard Zoral said, Guh, guh, guh, and still he must be playing train, dragging that miserable chicken. Then a real train came grinding past, and smoke blew all the way to the Tebbs house, for the wind was rising. This week was unseasonably chilly, for March.

Knowledge of that wind posed a new problem for Coral. Loose boards on the roof rattled, it would be cold in the swamp tonight, it would be cold everywhere. Touch and consideration of the haversack brought his comrades back to him. He saw them, lounging in column; far long twisty roads, stones bulging out of clay to hurt you, blackened skillets fastened to the rifles, the spittle rolling in a hard hot ball when you spat into the dust. *Rye whiskey, rye whiskey, rye whiskey so free, you done kilt my Pappy, God damn you, try me.* He began humming as he moved with caution about the room, he was not humming loudly enough to awaken his mother. Which barrel? One over here: that was where she kept stuff. He grubbed around in the barrel, brought out a torn pair of drawers, some old skirts of Zoral's, a gown which Laurel hadn't taken with her. Here, by Jesus God. Union army coat to wear in the rain—one of those kind of oilcloth ones. Some visitor had left it in The Crib the year before; it had part of the cape missing, it wasn't of too much account, but it would serve. And this here old quilt. Coral worked at the table, kneading quilt and raincoat into a familiar roll, passing the roll over his head and shoulder after

he had donned the haversack, after he had tied the ends of the roll
with raveling twine.

. . . Coral, she'd say some day, what went with that old green and
white quilt?

Don't know. Hain't seen hide nor hair of it.

He found his old canteen, also *U.S.*, and filled it with milk.

Canteen, blanket roll, haversack. *Foooorward, ha.* Jo Coppedge,
Bunny Teasley, Kyle Leftwich, Darius Voyles. Gettysburg, Chancellorsville, South Mountain, little place name of something or other where
they camped one night and where Darius Voyles shot himself through
the heart because he was careless with his gun and forgot to draw
the charge. *Foooorward.*

Once more Coral smiled his shameless smile. He recalled community
gossip at Uncle Arch Yeoman's.

—Yes, sir. Put you in jail.

—Worse'n that. Reckon they can hang you or shoot you.

—Says so in the lawbooks. Petey Rooks was a-telling me, and he
can read, and he seen it plain in print. They call it giving aid and comfort to the enemy; and him who disobeys that law is liable to get himself hanged by the neck until dead. So Petey says.

So there was a law, was there? . . . Hang him? By God, he was a
hero, kind of man senators and such talked about when they were
speechifying. . . . He'd say, O.K. (Kind of speech he'd picked up
when they was invading against the North: it meant, All right, mister,
that's so, that's true, that's right with me, or something of that nature.)
O.K. What you mean to do? Hack the other foot off'n me?

Nazareth Stricker. It *did* sound like Bible talk.

Coral, reared in a godless home, if he could have been said to have
been reared, and if it could have been called a home— Coral knew
naught of the Scriptures. Lot of the boys in the army were mighty
Scripturalish. Preacher came around sometimes, a-praying . . . and
then, they sang hymns too. Jo Coppedge came from a farm up in Bibb,
and he said his old man was a deacon of the church. Jo knew right
smart about Saviours and Apostles and Testaments and such. He said,
Cory, I'd admire to open the portal for you and make you see the
Light. If'n you should go to your doom, Godless and in sin as you
dwell, you will suffer in Eternal Torment forever and a day. *Cepting
you Believe on Me thou shalt not be Saved.*

Well, now, what about them Yanks? Reckon they Believe?

That hain't the point, Cory. *Him that hearest on the Word and Be-
lieveth Not, and Accepteth Not, him also shall be Crucified alongside
of Me.* Or something like that. What my Pap always says, and I reckon
they don't come no more Godlier than he.

Aw, Jo, go pound salt up your butt.

But that Nazareth was a— Was a— By God. That was it. Nazareth was one of those Apostles or Disciples that Jo Coppedge was always talking about when he got going on religion, dad fetch him.

And there was that boy name of Apostle, got killed— Where? Got killed someplace or other, when they were tearing down that rail fence in front of their lines, acting as skirmishers. Yank shot him with one of those fancy long-range rifles, maybe had a telescope on it. Apostle Epperson. That was his name.

. . . O long dead burnt dried pastures with no herds feeding, O long tall bristly woodlands with winds converging, O dead dark chilly swamp with wind seeming to lift and sustain itself amid higher dignified trees and not coming low enough to riffle the water in solid black pools.

—Hey.

—You still laying here on this log? Them catch-dogs come along, going to grab you sure.

—Hey. God damn Yank! You want some rations?

The voice repeated the word, the voice said dully, Rations, but the wild blue eyes did not open to glimmer at him.

Set up, dad blast you.

Naz Stricker twisted into a sitting position, his eyes opened and he glared about. The first thing he saw was the haversack beside him from which Coral fished a wad of soggy newspaper. The wet paper fell apart, peas and hog jowl splashed in a mass upon the mossy bark of the log. Naz Stricker gave a cry. His single hand came shaking forward, turning itself into a claw as it came. The glinting eyes touched Coral Tebbs's face in disbelief and then lowered again.

Well, you said you'd eat anything!

The claw dipped into food, peas and grease were dripping, the claw reached the mouth, a gnarl came from shrunken depths of Stricker's throat even while his jaws clacked together and he made sucking sounds.

Reckon all you damn Yankees eat just like hogs.

Stricker wept while he chewed. Tears drained down over his blackened cheeks, they could not wash the grime coated there, they licked over grime and kept sliding. He blubbered between his bites.

This here canteen's got milk in it.

The Yankee wailed in disbelief. Milk?

I hain't a-storying you.

Stricker tried to remove the cap from the canteen with his one hand. Oh, God, Fumble Buttons, cried Coral in annoyance. He took back the canteen, unscrewed the cap and let it dangle by its rusty chain. He pushed the flask forward and Stricker's dried lips opened trustingly. Coral had a dim thought of a baby seeking its mother's breast . . . he held the canteen, tilting it gradually as the weight lessened, and the Yankee's dark thin neck twitched with contractions of swallowing.

Needn't take it all to once't. It hain't all the milk in the world. Just one canteen-full, you hog.

Nazareth Stricker munched pork, potatoes, pone; he ate the rest of the peas, he scraped them from the log with dancing fingers. Throughout the madness of this meal he kept making little chirrups and moanings. Tears still flowed.

God damndest bawl-baby ever I see. Do all you Yanks bawl like that?

I don't know, mourned Naz Stricker, I don't know. But his shrunken stomach could not accept this load, could not retain it for long. He began to retch, his whole body was torn with the struggle, his shoulders went into spasm, he turned and bent away across the fallen tree, and lost everything while Coral sat scowling.

Too much, said Stricker when he could speak again, too much.

You hadn't no call to go a-wasting it.

Know what?

What?

The Yankee spoke with the astonishing vigor of those stockaders who lay on the boundary of death. Men scarcely able to wiggle their fingers had at times crawled up and belabored each other with clubs; yet within hours they were collapsed, they were cold.

In the stockade there's fellows go around—hunting for the stuff that—other fellows have thrown up. And what's passed—through them. Passed through their bodies.

What they want to do that for?

To eat it, you damn Rebel!

Don't you call me no damn Rebel!

Guess you are—are one, aren't you? Or were?

They sat staring; and it was as if the food which Stricker had wolfed and then rejected— The food had, in some odd way and in a matter of minutes— As if it had given him strength. He emerged from the status of a beast into the ranks of humanity.

If they do that, said Coral Tebbs at long last, then they got mighty dirty ways. Like a bunch of birds after horse-apples.

Reb—what's your name?

Coral Tebbs.

Did you say *Coral*?

Yes, I said *Coral*. Hain't I got a right to my own name? Here I go fetching rations to you, and right off you start making mock of me.

I wasn't making mock, Coral. It's—kind of—unusual—for a name.

Well, so's your'n.

Twas my father's name before me, and my grandfather's.

Coral imagined Naz Stricker's father and grandfather, he saw them as bearded Pennsylvanians peering dumbly from red farmhouses, watching in alarm the Confederates' advance, fearful for safety of their livestock; well might they be fearful.

How's your belly feel, Nazareth Stricker?

Feels better. Might— Could I have some more milk?

Coral offered the canteen, but this time Stricker held it for his own drinking. He stopped suddenly, lowering the canteen and saying, Don't you—want any?

I done made a meal.

Stricker ate again, he ate more slowly, there was painful leisure in his approach to the morsels which remained. He ate half of a boiled potato, two more scraps of the fried pork; he looked at the large chunk of corn pone which was left, then stuffed it inside his shirt.

I got some pie, said Coral.

I can't believe— Ain't any pie on earth.

Oh, yes, there is, and Coral exhibited in triumph the great crushed chunk of it.

Stricker shook his head wearily. Wish I could. But I can't.

Well, keep it safe till you can, said Coral gruffly.

Already, and in this limited acquaintanceship, a meeting of witches, Nazareth Stricker showed himself as a soldier. A thing was there: it was for him, he took it. A thing was not there: he went without. He did not pry and examine, he did not query, he accepted. Coral Tebbs had not summoned him to a Stated Communication of the fierce new Lodge . . . the Lodge went into session, though no gavel fell, and a mystic unseen sentinel gave the requisite number of knocks on the closed door, and announced that there was a Brother who desired permission to approach. The Brother was examined, he gave the Grip (it was a Grip to be managed with but one hand or foot, or perhaps with no hands or no feet); he responded properly to silent questions; he was found to be a Mutilated Militant in Good Standing, or in Good Sitting.

You live around here, Reb?

Out yonder. My old lady's got a little place.

Your wife?

Naw, naw, naw. My Ma! I'm scarce eighteen.

I'm twenty.

Yank, you got the shakes again. Here, I got this blanket roll . . . tain't much of a coat but . . . and this here coverlid for to sleep in.

If I stay, the dogs might pick me up. But I can't move. Yet.

I got to think about some other place for you. I'll reason out a place. . . . Can't take you to the house; Ma gets too many folks come a-calling. And then Flory trots himself over sometimes from the stockade. He's in them Georgia Reserves. He's my half-brother, the little scut. . . . Naz Stricker, I had a funny notion.

Such as?

Oh, spose like that smoke was all around, there by that wheatfield, second day of the battle. We was coming up on you, and you was trying to shove us back—

Guess I had the—same idea, Coral.

What was you a-shooting?

Springfields. Regular bullets, paper-cartridge type.

Reckon that's what hit me. See, you could have fired, I could have fired, did fire, practically the same second.

It's—unlikely.

But it could have happened.

Yes. Could.

Yank, you live in a brick house? When you're to home?

Yes, I do.

Got one of them big funny barns out behind, sticking clean over the hillside?

No, we haven't much of a barn. We—live in a little town. We've only a stable and buggy-shed, and the shop. Out back.

What kind of shop?

Where Father works, and Uncle Asaph.

Asaph? Dad blast these Yankee names!

Father's fond of telling—how Uncle Asaph got his name. Twas a few days after his—birth—and they didn't know what to call him. He was having his didy put on him, and he—kicked out, like babies will. Kicked over a pewter cup, and it—fell on plates and things. So they fell, all—a-clatter. And my grandfather said, It says in—the Book of Chronicles—it says, Asaph made a sound with cymbals. So we shall call him Asaph. You see?

I don't see no way. What they make in that shop?

Coral, I'm—tired. Want to go to sleep.

Then get back in that brush, where you was when the hawk fell down. Here. I'll help you fetch this stuff.

They staggered and mauled their way to the center of the thick-clad little island.

You—asked me something.

Oh, twas just talk.

Asked me what they make in the shop. And I—used to help. I—grew up in the shop. Ask me again, Coral.

Well?

Ask me—again.

I'm a-asking.

They make feet. And legs. Legs and feet.

Coral Tebbs crowed wordlessly.

As God's my witness!

Oh, they do, do they? They make them any hands too?

Usually just—hooks. But Squire Barth lost his hand in a sawmill, and they made him—a hand. Just for show. Twon't work. It's got a glove on it, with the fingers kind of—folded. Natural as life. But twon't work.

Coral Tebbs sat talking with Naz Stricker until the Yankee, a thin bent ragged seed within the pod of coat and comforter, became voiceless. His breath blew out noisily as he slept; Coral watched him; sometimes he gargled and groaned and gave little squeaks; once he said something about Uncle Asaph. Coral watched him for what seemed an hour, it might have been longer. Then Coral made his way home and dropped exhausted upon his bed and found his own sleep, disturbed by nightmares as was Naz Stricker's slumber. One trip into the marsh, a trip home, the trip back to the marsh, laden with haversack and blanket roll, his crutches slipping and catching . . . he had fallen twice, with those burdens . . . the trip back home again.

But in the middle of the night he sat upright, eyes staring into gloom, ears hurtfully alert. Dogs. The dogs were out. That free running pack, bound to hunt Naz Stricker in his lair, the catch-dogs bound to seize him when trail-dogs had smelt their way to the island. Then Coral laughed hoarsely, and lay back, head cradled under his arms. The dogs were over east, winding and tracking and baying across the Claffey plantation. Some other escaped prisoner must be their immediate quarry, not Nazareth. And it sounded as if the dogs were a solid mile and a half away from that sacred island, and going farther all the while. Coral reached out, got this trousers, found his plug, bit off his chew, and worked the spittoon out from under the bed. He propped himself comfortably on the bed, wishing only that his shoulders would not ache so strenuously, gnawed as they were by merciless wooden jaws of those crude crutches. Faintly he heard the music box playing in The Crib, and smiled to hear it, but he could not pick out the air. Those were all old foreign tunes on that spindle—someone had said that they were German tunes—and Coral did not know their names because the list pasted inside the music box lid was long defaced, and anyway the list was printed in a strange higgledy-piggledy script, and anyway he could not read well.

Zoral woke up in the next room and said, Maw.

She ain't here.

Mawwww!

She's over to The Crib, you blame grasshopper!

Jink.

Well, if'n you want a drink you come get it your ownself.

Jink.

You heard what I said, you Zoral. I ain't toting no water to you, not this night. You're big enough to wait on yourself. I hain't your nigger.

It was doubtful whether Zoral understood half of what was said, but finally he came into the room, trotting slowly, and made his way to the water bucket, and drank deeply, squinting over the gourd at his half-brother while he drank. Then trot, trot back through the shadows; and a train went past, and again Zoral started to make train sounds until Coral roared at him to shut up.

Coral considered the swamp, and considered Naz Stricker, and thought of the Union army coat and the green and white comforter, now touched with muck, but covering Naz Stricker, shielding his weak body, helping to keep warm the wizened stump of his left arm. He thought of Flory, and his grin spread. Flory would puke. Thirty dollars a head . . . Turner and his dogs, Harris and his dogs . . . Captain Wirz, sir, I got this here Yankee. Give me thirty dollars, please . . . Coral slept.

. . . But awakened once more (and long after the widow's callers had departed, and after she was bugling in the next room) to take notice of his own confusions, recollections and the hard stolid body of a single ambition which stood like a segment amid these other riffraff. *A foot.* Nazareth Stricker—in awful weakness, but mumbling still the answers which Coral sought—had said that they used special kinds of wood. One kind came from some foreign land, and it was light but strong, not weighty to tote around. It was costly. Couldn't find any wood like that around here. But— Gum, tupelo, oak, pine, magnolia, haw? Sure enough, what about haw? Coral could— No, he couldn't. He couldn't cut down a haw tree by himself. But he might go over to the Claffey place and say, Mr. Claffey, sir, it might be that you're pestered with chicken hawks? Well, I aim to rid you of them hawks. Set out still as a stump until Old Hawk comes, and then blast the daylight through him. But— Mr. Claffey, sir, if'n I'm successful a-doing it, it might be that one of your niggers could cut down a tree for me? Teeny little tree, not much account? That'd be one way to get haw-wood, if haw-wood could serve. Maybe peach, maybe apple? Ma had a rolling pin made of apple.

The rolling pin took him on the trail of a more magnificent idea. He saw a kind of rolling-pin thing, sticking up out of grass. Saw it clearly. But where? . . . It was in dry grass and blackberry spines, over next door on the Granny Rambo place. Granny Rambo's house had burned down, burned to smithereens, the winter before Coral went to the army. Folks thought she must have put hickory in her fireplace, and hickory sparked like mad, and maybe that was what caught the bed-clothes afire, and Granny sick beneath them. Black smoke boiling high, and men flocking with yells from the railroad train when they came past and saw the smoke and stopped to fight the fire. There wasn't much use a-fighting it. They dragged Granny out, what was left of her, and got out a few pieces of furniture; then the roof caved in, and

the woodshed and old smokehouse burned up too. Nothing left standing on the place except the privy with blackened pines towering sad
beside it. . . . It was there that Coral had seen that big kind of rolling-
pin-shaped apparatus, sticking up out of the weeds.

And the privy.

Nobody went there; no longer was there a path; the fence was down,
hungry whips of berry vines extended over the deserted soil and made
new bushes like a barrier. And you couldn't see the privy from the
railroad, couldn't see it from the Tebbs place.

You needn't worry about black people straying in that direction,
for all of them believed that Granny Rambo walked the jungle which
had been her dooryard for twenty-odd years, walked at odd seasons
and in odd guise. . . . Saw her in her bonnet. She had that old shawl
a-folded across her shoulders. She had a basket on her arm. She walked
young as once she had been, with golden curls showing, and in a white
gown, and she carried her youngest child in her arms. She walked old,
she leaned on her cane, her face was hateful and hating.

To tell the truth, Coral Tebbs had first heard these tales when he
returned in the fall of 1863, and had more or less believed them. But
his honest memory of Granny Rambo was of a gentle little body who
made gingerbread men to give to hungry children when she had the
wherewithal. He did not believe that she would actually harm a soul,
whether she walked or whether she didn't.

He wondered if Naz Stricker was afraid of ghosts.

Nowadays Coral himself feared few things. Scorn or pity directed
at himself: these he feared and resented. And he was afraid of bad
dreams, echoes of *nrrrrwhuck* and himself hooting under the knife
and saw.

Coral had another nap (brief deep rewarding nap, a soldier's sleep).
He went prowling round the yard in the first hollowness of dawn.
Maybe it was warmer in the swamp than it was here, warmer where
wind could not reach so easily. He searched in ordinary places: in
the broken hogshead lying on its side; in a mouldering wagon box;
he searched behind sheds and under dry vines, he peeked at nests of
leaves and straw and pine straw. No one had gathered eggs the previous evening, or possibly for two previous evenings, so now he found
eight eggs. Coral built a tiny quick fire under the kettle and boiled
all of the eggs. Zoral awoke and came running out in his shirt, he
dripped lather as a dog might drip. Coral gave him an egg, and gave
him corn bread. Coral was kind enough to offer milk to this loathsome
mite as well, but the milk had turned sour, and Zoral upset his mug
on the floor. Coral struck at the child but missed. Zoral fled shrieking
to his mother's bed. The Widow Tebbs awakened.

What you doing up so early, Coral?

Going a-hunting.

What you going to hunt?

Just a-hunting.

What you cooking?

Hen-fruit. I collected— He looked into the pot. Collected five. I give one to Zoral. He spilt his milk, the little bastard.

Coral, don't you talk so bout my baby boy. You saving an egg for me, sonny?

Saving two. There was five. I et two.

Well, thank you for a good boy, Coral, she said drowsily, and soon was raucous in her snoring once more.

Again Coral packed the haversack: three boiled eggs for Naz Stricker, more pone, the last of the cold potatoes, the last slab of cooked pork. He shook the empty canteen . . . the balance of that milk was no good, but wasn't there some wine in that keg yonder? He remembered that his mother had bought a cask of wine for future hospitality. Scuppernong wine, but just about the worst ever made. Coral opened the spigot and tasted, and made a face. Sour and muddy into the bargain, but it would be better than nothing for the invalid Yankee, so he filled the canteen. He left the house finally, weighted with shotgun and ammunition. These he hid as soon as he was out of sight, he wasn't going to lug them to the swamp, he had no intention of hunting. In highest excitement he made his way through the forest . . . it seemed that the gray world was grown immaculately bright, promising bounty, promising varieties of wealth. Coral chanted quietly as he went; he could not sing well, but he chanted. Only the few stark birds and field-mice heard him. *O baby, O baby, I've tolt you before, just make me a pallet, I'll lay on the floor.*

Nazareth Stricker had built himself a house; he said that he scratched it together in the late afternoon after he came from stupor. He was not able to tell Coral that he had been nerved as much by unexpected charity from a foe as by the few nourishing juices which strayed into his body; no more would Coral have been able to countenance the thought consciously; yet in secret fashion each youth was aware of the benefit offered, the goodness prevailing and digested, the warm human treasure accruing to the pair of them. Naz Stricker had drawn light twigs and flakes of old moss into a pile amid which he'd nested in the quilt. Overhead hung the cowl of the torn raincoat, held aloft by broken sticks, serving as cape and shelter tent. Naz said that he had been truly cosy for the first time in— For the first time in a long time. He thought that he had never been so cosy before. He remembered—but, again, could not tell Coral—that in sudden frantic awakenings he had felt a horror at the soundlessness, the detachment from that race of noisy monsters amid whom he'd dwelt. And then, throbbing through lone blackness and past a twitch of branches and the night cry spoken by some bird or animal, Nazareth had heard the ticking of the mantel clock in the kitchen-living-room at home. On this first occasion of his long separation from home, he had heard it. He had heard a doctor's buggy rattling away down Lilac Street, he had heard his eldest sister talking in her sleep in the next room as often she talked, he had heard and felt his shepherd dog Buchanan changing position under the bed. He had whispered, Buke. Good Buke. You want to go out? Go to sleep, Buke. Then he himself had gone floating, unhurt, unstarved, master of time and distance, loved.

Nazareth Stricker ate eggs and pone, he said that he would save the potatoes and the bit of meat and the rest of the pone, he drank greedily of sour wine.

Don't you go drinking too much all to once't. Twill put you flat.

I've been drinking this water beside the island.

Swamp water! No good for your innards.

It's better than in the stockade—much better. Cepting for the spring.

You got a spring in there? I mean, you had—?

It busted loose last summer. They said God broke it free of the ground. It was good water, but I only had a little cup—practically doll-sized—and then I'd have to stand in line again.

Yank. You feared of ghosts?

Nazareth Stricker said judiciously, I never met any.

You mind dwelling in a privy?

Would it stink?

No, it's mighty old, no smell left.

Couldn't stink as bad as the—stockade. Whose privy is it?

Next place to our'n, but everything else got burnt; and tis told that Granny Rambo goes walking there, but I hain't never seen her, and I don't reckon she'd hurt a flea. Naz Stricker, you tolt me about that queer kind of wood they used for legs. What might be its name?

I can't remember. It came by ship from some tropic port. Pa couldn't always get hold of it.

Could you make me a foot?

Me with my one hand?

Reckon I could help. Reckon I could hold things, and turn them, and cut, and shave away, if'n I was showed proper.

Stricker meditated on this. Finally he said, It's a question of tools and materials. Up home in Pennsylvania we had everything: Pa and Uncle Asaph have got a turning lathe they work with a treadle, and we've got tools galore. We fill orders from— Oh, New York, Philadelphia, Baltimore, places such as that. Guess Pa and Uncle Asaph are now rushed to death, what with the war and all.

He said later, Guess they think I'm dead.

Well, you hain't.

Guess I could try to make a kind of peg-leg-foot, granted we had the proper wood and some tools. With you helping. Let me see your— leg.

On no other occasion had Coral displayed his stump to anyone as an exhibition, as a deliberate act. His family had seen the thing necessarily in their intimacy . . . his mother crooned about it until Coral shouted for her to keep still. Once the exasperated Flory called him Old Stumpy-Stump, and that time Coral's crutch caught Flory between the shoulders and like to busted his back. Floral was nigh to knocked senseless. He blubbered in bed for a day and a half, and his back was lame for weeks. The Widow Tebbs beat Coral across the head and shoulders until she broke her broom, but he only sat laughing, saying repeatedly that he was glad he had not missed.

The amputation was effected about two inches above the nodule of his ankle bone at the narrowest portion of his left shin. Peel off the sock, you damn Rebel, said Naz Stricker. Meekly Coral obeyed, removing the dirty knitted woolen wrappings so that Naz might examine the stump. The flap had grown into place soundly. Naz Stricker pushed against the stump with his hand. Hurt?

Not too much.

Does it hurt, really? Sometimes my stump feels all a-quiver. Sometimes it feels like my hand—was still there. Then I try to grab something and can't.

Reckon I know. Same way. Oft I feel like I got a left foot.

Ain't it—funny? Both left? Funnier than if it had been me right and you left, or t'other way around.

It's just as blame funny as all hell, said Coral Tebbs. The two of them engaged in a tittering laugh; thus they were no longer Entered Apprentices, they had taken the Second Degree of their Lodge. They were Fellow Craftsmen.

Coral, I'm no surgeon. But I've watched Pa fit feet—fit feet, and more often wooden legs. And he's made some of cork-wood, cork-wood that comes all the way from Spain and places. But it has to be braced within.

God damn it, can you make me a foot or can't you?

Guess I—we—could fashion a peg-leg-foot. Granted we had the makings.

Would it work?

Straps—would be hard to manage. The fastenings . . . twould have to be thickly padded where the stump fits in. . . .

I said, Can you or can't you?

We'll see. That was all that Coral Tebbs could get out of him.

That day Nazareth Stricker lived on potatoes, pone, wine and the scrap of fried meat. He regretted the waste of food on the previous day, but was too much of a philosopher to torture himself idly with unhappy contemplations. He kept looking ahead, Coral had made him able to look ahead. Naz had slept well and in comparative warmth. Inside his skeletal frame the values of milk, eggs and other nobilities were enriching him. This night he might sleep with a board roof over his head for the first time since he had been hauled from Richmond to Andersonville (albeit a backhouse roof). His shrunken face turned into a black smile at thought of Granny Rambo's ghost. He had lain amid some thirteen thousand men while they died; many of them he had seen puffed to fierce proportions before they were removed from his sight; he had worked in the hospital, also he had been a patient there; he had worked Outside, he had languished Inside; and he should be afraid of Granny Rambo, he should recoil from fancied odors of an unused latrine? Were he not a philosopher he had never been able to crawl through the reek of the old hospital drain, to worm his cold wet way past shivering trigger-ready guards, to circle the stockade and embrasures so that folks might think he'd escaped to the east instead of to the west, to provide himself with pepper and to scatter it, to flounder in low places where the wet going was hard; and to collapse at last in wilderness, no matter how loudly the dogs sounded in other portions of this boundless Avernus; and then to have the hawk come toppling.

While in the hospital Coral Tebbs had traded a stolen watch for a broken pepperbox revolver and ten dollars in greenbacks. The money was long since spent, but he had managed to repair the revolver, and now it would shoot. Late in the afternoon he fired the revolver three times at a rusty codfish can and missed every time. Mag popped her head out of the house door and cried, You Coral, take care like I bid you if'n you go shooting at a mark, for Zoral's at play in the dooryard. Hell, he told her, I was firing towards the brush. Three revolver shots were the agreed signal for Nazareth Stricker to take up his journey, blanket roll and all. Naz must be established in the old Rambo privy before dark, because Coral could travel through brambles and ruin of the Rambo homestead only by daylight or in the edges of dusk. He could not travel there when it was black-dark.

Painstakingly the Yankee must walk his solitary path as directed: through the swamp to the sweet-gum thicket, off in a left oblique directly toward the tall twin pines which could be seen rising in the east . . . then, when arrived between the pines, he must scrooch down and work south until he reached the remains of a rail fence. That was the most dangerous part of his journey: the woods were open. But Coral had met not so much as a stray Georgia Reserve or a Negro through all his recent trips to the swamp.

Coral thrust the revolver in his belt and crutched leisurely behind a weedy brake as if bent on more target shooting; then he headed for the Rambo ruins as fast as he could travel. It was hard for him to negotiate the last fifty yards because of blackberry coils. Hè arrived at the privy cursing and scratched. He envisioned misfortunes—he saw Naz forgetting to scatter the last of his pepper, and thus he was pursued by the noisy hounds once more. Would Naz remember to cross the broken rails, and slink behind concealing dried-out vines until he saw the charred chimney on Granny Rambo's cottage site looming before him? Would he have sense enough to lie flat and motionless if he heard voices or the step of an approaching mule?

Coral pushed open the swollen door of the old bleached structure and nearly fell backward. Naz Stricker was lounging upon his rolled quilt.

Jesus God! You scairt the piss out of my bladder.

But ain't this the place? This backhouse—

Sure it's the place, but you ought to waited my signal.

You did shoot.

They had a lively discussion. It seemed that an hour earlier Nazareth Stricker had heard three shots and had started out. They did not know where the shots came from; Coral had not heard them.

Guards at Andersonville, said Naz. Guess they shot three more of our boys. Thirty-day furlough apiece.

They don't get that!

Devil they don't. Every time they shoot one of us.

God damn lie.

Well, said Naz judiciously, we won't get anywhere arguing about it.

Tangles grew high, the railroad was out of sight, so was the Tebbs place, so was any track traveled commonly by slaves of the region. Together the youths dragged an old plank and placed it across the privy holes, and on this the quilt and coat could be arranged.

Couldn't find much to feed you on, said Coral. He produced half a dozen raw turnips from the pockets of his ragged jacket.

These'll be prime, Coral. I'm fairly starved for greenery. Naz started gnawing.

Got anything left to wet your whistle?

I filled the canteen with swamp water on the way.

Reckon there's plenty water in Granny's old well. Tomorrow we can rig you a bucket. Too bad you can't build no fire, but smoke'd give us away.

So easily it became we and us.

Coral, two things I wish I could have. Strange things.

Like what?

A shawl and a bonnet. An old lady's bonnet. Maybe one of those big wide ones that hides the face?

Coral stared at him blankly until he saw Satan jumping in the splintery gaze of Naz Stricker's deep small eyes. Then their glee rose to-

gether. Coral laughed seldom, usually he only grinned when he was
sardonically pleased. Now he brayed in a choking anguish which had
not overwhelmed him since he was wounded. He said, Granny Rambo!
Shawl and bonnet! Well, by Jesus, Yank, you shall have them!

He provided these articles of dress the next day but not without
peril. He stole an old shawl which he had not seen his mother wear
in years, and found a crushed bonnet in the barrel. The slats were
bent, the bonnet was a tatter but it would serve. He was in the act of
stuffing the booty into his haversack when he was pounced upon by
Mag, who had been watching through the crack of the open bedroom
door, and he had thought that she was asleep all the time.

Coral. What you think you're a-doing?

He felt dizzy, he felt his face go hot and then felt strength and
color draining. Well, he said, sparring for time.

Set down on that bench. Look at me. Look at your Ma. What you
up to, anyway?

Well, he said.

You got my shawl that belonged to Aunt Eliza; and half that ham
is gone that was left this morning, and I don't know what's come with
all the corn pone and leftovers. Who you giving things to?

Well.

You speak up and confess to your Ma, or I won't give you nary a
cent for plug tobacco, not never more. Coral, you selling my property,
maybe to buy drink?

Hell, you know I don't scarcely never drink. Makes me puke.

You tell me, or I'll get the lend of a cattle whip off'n somebody.

Well. I'm helping somebody.

Who you helping?

His glance, sly and mournful and shamed, came to meet hers. He
looked away quickly. I got me a girl.

A girl? Whereabouts?

Back yonder in the swamp.

What's she doing there?

Living. I come acrost her whilst hunting. Member the day I shot
that chicken hawk? Twas then.

Mercy on us. Where she come from?

Up Atlanta way. You know. All these folks wandering here and
there, ain't got no home to go to, count of Sherman's army and them
Yankee bummers. She tells how they burnt the very roof over her
head.

Sakes. You never had you a girl before, did you? My sonny boy,
my eldest, never did I think— Astonishingly the Widow Tebbs lifted
her dirty frilled poplin apron to her face, then lowered it quickly.
When I think of all the menfolks I've done entertained, and how I'm

scarlet as they say, but I do love a-doing It— When I think about my own flesh and blood— First little Laurel with the boys a-slathering after her— And now you. Coral, you laying with her?

A mite.

Well, that dirty swamp hain't no place fit for a poor homeless girl. Coral, you go fetch her straight away to this house. She can sleep right here in your bed. Go fetch her as I bid you.

Ma, I can't.

How come you can't?

Cause she's black.

The widow fell upon him with open palms, striking blindly, vociferous but incoherent. Zoral, seated on a small vessel in the room beyond, witnessed the assault through the open door and stretched his throat in a scream. Coral was nearly overcome with amusement at the serious rage with which his fabrication was greeted, but he managed to ward off a few of the slaps, and at last had to slam his mother away from him. His arms had always been powerful if stringy of muscle; they had developed additional power through a year and a half of crutching. He did not wish to hurt Mag, he merely shoved her into a state of collapse on the floor, where she remained sobbing.

He took the haversack with him as he left the house. You know what the old saying is, Ma, he chortled over his shoulder. Man hain't a man till he's run a nigger girl down a cotton row.

Oh, sonny boy, sonny! Keeping a wench! Keeping a black girl—

He left her lamenting, and headed for the swamp, and eventually traversed a half circle through open woodland until he could come unobserved to the Rambo farmstead. You damn Yankee, what I suffer for the sake of you. The old lady caught me with this here truck, and she like to jump down my throat. I had to tell her I was keeping a stray nigger wench back yonder in the brush.

Nazareth's grimy face showed alarm. Think she followed you?

Hell, no, she'd never follow. Just set there and bawl.

Won't that yarn make a deal of trouble for you at home?

Hell, no, she'll just fret. And heap insults upon me, and then turn soft. Naz Stricker, I want to show you something.

Coral toiled away from the privy, manipulating his crutches slowly among vines. He began to circle the scraps of blackened timbers near the chimney. At first his search was unrewarded, but after much hunting he found the object he sought, the rolling-pin-kind-of-shape upon which he had seized in thought two nights earlier. It protruded from the wreckage, doubtless it had not been moved since the day when Granny Rambo died. It was a portion of the bed in which the old woman had been lying in her hour of doom. Foot-post or head-post, Coral knew not which. It was turned from a single length of timber, you could not tell what color the wood had been to begin with, you

would know only when you cut it. The knob which had reminded Coral
of a rolling-pin handle was about four inches in length, thrusting
smoothly out from a larger column. Coral got down on his knees and
tried to move the thing; he could not. Naz Stricker came to help him.

You ain't even quarter-witted. Never ought to stir from that privy
by daylight.

Coral, you can't manage this alone.

Together they loosened the burned-off post (it was two or three
feet long) and Nazareth cradled it until they reached shelter. The
privy was only forty-nine inches wide: they would find that out when
they came to measure. Naz kept a big broken crock in the corner to
put his feet on when he slept; thus he made a bed in an L-shape, thus
he slept in a foetal position. He declared that it was better than sleeping in Andersonville.

What say you bout this pole, Naz?

It's gosh-awful heavy.

But we'd only need a teeny mite of the thick part.

You're the one who'd have to lug it around . . . of course the core
of it would be reamed out to accommodate your stump . . . it's stout
enough . . . that'll cut like iron.

What nature of wood is it?

Could be teak or mahogany.

What's them?

From tropic lands. *From many an ancient river, from many a palmy
plain.*

Hain't you smart with your rhymes and truck!

It's a hymn.

Don't care if it's a her. Where'd Granny Rambo ever get such like,
to build her bed out of?

Devil knows. Doubtless twas carpentered by someone else, long ago.
Take teak—some of the ships load it for ballast in the hold; and I've
known Pa to buy bits in Philadelphia, where also he bought that other
light stuff I can't remember the name of.

Naz, would this serve?

It'll be a chore. You'd have to get hold of tools some way.

Just you leave that to Granddaddy.

Harness and straps and padding will be a chore even worse, said
Naz Stricker gloomily.

He was not at all sanguine about the prospect of success. That night,
instead of dreaming about Home or dreaming that he was besieged by
starvation and complaints and rotting men who labored after him
with outstretched hands and swelling eyeballs, he dreamed he had
contrived for Coral Tebbs not one wooden peg but two. Neither of
them fitted properly. Coral's face grew darker and darker. He took
his revolver and shot his mother—a neat but shrunken little white-

haired woman, in Naz's dream. Then he shot Naz. Then he shot him-self.

. . . Mr. Claffey, sir.

Ira Claffey looked pityingly from the verandah, and limped down to shake Coral's hand. Coral, what can I do for you?

Like to beg the lend of some tools off'n you.

You shall have them. You look tired, my boy. Does your limb bother you greatly?

No, sir, I get around pretty peart. But I've studied out a way to make me a peg-foot; but we hain't got the needfuls.

Let one of my hands help you. Jem has learned some carpentry, and we have a work-bench here.

Prefer to go my own gait, said Coral stubbornly, sullenly.

Ira looked into the stern young beetling face, and wondered at the almost infernal intent he recognized. Come along to the implement shed, Coral. He reached for his keys.

Saw, gouges, file, other things which Nazareth had declared they would need. These Coral carried to the Rambo place; he carried the saw slung upon his back. He was eager to begin work immediately in the slight period of daylight remaining, but Stricker looked at his shaking hands and said No. Naz was wiser than Coral. Rome, Nazareth told Coral Tebbs, was not built in a day.

Hell no. Nor Atlanta nor Milledgeville neither. But Atlanta got *burnt* in a day, as you damn Yankees ought well to know.

Oh, pull that ramrod out of your ass, said Naz pleasantly.

Naz gained energy by the hour. When the Tebbs family ate high on the hog, as now, the widow paid old Simeon, the Bile Negro, to bring her a hand-cart load of vegetables from time to time. Yams, cabbages, carrots, kale turned sweetly tender by the frosts: these were piled on the stoops, front and back, in profusion. Naz craved these things even more than he enjoyed the ham which Coral had served to him that morning, and there were plenty of goober peas. In days to come Naz would munch on birds and rabbits which Coral Tebbs sought and roasted for him.

The following morning they set to work in earnest. Coral said that his mother had fussed at him but little . . . there was small oppor-tunity to fuss, for men from the guards' camp appeared at sundown. Jollity ruled in The Crib. A railroad engineer came later, bringing liquor. Mag was sound asleep when Coral went to the Rambo site after breakfasting on ham and eggs; he brought ham and leathery fried eggs and fresh milk to his Fellow Craftsman.

Reckon she thinks I'm plumb silly bout that black wench.

Now, Reb, hush. We must fix a place to saw this post.

(A shame which seemed an unnatural figment of existence, when viewed in the light of his domestic surroundings, and his attitude

toward them— The same shame which prevailed upon him in the army
was active now when Coral spoke of his mother. He had said simply,
She's a widow woman. . . . Guess your Pa left her well off? . . .
Not too well. We contrive to get along.)

They broke a saw blade on the solid bed post in the first hour of
labor, and Coral must needs visit the Claffey plantation again to express regret and to ask the value of the blade. To Ira Claffey's notion
the blade had no value . . . it had a value far in excess of anything
which Coral might offer in recompense. The saw's worth was beyond
estimation in a land where no saws were manufactured except in some
crude smithy. Ira found another heavier saw for Coral and watched
the boy inch along homeward. Ira tried to envision his sons moving
in the same road. He could not envision them. Sometimes he found it
hard to assort their features, the individual characteristics of eyes, ears,
hair-tufts. The sons blended together, distant, filmy, without voice,
with only a hollow song rising, a mingling of drone and unidentified
words as in a Mass heard long before in Mexico.

The peg-leg-foot constructed by Naz Stricker and Coral Tebbs
resembled a potato masher with a short thick handle, and twin flat
staves protruding from the masher portion. Achieving the necessary
hollow space to admit Coral's stump was the work of tiresome hours—
Coral holding, Naz gouging with his one hand until the fingers
cramped; the peg jammed down between stones in the privy's ledge,
Naz steadying, Coral gouging out the hard dry powder, powder of
wood like the dust of metal. The thing was cumbersome. It had to be:
there must be sufficient space in the socket to admit padding—padding
soft but solid, and with an aperture tailored to the exact dimensions
of the mutilated leg. It was no mean task for anyone to perform, and
materials came to hand only as the fruit of ingenuity and long search
. . . raw cotton found in an abandoned picking-sack, and ginned by
the boys' own fingers . . . a flannel jacket which had been worn in
turn by the Widow Tebbs's babies.

Coral, you might as well go soot your face, said Mag. You spend all
your hours with that little black tramp.

She ain't no tramp, poor thing.

Who's she belong to, did she say?

Man by the name of—Puckett.

What? Some kin of Captain Ox?

I reckon not.

Whyn't you spend your sleeping hours at night with her, same as
your waking hours?

Ain't really room for me and her in the tent I done made.

You mean to say you built her a tent? Out'n what?

Pine branches and old canvas wagon-cover.

Why, where'd you find canvas?

Corner of the loft of our stable.

Why, there ain't— There wasn't no canvas there!

Yes they was.

Mag found the supposed situation easier to accept than she had thought possible. Throughout her life she had seen innumerable yellow people large and small; there was a slave child in Americus pointed out as the spit and image of Mag's elder brother Claudey; often her callers boasted about their high jinks on the other side of the color line. Only trust, she thought, that the wench don't bear Coral a child here and now.

I low you might fetch her to the house, at that, the widow said reluctantly. Folks might think she was a servant of our'n; and she could help see after Zoral, and keep him off'n the railroad track when I lose sight of him.

Folks know we don't own no niggers.

Somebody could of left her to us, like in a will. Coral, you never did tell me what is her name.

Ah—Nazareth.

Hain't that a queer one.

Her old master was mighty religious, so she says. It's a religious word.

So tis. I recollect that Pa talked of Nazareth constant.

Dimly, when she thought of Nazareth at all, Mag thought of her not as kinky-haired Afric, but as a comely brown-faced girl with a soft voice and round small breasts. When rain boiled coldly against the sloping roof at night and made its *tunk-tunk-tunk* in pans spread around to catch leaks, Mag was glad that Coral had built a hut to shield Nazareth from the elements, and that she was well fed. Poor little critter, said Mag in the ignorant depth of her warm misshapen spirit.

The true Nazareth, doubled on his privy bed, sloped the oilcloth above him to ward off steady streams which raced through wide cracks of the structure. Oh, better than the stockade, he thought. Growing peace, the soundness engendered by unspoiled food and plenty of it . . . he stretched in them luxuriously, turned over on the other side, got himself wet in the process, put his feet where his head had been, his head where his cramped feet had been, readjusted the coat and lay sly and happy. He yielded to creature comfort as to a vice. For he knew, in any serious consideration, that he should be up and gone if he hoped to reach the Union lines in Florida or on the Georgia coast. Catch-dogs, straying past on the trail of some other fugitive, could find him here; they could tear the calf off his leg, as they had torn the calf of a man he knew as Frenchy in Andersonville. Frenchy was an unpleasant sight, brought back all reeking. People said that Wirz took a shot at Frenchy when he was treed but didn't hit him. Frenchy descended under threat of Wirz's gun, and then the dogs grabbed him.

Perhaps most of all Naz Stricker lived in fear that some wayfarer, feeling an ominous qualm of nature as he wandered the ragged fields, might spy that privy and decide to make use of it.

One day—it was a Sunday, and Coral was gone to Uncle Arch Yeoman's for tobacco and news—Nazareth sat with the peg-leg between his thin knees. Laboriously he was repacking wadding in the socket for the tenth time. As yet he and Coral had been unable to combine the necessary comfort and staunch support needed. Naz became aware of voices rising beyond the fence. How long the voices had spoken he did not know. Men's voices, and they were coming closer. Shivering as if with malaria, he peeped out and over a low place in the bushes. He saw two Negroes approaching steadily. One was long-limbed and ruddy, the other blacker, more squat. The taller carried a shotgun in his hands. If they continued on their present course they would reach the privy area within a few minutes. Nazareth could imagine the shotgun's blast directed against him, but was assured that he must act before the blacks came nearer. He arose immediately, snatched the shawl and draped himself, shoved the broken bonnet upon his head. His face was lost in scalloped depths of the bonnet. He dragged open the privy door and took slow step after slow step across the weedy area toward the chimney and blackened house timbers. He had turned his back toward the Negroes; every second he could feel shotgun pellets stinging through his carcass; then he heard a concerted cry and scampering, and knew that he was safe. He did not know how big Granny Rambo had been—that was a prime neglect on his part, not to ask Coral—but Naz concluded that she must have been of average old lady size, so he bent and shrank within the shawl. He reached the chimney and from its shelter he peered at the running Negroes. They were far across the briary field, scampering toward eastern pines south of the Tebbs place; the taller man held his gun on high as he fled silently with ungainly leaps; the shorter man lumbered behind, but neither of them looked back. Naz returned to the privy, removed his costume, and sat sweating in the chilly air. Alternately he was shaken by the quivering collapse of hysterical relief and by sheer youthful mirth. What a thing to tell Coral when he came.

Ira Claffey had considered driving to Americus to hear a sermon by Cato Dillard, but gave up the idea when Lucy took to her bed (she did this rarely, and then only when she was overtired and perhaps had caught cold). Harry, of course, was gone to the hospital. Trays were brought up and Ira ate eggs and fried mush with his daughter. Lucy had discovered a little diary she kept when a child, and she persisted in reading sections of this aloud to Ira; they laughed together, and wept

a little in their hearts. Ninny came up and said, That Jem and Coffee
ask please to speak with Mastah. She always spoke of her spouse as
That Jem. Ira went down to hear their petition. Old Leander had
already conducted one of his primitive services for the hands . . .
the Claffeys had heard the songs while they breakfasted. Now the two
younger slaves asked permission to desecrate the Sabbath with powder
and shot. Ira doled ammunition out to them, presented the ancient
shotgun which was kept especially for their use, and bade them stay
within the requisite two miles of the plantation boundaries.

He returned to Lucy's room and read to her a chapter from the
Confession of Faith, according to weekly custom. It chanced to be
Chapter Twenty-one, *Of Religious Worship, and the Sabbath Day,*
with its indirect castigation of Catholics in Section Two, and this they
found dull indeed. Lucy fretted, and Ira read only as far as Section Six.
He picked up the Bible, began to read the Twelfth Chapter of Romans,
more to the Claffey taste. *Be kindly affectioned one to another with
brotherly love . . . rejoicing in hope; patient in tribulation; continuing
instant in prayer.* A hullabaloo broke forth among the people below,
and looking down through the window Ira saw Coffee and Jem trotting
into the yard in a state of excitement, groaning and voluble. Something wrong, he said in interruption. I trust they haven't shot someone's mule. He put the Bible aside and hastened downstairs.

Seed her, Mastah. We seed her!

What is the matter with you, Jem? Speak quietly—

Deed they seed her. Deed they did. Oh, oh, oh, oh— Jesus, Blessed
Jesus, save us from the fury! With their eyes they seed her—

Coffee, stop making mischief. What did you see? Did you shoot
somebody with that gun?

No, Mastah, never even *shot* the gun. But we seed her walking, like
folks say.

Who did you see? I've a great notion to shake you, you lout!

Old Mistess Granny Rambo, a-walking and a-walking.

At her old place where she done burnt up!

Bonnet on her head, she come a-walking!

Mastah, we get down on our marrows and pray to the dear Lord,
but she was plain!

They seemed terrorized beyond sanity. Ira reassured them, said
that Granny Rambo did not walk, that they must have seen a buzzard
flying low, that they must have seen a mule in the bushes. Ira introduced these suggestions firmly. Yet both Coffee and Jem were convinced that they had witnessed the ghost in broad daylight, and that
was all there was to it. Ira took the gun from them (finding to his
horror that Coffee had somehow managed to cock the weapon while
in full flight) and persuaded them that if in fact they had seen Granny
Rambo there was nothing baleful about her. She would not follow

them home, she would not creep down their chimneys or carry off any children. As the people calmed he ordered Naomi to fetch cakes all round; she had baked a batch on Saturday, using substitutes for this and that, but the cakes were delicious and tasted of caraway and ground sunflower seeds. Soon the rest of the blacks were merry, twitting Coffee and Jem about their scare. The two slaves mumbled stubbornly with their mouths full of cake. In the end Ira was convinced that they had seen something other than an animal or a buzzard. God knew that they were familiar with both; and Ira had never observed them in such panic before.

He was mounting the stair when a thought made him halt, halfway up. Perhaps some dangerous vagabond was encamped on the deserted Rambo premises. Heaven knew that the country was filled with drifters; every town held its wounded; the hordes who had fled from Atlanta and other north central war-torn areas were not all people who could be taken safely to the heart of more fortunate communities. There was the natural modicum of prostitutes, thieves, uncertain and light-fingered wanderers of all sorts. Ira had heard rumors of stabbings, rapes, robberies; he believed that such crimes were an inevitable result of war's upheaval, but was determined to protect his own household and community insofar as he was able. Better have a look at the Rambo place. No telling who might lurk there.

He gave Lucy a description of the occurrence which she greeted with glee, but Ira made no mention of his own disquietude. Lucy thought that the slaves had suffered some infantile delusion. She and her father were out of the mood for Bible reading; Lucy did a little sewing, and sipped a glass of wine; then she said that she felt sleepy, and her father left her to the ministrations of Ninny, who came with a soapstone to place at Lucy's feet. Ira went downstairs, loaded a pistol and put it in his jacket pocket. He strolled idly down the lane, seeing only a few lounging off-duty soldiers along the way. It could be that a guard might have deserted, and was hiding out in the Rambo ruins. No, he would make tracks away from there. So would any prisoner escaped from the stockade. But better go and make sure.

Soon he approached the suspect area under cover of the gloomy chimney, working forward with caution, applying the best of his woodsman's facility to advance in silence. Examining the ground, he saw that weeds had been trampled and fresh vegetable rinds lay exposed. A shred of newspaper blew in the breeze. Edging closer quietly, Ira saw a heap of wood shavings and sawdust in front of the privy. He cocked the pistol; holding it ready in his pocket, he stepped to the door which flew shut with a shaking slam.

Ira said, Come out, or I'll shoot through the door.

Nazareth Stricker emerged, quaking and miserable, turned pale under the pitch which still dyed his skin.

Ira Claffey studied the youth, then took out his pistol and released
the hammer. You frightened my people, he said. They thought you
were a ghost.

Stricker was wearing his ruin of a cap with its corroded Second
Corps badge. . . . After a time Ira asked, When did you escape from
the pen?

Week or so ago.

Why didn't you travel farther?

Stricker was silent.

Where did you lose your hand?

Gettysburg.

. . . *It behooves their officers to be nonchalant, even to the point of
suicide, in disclaiming any attitude which might suggest that they were
not invulnerable to minié balls.* Did Suthy shoot off your hand before
he fell? Ira asked it in his soul while his mouth said nothing. You were
there. Did you kill my eldest? You were there.

How long have you been at Andersonville?

Came in with one of the first batches from Virginia.

More than a year.

Yes, sir, whispered Nazareth Stricker.

I don't understand why you squatted here.

Well, I was—tuckered. And a fellow gave me rations. And—

Who gave you rations?

A keen blue blaze shot from Stricker's deep eyes. Won't tell, he said.

Ira looked past the youth's legs and saw familiar objects scattered
on the privy floor and leaning against the inner wall. Those are my
tools. He understood before he spoke the words, he understood still
more as he uttered them. . . .

What mockery of battle now remains to be fought? Ira inquired of
himself. The *Albemarle* was long since destroyed. It was weeks since
the news of Fort Fisher had turned souls to lead. Ira wondered if
smoke still drifted from the ruins of Columbia . . . and General
Preston, of the Bureau of Conscription, announced that at least one
hundred thousand deserters had slid from the ranks of the Secessionist
army. Aleck Stephens was said to have crept home to Crawfordville;
people said that Early's forces were whipped and scattered; Sherman
was striding through North Carolina; it was told that Lee might withdraw the defense of Petersburg at any moment, and retreat toward
Lynchburg. A man found his way down from Richmond; he reported
troops rattling purposefully about the streets of the capital, impressing
every horse they could find. They were impressing horses in order to
collect the stores of tobacco: one shred of wealth left to the Confederacy. They would burn that tobacco if the Federals entered
Richmond— *When* the Federals entered Richmond—

Well, sir . . . Naz Stricker discoursed in monologue, and why should Ira care to listen to him? Whyn't you get it over with? You got a pistol. Whyn't you march me back where I belong?

In the end Claffey told him, Hold your tongue, my boy. He pushed past Stricker, looked into the little structure, and found what he had expected to find: the peg-leg-foot with cotton protruding from the cavity.

You've been making this for Coral. A hard task, one-handedly.

Oh, God. I must have given him away!

No, no, you didn't give him away. I'm Neighbor Claffey from across the way—I've known Coral since he wore skirts. He borrowed these tools from me.

Nazareth sat down on the privy step, folding his arms across his knees, hiding his face so that Ira could not see him as he cried.

Brace up, lad. You're not going back.

The gaunt face came up, greasy with tears, mouth sagging in disbelief.

Twould be tantamount to murder, said Ira sharply.

He stood for a few minutes, scrutinizing fields and woods to make certain that no one else was near, and then he ordered Naz back into hiding. He took Stricker's place upon the step and sat examining the peg, asking many questions which Stricker answered haltingly, lugubriously. It was obvious to Claffey that the boy must doubt him still. Small wonder. The smell of the stockade flowed around him suddenly, as it had drenched over Claffey acres for so long. Ira closed his eyes and shook his head; and then realized that he had done so, and thought with weak amusement of how Lucy would crow could she see him.

Where did you think to get the harness? he asked of Naz Stricker. The straps?

Coral thought his Ma had some old shawl-straps.

Those would never serve. Tell Coral that I have taken the thing home with me, when he comes. Do you both wait here for me, and keep out of sight. There may be other hunters abroad, for this is the Sabbath.

Ira added with grudging humor, And I should advise no more masquerading as Granny Rambo, in the bonnet and shawl which I saw there. The next person might shoot before he ran away.

He arose heavily and stood turning the contraption in his hands. We are whipped, he told the world.

Nazareth stared from concealment with a veteran's challenge. Guessed that you would be, from the first. You could never beat the Union.

That is now apparent. But all three of my boys died a-trying.

I'm sorry, sir, Naz muttered.

How sorry are you indeed? Ira wondered as he went toward the plantation, carrying the peg-leg. But the enfolding humanity which his own torture had instigated would not be denied; he must perform this charity, perform it in the face of law and military conscience.

It occurred to him before he reached home that Badger or Moses, invalided home from the army instead of turned to bones, might have done the same thing. Suthy . . . no . . . Ira feared that Suthy might have remained stiff-backed to the last.

How far off was—the last?

He went to his work-bench and finished repacking the padding in the socket, conforming carefully to the shape which the fugitive young Yankee had said must be retained. Painstakingly Ira upholstered the broad-headed tacks so that none of them would abraid Coral's hide. He cut strong straps of soft leather, and fastened the buckles into place, and punched the holes . . . one strap encircling the leg immediately below the knee, and fastened firmly to the staves; one attached to soft harness and encircling the leg immediately above the knee. That must be the way of it, Nazareth Stricker had said in his apprentice's erudition. It seemed odd to be performing a service for a wounded Yankee and for a wounded Confederate in the same act and in the same breath. Ira wished that he might make a hand for the Yankee boy; but—God knew—if the youth reached the Union lines safely he might in time acquire a hand of sorts.

There came only Jonas, seeking a whetstone, and he gazed in curiosity. What you do with that thing, please, Mastah?

It's a peg-leg for Coral Tebbs. He's done most of the work himself.

That poor young cripple soldier-boy, said Jonas.

In the afternoon, having disregarded his mid-day meal, Ira carried the artificial limb back to the Rambo site, lugging it in a grain sack. Coral Tebbs, scowling and frightened and sulky, was there with Naz Stricker. Like the other boy he found it difficult to believe that Ira Claffey could award such traitorous benevolence. Coral thought that if he were Ira he should wish to kill all Yankees in wholesale revenge. Ira had not lost a limb, he did not belong to the Lodge, he had not been fighting at that wheatfield place. Ira recognized their mutual attitude but said nothing in explanation, because he could not explain the whole thing, not even to himself. He could not say, Yes, once I too was a soldier. In Mexico. I was wounded painfully; I thought that I would lose my leg; for years I had to tie dressings about the wound each day, and let them fill up, and throw them away; until at last a surgeon's probe brought out the remaining loose bits of bone, and those bits had turned black as coal.

To be frank with himself, this was all beside the point.

Coral sat inert while they strapped the thing.

Don't become too ambitious all at once, mind! Ira added, Your knee is weak, your leg shrunken from disuse. You must go slowly. Use your crutches at first.

On a level patch close to the burnt relics Coral crutched solemnly back and forth, putting the heavy peg down cautiously, lifting it again, resting more and more of his bodily weight upon the stump. It caused him a degree of pain . . . it would all take time, but Naz Stricker had warned him of this again and again. Tentatively Coral slid his crutches out from under his arms and used them as canes to hobble with. Oh, the peg was heavier than he had thought it would be; he hoisted his leg in labor, he perspired, but persisted as in a trance. At last he stood in the lowest weeds, resting his entire weight on his good right foot and on the spindle thrusting down from his left leg. He spread his arms wide, and dropped the crutches from his hand. He stood crutch-less for the first time since he was wounded. His black eyebrows rose up. I'll be dipped in shit, he said.

Ira forgave him the vulgarity, he would have forgiven him anything. He turned away and busied himself with the grain sack he had brought. He produced some of Moses's old clothing: jeans trousers for wear in the forest, a rough brown jacket, a shirt and shoes and socks (the shoes were Badger's; Naz Stricker's feet had appeared to be more the size of Badger's), an old black hat.

I'd get out of this, he told the Yankee, as soon as possible. Wait for dark, then travel the railroad. There were guards at the bridges, but I hear they've been removed. But take care; it might have been false information.

Sir, I don't know how to thank—

Coral and I have our secret . . . it won't be long . . . as I said before, we are whipped. Ira repeated it under his breath. Whipped, whipped, whipped. Beaten down.

He took a fold of currency from his pocket. Fifty dollars Confederate. All I can spare. We are very short of cash these days. But it will help you to secure food.

Sir, God bless you.

Ah. He moves in a mysterious way . . . you know the song?

Yes, sir. Used to sing it up home in Pennsylvania.

Goodbye, my boys.

They mumbled their farewell, they stood united and wondering. Ira went home and found that Lucy was sleeping the afternoon away, she had not rested well during the night. But were she awake she might not have appreciated the texts which Ira pondered over in the library. Ruin was here, but she was young, she had a love.

The field is wasted, the land mourneth; for the corn is wasted: the new wine is dried up, the oil languisheth.

Be ye ashamed, O ye husbandmen; howl, O ye vinedressers, for the wheat and for the barley; because the harvest of the field is perished.

. . . Gird yourselves, and lament, ye priests: howl, ye ministers of the altar: come, lie all night in sackcloth, ye ministers of my God. . . .

Ira had no sackcloth, but he lay down all the same; he lay on the sofa and turned away from his dread past; and thought of the scrawny mixed future, but it was a peril, a bewilderment. He slept; he was lucky in having no dreams. He slept into the dusk.

You can always take to the woods, Coral Tebbs told Naz Stricker.

That's so. But I mean to travel by night solely, unless I come to complete wilderness.

Coral stood beside him in the dark. The two shapes bulked dangerously, sometimes teetering close together, sometimes drifting farther apart as if washed by winds, though no wind stirred. It was chilly. A bob-cat made a kill in the distant swamp, and screamed in the process; a few scattered dogs preached their immediate alarm.

Wish you could take this here haversack, but twould attract notice.

Why not? If you want to let me have it, Coral. I could be a Rebel soldier bound for home. Guess that's what I will be, though I don't much talk like it.

Then that saves putting spare rations in your clothes!

Coral passed the sack to Naz, and the Yankee slid the strap over his shoulder. Coral said, Looky, and Nazareth poked his head forward through the gloom to see the other youth poised on his true leg and his false leg, crutches upheld in his hands.

Don't you get too gay, Reb.

Shan't.

Coral.

What?

That Mr. Claffey gave me fifty dollars Confed. I'd like to go halves on that.

Coral Tebbs was strangling. Hell, I got Ma to see after me, and she's got enough and plenty. Right now, anyways. You'll need what little cash you got. Twill be slim pickings along the way, though I reckon niggers might help you. All they got in their heads these days is that cusséd Yankee freedom notion, dad blast them! And fifty Secesh hain't no fortune.

(He would say to his mother when at last he went to the house, Old lady, I fibbed my head off. . . . What you mean, you Coral? . . . Bout that wench. I didn't have no wench, I wasn't a-keeping no nigger girl down a cotton row nor no place else. Twas a Yankee, skun out of that stockade, and I've helped him away; and look what he made for me. . . . Coral! You helped a Yankee. You ought to be blown dead! My own flesh and blood, helping a Yankee! . . . Oh, shut up. Look at the pin he fixed for me! Week hence I'll throw these God damn crutches to the crows.)

Guess I'll get along.

Their hands trailed through the night. Long would Coral feel the

clasp on his own hand, long would Naz Stricker poke his way southward, choking as he went.

Look out for Home Guards, you bastard Yankee.

Don't stick that peg of yours down a gopher hole.

Now I just won't.

Very softly, *Foooorward*— They parted.

At first each could hear the crunching pace of the other, going away,
soon they could hear nothing. Coral Tebbs toiled homeward. Emotion-
ally he was profiting from war as some wise survivors profit. He had a
dim notion of knights. When he was small he had looked long at a
picture-book someone gave him, and there was a picture of knights
carrying shields, with visors lifted to show their faces; he could not
read the story, and no one had read it to him, but he remembered
the picture, and it spread before him now in the lone cold black. Naz
was a knight, so was he; oddly Ira Claffey joined them, and the dead
sons paraded behind; so did Jo Coppedge, Apostle Epperson, Darius
Voyles and the rest of the expired Rebels. He thought of the nigh-onto-
thirteen-thousand dead who had been buried from the nearby stockade,
or so Naz declared . . . they put on their mail and walked in his
imaginings, even though they were Yanks and so to be despised. There
was something in the concentration of death and peril which had
occupied his young years, which quickened his sensitivity to a degree
unbelievable. It was as if he walked stripped of flesh, tissues exposed,
blood open to the night. No one might understand what he felt, he
could not speak of it, there was no one to know.

He was only eighteen, for all the angry barbarous maturity which
had become his through suffering. Release from storming emotion
came to Coral. Crutches slipped, fell from his open clutch, he lay in
burs and pea-vines in his mother's dooryard, kneading crushed little
sheaves of wire grass in his large hands, sobbing, momentarily without
hope. God damn it, Naz, don't go way. But Naz was gone with not
even a star to lessen the night into which he walked.

LVII

The weather warmed for Lucy. Her father would not have wished that she go dreaming alone, nor would her husband. There were chores to be done . . . she knew that Pet and Extra would laze at tasks she had set them to, perhaps they might ruin the entire batch of summer candles, might forget to put in the beeswax. Lucy felt that she did not care. Again she had become a disobedient child, when in fact in childhood seldom had she been disobedient. Yet with the rest of humankind she found spice in the forbidden.

It was late afternoon. She went past cabins, over the rise and down the long gentle slope toward a steeper ravine of Little Sweetwater. Frogs were crunching in some low place already shadowed permanently, forgotten by the drifting sun. A breeze came; the young woman saw the brushes of each separate pine tuft painting erratically on far sky, never leaving paint to mark the sky. Soon Lucy's small shabby mended shoes were slipping among old cornstalks, stalks of a field now let go to weeds because there was not the strength within this population to work an additional field. The stalks were sad about it. How could corn stems—once firm, containing fluid—become so dispirited, leaning sodden? She wanted to say, Be of better faith, old plants. I feel sure that your descendants will one day push up proudly in this same place. There were relics of ancient cotton in an adjacent field; through all this time they had survived, as exhibits contained in a museum . . . through summers, the mass of rain coming down repeatedly, winter freezing stiff. Still they exhibited themselves amid more perishable reeds, and bitter flakes clung to the dry cotton plants, burnt to wire by age. In a swamp delicate new leaves had come out into the warmth—they were widening, showing red-lipped colors. Leaves on taller trees held the pale tender green of new pea-plants. It was a good season . . . one perspired when active, but grew chilly in breeze if jacket or shawl were removed.

O frogs in the swamp. How odd that there could be endearment and promise in such rocky stuttering. (Lucy's frogs were not of the variety which beleaguered Henry Wirz: frogs which jumped and ached in his miserable arm.) They were like water birds, and in solid dark of evening they would be speaking thin-voiced, high-pitched, their vociferous persistent wail and whistle would be suggestive of robins . . . early the following morning they would be calling still, even after chickens began to call, although the frogs' chorus would be thinner. Forever springs had affected Lucy Claffey, as one time she prayed that the promised beauty of religion might glorify her. Yet she could not find the same provocative majesty in contemplation of the Hereafter, or in God's works apparent. The teachings were favorable, they had value; they did not choke her throat as she was choked when she beheld brown-chocolate pads of water plants motionless on silent pools. . . . She went on beneath pines, down nearer the frogs. She was safe here from insult or intrusion, from any ugliness which her menfolks suggested might result from the proximity of a disordered ignorant undisciplined soldiery. In memory she was reminded of the night when she had flown from her room, the white long-ago moonlight when she ran with Deuce the setter, and—yes—she had told her father of that recollection many months before. They laughed about it, then they went on to the cottage where Laurel Tebbs lay. Remembrance came gasping. Lucy closed her eyes momentarily and put her left hand against a tree to steady herself, to draw sustaining quality from the ardent life of that tree. She remembered clearly the dreadful room, the girl with puffed face, the misery. She remembered how she applied the muscles of her hands to squeeze alum, with mortar and pestle . . . and there was the business of the syringe, the tall stooped man with queer face . . . how she had grown to love that face!— then and there, amid that very intrusion, the shared intimacy. It was an act symbolic of the dangers and disgust of the act of love when love was perverted into cruelty. Thus people were made into beasts; some of them might not wash off the stain. Lucy prayed in her heart that the color of that memory would be washed in time from Laurel's parched little spirit. Then the young girl might find such magnificence as overwhelmed Lucy now. It was a magnificence of soul and body intermingled.

She invoked forces of generosity, she wanted all women to share a joy that burst within her like the great verdant pain of Nature itself.

Did my mother feel that way when she was carrying me?

Carrying. Odd word, for the mite must be so tiny—but a bare speck, a speck.

Human, and therefore of God.

Of the Heavenly Kingdom. There is a Heavenly Kingdom here on earth. It's embraced me, it stretches before.

In a thicket a cardinal grosbeak danced amid those twigs which would hold him. He was wearing mating colors redder than raw flesh, showing zest which was in him until the eyes hurt beholding as his song came out, sometimes squeezed, sometimes spilled free and loose, he was aflame with song. He knew every flute and lute and played them. He piped on intimate pipes other males might not handle, blew a whistle other males might not know how to blow. You did not need to remember his song consciously; because it stayed, suspended in air, after he had whisked to last burning in other thickets.

Magnolias' steady green, back at the place, back at the place.

Before too long our child may run beneath them.

Other children may run.

. . . Am I wrong? She prayed, Am I doing a wicked thing in worshipping the power of woods and of winds, power of the sexes? Is it disproportionate, my intense savoring of these matters? Should I not set my mind more acutely upon the matter of Godliness for my child to come? What am I—pantheist, hedonist?

Her soul laughed even while the original strictness of conventional early teaching was rejected. She had rejected it first in lying with Harry. She could not tell which she loved the more: the original experience, or the recollection and frequent repetition thereof. A spectacle of bereavement and war stood taunting, accusing also; but it had been there before, been there long, it was so wide-spread as to have become meaningless.

. . . What of the South, what of my State? Poppy says we are going down so fast. Why do I not cringe and cry, give myself up to perpetual weeping because of the youth I loved as a girl, the brothers I knew and loved and lost, the mother who went to ruin in dismal fashion? Yet those people are no longer thick around me, they do not persist. It is almost as if they never existed in fact, but are now become legend. Duty and respect and affection will cause me to teach them to the children borne in my body, once they are born from my body, once they have their growing wits, prankish hands, fond eyes turning gladly to me for what sustenance I may give.

It has been so long-drawn a conflict, so degrading and caustic a war.

How many other wars have there been?

I cannot recite history, I do not wish to parrot knowledge previously gained.

I fear there will be more wars.

Yea, but there will be women alive then, as well as men. Strangely they may emerge from doom with lips still able to love, wombs still eager to receive the seed pulsed into them. Yea, I know this to be true.

True as God.

A blinding thought struck her. Perhaps this is God. These matters are what make God.

She turned and floated back toward the plantation. Feel like I'd been to church, she told herself. And how Uncle Dayto might knit his brows over such an affirmation!

A squeaking undercurrent of tiny unidentifiable birds—warblers, no doubt—hid ahead among mats of vines, danced their way north as she

came on. Soon she would reach the black people's cabins, the dark
life of blacks flowing. She would pause and appreciate the garden,
look at bright lettuce; she would appreciate even crinkled leather of
old collards standing tall beyond. There would be her flowers (she
had so little time to spend with them). Yet perennials were hearty . . .
there would be japonicas to dazzle. She would take a single japonica
to put before Harry's plate, and say that she had found not a violet,
and hoped that someday he would fetch violets to her.

Here, she thought. Her hand went up to touch the fine-spun hair.
He loved me here, loved me and my hair. He has worshipped and
gladdened my lips, nostrils. His strong fresh male tongue has played
its game with the curl of my ear. My breasts, he has known them, will
know them again. Our child will know them, more children to come
will know them. And that other holy warm glistening orifice of my
body—that province which we women guard as we would guard all—
He has known that, occupied it well. He will know it again. Oh, dear
God in Heaven—again, again. One day there will be a mighty pain, and
the child shall emerge. Then my dear one may know me again . . .
know me long, know me while life continues to run.

I have never set myself to be a prophet. Now I burn unseen incense
in my ritual, cry my prophecy: this local ugliness shall cease. Shortly
the last scarecrow columns will come dragging from the gate; wagons
will freight out the last of the dead, wagons freight the last of the
living. I'll be given a glory. To me will be awarded power of the
conquering rescuing army.

Sakes alive, I shouldn't desire the power of *Yankees!* Yet I shall
hold it, and with it release those cords which have bound a burden
to the back of my brave dear one: a horny thorny pack of stench and
wickedness will slip from his shoulders, twill thud and be forgotten.
We'll love and cry and weep for joy and relief when it falls.

Sounds of the ragged forest fell behind her. I must know Nature
better, she thought, far better than I do. For there's urgency waiting,
the urgency of teaching my children.

Yet she knew that she might love Nature less if she knew her better.
For, like the capricious woman Nature was, a portion of her enfolding
charm lay in mystery.

Far overhead the pines were saying Hush in a determined admonition whenever long high wind moved against them.

LVIII

Jonas found Ira Claffey in the implement shed and said gently, Mastah, please hear me.

With sinking heart Ira looked into the grave brown face, and noted how afternoon sunlight pierced through the open door and found silver in grubby twists of wool on Jonas's head; ah, there was more silver, more each month; Jonas was aging as Ira was aging, though Jonas was believed to be not more than forty. . . . Twice Ira had come upon the Yeomans' mighty Scooper talking to Claffey people with furtiveness. The second time Scooper made off nonchalantly when Ira approached (as if he had merely stopped to pass the time of day). Scooper was bound to be the trouble-maker in this particular neighborhood, just as there must be trouble-makers, thousands, scattered elsewhere.

What is it, Jonas?

Mastah, we wants to walk off.

Who is we?

Me and Extra, Mastah.

Do Jem and Coffee wish to go as well?

Don't know bout that. Spect maybe so, maybe not.

Ira had assembled the people in front of Leander's door a few hours earlier, after Cato Dillard stopped by to confirm the news of Johnston's surrender. Original impulse and lifetime habit dictated that Ira should cope with any unpleasant task promptly; he should slay or bury that which must be slain or buried; he must not keep a rabid dog on the premises, he must delve with shovel and quicklime when a monstrosity was found with birds above.

He said to the people, Our General Johnston has surrendered to the Yankees, which means that the war is practically over. A few bands of Confederates may hold out until the death; I pray that they will not; we are defeated by the North, by the Federal Government, do you understand? All three of the young masters are dead, as you people know—

Promptly they began to moan, and Old Leander, nearly blind, propped in a cushioned chair beside the door, announced that he had seen the young masters in the night; he spoke of raiment—

Hush, all of you! I am talking, you hear?

When the blacks had fallen silent, Ira continued: Your mistress also
is dead. Miss Lucy may be here for a time, but I suspect that soon
she'll remove elsewhere; thus I shall be alone. I have little to tempt
me to remain here, myself; still it is my home, always has been, and I
know not where else to go. Now, as to you people: you have been
slaves all of your lives, you were born slaves, I had expected that you
would die in bondage. But the Nationals say—and they have won, they
have whipped the Secessionists, they have whipped Georgia, whipped
us—

His voice broke suddenly. All the black women had their faces
buried in their aprons except Extra; she was staring fixedly at Ira,
eyes bulging, nostrils distended, mouth open and dripping.

He continued, The National Government says that you are free.
You belong to no one except yourselves, and to God above. I may no
longer order you about except as one man orders another because he
is the supervisor, the boss; thus he orders him. But no longer as master
and slave.

Naomi burst out with a shrill, But you *is* our mastah—

I *was* your master; no longer; the Federal law says that you are
free, and now the Federal law prevails, it rules here. But I can still
be your employer, and as my employees you may still live here as
you've always done—dwell in the same cabins, eat the same food,
live as you have done before. But now I must pay you wages.

There was a general beaming as they began to appreciate this
statement. You pay us real money, Mastah? Cash money? We get hard
money?

If you work for me, and do your work well, you will receive real
money. But if you do not do your work well, done as I wish it done,
then I'll get some other people to work for me, to live in the houses
where you lived before. You will be turned out. I shall need to employ
other people in your stead. . . .

Old Leander was nodding pontifically throughout and he said
clearly as Ira paused: My children do work like you bid, Mastah. Yes
sir, I *make* them do it. We all belong to you, like it say in Scriptures.

Ira said, I provided for you people, just as I provided for the many
we had here before the war. You had no thought of the morrow;
I thought of that for you. If you were sick, I doctored you myself;
if I could do no good for you, and Miss Lucy could do you no good,
then I fetched the doctor, and I paid him money to make you well.
As with you, Jonas, when you broke your hip whilst lumbering; as
with you, Coffee, when the cotton bale toppled on your foot long ago;
as with Naomi and her tumor, and the doctor took it out and healed
her. You were clothed and fed, fed better than most black people,
even in parlous times. No one has ever gone hungry on my place. Is
that not true?

True! It true! You good mastah, Mastah—

But now the law says that you must take charge of yourselves. If I am to pay you wages, then with your wages you must buy food and clothing; for I cannot afford to give you these things if I am to pay you money. If you ask me to give you meat and meal, shoes and stockings, then must I charge them against you. You are to sell me the work you do, and I am to pay you wages; if I give you fruit or corn or bacon or a shawl or a blanket, then I shall write it down in a book, each time, and I must show that book to officers who might come and wish to see it, to make sure that I am paying you wages as the law says. And— And I may not keep you on the place against your will! If one of you wishes to leave, he may go elsewhere. You are free men and women and children.

Old Leander declared feelingly that he didn't want any old Yankee law. He said that all this was none of the Yankees' business.

Ira's heart had gone from him as he spoke. Enough, enough, I can say nothing more; I cannot make them understand this thing which has befallen; indeed, do I understand it myself? I fear not.

He managed to tell them that he would explain further, when and if they wished further explanation; in the meantime he must examine his accounts, find out exactly how much money he had, how much he might reasonably expect to make off the plantation, and thus what wages he could offer; and if he said eight dollars or ten dollars, if he spoke of ninety-six dollars a year, then he would try to explain to them exactly what ninety-six dollars might be and what it would buy.

Ira went to his desk and sat among ledgers until he was half blind, until his head rang each time he moved it. He unlocked his iron cash box and counted currency contained therein. He placed Confederate scrip in one pile, the few bits of gold coin in another, the silver in another; he had no greenbacks, the law had said that he might have none, and he had obeyed as few other individuals obeyed. He owned however a sheaf of bills, some issued by the Central Railroad and Banking Company, more by the Georgia Railroad and Banking Company, and these he had held since before the war began. Thank God that the best of the old Georgia banks had been connected with railroads. Ira knew that in 1861 his own State had a greater mileage of railroads than Alabama and Mississippi put together. He had heard that these bills were selling at the North for from seventy-five to ninety-five per cent of their par value. Thus he was not at the moment penniless; he might be penniless in another year if he did not manage cautiously. He shoved his small riches back into the cash box without counting all of the piles, locked the heavy box and put it in its cupboard, locked the cupboard. He went outside with a swimming head, trying to clear head and spirit in the ministration of sun and garden smells, for the day was fair.

Therefore he was in the implement shed, reassuring his hand with the feel of his favorite knife, and thinking vaguely of plum weevils, when Jonas approached.

So you and Extra are determined to go. To what place?

Mastah? murmured Jonas as in a dream, and his eyes were dreaming also, they were intense within narrowed lids.

I said, where are you going?

Savannah, Mastah.

But you've never been there. Why do you wish—?

Get all our back money, Mastah.

Back money? Damn it, said Ira fiercely (almost never had he allowed himself to curse before his blacks; even more rarely did he curse them directly), you damned idiot, what are you talking about?

Scooper say you owe us wage now, Mastah. All time you own us, you owe us wage every day. You own me how long, Mastah? He inquired as one making a most delicate plea.

So Scooper's at the bottom of this!

Scooper he done gone already.

Gone where?

Savannah. Done left at sun-up, take his woman, take all the children.

What? Had he a mule, a rig?

No, Mastah. They a-walking. Old Miss Barney Yeoman, she say she not give him no cart, no nothing. She say she not owe him no wage. But Atlanta niggers, they come through lass fortnight, they walking on the railroad, and they say all our old mastahs owe us money for every day we work, and they get that money in Savannah.

Jonas, you're my best hand. I don't want to see you believing this silly thing. Tis an untruth from start to finish! No one owes you money, not one copper cent—not until now. From this time forth—

Scooper say them Atlanta niggers say white folks ain't got no money give us now. But Linkum got money, and he send folks pay us all them dimes, them dollars!

Jonas, Lincoln is dead. He was murdered at the theatre! He—

Could Jonas appreciate a cruel fact so quickly (even now, after only a fortnight) turned into history? He could not appreciate it. Since he stood in the first sturdiness of young maturity Jonas had been owned by Ira, had been dutiful and obliging, had been able to cope with the complication of more demanding tasks better than most slaves. He had trusted Ira, appealed to him, begged before him, begged to have Extra as his wife, had had her awarded to him as a prize when Extra admitted her willingness. In an exceedingly humble way he had shared the rise and fall of Claffey fortunes as a dog might share: a fine beef bone with meat attached, on occasion—scrawny table scraps when the fare was thin. He lamented honestly when the stroke of death fell, bragged about the prowess of young Claffeys when he saw them in uniform, wept afresh when the stroke came down again, wept sincerely again, remembered with pride how he had pulled the toddler Lucy out of a Sweetwater marsh when she went floundering there, loved to read the time from a plated watch which Ira gave him as tribute for this feat, loved to impress his fellows by reading the time even incorrectly. Jonas had tended Deuce when the puppy was near to dying of distemper, had volunteered with Extra to assume parental duties when little Dick was orphaned—he and Extra had volunteered kindly, they did not have to be ordered to take the charge. Ira had never considered selling Jonas and Extra and their children as he had sold so many when it became necessary. Extra was indigenous to the place, Jonas very nearly so.

Yet he would heed the word of the massive bully Scooper, the word of idle strangers; and solely because they were black words, so now to be considered as gospel.

If old Linkum dead, Scooper say they got other folks give us money—

Jonas, no longer are you a slave. As a master I may no longer forbid you to go. But do you believe I am your friend?

You always good to us, and Jonas began to cry.

Then as your friend I forbid you to go!

Scooper say— Jonas blubbered softly, unintelligibly.

Don't mention Scooper to me again, you hear?

Mastah, we wants to walk off.

Ira cursed savagely. And, I presume, take your children with you? Take Bun and little Gracious—?

Mastah, they our—children. They ain't belong you no more, like you say. They *our'n.*

What of Orphan Dick? He's not your child, you shan't have him.

No—Mastah. Pet and Coffee—they say they—look after Orphan Dick.

So it seemed that Coffee, whose intelligence was less than that of Jonas (at least that portion of intelligence essential to the performance of successful labors)— And Jem, the lightest-brained of the three— They were not going, they would not walk off with their wives. This course gave Jonas grief, but he stood here now as a man, not a chattel; and this very transformation was a grief in itself. It did not kill the soul but it hurt the soul, and the wound was in Jonas's eyes as he cried.

For the last time, I tell you it is nonsense, nigger nonsense, you hear? You couldn't find your way to Savannah! How will you feed Extra and the children, where will you put them at night?

Reckon we sleep out by a fire.

And it rains, it blows, you're all drenched, you have no roof over you, nothing to eat!

But when we *gets* to Savannah—

This is his illusion, try to take it from him, you can't, he adheres to it like a seed in a boll. The shiny table is spread with dollars, dimes, quarters, gold. Linkum or Linkum's ghost or deputy sits behind the table and calls the roll. He says, What your name? and Jonas say Jonas, and Extra say Extra. Yes, Jonas. Certainly, Extra. I got all this hard money here for you! Clinkety-clink in the money bag. Whole great big bagful money you got now, and never have to work no more. Now you walk in town like white folks, go in the store where once white folks bought Christmas for the black people— But now you are just like white folks, and Freedom done come, this the day of Freedom, Jubilee time! Now you just like white folks, got great big bagful dimes and solid gold, you buy Christmas for yourself any day you wish—

There was nothing left but prayer. Ira heard himself telling the glistening stubborn brown face, I shall go into the house and pray that you do not go. I have appealed to you to no avail. I'll appeal to the Lord.

He did go into the house and immediately encountered Lucy, who was smiling wanly and gesturing with her finger toward her lips; and this reminded Ira of Veronica, naturally, although Lucy did not much resemble her mother in appearance. Poppy, let's be still as mice. My dear Harry is asleep on your sofa. He just came in, and I put him there —and soothed him— Praise be, he's fast asleep! Nineteen hours at a single ssstretch— On this last word her voice was shaking.

Lucy, the Yankees will soon be taken away.

But do the Federals know that many sick are still here?

Of course, child, of course they know. They'll be along soon.

He told her of Jonas and Extra, the weird belief which tempted them. Lucy's eyes snapped and she went flying out across the yard; but when she came back much more slowly, and with heavier steps, she said that it was no use, the people were packing their duds. Extra had clung to her and wet her old gown with tears, but it was no use; these two dreamers were free, they were bound to go dreaming along the byways.

When do they go? At once?

I persuaded them to wait until the morning. I told them they should have baskets of food to tote along. It seemed that, if they slept on it— Don't you think, Poppy, if they slept on it—?

I fear tis no earthly use.

Later Ira had a thought that Leander might prevail upon his daughter Extra to prevail in turn upon her husband— This was senseless: Leander had not enough strength left to persuade or adjure. He had been ailing for years, declining for months, Cousin Harry guessed that he suffered enlargement of the spleen, for the old creature wore an uncomfortable protuberance like pregnancy.

Harry Elkins allayed Ira's perplexity if not his doubts for Jonas and Extra and the two children. Late in the evening the young man awoke from exhausted slumber, and Lucy fed him cold bacon and cabbage salad, and warmed up a pot of soup over blazing twigs in the library's fireplace (no longer was there a drop of oil on the plantation, so she might not use her little lamp). Ira came in from a limping plunging walk; he had watched the crescent moon go down, had wandered nearly to the place where Veronica had babbled in slime; then Ira turned back in sadness if not in terror. He thought that there was no terror left. Of what might he now be afraid?

Daughter Lucy told you of my people, Coz?

She did.

Ah, that stupid Jonas!

You know, came Harrell Elkins's mild grating words, I believe I know why he's bound and determined to leave.

Ira bent closer, frowning. Then tell me.

Because he's the only soul upon the place who's smart enough to realize that he is free! He and Extra, perhaps. She was Lucy's playmate, sometimes even her confidante; think you not that it's possible that her association with Lucy has developed her imagination more than the other wenches'? And often I've heard you say that Jonas was smart as tacks. On certain subjects, pertaining—say—to husbandry? Then, you see—

Elkins's head swayed forward and Lucy pressed her shoulder against his to sustain him.

You see, he *knows* that he is free. The two of them know it. They have—you might say, graduated—into a state of rapture without bound. Thus they may see sights, hear sounds, tread among visions never glimpsed or heard or trod among by the other blacks. The notion of Linkum and the money to be given away— They don't believe it actually. They but pretend to.

Harry was silent for a while, so were Ira and Lucy. It serves as an excuse for this seeming descent into starvation and homelessness, said Elkins at last.

Ira gazed long at the young pair through candlelight. If what you say is true, there might be a hope for the future.

Hope? echoed Lucy. For whom?

For black people. All of them, in every place. I mean education. I had not thought of it in that way before; and regarded folks who preached such education as either vicious or demented. But if our slaves are to be set adrift, might it not be wiser and safer for all— for them, for ourselves—to develop their minds, to aid them in developing whatever power might lie within them? Suddenly I feel that it might.

Ira considered this revolutionary departure until he slept belatedly. He thought of it in many phases and ramifications. Would the National Government establish schools quickly for these dogged capricious beasts now designated as humans? The Government should. Our Government, he said very nearly aloud. No longer is it Their Government. What's in a possessive pronoun? Should I assemble the remaining people tomorrow and set them letters upon slates, and bid them copy? His last conscious thought was a thanks given to Cousin Harry. Son-in-law or not, Ira would always think of him as Cousin Harry.

Some two hours after sunrise Jonas and his family presented themselves at the rear yard gate to speak farewells. Elkins was off to the hospital an hour earlier, but Lucy and Ira came down and stood to receive embraces and handclasps while the rest moaned and muttered beyond the palings.

You will be delayed a trifle, Jonas, in departing.

Jonas's eyes widened and his nostrils twitched. You could see that he rose instantly to the willingness for rebellion.

For you are to harness Tiger to the cart. The two-wheeler which little Bun drives about his work.

Mastah? came the guttural shudder of the Negro's voice.

For you are to take Tiger with you. I'm lending him to you, with the cart. I shan't have children trudging, stone-bruising themselves over the miles. . . .

Also Ira had prepared a paper, he had risen in gray light to prepare it. To Whom It May Concern: This will certify that I, Ira Claffey, citizen of Sumter County, Georgia, in recognizance of the laws of the United States of America now prevailing since the recent surrenders by Confederate States' commanders, have given permission to my former slave, Jonas, now a freedman, to proceed with his wife Extra and children Buncombe and Gracious, also formerly my slaves and now freed, to a destination of their own choosing. Warning is given herewith that no person shall interfere with Jonas and his family so long as they proceed peaceably, or attempt to arrest or persecute them, or offer them bodily harm or threat, under penalty of such retaliation as I shall assuredly bring within a court of law, or, if necessary, outside the law. These people have the protection of whatever law now applies to the State of Georgia, and have my own protection as well. The mule and cart in their possession are my property and must be treated as such. Signed by me on the first day of May, 1865. Ira Claffey. Witness: Harrell Elkins, Surgeon, P.A.C.S.

The paper was folded, pinned within the pocket of Jonas's shirt, and baskets of food were put aboard the cart. Ira gave Jonas an old tobacco bag with strings drawn tight, containing dimes and quarters. He thought that Confederate scrip might suddenly be of no value whatsoever, but feared to have Jonas exhibiting dollars in some wayside store; quickly he might be robbed, indeed probably he would be robbed sooner or later. So goodbye to the Tiger mule and the cart as well. But could Ira sit down to a mid-day meal and think of these people wandering with empty bellies, the children wailing? No, no, his arm must reach to feed them over whatever distance it could reach, his wheels and hoofs should bear them forward.

Bear them to what place? They went squeaking down the lane, the blacks waved and jigged and shouted, Coffee announced that he knew which side of his bread had the grease on it, he wasn't going Savannah or no such place. Orphan Dick tried to run after the cart, and was brought back by Pet and jailed; but still he screamed; he thought that Extra was his mother, he remembered no other mother. . . . Bear them to a gaunt freedom wherein the free were never fed, wherein the free suffered a captivity worse than the worst of slavery itself? Again Ira thought of slums in long-ago New York, he was forced to close his eyes against the thought, fling it out of his brain.

Man in blue coat, he got gold buttons on he coat, ha, ha, ha; he got that jubilee money for every day we slaves. Mistuh Soldier Man, you tell me where I find Linkum, like folks say? Please, Mistuh White Man, sir, this here road take us Savannah? . . . No, I ain't run off—I *walk* off—my own mastah, he Mistuh Ira Claffey, I got paper say so right here.

What protection, what interest, what provender? The storm of May might rage . . . but where would they be when June thunders came booming?

I try not to think of them, said Lucy.

But they would go.

Shouldn't you have held them here?

How?

Of course you could not. . . . Extra tattled to Ninny, Poppy. She told her that if they found short commons, they'd be back. She'd counseled Jonas so.

And would they find the way?

Poppy, let me work with you today. There's much to do within doors as always; but somehow I just naturally can't direct Ninny and Pet and Naomi today. Are you killing plum beetles again? Let me put on my old gown and help you.

Very well. I shall save the fattest *Conotrachelus Nenuphar* for you. Ugh.

And mind, Miss—excuse me, *Mrs.*—Florence Nightmare, you're not to doctor wounded weevils.

Oh, Poppy, I'll *squash* them.

The sudden departure of his daughter Extra was the finish of Old Leander. He mumbled gloomily about it, refused food, tried to walk down the road in his shirt-tail, was helped back tottering and soon lay unconscious. He died quickly. They buried him in the slaves' plot adjoining the Claffey graveyard, the first free Negro to lie there.

LIX

Captain Ox Puckett gone, everybody gone; the engines of passing trains operated by strangers who did not know the Widow Tebbs, who sent no jovial whistle toots piercing in salutation through walls of the house. Hulsey gone, Quillian gone, Wingo gone, Camp gone, Isbell gone, all the Confederate soldiers paroled and gone off to their homes. The memory of the Widow Tebbs was confused but it was thronged, her past was a pushing active mingling of male feet kicking high, thin or fleshy male arms gripping, some of them hurting her (her standard objection and warning to such customers as these was, Now, mister, you please to take it more easy. You're a-hurting me, and if you don't quit a-hurting me I'm a-going to kick you, and I surely do know where to kick). She did remember how she used to call Isbell Is-a-belle; it was a joke between them, a small joke which her small mind could enjoy. Middlebrooks gone, Deadwyler gone, Strozier gone, Judge gone. The nameless gone, the ones she addressed merely as Bob, Jo, Fat, Bully, Baby, Frankie, Freck, Goose, Pop, Dick (he liked to have her call him Dick, but she did so with reluctance because the use of the name reminded her of her long-dead husband, Dickwood Tebbs, and she had no jolly memories of Dick Tebbs). Gone and paroled, trudged off with tattered haversacks swinging, gone away gun-less, saying that it was a hundred and seventy miles to Home and by God they surely did wish they could catch a ride on a wagon. Defeat and emptiness and neglect and loneliness and defeat and improvidence and defeat and defeat pounded hard against the ragged landscape, no matter how porcelain blue the sky on some fair days, how tender green the pines.

Listlessly Marget Tebbs stirred at her pot of stockpeas, and she felt a drudgery in even the simple unrewarding task of searching bare or littered shelves, hunting for salt, finding no salt.

I do wish, she said to Coral.

Huh?

Wish we had a chunk of meat to put into this mess of peas. Misfortune that we ate up all the chickens already.

Coral was out on the porch, Flory was gone to the depot to try to beg tobacco from passing Unionists. Flory had learned to chew while he was with the Reserves; now he had no tobacco, and there was no money in the house. Zoral was playing train in the yard. Coral came clump, step, thud, step, clump across the warped flooring and halted in the doorway.

You mean to say all that there fat-back is gone?

Twasn't much left, sonny. Flory and I had it to our breakfast.

Whilst I was a-hunting, and you didn't save me a smidgin!

I did trust, Coral, that you'd fetch home some game.

God damn, I never met up with no game.

I smell something awful, the widow said, wrinkling her plump little nose.

By gum, so do I. Coral went outside to investigate and a moment later hooted with rage and disgust, and there sounded a scream from Zoral. Coral shouted, I'm throwing it over behind them bushes, and don't you dast bring it back! Zoral crawled to his den under the house and lay kicking in fury.

He had him an old possum, Coral reported when he came back. Like he's always hauling them dead chickens around, playing like they're cars and he's a engineer.

Dead possum? The widow clucked, angry yells still rose through the floor boards, and finally she was compelled to stamp heavily to claim the child's attention. You Zoral! You stop that caterwauling right this minute or I'll throw water on you like I done the other day.

Zoral stopped.

Dead possum! Hell, he was fat as a skinned horse two days in the sun. Wish I could have met up with a live possum.

Well, said Mag in resignation, least the meat would be stringy at this season.

Coral said, I swear he's Satan cut to size.

Who, sonny? That there possum?

Possum, hell! That blame Zoral of your'n. Know what he done this very morning? I come out: there he was, big as life, standing on the well-curb, peeing down the well. I give him a lick he won't forget.

Oh, sonny! The widow added musingly, But I'm truly glad you done it, for he might have fell in and drownded himself.

I wasn't agonizing about that no way! I just don't want to drink no Zoral pee.

The Widow Tebbs sighed. Guess we can't blame poor little Zoral too much. You know, sonny, the gentleman caller I always took to be his daddy— He was a queer piece sure enough. I don't mind his name now, but he tolt me he used to work in a circus; and first off I liked that, count of all the red and spangles and solid gold carriages and truck. But guess what he done. He said he bit the heads right off of chickens. It fair to turned my stomach, but he just laughed.

She found a few splintery scraps of cinnamon on a high shelf where they had lain long forgotten behind a dusty bottle half full of castor oil and another of coal oil. She stirred cinnamon among the bubbling cow-peas, it would give the vegetables flavor of a sort.

This was not a fair day, clouds were solid above but creased and rolled, turning from tannish to ugly brown beyond the somber tree-swept horizon. Coral returned to the door and sniffed the breeze darkly. Dad burn, I just fear for a whirlwind, day like this.

Don't talk so, sonny. I mind how a hurricane took the roof plumb off our house when I was a girl.

I said whirlwind. Hain't no hurricanes in Maytime.

Well, maybe twas a whirlwind. I wasn't more'n six at the time.

Hadn't never lain with your first man, said Coral in good humor. Not till you was seven.

Coral, that hain't no way for a young man to address his Ma!

Well, maybe not till you was eight. He said suddenly and in a strictly different tone, Reckon I'll walk over Claffey way.

He loved to say, I'll walk, walk here, walk there. The meager squeezed but determined face of Naz Stricker rose before him each time he said the word walk. He thought of Naz Stricker, laboring doggedly off into black space, into the sky itself, into strange Northern cities and villages, walking solitary on a homeward path past over-hanging barns. Maybe one day Naz would write him a letter, and Coral could read a little, maybe he could read the letter. If not, maybe his mother could spell it out for him. If she couldn't, Mr. Claffey would read the letter.

Why you going over to Claffeys', Coral?

Oh, I want to talk some business. I been pondering it.

The widow said, My, I just don't cipher no way what business you could be speaking to Mr. Ira Claffey.

There was a note like eagerness in Coral's voice, that tone usually so disapproving, grim, strung with bitterness. Might as well tell you what I got on my mind. Some of Mr. Claffey's niggers have gone off already, though they might come back; but that leaves him short of hands. And you know Old Leander died, for I tolt you I walked past whilst they was a-burying him. Well. Mr. Claffey's got all that big garden in, like he always has planted, with just plain oceans of collards and carrots and onions and yams and Christ knows what all.

Mag smiled happily at the mere mention of these delectable things. You mean maybe you might ask him for a mite of garden truck?

God damn, old lady, did you hear me say ask? By God I'm a man, and by God I hain't no beggar like that little Joe-Brown's-Pet-Snot-Nosed Flory of your'n. I can work for what I fetch home.

Coral! You mean—work on his land? Like one of his niggers been doing all the while?

Reckon I could wield a hoe if'n he showed me what he wanted hoed

up or down. And lots of raising of garden truck you got to do hunched
on your marrow-bones.

I never! Just like a nigger—

Plenty white folks got to get out and dig, these days. I seen that
nephew of the old Biles a-raking and a-digging, and he was a officer
in Cobb's Legion.

Mag imagined a good stew, vegetables bouncing and turning in
broth, and plenty of salt and pepper; and she thought of vinegar to
put on greens, too, for she despised greens without vinegar. You know,
Coral, we been faring just like them Yankees what was in the stockade,
ever since the soldiers was sent away. Scarcely nothing to bite nor
break.

Well I know, old lady.

He sighed, he thought of days of plenty, winter days, he thought of
ham. So I reckon I'll walk over and put it to him boldly.

You might even be keeping us—

She sighed. Stead of me a-keeping us. Putting victuals on our table
for us, Coral! And Zoral's so puny all the while, just punier and punier.

Mag added brightly, You know, Mr. Ira Claffey is a real gentleman
and kindly too. If'n it struck his fancy he might give you a mite of
meat to go along with what garden truck you earnt.

If I go to doing a nigger's work on the Claffey place, said Coral
ominously, that God damn Flory is going to perform his share of toil.
I don't aim to feed him free out of hand.

Reckon Flory'd be willing. But you'd have to set him to the task
and keep him to it.

By God. The boy spoke with relish. I'd admire to do that.

He went clump-stepping across the porch, stepping across the yard.
Mag stiffened when he was near the railway, for sound of his whistling
came floating back to her. Vaguely she was amazed, she thought a
stranger must be there, she was not accustomed to hearing Coral
whistle. He had whistled constantly, with little birdy warbles, before
he went to war. He had whistled a time or two in the winter, when
she thought he was keeping a black girl in the woods. She thought, I
do love pretty music, and had a wish to go to The Crib and turn on
the music box; then she remembered sadly that the music box was
broken at last.

Pursley gone, Carden gone, Almond gone, Swancey gone. Mag owned
a soiled cloth purse decorated with glass beads and dried melon seeds
strung together in a manner she thought beautiful. In this purse she
had kept money, hiding the purse in various places about the house
during those seasons when she possessed greenbacks and scrip. But the
ragged bauble mocked her now, empty and cast aside beneath a bed,
Zoral had played with it, the beads and seeds were coming off. It was
not solely empty purse and destitution which taunted. It was the lone-

liness, the rust of the machine in which she was dressed, the bones and tissues and fluids surrounding her spirit, the body—so active and abused by over-employment. Yet abuse became a long necessity, and Mag had thrived on the juices (clean or tainted, and so all the clean were tainted eventually) poured within her.

She looked through the open door and saw her youngest child streaking across the yard. Cunningly he had come out from under the house and sought to retrieve the dead possum and resume his freighting, his imaginary railroad play, once Coral was departed. Either Coral was returning without ever having reached the Claffey place, or else a stranger approached; nothing else could have caused Zoral to scoot to refuge with such celerity.

Mag stepped into open air and saw not one stranger but two. They were in uniform, they wore blue pants with yellow stripes, short jackets piped with yellow. They sauntered between wheel ruts, glancing up at threatening clouds; one man was smoking his pipe, one carried a tough green weed in his hand and flicked this switch idly against his leg as he strolled.

The widow wished that she were properly dressed. She wished that she was wearing her poplin gown, her blue one, she wished even that she was wearing her wrapper with torn ribbon bows. Hastily she touched her hair.

Howdy, she said from the doorway when the soldiers were a rod away and still coming closer.

Hello, lady. . . . Good day. . . .

It does look like rain. Maybe like we might get a whirlwind?

The taller of the two was chuckling. He said, Guess we scairt your little boy, lady. He went under your house, hot blocks, minute he saw us coming.

They were slender, tight belted, they were young but not too young, caps were worn at jaunty angles on the close trimmed brown head and the longer-haired yellow head, the men walked with the leisurely grace of assured people enjoying a moment of holiday. They were well fed, well booted, the great flaps of their holsters curled beside their belts, one wore a haversack slung from his shoulder, he had a wide sliced scar on his cheekbone and bending down into his neck, the other man affected a well brushed mustache, they were young, not too young.

Mag let her hand steal across her faded calico bosom. My, I wasn't expecting no company. Would have tidied myself.

Lady, we ain't company. Just a couple of old coffee coolers and blackberry pickers spreeing around for a couple hours!

Said the widow, I do believe you two are Yankees. You talk so queerlike.

Ain't nothing else, lady. Fourth U. S. Cavalry.

What we want, missis—

They said that to put it baldly they were skirmishing for a bottle of liquor. They had been working hard and traveling far, and they didn't have to report to Captain Noyes until five o'clock, and what about a bottle of mountain dew?

Hain't no mountains hereabouts. Mag's loose soft mouth was smiling, and a slow dream began to occupy her eyes.

Oh, call it bog juice, bug juice, bull juice, mule juice, white mule or brown mule or red-eye or forty-rod: it was all the same. But not like we got up in Macon, said the sharp rapid voice of Corporal Nevis, the man with the scar. I vow you could taste the feet of the boy that plowed the corn twas made from. Feet of the boy? repeated Private Ewing with emphasis. Goll, you could taste the feet of the mule that pulled the plow. . . . Nope, nothing like that; but just a little something to smooth the hair on their backs. They'd pay well for it, too. Tried to buy some from that old man down there near the depot, man who ran that little store down there, but great Scott, he gave them a regular Cold Water Army sermon for their pains.

The widow's heart was weakening. I'm just plain sorry but I hain't got ary drop of anything.

But they'd pay well.

But she didn't have a drop of anything. She was mighty sorry. Times were hard, she'd been awful tight run.

They laughed sardonically. Tight run as the prisoners over in that stockade?

I never did know any of those. I heard tell they was mighty sickly. But I knowed some of the men a-guarding them.

Well, well, too bad, can't even get our whiskers wet. Lady, is your respected husband to home?

Hain't got no husband. He's long dead.

Five minutes later the pea pot had been moved from the fire, and water began to heat in its place. From his haversack Private Ewing produced a small sack of coffee, and he offered it to the widow with gallantry; he could get more; what was a little coffee? In the bedroom Mag changed hastily into her wrapper, but she called animated pleasantries to her guests while she changed, while she loosened her hair and rearranged it and pinned it, while she hunted for red candy and moistened the candy and colored her round cheeks. I got a nicer place than this to entertain folks in, she cried. Just over yonder behind the house. Tis called The Crib; and I did have me a music box but it's busted. And I got a real nice soft bed, she concluded with mischief, and felt a glowing pleasure through her flesh as she heard vigorous Yankee laughter which rang when she said that.

It was a good day for every member of the Tebbs clan. Had the others but known it, Laurel received the gift of an apron from Mrs. Dillard in Americus. Coral was engaged as an apprentice gardener by

Ira Claffey, and there would be work for Floral as well, if he stood willing to perform it. There were other cavalrymen idling at Anderson Station. From these soldiers Flory was successful in begging more tobacco than he could chew in three days, and he traded some of it to Uncle Arch Yeoman for the last scraps of candy in the horehound jar. Corporal Nevis and Private Ewing matched quarters to see who should first enjoy the favors of the widow; Ewing won. Rain came but lightly, the tornado did not strike, it struck Macon County instead. Mag put not two but four greenbacks into her purse, and her body was blissful, and so was her shallow thin soul, and she planned to send Flory back to Uncle Arch's for salt and pork and many other things as soon as Flory reappeared. Zoral found a freshly dead mole under the house.

LX

These were enemies . . . Wirz felt in his pained bones that they had come to take him.

At first hand he had known no uniformed enemies except prisoners. In Paris, in 1863, he had sat alone in a small café, listening idly—then with curiosity, then with bewildered horror and disgust—to the conversation of three men in citizens' dress who were at a table behind him. From their talk he recognized that they were officers of the Federal navy. Wirz's dinner was spoiled, dyspepsia or no dyspepsia. His trembling hand spilled coffee from the cup. He paid hastily, left a gratuity out of all proportion to the cost of the meal, hurried away. From a darkened street he peered back through the smoky pane and saw Them, Them, Them; saw their faces, heard faintly their laughter. Enemies. But they were not in uniform. . . . Frogs imprisoned in his arm hopped desperately that night.

These men at his door in noontime were enemies, with all the gaud of cloth, buttons, belts.

Is your name Wirz?

Ja, I am Henry Wirz.

You have been in command of this place, commanding Rebel troops?

Wirz tried to straighten his sagging shoulders. He lifted his voice, cords tense and visible at his throat. *Nein!* The troops I have not commanded. I have been superintendent of the stockade only.

The man with bars on his shoulder straps said, I am Captain Henry E. Noyes, Fourth United States Cavalry. Acting as aide-de-camp to General Wilson. I regret to inform you that you are under arrest. Will you please instruct me as to your rank, so that I may know how to address you?

Henry said, Of promotion I was informed, before I hear the news of surrender. So now I am a major.

Have you received your commission?

It has not come. It is somewhere. . . .

In that case I shall address you as Captain.

Wirz retreated into the small parlor ahead of Noyes. Noyes called over his shoulder, Where are Ewing and Nevis?

A cavalryman said, At the rear of the house, Captain. We were taking precautions.

It's obvious that we don't need to, Sergeant. . . . Then again, to Henry: Captain Wirz, may I trouble you for your side-arms?

Wirz's glance flicked toward the window, back to the officer's face. He lifted his left hand to tug at the beard around his lips.

Mein arms, they hang in the entry yonder. Also a pepperbox revolver I got. Not truly a pepperbox—but from Europe he was—

I'm supposed to take your arms. Where is the revolver?

In the bed chamber I keep him.

Any other arms, or weapons of any sort?

. . . No, no, no, he had no other weapons.

Is any member of your family in the chamber at this time?

Henry Wirz shook his head violently. It seemed that this fierce shaking might rid him of veils gathering in his fogged weary brain, veils gathering before his eyes. My wife, my girls, they are in the garden. Back. They make the garden there. His voice broke in a hysterical titter.

Which chamber is yours?

It is above us. That revolver— I have hanging by the bed—

Sergeant Howe, go up and get the weapon and remove it with other side-arms to the verandah. Wait there until Nevis and Ewing join you. I trust these troops haven't terrified your family, Captain Wirz.

They would not be afraid, said Wirz. We have so many troops here. I mean prisoners, of the Yankees. Some Paroles. They work for me about the place, they brought wood. *Ja,* very good I treat them: double rations.

His voice rose shriller. Why is it I should be under arrest?

The heavy tread of Sergeant Howe returned down the stair. He carried the revolver in its holster. Already he had unfastened the flap in order to draw the ammunition.

Better do that outside, Sergeant. . . . Captain Wirz, will you invite me to sit down?

Ja, ja. . . . They sat, one at either end of the settee. Wirz was sitting chiefly upon his left buttock turned so far out of the seat that he was in a half-crouching position. Why am I under arrest, Captain Noyes? There has been the surrender. Troops you do not arrest after surrender!

I have my orders directly from General Wilson. There seems to be a feeling at Macon that you are subject to examination of your conduct as prison superintendent.

Henry said dryly, as if to himself: This I do not understand.

His thin face brightened for a moment as he looked up into Noyes's solemn gaze. Captain, is it possible that you speak the German? My English is—

Sorry, no German. However we seem to be getting on tolerably well.

But I do not understand! Again Wirz's voice went near a shriek, a cry which broke in two and seemed to leave a ruptured piece of the sound hanging in air before it fell.

See here, said Noyes. He tried to make his speech as smooth and reassuring as possible. The sum and substance of my conversation with the general can be reported. To begin with, about the first of this month, General Wilson sent me to Alabama on a task concerning our forces at Eufaula. On my way I passed through this village of Andersonville, and the train stopped to wood up. Some of our Federal sick were at the station. I observed you there also, Captain Wirz. Wasn't there some business about trying to parole the Northerners? Some of your troops were there with you, and you were presenting little pieces of paper to those sick men, to sign. You should have known very well, sir, that it was unnecessary for them to sign anything! General Wilson's orders had been that all the sick should be brought to Macon as rapidly as possible, and that was that. . . . I heard a voice, Captain Wirz. It was to this effect: Hurry up; sign these paroles or you'll die here anyhow. I can't swear that you made that remark, Captain. But today I have heard your voice, and I think it was your voice that I heard at the depot. What business had you paroling our sick men, after the surrender? Certainly it would have been impossible for you to hear that the armistice was repudiated!

Wirz was swallowing rapidly. *Nein,* nothing do I hear of that.

Matter of fact, said Noyes, I was on the point of going to remonstrate with you. Just then the train whistle blew, and I had to get on and travel. But when I returned to Macon I reported the circumstances immediately to my superior, and was ordered to proceed to this destination, and bring you back under arrest. That's the story.

Wirz spoke in a coarse crawling whisper (certainly, mused Captain Noyes, he must be thinking of stocks and chain gangs). What— What should they do to me?

I presume that if General Wilson is satisfied that you have only been performing your duty, and acting in accordance with orders, you will probably be released.

Wirz lifted his china face with eagerness. He began to nod. That is true, Captain. That is what I do, all the times: I carry out orders! They tell me to be superintendent of the stockade, so I serve. I *am* superintendent. I do my duty, Captain. You are a soldier. That you should know.

For a minute or two it was very quiet in the small hot room, with little sound except the breathing of Henry Wirz.

You spoke of giving double rations to men who were paroled to work for you, said Noyes. What about the prisoners who remained in the stockade? Did they receive double rations? Did they receive *any* adequate rations?

Wirz shook his head briskly, put his left hand over his face, pressed his face down toward his knee. Captain—

His voice was forced out between spread fingers.

—I tell you, only my duty I have done! That General Winder, he give me nothing, nothing. I do what I can. That Sid Winder: adjutant, he was. That Dick Winder: quartermaster. He is bad. I think he steal much from the food. I think maybe they steal money, those Winders! No help do I receive from them. I am a poor man.

His face came up again, his hollow eyes tried to implore Captain Noyes, to tell him of woes, to make the captain believe how very poor Henry Wirz was indeed.

In the campaign west, Captain, they take my place. I have a small plantation, I have a house in Louisiana. All is gone. I am ruined. Now we are in defeat! What do I *do*? I ask you that. How feed I *mein* wife and children? Three children I have by this house. I mean, one is ours, the two elder girls are of my wife. . . . See you this arm?

He shook the relic within its sling, and made a face, and squealed again in the shaking.

This I get at Fair Oaks, what you call Seven Pines. It is very bad. The surgeons, they are no good, nothing can they do. So much pain I have. Always, always—

Sorry about your wound, said Noyes. Sorry about the whole blame business, the whole blame war. Who isn't? Thank God it's over now.

Wirz said softly, Is it not odd? I was thinking. My name, it is Henry; and now you come to put me in arrest. And you too—your name is Henry. Is it not odd?

Very odd, said Henry Noyes, and again there was silence. Silence gave way before the racket of a door being opened and closed at the rear of the house . . . spasm of high-pitched voices all a-whisper, the rapid treading of light feet. Pale and glassy of eye, Elizabeth Wirz rushed into the room. She stopped short when she saw the Federal captain with her husband.

Noyes arose quickly, Wirz got up with labor.

Elizabeth's three daughters were behind her; they pushed together, staring with terrified gaze. Susie had a hat of plaited straw (she had plaited it herself) tied on her head. The bonnets of Cornelia and Coralie were hanging on their shoulders. The two elder girls wore old gloves for gardening, but the child's hands were grubby. Elizabeth Wirz herself held a wooden trowel, and somehow to Captain Henry Noyes that whittled implement spoke volumes. He thought of manufactories at the North. The wife of this Southern officer had no trowel such as his own wife might have used in her garden. There it was:

cumbersome, stained, the edge worn blunt, a split up the middle; what slave had fashioned it? Or perhaps even Henry Wirz? No, no, certainly not Wirz, with his arm in a sling, and a pyramid of prisoners atop his shoulders.

Husband— Is it true—what those Yankee soldiers told me?

This captain, said Wirz. He has told me that with him now I must go.

But husband— Henry, you've done nothing wrong!

This captain, said Wirz. His name also it is Henry. In the Old Country, Heinrich it would be. Again his weak giggle crept out.

The plump woman came closer, confronting the Union officer. He looked down to observe and identify and contend against the defiance in her gaze.

Have you arrested my husband? Pray on what grounds?

Madam, I'm merely obeying orders! As, no doubt, your husband obeyed orders given to him. As I have just told Captain Wirz: I presume that he will be released, if he but make it clear to General Wilson that he was proceeding according to orders. I mean to say— fulfilling the duties of command.

Where must you take him?

The general is at Macon. I was instructed to fetch your husband there.

Tomorrow night I should be home, said Wirz hopefully.

Little Cora had thrown her arms around his thin body. She cried distinctly over her shoulder, Don't you hurt my Pa!

I shan't hurt your Papa the least bit, Noyes told her. He must soothe these people, he must avoid a display of hysteria. What is your name, my dear?

They chorused her name. Wirz and his wife said Coralie, the girls said Cora.

Noyes reached out with strong tanned fingers. There is something very pretty around your neck. Is it a locket?

No, tis a Bible. . . .

Wirz addressed the child in a stuttering whisper.

No, *sir*, tis a Bible. . . .

Never before did I see a Bible worn around the neck!

Cora murmured, although she feared to look at the man. Made out of bone. A prisoner gave it to me, and he made it his own self, and he said to my Papa, Give it to your baby.

Noyes drew gently on the creased ribbon from which the ornament depended. There was nothing else to do: he wanted no yells when he marched Wirz out of the house. It was a tiny thing: *Bible* carved on one side, a diamond-shaped hole on the other side filled with red sealing-wax. A hole had been drilled in one end to admit the ribbon. What piece of bone? thought Noyes. Recollection of that putrid tenant-less stockade was still cold and strong in him. What bone? A piece from a brute, or a piece from a human? *They are neither man nor woman, they are neither brute nor human, they are Ghouls. . . .*

And their king it is who tolls.

Who was king of the Ghouls? Wirz? He was unfit to be a king, he must be a courtier.

Noyes left off examining the queer little gaud and stood stroking the child's hair. Still she would not look at him. Her face was pressed against her father, she had squeezed her eyes shut.

Madam, he said again to the mother. Let me repeat: I know of no particular charges having been filed against your husband—no bill of particulars, so to speak. It is merely that the general wishes to question him concerning his role as superintendent of the prison. Also— He turned back to Wirz. We are to carry along all records in your possession. They must be examined.

Ja. The books, I have them.

And loose papers. All papers. My men brought carpetbags for the purpose.

For many bags it will not be necessary. So few records were kept by me. Many are by the Winders, somewhere— I have copies from my reports—

We have already requested the hospital records, said Noyes, again in the most reassuring tone he could muster. He wrinkled his nose. There is a delicious smell in your house, Madam.

Corn bread, said Wirz behind him. Every day we have him.

Elizabeth's trowel was shaking. She looked down, saw the trowel, saw her hands a-tremble. Gradually their shaking ceased. She had willed that she make it cease. Noyes felt a sudden respect for the woman. She was made of good stuff.

She said, Our repasts are extremely simple, sir, but I believe things are soon going onto the table. Eve has not yet rung the bell. Will you join us?

I'd be delighted, if I shouldn't be putting you out.

No, no, said Elizabeth rapidly. There is a sufficiency—I mean for you. I fear we cannot offer your soldiers—

They have their own rations, said Captain Noyes.

The simple luncheon—mainly corn bread and bacon, with a few green things from the garden—was eaten in silence. There was an undercurrent of sniffling from the daughters. Before the end of the meal, Cornelia jumped up suddenly and ran from the table. She burst into tears in the hall; they could hear her tears; they rattled their forks, broke their bread, pretending not to notice the young girl's departure as she went rushing to the second story.

Wirz felt an inexpressible tenderness for his family. There was nothing now which he could say to Captain Noyes. Oh please, he thought, dear God, do make him understand, make the general under-

stand also, when we arrive in Macon. Make them understand that I am
a soldier, I was a soldier. One does one's duty. When the prisoners
were bad, they were like naughty children, and naughty children must
be punished. So I punished the prisoners. I am not a bad man. Dear
God, make the Yankees who have now triumphed over us, make them
understand that I am a good man! I am not wicked, I have done
nothing wicked. That old General Winder (and dead he is now, and
a good thing for all that he is dead), he would not coöperate. He was
relentless; he did not wish to have the hospital moved to the Outside,
and it was a very wrong thing to have the hospital on the Inside.
Very little food could we get for anybody! Yes, the prisoners were
crowded. I could not conduct a neat and efficient prison; all the time
they kept sending more prisoners—train load after train load. More,
more, more! It was wrong of the authorities to do this. Oh, dear God,
please to make the Yankees understand how handicapped I was! And
my arm: how it pained me constantly; it is paining now, with little
hopping monsters therein begging to be freed. I should have let those
surgeons lop it off in the first place; but I thought that in time I could
be healed; I did not wish to have but one arm, I wished to serve the
South. I was kind to many of the prisoners. Yes, yes, I shall tell the
general how kind I was to them! They wanted clubs to hunt down the
raiders, so I gave them clubs. They wanted to hold a court; they asked
to have attorneys, so it would be a proper trial, and I let them hold
court, let them appoint attorneys. They wanted lumber for a gallows;
I gave them lumber. And what did they do with it? It melted away as
the fence melted away—seven hundred and eighty feet of fence, and all
in one night. Most of them could not be trusted, so I did not trust
them. Many broke their paroles, they ran away. There was no fair play
about it! They ran off, and some of them managed even to elude the
dogs. They were devils and they were bears, worse than the bears in
Bern! This also shall I tell to the Federal officials, and make them
understand the scorn and unfair treatment received by me. The Yankees
threw mud, they called me evil names. They were recalcitrant, disobedient; so I was compelled to enforce my discipline with the stocks
and the chains. They were dreadful prisoners, those Yankees. They
would not submit, they would not obey my rules. They were very, very
dirty. They even killed each other! And the Northerners must understand the worthlessness of the guards foisted upon me: old men and
little boys. They were no fit soldiers; they did not know how to be
soldiers. The Northerners must understand that in my heart I am a
very kind person! If I were not a kind person, I would not have been
kind to Little Red Cap. I was very good to Little Red Cap, and he, at
least, could be trusted not to run away. Why, my Ilse even gave him
gingerbread! And little Coralie trotted after him when he came here
to my house to perform errands. I have seen them sitting together on

the bench yonder—there is the very bench, out through that window, beneath the chinaberry tree—and I have heard Little Red Cap teaching a song to my Cora.

It was a song he had learned at the North.

He would sing, *Auralee.*

But he would make it instead *Coralie.* He would sing in his young soft voice—a mere boy's voice, because he was a mere boy— He would sing, *Coralie, Coralie, maid with golden hair. Sunshine comes along with thee. . . .*

Her hair, it is not truly golden—it is light brown. But, yes, I think it has a touch of gold in it. So he was right in calling my Cora a maid with golden hair.

Other songs I would sing myself to my little daughter. I have sung them often. Oh, I wish now that I were merely sitting with my child, singing to her the German! Honestly, I am a kind man. I love the old songs in the German! I love to sing:

> *Muss i denn, muss i denn zum—Städtle hinaus,*
> *Städtle hinaus, und du mein Schatz, bleibst hier!*

. . . Must I then to the city away . . . city away . . . and you, my love, stay here. . . .

. . . When I come, when I come, when I come back again, come back again, I'll return to you, my dear. I cannot always be with you, still you are my only joy. . . . So must I then to Macon away! I am positive that General Wilson will understand. I am *almost* positive. . . .

Whatever Captain Noyes might do in ease of the situation, there were tears and wailing when Henry Wirz left the house. Wirz kept babbling about the hospital records: Dr. Roy, who remained there still, had said that the records were not complete, that the Yankees must send him some clerks in order to complete the records. This Captain Noyes promptly agreed to do. But still Wirz kept babbling about it.

Noyes had spent the previous night in Americus, because of lack of accommodations in the Andersonville region. Two of his men—a corporal and a private—had seemed eager to remain at Anderson. That was odd; but they were trustworthy men in whom Noyes had the utmost confidence, so he yielded to their whim. They seemed suffering from lack of energy on this day, but he could smell no liquor. He wondered idly what they had been up to. Noyes himself, and the remainder of the men, had come to Anderson Station on a freight train. He had arranged for a later train to bear the party to Macon with their prisoner.

Thus they reached Macon a few hours later, and at once Noyes escorted his captive to General Wilson's headquarters. He was glad to be rid of this task; but a much more exasperating one awaited him some days later.

Orders came from Washington, requiring that Henry Wirz be fetched to the capital, bag and baggage, together with the records. General Wilson took advantage of the opportunity to send along a bundle of captured battle flags which he had taken from the Confederates during his recent campaign through Alabama and western Georgia. Captain Noyes was very glad to go to Washington; but was extremely annoyed at being burdened with the flags and with Henry Wirz; and still he did not know what was in store for him.

The trip had to be made through the central South, because of the more direct lines being out of commission. At Atlanta, Noyes permitted his prisoner to take exercise upon the station platform, guarded by Ewing and Nevis. He himself was in a toilet room when an unholy row burst forth on the platform. Noyes heard his soldiers' voices, he adjusted his clothing and hastened to the scene. He found a small riot in progress. Ewing's nose had been bloodied, Nevis's jacket ripped. The young men fought savagely to restrain several purple-faced soldiers who struggled to get at the person of Henry Wirz. Even the sharpest tones of command were ignored. Noyes was compelled to draw his revolver before he could quiet the men.

When the party reached Chattanooga, Noyes concluded to take no further chances.

We'll have to remain here the greater part of the day, Sergeant. There's bound to be a post prison: take the prisoner there at once, because otherwise you'll draw a crowd, and we may have trouble.

Yes, sir.

Guard him carefully. I don't want him to be mobbed. And report back here with the prisoner at four o'clock.

Yes, sir.

When Noyes saw Henry Wirz again the brim of his hat flapped, his coat was gone, his shirt dirtied and ripped; even his trousers appeared to have been half torn from his body. Wirz himself was close to collapse. He jabbered in German, he was talking also about his little daughter, and talking about a little red cap. He didn't even make sense.

What the devil, Sergeant Howe! I told you to guard this prisoner with care!

Well, by God, sir! Excuse me, sir— It's on account of all these damn troops. Some of them were prisoners down there, and they kept yelling, Let's kill the son of a bitch! Excuse me, sir. But that's what they said—exactly what they were yelling. Christ sake, sir—excuse me, sir— but we were almost done in! I got knocked down, and finally had to fire a couple shots in the air!

It happened again at Nashville. For Henry Noyes it was from then on a sleepless journey. By this time, the dilapidated appearance of the captive would have drawn a crowd, even if he had not been recognized as being Henry Wirz. He muttered now about a place in Kentucky called Cadiz. He said that that was where he had met his wife, years before. He thought he had friends in Louisville. Perhaps they would supply him with clothing.

The friends were found at Louisville, and Wirz was garbed in a suit of black and given a beaver hat.

Shave off his beard, said Noyes.

Mein beard, Captain? It is that I do not wish to be shaved! Always I have worn a beard.

Shave off his beard, said Noyes again. Wirz was taken to a barber.

When he returned his family would not have known him. And Noyes thought that his cavalrymen were escorting a stranger—even though he had ordered this alteration.

They had no more trouble after that. Soldiers trooped along the platforms, they passed the open window where Henry Wirz sat in dejection— They passed unheeding, although doubtless there were ex-prisoners from Andersonville here and there in the jingling throngs.

Smoke swished through the car, cinders settled. Wirz complained that his arm gave him anguish, it had been injured when the troops hustled him. He asked for sulphate of morphia, so a surgeon was found to furnish him with drugs, at Cincinnati.

The pain seemed to be somewhat relieved after this. But the freshly shaved mouth kept moving, sometimes soundlessly, sometimes making sounds.

What were you saying, Captain Wirz?

It is a song. It is from the German. I learn it in my youth. It goes— in the German: Must I then, must I then to the city away? . . . When I come, when I come, when I come back again, come back again, I shall return to you, my dear. That is the German: *mein Schatz*. . . . Captain Noyes, I tell you I am not a bad man. They should not wish to kill me! I was but doing my duty. And Little Red Cap: I was good to him. I was a kind man to many prisoners.

Then he fell silent and seemed to be in a stupor; but every now and then his thin hand stole up to clutch lightly at his throat.

LXI

ANDERSONVILLE

Around the walls of Ira Claffey's chamber was built a moving frieze. It was like marbles of Mediterranean and Aegean temples, wherein men with horses and chariots made eternal progression out to war. But figments cut in relief beyond the whirl of Ira's vision were parading away from a war.

They proceeded up out of a valley of death . . . they were moving, living. Confederate troops escorted them, first off; then came Federal troops into the picture. They were so fresh out of recent memory that Ira sat up in bed and swept blindly at his own eyes to wake himself, to get rid of the lurch and grinding. He could not drive them off, he wondered how long they would be sculptured before his gaze. Depart beyond recall! he tried to tell them. Yet that was sententious falsehood, truly he did not wish them to vanish, they must be accepted as reminder that some survived, some had been carried home. No chariots in this his frieze; but wagons, wagons, wagons with clean straw filling the beds, stretchers and blankets hoisted up, people saying, Now just hold quiet, old top, this is going to hurt a speck when we lift you. The weak shorn-off scream. Soon wheels jolting, rusty smoking engine waiting on the track beyond, Yankee sentries—*Yankee* sentries—strolling by the station where formerly Georgia Reserves had moved.

He thought he saw a Northern house. He was not sure where it might be situated; he had been in but two private houses at the North, and those were palatial. But small ordinary homes he had seen from the railway carriage—their gables peaked sharply, tiny porches, often the leaning plane of a cellar door to be seen. Ira counted it peculiar to think that there was a subterranean life beneath most Northern houses, and that most Southern houses had no cellars and were built high above the ground. . . . Such a house, then, and what shall we name the people sitting there?

A name came to him, echoed from a long-ago business transaction in New York. The name was Kearns.

The people are named Kearns—father and mother—they sit above the doorstep, it is late afternoon. Who comes creeping? A spectre wan, the loose jacket and trousers are too big for him, the head has been shaven, face and head are scarred. Bony hands slide from picket to picket of the white fence, the figure comes along. Who on earth is it? says Mother Kearns, and puts up her hand to shade her eyes against the lowering sun. The fence is perhaps a hundred feet away from the doorstep. Still she does not know, she does not know. . . .

Father Kearns sees blue cloth on the weak creeping figure, and he thinks sadly of Johnny who went off to war and perished there. Johnny vanished, they'd heard no more. Johnny has been dead, they believe, a year or two. Mr. Kearns sees faded cloth and says, Just some poor tramp, Metta, and sickly too; maybe one time he was in the army. Father Kearns fastens his pipe between his teeth and picks up the newspaper.

But Rex is lying on the door-mat, Rex pricks his ears.

Oh sad, sad, thinks Mother Kearns, a-rocking and a-rocking. She will not even lift her apron to cry into it, she has wet so many aprons in the past. . . . But still that stubborn figure worries along the wooden sidewalk, still its hands go from picket top to picket top, holding on. He must not fall again, he fell twice on his way from the depot.

The dog stands, his ears are high. He stretches up, his nostrils work, he begins to whine.

Now, Rex, says Mr. Kearns, don't go to barking, that fellow won't hurt no one. The figure halts at the gate and stares at them. Rex dives from the porch. Johnny, Johnny, they are screeching a moment later. Rex is bounding wilder than any wild animal, jigging on hind legs, leaping, trying to tell them that he knew all the time, from the very first, he knew, he alone. . . .

There was a Johnny in each of those wagons which went shuddering from hospital to depot. There were many Johnnies in mendicant columns which prowled forth from the gates in their last Georgia excursion.

Ira got up and dressed, he could sleep no longer. Silence battered his ears. No rifle shots puncturing the night, no yells from a bottomless pit of gangrene and decay; no burble, no mass of human poultry roosting in hospital or stockade. Ira went down into the library and warmed a bent candle in his hands so that he might straighten it before he lit the candle. He began to read his Bible. He'd tiptoed on the way, no one must waken Cousin Harry. Coz had earned his good long sleep, earned it a thousand times over. . . . In her arms, thought Ira. Oh, long may he deserve such sleep, and in my Lucy's arms, and she in his. I would not be surprised but that she owns a secret. I think the secret shines from her eyes, comes up out of her heart and through her eyes. She has told me nothing. He smiled, then tried to put his attention to Scriptures; but problems of Lucy and Harry seemed to come first. For his part Ira would have been happy to have them make their home permanently at the Claffey plantation. He had never enjoyed a harmony greater than his harmony with Lucy. Nor could he imagine that contention might ever rise between himself and Harrell Elkins, since each bore such respect and affection for the other, since they held a common pride and humor. But he knew that young men and women should make their way, a separate way from that of each elder generation, they should have their own roof-trees. As he grew older Ira might not find undiluted contentment in observing his own ways and manners tailored to needs of the young. But he knew that Harry did not have a dime, nothing but a faraway family patch where springtime weeds were tall and window panes were broken out of the house, where shutters were sagging, and steps gone, not a plow or a cart or a Negro or a mule on the place.

It would take doing but there would come a way, in time there would come one.

Again Ira hunted for specific reassurance amid the fine print held before him. He could find nothing at the moment. Vaguely he was reassured by the feel of the Book in his hands, by thought of young strength and intimacy above stairs.

It was almost full daylight at last; he should be out and doing. No Leander left to rouse the hands . . . he himself should ring the bell. *Clong. Clong. Clong.* He heard the notes echoing until they were swaddled in stronger silence rising now like a wall from Andersonville. The silence hurt to excruciation. Its very fact reminded you of the noise which had lived.

Ira put Coffee and Jem to their work. The Tebbs boys had arrived, and Ira instructed them in the art of setting bean poles and planting beans. Then he went off to make sure that Jem was not hoeing too closely to young cornstalks, that Coffee was using only old dried guano at the bottom of the cucumber hills.

Just as he had feared! . . .

No, that must be taken out, Coffee, and done over.

Mastah?

It's my own fault: I neglected to make it plain to you. The dry manure is in the smaller bin, not the larger. Remember when you scraped the floor of the hen house? Now that stuff's been bleaching and drying long enough, and will serve.

Old chicken shit better'n fresh chicken shit? Coffee asked in puzzlement.

Exactly so. With this fresh manure the plants would die out. Get rid of it, and use only old and dry.

As he came back to observe Coral and Floral he heard an altercation in progress. Before he reached the scene he saw the older youth strike at the younger with a bean pole. Dad blast you, you little scut! You won't do half what you're tolt to do.

You ain't my sergeant, yelled Flory in rage.

Let us have no more high words, said Ira sharply. What seems to be the trouble, boys?

Coral explained in indignation: He won't plant them poles nor beans proper. I mind what you said—put them in before planting, stick them deep and firm in the ground so's they're maybe ten foot long. And not more'n five or six beans to be put around each pole, and not more'n an inch and a half deep, neither!

That's exactly the fashion. And, Floral, let me tell you this: Coral *is* your sergeant in this case. I am captain over both. Proceed according to orders. Silence in the ranks, he cried over his shoulder as he went away, and was rewarded by a faint giggle from the two.

Silence in the ranks, silence in the valley, silence in the marsh. All quiet along the Sweetwater branch . . . all quiet along Stockade Creek.

Many hours later Ira walked hesitantly into the pen alone.

He stood in that infrequent but dread state of knowing that he had observed history with his own eyes, even that he had helped to make it or had attempted to unmake it. As a very small child he first became aware of the immutability of inanimate objects. He had looked upon them with grave suspicion because they were such blocks and hulks, unfeeling, uncaring, unknowing, left to sit and stare stupidly after the humans were borne off. There had been one of the numerous deaths in the Claffey family: Ira came into the room where the person had lain sick and finally had died (he could not remember which relative it was, it didn't matter) and there was that dresser near the bed, the dresser on which bottles and glasses had stood, on which pewter spoons had been placed with puddles of unabsorbed medicine congealing in their bowls. This debris was removed, servants were carrying out featherbeds to beat them in the sunlight. But the dresser stood; it was there; same knobs, burns on the scarred oaken surface, the split in the wood where some artisan had poked out a primitive keyhole with too heavy a hand. Ah, and clothing was removed from drawers, hung up, given away; a cousin had the handkerchiefs in her own drawer now, a slave named Aba had been given the stockings, a slave named Esther had filched the tippet. But the dresser stood. The dead person was gone with all her appurtenances. The dresser stood. The same piece of broken crockery lay shoved beneath a leg to fill in a depression in the uneven floor. Did the dresser feel? Nay, nay . . . when wood was alive in trees the wood had felt; trees had sorrowed, chuckled, breathed, dreamed. Ira Claffey squinted his eyes and shook his head, recalling this first shock of particular knowledge, particular realization (which brought enduring pain as all wisdom brings pain because the man who acquires wisdom may only watch and try to understand; he may not select, manage, alter). That was Ira Claffey's name in the original Hebrew. Ira: a watcher.

He stood watching.

Or was he engaged in mere observation, evaluation, estimation? You could watch an occurrence, a happening—you were said to be watching when events moved before your eyes. This place, however ruined and despoiled, was become static. Silence smoked up from the offended earth and struck your ears with force. Birds refused to visit here. They were occupied with family cares, with feeding in woods past the fence . . . Andersonville. They'd have none of it . . . Ira moved his shoe and hoisted a dripping wad on the toe of his shoe and let the wad fall off. Declare it to be blanket, jacket, jeans, shirt, drawers in its origin; it was none of these now, it was reek endeavoring to be made into soil. Try once more. A sandal—someone had constructed it pains-takingly—it was carved from leather scraps, the scraps had been stitched together (could it have been fabricated by a middle-aged saddler from Ohio? Somewhere good food was being cooked. Its scent came from the past and titillated Ira Claffey's imagination; yet he had never known a man named Gusset, he had known none of the prisoners excepting Nazareth Stricker). Take a homemade broom and with it throw the queer sandal aside. And why a homemade broom, with shavings cut into a bunch and tied with a thong? What might anyone sweep in this wide wild den, what manner of housekeeping had been carried on? Tin receptacle crude and long and flat—ho, he'd heard of those, Colonel Persons had told him a year earlier. They are very in-genious, Persons said. Like all prisoners in all times and places the Yanks are forced to make do with what they have. Some of them were confined in an old warehouse in Richmond before they came here, and those sheets of tin— Something to do with tobacco presses— They filched them and made them into cooking pans— Serve fairly well, or so the prisoners say. Which is fortunate, since we have no pots or cutlery to give them.

Rags, rags, what had they been? Trampled deeply into clay to spoil there, or lying dried by sun, wetted by many rains, dried by numer-ous suns again. Whittled ladle and broken cow's horn (powder-horn, drinking horn, horn to blow a blast upon? You couldn't tell: it was a scrap of horn) and half-canteen, and tin fork with one of the tines broken off and one sticking east and one sticking west, and wooden bucket with the bottom splintered out of it. These things wounded Ira not in their ugliness but in their silence and lack of life.

Again: the distressing implacable stubbornness of the inanimate which remained after the animate were gone away.

Oats, flour, rice, meal—something had been kept in that wooden pail in its original time and place. Perhaps Vermont maple sugar, perhaps sugar of the South? Certainly. Flinty cany bits had been

weighted up to the brim, and the wooden lid had molded the mound
flat when it was pressed on, and a woman or a slave (ha, slaves were
become women now; it must not be forgotten) had reached in with
smooth wooden scoop or teacup or gourd dipper to lift the sugar out,
to bake it in a cake, to stir it in a pudding. Sunlight had come kindly
through a window and had found the bucket on a shelf in its
accustomed situation, and sunlight had warmed through wood and
had made the sugar richer, or so you could imagine; and a little boy
had come tiptoeing to steal the sugar . . . the bucket waited in docility
upon that shelf when Bet whispered outside the pantry door and told
her mother bashfully that she was going to have a baby next April; it
stood there in February when the baby came too soon, when the
baby was born dead, when Bet died, when the preacher stood in the
front room and quoted sepulchrally, *I am the Resurrection and the
Life.* It stood there.

Hate the inanimate, expunge it.

Let there be but Resurrection and Life.

Whence, and by what power?

Was God strong enough?

What of the Nation? The Nation was mutilated and crippled, crippled worse than Coral Tebbs, crippled worse than Badger Claffey
might have been had he dragged himself homeward instead of contributing to cold loam in fabled mountains.

(Perhaps— No loam in the Chickamauga region? Naught but rocks
and the gravelly soil of hills, and clay, and clay again, and bones
and skin and young men's lungs and tongues turned into fresher
clay?)

Shebangs broken, many others unbroken and brooding in emptiness, yawning pits drilled deep—one must be careful not to fall into
them— Crushed metal cups, the sole of a boot, the fold of paper with
its more exposed portions flaking, and there were marks of penciling
upon soggy inner portions, and it had been a letter written from
one human being to another, and for some great purpose, but now
it could not be read: it was a letter no longer; its legibility had
strayed off into the elements as its original purpose had strayed into
space with the boy who'd treasured it—

Trudging solitary through this wasteland, Ira Claffey felt the indefinable disease of old age upon him. He feared that it would not
let him move his limbs and respire and keep his blood in motion long
enough for him to keep his body in motion, and so walk at last
through that open gate yonder, and escape the balefulness which
clung to every rotting rag and scrap of charcoal.

Nineteen months ago, he mourned, partridges were here. Nineteen
months ago the open pine forest was compassionate. What rare concentrated tragedies will have occurred within another nineteen

months—not here, for this place has bred a tragedy greater than any
recorded in the Nation's past—but elsewhere, all over the South,
through back roads and on wharves and in legislative rooms, in
foundries which rust because the fires have gone out?

He prayed wordlessly, felt no answer, heard none. Gone far into
his fifty-second year he felt that in fact he was a generation older
than that, two generations older. He was ninety, he was a hundred
and more. If grief made age then his hair was hoary and his flesh
pendulous, his tendons frailer than thread, his eyes sightless.

But finally the sun came out, burned weak clouds apart, the sun
said that the half-a-button lying here was a jewel, the piece of
buckle over there was another jewel, and dank hovels between were
nothing but manure needed by soil to fetch a future growth.

Let my age and my weakness fall away; and in some inverse
fashion weakness must decline within the Nation's body as its age
increases. . . .

Here was a truth to offer strength and—perhaps, later—courage.
This truth: any creed for which men are willing to die achieves an
historic dignity, and cannot be shamed, no matter how one hated
it. I hated the North, said Ira. Hated the National Government. My
sons warred against the Nationals, my sons were killed by the Nationals. Yet the youths who suffered within these walls have given
the National Government a greatness it did not possess before; and
in time that Government may be embraced, welcomed, respected,
worshipped by those who once were unwilling to love it without
stint.

A slender stiff stick was trodden up by the weight of one boot and
passed between his feet as if to trip him. Ira stepped back and nudged
the thing aside, then bent to pick it up. He held a tooled length of
hardwood, worn smooth by the dirt and touch of many hands. A
branded *C* was visible still, no matter how many centuries of soak-
ings and tribulations the broken fragment had endured since Ira
handed out implements to his black people in the home dooryard.

    . . . All of you watch these axes and shovels, to make certain
they're not stolen. Hear me?

    . . . Yes, Mastah, we watch.

    . . . May be some dishonest folk among the other laborers. And
such implements are valuable. Watch as I bid you.

    . . . Yassah.

    . . . I wish to pick up my shovels, sir. My hands did not fetch them
home last night.

    . . . Don't know anything about your God damn shovels! I can't go
around guarding every bastard's shovels in the land.

Fist swinging and smashing. He could recollect still his boyish
primitive satisfaction in that.

Who had used the broken handle as a crutch, who'd used it as a
tent pole, had it been a weapon, was a spongy corpse pried with it?

To what use might it be put at last? Might Coral employ it as
a bean pole? Ira moved on toward the gate, his knee suffered because of the uneven terrain; now he had a cane. But first and foremost the shovel-handle suggested agriculture, and agriculture had
been a prime necessity of men all the way back to those desert tombs
where peas of the past were found drying. Ira felt that his own
gardening must proceed indefinitely, though it was assuming a new
form.

But if he put mind and heart into the soil where his sons had gone,
and where the human wastage of Andersonville had gone, and where
that enormous blood-curdling fraction of America's young males had
gone, North and South— Eventually the stalks might rise, toughen;
beards would dry out, husks turn to parchment; and those hands
who'd made his crop might reach in memory to carry him in salute
to the crop, the fields, the earth itself.

. . . You had to pretend to be surprised, you did not know that
a toting was due. Secretly you arranged for Naomi and the wenches
to provide meats, cakes, sweets; these were hid and locked away,
and so was the cask of wine; you grew both religious and Masonic in
your thought and discussed with yourself the virtues of salt, wine,
oil, and corn. You sat with your own white flock upon the evening
gallery while a chanting came from cabins spread along their private
avenue beyond the outbuildings. Your white children giggled and
whispered as black children must be giggling and whispering. You
sat aloof, you fanned yourself idly with a newspaper, you pretended
not to heed.

Oh, that old moon, way up there.

Ooohhhh. . . .

Where he gone, gone, that old moon?

He gone in corn, that where he gone.

Ooohhhh. . . .

Where he gone, gone, that old moon?

The moon was behind a cloud for a while, but then the cloud
shifted with its gilt and blue and suggestion of other rainbow colors,
the low moon burned white again, and seemed to blister long sacred
fields with its oil and its salt and—God knew—also wine in the moonlight? For the intensity of hardening corn was in the air, it made you
think of coons and possums and the yammer of dogs, and pine knots
flaring scarlet as Negroes whooped.

They approached slowly, trailing banners of flame, the clattering
voices muted as the long troop of them passed under the driveway's
magnolias . . . men coming on ahead, the women next with torches
enchanting their plain garments, children gyrating as if they danced

to drums, twisting and turning and holding little arms aloft for sheer love of the twist and turn.

He gone in corn, he gone in corn.

Ooohhhh. . . .

No, sir, old coon, no sir, old coon. . . .

You never get the Mastah's corn!

We pick that corn, own selves, we pick that corn.

Oooohhhh. . . .

They issued from Nile and Congo and Niger, they had come a long way to grow Ira's corn for him and now to carry him in triumph amidst it. They jigged in orange and black and shadows, with eyes agleam, they came pirouetting, the fierce barbaric rank of strong men in the lead.

Now was the time for the planter to arise and step to the front of the gallery (as a general might have stood, as a Highland chief might have stood when pipes came screaming in the March Past). Silence chopping suddenly, the silence a pain from the second the master arose; and his woman and his children and his visiting aunt and cousin grouped behind, years of error stretching off behind them, years of other error staggering ahead with neither servants nor master able to evaluate them.

Mastah! That was before Leander was bent to helplessness, it was when his voice held the bronze timbre of a plantation bell.

Yes, Leander.

Evening, Mastah.

Good evening to you all.

Mastah, time right! Night all right, moon all right, corn all dry, ready now we pick it—

That is so. Some of you shall start the picking tomorrow. I'll be up early to tell you off.

No, sir, please, Mastah. Not up early. Up late! For tonight—

Why, what about tonight?

This was the ritual. It varied from year to year, yet in truth it never varied until a war loomed to dismember the plantation, dismember the Union, eventually dismember the new Confederacy itself.

Tonight—we wants—to *tote* you!

Yah, yah, yah, and suddenly he was festooned amid their babble, their rich smell came up around him, he loved it as he loved the odor of cows and horses which also were his property and paid the same domestic dividends. His haunch was on Jonas's shoulder, his other buttock sustained by Japeth's big hands, Nestor clutched Ira's ankle, Ira was riding high. Dudley had a cowbell, Putty a tin wash-basin, Putty was thrumming the thing with his knuckles as his grandfather might have stroked a jungle drum.

Toting time, toting time. . . .

Oh, woh, woh, woh, woh!

Tote our Mastah to the corn. . . .

Why we tote him? Corn all ripe!

Ah, wah, wah, wah, wah!

Younger women lifted their skirts as they skipped behind, children scuttled and scooted, and soon were chased out of the first cornfield. This was a rule enforced by Leander: he would not permit women and children to venture past the gate, they did too much damage in dry crowded fields, they tore down stalks and made it difficult to find the ears, they made more work for the menfolks and for themselves. A coon whickered over toward the McWhorter place (in pine woods become extended Hades, pools stirred by evil pitchforks; why, it might have been at this very spot that the coon called) and all the pickaninnies yipped to hear it; the bigger more ornery ones said that it was a Woogum. There was thought of autumn coming on, colder weather, potatoes roasting in ashes; birds whirring up as if they were cranked to the whirring; smell of burnt powder, the smoke blowing free, the setter racing, the setter bringing a bird in his mouth. Thought of cool mornings after cooler whiter nights, and Naomi fetched the biscuits wrapped in a red-checked cloth, and pine flames seethed on many a hearth. It was good to be alive and crush a biscuit and smell a fire. And always there was the thought of corn, and how men and beasts would feed on it, and they would profit from the grain because it was a good thing, made good by the earth and the labor of many hands.

Oh, that old moon stay so high. . . .

Why we tote our Mastah dear?

Corn all ripe. Pick, pick, pick! Corn all ripe.

Oohhhhh. . . .

(Here corn bread had rotted, but most of it was rotted away . . . most of the last prisoners had lain within the hospital enclosure, while the stockade itself took on an air of wide desertion. Ah, here indeed was a scrap of corn bread surviving as a paste! A bug was feeding on it, several bugs. Ira turned from the sight and walked on.)

His black people's song cried from the past, but Ira told himself that also he must listen to their lamentation. He thought that he had not caused them to lament, but others had done so. America owned its own Wilberforces, and *Laus Deo* said the poet whose poem had filtered down from the North. No blacks would ever tote Ira again in a triumphal circuit of the cornfields, no other man would ride on slaves' shoulders, because now there were no slaves (and little corn to triumph about). He must tell himself that the institution of slavery was evil because it had perished. He must persuade himself that a greater good was achieved when a thing vanished. For his own part he saw little difference between a legal slavery and an economic one, and he thought that his own people were better off than sickly whites he'd seen trooping through mill gates at the North. But perhaps the Claffey place was not the Confederacy, and God knew there must be happier children at the North than bobbin boys.

Here was the hillside, here the spring. Often he'd stood upon that sentry platform yonder and watched the prisoners filing for their drinks, with police of their number standing, clubs at the ready, to keep them in line, to discourage speculators, to give fair opportunities for drink to everyone. Police, he thought, may I have my turn? On an impulse he knelt and scooped up water; he closed his eyes and listened to Lucy talking about a fairy she'd seen among mossy places now not mossy but only littered and tattered. Ira Claffey got up blindly and went down the slope, crossed the narrow rotten cat-walk over the marsh (with its smell lessening but still a smell) and went up toward the South Gate past the place where gallows had stood.

Thought of the gallows brought memory of those specific dead— the giants slaughtered to bring them to time!—and also the recognition of the nigh-onto-fourteen thousand who lay past pines northwest of the stockade. How many other Yankees had gone to their sleep in cars bound for Savannah or Charleston, how many had jittered and then silenced themselves in pens at Millen and Florence because they held the evil of Andersonville in their bodies when they staggered through that gate ahead? Say another thousand, or two, or thousands more? What of the relics who were carried to their homes at last? Would they grow keen and sprightly, unblemished except in spirit?—or would they languish and continue the putrefaction which had begun within these acres? Had Americans ever brought so many Americans to death in such limited acreage before? Ira thought, No great battle was ever waged within the confines of a twenty-eight acre patch. It was said that seven thousand were shot dead at Gettysburg; there they fought over twenty miles of hills and orchards. . . .

He groped for a text and found none. Cato Dillard should be near to provide texts. But a great voice intoned somewhere, and Ira stopped to hear it. *Their memory has escaped the reproaches of men's lips, but they bore instead on their bodies the marks of men's hands.* Thucydides quoting Pericles . . . *their story is not graven only on stone over their native earth, but lives on far away, without visible symbol, woven into the stuff of other men's lives.*

He had a renewed sense of timelessness and its values. The song did not ring for a solitary moment, nor merely to enrich the spirit which had sung it, and to enrich admirers of that spirit; but it went echoing indefinitely. Thus the future became packed with a good accumulation. A vanished Pericles had lived anew when Thucydides counseled the listening Athenians to heed a forgotten funeral oration. Thucydides mixed his own dreams and opinions with those of Pericles; therefore the two became indissoluble, creatures in common, neither holding to his own part of the century. Rather they were the Fifth Century, they made it; so they and other honorable souls had manufactured the millenia.

Ira believed that a new Nation was made. It was one which he had prayed not to see; but here it was. His own fields, were he allowed to retain them, extended to Maine and Texas and to the Oregon country; because granule of soil lay next to granule of soil, and small roots were intertwined, and fences broke down in one patch of woods but rose in the next; and rivers were not bottomless, there were earth and rocks underneath, the rocks touched, it was the land, it was all the American land and the American waters belonging principally to America and not to individual planters, and not to New York or Georgia, as had been so cruelly demonstrated.

And now came the strophic echo of the Grecian past (which was not truly the past, and not solely Grecian), *when you have finished your lamentation, let each of you depart.*

There was no Each Of You about it. He was alone, with stains upon his shoes and the legs of his jeans, alone with the recovered shovel-handle for a cane. He moved toward the great gate with not another living man moving there. *For the battle . . . now to face is . . . against the foe in her own household, the desires and ambitions she herself has nurtured.* The Greek said America instead of Athens, and America was an undreamed wilderness beyond seas the Greeks never sailed; yet still he said America, because of the essential timelessness—once more—of clear thought and valuable deed. *Shall she welcome them in their fullness and seek to furnish them with all they need?*

. . . How are you doing with the final stages of Greek, dear Sutherland?

. . . I must say, Father, that you will hear the valedictory spoken in July—but not by me, sir, oh not by me—but by my beloved classmate, Sidney Lanier. He takes as his topic, The Philosophy of History. . . .

Find the philosophy in history if you can, Ira directed himself.

He passed through that gate and felt the eyes of the dead Yankees watching him as he retreated. Were the bulk of the dead too young or too degraded to concern themselves with desires and ambitions of the America for which they had fought and which in turn had slain them; or did the process of extinction award them wisdom? *Or shall she try to put them from her, lest they corrupt her and wreck her peace?* Ira felt that he himself held no desire or ambition, but this bruised collection of States must hold ambition, else the Nation was not fit for the sun to shine upon it; and the sun was shining. *Or, while*

she is seeking a middle course, will they lay her glory in the dust?
He went past abandoned earthworks, abandoned camps, going
directly to his plantation and into the future, and toward challenges
waiting there. When he had nearly reached the lane, birds rose before
him like an omen.

16 December, 1953.
25 May, 1955.

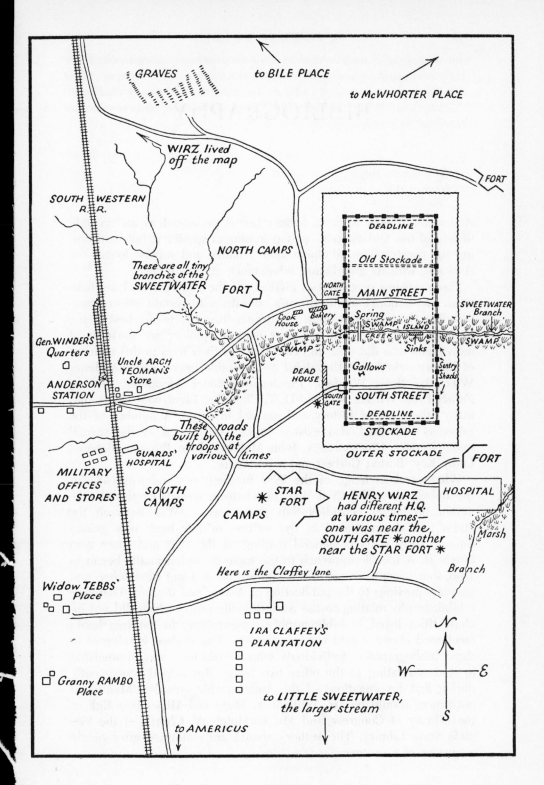

Chart showing approximate location
of various points and areas at Andersonville.

BIBLIOGRAPHY

Andersonville is a work of fiction, but is presented as an accurate history of the Andersonville prison insofar as specific details concerning the construction, administration, tenancy and supervision of the stockade, with its guards and inhabitants, are made clear.

Those persons portrayed as civilians of the neighborhood are fictitious. The majority of the prison's officials, with certain officers commanding Confederate troops, are drawn from life to the best of the author's ability; and, in his most earnest opinion, are portraits of individuals who did exist and contribute of their lives to this moment of history, whether with baleful or charitable intent. Captain Henry Wirz, the three Winders, Lieutenant-Colonel Alexander Persons, Father Peter Whelan, Colonel D. T. Chandler, Lieutenant Davis, and many others are of history and are not invented. A number of the prisoners described also existed in fact—such men as the several raider leaders, Chickamauga, John McElroy, John Ransom, Bateese, Leroy Key, Boston Corbett and a few more.

Whatever knowledge of the War for Southern Independence—or the Rebellion, or the Civil War, or whatever term is employed (the author no longer considers that there was a "War Between the States")—is demonstrated in the writing of this book was gained through forty years of general reading on the War and those who fought it. A specific approach to the topic of Andersonville began in 1930, four years previous to the publication of *Long Remember,* and six years previous to the publication of *Arouse and Beware.* Therefore a bibliography relating to the Andersonville prison which did not include titles listed in bibliographies appertaining to the two books mentioned above, would not be complete. The student is referred to those bibliographies. Individuals whose assistance was appreciated in studies relating to the other two books also helped concurrently during first investigations of the Andersonville complex. Mentioned once more should be Mr. William A. Slade and Miss Clara Egli of the Library of Congress, and Mr. Randolph W. Church of the Virginia State Library. The author's thanks are reaffirmed after nearly a quarter of a century.

More recently and more specifically again, relating to *Andersonville,* the author is indebted particularly to the following:

Mr. Edward W. Beattie, Jr.; Mr. Clifford Dowdey; Monsignor C. L. Elslander; Mr. Jerome Fried; Colonel W. A. Ganoe; Dr. Thomas C. Garrett; Mrs. Phyllis Gossling; Mr. Edgar Kimsey; Miss Jean L. McKechnie; Colonel William J. Morton, Jr., historian of the United States Military Academy; the Reverend Father John P. O'Connell, editor of the Catholic Press; Dr. William J. Petersen, superintendent of the Iowa State Historical Society, and Miss Mildred Throne of the same organization; the Reverend Mr. David H. Pottie; Miss Hester Rich of the Maryland State Historical Society, and Mr. Fred Shelley, director of that society; Mrs. Elizabeth Service; Miss Ella May Thornton, formerly State Librarian of Georgia, and now honorary librarian; Mr. F. F. Van de Water; Mr. Sylvester Vigilante, formerly of the New York Public Library and more recently of the New-York Historical Society; and Mrs. Mary Gladys Perrin Watkins, only surviving grandchild of Elizabeth and Henry Wirz.

There are general works, some of them original sources, some not: tried and familiar standbys such as *Battles and Leaders of the Civil War,* edited by Robert Underwood Johnson and Clarence Clough Bull, New York, The Century Company, 1884; the *Photographic History of the Civil War,* edited by Francis Trevelyan Miller, New York, The Review of Reviews Company, 1912; the Official Records, War of the Rebellion; and various executive documents published by various United States Congresses. Excerpts from the reports of Confederate officers contained herein are taken verbatim from Executive Document No. 23, Fortieth Congress, Second Session. There has been no tampering with any of the remarks attributed to Confederate officers such as General Howell Cobb, General John H. Winder, Colonel D. T. Chandler and Captain Henry Wirz, when those remarks appear *solidly italicized* in the text.

A great debt is owed to the diaries of John Ransom and John McElroy especially; to the books of General N. P. Chipman; and to the defense published after the war by a former Confederate Chief Surgeon, R. Randolph Stevenson.

A reasonably complete bibliography, each volume including some material employed by the author in the preparation of *Andersonville,* appears below:

A History of the 117th Regiment N. Y. Volunteers. James A. Mowris. Hartford, Conn. Case, Lockwood & Co. 1866.

A History of Popular Music in America. Sigmund Spaeth. New York. Random House. 1948.

A Journal of Hospital Life in the Confederate Army. Kate Cumming. Louisville, Ky. Morton Printers. 1866.

A List of Union Soldiers Buried at Andersonville. Dorence Atwater. New York. The Tribune Association. 1890.

A Memorial Volume of the Hon. Howell Cobb. Edited by Samuel Boykin. Philadelphia. J. B. Lippincott Co. 1870.

A Narrative of Andersonville. Ambrose Spencer. New York. Harper & Bros. 1866.

A Rebel War Clerk's Diary. J. B. Jones. New York. Old Hickory Bookshop. 1935.

A Yankee in Andersonville. T. H. Mann. New York. The Century Magazine, Vol. 18. 1890.

Adventures of an Escaped Union Prisoner from Andersonville. Thomas H. Howe. San Francisco. H. S. Crocker & Co. 1886.

Adventures of George A. Tod. George A. Tod. Edited by Mildred Throne. Iowa City, Iowa. Iowa Journal of History, Vol. 48, No. 4. 1951.

Andersonville. John W. Elarton. Aurora, Neb. Burr Publishing Co. 1913.

Andersonville. J. Frank Hanly. New York. Eaton and Mains. 1912.

Andersonville. John McElroy. Toledo, Ohio. D. R. Locke. 1879.

Andersonville, an Object Lesson in Protection. Herman A. Braun. Milwaukee, Wis. C. D. Fahsel Publishing Co. 1892.

Andersonville and Other War Prisons. Jefferson Davis. New York. Belford Co. 1890.

Andersonville, and the Trial of Henry Wirz. John Howard Stibbs. Iowa City, Iowa. The Clio Press. 1911.

Andersonville Diary. John L. Ransom. Auburn, N.Y. Published by the author. 1881.

Andersonville Prison Park. Compiled by James P. Averill. Atlanta. Byrd Printing Co. 1899.

Ante Bellum Southern Life As It Was. Mary Lennox. Philadelphia. J. B. Lippincott Co. 1868.

Billy and Dick from Andersonville Prison to the White House. Ralph O. Bates. Santa Cruz, Calif. Press Sentinel Publishing Co. 1910.

Captain Sam Grant. Lloyd Lewis. Boston. Little, Brown & Co. 1950.

The Capture, the Prison Pen, and the Escape. Willard W. Glazier. New York. United States Publishing Co. 1868.

Civil War Prisons. William H. Hesseltine. Columbus, Ohio. Ohio State University Press. 1930.

"Co. Aytch." Samuel R. Watkins. Nashville, Tenn. Cumberland Presbyterian Publishing House. 1882.

Collections of a Coffee Cooler. Samuel Creelman. Pittsburgh, Pa. Photo Engraving Co. 1890.

College Life at Old Oglethorpe. Allen P. Tankersley. Athens, Ga. University of Georgia Press. 1951.

Conscription in the C.S.A., 1862–65. Robert P. Brooks. Bulletin of the University of Georgia. Athens, Ga. 1917.

Contributions Relating to the Causation and Prevention of Disease, and to Camp Diseases. Austin Flint. New York. Published for the U. S. Sanitary Commission by Hurd and Houghton. 1867.

Country Life in Georgia in the Days of My Youth. Rebecca Latimer Felton. Atlanta. Index Printing Co. n.d.

The Demon of Andersonville. Anon. Philadelphia. Barclay & Co. 1865.

Doctor Chase's Recipes. A. W. Chase. Ann Arbor, Mich. Published by the author. 1860.

Escape of a Confederate Officer from Prison. Samuel Boyer Davis. Norfolk, Va. The Landmark Publishing Co. 1892.

Florida Plantation Records. Edited by Ulrich Bonnell Phillips and James David Glunt. St. Louis. Missouri Historical Society. 1927.

From Andersonville to Freedom. Charles M. Smith. Providence, R.I. The Society. 1894.

The Gangs of New York. Herbert Asbury. New York. Alfred A. Knopf. 1928.

Gardening for the South. William N. White. New York. Orange Judd and Co. 1868.

Georgia and State Rights. Ulrich Bonnell Phillips. Published by the American Historical Association. Washington, D.C. Government Printing Office. 1902.

The Gray Book. Published by the Sons of Confederate Veterans. n.p. 1920.

Henry Wirz and the Andersonville Prison. Mildred Lewis Rutherford. Athens, Ga. Published by the United Daughters of the Confederacy. 1921.

Historical Record of Macon and Central Georgia. John C. Butler. Macon, Ga. J. W. Burke & Co. 1878.

History of O'Dea's Famous Picture of Andersonville Prison. Thomas O'Dea. Cohoes, N.Y. Clark & Fister. 1887.

History of the 148th Pennsylvania Volunteers. Edited by J. W. Muffly. Des Moines, Iowa. The Kenyon Co. 1904.

The Horrors of Andersonville Rebel Prison. Norton Parker Chipman. San Francisco. The Bancroft Co. 1891.

The Horrors of Southern Prisons During the War of the Rebellion. Wm. Henry Lightcap. Platteville, Wis. Journal Job Rooms. 1902.

In and Out of Andersonville Prison. Wm. Franklin Lyon. Detroit. G. Harland Company. 1905.

Jefferson Davis at West Point. Walter L. Fleming. Baton Rouge, La. Mississippi Historical Society. 1910.

Letter from an Eyewitness at Andersonville Prison. Edited by Spencer B. King, Jr. Collections of the Georgia Historical Society, Vol. 38, No. 1. 1954.

Letters by Hurieosco Austill. Alabama Historical Quarterly, Vol. 7. Wetumpka, Ala. 1945.

The Life and Adventures of Sergt. G. W. Murray. George W. Murray. Minneapolis. Herald Publishing House. 1872.

Life and Death in Rebel Prisons. Robert H. Kellogg. Hartford, Conn. L. Stebbins. 1866.

Life Struggles in Rebel Prisons. Joseph Ferguson. Philadelphia. Published by the author. 1865.

Little Aleck. E. Ramsay Richardson. Indianapolis. The Bobbs-Merrill Co. 1932.

Major Henry Wirz. Lyon G. Tyler. Williamsburg, Va. The William and Mary College Quarterly, Vol. 27. 1919.

Martyria; or, Andersonville Prison. Augustus Choate Hamlin. Boston. Lee and Shepard. 1866.

The Martyrs Who, etc. Published by the Quartermaster's Dept. Washington, D.C. Government Printing Office. 1866.

The Melvin Memorial. Alfred Seelye Roe. Cambridge, Mass. The Riverside Press. 1910.

The Narrative of Amos E. Stearns. Amos Edward Stearns. Worcester, Mass. F. P. Rice. 1887.

Narrative of the Privations and Sufferings, etc. Printed for the U.S. Sanitary Commission by King and Baird, Ptrs. Philadelphia. 1864.

Necrology: or, Memorials of Deceased Ministers. John S. Wilson. Atlanta, Ga. Franklin Printing House. 1869.

Nineteen Months a Prisoner of War. Anon. Milwaukee, Wis. Starr & Son. 1865.

Out-Post. D. H. Mahan. New York. John Wiley. 1863.

Over the Dead-Line. K. C. Bullard. New York. The Neale Publishing Co. 1909.

Prison Life in Andersonville. John Levi Maile. Los Angeles. Grafton Publishing Co. 1912.

Prison Life in Dixie. John B. Vaughter. Chicago. Central Book Concern. 1880.

Prison Life in the South. A. O. Abbott. New York. Harper & Bros. 1865.

The Prisoner of War, and How Treated. Alva C. Roach. Indianapolis. Railroad City Publishing House. 1865.

Reminiscences of Andersonville and Other Rebel Prisons. M. O'Hara. Lyons, Iowa. J. C. Hopkins. 1880.

Report of an Expedition to Andersonville. Clara Barton. New York. The Tribune Association. 1866.

Secondary Education in Georgia. Elbert W. G. Boogher. Philadelphia. Published by the author(?). 1933.

Seven Months in Prison. David E. Russell. Milwaukee, Wis. Godfrey and Crandall. 1866.

Sherman: Fighting Prophet. Lloyd Lewis. New York. Harcourt, Brace and Co. 1932.

Smith's "Knapsack" of Facts and Figures. Frank W. Smith. Toledo, Ohio. Spear, Johnson & Co. 1884.

The Soldier's Story of His Captivity at Andersonville, etc. Warren Lee Goss. Boston. Lee and Shepard. 1869.

Some Records of the Winder Family of Maryland. Philip D. Laird. Baltimore. Maryland Original Research Society. 1913.

The South: A Tour of Its Battlefields and Ruined Cities. J. T. Trowbridge. Hartford, Conn. L. Stebbins. 1866.

The Southern Side, or Andersonville Prison. R. Randolph Stevenson. Baltimore. Turnbull Bros. 1876.

The Story of Andersonville and Florence. James Newton Miller. Des Moines, Iowa. Welch Printing Co. 1900.

To the Memory of My Brother, Edwin W. Niver. Emogene Niver Marshall. Sandusky, Ohio. Krewson Press. 1932.

The Tragedy of Andersonville. Norton Parker Chipman. San Francisco. Blair-Murdock Printing Co. 1911.

Travels in the Confederate States. E. Merton Coulter. Norman, Okla. University of Oklahoma Press. 1948.

The Trial and Death of Henry Wirz. Sarah W. Ashe. Raleigh, N.C. E. M. Uzzell & Co. 1908.

True History. Henry Hernbaker, Jr. Philadelphia. Merrihew & Son. 1876.

The True Story of Andersonville Prison. J. M. Page and M. J. Haley. New York. Neale Publishing Co. 1908.

Twelve Months in Andersonville. Lessel Long. Huntington, Ind. T. & M. Butler. 1886.

Vocabulum, or, the Rogue's Lexicon. Compiled by George W. Matsell. New York. G. W. Matsell & Co. 1859.

ABOUT THE AUTHOR

MacKinlay Kantor was born in Webster City, Iowa, February 4, 1904. His parents were separated before his birth, divorced soon afterward. The future novelist spent a chaotic childhood and youth in Iowa and in Chicago—years marked by poverty, hard work, and occasional moments of comparative luxury. He started to write seriously at sixteen, became a newspaper reporter at seventeen, and an author devoted exclusively to fiction at the age of twenty-three. Mr. Kantor's first novel was published in 1928. Since then thirty of his books in all have been appreciated by readers in America and abroad: novels, verse, collections of short stories and novelettes, juvenile books, and histories. He has come to be regarded as a foremost interpreter of the essentially American flavor and scene. He has lived actively, intensely in that scene. MacKinlay Kantor's accomplishments vary from the Hollywood motion-picture complex (he wrote the original story for the world-famous *The Best Years Of Our Lives,* which won thirteen Academy Awards) to a year and a half spent living the life of a patrolman in the New York City Police Department. He has achieved combat experience in two wars and was personally decorated by the commander of the United States Air Force. Mr. Kantor was married in 1926 to Irene Layne, an artist. They are the parents of a daughter and a son (the latter now a flyer in that same Air Force) and the grandparents of two small boys. The Kantors divide their time between Sarasota, Florida, and Spain, where much of *Andersonville* was written. The author began his intensive study of the Andersonville prison more than twenty-five years ago.